Collectors Edition #1, Books 1-10

Tail of the Dragon

Claws of the Dragon

Battle of the Dragon

Eyes of the Dragon

Flight of the Dragon

Trial of the Dragon

Judgement of the Dragon

Wrath of the Dragon

Power of the Dragon

Hour of the Dragon

Craig Halloran

Tail of the Dragon Collection
Collector's Edition #1, Books 1 – 10

TWO-TEN BOOK PRESS
P.O. Box 4215, Charleston, WV 25364

ISBN eBook: 978-1-946218-21-6
ISBN Hardback: 978-1-946218-22-3
ISBN Paperback: 978-1-724074-9-11

www.craighalloran.com

Publisher's Note
This book is a work of fiction. Names, characters, places, and incidents either are the product of the author's imagination or are used fictitiously, and any resemblance to actual persons, living or dead, events, or locales is entirely coincidental.

NALZAMBOR
Faalum Sea
Urslay
Marlun
Huskan
Artus
Riegelwood
THRAAG
Pool of the Dragons
QUINTUKLEN
Riverlynn
NARNUM
Shale Hills
MORGDON
Valley of Bones
ELOME
The Ruins
The Settlement
Stonewater Keep
Advent
DRAGON HOME
Old Hen
Lost City of Borgash
Slaver Town
Cherlon
Abblyn
Berglon
Karl Vesterberg 2017

TABLE OF CONTENTS

TAIL
OF THE
DRAGON

-Book 1-

Craig Halloran

CHAPTER 1

"COME ON, BRENWAR. HURRY UP," Nath said, staring down over the rocky edge of a mountainside. Below, Brenwar's meaty mitts tugged hand over hand at the rocks. Sweat beaded his forehead. The brisk winds tore through his gray-streaked black beard. "I'm getting hungry."

Brenwar glared up at him. "I'll get there in my own good time. Why don't you go scarf down some cattle or something?"

Nath's golden dragon eyes widened. "Are you taking a poke at me?"

Brenwar didn't respond. The powerful frame of a dwarf continued his agonizing pace up the steep mountainside. Below him were endless miles of lush green countryside. It would be an hour before he caught up with Nath.

"Great," Nath said, turning his serpentine head away and facing the top rocks of the mountain. He took his anger out on Brenwar, but they both knew he was really mad at Selene. After all they'd been through to stop Gorn Grattack, a year ago she'd up and left. It still deeply hurt him she'd done that. No explanation. Not a word.

On all fours, Nath weaved his way through the trees like a great cat, his dragon paws leaving deep impressions in the ground. He sat back on his haunches and leaned his scaled dragon frame against the tall rocks, eyeing his prints. "I don't think I'll ever get used to that."

Nath was all dragon now, from his smoking nostrils to the tip of his lightning-quick tail. He was bigger than a team of horses, and though still graceful as a gazelle, he wasn't entirely accustomed to his huge body yet. He puffed out a fiery smoke ring. It floated high in the air before descending over a tree and turning it into ash. "I'm big. I'm astounding. I love it."

He clicked his claws together in admiration. Some were bigger than a man's arm. Sharper than elven steel. His scales were alabaster flecked with bronze now. A flame-red streak raced down from the middle of his horns to the middle of his back. His wings were red and folded tight over his back. He lifted his chin toward the sky, thinking it was true, what his father, Balzurth, had once said: "The land was made for men, the sky for dragons."

Nath's stomach rumbled. "Guzan, I can't believe I'm hungry already. I ate ten cows yesterday." He rubbed the scales on his belly. "I like food as much as anyone, but this is ridiculous." He snorted some air into his nostrils. His scaly brow started to crease. "Nothing worth eating up here unless I rustle up a thousand squirrels and chipmunks."

Nath pushed off the rocks and flattened himself so that his iron-hard belly hung inches over the ground. Head low and with his horns flared out over his back, he approached the rim of the mountain again. Brenwar had made little progress. "I'm going to eat," Nath called down to the dwarf. "Eh, so don't fall or anything."

"Like you care if I fall or not," Brenwar grunted.

"Oh, it's not you I'm worried about. It's the mountain." Nath's chuckles rumbled. "I'm off." He pushed off the edge and darted down the mountainside, zooming by Brenwar. Hearing his friend let out a startled curse, Nath spread his wings out and took flight, laughing.

The wind ripped through his earholes. A split second later he was soaring high in the sky. The mountaintops and farmlands, far below, looked like little more than a map on a table.

Nath let out an exhilarating roar. "Mah-hoooooooooooo!"

Cutting through the clouds, Nath spun, dove, climbed, and dove again. There was nothing like flying. Even the best days walking the land were not even close. Minutes into the flight, miles away from where he'd started, his keen dragon eyes spotted a herd of cattle roaming the land.

"Ah, dinner."

Circling lower toward the earth, he looked to see if any people were tending these cows. Nath took no pleasure in eating what people had rustled for themselves, unless it was absolutely necessary. So far, it had not been. Ranchers from all the races needed meat, but there were still plenty of wild herds for him to go around and feast on.

A flicker of movement caught his eye. There were men. Some on horseback and others walking.

"Blast my hide!" he said, hovering just below the clouds. "And I'm getting really hungry too. Wait a second." He sniffed the air. "Oh, I know that foul aroma. Those aren't men. Those are orcs." He clutched his claws and dove toward the ground with a broad grin full of teeth showing on his maw. "Perfect."

Nath's shadow fell upon the orcs.

Their necks snapped up. Their yellow eyes filled with surprise.

Nath buzzed over the tops of two orcs' heads, knocking them both from their saddles.

The horses galloped away. The orcs scrambled.

Nath let out a roar so terrifying the ground shook.

Orcs clasped their grubby hands over their ears and fell to their knees. One of them found the courage to rise to his feet and face Nath with his spear.

It's always the stupidest ones that are the bravest.

The orc, little more than a morsel in Nath's midst, marched forward. Its head hung low, and its spear was gripped with white knuckles. It was stout and sweaty, more so than the common orc. A brawler.

Really. Nath shook his head. *Being king, I really think I should be able to kill them. It would almost be worth doing if they had some flavor to them. Ew! I really hope I don't get so hungry that I eat foul beasts.*

The orc continued his march through the tall meadow.

If I were a man, I'd gladly pummel you with my fists, but I don't have time for that. He unleashed his tail. *Swat!*

The orc flipped head over heels and crashed into the ground.

Nath prowled over. Using his clawed hand, he plucked the orc up from the ground by the leg and dangled it in front of his face. Nath shook the orc a few times and flicked him like a toy far aside.

And to think I used to struggle with those smelly things. Oh well. Nath dusted off his paws. He turned and gazed over the rolling hills. The cattle were grazing again, not too far away. There were hundreds of them. Nath's eyes glazed over.

Thoom!

Nath stretched up his long neck. *What was that?*

Suddenly, mounds of dirt exploded near the cattle. Great men emerged from the ground, taller than trees and hewn from mighty frames as big as Nath himself.

Great Guzan! Giants!

CHAPTER 2

ARTH GIANTS. BIG AND NASTY was an understatement for their kind. The towering men stood more than twenty feet tall. They were built like mountains, and their faces were covered in dark, coarse beards. The ground shook as they closed in on the cattle and began snatching them

up one by one. One of them, covered in furs for clothing, dropped a cow into his mouth and swallowed it whole.

"THAT'S MY DINNER!" Nath roared.

The giants froze and turned to face him, their eyes widening underneath their bushy brows and revealing an evil glimmer of yellow. The second giant stuffed a cow into his mouth, chewed it up, and swallowed. Then the pair of them rose to their full height and started to spread out, flanking Nath.

They're both as big as me. This should be interesting.

The cattle made their escape, pressing through the tall grasses and out of sight. The giants grumbled back and forth to each other, hands clutching in and out, eyes wary. It was only the dragons that ever rivaled them in size. The giants hated that. For the most part, they hated everything. They were the big bullies in Nalzambor.

Nath flashed his claws and let out another roar of warning. *I can at least give them a chance. They don't want to mess with this dragon.*

The giants pulled their shoulders back and closed in. Evil leers formed on their disturbing faces.

I expected as much.

Nath's golden eyes narrowed. He let out a small blast of fire.

Good.

The giants circled him. Their hands became monster-sized hammers. They started hooting at him. An odd sound. Weird, yet threatening. Brimming with confidence, their voices became louder. More disturbing.

Nath cocked his serpentine head. *Strange and ugly. I almost feel sorry for them. No wonder the dwarves hate them so. They remind me of oversized orcs.*

The ground rumbled beneath his feet. Hands and arms burst from underneath like massive tree roots. Powerful fingers locked onto his tail and jerked him backward.

Nath stumbled. *Blast!*

Another giant bearded head emerged from the ground and spat out a mouthful of dirt.

Nath tried to shake out of its grasp.

The other two giants leapt on top of him and began hammering away at his body.

Wham! Wham! Wham! Wham!

The first blow caught Nath square in the jaw. The next shots landed hard on his belly, knocking the wind out of him. Besieged by monsters just as big as him, he found himself in a fight for his very life.

The blows kept coming. Hard. Furious. All giants were brawlers. Fearless. Only the grave could take the fight out of them.

Great Guzan! I'm getting whipped!

Nath shook the stars from his vision. Out of the corner of his eye, he saw a giant fist coming down fast. Nath struck back like a snake, clamping his powerful jaws down on the giant's arm.

The giant let out a pain-filled yelp. Using its free arm, it started pounding on Nath's face.

That was a mistake.

Nath drew a deep snort of air in his nose and summoned his fire. The giant's arm that he clenched between his teeth erupted into flame and quickly turned to ash.

The giant staggered back, gaping at his missing arm.

That'll teach him.

The other giants were unrelenting. One still had Nath's tail locked up in its fists. The others continued to hammer away. Nath's scales shook under the force of the blows. A hundred mules didn't kick so hard. Every punch shook his dragon bones.

Enough of this!

Nath lashed out. His clawed forearms ripped through the skin and furs of one giant's chest.

It let out an angry grunt and locked onto Nath's neck. It put Nath in a headlock and started to squeeze.

The threesome thrashed on the ground, shaking the earth. The giants were great wrestlers. They had a natural knack for grappling. They tried to snap Nath in half like a twig.

Nath twisted and clawed. His muscles strained with effort.

Guzan! Nath's temper went red. *Blast it! I'm the King of the Dragons!*

With a tremendous heave, he ripped his neck free of the first giant's grasp. Rearing his head up eye to eye with the colossal man, he unleashed his inferno. A white-hot stream of yellow fire burst out of his mouth, covering the giant in flames.

In most circumstances, giants didn't burn. But in this case, Nath's fire, hotter than the hottest dwarven forge, could burn anything.

The giant's body turned into a pile of ash and bones.

Still seeing red with rage, Nath whirled on the giant that was still tugging on his tail.

Catching the fatal look in Nath's eyes, it dove for cover into the ground where it had come from.

Nath filled it with fire, and then eyeing the crater of flame, he let out a mighty roar.

"Mah-Roooooooooo!"

A rustling caught his ear. His head whipped around.

The last surviving giant, the one missing its arm, was trying to dig its way back into the dirt. It caught Nath's eye, and its one good arm started digging faster.

Nath shot across the tall grass, spread his wings, and dug his back talons into the giant's shoulders. Wings beating, he ascended high into the air with the heavy earth giant in tow. He rose high above the clouds, ignoring the giant's angry cries.

Oh, be silent!

Nath was out of danger now, yet his temper had not cooled. He wanted to drop the giant. Let the evil creature plunge to its death. That would be a far more merciful fate than what he had bestowed on its comrades.

After all, the giants would have killed him. Skinned him. Eaten him if they could have. The great monsters were killers, said to be irredeemable.

Still, deep inside, Nath knew that would be wrong. He heard his father's words.

Take the high road.

He shook his head and glanced down at the giant. There was no pleading in its eyes, just anger. Hatred. It lashed out with its only hand again and again.

Sometimes I hate the high road.

Nath flew mile after mile until he came to a high and snowy peak and dropped the giant deep into the snow-covered banks. Without looking back, he returned to where the cattle grazed. Now even hungrier than before, he stuffed himself full.

Still, letting that lone one-armed giant live lingered. It was a knot nagging under his jaw.

CHAPTER 3

"YOU DID WHAT!" BRENWAR SAID, jumping to his feet.

Nath didn't want to tell him about the giants, but the dwarf was always good at knowing when he was holding something back. "It was as if I'd gone looking for them. They just appeared. Erupted, rather, right in the middle of the field."

Brenwar gripped his war hammer in front of his chest and started to stomp around the woodland.

"You can't fight giants without me. You just can't. It's wrong. Wrong." His hand tugged at his beard. "You should've come back and gotten me!"

"It was leagues away," Nath said, trying to sound reassuring. "Besides, they jumped me." He rubbed his jaw with his paws. "It wasn't an ordinary scrap, you know. They were tough. Caught me off guard, but I handled them." He puffed out a fire ring. "They're Nalzambor fertilizer now. Well, except one."

Brenwar turned and faced him. He lifted a brow. "One? What one?"

Nath inspected his dragon claws. *Is that a chip? Blast!*

Brenwar marched over and poked Nath in the leg with his hammer. "What! One!"

"Uh, the one I dropped off in the snowcaps. It won't be much of a bother now. And he's only got one arm left."

"You fool!" Brenwar blurted out.

Nath reared up. "What did you call me?"

Brenwar took a step back, glanced up at him, then glanced back down. "I apologize."

Nath sighed. Certainly Brenwar meant well, but things had changed. Nath was the ruler of the dragons now and had to be treated accordingly. An outburst like that would be costly in front of others. "You're fortunate no one else is around, aside from the trees."

"Punish me," Brenwar said. There was a sad tone in his voice. "It must be done. I never would have spoken to your father like that. And if I had, I'd have been ash."

"True. Either that, or he might have told you one of his hundred-year-long stories." Nath nudged Brenwar with his tail, knocking the stalwart dwarf over. "How's that for punishment?"

Lying flat on his belly, Brenwar said, "You're too merciful."

"Oh, am I? I guess I'll have to make the punishment more severe, then."

Brenwar took a knee and bowed his head. "As you wish, Sire."

Nath raised his tail to strike. Of course, he'd never harm a friend, even in the worst of cases. But still, he was the King Dragon now. Even on a rogue adventure, there had to be some form of order. Even for Brenwar, and the battle-hardened dwarven warrior knew that. Still, it made Nath uneasy. His stomach fluttered. He had subjects now, so things weren't the same as they had been. Brenwar and many others treated him differently now. It left him feeling isolated.

"First, Brenwar, tell me, why did you call me 'Fool'?"

"Er, the earth giants, well, they hold grudges. And they are tight knit. They'll summon all their clans to avenge their fallen. It would have been better if you'd killed them all."

"Has anyone ever made the right decision every time?"

"Your father did."

Nath huffed. It was hard to argue that his father Balzurth hadn't always made the right decision every time, seeing how Nath had never really seen his father do much of anything at all. However, of one thing he was certain: his father's word was without question. "Not that you have seen, anyway," Nath replied. "So, perhaps I'll revisit the snowcaps and finish what I started, then?"

"Don't bother, Sire," Brenwar said with an increasing frown. "He's long gone by now. I'm certain of it. Besides, we have things to do." His dwarven breastplate reflected the sun's light when he turned and faced what looked to be an abandoned temple of some kind. There, large piles of rubble and stone pylons had toppled over and become covered in overgrown brush. Brenwar started toward it, stopped, and said, "With your permission, of course, Sire?"

"Nath, Brenwar."

"Aye."

"And Brenwar, what about the earth giants. Is there truly a dire concern?"

"No doubt there will be," he said, pushing through the brush. "But it will take time. They aren't quick about such things. They'll plan, then strike. And all of Nalzambor will know."

"That sounds severe. I'd just as soon prevent it."

"Pah. If you wanted to prevent it ..." Brenwar's voice trailed off.

"Oh come now, Brenwar. Speak freely. Though I've often wished you had a bridled tongue, I value your wisdom."

Brenwar climbed up on a pile of busted stones and met Nath's dragon face eye to eye. "The giants couldn't have eaten all the cattle, could they?"

"Their bellies were quite formidable."

"You should have left well enough alone. Let them have their fill and moved on. But you couldn't, could you? Itching for a fight you were."

"And you wouldn't have been?"

"Of course. But I'd have planned it better. Let them eat, get fat, and be slow. They just bury themselves in the deep dirt again. They rest for years, even decades, you know. But now, they have a cause."

"Are you telling me my actions might have cataclysmic consequences?" Nath asked.

"Probably." Brenwar hopped to the ground and headed back into the ruins.

Nath lumbered in behind him. With ease he pushed the piles of rocks and fallen trees aside. "I think you're exaggerating, Brenwar. Just trying to teach me a lesson."

"We'll see," the dwarf said. "We'll see."

CHAPTER 4

BRENWAR TURNED HIS HEAD OVER his shoulder and gazed up at Nath Dragon. Over the decades, he'd gotten accustomed to Balzurth's mighty dragon frame. The king dragon's presence was warm and radiant, but one had to be mindful in his presence. Balzurth's very voice could shatter a man's bones.

Things were different now with Nath. His friend, covered in supine armored scales, had grown into nothing short of the magnificent presence that his father was. Nath was a beautiful work. A giant lizard that moved with cat-like grace. His voice was strong and reassuring. Nath was all the right things in one. Still, Brenwar's chest tightened. His heart ached. His best friend had grown up on him, and it wouldn't be long before he'd move on. Spend more time with his own kind. Brenwar was certain of it.

"Sire, er, I mean Nath, I'm going to venture into the bowels of the ruined mess, if that's all right by you?"

Nath's armored frame eased to the ground, becoming one with the mountainside. He eyed Brenwar and said with a yawn, "You do that, Brenwar. Just yell if you need me. Whew, those cattle sure were filling. I think I'll sit and listen to the birds for a bit."

"Well, don't fall asleep. The last time you went out, more than a month passed by." Brenwar hefted the war hammer over his shoulder. "And I'm not getting any younger. I've only a few hundred years still in me, if that."

"Oh, Brenwar, you'll never die. Your bones are too bitter for the grave."

"If you say so, Nath." Brenwar marched off. After he'd gone a few hundred yards, he began chucking away the stones that lay over some kind of buried entrance. With a grunt he pushed away a rock bigger than him and found himself gazing at a pewter portal wide enough for a large man to fit through. It was round and marked in ancient script. He didn't know the writing. There were two handles on it. He clutched his beard. "I sense treachery."

"What was that, Brenwar?" Nath said from far away. "Treachery, you say?"

"Probably nothing, just a marker. I'm assuming there's another vault below. Probably filled with goblin bones or some other kind of stupid." He started to tug on the handles. "I got it." He strained and grunted. The pewter door groaned but didn't give. "Ugh!" Brenwar spat on his hand and renewed his grip on the handles. He put his back and short, powerful legs into it. "Hurk!"

The door didn't yield.

"Perhaps I can help," said Nath's voice.

Brenwar turned and jumped half out of his boots. Nath's nose was in his face. "Quit doing that!"

"Doing what?"

"You know, sneaking." Brenwar ran his eyes up and down Nath's huge body. "I don't know how you do that, but it's aggravating."

"Maybe you're losing your hearing, Brenwar." Nath tapped his dragon claw on his temple. "Too many blows to the head, perhaps."

I'd like to give you a blow to the head, Brenwar thought.

Nath's golden eyes narrowed on him.

Brenwar swallowed.

"Here, let me try," Nath said. He wedged one claw under one handle on the pewter portal and popped it off with a flick.

A rush of stale air burst out.

Nath dangled the portal door in front of Brenwar's eyes. "Here you go."

"I loosened it for you." Brenwar leaned over and peered down into the hole. He said to Nath, "Don't suppose you can squeeze down in there, too, can you?"

Nath took a snort of air into his nostrils. "Nothing but the malodorous dead down there. You might want to be careful." He flipped the pewter portal door like a coin and watched it land on the ground. He eyed the markings. "Huh, these runes have patterns similar to some we've seen before. How old is Nalzambor, anyway?"

Brenwar rubbed his forehead with his fingers. That same question had often been asked. No one knew the answer for sure, but the dwarven histories dated back a few thousand years—and no further than that. "So you're saying you can't read it?"

"No, I can't. But I can only assume that it's a warning. You'd better be careful."

Brenwar peered back into the hole again. The last time he'd crawled into one, he almost hadn't made it back out. "You could come too, you know."

"But it's so agonizing to change back into a human. You know that. Besides, we'd be able to cover more distance if you'd just ride on my back," Nath said.

"Dwarves don't fly."

"I could insist that you do it."

"Well, I'd prefer you didn't." Out of his rucksack, Brenwar produced a tiny lantern attached to a string. He tapped on its side three times, and its fire came to life. Hand over hand, he lowered it into the hole. "Besides, I like long walks. You used to, too."

With a matter-of-fact tone in his voice, Nath said, "Those days are gone, Brenwar. I'm a dragon now. And we have a lot of ground to cover in this search for my mother. At this rate, it'll be a hundred years before we even find a clue. Of which, well, we have very little already." Nath slumped down on his belly. "Oh, I don't even know why I'm bothering. If my mother really is out there, you'd think she'd try to find me."

"You can't think like that," Brenwar said, eyeing Nath. He noticed a deep crease forming between the eyes and horns of Nath's head. "I'm sure if she could, she would."

"It's futile. It's been a year, and we haven't found a thing."

"Nothing is futile, not for a dragon such as you, anyway. And we have found some things."

Nath rolled over on his back and gazed up at the sky. "Sure, a bunch of old pottery from civilizations long past. How exciting. Huff."

Brenwar's stomach started to knot. Sure, he didn't want to fly on Nath's huge dragon back, but he didn't want the quest to find Nath's mother to end too soon, either. He enjoyed his adventures with Nath, but now, he felt those grand times were fading. Times that would never come back again.

"If you like, you can scan for some other sights. I don't think we'll find much here."

Nath didn't reply.

So far, their journeys had been pretty exciting and eventful for Brenwar. He enjoyed traversing into places he'd never been before. And they had a great system going, too. Flying above, Nath would scour the mountain ranges and pick up anything interesting with his keen eyes. They'd already found dozens of ruins and temples that were long forgotten. Brenwar had even dug up some lost treasures, and he liked that. But their search for signs of Nath's mother was fruitless, and they only had one clue to go on. It was a message that Balzurth had left. It said, "What you seek is in the peaks." That was all.

"I'm going in," Brenwar said, glancing back at Nath. "Don't run off, now." He dangled his legs over and found footing on the iron rungs inside. He began his descent. Something shot out from below and snagged his leg. *Thwiip!* "What in the—*ulp*!"

CHAPTER 5

NATH SAT UP. "BRENWAR?" TILTING his head, he picked up the sounds of a violent rustling down inside the hole. "Brenwar!"

"Nath!" his friend bellowed out.

Nath leaned over the portal. Something big darted out and jumped on his nose. It was a tarantula-like creature, but it had scales and a dragon's tail. The fangs in its mouth dripped with venom that sizzled on Nath's scales. Its many eyes, deep red and beaded, glared at him. It struck, sinking its fangs into his nose.

The venom burned.

Nath's eyes watered.

He snatched the dragon spider by the tail and slammed it into the ground. "You little fiend!"

The monster, about the size of Brenwar, zinged spider silk into a nearby tree and started to scurry away.

"Oh no you don't," Nath said. Like a mighty whip, he unleashed his tail. He smote the dragon spider across its back and smashed it into the ground.

The spider spat a ball of venom on Nath, stinging his toes.

"Ow. Blast you, insect!" He snatched up the dragon spider in his claws and squeezed.

Its body squished and crunched.

Nath wiped the dragon spider off his paws and onto the grasses.

Its scaly skin was intact, but the goo was squished out of it.

"Yuck."

"For Morgdon!" Brenwar bellowed from inside the hole.

The ground shook.

Krang!

Wary-eyed, Nath looked back inside the hole. The lantern was out, but Nath could make out something still moving below.

Suddenly, the lantern was aglow again and Brenwar held it in his hand. His shoulders were sagging.

"Brenwar, are you all right?"

Brenwar started up out of the hole. He was moving slowly, even for him. He emerged. His armor was splashed with dragon spider guts. He staggered over and leaned against a rock. War Hammer hung loose in his hand, and his breathing was heavy.

"Brenwar, you don't look well." Nath took a closer look. Brenwar's skin was pale. Clammy. "By the Flames! Your hand!"

The skin on Brenwar's hand was purple and bloated.

"Just a little spider bite," Brenwar mumbled. I'll be fine."

But Nath could tell that the dwarf was not fine. His friend and oldest ally smelled of decay. Nath narrowed his eyes and focused. With his special dragon sight, he could see that the spider venom was eating Brenwar up from the inside. It was happening at a very alarming rate. Oh no! Brenwar's arm was beginning to disintegrate!

"Brenwar, the chest! Get the chest!"

The dwarf fumbled with his belt pouch. His eyes were glassy, his pupils wide and dark black. He collapsed face first on the ground.

"Brenwar!"

Nath's heart raced. He rolled Brenwar over and tried to open up his belt pouch. His claws were far too big. *I've got to change. I've got to change now! Guzan!*

Changing back into a man took time and a great deal of concentration. If he did it more often, it wouldn't be so bad, but it had been a long time since he'd been a man.

Think, Dragon. Think!

A thought struck him.

He let out a dragon squawk. A call for help. "*Ka-Kwak! Ka-Kwak! Ka-Kwak!*"

In times past, the cry for help wouldn't have done him much good. The dragons had ignored him for the first two hundred years of his life, but those fences had been mended. He was their king now. He nuzzled Brenwar's body close to his.

Brenwar's eyes blinked rapidly.

"Hold on, Brenwar. Hold on."

Brenwar's forehead burst out in beads of feverish sweat. He let out a painful groan. "Ooooh!"

I've got to change. I've got to change. Holding Brenwar tight, Nath closed his eyes and started to meditate. Despite all his power, Nath hadn't often taken the liberty of exercising his gifts. In truth, he had many that he still needed to discover for himself.

Right now, he could only hope some other dragons could come to his aid, because by the time he changed, it would probably be too late.

Brenwar's thunderous heartbeat had slowed.

Come on, Nath. Change. Change!

"Squawk-Chirble!"

Nath's eyes popped open at the unforeseen sound. A small dragon, little bigger than a dog, stood on its hind legs at his feet. It was a green lily dragon, rich forest green with a paler shade on her belly. Her eyes were lashed, a golden brown, and pretty.

Nath spoke to her in Dragonese. "I need you to open his pouches. Search for a small box in there."

"I'd be honored to assist the Son of Balzurth, my liege Nath Dragon," she replied in a very polished Dragonese voice. Her tiny paws rummaged through Brenwar's pouches and produced a wooden chest just big enough for a large ring. "Is this what you seek?"

"It is," Nath said, eyeing it. It was Bayzog who had shrunk it down to that size. There was a particular word that would make it grow back to normal size, and Nath hadn't been paying attention when it was said. "Ah, forgive me, Brenwar. I can't remember the word."

The green lily cocked her head and said in the direction of Brenwar. "Is this dwarf important to you?"

"Of course. He's my friend."

"Why?" she said.

"Oh, it's a long story and we're running out of time. He's been poisoned." Nath sighed. "I fear he doesn't have much time. Blast my scales. I can't remember the word."

The green lily turned and faced him with her little paws clasped together. She looked like a princess on her hind legs. "Is there anything else I can assist you with, Dragon Prince?"

"I need the chest open. I need a cure for that dragon spider poison."

"I'm sorry, I can't help you with that," she said. "It was a pleasure to meet you. May I be dismissed?"

"What? No! I need you to administer the potions once I get the chest open. Ugh!" He slammed his tail hard into the ground.

Boom!

Brenwar's heartbeat continued to slow and weaken.

If Nath could have perspired, he'd have been covered in sweat.

This is my fault. All my fault. Here I am the king of the dragons, and I'm not even paying attention.

He let out a roar. "Maaarrroooooooo!"

"Nath Dragon," he said to himself out loud, "what have you been doing?"

CHAPTER 6

THE CHEST POPPED OPEN.

It started to grow.

Nath gaped. What had he said that triggered it? "All I said was, 'What have you been doing?'" His thoughts were strained. A bright moment hit him. "Been! It was Ben! They sound the same. Ha! How simple! I'm such a fool." Relieved, he gave the green lily her next orders. "See those vials? I need the yellow one."

The green lily picked up one of the vials from the drawers that folded out like an old fisherman's chest. She held it up. It was yellow and milky in color.

Nath shook his head and said, "No, the golden one."

She picked up another and held it out for display.

"No, the more golden one."

She sighed and plucked out the last possible candidate.

"That's it, now carefully pour it over his lips. He has to drink it down, all of it. Plus, he needs another." His eyes scoured the chest that was still plenty tiny to him. "Oh, I need something to battle the poison. Which one is it? Which one is it?"

There were more than thirty vials, in a multitude of colors. Bright purples and lavenders. Velvety red. Orange that was swirled with black. Others cracked with tiny lightning in the bottle. In truth, Nath had little need for such things these days. There wasn't anything he knew of that he couldn't handle himself. "Ah, I think it's that one. At least I hope it is. Feed him that one."

The green lily slipped out a vial that was filled with a mix of pink and gray. "Are you certain?" she asked with a furrowed brow.

Brenwar's heart had almost stopped beating.

"I have to be," Nath said. "I have to be."

The green lily climbed up on Brenwar's chest, removed the cork, and pulled back Brenwar's lips with her free hand. Carefully, she poured the entire vial into his mouth. She replaced the cork and said to Nath, "May I go now, Sire?"

Most dragons had no attachment at all to the other races. Of course, much of that could probably be explained because of their persecution. Still, it rubbed Nath the wrong way. Fighting back the urge to rebuke her in some fashion, he said, "Yes, go. And thank you."

Her wings fanned out. Her lithe frame leapt from Brenwar's chest and into the air. A few graceful flaps of her wings followed, and she was gone.

Dragons. I hope I never feel as they do.

Brenwar coughed and sputtered.

Nath leaned down and propped him up against a fallen log.

His friend's heartbeat had steadied, but it was still weak.

Come on, Brenwar. Come on.

It was a long night. A long week. Brenwar hadn't awakened. He breathed, shuddered, and coughed occasionally. Nath stayed close the entire time. He pushed over some trees and started a fire. He did his best to keep Brenwar free of the chills. Still in the full body of a dragon, he wrestled in thought whether he should turn back to a man or not.

If I had been in the form of a man, as Brenwar requested, I might have saved him.

He lay near Brenwar, watching his every movement. Counting the heartbeats in his chest. They were slow and steady. A good sign. Good enough for Brenwar to awaken by now, but he hadn't. It was puzzling. Frustrating.

This is my fault.

Nath realized he'd taken for granted his own power and forgotten about the fragility of the other races. Perhaps that was why dragons were so distant from the men and women of the world. They just didn't last as long. They didn't have the same protection. Their thin skins were nothing compared to a dragon's steel-hard scales. Their lives could so easily be snuffed out in an instant.

He put his paw on Brenwar's chest and felt its rise and fall. There was a rasp in his breathing. Nath didn't doubt that the dragon spider's poison had gone straight to the heart. If anything, it was a miracle that Brenwar lived. He could thank his dwarven constitution for that.

Should I take him to Morgdon? To the elves, perhaps. They have the best healers, but Brenwar would want to kill me if I did that.

Nath batted the idea back and forth, a hundred times if not a thousand. Yet he remained where he was, certain that Brenwar would wake up. And he didn't want to fly with Brenwar, either. It might prove too much of a strain, and Brenwar would be furious if he did. "I'd rather die than fly," Brenwar had once said. Nath chose to honor that.

So Nath waited and waited. He pondered their mission. The search for his mother. His father Balzurth had told him that he'd have the power to find her, but he'd given only the one tiny hint beyond that. Traveling with Brenwar was slow, but for a dragon, a creature that seemed to have all the time in the world, it wasn't so bad. Nath wasn't even two hundred and fifty years old yet, and he had at least two thousand more years to go. But so far, this adventure hadn't been quite as exhilarating as the ones before. Of course, the battle with the earth giants had been nice. The battle with the dragon spiders not so much. He eyed the portal.

Dragon spiders. Of all the luck.

That was another mystery that Nath had to ponder. Dragon spiders were just as rare as dragons themselves. Even rarer. They weren't all good or all evil, either. In many cases, they were guardians of precious things and even used by the dragons themselves. Oft times they could be found guarding dragon eggs while dragons hunted. But it took a great deal of power to employ the service of dragon spiders. And Nath was certain that they weren't in the portal by accident. Something meaningful, perhaps more so for men than for dragons, was in that vault.

Not that it matters. I'm sure it won't have anything to do with my mother. Probably some withered lich's treasure hoard.

Nath studied the hard lines in Brenwar's face. He knew every weathered crease. He was certain he'd caused at least a dozen of them himself. He'd even seen three new ones form during one conversation. Nath chuckled. "Hah, Brenwar. You wouldn't have any gray at all if it weren't for me. It suits you well, though. Now, wake up. If you don't, I'm liable to do something stupid. And you wouldn't want that, now, would you?" He listened to Brenwar's heartbeat.

It was slow.

Thump-thump … thump-thump … thump-thump …

"Boy, I think I can hear some giants nearby. Oh my, I can see them. Lords no! They are juggling dwarves!"

Thump-thump … thump-thump … thump-thump …

"Oh my goodness," Nath continued, "I thought I'd never see the day. My, how the world has changed since you took your name. Your sister, Ellgall, is finally going to marry. But her groom isn't of the standard groomsman fare. No, she's different. Of course you always knew that. Aye, I can see him standing at the altar waiting for her now, except he's much taller than a typical dwarf. But I'm sure it will work out. I just never thought I'd see the day when a dwarven maiden, your sister Ellgall, married an *orc*."

Thump-thump … thump-thump … thump-thump …

Nath's head hung low.

CHAPTER 7

ATH FLATTENED HIS BODY DOWN on the ground with Brenwar between him and the fire. He listened to his friend's heartbeat. He could feel it in his bones. Every beat seemed like the last, leaving him restless. And then—

Thump-thump-thump-Thump!

Brenwar's eyes popped open. His mouth parted. "Orc! Ellgall!" He sat upright. Bleary eyed, he looked around. "Where is the rotten beast?"

"Brenwar!" Nath said with elation. "You're back!"

The old dwarf scrambled to his feet, only to teeter over and bump his head on a log.

"You'd better take it easy," Nath said. With his tail he helped Brenwar to his feet. "Don't overdo it."

Brenwar blinked and slowly spun around. "Harrumph. I must have been dreaming. I don't see any orcs. Or Ellgall." He clawed at his beard, looked up at Nath, and said, "What happened?"

"The dragon spider's poison took you. About a week ago. I thought you were through."

The chestnut eyes under Brenwar's bushy brows popped wide. "A week!" His hands clutched at his beard. "Blast my beard! Why didn't you wake me up?"

"You know I certainly tried, Brenwar, but you were sleeping like a petrified log," Nath said, stretching his wings out a little and folding them back. "How do you feel?"

"Mmmmm, I'm so hungry I could eat an ogre."

"That can be arranged." Nath's serpentine head twisted around. His eyes scanned the surroundings. "I'd be happy to fetch some goats, or a stag."

"I can do it myself—Oof." Brenwar's face turned sour. He rubbed one hand through his beard, then rubbed his temples with his fingers. "Something feels funny." He held one hand in front of his face. It was the one the spider had bitten. There was no skin or muscle, only bone. "Gah!"

"Easy, Brenwar," Nath said. "I can explain."

"I'm dead, aren't I! You brought me back from the dead! Why did you do that? I deserve a proper burial. A grand tomb and plenty of rest!"

"You aren't dead, Brenwar. Again, let me explain."

Brenwar's eyes studied his one hand beside the other. His left hand was just fine, filled with strong, stubby fingers. The other, his right, was pure bone with big knuckles. He opened and closed it. His eyes filled with astonishment. He tipped his head up toward Nath. "What did you do?"

"Well," Nath said, coughing a little, "I may have gotten the potions mixed up a bit. Or perhaps the application was wrong." He made a remorseful face. "Seems I had you swallow what should have been applied, but it wasn't easy, and there wasn't much time. At least you live."

Brenwar's hard eyes filled with surprise. His brows clenched up and down. His eyes fastened on his skeleton hand. He mumbled something.

"What was that?" Nath asked.

In a low voice, Brenwar said something again. In Dwarven.

Nath's dragon lips turned up. "If I'm not mistaken, I think you said, 'like it.'"

Brenwar's eyes searched the area until they rested on War Hammer. He strolled over and picked it up with his skeleton hand. With a spark in his eye, he held it high in the air and said, "Wait until they see me in Morgdon! There's not a single dwarf in the great hall with a wound like this. Har!"

Taken aback a little, Nath said, "So you do like it?"

"Like it?" Brenwar growled. "I love it!" He brought the weapon's hammer-like head down, pulverizing some rocks. "Ah, the fear in the eyes that me and War Hammer will bring. Let's go find some giants!"

"Sure, but let's eat first." Nath eyed War Hammer. Handcrafted by Brenwar himself, it was a magnificent weapon. A hardened oak shaft hosting a burnished head of rune-marked steel. An axe head on one end and a mallet on the other. It was impressive, but something was missing. "You know, Brenwar, don't you think it's time that you gave War Hammer a real name?"

"It has a name: War Hammer. Mrrummaah in Dwarven. It's a fine name."

"I think that cleric of Barnabus was right. Something so exquisite needs a little more original name."

Brenwar scratched his head.

"For example," Nath continued. "It would be like me calling Fang Sword. Or you calling me Dragon. Er, well, bad example. Or me calling you Dwarf."

Brenwar's brow furrowed. Creativity wasn't part of his makeup. He found details such as the names of things mundane, not oft so important. Which was odd for a dwarf, because they had many sophisticated names. And some of them were almost as long as dragons' names for things. "What do you suggest?"

"Well, how about," Nath drummed his claws on his chin, "Crusher. It crushes a lot of things, does it not? Is there a word for that in Dwarven?"

"Hmmm, not really," Brenwar said, raking his beard. His rigid lips formed a smile. "But I can make it work. Mortuun..." The word went on for hours.

Finally, Nath said, "How about Mortuun for short?"

Brenwar grunted. "Aye. Now that you've made me go and think on it, Mortuun it is. Mortuun the Crusher."

CHAPTER 8

"DO YOU SEE ANYTHING INTERESTING down there?" Nath yelled down through the portal he had opened. Brenwar had climbed in an hour ago. Now that he'd eaten, he had a bounce in his step and had been eager to head back down. "Brenwar?"

Brenwar didn't reply, but Nath could still hear him shuffling through the tomb. There was a lot of scraping of stone over stone and the sounds of stone being bashed in with Mortuun, but apparently Brenwar hadn't found anything interesting.

"Watch out for dragon-spider nests!" Nath yelled back down. "You never know."

"And you'll never know," Brenwar fired back. His voice echoed up the tunnel, "unless you come down here yourself ... Sire."

"Humph." Keeping his ears tuned to the hole, Nath sat back down. He didn't sense any danger. Perhaps the dragon spiders had been the only "price to pay" for intruders trying to loot the ancient tomb. Quite adequate, for most intruders. And the dragon spiders could have been inside there for centuries. Maybe a millennium.

"I'm sure you can handle it, Brenwar Bone Hand."

Brenwar's rustlings came and went. There were tapping sounds on stones. Heavy grunts. Objects being shoved back and forth. It seemed Brenwar was deep in his search but not having much luck. It was possible that whatever needed to be found had been concealed by a spell. Nath could help with that, but the likes of Bayzog and Sasha would be better. *I wonder how they are doing. I bet Bayzog's had his nose stuck in a book ever since he returned to Quintuklen. What's left of it, anyway.*

Nath hollered down the hole, "Why don't you try a potion of finding or something?"

In a distant voice, Brenwar hollered back, "I don't need no potion."

The vault was deep. Nath figured it to be at least fifty feet straight down. And in some cases, the ancient vaults and tombs could go a hundred yards. They'd already come across a couple like that. And it was not that Nath was impatient. Pretty much all dragons were very patient, but Brenwar's searches could take months. Dwarves liked it down inside the earth.

Maybe I should change.

Nath grimaced.

But moving on two legs is so slow. And no wings? No way!

He scratched his dragon chin with his claw.

Hmmm, maybe I could turn into a man, and keep the wings?

He pondered the idea until the day turned into night and back into the day again.

Nah. Then I'd look like Sansla Libor. Or a draykis.

He sat upright. Cocked his head on his long serpentine neck.

Brenwar's booted feet were echoing off the portal's rungs and getting higher. His black-haired head popped up like a gopher out of the hole. Straining, he climbed out with a very heavy strongbox, half the size of him, in tow. Using two hands, he gave it a heave and dragged it out of the hole and onto the dewy grass. Breathing heavily, he said, "Found something."

"I can see that," Nath said, eyeing it.

It had handles on each side, like a chest, but there weren't any latches, key locks, or hinges. It was made of bright polished steel, which reflected the sunlight. To a mortal naked eye, it looked like nothing more than a block of solid metal.

Nath could make out a very narrow seam that looked like the lid. "That's one strange treasure chest."

"It was well concealed." Brenwar put his hands on his hips and stuck his chest out a little. "But I found it. No creature on Nalzambor can read the stones better than a dwarf. No sir." He held up his bony hand, marveling. "And none with a hand like this."

"Nothing compares to you, Brenwar. That's for certain. So the question is, how do we get this thing open?"

"Maybe we shouldn't open it at all," Brenwar suggested.

"Then why did you bring it up here?"

"Why? So you could look at it."

Nath rolled his eyes. "I am looking at it. I have to admit it's not like anything I've ever seen before. The craftsmanship is unique. Did anything down there give you any idea who created it?"

"I saw some markings. The tombs were all sealed, but I busted one open. There was nothing but powder and dust in there." He scratched his nose. "Whatever fed on them, it fed on them long ago. There were worm holes, too, but most of them had refilled."

"How many tombs?"

"A few dozen. Judging by the size of them, I'd say they were men. Not for certain, but I'd say it's a tomb of the unknown." Brenwar started scratching his back with his bony fingers. "Mmm, that feels good."

Nath didn't really have his hopes up to find anything new. After all, there were plenty of strange things all over Nalzambor. They'd never find them all. And this location, well, it seemed much older than what he'd be looking for. As far as finding his mother was concerned, he should be able to find something, somewhere, that wasn't much older than him.

"Brenwar, are you certain that you've never seen my mother?"

"Of course not. I didn't come onto the scene until you were a mature young boy. Well, not exactly mature, but you know what I mean."

"Yes, I know," Nath said, drooping his huge dragon head down. "Surely my father knows where she is. Wouldn't he know?"

Brenwar shrugged his brows. "I think he likes to leave things a mystery until the time comes that you should know."

"You'd think I'd know enough already, but I don't know any more than I knew a hundred years ago." He balled up his paw and brought it down on the rectangular chunk of metal.

Whummmm!

"There must be a million peaks to search on Nalzambor." Nath hit the block again and again.

Whumm Whumm Whumm!

The odd strongbox hummed.

Mrrrruum mummm mummm!

Its cold steel finish swirled with life.

Eyes widening, Brenwar stepped back, readying his war hammer and setting his shoulders.

"What's this?" Nath said with wary eyes.

The steel box started to brighten, the sun's light feeding it with white-hot power. Its radiance became stronger and stronger.

Nath's neck coiled back. His scales tingled. There was power. Ancient. Ominous. Threatening. "You'd better get behind me, Brenwar."

"You'd better get behind me," the warrior said. He raised Mortuun over his head and rushed toward the strongbox.

"Brenwar, no!" Nath said.

CHAPTER 9

Nath's tail lashed out quicker than a snake just as Mortuun the Crusher came down. He was a split second too late. The war hammer smote the strongbox with all powerful authority.

Krang!

The burst of sound slammed into Nath and everything else in all directions around the strongbox.

Nath's claws dug into the dirt.

Brenwar was knocked off his feet and tumbled head over heels.

Trees buckled and branches snapped.

Nath's ears were ringing, but other than that, he was unaffected. "Brenwar, what did you do that for?" He surveyed the devastated landscape. "Brenwar?"

"Up here," said a gruff voice. Brenwar was hanging upside down from a tree with his feet caught in the branches. Angry and somehow with Mortuun still hanging in his grasp, he started chopping with fury. "Let go of me, leafmaker!"

Nath started to make his way over.

The branches gave way.

Crack!

Brenwar tumbled down through the air and hit the ground hard. "Oof!"

"Are you all right?" Nath said, brushing aside the bushes his friend had landed in.

"I'm fine," Brenwar said, rolling up to his feet.

"I wasn't talking to you," said Nath. "I was talking to the bushes."

"Hah."

Nath turned away and returned his focus to the chest. Someone or something sat on top of it.

Brenwar stopped in his tracks.

Nath froze.

It was a woman of sorts. Beautiful. Exquisite. No bigger than a child human's, her lithe body was adorned in pink, white, and black fabric in marvelous patterns that flowed with nature. There were wings on her back, transparent, that caught the light. Her eyes were black, her face expressionless. In a soft but strong voice, she spoke in a language that Nath did not understand.

"Pardon?" he said in Common, somewhat mesmerized.

"Who are you?" she asked in the same tongue.

"I'm Nath Dragon."

She rubbed her head with her dainty hands, tousling her long white locks. "And who is this one that smote me?"

"Brenwar," Nath said, edging closer. He eyed her up and down. He'd never seen anyone like her before. Her loveliness rivaled that of the most winsome dragon. "And may I ask who you are?"

She scoffed. "Hah." She fanned out her pretty pink nails and yawned. She hopped off the chest and started shoving it across the ground until it dropped back in the hole. A loud bang echoed up out of there.

Bang! ang ang ang ang!

Nath glanced at Brenwar and found the dwarf staring back at him. They both turned back to the winged woman, and Nath said, "Are you a fairy?"

"Hah!" she said. Her fingers began dancing in the air. Suddenly, the cover to the portal lifted up over the ground and dropped back over the hole, sealing the portal. She spoke indistinguishable words. The round cover glowed with hot light, and its edges sealed. She dusted off her hands and turned back and faced Nath and Brenwar with her hands on her hips.

"You're drinking in my beauty, aren't you."

"I'm just wondering who you are," Brenwar said.

"I am whoever I want to be."

"Why were you imprisoned in there?" Nath asked, narrowing his eyes on her. If she was a fairy, then she was a very powerful one. And fairies often tricked one into doing their bidding.

Approaching Nath, she rolled up on her toes and stood as tall as one of the claws on his dragon-clawed feet. It should have been funny, her being so small, but somehow it wasn't. "You should have gotten the answer to that before you freed me." She showed a smile full of bright white teeth. "But, still, I am grateful to be free from my bondage. So much so, I will share my name with you, and with it comes the answer to any one of your questions."

"You know the answer to everything? Hah!" Brenwar said.

"I do." Her eyes shifted up to the right. Her face creased in concentration. Her toes sank into the ground. "Ah, that's better." She faced Brenwar. "Yes, I do, Brenwar Bolderguild. Five hundred and seventy-five years young, is it? Son of Ballor Bolderguild the Forgekeeper. Shall I go on?"

Brenwar looked like he had swallowed his beard.

"It's not often I've seen you stumped. Ha-ha!" Nath laughed. "And dare I ask what you know about me?" he said to her. "Oh, and what is your name, as you mentioned sharing it before."

"I am Lotuus, Nath Dragon. The Fairy Empress."

"Empress?" Nath lifted a brow. "That sounds important. I imagine there are many that have been missing you."

"In due time, I'll know." Her transparent wings fluttered and she rose up from the ground, coming to eye level with Nath. "Ah, you're the son of Balzurth. Seems I've been imprisoned longer than I imagined. It's so hard to tell the passing of time when I'm in a suspended state." Now her dark eyes gave him the once over. "You certainly are a magnificent dragon. It seems much has happened since I've been gone. So, please, ask me a question. I can sense something deep is on your heart."

"It was Brenwar who freed you, not me," Nath said, eyeing his friend. "Answer a question of him."

Lotuus chuckled. Her laugh was as light as feathers. "Oh, no, no, no. It was your touch, not his, that lifted the seal from me. You are magical, Nath Dragon. You are power without end. It was you who freed me. Not him."

"And you can tell me anything I want to know?" Nath withheld the suspicion from his tone.

She nodded.

He didn't want to insult her, but he doubted she could tell him the answer to any question. He didn't even think his father could do that. Hm. Come to think of it, his father had long ago told Nath there was a spirit world that couldn't be trusted.

Balzurth had said, "Be wary of their tricks. Seek wisdom, not shortcuts. The key to knowledge comes from the paths less taken."

Lotuus seemed harmless enough, though. What harm could come from playing her game? Nath thought he had nothing to lose and only something to gain. At least this was entertaining. She was so marvelous and pretty.

"Give me a moment," Nath said, putting his clawed paw to his huge dragon forehead to indicate he was thinking of a question.

CHAPTER 10

LOTUUS HUFFED.

Brenwar scowled. "Nath. Come."

Nath walked his monstrous frame over. "What is it?"

"I smell treachery." Noticing Lotuus spying on them, Brenwar turned his back to her. "Maybe she was imprisoned for the right reasons."

"Maybe she was imprisoned for the wrong reasons."

"I can sense your doubt," Lotuus said. "As the Fairy Empress, I find it a bit degrading. I tell you what. I'll let the dwarf have a question and you as well. After all, how hard can a dwarf's question be to answer?" She floated closer and stared down at Brenwar. "I bet I can guess your question myself. Let's see. Aha! You want to ask which ingredients make the best ale!"

Brenwar shuffled back. His expression was priceless. "No I don't. No I don't."

"Come on, dwarf, then ask me something," she said.

"All right, fine then. Where is Nath's mother?"

Nath's heart pounded in his horns.

"Oh, that's easy," Lotuus said, drifting back down to the ground. "She's in Nalzambor, of course."

Brenwar slapped his face with his bony hand. "Gah! Sorry, Nath!"

Nath's excitement deflated. His swaying tail came to a stop. "Way to go, Brenwar."

"She could've answered more than that," Brenwar whined. "She's a clever one, she is. They all are. I say don't waste your breath, Nath. She doesn't know where your mother is."

Feet barely touching the ground, Lotuus walked through the forest and sat down in a small bed of flowers. She plucked a purple flower and gave it a sniff. "Any second now."

Be smart, Nath. She might be the Fairy Empress, but you're the King Dragon.

He started to weigh the pros and cons of his question. Perhaps asking where his mother was would be a selfish question. Maybe there was something more important that he should ask, such as "What or who is the greatest threat to Nalzambor?"

That wouldn't be a bad one. I could just take them out now, before they expected it.

Nath reflected on what his father had told him about his mother again: "What you seek is in the peaks." He glanced over at Brenwar.

The grumpy fighter slowly shook his head.

Just because you blew it the first time, that doesn't mean I'll blow it the second time. Besides, we've been searching for a year. This is the best opportunity we've had. Just don't waste it, Dragon. Ask your question carefully.

He cleared his throat.

Lotuus looked up at him. "So, the King Dragon, ha-hah, is ready to ask the question." She rolled her eyes. "Oh, how I can't wait to hear it."

"I am ready," Nath said in a strong and confident voice. He lowered his massive horned head and came face to face with her. "Are you ready?"

Lotuus's black pupils enlarged. "Oh, certainly." She rose to her feet and shuffled back in the flower bed. "My ears are to hear. My lips to assist. It would be an honor, King Dragon. Please, go ahead."

Nath fanned out his huge claws and studied them with admiration. Each claw was about as big as Lotuus. He caught her eyes on his paw. He saw her swallow and drift back a little farther. "Come closer, Lotuus," he said.

"Uh, why?"

"I want to make sure you can hear me. I wouldn't want my question to be misinterpreted." He opened up his paw and lowered it to the ground. "Hop on."

"My hearing is excellent. I'm fine right here."

Nath took in a deep breath. The furnace inside his chest started to glow. He put a little thunder in his voice. "Hop on!"

Head down, Lotuus floated over, saying, "Yes, Majestic Majesty."

Nath raised her up to eye level and said, "I like the sound of that. Now, I think you were about to reanswer my companion's question. A lot more specifically."

"I was?" Lotuus said.

Nath's eyes narrowed. His claws started to close around her. "I'm certain of it."

She made a pleading look toward Brenwar.

His stern expression was the same as a petrified stump.

"Southern Nalzambor?"

"That's awfully vague," Nath said, closing his claws around her even more. "Perhaps a landmark to go with it."

Eyeing the claws that had closed around her like a cage, she said to Nath, "Am I being threatened?"

"No, you're being protected," Nath said with deadly reassurance. "Very dangerous creatures lurk about. And I'd hate to see anything happen to you, Fairy Empress."

"I see. And I thank you, but I am quite capable of taking care of myself." She placed her hands on his claws. "And I doubt any hostile forces would dare threaten me with you around."

Nath's dragon lip curled back. Not by his own will but rather as a reaction.

There was magic power in Lotuus's touch. Formidable. Mysterious. It was said the fairies and dragons were the earliest creatures in Nalzambor. Both came long before the other races. And Lotuus was much older than he was.

But he was a dragon and she was just a fairy. He turned up his inferno within.

Lotuus's hands jerked back, and she winced. "Borgash," she said.

"I beg your pardon," Nath said, "I didn't quite hear that."

"The lost city of Borgash. What you seek is in there." Shoulders slumped, she said, "May I go now? I long to see my kin."

"You've answered his question, but you have not answered mine," Nath said.

"But," Lotuus stammered.

"But," Nath said, raising a brow. "If you agree, then I'll hold my question for you to answer when I summon you later. Agreed?"

Her little body stiffened. Finally, with a scowl she said, "Agreed."

Nath opened up his claws. "Be well on your journey."

Lotuus spread out her transparent wings and said with a sneer, "Good luck staying well on yours." Her wings buzzed, and up into the air she went, disappearing into the sunlight.

"Clever," Brenwar said, toting Mortuun over his shoulder. "I hadn't seen that side of you before."

"You don't think I crossed the line, do you?"

"With a fairy? Har! There is no such line with them. I think you did well. And she still owes you one. I bet she hates that."

I bet she hates me, too.

CHAPTER 11

"How about we get you a horse, Brenwar?"

"No."

"Aw." Nath shook his head. He'd spent the last three days slugging through the lands with Brenwar in tow. He could have flown back and forth to Borgash ten times by now. Easy. "Well, you can't blame me for being eager. If you'd never met your mother, wouldn't you be anxious to get on with it, too?"

"Sire, er, I mean Nath..." Brenwar stopped along the edge of the stream and began refilling his canteen. "Don't put your faith in fairies. Trust in what you know and see."

"Are you saying since I haven't seen my mother, I shouldn't believe she's there?" He dipped his head in the cool waters and gulped in some water and a few small fish. "I've heard of many things that I've never seen, yet I still trust that they exist."

"That's not what I mean." Brenwar put the canteen to his lips, gulped down the water, and started refilling it again. "Just enjoy the journey. Like you used to. Sometimes there are clues along the way. You might have great eyes, but you still can't see everything from up there."

"I think it's best that I maintain a low profile. I can't exactly pass through forests like a cat anymore."

"You could if you'd change," Brenwar argued. "Pah! Forget it. Tell you what, if you want to go on forward as fast as you can, then go ahead. I'll catch up. Eventually."

"No," Nath said, wading into the stream. It was almost deep enough in the middle to cover his entire body. "Hmm, maybe this is a good way to travel."

"Humph."

Nath pushed up the stream. Brenwar followed along on the bank.

I do want to hurry on ahead, but I won't. I've learned my lesson.

Nath certainly had the authority to get Brenwar to do whatever he wanted, but he wouldn't use it. For one thing, Brenwar wasn't a dragon, so he didn't really have to listen to the Dragon King. But the dwarf had given an oath to serve Balzurth, and that oath had been passed on to Nath. And at the same time, Nath felt obligated to keep an eye on Brenwar. The dwarf had a noticeable hitch in his step that hadn't been there before Nath's last long sleep. Brenwar's pace was almost a half step slower than it used to be. The dwarf, though just as formidable as any that lived, was so much more fragile than Nath.

"What are you staring at?" Brenwar said, glaring at Nath.

"Oh, was I staring? Sorry, Brenwar. I was just admiring your hand. I think your kin will glorify it."

Brenwar's shoulders lifted. He held his hand high and gazed at it. "It is something. Ha! I can't wait to show them. I bet they start a statue of me right away."

"I agree." Nath had a thought. "You know Brenwar, Morgdon isn't so far away. Why not stop by for a visit? You haven't even been home since Gorn Grattack has fallen. For all you know, they have a statue of you already. It wouldn't surprise me a bit if Pilpin jumped right on it."

Brenwar came to a stop on the bank. His boots sank a little in the sands. Hard eyes fixed on Nath's, he said, "What are you getting at?"

"Nothing. I just thought maybe you, or we, should celebrate, before we dive too deep into other things."

A swarm of pink-feathered swans swam by and honked at Nath.

Haaaank! Hank hank hank!

"I'm certain what we're about to get into will be treacherous. You had one really close call already."

Brenwar's eyes narrowed into slits. His good hand became white knuckled on Mortuun's shaft. "You're coddling me."

"No, never."

"You are!" Brenwar set his shoulders and marched away from the stream and back into the woods.

Under his breath, Nath said, "Well, maybe I was." He eased his way out of the stream and spread his wings. He yelled after Brenwar, "Well, I could use some fresh air anyway." After gathering his legs underneath him, he launched himself into the air. In seconds he was hundreds of feet up and soaring like a big scaly bird. "That's better."

Below, he couldn't see Brenwar, but he knew the dwarf's scent all too well. He was never hard to find, and Brenwar never tried to hide from anybody, either.

Nath spent hours up, traveling miles at a time, back and forth. He scanned the horizon and the landscape, too. He was very in tune with Nalzambor. More so than he used to be. His intuition was incredible. His senses were so acute he could tune into activity inside an ant hill.

Ah, it's great to be me.

He widened his circle, staying just within the belly of the clouds. He didn't want to terrify any townsfolk or farmers. They'd been through plenty, thanks to the likes of the armies of Barnabus. They were just getting their lives in order. Nath was privy to that. He could hear their hammers pounding. Saws cutting through the fallen timbers.

And stew was cooking somewhere always, not to mention the buttery biscuits. His mouth watered. Drool fell from his lips.

Now that, I do miss. I wish someone could make biscuits big enough for me. And it wouldn't be so bad gulping down a river full of stew sometime. I have to hand it to humans: they make the finest dishes.

A glimmer of movement caught his eye. A dark wink. A nasty twinkle. A small flock beat their wings nearby in a V formation. Thirteen of them.

Those aren't birds. Birds aren't that big, and they don't have tails like that!

Nath flapped his wings harder.

They have scales. Not the likes of which I've ever seen before, either. Great Guzan! What are they?

Closing in, Nath let out a squawk.

HrrAWk!

The dragon in the rear, the size of a long-tailed pony, turned its head. It was flat like a snake's, hornless, with slanted ruby eyes that glimmered with hate. It opened up its mouth and let out an angry hiss.

Hhusssssssssss!

A pair of forked tongues snapped in and out of its mouth. It turned away and squawked up to the others.

Hrawk.

I don't understand what it's saying.

One by one, the other dragon heads turned and stared at Nath. Their pulsating red eyes bore into him.

Brash, whatever they are.

The dragon in the rear let out another frightening squawk.

Hrawwwwwwk!

In the blink of an eye, they stopped in midair in attack formation. Claws and teeth bared, they made straight for Nath Dragon.

Sultans of Sulfur!

CHAPTER 12

THE WICKED BROOD OF DRAGONS darted straight into Nath's path.

He spat out a ball of fire.

The lead dragon veered right.

Half of the ranks followed.

The other section of the formation went left.

The fireball sailed in between.

They're quick!

Screeching, the dragon brood flanked Nath and started to close in.

Let's see how fast they really are.

Nath pointed his head toward the earth, pumped his wings, and dove. He cut through the air, a scaly knife in the sky, reaching amazing speeds. Folding his wings behind his back, he dove faster. The wind whistled between his horns, making an eerie howl.

Eoo oo oo oo oo

I'm fast. I like it!

Daring not to glance behind him, Nath focused on the ground rushing up to greet him. He aimed his body like a giant missile toward the rocky hilltops, where the hill goats began to scatter.

Get it right, Nath, or you'll be dragon goo.

Chin out and horns back, he watched certain death coming to greet him. Jagged rocks waited like a mouthful of broken teeth, enlarging in an instant.

Now!

He spread his wings and pulled up, straining with all his might. Rocks scraped over his belly and tail.

Made it!

Soaring away, he glanced back over his wings. Three of the dragon brood had slammed into the hillside. Rock and debris exploded.

Boom! Boom! Boom!

Nath found the other dragons hovering nearby in the sky. Their eyes were full of malice. They let out angry shrieks, and their mouths glowed like red-hot flames.

Beating his wings, Nath hovered in the sky, looking down on all of them. "I don't know what you are or where you came from, but wherever that was, I'm going to make you wish you had never left." He unleashed a geyser of fire. It streamed out of his mouth and exploded, coating some of the smaller dragons in white-hot flames.

Their pain-filled screeches could have shattered glass as they writhed in the sky.

Eeeak! Eak Eaak Eeeeaaaaaak!

"That's only a sample of what I have in store for—Agh!"

From out of nowhere, razor-sharp talons dug into his back. A knot of four dragons latched onto him like leeches. Fangs bit into Nath's hard scales. Liquid fire dripped like venom from their mouths, causing him excruciating pain.

Nath let out a tremendous roar.

"RAWR!"

And then he turned loose his own assault. The end of his tail coiled around one dragon's neck and ripped it free of him. Using it like a club, he started swatting away at the others.

Whop! Whop! Whop!

He knocked one more off his legs, but two more latched on. Wings beating with fury, Nath fought to keep up in the air.

Rising higher, two more dragons darted in and attacked his wings.

Nath lost control and tumbled through the sky. Battling for his life, he hit the hillside hard.

Whoom!

"Enough of this!" Nath yelled in Dragonese. Eyes hot with fire, he unleashed his vision heat on the first dragon he saw. The beams of light turned the creature's dark armored scales to ash, leaving only a pile of bones. Ignoring the burning sensation of claws and teeth digging into him, he reared back his head and struck like a snake. His jaws clamped around another dragon's neck. With tremendous force, he bit down and broke its neck.

The dragon brood went into a frenzy. They struck and bit. Spat out small geysers of flame. They latched onto Nath's chest and coiled their tails around his great neck.

Unrelenting, Nath and the brood thrashed through the hill. Trees snapped under their weight. The branches caught fire.

Nath stomped one dragon's face in the dirt.

Another dragon spat hot flames in Nath's eye.

Nath snatched it by the neck and with his breath, he turned its head to ashes. He huffed for breath. The strain of battle was starting to take a toll on him. His inner flame was going dim.

Don't these things give up or tire? I've already killed six of them!

The evil throng battled on. Their teeth and claws were tiny razors digging deep in between his scales. They were merciless, and Nath was covered in them.

He bit one's tail and slung it off his back.

Another dragon whipped his eye with its tail.

"Argh!"

Nath made it pay. He slammed it into the ground and pulverized it under his paws.

Back and forth they battled, the dragon versus the drag-ons.

Nath matched their savagery with his own. They were strong and quick. He was stronger and quicker. But their numbers gave them the advantage. They stayed latched onto his arms. His legs. His wings. They started taking him apart a tiny piece at a time. Their fiery venom crept in between his scales and into his flesh.

Nath unloaded one more blast of fire, vaporizing two more of them.

Eight down! At least I think so.

His great strength had faded. He felt drained. His sight started to dim.

This can't be happening to me. I'm the King Dragon.

CHAPTER 13

FIGHTING TO STAY AWAKE, NATH'S mind went through his known cache of abilities, but it was sluggish. Even the pain had begun to subside.

I have to get these things off of me before they drag me off somewhere. Or eat me!

He pushed up off the ground and belly-rolled over, crushing one of them underneath his girth. Still, his limbs became heavy. He flailed his tail but couldn't get a sense of where it was going. A dark shadow fell over them.

"Screeeeeeech!" the dragon brood cried out in unison.

Guzan! What now?

Through blurry eyes, Nath saw a black-winged bulk drop out of the sky.

It landed hard on the ground.

Oh no! They come in bigger sizes!

It closed in on Nath.

With tremendous strain and effort, he closed in on it.

One of the smaller dragons darted in between them and shot out some fiery breath.

The bigger dragon swatted it away with its tail and began pummeling it into the dirt.

Wap! Wap! Wap!

The bigger dragon finished it off with a blast of scorching fire.

"Huh?" Nath said, barely able to keep his eyes open.

The big black dragon's head whipped around just in time to confront another small attacking dragon. With its breath, it turned the little serpent into dust. Then the huge black dragon spoke to Nath in Dragonese. "Get up and fight, Lazy Bones!"

Nath's head perked up. His dragon heart began to race. "Selene?"

The big black dragon ripped a smaller one off his hide, smashed its bones into the ground, and said, "Do I really need to answer that?"

Charged up with renewed energy, Nath tore another small dragon away from his arm with his tail. He bashed it into the rocks until it moved no more.

Selene continued to rip them off of him and then crush them with her mighty paws or use her breath weapon and turn them into pixie dust.

In less than a minute, all the hostile dragons were dead.

"Gather them in a pile," she said.

"Why?" Nath said, shaking out the cobwebs inside his head.

Sarcastically she said, "Oh mighty King Dragon, will you please just do as I say." With her mouth she dragged one across the ground and into another, starting the pile. "And don't miss any."

Wary, Nath did as she asked. Strange dead dragons were piled up before them. "So, now what?"

Selene opened up her great mouth and covered them in flame.

The pile burned and popped. Nath fought the urge to cover his nose. The stench watered his eyes. The dragons burned—scales, horns, bones, and all—until there was nothing but ash left.

Finally, he said, "What did you do that for? Now I'll never know what they are."

"You almost weren't going to know anything else ever again, King Dragon."

Nath approached her with a smile.

Covered in black scales with a long, sensuous tail, Selene was the most beautiful dragon he'd ever seen. Her lashed violet eyes were radiant beneath her exquisite crown of horns, streaked with silver.

Heart pounding inside his chest, he said, "Thanks, Selene. It's good to see you. I didn't think you could stay away from me forever anyway."

"Hah!" she laughed. "Me, seeking you? Nothing could be further from my quest."

He frowned. "Quest? What do you mean, quest?"

Selene's violet eyes drifted onto the pile of ash. "Tracking down these vermin and killing them."

Irritated, Nath fixed his eyes on her. "So you know what they are, then?"

"Sadly," she said, neck drooping a little. "I do. They are called wurmers."

"Wurmers? What tongue is that?"

Without batting an eye, she said, "An ancient one. Long forgotten until … sometime around now."

Nath spread out his wings and winced. Turning his head around, he noticed one of his wings was dangling. "Blast!"

Selene's eyes widened. "That's a horrible wound. You should be more careful."

"Thanks, Selene. I'll remember that the next time I'm assaulted by a bunch of renegade dragons." He snorted. "Don't guess I'll be flying anywhere too soon. It should make Brenwar happy." He focused his attention on Selene. "You were saying these things had been long forgotten until sometime around now. So you knew of them?"

Sitting back on her haunches and clicking her clawed front paws together, she said, "Let's just say I've encountered them before."

Nath's eyes narrowed. "Is this something that Gorn Grattack had a hand in? That you had a hand in?"

"Yes and no."

"That's not an answer, Selene. And I don't like it. What do you know about these creatures? And how in Nalzambor did they get here?" He brushed his tail through their remains. "And is it bad that I killed them?"

"Don't fret, Nath," she said. "The wurmers are more dragon-like than dragon. They aren't flesh and blood like other life on Nalzambor. That I'm certain of."

Nath eased his tone. "Well, that helps a little. Keep talking." He half flapped his broken wing. "I'm not going anywhere soon."

"The wurmers are a creation of other evil mages and clerics who preceded Barnabus. They hated dragons, and through their collective efforts they created a creature to slay dragons. They used dragon parts and magic and turned them into bloodless, living things, like insects."

"Oh, I see," Nath said. "Isn't that pretty much what you did with the draykis? How many of them are still running around?"

"I'm pretty sure there aren't any."

"Pretty sure, well," Nath said, rolling his eyes, "that's reassuring."

"Don't be smug."

"I'm sorry, Selene, but this stinks of your old dealings, and let's face it. You haven't been around. There's no telling what you've been doing or who you've been doing it with."

Selene's eyes became bright as fire. "Nath! How dare you suggest?"

"I'm the Dragon King, and I'll suggest what I will. I have an entire world to protect."

"Well, you weren't doing a very good job of it a few moments ago—unless you were going to protect it as new fertilizer!" She spread her wings. "Good luck to you. I'll resume this quest on my own." Her feet started to lift from the ground.

CHAPTER 14

ATH SNATCHED HER TAIL AND pulled her back down. Calmly. "You aren't going anywhere, Selene. Sorry. Just tell me more."

The flames behind her eyes subsided, and she continued her story.

"Yes, the Clerics of Barnabus sought to employ the wurmers in our cause, but dealing with them proved difficult." She sighed. "Very difficult."

"How so?" Nath said, brushing his tail against hers.

"They're mindless things that don't discriminate. They'd attack any dragon, good or bad. Both Kryzak and I tried to find ways to control them, but everything failed. I even have some scars to show for it." She ran her claws over her side. There were some gashes in her scales that had never fully healed. "Kryzak actually saved me. After that, I came up with the draykis. They were my creation. I could control them. But the wurmers, they come from another time. A different magic. I told Kryzak to destroy them. Their larva. Their nests. I was very disappointed when I found out that he didn't."

Nath reached over his shoulder and plucked a torn wurmer claw out from between his scales. Eyeing it, he said, "They are nasty things. How many have you hunted down?"

"Thousands."

Unable to contain his surprise, Nath said, "Thousands!"

"Give or take a few hundred," she added.

"You should have sought me out, Selene. How many of these things do you think are out there?" He stomped his paw into the ground. "And being the King Dragon, I need to be informed of any dire threats to this world."

"Don't stiffen on me, Nath. If you were so worried about any threats, you'd be back at Dragon Home. Instead, you are on a personal quest—which," she said, eyes saddening a little, "I don't blame you for."

"Regardless, Selene, you should tell me, especially when you are putting yourself in danger." His tail glided up around her shoulders. "I wouldn't want anything bad to happen to you."

Her eyes drifted down over his tail and then found his. "Really? And why is that?"

Nath swallowed. Nothing in Nalzambor intimidated Nath, but Selene did. Not as a threat but as a woman. A grand one. And his attraction to her was powerful. But he didn't know how to tell her that. "Because … you're my friend."

Selene's eyes drifted away, and she let out a huff of smoke. She walked out from underneath his tail. "Oh, I'm elated to know that. And as for the wurmers, the amount I've destroyed isn't so big. As a matter of fact, these are the biggest I've seen." Her brow creased. "I've mostly found unhatched nests. You see, the wurmers start out in a larva stage. Much like insects. I find them and destroy them."

"How many more do you think are left?"

"Hard to tell. I found one of the original lairs, but I think there are many more. Especially after seeing a group as big as this flying around." She swatted her tail through the charred remains. "But these are drones. Which is good. The females lay the eggs. One female, rather. Perhaps a queen for every nest."

"So they are like the bees?"

"No. Bees produce honey; wurmers produce death." She continued, "Nath, now that the Clerics of Barnabus no longer hunt them, the wurmers will multiply fast. If they get out of control, they'll swarm all of Nalzambor like locusts. Nothing will remain."

Nath tried to get close again, but Selene shifted away. Aggravated, he said, "If it's so serious, you should take some other dragons with you, then."

"It's my responsibility. I'll handle it on my own."

"I insist," Nath said.

"I still have allies aside from yourself," she said.

"Really, who?"

"You focus on your mission, and I'll focus on mine," she said. "And I wish you well on your quest to find your mother."

"Selene, don't rush off. Please. You just got here."

"The wurmers are serious business, Nath."

"Just for a little while. Please?" he said, forming a long face. "All I've been doing is traveling with Brenwar, and it's not the same … as it used to be. It's hard being a dragon when all your friends are mortal."

"That's why dragons don't get so close to the mortals. But you'll get used to it."

"I'm not sure that I want to get used to it."

"You can't have the best of both worlds. You are meant to rule the dragons, not the other races as well. They'll be just fine without you, Nath."

"I suppose."

"And if you spent more time among your kind, I'm certain you'd be enlightened." She ran her tail under his chin. Her eyes smiled into his. "But I envy you, Nath. You understand what it's like to be both man and dragon. And you have true friends among all the races. Consider it a precious gift. It will give you wisdom that others have never had."

"If you say so." He flexed his bad wing again. "Honestly, please stick around. Not being able to fly is going to be hard enough. And I'm never going to hear the end of this from Brenwar."

"You're such a child sometimes," Selene said, "but lucky for you I like it. So I'll come along, but only for a bit."

Yes! Pulling his shoulders back and heading back down over the hillside with a bounce in his step, Nath said, "Well, come on, then."

On foot it took a few hours to get back to the general area where he'd last seen Brenwar. Putting his nose to the dirt, it wasn't long before Nath found his oldest friend's scent. "It won't be long now." But an hour later, Nath lost the scent. A sinking feeling crept into him. "Selene, do you smell anything?"

She shook her head. "I sense nothing."

CHAPTER 15

THE VANISHING OF BRENWAR MADE for a long day—and days were usually nothing to a dragon. Nath ripped another tree out of the ground and flung it away.

"Nath," Selene said, "You can't check underneath everything. Least of all the roots beneath the trees. I'm certain there's a reasonable explanation for it." She stroked his back with her tail. "Take a breath and let things come to you."

Nath pushed some moss-covered boulders aside. Worms and insects scurried deep into the dirt. "Ah!" He rolled the rocks back into place. "Blast!"

"Nath, we will find him," Selene said, being reassuring. "I'm certain of it."

He wanted to agree with her, he really did, but Brenwar's disappearance left him feeling empty inside. Guilt swelled inside him. He couldn't bear the thought of losing his friend again. After all, Brenwar had almost died once already. Looking at Selene, a thought occurred to him. He couldn't help but let it out. With wary eyes he said, "It's been a strange series of circumstances."

Selene sat back on her haunches, crushing the brush underneath her tail. "What do you mean?"

"Well, let me put it together for you. I get a clue about where to find my mother. Not long after that, the wurmers show up, followed by the sudden appearance of you, and now Brenwar disappears."

Selene's dragon face darkened. "Are you suggesting I had something to do with this?"

"A wise king wouldn't rule out the possibility."

"A wise king wouldn't insult his friends!" she fired back.

"Oh yes, a friend who created the draykis, who was willing to let loose the wurmers on dragonkind." He shook his head. "Huh. Not to mention that you don't want any help. Look, Selene, you have to admit, is that not the least bit suspicious?"

She leaned toward him and said with her razor-sharp claws extended, "I ought to rip your tongue out. I just saved your life, you fool."

"Fool!"

Nose to nose, she added, "Do I need to say it in the seven languages to you?"

He bared his teeth. "You do not speak to me that way!"

"And you shouldn't speak to anyone that way."

"Hah! Like you care! This, coming from someone who killed if someone batted an eyelash at you. And you dare to judge me?"

Air rife with tension, Selene cut loose. Her tail lashed out, smiting Nath across his cheek.

Whap!

Nath shook it off. His eyes blazed with fury. He rose up to his full height, towering over her. "Why did you do that?"

"Because if you unleashed one more insult like that, I was going to try and kill you."

"Really?" Nath growled.

"Really!" Selene said, bumping her horns against his.

Clack!

Nath's temper boiled over.

Somewhere deep inside him, his conscience said, *Nath, what are you getting so mad for?*

He couldn't control it, though. His inner volcano was erupting. The fires in his chest wanted to explode. "You better get out of here, Selene. I think I've had enough of you."

Taken aback, she scooted away. There was hurt in her eyes. She spread her wings. "Fine. Fine, then, Nath. Good-bye." In one powerful flap, she took to the sky.

Nath clutched the horns on his head. *What am I doing?* "No, wait! Selene, come back!"

She was little more than a speck in the sky now. An ash drifting away.

He spread his own wings and cried out in pain. "Ow! Blast my busted wing!"

Hours later, Nath had made his way deep down inside a ravine. He'd pushed himself far into the brush overhanging the creek. His temper had long cooled, and now he hid from the world with a belly full of regret.

What in the world got into me? That was no way for a king to behave. Selene was right about that.

Sulking, he raced through the scenarios on how to make things right.

How am I supposed to apologize to someone who will probably never want to see me again? I can't fly. I've lost Brenwar. Now that's two people I have to find. Him and my mother. Not to mention there is another threat to Nalzambor. What do I do?

He closed his eyes and let it all soak in. Everything had happened at once. A sudden storm. A turn of the tide. At the moment, missing Brenwar hurt even more than losing Selene. Brenwar was his rock. The dwarf would have something to say that Nath needed to hear. But hadn't Selene?

Aw, I mess everything up.

Things were different than before now that he was a dragon. He was still getting used to it. He needed to focus on the best way to find Brenwar first. Another part of him wanted to be with Selene.

Think, Dragon, think!

He recalled a conversation that he'd had a long time ago, before he and Bayzog had parted. The part-elven wizard had given him some advice. "When in doubt, ask yourself what your father would do."

Yes, what would my father do?

He envisioned Balzurth's mightier red dragon frame sitting on the throne within the great treasure chamber. His father's eyes were often closed, but he was always aware of everything around him. Not even a mouse escaped his attention.

Come on, Nath, you're the greatest tracker in all the lands. At least you used to be. Think of your father. Think of something. How hard can it be to find Brenwar?

He thought back to when he was much younger. Back when he spent more time with his father. It was just the two of them most of the time: hunting, fishing, and feasting together. Both of them would lie down with a bellyful and count the stars in the sky.

But every once in a while, another dragon would come by and share news with Balzurth, speaking into his father's ear. Balzurth would nod, grunt a little, and send the dragon messenger on its way. Those were good, good times.

Nath's eyes snapped open.

I've got it!

CHAPTER 16

ATH RETURNED TO THE SPOT where he'd lost the scent of Brenwar. There was nothing extraordinary about it. It was just another stretch of woodland and heavy brush.

All right, someone around here must have seen something.

He stretched out his senses. The pulse of life was all around. The birds perched high up in the trees. The vermin that scurried over the ground. The insects that crawled underneath the moss and through the branches within. All Nath had to do was ask them.

Nath opened up his paw and sat it down on the ground. Creating a gentle hum in his voice, he beckoned to all the life that was around. His melody gently massaged the leaves in the trees. Everything that crept or crawled stopped in its path.

Come now, come. Come and help me out. I seek. Help me find.

He kept at it for minutes. There was hesitation. Fear. Curiosity. Not one creature came forward. Nath continued, however. Even though he was a friendly force, he still looked like a giant predator—for dragons fed on all kinds of things. The world was their buffet. Some ate bugs, others fish of the waters and the fowl of the air. Some dragons only ate the flowers and leaves.

Come, Nath beckoned. *Come.*

Nothing came.

Blast!

Nath sat down, shaking his head. He didn't have anyone left to help him. No friends in sight, and he couldn't blame them. He'd run Selene off. He'd acted like a lousy king, and even the creatures of the forest knew that. He'd lost all credibility.

I'm a sad excuse for a Dragon King. And I thought things would be easy once I was a dragon. Out of the corner of his eye he caught some movement. *What's this?*

A raccoon approached, head low. It was a big one, bushy, with chestnut brown spots and rings instead of black. It stopped short of Nath's paw.

Nath hummed out a welcoming sound.

The raccoon lifted its head.

Now came the tricky part. Animals and insects couldn't speak, but they had their ways of communicating. Nath summoned his magic and released a spell. He had several he could recall that he'd learned when he was younger and walked the lands more. Speaking with animals was one of them, and it had helped him rescue many dragons.

"How are you?" he said in words the raccoon could understand.

It spoke back. "I am well, Mighty Dragon. How may I assist?"

"What is your name, little friend?"

"I'm called the Ringed Goose by my family," it said.

"I lost a friend, a dwarf. Bones for a hand and black bearded. Have you seen him?"

"Yes," the raccoon said. "He was here yesterday. He marched through and then was taken."

"Taken by what or who?"

Tiny clawed hands together, the raccoon looked back over his shoulders. "I'm scared to say for fear that me and my family might be eaten."

"I won't let that happen," Nath said. "Please, help me. He's my dear friend, and he means as much to me as your family to you."

The raccoon nodded. "A black, black dragon dropped from the sky and took him."

No! Not Selene!

"Can you describe this dragon in better detail? Did it have blood-red eyes and rough, dark scales, perhaps?"

"The scales were such as yours," the raccoon said.

"Did it have horns on its head?"

"The raccoon rubbed its chin. "Yes, I think so."

Nath's heart dipped. "Now think hard on this. Did you see the dragon's eyes?"

"Oh, most definitely, they were the prettiest and deadliest violet I ever saw."

Head filled with troubles, Nath burrowed his way into a nearby mountainside and blended in with his surroundings. The raccoon's news was deeply disturbing. Selene had betrayed him once again, it seemed.

After all we have been through, she's turned on me? Why?

His heart ached.

And why take Brenwar? She wouldn't kill him, would she?

Of course, if anyone wasn't as blind as Nath, it was Brenwar. Nath cared deeply for Selene, Brenwar not so much. He wasn't a very forgiving sort. And if the seasoned soldier suspected something, he wouldn't hesitate to let Nath know about it.

I can't believe this is happening. And it couldn't be more perfect. Here I am grounded with a busted wing.

He curled deeper into his spot. Mind filled with doubt, he ran over countless scenarios. Did Selene want his throne? Did Gorn Grattack still live? Was she trying to prevent him from finding his mother?

It seems my suspicions were right all along. That Selene. She's such an actress. I should have known better. Fine, I'll wait it out, Selene. My wing will heal soon enough, and then I'm going to hunt you down like a draykis.

Burrowed deep in the earth, he settled in and used his energy to heal up. All around him the plant life perked up, starting with new growth. Hours went by that turned into days. Before long he was covered in the brush and flowers. The varmints of the forest didn't notice him. The birds started to nest. The smaller creatures burrowed. Life traveled all around him and over the top of him. He was part of the mountain now. Many dragons did that.

He opened his eye.

His wing no longer hurt.

That ought to do it.

Red birds with long white tails were chirping in the thicket that covered his eyes. The sweet music turned to a squawk as Nath shifted his bulk, loosening the dirt. The wildlife that covered him scattered.

Sorry.

With a heave, he pushed his way out of his burrow and shook off the leaves and foliage. He pressed his way through the forest until he found a clearing. He stretched out his wings.

Ah! That's much better! Here I come, Selene.

CHAPTER 17

FLYING HIGH, NATH SET OFF in the direction Selene had been flying. She'd be hard to find if she wanted to be. She could transform, become big or small like he could. But her scent would linger. He had that to go on.

You won't escape me, Selene. I won't let you get away with this.

Of course, for all he knew, he might be playing right into her hands. A trap might spring. After all, she'd had plenty of time to set it. He wouldn't be one bit surprised if she'd left him a clue of some sort.

He dashed in and out of clouds filled with lightning and rain. He swooped over the land and his belly grazed the ground. There was plenty of ground to cover, but he sensed she was near. And he figured chances were that if he could find some of those wurmers, then he'd be about to find her as well.

Rising back into the air, he noticed a broken form unmoving down in the valley. There, a dragon lay still. He was citrine yellow with a red stripe across his back. Little bigger than a pony, the yellow streak dragon was dragging his belly through the sloppy rain with his head hung low.

Nath dropped out of the sky and down in front of him. "What happened, brother?"

"They're dead," the yellow streak said in a ragged form of Dragonese. His body had deep cuts in it, and some of his scales were missing. "All dead. I couldn't save them. I'm sorry, Nathlalonggram ...agh." He collapsed on the ground.

"No!" Nath cried out in alarm. The dragon's heartbeat was quickly fading. Nath scooped him up in his arms. The yellow streak's life was gone.

Chest puffed out, Nath picked up the dragon's trail. The rains were washing it away in the mud, but Nath's keen eyes still picked it up. He followed the tall grasses that were matted down. The dragon's path wound through a valley, and Nath found bits of blood along the way. His nostrils flared.

That doesn't smell good.

He pressed on. Up ahead, a small plume of smoke twirled in the rain. Patches of fire were burning the trees.

Oh no!

Dragons were scattered all over the ground, yellow streaks, a large family. Their bodies lay still, their scale hides ripped and torn. Wings broken. Teeth and horns busted. The battle must have been fierce.

Nath stopped short of the battleground and scooped up a small dragon that didn't even fill his hand. She was so young and beautiful. Her neck was broken. Nath's eyes watered.

Lightning streaked across the sky and thunder cracked.

He let out a roar.

"Maaaaaarrrroooooooo!"

Someone is going to pay for this!

He stepped in a pile of ashes that had begun mixing in with the mud. It was familiar. Scraping some of the goo up onto his finger, he eyed it closely and gave it a sniff.

It's from a wurmer. Hah, seems the yellow streaks put up a fine fight and took some of these dark fiends with them.

He picked his way through the carnage. There were scales and teeth he hadn't noticed before. He sifted through them with his hand, feeling the texture and absorbing the scent into his scales. The wurmers couldn't be far away. It wouldn't be hard to find them now.

And once he found them, he'd find Selene.

Selene has a lot of explaining to do.

One by one, he picked up the fallen dragons and laid them down side by side. He even returned and brought back the first one he'd encountered. There were seven in all. The father went first, being the biggest, and the mother, going down to the sons and daughters being the smallest. With a heart full of sadness, Nath dug into the soft dirt. His powerful hands scooped out the dirt and rock and pushed it aside, and the first grave was made.

This hurts.

He had thought these days were done. That there would be peace on Nalzambor for a long time. He slung a pile of mud aside.

This shouldn't be happening! Why can't everyone and everything behave themselves?

He kept digging, taking his time about it. And he started singing, a sad and ancient tune. It was one he had learned from his father when he was a boy. The other dragons used to sing it as well. It was about the first dragons who had fallen during the first dragon war.

Their scales were cherry, the fairest of their kind.

They drank deep of the waters and flew high in the air.

Fire came. Lightning struck. They tumbled through the sky.

It was the end of the crimson dynamos and the beginning of Nalzambor's despair.

There were hundreds of segments to the song, but Nath only made it as far as fifty. He'd finished his work, laid his kin in the graves one by one, and started covering them in dirt.

When he lifted his sagging head, a change in his surroundings caught his eye. He was encircled by the creatures of the wild. Mighty elks with curled horns. Chipmunks and rabbits with tiny bright fairies riding on their backs. There were owls in the branches. An old and aging centaur woman too. The woodland creatures closed in and began pushing the dirt into the graves as well. Beavers and pixies. A pair of bears bigger than Brenwar. In moments, the dragon graves were covered and new grasses and flowers were planted.

"Thank you," Nath said to them all.

Quickly they were all gone, leaving Nath alone in the rain.

CHAPTER 18

NATH SCOURED THE AREA FOR leagues. He did it in the air and on the ground. The scent of the wurmers was strong. Flying through the sky, he caught a distant flicker of movement down below. There was a clearing on a hillside. Its peak was covered in rough stone and loose shale. A plume of smoke rose into the air and dissipated.

I'd better check that out.

Wary eyed, he glided down and landed soft as a dove on the ground. The shale squeezed up between his clawed toes. He spied a faint series of caves in the light of the dusk. They seemed to breathe with life of their own. Warm yellow smoke oozed out of them. There were no other signs of life nearby.

Could be a lair.

Head low, Nath crept in for a closer look. His nostrils widened as he took in a deep draw of air. The yellow smoke smelled like acid. It was like the Lakes of Sulfur farther south, which had been formed by the lava rivers. They made great places to hide for dragons, who could handle the heat, much more so than men.

But this was different. This was in the forest.

Strange.

He inhaled again. There was more than sulfur or acid. The wurmers' scent was there, mixed in with the pungent cover.

Hah! I have them now!

The tufts behind Nath's earholes fluttered. He could smell them but not see them. The mouths of the caves were too small for his great girth. He climbed behind them, hung his head over the lip, and listened for any sound. There was a roar of wind that whistled through the jagged rocks. Deeper, he could hear something else. In a part of the world deep in its bowels, there was a groaning. Something flowed. Beat. Pulsed.

Nath rubbed his razor-sharp claws under his lip.

Hmmm ... can't help but be really curious. Perhaps I should change so I can go down there and check it out. No. Now is the time for patience. He envisioned the broken bodies of the yellow streak dragons. *Soon I'll have vengeance.*

Nath focused on blending in with his environment. His body became one with the natural surroundings. Part of the rock and soil. His thoughts wandered. What if Selene was down there? And Brenwar?

What if it's a trap? Another one of Selene's clever setups?

The hours went by, and darkness fell over the hill. Above, the moon's light was dim in the drifting and dreary clouds.

The caves gave off the faintest illumination. The smell of sulfur remained strong. Nath let his eyes close. He sank his talons deeper into the hard earth. He could feel all of the life of Nalzambor. The heartbeats of the sleeping creatures nearby. The feet of ants marching over the dirt. There was something else too that he felt. Distress. Nalzambor seemed worried.

The hillside suddenly quavered.

Thoom.

It was faint. Undetectable by many creatures of nature. The shale shifted the slightest bit.

Thoom.

Nath's eyelid slid back.

Thoom. Thoom. Thoom.

The bellies of the caves were coming to life. Angry sounds and shrieks erupted from within. Something was coming out.

Thoom! Thoom!

Shale and dirt poured out over the rims of the caves. Creatures who had been lying peacefully in the forest scattered. One of the caves glowed with bright orange light, and the roar of a dragon echoed.

Something fights within!

A slender black dragon snaked out of the hole.

Selene!

She was smaller. More svelte. The scales on her dragon chest were heaving as she backed away from the mouths of the caves.

Nath's claws pulled up out of the dirt.

I've got her now!

Selene snorted fire and smoke. Her long neck swayed from side to side. Her violet eyes were intent on the caves. She continued her retreat.

What's going on here?

One by one, wurmers emerged from the shadows of the caves. Ten of them, claws sharper than swords that twinkled in the night, flanked Selene.

This should be interesting. I'm no fool. I'll just wait and see what she says to them. She probably has them wrapped around her finger like she once had me.

Striking with uncanny speed, the wurmers plowed into Selene. Her body was covered in the scaly fiends. Only her whipping tail could be seen.

Selene!

"Maaaaaaarrrroooooo!"

With a fearsome roar, Nath tore his body out of the rocks and pounced into the fray.

The wurmers let out shrill cries.

With a bone-crushing stomp, Nath silenced several cries. Fully healed now, Nath tore into the wurmers. Fueled by his vengeance for the yellow streaks, he cut loose. Plucking wurmers from Selene like ticks, he pinned them to the ground.

They nipped and clawed at him.

Nath responded in fiercer kind. He took in a lungful of air and blasted them with flames that ended their existence.

"Save your breath!" Selene cried out. There was desperation in her voice. "Save it, Nath!"

"Hah," he said. "Like I should trust you." His tail coiled around a wurmer's neck. He lifted it up and slammed it repeatedly into the ground.

Wham! Wham! Wham!

"Nath!" Selene cried out. "Help me!"

His head reared up.

Four wurmers had latched onto her. Two of them sank their teeth and claws into her neck.

Her violet eyes popped open, filled with pain.

The hot glow of the wurmers' powerful maws ignited with fire. Lava oozed out, down Selene's neck.

She let out a horrifying howl that split the air in the sky.

"Haaaaaaarrrrrrrrlllllllll!"

Nath's scales stood on end.

Selene's supine body went limp, and the light in her eyes faded.

"Nooooooooo!"

CHAPTER 19

ATH'S GOLDEN EYES BURNED LIKE fire. Staring down the wurmers, he unleashed a blast of power from his eye sockets. The rays of light cut through one of the wurmers on Selene's neck, killing it. He let loose on another. Eye beams blasted into it and turned it to ash and powder.

The remaining wurmers detached themselves from Selene and launched into Nath.

Fueled by a desperate sense of urgency, Nath's massive body became a juggernaut of battle. He bit down on one wurmer and crushed it in his jaws. His claws smashed a second one into the ground until its bones became dust.

Die, you scaly vermin! Die!

The third wurmer pounced on Nath's head. Its razor-sharp talons tore at his eyes.

He reached up and grabbed the wurmer and squeezed it between his dragon paws.

A hot stream of fire shot from the wurmer's mouth, covering Nath's face.

"Argh!" Nath roared. "Enough of this!" He crushed it like a beetle in his hands and slung its corpse into the woods. Still tormented by the burning oil, Nath buried his face in the ground. The flames extinguished.

Need to be smarter than that, Dragon.

Shaking his head and slinging off the dirt, he quickly scanned the area. All the wurmers were dead.

A soft, weak, and desperate voice caught his ear.

"Nath." It was Selene. She lay flat on the ground, trying to push herself up. Her neck was sagging. Her chin rested on the ground. "Use your fire."

"On what?" he asked. His eyes narrowed on her. "You?"

"What do you mean?"

"I'm no fool, Selene. I'm certain this is some clever ploy to trap me. Where's Brenwar?"

Irritated, she pushed herself up off the ground. Her neck still drooped, and it had horrible gashes in it. Strength returned to her voice. "You are mad!"

Glancing at her wounds, he replied, "I see you are feeling better."

Selene, smaller and standing beneath him, looked up at him and said, "I can't believe you."

"Don't play games, Selene. Where is Brenwar?"

"I don't know where that bearded man-goat is! If he's lost, then it's your fault, not mine!" She craned her neck and winced. "Now, will you listen to me? We don't have much time!"

There was truth in her voice. Nath felt it. He'd always been able to discern the truth from a lie. But Selene had fooled him before. Still, her neck was in bad shape. Blood seeped between her claws that held it. Finally, he said, "What do you want me to do?"

"That's a wurmer lair," she said, pointing at the caves. "I went in and found the larvae, but the wurmer guardians found me before I could act. The wurmer eggs aren't too deep, but there are hundreds of them. You need to stick your head in there and turn loose the heat. Do you understand me?"

"And turn my back to you?" Nath objected. "I don't think so."

"Dragon King," she said, softening her tone, "you must listen. I'd do it myself, but I've nothing left. I can barely stand."

"Tell me where Brenwar is first."

"What in all of Nalzambor makes you think I have that dwarf?"

"Someone saw you fly away with him," Nath said.

"Someone who?"

"A raccoon."

Selene's jaw dropped. Then, with incredulity, she said, "A raccoon? Are you being serious?"

Taken aback, Nath said, "Yes."

Selene started to laugh. "Ha ha! Please, you are making me laugh! And it hurts. Heh heh! The Dragon King and his raccoon advisor. Haw!" She sucked her teeth. "Oh, it hurts."

"Stop it," Nath said.

"Ha ha! I wish I could," she said, slapping her tail on the ground. "Heh heh heh! But I can't. So, where is this advisor?"

Feeling like a fool, Nath filled his chest up with fire. He glared at her, turned, stuffed his head inside one of the caves, and unleashed his flames. The white-hot blast vaporized everything in its path. Nath let it all out. His anger. Humiliation. Frustration. His fire stopped. He pulled his head out of the hole and found Selene.

She had a wry smile on her face. "Well done, Dragon King. I'll be right back." With a hitch in her gait, she slipped back into one of the caves.

Nath sat down on his haunches. His head was light, and he saw spots in his eyes. He'd never let out so much fire before. All the cave openings were smoking brown now instead of yellow.

Huh, didn't know I had that in me.

A few minutes later Selene emerged. "That took care of it," she said. She held out her dragon palms, revealing an amber stone a little bigger than an egg. Something dark green wiggled inside. "Wurmer egg," she said. "It survived, but I dug it out. There's always a remnant that will survive if you are not careful."

The larva inside spun and rolled. It radiated evil. Its thrashings were revolting and vile.

"What are you going to do with it?" Nath said.

Selene squeezed it into goo in her claws. She rubbed the muck into the dirt. "I just wanted you to see it, so that you would know."

"Thanks. I still need to find Brenwar, though." He averted his eyes. "And I …"

"Nath, I understand why you might not fully trust me. After all, I did try to destroy you once. But I won't again. I promise." She sighed. "You gave my life meaning. Once I accepted it, I knew I couldn't go back. I'll die first. Trust me or not, you won't get any trouble from me." She sagged and swayed. "Ugh."

"Selene!" Nath said. "You are not well."

"It's the wurmers' poisoned flames. It will fade away. I just need to rest."

"You rest, then. I'll watch out."

"I'll be fine. The threat has passed." She lay down in the grasses by his feet and closed her eyes. "Besides, you need to go and find Brenwar."

Nath's eyes grazed over her form. She was so beautiful adorned in her sparkling black scales. Supine. Graceful. Mesmerizing. *She's amazing.*

"I can feel your eyes on me," she said with her eyes still closed. "Do you like what you see?"

"Huh?" Nath stammered out. "The truth is, you aren't half bad for a dragon."

"You're supposed to increase in charm as you get older, not lose it."

"Well, unlike you, I won't be older for a much longer time."

"Whatever you say, Dragon Boy."

"Boy?"

CHAPTER 20

SELENE SLEPT A WEEK, JUST as he had when he'd been poisoned by the wurmers. During that week, Nath found that his patience was not tried at all.

Too soon, she was up again. "I'll help out with Brenwar," she said. "Besides, I'm curious about this raccoon you met."

"Curious why?" Nath asked.

"Because I don't recall any raccoons being in that area of woodland. It's possible but atypical."

"The woodlands are full of varmints. Especially the raccoons."

"Did you see any others?"

"No," he said.

"But you do know that raccoons travel in families typically, don't you think?" She stretched out her wings and yawned. "Tell me more about this raccoon."

"He was big for a raccoon. White with brown eyes and brown rings."

She rolled her eyes. "A brown raccoon? You're certain?"

"Sure."

"Have you ever seen a brown raccoon before?"

"No, but there are plenty of things I've never seen. And what makes you such an expert on critters anyway?" Nath expanded his wings and took flight, and then he yelled back down, "Oh, come on. I'll show you."

Selene jumped into the air and flew after him. "Oh, I can't wait."

Nath and Selene were back in the woodland where he'd lost the scent of Brenwar. Pushing between the trees and bending them aside, he sniffed the air.

"Let me guess, you lost the raccoon's scent too."

"Just give me a moment."

"Sure, take all the time that you want." She shrugged her eyes. "But I smell many things, and a raccoon isn't among them."

Selene was right. Nath didn't smell a single raccoon, but there were plenty of squirrels, chipmunks, and other such things. If dragons could blush, his cheeks would be red. It was embarrassing. He'd missed something again.

"Just keep looking," he moaned.

The search continued, but it was futile. Though the woods were big, Nath was still too big for them. His presence unsettled everything. Finally, he eased back into a clearing and waited for Selene to return.

I hate being wrong, and I don't much like her being right, either.

Selene emerged into the clearing. "Giving up so soon, are we?"

"There has to be an explanation for this." He dropped his horned head into his hands. "Selene, have you ever encountered a fairy empress?"

"No, I can't say that I have. Why, have you?"

"Brenwar and I found one in a tomb. Her name is Lotuus."

"Tell me more, Nath. Don't leave out a detail."

Nath filled her in from start to finish, leaving them both in silence.

"I'd say there is a very good chance that *Lotuus* is behind this." She smacked Nath's leg with her tail. "And you didn't even consider this before? Instead you blamed me."

"But the raccoon said—"

"Oh hush it, Nath. Besides, I've forgiven you already."

"You have? Why?"

"Why? Because you saved my scaled back at those caves, that's why. If you hadn't shown up, I might very well have died."

"Well, I'd hate for that to happen, even though you are difficult …"

"What!"

"And irritating."

"You think I'm irritating," she said, rising up to full height.

"Not to mention beautiful."

"Oh." Selene's composure softened. "Now that's more like it." Slowly, she approached and nuzzled into his chest.

Nath's heart pounded harder and faster. Swallowing, he eased his tail around her waist and pulled her closer.

She kissed him on the cheek and said with a soft look in her violet eyes, "You're learning, Nath."

"Oh please," said an unfamiliar voice. "I don't think the two of you are married."

Nath and Selene stiffened into upright positions and eyed the owner of the voice.

A big raccoon, chestnut ringed, stood atop a small boulder, checking his claws.

"You!" Nath said.

"Me," the raccoon said, touching his chest. "Yes, I suppose it is me. What about it?"

"Where is Brenwar?" Nath demanded. Silently he snorted the air. The raccoon still didn't have a familiar scent. "Out with it now."

"I told you," the raccoon said, pointing at Selene. "She has him."

"I certainly do not!" Selene said.

The raccoon giggled. "Well, I might have been mistaken. These eyes aren't quite what they used to be. You'll understand when you get to be as old as me."

"Enough games, raccoon." Nath stomped his paw. "Tell me where Brenwar is!"

"Who?"

"You know very well who, you trickster." Nath crept closer. "The dwarf. Black bearded with a skeleton hand."

"What's he doing with a skeleton hand?" the raccoon said.

Nath slammed his paw down, shaking the ground. *Boom!* "Tell me where he is!"

"Eh, easy, big dragon. You might hurt something." The raccoon scratched his head. "Boy, you really aren't getting this, are you?"

"What do you mean?" Nath said.

"Come on, you know better than that."

"You are that trickster, Lotuus."

"No," the raccoon said, shaking his head. "I don't know who you are talking about."

Nath lowered his snout over the raccoon's face and sniffed him again. *Hmmm, he has no scent at all. He has to be made of magic, but who and what is he?* He snorted again.

"Hey, easy," the raccoon said, hugging the boulder. "I don't want to venture into your nose."

"Humph!" Nath said, eyeing the raccoon with continued suspicion. He stared deep into its eyes.

There was something there.

Something familiar.

"Gorlee!"

"Hah!" the raccoon slapped his knee. "It's about time. *Ulp!*"

Nath snatched the changeling up in his claws and squeezed. "Why the games?"

Eyes bugging out of his head, Gorlee shifted his shape into the human form of Nath Dragon. "I'm a changeling, remember. We don't do things the easy way. Besides, I needed you to track down Selene and bring her back." Struggling in Nath's clutches, he said, "Do you mind?"

Nath set him down and said to a human-looking version of himself, "So Brenwar is safe, then?"

"Yes, he is. He's back in Dragon Home. He's pretty slow, so I sent him back with a teleportation stone, but the two of you can fly there."

"Why would we do that?" Nath said

"Because Balzurth sent me to get you."

Nath's blood thinned under his scales. "My father is back from beyond the Great Mural?" He looked at Selene. Her eyes were as wide as moons. He turned back to Gorlee. "Why?"

"He didn't say," Gorlee said. He walked over to Selene and patted her on the back. "How have you been doing, Selene?"

"Fine," she said, glowering at him.

Gorlee backed away and slapped his hands together. "Glad to hear it. Now, which one of you grand beasts is flying me back to Dragon Home?"

For the moment, Nath's tongue was tied. Going home was one thing. Being summoned was another. He felt like a child again. *What is this all about? I can't stand it.* He lowered his head. "Get on, then."

CHAPTER 21

DRAGON HOME. ON THE OUTSIDE, things had changed. Dragons soared the nearby skies now. Colorful families of the scaly beasts huddled in the peaks. The deep valleys at the bottom of the mountain showed glimmers of the families hunting and frolicking with one another.

Lava flowed in small streams down the mountainside. The caves smoldered and sputtered out smoke.

A pair of blue razor dragons darted by, making friendly squawks. Several heads popped up at Nath's flying approach. They squawked hellos and welcomes. Fire Bite dragons the size of piglets swarmed the air and blew hot puffs of fire at him.

Nath was elated. In all his days before, he'd never received so much as a welcome, but he was accepted now. He was a friend. A fighter. A champion. He was their king to command them.

"They sure are making a fuss about you," Selene said as they flew, eyeing two columns of silver dragons that were guiding them toward the great mountain. "I guess they don't know any better."

"Funny, Selene. Hah-hah."

They dropped into the largest mouth of the cave and landed. The massive cave led to a very tall and wide passageway. Gorlee hopped down onto the carved stone path. "It's an awfully big place, isn't it?"

"You might want to shift shapes, Gorlee." Nath's heart was pounding as he eyed the passages that led to the throne room. "We wouldn't want to confuse anybody."

"Good idea," Gorlee said, "But who should I be?"

"Why don't you try being yourself for a change?" Nath suggested.

"Seems boring, but why not?" Gorlee made a face. "Uh, Nath, what do I look like?"

Nath gazed at the huge chamber doors towering over his frame. He studied the dragon images inlaid in the brass. Selene stood at his side, and Gorlee stood down between his feet. The changeling's skin was hairless and pinkish, his head bald, and his eyes big green baubles in the sockets. He was odd looking and lanky and wearing a set of loose cotton robes.

Nath raised his paw up and started to knock. "Wait a minute, this is my throne room." He shoved the door open and gazed upon the heaping piles of gleaming treasure. "After you," he said to Selene.

Inside, coins jangled and shifted under his feet. The throne room with its high columns didn't seem as big as it used to. Of course, he'd spent most of his time the size of a man before. At least that was how he had departed it last. He eyed the great throne, a backless chair plenty big enough for him and crafted from the finest metals. He made his approach, head moving side to side. "I guess I'll have a seat and wait then."

"Hold it right there," said a gruff voice. From behind one of the throne's legs, a stout black-bearded figure stepped out.

"Brenwar!"

"Aye," said the dwarf. "No need to get all emotional."

"I'm just glad you're well," Nath said, leaning down. "I was worried."

"Humph." Brenwar lowered Mortuun to the treasure floor and rested his hands on the butt of the shaft. He stood at attention, eyes forward. He didn't blink.

Nath looked at Selene and gave a shrug.

Her eyes were fixed on the gigantic mural behind the throne.

The painting always changed. The dragons and clouds in the sky moved in an endless and timeless scene. The changes were slow and subtle. It was like watching a very slow and massive hourglass with the sand draining. It took its time, but eventually it changed.

"So, I guess the waiting part begins. Say, Gorlee. Gorlee?"

The changeling was nowhere to be found.

"Well that's just great," Nath said. "He probably has the right idea, though. Wouldn't surprise me if we stood here for days." He tapped his claw on the treasure-coated floor. "Or weeks. And just when I was about to close in on my mother."

"Always be wary. Plans change. Be prepared for the unexpected," Selene said.

"I suppose."

I wonder what Father has in store for me now. He told me it would be fine to chase after Mother. Perhaps I should have completed the mission by now. Of course, I would have if Brenwar didn't slow me down.

"So, Brenwar, as I understand it, you teleported, but you won't fly? Didn't you use the old 'Dwarves don't teleport' line on Gorlee?"

Brenwar didn't move.

Oh great. He's assumed the position. Guzan, I'm liable to be standing here for weeks.

Nath gazed around the treasure room. There was nothing worse than waiting, even though he was a dragon and extremely patient. But this was different. He was waiting on his father—again—and he couldn't help but feel like he was in trouble. Still, he was looking forward to seeing his father again. He realized he might not see him again for a long time. It did his heart well.

But for Balzurth to come back, there had to be trouble.

Oh, I'll just give him a hug. Certainly he'll be as happy to see me as I am to see him.

Selene's tail swished into his. "I'm not sure I like this. Her eye grazed the vaulted ceiling tops. "Reminds me of my days with Gorn—"

"Let's not utter his name here," Nath interjected. "He shouldn't ever be mentioned in these hallowed halls."

"Noted," she said. "Let's just pray this has nothing to do with him or his ilk."

"I'm certain his existence is entirely wiped out," Nath said, with a sneer. "I felt it myself." He locked his eyes on Selene's. "You haven't sensed him again, have you?"

Flatly, she said, "No. But evil is so hard to destroy."

"As if we didn't already have enough of a problem with the wurmers."

The mural warbled, and a massive dragon stepped through. Balzurth came. The great horns on his head seemed to stretch to the top of the ceiling. The great muscles underneath his deep-red scales, flecked with gold, appeared more powerful than ever. His voice had as much thunder as it ever had. The room quavered, and the piles of coins shifted when he spoke.

"Welcome home, Son."

Nath pulled his wings back. "It's good to be home, Father." He stood eye to eye with Balzurth and butted horns with him. "You look as grand as ever."

"And you are quite the specimen of a great dragon yourself." Balzurth turned away and faced the other dragon in the room. "Hello, Selene. How are you?"

"Quite well, King Balzurth."

Balzurth's golden eyes examined her black-scaled body. "I sense that is not entirely true."

"What do you mean, Father?" Nath asked with surprise. "Selene is just as spirited as ever."

"No, no she isn't, Son. That's one of the reasons I brought you here."

"It is? Why, what is wrong?"

With a sad look in his eyes, Balzurth said to Nath, "Your friend Selene is dying."

CHAPTER 22

"DYING?" NATH SAID. HE SWATTED her gently with his tail. "I've never seen her better. You're fine, Selene. Tell him."

She looked up at Nath with weak eyes and shook her head. "No, I'm not. My time in this world has run its course." She turned and faced Balzurth. "How did you know?"

"I've always known. It's what Gorn does. If he goes, all of his closest acolytes go with him. It's in their bloodstream." Balzurth stretched his tail out and brushed it over her cheek. "You've been living on borrowed time, and now your time has come."

Nath's heart sank in his chest. "What? No. This cannot be. What are you talking about, Father?"

"Selene is a dragon the same as most, but more gifted, born black. Gorn found her at birth and took her under his wing." Balzurth cleared his throat. "He cursed her blood and blended it with his. She can't live in this world without him."

"I thought Gorn was a spirit."

"He was, but all evil spirits can taint things." Balzurth stepped around the throne and put his wing over Selene.

Tears dripped from her eyes.

Nath's eyes started to water. "What are you going to do?"

Balzurth then said to his son, "She's made the right choice: good over evil. She's one of us, and I'm taking her with me where she can live well—beyond the mural."

Nath was numb. Despite their battles, he'd become as close with Selene as anyone. Now she was going to be gone! He probably wouldn't be able to see her again for at least a thousand years. He turned and faced her. "Is this what you want?"

"This is the only choice I have." She shrugged. "But it's hardly a bad thing. It's just happening so suddenly. Quite frankly, I'm not ready. I feel my work here on Nalzambor isn't finished. That's why I've been working so hard to eradicate those wurmers. I'm partially responsible for that mess, and I knew I needed to clean it up. Now, it's going to be a burden for you and the rest of the world to deal with."

"Does she have to go right now, Father?"

"We need to be prudent about it, Son. I sense the poison could strike her heart at any moment. Can't you sense it as well?"

Nath shut his eyes. His heightened senses reached out. Selene's heart fought for every beat. She was strong, but the fight in her was weakening. There was a deep sadness in her, too. "Can we not heal her?" Nath suggested. "Perhaps the Ocular of Orray can help? It removes curses."

Selene brushed his cheek with her tail. "It's been tried. It worked for a time, but that time is up. Nath, don't be so sad. Without you, I never would have made it this far. I'd have been dead with no hope of life beyond the mural."

Nath stomped his paw. "Why didn't anyone tell me this until now? We could have been searching for a solution."

"Nath, you have to live your life and I have to live mine," Selene said. "Just let it be."

"Come now, Selene," Balzurth said. "We must go now. A new life will begin beyond the mural."

"Can't she leave, be cured, and come back?" Nath said to Balzurth.

"Only I can leave and come back, Son. And it's quite taxing to do so. Now, say your goodbyes so you can resume your quest."

Nath clasped Selene's claws in his. "We can beat this, Selene. There must be a way."

"This is my choice, not yours," she said. "And I fear I've done much more harm than good in this world." A giant teardrop dripped from her eye and splashed on the treasure. "Will you rid Nalzambor of the wurmers for me?"

"No!" Nath retorted. "You need to do that yourself. But I will help you." He turned on Balzurth. "Father, you've told me countless times that there is always a way to solve anything in this world. So tell me how to solve this. Please. What can I do to help my friend?"

Balzurth's voice darkened. "Don't ask questions you don't want the answers to."

"So there is a way?"

"One that comes at too great a price," Balzurth said.

"No price is too great, Father. I'd give my life for hers."

"Nath!" Selene said, gasping.

"Oh, don't be so dramatic, Son." Balzurth rolled his eyes. He leaned over and poked Nath in the chest. He ran his paws over Nath's horns. "You are as fine a dragon as there ever was, Son. Are you willing to give that up?"

"What do you mean?" Nath asked.

"Oh, you say you'll give up your life, but let's qualify that. Will you give up your life as a dragon?"

Nath swallowed. "I can't stop being a dragon, can I?"

"You'll always have a dragon's blood, as you did before you changed. But what if you gave up all of your other powers? The gift of flight. Your iron hide. Your humongous girth and awesome power. Hmmm?" Balzurth poked him again. "Can you give all of that up? Not to mention the crown of the dragon kingdom?"

Nath shrank inside his scales. "I can't give that up. I'm the Dragon King now."

"A Dragon King that has only spent minutes on the throne," Balzurth said. "You know, I was seven hundred and fifty-some years old before I assumed the throne from your grandfather, and it took another five hundred years to get used to it."

"But, it's my destiny to be king, is it not?" Nath said.

"Oh, destiny can wait. In the meantime," Balzurth said, taking a seat on the throne. "I can keep an eye on things."

"Nath, you can't do this. Not for me. I'm not worth it," Selene said, stroking his cheek with the back of her paw. "You love all of your dragon powers. It wouldn't be right for me to be restored and you to be the lesser of what you were before."

"You don't want to leave, Selene. I can feel it. And I don't want you to leave, either. Deep down inside, we both know we aren't to be separated."

"But it wouldn't be fair for me to have my powers and you to not have yours."

"Ahem," Balzurth interrupted. "Oh, but you would pay just as big a price as he, Selene. You both would be affected. You both have to want this. There is no other way."

"So, we'll be made human again?" Nath said to his father.

"I can't say exactly how it will work out. All I can say is that your powers will be severely limited. Notably so."

"Does this mean I can never be king?"

"You're a king already, Son. Always have been. Always will be. But, if you do this, you'll have to assume the title of Dragon Prince again. At least for now. And that won't be easy."

Nath looked down at Brenwar. The dwarf's eyes glanced up at him and quickly looked away. His friend seemed so tiny. Vulnerable. Nath didn't want to feel that way again: mortal.

"Now's not my time, is it, Father."

Balzurth sat there, deep in thought. His thinking lasted for days.

Nath and Selene stayed right there with him, figuring it was a good thing Brenwar had frozen, or the dwarf might have become bored.

At long last, the old Dragon King made his pronouncement.

"As a man, Nath, you defeated Gorn Grattack and ended the Great Dragon War, but I think Nalzambor still needs you, as a man. And the world needs Selene, too. And … you two need each other, I believe."

Nath's eyes found Selene's. "As I understand it, life is awfully nice beyond the mural."

"And life as a king can be just as delightful," she replied. "I wouldn't give it up for the likes of me."

"Well," Nath smiled and stared deep into her eyes, "then it's a good thing that you aren't king. Father, I'm ready."

Balzurth nodded. "What about you, Selene?"

"Can two bad decisions produce something good? I guess there's only one way to find out. I'm ready."

Balzurth leaned forward. "So be it. Now, clasp hands, close your eyes, and repeat after me."

CHAPTER 24

Nath's heart pounded in his skull. Darkness surrounded him.

Guzan! What's happened to me?

The last thing he remembered was his father saying some words. Ancient and mystical. Powerful and transforming. The words had felt like they were separating his bones from the marrow. They penetrated his very core. The essence of his being. He struggled. His eyes wouldn't open. His limbs wouldn't move. His entire body was hemmed in by warm goo.

How am I even breathing?

His heart beat faster and faster. It thundered in his ears.

Settle down, Nath. Certainly your own father wouldn't do you in. Would he?

Blood racing through his numb limbs, his body started to tingle. His strength grew. He pushed with whatever part he could feel. He hit something stiff. It was smooth to the touch.

What sort of prison is this? What has become of me?

Feet gathered into his chest, he stretched out. He kicked at the wall that held him fast.

Something cracked.

He kicked again and again.

The ooze around him began to spill out from the hole, and light crept over his eyelids.

Excited, Nath unleashed all of his limbs at once. Busting out of the strange shell, he started into a fit of coughing.

Yuck! What is this?!

Gagging, he spat up fluids until he could spit no more. Using his hand, he wiped the goo from his eyes and squinted them open. The light was painfully bright, and the surrounding sounds were muffled. A stiff breeze chilled his warm bones. Using his fingers, he cleaned out his nose and earholes. He rubbed his lobes.

"I have ears!"

"Yes you do, sleepy head," said a muffled voice. "And a tongue, too!"

Nath shook his head like a dog and wiped all he could from his eyes. On opening them up, he found Brenwar. "You're much bigger than before," he said, spitting ooze from his mouth. "So I guess that means I'm much smaller?"

"Well, you certainly aren't any smarter," Brenwar added, "but if I were ever happy, I'd be happy to see you."

Nath took in a deep gust of air. He was in the woodland, and a stream trickled nearby. His feet stood on large chunks of reddish-green shell and goo that reminded him of an … "Was I in an egg?"

"It looked like an egg to me, hatchling," Brenwar said with the grimmest of smiles.

Nath stretched out his arms and hands. They were that of a man, but they still had scales. Black scales and golden-yellow claws. Eyes wide, he twisted his head over his shoulder and spun around. "No tail. No wings." He thumped his chest with his fist and forced out more coughing. "I feel so weak. Vulnerable."

"If you were smart, you would've asked to come back as a dwarf. We never feel that way."

Nath stared at his hands. His body. His chest was skin with a slight mix of scales. The same went for his legs. He felt his face. His sensitive touch revealed nothing but smooth skin on his face. He smiled when he felt his long hair.

He let out a breath and gazed up at the birds chirping in the trees. One darted into flight, and others followed. He became aware of a hole inside of him. He used to tower over the trees. Over everything. Now he looked up to it all again. He held his head and sat down.

"What's wrong?" Brenwar asked.

"This will take some getting used to, that's all. Where are we, anyway?"

"South of Dragon Home."

"Say, where's Selene?"

"Getting something to eat," Brenwar said, eyeing the streams. "Been gone since dawn."

Nath jumped up. His head spun and his legs turned to jelly. He crumpled down on the ground. "Oof. I am weak."

"And whining. Now get up." Brenwar offered his arm. "Get up now."

Nath took Brenwar's arm. It was like grabbing an iron rung that pulled him up. "Hah. I guess my strength will come back soon enough." He surveyed his colorful surroundings. "So Selene is well, then? How long has she been up?"

"Two days."

"She got out two days before me? Really?"

"It hardly matters. You always slept too much."

Combing his fingers through his hair, Nath then asked, "So how long since we left Dragon Home?"

"A few weeks?"

"Brenwar …"

"Give or take a few months."

"Are you jesting?" Nath said in shock to Brenwar.

Brenwar eyed him.

"Guzan! A lot can happen in a few months." Strolling over the grasses, he noticed he had toes and not clawed feet. He waded into the waters and rinsed off. The goo was quickly shed from his muscular frame and washed away with the waters.

Brenwar handed Nath an off-white suit of commoner's robes and some boots.

Once he was dressed, Nath scooped up a handful of water and drank. "I guess I'll have to get used to drinking from cups and goblets again."

"And routine bathing will probably be in order," replied a voice much softer than Brenwar's.

Nath whipped around and found himself staring at Selene. She stood on the bank wearing commoner's robes like his. Her hair was long and jet black, her eyes violet fire. Behind her back, a long black tail swished over the grasses.

"How do you feel?"

Shrugging her eyes, she said, "As mortal as I ever felt."

"Yes," Nath agreed, "me too. Exciting, isn't it?"

CHAPTER 25

TRAVELING ON FOOT, NATH, SELENE, and Brenwar made it within a league of the Lost City of Borgash. Standing atop an overlook, Nath squinted his eyes toward the distant city. Its once-tall spires, now rubble, lay all over the barren and broken land.

"I don't see a sliver of life in there," he said, fading away from the edge of the overlook and standing alongside Selene. "What about you?"

"Though my vision is not what it was, I still see a few things that scurry."

"You do?" Holding his hand over his eyes to shade them from the bright sun, Brenwar leaned forward on the overlook. "My eyes are as good as any. I see nothing."

"Look closer. Scorpions crawl along the sand underneath that archway."

Brenwar scowled. "Poor eyesight, my hide. Pah!" He marched back and grabbed his gear. "You still see better than the eagles."

"I would hope so," Nath said. He had the urge to pick up a weapon, but there was nothing to grab. He and Selene had nothing on aside from their commoner garb. It was odd. The clothing itched a little. It was nothing like being covered in dragon scales. He sat down, took off his boots, and dumped debris out. His feet were swollen, pink and tender. He started to rub them. "Sultans of Sulfur! Is that a blister?"

Selene giggled. "Exciting, isn't it?"

"No, it's horrible. My feet hurt, and I swear there's a kink in my neck. And I can only imagine that my hair is a mess." With a sour face, he eyed the blister and extended his index finger's claw. Wincing, he sliced the blister open. "Ow!"

"Oh my, that's embarrassing, you scaly child," Brenwar huffed. "Perhaps I should get out a healing potion for you."

"Would you please?" Nath said, more ordering than asking.

"Absolutely not! That's not a wound."

"But it could get infected," Nath whined. "Great Guzan, what am I saying? I'm worried about a bloody blister. Shame on me." He punched the ground he sat on. "Shame on Nath Dragon!"

Playfully, Selene said, "I could carry you."

"No, we'd better make a stretcher and drag him," Brenwar offered.

"Be silent, both of you. Blast!" Nath got up and hopped away from the pair of them until they were out of sight. Being smaller and weaker was a horrible thing. He missed the grand power he'd had. The ability to fly. The power to take on anything. He'd been the most powerful creature in all of Nalzambor, and now he felt like nothing. "I can't believe I did this to myself."

Selene appeared from underneath the low-hanging branches and said with a guilty look on her face, "Having regrets?"

"Yes," he said.

Selene frowned. "I see." She turned away.

"No, wait, Selene," Nath said, hustling over and grabbing her arm. "Not about you. Certainly not about that. But losing all of that power. It's going to take some getting used to."

"You know, Nath, the first time I met you, there wasn't an ounce of doubt in you. You weren't scared of anything. And you were less powerful than you are now. Ask yourself, what is different?"

"About five tons of brawn and scales."

"Seriously?"

"Come on, Selene. Certainly you should understand. Don't you feel weaker?"

"Physically, yes. Mentally, no. I still have my wits. Have you lost yours?"

He kicked a fallen branch. "No. But I liked being a dragon. Now I might not ever be one again."

"You're still a dragon, Nath Dragon." She brushed her long locks behind her back. "Just a little smaller. You'll get used to it." She extended her hand. "Now let's go find your mother."

He took her hand in his. It was warm to the touch. Invigorating. The bounce returned to his step. After thinking things through, he came to a simple conclusion.

I'm a man once again. I have to live with the decisions I make.

Brenwar had already begun to forge ahead. He'd slid halfway down the steep hillside and had begun a determined trek into the valley.

The Lost City of Borgash was lost from sight and the wind picked up, howling through the half-dead trees. The area surrounding Borgash was eerie. It was heavy in overgrowth. Vines and roots jutted up like massive snakes, shooting from the ground and twisting around the trees. The berry bushes were barren. The leaves brown. The mosses weren't green but rather a sickly yellow. Soft and spongy on the ground.

Nostrils flaring, Nath broke the silence, "I'm not so sure about that smell. Not to be crude, but it smells like a giant defecated." He covered his nose. "It's foul."

"It's no more offensive than your words to my ears," Brenwar said, climbing into a corridor of fallen boulders. "Yer giving me a headache."

"Mind your tongue. I'm still—"

Selene tugged on his arm.

"What?" Nath stopped and looked at her.

"You might want to let that argument go," she said. "Things have changed, remember?"

"But I'm still the—"

"King? Prince? Does that really matter now?"

"I suppose not. It's just that—"

Selene pressed her finger on his lips and gently shushed him. Her nose twitched. Her eyes darted from side to side. "Let it go. We have more important things to worry about."

"Like what?" Nath asked.

Brenwar let out a yell. "Goblins!"

CHAPTER 26

HAVING SNAKED THEIR WAY INTO the path between the rocks, Nath and company found themselves pinned in now. Brenwar stood face to face with a knot of goblins pressed into the path.

Little taller than the dwarf, they stood brandishing crude swords, spears, hatchets, and knives. Their dark hair was matted and greasy. Carved bone jewelry rattled on their chests and necks. Their yellow eyes were wide with evil.

"Perhaps that's what I smelled," Nath said, lifting up his foot and standing on one leg.

"Uh, are you going to stomp them?" Selene said.

Nath put his leg down and gave a shrug. It was instinct. He'd gotten used to crushing many things under his powerful legs. Now all he had was muscle and claws. "Brenwar, let's see if we can come out of this encounter peacefully."

"Never," Brenwar said back over his shoulder. He held Mortuun out in front of the goblins' eyes. "If you value your lives, you dirty things, you'll be stepping aside."

The goblin in front, a small, hunchbacked knot of muscle, licked his lips and showed a mouthful of jagged teeth. "Dwarf. Mmmm. Lots of meat under that beard. Should be fun to kill. Delicious to eat."

"We'll see about that," Brenwar said, raising his war hammer high over his head.

Nath turned his ear upward. Scuffling clamored off the rocks that hemmed them inside the path.

Several more goblins appeared. Spears were poised in their sinewy arms. Their beady eyes hungered to attack. "I don't suppose you are open to negotiation?" Nath said in Goblin.

The lead goblin spat a wad of dark juice, wiped his mouth, and said, "We've not eaten in days." It set its eyes on Nath, then they shifted to Brenwar. "This dwarf should suffice. Leave him and you may pass."

"Let me think about that."

"What?" Brenwar said.

Nath made a quick count. There were ten goblins that he could hear and see. Their eyes were feverish with hunger. Desperation was in the leader's voice. Hearts pounded behind their bone breast-plated chests. *I can't believe I'm wasting my time with this. If I was still a dragon, they'd be fleeing into the hills. This is beneath me.* Summoning the authority in his voice, he said, "Tell you what, goblins, let us pass and I'll let you live."

The lead goblin made a face like he'd swallowed a large bug. In the next instant, his expression darkened and a rage-filled order burst forth from his sweaty lips. "Attack!"

Brenwar ducked underneath a slicing sword and charged straight into the leader.

Behind Nath, Selene's tail licked out and swatted two goblins across the face at once. Both tumbled headlong into the path.

"Nice move," Nath said, spinning around and snatching a spear that was flying toward his neck.

The goblin that threw it gaped, wide eyed. It went for the knife tucked into its belt.

Nath spun the spear around and busted the goblin's hand. "None of that, now!"

Clutching its hand, the goblin cried out in pain.

Nath slugged it across the jaw with the butt of the spear.

It stumbled into one of the boulders, knocking its metal helmet off. "That will … *oof!*"

A pair of goblins flung themselves into Nath and drove him headfirst into the ground. One wrapped around his legs and started biting. The other goblin locked one arm around his neck, squeezed, and started stabbing at Nath's chest with his free arm. The blade bit deep.

"Argh!" Nath twisted the knife free from the goblin, dipped his shoulder, and, with a heave, slung it off his neck. He turned his attention to the one latched onto his leg and biting it.

Its teeth sank deep into his calf.

Now realizing he still had his boot in his hand, Nath started beating the goblin with it. "Get off of me, you dirty tick!"

Selene's tail coiled around its neck and jerked it free. She hoisted it high in the air and slammed it into one of the nearby rocks. *Thud!*

Ahead, Brenwar had a goblin pinned down by the neck. He hammered it in the face with his fist. "Eat me, will you? Eat this!" *Wham! Wham! Wham!*

Chest heaving, Nath caught a flicker of movement out of the corner of his eye.

Above, on the rocks, a goblin and its spear were poised to attack.

Nath sprang high in the air, landing right beside the slack-jawed goblin.

It made a desperate lunge.

Nath caught the spear and ripped it away. He cracked the goblin upside the head with the shaft, breaking the spear. *Whap! Whap! Whap!*

The goblin fell to its knees and begged for mercy. "Please, stop! Please stop! No more hungry. Please!"

Nath picked it up by its ragged armor and trousers, and with a heave, he tossed the goblin far into the woods.

The party of goblins that survived quickly grabbed all the fallen weapons and fled in all directions, leaving Nath, Selene, and Brenwar alone once again in the crevice.

Looking up from the path at Nath, Selene said, "You're bleeding. Are you going to cry about it?"

Blood pumping through his battle-charged veins, Nath smacked his fist into his palm and replied, "Let's go find some orcs."

The Lost City of Borgash was anything but lost. However, it was a wasteland. Nath and company entered from what was left of the main gate that led into the city. A rusting portcullis—big enough for giants to enter—was torn asunder. The rocks that held it were half rubble, but many still stood firm. There were markings. Carvings in the stone.

Nath ran his fingers over the edges. "What do you think, Brenwar?"

"Well before my time. Not much in the dwarven archives, either." He ran his hands over a fallen stone column. "Clearly not made by dwarves, or it never would have fallen. Har. Probably elven or orcen."

"What about you, Selene?" Nath asked. "Any ideas?"

She ran her hands up and down her arms and shivered a little. "It's eerie. It's always been my understanding that there was an invasion and the people just disappeared. But that was hundreds, maybe thousands of years ago for all I know. I don't think anyone really remembers. Besides, there are several cities that have come and gone just like this."

"This was no small city," Brenwar said. He climbed up a pile of vine-covered rubble. "It rivals the likes of Quintuklen. If there is a clue about your mother here, it will take days, maybe weeks to search it out. And with the air so foul, it will take some getting used to."

"At least we're here, so let's get started. Perhaps we should split up," Nath suggested.

"There's danger here, Nath," Selene said, covering her shoulders with her hands. "I've no doubt we aren't alone. And there's a reason not many venture too deep into Borgash."

"Really, why is that?"

"Because most that go in don't come back out."

CHAPTER 27

BORGASH WAS BIG INDEED. THE abandoned city stretched for miles in all directions. Most of the city was nothing more than part of the landscape, but in places there were remnants of once-thriving stone buildings.

Nath climbed up a series of vines where dead-looking trees sprouted up like massive pylons. The bark was petrified and swallowed up by the prickling vines. He sauntered out on one of the branches and spied on his surroundings.

Not too far off in the distance, Brenwar stood on the ground, moving large rocks and boulders back and forth.

That should keep him happy. Well, "content" might be a better word.

Selene was nowhere in sight. Nath felt a little guilty about that. He'd insisted they split up. They didn't need to watch over him anymore, dragonman or not. If anything, Selene needed an eye kept on her. After all, her roots had once been steeped in evil.

They'll be fine. This place seems harmless enough. He reached up, dug his claws into a branch, and pulled himself up to greater heights. From his perch up in the dead and leafless tree, he could see all around, and so far as he was concerned, there wasn't much to look at.

I can see why no one leaves. They die of boredom.

He stretched his arms out and spread them wide. *Oh, if I could only fly!*

You can.

Nath froze with chills going up his spine. Finally, his lips moved. "Eh, is someone there?"

There was no reply. Just the soft howl of the wind. Nath spun around on the branch and looked everything up and down. There was nothing in the tree. No birds. No nests. But there were some holes bored into the wood. He shook his head. "I must be hearing things. My own imagination, perhaps."

Glancing back down at the ground, he noticed Brenwar was gone.

A chill wind slid over Nath's neck, standing his nape hairs on end. His body tingled, but not in a good way. He felt unseen eyes all over him. The warmth of the setting sun on his face began to fade. Shadows from distant mountains changed the look of Borgash's landscape. Nath rubbed his neck. *Perhaps splitting up wasn't such a good idea.*

Too impatient to scramble all the way down the tree, he hopped down the last twenty feet and landed soundlessly on the soft ground.

Not bad. Couldn't have made such a subtle landing before, I'll admit that.

He was headed in the direction he'd last seen Brenwar when Nath tripped and fell. "What in the world?" Glancing down, he noticed his feet were tangled in some vines. He started ripping the vines from his boots. "Stubborn things."

Finally, his feet were free, and he carefully backed away. Glancing up, he noticed the tree he'd just climbed from was different. The branches were bent downward, seeming to come right at him, but still stiff and frozen.

"Odd. Very odd." He took off at a trot, traversing the jagged landscape of the fallen city, and found himself standing where he'd last seen Brenwar. There was no sign of the dwarf. No tracks, either. "Oh, I'm not losing you again."

By taking in a whiff of air, Nath found that Brenwar's dwarven musk lingered. On cat's feet, Nath picked his way through the foliage and growing shadows. If Brenwar had passed through the direction Nath was headed, there wasn't any sign of him.

I don't like this. I don't like it at all.

Nath stopped and turned. Behind him, the grasses he had trodden on didn't show the slightest sign that he'd passed through there at all. He squatted down and pressed his palm into the moss- and grass-covered ground. After he lifted his hand there was an impression. It lasted only a moment, and then the grass and moss had returned to their prior places. "That's new."

Glancing up at the setting sun, he noted there was little light left in the day. With a twitch in his nose, he hustled after Brenwar.

Great Guzan. What if this place has eaten him?

Pushing through the overgrowth, Nath noticed that every fiber of life he touched seemed to scrape and pull at him. His boots got stuck in between some more vines, and he ripped his foot clean out of the leather. He reached down only to find the ground and foliage swallowing his boots up. "Sultans of Sulfur!" He grabbed them just in time and hopped over more vines while he put them back on.

Keeping to the trail of Brenwar's scent, Nath sprinted away.

I've got to warn Brenwar! Find Selene!

Jumping over fallen stone after fallen stone, he emerged in a barren spot of land and came to a sudden halt in front of a living and gaping hole.

His eyes were locked on Brenwar's.

The dwarf was bound up in the new tendrils of a vine just outside a monstrous maw in the hole, encircled with teeth. On the other side of the expansive monster, Selene was corded up and being dragged into the gurgling hole.

"Selene!"

CHAPTER 28

THE GAPING HOLE OF VEGETATION groaned. Deep in its middle, a ring of teeth chomped up and down. The vines gripping Brenwar and Selene dragged them downward toward the bone-crunching hole.

"Hold on!" Nath yelled.

There were no replies. Selene and Brenwar's mouths were encircled by vines. Their eyes were pleading and filled with desperation.

"Blast! If I was bigger, I'd rip this thing out of the ground!" Nath's eyes searched for something, anything that might aid his friends. He dashed around the rim of the monster. "Selene! Give me your tail!"

Her tail whipped out. Nath stretched his fingers as far as he could, but there was still a considerable gap around him.

Suddenly, more vines burst forth from the monster's mouth. Like venomous snakes, they came right for him. He backpedaled. His feet were snagged by a tangle of vines and grasses. "Blast!"

Selene and Brenwar continued to descend deeper into the hole. All of their struggles were in vain.

"No!" Nath ripped free of the foliage.

The tendrils from the mouth reared up and encircled his arms. The vines tugged at him with tremendous force.

Nath tugged back with all his might. He ripped a tendril clear of the monster's mouth. *Snap!*

The ground shook.

The monster let out a shrill cry. *Eaaerrrrrrrr!*

Nath ripped out another vine. *Snap!*

The earth buckled beneath him.

"Hah! You don't like that, do you."

More tendrils burst forth from the monster's mouth. Dozens of them surged for Nath all at once.

"Not good!"

Striking fast, the tendrils ripped at Nath's legs.

He leapt backward and bounced off a boulder.

The tendrils snaked over the rim and pressed after him. The other grasses and vines came to life, holding him fast.

"This entire place is alive!"

While he was pushing himself out of the tangles, the boulder in front of him inspired an idea. He darted to the other side, wrapped his arms around it as best he could, and hoisted it up onto his shoulder. "Argh!"

The tendrils coiled up his legs and squeezed.

Sweat beading on his brow, Nath fought for balance and shuffled forward. The skin on his legs started to burn. The tremendous weight of the stone strained every muscle in his shoulders and back. Using the tugging of the evil vines, he continued the slow march forward.

"This is it, monster," Nath said through gritted teeth. "I've got a bellyful for you." Standing on the rim of the sunken maw, he hunkered down. With a heave, he launched the huge rock off of his shoulders and down into the mouth.

The boulder smashed right into the snapping mouth.

The ground rocked and reeled.

The earth let out an uncanny shriek. *Rreeeeeeeeeee!*

The tendrils uncoiled from around Nath's legs and darted back down into the hole.

The rock covered the mouth entirely.

The tendrils attacked it. They bounced off the gritty surface over and over like snakes gone mad.

Without hesitation, Nath slid down the side of the hole and yanked Selene free of the tendrils. She was gasping for breath. Nath carried her in his arms and set her down on the rim.

Below and butted up against the rock covering the mouth was Brenwar. There was a disgruntled look on his face. Nath scurried back into the hole, broke away the clinging tendrils, and fetched him up and out of the hole.

"Is everyone all right?" Nath asked.

The ground tremored beneath them.

"By Mortuun! The cursed ground here is living!" Brenwar said. He raised the war hammer high.

"Stop, dwarf!" Selene said, staying his hand with hers. "This isn't some mountainside you can cave in. This evil breathes." She shoved into him. "Let me handle this."

"How dare you!" Brenwar growled, pushing back.

Selene's hands flared up with fire.

Brenwar's eyes became moons.

"Selene! How can you do that?" Nath said, gaping.

"I've been a priestess, have I not? My ability to craft magic is not gone. Does it make you uncomfortable?"

"Just a little surprised is all."

She shook her head and turned away. Mystic tones and arcane words spun from her lips. Fire rushed from her fingertips, driving hard into the monster.

The ground screeched.

The gaping hole spread with flame. The tendrils writhed, popped, and crackled. The expanse became a burning pyre where vegetable turned to ash. The rock inside its mouth collapsed out of sight. Gray ash drifted in the wind.

Leaning over the edge, Brenwar said, "All we had to do was set it on fire?"

Selene dusted her hands off. "Mystic fire. But I took a chance."

Nath eyed her.

"What?" she said, eyeing him back. "I'm a lifelong spell crafter."

"Then why didn't you use your craft before?" Nath asked.

"The same reason the dwarf didn't get in a swing of his hammer. I was surprised."

Nath nodded. "If you say so."

"Nath, now is not the time to doubt me again."

"Well, maybe if you didn't have those black scales, we wouldn't doubt you," Brenwar interjected.

"Black scales. Are you jesting, dwarf?" She pointed at Nath. "Have you not noticed his too?"

"Aye, I have, and I don't like them. Black is a sign of evil."

Nath put his fists on his hips. "Well, your beard's black. Does that make you evil?"

"What?" Brenwar clutched at his beard with his skeleton hand. "Why no." He rapped Mortuun's shaft down on the ground. "Like I said, 'Black, isn't it glorious!'"

The three of them had a little laugh.

Nath then turned to Selene. "I have to admit, I'm envious. It seems you have much of the power you once had. I don't appear to have anything."

Selene cupped his face with her hand. "Nath, be patient. I couldn't have lifted that boulder."

His eyes brightened like gold stars. He flexed his black-scaled arms. "No, I guess you couldn't."

"I could've," Brenwar said, staring down at the hole.

"With the gauntlets, sure, but look at that thing. It must have been a ton if not more."

"It wasn't that big," Brenwar said, still staring into the black hole. He reached down and found a piece of broken vine. He waggled it in front of Selene. "Do you mind, snake tail?"

"Oh," she said with smoldering eyes, "you are a bold one, Bolderguild." With a snap of her fingers, the tip of the vine was encircled in flame.

Brenwar tossed the makeshift torch into the hole. It landed with a crunchy sound that echoed upward. "By Morgdon, that hole is full of bones!"

CHAPTER 29

Nath stood inside the hole, surrounded by bones piled as high as his chin. Beside him, Brenwar pushed through the skeletons, making a path.

"Guzan, there must be hundreds of them," Nath said. He picked up a skull and held it before his eyes. "Look at these high cheekbones. This one is elven."

"It seems the creature took all kinds," Selene said, holding up a round skull with heavy bone. "I'd say this one is dwarven or orcen."

Brenwar snatched it away. "Orcen? Pah! It's dwarven. And it needs a proper burial."

"Don't be silly, Brenwar. We can't pick through all of these bones to bury your dead. They've probably been at rest for hundreds of years." Nath plucked up a sword out of the pile then dropped it again when he saw that its metal was long rusted through. There were hundreds of decaying things scattered all over. "The dead are at rest. Let them rest."

Brenwar tucked the dwarven skull under his arm. "I'll bury him if I want."

"Fine, Brenwar. Fine." Wading through the bones, Nath sauntered up to Selene. Her tail was brushing the piles aside. "So, what do you make of this? Do you think this monster is what made Borgash extinct?"

She held a head in front of her that still had some hair on it. It was long and showed canine teeth. "A gnoll. A shame they aren't all gnolls, but no, I don't think this monster was the demise of the city. All of the races seem to be represented here. This is just hundreds of years of victims. Treasure hunters, perhaps? Travelers. All victims of the guardian."

Nath cocked a brow. "Guardian?"

"One of many in this valley, I'd say. And if I'm correct, this plant monster is called a devourer, though this is the biggest one I've ever seen."

"Where did you see them before?" Nath asked.

She dusted off her hands and faced him. "I don't think that really matters now. Excuse me." She brushed by him and began shifting through the char that used to be the dangerous plant. "Ah, see this?"

"Guzan!" Nath said, jumping back. "Kill it!"

Out of the ground, a tendril with a white bud on the end was writhing about. Selene seized it with her hand. "These devourers have strong roots and grow back quickly. You have to destroy the root." She started to tug on it. "A little help, please?"

Nath wrapped his arms around her waist, dug his feet in, and started to pull her back.

"This isn't exactly what I had in mind," she said.

"Oh, hush and hang on." Feet digging in, he started to pull her back harder. "Guzan! How deep is this thing?"

Puffing for breath, Selene said, "I thought you were strong!"

Nath set his jaw, leaned back, put all of his muscles and weight into it, and said, "I sure hope you don't break."

"I won't!"

"Grrrrrr!"

Rip! The plant gave.

Nath stumbled backward and crashed into the bones. Selene was on his lap, holding the squirming tendril. At its end, a huge red tuber, bigger than an ogre's head, pulsated like a heart.

"That's creepy!"

Brenwar charged up with Mortuun.

"No, dwarf!" Selene said, stretching out her arms.

Mortuun the Crusher came down with ram-like force.

Splat!

Slime and goo covered Selene and Brenwar.

Jumping to her feet with fists balled up at her sides, she screamed at Brenwar, "Fool of a dwarf!" Her tail rose up behind her. "I'm going to kill you!"

Brandishing his war hammer, Brenwar fired back a warning. "Watch yerself, dragon lady."

Nath, shielded behind Selene, chuckled. "You two just aren't ever going to get along, are you."

Combing the gunk out of her long black hair, Selene walked away. "Probably not."

"You really should try being a little nicer to her, Brenwar."

Brenwar's eyes widened. "Me? Why?"

"She's a woman."

"With a tail, and not so long ago, she tried to destroy me, you, and the rest of the world."

"We're past that now, so try to put forth a better effort." Ignoring Brenwar's frown, Nath glanced up out of the hole at the darkening, star-filled sky. "It's going to be blacker than my scales before long. Hmmm." He picked up a skull and chucked it into the black expanse that surrounded the hole. The sound of it skipping off stone echoed back. "That's interesting. Uh, Brenwar, we could use a torch or something. Do you have your tinderbox handy?"

Selene slipped in between Brenwar and Nath. "So primitive." With a snap of her fingers, her hand glowed with a warm green light. Its wavering glow illuminated the entire hole and beyond.

Gaping, Nath said, "Looks like the Lost City isn't so lost after all."

CHAPTER 30

DEEPER INTO THE BOWELS OF Borgash they walked. It was an underground city with a sky made of dirt. Selene's light cut through the dimness, revealing remnants of paved streets and buildings. Dirt and a slick coat of grime covered most of the area. The sky of dirt and roots was suspended above them, looking to collapse at any time. Somewhere, water trickled inside the eerie expanse.

"What do you think, Brenwar?"

The warrior held a small torch now that gave off a warm, glowing yellow light. He climbed up on a half-covered statue of a centaur and poked at the dirt ceiling with his hammer. "Hmmm, seems to have held hundreds of years; no reason to believe it won't hold a few hundred more." He hit it harder with his war hammer.

"Is that really necessary, dwarf?" Selene said, backing up into Nath.

"If it falls, I'll dig us out. It just might take a few years."

"Come on," Nath said. "If there is anything to be found, I can only assume it's below ground and not above."

Venturing deeper into the buried realm, Nath rolled his shoulders. The tightness in his back remained. Something lived here. Something dark. He dusted off his nose with his thumb. There was a stench, too. Not dirt or mud. Not bones or rotting flesh. Something unnatural. A lurking of Evil.

There were plenty of normal creatures that lived beneath the ground. Dragons were one of them.

Gnomes and dwarves were well known for making league-long holes. But not too many creatures lived without daylight for very long. Hibernated, yes. Lived, no.

"What's on your mind?" Selene asked.

"Everything feels wrong." He kneeled down and began brushing off some caked dirt that covered a fallen statue. On uncovering its oversized visage, he discovered a monstrous face with multiple eyes and a mouthful of fangs. "Seem familiar?"

"I've never seen a carven image the likes of that before," she said, but…" She backed away and began clawing away hunks of dirt that covered the stony walls. Her efforts revealed painted images. Runes. People. Monsters. Violence. "I'm starting to think the devourer is here for a great reason."

The way she spoke made Nath's skin prickle. "You said it might be a guardian. A guardian of what?"

"A guardian that not only keeps things from getting in," she said, moving away from Nath. She kept the light of her hand pointed at the dirt ceiling. There was a higher spot above. The roots moved away from her light. "Nath, you know how you said this place was evil?"

"Yes."

Selène started back toward him. Standing by his side, she said, "I'm pretty sure you're right."

"Brenwar, did you hear that? She said I was right. See, Selene can be sensible."

Selene jabbed an elbow into his ribs. "Don't be foolish. We need to go."

"Really, why the rush all of a sudden?"

Selene knelt down beside the cruel and unusual face that Nath had revealed. She pointed at it and said, "Because I think I know what this is. It's an image of an old titan."

"Titan?" Nath said, making a quick shrug. "What's a titan?"

"The race that enslaved man. That tried to enslave the dragons as well." She started packing mud back over its face. "The race that would stop at nothing to enslave Nalzambor."

"Step aside," Brenwar said. With a quick swing of his hammer, he busted the image of the old titan face. *Bang!* "Humph. That's better."

"Will you quit hitting everything with your little hammer?" Selene said.

"We don't hesitate to deface the titans where I come from," Brenwar said, resting Mortuun back over his shoulder. "Ever."

Brenwar's tone was serious.

The truth was, Nath had never heard of the titans before today. He'd gathered from Selene that they were legend more than anything. Men and women of great renown, worshipped like deities, who had deceived the races in times past. Judging by the age of that statue, it had happened long before his time, just the same as Borgash. "So, are we staying in or going out? I'm opting for in. I'm not going to find my mother by being cautious. But if you don't want to venture any farther, I understand."

"Oh, please," Selene said, rolling her eyes.

"Shaddap," Brenwar added, holding his torch out and venturing deeper into the passage.

"It seems we're all in again. Great." Nath glided to the front. He could feel the heat from Brenwar's torch on his back. Using his keen eyes, he had little problem making out the deeper outlines of the cavernous passage. Here and there the old roads were revealed. There were still standing walls and columns with markings on them. Old wooden stables were petrified. The air was dank and musty. It would take days to search all of the cave city. Maybe weeks. They might have to dig, and digging wasn't very much fun.

"Seems like a strange place for your mother to be," Selene said. She stood by some stalactites and stalagmites that had formed around a small pond near her feet. "I'm not so sure that I'd trust a fairy. Certainly not a fairy empress."

"You didn't have to come—not that I'm unhappy that you did come—but this is all we have to go on for now." Nath came across a wide staircase of stone that wound deeper into the ground. Squinting, he swore he saw a wink of light down there. "Say, Brenwar, what do you make of this?"

Brenwar sauntered over and peered down the steps. "Looks deep," he said, bobbing his head. "I like deep."

A wink of light flashed.

"Did you see that?" Nath said in a whisper.

Brenwar replied in kind, "Aye, I did." He started down. "And I hear water, too."

"Coming, Selene?" Nath said.

Holding her glowing hand out, she stood behind Nath and said, "You first."

Nath took a breath and headed down after Brenwar.

One thing is for certain. Being small leads to many more interesting places.

The stairway was well over a hundred steps down, its hard surface slick with damp mud. Nath had been in caves all of his life. Even Dragon Home had been bored out of a mountain, and there were prisons more than a hundred feet deep. But this was different. It gave him a mysterious feeling that he couldn't shake. It clung to his scales. Rushed his breath.

"Bottom," Brenwar said. He stood inside a chamber the size of a small cathedral. The light did little to capture the full grandeur. Square columns and great arches held up the expansive ceiling. Colorful murals above glinted in the faint light cast from below. "Sound craftsmanship."

"Dwarven?" Nath asked.

"Not that sound."

A bright light, distant and wavering, appeared far away from them. Humanoid in shape, it glided forward. Nath's breath became icy. The shade closed in, getting bigger. Towering over them all, it came to a stop. Faceless, robed, and ethereal, its haunting voice froze Nath's bones.

CHAPTER 31

THE APPARITION SPOKE, TURNING BLOOD to ice water.

Nath felt Selene's arm entangle with his. Heart pounding in his chest, head gazing upward, he found it hard to keep his eyes fixed on the monster.

Haunting sounds came from its ghostly lips. Its language was unnatural and changing. A howling shriek burst from the veiled face of the apparition.

"Hoooowwww-eeeeee-hooooooowwwwww!"

Nath's knees buckled. His legs turned to jelly. Hair billowing, he covered his ears. Beside him, Brenwar dropped to a knee. Selene's sharp fingernails dug into his arms. "Selene, what do we do?" he asked, trying to shout over the howling shriek.

Shouting in his ear, she replied, "I don't know!"

The apparition's wispy veil lifted. Its face contorted and twisted, showing brief glimpses of all the races. Its shrill voice changed. The tones lifted high and fell back low. Its long-ranging arms stretched toward Brenwar.

The battle-hardened dwarf recoiled. His thick limbs remained rigid.

"Move, Brenwar! Move!" Nath yelled. At least he thought he did. He couldn't tell now. His own limbs were stiff and frozen. His tongue seemed to cleave to the roof of his mouth. Fighting against his frozen bonds, he reached down, grabbed the dwarf by the collar, and jerked him back.

The apparition's hands wavered to a stop. Its face settled into an image more readily seen. Its features sharpened. High cheekbones. Pointed ears. It opened its thin lips and spoke its first intelligible words in a deep and hollow tone. "Who are you?"

That's Elven! Nath's unseen shackles melted away. *An old dialect, but it's Elven.* He spoke back in the best Elven he could. "Nath. Nath Dragon."

The apparition's face shifted from elven to the face of a dragon. It spoke again, this time in Dragonese. "You are odd for a dragon."

Nath looked at Selene, only to find her eyes as wide as his. He turned back to the apparition and replied in Dragonese, "It's a long story. And who might you be?"

The haunting figure diminished somewhat in stature. Its foreboding presence eased. Its long hands stretched out again, cupping around them all but without touching. "Blood runs through your veins. Life-giving blood. Ah, so desirable. So delicious. How fortunate you are to live."

"Who are you?" Nath said. "What is your purpose?"

"Ah, to live again. To breathe. To taste." The ghost's hands lashed out and enveloped Nath. "So wonderful!"

Nath's head jerked back. His blood turned to ice and fire. A flood of memories washed through his mind, not his but someone else's. The apparition's. There were battles. Great titans ruling man and fighting dragons. Death. Life. Loss. Destruction. "Stop it! Stop it!" Nath screamed.

A blinding light flashed. Pain split through his skull. In slow motion he saw himself fall and crash into the cathedral floor, unmoving. Someone rolled him onto his back. Selene stared down at him. Her lips were moving, but no sound came out. Brenwar appeared. Gruff. Angry. Confused. He reached down and started smacking Nath's face.

Will you quit that?

Nath coughed. Finding a small reservoir of strength in his weakened limbs, he tried to sit up. Brenwar and Selene propped him up.

"Nath," Selene said, cupping his face in her hands. "Nath, can you hear me?"

Blinking away the pain behind his eyes, he said, "Yes, stop yelling. What happened?"

Brenwar pointed down at the cathedral floor and said, "That happened."

A man in white robes danced on the cathedral's floor, his bare feet slapping it. Hands on his towheaded hair, he side-stepped back and forth and was singing in a complicated common tongue that the old-timers used in more remote farms and villages deep in the valleys.

"Who is that?" Nath asked. He took Brenwar's arm and allowed the dwarf to help him to his feet. He stretched his aching back. "Gads! I feel like I've aged a hundred years." He caught Brenwar and Selene glancing at each other. "What?"

"Nothing," Selene said, showing an uncertain smile. "How are you feeling?"

Rubbing his head, Nath said, "I haven't been sleeping a hundred years, have I?"

"Why, do I look a hundred years older?" Selene said.

"No, it's just the pair of you have some very peculiar looks on your faces." He rubbed his beard and said, "Gads! What happened?" Nath clutched handfuls of red beard in both of his clawed hands. "I'm not a dwarf, am I?"

"What?" Brenwar growled. "Now you're dreaming. But the beard is a good look for you. Other than that, you look normal, aside from a few new wrinkles."

"Be silent, dwarf!" Selene said.

"Wrinkles!" Nath cried. He felt his face. His skin was tighter, and there were creases in his forehead that had never been there before. "What did that thing do to me?"

The dancing man in the robes came running up the stairs, leapt up the last few, and said, "Apologies and thanks!" He grabbed Nath's hand and shook it vigorously. "I could not help myself! Tee-hee! I breathe again!"

Nath's nostrils flared. The man was taller than Nath and big boned, but there was nothing powerful about his build. A strange, big man, a hair over seven feet tall. Human, but odd for that kind. He seized the man's wrists. "I'm only going to ask you this once. Who are you and what did you do to me?"

"Azorath is my name, I think. Azorath, the gatekeeper of Borgash." He grimaced. "Your grip is iron, liberator. You need not fear anything else from me."

"What did you do to me?"

"I merely stole some years from your life force." Azorath blinked at him. His eyes were black glass and spacey "Please, do not fret, you have plenty. A hundred years or so won't hurt you."

"A hundred years!" Nath started pushing Azorath back down the steps. "Give it back!"

"I fear I cannot! I admit, I would not. The flesh of life is in me again!"

"The flesh of life will be gone from you if you don't undo this."

"You would not kill me, Nath Dragon," Azorath said with a feeble smile. "It's not in your nature."

"It's in mine," Brenwar said.

Selene confronted the man. "It's in mine as well."

"Er ..." Azorath's eyes danced back and forth among the three of them. "Slaying me won't change a thing. It was worth it. And so will your sacrifice be as well, Nath Dragon."

"I didn't sacrifice anything," Nath said. "You stole it."

"The moment you ventured into the bowels of Borgash, you sacrificed everything to find your mother." Azorath tapped his finger to his head. "And I know where she is."

CHAPTER 32

AZORATH LED NOW. NATH, BRENWAR, and Selene followed. The former shade, now a man, picked his way through the subterranean levels of the fallen city. They climbed over huge chunks of road that had been heaved up. Passageways that weren't made by men. Their eerie guide talked the entire time.

"This was the square here," Azorath said, running his hands over a piece of twisted metal. "Many celebrations and ceremonies. Weddings. Feasts. Grand times, at least until the titans came. They had a different way of celebrating. They killed and ate people. Pitted one against the other. Horrible times, but the dragons liberated the races." He pointed at Nath. "You understand that. A brave and noble thing, fighting for the weak and saving them from the strong."

"Yes, you've said that before, shade," Brenwar said. "How much more walking and talking? You say you know where Nath's mother is. How much farther is she?"

"Almost there," Azorath said, climbing down over a ledge and stopping before a stream of water that trickled. He pushed his hands down in the water and giggled. "I have not drunk nor eaten. I thirst!" He stuck his face in the water and drank. "Ah!"

Brenwar stepped into Nath and Selene's path. "That thing is not right. Don't trust it."

"I know, Brenwar," Nath said, watching Azorath continue to drink and giggle. "But if he knows anything, we have to take that chance."

Brenwar shook his head and followed after Azorath.

"You've been awfully quiet, Selene. What do you make of this?" asked Nath.

She rubbed his shoulder. "It's not for me to decide. It's your quest. You lead, I'll follow."

Nath nodded. Despite the creepy feeling he couldn't shake out from under his scales, he found a ring of truth in Azorath's words. He wanted to believe the strange man knew where his mother was. *Why am I trusting someone who just sucked a huge part of my life from me? How did he know I was searching for my mother? Did he steal my memories as well?"*

After finishing off another handful of water, Azorath continued. "You're probably wondering if I'm the only survivor left of this once-great city."

"No," Brenwar said.

"Sure you are, so I will tell you. Yes, I am." Azorath ducked between two buildings that had collided and formed an unnatural archway. "I was chosen to be the gatekeeper. To be the last. You see, the titans were defeated, but their dark ways were not. Borgash broke out in civil war once the deity-like beings were out of the picture. This faction fought with that one. Everything began to come apart at the seams. The wizards and priests battled for rule and order. Earthquakes broke out. Tornadoes screamed. It went on and on until everyone fought and no one survived. It was madness."

"Still don't care," Brenwar said. He shoved Azorath forward. "Now get us to where we need to be getting."

"I can't help but share my speech. It's been so long since I spoke to anyone. Forgive me for enjoying your miserable company." He ducked his head underneath a low archway that led into a tunnel. "I find it delightful."

Nath rubbed his temples.

I feel like a fool. Just don't look like one, Nath. Be wary of a trap.

He trod over the grime-slickened stones, keeping Azorath in sight. The lanky man had a spring in his step. His whistles echoed, too.

That doesn't make my head much better.

Finally, the gatekeeper came to a stop in front of an archway that was broken in half. Above it, two massive rocks had collided. Pitch blackness was on the other side of the archway. "Through here," he pointed. "Answers to the questions you seek." He reached for Brenwar's torch. "May I?"

"Get yer own."

"Brenwar," Nath said, "please, oblige him."

With a grunt, Brenwar handed the torch over.

Azorath waved it back and forth and erupted in a short series of giggles then said, "I can't help it. I feel the warmth from it. It's delightful." He stuck it through the archway. The flames vanished in the blackness. He pulled it back out, and the flames were still alive. "I warn you. It's very dark in there, but not far." Showing a row of big, smiling teeth, he said, "Who goes in first?"

Nath didn't move, and neither did Selene or Brenwar.

"I see," Azorath said, "then I guess it will be me." He hopped into the blackness and vanished.

Selene let out a sigh.

"What was that for?" Nath said to her.

"He bothers me," she said.

"Me too," Brenwar agreed.

"Nath, now that he—or it—is gone, I'm more prone to speak freely. I'm not so sure there is anything to be gained from this venture. You don't have any evidence to go on about your mother, just the word of a fairy, and now this creature. They are both far from trustworthy."

"Aye," Brenwar said.

"I've considered that," Nath said, "But what if my mother is down inside this horrible place? I can't bear the thought of that. Not to mention I want my years of life back."

"But why would she be?" Selene said. "This place fell more than a thousand years ago. Your mother gave birth to you maybe two hundred and fifty years ago. Why would she come here?"

"Those are good arguments," he said, "but my gut tells me that I need to at least eliminate the possibility." He stepped up to the arch and stuck his hand in it. It felt like he had stuck his fingers in ice. "I'm going in." He extended his free hand. "Anyone else?"

Brenwar came forward. "I'm going, but I'm not holding your hand."

"I will take it," Selene said, taking his hand in hers. "But don't get used to it."

Head ducking down, Nath led them into the archway.

CHAPTER 33

EMPTINESS. THERE WAS NO WORSE feeling than nothing at all.

Guzan, what madness is this?

He tumbled through the blackness, yet there was no wind in his hair. Selene's touch was gone. His heartbeat was missing. Only his thoughts remained. A mind without a body. Soundless, he drifted in nowhere.

I've been deceived!

Struggling to find his own self, he noted a small window of light. He swam toward it. It became bigger, brighter, and it swallowed him whole. Wind rushed by his ears. His arms and legs flailed. "Gah!"

He crashed into a soft bed of sand. He spat the sand from his mouth and shook it from his hair. A shadow fell over him. He glanced up.

"Incoming!" Brenwar yelled. The dwarf landed on Nath's chest.

"Ooof!" He pushed Brenwar off and helped him to his feet.

Brenwar shook the sand from his beard. "This is a fine place."

They stood on a huge bed of cool, wet sand. Water trickled from all around, running down slick, polished cave walls. A soft green light illuminated the cavern like a spectral sky. It was humid and sweaty.

"This will probably be a regrettable decision," Selene said. She was standing behind Brenwar and Nath, dusting the grimy sand from her clothes. Her black hair was matted to her face. She parted it and brushed it back behind her shoulders. Hands on hips, she said, "So, where is your friend?"

Nath shrugged. There was nothing in the cavern but them, and the archway they had entered from was gone. "Any idea how deep we are, Brenwar?"

Brenwar rumbled a reply. "I can't say."

Nath kicked the sand. "Just great."

"Oh, stop being so grim. I was only scouting ahead. Frankly, I didn't think you would come." It was Azorath. He lumbered up a sandy hill where water ran like a stream below. "Time has a funny way of working down here, and it's been quite some time since I've been in this area. And with a body?" He felt himself. "Tee hee!"

"Listen, Azorath, enough of the games. Take me to see my mother like you promised," Nath said.

"I don't recall promising anything. But if it makes you feel any better, I promise to show you your mother."

Nath didn't reply. He'd spent almost all of his natural life wondering who and where his mother was. Other dragons knew, but he never did, and his father had never told him. Deep down it bothered him, severely, but he never dwelled on it for long. Now, to think he might find the answer to his question? He wasn't sure he was ready. He pulled his shoulders back, marched forward, and said, "Lead the way, then."

Shuffling over the strange landscape, they moved forward at a depressive gait. Never in his life had Nath felt so displaced. His surroundings were so unnatural and odd. Light without a source from above. An eerie tingle in the air. His heightened instincts choked back and waited to cry for danger. He had to see it through, though. Have faith that his heart would lead him to his mother.

I hope I am not deceived.

He recalled his father, Balzurth, often saying, "Be careful of your heart's desires. Sometimes it can deceive you. Seek wisdom first. It will always prevail."

Azorath slogged into the ankle-deep waters and forged away. The strange man's shoulders swung left to right as he moved. The oddness about him made Nath wonder about the people that had lived in Borgash and the culture they'd shared. He felt Selene take his hand in hers. Softly he said back to her, "You must feel as out of place as I do."

"I'd be lying if I said I didn't want to see Nalzambor's sun again. It seems we've been in here for weeks already."

"Almost there," Azorath said, picking up the pace. "Oh, that was quick. It seems we are already there. Now gaze, my liberators. Gaze at the Great Wall of Dragons!"

Selene squeezed Nath's hand and gasped.

Ahead was a great wall indeed. The most magnificent wall that Nath had ever seen. A wall made of dragons. It was expansive, too. It stretched up several stories high and was just as wide. The dragons were a tight cluster of scales, claws, tails, horns, and teeth. They were a colorful mix of stone and marble. Every detail was just as realistic as the next. Dragons, great and small. Nath could tell what they were by the shapes of their heads. There were dragon breeds from the large bull dragons to the smaller fire bites. Finding his breath, Nath said, "Who created this wonder?"

"Why, the dragons did," Azorath replied. He had his hands clasped behind his back and was studying the wall with adoration. "Quite the sacrifice, isn't it?"

"I don't take your meaning," Nath said. "Are you saying that dragons carved this?"

"No, no, you don't understand. Come, come," Azorath said, beckoning with his hand. "Touch it. Feel it. That is the best way to answer your question."

"I don't like this," Selene said, not hiding the concern in her voice.

"I've never seen stonework so grand as this," Brenwar added. "Not outside of Morgdon for certain."

Nath's heart beat faster. Drawn to the great wall, he ventured forward and stretched out his hand. With the slightest tremble in his claw-tipped fingers, he laid his scaled palm on the wall. It was warm to the touch. His jaw dropped, and then with amazement he said, "Sultans of Sulfur! It's beating!"

CHAPTER 34

"I CAN'T BELIEVE THIS," NATH SAID with incredulity. "Selene, you must feel it."

The raven-headed woman hesitated. "I don't know about this, Nath. How can they live such a fate? I don't understand."

Nath swallowed. Sweat dripped into his eyes, and his heart continued to race. Hundreds of heartbeats, slow and steady, thumped through his palm, igniting his entire body. So many dragons clustered together as one. *Why?*

Finally, Selene stretched out her hand and touched the wall of dragons. She took in a sharp breath. Tears swelled in her eyes. Her normal calm and cool expression switched back and forth between sorrow and joy. "This is madness. But I don't sense any torment. Do you?"

Nath searched his feelings. He searched the feelings in the life within the dragon wall. There was no sadness. Just duty. Honor. Comfort for one another. "They aren't alone in this. They have united together. But why, Azorath?" He tore his hand away. "Why?"

Rubbing his chin, Azorath said with sad dark eyes, "They formed a barrier to keep the titans within. Never to escape again."

"Didn't they kill them all?" Nath said.

"The dragons showed mercy in hopes that one day the titans might redeem themselves." He sighed.

"There was a time when they served the world for good, not evil. At least some of them. That is how I remember it, anyway."

Eyes fixed on the dragon wall, Nath said, "The price is too high. These dragons have lives to live. Certainly there must be a better way to seal those foul monsters within."

"I don't know the answer to that," Azorath said, "but dragons live a long time. And I've seen dragons take other dragons' places." He walked up to the wall and touched the face of a red rock dragon. Running his hands over its curled tail, he said, "See, this one is new. I'd guess he came here not fifty years ago, when another one left."

"You're telling me the dragons know about this, but I don't? How can that be? Selene?"

"I don't know either, Nath. It's a mystery to me," she said.

"It's a big world, and it's full of surprises." Azorath placed his hand on the wall. "How sad, I don't feel what you feel. It just feels like a wall to me. Interesting."

"You were a shade before. Have you ever been on the other side?" Nath asked.

"No, not possible. Nothing can pass through it. No shade, spirit, titan, nor dragon."

It made sense enough to Nath. Staring at the dragons, he began picking out the details of their faces. He knew every breed. Beyond the color of their scales, each dragon breed had a unique design to its claws, horns, and even the flecks of their iron-hard scales. There wasn't any type that he didn't recognize. "I have no idea what my mother looks like or what type of dragon she is. Have you seen her, Azorath?"

"I've seen many dragons come and go."

"You said my mother was here. How would you know that if you hadn't seen her?" Nath's brow furrowed. "Show me which one she is."

"Ask them yourself. It might take me years to sort through all of them. I'm not so bored that I note every detail."

"This smells, Nath," Brenwar said. "Smells really bad. This Azorath is a liar. A stealer. I wouldn't trust another word he said."

"Don't be such a dwarf," Azorath said. "I haven't done anything you wouldn't have done given my situation. Again, I'm grateful. I have flesh again, but I do miss my people."

Nath spread his arms out, held them in front of the wall, and said, "I'm going to ask them."

"Be patient, Nath," Selene said, walking in front of him and staying his arms. "We need to learn more about what we're dealing with. Let's study the histories and research it."

"You felt it, too, Selene. We can't just let them live like this. We must see what they need. Maybe we can help them."

"They might not want help," Selene said. "It seems they made their own decision."

"That's only a guess."

"It makes no difference to me. You wanted to find your mother. I care not if you find her or not. But if I could find my mother, I'd probably venture the extra step," Azorath said, stretching his arms and yawning. "Oh my, did you see that? My limbs tire. What a feeling!"

Nath glanced at Brenwar. The dwarf's stern expression didn't offer any advice. He found Selene's eyes. Beautiful and mysterious, there was doubt lurking deep within. It wasn't like her at all. Perhaps it was guilt. She'd unleashed something terrible with the wurmers. Sounding as reassuring as he could, he said, "It's only a question."

"Then I hope you are prepared for the answer." Selene stepped away and found a place behind him. "You might not like it."

Nath placed both hands on the wall. Life flowed through the structure like a living stream. A powerful network of dragons forming a cohesive unit. It was a marvel the likes of which he'd never seen. Without hesitation, he spoke to it with thoughts instead of words.

"Brothers and sisters, I am Nath Dragon, and I am searching for my mother. Is she here?"

The wall trembled. Dragon thoughts assaulted his mind. They probed. They questioned. Nath felt every bit of them. Patient and strong they were. Formidable. Dedicated. His body shook.

"Go away, Son of Balzurth," they said. "Go away!"

Nath felt them holding back. They protected something. Something that wasn't beyond the wall. He didn't back off. "I want to know where my mother is," Nath fired back. "I am the Dragon Prince. I demand it. Is she here or not?"

Boom!

The dragon wall shook, juttering Nath's arms. Something had slammed into it from the other side. Nath grimaced. He could feel the dragons' pain.

Boom!

The wall shook again.

"Go, Nath Dragon, go. We cannot afford this distraction," they said with fierce desperation. "We must stay focused."

Nath held on and said again, "Is my mother here or not?"

"I am, Son," said a female voice.

Every fiber of Nath's being came to new life. The warmth of her voice enveloped him.

"Mother?" he said, tears streaming down his cheeks.

"Son, you must go. You endanger all of us. You'll see me when the time is right."

Boom! Boom! Boom!

Something raged on the other side of the wall. It was fierce. Unrelenting.

Nath sensed confusion among the dragons. There was pain and worry. How often did the dragons have to endure this?

"Mother! Let me help you! Let me see your face!"

"Nath, you must go before it's too late. Trust me!" Her words were no longer soothing but worried. "Flee this place with urgency!"

"I cannot let you suffer!"

Boom! Boom! Boom!

Brenwar rammed into him, knocking him away from the wall. "We have to go! This entire place is coming down!"

"Noooooooooooooooooo!" Nath screamed, clutching at the wall. Selene and Brenwar hooked his arms and dragged him backward. Gaping, Nath watched the entire wall of dragons come to life. Their colors returned. They moved and shifted. Eyes snapped open. Dragon jaws grimaced. They squeezed into as tight a knot as they could.

Boom!

The entire wall buckled.

"Perfect," Azorath said. He found Nath's eyes. "We thank you for the long-overdue distraction."

Boom!

The center of the wall of dragons burst open. Dragons were flung from the air. Something evil and colossal emerged.

CHAPTER 35

THE TITAN WAS THE BIGGEST man Nath had ever seen. His head had two faces: one in front and one in back. The massive man was chest and shoulders on both sides, his body bronze and brawny. One face sneered. The other was shouting, "I am free!"

Nath's mother shouted an order. "Dragons, attack! Force Isobahn back behind the wall!"

Hundreds of dragons converged, coating the titan.

The huge man—so big he held a bull dragon in the crook of his arm like a pup—slung them off one by one.

The dragons released fire. Lightning. Everything shook. They flung themselves into the titan, driving him back inside the wall.

Nath watched the battle in awe. The dragons, with all their skill and grandeur, were no match for the titan's relentless power. His massive fist swatted the dragons down like flies. His feet stomped them between his toes. Isobahn was no man. He was pure monster.

"We have to help!" Nath said.

"Aye!" Brenwar said, spitting in his hands and rubbing them together. "Step aside. That giant is mine!" After a few seconds of winding Mortuun in a huge windmill circle, he released the hammer with all his might. The hammer flew and struck the titan between the eyes. A clap of thunder rang out.

Kapow!

Isobahn the titan teetered backward.

The dragons rallied with triumphant roars.

"Push him through, brothers and sisters. Push him through!" Nath's mother said.

Moved by his mother's words, Nath, little bigger than the titan's finger, charged. He hurled himself along with the throng of dragons and scaled up the titan. Clawed hands digging into its coarse flesh, he raced up its belly, up the shoulder, and launched both fists into one of its eyes.

The titan groaned and fell like a collapsed tower.

"Get out of there, Nath!" he heard his mother scream.

Fire and lightning blasted into Isobahn. The titan rocked and reeled. Dragons by the hundreds, all shapes and sizes, piled onto him.

Catching friendly fire, Nath dove away.

Guzan! Where am I?

The other side of the cavern glowed with a burning red light. Streams of lava flowed from the deep. Steam and sulfur tainted the air.

Nath's eyes watered and burned. Blinking, he watched the dragons reforming the wall.

"Run, Nath! Quickly!"

Nath sprinted for the wall. The dragons were reforming it with incredible speed. He took a quick glance over his shoulder. The titan was back on its feet. Its massive hand reached down and scooped Nath up from the ground.

Nath cried out. "Ahhh!" Pain exploded through his body. His breath fled. His face purpled.

The titan opened up its mouth and started to shove him in.

Sultans of Sulfur! I'm being crushed and consumed. Nooooo!

A gold dragon appeared. It slipped into the jaws of the titan's mouth and unleashed a firestorm down the titan's throat.

Nath slipped free of the titan's loosened grasp. He hit the ground with a thud. Reeling, he forced himself up to his feet, cried out, and fell. His leg was broken. He spat blood and clutched his sides. His ribs were busted.

How many bones did that monster break?!

Setting his jaw and ignoring the pain, Nath hopped on one foot toward the wall.

Behind him, the gold dragon, the most magnificent winged serpentine he'd ever seen, continued to let the titan have it. The monster's head was nothing but flames.

Still, it fought on, swatting oversized fists at the dragon. None of the heavy blows hit the mark. Roaring, it lowered its shoulder and charged for the wall.

Hobbled, Nath hopped as fast as he could.

The titan's foot overshadowed him and came down.

I'm going to be goo!

A golden streak whizzed in and scooped him up just as the giant foot came down.

Whoom!

Nath found himself being sped toward the small hole that was left in the wall and whisked through. The golden dragon gently set him on the ground and turned to face the wall. The dragons filled it in with their armored bodies. The final link was set. Their colorful skins and hides began to harden just as the titan on the other side rocked against it.

Boom! Boom! Boom!

"We are safe now," the golden dragon said. "The wall is secure."

Finding Selene and Brenwar back by his side, Nath used them to get back on his feet. Then, gazing up at the dragon, he said, "Who are you?"

"I am Grahleyna, Nath. Your mother."

Three horses tall, she towered over him. She was wondrous. Her pearl-white horns curled over her head, and long black lashes flicked over her golden eyes. Scales twinkled at the subtle movements of her muscles underneath. Nath reached over to touch her. Limping over, he wrapped his arms around her massive leg.

Grahleyna chuckled. "Oh, Nath, let me make this easier for us." With an utterance of mystic words, she began to diminish in size. Standing gold eye to gold eye with him, she said, "This is better. Is it not?"

She was a fair-skinned, golden-haired woman with a pearl crown on her head. Trembling, Nath reached over and hugged her with tears swelling in his eyes. Her embrace was warm as a campfire. "I was never sure if you were real until just now."

She stroked his hair. Tears ran down her soft cheeks. She sniffed. "I'm sorry, Nath. I never meant to leave. And I never intended to be gone so long, but I had to do what needed to be done. It was my turn, and the timing was bad. Besides, I didn't have any way of knowing that you were the one."

He eased back. "What do you mean?"

"There were many eggs. Some hatch in days, others decades. You certainly know that you have brothers and sisters." She squatted down and put her hands on his broken leg. "They just hatched dragons, and you a man."

Nath's leg tingled with tiny charges of fire. The pain eased. He shifted his weight on it and said, "It's better, but wait a moment. You said hatched."

"Yes, why?"

"So, I was born in an egg?"

She combed her fingers through his hair and said, "Certainly. How else would you be?"

"Hah! I knew you were hatched!" Brenwar said. "I knew it!"

Nath didn't want to think about it. Even though he was a dragon, he didn't care for the idea of being hatched. He never had, for some reason. Moving on, he asked his mother, "So, can you come with us? Or do you have to stay and help form the wall?"

Boom!

"Oh," she said, glancing over her shoulder, "Isobahn is secure. He's not the one we need to worry about. It's the others."

CHAPTER 36

"I DIDN'T SEE ANYTHING ELSE," NATH said to his mother. Brenwar and Selene looked around with wide eyes, too. "Azorath? What has become of him?"

There was a shuffle of movement underneath one of the dragons who had fallen to the wrath of the titan. It was a gray scaler, little bigger than Nath. A hand stretched up and around its belly. Brenwar jogged over and rolled the dragon over. He jerked Azorath's haggard form up to his feet. "Here is the wretched deceiver."

Clutching his chest, Azorath said, "I need to get used to this mortality. I think parts of me are broken. Weee! Ow! I hurt." His spacey black eyes drifted over to Grahleyna. "I see you found your mother. I told you so, Nath. Giving me life was worth it, now. Wasn't it."

"You took what wasn't yours, Azorath."

"Oh, you'll be fine," he said in his mysterious way. "Besides, with the titans free, you probably shouldn't plan a life of longevity. But I'm certain yours will be fuller than a hundred lives, for a spell."

Nath stepped toward Azorath and took ahold of his neck. "What do you mean?"

Grahleyna took his arm and pulled him back. Resting her hands gently on his shoulders, she said, "Finding me came at a price, Nath. You see, Isobahn was a bodyguard of the true threat. Now, the others escape. Crafty spirits they are. They couldn't penetrate the dragon wall, but little more than ethereal in form, they easily escaped when the wall was breached."

"So we can't see them?"

"They are harmless until they take host in other bodies, and that could be anybody," his mother said. "They prey on the weak. Divide and conquer. The threat they pose is not easily seen. That's why Borgash fell. The men and women were so divided that even after we vanquished the titans, they still fought among themselves. Once you plant the bad seed in men, it doesn't take long for their lives to unravel."

"How did you trap them before?" Nath said.

"In this last case, we trapped them, body and spirit, behind this barrier. Several brave dragons fought them on the other side, hoping to wipe them out of existence, but their valiant efforts failed." She rubbed his shoulder. "It's difficult to destroy evil. A remnant always remains."

Nath's throat tightened. Did Gorn Grattack still exist? Had Nath not wiped that monster out entirely? "Mother, there has to be a better way than this." He stretched out his hands toward the wall.

"Don't," she said, "else you'll have Isobahn trying to bite off our heads again. It's best such darkness lies in the deepness from where it came. Nalzambor's bowels can hold them without help. And the dragons understand their sacrifice, but a time may come when it has to be made permanent. That is a fate they must choose on their own." Grahleyna put her arm around Nath's waist and led him away. "It was destined that they should be let loose for a season anyway."

"Let loose? Why?" he said, incredulous.

"It's just the times we live in."

Long faced, Nath felt his blood seep into his toes. Finding his mother should have been a time of celebration. Instead, he'd loosed more menaces into the world. It didn't help that he wasn't in the full grandeur of a dragon, either. He was much weaker.

Selene found her way to his side. "Don't be hard on yourself, Nath. You couldn't have known."

"Your friend is right. Selene, is it?" Grahleyna said, fastening her eyes on Selene's.

"Yes, your majesty," Selene said, taking a knee.

"Oh, there is no need for that, my dear." She helped Selene up to her feet. "You have a great understanding of this darkness, don't you."

Frowning, Selene said, "More than I care to admit."

"Use that knowledge. You'll need it." Grahleyna turned back to Nath. "What led you here anyway?"

"Father gave us a hint: 'What you seek is in the peaks.'"

Grahleyna laughed. "Oh, and that was it. So like him. He gives you just enough information so it will only take one thousand years to find me. But here you are."

"So does father know that you have been here all along?" Nath said.

"Certainly."

Angry, Nath said, "Why wouldn't he tell me that? Why would he just leave you here like this? It's a terrible thing!"

"And boring, but it's mostly sleeping, so it's not so bad." She poked Nath's chest. "And don't you judge your father. It was my choice, not his. He didn't like it one bit. He had a fit like a one-hundred-year-old about it. He started stomping around and shooting up big puffs of fire. I was embarrassed for him."

"Father did that?" Nath said. He'd never seen anything like it from his father.

"Oh, don't be disenchanted. He's temperamental because he loves me." She checked her nails and pushed her hair up a little. "And that's probably why he endorsed your search."

"Couldn't he just come and see you?"

"By the Sultans, no! Balzurth would charge right through that wall and try to put an end to those titans. That's exactly what they want. Take down the Dragon King. End his reign. They were so eager to get out, they missed a golden opportunity. They overlooked you." Grahleyna turned her attention back to Azorath. "Now what do we do with you?"

"Me? I'm harmless. I just want to walk among men again." His eyes darted from face to face. "Just a man. One that can live and have a natural death."

"And a natural death you shall have." Grahleyna opened her mouth. Bright golden flames washed over Azorath. He turned to a pile of ash before he could even scream. "Never trust a shade, Son."

Nath convulsed. A river of life rushed through him. His blood coursed with a new spring of energy. "Thank you, Mother."

She patted him on the shoulder. "Evil—don't give it a chance. Now it's time for your first order from Mother. Find those titans. Bring them back or destroy them."

CHAPTER 37

GRAHLEYNA FLUNG HER HEAD BACK. "Ah! It's so good to be in the sun's light again. It warms me inside and out." She spread her arms wide and spun slowly around. The bright light enhanced her incredible beauty and elegance. "Come, walk with me, Nath, and bring your friends along, while I still have the time."

The Lost City of Borgash was still a barren place with strange and ugly vegetation. Nath carefully maneuvered through the thick vines. Brenwar's eyes remained fixed on the ground, Mortuun swinging at his side. Selene managed to find her own place over a dozen paces ahead on a broken path that led east and out of the forgotten city.

Grahleyna whisked them out of the catacombs. It was a confusing and winding path, but Nath could make it back and out again if he had to. He was sure of it. Walking stride for stride with his mother, he kept his chin up and chest out. The joy of having her by his side was incredible, but a frown started to crease his lips.

"You care for her much, don't you," his mother said to him, eyeing Selene.

"I care for you much, and now you are leaving?"

"Well, I'm going to leave you with good advice, and that will be much better than the advice I left you with the last time."

"Hah, well I suppose that is true." He laughed. "I don't want you to go, though. I want to stay with you. The titans can wait at least a decade, can't they?"

"Oh, a decade with our sweet mother. How flattering is that? You certainly get that side of you from me and not your father. Of course, he does have a dashing side."

"Father, dashing?"

She tousled his hair. "You are very handsome, like him, but more so."

Nath flashed a smile, "No doubt it's the part of you in me that shines."

"Tell me more about you and Selene. I want to know everything."

"Sh! Mother, she can hear everything."

"That's right," Selene said, waving her arm up over her head. "And I can't wait to hear what you have to say, Nath."

"Perhaps our time could be better spent talking about how you met Father, Mother?"

Grahleyna chuckled. "I'm not going there, but I will tell you this: we were in mortal forms when we met."

Nath's brows lifted and he said, "Like me. Like us now?"

"The same."

Nath's eyes glided toward Selene. She was staring back at him with a playful glint in her eyes.

His mother continued, "Balzurth roamed Nalzambor the same as you did. A hero among mankind with countless triumphs. He was so cocky." She sighed. "But I liked it. He picked the prettiest bouquets of flowers. And he could sing so soft the fairies would cry."

"My father?"

"Oh, think back, Nath. I'm sure you've seen a softer side of him."

There were plenty of lessons that Nath recalled, some harsh and others wise, but singing? He didn't remember any of that.

Grahleyna started humming.

Words formed in Nath's mind. He started singing.

"Ah praise the hills of daffodils, the kings, or run Tinny Lee. The dragons come, the fairies flee. Riding on the wings and scales came lightning from the clouds. Hondor the brave and ten thousand bannered warriors.

Run Tinny, run Tinny, run Tinny, run.

A thousand years, a thousand slumbers, comes the gentle crescent of night. Half for the light, half for the dark.

Run Tinny, run Tinny, run.

Home is there for the wayward son."

Nath came to a stop. "He did sing that to me, didn't he?"

"Yes, I'm sure of it. I never liked that song. It was sung by a drunken troubadour the day we met. The man's voice was awful as an ogre's, but your father made the song beautiful."

"What does it mean? Who is Hondor?"

"No idea," she said. "Just a silly song written by a sordid man who needed a button for his trousers. Not every song has to have a meaning. Sometimes it just needs to be fun to sing." She lifted her chin toward the sky. A flock of dragons streaked through the clouds. "What in the name of Morgdon were those?"

Not hiding the concern from his voice, Nath replied, "Wurmers."

Grahleyna's golden eyes became as big as saucers. "Please tell me my eyes deceived me? Those blasted things are an abomination." Fire sparked in her voice. "Oversized winged termites! Barnabus! They'll be perfect hosts for the titans!"

Selene rushed down toward them and said, "Your majesty, it is my error. A failure of my past!"

"Then I'd say you and Nath are made for each other. You let one terror out of the sack and he let out another." Grahleyna shook her head. "In the meantime, it looks like I'm going to have to deal with those wurmers myself. Stand back."

Nath and Selene stepped way back.

Wings sprouted on Grahleyna's back. Her body enlarged, and scales quickly covered her from head to toe. Within seconds, Nath gazed up at a most excellent gold dragon. "If I could only fly, I could go and destroy them with you."

"Hah, hah, hah," Grahleyna said, "if you could only fly. How silly you sound, Nath. I hope you figure that out soon, Dragon Prince." She spread her beautiful black-and-gold wings out. "Now, I must go. And you two need to figure out how to clean up your mess."

"But Mother, you can't leave. We just met!"

Grahleyna bent down and kissed Nath on the head. "I promise to see you again much sooner than the last time." Pushing off with her powerful legs, she launched herself into the air. Wings beating at a furious rhythm, she sliced through the air like a golden arrow and disappeared, pursuing the wurmers.

Shoulders slumped, Nath turned and faced his friends. "I can't believe she's gone already."

"Get yer chin up," Brenwar said, "I'm not of the impression that your mother would approve of you moping around."

"Me either." Holding her head, Selene said, "Gads, but now I feel even guiltier than before. We're going to have to finish off those monsters before it's too late."

Eyeing the sky and rubbing the back of his neck, Nath said, "You know, just once it would be nice if my parents gave me a little more information." He took a deep breath through his nose and pulled his shoulders back. "Well, I figured it out before, and together we'll figure it out again. Let's go."

"As long as there's a fight ahead, I'll always be ready." Brenwar swung Mortuun around with his wrist. "Where are we going?"

"It's time to visit one of Nalzambor's greatest historians."

"Aw, great! We're going to Morgdon," Brenwar looked elated and started marching away.

"I'm pretty sure Nath's not talking about Morgdon. I believe he's referring to Quintuklen."

Brenwar stopped and cocked an eyebrow. "Quintuklen? It's a pile of rubble. And that will be a long, wasted march, too. Morgdon is far closer." He eyed Nath and Selene up and down. "Not to mention the likelihood of danger. There isn't even a weapon between you."

"My wits are all that I need," Selene said, standing with her arms crossed over her chest.

Nath held his clawed hands out before him. Having battled the wurmers before in the body of a full dragon, his clawed fingers seemed wholly inadequate. He tapped his noggin and walked off with a shrug, saying, "I guess my wits will have to do as well."

But I'd feel much better if I still had Fang.

CHAPTER 38

IT TOOK OVER A WEEK on foot to find the tall hill grasses that surrounded Quintuklen. Nath stood shirtless, waist deep in a pond, with a long stick whittled down to a spear.

"What's the matter, can't you catch them with your hands anymore?" Brenwar said. The salty old dwarf stood on the bank running a rugged comb through his beard.

"You can always swim in here and fetch dinner yourself, you know," Nath said.

"You volunteered, not me. I said I could wait until we made it to Quintuklen anyway. It's you that has the growling tummy, not me. Pah." The dwarf picked up a smooth stone and skipped it over across the ponds and right by Nath's head.

"Watch it, Brenwar! My head isn't as hard as yours."

"It's gotten soft. I can attest to that."

Spying movement in the murky green waters, Nath jabbed his spear quicker than a striking snake. He pulled a fish bigger than his head out of the pond. Its big tail flapped back and forth and caught Nath in the face.

"Oh ho ho!" Brenwar laughed, holding his gut. "That fish has more fight in it than you!"

Nath waded out of the waters. "You keep holding that big gut of yours, because this fish is going to feed me and Selene."

"Gut!" Brenwar slapped the breastplate over his belly. "An iron gut, lad!"

"Lad!"

"Aye, lad! A big, scaly, flame-haired one. What are you going to do about it, strike me with that mighty fish?"

Nath swung the fish full into Brenwar's face. *Slap!*

Brenwar's eyes became big angry moons. "Never hit a dwarf with a fish!" He dropped his shoulder and charged.

Nath came off his feet and tumbled to the ground. "Blast it, Brenwar!"

Brenwar stuffed Nath's face into the soft bank. "Quit yer bellyaching, Nath Dragon!" He locked Nath's arm behind his back and pinned him half in the water and half in the sand.

"Have you gone mad? You'll pay for this!" Nath struggled against his friend's iron clutches. He didn't have any idea what had happened to Brenwar. They'd been bickering for days. Brenwar didn't have anything to be mad about, either; Nath did. He'd lost his power. Found his mother only to lose her again. Not to mention that he'd unintentionally turned a new menace loose on Nalzambor that he hadn't meant to. With a heave, he flung Brenwar over his shoulder and slammed him into the cattails and reeds. "Get off of me!"

Brenwar sprang to his feet and launched his head hard into Nath's chin.

His teeth clacked together and he saw stars exploding in his head. Staggering back, he felt his knees wobble, and he plopped on his butt into the water. While he sat shaking his head, his eyes became flame. "You're going to regret this, Bolderguild!"

Brenwar spat in the water. "Pah! I don't think you'll do anything with those tears in your eyes. Here, let me get a handkerchief. Maybe Selene will wipe them away for you."

Nath exploded into motion. His fists became striking hammers, fast and powerful.

Brenwar fought back, landing bone-jarring shots on Nath's ribs and chin.

Not holding back, Nath busted Brenwar hard in his breastplate, creating a dent. *Bang!*

Brenwar let out a wail. "Yer gonna fix that!" He rammed his elbow into Nath's groin.

Seeing red, Nath snatched Brenwar up high over his head and stuffed him head first into the waters. He held him down, ignoring Brenwar's flailing boots.

Zap!

Nath's hairs stood on end. His bones juttered from pure shock. His grip loosened on Brenwar.

Brenwar popped up out of the waters and dashed the water from his eyes with both hands. "What kind of trickery was that, Nath?"

"Have you two gone mad?" It was Selene. She stood on the bank. Her face was hot with confusion and rage. "Get ahold of yourself!"

Sitting in the water with his hands over his knees, Nath started laughing uncontrollably. He stopped abruptly and rubbed his jaw. "Oh!

Brenwar held out his forearm. "Feeling better?"

Rising to his feet, Nath said, "Thanks, Brenwar." It had been a long time since the pair romped. They'd done it plenty when Nath was younger. Brenwar had taught him all about fighting, clean and dirty. Nath's charging blood had him feeling better again. "I needed that."

"You both are mad," Selene said in astonishment. "But you are men, after all. What's next, hugging?"

"No thank you," Brenwar said, sloshing out of the water.

A dark shadow soared overhead and darted north toward Quintuklen.

"Shades!" Selene said. "You too buffoons distracted my intentions. I came to warn you: Quintuklen is under attack!"

CHAPTER 39

Hoofing it over the grassy knolls and hillsides, Nath sprinted as fast as he could, with Selene only a few strides behind him. Ahead, Quintuklen, at least what was left, was smoking. Dragons, flying above, were pelting it with fire.

"Those are wurmers!" Nath said, legs churning even faster.

Quintuklen had been all but destroyed in the last dragon war against the Clerics of Barnabus and Gorn Grattack. But now, from the distance, he could clearly see that it was being rebuilt. The stone walls that surrounded the town were almost entirely intact. Pulleys, bulwarks, and scaffolding had popped up all over the city. New stone buildings and wooden apartments. Fresh paint. The old roads were no longer mud and grass but filled with stone. And there were people. Throngs here and there, gathering stones and makeshift spears and hurling them at the dark-scaled dragons.

Fire came down on the valiant defenders.

Claws from the skies snatched people up and dropped them from high in the air.

"Noooooooooo!" Nath screamed.

He fought the helplessness that boiled inside him. If he could fly, he could rise into the air and battle the wurmers. Instead, he was stuck on the ground, racing over the expansive distance hoping he could get there in time and somehow help.

"Selene, have you any thoughts?"

"I was hoping you did!"

They made it to the first barrier wall that protected the city. It was more than ten feet tall. Rather than race down to the next gateway, Nath leapt clear over it. Five walls later, he was on the road that led straight into the city. A bright gleam of steel caught his eye. The midday sun shined off the breastplates of a squad of Legionnaires.

"What can I do to help?" Nath said, jogging up to the highest-ranking officer.

The commander had a long and wispy moustache that hung down past his chin. Stout and durable in his plate-mail armor, he looked Nath up and down and said, "Find some steel, and if one of those things lands, start swinging. Go for the wings. Their hides are as thick as, er," he looked at Nath's arms and said, "a dragon's."

"May I borrow a spear?" Nath said to the commander.

"Anything for you, Nath Dragon," the commander said. "Lieutenant, give this warrior your spear!"

Nath pulled back his shoulders and took the spear the soldier offered him. *They know me. They don't fear me. A good thing!* He scanned the faces of the Legionnaires. There was more duty than fear in their stern expressions. And there were less than twenty of them. All survivors who had returned to rebuild their city. Their determined looks filled Nath with greater courage. "Get those crossbows ready. We need to get their attention. Aim for the biggest one."

Counting the dragons, he noticed most of them were only about fifteen feet long. *Not too big, but still plenty deadly. If I can take the leader down, hopefully the rest will flee.* "Selene, can you bring some light? We need a distraction."

Selene's hands flared with bright purple light. "Like this?"

"It's pretty, but not exactly the attention getter I was looking for."

"Oh," she smirked, "you want something more like this." Lavender shards erupted from her fingertips and made bee lines toward a dragon latched onto one of the tower walls.

It let out a roar and crashed to the ground.

The legionnaires let out a triumphant cheer.

"Show-off," Nath said.

The dragon popped up off of its back. Snarling, it charged straight toward Nath and Selene. Nath lowered his spear and raced right into the face of the dragon. Finding a soft spot in its neck, he jammed the spear into its throat.

The dragon shrieked and thrashed. The spear shaft snapped in half. Its tail flicked out, catching Nath in the heel and pulling him off his feet. The fifteen-foot monster's head recoiled, and its chest filled with fiery breath. Nath started to roll.

Boom!

The wurmer exploded into scales and pieces.

Getting back to his feet, he found Selene and said, "Did you do that?"

"No. It wasn't me." She pointed toward one of Quintuklen's towers that was being rebuilt. "It was him."

Nath twisted his head around. A tall, rangy warrior stood at the top of a rebuilt staircase. Long brown hair with gray streaks flowing through it billowed in the wind. He took the arrow out of his mouth and fired again. The sound of the bowstring's snap was one of a kind. *Twang!*

The arrow caught a sky-cruising wurmer in the belly and turned it into dragon chunks with another thunderous *Boom!*

"Ben!" Nath screamed.

Holding the bow Akron high over his head, the old warrior saluted and cried out, "Dragon!"

Suddenly, a pack of three wurmers, wings beating, surrounded Ben. Their lungs filled with air, and fire gathered inside their jowls.

No, he'll be incinerated!

Nath looked for something to grab. Something to throw. There was nothing. "Let loose something, Selene! Soldiers, unleash those crossbows!"

"They might hit Ben," Selene warned.

Helpless and with bated breath, Nath watched Ben about to die. Without notice, the air crackled with new energy. From somewhere below, a streak of energy shot into the sky and struck the wurmers hovering over the tower. One beast turned to ash, and the other two let out startled cries. A fork of lightning rocked into both of them. They twitched, smoked, and plummeted hard into the earth. *Thud! Thud!*

With no more dragons in sight, the Legionnaires and city folk erupted into cheers. Coming down the street and heading straight toward Nath and Selene, two figures emerged. Ben, looking as tough and rugged as chewed leather, strolled, arms swinging, with a smaller person by his side. Bayzog was violet eyed, green robed, and looking calm and serious both at the same time.

With a broad smile on his scarred lips, Ben put Akron away. *Clatch. Snap. Clatch.* He gave Nath a hug. "Dragon, I never thought I'd see you like this again. Or at all again, for that matter. I can only imagine that something bad is going on."

"Thanks to you, nothing bad is going on at all here, Ben. You sure took it to those wurmers and saved my scales again."

"What did I miss? What did I miss?" It was Brenwar, rushing up to them, Mortuun ready, and huffing for breath. "Tell me I didn't miss all of the fighting."

"Of course you did," Bayzog said to him. "If we had to wait for you, we'd miss out on dinnertime."

"Watch it, part-elf."

Elderwood staff in hand, Bayzog patted Brenwar on the head. "I didn't miss you either, friend. Eh, nice hand. What happened, did you run out of hide jerky?" He gave a quick nod to Selene and then turned to Nath. "What have you done now?"

"Me?"

Selene interrupted the moment, pointing at the sky. "Look."

A white dragon, no horns, small legs, and with a very long body and tail soared high above.

"Strange," Nath said, "what would an ivory slider be doing here? They are messengers," Nath said

"Fascinating," Bayzog said. "It's quite a treat seeing a breed I have not seen before. It looks to be carrying something in its paws."

The ivory slider released something with a nice bright shine and disappeared in the backdrop of clouds in the sky.

"What was that?" Ben said. "Why did it drop it on the other side of the walls?"

"There's only one way to find out," Nath said. He took off at a trot.

"We don't have to run everywhere, you know," Brenwar said.

"Fine," Nath said. "We don't have to complain everywhere, either."

"You know, Brenwar, I could make you some boots that will make you walk faster," Bayzog offered.

"Why don't you make yourself some boots that will take you back to your homeland, part-elf."

"I love reunions," Ben said to Selene. "How about you?"

"I don't know. I've never had one before."

Eyes feeling a little misty, Nath started to round the gate at the outermost wall. There was no feeling quite like being around the friends that had fought for you again and again.

No feeling like it at all.

He came to a stop and gawked at the object sticking up out of the field. A beautiful sword pommel with dragon crossguards winked at him with gemstone eyes. "Fang!"

"I'll be," Brenwar said. "We really must be in for it."

Upon snatching the sword up, Nath began twirling it around in strokes that looked like lightning. New energy coursed through his veins. The handle was warm as an old friend's handshake. He kissed the grand and shiny blade.

"Looks like the pair of you have been reunited just in time," Bayzog said, eyeing the storm front coming from the south.

"Really, Bayzog, why do you say that?" Nath asked.

Everyone pointed where Bayzog was looking. Wurmers, wingless and big, were snaking through the tall grasses.

Nath raised Fang high, and with the fierce bellow of a dozen embattled warriors he yelled, "Dragon! Dragon!"

Epilogue

"How nice it is to see you again, Eckubahn. It's been too long," Lotuus said. The fairy empress hovered inside a portion of mountainside that looked to have recently been scooped out. Inside, three earth giants stood staring down on her with heavy eyes. The tallest, brawny and covered in coarse black-brown hair, petted the hairs on his forearms. He leered at her. "Does that body not please you, grand titan?"

Eckubahn scratched the scruff underneath his neck, wetted his thumb, and smoothed his eyebrows back. His voice was the sound of a rumbling volcano. "It will do, fairy."

Lotuus buzzed up and hung in the air right before his eyes. They couldn't have been more different. Her figure was grace and beauty that shimmered with seductive activity. His body was a raw-powered, stony-skinned abomination. She kissed him on the nose. "I've missed you, my lord. Have you missed me?"

"For centuries I've burned with vengeance. There was no time for pleasant memories."

She stood on his shoulder and spoke into his ear. "You are free now. Does that make you happy?"

"No, but soon it will." He formed a fist, cocked it back, and struck at the nearest earth giant with bone-shattering impact.

Boom!

The earth giant crumpled to the ground and lay dead. The other earth giant backed up a step, took a knee, and bowed.

Petting the giant's ear, Lotuus said with a thrill in her voice, "So powerful. So masterful. Oh, how I have missed you, Eckubahn. I must say, I was beginning to lose hope, but then Nath Dragon came along and I was freed. Hence, you were freed. I didn't hesitate to dupe him."

The titan's throat rumbled. "Make no mistake, you didn't dupe anyone. This was meant to be. Certain dragons want us gone." He punched his fist into his hand with a resounding smack. "I want them gone. And I pledge it will be done."

Lotuus clapped her hands. "Oh, how I can't wait to see you upend those arrogant lizards. I'd like to pluck the scales off of them one by one."

Eckubahn put his oversized finger under her chin. "I promise that you'll see it done." Feet shaking the ground, he headed out of the monstrous alcove. "This body hungers. Lead me to the nearest city so I can feast." He spread his arms out wide, tilted his chin up toward the sky, and yelled, "Then I will have my VENGEANCE!"

CLAWS OF THE DRAGON

-Book 2-

CRAIG HALLORAN

CHAPTER
1

URMERS—DARK-SCALED DRAGON-LIKE CREATURES LARGER THAN men with an evil glimmer in their eyes—were coming by the dozens.

Ben loosed another arrow.

Twang!

The feathered shaft ripped through a wurmer's chest and dropped it to the ground.

"It's never a surprise when you show up."

"What's that supposed to mean?" Nath swung Fang into an oncoming enemy and shore clean through the next.

Back to back with Nath, Ben continued to stretch his bowstring and fire.

Twang! Twang!

"Trouble is your mistress."

Twang! Twang!

Stepping forward, Nath twirled Fang around his body and carved down two more jaw-snapping wurmers. "Are you being serious?"

A wurmer bit at Nath's leg.

He jumped high and away, turned, and clipped its hindquarters with Fang.

It whirled on him, its mouth heated up with energy.

Ben crept in behind it and let loose a point-blank shot in its skull.

Thwack!

The glow went out of the monster's eyes.

Ben readied another shaft. "Well Dragon, everything *was* peaceful and quiet until you showed up."

"Quit yer jawing and start fighting!" Brenwar brought Mortuun the war hammer down with all of his might and clobbered the scaly skull of a wurmer that was clamped down on the metal legging of his armor.

Krang!

A pair of wurmers popped up in the tall grass and pounced on the fearless dwarf's back and drove him into the ground.

"Brenwar!" Nath exclaimed. Sword high, he leapt into action.

"Get these lizards off me!" Brenwar whopped one in the head with the side of his hammer.

Its jaws locked over the thick muscles in his arm.

Nath stuck it in the side and sent it to the grave.

"Get off me!" Brenwar beat it in the head with savage force.

The monster's mouth glowed with life. Fire spilled out.

Thwack!

Ben shot it in the gut. "It's a good thing these are moorite arrows. Are you sure that's dwarven?"

Pushing himself off the ground, Brenwar made a skeleton fist and shook it at Ben. "You've been spending too much time with that part-elf. Shaddup."

Kar-Roooom!

The ground shook. Brenwar lost his footing. Nath caught his fall.

"Sultans of Sulfur! What was that?" Brenwar bellowed.

A powerful magic force blasted away the wurmers and blew down the grasses.

A handful of wurmers survived and attacked. Another half dozen lay dead, except one in particular that stood out as it rose up out of the tall grass. It towered over the rest, standing eight feet tall at the shoulder. Its long neck was scale and muscle. The seams between its scales glowed with inner fire.

A heavily armored knot of Legionnaires rushed it with long spears and lances.

"No, don't!" Dragon yelled, knowing the brave men would be incinerated.

They already knew their weapons couldn't hurt the wurmer. But they were fighters. Soldiers. They wouldn't turn from a fight. Not of any kind, no matter the odds. Not once their blood got flowing.

Nath took off at a sprint, waving his sword high. "Over here, you ugly lizard!"

The wurmer paid him no mind. Its eyes narrowed on the oncoming rush of man meat, its neck coiled back and mouth dropped open. A billow of fire exploded from its monster jaws.

"Noooo!" Nath yelled. He'd get there, just too late.

The lances and spears of the first Legionnaires in the charge were incinerated in a wash of flame. Bodies turned into smoldering piles of ash.

A mystic shield of radiant energy appeared over the rest of the soldiers and cut off the flames. Selene stood underneath it with her arms spread wide and shaking.

Nath's own face felt the searing heat as the wurmer's flames bounced off in all directions.

The grasses caught fire. Flames spread.

Nath closed in, Fang down and ready to plunge into the monster's side.

Out of nowhere, the wurmer's tail lashed out.

Whack!

Head over heels, Nath landed and bounced off the ground. He scrambled to his feet and found himself face to face with the lava-dripping jaws of the huge wurmer. He started back into his swing and gaffed. Fang wasn't there. The grand sword lay nearby. He jumped for it.

Whack!

The wurmer's tail drummed his back, flattening him on the ground.

Whack! Whack! Whack!

Taking a beating, Nath clawed toward Fang's pommel.

Come on, Fang! Help me!

Whack! Whack! Whack!

Fighting through the beating, Nath's fingertips nudged Fang's bottom pommel.

Just a little closer!

The one-ton dragon stepped on Nath's back and drove his face into the ground. Its claws sank into Nath's shoulders.

He let out a muffled scream. Dragon heart thundering in his chest, hand spread wide, Nath fought through the pain and grabbed Fang's pommel. He jerked Dragon Claw free.

The dagger inside of the great sword's hilt shined with blue light. Its energy coursed through Nath's veins.

"Get off me, Lizard!"

With tremendous effort, he ripped away from the wurmer's claws, twisted around, and plunged the blade into the armored scales that coated its chest.

Sckreeeet!

The giant wurmer reared up. Flames shot out of its mouth. Its scaly body crackled and popped. Inch by inch, scale by scale, its body iced up and crystalized. In seconds, the entire beast became a solid sheet of ice.

Bleeding, Nath tore himself out of its grip and grimaced with his hands on his knees, sweat dripping from his brow, and caught his breath. "That was close."

The rest of the wurmers were dead.

Selene, Bayzog, Brenwar, and Ben gathered around.

The old dwarven warrior marched forward with his war hammer raised high and prepared to strike the great wurmer.

"Brenwar, don't!" Nath ordered.

The dwarf stopped and looked at him. "May I ask why?" Brenwar huffed.

Nath didn't have a good reason why not, and several had died because of the monster already. "Never mind. Carry on."

Brenwar brought back the hammer and turned it around full swing.

Krang!

The giant wurmer exploded into thousands of icy pieces.

The Legionnaires erupted in a cheer.

Ben held his hand out and caught some of the drifting ice on his leather gauntlet. "Look. It's snowing."

Chapter 2

"You need stitches," Selene said to Nath in a motherly kind of way. "Be still."

Nath stayed her with his palm. "I don't need stitches. It's hardly a wound." He glanced at the claw marks in his shoulders. His stomach turned queasy. "Guzan, I miss my scales!"

Brenwar chuckled under his beard. He wasn't in much better shape than Nath was.

"Laugh all you want, Brenwar. But it's only your armor that holds you together."

"I don't need this armor. It's just a uniform showing dwarven pride," he grumbled. Ben was stitching up a gash over his bushy black eyebrow. "Careful with that needle. I don't want my eye poked out."

"Maybe you should start wearing a helmet," Ben said. "You aren't getting any younger, you know."

"He doesn't need a helmet," Bayzog said, leaning on the Elderwood Staff. His ivy-green robes with gold trim rustled in the wind. "Dwarven skulls get thicker the older they get."

"Well now, that explains a lot!" Ben laughed.

"One of these days I'm going to bust you in the mouth, part-elf." Brenwar got up, grabbed Mortuun, and stormed away.

The daylight was beginning to fade, and the Legionnaires had started moving their dead and wounded. The only ones sitting still were Nath and company and the dead bodies of the wurmers. Their scales rotted quickly.

Nath covered his nose. "Those things reek. How come they rot? I thought they had to be burned."

"They still need to be burned. Don't leave a trace of any of them," said Brenwar, turning away his nose. "And I thought orcs smelled bad."

"Commander," Nath said to a Legionnaire with a long moustache. "You heard him. Get oil and some torches."

"You're going to reek as well if you don't sit still," Selene said to him. She tried to poke his skin with a needle. He flinched away. "Don't do that again, Nath. I'm trying to take care of you."

"Take care of me?" He snatched the needle from her hand. "I'll take care of myself, thank you." Grinding his teeth, he turned away. He hated asking anyone for help, but even more, he hated feeling mortal. The wurmer's claws had burned like fire on his flesh where the scales from his arms stopped around the shoulder. He pinched the skin behind his neck but couldn't reach it with his free hand. "Great Dragons!"

"Will you set your pride aside for a moment?" Selene said, plucking the needle from his fingers. "You can't do everything, you know."

"Not anymore. That's for sure." He frowned and stared off at the sinking sun.

I have to get used to this. Nobody else is complaining.

"Fine, Selene. You win. Stitch me up."

"That's better. Try to have a better outlook on things. You just got Fang back. Doesn't that make you glad?"

Nath held up the beautiful blade before his golden eyes.

Fang's steel seemed to absorb every ray of sunlight. The magnificent blade's pommel sent shivers of power through his blood and into his bones. Fang was more than some precious object. He was a friend.

Nath let out a sigh and nodded. "Yes, having Fang back is good." He ran his scaled fingertips over the exquisite dragon-headed cross-guard. "Very good."

Bayzog stepped into view. The half-elf wizard had a curious look in his eyes. "I'm at a loss. Care to explain?"

"You're at a loss!" Brenwar yelled from a distant spot. "Hah!"

As Selene stitched up his back, Nath began to explain everything that had happened of late. He explained how he gave up his powers to save Selene. How the wurmers were a cursed carryover from Gorn Grattack. There was the issue of rescuing his mother, Grahleyna, and the fight behind the Great Dragon Wall.

"All in a good day's fun, right Bayzog? And now it seems we have these titans to deal with. My mother warned me. Eckubahn is one of their names. It seems they don't get along too well with dragons. Can you believe that?"

Selene bit off the thread and patted Nath on the back. "All better. Just don't swing that sword for a while."

"Now that we're all caught up, Bayzog, perhaps we can eat and drink." Nath saw that Bayzog's violet eyes were filled with concern. "Bayzog?"

"I know something of these histories." There was tightness in the half-elf's voice. "This is horrible, Nath." Covering his nose up with his long sleeve, he walked over to a wurmer's corpse. It fizzled and popped. The scales and bones were turning to goo. He looked at Selene. "How many more nests do you think are out there?"

"I destroyed several, but as soon as I found one, I'd come across another." Her brow creased. "I'm all for new solutions. I think that's why we're here."

"So what do you think, Bayzog?" Nath said.

"I think I'm going to have to check the histories. Over the centuries, so much has been lost, buried, or destroyed." His eyes landed on Nath. "But your kind might have a better solution to this than us. They've dealt with this problem before."

"I assume. My mother seemed to know something about it and the titans. And then, she was gone." He shook his head. "I swear, my parents are aloof."

Selene chuckled and patted him on the back.

"Sorry about that, Nath. I'm sure she had her reasons," Bayzog said. "We'll just have to wait and see how things turn out when you have children of your own."

"Can we just stick with the titans?"

"Nath!" Sasha rushed into his arms and gave him a great hug. She had aged little since the last time he'd seen her. Her soft eyes had little crow's feet, but she was still beautiful. "I've missed you. Come, sit down."

They were back inside Bayzog's tower. Somehow the magic abode of the wizard had survived. The grand table—round, elven crafted, and exquisite—that Bayzog studied from was still there. He sat on a stool with his nose buried in a great tome.

Nath sat down beside Sasha. "Is he still reading too much?"

"So it seems," she said, picking up a crystal carafe. "How about some wizard water?"

Nath shrugged his aching shoulder. It still burned. "Sure."

"And how about you, Selene?" Sasha said with a forced smile.

Nath felt a bit of a chill in the air. Selene had deceived Sasha, and he could sense Sasha's unease with the woman.

Oh my. I sort of forgot about that.

"Thank you, that would be nice," Selene said. She took a seat on Nath's other side and rested her hand on his knee, eyeing the surroundings. "This is a lovely place."

Sasha poured three glasses and handed them over. Her hand trembled a little.

"Are you alright?" Nath shifted toward Sasha.

For some reason he missed Brenwar.

His old friend hadn't wanted to come inside Bayzog's place, so Brenwar and Ben had decided to stay outside and inspect the rebuilding of the town. That left Nath all alone with the women, who he was pretty sure didn't like each other. And Bayzog wouldn't be much help at all. He'd have his nose in the books for hours.

Nath sipped from his glass. The enchanted water quickly refreshed his parched lips. Raising his glass, he said, "A toast, perhaps. To old friends and new adventures."

Sasha set her glass down on the table and sighed. With a frown on her lovely face, she said, "I'm sorry, Nath. I can't drink to that."

"What? Sasha, what is wrong? Have I done something to offend you?"

"It's not you, Nath," she said, fixing her eyes on Selene. "It's her. How in Nalzambor can you trust her?"

CHAPTER 3

BAYZOG'S HEAD SNAPPED UP FROM his book. "Sasha, please, these are our guests."

Sasha was on her feet with her fists balled up at her sides. She fired back. "No. I cannot be silent. I'm sorry, Nath, but have you forgotten how many lives were taken on account of her? Thousands died because of her bewitching. Not to mention Ben's family." She pointed at Selene. "She was behind their deaths. The same for my own friends and family. Just look at this city!"

"Sasha, please," Bayzog pleaded. He got up off his stool and made his way over to her and spoke in a stern voice. "You're embarrassing yourself."

Sasha's eyes flashed. "What! You of all people! Don't stand beside me." Her eyes watered up, and her lip started to tremble. "How could you?" She glared at Nath. "And how could you?"

Selene got up, set her glass down, and said, "I'll leave."

"Yes, yes, do leave, you schemer! You plotter! Go ahead and try to wash the blood from your hands!" Sasha's chest heaved, and her body shuddered. Bayzog tried to steady her, but she pushed right by him and ran out of the room crying.

Nath opened his mouth to speak but closed his jaw. He didn't know what to say. He'd never seen Sasha so angry. It shocked him like a jolt of lightning. He turned and watched Selene heading to the spot that led them out of the apartment. Her chin that was always up was down a little. He cleared his throat. "Selene—"

She cut him off with her hand. "No. She has a right to be angry and not to trust me. I can't expect everyone to forgive me." She showed him a dejected look, shook her head, and sighed. "Why would anyone forgive me?" She stepped on an arcane symbol on the floor, shimmered, faded, and disappeared.

"I've forgiven you," Nath muttered. He felt empty inside. Forgiveness didn't come easy for some people. He was a dragon and a lot more patient than most. He knew that in the world of men, where life was short and highly valued, taking one away from another hurt the most.

It hurt him, but he also understood that people are often deceived and misled. Evil was often taught and bred. Gorn Grattack had raised Selene. It was a wonder she had broken free of his spell.

"Apologies, Nath," Bayzog said. There was a look of disappointment in his eye. "Sasha should have more self-control than that."

Nath put his clawed hand on Bayzog's shoulder and gave it a gentle squeeze. "You can't expect her to keep her feelings bottled up all the time. She has a right to vent. Don't be so hard on her."

"A sorceress should have more discipline." He had a blank look on his elven face. "But the sad thing is I never knew she felt that way."

"Then I'd say you need to talk to her more often."

Bayzog glanced at the tome he'd been studying. "I need to research."

"No, you need to go to your wife, and the first words out of your mouth should probably be, 'I apologize.'"

The part-elf stiffened. "For what?"

"Who feeds you, Bayzog?"

"Why, she does."

"Well, you don't want to starve to death, do you?"

Bayzog lifted a brow. "Perhaps you are right. Thank you, Nath." He headed after Sasha.

Nath resumed his place on the sofa and gazed at the warm glow of the fireplace in the corner. He sipped on the wizard water.

I think a lot more happened in the twenty-five years I was gone than I realized.

Shuffling through the rubble-filled streets of Quintucklen, Nath found himself liking his isolation. He'd hung around Bayzog's place until the quietness made him uneasy. It had taken Bayzog more than two hours to return from his talk with Sasha, and when he did, the dark-haired part-elf wizard had little to say. If anything, his face was a little ashen when he stuck his nose back in his book and began flipping pages.

Time to go.

Nath thought there wasn't much sense in him hanging around with so much tension in the air. And in a surprising way, he felt a little foolish. Was Sasha right in her suspicions of Selene? Had he missed something? He was incredulous that she'd gotten so upset over it. It gave him much to think about. Things to ponder.

A long walk should do me good.

It was late in the night, and the streets were dark. The lanterns that used to light the fallen city were scarce. Instead, there were catwalks, planks, pulleys, and stacked stone blocks—some large, others small. A few buildings were almost complete, but so many had been demolished.

Nath stopped beside a wheelbarrow that was filled with broken blocks and sighed.

What a mess war makes.

But as he continued on through the dust and debris, his heart swelled with pity. There were tents set up all over the city. Camps full of people. Some faces sat around campfires and grumbled. He got a better idea of what Sasha was experiencing. This was her home, and so many had lost everything.

Sure, to a dragon it didn't seem so bad. After all, the people would rebuild. It might take a few years, but they'd bounce back. But some of them wouldn't bounce back. They didn't have enough time for that. They'd die homeless and poor.

This is horrible.

Nath crossed from street to street, picking his way through the city. He heard sobbing. Through a broken window he saw a woman's face in tears. Listening carefully from a place of concealment, he realized one of the fallen Legionnaires was her husband. They'd come to rebuild. They had children. Two of them. Twin girls. A woman friend was there to console the upset woman, who said, "Just when things settle, more of those dragons come and kill. I hate the dragons. They all bring trouble."

Nath's chest tightened, and he moved on. Her voice wasn't the only murmuring he heard. People all over were frustrated, and the truth be told, most of them couldn't tell one dragon from the other. And now, they were threatened again. After all of their work, the peace had vanished almost as soon as it had come.

Will this fighting ever end?

Edging deeper into town, he came across the shambled wooden porch of a tavern. There was a lot of commotion inside the walls of the torch-lit room. He ventured closer, with the porch creaking underneath his foot.

Seems pretty lively. At least not all spirits are broken.

Crash! Boom! Bang!

Inside, a booming dwarven voice yelled, "For Morgdon!"

CHAPTER 4

ATH DASHED THROUGH THE DOOR. A host of men armed with clubs and tankards encircled Brenwar. Some of them had chairs. Nath saw Ben out of the corner of his eyes. The older warrior stood in the corner, leaning against the wall with his arms folded over his chest. He shrugged at Nath.

"Take it back!" Brenwar said. He hiccupped. He smacked his fists together. "Take it back, or I'll slaughter every last one of you!"

Nath pushed through the throng of angry men.

One man shoved him in the back.

Nath shoved him back.

The man eyed his scales and faded back.

"Get out of here, Nath!" Brenwar growled. "This isn't your business. Go away. *Hic.*"

Nath spread his arms out and slowly spun around. "Easy, men. What's this about?"

"I'll tell you what this is all about!" Brenwar spat through his beard. "They say they'll rebuild this city better than Morgdon! Hah! And to think, I was trying to help them. Stupid men!"

"Is this true?" Nath said, gazing at all the men. "I've never known a dwarf to lie."

"Quintucklen is better!" one man said, holding a chair in two hands. "The dragons didn't ever attack their city! We are better. We are stronger!"

"I'm going to rip him apart!" Brenwar surged forward.

Nath held him back for a moment, just long enough to unload a warning to the men. "You had better take it back, or he's going to fight every last one of you. And you don't want that."

"Nay! Let him fight. No dwarf is going to tell us who and what we are in this city," said the man. "Let the bearded cur loose!"

Hometown pride.

Nath had to give the men of Quintuklen credit. They loved their city as much as the dwarves loved Morgdon. He released Brenwar. "Have at it, then."

The grizzled dwarf stormed into the man with the big mouth and chair. The chair came down and splintered on his head. Brenwar tackled the man, and all the other men piled on.

Nath stepped away from the fray and headed toward Ben.

Gaping, Ben said, "You're letting him fight all of them?"

"I don't think I could stop him. Do you?"

Ben ducked under a tankard that whizzed over his head. "I suppose not." He slapped Nath on the back. "Say, you look a little long in the face. How about I get you some ale?"

Brenwar squirted out of the pile, charged through the screaming voices and tables, and plucked a keg of ale up from the floor. Hoisting it overhead, he hurled it at the rush of men. Four men went down, and the keg of ale cracked open and started to spill. "And your ale is lousy!" Brenwar said. He climbed up on the bar and jumped into the throng.

"I think the price of ale just went up. Do you think you can afford it?" Nath asked.

"Come with me," Ben said, leading Nath by the arm. They picked their way through the broken chairs, tables, and pottery and slipped outside on the porch. Taking in a breath of fresh air, Ben said, "It's good to see you, Dragon, but you don't seem well."

"What makes you say so?"

A man flew through the glass window on the other side of the door. *Crash!* Another one came out and landed on top of him. *Whup!*

Nath and Ben shuffled away.

Ben continued. "I can tell when you have a lot on your mind. Sure, I'm not some seer or anything, but when I met you, way back when, you never worried. There's a crease between those brows of yours now."

The swinging doors burst open, and Brenwar stormed out. "*Hic!*" He grabbed both of the men by their collars. "I'm not finished with these two." He dragged them back inside, and another clamor arose. Wood clacked and shattered. Men howled in triumph and pain.

As if nothing were happening, Nath said, "That's disappointing. I haven't really aged so many years, but sometimes I feel as ancient as my father. Aw, Ben, I shouldn't complain. The truth is, I lost a great deal of my power."

"You can't fly anymore, can you?"

Nath shook his head no. "And that's not all. I'd say for the most part, I'm right back where I was when you met me. I know I sound vain, Ben, but with the power I had before, I could do almost anything. Now I'm a shadow of that, and I think, 'How am I supposed to protect so many people from such great evil?'"

Ben rubbed his beard. The stern-faced man had an iron jaw and weathered skin. He'd seen a hundred battles and survived. There was a steely wisdom in his eyes. "You'll do it just like you did it before, Dragon."

"Really, and how did I do it before?"

"With boldness. It didn't matter if we were facing giants or dragons. Wherever we went, there was never anyone bigger than you. Larger than life, you launched yourself into the threat without a sliver of fear in your eyes. You are Nath Dragon, The Dragon Prince. Maybe you're a little smaller than you'd like to be, but I know you. Your ego's bigger than all the mountains in the world."

Nath couldn't stop the smile on his face, and he didn't want to. It felt good. And Ben was right. Nothing had really changed. He was still faster and stronger than any man alive. And what did he have to be scared of? He had Fang. And, more importantly, he had friends who believed in him.

"You know, Ben," Nath said, throwing his arm over Ben's shoulder, "I always knew you were going to grow up to be one of the wisest men who ever lived."

Ben looked him in the eye. "You know you're always right, Dragon."

Crash!

"I think we had better get in there before someone really gets hurt." Nath bustled through the door and stopped just inside.

Brenwar sat on top of a pile of bodies. Beside him sat the man who had insulted him to begin with. Both of them had smiles on their bruised faces. The man, a thickset laborer with a bald head, had a pair of teeth missing that hadn't been missing before.

Nath said, "So I guess the argument is settled, then?"

"Aye!" Brenwar said, clawing at his beard. "These humans and I have come to an agreement."

Nath lifted his brows. "Oh, and what might that be?"

"Men love Quintuklen as much as the dwarves love Morgdon! And that's worth fighting for any day!"

"Aye!" said the men on the floor. They were slowly getting back to their feet and crawling up on unbroken chairs.

Ben looked at Nath and shrugged.

"And better yet. *Hic,*" Brenwar continued, "They've agreed to let the dwarves come and help rebuild them!"

"Aye!" the men said.

"Now that the fighting's over," Brenwar bellowed, "let the singing begin! Aaaaaaah … Home of the dwarves—Morgdon! Home of the dwarves—Morgdon!"

Ben sawed his elbow back and forth and joined in with a big smile behind his greying beard.

Nath was about to join in as well, when he felt a tingle on his neck. He backed up through the door and stepped out on the porch.

Selene stood in her purple robes alone in the moon's shadows.

"Selene?"

"Yes," she said, sounding dejected.

"Look, don't you worry about what Sasha said."

"No, it's fine, Nath. I understand her concerns. I just came to tell you I'm leaving."

CHAPTER 5

HORNLESS WHITE DRAGON WITH GOLD flecks in its scales soared over the grasslands. It was an Ivory Slider more than fifteen feet long with beautiful wings and a very long tail. More graceful than an eagle, she glided from side to side in the air. Her long eyelashes blinked.

Ahead, a flock of wurmers dropped from the clouds and dove right for her.

Outnumbered and seeing the fire in their eyes, she turned and headed back in the direction she had come from.

"Oh no," she said in Dragonese.

Wurmers dropped from the clouds all over by the dozens.

Flapping her wings, she cut through the air, belly skimming the tall highland grasses.

Behind her, hungry shrieks howled out in pursuit.

She was fast, very fast. The Ivory Sliders were the messengers of Dragon Home. They cut through air like a knife through butter, and not many dragons could catch them other than the Blue Razors. Beating her streamlined body through the wind, she began to outdistance her pursuers.

Ahead, she saw a series of mountains with winding crevasses and ravines that would be the perfect place to lose them. Making a beeline for the rocky cliffs, she soared higher.

A spitball of fire whizzed by her ear. The wurmers were shooting balls of energy at her.

Head turned around, she barrel rolled and evaded.

Above her, another wave of wurmers dropped from the greying clouds and blanketed the sky. Balls of flame like tiny meteors showered her from above, singeing wing and scale.

Just as she turned to find a path of escape, a rock bigger than her head slammed into her chest. Spinning out of control, she crashed to the ground with balls of fire peppering her body, and she let out a tremendous roar that split the air.

The wurmers were scattered by the sonic wave of energy. They became disoriented and fell from the sky. Still more came.

The Ivory Slider let out another mystic roar, shattering the air. She shook off the flames and spread her wings once more.

One by one, wurmer after wurmer slammed into her and drove her to the ground. Jaws with sharp, jagged teeth bit into her legs.

She fought with all of her strength, thrashing and biting, but before long, her limbs gave out under the sheer weight of her growing foes. She let out a weak sonic sigh that flattened the grasses and stopped at a pair of massive feet. Pinned down, she still managed to lift her chin. Her eyes flashed.

A giant!

Dragons hated giants, and giants hated dragons. It always had been and always would be. But the wars between them had been quiet for centuries.

And here was one before her, almost twenty feet tall. A towering figure of brawn and muscle, covered in thick hair. But unlike the giants she'd known, this one was different. His entire head was covered in flame. In his mighty grip was a sling big enough to hurl a sheep.

Lizardmen appeared behind the giant with heavy robes in their hands.

She hissed at them.

They bound her up.

The flame giant's necklace of dragon bones shook when he spoke. "BRING HER," he said in a voice as deep as a canyon.

The Ivory Slider was dragged by the lizardmen over the grasses and into the belly of the mountain, where they marched until they stood on the edge of a small ravine. A pair of horned dragon skulls were on spikes that guarded the carved stone steps that led down.

"Take a long look," said the flame giant, pointing into the ravine.

Her nostrils flared. Her neck recoiled. The stench of death and decay was strong. But it was familiar too. Lifting her head, she peered down into the ravine. Her jaw dropped open. Her stomach turned to knots. *Nooooo!*

Down there, dragons lay dead in the brush and trees. Scales of many colors. Copper. Blue. Red. White. Yellow. Green. Their bodies were broken. Wings busted. Horns shattered. Even a massive Bull Dragon was down there.

She turned her fear-filled gaze toward the giant.

Head aflame, he said, "Fear not. You will be spared, messenger. What you have seen, report in every detail to Balzurth of Dragon Home. Tell him Eckubahn sent you."

Trembling, she nodded.

The giant wagged his finger in her face. "You will not fly." He slid out a dagger that was too small for his belt and dropped it point first in the ground. It was carved from a dragon's tooth, and it glimmered with enchantment. "You will walk. Lizards, cut off her wings."

CHAPTER 6

"SELENE, YOU CAN'T GO." NATH laid his hands on her shoulders.

She rested her palms on his hands, and with tear-filled eyes she looked deeply into his. "Sasha is right. I'm behind much of this. These people should kill me. I would if I were them."

"Don't say that, Selene. It's not true."

"It is true. Every last bit of it." She slipped out of his hands and stood on the edge of the porch beside the wooden post that held the ceiling. "I've been walking through the streets and listening to the conversations of men, women, children. You know, I never cared one lick for any of them before. They were rodents. No, not even that. They were bugs to be squished under my scales. Vermin to be chewed away at Gorn Grattack's order." She made a deep frown. "I hated them for their laughter. Happiness. I wanted to destroy it all. I still envy them."

"Selene," he said, looking at the sadness growing in her face. "Everyone can change. You proved that. Don't be so hard on yourself."

"What a jest, Nath. I'm sorry to be ugly, but I should be tried for my crimes."

Nath snuck up to her and tried to cover her mouth.

She slipped away.

He said in a harsh whisper, "Keep your voice down, will you? If someone were to hear you, it might just come true. There are tribunals, you know."

"I can't just wish my past away, Nath. What happens when people figure out who I am, hmmm? Do you think all of them will forgive me? Think of Sasha. She's a sweet and reasonable person, but she wants my head on a platter."

"No, she doesn't. Well, not on a platter anyway. Maybe mounted on the wall."

She glared at him.

"Er, it's a jest." He combed his hair out of his eyes and fell silent. As a stiff wind blew through the streets and stirred up tiny dust devils, his mind dove deeper into thought. Selene had made a good point. The world would not forgive her the same as he had. All over Nalzambor, grudges were still held that were centuries old. And now, it didn't seem fair that like him, she would have to walk the world as a human, knowing so many hated her. "Why don't we walk together?"

"No." She faced him. "Nath, I'm leaving."

A spark of anger flashed in his golden eyes. "I need you, Selene. We are in this together. To the end. You can't just go it alone!"

"Don't get testy. I'm not abandoning you or the cause, but I am getting out of this city. It makes me ashamed of all I have done. So many I have hurt. People I don't know. Family, friends, destroyed. Don't you see, Nath? Don't you see what I've done?" She pointed at some memory banners rustling in the wind that adorned many windows. "That's because of me. I really and truly wanted each and every one of these people dead! How and why," she said, exasperated, "could anyone ever trust me?"

"I trust you, Selene. You have to believe that. You saved me, and we stopped Gorn. If *you* hadn't done what you did, all of Nalzambor would have fallen." He stepped by her side. "You have to forgive yourself. And at least you care now."

"Yes, I do." She nodded. "And I'm not liking that so much either. Helping people is so … foreign to me."

"But it's rewarding."

"We'll see. I'm going north. To the high mountains. I think there might be a nest of wurmers there.

I'll stay in touch. You find out what Bayzog suggests, and maybe we can rendezvous there, say, in a week or two. Goodbye, Nath." She kissed his cheek and disappeared into the dark streets.

Don't leave.

Nath's heart sank. Every time she left, he couldn't help but wonder if he would ever see her again.

Please.

A few moments later, Ben stepped out on the porch. He had a turkey leg in one hand. Looking into Nath's face, he said, "Now what? I thought I had you charged up. Now you look like Brenwar would look if someone shaved his beard off."

Nath made a sour face. "I sure wouldn't want to see that. No, Selene just swung by and departed."

Ben nodded his grizzled chin. "I see. And that upsets you because you are so fond of her."

"No."

"Aw, I know you better than that, Dragon." Ben tickled Nath's ribs. "You want her for a bride, don't you?"

"How much ale have you had?"

"Oh, I'm more of a cider man these days. The ale's too hard on my gut. So tell me, why did she leave?"

"Guilt."

Ben stroked the rim of his moustache. "I see."

"Can I ask you something, Ben?"

"Sure, you can ask me anything."

"Do you have any resentment toward her? After all, she did lead the war that killed an awful lot of people."

"Hmmm, you know, I really haven't given it that much thought. As a soldier I learned that life is full of losses, and you have to move on. It's full of many blessings too. I just keep marching forward. I can't let the past slow me down."

"But your family, Ben. You lost all of them because of Barnabus."

"True, and I miss them every day. But I don't blame the likes of Selene, but I do think …" Ben's voice trailed off.

"Think what, Ben?"

He slapped his big hand on Nath's shoulder. "Nothing. If you've forgiven her, I've forgiven her too."

Nath eyed him. "No, you were going to say something else. What was it?"

Ben shrugged. "I do think, if justice is to be served, it will catch up with her."

CHAPTER 7

NATH STOOD FAR OUTSIDE OF Quintuklen's walls inside the valley full of stone markers. They were graves, thousands of them in rows as far as the non-dragon eye could see. Over the past couple of days he'd lain low, stayed out of the city, and begun noting each and every one of the markers.

He scraped some debris from one of the stones and revealed a familiar name. His eyes teared up. It was Ben's wife's marker, and beside it were two more, Ben's son and daughter. Nath's heart sank. Three names among thousands. He thought about all of the people who had suffered like Ben had. Men and women. Mothers and fathers. Not all of them could move on. Not when they had lost people they loved so much.

How many more must die for the sake of evil?

Clenching his fist, he rose up and walked a few miles, lost in thought. Eyes searching, he found something he was looking for. Wildflowers. He plucked some out of the ground and filled up his hands with three colorful bouquets. He marched back to the graveyard, set the flowers on the stones of Ben's family, then started the long walk back to the city.

It was mid-morning, and the laborers were hard at work under a hot sun. Hammers pecked and chiseled. Foremen shouted orders. Pulleys squeaked. Large loads of materials rolled down the main roads on huge wagons pulled by teams of horses. And there was a liveliness about the men. Some of them were whistling, even singing.

Nath pulled back his shoulders a little. Walked a little taller.

Their spirits aren't broken, so why are mine?

There was nothing like seeing men and women working together with such purpose. It kept their minds off the past. And that was a good thing. They could look forward to the future, and Nath wanted to make sure that future was a bright one.

Making his way through the maze of walls that surrounded the fallen city, he spied a woman on top of one of the ways, waving her arms at him. It was Sasha. She was in a pale-yellow gown, trimmed in flowers. Her platinum hair was pinned up with a fine silver comb. He jogged toward her. She came rushing down the steps to greet him.

"Nath! Where have you been?" Sasha threw her arms around him and held him tight. "I've missed you."

"Uh, I've just been wandering and waiting for Bayzog to call on me." He lifted her off her feet in a hug. "You seem well."

"Well? Why wouldn't I be?" She slipped off of him, took his hand in hers, and led him back into the city like a little child. "Come on, let's get back home and see Bayzog."

He followed her lead, but it wasn't long before he felt long stares and eyes on him. Nath had done little to conceal his ebony-scaled arms. They were mostly bare under the tunic that he wore. And it didn't help that his great height and flame-red hair were far from ordinary. A small group of children slipped in behind him with giggles. He turned to look at them, and they scattered.

Oh no, here we go again.

"Come on. Come on," Sasha said, prodding him along.

Once again the children fell in step behind him. He ignored them. Focused on the others he passed who stared at him. One man, a burly fellow with a limp, nodded a greeting at him. So did the woman behind him, and she smiled. He nodded back.

"Hail Dragon Slayer, welcome!" said a bricklayer on top of a catwalk, waving a navy knit cap like a banner. "Hail!"

Nath waved.

That's odd, them calling me a dragon slayer. Of course, they probably don't know the difference between the wurmers and a real dragon.

"Dragon slayer!" another man cried out. It was followed by another and another, and before Nath knew what was going on, people were filling the streets and shouting encouraging words to him.

"See, Nath?" Sasha said, rubbing his arm. "They embrace you now. You are their hero. You are my hero as well."

Arm high, Nath waved and nodded in return to the folks who watched his small parade.

Now this is more like it.

The streets thickened with people, happy faces one and all. Children were on men's shoulders.

"This is almost embarrassing."

"Hah," she laughed. "Not for you. No, your name has spread, Nath. In the good spirit that it should."

But as the people chanted 'Dragon Slayer!' over and over again, a dark memory crossed through Nath's mind. Of his time in Narnum, when the people had crowned him the Champion after he defeated Selene's war cleric, Kryzak. A dark and shameful time.

He didn't like the association, not one bit. It was contradictory and perverted to him. And this parade he had unintentionally created was growing behind him. A few dozen people at least.

"We need to end this, Sasha."

She looked at him. "Why? It's delightful." She started waving her hand. "Enjoy the moment, Nath Dragon."

He played along for another block as he studied Sasha. There was something odd about her. She wasn't one to get caught up in moments like this. Though she wasn't quiet, she was reserved.

"So Sasha, you are no longer angry?"

"Angry?" she said, looking at him somewhat aghast. "What in the world are you talking about?"

"Last time I saw you, you were fighting with Bayzog."

"Bayzog and I never fight."

"Well, maybe I'm not putting this right. But you were very upset with Selene. Are you over that now? I can't imagine you would be."

Still walking and with a confused look on her face, Sasha said, "Where is Selene? I would like to see her."

"She left."

"Why would she do that? I'd love to see her."

"You would?"

"Of course I would," she said cheerfully.

Either I'm lost, or I really don't understand women.

Nath then said, "But you had some very choice words with her. Are you not still angry?"

Suddenly, Sasha whirled. Anger filled her eyes. "Nath Dragon, quit playing games! I don't know what you're talking about!"

CHAPTER 8

BACK INSIDE BAYZOG'S APARTMENT, NATH stood at the great table. Books were stacked up in neat piles. Some of them still floated open in the air. With a wave of his hand, Bayzog sent one book floating away and pulled over another.

"So you enjoy reading, don't you." Nath was just making conversation. His eyes were busy soaking in the grand oversized room that was much too big for the small building it was housed in.

"So you've noticed," said the wizard. His eyes darted over the wording of the ancient texts, and the pages flipped faster than Nath could attempt to read them. "Study creates the building blocks of knowledge."

Sasha wasn't in the room. She'd said she was heading out to the market so she could prepare food for them later. She'd only departed moments ago.

"There isn't a lot that escapes me," Nath said. "Something's amiss with Sasha, isn't it?"

Bayzog's face drew tight.

"Talk to me, friend," Nath said to him. He reached over and shoved the hovering book away. "Come on, Bayzog. I can't help if you clam up on me."

With a dejected voice, Bayzog said, "You can't help anyway, Nath. She has the Wizard's Dementia."

Nath leaned forward and patted his friend on the back. "I'm not sure what that is, but it sounds horrible."

Long-faced, Bayzog said, "Horrible is an understatement. There's no cure for it."

"There's a cure for everything," Nath said, "but it would help if you'd tell me what you were dealing with."

"Nath, this is my burden. Not yours. You have bigger tasks ahead that you need to remain focused on."

"If I can't be helpful with small matters, then how can I give aid to the large ones?" Nath replied. "Please, confide in me, old friend."

"For all the good it will do, why not?" Shoulders sagging, Bayzog made his way over to the couch, poured some wizard water, sat down, rubbed his eyes, and yawned.

Boy, he must be whipped. I've never seen him yawn before.

Nath took a seat. "So, what are you dealing with?"

Bayzog finished a long drink. "Wizard Dementia is caused by magic. It's very, very rare, but anyone—particularly a human—who calls on the powers of Nalzambor can be afflicted. You see, Nath, magic is not as natural to all as it is to dragons and to elves. We have a stronger nature for it, which I can't even explain. But with humans it's different. Even though Sasha is a fine sorceress and well disciplined, the magic she has used has taken a toll on her mind." His lip quivered, and a lump rolled up and down his throat. "Her mind is eroding—slowly, but still eroding."

"That's horrible, Bayzog. Certainly there is something to be done?"

"Nath, I've searched. I've tried. It's just so rare that there isn't much material on it."

"What about the Occular of Orray?" Nath suggested.

"I've sent word," Bayzog said, taking another sip of water. "But it's unlikely. The elves are more protective of it now than ever. Truth be told, they'd be very reluctant to use its powers on a human."

"I'll go down there and speak to them myself."

Bayzog held up his hand. "Nath, for some things in life there isn't an easy fix. Death takes us all, be it at twenty-five years or one thousand. I will quietly deal with this."

Nath didn't push. He knew it wouldn't do him any good. And now wasn't the time to argue with his friend. Bayzog had opened up, so it was time to listen. "Does she know, Bayzog?"

The wizard shook his head no. "That's the hardest part, Nath. I feel as if I am deceiving her. Sometimes she gets so confused."

"Do Rerry and Samaz know?"

"They do. Why do you think they are away?"

"Ah." Nath leaned back into the cushions. "I see."

So, someone is *looking for a cure. Good for them.*

"The worst part is her love for magic, Nath. She wants to practice and train. I keep having to distract her with something else. I tell her I'm too busy, or make up some petty lie. It's horrible. But if she uses magic, it could be disastrous. Fatal. Not to mention it would accelerate her condition. I can't risk that, and yet she loves magic so much. She was such a talented pupil. It sickens my heart, Nath. Every bit of it."

Nath swallowed the lump in his throat. This was one of the most devastating things he'd ever heard. And Bayzog, who hardly ever showed emotion, had deep creases in his brow.

All Nath could think to say was 'There's always hope.' But he didn't. Instead, he sat with his friend in front of the warm fire in silence.

Sometimes being there and saying nothing is the best comfort of all.

"It's stuffy in here," Brenwar said. He had his arms crossed over his barrel chest and was eyeing every detail of Bayzog's home. He stood with his back to the fireplace adjacent to the sofa. "Horrible construction. Looks like elves did it. I'm surprised it survived the war."

"I'm surprised *you* survived the war," Bayzog retorted.

"Watch yer mouth, part-elf."

Bayzog shook his head and faced Nath and Ben, who were both sitting at the table. Sasha was back sitting at the table too. She had a smile on her face as she hummed and prepared a tray of food. She brought each man a plate.

"Thanks, Sasha," Nath said.

"Yes, thanks," Ben added with a courteous nod.

Brenwar frowned at his plate full of fruit, pastries, and cheeses. "Haven't you any meat?"

Sasha giggled and patted him on his head. "Of course. Anything for you, Brenwar, but that comes later."

Bayzog cleared his throat. "Ahem. If you don't mind, I'd like to discuss the business at hand."

"I'm not stopping you." Brenwar sniffed a handful of purple grapes. His face soured, and he set the plate down. He walked over and climbed up on a stool at the study table and shoved away the floating books that blocked his face. "Go on."

With a studious look on his face, Bayzog said, "The good news is that I have found some history of the wurmers. And like many insects, it seems they all function on the order of a queen."

Nath nodded. Selene had already alluded to how the wurmers were more of an insect-like culture that built hives and had nests. "I've seen their nests first hand. And we've destroyed some of them. I would think we must have destroyed the queen that was in there too."

"Which brings me to the bad news," Bayzog said. "According to the histories, the last queen—their true queen—was never found and killed."

Leaning forward on the table, Ben asked, "So what does that mean?"

"It means there are wurmers we know of—Selene has discovered those—and then there are those we don't know of."

"You mean there are even more?" Ben asked. He looked at Dragon. "Those things are hard to kill."

Bayzog continued. "I'd say it's highly likely that the queen has been hiding. Possibly hibernating." His face turned grim. "And if I were to guess, she's been laying eggs for centuries. And if I were a titan, I'd be trying to find them, wake them up, and turn them loose."

"And what if that happens?" Sasha asked.

Bayzog's reply was devastating. "They'll blanket Nalzambor like a plague of enormous insects."

CHAPTER 9

THE ATMOSPHERE WAS SOLEMN IN the picturesque room. Everyone's face was long and silent. Again, Bayzog broke the silence. "This isn't all on our shoulders, Nath. The rest of the world will help out as well. This affects everyone's lives, not just our own."

"I know. Sometimes good allies are hard to come by, but I know I can always count on my friends." Nath stretched out his long-clawed hands and squeezed Ben and Brenwar's shoulders on either side of him. "Right?"

Ben was looking away and whistling.

"Ben?" Nath said again.

"Only joking, Dragon. You know that. I'm always with you. It's just that I'm heavily committed to rebuilding this city. I have people here counting on me. You know, I don't just sit around and wait for adventure to come and get me. I have responsibilities. And I need to be here to protect this city. I hope you understand."

Taken aback, Nath said, "Uh, Ben, I feel foolish. And I certainly didn't mean to make you feel that you were required to come along. None of you need to feel obligated. I only meant that I know I can always count on you."

"And we you, Nath," Sasha said. She slipped in behind him and gave him a hug. "That's why I'm coming with you."

Nath's gaze froze on Bayzog's widening eyes.

Oh my!

"Now, Sasha," Bayzog stammered. "We can't leave. Not now."

"Oh, you can stay. I'm going," she said, petting Nath's arm. "Nath needs me."

"I need you too," the wizard said. "I need you here. Our efforts to aid Nalzambor are best served here. I insist."

"I don't care." She made her way over to an open closet and draped herself in a fine grey traveling cloak. She also took the Elderwood Staff in hand. "Come, Nath. Let's go."

Tension filled the room as the staff's gem glowed with life.

Bayzog was on his feet, hand extended toward Sasha. His face was drawn tight. "Sasha, may I please have my staff?"

She hugged it. "I would like to use it on our journey."

Gently, the wizard replied, "I would also like to use it on our journey. May I please have it?"

"Only if you promise that you'll teach me to use it."

The part-elf crept closer.

Nath eased out of his seat. The fire growing inside the gem made the scales on his arms tingle.

Bayzog inched closer to her. "Sasha, do you want to walk or ride? Shall I gather us some horses?"

Her usually sweet eyes bore into Bayzog with frustration. "Promise me, Bayzog! Promise me!"

"Sasha, it is elven. You cannot use it," Bayzog said. "Please, release the staff to me. You could hurt yourself."

Her eyes shifted to the radiant power emanating from the gem. "It seems to like me. Its power courses through my veins. Teach me how to use it, Bayzog. Teach me now!"

The staff's green glow lit up the entire room. It reflected in Sasha's eyes. She began to radiate power. Something was about to erupt.

"Sasha," Bayzog pleaded with his worried face bathed in green light, "I will teach you what I can. But please, hand it over. You could hurt yourself. Or others."

"No. You won't let me use magic. You want it all for yourself." She lowered the staff at him.

Nath stooped, legs ready to spring.

This is getting bad! Dangerous.

Bayzog eased ever closer. "Sasha, you must trust me."

"No, it's mine." She tapped the bottom of the staff on the floor. The entire room shook, sending fine pottery crashing on the floor. Sasha's eyes widened. "Whoa." Wild eyed, she brought the staff up and down again.

Nath sprang. He arrived a split second before Bayzog and wrapped his hands around the staff before it hit the floor. A charge of energy went through him.

Zap!

His limbs went numb. As he fell, he saw the horrified look on Sasha's face. He landed hard. Forcing his eyes open, he saw Bayzog on the floor as well. The half-elf's eyes were closed. He wasn't breathing.

CHAPTER 10

"I'LL WAKE HIM UP," BRENWAR roared. He hopped over Nath and landed alongside Bayzog. Using his thick, stubby fingers, he pinched the half-elf's ginger arm.

"Ow!" Bayzog screamed. He sat up and found himself face to face with Brenwar. "What did you do *that* for?"

"I saved your life." Brenwar gave him two hard slaps on the back. He helped Bayzog to his feet. "And I'll never let you forget it."

Sasha rushed into Bayzog's arms. Tears were streaming down her face. Her body was trembling. "I'm sorry, Bayzog. I'm sorry! What is wrong with me? Please tell me what's wrong with me!"

"Shhhh." Bayzog hugged her and gently stroked her hair. "It's fine. I forgive you."

She sobbed. "Something's wrong. I know it is! Help me."

He kissed her cheek and said in her ear, "Let's rest on this. Accidents happen." He said something in Elven. Sasha passed out in his arms. Misty-eyed, he carried her off to the bedroom.

Ben reached down to where Nath lay and put a hand on his shoulder. "How are you feeling?"

"Shocked." Nath flicked the numbness from his fingers and stared at the staff. Its gemstone was now dim. Brenwar was reaching down for it. "I wouldn't do that. It's elven. No telling what it would do to a dwarf."

"How about I do everyone a favor and take my war hammer and break it?"

Allowing Ben to help him up to his feet, Nath shook his head. "That was interesting."

"That was strange," said Ben. "What has gotten into Sasha?"

Nath gave Ben and Brenwar a brief explanation. Just as he finished, Bayzog re-entered the room with a very long look on his face. He picked up the Elderwood Staff. "That was too close."

"Too close to what?" Brenwar said.

"Our deaths."

"You *were* dead. I saved you."

"No, I was unconscious." Bayzog looked at his arm. "But thanks for the bruise." Holding the staff, he said, "Nath, you know that I can't take the journey with you."

"I never expected that you would."

"Listen, before you depart, we need to talk about the titans." Bayzog rubbed his head.

"Bayzog, you don't need to worry about this. You have enough to manage on your own."

"It is our burden to share, me and Sasha, husband and wife. We shall manage. And when she wakes up, we'll have a long and honest talk." Staff in hand, he took a seat on his stool. "Now, set us aside from your mind. We need to talk about the titans."

Nath wanted to press back and tell his friend 'Not now,' but he didn't. He knew Bayzog well enough to know that letting him talk about history would speed up his healing. He took his place at the table.

Silent, Brenwar and Ben did as well.

"It's interesting. There is no mention of the Great Dragon Wall in the histories. The dragons did very well concealing it." Bayzog scribbled some Elvish notes on some paper. With a bright look in his eye, he said, "I would have loved to have seen that. It's so fascinating. Perhaps you could draw or paint it for me one day."

"Perhaps," Nath said.

"Such a great secret, and in Borgash of all places," the wizard continued. "Well, according to the histories, the titans were worshipped by all. They'd attract throngs of men and women to them. Very charismatic. So, don't be surprised if it's not hard to find them. Or at least, find the bodies in which they host. They are arrogant. Proud. Deceitful. They love to boast and have no shame about them whatsoever. But they can take anyone's form. So, the goal is to trap that spirit. Return it behind the wall at Borgash and secure it. But killing the body is one thing. Trapping the spirit is quite another."

"Can the spirit be destroyed?" Nath asked. "I would think to find that easier."

"If that were the case, the dragons would have done that already. Unless of course they just haven't figured out how. But for the time being, we want to trap them. In order to do that, you will need this." Bayzog flicked his fingers at a book's pages and said a mystic word. An image of a smooth stone with a pale-pink fire appeared over the table. "A spirit stone."

Looking around, Nath said, "Well, I hope you have one squirreled away in here."

"Ha!" Bayzog laughed. "No, like the titans, these stones haven't been seen for centuries. So either you have to find one, or I have to make one."

"You can do that?" Ben said.

Bayzog waved the image away. "I can at least try. But if you want to find one, my guess would be that if the Spirit Stones still exist, they are kept by the dragons." He looked at Nath. "That's where your influence comes in."

"Let me see if I have this straight. I need to kill all of the wurmers."

"Aye," Brenwar agreed.

"Seek the aid of my kin and get these Spirit Stones." He spoke a little more sarcastic as he went.

"Aye."

"Kill the titans' host bodies."

"Aye."

"And secure them behind the Great Dragon Wall once and for all."

Brenwar continued to agree, "Aye."

"Oh, and if I figure out how to kill the spirit, I'll execute it as well."

"Aye!" Brenwar hopped off his stool and was practically frothing at the mouth. "What are we waiting for?"

"Nath, remember you can't do it all by yourself," Bayzog said with a nod.

"Well, of course not," he replied. "That's what I have Brenwar for."

"Aye!"

CHAPTER 11

Leaving Bayzog and Sasha wasn't easy. It was one of the hardest things Nath had ever done. On foot, he led his horse, a fine dapple-grey steed, toward the exit through the outer walls to the north. Brenwar was with him, leading a small chestnut horse, and Ben walked beside him, sending him off. Facing the stiff winds and some spitting rain, Nath swiped the hair from his eyes and took relief in knowing that Bayzog, Sasha, and Ben would at least be safer in the city than with him.

Ben was seeing him off. "Don't be so quiet, Dragon. It's not like you."

"Aw, you're making me feel like an old man," Nath said, smiling at him.

The older warrior raised an eyebrow. "Man, you say?"

"You know what I mean. Sorry, Ben, I'm just worried about Bayzog and Sasha."

"I'll be looking after them as best I can."

They made it through the first line of exterior walls that surrounded the city. A group of workers were making repairs on a busted section of wall.

Brenwar grunted. "I've got to get word to Morgdon, keep those walls from being crooked." He handed Ben a scroll of wax-sealed paper. "This will take care of it."

"Oh, yes," Ben said, taking the scroll, "After all, nothing in this world is straight that isn't dwarven."

"You got that right."

Winding through the maze-like formation of walls, they finally emerged. The distant snow-capped mountains of the north lay ahead. Nath wondered if Selene was out there somewhere, and if she was safe.

"I guess this is it, Ben," Nath said to his friend. "I'd be lying if I said I was glad to leave you here, albeit in safety."

"I can't say that I blame you. Of course, even a stone is better company than Brenwar."

"Don't you mean a bearded stone?" Nath said.

"Ha ha!" Ben laughed. "Dragon, you know I'd come, and I wish I could, but I made a promise to someone that I wouldn't leave them."

"Someone who?"

"I have a new betrothed. Her name is Rebecca."

"Ben!" Nath said with excitement. "That's great. Why didn't you tell me? I'd like to meet her."

"She's in Narnum now, and her journey doesn't bring her back until next week."

Shaking Ben's hand, Nath said, "I'm happy for you, Ben. Very happy. It's not often that a man can find true love. It seems it has struck twice with you. I can tell."

"Thank you." Ben unslung his quiver full of arrows and unsnapped Akron from his back. "Here."

"No, Ben, you keep it. You'll need it to help defend the city."

"Dragon, I've a feeling that you'll need it more than me. Besides"—he stuffed the magic bow in Nath's hand—"it's always been yours. I was only protecting it while you were gone."

"It couldn't have been in better hands," Nath said, trying to pull it free of Ben's grip.

The older man held it tight. "Sorry, Dragon," Ben grimaced. He held the bow firm. "Boy, this just isn't very easy." He closed his eyes and with a gasp, he released the bow. Opening his eyes, he said, "That really was as hard as I thought it would be."

Nath pushed Akron and the quiver back into Ben's hands. "Farewell, Ben."

"I'm going to miss you, Dragon."

Nath climbed onto his horse, and Brenwar did the same.

The dwarf said to Ben, "Well, don't get all misty for my sake, Ben. Just deliver that letter."

Ben slapped Brenwar's horse on its hindquarters and sent it off in a lurch. "Goodbye, Brenwar!"

As Nath rode off, the last thing he heard was Ben's voice, shouting with cheer from the top of the outer wall. "Dragon! Dragon!"

It rained the entire day's ride north. The harder it rained, the louder Brenwar sang. Black beard soaked with water, he sang one ancient dwarven tune after the other. And the songs weren't too bad either. They lifted Nath's spirits.

"You like this, don't you," Nath said in a loud voice that carried through the heavy rain.

The dwarf kept on singing.

"You know," Nath started to say, but he stopped.

No one would hear them coming over the rain. Instead, as the horses clomped through the muddy hillside they climbed, he held his tongue.

Let Brenwar be happy. He deserves to be.

Brenwar stopped singing. "What? Did you say something?"

"I said, do you think you could sing something in Elvish?"

Brenwar wrung water out of his beard, shook his thick head, and started singing in Dwarven again.

Nath continued to lead the way over the sloppy hills that met with a forested mountainside. Ducking under heavy branches and weaving through the trees, he searched for shelter. Night would soon fall, and even though neither he nor Brenwar required much rest, getting out of the rain until it passed seemed like a good idea.

Half a mile up the mountain, he came across a large rocky overhang. Water poured off it like a waterfall. Nath ducked under it and took a breath. The space was big enough for four men and horses. Brenwar followed him in and shook the water from his rain-soaked face. Nath wrung out his long red hair.

"Why are we stopping?" Brenwar said. "It's not even dark yet."

Nath slid out of his saddle. "I need a moment."

"A moment? What's a moment?"

Nath flipped open a saddlebag, removed a pair of orange fruits with a stem, and tossed one to Brenwar. The other one he fed to his horse. He scratched behind the horse's ears. "You're a fine steed."

The dapple-grey horse shook his head and nickered.

Nath froze. His nostrils widened. Something foul lingered in the air. His hand fell on Fang.

Eyeing him, Brenwar started to speak.

Nath put a finger to his lips.

Brenwar readied his war hammer, Mortuun the Crusher.

Golden eyes peering into the deep black where the rock jutted from the ground, Nath spied a small cave opening.

Silvery eyes flashed within. Scales slithered over the wet earth, and the hooded head of a great snake slipped out. It was bigger than Nath, and it reared back to strike. Its black tongue flicked from its mouth.

"That's an awfully big snake," Brenwar grumbled.

Two more monstrous snakes slithered out and flanked them. Venom dripped from fangs as big and sharp as a dragon's.

"Pardon," Brenwar said, shifting in his saddle, "I meant snakes."

CHAPTER 12

A green lily dragon half filled a wooden cage big enough for a large dog. Its snout was bound shut with leather cords. Its torn wings were folded tight on its back. Its scales shined like green pearls in the moonlight.

"I say we eat it," said an orc. He was large, as most orcs are. A tangled mess of greasy hair covered his bare back down to the waist. He poked the dragon with the back of his spear. He licked his split and puffy lips. "I've never eaten dragon before. They smell delicious, like baby deer."

"Leave our treasure alone," another voice said. It was a gnoll. A huge wolf-faced man taller but slimmer than the orc. He wasn't alone. The party of poachers was made up of orcs, gnolls, and the much smaller yellow-eyed goblins. There were nine in all. "Once we sell it, you'll be able to eat all you want and more."

The orc at the dragon cage grumbled in his throat. Sounding a bit stupider than his gnoll counterpart, he scratched his head and added, "Are they worth more alive or dead?"

"Alive," the gnoll said, filing his long fingernails with a sharpening stone.

Unlike the others, the gnoll had more flare on him: shiny breastplate made for a large man, heavy axe on his hip. All of the others—gnoll, orc, and goblin alike—carried spears or smaller weapons.

"Now get away and don't pester it anymore." The gnoll walked over and eyed the dragon. "It may lie quietly, but don't let it fool you. It's thinking, not dreaming."

A goblin hopped over the campfire. "Dragons dream?" The filthy humanoid's necklace of animal bones rattled around his neck. He was feisty, even more so than his ornery kin. "How do you know they dream?"

"I know," the gnoll assured him. His chin was up in an attempt to be dignified.

"You don't know that," the goblin retorted. "You're just saying that. Think you're smart?"

The gnoll huffed on his fingernails and dusted them off on his bloodstained sleeve. "Of course I'm smart. That's why I'm the leader. And was it not my trap that caught the dragon?"

Fingers fidgeting at his side and glancing around, the goblin said, "It was luck. Strange fortune. You set no trap at all. The dragon was sleeping." He pounded his chest. "And I saw it first! Told you about it, I did."

The gnoll bared his canine teeth in a snarl. His blades whisked out of his sheaths and found a new home under the goblin's greasy chin. The leader then said to the wide-eyed goblin, "Perhaps you don't want to share in my good fortune, then. The less of you, the more for me and the rest."

Everyone in the poachers' camp's eyes were on the gnoll. The two goblins that remained drew the crude hand axes at their sides. Their feverish eyes had murder in them.

The gnoll pressed his superior blade harder into the goblin's neck. He marched the little monster backward. "You do realize that if I kill you, I have to kill all of your kind." He shrugged his shoulders. "I like the nine. Three gnolls. Three orcs. Three goblins. It's a fortunate number. But minus one goblin, we have eight. Unlucky. Minus two, we have seven. That's the luck of a human's number." He spat. "Bad luck for gnolls. So that means I need six. I like six, but nine is better. Twelve, too big to control."

Gaping, the goblin continued to back away until he stopped a couple feet from the hot coals of the fire. Sweat beaded and dropped over the creases of his brow. Stammering and flapping his hand, he said with a crooked smile, "Nine is good. Nine is good. You say dragons dream, I believe it. Dragons dream. Yes. Dragons definitely dream."

"Mmm, you know, now that I think about it," the gnoll said, rubbing his chin and glancing skyward, "I don't think dragons dream. So, it seems we are once again in disagreement."

The goblin's mouth fell open.

The gnoll cocked his sword arm back. "Six is my favorite number." He started to swing.

"Dragons do dream," said a voice out of nowhere.

The gnoll froze and turned.

A shadowy hooded figure emerged from the woodland.

Every poacher in the camp readied their weapon. Narrowing his wolfish eyes on the figure, the gnoll said, "We don't share our fire with strangers. We kill trespassers."

"Oh, I'm not here to share your fire. I'm here for the dragon." Selene revealed her face. "And zero is my favorite number."

CHAPTER 13

Sliding his sword out of his scabbard, Nath backed up his mount. "The horses, Brenwar. We need to ride out of here."

"I hear you," Brenwar replied. Imitating Nath's, his mount started backward.

The snake flanking it struck. The reptile buried its fangs into the horse's hindquarters.

Throwing the dwarf from the saddle, the horse bucked and instantly fell down dead.

The snake flanking Nath's dapple-grey steed slithered after him. It coiled its hooded head and struck.

Fang's blade flashed quicker than the blink of an eye and shore the snake's head clear off.

Nath hopped off the saddle and scared his horse away. "Get!"

The middle snake, bigger than the rest, reared up right before Nath's eyes. There was deep hypnotic power in the massive cobra's eyes. Deep and evil, its hooded face swayed back and forth. Drops of burning venom dripped from its mouth.

"You think you're faster than me, do you?" Nath said to the snake—whose body was thicker than his leg. "Belly crawler, beware. I'll cut you down like your dead brother over there."

"You need to cut them both down!" Brenwar mumbled. His entire body was encircled by the cobra that had killed his horse. His eyes bulged in their sockets, and his face purpled. He spat out his next words. "Quit trying to make friends with that lizard, and kill it!"

The great grey-black snake hissed. Its tongues flickered.

"You've given me no choice," Nath said, brandishing the glimmering blade of Fang. He spoke in the ancient Snake tongue, unknown to most. "Crawl back inside your hole or die, Snake."

Head reared up eye to eye with Nath, the giant snake struck lightning fast.

Nath banged the tip of its nose with the flat of his blade, driving the reptile back. "I told you I was fast," Nath said in an ancient warning. "My next blow will be fatal."

The snake's eyes bore into him like ancient black pearls of evil. Its head feinted with short strikes and then recoiled.

"Quit playing games with it!" Brenwar blurted out. His face was beet red, and he screamed. "Nothing crushes a dwarf!"

Nath's sure feet slipped on the wet rocks.

The cobra struck. Dripping fangs bore down on Nath's neck.

When Nath snapped his arm up, the cobra's jaws clamped down hard on it. The snake's teeth broke off on Nath's black scales. Toothless, the reptile struck again and held on, chomping down hard on Nath's arm like a vice.

Nath started laughing. "Look at this, Brenwar! It busted its teeth on my scales. I should have known."

"Grrrr!" Though Brenwar flexed with all his dwarven might, the snake that constricted him did not give. "Will you get this thing off me?"

"Certainly," Nath said. Dragging over the snake that was clamped down on his arm, he picked up Brenwar's war hammer and clobbered the lizard in the head.

Its diamond-scaled body eased its all-powerful grip.

Puffing for breath, Brenwar squirmed out of the scaly locks, plucked Mortuun from Nath's grip, and whacked the snake again.

"No! No!" cried out a scratchy voice.

A small shambling figure squeezed out of the snake hole. It was a dirty little man with a full head of scraggly brown hair and a partial beard. He wore strange robes made of snakeskin and had a belt made from snake skeletons. "Don't kill any more of my pets. Please."

Brenwar slammed the man into the ground. "Why? They tried to kill us, and they did kill my horse."

Blue eyes blinking, the odd wilderness man said with desperation, "They were only protecting me. Just as a dog protects his master."

"We posed no threat," Brenwar stated.

The snakeskin clad man let out an inhuman hiss. The cobra released Nath's arm and slithered away. "See! See! I control them."

Holding the little middle-aged man by the scruff of the neck, Brenwar shook him. "Can you bring back my horse from the dead too?"

"Er … no," the little man said.

Nath sheathed his sword. "Who are you?"

"Ipsy the Snake Charmer." The scruffy man blinked a lot. "Ipsy the Hooded."

Brenwar toyed with the cobra-like hood hanging from Ipsy's strange robes. "He's a druid."

Fingers scratching at the air, Ipsy said, "I prefer woodland seer. Well, if one is being particular, I'm very keen on Ipsy the Hooded. Really draws the attention of the women in small villages." He winked at Brenwar. "What is your name, dwarf? Black Beard?"

Eyeing Nath, Brenwar shoved Ipsy to the ground and stepped on his back. "Druids can't be trusted, and I don't like the stink of this little man. Can I kill him?"

"Kill me?" Ipsy squeaked. "No, no, that would be fatal. It would bring a great curse upon you for the entirety of your days. Please." He eyed Nath's arms and changed his demeanor. "Er, how did you come across those scales? Are you cursed? A demon?"

Nath remembered a few other encounters with druids, in days gone by. They came in many shapes and forms. Men or women, they could be anyone from a halfling to a bugbear. They were loners, hunkered down in their territory, somewhat aloof to everything that was going on in the rest of the world. In a way, Nath envied them. But one and all, they were squirrely as a dryad or a fairy. "Let him up, Brenwar."

"This weird little man owes me a horse." Brenwar nudged his boot toe into the druid's ribs.

"Ow!" Ipsy whined. Gathering himself to his feet and eyeing Nath's arms with avid interest, he stretched out his eager fingers. "May I touch them?"

Flattered, Nath started to say yes.

But Brenwar cut in. "No."

"Let the flame-haired man speak for himself," Ipsy said to Brenwar. He pleaded. "Please? Please? You are so fast. I've never seen any man faster than a snake. And those scales. I marvel. They must be harder than steel."

Wary, Nath fanned out his yellow-gold fingernails on his clawed hand. "And sharper than steel as well."

With an awe-inspired gasp, Ipsy ran his grubby fingers over Nath's scales. "How is this possible? You are both man and dragon."

"It's a long story and one that you don't need to trouble yourself about." Nath watched the snake slither back into the hole. "You need to be more careful with your pets. And we are down a horse thanks to you. How do you propose to replace it?"

Ipsy's eyes enlarged beneath his unibrow. "Being a druid, I have no personal belongings. And if anything, that horse has been freed from a life of slavery." He sneered. "I should suggest that you free your mount as well."

"And let it starve to death? I think not." Nath closed in on the druid and glared down in his face. "Now, tell me, how will you compensate me and my friend?"

"I have nothing."

Brenwar hemmed the little man in from behind and growled, "Everybody has something." He slapped his hammer head in his hand. "Especially when their life depends on it."

Ipsy swallowed the lump in his throat, raised a finger, and replied, "I have knowledge."

CHAPTER 14

THE GNOLL LEADER LET OUT a rumbling chuckle from his throat. The others in his gang started to chuckle as well. Sliding out their weapons, they surrounded Selene on cat's feet. Stroking his chin, he eyed her up and down. "It seems that you are surrounded, traveler. But by the looks of you, I think more fortune has fallen into our hands. You might even fetch half the price of a dragon."

"Oh, you mean my dragon," she said, creeping closer to the dragon's cage.

The orc that stood closest blocked her view, looking down at her. "Perhaps I'll stuff you in that cage with it."

Selene's tail slithered from beneath her gown, coiled around the orc's neck, and jerked him up off his feet.

"Urk!" The orc clutched and clawed at her tail.

Effortlessly, she slung the orc far into the woods and out of sight.

Pointing his sword at her, the gnoll leader shouted a command to his ranks. "Kill her!"

The quicker goblins dove in with their weapons.

Selene's tail struck like the crack of a whip.

Whap! Whap! Whap!

She flattened the three little fiends, knocking two of them out cold.

Eyes filled with fear, the third's hands clawed at the dirt, trying to scramble away.

Selene's tail coiled around its ankles and lifted it off the ground. Using the goblin like a club, she swung the humanoid over her head and bashed the two charging orcs with it. *Whop! Whop!* Checking her nails, she pummeled them both some more. *Whop! Whop! Whop!* She tossed the goblin aside, sending him skittering across the ground in front of the gnoll's feet.

Canine snouts dropped open, the two remaining gnolls threw down their spears and ran. Looking from side to side, the gnoll leader said, "Cowards!" He narrowed his eyes on Selene and said with his sword raised high, "I'm going to cut that tail off and chop it into nine little pieces."

Without looking at him, and rubbing some smudge from one of her nails, she said, "There is zero chance of that happening."

Howling at the top of his lungs, heavy sword arcing high, he charged and struck.

Selene caught the blade in her dragon-scaled hand and jerked it free from the gnoll's grip. Her tail lashed out and knocked him clear off his feet. Holding the sword in both of her hands, she said, "I should kill you with your own sword."

"No, please. No!" the gnoll pleaded. "I'll do anything!"

"On your knees!" she demanded.

The gnoll did as she said.

"Hands on your head."

Shaking, he did as he was told and pleaded, "Please, don't kill me. I'll never touch a dragon again. I promise."

"Oh, after this, you're going to wish you were dead."

"Wh-what are you going to do?"

"Be silent!" Using both of her hands and squeezing the well-tempered blade, she bent it around his neck as easily as a man would bend a spoon. "Enjoy your new necklace. And when more of your filthy ilk ask why you have a sword wrapped around your neck, tell them the next poacher I find won't have a sword wrapped around their neck. It will be placed through their wicked heart instead."

Stammering, the gnoll tried to speak, but no words came out.

"Be gone."

The hairy, dog-faced brute quickly found his feet and, running full speed, vanished into the woods.

Pivoting on her heel, Selene headed for the dragon's cage.

The wooden crate was crude, but durable. The cage door-lock consisted of leather cords and a peg stuck through a latch. She plucked it out, opened the door, and with gentle hands she removed the lily dragon. Through her palm, she felt its heart racing. "There, there, little brother."

Using her nail, she slit the bindings that secured its wings and mouth.

The dragon slid from her grasp and strutted around the camp. It shook its head and hissed at her.

Taken aback, Selene said, "Excuse me?"

Spreading its grand wings, it pushed off with its rear legs and took flight. Seconds later it was gone.

Selene's eyes watered up, and she dropped to her knees, trembling. Her guilt and shame overwhelmed her. Tears streamed down her cheeks and dripped onto the ground. How many dragons, her own brethren, had lost their lives because of her? She had commanded the Clerics of Barnabus to have the dragons poached. She'd had them captured. Those who would not serve Gorn Grattack had been killed. Their parts sold.

Heart aching inside her chest, she started to pant and tremble. She was an abomination—both to mankind and to dragonkind. How could anyone forgive her? How could she replace all that she had taken? What about all the lives that were devastated? Families torn asunder. The innocent deceived.

Wiping the tears from her eyes, she glanced at the open cage. At least one dragon was free. It felt good, but it also reminded her of all her bad deeds. And that lily dragon knew who she was and what she had done. It had made that clear. No, she needed to pay for what she had done. She had to atone for it. If not, the past would catch up with her. She was certain of it.

Standing up, she dusted her knees off.

I need to turn myself in.

She resumed her trek to the north, chin down and heavy in thought.

I need to stop the wurmers too.

Using her powerful dragon senses, she looked for signs of the wurmers as she trekked through the changing terrain, scanning the misty night sky.

Does Nalzambor need me, or is it better off without me?

CHAPTER 15

"Knowledge, eh?" said Brenwar. "Well, it better be able to find me another horse. Nath, don't listen to what this fool has to say. We're better off going."

With the rain from the rocky overhang pounding at his back, Nath shook his head. "No, I'd be interested in hearing what this troublemaker has to offer."

"Excellent," said Ipsy, rubbing his hands together. "Excellent. Let me get us some food and some drink. You know, I don't have many people over. The snakes aren't too chatty, and the birds talk far too much." Eagerly, he turned toward the cave.

Brenwar barred his path. "We aren't hungry. I'm interested in hearing what you have to say that is worth more than a horse. Now talk."

The druid slid away from Brenwar and closer to Nath. His eyes kept attaching themselves to Nath's arms. "So fascinating."

Brenwar poked him. "Talk!"

"All right! No need to get testy. The world has shifted. The forest creatures' patterns change. Giants come down from their mountains and their massive caves. Though not one of long life, I'd not seen but one giant. Now, they pass and scatter the vermin constantly."

Brenwar's brows perched. "Giants, you say? Keep talking."

Ipsy rambled on.

Nath gave the druid his full attention, nodding and agreeing with what he said. There were giants roaming about more so than before, all right. Nath believed him. At the same time he wanted to test the druid. Catch a fib or lie—which their kind were known for.

But so far everything the druid said was at least half true. Of course, much of it was common knowledge. After all, it wasn't so long ago that Nath, then in the form of a dragon, had fought a handful of earth giants.

"So how many giants have you seen exactly?" Nath asked.

"A half dozen or so in the last few months."

"And where were they headed?"

"Oh, I can tell you that easy. You see, I followed them, I did. Heh-heh. They don't pay any attention to the likes of me. No, not at all. Too, too small." He grabbed some moss from a rock and rubbed it on his skin. "And my scent blends in. Giants are good smellers, you know. Like big hounds." He eyed Brenwar. "Smell your scruffy stink a mile away."

Brenwar drew his fist back. "Why you—"

Ipsy slid behind Nath and peeked around his waist.

"Let it go, Brenwar."

"I want my horse back," the dwarf said. He plucked a small spade from the dead horse's saddle. "And I'm not leaving until he buries this one."

Nath sighed. He understood Brenwar's point, but burying it? "We'll figure out something. Now, Ipsy, tell us, I haven't noticed any giants' tracks. Where did you follow them to?"

"Only a couple of leagues away they are, building in the Craggy Mountains. Dark and treacherous up there, it is. Nothing that giant slayers like yourselves can't handle. Are you going to kill them? I hope that you do. They attack dragons, you know. Kill them. Eat them. I saw some, dead, strung up like deer with purple scales. Two in all. Dead. Beautiful, but dead."

Nath's fingertips tingled. He grabbed Ipsy by the arm and squeezed it hard. "Don't toy with me, druid. Is this the truth?"

Holding up his hand, Ipsy said, "I swear it on my mother's mossy grave."

"Speaking of graves," Nath said, looking at the horse, "you need to get started."

"But it's raining!" Ipsy whined.

With little help from Brenwar or Nath Dragon, Ipsy carried rocks through rain and wind up and down the hill all night. One by one, he covered the dead horse with rocks. Many of them were bigger than his head.

Finally, the little druid had covered the horse's body in its entirety. Holding his back and stretching, he said to Brenwar, "Am I finished?"

The dwarf clawed at his black-grey beard. "A few more rocks would be better."

"I can't find any more. This is a hillside, not a quarry!"

"You should have thought of that before you killed my horse!"

Nath stepped in. "That will do, Ipsy. We'll be going now. I want to see if your story checks out."

With a sigh of relief, the druid said, "Thank you! Thank you! I did not deceive you!" He mopped the sweat mixed with rain from his eyes. "I promise."

Nath departed with a scowling Brenwar.

With a short maniacal laugh, Ipsy plopped down on the tomb of rocks and rubbed his aching fingers. "Guzan's feet, I thought they'd never leave. Hard men, the both of them. Love horses as much as a horse itself." He lay back on the pile of rocks and fell fast asleep.

While Ipsy lay snoring, a tingle at his feet awoke him.

He lurched up and faced a beautiful woman half the size of him, hovering over the ground. Long hair white as snow. Eyes dark as black pearls. Two violet wings beating gently behind her back. She was surrounded by a dozen dark and colorful hand-sized fairies. He dove to his knees and groveled. "Fairy Empress! Do with me what you please!"

"Arise, Ipsy the Hood," she said with a coy smile. "I see our little plan failed."

"I'm sorry, but my pets were not quick enough. And those two are quite formidable. I'm sorry. Punish me!"

She slapped his cheeks with her delicate hands and squeezed them. "Did you mention me?"

"No, they didn't ask. I just told them about the giants like you said. As a matter of fact, they walked right into it."

"And Nath Dragon didn't suspect a thing?"

"I wasn't lying, but his eyes were still wary." Holding his back, he grimaced. "They sure love horses. Ugh."

Her black eyes inspected the stone grave. "At least you killed a mount. That will slow them down and give me further time to plan."

Fingers fidgeting at his side, he asked, "So, I did well?"

"Of course, Ipsy." She caressed his cheek. "Of course. After all, you chose to follow me, the giants, and the titans. You'll be a part of our destiny to take down the dragons."

"What else can I do, Fairy Empress Lotuus?"

Glancing at the rocks, she said, "This pile of rubble is suspicious. You're going to need to remove it, and the horse with it."

His mouth fell open.

Lotuus waved her hand toward the small cave opening. The giant cobra with the busted fangs slithered out. "Come, come, sweet pet." The snake coiled up beneath her feet. She patted its head. "Ipsy, close your eyes."

"My eyes?"

Her face darkened. "Yes, your eyes."

"Uh, as you wish." He shut his eyes.

"You trust me, don't you, Ipsy?"

"Certainly."

"Good, now keep your eyes closed and don't move."

He swallowed and nodded. A new layer of sweat beaded on his brow. He felt his snake entwine itself around his body. The connection he had with it was gone, overpowered by a darker force.

"Now open your eyes," she said.

He did. He was wrapped from neck to ankle in the giant poisonous restrictor. Its muscles slowly started to squeeze the breath out of him.

"Fairy Empress, you said I did well."

"I lied," she said with a sneer. "You should have at least killed the dwarf."

"But–" he blurted out. Breathless, he could say no more. The snake began crushing his body.

Lotuus pinched his cheek and smiled. "Die knowing that your ultimate purpose was served." With the grace of the wind, she and her fairies departed.

All Ipsy could do was unleash a silent scream. "Noooooooo!"

CHAPTER 16

BRENWAR STOOD INSIDE A GIANT-SIZED footprint of pressed-down grass. Squeezing his war hammer, he said with a fierce grin, "There be giants."

Leagues away from where they had left Ipsy, Nath led his horse alongside his comrade. The footprints led straight toward the base of the Craggy Mountains. He hopped off the saddle and studied the prints in the grass. "I see three sets of them. Seems that the druid wasn't fibbing after all."

"He's not very good with distance. We're a good bit farther north than he suggested." Brenwar's eyes studied the mountains, whose peaks stretched up above the clouds. "And it's no surprise there'd be giants up in there. Probably be some mountain goats too. Har, he's fooling with us."

Scanning the ground, Nath said, "True." After all, he and Brenwar knew Nalzambor about as well as anybody.

Though he'd never ventured into them, the Craggy Mountains weren't so much of a mystery. Their high, jagged peaks were a coarse trek, and most men didn't go near, let alone bother to climb it. It was a great place to hide, for anyone, any size.

Nath took a knee and plucked up a handful of the flattened grasses. He sniffed it and made a sour face. "If it stinks like a giant, it must be a giant, right?"

"I thought it was obvious."

The sun gleamed through the grey clouds, but a light drizzling rain still fell. Nath's nose twitched. "How many days do you think, since they passed?"

"Three," Brenwar replied.

"Even with all this rain?"

"It's rained more south than north. I stick with three. Why?"

"Oh, that's my assessment as well." Nath eyed the mountain. "I say we go back."

"Back?"

"Let me rephrase that. Backtrack."

Brenwar clawed at his beard. "You mean, backtrack the giants?"

"Yes. I'm curious to see where they came from." Nath snapped off some grasses that were still standing high. Blood residue was on them. "I have a bad feeling about this."

"You should. It's giants."

Taking the horse by the reins, Nath followed the giants' trail over the rocky steppes.

For some strange reason, the land was quiet. Not a single bird crossed the sky. There was no rustle of vermin scurrying through the fallen leaves. Only the rattle and squeak of the horse's saddle accompanied them.

They'd made it about a league when Nath said, "I don't like where we are headed."

"Aye," Brenwar agreed.

"Why don't you get on the horse?" Nath suggested.

"Why?"

"So you can keep up."

Without hesitation, Brenwar climbed on the horse and took his place in the saddle. "You're that worried?"

"I feel trouble in my scales." Nath took off running, with Brenwar on the galloping horse behind him.

Based on the course they were following, he knew there was a large group of village communities only a few miles away. Good people, hardy and durable farmers and traders, and a mix of the races at that. They called the area Harvand, which was Elven for outcast. Nath never understood why it was called that.

The people were like the rest of the world, but they did seem to prefer additional isolation and were quite accepting of people who were a little different.

Nath's long strides kept an even pace with the horse that ran behind him. His flame-red hair was a banner behind him. It felt good running at the speed of a horse. There weren't any two-legged creatures in the world that could outrun him. At least, he'd never known one that could. Not even the fastest elves were fleeter of foot. Charging up one hill and down another, blood pumping, he started to feel good. He might not be a full-sized dragon anymore, but his body and what it could do was still incredible.

It's not so bad, Dragon. Not so bad at all.

He bounded up a steep hillside and came to a stop at the top. The dapple-grey horse snorted when it caught up with him. Nath rubbed its neck. "You enjoyed that too, didn't you?"

"Harrumph. Running's overrated. A dwarf never rushes anywhere." Brenwar got off the horse and handed the reins to Nath. "He's always exactly where he needs to be."

With Brenwar at his side, Nath focused his attention on the valley of villages ahead. Tiny houses and barns were stretched out on the fertile land around Harvand almost as far as he could see. Aside from the barns and silos, no building was taller than two stories. He could see people milling about the streets. They looked small, but his keen eyes could make out some of the faces quite well. The people were long-faced, and many carried tools.

"What's that?" Brenwar pointed west of the village.

It was a pile of rubble. Wood and stone. People were dragging materials over on carts and wheelbarrows. Some carried it by hand. They pitched materials into the pile of scrap.

Scanning the buildings, Nath noticed that many of them weren't even standing. Several were crushed. A barn had a grain silo stuffed through its roof.

Nath's throat tightened. "We need a closer look."

The closer they got, the worse it looked.

Following the sloppy road, they crept into the nearest village. No one paid them any mind. The last time Nath was here, dozens of years ago, the people had been nothing short of accommodating. Of course, that had often been the case with him back then, and he had enjoyed it. Now, the people were grim-faced, and heads were downcast. They slogged through the torn streets carrying tools and scrap. Few words were spoken.

A woman with two small boys was trying to fix the door to a small home that didn't have a roof or a back wall. A group of children splashed through a puddle made by a giant's foot, chasing after loose chickens. There was hunger. Pain. Depression.

Finally, Nath approached a group of three sandy-headed men with scruffy faces and small points on their ears. They were sawing down a tree. One on one handle, one on the other, and the third measuring with a strip of cloth. "Might I ask what happened?"

"Giants," said the one who measured, without looking at him. "Best that you move on."

Nath pressed. "Did they take anything?"

The half-elves stopped sawing.

The taller one said, "Just our livelihood." His piercing eyes scanned Nath. "You best keep going. No room for heroes around here."

"Sssh," said the half-elf on the other side of the saw, glancing at Nath. He looked back at his counterpart. "Just cut, will you?"

"Come on, Brenwar."

That might have been the most impolite and brief conversation I ever had with an elf of any kind.

"Sorry to bother you."

Walking along Nath's side, Brenwar said, "Something's still amiss."

Nath headed toward the heart of the cluster of villages. "And we need to find out what that is."

Chapter 17

In the center of Harvand was the grandest structure of all: a round stone building with a high cathedral-like ceiling. Smoke came out the chimney on the top. A pole stretched up taller than the chimney. On it, a checkered blue-and-orange flag bearing a wheat symbol flapped in the brisk wind. An archway covered by a sheepskin led inside.

Nath pushed through. "Hello?"

There wasn't much in the room. A rectangular table with long benches for chairs. Aside from the fire blazing, there was no life inside at all.

Nath spoke again. "Hello?"

The shuffle of sandals over the stone floor caught his ear. An old woman with long white hair and plain purple robes teetered out from behind the other side of the fireplace. She had a cane in one hand that clicked on the floor, and she held a horn to her ear. Her left eye was milky.

"Do my eyes and ears deceive me? Is that Nath Dragon I hear?"

"Marley?" He made his way over to her and took her wrinkled hands in his. "It's good to see you again."

"Oh, I can hear the disappointment in your voice." She rubbed his scales. "Oh my, that's fascinating." She coughed. "You've changed. But you're still the same."

"I could say the same of you."

She slapped his arm. "Oh, please. I've aged sixty years since you've been here last. I've more wrinkles than a prune. But it's good to know you're still a flatterer."

"Has it really been so long?"

"Oh, yes. The truth is, not a whole lot has happened since you left. Us old ladies still talk about the time you waltzed in here and dazzled us with your song and skills. And you got rid of the horrible bugbear, Mondoon. Blecht." She clicked her cane on the floor. "And you danced with all the women and even saved the last dance for me. I swear, my feet didn't touch the floor."

Nath remembered. He remembered everything, even though time often slipped by him unnoticed.

Marley had been the most beautiful gal in Harvand. Chestnut-haired and dark-eyed, her natural beauty had rivaled that of the elves. She couldn't have been more than thirty years old then. A widow, for her husband was killed by the bugbear Mondoon. A terrible time for the whole village town. After a hard-fought battle, Nath had vanquished Mondoon.

"And you never remarried?"

"No point really, at least not after dancing with you." She sighed. "No man in the village could measure up to my tainted expectations." She poked him with her cane. "And they're still pretty high, you know. No, I raised the kids, worked until my back couldn't take it anymore, and let them place me in charge of this city. Things were quiet until now."

"Please, Marley, tell us what happened. We want to help."

Marley shuffled over to the bench and sat down, eyeing Brenwar. "And who is this hairy little fellow?"

"I was here the last time too, you know," Brenwar said with a grumble.

She cocked her ear toward Nath. "What did he say?"

Nath sat down by her side. "He said it's good to meet you, too."

"I did not. Oh, never mind." Mumbling under his beard, the dwarf proceeded to tour the small building while Nath and Marley talked.

Nath took her fragile hand in his. "Marley, tell us what happened."

She shivered. "They just came. Three of them. My, they were taller than those tall buildings in the cities. They were hairy, brawny, and had a smell about them. Started smashing things, toppling one home after the other. It was awful. They then gulped down our livestock, and we thought that might be the end of it. Maybe they were hungry. So we tried to plead with them, and they just laughed. They said in huge baritone voices, 'This is just the beginning.'"

Nath put his arm around her shoulder. "How many people were hurt?"

"Oh, well, that's the oddly fortunate part. There were some injuries, but not one person was killed."

"That *is* odd." Nath caught Brenwar looking at him. Giants didn't leave survivors. "But that makes me happy to hear it."

"Oh, don't be too happy. They said they would be back. They said they wanted people to come with them. Serve them and their new leader. They have built a mountain city in the Craggies. I don't understand it myself, but they made it clear that if they got enough, eh, volunteers, the village would be spared. But only to serve them. I think they want us to raise livestock to feed them. Oh, Nath," she sobbed, "we were peaceful, and that peace is gone."

Brenwar walked over and spoke. "How long until they come back?"

Startled, Marley said, "Where did *you* come from?"

"Morgdon."

She looked up at Nath. "Where?"

"It's not important. Marley, how long until they come back?"

"They didn't say. And though we are terrified, I think many believe they won't come back. But I know they will. Nath, I don't think anyone will go with the giants. I've tried to have meetings. We have no volunteers. We'll all be killed."

It rankled Nath's scales. Clenching his fist, he said, "No one will be killed. Not so long as I am here. But perhaps, Marley, you and your people should hide. I know a place. And when the giants come, Brenwar and I will take them on."

"Aye!" Brenwar injected.

Marley jumped. "Excuse me, who are you?"

"Brenwar!"

"Be easy," Nath said to his friend.

"Easy? She hears me just fine, just doesn't like dwarves. She didn't the last time either."

Nath recalled Brenwar and Marley getting into a spat. She'd told him to shave his beard, and he'd said he would shave her head first. But Nath couldn't tell if she was being selective with what she heard or if she was that feeble.

His thoughts drifted to Sasha.

I hope we can make her better.

"Is it warm out?" Marley asked. "I'd like to walk. The sun warms my cold bones."

"I think there's enough sun out there for you, and what *it* won't do, *I* will." Nath helped her up and led her out the door and kept his hand on her shoulder. Sunlight crept through the clouds. "Which way?" he asked.

"Eh, this way," she said.

She moved slowly, but that was fine with Nath. He wasn't in any kind of hurry. Instead, he took in all of the busy activity. The workers were far from robust, and only a few eyes found their way to him. There were some children who hid and giggled at him as he passed by the split-rail fences.

Scanning the distant fields, Nath noticed some odd structures. "What are those, Marley?"

She stopped and followed where he pointed. "Oh, those are just silos. I'll take you to see them if you like."

"It's just odd that all of them are still standing. Did you rebuild them?"

"I can't remember. I guess it must be good fortune. Come on, let's go and see what's going on."

Four silos stood in a perfect square. Made of stone, they were over thirty feet high, with round shingled roofs.

Brenwar stood in the midst of the four of them. "That's a strange design for silos. They're too wide." He rubbed his bearded chin and eyed the ground. "And I don't see any evidence of grain. And those stones. Awfully big. Did your people build those, or did someone else?"

Marley slipped out from under Nath's arm and looked at him with a painful expression. "Nath, I didn't have any choice." Her chin trembled. "They said they'd kill all of us. It's a trap, Nath. Run!"

CHAPTER 18

"MARLEY! MARLEY! WHAT ARE YOU talking about?"

The old woman was suddenly more nimble than she appeared to be. She slipped away from Nath's outstretched grasp. "Run!"

Wary eyed, Brenwar growled. "I knew something wasn't right—with her or this hog hole—from the beginning. You should have listened to—"

Giant arms busted out of the silo walls.

Big, ugly bald heads popped out the tops of the silos.

"I knew it! I knew it!" Brenwar yelled. "They're stone giants, Nath! That's why I didn't smell them out!"

The stony makeup of the towering buildings crumbled away. Massive men stepped out of the debris and dust that rolled away from their feet. Four towering men almost thirty feet tall had them surrounded.

Marley ran screaming, but she was too slow.

The giant behind them lifted up his great foot and brought it down.

Nath screamed. "Nooooo!"

The ground shook.

Thoom!

Marley was gone, like a bug under a man's shoe.

Nath's heart sank. His jaw dropped. His hands were numb at his sides. So cruel and merciless it was, he didn't even notice the entire town scrambling in panic.

Evil. Such Evil.

"Fill your hands, Nath Dragon!" Brenwar roared. "Else you're going to be goo under their feet too." He raised his hammer high and banged it on the ground.

Krang!

The ground busted up underneath one giant's feet and knocked it to the ground.

"Woohoo!" Brenwar screamed.

Nath ripped Fang out of his scabbard and charged the stone giant who had smashed Marley.

The mountain of marble-like muscle sneered at him and laughed.

Summoning Fang's power, Nath struck the giant's ankle with all of his might. The blade bit deep.

Ice raced up the giant's leg and froze it fast to the ground.

The monster's eyes widened, and it screamed out in horror. Leg icing up, it lashed out. The monster's fingers clipped Nath's ducking head. The raw power of the massive man lifted Nath from his feet and sent him rolling through the dust.

Seeing stars, Nath lifted up his head at the sound of heavy footsteps.

The third giant charged right for him. Its huge fists came down together like a great anvil.

Nath sprang away.

The fists missed him by inches.

Boom!

Without hesitation, Nath whirled around and stabbed Fang through one of the giant's hands.

Its hand burst into flames. Slobbering from its jowls, the monster jerked its hand away, ripping Fang out of Nath's iron grip. The monster screamed at its burning hand with Fang still in it.

"Guzan! I need my sword back!"

"Take that, giant!" Brenwar climbed on top of the giant he'd knocked down and hammered away at it with Mortuun. The grand war hammer came down again and again with the sound of clapping thunder.

Boom! Boom! Boom!

The giant swatted at Brenwar with hands, forearms, and elbows.

Somehow, Brenwar slipped in and out of its efforts only to hammer it again and again with devastating effort.

Its ribs cracked. Its jaw and eye socket were broken.

"You'll regret the day you ever crossed me, giant!"

Boom! Boom! Boom!

Brenwar put everything he had into it. Stone giants were serious business. As their name suggested, they were stone and bone, not flesh and bone like most giants. Killing them was never easy, and plenty of dwarves had met the grave trying. He unleashed as much of Mortuun's power as he could.

"Come on, Mortuun! Come on!" Black-beardedly wild as a berserker, he unleashed all that his ancient dwarven bones had in him. "We've still got three to go!"

Boom! Boom! Boom!

Finally, the giant lay stretched out between the broken silos, dead.

Hammer in hand, chest heaving, and iron arms weary, Brenwar turned. "Whew, where's the next one?" He froze.

He was eye to eye with the next giant.

Bending down and clapping its hands together, it smashed Brenwar like a fly.

One giant fought the icy cords that tethered it to the ground. Another giant fought to put its flaming hand out.

Lucky for Nath, his sticky fingers had managed to snake Dragon Claw out of Fang's pommel. In a rush, Nath climbed up the distracted giant's back with Dragon Claw in hand and smote it in the temple.

The stone giant fell on its knees and collapsed face first in the muddy dirt.

Splat!

Nath surveyed the battleground.

The third giant was dead and sprawled out on the ground, but the fourth caught Nath's eyes.

"Oh, no!"

With Brenwar clasped inside the giant's hands like a little woodland creature, it leered down at Nath with a cold-blooded killer's gaze and said in long and loud words, "I'll take his life if you don't surrender, Nath Dragon."

Spitting through his beard with a great strain in his face, Brenwar said, "Don't surrender, Nath. Don't do it!"

Chapter 19

Nath retrieved Fang and stood before the stone giant. "Killing him will only bring you a swift death, giant. If you want to live, then put him down."

The giant shook his head and said in his long drawn-out voice, "And pass up killing this dwarf? No. I think not." He squeezed Brenwar harder.

Brenwar's eyes bulged. "Urk! Don't worry about me, Nath. Just kill him!"

With two giants down and only two remaining, Nath liked his chances.

Behind him, the one giant struggled and freed its frozen leg. Somehow, it managed to hobble forward toward Nath.

I can handle this. I have Fang, and Brenwar's plenty tough.

Brandishing the great sword, Nath said, "Just put him down, giant. Leave this village. It is under my protection."

"Oh ho ho," the giant said with a chill in its voice, "Nath Dragon, this trap was not sprung to fail. Be wise as a serpent and surrender, or the blood of every villager will be on your hands."

It was a trap, all right, but who had set it? And how had they known that Nath would be coming to this village?

I can't think of anything at all that led me here.

Uncertainty filled him. Someone somewhere was watching him. His thoughts raced back.

Ipsy!

Why had the druid set him up? He'd never met the druid before. He must have been working with somebody else, but who?

"I think you're bluffing," Nath said, creeping forward with his sword. "Now put the dwarf down so no one else gets hurt."

"You are a cocky little flea." The stone giant let out a strange hoot. "Howeet!"

Large stacks of hay that were scattered all over the villages came to life. Giant humanoids—ogres and bugbears—emerged from the hay and snatched up any screaming villager they could find. They wrapped them up in powerful arms and started to crush the life out of them.

The distraught people screamed and begged for mercy.

"Eeeeeeeee!"

"Oooowwwww!"

"Still feeling cocky, little dragon?" the stone giant said.

Aghast, Nath squeezed Fang's hilt so hard that his hand trembled.

How did I miss this trap?

It wasn't like him to overlook what should have been obvious details. But somehow his transgressors had deceived him. He'd missed the giants and dozens of burly humanoids. And the villagers of Harvand were so terrified, they'd played along as well. He should have listened to the half-elves.

Great Guzan! Those half-elves were trying to warn me.

"What is it you want, giant?"

"Just surrender, and all of them will live." He held Brenwar out in his long outstretched arms. "Including this bearded chipmunk."

"Am I to be your prisoner?"

"No, you are to be someone else's prisoner."

"Who might that someone be?"

"Surrender, and you will see."

That was a problem with the giants. They were liars. Their guaranteed word was no better than an angry orc's. For all Nath knew, he'd turn himself over, and they'd kill all of the villagers anyway. Which begged the question, how do you get a giant to keep his word? And this one wasn't even calling the shots.

"I need proof that no harm will come to anyone else, including the dwarf."

"Hmmm." The giant scratched its chin with Brenwar's head then showed a toothy smile. "You'll just have to trust me. You don't have any choice, little dragon."

Panicked cries of alarm and horror filled Nath's ears. The rough hands of the beasts that held the villagers were far from gentle. The message was clear. Nath could feel it. They wouldn't hesitate to kill anybody.

"Nath!" Brenwar said. "You are too important. Don't do it."

"If I think I'm more important than anybody else, then I'm truly not important at all." Nath stuck Fang in the ground and placed his scaly hands on his head. "So be it, giant. I surrender."

"Secure him," the stone giant ordered. A pair of bugbears marched forward. They were huge ugly men, somewhat bear faced, with huge muscles in their shoulders. They carried chains and shackles made from moorite. With rough hands they shackled Nath's wrists and ankles and put a collar on his neck. "That's good."

"I've submitted. Now put the dwarf down and leave these people alone."

The giant tossed Brenwar through the roof of a nearby home and wiped his hands on the muddy street. "Filthy little thing." He reached over and picked up Fang with the tips of his fingers. His stony skin started to sizzle. Grimacing, he ordered Nath, "Put it in a sheath."

Nath complied.

The stone giant picked up the sheathed sword and stuck it in his belt, which held up a roughhewn pair of trousers. "Let's go."

Escorted by the bugbears and the ogres, Nath followed the giant. Glancing behind him, he saw the village was left unmolested, but some of the people followed. Perhaps many of the people had already sworn a new allegiance to the giants or whomever the giants answered to.

A bugbear shoved him forward, almost knocking him down. "March," it growled.

Nath turned around and marched backward with the chains rattling around his ankles. "You mean like this?" he said.

It was a distraction. His eyes searched for Brenwar. Even though he didn't think the fall into the building would kill the dwarf, he could be seriously hurt.

He's fine, right? He always is, isn't he?

CHAPTER 20

SELENE STOOD ON THE NORTHERN shores of Nalzambor, less than a mile away from a small sea town called Dusky. The early-evening tide splashed over the rocks, creating pockets of sea-foam as the fishermen hauled in their nets and dragged them up the sandy banks. As the water chopped and smacked into the rocks, she finished braiding her long locks into a style more customary.

Perhaps I should go sailing.

For her entire life, she couldn't remember doing anything that she wanted to do. She'd been trained to fight, to conquer and deceive. But she was never taught to enjoy life.

Maybe there is peace for me somewhere out there.

"Peace. Hah. A child's tale."

Her tail snaked up under her robes, and she pulled down her sleeves. With sure footing, she traversed the rocks and headed down to the shore where the seafarers talked and joked. She envied them. Somehow, someway, they enjoyed the work they did, hauling in oily amounts of stinking fish.

"Ho there, Miss!" a man said, waving his cap at her. "What are you doing up there? You need to get down."

Stopping to survey her surroundings, she realized she stood on the jagged black rocks with strong waves smashing into the deep alcoves. Water was splashing up and soaking the hem of her robes. Clearly, for a mortal person this would be a dangerous position, standing on slick rocks where the slightest stumble would send a body into the cold water and dash it against the rocks.

Hand to her chest, she resumed her trek and navigated the dangerous path until she found herself in front of the wide-eyed sailor.

"Hello," Selene said.

The man wasn't old or young, and he wore standard attire of the seaworthy people: a white cotton shirt with long sleeves soaked to the elbow, brown trousers where the hem touched his bare feet. He had a mop of light-brown hair, thick side burns, and sea-green eyes. His features weren't handsome but fair.

He said, "Are you real, or do my eyes deceive me?"

She took his calloused hand in hers. "What do you think?"

"Real … real beautiful," he explained.

She almost smiled. "Tell me, what is your name?"

"Gavlin."

"Gavlin, may I ask you a question?"

He shook his head yes. "You can ask me anything."

"Do you ever see dragons over the sea?"

"Oh, sure, we see them inside the waters as much as above. Do you want me to take you out in the morning? You never know when you might see them, but I know a place where many roost."

He said it as if the dragons weren't any more extraordinary than big birds. He didn't have any worries about dragons at all.

It surprised her. "I just might take you up on that sometime, but I'm looking for a different kind of dragon. Dark and rough scaled, not smooth and polished like mine." Still holding his hand, she lifted it up in front of his eyes. "See what I mean?"

He gasped and tried to pull away.

She held him fast. "Gavlin, you have nothing to fear from me. Why do you try to flee?"

"You're a demon!" His face was full of strain. "Please, let me go!"

"But you said you would tell me anything." She looked deep into his eyes and used a hypnotizing effect. "I want you to tell me, Gavlin. Have you seen these dragons I speak of?"

The rapid beating of his heart started to slow. "Yes, they fly in thirteens. Heh, I've never seen purple eyes before. I've never seen scales on a woman before."

"Gavlin," she said calmly, "where do those dragons go?"

"Well, I don't follow them. That's trouble. No, no, no. Here in Dusky we avoid trouble."

She rolled her eyes, breaking the connection. "You're an observant man. Just tell me where they fly."

"Where all the wretched go these days. Down into the Craggies." Wincing, he looked at their interlocked hands. "Are you going to kill me, demon?"

"I am not a demon, so no, I'm not going to kill you. I'm trying to befriend you." She released him. "I thought you said I was beautiful."

He backed away. "Just because you're beautiful doesn't mean you're not evil. My wife's told me about women like you. Stay away. Stay away from here, and stay away from Dusky." He turned and ran away, shouting to his fellow sailors. "Beware! A she-demon is in our midst."

Angered, Selene started after the man. Nath didn't have this problem. Even with his scales, people accepted him. What was so different about her? Anger turned to sadness. Maybe she hadn't changed. Maybe she was still evil.

Approaching the men with her arms spread wide, she said to them, "I am a friend."

The fishermen picked up their fish and started throwing them at her. "Go away, Demon!" they yelled. "Go, go back to the Craggy Mountains!"

"And what if I don't, you stupid fish-throwing people?"

They kept throwing the fish with deadly accuracy.

She swatted them away.

But one of the men said, "Then we'll summon Nath Dragon to kill you!"

"Agghhh!" she yelled. She snatched a fish out of the air and threw it back so hard, it hit one man in the face and knocked him over.

All of the fishermen dropped their fish and ran away, screaming toward their town, "Demon! Demon! Demon!"

Disgusted, Selene lifted up the hem of her robes and let her tail out. "No wonder I never liked people. They're stupid."

She climbed up the rocks onto the tall grass and marched back south, watching the skies for any wurmers going toward the Craggy Mountains.

Of course they don't like me. Why would they?

CHAPTER 21

The march to the Craggy Mountains wasn't so bad, but the march up the Craggy Mountains was. Nath, one to pride himself on knowing the terrain of so many places in Nalzambor, didn't find any familiarity with the cold mountains at all. Shackled at the ankles, he slipped and bumped into the rocks of the narrow pass that winded slowly up the mountain.

A bugbear whacked him in the back with the butt of its spear. "Keep moving, Scales."

Scales. That was what they were calling him. An unpleasant little nickname full of spite and mockery. It didn't take much for the big, cruel humanoid races to take their shots at him. They tripped him. Bumped him. Threw small stones at him. They pulled and clipped off strands of his hair. They did everything they could to provoke Nath to anger.

Jaw set and teeth grinding, Nath bore it all. One insult after another.

I'm glad Brenwar's not here. He wouldn't make it. How am I *making it?*

Getting back on his feet, he resumed his march. All in all, it wasn't so bad for him. His limbs didn't tire. His extremities didn't freeze despite the frost and snow thickening on the banks. No, he could take it. He was Nath Dragon, the Dragon Prince. He could take anything.

Walking up the frozen road with the real world he knew a mile or more below, they ventured through a sheet of low clouds. He momentarily lost sight of the bugbears that pulled him by the collar clamped around his neck. But he could hear the rattle of their armor. Smell their unpleasant sweat.

I've a feeling where I'm going will hold a far worse fragrance than Orcen Hold.

He shook his downcast head.

I hope Brenwar is fine. And I hope he doesn't come after me. He hates climbing these mountains. And if those giants get ahold of him, they'll bounce him down the hillside like a ball.

"Come on, Scales!" cried an unseen bugbear. The moorite chain connected to Nath's collar snapped taut and jerked him clean off his feet. "Get up!"

Nath's eyes turned into burning golden flames. From his knees, he coiled his hands around the chain and tugged it back.

The bugbear appeared in the mist, stumbling.

Furious, Nath rushed the bigger humanoid and tackled it to the ground. In a split second he had the chain around the bugbear's neck and was choking it.

The bugbear let out a croak.

Biceps bulging under his scales, red brows furrowed, Nath put his back into it. Why not kill his captor? Now was the perfect moment to make his escape into the cover of the mist. Sure, he was shackled, but if anyone could escape these moronic fools, he could.

Whack!

A spear shaft broke on the back of his skull. Out of nowhere, the ugly, greasy faces of the orcs, ogres, and gnolls crowded him. They smote him with clubs and big fists.

Nath held on to the chain. He'd had enough of his tormenters on this long, cold, miserable march. He was a dragon.

No one messes with a dragon!

The relentless assault of his captors hammered away at his face and body.

Whop! Crack! Smash! Whump! Whump! Whump!

Blood dripped into Nath's eyes. A sharp blade pierced his skin. He lost his grip on his chain.

The bugbear he had been choking to death crawled away. It clutched at its throat, coughing and hacking.

Somehow, from beneath the pack of bodies, Nath managed to kick and break its nose. "You'll think again before you jerk *me* around, stupid beast!"

Something hard smacked right into the side of Nath's temple. Bright spots erupted in his blood-filled eyes. Sagging underneath the greater weight and getting hit time after time, Nath's valiant strength gave out. They beat Nath without mercy and dragged what was left of him up the mountain.

Half-conscious, Nath was uncertain how much time passed before they stopped dragging him. Parched, he spat out the grit from his mouth and forced himself up to his hands and knees. Through his swollen eyes he could see that the mist had cleared, but it was night, a black, moonless sky with not a star in sight. Some of his captors carried flaming torches for light. Snowflakes fell from the sky, and he caught one on his tongue.

Pretty, but not filling.

Rising to his feet, he stumbled and winced. One of his captors had stabbed him in his calf. Taking another step, he was forced to limp.

"Huh huh huh!" one of the bugbears laughed.

But it wasn't the one Nath had nearly killed. No, that one looked at him and glanced away.

Good. At least one of these stupid beasts got the message.

One of his captors shoved him.

Nath hobbled forward, acting a little worse off than he was.

If you fool these morons once, you can fool them again. Smelly morons.

The pass was wide enough for a dozen men to squeeze through side by side, and the cliffs were steep and jagged on either side. It was a one way in, one way out kind of thing.

Nath saw movement in those rocks. A glint of metal from armor and weapons. Black faces were hidden in those roosted shadows, but he could make out their breathing. Dozens of soldiers manned the rocks. But why? Why would anyone want to live in such a harsh, cold, and unforgiving place?

Hmmm, probably the perfect place for harsh, cold, and unforgiving people. Yes, the giants and their smaller, fouler little cousins deserve a place such as this.

Twisting around another bend in the road, Nath finally saw the stone giants he'd lost sight of long ago. The towering monster men weren't so towering now. They stood side by side in front of a pair of great iron doors twice as tall as them. The ironwork was something like you would see in a dwarven city, only bigger, cruder, and unwelcoming.

Lifting his chin up at the ever-so-high doors, Nath gawked.

Sultans of Sulfur! Those are just as big as the ones inside Dragon Home. What in Nalzambor lives in there, a city of giants? Or worse.

CHAPTER 22

Balzurth the Dragon King let out a roar that shook the Mountain of Doom. The great red dragon with gold glinting between his scales paced through the piles of gold and other treasure. His huge paws stomped the tiny coins and flung them aside. He shook the great horns on his head, and fire burst from his nose.

His voice was a rumble of thunder. "THEY WILL PAY!"

"Mind your temper," said Grahleyna the Dragon Queen. Her dragon body was covered in scales of old gold with traces of white. She was smooth and supine beside her bigger husband. She was a thing of beauty that outshone every bauble and trinket of treasure in the room. She brushed up against Balzurth. "You need to be statelier. You're setting a bad example for the rest."

Balzurth bumped up against her and said in his strong voice, "It's not going to be the end of the world because the king gets upset. Aw, that poor green lily. When I saw her, a she, with her wings shorn off…" His throat growled. "I don't know how I've been able to contain myself this long. Now is the time for action, Grahleyna. I need to strike now!"

She clocked her horns with his. "You need to stay here, Balzurth. This is where you belong. It's clear they are trying to draw you out so that they can kill you."

He stomped his clawed foot and rattled the coins. "Let them try! I welcome the challenge."

"Let me tell you something: I'm not letting you out of my sight, so don't try anything. Oh, and don't think I'm not still privy to your tricks. I know how you like to slide out of here, and just so you know, I have my eyes and ears everywhere. For now, we need to wait. Be patient."

"Grahleyna! You heard the lily's story. Those vile giants are decorating their chambers with dragon skulls! I can't sit back and allow that kind of mutilation. You know that!"

She curled her tail around his. "Yes, yes I do. And my heart aches as much as yours, but you have to have faith now. The word is out about the giants and the titans. I have seen to that. The dragons will be more cautious and careful from now on."

"Not all of them."

"No," she agreed. "But you can't be responsible for all of them."

He tightened his tail around hers and looked into her incredible eyes. "I'm glad you're back. Life's not the same without you by my side."

"You're sweet, Balzurth. And about that," she said, nuzzling him, "I find it very curious that our son, Nath, happened upon me. You wouldn't have had anything to do with that, would you?"

The grand dragon stammered. "The boy kept asking about his mother, so to keep him busy, I sent him on a quest. I only gave him one little hint."

"Balzurth!"

"I didn't think he would find you, though I hoped he would. Grahleyna, I missed you. A few hundred years without you was enough."

"A few hundred years is nothing to us, and don't try to play the romantic." She rustled her wings and shook her head. "You hate the Great Dragon Wall."

"No, I hate what is behind it. And WE SHOULD NOT HAVE TO SACRIFICE OUR LIVES CONTAINING AN EVIL THAT MUST BE DESTROYED! That wall cannot last forever, Love. You know that."

She uncoiled her tail from his. "Oh, so it wasn't really about me?"

Using his tail, he tried to grab hers again. "No, I didn't say that. You know how deeply I feel for you." His tail swiped through the treasure after hers, but she was quick, and he kept missing. "Grahleyna, don't be like this. I don't want to go decades without talking!"

"And you think I want to talk to someone who yells all the time?"

The massive chamber shook.

"I'M NOT YELLING!"

"Oh, really?"

Taken aback, Balzurth softened his tone. "Well, maybe a little. Grahleyna, please—"

She coiled her tail up with his again. "I forgive you. Honestly, Balzurth, you should know me better. I was only teasing you."

"I understand many things, but I have the hardest time with you."

"I know. But I like it that way. I find it … entertaining."

The closer she got, the more Balzurth's temper eased. He had plenty on his mind. Titans. Giants. Wurmers. His family was under attack again, and here he sat on his throne, feeling guilty. He wanted to take the fight to his foes. Vanquish the enemy once and for all. He glanced back at the Great Mural, where the images of the dragons moved at an impossibly slow pace. Time was so different on the other side.

"What are you thinking, Balzurth?" Grahleyna said, nuzzling him.

"Our son. It's so much to leave on his shoulders. It seems unfair."

"I know. I worry about Nath too. But I have faith he can do it."

"Yes, yes, I do too, but still … I just want to help him. He's so young, and the world is so full of ancient evil."

CHAPTER 23

The humongous doors swung open with an ugly groan coming from the hinges. Marching into the mountain, Nath noted a smaller set of doors, man-sized, were built into the ones that had opened.

Interesting.

The two stone giants led him right through the mountain with their great arms swinging at their sides. The road within was wide enough for a dozen carriages, and it stretched as far as even Nath's eyes could see.

It looks like they've carved a canyon out of this mountain.

On either side of him, crude structures jutted toward the sky. They were carved from rock and stone and merged with metal. Strange houses, open faced, were tiered up several levels. There were wooden ladders and stone staircases that all led higher and deeper into the strange new land.

Shuffling forward on his sore leg, Nath kept pace with his detainers. They had some swagger to them now, a strut in their step. People from all of the races were waving and greeting them, throwing dead branches and prickly rose stems on the road at their feet and cheering them on.

This is the oddest welcome I've ever seen. Men, orcs, halflings—ack! Is that a gnome? Oh my, a human boy is riding on a gnoll's shoulders. It can't be!

But it was. An eerie harmony pervaded these people. They were cheerful almost, one and all. Many chiseled at rocks. Others hammered metal inside the smithies Nath passed. The odd city seemed to have everything that a city would need. People. Livestock. Store fronts and shanty-like homes. There were coal-burning fire pits everywhere. And that wasn't all.

There were giants.

More than Nath had ever seen.

Brenwar's head would explode if he were here.

The giants, though outnumbered by the people, were monstrous men among them. Nath counted over two dozen of them. Hard bodied and bare chested, most of them stood between ten and twelve feet tall. They were the more common kind, unlike the stone and earth giants that towered around thirty feet high.

Nath stopped in his tracks.

Oh Guzan, I must be dreaming. No, it's a nightmare.

Four giant orcs strode down the street. Dark skinned and pig-nosed, with some canine teeth sticking out from their bottom lips.

Nath couldn't believe his eyes. He sniffed, and his eyes watered.

Oh, they are bigger and smell even fouler.

They walked right by Nath, flapping their jaws with chins held high, as if he weren't even there.

It was strange. Nath for a change was one of the smallest people there. He didn't like it.

What kind of an orc ignores me?

Nath stuck his foot out and tripped the one in the rear.

It stumbled into the others and knocked them all down.

"Ha ha! Stupid orcs. The bigger you are, the harder you fall!"

One of the bugbears turned around and took a swipe at Nath with his spear.

Ducking under it, Nath mocked him. "Nice try!"

One would think he'd learn his lesson from the last beating he took only hours ago, but the sight of the huge indifferent orcs infuriated him. He hated orcs.

I hate orcs! Certainly orc giants can be killed!

The giant orcs climbed back to their feet. Their dark eyes were hot with rage. Brows crumpled over their protruding foreheads. One of them yelled at Nath's guards. A bugbear started apologizing profusely over himself.

Huh, well if that isn't a twist. They're mad at my captors and not me. Maybe the bigger ones are smarter than the smaller ones.

A giant orc unhooked a metal hammer from its belt and launched a devastating swing. The blow crushed the pleading bugbear's face in and killed it.

Nath grimaced.

Bigger and meaner.

Every one of Nath's captors dropped to their knees, leaving him standing upright, front and center.

The orc giant faced him with its heaving hammer in its hands and glowered down at him with its nostrils flaring. It cocked the hammer back over its shoulder.

"Eh," Nath said, but he held his tongue. He wanted to say 'I didn't trip you.' He really did, but that would be a lie. And even though it was an orc, and his life was in peril, Nath just couldn't lie, so he said something else. Something positive. "Nice hammer. Can I hold it?"

The orc tossed it to him. Nath caught the massive thing with both hands. "Oof!" It was as heavy as an anchor. Straining, he lifted it over his head, teetered backward, and fell.

The orcs erupted in thunderous guffaws. Paying Nath no more mind, the one orc picked up the hammer, rejoined his group, and walked away.

"Whew!" Nath said, smiling. The hammer was heavy, but not so much as he'd led them to believe. He'd need to be more careful though. These giants were about as cruel as anyone he'd ever seen. They even killed their own kind.

Nath extended his hand to one of the bugbears on the ground.

It slapped his hand away.

For some strange reason, Nath almost said he was sorry. After all, it had been his actions that got the other bugbear killed. But the murder had revealed an awful lot to him.

These giants don't play around. They're stone-cold killers.

With him surrounded, his captors continued through the great but daunting city.

Nath, who had seen many things in his life, marveled.

This place was like the darker side of Narnum with all of its cultures, races, and sizes. Twenty-foot-tall ettins strolled the streets. Each giant traveled with a pack of smaller people that were enthralled by it. Huge slabs of meat cooked on monstrous grills and spits. There was the stink of sweat too. Filth and grime on every face. But the hard men and women worked with purpose and zeal. It was as if they wanted to help the giants. They enjoyed it. Hundreds of them. Maybe thousands. And they sang awful, ear jostling, horrible praises.

Bizarre. Yes. Bizarre.

Venturing into a great hall lit by great flaming urns bigger than ogres were tall, Nath stood before three empty thrones carved from black marble. Each one was about the same size as his father's. They chained Nath's links to the metal eyelets on the floor, and all of his detainers scurried away.

Skin crawling, Nath felt odd in his new isolation. There was an evil chill in the air that prickled the edges of his scales. Scanning the great vastness, his eyes glanced over the huge archways and columns where he found décor that was quite disturbing. Dragon skulls were mounted on the sides of the walls. Dragon skins hung like banners from poles.

Anger mixed with Nath's queasiness. The corded muscles in his arms strained against his chains. The moorite groaned, but it would not give. Sweat burst on his brow. It was futile, and he gasped. The sound echoed throughout the massive chamber. That's when another sound caught his ear.

Something hard pecked and scraped at the floor and echoed everywhere.

I've a horrendous feeling about this.

An enclave of wurmers snaked out from behind the bone-covered marble thrones. Eyes glowing and mouths dripping acid that sizzled on the floor, they made a beeline for Nath.

Did I say horrendous? I meant extremely horrendous.

CHAPTER 24

WURMERS. THEY WERE DRAGON-LIKE, BUT not dragon at all. They had scales and were dark colored and rigid. They had wings, functional but not graceful. And their claws and teeth made their appearance even less desirable. It was like comparing a hummingbird to a hornet. There wasn't anything admirable about them at all, unless you liked killers.

Nath stood tall with his chest out as the wurmers eased closer with a deep-purple glow in their snake eyes. If he was going to go down, be devoured or torn apart, he'd do it with his head up.

He spoke to the mindless things. "Come on, then. I'm a better meal than you deserve, and the best meal you'll ever have. Kind of sad really. I probably won't even give you a stomachache."

One of the wurmers in the middle, standing a head taller than Nath, snapped at him.

Frankly, he was getting tired of being smaller than everything in this city.

And father says size doesn't matter. Hah. Wonder how he'd feel about that if he were in my shoes.

He recalled Balzurth's oft-quoted favorite saying.

It's the size of your heart that matters most.

Inside Nath's chest, it felt like his pounding heart was as big as his head.

Easy for him to say. He's as big as a hillside. I used to be as big as a hillside. Great Dragons!

Clap! Clap!

The wurmers recoiled and backed toward the foot of the thrones.

With his view no longer obstructed by the wurmers, Nath noticed a small figure sitting on the bone-clad throne on the left. "Lotuus!"

"Oh, you remember my name. How special I am." Lovely as a bee, she flew over and hovered eye to eye with him. She was a little under half his size. Her features were as beautiful and exquisite as ever. Her white hair looked soft as cotton, her skin smooth, and she had a radiant smile that could melt the snow. She reached out and touched his swollen face. "My, you look much worse than when I saw you last, Nath Dragon." She poked her finger in his cheekbone. "Do these bruises hurt when I touch them? I wouldn't know. I've never been bruised."

Nath didn't wince. "You have a funny way of thanking your liberator, Lotuus."

She started toying with his hair. "My, your mane is so feathery and divine."

"Well, that it is," he said, starting to brim. But then he remembered who she was. "Hold on, get your hands out of my hair!"

From behind him, she tangled her arms up deeper in his locks. "I could sleep in it."

"Keep dreaming."

"No, literally. I *could* sleep in it. Not with you attached of course. No, I'd shear it off, mend it with other gentle fibers, and sleep for a decade in it. My, if I'd had this in my prison, I might have stayed." She spoke with elation. "I love it!"

"Get out of my hair!"

She untangled her arms and floated around him, poised in thought. "You know, I could shave it. Imprison you. Let it grow. Ah, yes. Shave it. Let it grow." She rubbed his chin. "I bet you can grow the softest beard. I want you to grow that too. My, how rare it is. I mean …

Dragon scales are valuable and rare,

But how many dragons actually have hair?"

She twirled around. "My blanket shall be marvelous!"

Straining against the moorite chains, Nath yelled at her, "That's not going to happen!" He huffed. And then curiosity got the better of him. "Now tell me, Lotuus, what are your motives?"

She stared at him with her round black eyes. "It's not my motives that you need to worry about, Nath Dragon. It's the titans. You see, you might have thought Gorn Grattack was a threat to mankind, but he was still a dragon. He just wanted to convert them. I personally never liked dragon kind. So pure and arrogant. Even the ornery ones." She huffed on her lavender fingernails and dusted them off with Nath's hair. "Oh my, look at that shine. It's too bad there's only one of you."

Irritated, he asked, "As you were saying?"

"Oh, yes. You see, I like the titans. They almost took this world over before, but the dragons defeated them. At that time, I thought maybe I had picked the wrong side, hence my imprisonment. But I always figured I'd get a second chance, and now we do. Thanks to you."

Nath frowned. It seemed that everyone spoke in riddles that he didn't fully understand.

His father had sent him after his mother.

That had led him to freeing Lotuus.

Which had led to him inadvertently freeing the titans.

He still didn't fully comprehend his father's reasons, but there had to be good reasons for it. One thing was for sure, it seemed everyone knew more than he did. It frustrated him.

"So, what makes you so certain that'll you'll be victorious this time when you were soundly defeated the last time?"

Her brows perched. "Soundly defeated?"

"Certainly. After all, my father has never been defeated, and never will be. Why do you think this time the outcome will be any different?"

She touched his nose. "Because we have you, Nath Dragon, and not only that, we have the wurmers as well. And with leverage and greater numbers, I don't see how anything can stop us."

"Let me ask you something, Lotuus. What is it that you wish to gain from all this?"

"Control."

"Control. Is that what pleases you, control? In all of your years of life have you not figured out that you cannot take away free will? I'm far younger than you—and I might add, comelier too—and I've figured that out."

Lotuus frowned. "What we cannot control we will destroy."

"Then you will wind up with nothing. What will you control then when only misery and emptiness is your company? How will you control that growing pit in your stomach that devours you from the inside out?"

With defiant eyes she sneered. "We will see." She flew backward and stood on the left throne, which was so big, he barely even noticed her on it.

The floor in the great hall started to shake under the thunder of footsteps. Behind the thrones a flaming ball of light appeared. It was a giant with a husky and roughhewn frame wearing breastplate armor like a man with his head afire with blue flames. His mighty frame filled the middle throne.

He gazed down at Nath and said in a cavernous voice, "Son of my enemy, I am Eckubahn. Welcome to Urslay. It is Giantish for *torment,* and your time of torment has come."

CHAPTER 25

Brenwar awoke only to find himself jailed in a stable. Hands and legs bound up, he rolled onto his belly, gathered his legs underneath him, and using the wall he pushed up to his feet.

A cow in a nearby stable mooed.

"Moo you," Brenwar replied. Legs and wrists tied up, he hopped on two legs and bumped into the stable gate. He peered in between the planks. The barn was typical. A ladder led into a loft full of hay, and about two dozen stables were inside.

Just outside of the barn's main doors, two of the villagers stood guard. One had a pitchfork. The other had a hand axe. They were talking to each other and not paying any mind to Brenwar at all.

He hopped backward, slipped in the straw, and tumbled down hard. He spat the straw from his mouth. "Great Morgdon."

Fortunately for him, his hands were bound in front of him, and it was a poor job at best. Clearly, the villagers didn't take many prisoners. Using his bony fingertips on his skinless hand, Brenwar started picking at the threads.

"Hmm, that's quite a trick."

The sensation was on in his bony hand. He could feel with it, but there wasn't any life to it. Still, he liked it and continued picking one tiny thread from another.

"No one but Brenwar has a hand like this. Ho ho!"

Though it was daytime, a few things escaped him. It wasn't often that anything had ever knocked him out before. As a matter of fact he didn't recall ever being knocked out before. He wondered how long he'd been out. Hopefully not more than a day. It couldn't have been that long.

"Certainly not."

Finally, the ropes on his wrists gave way. Using his dwarven strength, he snapped out of his bonds and undid the bindings on his legs. Wearing only his clothes from beneath his armor, he reached through the planks, unlatched the gate, and swung it open. He rolled his eyes as it groaned and the villager guards faced him with eyes filled with surprise.

"Where's my hammer?" He spat hay out of his mouth and started again, "Where's my armor?"

One of the villagers took off at a dead sprint.

The other one rushed up to him with a pitchfork and got dangerously close. It was a farmer, slack-jawed and slow-eyed, with some meat on his shoulders. He said, "Get back in that stable and tie yourself up again. You're going to stir up trouble."

Brenwar cocked an eyebrow at him. "Is that so, human? What are you going to do, poke me with that fork? Is that how you rump kissers feed those giants you're in league with?"

"We don't have a choice."

"Sure you do, you corn-shucking coward. It's called fighting, yellow belly."

"We can't even hurt them," the farmer said. He poked the pitchfork at Brenwar. "Now get back in there and be silent, before he gets here!"

When the pitchfork jabbed at him, Brenwar snatched it away. He broke it in half with his bare hands.

Snap!

"Now tell me where my gear is."

The villager swallowed. "The giant has it."

"There's just one giant?"

The man nodded his head.

Brenwar rubbed his beard. Sure, he could fight the giant, but they were tough to kill. He'd need the magic in his hammer or something bigger. He scanned the barn for a weapon of some sort. There was a horseshoeing station nearby with a large anvil in it. Brenwar marched over to the anvil.

The farmer eased in behind him. "What are you thinking? I can't help you pick that up."

"Did I ask fer your help?"

"No."

"Then shaddup. All I need you to do is lure the giant in here. Got it?"

The look on the farmer's face didn't give him any confidence. Shaking his head, Brenwar wrapped his arms around the anvil and lifted it off the pedestal. Then, in one quick cling and jerk motion he hefted it onto his shoulder.

The farmer marveled.

Brushing by the dumbfounded man, Brenwar made his way over to the ladder that led up into the loft. With his free hand he tugged on it and grunted. Rung by rung, he climbed the ladder like a bearded ape. Forehead bursting with sweat, he walked over the groaning planks.

Once he was in position, Brenwar glanced down at the farmer. "Did you build this barn?"

"No."

"No surprise there."

The barn tremored. Heavy footsteps approached from outside.

The lazy farmer started to shake.

"Just stand where you are and wait," Brenwar ordered him.

The man was frozen.

Through the barn's large doors appeared the figure of a giant. A full head taller than the opening, it stooped its head and stepped beneath the doorway. The giant was bald aside from a long ponytail that rested over its expansive back.

Mortuun was tucked between its bearskin loincloth and waist.

The giant eyed the villager with fearsome eyes.

The man glanced up and started pointing at the loft, screaming, "He's up there! The dwarf's up there!"

The giant's head snapped up.

"Hello, stupid!" Brenwar roared. Anvil hoisted over his head, he hurled the hunk of steel with wroth force. The huge missile smote the giant right between the eyes.

It stumbled around a few paces and fell flat on its back.

Boom!

Brenwar hopped down from the loft and landed on the dead giant's chest. After he retrieved Mortuun, he walked down the giant's chest and hopped off beside its head.

The farmer gawked. "What do we tell them when they come back and see his body?"

"Tell them Brenwar is coming—and Mortuun is coming with him."

CHAPTER 26

"SO I GUESS YOU WON'T be unshackling me." Nath rattled his chains. "Well, it's not so bad. At least it's moorite, so it doesn't chafe my scales. Well, what exactly is this torment going to consist of? As you can see, I've had a pretty rough day already."

Eckubahn's fingers dug into the wooden arms of his throne. He leaned forward. "I should devour you right now."

"No need to be hasty. I saw goats aplenty on my way in here." Nath searched for the titan's eyes.

His face could still be seen behind the flame-like aura that guarded it. The mystic flames flickered between deep-purple and bright-orange colors. Perhaps they revealed the mood the titan was in.

Still, Nath could make out enough to see that it was an earth giant by its big facial features. A flat, broad nose and long earlobes. It was just like the ones Nath had fought as a dragon months ago. The giant was still in there but was now possessed by the spirit of a titan. Nath didn't have a very good understanding of them still.

Aw, I wish Bayzog were here. Well, what he didn't tell me I guess I'll just have to find out for myself.

"I notice one of those thrones is empty. Did your wife leave you? Oh wait, I bet she caught on fire when she tried to kiss you."

Eckubahn slapped his hand down on the arm of his chair. "Silence!"

Nath held his tongue.

Fine, I'll let him do all the work, then. Keep talking, giant mouth.

The titan continued. "Torment is tearing someone apart a small piece at a time. That is what I am going to do to you. That is what I am going to do to your father. Just imagine the shock that will fill his eyes when a piece of you is delivered each week. Or each month. Perhaps once a year. So far as I am concerned, it might take forever. I'll start with something small at first. One of your precious scales. Maybe a fingernail. A lock of your hair."

"I think Lotuus has dibs on the great mane," Nath said, winking at her.

"Quiet, you fool!" Eckubahn said. His flames turned a deep red. "This is no place for your boasts or your jests. This is the place of your inevitable death."

Nath's shoulders sank. It was clear that the titan meant business. He could feel the deep hatred from where he stood. The titan's passion for destruction seeped into his bones. Eckubahn and his followers would execute their diabolical goals and would destroy anything that stood in their way. And Nath would be his pawn.

He wants to use me to draw my father out.

Tapping his fingertips together, Eckubahn said, "It is going to be a delicious time. Unlike the last time, this time we have the numbers, and Balzurth will come out and fight his final battle. But it won't matter. He won't stand a chance." He waved his hand.

The stone giant who had taken Nath into custody was coming down the hallway. It walked past Nath and took a knee in front of Eckubahn. Though little shorter than the titan, the stone giant seemed much smaller by comparison. It reached into its vest and handed over Fang.

The titan took the blade by the scabbard, studied it, put his fingers on the tiny pommel, and pulled out the sword. His fingertips sizzled and smoked. He eyed the glimmering blade, slid it back into the scabbard, and handed it over to the stone giant. "Interesting work. Take it to the Chamber of Contest. Let's see if I have a champion who can destroy it."

The stone giant slid the grand sword back into his belt and started to walk away.

On impulse, Nath stretched his hands and rushed toward the giant's feet. The chains snapped back his neck and held him fast. He squeezed his eyes shut and thought on instinct.

Fang! Come to me! Come!

The stone giant's hand fell to the sword on his belt and stopped. Glowering at Nath, he kicked him in the gut. After knocking Nath flat to the ground, the giant strode off.

Nath pushed himself up into a sitting position and clutched his gut. He started into a fit of coughing. Gathering his thoughts, he watched the giant's great form diminish down the hall. Subtly, he stretched his tingling fingers out again. He could feel Fang's presence.

The giant vanished from sight, and the sensation was lost.

Rubbing his fingers together, Nath pondered what had just happened.

Was that Fang I felt?

"Do not hope, Nath Dragon," Eckubahn stated. "There is no hope for you here."

Turning to face his captors, Nath said, "Yeah, I've had that feeling for some time now. So, what is next? What is to become of me now?" He patted his belly. "I'm a bit hungry."

"Interesting that you should mention it. The wurmers are hungry as well."

"I think you've made it clear you aren't going to dispatch of me anytime soon. So what are the wurmers to me?"

"Oh, I was not planning on letting them feast on you. Rather, I was planning on having you as my guest at their dinner. I think you will find it quite salivating."

Lotuus giggled.

Nath felt his scales start to crawl. Whatever they were implying, he had a gut feeling that he didn't want to see it.

Eckubahn motioned again.

Another figure emerged from the shadows behind the urns. It was the biggest lizard man he'd ever seen. It stood almost twice as tall as Nath.

The bigger they are, the more I hate them. What is going on in this place? Why is everyone so humongous but me!

The lizard man unhooked Nath from the rings on the floor and held the chain attached to his collar like a leash. With a powerful tug, he jerked Nath off his feet and onto the ground and started dragging Nath down the hall.

Nath, ever deft, fought to get back on his feet until he was finally walking again. He glanced over his shoulder.

Eckubahn still sat, but Lotuus was on the move. She floated after him with a ruthless smile on her lips.

How can someone so beautiful be so ugly within?

"I guess I'll be having the displeasure of your company?"

"You'll be having displeasure for certain," she said. "And this is only the beginning of your suffering."

"For the life of me I cannot grasp why people like you are so intent on harming people like me. And I've known plenty of fairies to be contrary. This spite that you share is a shame to your kind."

"You dragons are so arrogant. You think you are so much better than everyone. A little humility would suit you quite well."

"Do me a favor, Lotuus, please. Give me an example of a dragon wronging you."

Her pleasant features hardened with concentration.

"Funny, I didn't hear you say anything," Nath said. "Could you speak a little louder?"

I knew she didn't have anything. They never do!

Lotuus then blurted out, "You think you are so perfect!"

"I don't think I'm perfect. I mean, sure"—he flicked his mangled mane—"I look perfect on the outside, but I have flaws on the inside. I just keep them to myself. Unlike your kind, that lets all the ugly out."

"I embrace my passions. Why shouldn't I?"

"Because they are misdirected and harmful," he replied.

"Says your kind." She sneered at him. "My kind says, 'I'll do whatever I want, whenever I want, *to* whomever I want. If it is my heart's desire, so be it.'"

"You're a bitter little thing with a wicked little heart."

"Says you. Who cares?"

Nath sealed his lips shut as the giant-sized lizard man led them back into the streets. It was clear that arguing with Lotuus wouldn't get him anywhere. She was no doubt a petty and stiff-necked thing. It reminded him of how Selene used to be. He decided to change the subject. Watching the influx of oversized people in his life, he asked, "Lotuus, honestly, where are all these giants coming from?"

She showed a smiling sliver of teeth. "Oh, you are a wonder, aren't you Nath Dragon? Noticed that all by yourself, did you? Well, I'll let you in on a little secret that just might ruin your trousers. Not only do the wurmers populate fast, but the giants are populating fast as well."

"You're joking."

"No, not at all."

Loud chanting came from inside a humongous archway where the lizard man stopped and tugged on Nath's neck chain. It led him to an indoor arena. The seats went downward and were carved from hard stone.

Nath's head sagged. He could smell it. The greasy skin and sweat build-up and foul moisture in the room.

Oh, surprise, another arena.

CHAPTER 27

THOUSANDS OF PEOPLE FILLED THE seats, with a minority of giants scattered all about. They all pounded on their chairs, chanted, and smacked their hands together.

Blood was in the air.

They wanted it.

Nath and company took a seat in a balcony that jutted out ten rows higher than the caged arena below. Nath got his first glimpse at the dragon inside. It was a red rock dragon, a big one too. It was bigger than a horse. He used to see them from time to time swimming in the streams of lava near Dragon Home's sulfurous springs. They were wingless and deep red with hard fireproof scales that covered their entire bodies.

"Good luck eating him," Nath said.

Lotuus scoffed. "It will be interesting."

Though the red rock dragon was a big one, it seemed small in this strange city of Urslay, where everything was bigger than it was supposed to be. The arena itself was a massive cage of steel big enough to hold many giants.

It was a setup that Nath had seen over and over during his years of rescuing the dragons. For reasons Nath could never comprehend, people had a zeal for tormenting dragons.

"Ah, I see the champions are arriving." Lotuus grabbed his chin and turned it. "Look."

A parade of four warriors rode down a runway toward the cage. They were heavily armored people—orc, gnoll, bugbear, and ogre—stuffed inside plate armor. They carried spears and halberds that gleamed with a mystic silvery energy. They rode on the backs of four wingless wurmers.

Nath's jaws clenched. His brow furrowed.

"What's the matter, Nath?" Lotuus said to him. "You seem a tad worried."

The warriors entered the cage, and the door was slammed shut behind them. An incredible roar burst forth from the crowd. Inside the cage, the fighters spaced themselves evenly around the red rock dragon and dismounted. The odds seemed to suddenly change from four against one to eight against one.

The red rock balled up into a heap of scale and muscle that resembled his name.

The warriors turned toward the crowd and raised their long weapons up in salute. The throng went wild. They stomped their feet and shouted like madmen.

Nath's frown deepened. Just when he thought he'd managed to lead his kind to safety by defeating Gorn Grattack, in no time another enemy had taken Gorn's place. It was one that seemed far deadlier than the first. Subtly, he tried to break his chains. The links had no give in them.

Still standing, Lotuus leaned on his shoulder. "Oh, you want to go and help your little dragon, don't you? Well, that is too bad. Instead, you must watch. But I'm sure you will get your chance."

"I never should have freed you," Nath said.

"I couldn't agree more." She stroked his cheek. "But I'm so happy you did."

A horn sounded that drowned out all of the shouting in the room. The crowd fell silent. Inside the cage the warriors turned, faced the dragon, and lowered their weapons.

The horn sounded again. The warriors charged. The excited audience jumped back to their feet and urged them on.

The deep-red ball of dragon mass burst into motion. Tail lashing out, it spun in a full circle. The warriors, weighted down in heavy armor, couldn't move out of the way in time. Each and every one fell and crashed in a pile of metal.

"Hah!" Nath cheered.

The wurmers, quicker than the men, pounced. Teeth and claws latched onto the red rock's body, covering it entirely. A burst of flame billowed out from under the pile, catching two of the four wurmers on fire. Rearing its thick neck, the red rock shook the other two off its back. Without hesitation, it plowed into a wurmer, pinned it down, and shot lava-like flames all over it.

The monster screamed and sizzled.

Back on its feet, a gnoll wielding a glowing halberd struck the red rock on the back of his scales.

The dragon let out a roar, spun, and slapped the gnoll with his tail from one side of the cage to the other.

Nath pumped his fist. "Ah-hah!"

The battle raged inside. The red rock was quicker and stronger. His speed belied his husky girth. He toppled the warriors. Pounded the wurmers.

The brood of insect-like dragons spat balls of bright fire at the dragon.

The red rock shrugged it off and spat scorching flames back.

The wurmers' hard scales crackled.

The dragon crushed their flesh.

The battle that had started with eight was down to three.

"Are you sure you want to side with the titans, Lotuus? To your folly, I fear that you underestimate the dragons."

Arms crossed over her chest, she said, "It's not over yet."

The ogre chucked a spear deep into the red rock's side.

The dragon let out a blast of fire, turning the ogre into burning flesh and melting metal. Spear buried in his side, he attacked the two wurmers. His jaws clamped down on one's neck, shook the life out of it, and slung it away. The last one he rendered into pieces with his claws.

All eight of the enemy were dead, and the battered and bloodied red rock dragon resumed his spot and balled up in the middle of the circle. He closed his eyes, paying no mind to the silenced crowd.

Brimming, Nath said to Lotuus, "Never underestimate a dragon."

She replied with, "And never underestimate evil."

A stir rose in the crowd. The cage doors were split open, and down the runway at least twenty wingless wurmers surged from the tunnel.

The red rock's eyes snapped open. Quickly, he was back on his feet.

The horde of charging wurmers consumed him.

Nath's gaze froze on the horror. The feverish crowd's cheers shook his very core. They chanted praise as the wondrous hard-fighting dragon was torn apart and devoured in pieces.

He shook his chains.

Unable to contain his anger, Nath whirled on Lotuus. 'You are depraved!"

"I know." She nodded to the giant lizard man. "Take him to the dungeon and triple the guards. Oh, and one more thing." A pair of scissors appeared in her hand. She cut off a lock of Nath's long red hair.

Snip!

"An heirloom for Balzurth." She started floating away. "Once we've conquered Nalzambor, I'll see you at your execution. Until then, enjoy the misery that is coming. Bind him!"

Chapter 28

Avoiding the road that led into the Craggy Mountains, Brenwar opted to make the climb with his own hands and feet. As much as he wanted to storm right up the path into the unknown hills and battle every monster he faced, the wisdom within let prudence intervene. Now, he hung by his meaty but strong fingers off the rim of a narrow ledge. Puffing through his beard, he hauled himself up on the ridge, staring up into the dark sky that seemed to seep into the mountainside.

"One hundred feet up, and only three thousand more to go. Now that's living. Hah. And that only took a couple of hours."

Brenwar sat up, spat on his calloused hands, then took out a pick he'd borrowed from the village and started the climb to the next bench. Though climbing wasn't his favorite thing, he and his kind weren't half-bad mountaineers with the right equipment.

Inside the caves and tunnels they carved out there were plenty of hazards to face. In Nalzambor there were just as many jagged cliffs to face inside the world as out. Some fascinating marvels to behold, too. Waterfalls, underground streams, and lakes. A magnificent world hidden in the darkness.

He climbed, walked, slipped, and fell a few more hours and managed a couple hundred more feet.

"The things I do for a dragon," he muttered.

Of course, he'd do anything for Nath, and not just because Balzurth had charged him with it either, but because he was his friend. And the truth was, things were always exciting with Nath around, even though Brenwar often bickered at him. Nath was fun to bicker with. It bothered the dragon prince. Bickering among dwarves didn't matter at all. It was their way. Pushing. Suggesting. Perfecting.

The aging dwarf took a seat on a narrow tier and mopped the sweat from his brow. He uncapped his canteen and drank.

Some white night owls bigger than hounds flew through the night. Wings stretched out like great fans, they glided through the night sky with ease.

This would be one of the rare times Brenwar would consider riding a dragon.

But only because time is pressing and I need to find my friend.

Out of the corner of his eye he noticed a shadow swooping down the mountainside in pursuit of the owls. Still as the stone, he only moved his ancient eyes enough to make out the sleek dragon forms of the wurmers cutting through the air. Three in all, they gave the agile owls chase until all of the flying parties vanished in the night's chill air.

"Morgdon's Toes," he said under his breath.

He reached over his shoulder and patted Mortuun the Crusher, who was secured to his back.

"As if this climb wasn't bad enough. This is why dwarves go *through* mountains, not up and around them. That's what the other knuckleheaded races do."

Frost covering his armor, Brenwar resumed his climb. His cold breath and iron will were his only company. He fought his way up the least likely path a dwarf would ever take, carefully keeping his ears pricked for any signs of wurmers that could be roosted in the rocks.

The night turned to day, and the day back to night as he clawed his way to the top.

It wasn't a straight climb either, but one where he might have to traverse a narrow ledge horizontally for a mile before he could find another way going back up again. The footing was slick, the effort hard and strained.

He ignored the gnawing in his gut. Finally, almost three days later he found himself on the top. He wanted to scream but held his tongue.

Bushed, he took a knee. The top of the mountain revealed little about the location that he wanted to find. At best, he was miles away from where the giant road led up into the mountains. With the cold wind biting at his frozen face, he closed his eyes and listened. There wasn't much to be heard aside from the wind howling through the icy mountains. No life stirred.

His nostrils widened. "Ah."

Something akin to nature drifted into his nose. Somewhere, meat cooked. There was no hiding that from a dwarf hungry enough to eat a boar. He untethered one of the strings on his pouches and pinched out a strip of jerky and chewed on it.

"Hmmm," he grunted. "Where there's meat there's ale."

He knocked the frost from his eyebrows and beard and unhitched Mortuun from his back. He was topside now. If there was life about, it lurked in the direction he was headed. Toward the warmth. Toward the food. Following the scent, he marched through boot-deep snow, between treacherous crevasses and ravines. There were some modest climbs too, and the pace was slow, but at the dawn of the next day he saw firelight in a distant tower.

"I'll be."

Through the bitter snow he spied a ring of tall stone towers spread out with at least a mile between them. It was clear that wasn't all of them either.

"Why in the world would there be towers all the way up here? No one can see them."

Brenwar made a climb to a higher elevation to get a better look above the towers. It took a few hours, but when he made it, his eyes filled with wonder. The towers overlooked a canyon, and inside that canyon was a city with giant-sized activity.

"By my beard."

He squeezed Mortuun's handle.

"There be too many giants in there."

He cocked his head. His eyes narrowed. Soft footsteps crunched down the snow behind him. He turned his shoulder and started to swing.

"No one sneaks up on a dwarf!"

Something knocked his feet out from under him.

As he rose up on his elbows, Brenwar's eyes widened. "You!"

CHAPTER 29

Head down between his legs, Nath sat with his eyes shut and tummy rumbling. He was a dragon, and dragons were patient, but at the moment, days into it, he was unsettled. Not that anyone would be comfortable in prison, but he wasn't used to misery being his only company. He was alone. Entirely. Forgotten. The giant lizard man had thrown him behind the metal bars and left him there. He hadn't seen anyone since.

He lifted his chin up and studied the same grey walls he'd been looking at for days. They were moldy. Ancient. Water and filth from the streets above dripped through the cracks.

He wondered what this strange city of Urslay really was. If anything, it was a city built on top of another city. And maybe this subterranean part of the city was built on another city. That was entirely believable. After all, the lost City of Borgash was mostly buried in the bowels of the earth, and in all of Nalzambor's thousands of years, empires of men, orcs, and dwarves must have fallen from time to time. Nath had found evidence of that everywhere.

His belly groaned so loud it echoed in the chamber. He laughed.

With my luck I'll go into a cocoon again. There's no telling what I'll be when I wake up next. Ah, those were the days. Sleep, wake up, get more scales. Sleep, wake up, get more scales.

He rubbed his eyes and yawned, though he wasn't really tired. There had been quite a few times, when Nath was younger, that he'd been in jail. He'd never really worried about it too much before. But now things were different. The world had ended up much bigger than he thought it was. And the giants, he'd never thought of dealing with more than a few of them at a time, but now it was clear there were hundreds, maybe thousands—and they were united against the dragons.

"Humph."

Keeping his ears open, he got up and put his hands on the steel bars. They were thick. Not moorite, but thick. A solid inch of spring steel.

"Hello?"

His voice echoed down the great hall that ran between his cell and all the rest. There weren't any replies. Not a shuffle. Not even a rat. At first, he had figured there would at least be some tormenters that would pester him. That maybe they'd put him on the rack and stretch his limbs as long as the giants'. But no. Nothing.

He gazed up and down the row again. Perhaps there was some other type of guard lurking in the cells. A monster or phantom of some sort. It seemed very strange that no one was there to keep an eye on him at all. The giants were often stupid and cocky. But careless? No.

Nath lowered his shoulder and rammed it into the cell door.

Wham!

A solid rock wall would have been softer.

So what if they hear me? I could use some company.

He hit it again, and again and again.

Wham! Wham! Wham!

Huffing for breath and shoulder aching, he pressed his face to the bars. "Come on now, somebody somewhere has to be listening. Someone? I'll even take an orc if you have one."

The silence was almost as annoying as his stomach aching. He was hungry. Very hungry. And it seemed to sap his strength and will.

Oh, don't start flailing like a fitful child, Nath Dragon. You're a prince. Stick with the plan. Bad as it must be, it's still a plan.

It was clear that his captors wanted to wear him down, and if that was the case, then so be it. He wanted to wear them down. Feign being weak and defeated. When he saw an opening, he would strike. The trick was getting out of his moorite chains. He was strong, but perhaps not that strong.

That led him to another plan. This city, Urslay, if it was built upon another city, perhaps there was another way out. Another place to hide and escape. There always was.

But after escaping, most important was the retrieval of Fang. Like any friend, he wouldn't want to abandon his blade. He could feel its presence. And he'd felt something else for a while now. A bond that was growing between them. Fang had a lot of power that Nath didn't yet understand. Perhaps he had taken it all for granted.

Instead of making the most of what I have, I've been making the most of what I've lost. That's no way to be a leader.

If anything, Nath's isolation had some benefits. It gave him time to think about how he dealt with things and how he could handle them better. He had so many advantages over others! But oft times he didn't plan, just winged it. His talents and skill prevailed in times of need. But now, with the stakes so high, he needed to be less reckless and more careful. A patient planner. One who paid attention to the details.

Certainly I have it in me to be wise?

As he tapped his fingernails on the bars, his mind picked away at what Eckubahn and Lotuus had said. Fang had been taken to the Chamber of Contest. There, the giants would try to destroy Fang. And Lotuus had hinted that Nath would battle inside that arena. It would be there, if anywhere, that he would make his escape.

No doubt they wanted to wear him down as much as they could before they turned him loose in the cage. And the goal wasn't to kill him. They'd made that clear. Or was it? Lotuus and Eckubahn were both liars. One could never trust a word that evil said.

Mind games. It's all mind games.

CHAPTER 30

"Are you lost, Dwarf?" Selene stared down at Nath's pet dwarf. At first she had thought he was drunk, the way he stumbled around in the snow so far away from everything. But no. The little bearded ape was just spying on the giant city. Like she was. Interesting.

Brenwar kicked at her tail. "Just when I thought it couldn't get any colder, you show up." He got up. "So, what brings you here?"

"Wurmers. You?"

"Nath."

Oh no! Does he know where Nath is?

Keeping her worry off her face, Selene just lifted her brows in what she meant to look like curiosity. "So, he's lost and so are you, it seems."

"No one is lost." He eyed her as he dusted the snow from his armor. "Let's hope anyway."

"What is that supposed to mean?"

"Nothing," he said.

"You don't trust me, do you Dwarf?"

"I didn't say that. But I will say this, I don't like you much."

"Perfect, I don't like you either."

"Good."

It was an awkward moment. Selene actually was happy to see Brenwar, but sad that Nath wasn't with him. "Tell me what happened."

Begrudgingly, Brenwar spilled out a disturbing story about giants tricking Nath in the nearby village cluster at the site of the old city of Harvand.

In this case, Selene agreed with Brenwar. She would have left the fate of the people in those villages to the giants in exchange for keeping Nath. Why he fought so hard for people that were far inferior she didn't quite understand. "I see."

"So glad your eyes are open and that you can see, Selene." The annoying little dwarf glanced over his shoulder. "So, you've tracked the wurmers here?"

She relayed what she had encountered in the fishing villages. "Seems there is quite a nest here. So, should I wait here while you go in and rescue Nath?"

"You know, you're as funny as you look. But I'm doing just fine without you. Still, if you want to come along, I won't stop you."

"Oh, thank you for your generosity. A smallish escort is just what I need."

"Smallish?"

She gave him her best condescending smile.

Obviously choosing not to notice, Brenwar took the lead, making a wide trail through the snow, until they were less than a mile away from the first tower. "We need to be wary. There's no telling what kind of eyes are in those towers."

"Those are dragon towers," she said.

"How do you know that?"

"I know. This is Urslay, place of the giants, though it was fairly dormant during the time of Gorn Grattack. We sought their aid in the Great Dragon War, but they weren't interested. Giants aren't a race that wants to be unified with dragons ever. Those towers go back to the last battle the dragons fought against the titans and the giants. I know that much. They are there to watch the skies, not the ground. I don't think they'll be looking for us."

"Don't you think you should have mentioned this place before, back in Quintuklen?"

Uh, I didn't know it was active back then, stupid.

"No."

The little dwarf huffed, turned his eyes forward, and plowed through the snow.

Good, we've found a use for you: snowplow!

In the night, they could see silhouettes against the fires burning at the tops of the towers. Two people were within each hundred-foot-high tower, manning the ballistas that were mounted up there. To shoot at flying dragons.

Brenwar led them midway between the closest tower and the next tower. The wind blew his beard straight up in a very undignified way when he turned to speak to her. "Since you aren't very forthcoming, tell me, have you been inside Urslay before?"

Selene bit the insides of her cheeks so she wouldn't laugh at the funny picture he made.

No sense getting him all riled up. That will waste time that Nath may not have.

"Yes."

But the pesky little dwarf got all riled up anyway, running ahead of her as if he could leave her behind. He was such a child.

"You long-tailed giant-loving witch!"

"Oh, don't be so dramatic. I didn't have much of a choice then," she said, catching up to Brenwar, who was only a few steps from the canyon's edge. "And I only had a glimpse. Show some mirth. Who would have thought it would be something that could serve our cause now?"

Brenwar hurried, apparently thinking she couldn't pass him, came to a stop at the rocky edge, and leaned his head down. "That's quite the canyon."

Selene found her place by his side. "Yes, a very unique city."

The canyon was hundreds of feet deep and went on for miles. There was firelight coming from the small and large stone carved alcoves that made up the strange city. Tiny figures shuffled over the roads, and livestock in mass quantities were herded into pens.

Selene could smell everything. Hay, orcs, humans, halflings, cooked meat, coal, and wood smoke.

The last time she was there, it had only been giants, and not so many. For the most part, it had been abandoned, but now it was quite different. There were hundreds, maybe a thousand people, and they thrived. Their voices lifted up over the rocks with wild songs of praise.

"What are those people so happy for?" Brenwar asked.

"The titans have a uniting effect on weaker people." She started down the side. "Stay here. I'll take a look."

Brenwar seized her arm. "You'll do no such thing. I'm not going to sit here like a yeti while you go and reminisce with old friends."

She jerked out of his grip. "So you're coming, then."

"No."

"Then what do you propose we do, sit here and wait for Nath to greet us?" She searched Brenwar's hard eyes. "Brenwar, you will need to trust me."

His eyes pierced hers. "I don't."

She had tried to be nice. She had even called him by his name. Aggravated, she fired back, "And what was your plan? Did you think a dwarf could infiltrate the giants? They would sniff you out as soon as you set foot in there."

"I'm not worried about putting my life in peril."

"I'm not either, but you can't just go waltzing down there with me. It would be stupid."

"Are you calling me stupid?" he growled.

She shook her head. "No. I think you are well aware of your limitations already."

"I'm going to cut your tail off!"

"Try, and I'll strangle you with your own beard!"

Red-faced, Brenwar replied, "Leave my beard out of this." He drew Mortuun back. "Go ahead, say it one more time!"

"Will you keep your annoying voice down? The guards are distant, not deaf!" Finally, she sighed, leaned over, and kissed him on the forehead.

Brenwar shuffled in the snow, his temper cooled. "What was that for?"

She shrugged. "I just realized I'd do anything to shut you up."

"Ho ho ho!" Brenwar rumbled. "I don't like you, but I like your spite." He lifted his brows, reached into one of his pouches, and pulled out a colorful potion vial. "I have an idea that should satisfy us both."

CHAPTER 31

Hours were usually like minutes to a dragon, except now. No, now the minutes felt like long, agonizing hours as Nath's insides gnawed at his outsides. He was hungry. He was angry. Typically, a dragon would sleep through a wait like this, hibernate like a bear. Instead, Nath paced and fought to keep his weary eyes open. Something had to give.

He yelled through the bars.

"Hello? Hello!"

His loud voice echoed down the hall.

Nothing replied.

He banged his fists on the bars and screamed at the top of his lungs.

"HELLO, I SAY!"

He followed it up with a roar so loud it rattled all the locks in the dungeon.

"RAWWWWWRRRRrrrrrr!"

He shuffled backward and touched his throat.

Was that me?

He let out another cage-shaking roar.

"RrrrrrrAAAWWWWWWRRRrrrrrrrr!"

Huh! It was *me! Seems I still have some dragon pipes in me.*

Suddenly he belched. "Urp."

A puff of grey smoke rolled out of his mouth. There was a charred taste on his tongue. His golden eyes lit up.

He blew smoke from his nostrils.

Can it be?

Stomach growling, he eyed the bars that caged him in. He rubbed his chin.

Hmmm, if I can summon my flame, then I can melt these bars. Hah! Wouldn't that be something?

He focused and concentrated on his fires within.

Come on, Dragon. You can do it.

His stomach burned like fire and surged up his throat. A blast of hot, smoky air spilled from his mouth. The plume of hot smoke filled his dungeon cell and the hall. Within seconds, the air was thicker than dwarven stew and he couldn't even see himself. He fanned away the vapors, coughing a few times.

"Well *that* was pointless!"

He coughed some more and screamed. His muscles ached, and weakness assailed him. Whatever he had done had sucked the life out of him. He sagged down onto his knees and stretched out on the floor. His heavy eyelids felt like they were filled with sand.

Maybe I should try and take a nap until the smoke clears. What a useless trick for a dragon. Who needs a dragon that blows smoke instead of fire? Such a joke.

Nath was drifting into slumber when the scuffle of soft feet caught his ear. He lifted his weary head, cocked his ear.

I must be dreaming that I have a visitor coming.

He lowered his head again and shut his eyes. Again, the scuffle came. Footsteps were making their way down the dungeon hallway. He sat up and peered through the dissipating smoke.

A man appeared in the smoke just outside the bars. The build of the man was very strange, thick, but with gingerly moves.

Am I dreaming?

"Where did all this smoke come from?" the man said in an irritated but friendly tone.

The sound of the man was very odd to Nath's ears, not rough and husky like most of the over-sized people.

"And what was that racket I heard? It sounded like a dog choking."

Nath made his way to his feet, rubbed his gold eyes, and sauntered over to the bars. There, he got a better look at the man, who was broad and round faced. Nath blinked his eyes and said to the unique man, "Are you a *halfling*?"

"What?" the man said really loud. He pushed his frosty locks from his eyes, fanned more of the smoke away, and stared at Nath. "Yer that dragon fella they talk about above, ain't you?"

"Are you a halfling?" Nath repeated with astonishment.

"You say that like you've never seen a halfling before." The giant halfling wore navy-blue trousers with a maroon shirt. He stuffed his long and slender fingers into a big pocket in the middle of his overall and withdrew a pouch. He loosened the strings and removed a pinch of snuff and snorted it. His eyes brightened. "Woo Wee! Now that is dandy!"

Gently shaking his head, Nath said, "Who are you?"

"What?"

Nath spoke louder. "I said, who are you?"

"You heard a moo?"

"No!"

The old halfling reached behind his back and brought forth a brass horn with a bend in the smaller portion of its neck. He held it to his ear and tilted it toward Nath. "Speak into my good ear."

"What is your name?" Nath asked.

"Pepper." His forehead crinkled, and his button nose sniffed. "Where'd all this smoke come from?"

Nath didn't want to lie, even though his first urge was to say, 'I don't know.' Instead, he changed the subject. If there was one thing he knew about people, especially halflings, they liked to talk about themselves. "How'd you get so big?"

"Speak up, flame mane."

Nath huffed and spoke directly into the earpiece. "Why are you so big?"

"Well, you don't have to yell! My name's Pepper."

"You told me that already. Sheesh. Pepper, why are you so big?"

"Oh, I see," Pepper said. "You want to know why I am so big. We are all big in my family. Well, most of us mostly." With soft eyes he stared down at Nath. "I just remembered. I can read lips. Go ahead and speak at your common loudness." He lowered his ear horn.

"Pepper, halflings are half as big as men. Why are you and so many others in this city so big?"

Rubbing his chin, Pepper studied Nath's lips and replied, "No, you can't marry my daughter."

"I didn't ask to marry your daughter!"

"Oh, so you are asking me—wait a minute, you're that dragon fella everyone is making a fuss about, aren't you?"

Unable to restrain himself, Nath slapped his forehead. He was dealing with an eight-foot-tall elderly halfling who was nearly deaf and enfeebled. Nath's claws dug into his long locks of hair and pulled on it.

Pepper cocked his head sideways. "What are you doing? Does your flame hair burn? Must you pull it out, eh? Oh, you want to put it out. Yes. Put the fire out. I'll fetch some water."

"No!" Nath said, trying to snatch Pepper through the bars.

Pepper scurried down the hall, weaving right, then left, then right again and out of sight.

Nath banged his head on the bars.

By the time he gets where he's going, he'll forget I'm here!

CHAPTER 32

"WILL YOU PUT THAT AWAY, Dwarf? What is it, anyway?"

"Don't you worry about that," Brenwar said as he put the potion to his lips.

Selene snatched it away and resealed it. "You're being hasty. I thought your kind were better planners than that. I think it will help if you at least tell me what this is going to do."

"Gimme my potion!" Brenwar leapt up for it.

Selene, much taller, dangled it over his head.

Ha ha! Dwarves are horrible jumpers.

"I'll bring you down to my level if I have to!"

"Potions don't last so long. We might be in there for days. Maybe longer." She shook the liquid in the vial. It swirled with a twinkle. "What are you hoping to accomplish?"

"It's a changer. I've taken it before. I'll blend in down there."

Fat chance, the way you stink! Ugh!

"Oh, and what were you going to change into?"

"Human, I suppose. And how exactly were you going to blend in with that tail and those scales?"

"I can control that." She held out her arms and concentrated, turning her scales to skin and making her tail vanish under her robes. "See?"

"And how long can you keep that up?"

"Long enough. Listen, you need to trust me, and I need to go it alone."

But the little dwarf just glowered at her. "No."

Such a little child! Even if I do leave without him, he'll just follow me on his own later. And get caught. And Nath won't leave here without him...

She dropped the potion.

Brenwar snatched it in his skeleton hand.

"Have it your way," she said, "but I'll be curious to see if it conceals that."

"Don't you worry about that. I have plenty of tricks up my sleeve."

She lifted a brow. "Really, so you have more magic at your disposal? That's odd for a dwarf."

"Well, I'm no lover of magic, but on occasion it's served me well."

"Oh, you like it, do you? How exhilarating."

He does like magic! He's trying to conceal it, but there's a glimmer in his eye! Ha! He needs magic to keep up.

She filed that information away for future use.

As Brenwar put the vial to his lips, she held up her hand to halt him.

He started to draw back his fist, but she rushed to explain.

"Why don't you hold off until we hit bottom and enter the city? We'll need every second of time that potion can last. I'm certain."

"Agreed."

CHAPTER 33

SITTING IN THE BACK OF the cell, Nath watched a steady drip of murky water splatter on the floor. He'd counted five hundred and sixty two drops. Each just as annoying as the last. He focused on that water.

Splat. Splat. Splat. Splat.

Water. That was what Pepper had said he was going after hours ago. There hadn't been any sign of life in the dungeons since he left. There was only the drip of water. It wasn't just in Nath's cell either. It was all over the place. A steady, unrelenting, tormenting harmony.

Everything in his life was out of order. Everything he knew had been twisted upside down. Giant-sized orcs, lizard men, and halflings.

"Ugh, how can this be?"

Nath wanted to sleep. To wake up in a better time and place. Even Dragon Home perhaps.

The mountain home of the dragons wasn't really that bad. He just didn't fit in. The dragons didn't like him. That was supposed to have changed, which, to some degree it had, but other than Selene, he still hadn't really bonded with any of the dragons. He rubbed his nose and yawned.

Why is that?

He studied his scaly hands and long fingernails. Not so long ago he could have torn this entire dungeon apart. Not that he'd ever have been caught to begin with. In dragon form, he would have ripped those stone giants to pieces.

I have to have more power than just these clawed hands.

His stomach growled.

If only being hungry was a power! I could destroy anything!

He clutched his head.

Come on, Nath. Get it together and think. I have to have more powers. I have magic, because Selene has magic. I need to explore it. Let's see.

Twirling his finger in his hair, Nath made a mental list of things he could do.

I can grow gorgeous hair. Hah! Oh, am I not the envy of all dragons. Let's see, what else? I can yell really loud. And I can blow smoke. Yes, blow smoke. Such a terror I can become. Beware of the terrifying smoke-blowing dragon. I can complain. Be hungry. Oh, I'm useless without Fang!

He snapped his fingers.

Maybe I can summon the blade.

He closed his eyes and envisioned the magnificent blade. His stomach moaned. He slammed his fists on the ground.

Oh, this is useless! I can't even concentrate!

He stood up and eyed the metal bars that caged him in.

I can bend those. I know I can. I just have to believe that I can.

Stomach rumbling, he walked over to the bars and wrapped his fingers around the hard steel.

Clatch.

Somewhere, a door opened. Nath pressed his face against the bars.

Coming down the hall from the direction opposite where Pepper left, something rolled on squeaky wheels. It was coming straight for Nath. The loud, annoying sound would have woken up anything that slept. Wheels rattled and clanked over the cobblestone floor.

Nath's nostrils widened. His mouth watered.

Food!

Pepper the giant halfling came into full view. He was pushing a cart filled with huge amounts of food. Roast turkey. Baked hams. Hot rolls and steaming potatoes.

"Chow time," the halfling said to Nath. "You are lucky. There are no other prisoners to be fed. You can eat all of this."

Nath stretched his hand out through the bars.

Pepper slapped it. "A moment, please. Eh, put this on." He handed Nath a checkered bib that was the size of a small blanket. "Now, scoot back. Scoot. Scoot."

Staring at the food and licking his lips, Nath did as he was told. In the back of his mind he felt maybe it was a trick.

I don't care. I'm so hungry I could eat a giant's leg!

With a rattle of keys, Pepper unlocked the door and swung it open.

Nath fought the urge to make a dash for it. He was so hungry though.

Just see how this plays out.

The halfling shoved the cart inside and blocked the entrance. "Hold on. I have to bless the meal." He closed his eyes and spoke some pleasant words in Halfling and reopened them. He closed the door back into place with a loud clank. "Enjoy."

Casting all the etiquette he'd ever known aside, Nath dove in.

Chomp. Chomp. Chomp.

The meal was a far cry from elven cuisine. There wasn't much flavor, but it was sustenance. Greasy, claw-licking, stomach-filling food. He tore off a turkey leg and gnawed it down to the bone. Huge chunks of ham were stuffed in his gullet. The bread was hard as a log, but Nath didn't care. He tore it in half and devoured it.

"Eh, Flame Hair, wash that down with that jug down there. And don't choke on the bones. You eat like a giant."

Nath grabbed the clay pitcher and gave it a sniff.

Honey mead!

He guzzled it down, wiped his elbow across his mouth, and said, "Ah!"

There was enough food to feed a dozen hungry dwarves. He must have eaten half of it before he was finished. He let out a long, loud belch. "Buuuurp!"

Fanning his huge button nose, Pepper said, "Oh, my. You might not be a giant, but you act like one. Sheesh. And I thought I was going to sit down and have a nice dinner with somebody for a change. How rude."

Nath wiped his mouth and fingers on his bib, walked over to the bars, looked up at Pepper, and said, "Thank you."

Pepper cupped his ear. "What?"

"Thank you!"

"You are welcome. So, is your belly full?"

Nath patted his bulged-out stomach. "I think I have some room left, but I'm not going to push it."

"You aren't feeling sleepy, are you?"

"No, why?"

"Oh, I always like a nap after a big meal. It settles the tummy, and the dreams are pleasant as a trickling stream." Pepper reached into his big pocket and retrieved his snuff pouch. "This here is what you need. It'll open up those heavy lids of yours."

"You don't say? No, I think I'll pass." Nath glanced at the door. "So, what now? Are you fattening me up for the giants?"

The halfling took a deep snort of the tobacco and shook like a wet dog. "Woo! I like that! Er, you said something?"

"What now?" Nath yelled at him.

"Oh, I think I need to get that cart out of there." He unlocked the door, reached inside, and dragged the wooden cart out. He eyeballed the wide-open door. "Well, aren't you going to run for it?"

Nath sidestepped over to the right, preventing the door from closing. "Are you helping me escape?"

"Oh no, I'd never do that. Ho ho, never. I mean, those giants would put me on a spit and eat me alive. No, never, never say such a thing." He got behind the cart and started pushing it down the hall toward where he came from. He stopped and looked back at Nath. "Are you coming?"

Nath trotted up to the big halfling, who led the way down the halls. He glanced in every cell that he passed by. There were bones. Tusks. Bodies mummified and petrified in armor. Chains hung from walls with hands and wrists still in them. The bodies were piled-up bones. There were no signs of life in any of them.

I sure am glad I'm getting out of here.

The food cart came to a squeaky halt. Pepper stood in front of a twenty-foot-high door. The wood was ancient and grey and the iron hinges tarnished. He grabbed the handle designed for a man even taller than him and pulled it open. To Nath's surprise, the hinges were silent.

Pepper put a finger to his lips, turned toward Nath, and said, "Wait here." He slipped inside the crack in the door.

I'm not waiting.

Like a shadow, Nath fell in step behind Pepper.

The halfling turned, saw him, and jumped back. "I told you to wait!" He pointed at something behind him. "Ssssh!"

Nath froze. Three giants were in the room. Each was more than ten feet tall, and they all had swords on their belts. They sat at a huge table fit for them, but small by their standards. Food was piled as high as their chins. One was leaned back, head dropped over his shoulder, snoring. It was a three-eyed cyclops. The other two's heads were resting on their arms.

"They ate too much," Pepper said with a little grin. "Come on now."

Nath scanned the room. It was a crude office, dining room, storage room, and barn. It smelled like sweat and stale ale. There were barrels and a pen filled with livestock. A huge goat bleated. Some oversized chickens clucked. With his dragon eyes, Nath searched the walls and the tall slime-coated ceiling above him.

Pepper came back and nudged him. "What are you waiting for?"

Nath held up his moorite chains. "I can't be hindered by these."

"What?"

Nath raised his voice. "I can't—" He shook his head.

Pepper scratched his eyebrow. "You'll make too much noise in those. Hmmm, moorite. My, you must be important." His slender fingers searched the soft curly locks of his grey hair and plucked out a sliver of steel as thin as one hair. "Stand still."

Nath didn't move.

The halfling's hands were as big as Nath's own head, but the fingers moved with the ease of a fairy in flight. The lock on his collar popped off. Seconds later his arms and legs were free.

Nath cocked his head from side to side and smiled.

Pepper patted him on the shoulder. "Feel better now, I figure."

"You have no idea."

"So, do you feel like running?"

Nath shrugged. "Not really, why?"

Gazing over Nath's head at the table full of guards, Pepper said, "'Cause I don't think I put enough sleeping lard in that cyclops's muffins."

Nath twisted around. The cyclops, the brute sitting in the middle, was wide awake. Soft footfalls caught his ear. He turned back. Pepper was off and running.

CHAPTER 34

Selene and Brenwar had managed a slow trek down the canyon into the city undetected. Now, they stood in a quadrant filled with huge cattle and other oversized livestock. The animals stirred little, and not many people were around that she could see.

"Seems you found a good spot to drop into." Her nose crinkled. "I imagine it's just like your home in Morgdon."

"Hah hah." Surrounded by goats and lambs, Brenwar scooped up a handful of the dirt and rubbed it over his clothes and armor.

"This is no time for a bath, Dwarf."

"I'm covering my scent." He slapped some mud under his armpits. "And you aren't exactly looking inconspicuous either."

"I hope you don't think I'm going to mimic you."

"It would do you some good."

They were hemmed in by sheer canyon walls hundreds of feet tall. Animals were everywhere, but the people scarce. Not too far away were some barns and storehouses. They were bigger than what one would see in Nalzambor, but not exactly fit for the giants. Just big.

Selene wasn't surprised by any of it. The giants often kept throngs of people as willing servants. Those people handled the chores. Tended the herds and gardens. But the men and women had to be careful. If the giants got too hungry, they would eat them.

"Follow me," she said, making a beeline for the outer fence.

Pushing through the livestock, Brenwar followed.

"I'll be right back."

"No—" Brenwar objected, but it was too late.

Selene hopped the fence and scurried to the nearest barn and slipped inside.

A pair of long-faced country boys stood there in heavy cloaks, warming their hands over a crude stove.

She approached on soft feet.

One of them turned and faced her. "Who are you?" His eyes were filled with wonder.

"I'm new, and I was hoping I could borrow some cloaks for my family." She hugged her shoulders and shivered. "I'm not used to this mountain air."

The man stripped off his cloak. "Here, you can have mine."

"No," the other man said, removing his cloak. "Please, take mine. Much warmer than his. It's oxen wool. The best."

The first man shoved the second. "Don't listen to this pig farmer. Please, take mine."

Selene offered an enticing smile. "Oh, you men are so kind. It's such good fortune I have run into you." She grabbed both of the warm woolen cloaks. "May I bring my family in to warm by your fire?"

The second man smoothed back his hair, licked his lips, and said, "Are you spoken for, milady?"

"No, I am a lone widow traveling with my uncomely child. He's most comfortable among the animals. It puts him at ease. That's why we've ventured so far from the main city."

The first man stepped in front of the second, and with a toothy smile he said, "You'll find just as much hospitality here as you will in there. What duties will you be assigned?"

"I'll be a seamstress for the giants."

Both men scratched their heads. Finally, one spoke up and offered, "Please, bring the child in, and don't be ashamed." The man was poorly featured and built. "The child will be welcome here. I've got a daughter a bit long in the tooth as well." He winked. "She gets it from her mother. Yep, can't say what it is, but the men in my family don't marry well."

The second man shoved him. "Say, you're talking about my sister!" He drew back a fist and punched the first man in the face.

Selene spun on a heel and started walking away. "I'll be back, and when I return I'll grant a kiss to the winner."

The raw-boned country men let loose on one another.

As soon as Selene cleared the barn, she heard a gruff voice speaking from the shadows. "Uncomely child, huh?"

She tossed one of the cloaks to Brenwar and put the other one on. "I'm sorry, was that too much of an understatement?"

He covered up in the cloak and covered his head. The hem and sleeves were way too long. He grunted. "Worst disguise ever."

"Come on." Selene led the way.

As they walked, Brenwar said, "This is a big place. How do you suppose we track Nath down?"

"There's a chance that I'll catch his scent. And we can always ask. Well, I'll ask, anyway. I don't think too many people will be interested in talking to you. So for the time being, just be my uncomely mute boy and pray the giants don't get a good whiff of you."

Now dressed to blend in, the odd couple ventured forward toward the heart of the city.

Aside from the influx of people, not much had changed in Urslay. The alcove stone homes made the place look like an inverted honeycomb. People of all races and sizes worked along the streets and traversed the roadways above.

Brenwar brushed against her when an ugly giant walked by and leered at them and passed, and then the stupid little dwarf bustled in front of her with his long sleeves flapping.

She caught him by the sleeve.

He jerked away.

"What are you doing?" she hissed.

"I'm trying not to explode," he said. "In case you didn't notice, there are giants everywhere."

"I count three," she said, gazing up.

The towering men, ten to thirty feet tall, pranced throughout the city like overlords. Some carried whips, others swords and lance-sized spears.

She noticed a few more posted on the alcove terraces above. "We'd better look busy. Grab that wheelbarrow."

"You grab it." Brenwar scurried over to a stack of grain sacks and hefted one up on his shoulder. He grabbed another by the neck and tossed one after another into the wheelbarrow. He eyed the cart. "Well, put those hands to work. Push."

With a huff, Selene grabbed the handles, and with her head down she followed Brenwar. Shuffling through the streets, she said, "Where exactly do you think you're leading us? I was of the impression you'd never been here before."

"Just because I haven't been here don't mean that I don't know where I'm going." He cocked his head. "Hear that?"

Somewhere in the distance was a very loud hammering of metal striking metal. The banging was quite unique.

She nodded her head. "Yes. Iron strikes iron. So what?"

"That ain't iron, lady. That's someone trying to destroy Fang."

Chapter 35

Nath took off at a sprint after Pepper.

Halflings are fast, but giant halflings are even faster.

No longer shackled, Nath ran like a horse down the hallway before finally catching up with Pepper, who had ducked out of sight in an archway. Nath skidded to a stop. His toes hung over the edge of a bottomless pit. "Sultans of Sulfur!"

Pepper caught his arm and pulled him back. "Don't fret. It's not so bad as it looks. They say it's a hole from one side of the world to the other."

Gaping with his back pressed against the wall beside the doorway, Nath stared into the black expanse. There was nothing except a lone light more than two dozen yards away. It looked like a tiny doorway.

"I think I'll take my chances with the giant." Nath turned and found himself face to face with the cyclops stabbing at him with a sword. He sidestepped the blade's edge. "Gah! That was close."

"Oh my," Pepper said, sliding up behind the much taller cyclops. He tapped him on the shoulder. "Get away from my prisoner, one-eye!"

The cyclops grunted and unloaded a hard chop at the halfling.

Pepper skipped away and stopped with his heels on the edge of the crevice.

The cyclops spoke. "Your fun and games are over, Pepper."

The halfling cupped his ear. "What?"

The cyclops lunged.

With the ease of a dancer, Pepper back spun around the blade's edge. He fastened his hand on the cyclops's thick wrist and, using its momentum, flung him forward over the edge.

Shocked, Nath listened to the cyclops's outraged and fading scream. He studied Pepper. "Aren't you going to get into a lot of trouble?"

"Nah. I never liked that one-eye much. A big complainer, he was." Pepper dusted off his hands. "Besides, I'll just blame it all on you. Prisoner escaped, and that ugly feller died trying to catch him. Now, where to?"

"You're asking me?"

Scratching his head, Pepper said, "I see your point. Uh, where did you want to go?"

"I want to get out of Urslay, but I need to find my sword first."

"Sword, you say? What's so special about a blade? There are plenty of those around here."

"No, not like this one. This one is a friend." He recalled what Eckubahn said. "They took it to the Chamber of Contest."

Pepper made a leery face. "Ooh, you don't want to go there."

"I insist, Pepper. And you know what, you aren't having too much trouble hearing me now."

"What?"

Nath waited.

The halfling shook his head no. "I'm not helping you. I serve the giants. Yes. Yes. Serve the giants." He teetered back into the hall. "Come on, the coast is clear now. I'll show you to the Chamber of Contest, but I warn you, there are much safer paths out of here."

Nath caught him by the elbow and fixed his eyes up on the halfling's. "Pepper, why are you helping me?"

The giant halfling tried to pull away, but Nath held him fast. Finally, with a huff, Pepper said, "Everyone who knows good is obligated to do it."

In his heart, Nath knew that Pepper was good and truthful. "You couldn't be more right."

"What?"

"Just get me out of here."

With a confused look, Pepper shook his head. "Let's get you out of here."

On ginger feet, the giant halfling led him back into the stone carved corridor designed for giants as big as thirty feet tall.

They ran for minutes, and Nath marveled with every stride. There weren't many things that made Nath marvel, but this did. The world he'd known so well had become bigger and deadlier than he ever imagined. He'd taken too many things for granted. He was used to really tall trees, but he wasn't used to so many men bigger than he. It bothered him. Giants were rare, but apparently not as rare as he thought. Perhaps, long, long ago, the giants had dominated the world of Nalzambor.

"You know, we ought to be out of here by now," Nath said.

"Almost." Pepper stopped in front of a door and pushed it open. Inside was another storage room, abandoned and dusty, with a stairwell at the far end. "This will take us up into the city. Just below the Chamber of Contest that you seek. I don't recommend it though. The worst of the worst giants will be there proving themselves. It wouldn't surprise me a bit if they swallowed you whole. They eat a lot."

"I'll manage, somehow. Pepper, I have a question. Do you know where the hive of ugly dragons is, the wurmers?"

"What?"

"Dragons!"

Pepper's face turned sour. He shook his head no. "No, not taking you there. There is death."

"Tell me where, then."

"No, you just need to leave. Get your sword and go. You've caused a big enough stir already."

"Just a hint, please!"

"The eastern part of the city. There is a nest. But those things, brrr, are nasty. I'm nosey, but not that nosey. Beware. They will pick the flesh clean off of you."

Nath patted Pepper on the back. "Thanks. Every bit helps." He jogged for the stair and bounded up several steps then stopped and turned. "Aren't you coming?"

"By the giants, no. I have to round up a search party."

"A search party for what?"

"To find you." He saluted. "Got to go. Good luck, flame hair. I aim to not see you too soon. And if you make it, come back to where you came in to get out of here." He vanished through the doorway.

Where I came in? Strangest rescue ever.

While Nath was rushing up the steep flight of stone steps, an unseen force jolted him.

Bang!

Nath doubled over. His senses were jangled. Blinking, he searched all around him. It was just him inside the lonely stairwell.

What was that?

Clutching his chest, he resumed his climb and raced up the steps.

Bang!

He fell to his knees. Searching all around, he didn't see anything.

But he heard something.

It was the sound of metal hitting metal, but it wasn't any kind of metal. There was a unique sound to it. Almost like a tuning fork being struck. And the sound was echoing down the staircase from above.

For some reason Nath searched his feelings. Like a hard punch in the gut, he felt it again.

Bang!

His eyes widened. He realized what was happening.

Fang!

Chapter 36

“Drink your potion,” Selene ordered Brenwar.

“What? Why?”

She pointed at the giants coming their way.

Shirtless heavy-eyed brutes were eyeballing and harassing the line of people trying to enter the chamber where the banging was coming from.

Reluctantly, Brenwar slipped into a storage alcove filled with cut stone. He took out the vial and drank the potion down. His stomach turned. His skin and bone stretched. The blocks of stone lowered in his sight. He slumped back against the wall and shook his head.

“Are you well?” Selene asked.

Brenwar steadied himself and looked at the slender hands that hung out of his once-too-long sleeves. “I’ve been better.”

“You look much better, aside from the beard.”

He looked down at her. “I wish I could say the same for you. Let’s go.” Brenwar made his way out of the alcove and merged with the crowd of people heading down the street toward the banging sounds that echoed throughout the city. Half a head taller than Selene, he led the way with a lengthy step and swagger to his gait. He kept his chin down as he approached the giants.

One of them, a ten footer with a fuzzy red unibrow, shoved him in the shoulder. It eyed him and said with a sniff, “You smell bad.”

Head down with his fist balled up at his side, Brenwar replied, “Er, not everyone can smell as good as you.”

The giant’s head reared back, and a deep scowl formed on his ugly face. “You jest with me?”

Selene wedged herself between them. “Forgive him, master. My brother is addle-minded and not in the city much. He meant it as a compliment. He admires the giants. Pure admiration.”

“I can speak for myself,” Brenwar said.

Selene elbowed him in the chest. “Be silent.”

The giant’s hand went to a hammer at his side, started to remove it. “No, still don’t like him. I think I’ll crush him. It’s been days since I’ve crushed anybody. And he smells funny.”

“I’ll crush—*umph*!” Brenwar’s mouth was sealed by Selene’s hand.

She then said to the giant, “My, you have such marvelous shoulders. I am a seamstress, and I could fit you in a most handsome cloak. You know, a little gold-and-silver trim. I have some leftover material that I could share with you if you spare my ignorant brother.”

The giant stuck his face in hers. “I’ll crush your brother, and you’ll make it for me anyway.”

“Sure, sure,” she said, “go ahead and crush him, them. He’s nothing but trouble.” She winked at the giant. “I’ll just need to explain to Eckubahn what happened to my assistant.”

The giant swallowed and said with a stammer, “Go, go along. I will drop this matter.”

“No, please, it’s not a problem. Smash my brother. I’ll make you a cloak so fine that everyone will notice.”

“Go away!” The giant moved on down the street with the other one in tow. Neither looked back.

“My, you really want to get rid of me, don’t you?” Brenwar asked.

“It’s a risk I’m willing to take.”

“Ha ha.”

Following the throng, they finally entered through the archway that led into the massive chamber big enough for hundreds of giants.

Brenwar got his first eyeful of a ten-foot-tall orc and a nine-foot-tall goblin. He nudged Selene. "By the Sultans, what in their fiery flames is going on here?"

"Indeed, it is strange."

Brenwar knew all about the giants. There were cyclopes and ettins. Earth giants, stone giants. Those were the rare ones. Normally bigger than the rest. Then there were the others. They lived in clans. Brutish men, crude and hairy. The dwarves considered them pure bloods. The others were abominations of flesh and magic.

Now it seemed there were giant races too. Orcs, goblins, gnolls, bugbears, the biggest he'd ever seen. It didn't make sense. What could be causing this? He hated the idea of a world filled with giants. He relished the idea of killing them.

Bang!

The sound of metal on metal jolted Brenwar. He picked his way through the crowd toward the front.

Several giants stood inside a grand ring. Its flooring was a dark-red tile. In the middle was a huge anvil, bigger than a mule. Fang lay on top of it, like starlight in a night of grime. Hovering over the sword was a balding brute of a giant missing one eye. The twelve-foot pure blood held a blacksmith's hammer in two hands. Sweat dripped down his face. Packed with thick muscle, the barrel-chested monster brought the hammer down on Fang.

Bang!

The crowd cheered.

Bang!

Sparks flew. Face filling with red rage, the giant hammered away.

Bang! Bang! Bang! Bang!

Sweaty lips puffing and broad chest heaving, the giant dropped the huge hammer on the ground. Another giant, a little bigger, walked up with his arm swinging. He was chuckling under his grubby beard. With a sneer, the first giant drew back his fist and punched the second one in the face, knocking it down to the ground.

The people erupted with feverish excitement.

"I like it," Brenwar said in Selene's ear. "Let them kill each other."

As the pair of giants slugged and wrestled, a third giant took center stage. With one hand, he picked up Fang and eyeballed him.

Fang was a big sword, with a two handed pommel. He fit in the giant's huge hand like a glove.

Suddenly, the giant's pupils turned into huge pearls. His hand smoked. His skin sizzled and fried. He dropped the sword on the anvil with a clatter and let out a howling cry. He ran around holding his smoking hand, knees pumping and screaming.

The audience laughed.

Brenwar found himself caught up in it as well. There was nothing quite like watching a giant making of fool of itself. As stupid as they were, they could still be entertaining. He guffawed and guffawed and guffawed.

Over the next hour, the giants tussled back and forth in odd contests. They punched. Tugged. Head butted each other and the anvil. For the most part they beat themselves senseless and dizzy, all to the thrill of the crowd. But not a one of them could make a mark on the sword.

With a straight face, Selene said, "So glad you are amused. Need I remind you why we are here?"

"Of course not." Brenwar swiped his thumbs over his eyes. "We just need a distraction."

Someone jostled him.

Brenwar turned.

A pure bred giant stood behind him. It wasn't as stout as the one bragging and brawling front and center.

Not thinking, Brenwar blurted out, "Watch yerself, giant!"

The monster man looked down on him with an astonished look in his eye. Its nostrils flared. Muscles in its jaws clenched.

Astonished himself, Brenwar watched the angry giant get bigger and bigger. He looked up at Selene.

Her violet eyes filled with surprise. "Oh, no."

The giant screamed, "Dwarf!"

CHAPTER 37

NATH SAT AT THE TOP of the steps, clutching himself. Every hammer to Fang's steel was a blow to the gut. "Sultans of Sulfur," he muttered.

He had no idea why he had such an attachment to Fang. They'd been together for a long time, but they hadn't ever bonded like this before. It was very weird. So far as he knew, Fang still didn't obey him most of the time. The battering of metal came to an end, and he forced himself back to his feet.

A chained door made of barred metal stopped Nath on the top step.

Peering between the bars, he could see a room filled with oversized people with their backs to him. They were shouting and cheering. There were grunts and oomphs and the hard smack of fists on faces.

Sounds like the Chamber of Contest to me. How did that halfling expect me to get in there without a key?

But now that his belly was full, Nath discovered that his strength had returned. The bars and chains weren't as thick as the ones in his prison. They were aged and coated in green tarnish. He stuck his hands through the bars and grabbed the padlock on the other side. He gave it a hard tug.

Pop!

The lock and chain fell away.

"Huh, that was easy." Wary eyed, he pushed the door open and made his way into the chamber.

A well–built man staggered out of the crowd into Nath's path. His eyes filled with alarm.

With a quick punch, Nath knocked him out, and then he dragged him out into the hall, stripped off his heavy cloak, and put it on. He covered his head and ventured deeper into the chamber.

The giants inside the arena were brutes. Each was thick skinned and padded in heavy muscle. Nath shuddered at the thought of an army of them. On the humongous anvil lay Fang, like a twinkling gem.

This should be child's play. All I need is a distraction.

He closed his eyes and summoned the fire in his belly. It came surprisingly easily. He spat a small puff of smoke out of his mouth.

Ah, yes, a monumental plume of smoke should do.

He caught a pair of gap-toothed women staring at his lips. He thumped his chest with his fist, winked at them, and said, "All of this excitement gives me bad gas."

The women turned their backs, threw up their arms, and cheered with wild spirit.

Nath filled his lungs and focused on his goal.

Smoke. Snatch Fang. Vanish. Easy.

When he was ready to unleash his plan, a clamor arose from the crowd. A giant fell into the arena screaming and holding his leg. The startled crowd scrambled away and bustled one over the other to get out of the grand chamber.

The wounded giant kept saying the same thing over and over. "Dwarf!"

Two cloaked figures stood on the opposite side of the arena from Nath. One was Brenwar, the other Selene.

It can't be!

Before Nath could act, the chamber's main door dropped in place with the thunderous boom, crushing a handful of people and trapping others inside.

Nath made a quick count.

One, two, three ... fourteen giants!

"Dwarf! You got that right!" Brenwar yelled in a thunderous voice. He waved Mortuun over his head. "Come and kiss my hammer, giants!"

The entire chamber exploded into battle. The snarling giants charged with rage-filled eyes.

Selene slipped through the giants' clutches time after time. Giants fell and toppled hard. Frustration cried from their lips.

Brenwar's hammer swung and connected with bone-busting blows. The skittish dwarven fighter popped between legs, hammered feet, and broke bone after bone. But only a few suffered the wrath of Mortuun forged in Morgdon by Brenwar the dwarf.

The tide turned.

The hulking throng was overwhelming.

Within seconds, the giants—big, but still quick as men—had Brenwar and Selene in their clutches.

On instinct, Nath rushed to snatch up his sword and then stand atop the anvil.

Power surged up his arms and down his back.

He struck Fang's tip on the anvil.

Ting!

Nothing happened. Nath fully expected the sound to grow, fill the giants' ears, and drop them to their knees. He struck Fang on the anvil again.

Ting!

Nothing happened. Well, not entirely. Now, he had the attention of every last one of them, including the ones with their hands filled with the struggling forms of Selene and Brenwar.

"Is this the thanks I get for rescuing you?" Nath said to the sword. He looked at his friends. "What are you doing here?"

"Saving you!" Brenwar growled.

"Well, you're doing a fine job of it."

Kicking her feet and gasping for breath, Selene yelled, "Will you shut up and do something?"

A giant reached for Nath. He swung Fang and clipped off the tip of its finger.

The giant's bellow permeated his ears.

Still feeling a surge of power, Nath burst into action just as the giant blacksmith hammer came down and smote the anvil where he'd been standing before he leapt. Metal smote metal.

Clang!

Nath didn't hold anything back. The giants were cold-blooded killers. Any hesitation would leave him and his friends dead. He sprang at the giant who clutched Selene and chopped it through its wrists.

Selene landed like a cat and skirted away.

Ducking underneath the swing of a sword, Nath plunged Fang into the side of the giant who held Brenwar.

"RR-Rah!" the monster screamed.

"We need to get out of here!" Nath said, still chopping and hacking with intensity.

Brenwar was at his side, clubbing away.

Selene shot bright and tiny little missiles from her fingers. "There's a stairwell. Follow me there!"

"Lead the way!" Brenwar said.

To the tune of metal ringing against metal, they battled their way to the tunnel from whence Nath came.

"Great Guzan!"

The tunnel was filled with more giants. And there was a familiar face as well. Pepper.

The giant halfling was pointing at Nath. "There he is! There he is! I told you I'd find him. I told you so!"

"You rat!" Nath yelled at him.

Pepper shrugged at him. But the look in the halfling's eyes told it all. It hadn't been his choice to lead them to Nath. He was in over his head.

"What do we do now?" Selene said.

"Keep fighting!"

"Aye!" Brenwar replied.

They battled through the giants, downing one after the other, but it wasn't enough. Brenwar's iron endurance was puffing for breath. Selene's own fires had fled her fingertips.

Furious and relentless, the giants kept swinging. Their blows were taking a toll. All three friends were bruised and bleeding. Nath had no idea how he was going to get out of this. The doors were sealed. More giants filled the room from the tunnel.

Circling around the anvil, Nath said to his friends, "This is a horrible rescue."

"I told you not to give yourself up!" Brenwar replied.

"It's no one's fault," Selene added. With a whisk of her tail, she tripped a giant. "Just shut up and fight!"

They did. Nath cut one giant down only to face two others.

Where are they coming from?

Finally, after endless minutes of agonizing battle, the giants backed off.

Panting for breath and sword steady in his grip, Nath said, "What's happening?"

All of the giants took a knee and faced the gated entrance.

Eckubahn stood on the other side of the bars, his great head aflame with mystic green fire. Two ogres cranked the iron wheel that lifted the iron gate. Eckubahn stepped inside. Hundreds of wurmers flew inside with him. They covered the floor and attached themselves to the archways and rafters above.

Nath gazed up with wonder. "I hate those things." Out of nowhere he noticed Pepper was standing alongside him.

The giant halfling said, "You sure do fight a good fight."

Nath started to speak but didn't bother. He was too tired. Pepper wouldn't hear his last words anyway.

Finally, Eckubahn spoke. "Nath Dragon, you are too much trouble to keep around."

"I thought you wanted to keep me around to torment my father."

"No. I've decided I'll just send him your scales and draw out his vengeance. And what a delight it will be to have you watch me torment your friends before you go. I think we'll start with that dwarf. I see he needs more flesh taken from his bones."

Brenwar yelled at Eckubahn. "Come take it yourself, then!"

"No need for that. I'll let the giants handle it."

"Roast him like a sow, we will!" one true-blooded giant said.

Head downcast, Nath said to his friends, "I'm sorry."

"What?" Pepper replied.

A tingling sensation raced from Fang's grip up into Nath's arms. He didn't know why he did what he did and said what he said, but he tapped the tip of his blade on the anvil again and said, "Fang, get us out of here."

Ting!

The blade unleashed a gush of hidden power.

Zip!

Nath found himself standing in the middle of a flowered field with more colors than he could imagine. In an instant he knew exactly where he was. The Elven Field of Dreams. He wasn't alone either.

Brenwar and Selene were there with jaws dropped.

Filled with elation, Nath threw his sword up high in the air. "Ah-hah! Fang, you are wonderful!"

All of them burst out in sheer joyous laughter. Brenwar and Selene briefly hugged each other. Finally, with his emotions settling down, Nath noticed someone else was laughing. It was Pepper.

The giant halfling said, "Now that's my kind of rescue."

Epilogue

Sitting on his throne, Eckubahn's head had a deep-crimson afterglow. His hands clutched the stone armrests and crumbled one of them to pieces.

There was blood on his hands.

Outraged, he had slaughtered half a dozen of his own giants. Two more he had hung by the neck in the streets. That didn't include the many that Nath Dragon and his company had killed. Now, the entire city of Urslay was silent. The howling wind was the only life in the abandoned streets.

Sitting on the throne beside his, Lotuus said, "Don't fret, Milord." She toyed with a tassel made from Nath's lock of hair that she'd had mended to a wand-like stick. "We won't have any trouble finding him. Shall I give the order?"

"Yes."

Wings coming to life, the tiny woman floated down to the floor, where dozens of wurmers lay. She fanned her tassel under the lead wurmer's nose.

Its deep-purple eyes filled with a hungry radiance.

She gave it two commands. "Seek. Destroy."

BATTLE OF THE DRAGON

-Book 3-

CRAIG HALLORAN

CHAPTER 1

The Elven Field of Dreams. Nath lay face down in a pile of yellow and pink lilies, waving his arms and letting the fragrant flowers tickle his nose.

"Ah-hahahahaha!"

He rolled, hugging and kissing Fang. If there had ever been a time in his life when he had doubted his survival, it had been today. Surrounded by giants, wurmers, and the titan king Eckubahn, he'd cheated death once again.

That he was elated was an understatement. He rolled on his back and kicked his legs.

"Fang, you are amazing!"

"Tang is amazing!" said Pepper, the giant halfling. "What is Tang?"

"Fang," Nath said, sitting up and correcting the gray-headed halfling. "With an 'F'!"

Pepper cupped his hand to his ear. "Who's Jeff?"

"He said 'F' for Fang!" yelled Brenwar the dwarf, looking up at Pepper and then glancing at Nath. "Where in the world did you dig up this oversized mop top, Nath?"

Coming to his feet, Nath said, "The Urslay dungeons. He came to my aid, sort of."

With one eyebrow cocked and his nose twitching, Brenwar said, "Sure he did. Seems a bit shifty to me. Those beady eyes." His grip tightened on his war hammer's haft. "I don't like him."

Looking down at Brenwar, Pepper said, "I like you too." He wandered away, staring at all the lush greenery.

Brenwar yelled after him, "I said I didn't like you!"

"You don't like anybody," Selene added, rolling her eyes. She sauntered over to Nath and ran her thumb over a bloody scratch on his cheek. "You look terrible."

The nearness of Selene's beautiful face revealed a swollen eye and a bruise on her chin. Nath took her hand in his. "And you've never looked better. Didn't I tell you two not to come after me?"

"Yes," Selene and Brenwar said together.

"I just wanted to make sure you were each just as hardheaded as the other." Nath stuck Fang tip first in the ground and marveled. "Sultans of Sulfur! I don't know what made me do that. I didn't know he was capable of such a feat. My scales are still tingling." He turned his head.

The Elven Field of Dreams was a place of wonder and marvel. Every imaginable flower and bush of beauty was there. Lavender and sage splashed the tree line in the distance. Pink-, blue-, and white-spotted roses and knee-high daffodils spread as far as the eye could see. The fragrant aroma was intoxicating, energizing, and soothing. "I wonder why he brought us here."

"Morgdon would have been far better." Brenwar flicked Fang with his finger. "Take me to an ale house."

"Don't do that," Nath said, shielding the blade.

"Oh, pardon me." Brenwar patted the blade on the pommel. "Apparently everyone else can have a sense of humor, but I can't."

"Oh, the dwarf made a jest." Selene had bent over to pick some flowers. "How unfunny."

"You're one to talk, frostbite queen," said the dwarf.

"None of this bickering will make our wounds any better," Nath replied.

"Maybe not you, but I'm feeling better already." Brenwar rolled his burly shoulders and grimaced. "Ooh!"

Selene chuckled.

"No, but seriously, why did Fang bring us here?" Nath cocked his head. Nearby was the sound of cascading water. He pulled the great blade out of the ground and started heading in that direction.

Alongside him, Selene said, "Isn't that blade of elven craftsmanship? Perhaps that's why."

"Pah!" Brenwar scoffed.

"Perhaps the elves had a part in it, but Father was always clear that he made Fang for me himself."

"Pah!" Brenwar said again.

Nath turned around and walked backward so he could face his friends. "What are your thoughts, Brenwar?"

"Only a dwarven forge could have sired that blade. Your father used the fires of Morgdon to temper it."

"And you know that for a fact? Didn't Laedorn say he was there for its making?"

"I know what I know!" Brenwar stormed forward right by the both of them. "Now get out of my way. I'm thirsty. And if I can't get any ale, I guess I'll have to make do with this elven pond water."

The three of them approached a pond so clear you could see to the bottom. Bright fish darted back and forth underneath. There was plant life too, like mushrooms with a soft radiant glow to them. On the other side, water cascaded over rocky falls, plunging into the pond to create foaming bubbles. It didn't make any ripples.

Seeing the looks on his friends' faces, Nath turned to look. "That's odd."

Selene lifted her brows. "That's magic."

"Hi-Hoooo!" Pepper yelled from out of nowhere. He was standing on some rocks to Nath's left, gazing at the waters. He was waving his arms and only wearing his trousers. "Watcha waiting for? Get in!"

"No, Pepper, wait!" Nath cried.

Knees up and jumping high, Pepper cannonballed into the pond.

Splash!

On his knees, scooping a mouthful of water into his bearded face, Brenwar glowered. "Dirty halflings aren't good for anything. Now the entire pond is ruined."

Floating on his back and paddling with his feet, Pepper waved his hand in the air. "Get in. This water is unlike anything I've ever felt before. So exhilarating!"

Nath lifted up his foot, tried to tug his boot off, and fell down. "Perhaps I'm a little wearier than I expected." He rubbed the scales on his shoulder. He was aching all over. More so than he'd realized. With a grunt, he tugged at his boot again, but it didn't come off. "I'm going to have to cut them off."

Selene approached. "Maybe your feet grew." Her tail snaked over and coiled around Nath's ankle. She grabbed his boot by the heel and pulled it off. She did the same with the other. "You just needed a woman's touch."

"Apparently so." Nath removed his chest plate and the tunic underneath. He moved toward the water and said to Selene, "Coming?"

"Perhaps."

Nath waded in. The cool water cleansed every pore and filled his body with a tantalizing sensation. The throbbing in his sore muscles and bones subsided. Elated, he submerged himself. A school of fish swam past his eyes. They were a brilliant lime-yellow with green stripes. One of them winked at him. He gaped, choked on some water, and resurfaced, coughing and laughing. Finally, he said, "This feels great! Get in, Brenwar!"

Arms crossed over his barrel chest and sporting visible cuts on his arms and legs, the black-bearded dwarf said, "No."

Nath splashed him.

Backing away, Brenwar said, "Cut that out!"

"You really need to get in. There's nothing to fear here. It's the Elven Field of Dreams. A place of sanctuary." He eyed Selene. "Join me?"

Eyeing the surroundings and settling her gaze on an arm of the pond that jutted into a grove of trees, she picked up the hem of her robe. "I could use privacy."

Nath nodded. "As you wish."

Selene disappeared into the trees.

Nath shrugged and splashed through the waters. He swallowed a mouthful and smiled. He'd been to the Elven Field of Dreams before, long ago when he was much younger. There was no other place like it in Nalzambor. The creatures were friendly, not one bit shy. Two stags with black coats and white horns drank from the waters on a nearby bank. Blue birds with red wings skimmed the surface. A family of pink-feathered swans swam nearby. As he lay floating, all of Nath's worries faded away.

This is how life should be—for every creature in the world.

"Ho! Fighting Dragon, come and feel this!" Pepper sat beneath the small waterfall that ran over the rocks and fell into the pond. Its foaming bed now formed around him. "It makes me ticklish. I'd forgotten what it was like to be tickled. It's funny."

Nath found a spot near the giant halfling and soaked up the refreshment. He couldn't remember the last time he'd felt so good. At least, not in the form of a man. Being in dragon form was different, oh so different.

"I want to thank you for coming to my rescue," Pepper said.

"To be clear, saving you wasn't part of the plan."

"You never know what the true plan is until it plays out." Pepper rinsed his puffy face off. The giant halfling's bulk still dwarfed the gilded frame of Nath. "You can count on that."

"It seems the waters have improved your hearing, Pepper."

The halfling cupped his ear and said, "What?"

"Uh-huh."

Nath soaked up the cool waters and enjoyed the warm sunlight.

I could sit here forever.

But out of the corner of his eye, he noticed some movement cutting through the cove Selene had vanished into.

Maybe I should check on her. Just to be safe.

He scooted out from under the falls.

"Where are you going?"

"Uh, just checking things out."

Pepper pointed his huge finger toward the cove and winked. "Checking things out that way, I reckon."

Nath's throat tightened. "No, just…"

Pepper leaned behind the falls and disappeared from sight.

Shaking his head, Nath paddled toward the grove. The waters were a little mistier below the surface once he crossed beyond the jetty of trees. Neck deep, he slipped through the coolness, but he saw no sign of Selene. The pond didn't extend any farther, it just ended. Other than a distinct lack of wildlife, there weren't any signs of Selene at all. He headed for shore with his heart racing. He spun around in a full circle.

She'd better not have abandoned me again.

"Brenwar," Nath called out. "Brenwar!"

His gruff friend wasn't anywhere to be heard from. He hurried up the bank, hoping to find a sign of her tracks.

Something seized his leg and pulled him under.

He started choking.

Ulp!

CHAPTER 2

Legs bound by an unseen force, Nath was pulled deeper into the pond. Thrashing and flailing his arms, he swam for the surface to no avail. A strong arm locked around his neck and squeezed his throat. He clutched at it. Without the use of his legs, his desperate maneuvering was futile. A strong supine figure had latched onto him, pressing its body into his and with angry force, dragging him up above the waters. He gasped and choked from his constricted throat.

A familiar voice with a sharp and biting tone spoke harsh words into his ear. "What kind of Dragon are you that spies on a bathing woman? Do you not know the meaning of privacy? Discretion?" She tightened her lock on his neck. "Hmmm, Dragon Prince?"

Coughing, he forced out his words. "Sorry. I was worried."

"Worried? About the likes of me, in this place of refuge? The safest spot in all the world? Don't toy with me, Little Dragon."

"I thought you might have departed. That's all."

Her strong grip eased. "And why would I do that?" Her voice became more of a purr. "Especially after all we've been through."

Nath swallowed. The mood had changed. The taut muscles of Selene's majestic figure had softened into something else. His throat turned dry. He turned his body into hers. Her long arms no longer held him in her grip. Instead, they draped over his shoulders.

His eyes searched her face. He'd never seen Selene look like this before. Her hard features had softened. A playful smile was on her maroon lips. Her dark wet hair lay on the waters like black lily pads. The violet in her eyes sparkled. She was glowing. Happy.

His heart started pounding in his chest.

"What?" she said to him.

"Nothing, it's just that you look so … beautiful. A hundred ballads from Helflim wouldn't do your radiance justice. I'm at a loss for words."

Her tail came up out of the waters, pushed the hair from his eyes, and touched his cheek. "How flattering." She eased into him, chest to chest. "I can feel your heart, Nath. Tell me more."

Nath's hands found her waist. He'd never felt like this before in Selene's presence. He was excited and uneasy. Maybe it was the waters or the sanctuary, but she was different, in a very good yet confusing way. "Uh—"

She put her fingertip on his lips and said with dreamy eyes, "No, let me speak. Nath, I don't think I ever properly thanked you for all you've done for me. Nath, will you kiss me?"

Nath could barely remember the last time he kissed a woman of any kind, but it must have been at least thirty years, aside from Sasha kissing him on the cheek. He closed his eyes and leaned in.

Someone interrupted. "Ahem."

CHAPTER 3

Nath's eyes popped open. Selene's were still closed. Slowly, they fluttered open.

"Ahem." A voice repeated.

It was Brenwar. Nath was certain of that.

Go figure.

Wrapped up with Selene, Nath turned. "You always have to spoil every—"

Brenwar wasn't alone. He was surrounded by a host of elven soldiers clad in light but ornate black-and-green armor. Each had a tall spear. The slender-faced elves looked even taller alongside the bulk of Brenwar. They didn't wear helmets. Instead, their handsome facial features were distinguished by their long, wispy moustaches.

"See what happens when you fool around?" Brenwar said. "These lanky predators show up."

A pair of elves lowered their spears on Brenwar's ribs.

Another who was a half head taller than the others, with silvery hair, stepped forward. "You are trespassing on elven land, strangers. You taint our waters. There is a high price to pay for that."

"Get those toothpicks away from me," Brenwar growled. "Don't point things if you don't aim to use them."

"Oh, we will use them," the commander said to Brenwar, but he was looking at Nath. "On all of you."

Selene slipped out of Nath's arms. "Strange, but I think they mean it." She whispered to Nath, "Something doesn't seem right." She eyed the commander. "I hope the elves haven't lost all of their manners to the point where a woman would be deprived of the chance to clothe herself upon getting out of the water. A moment of privacy, if you please."

With the distinguished haughtiness of an elven commander, the leader said, "As soon as the red hair steps out of the waters and into our custody, you can dress yourself." He let out a whistle. Another pack of soldiers came forward, shorter. They were hard-eyed elven ladies with blue meshed into the black of their armor instead of green. "Don't let her out of your sight."

Nath sloshed out of the waters. Trousers soaked and dripping wet, he said to the commander, "You wouldn't happen to have a towel on you, would you? I'd hate to catch cold from this sudden frost."

The elven commander looked around but zeroed in on Nath's scales. "Oh, you jest. You can rely on your jokes to keep you warm, then. Bind them."

"Now, now. Hold on." Brenwar backed away. "Wait until I get ahold—"

"Do as they say," Nath ordered Brenwar, "and please, keep your thoughts to yourself. We don't want any trouble."

Brenwar looked like his beard was going to explode, but he fell silent.

The elves marched them to the other side of the pond, where Nath gathered his tunic. His breastplate was seized, along with Fang and his scabbard. Brenwar's war hammer, Mortuun, had been gathered up as well.

Nath scanned the pond and the surrounding area, but Pepper was nowhere to be found. He felt Brenwar's eyes on him. It was clear that the dwarf was at a loss too.

How does the biggest one of all of us evade the elves? Halflings never cease to surprise me.

"You know," Nath lifted his bound wrists before him, "I can't put my shirt on with my hands tied like this, and I just don't feel right strutting around half naked." He pulled his shoulders back, flung back his long, wet red hair, and smiled. "I fear I might distract the elven ladies from their duties."

The commander gave a nod to one of the guards. The wiry elven warrior rammed his spear butt into Nath's gut. It dropped him to one knee.

Nath's golden eyes burned like flames when he said to that elf, "I wouldn't ever do that again if I were you."

"Then you had better mind your comments," said the commander.

Nath took a stand. The waters had completely refreshed him, healing up his wounds, but now he had a throbbing in his gut and was surrounded by elves with bad attitudes.

Can't win for losing.

"Point taken."

"Let's go," the commander said. "Onward."

"Er, I can see by the insignia on your armor that you are a high commander, but I don't recognize your crest. Do you care to identify yourself? Or selves, rather."

"We are the guardians of the Elven Field of Dreams. Wilder elves. I am Slavan Fonjich, the leader." He stepped up alongside Nath with his hand on the pommel of his elven-crafted sword. "I'm curious how you came here undetected. No one, especially a dwarf, has crossed into the fields for a decade—and hopefully not another stubby foot ever will."

Brenwar puffed hot air out of his beard. "Nath."

Selene and the female warriors met up with them. Her playful gaze was still there. She winked at him.

"Uh," Nath stammered to Slavan, "if my memory serves, the fields have never been guarded. Anyone who could find them was welcome to them. They were the reward at the end of the long journey for those who dared to seek them. Of course, that always made me curious. Why would travelers who came here ever leave?"

"Not that many travelers make it in the first place," Slavan said, ducking under some branches. "And the fields have a way of sending one off with a renewed purpose. It's not so remarkable to the elves. We already maintain the loftiest of standards."

"Pah!" Brenwar clawed at his beard with his skeleton hand. "The problem with you elves is you think you're better than everyone. But you're not. Every good thing you ever did, you learned from us."

"It's beneath me to argue about it with your kind," Slavan said. "I'd be better served talking with hogs in pens."

"Why, that impudent, scrawny, pointy-eared jackal!" Brenwar strained at his bonds. "I'm not putting up with this, Nath, and why are we captives anyway? Pah! There's treachery afoot!"

Slavan let out a command. "Gag him!"

"What!" Brenwar said.

"Slavan," Nath said, standing a full head taller than the commander, "this treatment is below your kind, and you can't be foolish enough to believe we are enemies of the elves. We are well known among your kind. Just send word to the High Council, to Laedorn himself. He will certainly vouch for Nath Dragon and Brenwar Bolderguild."

Slavan stayed his elves with his hand, faced Nath, and looked him in the eye. "It grieves me to inform you, but Laedorn is dead."

Nath's chest felt like it was collapsing within itself. Elves could die of old age, certainly, but that would take centuries, and Laedorn was far too young for that. He could still see Laedorn, noble and friendly, an exemplary example of the proud elven heritage.

With dread, Nath asked, "What happened? Was it a battle? Please don't tell me it was the titans."

"He was murdered," Slavan said.

CHAPTER 4

"MURDERED!" BRENWAR SAID WITH ALARM. He grumbled. "Where did such a crime take place?"

"In Elohim, in the very heart of the city, right in front of everybody. His heart was pierced by an arrow, straight and true. It happened while he spoke to the people, warning them of the dangers to come, the power of the titan Eckubahn. He was telling us how Evil can turn one elf against another. To be wary. Hold fast and stick together."

Still marching through the meadow of flowers, the troupe veered down a steep hillside that led into a valley. "His words couldn't have been more true. Since his death, the elves have been divided. Without his leadership, many seem lost."

"Who killed him?" Nath said.

"No one was ever captured. The assassin escaped." Slavan motioned to one of his guardsmen, pointed deep into the ravine where the meadows merged with a dark forest, and said, "Take us in."

"What do you mean you never caught the assassin? How is that possible? There must have been thousands of elves present," Brenwar said. "I tell you what, no dwarf has ever been assassinated in Morgdon."

"What do you mean?" Ginger footed, Slavan skipped over the rocky steppes that led into the ravine. "Uurluuk was killed just the same."

"You're a liar! Uurluuk Mountainstone is not dead!" Brenwar blustered through his beard. "It's not possible! No single arrow could kill our top general."

"He died by the same means: an arrow, straight through the heart." Slavan's face was a mask of confusion. "The entire dwarven realm, much like the elves, mourned for months. All of Nalzambor knew of it."

Brenwar looked at Nath. "He's talking madness."

"Agreed," Nath said, eyeing Slavan. Everything the elf was telling him was bizarre. Out of place. Still, Nath felt deep sorrow inside his heart. Slavan's words rang true, even while none of what he was saying made any sense. If Laedorn and Uurluuk were dead, Nath certainly would have known about it. "You say the elves and dwarves mourned for months, Slavan, so how long ago did all this happen?"

"It's been all of a year and a month since Uurluuk was slain. Almost a year to the day for Laedorn," the elf replied.

The elves were leading them along a creek bed in a ravine that was thick in green foliage and shadows. It was a place where the day felt more like night. An odd still quiet prevailed. No vermin rustled over the ground they passed.

"Ever since," Slavan went on, "a host of guards has been stationed at every corner of Elven lands. It is the same for the dwarves. Everyone is on guard—including the humans and even the orcs."

"Have there been other assassinations?" Nath asked.

"No. That was the end of it, for security has become tight."

Brenwar forced his way to Nath's side and puffed under his beard, "These elves are quite mad. I've been to Morgdon since then. Crossed the dwarves. There's been no mention of any of this over the past year. It's not possible. Maybe within weeks, but months, a year? Preposterous."

"I assure you my words are true, Dwarf. I don't know what mountain you crawled out from under the past year, but you've clearly missed out on the madness that is upon us. Upon all of Nalzambor. The titans have a presence in almost every known city. They now rule from the center of Narnum."

"Narnum!" Nath gasped. "That's not possible. They barely had a presence in the world just a day ago. They hold up in Urslay of the craggy mountains. Everything you're saying is preposterous."

"Agreed!" Brenwar said.

Nath found Selene's eyes. She didn't seem alarmed. Instead, there was a cattish playfulness in her eyes. He tore his gaze away, wondering what in Nalzambor was going on. It seemed his entire world had been turned upside down. Again. "Slavan, where are you taking us?"

"I'm taking you where we have arrived," the elven commander said. He stroked the fine long hairs of his moustache with the leather gauntlet on his hand. "The Inner Sanctum of Lheme."

They stood before a wall of overhanging vines coated in white and yellow flowers. With a word—an enchanted Elven word from Slavan—the vines parted with life of their own, revealing an archway of rune-carved stone. The elves marched into the dark passageway. The lady elves went next, along with Selene. The guards behind Nath and Brenwar pushed them forward.

"I'm going!" Brenwar said. "Humph, at least it's underground. A little cold dirt will do my bones some good."

In the front, middle, and back of the ranks, elven warriors lit and carried small torches. The tunnel was nothing more than packed earth held up by wooden beams, much like the miners used. It didn't slope up or down, but had hairpin bends left and right, and it split off in many places.

They walked for an hour, then two, before winding up in a cavernous chamber. Its floor was checkered tiles in different shades of jade. The walls were sandstone, and archways that supported the roof and ceiling were made from blocks of marble. The elves with torches lit the iron lanterns that hung on the walls. The room filled with a soft glow.

"Hah!" Brenwar lifted a brow. "I should have known. This place is dwarven crafted."

"And elven crafted as well," Slavan added.

"So you say," Brenwar grumbled. "And what is the point of bringing us into these catacombs? Did you want to ask me how we built it?"

"Subdue your bickering, Brenwar." Nath pushed his now dry hair out of his eyes, briefly enjoying how clean and silky the waters had made it. "But why *are* we here, Slavan? And why are we bound? You must know we are no threat to the elves, nor to any of Nalzambor's people. What is the meaning of this?"

Slavan pointed at his chest and said with an angry voice, "Because you are a suspect, Nath Dragon!" His voice echoed.

"Suspected of what?"

"Killing Laedorn and Uurluuk!"

"Madness, I say! Impossible!" Brenwar said. "I'm a witness to that!"

"I'm my own witness," Nath replied, "and so is Selene. I haven't been anywhere close to Morgdon or Elohim. Surely you jest."

"I wish that I did, but I do not. Witnesses place you at both spots." Slavan walked over to a large, round stone pedestal that was waist high. "It happened at the four hundred and tenth Festival of Raye. That is where Laedorn addressed his kinsmen, only to be shot down in cold blood. Witnesses recall a red-haired man with scales on his arms. When they gave chase, the assassin left his weapon behind." He waved his hand over the pedestal and muttered some words. An image appeared hovering above the stone. He turned to Nath and said, "Does this look familiar?"

Nath's face turned white as ash. The image he beheld was of Akron.

CHAPTER 5

NATH GAZED AT THE EXQUISITE bow. It was of the finest craftsmanship he'd ever seen. A glorious weapon indeed. "Where is the bow now?"

"It is safely kept in Elome now." Slavan shook his head. "Such treachery, Nath Dragon. That bow was a gift to you and your father. Laedorn carved it with his own hands, and now your betrayal has slain him."

Nath felt Selene's eyes on him. There was confusion in them. Worry.

The elves who surrounded them were not vengeful people, but they would want retribution. They would need answers. Like the dwarves, they would have justice, find the murderer.

Nodding his head, Nath said to the commander, "You say it was the four hundred and tenth Festival of Raye. I'm not crazy. I know the four hundred and ninth festival has not even occurred yet. Judging by the stars in the sky, it will occur this year, and soon at that."

"You are confused, Nath Dragon. Perhaps an illness has taken your thoughts. Maybe that can be your case when you stand trial."

"Trial!" Nath said.

"Lock them up!" Slavan ordered.

"No elf is about to lock me up!" Brenwar stormed into a pair of elves, bowling them over.

Quick as serpents, the elven guard pinned him in with spear tips at his throat. "Go ahead, try and kill me!"

"Stand down, Brenwar!" Nath said. "We can't be found guilty of something we didn't do."

"You'd better hope for your sake you speak the truth." Slavan pointed to the other side of the chamber, where iron doors led deeper into the cavern. "Of course, death would be a better recourse than what the elves have in store for you if you are found guilty."

"And what about my friends? What are they being accused of? Let them go."

"Aiding and abetting, allegedly. And we can't risk someone trying to break you out. Think about it this way, Nath Dragon. You are safer with us than you are outside. The elves and dwarves have not stopped their search for you since the incidents occurred. If you cross any of those armies or militias … you will be killed." He lifted his chin. "You should thank me."

"Sure," Nath said. "Thanks. In the meantime, with me in here—who is fighting the wurmers and the titans? I'm warning you, a plague is about to happen out there."

Slavan scoffed. "That has already happened. Take them away."

The elves marched Nath, Selene, and Brenwar through the iron gates and locked each of them in their own cell. The dungeon was small, with a thick iron door and barred high portals. Cramped inside a stone cell that just had bars above his waist in the front—with a solid iron door—his head brushed against the rock ceiling. Brenwar was across the way. Selene he could not see. Nath crouched and sat down, staring at the heavy steel bars that closed him in.

Great Guzan, what's going on?

"Out of the fryer's pan and into the pyre, eh Nath?" Brenwar's voice boomed inside the small space. Their only company aside from one another was the glow of the torches they had passed when they entered. There was a rattle of bars. "We need to get out of here, you know. These elves, they are shifty ones."

Arms clasped over his knees, Nath said, "We need to get a handle on what's going on. How can anybody think I would ever kill Laedorn or Uurluuk? That's insanity. Selene. Selene? It's quiet over there. Are you all right?"

"I'll be fine so long as I am always near you, but I would be far better if you were in my cell with me," she said, not shielding the desire in her voice.

Nath's neck hairs stood on end. His scales tingled. Selene wasn't anything like her normal self. The allure in her voice was almost opposing. "Er, they didn't hit you in the head or anything, did they?"

"Quite the contrary, my love. My head only aches because I'm away from you."

It sounded like Brenwar smacked his hand into his head. The dwarf said, "What is wrong with you, Dragoness? You're all daffy in the head. Did you swallow too much of that pond water?"

But Selene's words stirred Nath. He crawled to the cell wall and reached his hands through the bars, stretching his fingers out. "Can you reach me?"

"No, no, Nath my love, I cannot."

"Will you two get ahold of yourselves?" Brenwar said through the bars that held him in. "She's one cell over, looking like a dragon about to eat a herd of lambs. I think you're in more trouble than you bargained for!"

Nath's chest tightened. In a good way. He'd never felt so bonded with Selene before. A closeness was growing within his heart like a fire spreading. He'd felt love and passion with women before, but never anything quite like this. He grasped the bars and tried to bend them. The biceps underneath his scales bulged. The cords in his forearms knotted.

Across the way, Brenwar's eyes widened. "You can do it, Nath."

The metal, thick elven steel, would not give. Nath gasped. He wiped the sweat from his brow. "Not this time, I can't." His passion for Selene eased. "We need to figure out what has happened. I'm worried. Really worried. Ben had Akron. Something might have happened to him. To Bayzog and Sasha. And the elves say they and the dwarves have been searching me out for over a year! How is that possible? Where did the time go?"

Brenwar started banging his head into the bars of his cell.

Bang. Bang. Bang.

"What in Nalzambor are you doing?" Nath asked.

"It helps me think," the old warrior replied.

Bang. Bang. Bang.

Sounding a little bit more like her normal self, Selene commented, "Perhaps your sword did it."

Nath lurched up. His golden eyes widened. The scales on his back shivered. Had Fang teleported them through time and space? "It can't be possible."

CHAPTER 6

"Anything is possible," Selene said. "And it would explain why I'm feeling how I'm feeling. I've never been so out of sorts with things. A female dragon's life cycles differently than a male's. Perhaps that's why I'm so—"

"Spare my ears from it," Brenwar barked. "I don't need to know." He pillowed up a handful of beard in front of his eyes and grunted. "Seems I have a tad more gray than what was there yesterday. By the Sultans, Nath! You managed to age us all a year in a day."

"It looks more like ten years in your case," Selene remarked.

"Great Dragons, we have been gone a year." It was Nath's turn to bang his head on the cell bars. "Why did Fang do that?"

Selene calmly said, "He saved us, remember? Assuming this is the truth, he took us all as far away from titan town as possible. I don't blame him. I doubt we would have lasted a moment longer, surrounded by all those giants and wurmers. The funny thing is, Eckubahn has probably been looking for you all this time, and finding no sign of us at all. That must have been frustrating. It's troublesome too. Just think of the power Fang must be able to unleash."

Nath clutched at his skull. "And I don't have Fang anymore! The elves do!" He staggered back, feeling all clammy inside. His greatest treasure was gone. It was unsettling. And being cooperative seemed to have only made things worse. If nothing else, he needed to secure his sword. A sinking feeling crept into his stomach. "Guards!"

Brenwar yelled too. "Guards!" And then he turned to Nath. "What are we yelling for?"

"Something about Slavan and this particular pack of elves bothers me. Does he not bother you? He was truthful in his words, but I sensed he wasn't telling it all." Nath grabbed onto the bars. "There was a shiftiness about him that made me very wary. Am I the only one who sensed it?"

"All elves bother me!" Brenwar threw up his arms. "I told you they couldn't be trusted. A dwarf, now, a dwarf you can trust. We don't lie about anything. We'd die first."

"This isn't about lies, this is about half-truths," Selene said, "And not about your blind loyalties to yourselves. You're a proud and stumpy little fool, no less corrupt than the high-and-mighty elves themselves."

"You watch your tongue. You're the last one who should talk about honesty!" Hands clutching the bars, Brenwar pulled himself up to see out and banged his head again. "Guards! Get me away from this scaly woman!"

Nath ran through his thoughts. Everything Slavan Fonjich had said rang true, but there were things Nath deduced from what the elf had avoided discussing. The elves fought among themselves. There was discord. A divide. The titans' presence filled the cities abroad, and people had flocked to them.

Hah! Eckubahn is no fool. He hasn't just been searching for me, but me and the sword. He sent the word out to every bounty hunter, cutthroat, and murderer all around, trying to manage my capture. I bet he's promised them the world.

A pit formed in Nath's gut. He hit the bars. "Guards!"

There was no response. Only the gentle flicker of the torches answered. The three of them were all alone, sealed away in the twist of the catacombs where no one would ever find them if they weren't wanted to be found.

"They'll be back. I'm sure they'll be back. No elf can do without taking a jab at a dwarf. Well, I've got some words for them. Plenty." Brenwar mumbled insults in Dwarven.

Fang had done his thing, had gotten Nath and his friends as far away as possible, but the plan had backfired. The Elven Field of Dreams should have been safe. It wasn't. The world had changed, and in his heart Nath knew Slavan and the elven guard had changed with it.

"Guards!" Brenwar said. "We need some food and fresh air! It smells like dirty elf down here."

Nath broke out his conclusion. "There aren't any guards, Brenwar. They took Fang, and they're gone."

"Gone! What about Mortuun!"

Nath closed his eyes and concentrated. He and Fang had become closer, and he didn't have to worry about the blade operating in the wrong hands. It could protect itself, but without the blade, he was almost defenseless against the giants and wurmers. That was hardly the problem now. He needed a way out of this cell.

Brenwar started ramming his shoulder into his iron door.

Wham! Wham! Wham!

"Will you stop doing that, Dwarf?" Selene said. "All you do is make noise."

"Perhaps Pepper will come for us," Nath said with a sigh.

Brenwar stopped his charge. "Pepper? He's too big to stuff his chubby behind through those holes. No chance that he will find us." He lowered his shoulder and started ramming again.

Wham! Wham! Wham!

"Selene," Nath said over the loud noise, "can you cast a spell to get us out?"

"I'll try." She muttered an incantation.

Zzzz-pap!

Pressing his face to the bars, Nath said, "Selene?" He looked at Brenwar. "Can you see her?"

"It's all smoky."

Nath bent his ear. He couldn't hear anything. A green smoke rolled by his eyes. "Selene, say something!"

"Something," she replied in a little bit of a moan.

Nath exhaled. "What happened?"

"I shot a charge into the bars, but they're too thick. Other than that, I'm all out of ideas. I'm sorry."

Squeezing the metal rods in his clawed hands, Nath said, "Yes, they are pretty thick. Perhaps..."

"Perhaps what?" Brenwar coughed and fanned the smoke from his face.

"I might be able to melt them."

"With your breath?" Selene said. "Can you do that now?"

"I can at least try. I know I've melted metal thicker than this before. But it was different then."

Not so long ago, he'd had dragon breath like a thousand infernos. He'd been a flying volcano. All-powerful. Capable of anything. Bars like this had been nothing. But he'd given all of that up. Given it up to save Selene. It was worth it, yet it still made him angry. He wanted to fly again. Have the dragon breath back.

Something stirred behind his breast. He took in a lungful of air, closed his eyes, channeled his energy, and envisioned turning the bars into liquid metal with a single huff. His lungs warmed.

Here goes!

He exhaled. Grey smoke rolled out of his mouth, filling his cell, filling the dungeon. In seconds, they all were covered in smoke so thick they couldn't see a hand in front of their face.

Everyone was coughing. Nath groaned and struck the bars. It hadn't worked. There was no way to escape, and it felt like time was running out.

CHAPTER 7

It was quiet. Stark. Lonely. The minutes were long, the hours like eons. Nath, being a dragon, wasn't bothered by the passing of time so much, except now. Now, he and his friends were trapped and left for dead. His stomach rumbled.

"Don't do that, Nath," Brenwar said from his cell. "I'm trying not to think of food. I'm a bit hungry, you know. A little parched. That battle with the giants expended my reserves."

"Sorry," Nath said, holding his stomach. Being hungry was hardly the immediate problem. He, Brenwar, and Selene could last for weeks like this, he figured. Being a dragon, chances were he'd hibernate.

Perhaps if I sleep, I'll wake up and have more dragon powers. It's happened before.

He couldn't bear the thought of anything happening to Brenwar, though. He'd have to think of something.

"Don't blame yourself, Nath." Brenwar's voice echoed in the chamber. "You need to focus. Think of a way out."

"We aren't all sitting here twiddling our thumbs, you know," Selene said with irritation in her voice. "Not that you could bring anything useful to the table."

"I can argue you to death anytime if that's the way you want to go! Have at it, then, you sorceress from the gates of the under realm!"

While Selene and Brenwar bickered back and forth, Nath closed his eyes and went into deep thought. His concern for his friends was heavy on his mind. The whereabouts of Bayzog, Ben, and Sasha worried him. And what of Sasha's condition? She wasn't well. Unstable. And then there was his father, Balzurth. Eckubahn was trying to bait the Dragon King. Draw him into a huge fight. Finish their rivalry once and for all. Without a doubt, all of them were in danger. Nath dipped his head into his hands.

And to think a year has passed! Eckubahn is the host in Narnum. People have started to worship him. So quickly? It's inconceivable.

Those were only a few of the items weighing on his mind. If he had to guess, Slavan and the rogue wilder elves had fallen in league with the enemy. Why else would they abandon him here? Would they come back and kill him and his friends? No, not even a fallen elf would have such blood on his hands. Instead, Nath and company were left to their own fate. And there was yet the major issue at hand. He'd been accused of murder! But Laedorn and Uurluuk' s assassin was still out there. The dwarves and elves were hunting for him. But who had posed as him? There was only one creature on Nalzambor whom he knew for certain could do such a thing.

Gorlee!

The changeling knew about the bow, Akron. He was familiar with Ben and Bayzog. That was whom he had to find for answers. But Gorlee had been working with his father, Balzurth. Nath rubbed his temples.

See what a fine mess this world gets into if I'm not around? Maybe I'm useful after all.

He sulked in the darkness. Selene and Brenwar's bickering subsided. Nath counted down the hours that became a day. On and off, Brenwar would sing dwarven chants.

With an axe in one hand and a hammer in the other,
Uurluuk slew the giants.
With a brown beard filled with a jaw made of iron,
Uurluuk slew the giants.
With a tankard of ale and chest plate armor,
Uurluuk slew the giants.
He slew them, he slew them, and made a mighty stew of them!
He slew them, he slew them, and it wasn't hard to chew them.
With a missing eye and a belly full of ham,
Uurluuk slew the giants.
With a host of dwarves clad in nothing but muscle,
Uurluuk slew the giants.
With the sun in his eyes and the ogres at his back,
Uurluuk slew the giants.
He slew them, he slew them, and made a mighty stew of them!
He slew them, he slew them, and it wasn't hard to chew them.

The chant went on like that for half a day. Nath had his own songs that he could sing too, but he wasn't in the mood. It wouldn't do his mood a lot of good right now anyway. Back against the wall, facing his cell door, his eyes would open and close as he caught small naps between blinks.

A child-sized head appeared in the portal, between one blink and the other.

"Huh?" Nath leaned forward. There was nothing there.

I must be seeing things.

He leaned back against the wall, eyes open. A soft scuffle caught his ear. Two childlike hands grabbed one bar, and that small head came into view. A pair of little eyes was squinting, peering into the darkness of Nath's cell.

"Pepper?"

The figure dropped from sight.

Nath rushed for the door and grabbed the bars. "Pepper!"

"What's going on?" Brenwar's face was pressed to the bars. "That halfling wouldn't fit in here. Are you seeing things?"

"I see everything," Nath said with excitement, "and I saw Pepper. He was smaller."

"You dream, perhaps."

"I don't dream, at least not like that. No, it was him. Pepper! Pepper!" Nath's nostrils flared. He could smell the halfling now. Sense his warmth. "Where are you? Reveal yourself. Selene, can you see him?"

There was no answer.

"Selene?"

"At least she's quiet," Brenwar said.

Nath sniffed. "Pepper, I know you're in here. Please, reveal yourself."

"I'm here," said a little voice. It came from right outside Nath's cell door. "But how do I know that's you in there?"

"Pepper, it is me." Nath tried to peer downward. The halfling must have been right up against his door and out of his line of sight. "I'm the one who brought you to the Field of Dreams, by my sword, no less."

Brenwar managed to pull his face up to the bars. "I see him! I see him! Get us out of here, you walking mushroom!"

Backing up, Pepper stepped into Nath's view. He was barely three feet tall, if that. Just a little man with a mop of salt-colored hair and long, fuzzy sideburns. "I can see your eyes now. It is you." He reached over to the latch on the iron door and pulled the pin out of it. "Eh, there's still a lock on it. I'll go and find the key."

"No, wait!" Nath could see the fearfulness in Pepper's eyes. There was danger out there. He didn't like the thought of Pepper going beyond the threshold. He might not see Pepper again. He couldn't risk it. "Don't go just yet."

"But you need to get out. I need you to get out so I can get out. I'm lost."

Pepper vanished from sight. Nath's jaw tightened.

Please come back. Please come back.

CHAPTER 8

"WHERE DID HE GO?" BRENWAR asked. "Stupid halfling, where did you go?"

A strange groan of the living came from deep within the caverns. Dark and disturbing.

"What was that?" Brenwar said.

"I don't want to know."

Moments later, Pepper reappeared. "I can't find a key, and we ... we need to get out of here."

"What's out there?" Nath asked.

"I don't know, but I think it wants to eat me." The halfling eyeballed the lock, rubbed his chin, and tapped his foot. "You know, I used to be a locksmith. I think I can pick this." He reached into his trousers and produced a leather satchel. Gingerly, he unfolded the flap, revealing some metal utensils. He eyed a long, sharp, slender rod with key-like teeth on the end. "That should do it."

Nath heard the tool fishing around inside the lock.

Pop.

The door swung open.

"Well done, Pepper!"

The deep moan from the tunnels started again.

"Hurry, get the others out."

"Start with me," Brenwar demanded.

As Pepper worked the lock, Nath asked questions. "Pepper, why are you so small? What happened?"

"I don't know. One moment I'm sitting in the pond, big as a boulder, and the next thing I know I'm buried underneath a bunch of lily pads. That's when those elves showed up. They had a look about them, so I hid and watched them march you off. Huh, I don't think I can pick this lock open. It's stubborn." He looked up at Brenwar's face through the bars. "Go figure. Perhaps I should try the other."

The moaning came again, louder this time.

"You will open this one now!" Brenwar said with wide eyes.

Pepper started picking at the lock again. "Be silent. You're making me nervous. Anyway, I followed those elves to this place. Saw them depart and everything. Thirteen in and thirteen out, ladies included. My, they are something pretty. I snuck in to look for you, fell in a pit, climbed out, fell in a pit again, climbed out, got lost, and somehow found myself here." The lock popped open, and he let Brenwar out. "Whew, what a relief. Come on out, Grumpy."

Nath made his way over to Selene's cell and peered inside the barred portal. "Selene. Selene." He could see her body huddled in the corner, as if she was sleeping. "Selene, wake up."

She didn't stir.

"Pick it. Pick it now, Pepper."

A howling moan tore through the tunnels.

Pepper dropped his pick and snatched it up again. "I don't like the sound of that."

"Me neither," said Nath.

Working the lock, Pepper added, "It sounds big. Really big. But the tunnels are small. Maybe it's not that big at all." He twisted his tool in the keyhole. A click followed. "Got it. Three for three, not bad for an elder rogue, er, I mean an elder halfling."

Nath flung the door open and rushed inside. Selene wasn't moving, but she was breathing. He gave her a firm shake. "Selene. Selene. Wake up."

"She must be really, really tired." Pepper put his tools away. "And she looks heavy."

Nath scooped her up in his arms and tossed her over his shoulder. "Let's get out of here. Brenwar, lead the way."

"That's the best advice you've given in months." The dwarf marched them straight through the grand chamber of the Inner Sanctum of Lheme. The gorgeous room was far from threatening. If anything, it was peaceful, and a pair of torches still flickered. He cut right through the middle of it and made a beeline straight for the archway that they came through to begin with. "This way."

From down the dark corridor, a loud moan hit Nath right in the face, jangling his nerves.

Pepper covered his ears.

Spinning on his heel, Brenwar pointed to another exit on the right side of the chamber. "That way sounds better."

With Selene over his shoulders, Nath followed the dwarf. "We don't know where that goes."

"It's got to go somewhere, and if I can't find it, by my beard, I'm not dwarven."

Nath snatched a torch off the wall and handed it to Pepper. He had plenty of faith in Brenwar. None knew their way underground better. Facing whatever guardian roamed the tunnels was a different matter entirely. Aside from his claws and his tail, they didn't have any weapons to defend themselves.

Selene was out of commission. Out in a strange way.

Ahead, Brenwar marched through every twist and turn, choosing the way at forks instantly. "This way. This way." The only time he came to a stop was at a triple fork in the corridor, and even then he only scratched the back of his head with his skeleton hand before he headed into the one in the middle. "This way."

They were moving along at a brisk pace when Pepper, looking side to side and back and forth, gave a warning. "There are pits. Be wary. You move too quickly."

"If there's a pit, I'll find it before it finds me." Brenwar argued. "Come on, then, I sense a twinge of fresh air this *gaaaaaaaah*!"

The floor opened up underneath them, and the company plummeted down. Nath hit the bottom hard, with Selene landing on him and knocking the wind from him.

Pepper lay on Brenwar's broad chest. "I *told* you about the pits. But you didn't listen. I knew it. I knew it." He glanced up. "My, this is a deep one. Really deep. I'd say fifty feet at least."

Pushing himself up onto his elbows, Brenwar replied, "More like thirty."

"Heh, look at this." Pepper held up a skeleton's head. "It matches your hand."

Nath propped Selene against the wall and stood up. The pit floor crunched beneath his toes. Bones were everywhere. The walls were sheer and high. He stuck his claws into the rough-hewn stone. "I can't jump to that ledge, but I think I can climb out. No worries. Hauling Selene out will be the difficulty."

The howl returned. It was right on them, a thunderous moaning that brought out the goosebumps on every inch of Nath's skin.

Pepper's lips peeled back in a horrified smile. He covered his ears once more.

Brenwar stood up with a grunt. "I've never heard a sound like that before. It's as awful as an elven accordion."

The death moan continued. Louder. Closer. Debris and dirt from the rafters high above rained down into the pit. The vile and horrible sound cut to the bone.

Nath balled up his fists. Whatever it was, spirit or beast, he'd fight it with everything he had left. "Pepper, get behind me."

"I already am."

CHAPTER 9

THE EAR-SPLITTING MOAN CAME AGAIN. It was right on them. Nath feared nothing, but that sound made his skin crawl and his stomach churn. Whatever it was should've woken the dead, but Selene didn't stir.

Pepper clamped onto Nath's leg with his eyes squeezed shut. "Save me, save me!"

Head tilted toward the clamor above, Brenwar picked up a thighbone and walked backward.

Two huge sets of claws appeared on the lip of the pit's edge. They dug into the stone. A frightening howl started up again, shaking the very earth, weakening Nath in the knees. He set his jaw and prepared himself for an epic battle against the monster that waited above.

The horrifying sound came to a stop. Over the ledge, a head on a long neck revealed itself. It had four long horns stretching along its neck. A beard of skin and scales started underneath the monster's jowls and ran down its neck. It cocked its head and looked at Nath with bright-green eyes, opened its mouth, and said, "Urp?"

The pounding in Nath's chest slowed. He said in Dragonese, "Hello, thunder beard."

The dragon's tongue flicked out of his mouth. His head was small, compared to his claws. He hissed at Nath, lowered his head into the pit, and said again, "Urp?"

"Come, come down," Nath said in Dragonese. "Come, friend, please."

The dragon shook himself, flapping his beard.

"What *is* that thing?" asked Brenwar.

"A dragon. A thunder beard. They make excellent guardians. Not too big or violent, but their roar can scare a hundred bull dragons away." Nath extended his clawed hand upward. "Come, come down, little brother."

The dragon slithered over the edge and stuck to the wall of the pit like a great lizard. His body was long and lean, his feet very big and awkward. He had no wings, but a very long tail. His scales were green and blue with some pink mixed in. He climbed down the wall and crept by Brenwar, flicking his tongue at the dwarf.

Nath kneeled down and petted the dragon's head. "You had us terrified, little brother."

The small dragon batted his snake eyes. "Urp."

Stretching his small hand out, Pepper said, "Will he bite?"

"No, not now at least. We're in good company. As a matter of fact," Nath said, picking Pepper up, "I think you're just small enough to ride him, if he'll let you."

"Hey, wait," Pepper objected, "I'm too old to start riding dragons!"

"Just hang on to his horns," Nath said, "and have a go at it."

Pepper clenched his teeth and hung onto the horns of the dragon. The beast lurched forward and then, smooth as spider silk, it raced up the pit wall and vanished.

"Harrumph," Brenwar said. "You don't see *that* every day, but the rest of us are still stuck in here."

"I'll be back. Just keep an eye on Selene." Nath dug his claws into the stone wall and made his ascent.

"It's not like she's going anywhere. Just make it fast. I don't want to be stuck down here when she wakes up."

Nath pushed up over the lip of the pit and found Pepper still on the back of the dragon. The old halfling had a smile on his face. "Aw, you like it, don't you?"

"As long as it keeps its mouth shut, I think I could get used to it."

Nath started to yell down into the pit just as Brenwar flung the torch up. Smiling, he called down to his oldest friend, "You read my mind." He found another torch in the tunnel and lit it along with a couple more. "We need some rope, or a ladder or something."

"Do you think he can help?" Pepper said of the bearded dragon.

"Perhaps." Nath spoke in Dragonese some more, asking the dragon where the materials he could use might be. The dragon made a rattle in his throat and took off with Pepper.

"Eeee! Where is he taking me?"

Nath didn't answer, just watched Pepper's torchlight disappear around the bend. And then he dropped one of his torches down into the pit. "Heads up."

Brenwar snatched it out of the air. "What do you want me to do with this?"

"Stay cozy."

"Pah."

It was more than an hour before Pepper and the dragon returned. The halfling held a coil of rope—and Nath noticed a shiny new ring on his hand. He took the rope from Pepper. "Where did you get that?"

Pepper covered his ring with his free hand. "The rope?"

"No, the ring."

Cupping his ear, Pepper said, "Huh?"

Lowering one end of the rope into the pit, Nath said a little louder, "I said where did you get the *ring*?"

"Pardon?" Pepper said.

From down inside the hole, Brenwar yelled, "What ring are you talking about?"

"I'm not talking to you," Nath said down to Brenwar. "I'm talking to Pepper."

"Oh."

Holding the rope tight in one hand, Nath grabbed Pepper's ring hand with the other. "Where did that come from?"

"Oh, *that* ring. Well, the dragon led me to the most marvelous place… Actually, it's not anything you should worry yourself about, but that's where the rope came from. We really need to get out of here." Pepper rubbed his narrow shoulders. "It's chilly."

Nath noticed a bulging leather pouch tied to the back of Pepper's trousers. He snatched it.

Pepper objected. "Hey!"

Nath emptied the pouch on the ground. Gold coins and gemstones spilled out. "Did this dragon take you to its trove?"

Pepper scooped up the treasure and shrugged.

Brenwar emerged from the pit, sniffing the air. "I smell gold."

Nath looked down at his friend. "Aren't you forgetting something?"

"No."

"Selene. You were supposed to tether up Selene."

Brenwar leaned over the hole. "I didn't see the point in it. I say leave her here. Let her sleep."

"Guzan!" Nath stuffed the rope into Brenwar's hands, glared at him, and hopped into the pit. He loaded Selene over his shoulder, and hand over hand, he climbed back out of the pit. When he got to the top, he said to Brenwar, "You really should know better by now."

Brenwar grumbled and turned away.

Nath then said to Pepper, "Were there any weapons where you went?"

Looking up and seeming to see far away, Pepper said, "Yes, I believe so."

"Good, because we're going to need them."

CHAPTER 10

The small bearded dragon led them to a cave full of supplies. Everything from weapons and armor to dried rations and kegs of wine. Brenwar sat on a bench at a table, helping himself to some jerky and remarking at the horrible taste of the elven wine as he guzzled one goblet after the other.

"We are most fortunate," Nath said, strapping on a belt and scabbard. He had an elven longsword in his hand. He cut the air. It was well balanced. Finely crafted. He tried to find some clothing in some chests, but everything was too small for him. He grabbed an oblong shield. "Why not?"

Finishing his food, Brenwar came across some dwarven arms. He hefted a battle-axe with a handle carved from black wood. "Not bad."

Nearby, standing atop a table, Pepper managed to make a fitting shirt from an elven jerkin. He cut the sleeves down and stitched up the neck. Spinning on the table, he said, "How do I look?"

"Old and stupid," Brenwar said.

Pepper shook his head. "It's a good thing I don't understand Dwarven."

"I didn't say it in Dwarven." Brenwar turned to Nath. "Now what?"

"I'd be lying if I didn't admit I was a tad fearful of what we might face out there. One year gone, and now it sounds like the entire world hunts me again." Nath sighed. "We need to get our weapons back. But even more, we need to clear my name."

"The dwarves won't stop until they find you. That's for sure." Brenwar rubbed his beard. "And I don't think those rogue elves are angling to turn you in, either. No, they have something else up their sleeves."

"I'm of the impression they're trying to appease the titans." Nath pushed the hair out of the pretty closed eyes of Selene, who was lying on a bear rug on the floor. "I do wish you would wake up. I could use some of those thoughts of yours."

"I know you don't like it, but she might be safest here. She'll just slow us down." Brenwar swung his axe around his head. "Let your dragon friend keep an eye on her."

"That's what you did for me, isn't it?" Nath was referring to what had happened to him. He had slept more than twenty-five years—the longest slumber of his life, but not the only long one. What if this was a long sleep for Selene? He placed his hand on her cheek. The skin was smooth and warm. It stirred him. "I just can't do that. Not here anyway. Perhaps somewhere else."

"The Mountain of Doom, perhaps?"

"They'll be watching, that much is for sure." Nath picked Selene back up and placed her over his shoulder. "Let's get out of here."

"Where are we going?"

Nath had to make a decision. It wasn't easy. He was worried about his friends Ben and Bayzog. His father, Balzurth. But the other mystery bothered him most in the moment. It fluttered in his guts. Slavan and the rogue elves. They'd taken his sword, and wherever they had gone with Fang, that was where he would find answers. "We're going after the weapons."

Brenwar slapped his hands together. "That's what I like to hear. They're no more than a day off. We can catch them."

"Only if they don't catch us first. And remember, we're deep in elven territory. I'm sure we'll be noticed if we're not careful."

Brenwar dug some traveling cloaks out of a chest.

"I don't think that's going to work," Pepper said. "They're too small for him."

Brenwar tossed one to Nath. "Just try it on."

Nath slipped it on. The elves were skinny, so it was snug, but it fit. He wrapped Selene in one against the cold and put her gently back over his shoulders. "Let's give it a go, shall we?"

Getting out of the Inner Sanctum didn't prove to be too difficult, and to Nath's surprise, the bearded dragon agreed to come with them. Pepper never even left his back. Before long, they found the trail of Slavan and the rogue elves. It led them right out of the Elven Field of Dreams.

That's where the trouble started. Less than a league west of the fields and having avoided any scouting eyes, the rogue elves' trail took a new form.

"That's just great," Brenwar said. He was kneeling down with his hand in the impression of a hoof print. "They took up on horseback."

It was another one of those times that Nath regretted giving up the ability to fly. But not really. Saving Selene had been worth it.

No, that would make things all too easy.

Standing among the small bushes that popped up like mushrooms in the rolling greenery of the elven lands, he scanned the horizon. It shouldn't be too hard to follow them. So he walked. They all trotted all day long and through the night with no sleep, until the next morning. They were still a day's journey from escaping the territory of the vigilante eyes of the elves. Cutting through the tall grasses, they kept their distance from the villages and farmlands. Though peaceful, the elves didn't take in strangers. It was uncommon for anyone without elven blood to pass through without elven company.

"I can't wait to get out of this place," Brenwar said, looking from side to side. "Every step is dreaded. I feel like an elf is about to pop out of the grasses at any moment."

"Agreed," Nath said, but he was confident that his keen sight and hearing would pick up any sign of trouble. He'd noticed very little so far. "Huh."

"Huh, what?" Brenwar asked.

Ahead a few hundred yards was a stretch of farmland. The cornfields should have had a golden hue among the green this time of harvest, but what Nath spied was dingy and gray. He headed in that direction. The closer they got, the more the fields were in decay, and the rot continued as far as the eye could see. The aqueducts that watered the fields were dried up as well. The storehouses and sheds were disheveled and in disorder.

A morbid feeling crept between Nath's shoulders. "It's no wonder we haven't seen any elves about. Their lands have been poisoned. They've fortified closer to Elome, if not within. This is dreadful."

Brenwar picked up a husk of corn and chucked it away. "I hate to admit the same, but I agree." He raised his battle-axe with a white-knuckled grip on the haft. "Do you hear that?"

"I hate to admit that I do," Nath said. He could feel the ground moving under his feet.

Pepper stood on the back of the bearded dragon, cupping his ear. "Hear what?"

"Hooves. Dozens of them, but I don't see anything coming," Nath said. "I can only feel … oh." Coming from the north, a cloud of dust stirred up like a storm. A row of horsemen came, the likes of which Nath had never seen before. He uttered a command. "Hide!"

CHAPTER 11

NATH AND COMPANY DUCKED INTO a storage shed. Through the cracks between the planks of wood, he watched the horde that thundered their way. It was massive men on massive beasts. Orcs by the looks of them, on horse-like creatures the size of two stallions with curved tusks on the sides of their heads.

"Barnum's beard! Those orcs only have one eye!" Brenwar exclaimed. "And I've never seen horses like that before. I guess you'd have to be awfully ugly to allow an orc to ride on you."

The knot of brutes approached at rapid speed, over a dozen in all. The orcen cyclopes were powerfully built and ugly, carrying lances and spears. Armored from head to toe in heavy gear and approaching the fields Nath and his friends hid within, they slowed to a trot less than one hundred yards away.

"What are orcs doing on elven land?" Nath said. "One eyed or not, they should be cut down."

"Aye. Those hounds would normally be cut down if they came so far as an inch over the borders," Brenwar said, clawing at his beard.

"It explains why we haven't seen any elves this far out, I guess."

"What do we do?" Pepper asked. "I'm not much of a fighter, but I'm a good hider."

"If we get into a scrap, you ride on that thunder beard and get out of here, Pepper," Nath said. "That dragon can't fly, but he's fast. Really fast. Just be sure to hang on tight."

"I wouldn't feel right, leaving you fellas behind."

Nath patted the old halfling's shoulder. "Don't worry about it. I'm sure you have a family or village you should seek out."

"No," Pepper replied. "I'm a loner. Have been a long, long time."

"Well, you aren't anymore, so worst case scenario, run and get help."

Pepper objected, "But—"

With his eye to a hole in the wall, Brenwar hissed, "Keep it down. They're upon us."

The horse-like beasts' heads were down to the ground, sniffing the earth like hound dogs. A rattle of metal sounded from the weapons harnessed to their large saddles. The orc cyclopes, burly and battered, towered in the saddle. They studied the land before them with hard beady eyes. They were hunters. Killers. One looked as dangerous as the other.

"Oh my," Pepper said in a hushed voice. He was trembling. "They seem much more intimidating now that I'm so much smaller."

"Be silent. It doesn't matter how big they are—they're orcs," Brenwar reminded them. "I'll take every last one of them if I have to. You'll see."

"Now's not the time to be stirred up." Nath's hand fell on his sword. "Lie low. Pray they don't notice us."

It couldn't have been a worse situation. There wasn't anywhere to run or hide. They only had the cover of the old storehouses and barns, and that was little. No, they were surrounded by endless farmlands and meadows without a better place to hide in sight. No river or stream to hide their trail. No mountains to lose the cyclopes in.

Nath was more than ready to fight. And even carrying Selene, he and Pepper and the bearded dragon could run. They would be fleet enough. But not Brenwar. The dwarf couldn't outrun a one-legged elf on his best day. And Nath feared Brenwar's loud protests if he offered to carry the dwarf or suggested he ride with Pepper on the bearded dragon.

Eyes on Nath, Brenwar said, "Take her and go. I can handle them."

"No, whatever happens, you and I stay together." Nath extended his hand. "To the end."

Brenwar clasped his hand. "Aye, I like it."

One of the beasts snorted. The monster mounts were right next to the shed they were in. Nath's heart raced. Once again, he was small among a new world of bigger men. He didn't like it, but sometimes the small can be overlooked.

Breathless, Nath watched the heavy-hooved beasts stomp toward them. One shook itself and let out an awful nicker.

"HrAAAAA huh huh huh huh huh."

"Grah! Grah!" the orcen cyclops rider said, tugging at the reins. The troupe of ghastly riders was only a few steps away. Alongside the shack, the rider brought its mount to a stop. It sniffed the air. "I smell. I smell foulness in the air."

Looking at Pepper, Nath put his finger to his lips.

The halfling nodded.

The cyclops poked the shack with its lance. *Tap! Tap! Tap!* It grunted. Its beast snorted. It pulled the lance up. "Onward."

The orcen cyclopes were moving on. Ten yards away. Twenty. The tightness in Nath's chest started to ease. He smiled at Brenwar.

"Hold!" the huge orc suddenly yelled. It snorted the air again with big, wide nostrils. Its horse did the same. It turned its mount back toward the shed. "I smell. I smell a dwarf in there! My nose does not fail me! Surround it! Dwarf, I say, come out!"

Gripping his axe in two hands, Brenwar said under his beard, "I'll come out, gladly."

"Just a moment," Nath said, pulling Brenwar back. He looked at Selene. "We can't just dive into this. Pepper, don't hesitate to run. Just go. We'll offer you a distraction for getting away. And don't look back either."

"I'm no coward," Pepper said.

"Dwarf! I smell you! Come out! Your bearded face will adorn my lance!" yelled the giant one-eyed orc.

Shrugging, Pepper added, "Well, not a full-blooded coward, that is."

"You stay here, both of you," Nath said, getting up. "Perhaps I can talk us out of this."

"Are you mad? Why don't you just let me cut off your head and throw it to them?" Brenwar said.

"Because that would defeat the purpose of me talking to them." Nath plucked away Pepper's purse. Hands and head concealed within his cloak, Nath stepped out into view. The entire shack was surrounded by the extra huge orcs on their enormous beasts.

I must look like a child to them.

"We are weary travelers, just passing through. We don't want any trouble."

The cyclops with its face adorned with small chains and a bone through its nose said, "Your travels are at an end."

"I plead for mercy. We are of no consequence. Just migrating from one safe hovel to another." He held out the purse. "I can pay for safe passage."

The orc leaned forward in his saddle. "I smell a dwarf. I hate dwarves."

"I can't say I blame you," Nath agreed. "They are irritating people, but he is our guide in these treacherous times."

"Send him out, and we shall relieve you of him and your gold. Then, I shall consider whether or not I let you live."

Under his cloak, Nath sneered. He hated the orcs as much as Brenwar did.

Stupid. Arrogant. Smelly and difficult. There was nothing noble about a single one of them. Despite the one eye, these weren't different than the average orc in demeanor, just bigger and more amplified. They were eight feet tall, solid in build, and hardened by raids and battle. Their strange beasts were something different altogether—flat headed, hard skulled, and deadly. A single one of them could trample an entire halfling village.

Nath shook his head no. "Take the gold. I offer you no more and no less."

The orc's canine teeth jutted up from its bottom jaw in a cruel smile. "I'm going to enjoy this." It barked an order to the other orcs. "File in. We're gonna run these trespassers through!"

CHAPTER 12

"Aw, fine then!" Brenwar emerged from the shack. "You want to fight me? I'll fight every last one of you spangbockers!"

The orcen cyclopes turned and rode away a little ways on pounding hooves. One hundred paces away, they turned and paused. The wind pushed down the high grasses, and their black-and-silver streaked flag waved like a banner of death.

Brenwar set his feet.

Nath took his hood down and drew his elven sword. "Guard the shack."

"To the death," Brenwar replied.

Nath had been in plenty of scrapes with orcs before, but this was different. He didn't have Fang, nor most of his powers. The orcs had been more manageable back then. Nath had been quicker, smarter, and able to outwit them most of the time. But this battle? It was going to be brute force against brute force. He didn't have any more dragon fire or extra scales to save him. And to top it off, these giant one-eyed versions were an abomination.

Raising his lance high, the orcen cyclops leader bellowed a command. The entire row of riders lowered their spears and lances. All at once, they charged.

The ground quaked. The boards of the shack rattled. Nath braced himself for the oncoming wave of terror. Fifty horse lengths. Forty horse lengths. Thirty lengths. Twenty.

"Nobody tramples a dwarf!" Brenwar yelled.

Pepper squeezed between Nath and Brenwar on the back of the thunder beard.

"I told you to run, Pepper. Run! Get out of here!" Nath said.

"It's not me, it's him," Pepper said.

The thunder beard eased in front of all of them, coiled back his head, and opened his jaws wide. He let out a ground-shaking roar that filled the valley.

"RRRRRRRAAWWRRRRRRRRR!"

The demonic horses reared up. Some halted dead in their tracks. Others skidded. The giant one-eyed orc riders were tossed and toppled. Several of the strange horses bolted, dragging their riders by the stirrups. The terrifying squad of blood-mad soldiers had been turned to chaos.

Sword high, Nath charged and cried out, "Dragon! Dragon!"

"For Morgdon!"

It's me against them! There's no other way!

He had to strike, and strike fast. Nath swatted a jabbing spear aside and ran a giant orc through. Other cyclopes were scrambling for their gear. Using what quickness he still had in him, Nath attacked. He caught one orc in the backside and sent it howling. Another he stuck in the chest.

Wham!

Something heavy clobbered Nath in the back. Shooting stars blinded his sight. A boot stomping in the ground caught his ear. The sound of a heavy weapon descending on him urged his desperate movement. He rolled to the left, evading the huge hammer that bit into the ground. He hopped to his feet and swung. Metal bit into metal, and a monstrous voice wailed. A giant orc fell. Regaining his sight, Nath waded into an angry knot of fighters that had surrounded Brenwar.

The husky dwarf was bleeding and yelling, "Come, you smelly two-legged trees!"

Nath propelled himself into the back of one giant orc and stabbed the arm of another. The orcs fought back with fury. Obstinate and angry, they were born fighters. Even if they were overly matched, they'd fight to the end, most of the time. That wasn't the case this day. Big and strong, they had numbers. The clash of steel on steel and flesh and bone shifted back and forth.

Back to back, Nath and Brenwar kept the horde at bay.

Clang! Bash! Glitch! Slice!

Nath and Brenwar were holding up just fine, out-quickening the lesser-skilled orcen fighters. Together, they had just brought one down with a pair of heavy chops when a pair of riders burst through their own ranks and plowed right over the both of them.

Flat on his back, Nath fought to rise again. One of the demon beasts pinned him down with its hooves. The orcen cyclops leader lorded over him with a crude sword in one hand and Selene's limp form hanging by the hair in the other.

The cyclops orc rumbled a wicked laugh. "Scales, scales, scales. Tsk, tsk, I know someone who will give a kingdom for the people that walk with scales. The question is, are you worth more dead, or alive?" He kicked Nath's elven sword away, pulled down his hood, and rolled up his sleeve. "My, my, it's the one and only Nath Dragon. Har! The titans will be pleased!" He slugged Nath in the jaw. "Very pleased."

CHAPTER 13

ATH AND BRENWAR WERE BOUND up with chains and marched toward the orcen city of Thraag. Selene was still in her deep sleep, slung over one of the demon horses' saddle. Pepper and the thunder beard were gone. Long gone, Nath hoped.

At least he was finally smart enough to listen.

"Orc," Nath said to the leader, "what do you call your beasts? And yourself. I like to have some familiarity with my captors. The rapport can be soothing on both sides."

Jaw jutted out, the orc glanced back at Nath. "I am Gaak. One of the nuurg. The steeds are wrathhorns. We orcs now breed them."

Brenwar stared up into the cyclops orc's one eye. "Breed with them, is more like it."

"Go ahead and delight, dwarf. We'll see how much you have to say after we shave your beard and make you eat it."

"What's a nuurg?" Nath asked.

"We are the nuurg. The new giants. The usurpers of lands. Servants of the great titans." The huge one-eyed orc spat. "Conquerors we are. Invincible."

"No one is invincible. You've certainly heard of Gorn Grattack and the Clerics of Barnabus?" Nath inquired. "He was quite mighty, I assure you."

The orc growled in his throat. "Not mighty enough to win. The titans will never lose. They will defeat Balzurth. We will inherit all the treasure in the Mountain of Doom. You'll see soon enough."

"I'll never understand why orcs are so overconfident," Brenwar whispered to Nath. "They've never won a major battle in all my centuries."

It was true. The orcs, though many, fought among themselves as much as with the various races. They had never been fully united. But Nath knew that strong leadership could change all that. It had just been a long, long time since they had any. Under the guidance of the titans, the orcs could be galvanized and turned into a great weapon of destruction.

It started to rain. The dirt road became sloppy, and before long they were trudging through the mud into a land where the trees had more bark than leaves. The orcen land that surrounded Thraag was mostly briars and stone. The brush was thick, and hungry vermin cawed and hissed as they passed by. Nath wasn't so much worried about himself as he was his friend. Brenwar would be killed. He was certain of it. And it wouldn't be quick. The orcs would torment and humiliate him. *I can't think of a much worse scenario than this. I have to find a way to save Brenwar and Selene.*

Tethered to the wrathhorns, their march was hard. Yanked by one of the beasts, Brenwar stumbled and was dragged. With a face filled with mud, he climbed up on his feet again and jerked back. It was futile to fight against the pull of the powerful beasts. They were thrice as strong and just as ugly as the orcs that rode on their backs.

Nath had a natural affection for all living creatures, but the wrathhorns were something else entirely. An evil breed. Bone-crushing war rides. There were bloodstains on their tremendous spiked hooves. He made a count. There were just eight riders left, but it wasn't likely he could take them all while tethered like this. Not and protect his friends too. The only option was to find a narrow break in the terrain where the huge mounts and orcs couldn't go—and hide. The problem was Selene.

How am I going to get her?

Selene's body was draped over the front of the leader's saddle.

Don't lose hope, Nath. Just think of something.

Doubt crept into his mind, and the pounding rain seemed to weaken his limbs. He didn't have the power he'd had before. In the form of a dragon, he could level mountains, cities. Now, he felt like an insect. He still hadn't adjusted to it. He thought he had, but had not. When he was young, there had been giants running around everywhere, but life had been more manageable. Now, it had all changed. He was the little fish in the big pond. He ground his teeth.

This stinks.

The nuurg leader raised his hand up and came to a stop. "Ho." He eyed the sky and all around.

"Problem?" Nath said, walking up alongside the giant orc leader's saddle.

Rain running down his furrowed brow, the nuurg leader said, "Something stinks."

"Yes," Nath said, looking at him and his dirt-marred skin, "I'd think you'd be used to that by now. These rains present an excellent opportunity to wash yourself."

The orc cyclops leered at him. "Quiet." He pointed at two of his followers. "Ride up. I sense an ambush near."

The riders on the wrathhorns thundered by Nath, splashing him with mud and bumping him down to one knee.

It was Nath's turn to look around. With all the heavy rain it was difficult to see anything, but nothing seemed out of the ordinary. It was strange. Why would the orc cyclopes be worried about an ambush on their own land?

It doesn't make any sense. Perhaps even these monsters are divided against one another. Interesting.

Minutes passed.

"So are we going to stand here all day?" Brenwar said.

"You're safer here than where we're going," Nath said, wiping the rain from his eyes. "And it's not like you to be in a hurry."

"Hanging around you makes me rush things." Brenwar looked at the huge cyclopes on the backs of the beasts and shook his head. "It's not right."

A few minutes later, one of the riders reappeared and said to the leader, "It's clear. Holorf still scouts ahead. He'll await us at the next fortress. Send up fire if there is trouble."

The leader, Gaak, nodded. "Let's go, then. We have great treasure. Ale and females shall meet us at the gates!" He snapped his reins. The beast lurched forward. Gaak slung forth his hand. "Howhaho!"

"Well," Nath said to Brenwar, "at least you're going to get a closer look at a city you've never seen before. They say it's not half bad once you get used to the smell."

Brenwar shook his head no.

Out of nowhere, an arrow rocketed through the rain and impaled Gaak's sleeve.

He roared and cried out, "Ambush! Ride hard for the city!"

Nath ran apace.

Brenwar was jerked off his feet and dragged by the wrathhorns. With a mouthful of mud, he yelled, "No one drags a dwarf!"

Arrows whistled through the air.

Zing! Zing! Zing! Zing!

A cyclops toppled from his mount with an arrow in his side. An arrow struck another rider in the skull, but that nuurg fighter kept riding.

Still tethered, Nath kept running.

It was a crossfire. Beasts and riders went down. Three arrows feathered an orc in the chest. Another arrow struck a beast in the hide of its hindquarters, rearing it up and toppling its rider.

Nath hopped on the chest of a cyclops that was being dragged by one of its feet, which was caught in the stirrup. He found his elven sword harnessed to the beast's saddle, drew it out, and cut his bonds, yelling, "Brenwar! Brenwar!"

Being dragged behind a wrathhorn, the dwarf managed to sit up. "What?"

Nath flung the sword end over end. It sliced through the taut rope that secured Brenwar.

The dwarf diminished in the distance but was up and running after him.

Nath hauled himself up into the beast's saddle and took the reins. With the beast still dragging the dead cyclops, he dug his heel into the mount's ribs. "Yah! Yah!"

The wrathhorn reared up, clawed the air with its hooves, landed back on its front hooves, and stopped. Its head swung around and bit into Nath's arm.

"Sultans of Sulfur!" Nath cried out. Ahead, Gaak and the surviving riders were getting away in long, fast strides. "Release me, beast! I have to get Selene."

A heavy fog rolled in. Selene and the riders were gone.

CHAPTER 14

THE WRATHHORN BUCKED, TURNED ITS head, and slung Nath out of the saddle by the arm with its teeth. Wrist deep in the mud, Nath got up. The beast lowered its head with the curved horns out and charged. Spiked hooves splatted through the mud and water and bore down on Nath.

At the last moment, Nath jumped high, sailing over its head.

The wrathhorn kept going, making a startling whine and not looking back.

Puffing for breath, Brenwar caught up with Nath. "There goes your ride."

Nath scoffed. "They still have Selene. You stay here. I'm going after them on foot." He started to run. A huge winged creature dropped out of the sky and onto the road, cutting off his path. "Sansla Libor!" Nath said.

Half a dozen roamer elves emerged from the rough woodland and encircled them. They were tall and hardy, long haired, with swords strapped beneath their round bellies. The tallest of them all was Shum, and his brother Hoven was there too. Their piercing eyes bore into Nath and Brenwar. "Hail and well met, old friend."

"Hail nothing, Shum," Nath said. "I don't have time for chatter. The nuurg have Selene! I must rescue her."

Shum and Hoven blocked his path. Hoven spoke. "You must come with us immediately."

Nath busted right between them.

Head to toe in mud, Brenwar was right on his heels. "Out of the way, elven bellies!"

Nath found himself face to face with the great white winged ape, Sansla Libor the King of the Roamers. The cursed elf was as big as ever, layered with bulging muscles under his fur. His chest was broader than those of three strong men. His eyes were sky blue, but with a savageness behind them. He held out his oversized hands, and towering over Nath, he said, "Stop, Nath Dragon."

Not hiding the urgency brewing within him, Nath said, "I'll do no such thing. Now get out of my way."

"Aye!" Brenwar agreed.

"I cannot. You must come now."

"No, I must *go* now." Nath got a run and jumped over the great ape.

Sansla, quick as a big cat, sprang into the air and dragged Nath down by the ankles.

Floundering in the mud, Nath kicked the gorilla-like beast in the chest. Sansla slammed him to the ground. Nath flipped Sansla off his back, drew back his scaled fist, and hit Sansla square in the face.

A savage snarl erupted from Sansla's black lips. He attacked Nath with savage fury. Fists the size of hams hammered into his body with bone-jarring ferocity.

Nath's temper ignited. He'd been holding back—against the rogue elves, the nuurg, and the wrathhorns. Selene was being taken. He'd hold back no more. He cocked back his fist and hit Sansla as hard as he could.

"Oof!" The mighty ape doubled over, clutching his belly.

Nath whaled on him, blow after blow after blow. "Stay out of my way!"

Sansla balled up and covered his face with his fists. He got peppered with lightning-quick jabs. Harder and faster they came.

Wham! Wham! Pap! Pap! Pap!

With fire in his eyes, chest heaving, Nath backed off. "Leave me be!"

Standing in the pouring rain, nose bleeding, Sansla rose to full height and spread his wings out and back in, and with seriousness he said, "I cannot." His head ticked left. He tensed up, visibly fighting the growing rage within. "You must listen."

Nath wanted to fight. To finish it. He could not tell if Sansla was being truthful or just a thorn in his side. He pointed at the winged ape. "You'd be wise to leave me be." He turned and ran. The elves closed in and piled on him.

"You must listen to us," Shum said, grappling Nath by the arms. "It is urgent!"

Covered in elves as big as he, Nath slung them off one at a time.

They kept coming.

Brenwar dove into the fray. "Foolish elves! I'll snap your bones like twigs."

In a brutal moment, Nath and Brenwar were swinging hard in a tangled knot of bodies. The elves, skilled and quick, wrapped up Nath, time after time. He slung them off again. Brenwar busted faces and bruised bones with powerful punches. The roamers would not give. Limping and bleeding, they pulled both fighters down into the slippery mud, time and time again. Nath's restless energy fueled his might.

Quicker and faster, he wore them down. Brenwar, a battle-tested iron tree stump, fought with the fury of a dozen storms. A loyal hound, fighting to the death.

Pinned down in Nath's grip, Hoven choked out, "Nath, you must listen."

Nath shoved him face first into the mud. "I'm done listening!"

Brenwar slammed his shoulder into another one of the elves, freeing up a path.

Hair streaming like a banner behind him, Nath dashed down the muddy road, leaving the elves to battle the angry dwarf for themselves. Moving with the speed of a great antelope, he traversed the sloppy trail ahead of him, determined to track Selene down and finish off her captors.

Sansla Libor swooped down through the rain and plucked him up off the ground and soared back up into the air. "You must not resist, Dragon Prince! A moment, listen, please, listen!"

"There's no time!" Nath screamed from a hundred feet in the air. He could make out Gaak and the other nuurg fighters charging toward the great stone outposts of the city of Thraag. They were much closer than he realized. The fortress was heavily fortified and guarded. "Sansla, do as I say and let me save Selene!"

"I cannot. I have my orders," Sansla said. He started flying away from Thraag. "You are coming with me."

Fighting to free himself, Nath kicked and yelled, "Whose orders?"

"Your mother, Grahleyna, sent me with the utmost urgency."

Nath was so worried about Selene that his mother's name almost didn't register, but he asked, "Why?"

"It's your father. Balzurth has gone missing."

Wind and rain tearing at his face, Nath said, "It will have to wait."

"It cannot," Sansla argued. "You must come, and come now. Time is precious. We cannot lose it."

"I cannot lose *her*!" Nath pulled his legs up and walloped Sansla right in the face.

The great winged ape's grip loosened.

Nath twisted away and plummeted to the ground. He smashed into a pile of heavy brush. Charged with desperate energy, he sprang back to his feet. Knees jarred, he nevertheless bulldozed through the brush and down the road after Selene. He gained ground, just enough to see Gaak and the riders vanish into the sanctuary of the fortress's ominous gates. From the twenty-foot-high parapets, the orcen cyclops soldiers on the wall unleashed a volley of heavy crossbow bolts at him.

Zip! Zip! Zip!

A new squad of pure-blooded orcen riders, at least twenty, charged. They were accompanied by three of the one-eyed orcen nuurgs riding on the backs of wrathhorns galloping out of the fortress.

Nath sank to his knees. Selene was gone. His eyes lit up like molten lava. He charged the overwhelming oncoming horde of riders. "Nooooooo!"

CHAPTER 15

CHARGING UP THE RAIN-SOAKED ROAD, the riders lowered their lances and spears. The terrifying gigantic beasts and their over-sized riders would have frozen a hardened soldier's limbs. Not Nath's. Defying reason, ignoring logic, and with bolts soaring past his head, he rushed toward the oncoming horde. "Have at me, then!"

The wrathhorns snarled. The orcs roared. "Kill him!"

Ten feet from certain impalement, Nath sprang into the air, snatching a bolt midflight and burying the bolt into the lead orcen cyclops.

The nuurg rider gawped and clutched at his chest.

Standing on the saddle, Nath snatched the reins and jerked them back.

The wrathhorn reared up. The ranks of riders behind it crashed into its haunches and one another. A rending of flesh, bone, and metal filled the air with a chaotic sound of confusion and butchery.

Nath sprung from the back of one beast to another, punching the orc cyclopes in their faces and toppling them from their mounts. He was an angry hornet, stinging the ravenous bears. His claws raked across their faces. His iron-strong limbs broke jawbones. His clawed hand filled with heavy steel and took on a life of its own. One towering long-limbed monster after another fell under his wrath, but the brawl was far from over. It was just beginning.

Nath was locked up with a cyclops when a hammerhead of steel clipped the back of his head, shuddering his scales and drooping his eyelids. Dazed and bloody, Nath staggered into the path of a spike-hooved beast. It plowed over him as if he were dirt. Elbow deep in the mud, he fought his way to his feet and set himself for the oncoming charge. He was busted up bad. Bright spots were in his eyes. "Come on, dogs! Come *at* me!"

Sansla Libor darted out of the sky and locked his steel-strong fingers around Nath's wrist. He pulled Nath up into the air and out of the dangerous path. With crossbow bolts still ripping through the air, Sansla shielded the stunned dragon-armed man.

"No, Sansla, no!" Nath's lip was busted, and his head was throbbing. Below his feet and vanishing in the rain was the impenetrable fortress that held Selene captive. His rescue had failed. He struggled with his captor. "Take me back, Sansla. You must take me back!"

"I cannot." Sansla continued his flight into the misty gray clouds above. The world below was lost from sight. "I cannot."

It was futile. Nath's heart sank. Selene was lost. Alone. Imprisoned.

Someone will pay for this!

Clouded by anger, it took his thoughts quite some time to subside into sense.

Meanwhile, Sansla flew with Nath for hours, staying above the meadow of dark clouds below them. The day turned to night and the night to day. Finally, a break came in the field of storms below, and the winged ape soared down through the gap.

Below were lakes of fire and sulfur. A torched landscape. Sweltering heat rose with the steam. It was Dragon Home—not the mountain itself, but the lands just west of it, a bitter stretch of land that stretched for leagues around the great mountain in all directions. Landing, Sansla set him down on the ground.

"Why did you bring me here?" Nath said.

"It is where I was ordered to bring you." Sansla said, grimacing. He peeked over his shoulder and spun around. A crossbow bolt was stuck in his back between his wings. "Be a friend, will you?"

"Guzan, Sansla! You flew all this way with this in your back?" Nath grabbed the bolt. "Hold on." He yanked it out.

Groaning, Sansla dropped to a knee and sighed. "Thank you."

Nath pitched the bolt into a nearby pool of lava. The bolt sizzled and sank. "I'm still angry with you."

Turning to face Nath, the great winged ape said, "I would be too. I'm sorry Nath, but I had my orders."

"Yes," Nath nodded. "I know you did. From my mother. Since when do you work for my mother?"

"Since you disappeared."

The Mountain of Doom stretched into the clouds leagues away. Nath and Sansla were on the outer edge of its natural barriers of protection, where the hot streams slipped into the earth again.

"Why here? Doesn't my mother want to meet me inside?"

"She did not say."

"You know Brenwar is not going to be too happy being left behind with the roamer elves. Was it so necessary that we leave them all behind?"

"They'll be safe."

"They are in orcen land!" Nath said. "How safe can they be?"

"I'll go back, if I can. We'll see." Sansla's wings collapsed behind his back. He sat on a pile of stones. "This place makes me thirsty."

Nath brushed his sweaty hair from his eyes. His face was dripping with sweat. "It's better than frost that freezes the bones. You seem to be doing quite well. No issues with your temperament."

"The curse is what it is. As long as I stay focused on what is right, I can control it."

A bright light appeared out of nowhere. Nath shielded his eyes. The light faded, and a mystic doorway appeared. A woman stepped out. She was as beautiful and radiant as the morning sun. Hair of golden light. Eyes the color of honey. She wore powder-white robes trimmed in silver.

"Mother," Nath said.

"Yes, my dear son, it is me," Grahleyna said.

Sansla took a knee.

"Please stand, Roamer King," she said, beckoning at the shimmering door. "Now come within. It is not safe out in the open like this."

Sansla went through the door.

Nath followed. Immediately, he knew he was back inside Dragon Home, but the room he was in was an entirely different one than the throne room. Amazing and wonderful carvings filled it with colorful pictures—people, dragons, and landscapes. The chamber wasn't large, but it was tall, and big enough for a pair of large dragons. Humongous pillows covered most of the floor. Every detail in the room, though simple, was exquisite, but with no furnishings other than the pillows at all.

"This is my spot," Grahleyna said, offering a pretty smile and a healing potion to each of them, "a place where I hide from your father."

"I'm sure this isn't your only option." Nath drank down his potion, recalling many memories. Dragon Home was an enormous city within the great mountain. Not even the work of the dwarves could rival it. There were thousands of rooms and caverns as well as roads, wide and narrow, that twisted and turned. Some of the places were very small, made for the little dragons, and the others were quite huge, big enough for a sky raider to squeeze through. All in all, it was a marvel. Amazing. When Nath was young, he had made it a goal to search out every place there was. He never found the half of it. The room he was in now was new to him.

"Selene, Mother," he said to her. Chin high, fists clenched, he stepped forward. "She's been captured by the nuurg. I was attempting to rescue her when Sansla arrived and fouled everything up!"

"Watch your tone," she said softly. She took his hand. "It is unfortunate about Selene, but she can take care of herself. You know that as well as I."

"She's in a deep slumber."

Squeezing Nath's hand hard, she said, "You cannot wake her?"

"No, Mother. She's defenseless. I was in the middle of saving her when I was rushed back here against my will. What is so urgent and pressing that I had to appear here this instant?"

She held his cheeks and said with great sympathy, "I am so sorry, Nath. Forgive Sansla. He was merely following my direct order as he should have been. I did not suspect it would be in such a moment of peril. Forgive me."

He hesitated, then said, "I do. But I must save Selene—among other things. Fang is stolen, and the elves and dwarves think I killed Laedorn and Uurluuk. How can all this be? And Father, what of him? He's gone?"

Grahleyna guided him to a seat on an orange-pink pillow. "He was angry. The titans had sent rather cruel messages. The bones and skins of dragons. They taunted him. Realizing that you were missing, Balzurth went after you."

"Me?" Nath pointed to his chest. "He's like a flying city in the sky. The giants and wurmers will be all over him. Please tell me he took an enclave of dragons for protection?"

Shaking her head with a face filled with worry, she said, "He is alone."

Nath jumped up. "Alone? That's insane!"

CHAPTER 16

"YOU ARE SO MUCH LIKE your father," Grahleyna said. "You, like him, always want to solve Nalzambor's problems on your own. Things would be so much easier if you learned to trust others."

"I don't like putting others in harm's way," said Nath, looking in the direction where he thought Selene lay, helpless and surrounded by monsters. "Not on my account. But Mother—"

Grahleyna held up her hand for him to listen. "People do what they want to do. If they want to help, let them. It's their lives, and they have to live them. How would you feel if I tried to protect you all the time? Never let you leave here, not even to help in times of dire need?"

What! No! She can't mean that! I have to go rescue Selene! Better not make Mother angry.

"I suppose I wouldn't like it."

"No, you wouldn't. So you left here with Brenwar—and left a good bit early. I don't think you were ready, but I think you are the better for it now." She poked his noggin. "Just a little hardheaded. There is so much you can still do. You just haven't learned how."

So tell me, already! Enough with the hints! Tell me how to fly again so I can go back this instant and rescue Selene!

But Nath couldn't speak to his mother that way, especially not when she had just threatened to ground him. She had the power to enforce that. If she ordered it, he really would not be leaving Dragon Home.

Shaking his head in frustration, Nath chose his words carefully. "Is there something I should know that you could tell me? Wouldn't that be helpful?"

"It's best that you learn these things for yourself. Your own trials and tribulations will purify your golden spirit. Just keep doing the right thing, Nath, no matter how hard it might be." His mother gave him a sad smile that made her years show in her face, and the look in her eyes was faraway.

Guzan, she's more worried about him than I thought.

Nath took his mother's hands. "So how long has Father been gone?"

"In secret, he managed to storm out of here weeks ago. He was insistent that no one go with him or after him. I pleaded with him," she said, squeezing his hands tight. "I fear I may not see him again. When I got word that you had been spotted and Sansla was already searching, I sent him after you immediately. Nath, you have to find your father. You have to find him now. If Eckubahn comes across him, captures him, kills him, the entire Great Wall of Dragons will come down. Every evil spirit will be unleashed. And the races will fall. The dragons with them."

"With all the dragons at our disposal, can none of them find Father?"

"Since you've been gone, the wurmers have grown to outnumber the dragons at least five to one. The dragons are maintaining a low profile, to say the least."

"We can't hide forever. At some point we will all have to fight." Nath turned, dropping his mother's hands to push his hair back. He wanted to hit something. "If only I were still a dragon."

"You still *are* a dragon," she reminded him.

"But I've lost so much power. Everything's bigger than me. The giants. The wurmers. Now even the orcs out-size me. They were big enough and obnoxious enough already."

"Don't lose your composure, Nath. Now is the time to plan and think."

"Ugh!" He flung his hands to his sides. "It makes my head hurt."

"Yes, you are your father's son." She let out a small chuckle.

Still, Nath could tell she was sad. He didn't know his mother well. He'd hardly spent any time with her at all. He needed to be strong and console her. "What do you think I should do?"

"What is best for the future of Nalzambor?"

"Your question comes across as a riddle," he said. "I've a feeling you know the answer."

"No, I have an opinion, but I'm not going to share that." She smoothed out the ruffles in her robes. "I shouldn't influence your decision. I can offer you this." She held out a knuckle-sized gemstone that shined like a blue star. "This will help you find your father. It will only work in your hands."

Nath took the stone. In his palm it pulsated with a life of its own. "What is it?"

"A searcher. It bonds mystically with the one it touches. It is tied to us—me, you, and your father. See how it gleams when I am near? It knows me. In my hands it will know you. Near your father, it will come to life again." She reached out and closed his hand over it. "Its magic is limited. You'll need to be close, but if you are close enough you will know he is near."

"How near?"

"It's difficult to say. A few feet? A hundred yards?"

"What will Father look like?"

"It's quite possible he looks like us. Or an elf. Maybe a dwarf," she said, rising to her feet.

"He can do that? Like a changeling?"

"His powers are mighty."

Nath's thoughts went to Gorlee. "They say someone who looked like me killed Laedorn and Uurluuk with Akron. It must have been a changeling."

"I know about the horrible demise of our allies, Nath, but are you assuming everything you hear is true?"

Nath certainly had his doubts about the rogue elf, Slavan Fonjich. After all, he had imprisoned him and left him for dead. "Do the elves and dwarves not hunt for me?"

"They do, but that doesn't mean what they heard was true. Perhaps witnesses lied about what they had seen."

"But they have my bow. Ben had my bow, and I need to know if he lives." Nath wanted to pull out his hair. "Everything's upside down since Fang took me away! And he's gone too. I don't know where to start."

"You need to realize you can't be everywhere at once, Nath. You need to remember you aren't a man. You are a dragon. The Dragon Prince. You have power at your command. You just haven't figured out how to use it." She hugged him tight. "Think like a dragon, not like a man."

"You're leaving me again, aren't you?"

"No, I'm staying here. I have to keep everyone convinced that your brazen father is brooding in the throne room. You're the one who's leaving." She snapped her fingers. A new mystic door appeared and opened. "Where do you want to start, Nath? The door will take you there. Just think of it. I have faith in your journey."

He looked at the gem in his hand. Where would his father be? He had no idea. He kissed Grahleyna on the cheek. "Goodbye, Mother."

CHAPTER 17

BLACK EYED AND WHITE HAIRED, she was beautiful and small, standing just over three feet tall and fluttering her black-and-pink wings. She stood on a tree stump, surrounded by dozens of fairies. They were all black eyed and covered in leaves, like the surrounding forest. One fairy was just as adorable and deadly as another. Encircled by her mystic people, Lotuus had a twinkle in her dark eyes.

"I have brought you gifts, Fairy Empress," said an elf. He took a knee and bowed. It was Slavan of the rogue wilder elves. A long object was wrapped up in cloth. A sword with a sharp tip that pointed out. He stuck it tip first in the ground and tore away the cloth.

Eyes wide, Lotuus gazed at the magnificent blade.

"Does this please the empress?" Slavan held his palm out. The skin was red and blistered. "I paid quite the price when I grabbed it. Be careful of its steel."

Wings coming to life, she floated around the sword. "I'm well aware of its powers."

"I have another present, though lesser than the blade," Slavan said. He outstretched his hand behind him. Another rogue elf handed him Brenwar's hammer. "I've not only disarmed your enemies, I've captured them too."

"Where?" she demanded. Her small hands locked around Slavan's collar. "Where is Nath Dragon?" she yelled in his face.

"He is secured," Slavan calmly said, "Empress."

Up in his face, she said, "Why did you not bring him here?"

"And risk his escape? No, the farther I separate him from his weapons, the better. I was not going to chance it. He is quite secure, I assure you."

"You had better be right," she said. Her eyes glowed with bright-green light. "Or I will kill you."

"You know I aim to please you, Empress. I would rather die than let you down." He reached for her.

Lotuus slapped his hand. "Don't you dare, Elf. Now tell me, where is he?"

"The labyrinth in the Elven Field of Dreams. The Inner Sanctum of Lheme. He's quite secure. No one knows he's there. And there's no escape for him—or for his friends. Are you pleased?"

"So he lives?"

"I wouldn't call it living, but he breathes quite well. As a matter of fact, he gave up quite easily."

Lotuus picked up a wand from her tree stump throne. It had a lock of Nath's hair on it. He had disappeared without a trace more than a year ago. Even the wurmers hadn't been able to find his scent. Now, she had him right where she wanted him. She sniffed the clipping of Nath's flame-red hair.

"Are you going to share my achievement with Eckubahn?" Slavan asked. "I want audience with him myself. I believe I have earned it."

"Now is not the time," she said.

"I disagree." Slavan poked at his black chest plate. "I didn't have to bring this gift to you. I could have taken it straight to Narnum. Sought the audience with Eckubahn myself. What I have done is worthy of my desires. I want full authority over Elome once it falls. I deserve it. I demand it!"

Tapping the tassel of Nath's hair in her hand, she said in a sweet voice, "And you will have it."

"Really, well, uh, that's much better." He adjusted his composure. "Me and my elves are ready for the journey."

Lotuus's eyes flashed. Green bolts of power shot from her eyes and cut a hole in Slavan. "Your journey is over." She twirled the wand over her head. Concealed wurmers, at least a dozen, appeared in the woodland. She pointed at the remaining rogue elves—who had drawn their swords. "Kill them."

The Elven Field of Dreams was not easily accessed by just anyone. The wilder elves were the guardians of it. And there were more of them, many, many more. The sanctuary was known by very few, including the elves. Lotuus and an entourage of fairies made their way through the lands of the elves, but they looked different. Using their dark magic, they had transformed themselves to appear as the wilder elves the wurmers had slain.

Posing as Slavan, Lotuus led the way. They came across more rogue elves—who were easily convinced—headed deeper into the Elven Field of Dreams, and slunk through the ravine into the Inner Sanctum of Lheme. It took hours to traverse the labyrinth.

Finally, they found the open cells.

Lotuus shook her head and screamed. "Aaaaaaaeeeeeehhhh!" Leaving the sanctum, she said, "Now I'm truly glad I killed that failure."

Outside the elven lands, she headed back into her forest sanctuary. Sitting on her tree stump throne, she toyed with the wand and tassel. Nath Dragon was alive and well.

Should I send the wurmers after him now?

She snapped her fingers. A wurmer glided over. It was the size of an ox and had deep-grey scales. A purple fire was in its eyes. She waved the wand under its snout. "Find out where Nath Dragon is, and report back to me."

The dragon spread its wings and departed.

She stared at the sword, Fang. Its steel shimmered with silvery life. "Humph, what Eckubahn doesn't know won't hurt him right now. My secret's safe with me."

CHAPTER 18

"YOU'RE CERTAIN NO ONE HAS left?" Nath said to Hoven. He had made his choice and departed from his mother. He was rescuing Selene. He arrived a mile from the fortress on the path to the city of Thraag. It was his choice. His father would have to wait. He couldn't leave Selene helpless like that. "You've had eyes on it the entire time?"

Hoven pushed his braided hair back over his shoulders. "The dwarf insisted on it. It was our desire to depart, but he managed to convince us otherwise." He glanced down at Brenwar. "It would have been easier to pull a tree stump out of the ground with my bare hands than move him."

"Well now," Nath said to Brenwar, "it seems someone has taken a shine to Selene. I knew you liked her."

"Pah." Chin up, head turning, Brenwar crossed his arms over his chest. "I like her as much as I like the porridge of bugbears. I stayed only because I knew you'd be back."

"Sure, sure," Nath said. Concealed in a high spot among the heavy brush and thickets, he gazed at the fortress beyond. It was square, twenty feet high, and made of heavy stone. It had a tower at each corner like a castle. The red-and-black banner of Thraag waved from the highest tower. Soldiers guarded the wall on every side. "How many do you think are inside?"

"At least a hundred," Hoven said. "That would include the nuurg. Of course, you did manage to whittle them down."

"*We* managed to whittle them down," Brenwar reminded them.

"Oh, but of course," Hoven said.

Standing among the present company of Hoven, Sansla, and Brenwar, Nath said, "I don't suppose anyone has ever been inside an orcen cyclops stronghold before?"

No one replied.

"That's what I thought. Well, I'm going to need to get in there," Nath said.

"You can't be serious?" Brenwar said, puffing through his beard. "They'll be waiting for you in there. It's what they want."

"It's what they expect," Sansla added.

"I suggest we wait them out," Hoven said. "It's possible they'll move her. They were heading toward Thraag, were they not?"

Nath was torn up inside. He knew in his mind that caution was the best option.

I want action! I cannot just leave her in there.

"I need to go in, and go in soon. I can't just stand here while she's helpless in there. I cannot."

Putting his hand on Nath's shoulder, Sansla said, "Give the orcs time to reveal their hand. After all, they are quite stupid. It won't be long before they squirm around in there."

"True." Nath rubbed his chest. It had been healed by the potion his mother had given him, but he still remembered what it had felt like, being trampled by a wrathhorn. "Let's keep our eyes open, then, shall we? I'm going to get a closer look."

Brenwar bumped up against him. "Not without me, you won't. I know what you're thinking."

"I won't rush in," Nath said.

Not in the daylight.

"I know better. Where you go, I go." Brenwar pointed at Hoven. "And if I don't have an eye on him, then you'd better have one."

Hoven nodded. "We will."

Consumed, Nath watched the fortress like a clock, day and night. Brenwar hung close to his side. Quiet. Alert. Nothing came or went out of the fortress, which was odd. The orcs should routinely send patrols out, surely, like the nuurg Nath had encountered. The fact that they weren't moving told him something. The orcs suspected he was out here. Watching. Waiting.

It was dusk. Sitting in a grove of large stones, with a full view of the fortress, Brenwar said to Nath, "So what did your mother have to say?"

Nath gave him most of the details and went on. "The sad thing is that the elves and dwarves truly are after me. They think I'm a murderer. Or a madman."

"Do you think doing this is wiser than looking for your father?" Brenwar said.

Nath shrugged. "I don't even know where to start with him. I can't say for sure if I'm doing right, but in this case, I do at least know where Selene is. I can do something." He picked up a stick and doodled in the ground with it. "And at the last moment before I departed, I got to thinking on going after him, but then I thought, 'What would Father do if Mother was in the same situation?' Then it was easy."

Brenwar nodded. "Aye. Even I can't disagree with that logic, but then again, Selene is not your mother."

"Brenwar…"

"Fair is fair," the dwarf said, taking a bite of some elven jerky. "She has quite a past."

"You need to move on."

"Tell that to the families of the dead she left in her wake."

Nath tried not to think about it and didn't very often. To some, everything Selene had done was unforgivable, but he'd been taught that on the higher road, everything could be forgiven if there was a true change of heart. He believed that. He pitched the stick. "I think she's trying really hard to make up for it. Many more would have been lost without her."

"Aye."

"Brenwar," Nath said, "you've spent time with my father. Where do you think he's looking for me?"

Rubbing his beard and gazing at the sky, Brenwar said, "Good question. I know your father likes to fly. Explore. He likes to be alone. I honestly think he would walk the world as a man and do good things. It's just a theory, though. What about you? You were close when you were young. He took you all over, did he not?"

Nath showed a smile. "Yes, he did. They were grand times too. Riding on his mighty back and soaring the air like a bird. It was the greatest feeling in the world. Me and him felt like one. He told me I could always fly, but look at me now." He lifted his boot and laughed. "I'm a landlubber."

Brenwar stomped his foot. "I like it. There ain't no worse feeling than nothing underneath you."

"You never know. One day bearded dwarves might fly—" Nath sat up in his perch. A flicker of movement had caught his eye. A violent act in the brush erupted in a patch where a roamer elf once stood. Nath took off running.

Brenwar yelled after him, "Where are you going?"

Crashing through the thickets, Nath burst into a clearing.

Down on the ground, Hoven fought the wurmer tearing into him.

Chapter 19

Hoven the roamer elf fought for his life. A huge gash was on his chest. His hands pushed up against the wurmer's snapping jaws.

Nath collided with the scaly beast, pushing it off Hoven.

Brenwar grabbed the elf's arm and dragged him out of the way.

The wurmer's tail whipped around, caught Nath in the chest, and knocked him off his feet. He sprang back up and braced himself for attack.

The scaly beast squared off on Nath. It sniffed the air. Its purple eyes narrowed in recognition.

Nath advanced with his elven blade. "What are you waiting for, insect?"

The wurmer darted forward and spun around, flicking out its tail.

Nath jumped backward.

The wurmer ran into the brush, cleared a path, and spread its wings.

"He's running," Nath said, sprinting after it.

The wurmer took to the air.

Nath dove for its tail. His fingers stretched out at full length, grasping for the flying monster. He whiffed and crashed into the ground.

The wurmer ascended toward the setting sun.

Nath slammed his fist in the dirt. "Guzan!"

Sansla landed beside him. "What happened?"

Gazing at Sansla's great wings, Nath yelled at him, "That thing's a scout. It knows me. Get after it, Sansla." He pointed at the sky. "You must stop it now!"

Without hesitation, Sansla leapt into the air and took off like a giant bat, making a straight line for the wurmer. Within seconds they were both gone.

On his feet again, Nath trotted back to Brenwar and Hoven. More roamers had formed a circle around the fallen roamer. Brenwar had Hoven's head in his lap. The long-limbed elf's chest was bloody and still bleeding. His complexion was turning a deep purple. He coughed and spat blood.

Taking a knee, Shum said, "I must get him out of here if he is to live."

"Where will you take him?" Nath asked. "The Elven Field of Dreams?"

Shum picked his brother up in his arms. "That's an option." He let out a sharp whistle. Two of the magnificent horses bred by the roamers showed up. One of them lay down. Shum climbed on with Hoven in his arms. The horse rose up. Checking the sky, Shum shook his head and said to one of the roamers, "Liam, you have my charge."

"Dragon speed," Liam said.

Shum nodded, nudged his heels into the horse's ribs, and galloped away.

"Well, that was awful," Brenwar said.

"Awful indeed," Nath replied. His eyes remained fixed on the sky.

Liam came alongside him. "I'm ready to go in if you are."

"Huh?" Nath said, lowering his gaze on the roamer elf. Liam was much younger than Shum and Hoven. His potbelly was not so pronounced, his long bones not quite as heavy as those of his elders. As another sign of his youth, his gray eyes were eager and energetic. "What are you suggesting?"

"We go in and rescue your friend Selene. Time is wasting."

Nath smirked at the long-haired rangy elf. "Let's see what Sansla has to say when he returns."

Bouncing up and down on his toes, Liam said, "And if he doesn't?"

"Have some faith in your king," Nath said with surprise.

"I do, but he can be inconsistent. You know, when he gets all excited, the curse, it will run away with him."

The other roamers crowded in.

Quick to order, Liam said, "Resume your posts."

Like apparitions, the roamers vanished into the falling darkness, leaving Liam, Nath, and Brenwar all alone.

Chin high, Liam said, "We can speak freely now."

"You were speaking freely," Brenwar said. "Quite clearly."

"Yes, you do seem quite eager to take charge of things," Nath added.

"But I *am* in charge of things. You heard Shum. He trusts me. I say we get moving. Strike in the night. The time is right." He rubbed his hands together. "I'm ready for some action."

Lifting a brow, Brenwar said to Nath, "Remind you of anybody?"

"I believe so," Nath said. "So Liam, tell me, what is your plan?"

"Oh, it's simple." Liam kneeled down and motioned them in. With his finger, he drew in the dirt. "This is the fortress. I noticed on the western wall there is a small entrance. We sneak inside, kill all the orcs and cyclopes, and rescue your friend." He dusted his hands off. "See? Easy."

Nodding, Brenwar said, "I like it. I like it a lot."

Nath rubbed his temples. "Oh my."

"What's wrong?" Liam asked.

"I sense the world ending," Nath replied.

Brenwar stood up with his battle-axe, looking all around. "Why's that? I don't see anything. Why is the world ending?"

"Because you're agreeing with an elf."

Brenwar shrugged his shoulders. "Even elves have their moments."

Sansla Libor dropped out of the sky. His fur was torn and bleeding. He huffed for breath. "I'm sorry. The wurmer escaped me."

"Do you think it was a scout?" Nath asked.

"Aye." Sansla shook his jaw. "I came back to warn you. They'll be coming. Soon, they'll be coming."

CHAPTER 20

"HOW MANY?" ASKED LIAM. He pulled his quiver off his shoulder and started counting the arrows. "I can take at least two dozen."

"I don't know," Sansla said, keeping his attention on Nath. "In the case of the wurmers, they often come by the dozens. In some cases we've seen them in the hundreds. Valcatrine was wiped out by a horde of them."

"Valcatrine?" Nath said with surprise. It was a small elven city where a few thousand farmers and tradespeople lived. "When did this happen?"

"Months ago," Sansla replied. "Nath, I'm sorry. It might be best to abandon this mission if we want to get out alive. If there's too many, well, we aren't capable of handling too many."

"I've fought wurmers before. We can handle them," Nath said, gripping his sword tight in his hand. "I'm not abandoning Selene."

"I'm all for going in and getting her," Liam said. He tested the string on his bow. "Every moment is precious."

"Yer a good bit more eager than your kin," Brenwar commented.

"Yes, much unlike his father, but his father trusts him. So do I," Sansla said.

Looking at Liam, Nath asked, "Who's his father?"

"Shum. He's a bit too cautious, if you ask me. Says I need more wisdom." Liam drew both of his swords, twirled them around his fingers, and slid them back into his sheaths. "But he also admits my skill and instincts more than make up for it. So, are we doing this?"

Nath weighed his options. He could possibly shake the wurmers from his trail and come back. But they were after him. Perhaps he should leave Selene's rescue to someone else. If anyone could pull it off, it was the roamers. They were the most-skilled fighters and rangers in the lands. He knew this. He'd fought alongside them often enough. They could handle the orcs, even the big ones. They, like the dwarves and so many other rangers, were giant killers.

Staring at the fortress, Nath remarked, "There must be a hundred soldiers in there, not to mention their beasts."

"I can take half on my own," Liam said.

"Aye, and I'll take the other half," Brenwar agreed. "You just focus on getting Selene out."

Sansla rubbed his fist in his palm. "I'm up for a good scrap as much as any."

With the evening breeze rustling his red hair, Nath nodded. "By Guzan, let's do this."

As everyone else readied themselves for the rescue, Nath stood alongside Brenwar, eyeing the fortress. They were less than fifty yards away. Torches cast flickers on the top wall. The orcen banner in the top tower waved in the stiff winds. Nath counted ten orcs with heavy crossbows guarding the walls. They wore full metal helmets and chest plates of iron.

Battle-axe over his shoulder, Brenwar said, "Any day you fight orcs is a good day. Let's take them."

Nath agreed, but he wasn't in it for the bloodshed; he was in it for Selene. However, he'd do everything in his power to get her. If orcs went down, so be it. "This assault will be considered an act of war, you know."

"There's a war already."

Liam appeared from the brush. "We're ready."

"Go, then," Nath said. "I'll await your signal."

With a smile, Liam vanished into the woodland.

"You know, it would be better if there were dwarves instead of elves," Brenwar said.

"Sometimes you have to make do."

"Humph."

"Let's go." Nath crept through the brush until he got close enough to the entrance at the bottom of the western wall that Liam had mentioned. It was a solid iron door with a narrow road that led out onto another roadway.

Nath climbed up into a tree. He could see the walls now and had a closer look at the orcen faces of the guards. Even at night, he could see the yellow of their eyes.

At least I still have my dragon vision.

Brenwar whispered up at him. "What's happening?"

"Nothing yet," Nath said. "Be silent."

Looking up at the fortress from down on the ground, Brenwar popped up on his toes. "Something should be happening already. The elves are slow."

"Give it a moment."

"I've got enough gray in my beard already."

Nath sat perched like an owl amid the sounds of wind whistling through the tree limbs. Cocking his head, he closed his eyes. A faint unnatural sound caught his keen ears, coming from the other side of the eastern wall.

Ah, the sweet sound of a stretching bowstring.

An orcen soldier fell over with an arrow stuck in his chest. Another volley cut into the ranks. Orcs clutched their chests or necks, teetered, and fell.

Inside one of the towers a bell rang.

In Orcen, one of the defending soldiers yelled, "Attack! Attack!"

"So it's finally started," Brenwar said with excitement. "It's about time."

The orcs abandoned this section of the wall, running to defend the eastern side.

"Perfect." Nath hopped out of the tree, landing on cat's feet by Brenwar. "Wait for me to get that door open."

"Make it quick. Can't let the elves have all the fun." The dwarf's eyes were fixed on the orcs that had deserted their posts. "They're so stupid. A dwarf never abandons his station."

"Wait for my signal," Nath reminded him. He darted for the wall.

The plan was simple. With the orcs' attention turned, he'd climb the wall and open the fortress's service door from the inside to let in Brenwar and the roamers. They would infiltrate with him, battle their way to Selene if needed. Though stealth was ideal, battle might be the only option.

Bursting through the brush, Nath made his way to the wall.

A giant orc cyclops, a nuurg, rushed out of the tower onto the western wall.

Nath hunkered down behind some long-abandoned quarry stone and peeked up.

The nuurg had spoiled his plan. There was no way he could sneak in there now.

Great Guzan!

CHAPTER 21

"THERE!" THE NUURG FASTENED HIS eyes on Nath and pointed with his sword.

Flying at full speed, Sansla appeared from around one of the towers and blindsided the nuurg. The powerful impact sent the brutish giant falling over the wall and crashing hard, armor and all, onto the ground.

Brenwar stormed out of the brush and said to Nath, "You go! I'll handle this!"

The one-eyed orcen eight-footer climbed to his feet and straightened his helm.

Brenwar took a whack into its knee.

Howling, the orc collapsed.

Brenwar didn't stop there.

Without looking back, Nath leapt high up on the wall. His hard claws dug in, and he ascended like a squirrel. Reaching the top, he slid onto the landing. A battle raged on the other side, in the fortress courtyard. The orcs fired crossbows. The roamers fired into their ranks with deadly accuracy. Reinforcements came storming from the ground level up the stairs. At least a dozen held the eastern wall, launching crossbow bolts from behind the stones that protected them.

Nath looked at the ground level.

Orcs had gathered weapons and were feeding more crossbow bolts to the upper wall. The nuurg were shouting orders. Nothing was right below him. Assured that no one saw him, he jumped down into the courtyard and turned toward the outer wall, searching for the service door. It was there, but it wasn't alone. A nuurg stood tall, swinging a long-handled stone-headed mace. It was Gaak.

Nath caught the hammering blow in his shoulder and fell to the ground. "Gah!"

In an instant, the giant orc was upon Nath, stepping on his foot and bringing down another swing.

Nath rolled to one side, evaded the first blow, and dodged another.

"Be still, scaly one." With two hands, the orc cyclops brought down the oversized mace with wroth force.

Nath captured the handle with both hands.

The pair wrestled over the hard ground, rolling back and forth.

The orc was bigger and heavier, his strength impressive, his leverage an advantage. He pinned Nath on his back again. "I'm no fool. I knew you would come here. You fell into my trap. This is where you die and I scale you like a fish."

Nath's nose crinkled. "Your breath is awful. Just awful. Is manure part of your diet?"

Brows buckling and face in a vicious snarl, Gaak put all of his crushing weight on Nath. He got the mace handle over Nath's neck, pinned him down good, and leaned into it. "Heavy, aren't I?"

Choking under the orc's weight, Nath pushed back with all of his might. With his face red as a beet, he managed to choke out, "Your mother must be proud. Did you know her?"

"You're a dead man!"

"Dragon, actually."

Hands on the handle, jaw clenched, Nath pushed back. A vein popped out in his forehead. His dragon blood surged. "Get off of me!" he growled.

"When you're dead!"

Slowly, with shaking arms, Nath started to lift the handle, watching Gaak's eyes widen. Sweat dripped from the nuurg's brow into Nath's face. "Yech!"

Gaak put his full chest over the weapon's haft and forced his weight with more effort.

Nath's arms locked in place. Then, he started pushing the huge orc off of his chest again.

"Impossible!" Gaak shouted.

With a heave, Nath shoved Gaak off, ripped the mace from his hands, and lorded over him. "Nothing's impossible when you're a dragon."

Laboring for breath, Gaak said, "Is that so?" He launched his foot into Nath's groin.

"Oof!" Nath sank to his knees.

Gaak gathered his powerful legs under himself and pounced.

Striking quick, Nath smote Gaak in the jaw with the head of the mace.

Krang!

The hardheaded giant stood dazed.

With the mace, Nath walloped him in the belly and crowned him in the head. "You'll never hit me there again."

Gaak was out. Dead maybe.

Nath didn't try to find out. His skirmish had caught the attention of the other soldiers. With angry cries and barking orders, they charged across the courtyard toward Nath. He found the door. Two steel crossbars sealed it shut. One by one, he shoved them out. He flung open the door.

Brenwar stood just outside. "Duck."

"Why?"

"Just duck!"

Nath squatted down. From outside the door, arrows zinged over his head.

Twack! Twack! Twack! Twack!

Behind him, Nath heard the thuds of four orc soldiers dropping dead on the spot.

Five roamer elves rushed in, led by Liam. He was shooting one arrow right after the other. "Find your friend. We'll keep these brutes off your back. Go!" He pointed at the tower and said to his men, "Take it."

"Don't order me around," Brenwar said, swinging his axe into an orc that charged from the side. "I like the ground level. That's where battles are won!"

Liam tossed his bow aside and drew his swords. "I couldn't agree more."

Together, Brenwar and Liam waded into the fray, with Brenwar screaming, "For Morgdon!"

CHAPTER 22

AVOIDING THE BATTLING TROOPS, NATH snaked through the chaos. The fortress had a simple layout, with the barracks, stalls, storehouses, and other needed areas built out of wood underneath the wooden catwalks between the stone outer walls where the orcs were posted. There was plenty to search. He ducked into a room where the orcs ate. The wooden tables were covered in stacked-up dirty plates. He covered his nose.

"Awful here. Awful everywhere."

He moved out to the next building. It was the barracks. There weren't any beds, just blankets piled up on the ground. Some loose weapons were left behind. Bones from leftover foods stank. The orcs didn't have much discipline, and the word "tidy" wasn't part of their vocabulary. The barracks butted up against and used the stone fortress wall.

Brenwar would have a laugh if he saw this. It's a wonder they built this fortress at all.

Nath could make a case for the orcs to some degree. They didn't care for comfort like many races. The hard ground and dirt were just fine with them. Also, to them, the more they stank, the better. It wasn't uncommon that the leader was the smelliest and ugliest of all of them.

It was part of the reason Nath hated them. They relished filth. Their hard hearts were filled with destruction. They were impossible to get along with. Always.

He abandoned the barracks. A battle raged outside. The roamers and Brenwar cut into the ranks of orcs but vanished in the knot of pig-nosed men. He wanted to help, desperately he did, but a voice in his head said, *Have faith.*

Blocking the clamor out, Nath snuck into the stables.

Immediately, something beastly snorted.

Liam was young for an elf. Barely a hundred years old, he fought like a ranger with five hundred seasons. His elven steel flashed in the night, cutting down one orc after the other. His two swords struck like lightning. Both blade tips bit deep into an orc's chest, sending it to the grave.

A broad machete-like blade cut at Liam's head.

He ducked.

Swish!

The young roamer cut away, removing the attacking orc's machete hand at the wrist.

Slice!

More orcs fell. More orcs came.

"I can do this all day!" Brenwar roared. In one hard swing, he brought two orcs down at once. "All day!"

From the tower above, the feathered shafts of the elves dropped the orcs one by one. The roamers on the ground fought hard and struck fast. Their skill and speed overwhelmed the heavily armored inferior orcen fighters.

A crossbow bolt clipped Liam's shoulder. He cried out, "Zauass!" Bleeding, he noticed the orc crossbowmen up on the catwalks. They shot at everyone, even their own kind.

Ducking and dodging dozens of arrows, Liam ran up the steps and stormed the catwalk, swinging his sword left and right. Orcs pitched over the catwalk rail and bounced off the ground. The orcs tossed their crossbows aside in order to draw their bladed weapons, but before they could pull them out, Liam engaged.

Slice! Slice! Hack!

In a matter of seconds, the bloodied orcs were fighting for their lives. Cut, slashed, busted, and bleeding, the orcs that survived Liam's onslaught fought on. They weren't brave nor valiant, just angry, stubborn, and stupid. Orcs hated to lose—and even worse, they hated elves. In a knot of blood and sweat, they poured it on.

Their anger was their downfall. Taking advantage of their rage and confusion, Liam carved them to bits. Out of breath, skinned, scratched up, and bloody, he peered over the wall and shouted out to the remaining roamers in the woods.

"To me!"

Suddenly, the catwalk shook.

On both sides of the catwalk, the monstrous one-eyed nuurg fighters appeared. Each carried a halberd—an axe head on a spear shaft. The single eye in the middle of each of their heads was intent on murder.

Roamers in the tower tops fired at the huge orcen cyclopes. Arrows stuck into their backs like the spines on a porcupine. The nuurgs didn't even grunt. Their skin was leathery. It took special magic to cut them. Liam made a signal to the tower. The volley of arrows was redirected.

Liam flipped his sword and beckoned the cyclopes into battle. "What are you waiting for, an invitation?"

The cyclopes charged.

Chopping the orcs down like saplings, Brenwar caught up to Liam on the catwalk, hemmed in by two giant cyclopes. He buried his axe in one's belly, pushed off, and shouted up at Liam, "Wait for me! Wait for me!"

A cyclops swinging a chain with spiked heads stepped into view. The chain whistled over his head.

"What kind of silly weapon is that?"

The chain licked out and wrapped around Brenwar. He looked down at his constricted legs. "Nobody tangles a dwarf!"

Putting his shoulders into it, the cyclops gave the chain a heave that jerked Brenwar off his feet onto his back. Hand over hand, the cyclops pulled the dwarf forward.

Chopping at the chain, Brenwar said, "Nobody drags a dwarf!"

The surrounding orcs swarmed him and piled on.

CHAPTER 23

WRATHHORNS. THEIR NICKERING WHINE COULD freeze a man's blood. One reared up as soon as Nath walked into the stable. Its hooves clawed at the iron gate that penned it in. It was just one of many—all of which were growling. Two of them butted their gates with the horns on their heads.

Nath forged ahead. There were plenty of stalls, and many of them were empty. He peeked in each one. There was nothing but hay, straw and stubble, and water troughs. Clothing was in one of the barrels, grain and burning oil in others. Casks of ale filled the entirety of one stall all by themselves. Moving quickly, he didn't find any sign of Selene.

He hit the back wall. "Sultans of Sulfur!"

There wasn't much to the fortress at all. Nothing mysterious. A simple layout. There were supplies and soldiers. It being a fortress of orcs, there wasn't any place for discipline or detention. If there was a problem in the ranks, they'd just fight it out. Maybe to the death. Hence, no dungeon cells nor any sort of brig. He kicked the hay piled at his feet.

"Come on Selene, where are you?"

The wrathhorns continued to buck, claw at their iron bars, and whine.

"Oh shut up!"

Starting to depart and scanning his surroundings, he slipped on the straw floor and caught his balance. Kicking the loose straw away, he said, "What's this?"

A flat piece of metal lay under the hay. He dusted it off with his feet, discovering the outline of a trapdoor. Kneeling, he found an iron ring and pulled on it. A stiff breath of stale air caught his cheeks. A stone staircase led down into the darkness.

Hemmed in by giants and halberds, Liam danced in and out of the jabbing blades. The cyclopes were cunning. They poked and stabbed. Liam ducked and shifted from side to side.

"Stand still!" roared one of the nuurg fighters.

Ducking under a slicing blade, Liam popped up again. "And let you skewer me like a pig on a stick? No way!" Swords up, he batted another lethal strike aside. "How about you hold that sticker of yours still?"

Working as a team, one cyclops struck high and the other low.

Twisting in midair, Liam dove between the blades and landed on his feet.

One cyclops counterattacked with a powerful chop Liam hadn't anticipated. The head of the ogre's halberd caught him flush in the chest and slammed him back into the wall. Liam lost his wind.

The halberd's blade came in with a decapitating blow.

Liam parried.

Clang!

The savage blow knocked his arms and swords back so hard that one of Liam's sword pommels clipped him in the head. Another heavy chop followed. Liam rolled aside. The halberd's axe head bit deep into the planks of wood inches from his cheek. Eyeing the blade with blood dripping in his eyes, Liam said, "This is getting serious."

The one cyclops tried to pull his halberd out of the catwalk. The other drew back to take another swing.

Liam jumped up and landed on the stuck halberd's handle.

Tugging at the handle with both arms, the cyclops said, "Get off of there!"

In a single bound, Liam landed on one monster's shoulders and waved at the other one coming his way. "Come and get me!"

The second cyclops zeroed in on Liam, charged, and unleashed an over-the-head chop.

"No! No!" yelled the first cyclops.

Liam back flipped off the one cyclops's shoulders just as the other's halberd cracked its skull. The cyclops's eye widened to the size of a moon. "No! Sorry! No!"

The dead cyclops fell over, crashing through the catwalk's rail and onto the ground below.

Liam was face to face with the shocked cyclops. "You really should work on your aim."

The cyclops's ugly face turned into a mask of rage. "I'm going to kill you!"

Twirling his swords, Liam said, "No, you aren't. You're dead already."

Halberd pointed at Liam's chest, the orcen cyclops charged. "Raaaaah!"

Liam shifted to one side and stuck the cyclops in the chest and belly with his swords.

The huge orc moaned, "Urk!"

Liam shoved the brute off the catwalk. "And that's how you kill a giant."

Brenwar punched, but he couldn't kick. His feet were still tangled, and the orcs were trying to pummel him to death. He socked orc after orc in the nose, ribs, and face. All the while, the nuurg fighter drew him in closer, hand over hand, link by link.

"I smell a dwarf!" the nuurg would say. "A dead dwarf! Save his beard for me!"

Brenwar bent an orc's arm and twisted until it snapped. The orc let out a howl, startling its fighting kindred. It gave Brenwar some breathing room. He snaked a dagger out of an orc's belt and poked over and over. The deadly jabs sent them away—dying and screaming. Still being dragged, Brenwar sat up again and chucked the dagger at the cyclops. It bounced off the cyclops's chest.

The cyclops smiled. "It takes a sharper blade than that to harm my flesh." The cyclops hauled Brenwar up by his tangled feet, leaving the dwarf suspended upside down. The cyclops leered at Brenwar. "This will be fun."

"Fun!" Brenwar spat back. "I'll show you fun." He took a swing that wasn't even close.

Still holding the chain that held Brenwar up, the cyclops spun around. The momentum lifted Brenwar's head higher off the ground.

"What?" he said. "What in Morgdon are you doing?"

The cyclops spun faster and faster. "I'm going to sling you like a rock into that wall."

Brenwar objected. "Nobody slings a dwarf! Nobody!"

The cyclops let him fly.

Brenwar sailed through the air, bunched himself like a cannonball, and smacked hard into the wall. The stones loosened under his stout weight and popped out on the other side. Shaking it off, he marched out from under the catwalk.

The cyclops gawped.

Brenwar lifted his arm up. "Liam!"

On the catwalk standing above Brenwar, the elf replied, "Yes?"

"Lend me your steel!"

Liam dropped it right into the dwarf's open mitt.

Sword in hand, Brenwar stormed toward the cyclops. "I've had my fill of you!"

The giant orc tossed aside his chain and rushed right for Brenwar. "I'm going to fill my pots with your hide!"

With hundreds of years' experience to his favor, Brenwar cut the cyclops to ribbons. The monster was dead in seconds.

"Well done!" Liam yelled to him.

"Aye." Brenwar marched back into the fray. The rout was on. The orcs were dropping like flies, second after second.

CHAPTER 24

COLD, DAMP, AND DARK WOULD describe the dungeon cellar Nath crept into. At the bottom of the steps under the hatch was a high and wide tunnel dug out of the dirt. Wooden beams held the earth in place, and oil lanterns hung on the posts, giving off a dim light. Nath sniffed the moldy air. A familiar scent wafted into his nose.

Selene!

He hurried down the tunnel and came to a stop at an iron door that barred his path. It was solid and without a portal for him to see through. He put his ear to the door. Something scraped on the other side. It was like the sound of a varmint clawing on a stone floor. He tugged on the handle, but there wasn't any give. That's when he noticed a set of keys hung on a peg nearby.

The first key he tried turned the lock, and with a tug, the heavy creaking door swung open. A moth bigger than his head flew out. A strange raccoon-like critter bolted out of the room and vanished down the tunnel. Nath pulled the door open wide and went in. Steel bars and doors decorated both sides of the tunnel.

Venturing into the dungeon, he noted some of the cells were empty, but not all. Locked up in one cell, a pair of halflings huddled in the corner. They were small, young, and shivering like leaves. A brown-haired male and female. Their round eyes fixed on Nath then looked away.

"It's going to be fine. Come on," he said, unlocking the door and opening it up. "You're free now."

The male halfling stirred and came his way. The female tried to tug the male back by his tattered clothing. Without looking at Nath, he grabbed the door and shut himself back inside. "Go away. You bring certain death upon us."

"The orcs will be defeated. You are free. The nuurg have fallen."

The halfling huddled back with his female and said as he tucked his head away, "They are not what we fear. Go, go away."

"There is nothing to fear here," Nath said. "The path is clear."

The halfling said nothing.

Nath unlocked the cell again and proceeded to the next. There was a skeleton with the bones picked clean. It was empty, and so was the next, but for more skeletons. The only living things he saw were the halflings. Otherwise the entire place was abandoned. At least it looked to be. There were still a few cells left at the end.

Selene, you must be here. I can smell you. My nose doesn't lie.

Debris fell from above.

Nath glanced up. The dirt in the ceiling was moving. At first he thought it was from the battle above, perhaps the giants shaking the ground.

No, it's not that.

His hand fell to his elven sword.

A mouth full of teeth burst through the dirt ceiling, swallowing Nath's arm up to the elbow.

"Gah!" Nath tried to shake the creature off. It was a ghastly huge centipede thing. Its sharp teeth chomped down on his scales. It continued to inch up his swallowed arm, farther and farther. "Sultans of Sulfur! Get off me!"

The monster's tail looked and shook like a snake's rattle. It was one of the weirdest creatures Nath had ever seen.

He started banging the creature into the metal bars.

Bang! Bang! Bang!

"Get off of me!"

The insect held on. Nath kept on hitting it. Like with a tick, the harder he hit it, the deeper it bit. The only thing saving his arm was his scales. He grabbed it by the tail and started pulling it off. "Argh!"

The insect wouldn't give.

"That's it!" Nath said. On his free hand, he bared his claws. "Two can play at this game!" He plunged his fingers into the crunchy armor of the insect and ripped it off him, hunk by hunk. Finally, the insect's jaws gave way, and Nath slung it down the corridor. Slinging the insect's remaining muck off his arm, he said, "That was gross."

Eyeing the ceiling, he backed toward the last two cells at the end of the row. The one on the left was empty. The one on the right had a body. He grabbed the bars. "Selene!"

Selene lay on the cell floor, huddled up but breathing. She was still in the deep sleep and otherwise unharmed.

Nath tried the keys in the lock. There were several. None of them worked. "What's going on?" Again, he stuck in key after key after key. Nothing worked. "Great!"

The steel bars were thick. "If I could just breathe fire on them, I could melt them." He clasped his hands around the bars. "I guess I'm going to have to try and get you out of there the hard way." He tried to pull the vertical bars apart. Muscles bulged in his arms. Sweat dripped down the side of his cheek. "Come on!"

The metal started to bend. It began to groan under his power. Nath took a breath, held it, and pulled with raw power. The steel stretched. The bars parted wide.

"Yes!"

He squeezed through the metal and picked Selene up in his arms. After brushing her hair from her eyes with his nose, he whispered in her ear, "Selene? Wake up, Selene."

Lips parted, she said nothing.

Nath noticed that other than being scraped up a little, she was in good condition. He slipped himself and her out of the cell and headed back toward the main tunnel. The halflings were still in their cell. Nath kicked the insect monster's teeth toward them. "Are you coming? I don't think there's anything to fear now."

Eyes fixed on the teeth, the halflings squeaked. They looked at Nath, and the little halfling man said, "There are no more?"

"No more."

The male halfling took the female halfling's hand. "Lead the way."

Seconds later, they emerged topside of the tunnel and were back inside the stables. The wrathhorns were quiet. Perfectly still. Nath headed toward the exit. No sounds of battle were heard on the other side. He set Selene down, drew his sword, and—fearing the worst—he headed outside.

Brenwar stood in the center of the courtyard along with Liam, Sansla, and the rest of the roamer elves. The orcs and nuurg had been defeated. The survivors were bound up and had surrendered.

Crossing the courtyard, Nath called out, "Brenwar, where's the celebration?"

The dwarf's bearded frown didn't change. He pointed at the high walls and towers.

Like a giant flock of scaled pigeons on the walls, parapets, and tower tops, wurmers perched side by side with each other by the dozens.

CHAPTER 25

HOVERING ABOVE THE MIDDLE OF the courtyard for all to see was Lotuus the Fairy Empress. Her black eyes landed on Nath. "Hello, Nath Dragon. We meet again."

Nath sheathed his elven sword. "The pleasure is all yours."

"Hah-hah-hah-hah-hah. My, you have such a charming wit. Too bad it hasn't done you any good." She glided down in front of his eyes, bouncing the wand with his tassel of hair off her cheek. "You really should be more careful with that lovely hair of yours. This led me right to you. Well, it led the wurmers, anyway. They make excellent bloodhounds."

"If they're so good, then why did it take you a year to find me?"

"I think your little sword had something to do with that. Oh, that escape you pulled off at Urslay was really something. Eckubahn is still furious. Poof. You were gone." She rapped him on the head with her wand. "But that will never happen again, now that your sword is in my possession."

Nath nodded in agreement, but his mind was racing. It was good news that Lotuus had Fang. That solved one of the mysteries. "You know, I don't think you have it. It's not possible. Fang doesn't play well with fluttering foul ilk."

"Fluttering foul ilk?" She touched her chest. "Me? How unflattering for you to say."

"There's more to come. It's sad, though, you being such a beautiful fairy. One that I alone freed. Only to have you turn on me."

She flipped him in the head with her tassel again. "You are such a pawn."

Fastening his eyes on hers, he spoke in a sweet and gentle voice. "Lotuus, you are far too marvelous to be so evil. Why not side with the dragons? Why the wicked spirits of the titans? You are a creature of magic and dignity. You know that, yet you defy it. Why?"

Long-faced, she said, "Because."

"That is not an answer. How about you and I talk? Just talk. I sense the hurt inside you. I want to help take it away."

"No!" Wings buzzing, she drifted backward. "I like my anger. It makes me strong. It reminds me that the fairies don't have to rely on anybody—not you, not your father, nor even the titans. But at least they will destroy everything I hate."

"Like the living?"

"Especially the living. They're the ones ruining everything! They fight. They steal. They lie. Who needs them?"

"It's not the races stirring the pot this time, Lotuus. It's the titans, and you know that. Now more people die because of it."

"No, the dragons caused this long ago. They imprisoned me and the titans. Wrongly. It is your kind that causes the problem, not mine."

"The titans destroy. The dragons preserve. Even an orc knows that." Palms up and out by his sides, he pleaded with her. "Your kind are not evil. At least not all of them. They follow your lead. You can change their path."

Hovering around Nath, she replied, "You say your dragons preserve life? Then where are they? Hmmm? People fall prey to the titans every day by the hundreds, and not a single dragon has shown up to stop them. They don't care, and I'm curious. Why do you?"

"They care," Nath said under his breath.

Lotuus made a good point, though. Her captivating eyes and voice made her argument quite convincing. If the dragons cared about the people so much, then why didn't they help them more?

"The dragons did help the people. And the people turned on them," Brenwar blurted out. "That's why!"

"That's not how I recall it," she said.

"While you live, it's never too late for redemption, Lotuus," Nath said, offering his hand. He had to try to win her over. Be sincere. There wasn't any other way out of the situation they were in. On a single word from her, the wurmers would strike and kill them all. "Why not change?"

"I tried it the other way before, and it just didn't suit me. I'm more suited for what I do now."

In a warning tone, Nath said, "You'll lose. And this time you won't be locked up again. This time you'll be destroyed by dragon fire."

"What dragon fire? Yours? You don't have any, Nath Dragon. And you don't have that sword to get you out of this bind. No. You're coming with me. We're going to see Eckubahn."

Nath nodded at his friends. "And what about them?"

"You and I are going to watch the wurmers kill them."

CHAPTER 26

A SHADOW COVERED THE FORTRESS AS if a cloud had rolled in above. Looking up, Nath said, "You might want to rethink that!" He pointed at the sky.

Staying the wurmers with her hands, Lotuus peered above. Her lips curled into a sneer. "No, no, no!"

Circling above them was a mountain of scales with wings. A flying fortress with claws and teeth. A dragon. And not just any dragon, a sky raider with horns on its skull the size of twisted oaks.

"I'm guessing he's here to help *me*, not you," Nath said. "And judging by the look in his eye, well, he won't be taking any prisoners. So what will it be, Lotuus? Do you want to surrender?" Nath hitched his leg up on a barrel of grain. "I tell you what, give me back my sword—"

"And my war hammer!" Brenwar blurted out.

"Yes, and that," Nath continued, "and I'll let you go free. See, I'm reasonable. No bloodshed. No violence." He cleared his throat. Nath was buying time.

Where in the world did that sky raider come from? His timing couldn't have been better. Good thing she doesn't know that. I'd better pour it on.

"I know what you're thinking, Lotuus. Certainly a dozen of your wurmers can take down the raider. But that would divide your forces. I don't mean to brag, but more dragons are on the way. He just happened to be the closest one in the area."

Fists balled up at her sides, Lotuus replied, "You're a horrible liar, Nath Dragon."

He shrugged and glanced up. "Am I?"

A second shadow fell over the crowd of onlookers below. Another sky raider had appeared. Saliva dripped from the jaws of the wurmers. Their throats rumbled like rattles. Death filled their bright eyes. Their sharp teeth chomped and grinded together. They wanted to fight. They wanted to kill. It was their only purpose.

"Impossible," she said through her teeth.

"Am I not the Dragon Prince? You shouldn't be surprised." He stretched his hand toward her and clasped his fingers in and out. "Return my sword."

Eyeing the sky, Lotuus chewed her lip. Her eyes glided between Nath and the sky raider dragons. She swallowed a lump in her throat. "I don't have your sword."

"Now who's the rotten liar?"

"Well, not on me," she said, displaying her lovely figure and spinning in the air. "Do I look like someone who would adorn myself so heavily?

"Where is it?" Nath demanded.

"Oh, you'll find it." She pointed. "It's in the woods, over there somewhere."

The two sky raiders started to descend.

"I think you need to be more specific."

"Do I need to draw you a map?" she yelled.

"Yes," he replied. "And I want my lock of hair back."

Hugging it, she said, "But I'm so fond of it."

"Hand it over."

"Fine." She threw it down on the ground. "Your sword is with the dead wilder elves a league that way. Just follow the stench." She motioned to the wurmers. "Come."

She darted off into the sky, looking over her shoulder, heading north and away from Thraag. The wurmers took right in behind her.

The sky raiders' roars were louder than thunder. Their voices shook the walls like great brass horns. "MAAAAAOO-OOOOOOOO! MAAAAAOOOOOOO!" The pair of great dragons gave chase after the wurmers.

"They're going after them!" Nath ran for the steps that led up the catwalk and watched from the walls. "Look!"

The huge sky raiders tore through the sky and descended on the wurmers. The wurmers turned and attacked. Flames gushed out of a sky raider's mouth, enveloping the wurmers in a great ball of fire. They screeched and burned. Tumbled from the sky. The second sky raider smashed through the wurmer ranks. The wurmers pinned themselves to its body, scratching, clawing, and biting. The sky raider took the dragon insectoids to the ground and ripped them to pieces with its claws. It gored them with its horns and tore them apart with its tail.

The wurmers fought in a knot of fury. They spat balls of fiery energy. They dug in with claws and teeth. The sky raiders, mighty and strong, brought the heat. The entire valley turned into dragon flames. Pillars of black smoke went up in a huge plume.

Nath lost sight of the battle in the all-consuming smoke and fire. Only the angry roars were heard, so loud that they seemed to shake the entire world. He could feel the searing heat on his face. He smiled.

A minute later, the sky raiders burst out of the flames and let out a roar of victory.

"MAAAAOOOOOO! MAAAAAOOOOOO!"

The grand dragons circled once, and upward they went, vanishing into the clouds.

Standing beside Nath, Liam said, "That was awesome."

"Where did they come from?" Brenwar said to Nath. "Did you summon them?"

"I wish I had, but no." He shook his head and shrugged. "I guess today just happens to be my day. Selene!"

"What about her?" Brenwar said. "Did you not find her?"

"No, I did." Nath's eyes searched out Sansla. He saw him on a tower and motioned for him to come down. The great ape glided down and landed by Nath's feet. "Sansla, I need you to take Selene somewhere safe. Can you take her to Dragon Home for me?"

"I will," Sansla agreed.

Nath went into the barn. Selene and the halflings were gone.

Chapter 27

"Selene! Aw, what am I yelling for? She wouldn't hear me anyway." Nath kicked up some hay. "She sleeps like the dead." He raced from stall to stall and searched high and low. He looked in every spot he could find.

Oddly, the wrathhorns were silent within their stalls. Not a single one of them nickered. Nath spun around. There wasn't anywhere for Selene or the halflings to go, and the halflings certainly couldn't have carried her off.

"Everyone search," Nath said to Liam.

Brenwar marched in and said, "What are we looking for?"

Aggravated, Nath said, "Selene!"

"Oh," Brenwar muttered.

"They couldn't have gotten far." Nath stormed out of the stables. Eyeing the towers, he said, "Search them too!"

A pair of roamers sprinted up to each tower. It was absurd to think the halflings could have taken Selene into the towers. Even in human form, she was twice as heavy as them. They wouldn't have been able to carry her away. And the battle hadn't lasted that long, so they couldn't have gotten that far anyway.

What if they weren't halflings? What if they were something else?

"Sansla!" Nath yelled to the great white ape who was perched on the catwalks looking over the walls. "Will you check from the sky?"

In a single bound, Sansla leapt into the air with his wings beating and took off into the sky. Nath sighed.

Brenwar stepped into view. "You need to settle yourself down. You're going about this all wrong."

"Am I?"

Fists on his hips, Brenwar gave a matter-of-fact, "Yes."

"And what would you do differently?"

Rubbing his bearded chin, the dwarf replied, "First, I'd go and secure my hammer, but I guess we can try to find your long-tailed woman."

"Brenwar, don't start—"

"You're a tracker, aren't you?"

"The best."

"Then track! You've got me and the roamers, all of the best trackers in the world, and all you are doing is running around and screaming."

Nath's boiling blood started to cool. Taking a breath he said, "You know, you're right."

"Of course I am. I'm a dwarf."

"That's clear." Nath headed back into the stables where he left Selene. He took a long draw through his nose. Among the straw and manure and other things, Selene's scent still lingered. There was an impression in the ground where he had left her. There were signs of her body being dragged over the dirt and straw.

"The trail seems pretty clear to me," Brenwar said. "I'm not sure how you missed it."

"You missed it too."

"I did not. I wasn't looking."

The trail came to a stop in front of one of the wrathhorns' stables. The huge beast eyed Nath from the other side with intent eyes. Nath had to get up on his toes to gaze within. The wrathhorn shuffled into his path, blocking his view.

"Will you get out of the way?" Nath argued.

The beast-like horse snorted all over him.

"Hah!" Brenwar laughed, slapping his knee.

Wiping the monster snot off him, Nath glared at Brenwar.

"Well, that was funny. 'Humor is good in sour times.' The great dwarven philosopher Puukiin said that."

Nath grabbed the stall's latch handle and pulled it back.

"What are you doing?" Brenwar said, dropping back with his elven battle-axe. "Pardon me for not wanting to get stomped on again."

"Are you telling me you can't take it?"

"I'm telling you I've been trampled enough for one day and I'm not keen on it ever happening again."

Metal scraped against metal, and the latch was pulled back. Slowly, Nath pulled the door open.

On the other side, the wrathhorn's spiked hooves clawed at the dirt. It nickered and shook its great head.

"Stay here and secure the door behind me," Nath said, glancing back at Brenwar.

"Somebody must have hit you in the head today, but I'll do it."

When he stood face to face with the wrathhorn, the gate clanked shut behind Nath.

"Are you still breathing in there?" Brenwar said.

"Yes."

Nath reached out and softly placed his hand on the bridge above the horse creature's nose. He traced around the curves of its horn. The wrathhorn stood a full head taller than a normal horse. It was built stronger too. Though it lacked the grace and refinement of its smaller, less formidable counterpart, there was still something remarkable and beautiful about it. Staring into its eyes, Nath saw a deep horse-like intelligence lurking within. He petted the shag under its chin and wondered if it had indeed been just a regular horse once or if it had always been something else entirely.

"Excuse me," said a soft little voice. It was the female halfling whom Nath had rescued. She stood right underneath the belly of the dangerous monster stallion. "Are you looking for your friend?"

Squatting down, Nath said to the pie-faced, toe-headed little halfling, "You shouldn't be under there. It's dangerous. This beast will trample you. Turn your bones to meat."

The halfling giggled. "No, it won't." She had a coarse horse brush in her hand and started stroking its belly. "We take care of the beasts. We feed them. Brush them. Train them. They won't hurt us because they know we wouldn't hurt them. Boy, you sure had them stirred up earlier. It's a good thing we arrived in time to calm them down. They can smell those gates. One charge. One kick. I've seen it happen before." She grinned. "It killed two orcs. That was funny. Orcs are stupid."

"Can you tell me where my friend Selene is?"

Out of nowhere, another voice chimed in. "She's in the back." The male halfling was sitting backward on the wrathhorn's neck. His eyes were brown, but bright. There was more life in them than there had been before. "Safe, thanks to us. Are all the orcs dead?"

Squeezing by the beast and toward the back, Nath said, "Yes."

"All of them?" asked the female.

"We're double-checking." Nath ventured to the very back of the stall. In the back was a trough, and on the other side lay Selene, fast asleep. He rushed to her side.

"Why is she sleeping?" asked the female halfling, standing on the lip of the trough to look over Nath's shoulder.

"Yes, how can anyone sleep in the middle of all this excitement?" asked the male halfling on the other side of Nath.

Picking Selene up in his arms, Nath said, "I wish I had an answer to that."

"She has a tail," said the female. "Do you have an answer to that?"

Rubbing Nath's arms, the man said, "And why are your arms so scaly? Are you a demon?"

"No!"

The halflings scuttled underneath the wrathhorn, clinging together and eyeing Nath. "Don't smite us, demon."

"I'm not a demon. No one is going to smite anybody, not anybody non-orcen at least."

"Oh." Resuming their friendly and curious demeanor, both halflings asked, "So why does she have a tail?"

"Nath!" Brenwar yelled from the other side of the gate.

"What?"

"Get out here! We've got a problem!"

CHAPTER 28

With Selene in his arms once more, Nath followed Brenwar into the courtyard, where Sansla and Liam were talking. "What's going on? As you can see, I found her."

"More company is coming," Sansla said. Liam nodded beside him and added, "Yes, come see for yourself." He led them up the catwalks to where they could gaze over the western wall.

"Oof," Brenwar remarked.

Well over a mile out on the open plains that led to Thraag, an Orcen army marched. It wasn't a small army. Orcs by the thousands. From the long distance, Nath's keen eyes watched the orc banners wave. There were heavily armored foot soldiers along with riders in the dozens.

"Excellent," Liam said. "I like a challenge."

"I don't imagine they know we're here, but they will know, soon enough," Nath said. "We need to move on."

"But this is a victory," Liam said. "This fortress is our prize. I see no reason to give it up."

"We didn't come here to take the fortress. We came to get Selene. Now that we have her, we must go."

"I want to stay. We have the wall, the towers. We'll pick them apart," Liam said. He wasn't being argumentative, just passionate.

"And what will you do when you run out of arrows?" Brenwar said, poking Liam's quiver. "Will you play the lute for them until they go away?"

"There are plenty of crossbow bolts in that armory. As I said," Liam replied, "we can hold them off for days."

"Liam, our mission here is accomplished," Sansla said. "It's time to depart."

"I need a favor, Sansla," said Nath.

"What do you wish, Dragon Prince?"

He handed the winged ape Selene. "Take her somewhere safe. Dragon Home would be best. I cannot continue to carry her with the journey ahead."

"In case I cannot make it to Dragon Home, I know another place of safety to secure her." Sansla eyed the roamers. "We shall guard her with our lives. Roamers, it's time to depart."

Liam took a knee. "My King, perhaps I could render aid to Nath Dragon on his journey."

"That is up to him." With Selene cradled in his arms, Sansla took off into the sky with a powerful leap.

"Liam," said Nath, "I need you to lead the orcs off our trail. Surely they will be in pursuit, and Brenwar and I need to make haste to find our weapons."

"The roamers will handle that chore just fine without me," Liam said.

"I don't think your father would be pleased if you left your men. Especially with your uncle Hoven in such peril." Nath put his hand on Liam's shoulder. "I appreciate the offer, but what's the right thing to do?"

"Stay behind and kill the orcs?"

"No."

"Fine." Liam made a hand signal and let out a sharp whistle. The roamers lowered the front gate, and their horses came in. Liam's horse stopped just below the catwalk. Liam patted Brenwar on the shoulder. "You're not a bad fighter, for a dwarf." He jumped onto the horse's back. "Soon again, Nath dragon. Soon again." He galloped off after the roamers.

"Stupid elf," Brenwar grumbled. "He's got spirit, though."

Eyeing the oncoming army, Nath noted a cloud of dust that had come up. The orc riders were galloping their way. "Guzan!"

"What?" Brenwar asked.

"If I were to guess, I'd say the orcs were waiting for a signal and hadn't received one. We'd better get moving."

"I'll never outrun those horses on these short little legs." Brenwar leaned his axe against the parapet wall, spat in his hands, rubbed them together, picked the battle-axe back up, and said, "No. I guess we'll have to stay and fight. I'll go close the gate."

"Don't be silly. We can ease out of here and be on our way just fine."

"You know those orcs can smell me from a mile away."

"Excuse me!" the halfling man called up to Nath from below the catwalk. He was riding on the back of a wrathhorn. Two more wrathhorns were being towed behind him. "If you want to outdistance the orcs, you should ride on one of these."

"I'm not getting on one of those things!" Brenwar yelled.

"I don't think you have a choice."

"I do."

"No, you don't," Nath said. "I'm getting on. You're getting on." He hopped off the catwalk, eased up to the middle beast, put his foot in the oversized stirrup, and climbed on. He looked up at Brenwar on the catwalk. "Come on. Those orcs are closing in fast. Can't you hear them?"

"I hear them, I hear them, already!" Eyeing the beast with wary eyes, Brenwar jumped down into the saddle and grabbed the reins. He stared at the female halfling, who was smiling at him. "What are you looking at?"

"Why is your hand so bony?"

Brenwar glowered at her. "Why is your pie hole so big?"

"What's a pie hole?" she asked.

"Let's go," Nath dug his heels into the beast's ribs. It took off at a thunderous trot toward the gate that led out of the fortress. A soft clicking sound caught his ears. In the saddle he turned. The orc cyclops Gaak stood underneath the bottom of the catwalk where they had fought. He was taking aim with a heavy crossbow in his arms. "Nooooo!"

Clatch-Zip!

The bolt rocketed through the air and plunged into Brenwar's back.

The dwarf pitched forward in the saddle. "Aargh!"

"Hang on, Brenwar!" Nath turned his mount and rode back for his friend.

Gaak was running right for him with a sword in his hand. "I will kill you, Nath Dragon. I will have your head!"

Nath scooped Brenwar out of the other saddle onto his. He shouted at the halflings, "Ride! Ride! Ride!"

Chapter 29

In tremendous strides, the wrathhorns thundered down the road faster than any horse could run. "Where are we going?" the halfling yelled back at Nath.

Snapping the reins, Nath rode up alongside him. "West, toward the forest."

At least, that was the impression he'd been given by Lotuus. She could have been lying, but he had sensed she was defeated. "Brenwar! Can you hear me?"

The dwarf didn't reply. The bolt still protruded from his back, and it was buried deep, right near the spine.

"Brenwar!"

Even with a bad wound it wasn't often that a dwarf stopped fighting. Perhaps there was something worse in that bolt. Poison maybe. Nath wouldn't put anything past the orcs. Especially one that had been turned into a nuurg.

Suddenly, the female halfling started screaming from behind them. "He's coming. Gaak's coming!"

The cyclops rode hard and right after them. He was on the back of a wrathhorn with a hungry look in his eye.

I should have finished him.

Brenwar shifted. His head popped up. "What's going on? Ow! What did you stick in my back?"

"It's a bolt. A cyclops shot you," Nath replied.

"What cyclops?"

On the back of the galloping wrathhorn, Nath spoke above the rushing wind, "The big one with one eye. The nuurg called Gaak!"

"A slimy orcen one-eyed coward shot me in the back?" Brenwar puffed through his beard. "I'll kill him!"

"Just hang on. I told you to wear armor that covered your back."

"Why would I do that? Dwarves advance, they don't retreat. Back armor is for cowards!"

"And so is shooting people in the back," Nath reminded him.

Brenwar squirmed in the saddle.

"Be still!" Nath said.

The dwarf twisted away, fell off the saddle, and bounced off the ground.

Nath wheeled the monster horse around. "Are you mad?"

Brenwar popped up on his feet and with the bolt still sticking out of his back was off and running toward the oncoming nuurg.

Seeing his dwarven prey, the nuurg bore down on Brenwar. The wrathhorn's thundering hooves kicked up the dirt. "Hahahaha!" the cyclops bellowed from his saddle. "The dwarf and the dragon both will die!"

Still barreling forward, eyes up and lowering his shoulders, Brenwar shouted, "For Morgdon!" He tackled the wrathhorn in the legs.

The beast pitched forward with a frightening whine and crashed to the ground.

The cyclops Gaak tumbled head over heels over the beast's head, popped up on a knee with a mouthful of grass, and wiped the mud from his eye.

Brenwar plowed into him. His powerful arms, like balls of muscle, punched away.

Whop! Whop! Whop!

The cyclops recoiled. His arms were flailing. "Get off of me!"

Brenwar didn't let up. There was blood in his eyes. A deep, angry hatred. Every punch he threw was as fanatical as the next. He climbed up on the dazed giant's back and locked his arms around his neck. The small grizzly of a dwarf squeezed.

"Urk!" The cyclops clawed at the air. His eyes popped open wide.

"This is what you get for shooting me in my back!" Brenwar yelled. He squeezed the life out of the cyclops Gaak.

The orc breathed no more. His giant body lay limp on the earthen floor.

The dwarf shoved the body to the side and rose back up on his feet. "For Morgdon."

Not hiding his amazement and excitement, Nath said, "Aye, for Morgdon. I've never seen anyone tackle a horse before. A giant horned one at that."

"And you probably never will again." Brenwar marched forward and teetered. "I feel odd." His eyes fluttered in his head, and he fell face first in the grass.

"Brenwar!"

CHAPTER 30

ATH, THE HALFLINGS, AND THE wrathhorns rode about a league to the general area where he thought Lotuus meant. They had dismounted and were resting in the deep woods. Nath sat on a fallen tree, and Brenwar lay at his feet on his belly. The bolt was still in his back. The halflings were on either side of him.

"Is he dead?" asked the female halfling.

"No, he's not dead. See how his back rises and falls? He's quite alive," Nath said.

The male halfling poked Brenwar with a stick.

Nath snatched the stick away. "Don't do that."

The female halfling hopped off the log. "How come your friends sleep so much? Why does he have a hand made from bone? Where is the skin? And you never told us about your scales. Or her scales."

"Yes," the male halfling agreed, "tell us about the scales. Are they fish scales? Do you come from the water? Are you a merman? I've heard of mermen in the sea. They have scales and fins." He inspected Nath with his eyes. "I see no fins on you."

The female halfling crawled back on the log. "Look for gills. He should have gills like a fish." She piled up his locks of long hair in her tiny hands and lifted them up and tilted her head. "I don't see any gills either."

"I'm not a fish!" he said. "I'm Nath Dragon!"

"I thought Nath Dragon was a dragon," said the female halfling.

"Yes, bigger than the biggest clouds, he is," the male halfling said, nodding his head eagerly.

Nath stuck his face in his palms.

Halflings. How did I get stuck with halflings?

Nath sighed and asked, "What are your names?"

"I am Zoose," the male halfling said, coming to his feet and sticking his chest out. "And my sister is called Goose."

"Zoose, huh? You seem awfully small to be called Zoose." Nath glanced at Goose. "And you're named after a bird?"

"No, my greatest grandmother Goose." She ran her hand over the scales on his arm. "So, you aren't a dragon, you're a fish."

"No, I am a dragon."

"But you don't have any wings or any tail," Zoose said.

"Not all dragons have wings or tails. Most dragons do have tails, except for the tailless dragons. But they are mean. Very mean. They'll swallow the both of you in one bite."

Face drawn up tight, Goose said, "That would be horrible. Do all dragons eat people?"

"It depends." Nath kneeled down by Brenwar and wrapped his hand around the bolt in the dwarf's back.

"Ooh, are you going to pull that out?" Goose said. "Won't that be painful?"

"He could bleed to death," Zoose added. "But I've heard that dwarves have sand for blood. Is that true?"

"No," Nath said, "can't you see the blood on his back? It's his, not someone else's."

Together the halflings said, "Eeeeew."

The wound in Brenwar's back looked bad, but he had been through worse, Nath was certain. Brenwar's last effort when he let loose against Gaak had been something else—a demonstration that proved his friend's will outweighed the dwarf's powerful constitution. Brenwar had tapped out all of his reserves. The dwarf was exhausted.

"Uh, Zoose and Goose, can you fetch me some deckle leaves and pine needles? A few handfuls of dirt would help too. And some water if you can find it."

They nodded eagerly. "Sure, sure," Zoose said. He and she darted into the brush and out of sight.

"That's better," Nath said. He let go of the bolt and leaned back against the fallen tree. His limbs were achy, and he was weary himself. He tilted his head back far enough to where the sun crept through the trees and warmed his face. "Ah."

There was plenty on his mind. Number one, the orcs would be hunting after him. He could only hope the roamers had managed to lead them away from his trail. Number two, Selene was rescued and in safe hands now. At least he hoped so. He'd gotten off to a rough start with Sansla Libor years ago, but he knew the Roamer King could be trusted now. It gave him some relief. And three, his best friend, Brenwar, was down. He wasn't used to seeing the dwarf laid out. It was easier to knock out a tree than a dwarf.

"I hope you aren't going to be out for years, like I was."

Nath felt guilty recalling all those years he'd been in a dragon coma. Twenty-five years at one time, even. Brenwar and the dwarves had guarded him that entire time in the snow-filled banks, high in the mountains. His eyes popped open.

"Sultans of Sulfur. Selene!"

What would it be like if she was going through such a change like he did? He might not see her for decades. And at the rate the titans were going, there wouldn't be anything left of Nalzambor in another decade. He sat up.

"I have to stop them."

"Stop who?" Goose said. She was standing right behind him with her hands full of deckle leaves and her pockets full of pine needles. "Oh, and Zoose is bringing the dirt. Or mud. Or water, was it? What is all of this for?"

"It's to stanch the bleeding."

"Oh." She cocked her head. "Who's bleeding?"

"Bleeding?" Zoose had arrived. He had made two bowls out of green leaves and twigs. One was filled with mud and the other water. "Who's bleeding?"

"Brenwar," Nath said.

Scratching his brown locks, Zoose replied, "Who is Brenwar?"

"Just bring over what you have."

The halflings laid out their supplies by Nath's side.

Nath rubbed his hands together, grabbed the bolt in Brenwar's back, and said, "You might want to get back, in case he kicks."

Neither of the halflings moved. Their eyes were filled with anticipation.

Nath yanked the bolt out.

Brenwar jumped up and cried, "Yeouch! What in Morgdon are you doing? It felt like you just ripped my spine out!"

Staring at the crossbow bolt, Nath noticed tiny barbs on it. It was meant to go in but never come out. "Sorry, Brenwar."

Brenwar snatched the bolt out of his hand and huffed through his beard. "I hate those dirty orcs." He turned his back to Nath. "All right, all right. Stick some dirt in that pothole you just put in me."

"Just lie down again," Nath said, looking at the wound in Brenwar's back and grimacing.

"I don't like lying down." Brenwar said, stretching out flat on the grass. "Sleeping is for the weak."

CHAPTER 31

"THIS IS HORRIBLE," GOOSE SAID. The little female halfling was aghast and covering her nose with her shirt.

Nath had found the area that Lotuus had mentioned. The rogue elves lay dead. Slaughtered. The claws and the teeth of the wurmers had torn them to bits, but not without a fight. A couple of wurmers were withered husks. Their decaying bodies wilted like acid had eaten them.

Nath took a knee where one body had been destroyed by an unknown energy. He plucked a metal pin from the ashes. It was the mark of the rogue elf leader, Slavan. He clenched it in his fist. "Lotuus."

Brenwar lumbered through the nearby woodland, a little gimpy and grumbling. "She's a liar. All fairies are liars. It wouldn't surprise me one bit if my hammer was sunk in the sea."

"I don't think it's made it that far," Nath said. Rising up to full height, he scratched his head. It didn't really make a lot of sense that Lotuus would leave the weapons out in the open. They were too big for the fairies to carry, and the wurmers didn't have the means, but she would have hidden them with magic, and they could be anywhere. Inside a rock or a stone. Maybe inside a tree—or just invisible. He put his foot up on a stump that looked a little like a throne. "Where are you, Fang?"

"Who is Fang?" Zoose asked.

"That's the sword we're looking for, you fluffy-headed little iggit!" Brenwar yelled.

Appearing at Brenwar's side, Goose asked, "What's an iggit?"

"Nath, can't you dismiss them?" Brenwar said.

"I suppose I could. Zoose and Goose, you are both dismissed. Free to go home. Wander. Roam." Nath shooed them away. "It's been nice to meet you. Now move along."

Standing with each other, Goose said, "Go where?"

"To your home."

"Oh," Zoose said, "and where might that be?"

"You don't know where you're from?" Nath asked.

"We were born inside the orc fortress," Goose said, picking a wildflower and stuffing it in her mouth. "But we like it out here. It's pretty."

"Brenwar, I think you're stuck with them for the moment."

"Great," the dwarf grumbled. "Now I've got a pain in my back and two more pains in my behind."

"Brenwar!" Nath tossed his head back and laughed. But something caught his eyes. There was a faint trail of blood leading away from the scene. Taking to his feet again, he said, "I think we just might have a witness."

"What's a witness?" Goose asked.

"I tell you what. You two stay with the wrathhorns and wait here until I come back. I shouldn't be gone too long." He patted their little heads. In a comforting way, the halflings made Nath feel bigger again.

If they can survive in this world at such a wee little size, then certainly I can.

"So, will you do that for me?"

The halflings gave excited nods.

"Let's go, Brenwar."

"Gladly."

It appeared that one of the rogue elves had survived by crawling away and then jogging off into the woods. The footprints were staggered and small.

"A female elf," Brenwar said, eyeing the ground.

Nath noted a smear of blood on a tree branch. "It seems a remnant always survives, no matter how bad the devastation is."

Brenwar pointed his thumb over the patched-up wound in his back. "Case in point."

They followed the blood trail over a mile. The rogue elf had done a decent job covering her tracks, but not good enough to avoid Nath's keen eye. Traversing the woodland another two miles, the tracks led them up a hill with a fairly steep incline.

"Whoever it is will run out of blood at some point," Brenwar said, puffing up the hill. He pointed at the ground. "Look."

A bloody handprint was on a sliver of stone that jutted up out of the ground. The rogue elf had started to crawl, gotten up, and fallen down.

Nath caught Brenwar's eye and put his finger to his lips.

The dwarf nodded.

On cat's feet, Nath proceeded forward. His scales tingled from his fingertips to his elbow. Someone was close. He could hear ragged breathing in the brush ahead. He pushed through.

Clatch-zip!

He jerked his head down. A crossbow bolt zipped over his head and lodged itself in a nearby tree. Before him, a wounded lady elf tried to load the crossbow again. Nath closed in and took the crossbow away.

She jerked a dagger from her belt and took a jab. The blade skipped off the scales on his arm. She moaned.

Nath took the blade away. "Enough of that now. You've got enough trouble already." Her wounds were severe. There were gashes in her abdomen, arms, and legs—clear through the black-and-green armor that she wore. Her fine elven features were exhausted, her breathing rough, and her limbs trembling. "Find her some water, Brenwar."

The lady elf's dark eyes found his. "S-Sorry, Nath Dragon. We betrayed you."

He took her in his arms and propped her up.

She coughed and grimaced in pain. "Slavan was not himself. He was deceived." She reached behind her and stuck her hand in the brush. "I secured it."

There was a glint of metal in the brush.

He dusted the woodland debris away. "Fang! And Mortuun!"

"Again, I am sorry. I only followed orders. It was my obligation."

Zoose and Goose popped into the clearing with large leaves filled with water. "Is somebody thirsty?"

"Have you been following us all this time?" Nath asked as he took a leaf and put it to the lady elf's lips.

"Certainly," Goose said.

"What about the wrathhorns?"

"We let them go," Zoose said.

"Let them *go*? There is an army of orcs in pursuit of us. Why would you do that?"

In a cheerful voice, Goose said, "It just seemed like the right thing to do."

"Sure, it was, just the wrong time to do it." Nath grabbed Fang in one hand and picked up the lady elf with the other, laying her over his shoulders as he had done with Selene. "We have to go."

Brenwar appeared. "Did someone say Mortuun?" He noticed the halflings. "And where did you two iggits come from?"

"Don't ask," Nath said. "Grab your hammer."

Brenwar picked his hammer up and gave it a hug. "Mortuun."

CHAPTER 32

"I AM LAYLANA," SAID THE LADY rogue elf. "I'm new to the order that protects the Elven Field of Dreams. Less than five years."

Nath had managed to patch her up good enough that she could walk. Still, their pace was slow. He'd offered to carry her, but once she was able, she refused. She ambled along using a cut branch as a staff to lean on. The lady elf was tough and yet very pretty. Chestnut-brown hair and light-green eyes, trim and captivating.

"You really should rest as much as possible," he said to her. "Everything will mend better."

Eyes forward, she replied, "I'm getting stronger with every step."

"Well, the orcs aren't getting any slower," Brenwar remarked. "I can tell you that." The burly dwarf marched past them both. "We'll be up to my beard if we don't move any faster."

"Pay him no mind," Nath said to Laylana.

"I don't," she replied.

Nath was taking them far north of Narnum into Quintuklen. The hills and dales were easy to travel, and there were plenty of villages where they could get food and rest. Possibly some horses to continue their travels. It was far out of the way of the dwarves and elves that were hunting after them. Nath was curious about that. The deaths of Laedorn and Uurluuk still seemed so unlikely.

"Do you think me guilty of the crime of which I'm accused?" Nath asked Laylana in Elven.

"No," she said.

"Why not?"

"There was no motive. Why would you assault the elves? Of course, it's not my place to question my orders. I am bound by my duty. I'm not a fool, but some of my brethren are. How quickly they've forgotten that you saved the lands from the hordes of Barnabus."

Nath smiled. It felt good to hear someone say something nice for a change. After all, Nath had put a lot of work into saving the land. "Yes, it's awfully strange that the races forget things so quickly."

"That's how it is. People are forgetful, and they seem to always blame someone else for their problems."

"You are awfully wise for such a young elf. Where does that come from?"

"My mother says I get it from my grandfather."

"And who might that be?"

"Laedorn."

Nath stopped in his tracks. His heart sank. It hurt, even. Though he'd had nothing to do with Laedorn's death, he felt guilty for some reason. "Laylana, I'm so sorry. We will find the murderer."

She came to a stop a little bit ahead of him and turned around. "You don't need to apologize, Nath. My grandfather and I were quite close, and he told me a great many things. He knew much about the dragons and told me I could trust them more than the races. Just that I shouldn't poke around in their business."

"There are bad dragons too."

"But you'll know them by their scales, won't you?"

He stuck out his arm. "And what do you know of black-scaled dragons?"

"Nothing, but you're far too handsome to be bad." There was a playful look in her eye. "I've never before seen a person more attractive than an elf."

"Yes, well, don't be deceived. There are many forces that can change the color of scales." Concentrating, he turned his scales from black to white with gold stripes. "Don't judge a dragon by their color. We know what they are by what they do." His scales reverted back to black.

Resuming her trek forward, Laylana said, "Can you change into anything?"

"No." He frowned.

I use to be able to turn into a dragon that could blot out the sun in the sky.

"Just my scales right now."

"But you have other powers, don't you?"

"I can blow smoke." He puffed out a few rings.

She giggled. "That's it?"

Zoose and Goose came rushing out of nowhere, yelling, "Do it again! Do it again!"

"No," he said.

Bouncing up and down like children, they said, "Please! Please! Please!"

Brenwar came storming down the bank. "Don't give in to them. Go away, you silly little things."

Seeing that Laylana was entertained, Nath puffed out some more smoke that covered the halflings.

The halflings started rolling around on the grass, coughing and holding their throats. "No more! No more!"

"That ought to do it," Nath said, tapping his chest with his fist. "I use to be able to puff out fire."

"What happened?" Laylana asked.

"It's a long story."

"Well, I'm sure you have a lot more power within. Be patient. You'll find it again."

"Time will tell." Nath believed it, though.

They walked through the tall grasses for a few more hours. The sun was setting behind the distant mountains. From their high point, the hills rolled down into the river valley.

Brenwar pointed far up ahead. "Village."

Gathering around the dwarf, everyone looked at the village in the valley below. It was a network of small wooden buildings surrounded by split-rail fences where countless livestock grazed. Gardens stretched as far as the eye could see.

"Holbrook," Nath said.

There weren't many places he didn't know from his travels. Holbrook was on the edge, just far enough away from where the orcs travelled. But that might have changed. Holbrook was a place of men with but a smattering of the other races. If anything, it was an extension of Narnum's multicultural environment. "We should be able to find some supplies there."

"I'm not so sure about that." Brenwar swung Mortuun over his shoulder and pointed at some movement just outside the city. Huge men walked among the people, who looked like ants in comparison. "There be giants."

Laylana swooned and collapsed.

CHAPTER 33

NATH BRUSHED THE HAIR OUT of Laylana's face. Her skin was burning hot. "She's got a fever. That's not good."

Some of the wurmer bites were poisonous. Their claws could burn. Laylana seemed to have avoided the worst effects, but now it had caught up with her.

"We need a healer, Brenwar."

Clawing at his beard with his bone hand, the dwarf said, "Of course we do."

"We'll need supplies from that village. I'm certain they have what I need. Or we can at least find somebody."

"We can go," Zoose suggested.

"You've never been outside the fortress, you said," Nath replied. "I think it's best that you stay here with Brenwar."

"I'm not staying back here with them," Brenwar said.

"Yes, you are. You know you can't get within wind of those giants." Nath spied the colossal figures in the small town. They stood at least twenty feet tall. Three in all. He needed to slip in and slip out quietly. "You'll wait, won't you?"

"Aye, but you better make it quick." Brenwar looked at the halflings. "And I won't be answering any questions from you two chatterboxes."

"Where is the skin from your hand?" Goose asked of Brenwar.

Brenwar glared at Nath. "Just hurry."

Nath tossed Fang on the ground.

"What are you thinking? If those giants find you unarmed, it's all over."

"I won't fit in so well with a giant sword on my back. It'll be hard enough to get around anyway."

"Well, don't be so careless." Brenwar stooped over and pulled Dragon Claw from out of Fang's hilt. He tossed it to Nath. "Something is better than nothing."

"Good thinking." He tucked the dagger in his belt. "Thanks."

Nath took off running. He made it into the valley in no time and used the cover of the outlying buildings to stay out of the giants' line of sight.

Night had fallen, and very few people were milling through the streets. With the weather being warm, there were plenty of people that sat and talked on porch fronts. By the sound of their voices, it was men and women, maybe some half-orcs and part-elves. Some halflings skittered through the streets carrying buckets. Back pressed to the wall in one of the alleys, Nath peered farther down the street.

Villages of a few thousand people were always quick to spot a stranger. Though not a giant, Nath would stick out like a sore thumb. He noticed something else that was different from before. There were armored patrols walking around in twos. They wore steel caps and carried long wooden clubs.

Great.

Finding a healing ward wouldn't be difficult, but getting inside one without being seen would be a problem. If he was caught, someone would ask questions. If the giants were called, there wouldn't be a place to run, and he had to get some potions or ointment to take care of Laylana. If only Brenwar still had his chest, but that had been left in the care of Bayzog.

Something tugged at his cloak. He snatched a tiny hand in his iron grip and drew the small body that was attached to the hand off the ground. It was Zoose. "What do you think you're doing?"

"I wanted to see the city. I've never been to a city before. It's marvelous."

"You need to go back."

"But I want to help."

"Then go back," Nath said, setting the halfling down.

Rubbing his wrist, Zoose replied, "That doesn't sound much like helping. Please, let me do something. I owe you."

Time was pressing, and discretion was needed. Glancing down the street at all the people on the porch fronts and the patrolling guards, Nath knew he would be noticed. He had a few acquaintances here, but from a long time ago. Things had changed. For all he knew, the people in Holbrook village were under the influence of the titans. It was safer to assume they were.

Nath kneeled down and said to Zoose, "So you want to help?"

Little hands clamped together, and nodding, the halfling said, "Desperately."

"Listen to me, then, and do exactly as I say. Do you know what a sage is?"

Zoose shook his head no.

"A sage is someone who helps the sick. They have potions, balms, ointments, salves, many things like that. Well, every town has a sage of sorts. There is one in this town, as I recall. There is a yellow lantern that burns a green flame from his porch. You will smell incense."

Zoose held up his hand.

Aggravated, Nath said, "Yes?"

"What is incense?"

"It's a pleasant smell, like perfume."

"What is perfume?"

"You've been with the orcs too long," Nath said. "Look, the building will smell different than the rest. A nice smell. The place you seek is several buildings down and across the street." He turned Zoose toward where he wanted him to go. Nath then turned him in another direction, pointed at a barn, and said, "I will wait for you there. Do you understand?"

"What do I tell them?"

"Tell them you have a friend who has a fever, but you'll have to pay them later. If he doesn't help, tell him it's for a man called Nath and that a wurmer got his friend."

Zoose saluted. "I'll see you soon." He skittered into the street and hustled right down the middle. A pair of soldiers stopped him.

"Oh no." Nath dug his nails into his palms. "They're going to skewer him."

One of the soldiers kicked Zoose in the back of the pants. The other shooed Zoose away and started laughing. Zoose hustled down the street rubbing his backside and vanished onto one of the porches.

Talking to himself, Nath said, "I hope this works."

CHAPTER 34

THE BARN NATH OCCUPIED WAS empty of life. No stable hands or farmers. No livestock. Just piles of hay and other farming supplies. Plows. Harnesses. Pitchforks, picks, and shovels. It was dark too. Quiet. Nath climbed up into the loft. There was a window overlooking the village where he could keep an eye out. The soldiers slowly walked the streets. The villagers talked quietly in the shadows of their porches. There were a couple of small taverns where fires burned within, sending smoke up through the chimneys. The people weren't lively like Nath remembered them, but oppressed. He could feel it.

People shouldn't be so miserable. They should be free to think and do as they please.

Spread out among the fields just outside the village were the giants. They stood as statues. They were ugly brutes, bald headed and hairy chested. They wore animal skins for clothes. They had no weapons, just hands that looked like they could crush boulders.

And I thought I got rid of all this treachery.

Nath pulled up a hay bale and took a seat. He figured it would only take a few minutes at most for Zoose to fetch the supplies he needed. It was a risk. Perhaps the help he sought would not come. A sage would help just about anyone. They were like that, finding the good in even the worst of people. They were curious that way. Many long minutes passed into the next hour. Nath got up and started to pace.

I should have gone after it myself. It's taking too much time.

He was worried about Laylana. The sooner they treated her, the better. Wurmer strikes could not only be lethal, but toxic to others in some cases. The lady elf was strong, from a great family. With Laedorn dead, Nath couldn't bear the thought of anything happening to his granddaughter.

I can't wait any longer.

A commotion occurred down the street. Zoose was talking to one of the soldiers. He had with him someone in robes. A wizardly figure, older, with a crown of white hair around the bald top of his head. The older man started talking as well. The soldiers nodded and departed the other way down the street. Zoose and the man Nath assumed to be a sage skittered down the street and into the barn. Nath remained in his spot.

"Nath. Nath," said the soft voice of Zoose. "I've come and brought help."

Nath didn't reveal himself. He waited. Something prickled his scales.

"He said he would be in here," Zoose said to the sage. The halfling rattled a sack of goods the sage had in his hand. He spoke louder. "I have treatments for the lady elf. We need to hurry."

Nath eased his way through the loft, stood on its edge, and said from the darkness, "Who is this with you?"

"I am Leander." The old man spoke with his hands. "A sage, as you requested. I've only come to help and to warn you."

"Warn me of what?"

Leander threw the bag of goods up to Nath. "This halfling has betrayed you. Run, Nath Dragon. Run!"

A knife appeared in Zoose's hand. He stabbed Leander in the side.

Glitch!

"No!" Nath yelled. "Zoose, what have you done?"

The halfling's eyes narrowed, and he waved his knife high. "Praise Eckubahn! Hail the death of Nath Dragon!" He ran out of the barn, sounding the alarm. "He's in there! He's in there!"

Nath peeked through the loft's opening. Soldiers were storming toward the barn. Two of the giants were moving in. One was heading up into the hills where Brenwar and Laylana hid. Nath hopped down, closed the barn door, and barred it shut.

The old sage was coughing and bleeding. He beckoned for Nath.

Nath embraced the man in his arms. "Hang on."

"The halfling came," Leander said, coughing and wincing in pain. "I knew he would deceive you. He told me. Wanted to turn you in. I played along. That's why I came. To warn you. Long ago you saved my father. My mother. I was a boy. I remember. I owe you my life." He patted the sack of goods gripped in Nath's hands. "The magic is good in this. Use it." He looked up into Nath's eyes with one last gaze. "I had a good life, Nath Dragon. I owe you my thanks."

Leander the sage died in his arms. Nath's eyes watered up. He didn't know this man at all, yet the sage had given his life for something Nath had done long ago. With his palm, he closed the man's eyes.

Something whacked the barn door. Axes were chopping into it from the other side.

Chop! Chop! Chop!

Nath carried Leander to a spot in the barn that had a thick bed of hay to lay him in. He set him down. "Thank you, friend." He wiped the tear from his eye. He was still stunned at what Zoose had done. The little halfling had murdered the man in cold blood. How had the halfling deceived him so easily? He hadn't detected anything evil from Zoose or Goose at all. It made him angry inside. He drew his dagger, Dragon Claw, and faced the barn door.

I've got to get to Brenwar!

The chopping stopped. A silence fell. Suddenly, the ceiling groaned and popped. A giant ripped part of the roof off and glared at Nath.

Great Guzan!

CHAPTER 35

FINGERS OUTSTRETCHED AND HUGE FACE snarling, the giant reached for Nath.

Dragon Claw poised to strike, Nath plunged the mystic dagger into the giant's hand.

The monstrous man jerked his hand back and let out a pain-filled bellow. He gaped at his hand. It was disintegrating right before his eyes. "No! Nooooo!"

Nath watched in awe. The disintegration spread up the giant's arm to the shoulder and then across his chest. Through the gaping hole in the roof, Nath watched the giant's screaming face turn to dust and take flight with the wind. He gazed at Dragon Claw. The blade had a violet gleam in the metal. It pulsated in his hand. Nath jerked the bar off the barn door and swung the door open. Holding the dagger out for all of the wide-eyed soldiers to see, he said, "Who else wants to taste my blade's fury?"

The soldiers backed away.

Behind them on horseback was a soldier wearing a full helmet of iron, with a red plume on top that billowed in the evening breeze. He had the insignia of an officer on his chest. "He is only one. We are many!" he said. "Kill him."

"Easier said than done!" Nath tucked Dragon Claw away. He didn't want to kill anybody, but he couldn't waste any time. Surrounded by the advancing club-wielding soldiers, he exploded into action, disarming two men at the same time and using their clubs against them. He sent them to the ground cradling their ribs.

Crack! Crack!

One bludgeoning blow came right after the other. Nath sidestepped and ducked. He parried and twisted. Wood clocked off wood with a crisp resounding effect. He busted knees with hammering blows.

Soldiers wailed as he popped their elbows. In less than a minute, all ten soldiers were down on the ground grimacing in pain. One gazed at his broken and swollen hand. Another held his bleeding mouth.

Nath spun the clubs around. "What about you? You on the horse. You started this. Now finish it."

"I'd be happy to!" The commander drew a sword from a scabbard on the saddle. Its blade shimmered like blue lightning.

Nath took a step back and drew his dagger.

Maybe I should have brought Fang.

The commander in the iron helm cracked his reins. "Yah!" The horse charged straight for Nath. The long, bright sword was cocked back, ready to strike.

Eyeing the razor-sharp blade and the galloping horse snorting with fury, Nath gathered his legs underneath him, ready to spring in an instant. The horse closed the gap. Nath hunkered down and sprang away from the cutting blade.

Slice!

"Argh!" Nath yelled. The commander hit him. Right across the back. It burned like fire.

The commander turned the horse around and prepared for another run. He held the sword high. The blade was longer than it had been before. It seemed to stretch like fire toward the dark sky. "You look surprised, Nath Dragon. You should be!"

The man had spoken with vague familiarity. Behind the horse and rider, Nath could see a giant still climbing the hill. He'd lost track of the third one. He eyed the mystic blade again.

And I thought I only had the giants to worry about.

He pulled his shoulders back. "You'll miss."

"With this blade," the rider said, "I never miss!" He dug his heels into the horse. "Yah!"

With thoughts faster than movement, Nath had to consider the possibility that the soldier wasn't lying. The blade he carried must have had a special power that made the man so sure of himself. Nath had Dragon Claw, but like Fang, its powers were unpredictable. And its length was much too short. As the oncoming horse and rider came closer and got larger, Nath made an instantaneous decision that he hadn't considered before.

Run!

He ran back into the barn and bolted the door behind him.

Whew! That should buy me some time.

Outside the barn door, the horse nickered.

Nath started for the other side of the barn. He could cut through there and make a run for the hills and find Brenwar. He jogged to the other side and swung the big door open. He was greeted by a pair of giant legs and was eye level with the knees. He backed up. "Not a good idea."

Slice!

He turned. The man in the iron helmet had sliced through the secured barn door. He kicked it open and marched inside. "Going somewhere?" he said with a confident voice.

"No, but I was hoping you were." Nath studied the man. There was something familiar in his walk. It had a slight hitch in it. The iron helmet was different. It had two metal horns that pointed down on the sides. The eyes were rectangular slits. The mouth was small bars of metal. "Who are you?"

"You would like to know that, wouldn't you?"

"Actually, no, I was just buying time." Nath backed up into one of the stalls. "And I'm certain there's a really good reason why you hide your face so well."

"So brazen. So bold!" Twenty feet away from Nath, the warrior cranked the sword back and swung. An arc of energy cut through the barn and knocked Nath Dragon from his feet.

Nath clutched at his chest. The force had sheared through his clothes and seared the material.

Guzan, what kind of sword is that?

He rose to his feet with wary eyes.

The warrior sliced the blade back and forth over the ground. It made a strange humming sound with each ground-dusting swipe. "I never imagined a day when you walked right into my hands. But you did. How delightful. Revenge is such a tasty, tasty dish."

Now Nath really was curious who the man was, but he wasn't going to ask. He shuffled back. There was a stir behind him. The giant. Caught up in the moment, he'd forgotten about the other giant. His head whipped around too late. The giant caught Nath in its massive steel-strong grip. "Gah!"

"You killed my brother," the giant said, bringing Nath up into his face. "I will feast on your bones one at a time."

CHAPTER 36

GRIPPED INSIDE THE MONSTROUS HAND of the giant, Nath squirmed and gulped for air. The giant's fingers were crushing his ribs. Arms still free, he held out his glowing dagger and said to the monster's face, "You saw what happened to your brother. Do you want to suffer the same fate?"

"I just want to kill you," the giant said. His jaw dropped open, and he brought Nath toward his mouth.

"I warned you!" Nath stabbed the giant in the hand. The blade sank deep and drew blood.

The giant's hairy eyebrows buckled. A sneer curled on his lips. He said, "Ow."

Nath stabbed the giant in the hand again and again. The blade bit deep and drew blood.

The giant's grip tightened.

Nath's eyes bulged. "Thanks for nothing, Dragon Claw," he spat. "You're just like your brother."

Using both hands, the giant tried to stuff Nath in its mouth.

Nath braced his free hand against the upper row of the giant's teeth. "I am not a meal!" He gagged. "And your breath is horrible!"

The giant jerked his head back and brought it right back forward, head-butting Nath.

Blurry-bright stars exploded behind Nath's eyes. His limbs loosened from head to toe. Dragon Claw started to slip from his fingertips. Head rolling on his shoulders, he watched the giant's gaping maw open up once more. It had a second row of teeth in its huge mouth. Its red tongue was like a spongy rug beneath his feet.

Nath's inner fire ignited.

He caught his breath and unleashed it.

A stream of gray smoke poured out of his mouth and filled the entire barn in seconds. The giant started coughing and choking. Nath's grip refastened on the dagger. He plunged it into the giant's wrist again, but this time with all his dragon might.

The monstrosity screeched in pain. "AAAAIIIIEEEEEEEEEEE!" Its grip loosened.

Nath twisted free and landed flat on his feet. He fumbled through the barn and snatched up the sack of goods Leander had brought him, now glad he had set it down before the giant grabbed him. He dashed through the blinding smoke and out of the barn. More soldiers approached, shouting and yelling. Nath raced up the hill, making a beeline for Brenwar and Laylana. He glanced over his shoulder.

The man in the iron mask staggered out of the barn and fell to his knees. His chest heaved. He gave a sharp whistle. His horse trotted to his side. The man pulled himself up into the saddle, snapped the reins, and galloped after Nath.

Ribs aching, Nath sprinted at full speed. He could run faster than most four legged animals, including horses. Aside from the roamer steeds that were much faster than most, he could outrace almost anything.

I might not be able to fly, but at least I can run like I have wings on my feet.

Brenwar stood over Laylana. The elven princess's breathing had become ragged. She trembled. He put his calloused hand on her head. It was hot. "You'll have to forgive me. I'm not much good at helping elves."

She reached up and grabbed his hand. Her eyes were open, but she wasn't there. She squeezed tight and let go again.

Brenwar's throat tightened. Seeing the lady elf hurting hurt him. Even though he had little love for the elves, he did have love for life. "Goose," he said. He hadn't seen the female halfling in a while. He'd told her to keep a lookout over the village. "Goose?"

He and the elf were surrounded by the cover of trees, tucked away out of sight. He clawed at his beard. Sniffed. Something somewhere was burning. Wood. Brenwar headed out of his hiding spot in search of the halfling. On the nearby hilltop overlooking Holbrook, the orange glow of a fire caught his eyes. He spied Goose dropping branches on it. The small blaze was catching fast in the wind. "By Morgdon, what the gallows is going on?" he yelled at her.

Startled, she dropped the wood she held in the fire.

"Put that out, you little fool!" he said.

"No," she replied. There was a devious glimmer in her eye. "If I do that, the giant will have a hard time finding you. And he might need the fire to cook you on."

"Are you mad?"

"No, I'm Goose. Long live Eckubahn! May the giants feast on you!" She fished something out of a little pouch and tossed it on the fire. The blaze shot up toward the sky, lighting up the hillside like day.

Brenwar shielded his eyes behind his forearm. Once the bright blaze went down, he rushed up the hill toward it. Goose was nowhere to be found. "Halflings! I knew they'd do something stupid."

The ground shook.

The town below was alive with activity. Soldiers charged down the dirt roads in a clamor. A hundred yards away and storming up the hill was a bigger problem. A giant was on its way with a hammer the size of a man in each hand. At least a dozen soldiers were behind him.

Brenwar's face scrunched up. His grip tightened on Mortuun. He butted the war hammer with his head and yelled down the hill, "You want to dance? Then let's dance! For Morgdon!"

CHAPTER 37

A BLINDING FLASH FROM THE HILLTOP smote Nath's eyes. His pace slowed. A horse nickered way behind him.

What was that?

He forged ahead. Behind, the man in the iron helm had lost control of his mount. A fire blazed ahead. A giant was charging up the hillside a ways away with a knot of well-armed soldiers following behind him.

That's when Nath heard Brenwar's battle cry. Against the night sky, the dwarf's silhouette appeared in front of the blazing fire. Brenwar was winding up the hammer like a windmill. A second later he let it fly.

A thunderclap rocked the summit.

Kraa-Booooom!

The charging giant's head snapped back. He teetered backward and stumbled on two soldiers, smashing them into the grass. His oversized limbs were still moving. He shook his head, stuck his hand in the earth, rubbed his chin, and rose again. The soldiers surged by and stormed Brenwar.

Nath cut through the grasses like a knife through butter. He blindsided three soldiers, knocking through them like a stampeding bull. Still running, he snatched Mortuun off the ground and tossed it over to Brenwar, saying, "Fang?"

Snatching the hammer from the air, Brenwar said, "Right where you left him." He started winding up again.

"I'll be right back. Hold them off until then."

"They'll be dead by then," Brenwar replied.

Nath dashed into the deep woods. The rider in the helm had almost crested the hill. Nath weaved through the trees into the hidden clearing. Fang was stuck in the dirt several feet from where Laylana rested. He carefully dumped the sage's gifts onto the ground next to her. Not sure what was what, he popped off the lid to a jar of salve. It was cool and soothing to the touch. He rubbed it on her forehead.

The horse and iron-helmed rider erupted from the brush. The rider hopped off the horse and slapped its hindquarters, sending it charging into the woods. He cracked his neck from side to side and flexed his powerful arms with the incredible blade gripped tight in his fingers. He tipped his chin at Fang.

Nath glided over to his magnificent blade, took the hilt in both hands, and pulled it free of the ground. "I take it you want a duel with me?"

The rider nodded. His build was powerful and familiar. The height of the man matched Nath's own. His shoulders were that of a bull, and the muscles in his arms were hammered iron. The blade glimmered with angry energy.

"It's seems you know who I am, but I don't know who you are," Nath said while he stuck Dragon Claw back inside Fang's pommel. "Care to share?" He rested the sword on his shoulder.

With one hand, the man removed his iron helmet and dropped it on the ground.

Nath lost his breath. "Kryzak!"

Brenwar's next swing sent two men flying back down the hill. "That's what we call a dwarven kiss!" Mortuun busted, dented, or popped the rivets of every armored soldier that crossed his path. Soldier after soldier fell. Brenwar battered a path of bodies to the giant, who had finally regained his feet and secured his grip on his hammers. Gazing up at the huge man, Brenwar said, "Now it's just you and me, big belly!"

Striking as fast as a normal man, the giant's hammer came down.

Brenwar spun aside.

The giant's hammer left a huge divot in the ground. The second hammer did too. Moved by arms like pistons, the heavy hammerheads dropped like drumsticks off a plate, tearing and shaking the ground.

Bam! Bam! Bam! Bam! Bam!

Brenwar slipped away like a bearded mouse scurrying from the falling keys of a piano. He snuck between the hammer strikes and busted the giant in the shin. The head of Mortuun, forged in the great fires of Morgdon and enchanted by the dwarven Mystics of the Mountainside, splintered the bone like it was dry-rotted kindling.

Letting out a tremendous moan, the giant dropped to a knee. Its eyebrows buckled. Its face hardened with rage. Giants were cocky. Not so smart, but when wounded they fought like wild animals. A wild swing took Brenwar from his feet and skipped him down the hill.

He rolled to a stop and charged up the hill again.

The giant chucked one of his hammers at Brenwar.

The dwarf flattened on his belly.

Two men piled on him and hammered away with fists and elbows. Something sharp bit into his leg.

Brenwar popped one in the forehead with the head of his war hammer. He kicked but couldn't free his legs.

The giant was coming.

The dwarf was tangled up in a knot of flesh.

The giant scooped the three of them up off the ground and started stuffing them into its oversized mouth.

Struggling frantically, Brenwar yelled, "Nobody eats a dwarf!" He shoved one soldier forward.

The giant's jaws clamped down on the screaming man.

Crunch!

Arms free, Brenwar unloaded on the giant and busted out a row of teeth.

The giant dropped him and growled.

Brenwar wound up and turned loose a mighty swing that collided with the giant's other knee.

The giant fell to the ground.

Without hesitation, Brenwar unloaded the wrath of Mortuun.

Whop! Whack! Boom!

The giant died from the final divot Brenwar put in its head.

Puffing for breath, the dwarf looked down the hill. More soldiers were coming, and giants too. "I don't suppose they're coming to congratulate me. Humph."

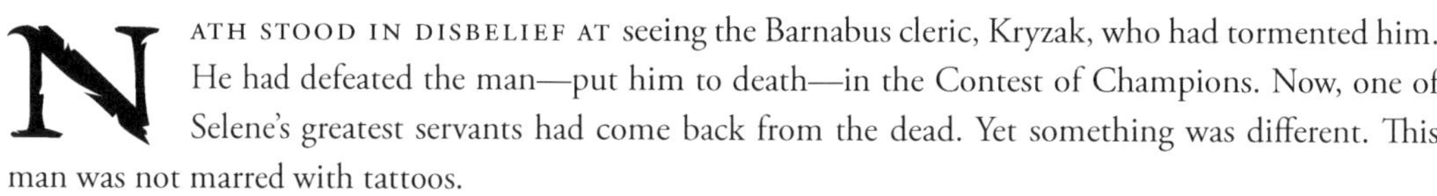

CHAPTER 38

NATH STOOD IN DISBELIEF AT seeing the Barnabus cleric, Kryzak, who had tormented him. He had defeated the man—put him to death—in the Contest of Champions. Now, one of Selene's greatest servants had come back from the dead. Yet something was different. This man was not marred with tattoos.

"Your keen eyes do not deceive you, Nath Dragon, at least not how you think they would." The hard-faced warrior circled. "Yes, my face is familiar, the same as my brother Kryzak's, but I am not he. I am Rybek."

"Your brother was an evil fool, and I take it you're just the same."

"Worse. My brother let his love for Selene blind him from his mission. It made him weak." Rybek sliced clean through a small tree with his sword. "Though he was a fool, I still feel compelled to avenge him. You see, I was there the day you took him down in your monstrous form at the Contest of Champions." His voice became angry. Deadly. "I saw your woman, Selene, turn him inside out and made a pawn. A sacrifice. I vowed revenge not only on you, but on her. And her execution, if it has not already happened, will happen soon enough."

Eyes narrowing, Nath demanded, "What do you mean?"

"The eyes of the titans are everywhere. Surely, you have encountered the betrayal of the halflings. There is nowhere you can go where we will not see. We know that Sansla Libor has taken her. The wurmers, I'm certain, have hunted them down. Hah, one winged ape versus a hundred wurmers? She's dead by now."

"Who is we?"

"It doesn't matter. All that matters is that you die!" Rybek swang. An arc of energy sliced through the air, wiping out everything in its path.

Nath brought Fang around in front of him. The great blade collided with the great energy, jarring his arms and knocking him back. Fang's metal let out a moan. The grip filled with wild energy that coursed through Nath's veins. Nath's eyes flashed like golden lightning. "You say you're a warrior! Then let's fight, steel on steel!"

"Gladly!"

Man and dragon charged one another. Nath turned loose a devastating swing.

Rybek parried.

Clang!

The surrounding branches on the trees bent. The mystic blades danced an angry dance. Mystic sparks sizzled off the metal.

Nath brought his blade forward, blow after blow.

Rybek ducked, dodged, and dived. He countered with surprising speed. Struck with the strength of many men. He matched every move Nath had—and snuck in some moves of his own.

The blades sang out songs of clashing steel. Back and forth the fighters went, toe to toe, blade to blade, pushing back and forth against one another.

When the two of them were locked up by the cross guards, Rybek said in Nath's face, "I will kill you. I will kill your woman! The titans will slaughter the dragons!"

The cold-hearted words from the killer jarred something loose in Nath. He was tired. Tired of the evil that wanted to kill him and wipe out his friends. He was tired of it all, and he wasn't going to hold back anymore, waiting for people to have a change of heart. He shoved the powerful Rybek back so hard that the man's back smashed into a tree. Nath rushed him and let loose his speed and power. He and Fang became one. He swung with wroth force.

Rybek brought his sword up to block.

Steel collided with steel. Metal snapped. A mystical explosion knocked Nath backward onto the ground.

Still charged up, he sprang to his feet.

A section of the forest was missing. Leaves were falling.

Rybek lay on the ground, unmoving. His sword was broken in half.

Fang still burned with exhilarating fire in Nath's hand.

On instinct, Nath found Laylana, half-covered in leaves. Her eyes were open. He slung Fang over his back and picked her up in his arms. "How are you?"

"What happened?" she said.

"Nath!" Brenwar yelled.

With the lady elf in his arms, Nath rushed out of the devastated woodland onto the hilltop. Brenwar was surrounded by soldiers and a dozen giants. That wasn't all. Wingless wurmers the size of small horses snaked through the grass.

"Are you going to swing that sword or that elf?" Brenwar said, backpedaling toward Nath.

"Hello!" said a voice from the shoulders of one of the giants. "Up here, Nath. It's me, Zoose!"

I wish I had Akron. I'd blow a hole clear through him.

"I can see that, Zoose."

"Yes, you do have awfully keen eyes, don't you?" Zoose said. Goose popped up on the other shoulder and smiled a smug little smile. "Too bad your sense of character is not as good as your eyes."

Nath wanted to kick himself. He couldn't understand how the halflings had fooled him.

I can't let that happen again. Ever.

Zoose continued. "This is the part where you surrender. And that would be wise. No one can hide from the titans. They have eyes everywhere."

"I know. I've heard that before. It's getting old."

"We can take them, Nath," Brenwar said.

"No, we can't, but I'm not surrendering." Nath held his sword in front of his eyes. "Fang, get us out of here." He tapped the blade on the ground.

Ting.

Nothing happened.

Brenwar let out a breath. "Thank goodness. I didn't want to wind up in the next century."

"Enough games." Goose pointed at Nath and company. "Just kill them."

Not knowing what to do, Nath let out a cry for help in Dragonese that sounded like a great roar that sent shockwaves through the valley.

"HAAAaaaaAAAAaaaaght!"

The advance of the giants stopped. Zoose and Goose covered their ears. The massive men looked at one another dumbfoundedly, but then on Zoose's new order they advanced once more.

Nath set Laylana down. "Stay close."

"I will, but I'm going to fight." She drew her sword. "It will be a great honor to make my last stand with Nath Dragon."

"Well, let's hope it's not our last stand, but it sure looks like it."

CHAPTER 39

buzz in the air caught Nath's ears. His head snapped up. A dozen blue streak dragons the size of big dogs darted out of the sky and surrounded Nath and his friends. Their blue wings shook like rattles and glowed with energy. Their mouths dropped open, and lightning shot out.

Ssssrazz! Ssssraaa! Ssssrazzz!

The bolts of energy shot into the wurmers. One by one, their scaly hides lit up like the day, sizzling and exploding. Rocked by the moment of surprise, the giants completely overlooked another terror. Four bull dragons, red as brick and as big as the towering giants, dropped out of the sky.

Whump! Whump! Whump! Whump!

Horns lowered, the bull dragons charged into the first wave of giants. They pinned the huge men down, and fiery infernos exploded from their mouths.

Filled with shock and elation, Nath let out a cheer. "Yes!" In all his life, he'd never expected such a rally. The dragons, even after the battle against Gorn Grattack, still seemed to shy away from him. Perhaps after all these centuries, that had changed. He certainly felt something, a new attachment, deep in his bones.

A giant hammered away at a bull dragon with thunderous blows.

A second giant pinned its wings.

Nath charged in and sliced one of the giants in the backside.

The dragon ripped into the other giants with his claws. His tail lashed out and knocked the huge man down. The dragon pounced and unleashed more fire.

The giant's skin turned to ash. Only the smoking bones remained.

The blue streak tore into the wurmers.

Bull dragons slugged it out with the giants, but the battle was far from won. It was a savage battle of teeth and scales, claws and fire. The iron and steel of men striking and howls of pain filled the air. The giants and wurmers, hardened, mindless and savage, recovered fast. They still had the superior numbers.

A dragon of golden-bronze scales slipped out of the darkness of the sky and landed on two wurmers the size of Nath Dragon.

Nath whirled around to face him.

His head was huge, and he had a magnificent set of horns. Golden eyes boring into Nath's own, he said in Dragonese in Nath's mind, "This isn't a battle. It's a rescue. Get on!" His tail cracked out and struck a giant instantly dead.

Nath called out to his friend, "Brenwar, quit swinging that hammer and get over here. Right now!"

The dwarf clobbered a wurmer's skull and froze in his tracks. He eyeballed the huge dragon. "Balzurth?"

"Father?" Nath said with shock. He gestured to Laylana, and together they climbed onto the great dragon's back.

Brenwar's stumpy legs powered over. It was one of the few times Nath had ever seen the dwarf do anything without arguing.

He helped Brenwar up. "You never cooperate so easily with me."

The dwarf grunted.

The monster bronze-gold dragon's wings beat and lifted them into the air. Balzurth let out a roar.

The bull and blue streak dragons broke off their attacks and took to the air.

Nath felt his father's lungs fill and the scales beneath him heat up.

A gush of fire exploded from Balzurth's mouth.

The giants and wurmers turned to ash. The hillside burned with fire. As they rose higher into the air, the burning hillside was a bonfire below them.

In astonishment, Nath said, "Father, I can't believe it was you who came!"

"Lucky for you I was in the area."

Epilogue

Zoose and Goose stood far away from the burning hillside. The flames crackled and shot up into the sky. All of the giants and wurmers, along with what was left of Holbrook's soldiers, were nothing but burning pyres that would one day fertilize the scorched soil.

Goose stared into his sister's eyes. They were black pearls that shined with the orange blaze that reflected in them. She was no longer who she once was. Neither was he. Now, they were spies controlled by the spirits of the titans.

"Are you well?" he said to her.

She nodded.

Zoose saw a struggle within her. The dragon that came. Its fire had not only been destructive, but also cleansing. Those flames had destroyed the giants and wurmers and all of the evil within. He saw his future in those flames. He trembled. He stared at his bloodstained fingers.

I killed that man. Why?

A huge man marched out of the smoke and flames. It was Rybek. He carried his helmet in his hands. He stopped in front of Zoose. "Did I hear correctly? They called that dragon Balzurth?"

Zoose didn't want to nod, but the evil that prodded him did it anyway.

"Good, then we have succeeded." Rybek put his helmet back on. "It's time to let the titans know that Balzurth is out in the world, just as they planned. Let the hunt for him begin."

EYES OF THE DRAGON

-Book 4-

CRAIG HALLORAN

CHAPTER 1

The mountaintop was a beautiful vision of tall grasses and bright, long-stemmed wildflowers. The massive rocks were covered in soft blue-green mosses. The swirling winds bent the branches and rustled the leaves in the trees, giving them an animated life of their own. It was one of the most picturesque places Nath had ever seen in Nalzambor and one of the many places he'd never ventured to before, a high precipice overlooking the distant Pool of the Dragons.

"It's always so peaceful so far away from everything," Nath said, gazing at his father, Balzurth.

The titan-sized dragon's armored scales of bronze and gold gleamed in the sun. His monstrous body crushed the vegetation beneath him. Balzurth scratched his great dragon horn on the rock as if he was sharpening its tip. His jaw, with teeth as big as men, opened up into a yawn that let out a hot burst of steam. He eyeballed Nath and replied, "The farther away from men, the better. I've been trying to teach you that."

"Me too." Brenwar's arms were crossed over his barrel chest. He looked like a bearded chipmunk beside Balzurth. He clawed at his beard. "He won't listen to me."

"The youth never do." Balzurth stretched his long neck around and faced the elven woman on his back. It was Laylana, the dark-headed, green-eyed elven daughter of the murdered Laedorn. "You seem to be enjoying yourself up there, pretty princess. Do you find my scales divine?"

Traipsing over Balzurth's back as if it were a bridge, she nodded with wide-eyed excitement. "Yes. Fascinating. Can we fly again? Soon?"

"Certainly, young lady. Certainly," Balzurth said in his powerful and reassuring voice. "I have a bit of an itch between my scales. Do you think you could scratch it for me?"

Clasping her hands together, she replied, "Oh, could I?"

"Of course." Balzurth wriggled his neck and added, "Over here where the horn meets the scale. That would be wonderful."

Without hesitation, Laylana climbed over to the back of Balzurth's head, dropped to her knees, and started scratching where he'd said. "Is this good?"

"Perfect." Balzurth turned his attention back to Nath. "You look disappointed. What's on your mind, Son?"

Nath should have been elated, but his father was right, he was disappointed. He didn't understand why. At least, not that he wanted to admit, but seeing his father in full dragon form bothered him. His father had wiped out a mountain full of giants in a single breath, but as much as Nath had enjoyed seeing it, he wished it had been him. Finally, he responded, "You've abandoned Dragon Home, Father. Why?"

Checking his claws, Balzurth said, "I can do as I wish."

"Oh, so you can do as you wish, but I can't?" Nath approached Balzurth and stood in his face, looking up at him. "Mother is worried, and you're placing yourself in danger. You're playing into the titans' hands. It's only a matter of time before they find us."

"I highly doubt your mother is as worried as she makes herself out to be. If anything, she's elated that I'm gone for a spell. You know how she loves decorating."

"Actually, no, I don't," Nath replied. "I only met my mother a short time ago, remember? She was imprisoned in the Great Dragon Wall all my life before that."

"Of course I remember," Balzurth scoffed. He poked a claw into Nath's chest. "I remember everything.

And don't you dare get on your high horse and worry about me. I don't need to be worried about. I'm the King of the Dragons, am I not?"

"Aye!" Brenwar shouted while hoisting his war hammer Mortuun up in the air. "Aye! Aye!"

Seeing the dwarf's enthusiasm, Nath felt a little bit foolish. His father could clearly take care of himself. Still, he sputtered out, "Well, you should still be more careful. It's been awhile since you last trekked through the world of men."

"Careful? Pah." Balzurth let out a puff of smoke. "I've handled the titans before, and I can handle them again. And I won't let them survive at all this time. No. There won't be any banishment." His voice filled the mountaintop with thunder. He stomped his paw and shook the ground. "It will be obliteration!"

Nath stepped backward. The power in Balzurth's voice shook the marrow in his bones. Laylana froze on Balzurth's back, and Brenwar stood stiff as a board. Nath found his breath again and said, "Father, thanks."

The furnace in Balzurth's eyes cooled, and he asked, "Thanks for what?"

"Saving us."

"Yes, well, you are my son and my friends." Voice softening, Balzurth scanned the three of them. "And as wretched as people can be, they are all still worth saving. Son, I've sat on my throne doing nothing long enough. I cannot stand it any longer. They take the dragons, they slaughter their own, and it's time for action. Do I think it will be easy? No, it never is. But it must be done." He sighed.

Looking deep into his father's eyes, Nath could see a hint of regret. Something was eating at Balzurth. He approached his father and laid his hand on his snout. "What is it, Father?"

"My selfish actions have led to all this, I fear," Balzurth said, not hiding his regret. "I sent you to find your mother. Alas, I did miss her, and I knew if you freed her, there would be consequences. Letting out the spirits of the titans had a much more rapid effect than I expected. Their anger and hatred made their evil spread faster than I imagined. I thought they could be contained, but I underestimated them. Yet I knew it would have to come to this eventually. I could not let our kin hold the Dragon Wall intact forever. It just wasn't fair."

"Don't be so hard on yourself, Father," Nath said, patting his father's huge snout. "I'm sure I would have done the same thing for Mother that you did."

"No doubt you will do the same for those you love, Son." Balzurth nudged him with his nose. "Besides, I feel that you are ready. Actually, I know it. You are ready to take down the titans."

Nath's eyes enlarged. He swallowed and said, "Me? What about you?"

CHAPTER 2

It was Zoose the halfling's first trip to the City of Narnum. He walked stride for stride with his sister Goose behind the powerful armored build of Rybek the war cleric. The towering warrior walked with huge steps that made it difficult to keep up on his much shorter legs, but he and Goose pressed on. He nudged Goose with his finger and pointed up.

"Stop doing that," she said, slapping his hand away. Her once-amiable face was pinched into a grimace of evil. She tugged at the long brown ponytail that hung over her shoulder. "I've seen plenty of wurmers already, and the colorful tile tops too. Get control of yourself and act like you've been here before."

That wasn't easy to do. Instead, his eyes searched over everything at once. The wurmers, dark and scaly with their purple eyes aglow, hung in the nooks and crannies of every building. Their eyes seemed to scan for any suspicious move. The people fought and haggled over food, weapons, and clothing. A burly roughneck shoved an elderly woman down, and not a single person helped her up. Heavy boots trampled by her instead. Zoose gravitated toward the fallen woman.

Goose grabbed him by the elbow and jerked him back into step. Under her breath, she said, "What are you doing, fool?"

Zoose's nostrils flared as he took in a deep draw of air. The scent of meat cooking filled his nose. Patting his belly, he said, "I'm hungry."

Goose punched him in the arm. "Be silent."

Rubbing his shoulder, he hunched down and kept the pace but continued to survey his surroundings. There was a festival in the market square they were passing through. Men and women frolicked with wickedness. Shouted and screamed with shameless glee. They'd made giant masks painted in vibrant colors that covered their faces. The images were wicked and evil. Dark and disturbing. Drums pounded. Songs were sung, strings were plucked, and horns blared. It shook Zoose to the core. Evil members of all the races had gathered, including many elves. He'd never seen or imagined such a thing. The grand City of Narnum was deteriorating into a depot of ruin. He hugged his shoulders, rubbed the cold seeping into his limbs, and cast down his eyes.

Goose gave him a firm shove. "Buck up, Zoose. We have arrived, and arrived on the right side."

I don't know about that.

Something had stirred inside him when he saw Balzurth's flames consuming an entire hillside and everything living on it turned to ash. The wickedness inside him that allowed him to commit crimes against his nature had fled. His rationale and humble halfling consciousness had returned. The distorted world he was now living in had been revealed to his once-tainted eyes. With his little heart pumping in his chest, he decided to play along.

There's nowhere to run anyway.

Marching through the cobblestone street, Rybek led them straight toward the tallest building in the city. It stretched a thousand feet into the air. A walkway wrapped around its massive column like a snake, level after level.

Zoose had never imagined anything so huge and vast in his life, but there it was in the heart of the city, a marvel of architecture. Head tilted back and eyes up, he said, "Are we going up there?"

His sister shushed him.

Rybek's head turned over his armored shoulder. He lifted his massive arm and pointed at a stone temple being built around the base of the tower. The stones were huge. The people who moved them were monstrous. Giants, dozens of them, men and orcs, shoved stones over logs and stacked them up on top of each other to form a temple with a huge thirty-foot archway that was near completion. "Eckubahn awaits. Come with me."

On each side of the archway that formed the temple's entrance, a giant sentry stood. Bare-chested and hairless, their alabaster skin blended in with the stonework of the black-eyed brutes. Each sentry held a leaf-tipped spear that rested on the ground and stood up to his neck.

One of the expressionless titans glanced down at Rybek and waved him in.

Staying close, Zoose and Goose followed after.

Inside the confines of the temple, the stone archways crisscrossed more than fifty feet above. Flocks of worshippers were stuffed inside. They wore masks and plumes full of feathers and black flowers. Among them were giants dressed in clothes like men, who towered over all of them. They lounged in great stone chairs chiseled by the hands of giant masons. The people laid trays of food and ornate gifts at their massive feet.

Zoose had never felt so small and insignificant as he did now.

This is twisted. I want to go home.

Unable to see beyond the hordes of jaded people, he heard a voice cut through the room like a crack of thunder. "People, go. Rybek and company, come."

The enchanted people departed in a stream. Seconds later they were all gone, leaving Zoose and his sister alone with Rybek among the giants.

"Come," the loud, canyon-like voice said, "and tell me what you know, Rybek."

Sweating from his brow, Zoose managed to peek around Rybek's legs at the source of the voice. A titan sat on a throne made of stone. His enormous hands squeezed the stone arms of his seat, and his head burned like an urn of flame. Zoose squinted and dashed the sweat from his eyes. He wanted to run, but he dared not. He was in the presence of the most powerful of all titans, Eckubahn.

Rybek took a knee and bowed.

Without hesitation, Zoose and Goose did the same, but unlike his counterparts, Zoose shivered and dripped with sweat. It took the life right out of him when Eckubahn said, "Why does that tiny one shake?"

CHAPTER 3

INSIDE THE GARDENS OF QUINTUKLEN, Bayzog sat on a bench alongside his wife Sasha. The beautiful human woman was dressed in a fine white-linen gown. Her stare was blank but fixed on the arrangement of flowers blooming behind the pathway. The half-elf wizard waved his hand in front of her eyes. "Sasha, it's time to go."

The gentle woman didn't stir.

Bayzog's heart sank. He'd been bringing her to the gardens every day in hopes that she could regain some of her memory and return to her normal self, but the magic within her was eroding her mind. He'd hoped watching others rebuild the war-ravaged gardens might rejuvenate her. It had not. There were only glimpses of her former self that surfaced from time to time. Now his hope rested in their sons, Samaz and Rerry. The young but formidable pair had set out on their own to find a cure for their mother, and he'd not heard from them since they left.

He took her warm hand in his. "It's lonely without you, Sasha. If I never appreciated you as much as I should have, I hope you'll know how much I appreciate you now." He reached behind him and plucked a purple flower and held it under her nose. "One of your favorites."

Sasha's chin shifted and her gaze changed. Wurmers streaked through the sky in flocks like birds. With effort she lifted her hand and pointed, saying, "Birdie. Birdie. Ugly birdie." Her hand dropped, and she became listless again.

Bayzog's chin sank into his chest. It was agony watching her deteriorate. Her beautiful life was withering away like a flower that blooms in the day and dies in the night. It was even worse with him being part elven. To him, her life was already fleeting, and now that process had accelerated. It was heartbreaking. At one time in his life, he'd felt himself free of such burdens, but now with a family, it was different. He had even caught himself wondering, *Will I even outlive my own sons?*

Night began to fall as the sun sank behind the buildings. The shade started to cool his bones, and Sasha's teeth began to chatter. He picked up his cloak, which was lying at his side. It was a rich forest green with golden leaves that traced over the hem and sleeves. Sasha had woven it for him when they met long ago. He covered her shoulders with it. "Sweetest Sasha, it is time to go."

Her stare remained deep and spacey.

He took her hands and tried to pull her up.

She stiffened and pulled free of his grip.

This was the hard part. People were walking about, staring. The last thing Bayzog wanted to do was draw attention to himself. Attention was dangerous. If the leadership of the city had any concerns about the state your family was in, they wouldn't hesitate to throw you out. He tugged at her again. "Please, Sasha. Come."

She rose to her feet without looking into his face. Instead, it seemed as if her stare was in a world beyond. Bayzog hoped that if she saw anything at all, it was pleasant. He wrapped his arm around her waist and guided her down the path beneath the archways of tree branches and leaves. The night birds started to sing the last song of the day, darting back and forth through the branches before they settled in.

A tear formed in the corner of Bayzog's violet eye. He wiped it away with his sleeve, remembering how the night birds' songs had so often made Sasha giggle for no reason. He'd never understood why the little speckled birds made her laugh. All she would say was, "It's joy, pure joy that they sing, and it gives me the tickles."

Oh, what I wouldn't do to hear that laughter again. I'd do anything.

Exiting the garden through the gates of iron, Sasha pulled him back. He whirled around in disbelief and found her eyes on his. She was blinking. His heart started racing inside his chest. "Sasha, can you hear me?"

"Of course, husband. Why wouldn't I?" She twisted around on her feet, glancing up, down, and over all of her surroundings. When she stopped, she said, "Where have Samaz and Rerry gone? They were just here. They must be hiding from the danger." She called out, "Rerry! Samaz! Come to the voice of your mother. I'll protect you!"

"Easy, Sasha. The boys are fine," Bayzog assured her. He pulled her into his arms. "Let's go home. Soon we will see them there."

She tore out of his grip. "No, Bayzog! They are in danger. I saw it with my own eyes. Those horrible birds in the sky will devour them if we don't help them!" Dashing into the gardens, she continued to call out for them. "Samaz! Rerry!"

Chasing after her, Bayzog broke out in a cold sweat. What Sasha had said was so convincing that it all seemed real. He'd known the hallucinations from the wizard's dementia would be powerful, but this bout she had shared tightened around the heart in his chest. A deep nagging feeling bore its way into the recesses of his mind. Somewhere, something was wrong.

"Aaaiiiieeeeee!" Sasha screamed.

Fighting his way through the now flourishing garden, Bayzog found Sasha on her hands and knees. She faced two oversized stones the size of men that lay silent on the soft ground. Tears started to stream down her face and she said with riveting meaning, "They're dead. My sons are dead!"

CHAPTER 4

"YOU KNOW, FATHER," NATH SAID to Balzurth, "you said that as if you weren't planning on helping me with it."

"Oh, so are you telling me the Dragon Prince isn't up to it?" Balzurth chuckled in his throat. "And I thought my son was up for anything."

Backpedaling, Nath swatted at some leaves in a nearby tree. "And I certainly would be, if I were in your condition. But alas," he said with a shrug of his shoulders, "I'm just this."

"Oh, I see. You're pouting because you can't turn into a dragon like me." Balzurth leaned his head toward Brenwar. "What do you think, old friend?"

"He's pouting for certain. If I've seen that lip stuck out once I've seen it stuck out a hundred times." Brenwar shook his head. "It's the redheaded ones that always seem so fragile."

"I'm not fragile," Nath objected. "And the both of you know I'm in no condition to take down the titans. We'd be dead ten times over if not for Fang bailing us out. I can't always count on Fang, though. Sometimes he's on it, and sometimes he's not."

"Oh, don't bellyache, Dragon Prince," Balzurth replied. "You're only upset that you haven't turned into a dragon yet."

Nath perked up and approached his father. He grabbed one of the long claws on his father's feet and held him fast. "You said *yet*? Does that mean I'll get my powers back?"

"Not if you hide up here on this mountain, you won't." Balzurth tried to pull his foot away from Nath's grip without hurting Nath. "Will you let go of me before I boil you like a fish?"

"Tell me how to get my powers back. I want to be a dragon again."

"Don't be so antsy. You made a sacrifice for Selene, and you should respect that. In the meantime, make the most of what you do have." Balzurth looked up over his back at Laylana. "That will do, Princess. Thank you."

She climbed down off the grand dragon's back onto the ground and said, "My pleasure."

Nath kicked at the dirt. One of the things that bothered him so much about his father being back was having to see a reflection of what he could be but no longer was. He didn't have any regrets for saving Selene, but my, how he missed his powers. If he had them back, he'd take it straight to the titans in a heartbeat. He took a breath, pulled his shoulders back, and faced his father. "So what is it I need to do?"

"Stay the course, Son."

"So you want me to go back to doing what I was doing before you arrived, which was essentially dying. Perhaps I should just turn myself over to the titans." Nath shook his head. "Great Guzan."

"Son, you called for aid and it came. Me and the dragons. Victory was snatched from the jaws of death, and you should be happy." Balzurth lowered his head. "I know I am."

"So what are you going to do while I'm doing what I'm going to do? I thought you were ready to take down the titans now." Nath said.

"I'm not going to rush in there without a plan. I still need to gather one. While I do that, you and your friends can do what you need to do. Just think about it." Using his tail, Balzurth uprooted a tree from the ground and started eating its leaves from the branches. "Mmmmmmm. It's not cattle, but it will do."

Nath tried to recollect where he'd been before his last adventure. What was going on in the wide world of Nalzambor?

Hm.

The giants were filling the cities and poisoning the minds of the people. Selene was comatose and hopefully safe with Sansla Libor. She should be in Dragon Home. There was the other item of issue too. The elves and dwarves were trying to hunt him down. They thought he'd murdered Laylana's father Laedorn and the hero of the dwarven people, Uurluuk Mountainstone. He needed to bring the real menace to justice and clear his own name. He needed to find out how the assassin got his hands on his bow Akron. He needed to visit Bayzog and Ben to see what happened. Who stole Akron?

Crunching on the branches, Balzurth peered down at Nath. "Have you decided what you want to do yet?"

Aggravated, Nath said, "I guess we'll just hustle off this mountain, leagues from where we need to be, and visit our old friend Bayzog. Of course, you could give us a ride and move our destiny along a little bit quicker."

"No, the walk will be good for you, won't it, Brenwar."

"The only thing I like better than walking is fighting." Brenwar was beaming. "Well, drinking and brewing ale aside, of course."

"Of course," Balzurth said.

Dumbfounded, Nath looked at his father and friend and said, "I suppose we should go then. It's been good seeing you, Father, if brief." He started to walk away. There was nothing quite like being in the presence of his father. Despite some understandable jealousy, Nath's best times were with Balzurth, even though on occasion they could be boring. There was something different about his father now, though. That liveliness he'd known as a boy was back. He liked it. He wanted to bask in it. Boots marching over the ground and without looking back, he carried on.

"Oh, I can't stand it," Balzurth blurted out just as Nath and Brenwar headed over the mountain's crest and down the bank. "Hold on."

There was a rattle and snapping of branches. Nath whirled around.

The tree was there, but the dragon was gone. Only a rustle remained under the branches. Suddenly the tree moved and Laylana gasped. A man appeared under the thirty-foot oak tree, pushed it up over his head, and tossed it aside like a log for a fire. He dusted his hands off. "I need to be more careful next time I shape change. It's been awhile."

Gaping, Nath watched as Balzurth changed.

No longer a dragon, a broad-shouldered statue came to life. His eyes were as golden as the sun, with long red hair that flowed over his shoulders like the ripples in a river. He tugged at the fiery locks cascading under his chin.

Brenwar nodded and said, "That's a fine beard. You wear it like any dwarven king I ever saw."

Putting his arm around the dwarf's shoulders, bearded man Balzurth said, "That's a fine compliment coming from you, Brenwar." Balzurth draped his other arm over Nath's shoulders. A hair taller, he said to Nath, "Any objections to me coming along?"

With a smile as broad as a river, Nath said, "No sir!"

Balzurth smiled in return. "We're off to see the wizard then."

CHAPTER 5

HEAD AFLAME, ECKUBAHN THE TITAN said, "It seems we have a deceiver among us. I do not sense the spirit of evil within this flea of a halfling." He pointed at Zoose. "Come to me, insignificant one."

With every one of his limbs shaking, Zoose tried to rise and shuffle forward but could not move. His shoeless feet were stuck to the floor.

Rybek reached around and grabbed him by the scruff of his shirt collar and pulled him forward. The warrior gave him a hard shove straight into the foot of the stone dais that held up the titan's throne. Zoose jammed his knee on the step's edge, sending a sharp pain through his limbs to his eyes.

"I sense this one's fear. It is great." Eckubahn reached down with an arm the size of a tree and scooped up Zoose into his palm. He lifted the halfling into the air, holding him like a wingless bird. "Who do you serve, half-a-man?"

Soaked with perspiration and drenched in fear, Zoose pulled his knees into his chest and balled up like a clam. The searing heat from Eckubahn's burning face made steam rise up from Zoose's sweat-drenched clothes.

I want to go home. I want to go home. I want to go home.

"This halfling is not one of us. He has defiled the temple." Eckubahn's fingers closed around Zoose. His huge hand was slowly crushing Zoose's little body like a walnut shell. "Do not allow such vermin into my temple again, Rybek."

The warrior nodded.

"As for this tiny defiler, let his life become an example of what happens to those who do not succumb to my power. I am Eckubahn. I will reign over all Nalzambor. Those who resist me shall be destroyed." His hand continued to slowly, agonizingly close.

Zoose felt immense pressure building around him. Squeezed fiercely in the titan's palm, he couldn't even peep. And then a warm light pierced through the veil of his eyelids. It became brighter and hotter until he finally let out a horrible scream.

Goose watched in astonishment as her brother Zoose was enveloped in the titan's hand. The giant's hand glowed with a fiery light, and a muffled scream from within pierced the center of her heart. Eckubahn opened up his fingers, tilted his hand over, and the fire-charred remains of Zoose spilled out onto the temple floor. Her throat tightened, but there were no tears. All she could think was, "What a shame, what a shame."

Eckubahn turned his attention to her. "Clean this up, half-woman. And be hasty about it. I don't care for the dust of fleas."

Scrambling forward, she dropped to her hands and knees and started scooping the cremated remains up into the lower length of her dress. The dust of her brother filled her nose, and the smell was awful. She sneezed, scattering halfling dust everywhere. Wide eyed, she glanced up at Eckubahn just in time to see his foot lift up and stomp right back down on her head.

Squish!

Rybek watched Eckubahn stretch out his hand over the remains of the halflings. An orange glow emanated from his fingertips and scorched the steps with a cleansing effect. No sign was left of the halflings. They were gone.

"Rise," Eckubahn said to him. "What do you have to report?"

Rybek stood, keeping his chin down. "Balzurth roams the land again. I have seen him with my own eyes."

"And you are certain of this?"

"Aye," Rybek said. "Our enemies confirmed it in our very presence. You have drawn him out, my lord. Your plan bears the fruit of everything you have wanted."

Eckubahn leaned forward. "Tell me what happened. What did you see?"

Rybek's gauntleted fingers twitched. He lifted his head to face the titan's fiery gaze. "We had Nath Dragon trapped by giants and wurmers with no chance of escape when Nath Dragon called out for his brethren. Within moments, dragons dropped out of the sky—and one of them was Balzurth. He turned the giants and wurmers into fire with one hot blast that set the mountain ablaze. Not a single giant or wurmer survived."

Eckubahn pointed at Rybek. "But you did. How is that?"

Throat tightening, Rybek replied, "Nath Dragon had defeated me earlier, shattered my blade, and I lay woozy in the forest. By the time I came out of my fog, the battle was over and the hilltop aflame." He glanced at the spot where the halflings once were. "I beg for another chance, milord."

Eckubahn lowered his hand. "Let me see this shattered blade."

Rybek took the scabbard out of a sack he carried, slid the broken sword blade out of the scabbard, placed it in the titan's palm, and stepped back.

"With evidence comes truth," the titan said, closing his grip around the weapon. "I hate the truth."

He opened his hand again, revealing the sword fully intact. "But I appreciate loyalty. You, Rybek, will be given the chance to redeem yourself, but not without superior help."

Rybek took the sword. "It will be my pleasure to accept any assistance you offer."

From behind the throne, an ominous figure emerged. Standing over twelve feet tall, a pasty green-skinned humanoid stood beside the throne. He was a ghastly giant, ugly from head to toe, covered with knots on this arms and legs that looked like boils. His arms and legs were long. He was broad chested but appeared out of shape. The wild hair on his head was shoulder length and his nose long. He wore a brown tunic with a huge brass-buckled belt wrapped around it. Deep, spacey black eyes resonated with evil.

Eckubahn made the introduction. "This is Bletver, a triant. He is going to aid you."

Rybek nodded. He was used to seeing giants, but he'd never seen anything quite like Bletver before. The oversized hands and long nails at the end looked like they would tear a grizzly to pieces. There was something disturbing about how the triant carried himself. He stood with cunning in his eye and his own air of dignity.

Bletver said to Rybek, "A pleasure."

Anticipating a little more company, Rybek said, "Who else will accompany me?" A sliver of ice raced down his spine as a shadow fell over his shoulder, and he turned.

A black shadow with a glow for eyes hovered right behind him.

Unlike his twin brother Kryzak, Rybek was more fighter than cleric. He wasn't as accustomed to the supernatural, but he knew a phantom when he saw it.

"The phantom and the triant will accompany you as you seek out Balzurth and his son, Nath Dragon. Separate them. Destroy their allies. Their friends. Trap them. Hunt them. You will need this." Eckubahn stretched out his hand to reveal a silver amulet on a wrought iron chain. A purple gem sparkled in the center of the amulet with the fire of a moody star. "Place this around the dragon's neck, and you will be finished."

Rybek took the amulet in his hand and tucked it away. "Anything else, milord?"

"All of my resources will be at your disposal. Make good use of what you have, and do not fail me again," Eckubahn warned. "Remember the halflings. Your fate will be far worse than theirs, which was merciful."

CHAPTER 6

Bayzog was back in his tower, eyes scouring his texts at his center table. Books floated all around as he shoved one book aside and replaced it with another. He hadn't slept since he'd returned with Sasha. She'd spaced out just after she wailed over her hallucinations of the deaths of Samaz and Rerry. Now, his problems were twofold. Perhaps his sons had died—and his wife still needed a cure for the wizard's dementia. He needed help and answers, and he had only one place to go.

"Umph!" a voice cried out. A man appeared inside the living room on a pile of pillows. The rangy, bearded man shoved the pillows aside and rose to his feet, shaking his head. "There has to be a better way to make an entrance in here."

"Thanks for coming, Ben," said Bayzog. It had been less than a year since the last time he saw Ben, but the man looked like he'd aged a decade. Brow perched, Bayzog asked, "Are you well?"

Checking the buckle on his sword belt and straightening himself, Ben approached with a little wobble in his legs, holding his stomach. "I will be once my tummy turns right side up again. Really, Bayzog, get another entrance. It's no wonder you don't have many visitors." He headed toward the nearest sofa and flopped down, facing the fireplace. "It's cold as the peaks in here, too."

With a twitch of Bayzog's fingers, the fireplace burst into flame, and ambient warmth filled the room.

The old rugged warrior clasped his hands behind his head and leaned back into the sofa. "Ah, that's better." Peering around, he asked, "How's Sasha?"

"Asleep, but not well." Bayzog grabbed a pitcher of wizard water and a pair of fine glasses and took a seat in a padded chair. He poured two glasses and said to Ben, "Again, are you ill?"

"Why, do I look ill?" Ben took the glass of wizard water and drank. "Perhaps this will make me feel better."

Ben tended to be as refreshed as any human could be, positive and engaging, but now the creases in his forehead and the sacks under his eyes were a cause for concern. Ben's eyes were avoiding his, too. "What's happened, Ben?"

The man tensed up and closed his eyes. "Nothing."

"Ben?"

Finished with his drink, Ben set the glass down. "You sent for me, I didn't send for you. I came, so what do you want, Bayzog?"

Bayzog took a sip of the wizard water. It wasn't like Ben to be so defensive. Something was bothering the man. Deeply. "Fine. I need you to go track down my sons."

"You know I'd love to help, but I'm too old to do that." Ben rubbed his hands on the thighs of his pants. "And I've started another family of my own, you know."

"Ben, this is serious. I need you. Your family can stay with me. I can't leave Sasha. You know that."

"It's too dangerous out there for me. Giants roam the world like common men, and wurmers flock like fleas. It's taking all we have to hold this city."

Trying to sound reassuring, Bayzog said, "You'll be fine. You have Akron."

For the first time, Ben's eyes found his. The man's face filled with strain. With a heavy sigh, he said, "I lost it."

Scooting to the edge of his seat, Bayzog asked, "You lost what?"

"Akron. I lost Akron."

Bayzog scooted back into the cushions of his chair and sat quiet for a moment as if he was frozen in time. He'd come to expect the unexpected in his life, but the loss of Akron was disheartening—especially coming from Ben, who was as responsible an individual as you could get. Softening his tone, he asked, "What happened?"

Ben lifted his shoulder and shook his head again. "I hadn't used it for quite some time, so I locked it up. This was years ago, and I hadn't even thought of the bow in a long time. Then, a few weeks back, there was talk in the streets. You probably heard it."

"Forgive me, but I haven't heard anything of late. I've been very distracted. Go on."

"Word came to the Legionnaires that Laedorn had been assassinated. A moorite arrow right through the heart." Ben's gaze landed right on Bayzog's. "Witnesses say that a man fitting Nath Dragon's description fired it."

"Impossible!" Bayzog exclaimed. His fingers dug into the soft cushions of the padded chair. He glanced toward the hallway that led to Sasha's room. "Sorry, but this news actually startled me." He grabbed his glass and took a long drink. "My heart beats in my chest like a galloping horse. How did I miss this news?" He drank again. "Please continue."

Resting his calloused hands on his knees and sitting up straight, Ben added, "It was elves that came, and they didn't want to make anything public about it. It's been very quiet, but they asked for me. I told them what I knew and everything about the last time I saw Dragon, er, Nath. They caught me completely off guard, but when they departed, they seemed convinced of everything I knew. And why shouldn't they be? After all, I told them the truth."

"Of course you did," Bayzog said, pouring Ben another glass of wizard water.

Ben drank again and set the glass down with a throaty "Ah!" He shook his head. "This seems inappropriate. That brew makes me feel better for telling the horrible news I had. I shouldn't feel good, but I do. Is that bad?"

"Ben, don't worry about it." Bayzog reached over and patted him on the back. "You carried this guilt too long and needed to get it off your chest."

"That's a true statement if I ever heard one." Ben let out another heavy sigh. "So as soon as the elves left, I rushed back home and opened the chest where I'd stored Akron. It and the quiver were gone. I swear I felt my heart sink straight into the very heart of Nalzambor. I was sick. Mortally sick. I wanted to tell you, Bayzog, I did, but I was so ashamed." He sank his face into his hands and sobbed. "I've been a wreck ever since."

"I hate to ask, but was the chest locked?"

Ben nodded. "And it was still locked when I opened it. I don't understand how this could happen. My wife and children…none of them saw anything. And the lock is dwarven, and I always keep the key on me. There are but a very few who can pick such a lock." He sat back up and leaned into the sofa. "It's my fault. All my fault, and now they're hunting for Dragon. Can you believe that?"

Rubbing his finger under his chin, the half-elf wizard said, "There isn't much I don't believe can happen these days. I don't suppose you've heard from Nath, have you?"

"Nothing. I wanted to search him out myself, but I won't leave my family—and if anyone can take care of himself, it's Dragon. But deep in my bones, I feel like something is greatly wrong. Do you ever get that feeling?" Ben asked.

"All too often." Bayzog rose to his feet and started over toward his large, round study table. "You are aware that plenty of eyes have seen you use that bow. It's far from a secret, and you are one of Quintuklen's heroes. Have you noted anything suspicious? Perhaps someone is avoiding you who didn't before?"

"No. Everyone's too worried about the giants, and I haven't been fool enough to speak about it. Even my wife doesn't know." Ben punched a pillow. "I'm a fool!"

"Easy now." Bayzog wanted to say whatever he could to bring Ben relief, but these troubles were even worse than he'd suspected. The elves would avenge Laedorn. Certainly they would try to capture Nath and bring him to justice—and they would have it one way or another. That was one problem, but the other was finding out who had taken Akron. There were two possibilities. In one, Nath was possessed, and he took it. Or in the second possibility, an imposter was setting Nath up—which was more likely. But there were very few who could pull off such a feat, and the only one they knew personally capable of such a crime was Gorlee.

So little is known about the changelings. Perhaps they have sided with the titans. After all, they're a neutral breed.

Ben got up and started pacing around the sofa while tapping the glass in his hand with his finger. He made a few rounds before stopping at Bayzog's table, looking right at him, and saying, "Bayzog, you have the power. You need to go after them."

"Go after who?" he said with mild astonishment.

"After your sons and Dragon. Can't you see it has to be you? You can get word out and warn him. Find your sons and bring them back before things get even worse."

"I can't leave Sasha."

"We can take care of her, me and my family. It would be our honor." Ben took Bayzog by the shoulders and squeezed them. "You know it has to be you."

"No," said another voice that had entered the room. It was Sasha. "It has to be us."

CHAPTER 7

BALZURTH WALKED WITH HIS ELBOWS swinging and a grand smile on his face. His strides were long through the tall grass, making it tough for Brenwar to keep up. The grim dwarf was like a child around Balzurth, having to rush forward to keep up from time to time, only to fall to the rear again. "It's good to walk. My feet on the earth have meaning," said the Dragon King. And then he turned around to yell, "How are you doing back there, Brenwar?"

"Never better," the dwarf yelled back. "I like stretching my stumpy legs."

In step with Balzurth, Nath beamed with admiration. There was nothing like being in the presence of his father, especially when he was showing his lighter side. The Dragon King wore a tunic crafted from leather that was a dull shade of emerald. He'd created the dye from the bark of trees combined with the local grasses. There were boots on Balzurth's feet formed from the skins of lizards and snakes and the hide of a boar. Though he was human in shape and form, there was an uncanny quality about him. An air. It lifted the spirits of them all.

"It's good to be with you, Father." Nath stretched out his clawed hands and compared them to the bare arms of his father. "No scales?"

"There should be," Balzurth said, glancing at the black scales on Nath's arms. "But you picked an interesting color. Why is that?"

"I like it, but I can change it," Nath replied.

"No, that won't be necessary. I know your heart is as red as mine, and that's what counts. Besides, the black looks good on you." Balzurth clamped his hand over Nath's wrist. "But be reminded, Son, that there is more to your scales than meets the eye. They do more than protect you like armor from piercing weapons, and they aren't for show or decoration."

Nath felt his father's strength coursing up his arm. It was as if the strength of an entire dragon was in the palm of a man's mighty grip. It was the power he'd once had and ever longed for. "What else do the scales do?" he asked, trying to distract himself from his oppressive feeling of loss.

"They're stronger than flesh in more ways than one. They protect you from many of the temptations men suffer. Have you not noticed that?"

Nath had never thought about that before. Thinking back, he realized the ways of men weren't as appealing as they had been before. He had better control over his emotions and urges. "I suppose I have been different since I got my scales."

"Yes, you are, and that's why dragons don't get caught up in the affairs of men. They have no desire for all the drama." Balzurth reached down and scooped up some wildflowers from the ground and handed them back to Laylana. "For you."

She sniffed the flowers with a thrill in her light-green eyes. "Thank you, Balzurth."

"The pleasure is mine, elven lady." He turned his attention back to Nath. "You were about to say something, Son?"

"Aren't you at risk without your scales?"

"I'd be lying if I denied I was tingling all over. It makes me think of the times when I was free like you, adventuring from town to town and freeing one damsel in distress after the other." Balzurth smacked his lips with a gleam in his eyes. "Those were adventurous times. One does silly things when he thinks his life is only mortal. But the greater treasures are rewarded through patience and discipline. You're doing good things, Son, and I'm proud of you. You wear those scales quite well."

"Not as well as you, apparently."

"In time it will come, so long as you do the right thing." Balzurth reached his hand into the air, and a blue bird landed on his finger and began singing. He hummed along.

"You know, Father, I've been trying to do the right thing, but the world is still a mess."

"Yes, and we journey to remedy that. For now. I'm not saying it will be easy. It never is, and it never lasts. But we must do it. Besides, we want to."

The four of them marched for hours toward the setting sun like an invincible army. On their journey, Balzurth revealed many things about his youth that were similar to Nath's. It seemed his father had had his own pitfalls. Nath felt a closeness between them begin to build, and the stories Balzurth told weren't as long and boring as they used to seem.

These stories are fantastic. Was I really so impatient?

They were still days away from Quintuklen when the skies began to darken. Night fell, and as they walked on, the sound of war drums caught Nath's ear.

Balzurth stopped and said, "That sounds interesting." He tilted his head. "Sounds like orcs are in our midst and having a party without me." He slapped Nath on the shoulder and looked back at Brenwar with a broad grin. "Let's go give them a greeting they'll never forget."

"Aye!" Brenwar replied.

With his long red locks waving in the wind, Balzurth made a beeline for the thumping sounds that stirred the menace of the night. The drums were a warning that orcs would often beat. It was their deranged custom to instill fear in their enemies and to let the weaker people in the world know they were coming. Nath always thought it was stupid to make so much noise where stealth should be applied, but they were orcs. Everything they did was offensive and brash.

The drumbeats were joined by howls and cries after they'd walked a mile to the drumbeats. Soon, they were overlooking a band of orcs that had formed a camp nestled in the woodland. Hidden among the trees, they watched the orcs beat their armored chests and guzzle wine from flasks. A huge campfire blazed, and beyond its flames were two husky orcs pounding on their drums as the celebration and clamor rose among them.

"Hmmm," Balzurth said. "They seem happy. Happy orcs mean trouble. I'd better see what's going on. All of you stay here and watch."

"No, Father, wait," Nath said.

But Balzurth slipped free of his grasp and cut for the camp with the ease of a leopard.

Brenwar, war hammer in hand, rushed to Nath's side. "What's he doing?"

Laylana pressed into Nath from his other side and added, "He's going to fight them all, isn't he."

"I have no idea what he's doing. I never have any idea what he's doing." Nath crept forward from one tree to another, with Brenwar and Laylana on his hips but with his eyes never leaving his father. Balzurth was moments away from wading into the middle of the orc camp. Nath knew in his head it wasn't anything he needed to be worried about. After all, they were orcs, and they were about to face Balzurth. Still, his scales tingled.

"Nath," Brenwar said, nudging him in the back. He pointed in another direction. "Look."

Beyond the fire and back against the clearing tree line were cages. Long necks lifted up with serpentine heads, and bright eyes locked on Balzurth, who had just waded into the middle of the orc camp.

The pounding on the drums stopped. The orcs, at least ten that Nath could see, stopped in the middle of their celebration. Discovering Balzurth standing among them, they dropped their drinks and drew their knives and swords and advanced.

Balzurth froze them in their tracks when he said in a dangerous voice, "How dare you cage my dragons? You'll pay for that!"

CHAPTER 8

"SASHA, PLEASE, YOU NEED REST," Bayzog said, taking her hands in his and trying to sit her down. "Let me get you something to drink."

"No!" She jerked away from him. "I heard everything, Bayzog. I know I have the dementia now, or at least I've put it together when I'm in my right mind. But I know what I saw. Our sons are dead if not in horrible danger. I can feel it in the marrow of my bones!" She walked over to an open closet and grabbed a backpack and threw it at Bayzog. "Let's go!"

"As you wish." Bayzog glanced at Ben, turned, and headed to a wooden chest that sat on the floor and opened up the lid. He began placing items inside the pack that she'd given him, one by one.

"Hello, Sasha," Ben said, approaching with open arms. "It's good to see you again."

Sasha burst into tears and rushed into Ben's arms. She clutched him, and with heavy sobs, she said, "Oh Ben, you must help Bayzog and me find my sons. I can't bear to not see them again while I rot away." Her body shuddered. "I know I need help. Bayzog needs help. The evil in me is destroying me."

"I will help," Ben promised. "I will help." He gave Bayzog a feeble glance. "You know you can count on me and Bayzog. And I know Rerry and Samaz can take care of themselves until we find them." He separated himself from her a little. "It wouldn't surprise me one bit if they were on their way back with a cure right now. Sasha?"

The woman stood staring back at him as if he weren't there. Her vibrancy was gone, and the tears began to dry on her face.

"She's gone," Bayzog said with a sigh. He wiped his eyes on his sleeve. "Every time that happens, I fear it will be the last I ever see of her again. I swear my heart is imploding in my chest."

Dumbfounded, all Ben could say was, "I can't imagine."

Bayzog carefully emptied the contents of the rucksack back into the chest and closed the lid. He hung the pack back up in the closet. "Did you believe her when she said our sons were dead?"

"I know a mother's instinct is far greater than a father's. So yes, I'm convinced they are in great peril." Ben put his arm around Sasha's slender waist and led her to the sofa. "Do you have any way of finding them?"

"I can attempt to find them with my resources, but I've tried that and haven't had any success as of yet." Bayzog grabbed the books that floated over his desk, closed them up, and stacked them on the edge. He made his way back over to the closet and grabbed the Elderwood Staff, which leaned back in the corner. "Ben, I'm going to have to take you up on your offer. Is it still available?"

"Of course it is, Bayzog," Ben said. "But I can't let you go it alone. I must come with you. You're no tracker. You'll need me."

"Who will take care of Sasha? I can only trust you."

"My wife, Margo, can handle it." Ben showed a confident smile. "Trust me, she and the girls can handle anything. They'll thrive at this. They're wonderful caregivers. The best. Just ask the Legionnaires. My family's stitched up more men than dragons have scales. I promise, Sasha couldn't be in better hands. Besides, I promised her."

Bayzog got on his knees in front of Sasha. Her face was so thin, and her eyes were listless and weak. He couldn't stay put and do nothing any longer. It was time he took matters into his own hands, and he'd have to trust some friends to do it. He kissed her hands and said, "I'll find a cure for you, my love. And I will find our sons and bring them back. I promise."

CHAPTER 9

AN ORC WITH A BIG body and a little head stepped into Balzurth's path. The ugly humanoid was half covered in iron armor that rattled and squeaked. He had a horrible underbite, and two canine teeth popped up on both sides of his nose that gave him a menacing look. "Fool! What are you doing in my camp? Have you come to be slaughtered?"

The snickering orcs formed a tight circle around Balzurth.

Nath's grip tightened on Fang's hilt. His father had told him to wait and he was obeying, but it didn't seem natural. It was uncomfortable, and it didn't help that his blood was rising. He eased forward.

Brenwar caught him by the elbow and tugged him back. "I'm as ready as you are, but we have our orders."

Balzurth stood face to face with the orc. "You have my dragons. I suggest you let them go, but if you'll allow me, I'd be glad to do it myself."

"No dragons will be freed, old man," the orc said with a sneer. Spittle dripped down his chin. "If anything, you'll be joining then in your own cage." He gave Balzurth the once over and stared hard into his eyes. "Your eyes are like gold. Perhaps we should cut them out, orcs. What do you say? Seize him!"

Surrounded by weapons, Balzurth watched with muted interest as the orcs bound his wrists up in heavy ropes.

"Put this fool in a cage," said the leader of the orcs, and then he leaned into Balzurth and added, "Keep quiet, too, or we'll have you for dinner."

Nath watched the rough-handed orcs shove Balzurth into a steel cage barely big enough to fit him in, and they padlocked it.

Laylana pushed Nath in the small of his back. "We need to free him. Oh, I'd like to show those orcs a thing or two."

"Great Guzan, what is my father doing? Is this what he wanted us to see, him getting captured?"

"He doesn't seem to be in any danger," Brenwar said. He had a stern look on his face. "Just give it a moment."

Concealed in the forest, they held their position for several long minutes. The drums started to beat again, and the orcs renewed their celebration, drinking and singing horrible songs that would make the deaf cringe.

Taken up in the scene of orcen frivolity, Nath momentarily forgot his father, so that when he looked back, his father's cage door was open.

Balzurth's mighty man frame was twisting the padlocks off the dragon cages and letting a small orange blaze and a green lily dragon go free. Both of them nuzzled into Balzurth as he stroked their long necks and the tiny horns on their heads.

"Hold there!" an orc yelled at Balzurth. The drums came to a stop again. The orc snatched up a spear and hurled it at Balzurth. The drunken throw sailed high and vanished into the forest.

The small cat-sized dragons' wings beat, and they took to the air and were out of sight through the tree branches that hung over the camp.

The orcen leader gaped and screamed. "Who let him out of there? I'll have your head!"

In a voice that rose over all of the weapon-drawing scuffles, Balzurth said, "No one let me out, you fool. I let myself out." He stepped back and opened up the door of his cage once again and said to the leader. "Now you get in there! Come on. I don't want to be standing here all night. I have better things to do than teach orcs a lesson."

With narrowed eyes, the orcen leader stepped over toward a stump that was in the ground with a battle axe stuck in it. He ripped it out and stormed toward Balzurth. Chest heaving, he said, "You're going to die for that, human."

"First, I'm not human. And second, well, there is no second, but if you want to try and kill me, then try and kill me." Balzurth spread his arms out wide. "Come on, you can have the first shot."

The orc lifted his battle axe over his head and brought it down with wroth force.

Balzurth sidestepped.

Swish!

The axe bit into the ground.

Using the orc's forward motion against him, Balzurth grabbed the orc by the scruff of the neck and shoved him into the awaiting cage. He slammed the door shut with authority and latched the lock. He said to the orc leader, "You are as slow as you are stupid." He faced the others. "Now, how about the rest of you?"

The dumbfounded orcs looked back and forth at each other.

With his lower jaw jutting outside of the bars, the orc leader yelled, "What are you idiots waiting for? Kill him and get me out of here."

The nearest orc took a stab at Balzurth with his sword.

The Dragon King snatched him by the wrist and pulled him around and swung him with ram-like force into two of his comrades.

The next orc jumped on Balzurth's legs.

Two more piled on.

Balzurth was half laughing and half struggling to keep his feet. "Same old orcs, same old tactics." He wrapped his arms around one of their waists and flipped the orc back over his head, sending the husky body smashing into the trees.

At the same time, the leader of the orcs was yelling, "Get me out of here! Get me out of here!"

An orc warrior shoved his dagger into Balzurth's chest, puncturing the tunic.

The Dragon King replied, "Your orcen steel cannot harm me." He slapped the orc in the face so hard his canine teeth fell out. "Don't ever try to scathe me again."

The drunken orcs turned into a knot of clumsy ferocity. Teeth and weapons bared, they piled onto the big man in a frenzy.

"We need to get in there!" Laylana urged Nath.

He couldn't even see his father now. It was just a pile of orcs swinging and punching with wild-eyed ferocity.

"I agree," Brenwar said, nodding his head. "Let's go."

"You're the one who's so eager to follow orders," Nath argued.

"I know, but this is killing me," Brenwar replied. "I can't stand it anymore. He's having all the fun."

"Look!" Laylana said.

A pair of big hands popped out of the angry knot of orcs and grabbed two of them by their heads of mangy hair. The heads were yanked back and the faces slammed together. The same hands made fists and started punching the orcs in the jaw and hammering them on the head. As the orcs sagged into the dirt, Balzurth's handsome face appeared unscathed, saying, "They stink. My, they stink so bad. Dragon fodder smells far better than them."

An orc snuck up behind Balzurth and whacked him in the back of the head with a hammer, rocking his head downward.

The Dragon King's head snapped up, and his gold eyes were ablaze. He twisted around with the speed of a striking viper and ripped the hammer free from the orc's hand.

"Guzan," Nath muttered. He'd seen that look in his father's eyes before. The fires in the center of a volcano were nothing compared to it. The orcs had aggravated Balzurth. "He's going to kill that orc."

"Good," Brenwar nodded. "Take out those spangbockers!"

"Aye," said Laylana. "Let's help him."

Slinging off the disheveled orcs that lay scattered at his feet, Balzurth snatched up by the neck the one that had hit him with the hammer. He lifted it from the ground. Instantly, eyes bulging from the sockets, the orc started to choke, flail, and gasp.

Nath burst into action. Crossing from the forest into the camp in three quick strides, he rammed his shoulder into his father, jarring the orc loose from his grip.

Hot eyed like a god gone mad, Balzurth glared at Nath. "You dare!"

"We're not supposed to kill them!" Nath replied.

An orc rushed him with a spear.

With ease, Nath sidestepped and drove his boot into the orc's belly, dropping it on the ground and gasping. "We just beat the stupid out of them."

"They're orcs, they don't matter," Balzurth said. Fierce as a charging bull, he lifted a woozy orc over his head and shoulders and hurled him like a stump of wood into the upper branches of a tree. "Now get out of my way!"

Nath shoved him back and said, "So you lied to me?"

"I don't lie," Balzurth said.

"So I can kill orcs then?" Nath fired back.

Balzurth hesitated. The hot glare in his eyes cooled. Clenching his fists, he shook them and said, "My flesh lusts for battle! But no, Son. You are right. I should not be slaying these impudent things, regardless of how stupid they may be. Unless of course my life is in peril." He took a glance at his surroundings. "Which it clearly is not."

A banging of metal resounded on the cage the orc leader was trapped in. One of his brethren knocked the lock off, and in a wide-eyed hustle they scurried away.

"Aren't you going after them?" Nath said to his father. "After all, it *is* pretty fun throttling them from time to time. And I must admit it was a delight seeing you in action. I've never seen you like this before."

"Aye, but I got carried away." A long look formed on Balzurth's bearded face. He raised his fingers and studied the specks of orcen blood on them. "This flesh is weak. Son, it's been so long that I've forgotten how hard it must be for you to be you. It's exhilarating but dangerous. Perhaps this form I've taken is not for me." He scanned the fallen orcs with a sneer. "So many are soaked in evil that it's impossible to avoid it. A shame."

"What do you want us to do with these orcs, King Balzurth?" Brenwar had an orc locked up with the war hammer handle under the orc's chin. "I'd be glad to vanquish these poachers on your command."

Nath awaited his father's answer. There had been a time in Nalzambor when poaching dragons was a crime, but those days were gone. How were they supposed to deal with orcs that committed crimes against his kind? There wasn't any way to enforce those laws nowadays without killing. There was no longer anywhere to imprison simple poachers.

"Destroy their weapons and belongings. That's going to have to be punishment enough for now. We have our own mission." Balzurth picked up the orc leader's axe and spun it around with a twist between his fingers and said to the orcs, "Just because you receive mercy today does not mean you will receive mercy tomorrow."

Deep in the bowels of the forest, a horn blared.

A tremor shook the ground under Nath's feet, and the branches shook though there was no wind.

Rising up with Laylana at his side, Brenwar said, "What in Mortuun's beard is that?"

The sound of branches snapping could be heard in the distance. It came closer and closer. A lone orc, the one Balzurth had hurled, fell out of the trees, hit the ground hard, and scurried away. Nath knew the sound. It was footsteps. Giant footsteps that shook the ground. And it wasn't just one set but many.

Balzurth looked at Nath and said, "It seems the fight is just beginning." He lifted the orcen axe in front of his face and with a single breath he turned the twin blades to flame. "I hope Fang is ready. We're going to need him."

CHAPTER 10

A STEADY DRIP OF WATER BOUNCED off Rerry's head. The icy water ran down his back under his clothes and plopped into a puddle. The pool of liquid made its way down the rocky cavern floor like a tiny river that winded around the cave wall into the black out of his sight. It had been going on like this for hours while the limbs of the part-elven son of Bayzog burned with agony.

"Ugh…I don't know which is worse, the water or the stretch," he said in a gravelly voice. Licking his cracked lips, Rerry wriggled against his bonds. His wrists were bound over his head by chains, just barely allowing his toes to touch the floor.

"The water wouldn't be so bad if I could only taste a drop. Ugh!"

In the corner opposite his was Samaz. The stouter brother of the two hung the same way as Rerry: upright and uncomfortable. But Samaz's hair hung over his eyes. His bare chest had bruises and red marks all over it. A nasty cough revealed the taut muscles of his abdomen.

Rerry let out a light laugh. "This is fitting for you, Samaz. You have lost some of that baby fat that guarded your ample belly. Just think, a few more days and you'll be as skinny as me."

Samaz coughed and convulsed. It was a sick cough, not some annoyance that comes with a dry throat. Something worse.

Rerry squinted. A single torch just outside the cavern of their prison was the only source of light they had, and it was very little. Just enough to make out his brother's body but not enough to provide any kind of warmth. "Samaz. Samaz? Are you sick?"

Samaz shivered in his shackles, and the wet cough came back again.

"Great Guzan, you are sick." Rerry tugged against the steel links of his bonds. The fire inside him had far from dimmed, but his wiry strength was lacking. His hands bled from trying to squeeze them through the steel cuffs that held them. The bonds were secure. "My captors are clever. They know better than to take a chance with a brilliant swordsman like me, eh Samaz? Rerry the Ravager. No, Rerry the Rage." He blew his sweaty blond locks from his eyes. "If only I had red hair, I could be Rerry the Red."

"Rerry the Rooster," Samaz sputtered out in a raspy voice.

"You speak!" Rerry beamed and then frowned. "Uh, why rooster?"

"Because you're clucking all the time." Samaz broke into another fit of coughing.

Rerry grimaced and said, "I need to get you help. You are very ill with hallucinations. Do I look like a chicken to you?"

Samaz shivered so hard that his teeth clacked. Gulping for air, he said, "It's a fever. It will break."

"You will break if you don't have nourishment." Rerry let out a sharp whistle. "Guards! Guards!" His voice echoed down the tunnels and came to a stop. He shouted again. "Guards! Guards!"

It was as if they were the only ones in the caves. Rerry wasn't even certain where they were, because they'd been hooded when they were brought in. And now, after days in the dark, the grim, damp cave was taking a toll on Samaz. And Rerry feared it might take a toll on him as well before long. He glanced down at the skeleton that lay on the floor with its mouth hanging open. It had long, wispy black hair, and its clothes were finely woven. Judging by the hair and the narrow features of the skull, Rerry was certain it was elven.

How long did that elf live in this cavern before he died?

A scuffle of soft steps splatting over the damp waters that ran through the cave caught his ear. Whoever was coming moved with the gentleness of the falling night. Gazing at the tunnel, Rerry waited for his captor to emerge. Limbs still burning, he struggled in his shackles. He blinked away the sweat that dripped into his eyes, and when he looked up again, an elf was there blocking the torchlight and casting an ominous shadow over him.

"It's high time you stopped disturbing the gloom," the newcomer said. Tall and slender, the elf was handsome in his features, but his brown hair was shorter than that of most of their kind, cut neatly just above the shoulders. An eye patch covered his left eye, and a white scar split the dimple in his chin. He wore a leather tunic dyed black over a white shirt the covered him from the knees up over his trousers. The feathered insignia of an elven officer was on his collar, and he carried himself with a sinister air. "So I take it you are needing something?"

"I don't, but my brother needs care, Scar," Rerry said. "He's sick."

"It makes no difference to me. Suffering is part of your punishment," Scar said. "It goes hand in hand with your imprisonment." He glanced at the skeleton on the floor. "Just ask him."

"I did. He's not answering."

"Your tongue is awfully sharp, little Rerry. You sound strong. I need to remedy that." Scar grabbed the chains that hung over Rerry's head and gave them a yank. Rerry let out a groan. Scar added, "Perhaps they need to be a little tighter."

"This is not right. Where is our counsel, Scar? We are entitled to counsel. I might not be a full-blooded elf, but I know the elven rules. You cannot hold us like this against our will. It's not the elven way!" He stretched out toward Scar. "Help my brother!"

"Oh, your brother will be fine." Scar made his way over to Samaz, took him by the hair, and pulled his head up. Samaz's face was pasty and white. His eyes were sunken into their sockets. "He looks fine to me, for a human that is."

Voice straining, Rerry said, "We might be part human, but we are still entitled to our elven heritage. I demand our counsel now, Scar!"

Scar slipped his well-honed rapier out of his sheath in the blink of an eye and held the blade against Rerry's throat. "It's Captain Scar, and you bastards are entitled to nothing. Your kind is poison to the elven world. Your father is an embarrassment, and it's no surprise that his atrocious sons are nothing but common thieves. I should cut you both open right now and be done with it."

Showing his teeth, Rerry replied, "Then what is stopping you, Captain Scar?"

"Unlike you, I have orders that I follow. Otherwise, I would have finished the both of you off the moment we met."

Staring down Scar—who looked middle aged for an elf—Rerry replied, "Why don't you give me a blade so we can see who'll finish who off fairly?"

Scar smacked him on the cheek with the flat of his sword and said, "You whelp. Do you have so little value for your life that you'd let me cut you down in a moment? I'd carve you to ribbons. Pah. I bet you've never even killed in battle."

"I doubt you have. Cut me down, Scar. Let our swords dance, and we will see what happens."

"You'll never get the pleasure. You're dead already." Scar slid his sword into his scabbard and walked away.

CHAPTER 11

THE FIRST GIANT SHOVED TWO smaller trees aside, snapping them both at their bases. It ripped another tree out of the ground and lifted it high over its head like a club. Standing at fifteen feet tall, the ugly brute was nothing but thick layers of fat over muscle. Its neck was as wide as its head, and it opened up a mouthful of teeth that numbered more than the hairs on its head.

Covering his nose, Balzurth said, "And I thought the orcs were smelly."

Two more giants emerged from the startled black of the forest. Like the other giant, they were bestial men with hides and furs for clothes.

Flipping his flaming axe around his wrist, Balzurth said, "I'll take the one in the middle." To Nath he said, "There will be no mercy to these unnatural beasts."

Without hesitation, Nath rushed in with Fang arcing high. He swung the great blade into the giant's leg with authority.

The giant let out an angry bellow, and its fingers clutched for the locks of hair on Nath's head.

Nath stepped under the giant's legs and cut deep into the back of its knee, sending it sprawling to the ground.

Wham!

There was a clap of thunder, followed by the moaning of a giant that Mortuun the war hammer sent staggering into the trees. Brenwar was yelling, "For Morgdon!"

Balzurth's flaming battle axe sliced off the fingers of the outstretched giant's hand.

Letting out an ear-splitting howl of anger and anguish, it brought the tree it carried like a club down at Balzurth's head.

In human form, the Dragon King knocked the tree club aside with his blazing axe, bursting the branches into flames.

The trio of warriors pressed the giants back into the forest, hacking, stabbing, and chopping the bewildered giants down. The battle raged, and the forest turned to flame. Smoke stung Nath's eyes as he gave chase to the giant he'd toppled, which had gotten up and was running for its life through the branches. Nath clipped it right behind the heel, and it crashed headlong into a tree. Dazed, the giant turned, just as Nath ran Fang straight through its heart, ending its life. Surrounded by smoke and the burning haze of the orange fire, he heard Laylana's voice calling out.

"Nath! Nath!"

Rushing straight for the sound of the elven woman's voice, Nath picked up a rattling sound in the woods that sent shivers down his spine. The giants were not alone. Wurmers snaked through the smoky murk.

When he caught sight of Laylana, she was surrounded by wurmers. The rogue elven fighter chopped with the ferocity of an attacking lion, keeping the wurmers at bay, but then a tail lashed out and struck her square in the back of the head, taking her down.

"Laylana!" Nath screamed. Charging with amazing speed, he attacked the slithering knot of wurmers. His great sword Fang cut off a wurmer's head at the neck. With a stamp, he punctured another wurmer in the chest, turning the purple gleam in its eye cold.

Jaws clamped down on his free arm, and he drove Fang's pommel into an eye, jarring the creature loose.

Claws slashed into him.

Jaws snapped at his knees.

Nath fought on, tearing through the wurmers one by one, trying to reach Laylana. His powerful sword strokes swept the wurmers aside until he found himself standing over the elven princess. She was on her hands and knees, bleeding. "Laylana! Can you fight?"

Clutching her sword and rising to her feet, she said, "Do I have a choice?"

Back to back, they fought off the wurmers. The man-sized lizards moved in, one right after the other, swarming them from all directions. Fang bit through scale and bone.

"There are so many!" Laylana coughed, and tears from the smoke were streaming down her pretty face.

Nath sensed her strength was beginning to wane. Blood pumping, he redoubled his efforts and chopped deeper into one wurmer after the other, killing them instantly. Like an angry flock of hissing birds, the wurmers kept appearing. It was only a matter of time before the monsters consumed them. "Guzan! Where are they all coming from?"

All around him, the forest was blazing. Crashes and cries of alarm erupted from the haze. Brenwar was letting out battle cries, and Balzurth blurted out boasts. Giants growled and howled. A huge hunk of rock soared through the air and crashed into the branches behind Nath's head.

Nath screamed out, "Father, you're setting the entire forest on fire!"

Out of nowhere, a giant backpedaled through the smoke and smashed into the trees. A flaming axe burned in its forehead.

Balzurth spurted out of the chaos with havoc in his eyes. He stormed toward Nath and grabbed two wurmers by their tails. With a tremendous heave, he slung them into the smoke and out of sight. "These nasty insects are many!"

Revved up in the presence of his father, Nath unleashed everything he had left. Fang splintered scales and skulls. The nasty, inky blood of the wurmers burned through his scales into his flesh, but his battle-raged mind didn't care. With one sweeping swat after another, he poured it on until all of the wurmers were dead. Finally, chest heaving and fighting for breath, Nath caught Laylana by the wrist and dragged her out of the forest.

Brenwar stood several dozen yards outside of the forest's edge, patting out the flame that was burning a hole in his beard. "Blasted giants!"

Nath heard a gusty laugh coming from behind him, outside of the flames.

"My, that was fun! Was it not, Son? We need to seek these giants out and do that again."

Coughing, Laylana replied, "I'm ready."

"You were a bit careless, Father. The smoke could have suffocated us in there," Nath said, watching the flames rise into the night sky. He stuck Fang in the ground. "Not everyone is accustomed to smoke for breath."

"Noted," Balzurth said. The glow in his eyes started to dim. "I suppose I did get carried away, but this body wants to work without the mind. It's so lively." He approached Laylana and took her by the hand. "Are you all right, my sweet elven lady?"

"I'll be fine."

Balzurth patted her hand. "I'm sorry for my carelessness. I hope you'll forgive me."

"Most certainly," she said. "No regrets on my end. You men certainly know how to show an elf a good time."

"You mean dragons," Balzurth said.

"And dwarves," Brenwar added.

"Of course," she said, wiping her hair from her eyes.

"Well, if someone is looking for us, they shouldn't have much trouble finding us now," Nath said. "And it would not surprise me one little bit if there were many enemies nearby beyond that blaze. I don't suppose the fire will burn itself out anytime soon. It's a bit of a shame."

"Oh, I can take care of that." Balzurth reached over and grabbed Fang by the hilt, pulling him free of the ground. The wondrous blade twinkled with bluish light. Balzurth marched into the flaming forest and stabbed a tree.

Nath's jaw dropped.

Ice spread from the tip of Fang's blade. With crackling movement, the veil of ice covered the ground and raced up the trunks and limbs of the trees. A sizzling hiss followed as the flames were extinguished one by one, leaving a twinkling, white-blue ice tree city shimmering in the moonlight.

"Whoa," Laylana said, "I am without words."

Hefting Fang over his shoulder, Balzurth walked over and offered the sword to Nath. "Fang is quite something, isn't he?"

Taking the sword in hand, Nath replied, "How did you get him to do that?"

"I just asked Fang to do what I created him to do, and he did it. Next time there's a fire, you might want to give it a try."

Nath stood there gawping while Balzurth pivoted around on his foot and faced north toward Quintuklen, saying to Brenwar, "Is it time to resume our walk again?"

Slinging Mortuun over his shoulder, Brenwar said, "After you."

Nath and Laylana tagged along behind through the chill wind of the night, silent for several miles.

Crossing over the rocks that made a path over a babbling brook, she eyed Nath and said, "You look troubled. It's disturbing. What's wrong?"

"So many things are going on that I don't know where to start. Those giants came out of nowhere, not to mention the wurmers. I don't know that we can travel a day without fighting something." He reached out his hand to help Laylana over a fallen tree. "It's depressing, really. I can't help but wonder how this few of us can defeat so many."

"Oh, I don't think that's the only thing bothering you. You have no fear of these hordes of dangers. I think it's your father who's getting to you." She twisted her hair around her finger. "He's so confident and wily. And the things he does are so amazing."

"Yes, and I should be able to do those things too, but I can't. It's frustrating."

"Give it time," she said, "I'm sure you'll figure it out."

"That's the problem. I don't think there is much time left to figure it out. I just hope Quintuklen still stands by the time we get there. I swear I feel as if all of Nalzambor has gone mad." Sidestepping a rock, he bumped into her shoulder, almost knocking her over. "Sorry."

She ran her fingers down his arm and replied, "It's quite all right, Nath."

The twinkle in her eye made him think of Selene.

Sultans of Sulfur. I wonder how she's doing.

Nath picked up the pace, catching up with Brenwar and Balzurth. "You two are doing a good job steering clear of any trouble."

"We hope not," Balzurth said. "This is the most fun I've had in centuries."

"I don't recall saving Nalzambor being very fun the last time," Nath said.

"Oh, it's all about making the most of the journey, Nath," said Balzurth. "Being in the company of your friends when the stakes are so high that you can barely sleep at night. Ah… Nothing worth fighting for is ever easy. Eh, Brenwar?"

Combing his fingers through his beard, Brenwar replied, "I've never had fun doing anything easy."

"Well said, well said, my stumpy little comrade." Turning around to walk backward, Balzurth said to Nath, "I'm glad you joined us. Now put a smile on that grim face of yours. There's no apparent danger at the moment, and we live, we breathe, we'll fight again."

Nath didn't get caught up in the high spirits of the others. He wasn't used to seeing his father this way—jolly, laughing, or even smiling. Sure, there had been some frivolous times when he was younger, but for at least the past hundred years, Balzurth had been … serious. Downright stern, even. And now the dragon-turned-man had become something else. If Nath didn't know better, he'd swear that some dangerous spirit had entered his father.

He couldn't possibly be this happy.

Finally, Nath gave in. "Fine, Father, but will you please be more mindful of the mortal company we are in?"

"Certainly, Son, certainly, but I heard you clearly the first time. No, I think Laylana will do just fine."

Onward they went, laughing, joking, and carrying on as if nothing could stop them.

CHAPTER 12

BEN SAT ATOP HIS HORSE, looking back at Quintuklen. The men worked day and night fortifying the mighty human city that had been turned to rubble by the Clerics of Barnabus not so long ago. Now new fortifications and buildings began to rise toward the sky again, thanks to the help of the dwarves. In each high tower were soldiers manning a ballista to fend off any flying terrors.

He filled his chest with air, sucking in the morning mist that covered the grasses and daisies. He was proud of these people. Even in the face of such adversity, they never gave up. He was proud to be among them. In the distance, stout men carried stones up ladders and set them down on scaffolding. They'd learned much from the dwarves and the dwarves some things from them. It was a joy to see them working together. It reminded him of Dragon and Brenwar. It seemed so long since he'd heard from them.

Considering the journey ahead, Ben thought to himself, *I wonder what they're doing now.* Noting the rising sun warming his face, another thought came to mind.

Bayzog ought to be out here by now.

The part-elven wizard had said he'd need ample time to prepare himself for the journey ahead. The violet-eyed scholar had seemed a bit rattled when Ben left him last night to be by himself. Leaving Sasha wouldn't be easy, but it was the right thing.

Come on, wizard. I'm itching to get going.

Ben unslung his bow from his back. He ran his fingers up and down the string. It was a fine bow, but nothing like Akron. His quiver of arrows rattled when he shifted in the saddle. There was a distinct sound to the arrows he shot. They were made from ash wood and tipped with tempered steel. He slipped an arrow out and nocked it on the bowstring. The thick callouses between the joints of his fingers were as hard as ever. He pulled the string back, aimed for a distant dogwood tree, and let the arrow fly. The arrow sailed high in the air and missed the mark by ten feet.

A little late to practice now.

He slung the bow back over his shoulder, longing for the *snap-clatch-snap* sound of Akron. There was already sweat forming on his brow, and his butt felt a little sore in the saddle.

Please don't tell me I'm too old for this, but I've barely made it out of the city.

Finally, Ben saw Bayzog come out through the outermost of the city's rebuilt white catacomb walls.

The half-elf wizard's expression was grim, but it perked up a bit upon seeing Ben. Riding up to the veteran warrior, he said, "Sorry for the delay, but I have something for you." He patted the bulging blanket behind his paint horse's saddle. "Take it. We will need it."

Ben lifted the blanket, and his eyes popped wide open. With astonishment, he said to Bayzog, "This is Brenwar's chest!"

"Indeed."

"Can we even open it?"

"See for yourself. I don't think it cares for elves. If you can't open it, I'm leaving it."

"No, no, no." Ben couldn't hide the thrill in his voice. He loved magic. It fascinated him, and he regretted not having an opportunity to experiment with the chest before. He took the strongbox by the outer handles and lifted it into his lap. "My, it's a lot lighter than it looks."

"Dwarves make everything appear stronger than it is," Bayzog said.

Ben's fingers searched the whole chest for a latch of some kind, but the area around the lid was almost seamless. "Bayzog, I can't open this up."

Bayzog stuck his staff out and poked the front of the box with the end.

Ben took a second look and discovered the face of a dwarf gilded in iron, flush on the front of the chest. It looked vaguely like Brenwar.

Raising his chin and wrinkling his brow, Bayzog said, "Stick your finger in the dwarf's mouth, and hope it doesn't bite."

Studying the gilded face and looking at his finger, Ben said, "You'd think there would be latches or something."

"Get on with it," Bayzog said with an arched brow.

Heart pumping in his ears, Ben poked the dwarf in the mouth.

Clatch.

The chest's lid popped up a hair, and a golden light peeked out.

"It opens!" With both hands, Ben started to lift the lid.

Bayzog reached over and closed it back. "It works. Good. Now let's get moving."

"No offense, Bayzog, but I'm going to take a look."

"Now is not the place or the time." Bayzog pointed the Elderwood Staff south. "Onward."

"Am I leading, or are you?"

"You're the one trained by the best tracker in the land. I trust your instincts."

Securing the strongbox on his horse, Ben tied it down and said, "Fine, but the next time we stop, I'm taking a longer look in this chest."

CHAPTER 13

BLETVER THE TRIANT TORE THE roof off a shed. A man shielded a woman inside. In a grisly but polite voice, Bletver said to them, "Have you seen a man with flame-red hair?"

The woman screamed, and the man fought to cover her mouth with his hands. He kept saying, "No, no, no, we haven't seen anyone like that!"

"Are you certain of that?" Bletver said, showing off his rows of teeth.

"I wouldn't lie! I wouldn't lie!" the man yelled back.

"Well, there's no reason to yell at me. It's impolite. After all, I am a guest in your quaint little farm town." Bletver licked his lips. "The smell of livestock is simply delightful. You know, I've been a thousand feet deep in a hole. I'd completely forgotten how salivating this world can be." He dipped his monstrous head deeper into the shed.

The man covered his face and gagged.

"Uh, are you absolutely, positively certain you have not seen a man with golden eyes and flame-red hair?"

"No, no, no," the man said. "I swear it on my life."

Bletver gave them a nod. "And I believe you. Thank you." He pushed the shed, collapsing it under his power and crushing the people within. He stepped on top of it and hopped on it a few times. The wood planks snapped under his weight, and that wasn't all that gave. The man's hand jutted between the boards and went still. Bletver dusted his hands off and eyed the goats that were crying behind the distant fence. "Ah, it's time to dine."

Taking his time to cross through the small farm village, he noted the withered husks of the once-vibrant bodies of people who had once nourished their surroundings for a hard but simple living. Faces of men, women, and children were frozen in horror. Their fragile lives had been sucked from the very marrow of their bones.

Nearby, the phantom swallowed up a man in the black shadows of his being. The blood quickly drained from the choking man's face. He dropped to his knees, frozen and lich-like, and then finally dead. The phantom's glowing eyes grazed over Bletver, then it passed through the stone walls of a well and moved toward the hidden voices that sobbed in terror.

"Bletver!" said a stern voice.

The triant turned.

Rybek had two well-knit men by their arms and was dragging them face first over the dirt roads like children. The men were busted up, and their spirits were broken. They didn't even cry out when they saw Bletver.

"What do you want me to do with them?" the triant said. "Crush them? Eat them?" He hitched his head over toward the fence that wrapped around the barn. "I'm thinking those sheep would be more succulent. These people tend to be a bit chewy."

One of the men gulped. His feet dug into the ground as he tried to pull free of Rybek's iron grip.

Rybek kicked the man in the ribs. "Be still." Drawing his dagger, he looked up at Bletver. "If you don't want to eat them, I'll kill them myself."

Lifting up his foot, Bletver stomped the life out of the nearest one. "Just because I don't want to eat them doesn't mean I don't want to kill them. They're humans. I can't stand them."

Rybek stabbed the second man in the heart, cleaned the steel on the man's shirt, and eased the blade back into its scabbard.

With a disapproving look, Bletver said, "Are we keeping score on the dead? Because I just added two other bodies over there. That gives me a count of ten—no, eleven, counting this one."

"Well, I'm not chasing down everyone that fled just to catch up. Besides, the phantom has doubled up on the both of us." Rybek picked up a stone from the ground. He chucked it at a husk of a woman on her knees clutching a bucket. His aim was true. The rock smote her in the face, and her body crumbled into a billow of smoke and a pile of ash.

"Humph, that was mildly amusing." Bletver sauntered over to a nearby fence post and yanked it one-handed out of the ground. He hurled it into a pair of phantom-struck bodies and turned them into a puff of smoke. "Not as thrilling as it looked. So you don't want to kill them all? I can smell their fear-filled sweat, you know."

"No," Rybek said. "Let them spread the news of our terror. It should draw out heroes like Nath Dragon. Eventually someone will show up. Someone that knows something will come. They always do, and we'll be waiting."

"Seems like an odd way to get results." Bletver gave a nod and headed for the barn. "If you'll excuse me, dinner is calling."

Rybek watched Bletver step over the barnyard fence, scoop up a whining goat, and devour it down in crunching chomps.

With a bitter expression on his face, Bletver tapped his chest with his fist and let out a disturbing belch.

Bllaaat!

"My, pardon me." Winking at Rybek, Bletver reached down and scooped up a sheep. Jaws wide, he stuffed the sheep into his mouth like a pillow into a case and swallowed it whole. "Mmmm…that's better."

Rybek's stomach gurgled. The thought of eating live flesh and bones wasn't something that sat well with him. He was human, after all, just evil to the core. Still, he wondered why the goat had cried out and the sheep hadn't. He'd noted that before in his conquests, where in some cases even people didn't have the slightest fear of their eminent death. Much like the sheep, they faced their fate with dumbfounded innocence. With life being so fragile, he wouldn't have thought they'd be so silent when it was about to end.

Venturing out of the town, he noted the crows circling overhead. The dead in the dusty streets were ripe for plucking. Grim faced, he set his sights on another conquest. Eventually, someone would stand up and face him, and his hope was that it would be Nath Dragon. He fingered the pouch that held the amulet he'd been given to capture Nath Dragon. The soft leather was cold and stiff to the touch. Rolling his stiffening fingers, he lowered them to the pommel of his sword. The blade's metal offered another reassuring feeling.

Eckubahn wants him alive, but I'll take his head. I'll have that betrayer Selene, too!

Rybek recalled the defeat Nath had given his brother, and a raging fire burned within him. Selene had taken full advantage of Kryzak's worship for her and turned him into an abomination. His brother had become a monster. The very essence of the man had been lost and was gone forever.

Rybek whipped out his sword and cut through the husk of a withered corpse.

I almost had her!

Indeed, he had tracked her as far as the seashore cities of the Pool of the Dragon, but he had lost her when she disappeared into the giant home of Uurluuk. No one had seen a trace of her for more than a year—not until what he'd discovered recently. She would surface again, along with Nath Dragon, and when they did, this time, now that he'd tested Nath's mettle, he'd be ready.

No mercy.

CHAPTER 14

After traveling a day and a night without incident, Nath found himself on a hilltop with his father and their friends, gazing down at the City of Quintuklen. The humans had made grand progress since the last time he'd been here, which seemed like only weeks ago. He still hadn't adjusted to the year they'd lost when Fang had teleported him and Selene and Brenwar, but it could have been worse.

"There's an awful lot of soldiers," Brenwar said, shielding his eyes with his hand. "That outer wall has been rebuilt. No doubt there were many dwarves working on that. I imagine word has spread regarding Uurluuk's treachery. Perhaps I should go in by myself and see Bayzog."

"I can go," Balzurth offered. "No one's looking for me."

"No, but you and I look so much alike, I doubt you'll avoid suspicion," Nath said. And it was true. If it weren't for all of Balzurth's hair and long beard, he could almost pass for Nath. "As for you, Brenwar," Nath continued, "they know how close you are to me. You'll be interrogated instantly."

With a grumble, Brenwar agreed, saying, "Perhaps."

"I can try," Laylana offered. "So far as I know, no one's looking for me."

"Judging by the soldiers," said Nath, "I have a feeling they aren't going to let any outsiders within. I'm still surprised they're working with the dwarves."

"Oh, this is silly," said Balzurth. "I can get us all in. We just need to be quick about it." He pushed up the sleeves on his arms. "Come closer, everyone."

They formed a tight circle.

With a twinkle in his eyes, Balzurth said, "Now hold hands."

"Dwarves don't hold hands."

"Brenwar, if you please," Balzurth replied.

Standing between Nath and Laylana, the dwarf took their hands, but he said, "Don't get used to it."

Standing before them like a priest, Balzurth laid his hands on their shoulders and muttered words in Dragonese. A prickle of energy shot through Nath's shoulder into his hand.

Laylana giggled.

Brenwar blurted out a stifled grunt.

"That should do it," Balzurth said with a nod. "Let's go."

Nath lifted his hands. All of his glistening scales were intact. Balzurth looked the same, and so did Brenwar and Laylana. He had fully expected some sort of transformation, but the only thing he'd gotten from it was a tickle. "Father, I hardly see how whatever you did is going to help."

"That's because I didn't change you. My spell will change the others' perception of us. We know what we look like, so we cannot fool ourselves, but we can fool the ones who don't know us," Balzurth assured him. "Now lead the way, Son. I'm excited to meet your friends who you've spoken so highly of."

Rolling with the odd sensation that was rolling underneath the skin of his body, Nath gave a shrug to his friends, who did the same. He wasn't sure what his father had done, but he felt confident that it would work. He'd have to trust him.

The soldiers met them on their approach just outside of the first gap in the wall. Dressed in full suits of chain mail and wearing skullcaps, the formidable men let out a giggle when they saw Nath. There were broad smiles on all their faces. One of them, a stern-looking man with bushy eyebrows bursting out from under his helm's metal frame, asked, "What is your business in Quintuklen?"

"We are meeting with my sister," Nath replied in a voice that wasn't his. He looked down at Brenwar. The brows on his comrade had lifted into his hairline. Laylana's lips were parted in an O. Nath cleared his throat and added, "It will just be a short stay."

Great Guzan! I sound like a woman!

"Oh," the soldier said. The broad-faced man took off his helmet and offered a generous smile and looked Nath up and down. "Is she as fair as you? And so tall?"

"Uh... oh sir, it's difficult for me to say," Nath stammered. He broke out in a cold sweat.

What did Father do to me?

"I'd be honored to give you and your family a personal escort," the soldier said.

With all of the soldiers' eyes fixed on him, Nath replied in his woman's voice, "Er, that won't be necessary. I know the way." He swallowed. "But, perhaps you could share a meal with my other sister later. She's a fine lady and has a penchant for ale."

"Oh really?" said the soldier. "I'd be quite eager to meet her."

"She's right here." Nath walked over and put his hands on Brenwar's shoulders. "Please, dear sister, introduce yourself."

The soldier's face soured, and the other soldiers blanched. Noticing Brenwar for the first time, each of them looked as if he had swallowed a frog. Sputtering for words, the soldier said, "Perhaps the next time you visit." He waved his arm at the men guarding the gates. "Let them in. Quickly."

The iron gates split open.

Nath bowed his head slightly and said, "Thank you."

Passing through the gates, Brenwar smiled and waved at all the soldiers. Each of them looked away, and one of them laughed.

Cheeks warmed, Nath said to his father, "They think we're women?"

"Yes," Balzurth replied.

"Why don't you sound like a woman?"

"I wasn't planning on speaking."

"Change me back," Nath demanded. His voice was that of an angry woman. "Oh, I can't take this. I sound ridiculous!"

Laylana burst out laughing like a man. Her guffaws were as baritone as Brenwar's. Wiping the tears from her eyes, she said, "Oh, I hope I don't look hideous."

"Clearly, I do," Brenwar said proudly. He took the lead and marched straight for the next break in the second outer wall.

The wall that encircled Quintuklen was made up of five rings with a break in each at different points. Designed like a simple maze, it made travelers walk a mile before they made it into the city.

They passed by several sets of secure gates before making it to the next open break in the wall. Lips sealed tight, Nath overtook Brenwar and led them through the next two walls. His breathing eased as they approached the final pass, but unlike at the three rings inside the circle, here more soldiers were gathered.

Nath stopped, turned, and faced his friends. "I suppose I'll do all the talking again?"

Balzurth's face twisted up. Laylana cocked her head.

"What now?" Nath said.

"Your voice," Laylana said in her own voice, which had returned. "It's back."

Nath clutched his throat. Incredulous, he said, "No, it can't be back so soon?"

CHAPTER 15

"FATHER, ARE YOU TELLING ME the spell has worn off already?" Nath rubbed his throat. Indeed, his voice had returned.

"I'm afraid so, Son," Balzurth replied. "But you have to admit it was fun while it lasted."

Flicking his fingers out, Nath said, "Fun? Pardon me, Father, but you have used that word far too many times."

"Entertaining," Balzurth offered.

"Same difference."

Brenwar chimed in with, "Merry. Dwarves like the 'word merry.'"

"And the elves consider such moments convivial," Laylana said. "Or witty."

Nath locked his hands behind his head and took a breath. "It's annoying. But please, allow me to take a moment to refresh everyone's memory on where we stand. I am being hunted by the elves and dwarves of Nalzambor."

"Yes, you're a fugitive."

"That's not helping, Father!" Nath threw his hands up. "If I were to guess, half of this city knows what I look like. Brenwar too, probably. We need to get inside undetected. Without trouble. I can't just go waltzing in there, and now I don't have anywhere else to go."

"Perhaps we should have traversed the wall in the dark of the night? Blended in with the shadows and avoided the light?" Balzurth said. "Now that would have been lively."

"You said you could get us through this, Father. That's why I did what I did. I like the night plan. That would have been easy." He held his head down and squeezed his eyes shut. "That would have been much easier than doing this in broad daylight. Sultans of Sulfur!"

As assuring as Balzurth seemed, it was complicating things with Nath. He was used to being in charge and doing what he could with what he had. Now, Balzurth had changed all that. Following his father's lead was not easy. If anything, it was the opposite.

Balzurth threw his arm around Nath's shoulder. "Son, let me do the talking. We've made it through the first gate, so I doubt they'll be worried about us passing the last. The goal is near. Just keep it in sight." He took Nath by the arm and rubbed his scales. "Besides, you have magic. Use it."

"Fine, Father, fine. I guess I can try it."

"You can do it, Son."

It had been a while since Nath had tried to use any of the magic in him at all. He'd come to rely on the skills he'd been used to having before, but back when he and Brenwar set out to find his mother, he'd changed the color of his scaled arms to all black with no white in between. Now, if he could, he'd like to conceal his scales with flesh. Closing his eyes, he envisioned his arms turning to skin. Something caterpillar-like crawled over his arms. On opening his eyes, he beheld the diamond-shaped scales rolling over to become flesh. The naked splendor of his forearm caught the light of the sun. "Huh, I did it!"

"Of course you did," Balzurth reassured him.

"Here," Laylana said, stepping behind him. Her ginger fingers tied his long red hair behind his head and tucked it in behind his shirt. "Now you look human."

In return, Nath took the tiara off her head. He adjusted her silky locks with his fingers to make her hair cover her pointed ears. "Now you do too, and a very beautiful one at that."

She blushed.

"Come on then," Balzurth said. Arms swinging at his sides, the grandly built man with his red hair flowing over his great shoulders sauntered right up to the soldiers. "Hello."

Hanging back a little with Brenwar and Laylana, Nath observed his father striking up a wonderful conversation with the soldiers. Two of the armor-clad men leaned on their spears, and the third one was laughing. For more than ten minutes, Balzurth spoke to the men as if he'd known them all his life.

Brenwar nudged Nath in the back and under his beard he whispered, "Don't just stand there waiting to sink."

Nath took Laylana by the hand and dragged her over to Balzurth and the soldiers. "Excuse me, but without sounding rude, we have an urgent matter that needs attending to. It seems our water has built to the top of the dam, and it seeks relief."

The soldiers gave Nath and Laylana a quick look then waved them inside, saying, "Stop in the Highside Tavern. Tell them Josh sent you, and they'll take care of you."

Giving Laylana's hand a squeeze, Nath scuttled into the busy streets of Quintuklen with her and Brenwar. The people milled about so quickly that they didn't even pay them a glance of notice. He stepped onto a boardwalk that ran along an unending row of marketplace stores, finding shade beneath the colorful awnings.

"Whew!" Nath said. He gave Brenwar a gentle shove. "We did it."

"My heart is still racing," Laylana said. With avid interest, her eyes searched her unfamiliar surroundings. "A busy place. Very intriguing. Do your friends live very far?"

"No." Nath could still see his father talking to the soldiers. "Oh no. He's going to talk to them until their ears fall off. Poor men. Humans would die of old age before he finished one of his stories."

Giggling, Laylana ran her hand over Nath's back and said, "I've heard you're quite the storyteller too."

"I've been known to spin a yarn or two." Laylana's caressing hand on his back sent a delightful shiver up his spine. He backed into her, allowing her hand to glide further up his back and massage the steely muscles underneath. The mild attraction he'd felt before had turned into something exhilarating. "Perhaps I'll tell you one later."

"Perhaps we can stop standing around and swooning over one another!" Brenwar said.

Catching his breath, Nath turned toward Laylana and backed away. Her eyes had a desirous sparkle in them. It was a growing temptation.

What's going on?

"Nath, is something wrong?" Laylana said, coming closer. She rose on her toes and touched his cheek. "You're sweating. I've never seen a dragon sweat before."

Unable to control his desire, he swept Laylana into his arms and kissed her.

CHAPTER 16

Ben's horse's hooves came to a stop inches from the stream. He swung his leg over and hopped to the ground. Putting his hands on the backs of his hips, he stretched and said, "Great dragons, my back aches. I can't be this old and this stiff. How are you doing, Bayzog?"

"I've never been very comfortable in the saddle, but it's not any worse than it's ever been." Planting the Elderwood Staff on the ground, he climbed off the horse onto the grass. "And I always chafe."

Both horses nickered and shook their heads, flipping their tails and drinking from the water. It was a little past midday, and the skies were cloudy. "Looks like there's a heavy rain coming, but we should make it to Quinley by then."

"If you're too weary, I can make other arrangements for us to sleep comfortably." Bayzog lifted the hem of his robes and dipped a canteen in the water. "I don't want you to overdo it."

With both hands, Ben guzzled down the remaining water in his canteen. "Ah! Glad we're right near a fill-up. You know, I'd like to take you up on whatever magic quarters you're offering, I really would, but I need to get on another layer of dirt to thicken my skin." He scratched his chin and swatted at a buzzing insect. "I can turn old, but I can't let it turn me soft. I need to rugged up."

"You aren't that old, Ben. You're not even Sasha's age." Bayzog tossed Ben a canteen. "Drink more. Heartily. Perhaps these streams will return your youth."

Ben hung the canteen on his saddle and said, "I envy you."

"Why is that?"

"You elves live so long, and you can even use magic. But the long living part is the hard thing. I know life can be hard, but I still enjoy the challenge I have when I wake up every day."

Bayzog corked the second canteen and hung it over his shoulder. Standing at full height but still several inches shorter than Ben, he said to him, "And that's why I envy you. You in particular, and many humans, are never complacent. I envy how you live every day to the fullest. It's why I was so attracted to Sasha. There was so much life in her."

The pair of them stood silent, watching the stream flow over the shallow rocks.

"We're going to find a cure for Sasha and find your sons, Bayzog. It won't be easy, it never is, but we can do it." Ben gave Bayzog a soft pat on the back. "Have faith."

"Perhaps it's time you took a look inside Brenwar's chest. Balzurth set him up with many wondrous gifts. I'm certain there's something that will make you feel younger."

Ben felt several years fall away. "Really? No, don't answer that." He untied the chest from his horse and set it down. On his knees with his fists on his hips, he said, "I haven't stopped thinking about this for two days."

Standing behind him with a soft breeze rustling his black hair, Bayzog said, "Me neither."

Ben popped the lid and pushed it wide open. Vials filled with a mosaic of colors were lined up in neat little rows. The entire tray of potions was on a single rack that he lifted back over the lid. It hung suspended on the folding arms that held it like some jewelry boxes he'd seen before. Underneath the tray of potions were several items. What caught Ben's eye was a pair of leather gauntlets woven with metal chain and a folded sheet of black cloth. He picked up the cloth and handed it to Bayzog. "What's this?"

Bayzog unfolded it and tossed it over the chest. The chest vanished.

"Great Dragons!" Ben said. "What did you do?"

Bending over, Bayzog seemed to pick at something out of thin air. He lifted something that reflected everything around and behind it, and before Ben's eyes the black cloth reappeared. "I believe it is called a Cloth of Concealment."

Touching the fabric as if it was an apparition, Ben said, "I like it!" Placing the Cloth of Concealment back inside the chest, he started taking count of the potion bottles with his finger. "There are so many. How do you know what they do?"

"Good question." Bayzog plucked a vial out with orange liquid that had sparkles swirling through it. There was tiny lettering on the bottle.

"What does it say?" Ben was squinting at the vial. "And what language is that?"

"It's called Scrollhewn, mystic lettering that magic users like myself often use. It certainly does take a discerning eye to read it, but it deters foolish abuse of what is within. This potion I think is one you'll like." He handed it to Ben. "It's dragon fire."

With both eyebrows arched, Ben said, "You mean if I drink this, I can breathe fire like Dragon?"

"Assuming it works."

Ben felt like a child again. When Bayzog looked away, he shoved it into his pouch.

Without looking at him, the wizard said, "Ben, it's fine if you take it. I'd tuck away some of those yellow ones too. They're for healing."

Ben picked out a few more vials, filling his pouch and buckling it up. The stiffness from the long ride began to ease, and he didn't feel so bad about the long journey now. Spying the gauntlets in the chest, he couldn't help himself and put them on. He stood up straight as an arrow. "Whoa!"

Clenching his hands, he said, "Bayzog! I feel like ten men in one." He strolled over to his horse that was still drinking from the stream and stroked its mane. "Be still. Be still." He bent down, braced his shoulders under the horse's belly, and heaved it up over his head. "Haha! Bayzog, look!

One of the corners of the part-elf's mouth turned up. "Perhaps the horse should be riding you?"

Ben set the horse down. Excited, he said, "Oh my, oh my!" He fetched his bow and quiver and loaded an arrow. He took aim at a distant tree farther away than his customary targets. He pulled the bowstring back along his cheek in one smooth motion. His arm didn't quaver. He released the bowstring.

Twang!

The arrow sliced through the wind, sailing true to the mark and burying itself in the distant tree.

Thunk!

"I never could have made that shot before!" Ben exclaimed. He nocked another arrow and pulled the string back.

Snap!

"Oops."

"It looks like someone got a little carried away," Bayzog said. "Be careful, Ben. Power like that is something you don't want to get used to."

Ben slipped off the gauntlets, walked over, and dropped them back into the chest. "I know. I think that's why I feel so horrible for losing Akron." He closed the lid on the chest and loaded it back onto his horse. "Come on. Let's hurry up and get over to Quinley. All this fooling around made me hungry. And besides, they make the best fish and biscuits in Nalzambor."

With a nod, Bayzog said, "I look forward to it."

While they crossed the stream on horseback, the wind picked up, and the rain-clouded sky started to darken on the horizon.

"The rain's coming sooner than I expected," Ben said. "But don't worry, Bayzog. A little water never hurt anybody. Try not to slip out of your saddle."

Eyes cast upward, Bayzog said with a grim look on his face, "It's not the rain I'm worried about."

Following Bayzog's line of sight, Ben lifted his chin to the heavens. High in the sky, a formation of birds soared toward them beneath the clouds. His chest tightened. "You don't think those are birds."

"No, I think they're wurmers."

CHAPTER 17

BRENWAR STROKED THE WHISKERS ON the corner of his mouth. Minutes ago, he'd grabbed Nath—who'd been lip-locked with Laylana—by the belt of his pants and pulled him free and into an alley.

Nath paced back and forth in a narrow passage between the storefronts. "I don't know what got into me. I've never acted so impulsively before."

"Hah. Your memory can't be that bad." Brenwar gave Nath the eye. "I recall plenty of times in your earlier days when you sucked face with ladies who were little more than strangers."

Nath pulled up a wooden crate and sat down. "I did, but that was so long ago. Another time. Was I that bad?"

"I hardly ever saw you pass up a pretty woman who batted an eye at you. It's not any of my business, but you've come too far along to go back down that path." Brenwar showed the calloused knuckles on his fist. "I'd hate to have to throttle you if it happened again."

"It was just a kiss."

"It looked like more than a kiss to me. Even I haven't forgotten about Selene. Imagine if she saw that. She'd tear those golden eyes out of your head." Brenwar gave a huff, flipping some of the hair of his moustache up. "Don't just sit on your hind end sulking. We have things to do. Important things. Now straighten this out with Laylana. I don't want to be around any awkwardness. It's bad enough being a dwarf in a human city."

Nath leaned over, peering around Brenwar. He didn't see Laylana at the end of the alley. If he could, he'd rather avoid the apology. Not that she didn't deserve one, but rather because he was embarrassed.

How could I do such a stupid thing?

Laylana was a beautiful elf with fine features. It was quite natural that any man who saw her would desire her. But he wasn't a man, he was a dragon. And she hadn't had such a profound effect on him when he'd first met her. What happened had come on so suddenly.

With a sigh, Nath said, "Why don't you give me a few minutes, Brenwar?"

"A few. No more." The dwarf turned and started down the alley, but when he neared its end, Balzurth emerged, blocking his path. "Pardon, sire."

Balzurth stepped aside and Brenwar was gone, leaving him alone with his father. With bright eyes, his father said, "So, I understand you had yourself a little kissy-kissy."

"She told you!" Nath exclaimed. His head fell back between his shoulders. "I can't believe that."

Pulling up a crate, Balzurth sat down in front of Nath. "She doesn't have anyone else to talk to, and most women like talking. Particularly about their feelings. Speaking of which, how are you feeling, Son?"

Gaping at his father, Nath replied, "We aren't really going to do this, are we?"

Balzurth's heavy stare didn't change.

Nath knew when his father meant business. They weren't going to move an inch until he opened up about it. He didn't want to sit in this smelly alley for a decade. He remembered the last time that had happened. "Guilty and embarrassed."

"Good." Balzurth gave him a little pat on the knee. "You should feel that way. But you aren't the only one feeling embarrassed. You left Laylana standing on the porch all alone. Poor girl looked like a frightened rabbit."

"Brenwar dragged me back here. Father, I was going to apologize." He gave his father's crate a little kick. "What happened? I just lost control."

"You let your guard down."

"What guard?"

Balzurth took him by the skin of his arms. "Your scales are gone. I told you they protected you in more ways than one. You're all flesh now. When that happens, it doesn't take long for your carnal instincts to surface."

Nath rubbed the fine hairs on his arms. "Flesh is awfully weak, isn't it?"

His father nodded.

"But you don't have scales at the moment," Nath said. "How are you coping with it?"

"I've got thousands of years of coping under my belt, so to speak. Come on." Balzurth stood. "Like the fifer gnomes say, let's nip this in the blossom's bud."

Nath found Laylana sitting on the porch, leaning against a post, and took a seat beside her. Her chin was down when he opened his mouth to speak.

At the same time, they both said, "I'm sorry."

"Please, me first," Nath insisted. He took a little breath. "I apologize for kissing you. It was very forward of me to do that, and it shouldn't have happened."

Showing a faint little smile, she replied, "It was a grand kiss, and I have no complaint. I've never kissed a dragon before, but I understand, Nath Dragon. The fault is not all your own. I did welcome it."

He swallowed. Her warming way with words was enticing him anew. Taking control of his impulses, he said, "Let's just shake hands and move on from it."

She extended her hand. "Certainly."

"I'm relieved." He saw the disappointment in her eyes. "Laylana, you are a magnificent woman, but I need to stay focused—and I can't forget about Selene."

Clasping his hands in both of hers, she said, "I'm a fighter, Nath. I'll be fine." She rose. "Let's go see these other friends of yours."

CHAPTER 18

DRIPPING WET, BAYZOG STOOD BY a stone fireplace inside a small home in the village of Quinley. As the logs crackled and popped, he wrung out the sleeves of his robes, splattering drops of water on the floor. He and Ben had been half a mile from Quinley when the rainstorm hit, the downpour so bad he could barely see ten feet in front of him. If it weren't for Ben, he'd have been lost.

"Bayzog, take off those robes," said Ben. "It will take you too long to dry if you stand there in wet clothes." He sat at a candlelit table nibbling at a plate of food with one arm hitched over the back of his chair. His brother Jad—much older but similar in demeanor—was at the table with his wife beside him.

They were thrilled to see Ben and hadn't stopped talking and feeding him since they'd arrived. "Make yourself comfortable and join us."

The quaint home offered very little in terms of privacy. It was one big room, with a window on every wall. The wind whistled through the planks of the boarded walls. A bucket caught a steady drip of water that streamed down from the rafters.

Not having a change of clothes with him, Bayzog smiled and said, "I'll be fine."

"He'll be fine," Ben reassured his family. "Just a little waterlogged."

Laughing, Ben's family resumed their talking. Ben had been quick to ask if they'd come across Rerry and Samaz, but they hadn't. The older couple were concerned about some of the other rumors that had spread, about the giants and the wurmers. That's when Ben had started making his case. "I wish you would both come to Quintuklen. You'll be safer there."

"And abandon my sheep and cattle?" Jad rapped his knuckles on the table. "Why, they'd never forgive me for it."

"They wouldn't miss you one lick," Ben said, joking.

"Oh yes they would," Jad said.

His wife nodded, saying, "He spoils them. How can a man spoil a cow? Yet he does. He walks out into the field and they come mooing. Silliest thing I ever saw."

"It's not silly," Jad said. "They like the attention."

"I'd like some attention too, you know," she said. "I shouldn't have to play second fiddle to the cows."

The light conversation went back and forth, creating a grand atmosphere of simple comfort. Bayzog cast a small spell that dried his robes, leaned his staff by the front door, and finally took a seat at the table.

Jad's wife filled him a clay cup of water. She stared at Bayzog and said, "I've never seen eyes like that before. I have that violet in my garden. It's beautiful."

"Thank you."

After a couple of hours of talking without ceasing, Bayzog made himself comfortable in the corner of the cabin. He pulled his legs into his chest, closed his eyes, and listened to the rain that continued to pitter-pat on the roof. The long ride had finally caught up with him, and he drifted off to sleep.

A startling crack woke him. Blinking, he noted the room was almost pitch black aside from the faint glow of some of the embers in the fireplace. There was a rustle of movement on the floor. Ben was under a blanket, starting to stand. His brother crept along Ben's side.

"What was that?" Ben said. He was up on his feet and slipping his trousers on. "Do you think a tree has fallen?"

"That wasn't a tree." Jad buckled his pants and grabbed his boots from beside the door. "And the rain and wind have stopped. It sounded like a beam cracked."

Outside, horses had started to whinny. Some of the livestock were crying out, too. Bayzog's ears prickled. Eyes now alert, he stood up and reached for his staff.

Whoom.

The small home shook. The clay goblets on the table rattled.

Whoom.

Bayzog noted the whites of Ben's eyes were huge. Ben whispered to him, "What in Nalzambor is that?"

Jad's wife slipped through the cabin, hugged him, and said with a tremble in her voice, "I'm scared."

"Don't be," Jad reassured her, "It's probably just some wolves or something."

A woman's cry screeched through the night. An agonized man cried out and fell silent. Buckling on his sword belt, Ben donned his leather armor and pushed his brother back. "Stay here."

Elderwood Staff in hand, Bayzog followed Ben out the door. In the center of the courtyard two foreboding figures stood, as out of place as an orc at a dwarven Festival of Iron. At fifteen feet tall with a back as wide as a stream, an abomination stood with his great hands hanging down well past his knees. He held up a length of fence post in one hand and snapped it in half.

Beside the giant was a man with a powerful build, wearing an iron helmet. His arms were bigger than most men's legs, and in the sinking moonlight they bulged with muscle. There was a dead body beside him. Blood was on the ground. He spoke with thunder in his voice and said, "Wake up, village. Your time to die is at hand."

CHAPTER 19

IT TOOK A LONG CONVERSATION, but finally Nath convinced Ben's wife Margo to let them into Bayzog and Sasha's apartment. The wizard's place was as neat as ever, but the mood was somewhat dark. Sasha sat on the sofa, staring into the corner firelight. Her sunken eyes were distant, but her natural beauty was hanging in there.

"Ben's going to be so disappointed he missed you, Dragon," Margo said. She was a pleasure of a woman to be around. Her hair was strawberry blond and short. She had the sunny personality of a country girl, simple in her clothing and a smile of beautiful white teeth. "But I never imagined you'd be even more handsome than he spoke of. And your father, too. It's uncanny." She rubbed her eyes with her finger and thumb. "Yes, you're real. I hope the food I prepare is worthy."

"Please, Margo, you flatter us. I'm certain that whatever you prepare will be more than sufficient."

"Without a doubt," Balzurth said, taking a seat on the sofa beside Sasha. There were two young dimple-cheeked girls hiding behind Bayzog's circular table and staring at Balzurth with eyes as big as the moon. They were very little. One favored Margo and the other Ben. He caught them looking. "Who are these two little delights? Come over here. I have something for you."

With a nod from their mother, the girls hopped up into Balzurth's lap.

"That's Trista and this is Justine. They're Ben's pride and joy."

"You have a handsome family, Margo. I say Ben did well to come by you," Nath replied.

"I'm just glad I found him. Things were very hard before he came." Her eyes watered up a little. "I'm not used to being without him. He never leaves my side for long, and I'm just not used to it. I didn't think it would be so hard after only a couple of days."

Nath felt that guilty nagging in his gut again. Ben had lost his first family during the war, so it only made sense that he would stay close so that it didn't happen again. Nath had never even gotten to meet Ben's first family. He'd been in his decades-long dragon sleep when they were around. Rubbing Margo's shoulder, he said, "We shall catch up with them soon, and I'll send him right back."

"No, no, I understand. You have to do what you have to do, and I feel horrible for Bayzog. Sasha is a sweet woman. Though I don't know her, I can feel it. She needs her family close. Ben is doing the right thing. He's a brave man. You taught him well."

"He was born brave," Nath said.

"These young little things are adorable," Balzurth said.

Laylana walked over to the dragon of a man and picked up one of Ben's little girls in her arms. She tickled Trista under the chin, bringing forth some giggles. "I've never held a baby human before. They are heavy."

"If you think *they're* heavy, you should try holding a baby dwarf," Nath joked.

"We're built to last," Brenwar said.

"If you'll excuse me," Margo said, "I'll finish preparing something to eat. Come, Trista and Justine. I need someone to sample the pudding before I serve it."

The little girls squirted out of Laylana and Balzurth's grasps.

The Dragon King started laughing. "If only people could remain childlike in their worries, Nalzambor would stay a better place." He turned his attention to Sasha. "This is a sad predicament. What did you say happened to her?"

"Bayzog calls it the wizard's dementia. It's rare, but it affects humans who use magic. She was a fine sorceress at one time."

Brow furrowed, Balzurth placed his hands on Sasha's face. He pulled the skin under her eyes down. "Hmmm. And you say they're on a quest to heal this? This is deep. Dark. There is no cure for this that man can find—that I know of."

Nath's heart sank. He knew there wasn't a cure for every ailment in the world. Life was hard. People were mortal. Old age and tragedy weren't the only ways people died. There was sickness, too. The flesh was weak, and it didn't hold up forever. "We hoped the Ocular of Orray might help, but it's closely guarded by the elves."

In a serious tone, Balzurth said, "I believe you experimented with that before, Son. How did it turn out?"

"It didn't." Nath reflected on the time in the elven city of Elome when he'd tried to rid himself of the black scales. It wasn't favorable. "That doesn't mean it won't work for her."

"No, this woman doesn't have long, I fear." Balzurth's big hands covered her shoulders. "Buried deep inside is a love for family that has let her hold on this long, but her attachment to life is hanging by a thread. Her hope and her very essence are fading. It's a good thing we arrived when we did."

"What do you mean?" Laylana took a seat on the other side of Sasha. "So we can comfort her?"

"Why no, so she can be cured."

"Father, I thought you said she couldn't be cured."

"Not by any human means." Balzurth rubbed his hands together. "But I'm not human."

The room filled with new warmth. The hairs stood up on Nath's arms, and as a soft golden glow formed around his father, he closed his eyes. The entire room was bathed in new light. Brenwar and Laylana were transfixed. Deep inside Nath's belly, he was uneasy.

Should Father be doing this, whatever it is?

But Nath's feet were glued to the floor, and all he could do was watch.

The heavy lids over Sasha's eyes lifted. New life gleamed in her eyes. Raising her wrinkled hands, she rested them on Balzurth's forearms. Her head tossed back, and she gasped for air. Head still back, her mouth was hanging wide open. Something dark began to seep from her pores, like tiny black droplets of rain. It gathered above her like a small cyclone in the air and floated over Balzurth.

No!

Nath wanted to stop whatever was happening. His raw instincts told him something was horribly wrong. He shifted his gaze from his father back to Sasha. She was refreshed and rejuvenated. Decades of life had returned. Her eyes watered like a new rain.

Just then, Balzurth lifted his hand into the dingy swirl. Like a hive of angry bees, it attacked and burrowed into his skin. The golden light faded to nothing, and the warmth was gone.

Following a long moment of silence, Sasha said in a voice like honey, "Nath, is that you?"

He rushed over to her and clasped her hands. "Yes, yes, Sasha, it's me."

She did a double take between him and his father. "Then who's this?"

The gold in Balzurth's eyes had turned to black, and he sat still as a stone.

"It's my father," Nath replied, but the cold expression on Balzurth's face sent spiders crawling down his legs.

CHAPTER 20

"BEN," BAYZOG SAID UNDER HIS breath. "Get to the chest. Now." He watched as Ben darted for the stables.

The door to the small house cracked open, and Jad peeked out.

Bayzog pushed his head inside and said, "Please. Stay quiet and stay in there." The door creaked to a close. As he turned away from the house, the man and the hideous troll-like giant turned and faced him.

"What do we have here, an elf?" It was a humongous giant who spoke in a polite, measured tone contrary to his face. "Strange place for an elf."

"Strange indeed," said the warrior wearing the iron helmet. He slid his sword out of the scabbard. The blade had a living shimmer swirling in the metal. "What brings you to these parts, elf?"

"I'm just passing through," Bayzog replied. He moved away from the house, positioning himself between the aggressors and the open fields behind him. He ran his fingers down this staff and added, "Perhaps you monsters should do the same."

Placing his fingers—which were unnaturally long even for his size—on his chest, the monster said, "I was only stopping in for a bite. I get very hungry moving from town to town. And my ears are still ringing from all the screaming."

"There will be no more screaming here," Bayzog said.

"Oh?" The giant troll lifted a brow. "Are you sure about that?" He hurled the fence post across a field into one of the nearest neighbors' homes. The beam crashed right through the window. Startled voices cried out. Cupping his ear, the monster said, "That sounds like a scream to me."

"What do you want with these people?" Bayzog said. "They're no threat to you."

The warrior came forward. "Perhaps they should be. The weak deserve the slaughter."

"They're not weak," Bayzog defended. "However, it *is* weak to take advantage of hardworking people."

"Oh, we have a *politician* among us." The giant clapped his hands together and bowed a little. "Tell us your name and your platform. Maybe we'll vote for you."

All Bayzog was trying to do was buy time in hopes that the people of the town had enough sense to slip out and find safety. The man and monster before him were killers. He could see it in their black eyes. He could smell it on the giant's rancid breath. They had no guilt. They sought devastation. But why? Even the giants that were taking over the towns weren't slaughtering people en masse. They were just controlling the masses with fear. Now this. "Why don't you tell me your names? After all, you're our guests."

"There's no point in that," the warrior said.

Taking a long step forward, the giant said, "I am Bletver, a triant. This is my boss, Rybek the Devastator. We are servants of Eckubahn, here to spread his blessing throughout Nalzambor."

"By killing people?" Bayzog said.

"We like to consider them mercy killings," Bletver said.

"Be silent, triant." Rybek blocked Bletver with his arm and stretched out his sword. "Elf, if you're going to attempt to stop us, I suggest you get on with it. But I'll show you mercy if you hand over that staff of yours."

Bayzog planted the staff in the ground. The wind picked up, blowing strands of his hair in his face. "The only way you get this staff is if you pry it from my part-elven hands."

"I'd be delighted." Rybek started his advance.

Bayzog pointed the staff at the triant Bletver. The gemstone centered inside the nest of wood that cradled it flared with amber light. A bolt of energy shot from the Elderwood Staff and smote Bletver in the chest with a clap of thunder.

The triant toppled over and fell hard to the ground. His chest was smoking, and he lay still.

Bayzog pointed the staff at Rybek. "Don't take another step."

Resting his sword on his shoulder, Rybek said, "And if I do?"

"I will turn you to dust."

"And here I was planning on turning this entire village to dust." Rybek lifted his shoulders. "Well, plenty of things will be dust once this is over."

Bletver rose to his elbows. Looking down the length of his nose, he saw his smoking chest and said, "What in a bearded wart hit me?"

"Stay down, triant," Bayzog warned. He pointed the staff between the two of his enemies. "Stay down or just crawl away."

"It's going to take more than your little stick to stop me," Bletver said. "Now the fight becomes interesting." With speed that belied his grotesque girth, the triant sprinted away, making a beeline for a nearby house and calmly announcing, "Incoming."

Rybek attacked.

Bayzog pointed the staff at the armored warrior and turned loose its power. A bright beam of energy struck the fighter's striking blade, which turned aside the blast.

Rybek shuffled back several steps, regained his balance, lowered his head, and charged.

Without hesitation, Bayzog loosed the staff's firepower again.

Sword swinging, Rybek knocked the bolt aside, kept churning, and powered his body into Bayzog's. The jarring impact knocked the staff loose from the half elf's fingers.

Bayzog moaned under the weight of Rybek's crushing body. The warrior was a big man, and with the armor, he felt like he weighed a ton. Fighting, wrestling, and punching weren't Bayzog's ways.

In an instant, Rybek had him pinned down on the muddy ground with the blade at his throat. "It seems I didn't have to pry the staff away from you after all, now did I?" Rybek clamped an iron grip over Bayzog's throat and squeezed. "Now tell me, bastard elf. Who are you?"

A crash of wood followed by screams caught Bayzog's ears. The triant's reign of terror had begun. The horrified cries multiplied. Choking out the words, Bayzog replied, "You are not worthy of my name, you murdering monsters."

Applying more pressure to Bayzog's neck, Rybek replied, "You are right about two things. We are murderers and we are monsters. Prepare to die, nameless bastard that you are."

CHAPTER 21

"How are you feeling, Father?" Nath asked.

Balzurth didn't reply at first.

Instead, Sasha embraced him. He patted her back without speaking as she thanked him several times. Her body was shaking against his, and finally she broke off her embrace.

That's when Balzurth said, "Eh, I'm quite well, Son."

Nath watched as the gold in Balzurth's eyes overtook the black, driving away the inky murk that had been there. "Are you certain?"

Hands on his knees, Balzurth said, "I think I would know if there was something wrong with me." The richness returned to his voice. "But what's important here is for nothing to be wrong with this young lady. How do you feel?"

"Exquisite." Sasha hugged Balzurth again.

Nath didn't think his father had been all there the first time Sasha hugged him. No, while what his father had done for her was wonderful, he couldn't help but think a price had been paid. His father, though vibrant in appearance, sat hunched over a little bit.

He'd better be fine.

Margo entered the room with a tray filled with food. "What's all the commotion about? Why is everyone so excited?"

"Margo!" Sasha said. "What are you doing here?"

Staring over Sasha's shoulder, Margo said, "Is this another episode?"

Smiling, Nath shook his head and said, "No, my father has healed her."

Brenwar made a skeleton fist and pushed it up in the air, saying, "We need to celebrate!"

For the next couple of hours, the friends gathered around the table, talking and enjoying themselves. Everyone was thrilled for Sasha, and she couldn't stop thanking Nath and Balzurth.

Now refreshed and with the color back in her cheeks and her pretty eyes as bright as the moon, Sasha became serious. "I remember terrifying dreams about my sons. You know I have to go find them."

"Ben and Bayzog are only a couple of days away from us. We'll catch up with them in no time and continue our search for Rerry and Samaz from there," Nath said to her. "I'm confident we will find them."

"When you catch up with them," Margo said, "will you please send Ben back home? I'm sorry, Sasha, but I miss my man. And the girls are sick without him."

"I insist on it," Sasha replied. "Don't you fret. Families need to be together during these dark times." She placed her hand on one of the spell books stacked on the table. "Now, if you'll excuse me, I have some preparation to do."

"Sasha, are you certain you're ready to venture out so soon?" Nath asked as he stood up from the table with the other men. "You might need more time and rest."

"I'll never rest until my family is back."

Getting back out of the city proved easier than getting inside had been. Sasha merely read a scroll, and they popped over the wall to the outside. It was early morning, and the dew was heavy on the grass. Balzurth was ahead, but he wasn't leading. Nath was. His father had been quiet since they'd begun the next leg of their journey. The weird thing was that Balzurth was talking to himself in Dragonese. His words were faint, and Nath couldn't quite catch them enough to understand.

Marching alongside Nath, Brenwar said, "What's wrong with your father?"

"You're asking me? You know him better than I do."

Brenwar had a more serious than normal look on his face.

"I'm joking," Nath reassured him. "But no, I do have a strange feeling about him."

Pawing his black-and-gray–streaked beard, the dwarf replied, "I've got that tickling the hairs on my toes feeling, too. He's off. The ever slightest, but enough."

Nath adjusted the strap that held Fang between his shoulders on his back. "I can only imagine he's adjusting." He scratched his arm with his golden-yellow claws. His black scales were back. True enough, they seemed to have restored the air of purity he'd earlier lacked. Taking a look behind him, he noted Sasha and Laylana chatting away. The fire that had burned inside him for Laylana was now gone.

Perhaps I should suggest that Father restore his scales.

"Take the lead while I have a moment with you know who?"

"Aye."

He glided back past his father.

Balzurth's stare didn't change its course. It was half in the trees and half in the sky, searching for something. His arms were swinging like he was in a grand parade.

Nath snapped his fingers before his father's eyes.

Balzurth swatted at Nath's hand, came to a stop, and said, "Huh?" He gave Nath a spacy look. "Oh, yes, Son. What is it I can do for you?"

"That was really incredible what you did for Sasha."

"I know, I know. It had to be done."

"I'm feeling better, myself," Nath added.

Staring at the clouds that drifted overhead, the Dragon King said, "What was wrong?"

"My scales. I have them back."

Balzurth nodded.

Nath took his father by the elbow and pulled him to a stop.

Balzurth jerked away, saying, "Unhand me, boy!"

Pheasants that had been hunkered in the tall grasses scattered into the air. Standing with the distant woodland at their backs, everyone in their party came to a stop. They stared right at Balzurth.

Balzurth's face became angry. His frown deepened. Casting a glance at all of them, he took a deep breath and let it out again. His stern features eased, and the slightest smile formed when he said, "Apologies. I am deeply distracted with our situation. It troubles me." He lifted his hands in a gesture of surrender. "Lead on. I'll follow. Please, it will do my heart good."

With a nod, Brenwar resumed his trek, pushing through the waist-high grass. The women followed.

"Son, what is it that you were trying to say to me?"

"I was trying to suggest that you might need your scales back in case this world is getting too deep for you. And I say that with the utmost respect." Nath patted his father's wrist. "My scales certainly made a change in me. I'm glad you shared that with me. Otherwise, I might not have known."

"You know, Son, sometimes even I can forget myself. You help remind me of the mistakes I once made, and that's not a bad thing. As a matter of fact, you remind me of a mistake that I'm making now."

"You, a mistake? Give me a moment while I have Brenwar hammer it out on a tablet." Nath was a little astonished. "I really don't know what to say, but what do you mean?"

"My power is not a frivolity. Even I can get carried away with it. I'm a dragon, not a man. I need to act like it."

"So, when you healed Sasha…did you harm yourself?"

"No regrets, Son." Balzurth changed the subject. "So where are we off to, exactly?"

"Quinley is the first stop. It's where I met my dear friend Ben."

CHAPTER 22

Inside the stables, Ben opened the creaking lid of a wooden storage box. He hustled out Brenwar's strongbox and laid it on the ground. He was dripping with sweat. It had been a long time since he faced men and monsters the likes of those he'd just seen. The ugly one was bone chilling. The iron helmet on the other sent a wave of terror straight through him. Depressing the dwarven medallion on the box, he popped the lid open.

Sssray-Boom!

An explosion outside shook the hay from the loft, dropping filaments over his clothes.

"Gut up, Ben. Gut up!" he said, encouraging himself. The phrase was something they'd said in the Legionnaires during their rigid training. "Oh, I wish I had Akron."

All around Quinley, his people started to shriek and yelp.

He grabbed the gauntlets and slipped one on. His sweaty hands were sticking to the leather. Using his teeth, he pulled on the second one. Power filled his limbs. He found his bow hanging on a wall, snatched it up, and grabbed his quiver. In two long strides he was back outside, surveying the chaos.

Bayzog was down on the ground, with the iron warrior holding him down by the throat. Ben nocked an arrow, pulled back the string, and let the missile sing. The arrow struck the warrior in the helmet's temple, knocking his head. Bayzog's hands charged up with white light and knocked his assailant aside.

Scrambling to his feet, Bayzog yelled at Ben, "Help them! Help them! Get them away from Bletver!"

"What's a Bletver?"

The wizard pointed at the triant that was running roughshod through the houses and crushing Ben's frightened people.

"Noooooo!" Ben cried. He fired arrow after arrow into the monster's bulk. The arrows stuck like cactus needles.

But Bletver paid them no mind at all. He continued on the warpath.

Ben took off at a dead sprint right at the horrible monster that was yards away from tearing another innocent home apart. With the force of a charging steed, he tackled the monster by the leg and drove it to the ground.

"Ugh!" Bletver said. "What in the deep well hit me?"

Ben planted his feet on the ground, tangled Bletver's greasy hair around his wrist, and with his free fist started punching the triant in the face.

"Leave"

Whack!

"my"

Whack!

"people"

Whack!

"alone!"

Whack!

Bletver's skull was as hard as a rock, but Ben kept on hitting it anyway.

"Quit hitting me!" Bletver said. The triant flailed on the ground like a spoiled child. "It stings something ghastly!"

Ben punched the face that was almost as big as him in the neck and nose. He drove his fists in hard with the gauntlets of power. Jumping onto Bletver's body, he smote him in the belly, sending up ripples of fat that shook Bletver's sagging chin.

"Ooooof!" the triant cried. And then in a speech more formal than his face, Bletver said, "This is getting out of control, little man!"

Ben punched like a mule kicks.

Bletver sat up. "I don't know what's gotten into you, but I'm going to make you pay for it!" He scooped Ben into his hands and gave him a squeeze. "I'm going to make you pop!"

"Never!" Ben said, flexing his iron-powered muscles. Veins bulging in his neck, he began to wriggle free. "And by the way, your breath stinks!"

"Impossible!" Bletver hoisted Ben over his head and tossed him away.

After sailing through the air for what felt like a long time, Ben crashed head first through his brother's roof and landed on the table at which they were just talking earlier. He pounced onto the floor. His eyes rolled up. Rods of pain lanced through his eyes, neck, and shoulders. He blinked, and his brother and sister-in-law were there. He tried to move but couldn't. Hearing the terror erupting all around him, he said, "Quick, find everyone and get them out of here!"

Ben's crack shot couldn't have come at a better time. The arrow glancing off the iron helmet was the perfect distraction Bayzog needed. With a quick-lipped incantation, the half elf turned loose his mystic juice and stood every one of the warrior's hairs on end.

"Gagh!" Clutching his helmet, the fighter practically jumped out of his boots before dropping to his knees on the ground.

Bayzog wiped the blood from his split lip. He didn't know what had gotten him, but he summoned more of his power into his legs and marched right at the warrior—who was trying to stand up—and kicked him square in the gut.

The tremendous impact sent Iron Helmet Man skipping through the mud in a splatter.

Rain started to come down in heavy drops.

Bayzog reached down for the Elderwood Staff and picked it up. Its gem-light rekindled. The wizard's eyes flashed. He began spinning the staff's head in a tiny circle.

The warrior's body spun and flopped in the mud.

Soaked in the muck, Bayzog used telekinetic power to fling the fighter hard into a stone well in the center of the farm town.

Mud oozed down the iron helmet and plopped in a puddle. The man hitched his arm over the well's wall and with a groan got back to his feet. His sword dangled in his grip, tip first in the mud. "Who are you?" he demanded in an angry voice.

"It's not a matter of concern," Bayzog replied. "Drop your weapon."

Slowly, the warrior lifted his hands above his head with the sword still firm in his grip.

"I said, drop it," Bayzog repeated.

"I'm not keen on taking orders from half-breeds. If you want it, come and take it."

Another round of melee was out of the question. Bayzog knew he'd been a moment from getting pummeled the last time.

I need to end this standoff, quick.

He absorbed more power from the staff. Deep inside, he knew he needed to destroy this man, that mercy would be too good. But the man needed to be held accountable, too.

Try something different.

He began casting a spell. As soon as he muttered the lengthy words of the incantation, the warrior burst into action.

Twisting his hips and shoulders with a fierce sword swing, he sent an arc of energy ripping through the village. It tore two homes apart. He swung again, unleashing more of the lethal force, turning more homes into rubble. "This is just the beginning! Nothing will be left standing when I'm finished."

Bayzog finished the last syllable of his spell.

The ground beneath the warrior came to life. The mud oozed up to his waist. He yelled at Bayzog, "What cowardly witchery is this?"

"Elven," Bayzog replied.

The mud and dirt gobbled the man into a sinkhole until he was shoulder deep in the earth. The sword vanished into the mud. The warrior looked like an iron statue covered in a mudslide. Spitting grit from his teeth, he said, "You have won. Now tell me, who are you?"

Squatting down in front of his foe, the wizard said, "If you insist, I'm Bayzog. And I'm no half-breed. I'm part elven."

"Bayzog..." The whites of the man's eyes behind the eyelets of the helmet showed recognition. He grunted a laugh. "Nath Dragon's ally. Perfect. And I am Rybek, the brother of the man Nath Dragon murdered."

Rising, Bayzog put his staff in Rybek's face. The staff's jewel was hot with dangerous light. All of Bayzog's senses screamed in warning that something even more sinister was afoot. "You know me how? Speak!"

"Heh heh," Rybek said. "I'm tired of talking, but maybe the phantom will speak."

An unseen force fell from the wet night sky, covering Bayzog in darkness from head to toe. His skin tightened, and all of his sinew seized up like a man struck by lightning. The Elderwood Staff went dark.

Something was sucking the life out of him, and he couldn't even scream.

CHAPTER 23

QUINLEY WAS A DISASTER WHEN Nath and company arrived late in the day. Half of the small houses built from wood and stone had been torn asunder. The barns had holes in one side and out the other. A carriage was turned upside down. A cow lay on the other side of a broken fence, crushed as if it had been squeezed to death.

Nath kneeled down and placed his hand on a footprint in the ground. It was humongous, the size of four men. He sniffed his fingers. "This doesn't smell like any kind of giant I've smelled before."

Brenwar took a whiff. "Triant."

"A what?" Laylana asked.

"Their mothers are trolls and their fathers are giants. Filthy things, even for giants." Brenwar scooped up a handful of dirt and rubbed it between his hands. "The vile creature won't be so hard to find now. The strange thing is, they usually stay underground."

"Way underground," Nath said. He recalled Gorlee recounting his imprisonment in the city of Narnum and how he was held in a place called the Deep by a similar creature named Bletver. He'd shared it with Brenwar.

It has to be a coincidence.

"Where are all the people?" Sasha asked.

Glancing around, Nath said, "I'm not sure that I want to know." The sound of voices softly singing caught his ear, and he turned. Facing the rolling hills just beyond the village, he recalled a graveyard he'd passed through when he'd met Ben long ago. Balzurth was already heading in that direction. He and the others followed.

A ceremony was taking place inside a cemetery that was hundreds of years old. Most of the tombstones were covered in moss and overcome by grass. A pair of stonemasons chiseled on a new flat rock while people held hands and sang. There was a black wagon pulled up to the cemetery entrance, which was marked by a modest iron archway. Bodies wrapped up in burlap bags lay in the back of the wagon, and two men loaded one body off and carried it to a grave in the ground and lowered it inside.

Keeping their distance, Nath felt Sasha wrap her arms around his and hang on as if she was about to fall. "I'm so sick of all this death. Innocent people die for nothing. My blood boils."

Her words brought Nath some comfort. The woman had much passion within, and it was good to see it back. The warmth of her body was comforting too. He hated to imagine the day that would come when Sasha's body turned cold. Thanks to his father, she had much life to live yet.

The citizens of Quinley had a humble ceremony. They prayed over the graves. They sang as the shovels dug in the dirt and buried their loved ones in Nalzambor's soft earth. Once the last grave was covered, each person lit a candle. One by one, they placed the candles on a stand made from stone until they all burned as one. There were many, too many.

Nath wondered if two of those candles were for Ben and Bayzog. It just didn't seem possible.

The long-faced people of Quinley dispersed back toward their fallen town. Women clung tight to their children. Men wore slings and other bloody bandages. One fellow was being pushed uphill in a cart. His legs were missing. Hardly any of the people gave Nath or his friends a single glance when they walked by. They'd seen the worst. Now they feared nothing.

One of the last people up the hill was a man in trousers and a woven canvas shirt. He was tall and lanky and looked like Ben but older. Tears had long dried on his cheeks that had cleaned some of the dirt from his face. He said to Nath, "They said you would come. I just didn't think it would be so soon."

Nath's chest tightened. "Pardon," he said. Taking the moment into consideration, he didn't want to just jump in and ask about Ben and Bayzog. "Er…I'm sorry for your losses, I'm—"

"I know. You're Nath Dragon. My little brother Ben has talked my ears off about you." He extended his hand. "I'm Jad. It's good to meet you. All of you. I just wish it was under better circumstances." The man's eyes welled up with water. Wet sobs and tremors shook his body. "I'm sorry. My wife is gone. Crushed." He glanced back down the hill at the cemetery. "Those aren't even all the bodies we need to bury."

Nath caught the sagging man by the waist. Sasha assisted. Together, they walked Jad back into town and sat him down on some busted boards and stones that had been set up like a bench.

Hands on his knees and still crying, Jad said, "Ben and the elf, Bayzog—they took them. Said if you came around to let you know they have them." He blew his nose in a rag. "I don't have any other family left. Just Ben."

Sasha intervened. She took the man's hand and said, "Who took them, Jad?"

"Their names were Rybek and Bletver." He looked up at Nath. "The one, Rybek, said you'd know him. He said to *come alone* if you want Ben and Bayzog to live."

"That won't happen," Sasha said. She took Nath by the wrist. "You aren't going anywhere without me."

"Or me," Brenwar added.

Even though Nath felt that Jad was being truthful, he wasn't certain about his story. "How could Rybek possibly know I would come here? What did he say?"

Sniffling, Jad said, "He said you'd probably ask that because you aren't as stupid as you are arrogant. But he wanted me to let you know that it was a hunch is all. He figured you'd come across his handiwork at some point. He said that seeing how he has your friends, he'll have plenty of time to play with them. If he didn't get word of you coming, or when his patience ran out, he'd just kill them and move on. He doesn't seem like the patient kind."

Sasha's fists balled up at her sides. "I'm not the patient kind, either. I'm going to find this scoundrel and put an end to him. All of them!"

Jad's eyes widened.

Nath laid a soft hand on her shoulder and nudged her back. "That's what we all want, but I've crossed Rybek before. He's truly dangerous, as you can see. What else did he say, Jad?"

Jab blew his nose again. "He said he'd be at the Temple of Spirals. I've never heard of it."

"If they've only been gone a couple of days, I'd say they just made it there by now," Nath said to Brenwar.

"Where is this Temple of Spirals?" Laylana asked.

"It's south of here, nuzzled between the Shale Hills and the Ruins of Barnabus." Nath noticed that Balzurth was no longer there. He'd forgotten that his father actually had been Barnabus to begin with, the one who as a man had slain black dragons. Perhaps the ruins had been named after him before his name had been corrupted by the foul acolytes and clerics that twisted it into a dragon-hating abomination. "Where's my father?"

Everyone looked. It didn't take long to find him. Balzurth was carrying two heavy wooden beams on his shoulders. He was following a pair of villagers, who were carrying one of the support beams together. Balzurth yelled back at Nath, "I heard you. Work now. Plan later."

"I'm not waiting," Sasha insisted. "If you know where it is, we go now." She turned her attention back to Jad. "What condition was Bayzog in?"

"I only got a glimpse, but his skin was shriveled and his hair white. It was as if he'd aged decades in moments. He barely moved, but he breathed." Jad let out a ragged sigh. "That giant thing carried them off on its shoulder. A nasty thing. It's what killed my wife." His head lowered.

Sasha pressed him. "Know how sorry my heart is for all this tragedy, but I must ask. Did they leave anything behind? A staff, perhaps?"

Jad shook his head, "No, it was taken." He perked up, shoulders back. "Ben told me to take these. He said if you came, you'd know what to do with them." He reached behind his back and produced the leather-and-chain gauntlets. "I fashioned it as a keepsake of him. There is a chest back in the stables too." He glanced at Brenwar. "It has a face that looks like you."

Nath handed the gauntlets to Brenwar.

Brenwar slid them onto his meaty hand and his skeleton hand and punched the first into the latter with a loud smack. "Let's go find that triant."

Nath held his tongue. Rybek had made it clear that Nath was to come alone. The last thing Nath wanted to do was jeopardize Ben and Bayzog. "Like my father says, we need a plan. At least we know what we're up against."

"A triant and a man you defeated before," Brenwar said. He twirled Mortuun around like a stick. A gleam was in his eyes. "I can handle the triant. You know that. This Rybek, I'm sure you'll see to it he has another bad day. Perhaps his last day."

"I wish I could come with you to help," Jad said. He stood up. "But I'm a farmer, not a fighter. My village needs me now, but please, bring Ben back like you always do, Dragon. Alive and as talkative about you as ever."

"I will."

"Oh, and one more thing I forgot to mention. Come, you must see."

They all followed Jad over to one of the barnyards, where no more animals were alive. Inside the barn was a figure of a man with his clothes hanging off of him. He was nothing but flakes and withered skin layering his bones. His fingers were outstretched, and his mouth hung open in agony.

"I don't know what did this, and he wasn't the only one. The others perished in the wind."

When Nath gave the figure a light touch fingertip to fingertip, the dead man's hand crumbled.

"But I can tell you this," said Jad. "He used to be the fattest man in the village."

CHAPTER 24

Rerry had completely lost track of time, but hanging by his arms was more agonizing by the minute. Spikes of pain lanced through his back, waking him up from what mild slumber he was able to steal between gasps of suffering. He stretched out his tongue, straining to turn and sate his horrible thirst with the water that trickled down the wall. The corners of his mouth burned from the dehydration that had set in.

If I feel this bad, I can't imagine how my brother feels.

He had been calling to his brother, Samaz, with no response for what had seemed to be days. His brother quavered and coughed. It was the only sign of life in him. As hard as it had been for Rerry to get along with his brother in the past, he'd now come to regret every bit of their bickering. His brother had been good to him, but Rerry had been nothing but ornery toward him. Samaz was an odd and quite deep thinker. He didn't act out, and he talked very little. There was no reason to punish him for it. He and Samaz were just different.

"Samaz, if we ever make it out of this, I hope you'll forgive me. You're a good brother. I should have treated you better."

Samaz shivered in his shackles.

"Lords of Knollwood, don't die on me, Samaz. Don't die."

Something brushed under Rerry's bare toes. Feet dancing in his chains, he said, "Eep! What was that?" Straining, he tried to get a look at what was under him. Chin buried in his chest, he got a gander at something that shimmered like the scales of a fish and disappeared. "Samaz! Samaz! Wake up! Something's in here with us!" Head pounding, Rerry jerked at his chains.

Something was crawling up his leg.

"Scar! Scar! Where are you, Scar?" Rerry hollered for the jailer.

Rerry had once prided himself on not being scared of anything, but with the unknown, that had changed. He'd heard tales about what huge bugs had done to people. There were some that could poison or paralyze. They'd come in the thousands, devouring man and elf tiny bit by tiny bit.

"Samaz, do something!"

Tiny prongs dug into his legs and inched toward his body.

"Oh, I don't want to die like this. I'm a sword fighter. I deserve a better death." Rerry flailed his arms and legs against the chains. "Get off me, you cowardly vermin! Get off!"

Something that felt like sharp, tiny fingers dug into his toes and crept up his other leg.

"No! No! No!" Rerry cast his gaze from side to side, straining to see the unseen enemy.

A fierce prick stabbed into his knee.

"Aaaah!"

Samaz sputtered. His head lifted and turned toward Rerry. In a weak voice, he said, "Will you quit screaming? You're giving me a headache."

Voice echoing in the prison chamber, Rerry shouted, "Samaz! Samaz! You wake!"

"The dead have wakened. Put a pipe in it, won't you?"

"What?" Rerry exclaimed. "Can't you see I'm being devoured?"

Samaz's face barely showed in the weakening torchlight. He squinted at Rerry. "I can barely see anything—it's too dark—but I can assure you I hear everything."

"Ow!" Rerry cried out. Moisture his dehydrated self would have sworn moments ago that he couldn't possibly contain beaded his forehead and started to drip. Rattling his chains, he tried to lick the sweat from the tip of his nose. "Clearly not! I've been trying to wake you for days."

"I heard what you said. You said you were sorry," Samaz replied.

"You're delusional!"

"You're the one who thinks something's crawling up his body," Samaz retorted. "I don't see any—oh!"

"What?" Rerry's cracked voice was shrill. "What is it?"

"You seem to have something crawling up your pants leg."

"I know that! Do something!"

Samaz replied in his usual matter-of-fact tone. "I can't. My hands are tied."

Rerry jerked at the chains. "And you wonder why you drive me out of my skull, you emotionless sack of human parts and elven bones."

"I never wonder."

Veins bulging in his neck, Rerry retorted, "I'm not sorry for anything, and I hope you never forgive me for anything I've done. Ow!" He started to whine. "Oh, ho ho, will you do something, brother of mine?"

Samaz's head sank back into his chest. He started snoring.

Tiny claws, more than Rerry could count, dug into his body.

"Nooooooooooo!"

CHAPTER 25

Nath's company rode on horseback without stopping except to rest the horses. He'd been trying to sort out a few things in his mind on the trip. According to some of the people they encountered, Rybek and Bletver had been wreaking havoc everywhere. It didn't take long for Nath to put it together. They wanted him. It wasn't a surprise.

Ahead, Balzurth brought his horse to a gallop just outside the ravine that cut through the mountains. It seemed so unnatural to see his father riding a horse. It just wasn't anything he'd ever imagined he'd see. "What is it, Father?"

Balzurth dismounted. "My horse tires. Let's all rest a spell, shall we?"

They made a camp with no fire. Brenwar whittled on a piece of wood with a buck knife. Balzurth dropped a pile of rocks on the ground. When he placed his hands on them, the rocks glowed, and the immediate area filled with new warmth. Sasha and Laylana cozied up to it. Nath sat down just as Balzurth started to speak.

"Son, I'd care to know what your plan is."

"And I was curious to know yours, Father."

Balzurth squatted, warming his own hands. "I'm fully prepared to eradicate them all, but my concern is our friends in peril. Those who hold them hostage do not value life. They are controllers. They use the flesh of others to manipulate people. We must be careful."

"And that's my concern, Father." Nath swallowed. "If we all go in at once, we might not see Bayzog and Ben alive again. I'm willing to go in and take my chances on my own."

"We can't let you do that, Nath," Sasha said, staring at the orange glow of the rocks and twirling her hair on her finger. "It would be unfair."

"They want me. They're using Ben and Bayzog to get to me," Nath said.

"And they only want you in order to get to me." Balzurth pushed the sleeves up over the cords of muscle in his forearms. He was a king if there ever was any. "You're bait. Your friends are bait. It's one of evil's oldest and best-working tricks. I can foil it. I can put an end to this once and for all." He plucked a stone from the pile. "I'm angry. The suffering must end."

"I've seen you angry before," Nath said.

"No, you've seen me pretend to be angry." Balzurth dusted the debris from his hands. "That was nothing."

"Oh, it was something. Your voice shook everything in the mountain when you raised it." Nath nudged Brenwar. "You heard it."

"Aye." Brenwar held a carved wooden figurine in his hand and walked it over to Sasha. "For you."

She took it and said, "It's Bayzog."

"It's the best I could do. I've never done an elf before, let alone a wizard."

She gave him a hug. "Thank you, Brenwar."

"All right, all right now, nobody hugs a...oh, never mind." Brenwar hugged Sasha back.

Nath continued talking with his father. "So you're telling me you weren't ever mad at me?"

"Disappointed, yes. Mad, no."

"But the yelling?"

"Raising my voice isn't the same as yelling. If I had ever yelled, you'd still be crying on the golden floor."

Laylana let loose a giggle.

Nath picked up one of the stones. It was warm to the touch but far from scalding. "I don't know. You were quite stern with me."

"Stern? That's because I was trying to scare the human out of you. There's nothing wrong with a stern talking-to. Wait until fatherhood happens to *you*."

Nath caught Laylana looking at him. She covered her mouth but still laughed.

"Quit that," said Nath to the elven princess. "I'm sure motherhood won't be any better for you. It's easier to keep up with jackrabbits than baby elves."

Balzurth looked up into the stars. "Why don't we all just sit and listen for a moment? Enjoy the world that surrounds us. Ease your mind, and don't worry so much about the journey ahead. Let nature run its magic through you."

The harmony of the woodland comforted Nath. The scuffles in the branches were soothing. The insects sang their songs. Not far away, beavers chewed into the wood to build their dams. Balzurth started to hum a tune in dragon song.

Nath wanted to enjoy the moment, swim in the peace, but he couldn't. So much was on the line, and his father had something up his sleeve. He envisioned Balzurth storming into the Temple of Spires and wiping Rybek and his brood of fiends out. He'd seen his father turn a small army of giants into a smoking graveyard. He wanted to see Balzurth turn loose the cleansing flame again—against all the giants—but more than anything, Nath wanted to do the same. Be a dragon who controlled the great flame that destroyed the evil that it burned.

At least Father seems to be back to normal, for now.

Laylana stretched out her arms and yawned. "What's this song he's singing?"

Nath knew it, but it had been so long since he'd heard it that he wasn't certain.

Sasha curled up on the ground and cuddled with her figurine of Bayzog. "It's wondrous, whatever it is."

Standing on his feet, Brenwar's eyes blinked open and closed. He started to sway, caught himself, and said, "Aye."

Nath's eyelids became heavy. He yawned.

I'm not supposed to yawn. What is this song that father sings? I usually don't forget such things.

He watched his father's lips. A sparkling swirl gathered around the Dragon King's body and twinkled to the rhythm of his words. Some phrases in Dragonese briefly pricked Nath's ears.

Sleep, little dragon, sleep.
The fairies come,
The giants run,
The wings of the goldlings beat.
Sleep, little dragon sleep,
For on the morrow a new world is at hand…

Nath's eyelids became impossibly heavy. He sank to the ground.

Great Guzan, he's singing my lullaby. Why?

Balzurth took on the form of Nath Dragon, black scales and all. He kneeled, brushed Nath's hair aside, and kissed him on the cheek. Rising with a black fire deep in his golden eyes, he whispered, "Sorry, Son, but I'm going to handle this."

Chapter 26

Claws dug into Rerry's skin and climbed over his belly. That's when he saw them, two lizards with a soft illumination in their green eyes flicked out their tongues and licked his chin. "Gah! What are you things?"

The lizards raced up to his shoulders, and their eyes bored into his. Their heads swiveled from side to side, slowly winking one lizard eye after the other. One of the lizards had eyelashes. It licked Rerry's nose. The other one revealed rows of teeth that looked too big for its mouth. It climbed up his arm, claws digging in until Rerry bled, and started nibbling on the chains.

Frozen in horror, Rerry watched a lizard the size of a kitten chew through the metal like it was bark on a tree.

These lizards won't have any problem devouring me! Sultans of Sulfur! Must I die like this?

The other lizard, the one with the eyelashes, climbed onto the top of Rerry's head and slammed him in the mouth with its scaly tail.

"Watch it, will you!"

The tail cracked him over the eye.

"Ow!"

The lizard on his head stretched out for the chain on his other arm, grasped it with its claws, and started chewing through the metal. The grinding and crunching sounds hurt Rerry's ears and bored into his brain. There was nothing he could do to fend off this new torture. Pushed to the limits of his stamina and beyond, he had almost no strength left.

In defiance of his fate, Rerry said, "I knew that some lizards were stupid, but I didn't think they were so stupid they would miss a fresh meal. You're supposed to eat me, not the chains. What happened, did orcs train you?"

The lizard without the eyelashes stopped chewing. Swiveling its head, it glared at Rerry and spat a tiny ball of metal into his eye.

"Ow!" With his eye closed, Rerry said, "Spit all you want, but if you keep this up, all you are going to do is free me, and when that happens, I'm going to stomp you under my heels."

A tail whipped out and cracked him across the mouth.

Fwap!

"Ow!" Rerry winced. "It even hurts to say 'Ow.' I swear, if I didn't know any better, I'd say you lizards could understand me, but I know better. You're just a couple of hungry—"

He got struck in the face by both tails this time.

Fwap! Fwap!

Somewhere in the tormented recesses of his mind, an uncanny thought registered as he watched them continue to nibble at the chains, little hunks at a time.

Maybe they do understand me?

In the dim light, he couldn't see too much color or detail on the lizards, but he took note of their scales, which were more rigid than those of most lizards. Like small suits of armor. And lizards didn't have eyelashes, but one of these creatures did. Rerry's head toggled between the two. He gasped with elation.

"You're not lizards. You're dragons, aren't you!"

The tiny gray metal dragon with the eyelashes turned her head around on her long neck and winked at him.

"Hah! You're freeing me?" He was incredulous, then he blurted out, "But you don't have dragon wings."

Their tails swatted his face again.

Fwap! Fwap!

"Oh, that's right. Not all dragons have wings. Father told me that. He's an expert, you know. Oh! And we are friends of Nath Dragon."

The dragons—little bigger than his feet—continued to gnaw at the chains.

The first link popped through.

Rerry's arm dropped to his side.

"Oh," he moaned. "That feels wonderful."

The second chain link gave, and both of his arms were free. Blood rushed there, bringing forth a stinging pain. He rubbed his sore arms and shoulders, hugging himself.

The dragons crawled down the wall and went to work on the shackles on his feet.

"Oh, thank you, thank you, thank you, you mighty little dragons!"

The dragons smiled up at him.

He leaned back. "With incredibly large but delightful teeth." Feeling a new lift surge through his sore limbs, Rerry shook his fingers and wriggled his toes.

I'm so thankful.

The dragons finished off the links on his feet, and the one without the eyelashes let out a burp. Rerry assumed that was a male, based off what he knew.

I wonder what kind of dragons they are.

He reached down and patted the tiny horns on their heads and stroked their chain mail–like skin.

They scurried away to his brother Samaz and began chewing on his shackles.

Rerry touched his brother's forehead with the back of his palm. Samaz's body was hotter than a biscuit that had just come out of the oven.

"How were you even talking to me earlier?"

After a few more minutes, the chains gave way to the iron-eater dragons.

On shaky limbs, Rerry managed to hoist his brother over his shoulder. "At least you're lighter now." He glanced down at the dragons at his feet. "I really hope you'll lead me out of wherever I am."

The dragons lifted their chins, and then, with their tails sliding behind their bodies, they led him through the dark caves until he found himself face to face with an arched wooden door, strapped in metal, that was sealed shut.

To the dragons, Rerry said, "I don't suppose you have a key, do you?"

The iron eaters blinked at him and left through a crack in the stone wall.

CHAPTER 27

DISGUISED AS NATH, BALZURTH SPROUTED wings and quickened the journey to the Temple of Spires. He landed little more than a mile north of the rigid peaks that jutted toward the sky. The black wings on his back collapsed and disappeared into his body until he was in the human form of his son Nath once more.

Brow furrowed, he marched over the rocky landscape where the edge of the Shale Hills ended in a nearby stream. He splashed through the waters knee deep and continued on from the other side. He pushed through the branches and cut through the rough. Nothing slowed his pace.

Guiltless, he'd made his decision to leave Nath and his friends behind. He needed to take matters into his own hands and get to the bottom of this himself. Eckubahn and his servants had to pay, and it was time for Balzurth to get to the heart of the matter and put an end to the evil spirits once and for all.

Walking at a brisk pace, the Dragon King ducked under the woodland branches and stepped out into a clearing.

The Temple of Spires waited.

Stark like a black monolith against the dawn of a purple sky, the temple sat with the wind howling through its peaks. The entire temple, vast in size, had once been just a hill made of stone. It had been crudely carved out from top to bottom, leaving the peaks like a crown on a small castle's forehead, unique in design. A narrow roadway curved toward the mouth of the long-abandoned temple. An arched bridge crossed over a foggy, bottomless canyon that was the only way in or out. The urns that adorned the high walls and edges were cold, but inside the temple's yawning entrance was light.

Balzurth headed toward it.

Heading down the long path toward the temple, he came to a stop. Two stone giants, twenty-footers, stepped out onto the road from their concealment behind some boulders. The long-faced humanoids were skin headed, with heavy brows that shadowed their eyes. They wore nothing but loincloths around their waists and carried no weapons. They peered behind Balzurth, glancing from side to side, searching.

Continuing his walk, Balzurth said in a voice the same as Nath's, "I'm alone."

One giant stepped behind him and the other in front. The humongous escort crushed the ground beneath their heels, footstep after footstep, flattening the overgrowth.

Balzurth's fingers twitched. He wanted to set their heads on fire and send them running for the lakes. He hated giants. He'd put an end to the lot of them right now if he could. But there was more movement against the rocks that made up the temple. Wurmers had nuzzled into the stony nooks.

The giants separated and stood to the sides of the temple's entrance.

Without looking at them, Balzurth said, "I'll be back for both of you later."

He entered a rough-cut hallway hewn from the rock big enough for giants to stroll through. Torches flickered beyond the hall's end, which opened up into a grand ceremonial chamber. Support columns were not as they seemed. They had been cut out by working hands and chisels, with warring images of the races carved in them. There were eight, merging with the temple ceiling that seamlessly merged with rock beams the shape of snakes. The entirety of the chamber was cold, and the shadows of the torchlight gave the engraved images a life of their own.

Balzurth walked between the columns and came to a stop.

A huge slab of stone lay on a massive pedestal in the center of the chamber, big enough for one of the stone giants to stretch out on. Ben and Bayzog were shackled there, on the bloodletting stone. They lay silent. Unmoving.

Lording over them was Rybek, the man in the iron helmet. His sword was sheathed, and he rubbed his hand on the pommel. Behind him, all smiles, was the triant Bletver, who fondled the grimy whiskers on his shaggy chin.

"You have arrived much sooner than expected." Rybek slid his sword out and lowered the tip onto Ben's cheek. "Your promptness suggests trickery."

Balzurth, in the form of Nath, said, "As you can see, I am unarmed."

"You might be unarmed, but I am certain your allies are near." Rybek flicked the sword tip over Ben's cheek, drawing a spot of fresh blood. He smeared it on his fingertip. "Do not toy with me, Nath Dragon. The only way they will live is with your full cooperation."

"And if they die, you won't get any cooperation. I am here. Let them go."

Bletver stepped around the sacrificial slab to the front and leaned against it. He had a cleanly picked skull that he was rolling through his fingers like magicians did with coins. "I suggest that Nath Dragon needs to have a go at me before we release his friends. If he loses, I get to eat him."

Balzurth balled up his fists. "I promise you this: I'll give you a sore jaw and a sore belly if you come one foot closer to me."

The triant pushed his flabby back off the slab, leaned closer, and stuck his chin out. "Oh? Try me, little dragon. Nothing can knock out a triant."

"I'm not nothing," replied the disguised Dragon King.

"You're like a fish." Bletver licked his lips. "A meal with scales."

Balzurth sprang forward, launching himself at the triant. Arm cocked back, he slugged Bletver in the jaw. The blow snapped the monster's head back.

Stumbling on his short legs, the triant staggered into one of the columns head first and sank to his knees on the cold stone floor.

Rybek raised his sword. "I warned you, Nath Dragon." The sword started to fall.

"You expect me to put up with that?" Balzurth said. "We are here for an exchange. Me for them. The blot of foulness over there does not factor into it, Rybek." He slapped his chest two times. "You are so close to what you want. Don't miss out on it now. I'm here. I've surrendered. Shackle me if you have to."

"It's too simple." Rybek glanced from side to side and let out a strange whistle.

"You have the advantage, Rybek. Your plan has worked. You have won." Still disguised as Nath, Balzurth shook his black-scaled arms. "You can see there is nothing up my sleeves, and you know I pride myself on honesty."

A shadow entered the ceremonial chamber and hovered beside Rybek. A phantom. Its head and eyes conversed silently with Rybek. On Rybek's nod, the phantom lifted off and disappeared through the cathedral ceiling.

"It's confirmed that you're alone. Interesting." Rybek unshackled Nath's friends and gave them each a firm kick. The man and part-elf were disordered, and mud covered their clothes. They looked like they'd been dragged the entire way. Bayzog looked old enough for his death bed. Ben was hunched over. "Get out of here." Rybek shoved both of them off the altar.

Ben supported Bayzog. They hobbled over to Balzurth, thinking he was Nath.

Bayzog said, in a gravelly voice, "I need my staff."

"Keep going," Rybek shouted. "The staff is mine to keep. Any tricks Nath, and your friends will be slaughtered out there by the phantom or the wurmers. I've seen to it there won't be anyone to save them no matter what."

Balzurth gave Ben and Bayzog one last look over his shoulder.

Ben nodded and said, "You don't have to do this, Dragon. Our lives are ours to give."

"Go," Balzurth commanded in a voice that sounded like Nath's. "I'll see you soon."

CHAPTER 28

N THE PATH OUT OF the Temple of Spires, Bayzog collapsed, dashing his knees on the stones. Ben scooped him up in his arms and continued, glancing back from time to time, eyeballing the stone giants that guarded the entrance.

"Stay with me, Bayzog."

He shuffled down the path, grimacing. His legs were wobbling and his arms shook. The journey to the temple had been nothing short of harrowing. Bletver had carried the both of them over his shoulder at first, but then for fun he'd dragged them through the mud, laughing and saying he liked his food with a little muddy seasoning on it.

Despite the jostling trek, Ben had been relieved.

Bletver had thrown him against a wall so hard, Ben had thought he shattered his back. The stunning shock had faded barely in time for him to gather his senses just enough to tell his brother Jad about the gauntlets and the chest. He'd been urging Jad to find safety just when Bletver tore back through the house and scooped Ben up. Lucky for him, the paralysis had been only temporary, and he now felt his limbs again.

"Let me walk. Let me walk," Bayzog said. The hollow eyes of the half elf burned with life, but his body was as feeble as a newborn baby's. His skin was wrinkled, and the long strands of hair were ghost white. "I live. I live. I need my staff, but I live."

"We aren't going back for the staff. I'm getting you to safety."

"Need to help Nath," Bayzog rasped.

"I know, but there isn't much we can do to help him right now. We're just going to have to hope he can take care of himself."

"Not right," Bayzog said, shaking his head. "Not right."

"I know it's not right, but I can't go back and fight all those wurmers and giants by myself now, can I? We need help." He stumbled on a loose rock and fell to his knees.

Bayzog fell out of his arms.

Gasping, Ben said, "I'm turning out to be a fine help, aren't I?"

From the ground, Bayzog pointed at something crawling behind Ben.

Head low, a wurmer came, moving slow but chomping its teeth.

Ben broke out in a cold sweat. "So much for Rybek keeping his word. That doesn't look like an escort." He crawled backward like a land crab until he bumped into Bayzog.

The feeble mage's bony fingers plucked at his belt pouch.

Ben had forgotten about the potions. He fumbled through his own mud-coated pouch and produced two vials of yellow liquid. He popped the cork from one and handed it to Bayzog, then drank the other. The tantalizing nectarine flavor coursed new life through his body, washing away the aches and pains in his bones. "That's more like it!"

Head lowered, eyes slit, and jaws slavering, the wurmer came.

Chapter 29

Water splashed on Nath's eyelids. A storm cloud drizzled cold drops over his face. He sat up with a gasp. "Balzurth!"

Brenwar, Sasha, and Laylana lay fast asleep.

Going from one to the other, Nath shook them all. "Wake up! Wake up!"

First to his feet, Brenwar smacked his lips and with woozy eyes said, "I feel like I've woken from the dead."

Rubbing her eyes, Laylana added, "My head aches." She peeled off a leaf that had stuck to her face.

Yawning, Sasha asked Nath, "What happened? Where's Balzurth?"

"He's gone."

"Gone?" Brenwar clawed his skeleton hand through his beard. "And where do you think he's gone to?"

Judging by the sun's position in the sky, it looked like they'd been asleep for the better part of a day. Balzurth had a long head start on them. He'd wanted it that way.

The horses whinnied.

"He didn't take the horses," Sasha said. "Can't we track him down and catch up with him?"

Using his keen sight, Nath searched for footsteps or any other signs of his father's passing. He circled the camp. There were only signs of his coming, but not his going. "It seems he's abandoned us." He kicked up the dirt. "How could he do that do us?"

"Now we know where you get it from," Brenwar grumbled. He strapped his war hammer over his back. Looking above, he said, "Do you think he turned back into a dragon? Did he fly to the Temple of Spires?"

Nath's nostrils flared. Certainly his father wouldn't have risked the lives of his friends. No, Nath had to figure out what he would have done if he was in Balzurth's place. While he thought, everyone else mounted up.

Brenwar opened his strongbox. "I'd say he got to the Temple of Spires hours ago." He arched a brow. "Of course, that's assuming we only slept through the night. If we want to catch up, these horses have some hard work to do. They're going to need something." He flicked a vial over to Nath. "Give each one of them a little bit of that."

Nath poured a little bit in his hand and administered the potion to the horses one by one. They nickered and reared up.

"Whoa! What does it do?" Laylana asked.

"They'll run hard and fast all the day long, so you'd better hang on tight. They won't be stopping," Brenwar said. There were only three horses though. Brenwar turned to Nath. "I'm assuming you can keep up?"

"No, you need to hope the horses can keep up with me. Let's go." Nath took off for the temple with fast and lengthy strides. His mind was racing. What had gotten into his father?

What's his plan? If I were Balzurth, what would I do?

The answer smote him like the clapper striking a bell.

I'd do what I always do, show up as me.

Darting through the grasses, he sped up his pace.

CHAPTER 30

"It's down to just the two of us now, Rybek, speaking from a general point of view of course. I'm not counting the flock of wurmers and giants at your disposal." There were more stone giants backed into the shadows standing as statues against the walls. Wurmers snaked through holes in the ceiling, positioning themselves in the rafters. "What's your end game? Or should I say Eckubahn's end game?"

Rybek jumped off the end of the slab. "Certainly you know you're the bait for taking down Balzurth. Eckubahn wants you alive, but I want you dead." He swung his sword, and an arc of energy knocked Balzurth from his feet and skipped him over the stones into one of the pillars. "But if I can't have you dead, I'll turn you over to him severely damaged."

Balzurth didn't even try to stand. He said to Rybek, "Oh, you're giving Eckubahn the glory. Why not the glory for yourself? You don't need him. Go ahead, take me down all on your own."

"Humph. You fight back with words and not fists. I'm surprised." Rybek sheathed his blade. "It seems the cocky dragon is humbled."

"Humility comes with age."

"I'm no spring fairy. I don't feel humble in the slightest, but I do enjoy humbling people. And by humbling I mean killing."

"Get on with it, then," Balzurth replied.

"As much as I hate you for destroying my brother, you and Selene both, I'm still a faithful servant of the new ruler of this world. I can wait for my reward."

"Your reward, if you don't change, will be fire when the end comes, one way or the other." Balzurth took a look at his surroundings. The giants and wurmers began to stir. Something was happening or about to happen. "You stall, Rybek. Why?"

"I don't need to stall. I'm being wise with my time. Turn around."

Balzurth did so.

Rybek bound his wrists behind his back with a silk rope that tightened with the power of a great snake. "You're making this entirely too easy. I expected a fight, not such cooperation." He spun Balzurth back around. "Still…" He punched him in the face. "Ah, that feels better."

Balzurth spat a tooth out. "Well, at least one of us isn't disappointed."

"Tell me, Nath, before I turn you over, where is your father Balzurth?"

Balzurth wouldn't lie, so he said, "My father is where my father wants to be."

Rybek tossed his head back and let out a little laugh. "And Selene?"

"I can't say, because I don't know." Both of the statements were true. It was important to Balzurth that even in the worst of circumstances, he still was honest. He just didn't want Rybek to catch on.

The warrior head butted Balzurth, helm first, in the chin.

Disguised as Nath, the Dragon King staggered back and gave his head a hard shake. "Are you quite done with that? You won't ignite my ire, if that's what you're attempting."

From a pouch strapped to his side, Rybek produced and amulet on an iron chain. Its yellow stone was the eye of a cloudy storm.

"Jewelry for me? You're vastly more thoughtful than you look. Vastly." Balzurth tilted his head. "What does it do?"

Dangling the amulet by the chain and swinging it gently from side to side, Rybek said, "It teleports you to Eckubahn."

Balzurth's heart raced. His eyes fixed on the amulet. "Why hesitate? Give Eckubahn the prize he wants. Receive your glory."

Rybek pulled the amulet back from Balzurth's burning eyes. "No, something's wrong. I sense it. There is no reason you should be so eager. What kind of fool rushes into certain death?"

"I'm bait. Eckubahn won't kill me."

"You don't know that. I don't know that." Rybek swung the chain around his wrist and back. "What are you up to, Nath Dragon?" His boot kicked something white over the granite floor. He went over and picked up a tooth as big as his hand. It was Balzurth's, the one he'd spat out. No longer a part of his body, it had resumed its normal dragon tooth size and shape. "What's this?"

"Perhaps I knocked that tooth out when I walloped Bletver. You really shouldn't let the little things distract you in the midst of a moment. Focus. The moment might slip away."

Rybek glanced between Balzurth and the tooth. He bent his head down. "I don't see the tooth you spat out." He scraped his foot over the ground. "What treachery is this, Nath Dragon?"

Eyes transfixed on the amulet of teleportation, Balzurth said, "You certainly should be the one to lecture about treachery, but no one lectures me." Balzurth snapped the cords that bound his arms behind his back. He lunged for the amulet.

Rybek jerked the amulet away and cradled it with his whole body. "This is madness. Why do you want the amulet?"

Balzurth wrestled the fighter to the ground.

Rybek, strong as a man can get and a seasoned fighter but no match for Balzurth in strength, squirted out of his grip.

"Give me that amulet!"

Rybek scrambled over the floor.

Balzurth snatched the man's ankle and dragged him back. He punched Rybek in the chest, denting the plate armor.

With the amulet tucked tightly in his muscular arm, Rybek groaned, "No."

Balzurth-Nath pinned Rybek's face down by the helmet, holding him tight while using his free hand to fish out the amulet. A shadow fell over his shoulder. "Huh?"

Bletver had walloped Balzurth with an uppercut that practically lifted him out of his shoes. It sent him colliding into the legs of another giant. "That's payback, Nath Dragon."

Shaking off the blow, Balzurth lifted his eyes to the triant, who stood as tall as a tree behind him. The wurmers climbed down the walls. More giants stepped into full view. It was him versus an army. He snorted. "I've got bad news for you. All of you. I'm not Nath." His hands and feet sprouted into dragon claws. "I'm Balzurth, and I'll be having that amulet."

CHAPTER 31

BEN PICKED UP A ROCK and chucked it at the wurmer. The stone skipped off its snout. "Just run if you can, Bayzog. Run. I'll hold it off as long as I can."

The giant lizard streaked toward him on all fours. Its claws scraped over the stones, flicking up the dirt and moss between the path of flat rocks.

Energized, Ben braced himself to make his last stand. Man with hardly a stick of clothing on versus a monster fully covered in natural armor.

Jaws wide, the wurmer scuttled in and bit.

Ben bounded up over the beast, clearing its snapping jaws and landing on its back. He wrapped his arms around the creature—which was just as big as him—and held tight. "Run, Bayzog! Run!"

Man and twisting scales wrestled in the dirt.

The creature let out bestial hisses. It stretched its neck to bring its head around, snapping at Ben's ears but missing.

Ben tucked his head down and held on for the ride of his life.

The wurmer's tail flogged every bit of Ben's body that it could hit.

Each lick brought the pain of a leather whip. Fighting the odds and the pain, Ben wouldn't let go of the tireless monster. No, this was his last stand. He might lose his life, but he could save another.

Whap! Whap! Whap!

The tail beat him without mercy. The wurmer would twist one way and Ben, feet digging in the dirt, would twist the other. Pushing himself to the limit, hand locked over his wrist, he cranked up the pressure. "I'm going to squeeze you to death, wurmer!"

The monster spun in a version of an alligator roll on land.

Ben's head cracked against a stone. His grip broke. The next thing he knew he was flat on his back with the wurmer's claws at his throat. His strength was gone. He thought of Margo and his girls. He said to anyone that could hear, "Tell them I'll miss them."

Sssssrazzzzz!

A jolt of light struck the wurmer, sending shivers through its scales. Smoke came from its eyes, and it wriggled and jerked and collapsed on top of Ben, dead.

With a grunt, Ben shoved it off. Huffing for breath, he said, "I don't know how I did that, but I knew I had it in me. I beat the smoke right out of it." But then he noticed Bayzog leaning back against the rocks. The wizard's withered skin had thickened after he drank the healing potion, and streaks of black were now layered into his greying hair. "So you did that?"

"I might have had the elf beaten out of me, but I still have my spells." Bayzog closed his eyes and shook his head. "Oh, that wasn't easy."

Ben got up with a grimace. "Well, thanks." His body stung all over. "I have a feeling I look as bad as you."

"You do." Bayzog opened his eyes. The violet fire had returned. Scanning the area, he said, "Odd."

Following his gaze back toward the temple, Ben said, "What's odd?"

"When we fight wurmers, we usually fight them all."

Holding his hip, Ben said, "Well, I'm not disappointed."

Loud noises came from inside the temple. Heavy booms and thuds. Angry howls so loud only a giant could be making them. "We're going in there, aren't we?"

"I need my staff," Bayzog said.

"We need Nath Dragon," Ben replied. He started forward. "Nath can't handle all of them at once."

"No, he can't. But that's not Nath Dragon in there," Bayzog replied.

"Sure it is. I saw him for myself."

"No, it's someone else. That's why I wasn't so worried."

The rocks shook at the top of the temple's spires, and a piece of rock broke off. It bounced off the temple roof and slid, spinning, into the canyon.

"So if that wasn't Nath, then who was it? Gorlee?"

Making his way to the bridge, Bayzog replied, "I don't know, but I'm going to find out."

Ben was relieved to hear it wasn't Nath in there, but he didn't want to go back inside. The temple was filled with giants and wurmers. He and Bayzog didn't stand a chance. And whoever was posing as Nath had made a great effort to save them in the first place. He held his hands up in front of his face and made two fists. "I guess these are going to have to do."

Robes dragging the ground, Bayzog didn't stop his trek back to the temple. "I have spells. I can handle this myself. You should wait."

The word "spell" triggered a thought. Ben reached into his pouch and produced a vial filled with a sparkling orange liquid.

A raucous, painful sound echoed out from the temple's entrance.

Ben said to the vial, "Bottoms up, 'cause they're going down."

CHAPTER 32

Slumped against the wall, Samaz's head rested on Rerry's shoulders. They'd been sitting in the same spot for hours. Feeling his brother's forehead, Rerry said, "I don't know how a person can be so hot and live. Of course, I don't know anyone as stubborn as you. In this case, it's a good thing."

He eased his brother to the floor. Still weak and dying of thirst even after drinking some sour cave water, he pressed his eye to the keyhole of the door.

If only those iron eaters would have gnawed out this lock, we could be out of here by now. Look at those hinges. There's plenty of good metal right there.

He slapped his forehead. "Aw, the hinges."

His fingers worked at the pins. He cracked his nails with the effort, but none of the pins would budge. He needed a tool, but even after searching all the chambers in the strange prison, he didn't find anything of use at all.

Rubbing his wrists, he sat back down and said, "Someone will come. Someone." With the cool rock against his back, he relaxed. He'd been so uncomfortable in his shackles that he'd barely caught any sleep. Leaning a little on his brother, he drifted off into a deep sleep.

A ring of keys jingled. Rerry's mind started to awaken, but he didn't register what was happening. His eyes peeked open, and as if he was in a dream, the door swung open, concealing them behind it.

Is this really happening? I can't move. I don't want to move. I want to sleep.

Two elven guards appeared in the crack between the door and the cave. With swords on their hips and wearing the cloth tunics of soldier's uniforms, they ventured forth with a bucket of water and a tray of food.

Rerry's nose twitched. The smell of food aroused his senses.

I smell meat on the plate.

His stomach groaned.

The elven guardsmen set the food and water down and turned.

In Elven, one said, "What's that?"

At the same time, the other elven guard said, "Who's there?"

Finding new strength, Rerry burst out of his corner. Just as the nearest elf went for his sword, Rerry hit him in the jaw and knocked him out.

Whap!

Desperate for freedom, Rerry used his bigger body to overpower the second, smaller elf. Using a move taught to him by his brother, he locked the elf up by the neck and silenced him in a sleeper hold. The elf's kicks subsided, and he too went out. Chest heaving, Rerry shoved the elf aside, grabbed the bucket of water, and guzzled it down.

"Ah!"

He scarfed down some of the hard bread and dried fruit. After taking care of himself, he did what he could for Samaz. Surprisingly, his brother—asleep with fever for all intents and purposes—nibbled down the food. Rerry poured some water down his brother's throat, too.

Sputtering and coughing, Samaz sat up.

"I thought that might wake you from your nap," Rerry said.

"Yes, a dream of drowning usually does." Samaz grabbed the bucket and guzzled between gasps. "Thank you. How did we escape here?"

"Don't you remember the dragons?"

"I hardly remember anything."

"Figures." Rerry made his way over to one of the guards and buckled on the sword belt. He slid the sword from the sheath and cut it through the air in a few intricate patterns. Eyeing the blade, he said, "At least it's elven."

Samaz crawled up the wall to his feet. He looked through the open door and back at the guards lying on the stone floor. "You didn't kill them, did you?"

"Yes."

"Rerry!"

"Will you keep your voice down?" Rerry put on one of the guards' uniforms, but the cloth tunic was very tight on him. The almond-shaped steel skullcap fit fine. "No, they're only out cold—and just so you know, I used one of your moves."

Donning the other tunic, barely, Samaz said, "Ah, you used the sleeper."

"Begrudgingly. So are you fit for the journey?"

"No." Samaz coughed. "But I'm not going to let feeling like ogre stew warmed over stop me."

Rerry tried to hand his brother the other elf guard's sword.

"No."

"Just strap it on. We'll need to blend in at some point, I imagine." Rerry planted the other elven helmet on Samaz's head. With effort, he got it down to his brother's ears, but it still looked too small. "You and that melon head. If I didn't know our parents for certain, I'd swear you were part orc. You're built like a chimney. What kind of elf is built like that?"

"A durable one." Samaz stepped aside. "Lead the way, Rerry."

"And am I to assume we're going back after the Ocular of Orray?"

"Do ducks have feathers?"

"It was your wild idea that got us captured in the first place."

"Oh, you like it."

"Well, I do, but only because it actually sounded like something I would do, not you," Rerry said. "So, shall we attempt to defy all odds again?"

"Anything for Mother," Samaz replied.

CHAPTER 33

BALZURTH CAUGHT THE STONE GIANT's fist coming down at him like a hammer. He had popped his dragon claws out of his human fingers, and now he dug them into the giant's hard flesh and yanked the giant face first into the stone slab.

BLAM!

"Don't you run, Rybek! Don't you run!" Balzurth ducked under a metal urn that whizzed over his head.

Bletver was throwing everything he could get his hands on at him.

"You stay out of my way, triant! I'll turn you into cinders." Balzurth caught Rybek creeping behind the stone slab with his sword out. "Surrender and find mercy, Rybek. This is your last chance."

Wurmers dropped from the ceiling. Fierce and nasty, the mindless things clawed and slashed.

Chest-high in wurmers, Balzurth poured it on. Now transfigured into part dragon and part man, Balzurth had covered himself in red and gold scales from head to toe. He busted the wurmers in their snouts and slung them away by their tails. Nothing was going to stop him from getting Rybek and the amulet. No, he wasn't going to let his plan fail. He was so close, he couldn't let this chance slip away.

A stone giant closed in, lifting its man-sized foot to stomp Balzurth into the floor.

The Dragon King pulled a wurmer by the tail under the giant's foot in his stead.

The wurmer's scales crunched and squished. Black ooze squirted out.

Hopping on one foot, the giant wailed. His skin sizzled and crackled from the acidic blood of the wurmer.

A wurmer pounced on Balzurth. Claws raked his scaled chest.

He laughed. "You mindless thing." He threw his arm around the wurmer's neck and snapped it like a twig. He caught Rybek running for one of the temple's many exits. He plowed through the sea of wurmers, shoving and throwing them aside.

But when Balzurth veered for the tunnel, the entrance was blocked off by Bletver's surprisingly agile bulk.

"Let's have a go at it again," Bletver sneered. He beckoned with his finger. "I'd love a trophy from the King of the Dragons. My, those scales and claws will look fantastic about my neck."

"You had your chance, triant. Now your doom is at hand." Balzurth filled his lungs with air, stoking the furnace inside his belly. Smoke puffed out of his nose, and Bletver's narrowed eyes widened. "Goodbye, Bletver. So long, evil one!"

But just then, the phantom dropped onto Balzurth, clouding his eyes and dousing his flames.

He dropped to his hands and knees, clutching at his throat and fighting for breath. The essence of the phantom's power attacked his mind and spirit. Probed his weaknesses. Exposed his failures. A flicker of doubt entered Balzurth's mind, and the phantom drove its poison deep into his heart. He saw his plan slipping through his fingers. He wanted to use the amulet to appear right in front of Eckubahn, turn his full powers loose, and destroy the unsuspecting titan once and for all. He let out a roar!

CHAPTER 34

A LOUD ROAR ERUPTED FROM INSIDE the temple, shaking the bridge. Bayzog stumbled.

At his side, Ben helped him up to his feet. "What was that?"

"Pain," Bayzog replied. "Anguish." He found new strength in his legs after hearing the desperate cry.

Ben had him by the arm, and stride for stride they were racing up the bridge. Carefully, they hugged the entryway wall and slipped unnoticed into the chamber.

A fierce battle was on. Wurmers agitated together in an angry hive. Two stone giants slammed huge clubs down over and over with wroth force. Perhaps most ominous of all, a cloud of blackness lingered in the air.

Ben inched forward.

Bayzog grabbed him by the arm. "Too dangerous. That phantom has him. I need my staff."

Puffing out smoke, Ben said, "I can't hold whatever's in me much longer. I'm about to explode."

"What did you drink?'

"That fire-breathing potion." Ben's eyes glowed with the fires of a volcano. "I have to do something."

"True, you cannot hold that fire in for long, or it will incinerate you from the inside. Hold it for just a moment." Bayzog closed his eyes and narrowed his focus, blocking out the clamor of battle that filled the chamber like the inside of a ringing bell. He sensed his staff. It was within the temple, but the temple had many chambers. Several paths. He opened his eyes and touched Ben. "You should come with me."

"No, I have a feeling I need to help whoever that is in there." Ben clasped Bayzog on the arm, shook it, and said, "You're just going to have to go your way and I'll go mine. Best to you, Bayzog."

"Best to you, Ben."

CHAPTER 35

A ROAR OF ANGUISH ECHOED THROUGH the valley. Flocks of birds scattered out of the branches. The horses came to a stop and reared up. Brenwar and the women were staring at Nath, who said, "Father!"

Dragon heart pumping, Nath doubled his pace, racing through the valley toward the Temple of Spires at full speed. He had heard plenty of sounds from his father, but never any of pain. It didn't seem possible. He veered off the path and cut into the forest, bursting through the low-hanging branches and leaving the others far behind him.

I might not be able to fly, but I can certainly run like the fastest gazelle. Hang in there, Father. Hang on!

It was surreal, his father being in peril. The Dragon King was invincible. Wasn't he?

Nath hit the bottom of the hill and was back on the overgrown path to the Temple of Spires. He could see the temple's jagged peaks stabbing at the clouds. That wasn't all. Nath wasn't the only one who had been attracted by Balzurth's roar.

A gigantic wurmer as big as Nath ever saw circled above. It landed on the other side of the temple's bridge. Its eyes glowed with red fire that bored into him. Behind the ancient archway it waited, opening its mouth to roar every so often.

Nath slid out Fang, shouting, "Dragon! Dragon!" Shoulders set, he charged.

Chapter 36

Filled with the same fear every warrior gets before battle, Ben hurried across the chamber toward the sacrificial slab. His body was so hot he felt as if he might burst into fire at any moment.

I can't hold this in.

Stepping out from beyond the phantom's blackness and the battling throng of wurmers, Bletver emerged. The triant's face was filled with a bestial delight. "You again? Mmm, another morsel for my belly. And the timing couldn't be better. All of this fighting makes me very hungry."

Swallowing down the flaming butterflies that stirred in his stomach, Ben pulled himself up onto the stone slab and faced Bletver. Forcing down the stammer in his throat, he said, "If you're so hungry, then what are you waiting for?" He did a little jig, feet tapping and elbows swinging. "Come and eat me, ugly!"

Bletver's brows buckled. He bared his teeth, chomped them, and said, "I've had all I can stand of you idiotic people. I don't know what trick you're up to, but I'm not taking any chances with delay." He reached for Ben.

Ben huffed a big breath and blew it, but no fire came out.

Bletver seized him in his powerful grip and jerked him up off the slab. "This time I'm going to ensure you are dead." He smashed Ben down onto the stone table.

A whoosh of fire came out of Ben's mouth.

It spread up the triant's arms, and he let go. "Agh! What have you done to me?"

Gulping in another lungful of air, Ben let out another flaming burst, covering Bletver's bulging body in flames.

The triant flailed and screamed wildly, but somehow, he caught sight of Ben and came right back after him again, shouting in rage at the flames that sizzled the skin on his body, "I'm going to kill you!"

Ben let out another gust.

A stream of fire covered the giant's face.

"Nooooooo!" Bletver yelled.

How that bloodthirsty giant saw him through the flames on his face, Ben didn't know, but somehow it came right at him. Ben dove off the sacrificial stone slab.

Bletver caught Ben's leg and held him fast. "I might die, but you will die with me." Drawing him in with Ben's pants catching fire, Bletver let out another phrase. "Let's burn together!"

With all of the commotion, Bayzog pressed his advantage. He muttered a spell he'd not used in a long time. It wasn't an aggressive one, rather something passive but helpful. Feeling endowed with new powers, his vision sharpened and refocused. His keen senses were all enhanced. Moving quickly, robes dusting the ground, he followed the beacon of magic he sensed into one of the corridors that branched off from the main chamber.

There it is.

A slightly translucent trail lingered in the hall like a dying will o' the wisp. Careful not to be followed, he chased after it. The corridor led him into another passage cut from the stones and ended in a chamber that spread out into many alcoves. The mystic vapor trail came to a stop inside the blackness of a small cavern.

Breathing softly, Bayzog advanced into the darkness. If not for his elven vision and the help of the spell, he'd have been as blind as a bat and not nearly as effective. Shoulder grazing the wall, he followed the trail. His toe clipped something that rattled on the floor.

I'm as good at sneaking as I am at hand-to-hand fighting.

It was a skeleton, one of many that were strewn over the chamber floor. At first, the wizard thought they'd been dead for centuries, but the tang of blood and the stench of rotting flesh lingered in the air. He covered his nose with his hand and ambled on. Inside the alcove, the Staff of Elderwood leaned back against the wall. Ghost white from the spell, he saw it and not much of anything else to note.

Inching forward, testing the hard floor with his toes, he thought, "It can't be this easy."

Arms outstretched, he reached for it. His fingertips stroked the smooth elder wood. He wrapped his fingers around the long shaft, and his old friend felt alive in his hand. He shuddered. He had never hugged his staff before, but he wanted to now.

Scraping caught his ears, and he turned back.

Wurmers slithered out of the other alcoves. Their purple eyes were a burning haze as their talon-covered paws scratched toward him. Heads low and teeth clacking, they converged on him in a frenzy.

CHAPTER 37

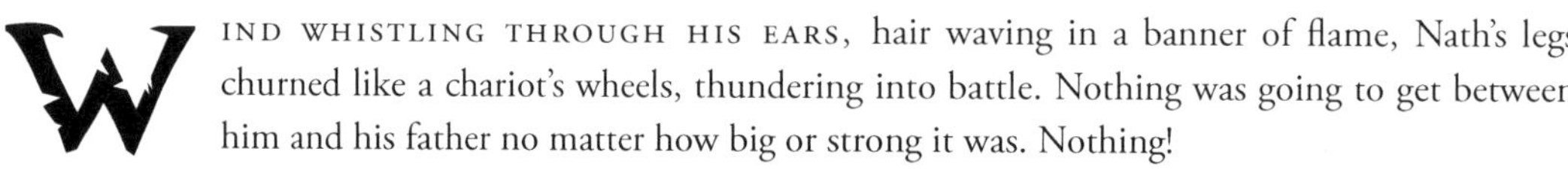

WIND WHISTLING THROUGH HIS EARS, hair waving in a banner of flame, Nath's legs churned like a chariot's wheels, thundering into battle. Nothing was going to get between him and his father no matter how big or strong it was. Nothing!

The monstrous wurmer's long neck coiled back. Black smoke spilled from its nostrils. Its horned head shot forward and turned loose a radiating pulse of energy. The scale-searing blast took Nath's feet out from under his body and sent him sailing over the railing and into the mouth of the bottomless canyon.

In midair, he clutched at anything he could get his hand on and caught himself on a beam that dangled beneath the bridge. Squeezing, his fingertips dug in. With one arm he hoisted himself up and managed to crawl up the beam with Fang still secure in his other hand. Taking a glimpse below, he saw nothing but a black abyss.

I've never wanted my wings back more.

He shimmied up the beam and into the arch under the bridge. Wedging himself into the stonework, he caught his breath.

Whew.

The wurmer's head lowered from above, twisting from side to side. Its nostrils snorted and flared.

Nestled in his spot between the beams, Nath pressed as deep into the crevice as he could. All he could do was hide. Without any footing underneath, he couldn't risk taking a swing. He would fall into the abyss.

What a predicament.

He started to ease Fang into his back scabbard.

Just then, the wurmer slipped off the bridge with a roar and vanished into the fog that spiraled like a tornado, its growls echoing deep in the canyon.

Nath made his move. Feet dangling over a certain death, arm over arm he climbed from beam to beam, making his way to the top.

Hurry, Nath, hurry. You're faster than this.

A wild ape couldn't have climbed any faster. His hands gripped the stones, and he began pulling himself up onto the bridge.

The wurmer exploded from under the mist with its jaws wide open, a huge fish chomping at the bait.

Fastened to the rail of the bridge, there was nowhere for Nath to go as the wurmer's maw closed in. He flung himself off the bridge and into the dragon's mouth.

Chomp!

CHAPTER 38

CLASPING THE ELDERWOOD STAFF WHERE it stood in front of him, Bayzog stretched out his fingers. Tendrils of lightning exploded from his fingertips into the nearest wurmer. The white-hot bolt of energy shot right through its scales and spread from wurmer to wurmer in an expanding chain of light.

The monsters screeched and howled. Their scales smoked. The first one exploded, and the others dried up and crumbled to the floor.

Head sagging, the half elf panted. His own magic was gone for now. And all he had was the staff. He slogged forward, brushing by one of the wurmers.

There was life in its eye, and its tail twitched. Its neck stretched out and its mouth opened. The bottom of its jaw fell off.

He poked it in the nose with his staff.

Its body quavered and fell into a pile of scale and bones that finally turned to dust.

I hate those things.

Bayzog trudged back to the chamber with heavy shoulders and legs that felt like lead. He felt old. The phantom's drain had cost him, yet he lived. Staff in one hand, braced against the wall, he peeked into the chamber. The blackness still lingered in the back end, yet there were fire and screaming near the slab.

Ben!

His friend was in the fight of his life. Half underneath the sacrificial altar, he kicked and screamed at the flaming giant. "Get off me! Get off me!"

Summoning his strength, Bayzog shot across the room like a wild berserker. With the tip of his staff lowered like a lance, he drove into the back of the burning Bletver.

Crack!

The triant's back arched, and his arms flung wide. Dripping hunks of flaming flesh, he teetered, swayed, and fell backward.

Wham!

In a moan of defeat, the triant's flesh boiled its last and died.

Ben rolled over and over on the floor, yelling, "Get it out! Get it out!"

Springing to his friend, Bayzog covered the man with his robes and patted him out. Ben had boils and burns all over him. His face was a mask of pain.

"Will you die?" Bayzog asked.

"And miss all this suffering?" Ben coughed and grimaced. "I'll live."

On the other side of the slab, the battle in the phantom's blackness yet raged. The wurmers dove in, only to be tossed out again. A stone giant hammered at something with its fists. Another giant turned, and its gaze fell on Bayzog. It came.

CHAPTER 39

INSIDE THE WURMER'S JAWS, NATH took matters into his own hands. He braced himself between the clenching jaws and shoved back. "Yuuurgh!"

The beast shook its head. Its throat muscles swallowed, and its tongue rolled under Nath's feet.

"You can't swallow me unless you kill me!" Nath buried his claws deep in the soft flesh of the wurmer's mouth. He pushed harder.

The creature gagged and spat Nath out.

Caback!

Free falling through the air, all he could see was the wurmer's face. "Oof!"

He was back on the bridge, covered in slime and with the wind knocked out of him.

Above, the wurmer's wings flapped, and it barreled through the sky, letting loose a mighty shriek. "Reeeeeeck!"

Nath sprang to his feet and dashed toward the temple entrance.

The wurmer swooped, landing in front of the gateway to cut him off.

Not slowing, Nath drew Fang and churned forward, giving the blade a single command. "Fang, destroy!"

A radiant burst of energy exploded from the wurmer's mouth.

Nath plowed straight through the searing heat and buried Fang hilt deep in the wurmer's body.

The wurmer exploded.

Boom!

Scales, flesh, and claws scattered through the air and rained down on the bridge.

No longer on his feet, Nath brushed a hunk of wurmer flesh from his shoulder and wiped some soft grit from his eyes. He studied the shimmering blade and felt the throbbing in his hand. He and Fang were one at last.

A clamor filled his ears. Springing to his feet, Nath rushed through the smoldering wurmer lumps into the temple.

Bayzog was standing over Ben with his staff raised over his head. A citrine dome of energy covered them in a sizzling glaze. Lording over the dome, a stone giant hammered at it two fists at a time. Bayzog was staggering on his feet, and the shield was blinking in and out.

Waving his arms, Nath yelled, "Over here, giant!"

But the monstrous man continued his focused assault on the dome.

Wham! Wham! Wham!

Closing the gap between him and the giant, Nath angled for its leg and chopped high. "Destroy, Fang! Destroy!" The great blade bit deep into the giant's knee, drawing forth an angry cry. But there was no explosion. No boom. Just a giant that wanted to kill him.

The raging humanoid clutched at Nath and screamed, "Die!"

Nath turned his hips into the swing of his sword and sheared the giant's hand off at the wrist.

It let out an awful howl so loud that Nath's teeth tickled.

"EEEEAAAAAAUUUGHHHHHH!"

Not backing off, Nath seized the moment and pressed his attack on the bewildered giant.

Slice! Slice! Slice!

Clutching at its wounds, the giant collapsed on its knees and died. Still upright, its limbs transformed into stone with a fast then slowing crackle. It was a statue now, a memory of a monster that lost its final battle.

Nath rushed over to his friends. Ben was a horrible sight, and Bayzog's face looked sickly. "Are you well?"

"Dragon, it's you!" Ben exclaimed. He hitched his chin over his shoulder at the blackness that still whirled around the room, fighting someone else. "Then who's that?"

Giving Ben a hand up, Nath said, "My father, Balzurth." He started forward, eager to rip his father out of the raging darkness and enemies that surrounded him.

But Bayzog held Nath fast. "Wait. That phantom will steal your powers. It's absorbing your father's powers now." The Elderwood Staff's gem winked with new fire. "I can stop it, but not if I'm interrupted."

"But Bayzog," Ben said, "the phantom almost killed you before."

"I wasn't ready for it then. Now that I have the staff and know what I'm up against, I am."

"What do you need?" Nath said, glancing over at the fracas.

"Just stay close and don't let anything interrupt me." Gripping the staff in both hands, the wizard planted one end of it firmly on the stone floor and raised his face to the ceiling.

Nath slipped Dragon Claw out of the bottom of Fang's hilt and handed it over to Ben. The silvery blade swirled with a mix of red and purple within.

Marveling, Ben said, "It lives."

The Elderwood Staff flared up in a white wash of light. Its brilliance lit up the entire chamber, driving the shadows and darkness away as the rising sun does to the night. Bayzog's white-knuckled hands were glued to the shaft. His eyes were white as snow. His mouth hung open, but somehow his voice was calling in a deep Elvish form of ancient song.

Above them in a swirling storm, the white gathered and took form. A white phantom-like creature grew with a distinct head and hulking shoulders. It pulsed and drifted toward the blackness. Then, like a snapping bowstring, it attacked.

A shrill whine shattered the clamor of battle. The night and the day had collided. The phantoms went at it with a howl.

The flock of wingless wurmers was quick to find new prey. The mindless creatures fixed their eyes on new blood: Nath and Ben. Slithering over the floor, they advanced with startling speed.

"Have at them, Ben!" Nath decapitated the first wurmer that came into his path.

Ben buried Dragon Claw in another's skull.

Pushed to the limit, Nath struck as hard and fast as he could. Anticipating every mindless move, he hacked the swarm of wurmers one by one, but it wouldn't be enough to stop them from clawing down Bayzog—who controlled the fighting white phantom above.

And Dragon Claw or not, Ben was overwhelmed.

"Get behind me, Ben! Just guard Bayzog!"

Splintering bone, teeth, and scales with his own might added to Fang's, Nath battled down the horde. Desperate for another plan, he gave Fang another order. "Repel, Fang! Repel!" He hoped a sonic wave would toss the slithering legions away. Between scale-rending swings, he banged the tip of the blade on the floor.

Ting.

Nothing.

A wurmer burst through the opening in Nath's defense and bit into his leg.

"Argh!" Nath cried. He beat the thing in the head with Fang's pommel, but its jaws were locked on his leg. He was practically immobile.

"Dragon!" Ben called. "I can't hold them off any longer! And look!"

Another storm giant was coming up from the recesses of the temple, headed right for them. Its coal-black eyes were intent on smashing Bayzog. The bestial man with skin of stone did something clever and unexpected. It picked up a wurmer and slung it straight at Bayzog.

Locked to the stone by the jaws of the wurmer, all Nath could do was watch the scaly missile soar.

CHAPTER 40

INSTINCT. SURVIVAL. NATH DIDN'T KNOW what, but for some reason Ben flicked Dragon Claw at the flying wurmer.

On impact, the scaly creature exploded into shards of ice.

"Ben!" Nath yelled, just as two wurmers tore into his defenseless friend. "No!"

The giant reached down to scoop Nath up.

Nath cocked Fang back to swing. "You'll pay, giant!"

A huge projectile smote the giant in the skull with a thunderclap.

Kraaang!

The enormous man's knees buckled under its body, and it fell face first on the slab.

"Brenwar!" Nath shouted.

Storming into the temple on horseback came Brenwar, with Sasha and Laylana close behind. "Don't be fighting giants without me! You owe me!"

The three warriors ran roughshod into the wurmers. Fiery missiles streaked from Sasha's fingers, puncturing one wurmer after another. Laylana's elven steel cleaved wurmer after wurmer in twain. Brenwar, powered by the gauntlets, punched with bone-snapping effect.

Nath locked his fingers into the jaws of the wurmer locked on his leg and began pulling them apart. Face reddening, arms bulging, he freed his leg and shoved the now dead but formerly vise-like clamp aside. Limping, he made his way over to Ben and hacked through the two wurmers attached to him.

"No, Ben, no," Nath sobbed, cradling his friend in his arms. Ben's face was marred in blood and burns. He'd never seen a man in such sad shape before. "Stay with me, Ben. Stay with me."

"I've been through worse," Ben said. He pawed at his side with a broken wrist. "Give me, give me the magic." His eyes rolled up in his head.

Nath fumbled through the belt pouch, found a restoration potion, and poured it into Ben's mouth. "Ben. Listen to me, Ben. You aren't dying on me."

Brenwar found his way to Nath's side. "I think that's the last of them."

Above, the phantoms continued their battle of darkness and light. Howling and shrieking back and forth in a knot of mystic sheets, the ghosts raged.

Bayzog's body trembled. His feeble frame seemed to be crushed under some unseen weight. The blackness of the phantom began to absorb the luminous white light.

Nath's chest tightened. He could barely breathe. Ben was dying and Bayzog was fading. He felt helpless.

From the heap of dead wurmers piled up all around, Sasha appeared. As lovely as ever despite the dirt on her face and robes, she gracefully made her way over to her husband. With the gentleness of a dove, she locked her arms around his waist and whispered in his ear, "I'm here for you, my love."

Bayzog straightened. The yellow in his eyes turned whiter than the snow on the peaks. The phantom he had summoned snaked out of the darkness. In an odd hand-over-hand movement, the white phantom reeled the black phantom in as if to swallow it whole. The black thing wailed and stretched. Its essence clawed at the air. Pawed for life. In two more tremendous gulps, the black phantom was gone and only a warm white ghostly light remained.

Bayzog collapsed into Sasha's arms and the Elderwood Staff's light went cold. The white phantom disappeared, and only the wavering torchlight illuminated the temple.

Weakly, Bayzog said, "Sasha, you're well?"

Brushing his sweat-drenched locks from his eyes, she said, "Aye."

"Dragon," Ben said, still cradled in Nath's arms. His color began to return and his heartbeat steadied. "I want to tell you something."

"Absolutely, Ben. Anything."

"I'm retiring."

"Oh? Ha ha! It looks like you're going to be fine after all." Nath brought Ben up to a sitting position. "Wait here."

Ben fell back down again, but Nath was on the move. He had to find his father. Brenwar followed right behind him, and as soon as they rounded the massive slab, they came across a startling sight.

CHAPTER 41

Rybek stood behind Balzurth, who was sitting on the temple floor. The Dragon King's head was down on his chest. Haggard and drained, he breathed short, raspy breaths. Rybek had a chain wrapped around Balzurth's neck, with his sword poised to pierce the dragon man's heart through the back.

"Ah," Rybek said. "It seems the true Nath Dragon has arrived. Such a joy. I've had no fun dealing with this imposter. Oh, it's not what I want. It's what Eckubahn wants, but I feel that today, we can both have what we want." He tugged on the chain, choking Balzurth. "You see, Eckubahn wants him, and I want you. Your father, so clever and wise, hoped for me to send him to Eckubahn at full strength and give him a deadly surprise. He nearly pulled it off."

"And how was that to happen without Eckubahn knowing?" Nath asked, buying his father time while he desperately looked for a way to free him.

Rybek dangled the amulet before them. "This will take you right to Eckubahn. Oh, he would be more than ready for the likes of you, but not Balzurth. No, I have a feeling Balzurth would destroy him. But now, with Balzurth in such a weakened condition, he'll be ripe for the picking. A veritable sheep for the slaughter."

"If you do that," Nath warned, "there will be no escape for you. Look around. You'd be smart to use that amulet on yourself." He stepped forward.

Rybek pushed his sword into Balzurth's back, drawing forth a moan. "Nah ah ah. Stay right where you are. If anything smells like a trick, I'll end him myself."

Nath took a half step back. "You won't win this if you stay, Rybek. Let my father go, or I'll end you."

"No, you won't end me, Nath. The dwarf might, but you won't. I know that about you."

"You'll die for all the innocent blood you've spilled one way or the other," Nath said. "Let go of my father and live to fight another day."

"That's out of the question. Eckubahn would kill me," Rybek said.

"Eckubahn won't know what happened here," Nath remarked.

Everyone in Nath's party had flanked Rybek. There was nowhere for him to go. And it was quite possible that Brenwar would kill him. The way the dwarf's hands twisted on Mortuun's handle suggested he wouldn't hold back.

"So you can take your chances with us," Nath said, "or with your leader. If you are so cherished, then I'm certain he'll need you later. Just do what your kind does: lie and curry his favor. You'll find no favor with us."

Rybek scanned all of their faces. He stepped back but kept the sword needling into Balzurth's back. "Perhaps you're right." He gave his helmet an angry shake. "You played well today, Nath Dragon. It won't happen again. Now back away."

The party spread out.

Easing his sword away from Balzurth's back, Rybek stepped away.

The tightness in Nath's chest subsided. He'd won. His father was safe. There wasn't anything Rybek could do to harm any of them now.

Sultans of Sulfur, that was close.

In the blink of an eye, Balzurth came to life. In a blur of motion, he twisted around and smacked the blade from Rybek's grip with one hand and snatched the amulet with the other. Standing up at full height in a body of restored strength, the Dragon King said to an awestricken Rybek in a voice filled with raw power, "Justice for you. Vengeance for me." He shoved the man to the floor.

"Father!" Nath cried out. "What are you doing?"

Balzurth turned. He'd transformed into a mirror image of Nath. "Playing possum." He dropped the amulet over his neck and said, "I'm sorry, Son, but what must be done must be done." He vanished.

Flight of the Dragon

-Book 5-

Craig Halloran

CHAPTER 1

"LET ME BUST HIM UP." Brenwar had Mortuun shoved in Rybek's face. The evil warrior was bound up with his hands behind his back and sitting on the stone floor. There was a victorious sneer on his face. "I'll remove the snide look from his jaw forever!"

Rybek's broad shoulders heaved with his chuckles. His dark eyes moved back and forth between Nath and his company with nothing but a taunting look in them. His voice was a dark rumble when he spoke. "Look at you. Look at all of you! You've fought so hard and lost. Now your father is lost. What a fool! Eckubahn will have been ready for his ploy, and it wouldn't surprise me one bit if Balzurth was dead already." His nostrils flared. "Victory. I smell victory. The world of dragons falls."

Brenwar cocked back his elbow and made a fist. The leather of his gauntlet squeaked. "I'll show you victory!"

"Enough, Brenwar. You'll get your chance to question him later." Nath was standing by the sacrificial slab of stone, tending to Ben and Bayzog. Both man and part-elf looked about as bad as he'd ever seen them. Ben's face was burned. Laylana, Laedorn's elven daughter and a fine warrior, was treating the red blisters on Ben's cheeks with nimble fingers. Sasha and Bayzog were reunited. Bayzog lay in his wife's arms, eyes closed, with a wheeze behind his breaths. His hair was almost all white, but some of the color had returned to his face. Nath watched Sasha stroke her husband's cheek and looked into her soft eyes. "I don't think I've ever seen him sleep before."

"It takes much to get him to rest," Sasha replied with a faint smile. "Don't feel responsible, Nath. He's going to make it. He just needs his rest."

Nath nodded back. Moving away, he picked Rybek's sword up off the cold stone floor. It was a magnificent weapon. The steel was smooth and polished so fine that he could see his reflection in it. The leather on the handle made for a fine grip, and the weight was near perfect in balance. He thumbed the edge. There wasn't even a notch in it. He cast his eyes down at Rybek. "I bet you could chop down a stone tree with this."

Broad jaws clenching in his hard-featured face, Rybek nodded sideways at Brenwar and said to Nath, "No doubt it could chop down this stump of a man." He leered. "In time, I'll chop you down as well."

Brenwar popped Rybek in the forehead with his knuckles. The back of the man's head smacked hard into the column of stone with a *crack*.

Eyes squeezed shut, Rybek shook his head and spat.

Nath said to Brenwar, "What did I say?"

Puffing through his beard, Brenwar said, "I can't help that. It's instinct. Nobody threatens a dwarf." He swung his war hammer from side to side. "Just let me knock his head off. We don't need him to find your father."

Nath held his left hand up, palm out, and flipped Rybek's sword around with his right wrist. He shuffle stepped and jabbed. Parried. Twirled.

Rybek's eyes followed every precise and quick move.

Nath swished the blade through the air in a masterful display of the swordsman's craft. "It's an amazing blade, no doubt." He chopped into the stone column just above Rybek's head. Hunks of stone and dust fell on the man's tattoo-covered head. "It really can hew through stone."

"Just imagine what it could do to a skull," Brenwar added. "Heh-heh."

"You need to leave my blade alone, Nath Dragon." There was an edge in Rybek's voice. "Put it down."

Nath started banging the flat of the blade hard against the pillar. The sound echoed through the

Temple of Spires. "Why, do you fear I might break it again?" With two hands, he smacked the blade hard into the stone.

Bang!

Rybek winced.

Nath struck the stone again.

Bang!

"Stop that!" Rybek shouted.

"Oh, I see someone is very fond of his blade." Nath squatted down and said in Rybek's ear, "Do you fear I might warp it?" He held it out for Rybek to see and turned the blade from side to side with his wrist. "It's still straight, for now, but I notice an imperfection."

"There is none."

"I disagree." Nath ran his fingernail over a hairline fracture just above the middle of the blade. "See that? It's where I broke it before. It's where I'll break it again."

"If you break that blade, you'll kill us all," Rybek said.

"I'm curious, Rybek. How did you manage to mend this sword so well?"

"You fool. Eckubahn did it with his bare hands. Such power he has, it's unrivaled. There might be a crack in the steel, but believe me, it's stronger than ever." Rybek's dark, hollow eyes caressed the blade with a passion only a warrior could understand. "You and that cleaver of yours could never break it again."

"Is that so?" Nath asked with an unbelieving tone. He rose back up to full height. "I really find it hard to believe." He waved Rybek's sword back and forth like a conductor's baton. "It's out of balance."

"It was made for my hand, not yours."

"I see." Nath rested it on his shoulder. "Why don't you tell me where my father is, Rybek? It would be the right thing to do."

"I'll tell you when you are dead." Rybek glanced at each person in the room. "And that goes for the rest of you as well. Including the women."

Brenwar launched another punch.

But Nath caught the dwarf by the meat of his upper arm. He changed places with Brenwar and turned loose a punch of his own. His fist connected with Rybek's jaw, snapping his head to the side. "You overestimate my capacity to show mercy."

Rybek's tongue fished through his mouth. He spat a bloody tooth out. "Perhaps I do. But mercy is your weakness. It's your father's, too. Eckubahn preys on it even as we speak."

Nath had to have some measure of faith in his father for knowing what he was doing, but the risk was so great, and his mother had warned him about his father taking those risks. He couldn't just stand around and hope his father's plan would work out. Deep down in his gut, he knew his father needed help.

Strength comes in numbers.

He stuck the sword tip first into the stone between Rybek's legs. "As evil as you may be, you still fight by the warrior's code of honor. How about one last fight, metal against metal? I win, you tell me where my father is. You win, I die."

Rybek lifted his head, sneering. "I'll take it."

CHAPTER 2

BALZURTH ARRIVED IN ANOTHER PART of Nalzambor on his knees, trembling. The amulet had done more than just transport him. It had drained him, somehow. His stomach gurgled and moaned. His limbs were heavy.

Chains rattled on his ankles, wrist, and neck.

How did those get there? Clever.

Balzurth lifted his hands up to his face. His scales were still midnight black, his clawed fingernails still sharp and golden yellow. He tossed his head. The flame-red hair cascaded over his shoulders.

At least my disguise is intact.

He surveyed his surroundings. He was outside in a misty smoke that covered jagged rocks. Colossal stones surrounded him in what looked to be the cold, dead mouth of a volcano. Somehow, sunlight illuminated the vast gap through the dimming gray mist. He rose to his feet and walked.

The heavy chains scraped over the stone. The iron of the chains was dense, the kind fashioned by men with a heavy ore mined by the dwarves in Morgdon.

It seems Eckubahn isn't going to take any chances with me. Or Nath, rather.

Balzurth walked outward until the chains brought him to a stop. He stretched them to their limit, about twenty feet, where they hung suspended, secured by the other end to a metal ring big enough to go around a horse's neck. It was mounted to a huge slab of square-cut stone at least ten feet tall and just as wide. He strained his arms and legs against his metal bonds. They held fast, like extensions of the world itself. He backed up, letting the links go slack. "Huh."

Accompanied by the wind whistling through the cracks in the stone mountain that was now his prison, he sat down. Crossing his legs, he lowered his chin onto his fist and waited. Balzurth's plan hadn't turned out the way he had hoped. He'd figured on landing right before the king of the titans, Eckubahn himself. From there he'd meant to take it right to him. A full onslaught. One swift stroke. He wanted to end it quick in a final stand. One last battle. But it hadn't happened the way he'd envisioned it. And that was a problem.

Now time has become my enemy.

With his clawed finger, he etched some patterns in the dirt and began to hum. His rich sound filled the expansive chamber. His thoughts landed on his son Nath. He was proud of Nath, what he'd done, how he'd overcome his trials and stayed faithful to the right cause. It hadn't worked out that way with his other children. But Nath was special, and no doubt his youngest son would be trying to find him. Balzurth just hoped to end this war before his son arrived in the thick of it. Now was the time to save lives and put a stop to Eckubahn and his mad reign.

I should have destroyed that titan when I had the chance. Let evil live and all it does is thrive.

He eyed his claws.

Next time I'll put it out of our misery forever.

Balzurth was still humming when a scuffle stirred the rocks. His keen dragon sight pierced the wavering mist. As he scanned the rock walls, the shapes of men formed in his eyes. These weren't average men but the larger sort: giants. Their huge frames eased between the rocks as they moved. Given the mist, the average person wouldn't detect them, but Balzurth could see all sorts. Mighty limbs came to life on legs of iron. They were fifteen feet tall and shaggy headed. Their noses were broad and flat.

And then their moans and huffs echoed through the strange canyon. On giant feet, they came forward, shaking the ground and surrounding Balzurth.

"I was wondering where the smell came from," said Balzurth in the guise and style of Nath as he counted their faces. There were fifteen of the monstrous men. They were bestial and savage, yet there was cunning in their beady eyes. Cruelty. "You know, Nalzambor is full of lakes you could bathe in. The fish might not like it—actually, they wouldn't like it—but the deep waters are said to take the stench out of anything. I know a great place I'd be happy to show you. It's just below—"

A powerful, echoing voice split the air.

"SILENCE!"

A giant emerged from the ranks. He was a head taller than the rest, more man than monster, with a green fire in his eyes. He was adorned in dragon skins hung like armor over his brawny shoulders and part of his chest. Bones rattled on his neck. Dragon bones and teeth. A belt fashioned from the same white bones hung from his waist. His head was mostly bald, and what hair he did have formed a long ponytail.

Balzurth rose with fire in his eyes. His heart thundered behind his breast. The atrocity enraged him. Many dragons had died to make this arrangement. Good ones. Blues, greens, and even a gold. It was just like the horrifying message the giants had sent to Dragon Home. A dragon's corpse. Broken. Mangled. Balzurth strained against the chains. "Who are you that defiles my kindred?"

"I am the spirit Isobahn, brethren of Eckubahn, the king." He stomped the ground.

Thoom!

Balzurth lost his footing and dropped to his knees.

"You will bow in my presence."

As much as he abhorred to do so, Balzurth fought back his commanding voice, popped up again, and continued in Nath's voice with a defiant tone. "I will not!"

Isobahn nodded his tremendous square-cut chin.

The other giants converged on Balzurth. Taking turns, they swatted, punched, stomped, and shoved him between their ranks. The blows were hard and heavy. The giants giggled like maniacal children. They tugged at his chains. Jerked him off his feet, dangled him, and patted at him like cats playing with a ball of string.

It was futile, but he fought back as best he could in Nath's form and chained. "You'll pay for this!" Balzurth yelled. Shaking his fist, he yelled even louder. "You'll all pay!"

By the chains, a giant swung him hard into the stone to which he was tethered.

Wham!

Balzurth absorbed all of the punishment he could endure. He couldn't break his cover. He just hoped his body could hold up, but his magic hadn't ever been drained before, so he didn't know how long he would need to rest before enough magic came back for him to change into his dragon form.

It could take years. Years of sleep! Let's hope not.

He took several more lumps.

Now I know how Nath must feel.

The beating continued until all of his physical strength faded. It stopped when he was face down and bleeding in the dirt. Two of the giants unhooked his chains from the stone pillar. By the chains still linked to his body, they dragged him over the hard ground through a slit in the rocks into the darkness.

Scraping along, he regained his feet—only to be jerked down again. It was futile. Miserable. They strung him along, and he had no idea where he was going.

CHAPTER 3

"CAN YOU MOVE ANY FASTER?" Rerry said, looking over his shoulder at his brother. "A one-legged orc could pass you!"

Samaz hobbled up the path. They'd managed to make their escape from the dungeon hours ago, but his legs were like noodles. "I'm pacing myself."

"Ah, pacing yourself. Makes perfect sense for a pair of men trying to escape." Rerry pushed some low-hanging branches aside and waited for his brother.

Samaz ambled up the incline.

Rerry let loose the branch, which slapped his brother in the face. "And let's hope our pursuers are pacing themselves as well."

Samaz slunk under the branches. "You have such an annoying way with things." He laughed.

"What's so funny?"

"I don't know, you just look funny with a metal almond on your head." Samaz peeled off his own elven helmet and chucked it aside. "I can only imagine how silly I must look."

"You always look silly." Rerry picked Samaz's helmet up. "Now put this back on. We need to blend in, just in case we run into anybody. Now you blend, you bulging misfit."

With a huff, Samaz took the helmet, but he didn't put it back on. "I'll carry it for now."

Mocking him, Rerry said, "I'll carry it for now."

For some reason, the banter that had gone on and on between them since birth lightened Samaz's spirits. Some strength returned, and he pressed on, keeping pace while his brother navigated the woodland like one of the forest's own creatures.

Ahead, Rerry was a strapping figure of grace and warriorhood. Adorned in the elven armor with his light hair spilling out from under his helmet, Rerry carried the look of a soldier quite well. Light footed, he moved on top of the stumps, fallen trees, and flat rocks, careful to avoid leaving any kind of trail.

In truth, neither of them had much experience in the woodland, but it came naturally to them, unlike it did to their father, Bayzog. And they had less elf in them than their father did, which was odd.

"What do you make of Captain Scar imprisoning us? Or any of the elves doing so? They swarmed us. They threw us in a dungeon." Rerry adjusted his helmet. "It's so hard to get used to this thing. As I was saying, what do you make of that? Elves aren't supposed to imprison elves."

Samaz hopped from one rotting log to another. "I don't think they took us in because we're elves but because we are part-elves. But I was sick when you did most of the parlaying, remember?"

Rerry led them down into a ravine, where a stream trickled by. He scooped up a handful of water and slurped it down. He wetted his face. "Everything was fine until you mentioned Father's name," he said.

"Me?" Samaz straddled the stream and sloshed some water on his own face then drank. "You're the one who said 'Bayzog,' not me. I tugged the back of your shirt, but you didn't listen. Those gums kept flapping."

"They asked. What was I supposed to say? I thought it would be a good thing, seeing how Father is known as a hero in this realm. Instead, we received a throttling and days in the clink. What kind of elves treat other elves so poorly?" He plucked a stone out of the water and chucked it down the stream. It skipped once and splashed to a stop. "It was as if they were looking for him."

"We aren't full bloods. That's problem one. Father lives outside the elven lands. That's number two. Nalzambor is under duress. That's number three."

"Oh, enough with your numbers. The world's a mess. I get it." Rerry unsheathed his sword and cut through some of the reeds growing along the bank. "But as long as I have a fine piece of steel, I can handle it." He eyed Samaz. "Seriously, when are you going to master some sort of weapon?"

Samaz poked his temple. "As long as I have a sound mind matched by my quick feet and hands, I'm never defenseless."

Rerry rolled his eyes. "That's so encouraging."

At the top of the ravine rim came a sound of branches cracking, followed by heavy footsteps. Something or someone was up there. It was big and not ordinary big but beyond. It dragged something through the brush.

Rerry's eyes met Samaz's. Both of his thin blond eyebrows perched. With a nod, he darted after the sound.

Samaz ran after him, bounding from one side of the stream to the other and racing up the hillside. Rerry was climbing over the rocks, still focused on not leaving a trail. One thing was certain: the trail of whatever was up there couldn't be missed. He crested the top alongside his brother. The soft-footed brothers edged into the foliage until they came across a path of crushed and snapped saplings.

Rerry kneeled down inside a footprint as big as him. He crinkled his nose. In a whisper, he said, "It smells awful." He flashed a row of white teeth. "I bet it's a giant."

"There's no need to pursue it," Samaz warned. He bent over and picked up some animal hair grafted to the bark of a tree. "It feeds, whatever it is. Leave it be. Pursuit will only draw its attention."

"I won't bother it." Rerry crept forward.

Samaz followed. There wasn't much of a choice in the matter. Rerry wouldn't listen. They'd just have to resume their quest to find the Ocular of Orray and help their mother later.

Rerry came to a stop. He turned to face Samaz with his blue eyes the size of the moon. He pointed.

Samaz came alongside his brother and stared along the path Rerry indicated.

There it was sitting on the ground, a giant. Sitting, it was still much taller than them. The expanse of its back was just as wide too. Coarse brown hairs like fur covered the giant up to its neck. The head was bald, knotted, and scarred. It was eating. Samaz moved closer and watched from another angle. It was eating a bear. Its jaw moved up and down, making a horrible crunching sound that threatened to turn Samaz's bones to jelly. "Let's get out of here," he mouthed to his brother.

Rerry nodded and backed away.

But the giant took in a deep draw of air through its nostrils. It sounded as if it was going to inhale the entire forest. Its bullish neck snapped around. Mouth still full of bear, the giant locked its eyes on them. Nostrils flaring, it licked its lips and got to its feet.

"Samaz, it's got horns. Horns on its head. I didn't think giants had horns. Why would they need horns on their heads?" Rerry finished with his jaw hanging.

Samaz watched the giant rise to its full height. It did have horns, like a ram's, on either side of its forehead. Its face was ugly, almost like a beast's, but more like a wild man's.

The giant smacked its lips and, with a bellow, filled the forest as it came right at them.

CHAPTER 4

"HAVE YOU GONE MAD?" BRENWAR was blowing the layers of moustache that had become one with his beard. "This vermin doesn't deserve the opportunity."

Nath eyed Brenwar. "Mind yourself."

"But..." Brenwar's heavy shoulders slumped. Head down, he backed away.

Without any notification, Nath brought Rybek up to his feet and cut his bonds.

The powerful warrior, as tall as Nath, stretched his limbs and rubbed his wrists. With wary eyes, he said to Nath, "A straight fight then?"

Still holding Rybek's sword, Nath picked up the man's iron helmet. It was crudely crafted—not from a lack of skill but by intent. It was designed for intimidation more than protection. He tossed it to Rybek and said, "You'll need this."

Laylana appeared at his side. "Nath, this crude man will not fight fair. His word cannot be taken. In this instance, I concur with Brenwar. Let me beat the information out of him."

"He'll die first," Nath said. He faced off with Rybek. The cold look of a murderer was in the man's eyes. Vengeance was behind them too. Rybek blamed Nath for his brother's death. He blamed Selene as well. He would never stop until they were both dead. Nothing Nath could say would change the man's mind, but he spoke anyway. "Your brother had choices in life, Rybek. You do too. You don't have to race down the same path of destruction your brother was on. He cannot witness your accolades in the grave, no matter how large."

"Oh, he might not see it, but from the grave he will feel your blood when I spill it into the ground."

Rybek stretched out his hand. "I accept your offer. Your head against my information on the whereabouts of your father. I swear it on my sword in front of witnesses and fellow warriors—a bond in blood from the blood we've shed from battle. If I lie, take my hands, take my skill, forever."

A thunderclap boomed in the skies above. A heavy rain came down. The Temple of Spires was an ancient place, and its dome was filled with cracks. Water wetted the floor.

Rybek stepped into the rain and spread his arms wide. He was a hulking man layered in bulging muscles. "Eckubahn, aid me! Grant my revenge!"

Ben made his way to Nath's side and handed him Dragon Claw. "Just finish him."

Nath locked Dragon Claw back inside Fang's pommel. He moved away from his friend and into the litter of dead surrounding them: slaughtered wurmers from the earlier battle, chopped up into bits. Giants who had fallen and turned into stone, parts of them already busted up into rubble. Then there was Bletver, the triant. His huge body was still a smelly mound of burning flesh on account of the potion of fire breathing Ben had drunk. Rain drops sizzled on his dead hide.

Nath motioned with his sword. "Come, Rybek. Let the battle commence."

Rybek pulled his sword from the stone floor and wiped the water from his face. "It will rain your blood today."

Nath readied into his stance. Rybek was as good a swordsman as he'd ever faced. He'd about gotten him the last time, but perhaps he was underestimating the man, so he wasn't going to take any chances. He set his feet and lifted his sword. "Come then, make it rain."

Rybek kicked the head of a wurmer out of his path and moved in. He stood tall, sword at the ready, with his free hand fanned out. Raindrops bounced off the steel. The sword he carried was an exquisite blade with a grip made for two hands. Its length was shorter than the long blade of Fang, but it was just as broad. Rybek waded in and unleashed the first swing.

Both fine blades appeared to be otherworldly when they met. They collided in a clash of steel. Mystic sparks flew.

Clang!

Fang's energy flowed into Nath's hand with an angry hum.

Back and forth the warriors went, each fighting one handed.

Rybek jabbed his blade at Nath's eyes and legs.

Nath slid his head aside and swatted the blade away.

Rybek broke off and backed away, saying, "What's the problem, scared to attack me?"

"Not at all." Nath jumped right at him and let loose a chop at Rybek's side.

Rybek caught the swing on his sword and countered by spinning back into Nath, cracking him in the jaw with his elbow.

Nath stumbled back with spots in his eyes. A flash of metal came down. He brought Fang up, parrying the blow before it could cleave into his shoulder. He backpedaled. He defended himself against Rybek's assault of steel. The taste of his own blood was in his mouth.

Clang! Bang! Clang! Ting!

Mystic sparks flew.

Nath shook his mane of red hair. He parried one blow after the other.

Rybek assaulted—quick, deadly, and unrelenting. The warrior's blows weren't trying to cut him in half and overpower him. No, Rybek was a true master swordsman. He was determined to wear Nath down with skill as opposed to strength.

One thing is for certain. He's an excellent fighter.

Nath got the hang of the man's routine. Within moments he timed every blow, every stroke. He played along. Let his footing slip, only to desperately catch one fatal blow after the other.

"What's the matter, Nath Dragon? Why don't you attack? Do you feel my arm will tire and you shall vanquish me then?" Rybek stepped and jabbed. "I don't tire. My will of steel won't allow it."

"No, Rybek, you're a fine swordsman, one of the best I've ever encountered. Just not better than me." With that, Nath smacked Rybek's sword aside in a vicious counter rather than a parry. The warrior's arm was flung wide, exposing his chest. Nath back swung at the mark in a strike sure to end it, but at the last moment he held back, aiming to wound rather than kill by slowing the strike of his sword.

Rybek dropped beneath the swing in an uncanny move with surprising speed.

Nath missed.

Swish!

Overextended, Nath glanced down at the man lying beneath him.

Rybek swept Nath's legs out from under him with his booted foot.

Nath fell onto his back. Before he even realized what was happening, Rybek's blade was on a collision course with his face. In a fragment of thought, he knew he could not bring Fang around to stop the blow in time. His free clawed hand lashed out, trying to stop Rybek's attack at the wrist. The effort didn't match the goal. Rybek's blade cut through scales and bone.

Rybek let out a triumphant bellow.

"YYYyeeeeaaaaaahhhhhhhhhh!"

Nath looked for his fingers. Half of his hand was gone.

CHAPTER 5

RERRY SHOVED HIS BROTHER SAMAZ back down the path. Fueled by fear, the pair of part-elves careened over the embankment and down the ravine they'd just climbed up. He was yelling to his brother, "I always wanted to see a giant, but not like this!"

"I told you we needed to go around!" Samaz said, but his foot became tangled, and he tumbled over and down the hill.

Rerry rushed after his brother, stretching his arms out, fingers clutching for his brother's clothing.

But Samaz balled up, probably to protect himself. Rolling like a boulder, he hit the rock bottom and splashed into the ravine creek.

Rerry scooped his brother up by his underarms. "You're so clumsy!"

"I beat you down the hill, didn't I?"

"ELVEN MEAT! I SMELL ELVEN MEAT!"

Both of the brothers glanced up the hillside. The giant's tree-trunk legs pumped down the hill. Its yellow eyes were still locked on the both of them. Humongous and hideous, it came like a rampaging one man herd.

Gaping for a moment, Rerry said, "That stupid thing can talk."

"It's startling," Samaz replied.

Side by side, the brothers took off at a dead sprint, ankle deep in the water.

Behind them, the giant's feet shook the ground in heated pursuit.

"What's your plan, Samaz?"

"Run!"

Rerry bounded over the water cascading over the stones. "Run where?"

"Until we lose the giant!" Samaz leaped over a fallen log and landed in the shallows. "Just keep moving. Surely he can't keep up with us."

"Not me, maybe." Rerry took a quick glance over his shoulder.

The giant moved through the pass like a charging bull. Head lowered, it picked up steam. Using one of its massive hands, it scooped up a handful of stream stones and dirt and flung it at them.

"Duck, Samaz!"

The rocks, some as big as a man's hand, pelted both of them in the back.

"Augh!" Rerry cried out. One stone clonked off of his helmet, knocking him sideways. He caught himself, hand out, on the trunk of a tree, retaining his balance. His legs churned. He'd always been confident he could outrun anything, but the giant's legs were longer than he was tall.

It was gaining, and gaining fast.

"I FEED!" the giant said. "I FEED ON FLESH AND BONES!" It flung another handful of dirt and rocks at them.

The heavy debris pelted Rerry's back, sending lancing pain from his shoulders into his eyes.

Samaz dropped to a knee, dashing it on a jagged rock and tearing his clothes at the knee. His brows buckled between his eyes. Jaw clenched, he forced himself up and resumed his run.

Sword in hand, Rerry said, "You run! I'll stay and slow the beast until you get to safety. Who knows, maybe I'll get lucky."

"Most likely you'll get dead, and I'm not ready to part with you yet." Samaz snatched up a smooth stone from the water and closed his fist around it. "I need you to steal me a few moments."

"For what?" Rerry turned his chin over his shoulder.

The horned giant filled both of its hands with more gravel from the creek. Its arms cocked back. It flung the debris like a sea of sling stones.

"Duck, Samaz!"

The gravel ripped through the air. The hard pellets of rock pelted both of the brothers. Rerry had been hit with rocks before in some strange games he and his brother used to play, but never dozens of stones at once. They struck like a hive of hornets stinging all at once.

"Now I know why so many prefer to wear armor. Thank Guzan I have at least one coating on," he said, flapping his arms. "Dear mother, it hurts!"

Samaz didn't reply. His eyes were closed, but his feet still navigated the path over the stream of water. Both of his hands were clutched over the stone he held, and a mystic light seeped out from within it. His pace slowed. "Buy us some time, Rerry." He halted in the middle of the stream.

"Have you gone mad?"

Samaz stood with the waters rushing around his ankles. His eyes were up in his head. "Hold the giant off a few moments longer."

With his lip curled up under his nose, Rerry said to his brother, "You're so weird." He faced the oncoming giant and started waving his sword high over his head. He yelled out loud. "Halt, giant! I am Rerry, and this is my mystic sword...Giant Killer! One strike from its keen edge and you'll be instantly slain!"

Hands filled with mud and rock, the giant came to a stop. Its massive head tilted to the side as it squinted and eyed the blade held by Rerry. Its throat growled in a strange but giant-like thoughtful manner. It chewed something in its mouth and swallowed.

Rerry guessed it was part of the bear it had been dining on. He swallowed and said, "I see you are as wise as you are big, giant. You fear my blade, and you should." He poked the sword in the air. The giant eased back, eyes narrowed. "Be gone, giant. There is no meal for you to have here. Be gone and finish the bear."

With its eyes still fixed on Rerry's blade, the giant replied, "The entire world shall be mine to devour." It snorted. "Man and part-elf alike. I shall suck the marrow from your bones, you little liar."

And I thought giants were big and stupid. This one is certainly not.

Rerry took a quick look at his brother.

Samaz hadn't moved.

Facing the giant again, Rerry stuck out his chest. "Only a fool would dare trifle with Rerry the Great. I offered mercy. You passed up my offer. Now I can only offer death." He advanced.

The giant took a huge step back.

Speaking as loud as he could, Rerry said, "Having second thoughts, are we?"

The fifteen-foot-tall giant blinked its immense eyes. Thoughts were being processed somewhere behind the horns of its brutish skull. It was like an animal, a smart one, fighting against its instincts. Its belly moaned and gurgled. Its monumental jaws widened. Saliva dripped from its huge teeth.

"Elven meat's the best kind of meat. Tender are the bones." It leaned down. "I smell no danger in your steel. Like a flea, you cannot harm my thick hide. No mortal blade can."

"Uh," Rerry said, easing back a little, "you sound very sure of yourself. If I were you, I wouldn't take a chance."

"If you could kill me, I'd be dead. But you can't. Now, no more chatting. I hunger. It's time to dine." It allowed the rock and sludge to spill from its hands. Its arms slowly closed in on Rerry. "Make it simple, little flea. Get inside my belly."

The rancid breath of the giant soured Rerry's stomach. He covered his nose and tried not to gag. He wanted to move, but his legs seemed frozen into the water.

Dear Mother, this thing really is going to eat me! I-I-I can't move!

CHAPTER 6

ATH'S THOUGHTS RACED THROUGH A suspended time. He gazed at the part of his hand that lay in a puddle on the stone floor. What had happened? He'd been careful, testing Rybek's skill. He'd had a chance to end it. Finish the man. He'd held back. Why?

Now his enemy was on the verge of finishing him.

Jaw hanging on the ground, Nath caught the flash of Rybek's blade.

With two hands clutching the handle, Rybek brought the blade down with wroth force.

Nath rolled out of harm's way.

Rybek's blade bit into the stone floor and stuck.

Brenwar started forward with his war hammer ready to go. His bearded face was a mask of worry. Laylana was right beside him with her sword poised to strike at Rybek.

Sword out before him, Nath said, "No! I can handle this." There wasn't a mortal in the world who had undone Nath in a long time. There'd been close calls when he was much younger, testing his skills in the world of men, but he'd always overcome the odds.

This was different.

The feeling in Nath's gut now was not the same. He bled. He was maimed. Rybek, somehow, had shown more skill and outwitted Nath.

Don't let him get in your head, Dragon. There's too much riding on this. Your own scales, for example.

Rybek yanked his sword free of the stone floor. With the rain dripping over his body, he said, "Oh, what a glorious day for victory."

Nath could have sworn the evil man's ugly iron helmet was smiling. Nath pulled his wounded hand to the side. It dripped blood. It burned as if it was a torch on fire. His jaws clenched. "I'll grant you a small victory, but that's it."

Rybek swiped his sword back and forth, scattering the rainwater that was filling up the floor. "I can see the anguish in those golden eyes. The doubt. The pain. Your cocky voice trembles. You are lost, Nath Dragon."

Nath planted his feet and readied his stance. "No, I know exactly where I am." He beckoned Rybek over with the stump of his hand. "What are you waiting for? Come on, then."

Ben's heart pounded in his chest. It took everything he had in him to not rush out and try to battle alongside Dragon. Ben himself gasped for breath. The healing potion had restored him, but he wasn't getting any younger. He was beyond tired, yet his fingers were wrapped around the pommel of his sword, gripping it tight. He slid the blade a little into the scabbard and out again, snapping it in and out of place.

Click. Click. Click.

Eyeing the fight, he made himself breathe deeply and stop gasping.

If I had Akron, I'd blow Rybek away. One shot. Boom! Dragon would forgive me. Eventually.

The battle between Dragon and Rybek raged on. Rybek was a gorilla of a man with hard muscles bulging in his arms. Two handed, he swung his sword in tremendous swings meant to cut a man in half. Nath backed away. Ducked. Dodged. Parried. He climbed over the dead wurmers and fallen giants, changing the ground where the men battled.

Clever, Dragon. Clever.

Ben had never seen two men fight so hard. Rybek was a force. His sword skills were nothing short of a marvel. Tirelessly, he took it to Dragon. Every strike was powerful, determined, and precise. Even for a man his size, it seemed impossible he could keep up the pace at which he attacked. Deep creases formed in Dragon's perfect face. He'd parry one blow only to defend against another. Rybek's sword licked out like a striking snake. Its point grazed the outermost skin of Dragon's forehead.

Laylana gasped. Brenwar stirred.

Ben's heart jumped.

That was close!

He ground his teeth.

Too close!

Blood trickled over the bridge of Dragon's nose, washed away by the pouring rain that came down in sheets through the cracks above.

Rybek continued to taunt Dragon. "I'm going to take you down one piece at a time. Fingers, toes, legs. Once I'm finished, I'll feed you to the wurmers." He struck. Swords collided with jarring impact, sending anguish through Dragon's face. "You're losing precious dragon blood. You weaken. Your fall will come fast."

Dragon's grim face remained silent. Normally, he'd have something to say even in the worst of situations, but not this time. No, his eyes were fastened on Rybek's, and his face was a mask of agony and concentration.

Come on, Dragon! I know you have something up your sleeve. Use it!

Ben watched in helpless fascination. Two monumental swordsmen seemed equally matched in power, skill, and strength. Ben never thought any mortal could stand a chance in a one-on-one fight with Dragon. He was too strong. Too fast. Yet Rybek impossibly did. The warrior's iron helmet had a living glow to it. The eyelets in the helmet pulsed with a life of their own. As the sparks flew between the wondrous swords, Ben got a sense Rybek's power was not going to fade, but Dragon's was.

"Keep those elbows up, Dragon!" Ben yelled.

Brenwar looked up at Ben and snorted. Then the dwarf yelled, "Quit fooling around, Nath, and just kill him!"

Dragon kept his wounded arm pinned to his side. His broad shoulders sagged. His jaw hung open. He swatted at Rybek's strikes desperately.

Clang! Clang! Clang!

Ben clutched at his chest. Dragon continued to retreat, now at a faster rate. He moved toward the temple exit, outside, and into the pouring rain. Ben and his companions followed the battling men outside. They stood at the top of the steps watching the two fight on the bridge.

The sheets of rain pounded the fighting men, but even the pouring rain couldn't drown out the sound of colliding steel.

Rybek's voice cut through the torrent of nature, saying, "Did you come out here to drown before you die by my blade?"

Lightning flashed. Thunder clapped. The bridge shook.

Rybek pounced. Swinging his sword in windmill-like circles, he beat Dragon and Fang down in strikes coming one stronger than another.

How Dragon managed to hold onto Fang Ben did not know, but he did. Dragon was down on a knee. His arm juttered beneath every bone-jarring blow. It rang out so loud it tickled Ben's teeth.

Do something, Dragon! Do something!

Clang! Clang! Clang! Clang! Clang!

CHAPTER 7

THE HORNED GIANT'S HANDS CLOSED in.

Rerry's locked-up joints came to life. He stuck his sword in the giant's eye.

It lurched back, clutching at its face, and let out a tremendous bellow. "YOWOOOOOO!" It stood with its shoulders heaving up and down. The sword protruded from its eye. It said, "I was just going to eat you. Now I tear you apart, bit by bit!" It stomped the ground.

Rerry fell.

The giant came right at him.

A blue ball of energy streaked by Rerry's head and smote the giant in the chest with a mighty explosion.

Ka-BOOoooooooM!

The ram-horned giant teetered backward. Its arms flailed wildly at its sides. It stumbled backward, groaning and clutching at its chest … and fell.

Boom!

The giant lay on its back. Smoke rose from its expansive chest.

Rerry looked back at Samaz. "What did you do?"

Eyes no longer rolled up inside his head, Samaz dusted off his hands. "Just a spell Mother showed me. I've had it mastered for quite some time, but I've never had the chance to use it."

"You could have used it sooner!" Rerry crept closer to the giant. Standing beside its massive foot, he said, "Did you kill it?"

Samaz shrugged. "I don't think we should wait around to find out. Let's just get going."

With bright eyes, Rerry said, "Samaz, do you know what this means?"

Staring at the foul monster that lay strewn out on the creek bed, Samaz replied, "No."

"We killed a giant!"

"You mean *I* killed a giant."

"No, if I hadn't stalled it—extremely bravely, I might add—you never would have gotten around to casting that sorcery." Rerry lifted his chin. "It was a team effort we can both take the glory in, even though I did the hard part."

"Do you have any idea how hard it is to cast a spell while running through a forest? No, of course you don't. You don't have the ability in you." Samaz pulled his helmet off and dropped it on the ground. "With this ugly helmet on, no less. But it's not a competition, Rerry. We live. That's what matters, so let's get moving again."

Rerry crinkled his nose. Eyeing the body of the giant, he said, "I need a souvenir, a trophy or something."

"Don't be foolish."

Rerry bent over the giant's crusty hand. It was almost big enough to pick him up with. He spied a ring on its finger. "I'll be!" Using both hands, he wiggled it loose and tugged it off. With his back to Samaz, he held it up over his head. "Looky looky what I found. I think it's gold." He spat on it and rubbed the grit off with his sleeve. The metal twinkled in what sunlight cut through the trees. "Yes, it is gold. Hah, what do you think of that, Samaz?" He stuck his entire arm through the hoop. "Now that's a trophy we can be proud of. Right, Samaz? Right?"

The forest was oddly quiet.

Rerry turned, eyes searching for his brother.

Samaz was nearby, but he wasn't alone. He was surrounded by fully armed elves. His hands were above his head. Rerry didn't recognize any of the elves—except for one, Captain Scar. The edge of his rapier was at Samaz's throat.

Wearing the standard black tunic of the elven guard, left eye covered in a patch, the fit, brown-haired elven soldier said to Rerry, "That is a fine trophy. It will look great hanging from my wife's neck."

Rerry made a move.

More elves emerged from the woodland with bows nocked with arrows pointed at him.

Captain Scar motioned to him. "Please, toss the bauble over. Finders keepers, eh?"

"I tell you what, Scar. How about this? I keep the ring. You keep my brother."

Samaz's eyes widened.

Scar showed a cocky smile. "Why settle for one when I can have both?"

With a shrug, Rerry said, "I see your point." He rubbed the ring, shining it up a bit, caressing it with his eyes. "How about I fence you for it?"

"No."

Holding the ring in both of his hands, Rerry looked at the golden object and said, "I promise I will see you again."

Birds scattered from the trees. Many of the elven soldiers clad in black tunics trimmed in silver glanced up.

Without warning, the horned giant's hand came to life and smote one of the elves dead with a single strike. With an angry groan, it sat up, saying, "Ah! A feast of elven meat is upon me! I'll relish all of your bones!"

Every elven warrior sprang into action. Bowstrings were pulled back. Arrows were let loose.

Twang! Twang! Twang! Thwack! Thwack! Thwack!

The arrows skipped off the giant's horns. Some of them pricked its skin. Their efforts were futile. The giant brushed the missiles aside and attacked. It snatched an elf in each of its hands and snapped their spines, making a horrible sound.

The elven ranks ripped out their swords and swarmed the giant. They chopped and hacked. Their blades hacked at the giant's fingers. They climbed up its body like stinging ants and smote it in the face.

But one by one, the giant slung them off. It grabbed one elf and tossed it into the trees. It rammed its horns into two elves, grinding them into the ground.

Scar shouted out, "Take the legs! Take the legs!"

A pair of elves worked a coil of rope and entwined the giant's legs.

The giant's foot snagged. It stumbled. Its angry eyes found the rope. It snatched up the coil.

The elves hung onto the rope just long enough for the giant to dangle one of them toward its mouth. It bit into one of the elves' legs, making a loud crunching *chomp*.

The elven soldier screamed. "Aaaaaugh!"

"Enough of this!" With his blade still under Samaz's chin, Scar said, "Don't you go anywhere, because if you do, I'll track you down and kill you!"

Rerry, who had concealed himself away from the fray, saw Samaz nod. Instantly, Scar's eyes somehow found his. "And don't you try to run either, prisoner!"

With a wild look in his elven eyes, Scar charged the giant at full speed.

The giant took a swipe at him.

Scar slipped beneath the swing, jumped onto the giant's chest, locked one hand in the scruff of its facial hair, and said, "You've brought enough death! Now it ends!" He pierced the giant's chest with his rapier. The blade sank deep, right where the heart should beat.

The giant's eyes enlarged. Its great limbs drooped.

The surviving elves, two of them, chopped into the heel of the giant.

The horned monster fell like a great tree and splashed into the creek. Giant blood mixed with the waters.

Still standing on the giant's chest, Scar yanked his sword free. Without a drop of sweat in his eyes or stain on his uniform, he said, "That's how you kill a giant. No dwarf could do any better." He wiped his sword on the giant, checked its clean edge, and slid it back into his sheath.

Rerry approached from the brush. He couldn't believe Scar had killed the giant with a single strike. "You have my admiration, imprisoner or not. That was—impressive."

Hand out, Scar said, "I'll be taking the giant's ring now."

Without a word, Rerry tossed the ring to Scar. The elven fighter had earned it.

"Hands up," Scar said.

Rerry and Samaz both surrendered their hands.

Only two elves out of the small band remained alive. The rest were dead, their bodies scattered and broken. One hung in a tree, and the others were smashed into the ground. Even though Rerry wasn't a full-blooded elf, he still felt great loss. He said, "You could use our help caring for the dead. It would be our honor."

Rolling the giant's ring like a bracelet around his wrist, Scar said in a nasty tone, "If you hadn't run away, none of them would be dead, now would they?" He shook his head. "I'll think about it."

But in the wink of an eye, the giant smashed Scar between its hands so hard his helmet popped off his head.

CHAPTER 8

THE BATTLE WITH RYBEK WAS the longest sword fight Nath had ever been in. Regardless of the outcome, the unrelenting warrior had gained his respect. Rybek's mighty blows would have burst the elbows of a lesser man. The jarring impact felt as if it could shatter bone.

Where does he get his strength?

Nath deflected another devastating blow.

Clang!

And yet another.

Bang!

No one of any race but dragonkind had ever before matched Nath's speed and strength, not even when he was young. He was a dragon, with a dragon heart the size of four men's. Nath suspected Rybek possessed supernatural powers like his brother Kryzak had, probably from the sword but possibly from that helmet. He already knew Rybek's sword had magic within. He'd seen its power level the trees in the forest when they'd first clashed.

He's got to have a weakness. Find it before his sword finds your neck!

Rybek cocked back to uncoil another bone-shattering swing.

Nath rolled backward, pushed off the ground with his powerful legs, sprang high in the air, and did a back flip. He landed on his feet a dozen yards away.

"Buying time, Nath Dragon?" Rybek scraped the edge of his sword over the bridge. "I can't blame you. Your death is inevitable, for I am invincible."

"You sound too sure of yourself, Rybek." Nath gulped down some air. "You should know nothing in Nalzambor is certain. Not even death." He glanced at his missing hand. The bleeding had stopped. His hand was a stump of ebony scales, but his thumb remained. He wiped the gash on his forehead. The wound Rybek had cut open had healed up.

Thank Guzan!

Pointing his sword at Nath, Rybek said, "Stand your ground! No more dancing! It's time to finish this!" He stormed forward, feet splashing in the puddles on the bridge. "Now it ends!"

Fang pulsated in the palm of Nath's good hand. He pulled his shoulders back. His blood churned. He'd bought enough time. Saved his energy. The bleeding had stopped. The loss of his hand had frightened him. Shaken his confidence. Now the fighter within was coming back. Confident. Certain.

I am Nath Dragon. I am the Dragon Prince. I could beat this man without any hands. Well, maybe I do need one.

He set his sight on Rybek. Locked his jaw. Narrowed his golden eyes. "Dragon! Dragon!" He charged.

Rybek laughed. He lowered his sword and shoulders and rushed at Nath in giant strides. "You're a dead dragon!"

The great blades collided. Thunder clapped.

Boom!

Rybek poured it on. His eyes behind the helmet were ever intent to kill. Metal scraped against metal. The men battled back and forth with lightning-fast strokes that were the stuff of legends.

Nath parried.

Rybek counterattacked. The warrior's magical blade came dangerously close to Nath's vitals.

Nath fought back. The strength in his arm renewed. His power seemed everlasting. The weakness from the loss of blood was gone. One handed, stroke after stroke, he pressed back against Rybek's fierce attacks.

"You might have a second wind, but it will still be your last."

"Will it?" Nath brought Fang down on Rybek's awaiting blade. In an impossible move, he shifted his swing. Fang slipped by Rybek's guard and slapped the man upside his iron helmet.

Krang!

Rybek staggered backward. His head wobbled on his shoulders. He shook off the blow.

Nath hit him in the head again.

Rybek fought to parry Nath's striking edge. His parries were too slow.

Nath weaved around Rybek's defense, Fang striking like a metal snake. He skewered the man in the meat of his shoulder. He jabbed him in the thigh. He punched Rybek in the helmet again, knocking him backward.

Rybek fought back more slowly.

Nath attacked faster. "Give it up, Rybek."

Hobbled, Rybek said, "Never!" He swung.

Nath sidestepped with ease, and with the tip of his sword, he flicked Rybek's helmet off his head. The helmet sailed over the bridge and into the canyon.

"Nooooooooooooooooooooooooooooooooooooooo!" Rybek screamed. He bull rushed Nath, sword arching high. It came down like a bolt shot from the sky.

Nath's instincts saved him. He twisted out of harm's way at the last moment.

The blow would have split him in half. Instead, it dug into the bridge. The sword's magic powers were unleashed. The rock of the bridge exploded. A gaping hole formed, and the heavy stones of the bridge fell through.

Nath backpedaled away.

More of the bridge collapsed. The distance between him and Rybek expanded. The bridge cracked and buckled.

Nath yelled to Rybek, "Get away from there!"

The warrior stared down into the abyss between them then held his sword up to his head in a salute. "Remember this, Nath Dragon. You did not beat me." The bridge floor gave way right underneath the huge warrior. He plummeted through the gap into the abyss.

"Noooooo!" Nath screamed.

The bridged trembled a few moments longer before it finally stopped crumbling. Numb and one handed, Nath stood empty in the midst of the storm's pouring rain, gazing down into the gaping hole.

CHAPTER 9

SCAR WOKE UP WITH AN aching head and a burning shoulder. He was sitting on the ground with his feet bound up together at the ankles, leaning against a tree. His sword arm—not on the broken side—was tied down to his waist. The last thing he remembered was talking to Rerry, then blinding pain, followed by blackness.

"Oh ho ho, look who has awakened." It was the sprightful voice of Rerry. The part-elven swordsman stood between the shallow stream and the fallen giant. He had Scar's rapier in one hand and the giant's ring in the other. He was tossing the ring in the air and stabbing the sword in and out of the hole. Rerry looked at Scar. "This is the finest steel I've ever held. Enchanted, isn't it?"

Scar let out a muffled groan. A strip of cloth sealed his mouth shut. The cloth tasted awful. He wanted to spit but couldn't.

"Oh, you can't speak just yet," Rerry said, twirling the giant's ring on the blade of the sword with acrobatic ease. "But we'll get to that when you're ready to cooperate."

Scar's eyes beheld the other two elven soldiers from his unit. Both of them were bound up tight and sitting on the ground on the other side of the stream. It was clear they weren't going anywhere. A rustle caught his ear. Samaz emerged from the woodland bank of the stream with a dead soldier in his arms. The husky part-elf gently lowered the corpse to the ground, setting the soldier beside the others. All of the fallen elves were there. All seven of them. Scar's throat tightened. Those were his soldiers. He was responsible for their lives. Though he wasn't close to any of them and he never showed it, he cared.

Rerry squatted before him, sword over his shoulder. "It seems the giant had one last effort in it.

Squished you like a fly, it did. A last-ditch effort from the grave." He glanced at the massive humanoid. "It died after that. We overtook your soldiers. Now this is where we stand, Scar. We bury the dead. Then we talk. But we'll need the help of your two remaining soldiers to get it done quickly. My brother and I will need to move on. Without pursuit."

Rerry might have been young, but Scar knew that at the moment, Rerry had the upper hand on him. He nodded.

Removing the gag from his mouth, Rerry said, "Give me your word in Elven."

"On the leaves from the limbs of Elome, I swear it," Scar said. He spat the foul taste from his mouth. "Where did you get this cloth from?"

"It was something I found on the giant."

"Blech!" Scar spat again. "You're no swordsman. You're a trickster." He surveyed their surroundings. "How do you propose we bury them? We did not pursue you with shovels."

"No, but soldiers should always bring a spade, now shouldn't they?"

Scar frowned. Rerry was right about that, but Scar liked to move quick and light, unencumbered. "What do you know about an elven burial? You're barely an elf. Neither is your father. A family of abominations."

"I am what I was intended to be and proud of it. The human blood in me makes me all the person your elven blood makes you. And it doesn't come with all the snobbery. I like the strength and passion it lends." Rerry stood. "Besides, my father Bayzog—the most powerful mage in the world who was gifted the Elderwood Staff from Elome's council of full-blooded elves—has taught us all about the claims and customs of elven kind. The stones of these waters will make for honorable graves."

Rerry had made a good point about his father Bayzog. Still, Scar's orders came from a higher authority, and, being a good soldier, he did not question them. But for the time being, he caved in. "Agreed."

Rerry cut him loose. "Let's get to work then."

Seven graves made from thousands of stones, large and small, were stacked neatly over the fallen elven bodies. The graves lay several yards up from the stream, nestled at the top of the bank where it leveled off in a small, flat spot of wildflowers. Helmets off, the three elven soldiers stood with their heads down, eyes closed. Rerry did the same.

Samaz sang. It was an elven hymn—sad, dreary, and long, but not without hope in it.

They say the winds can speak.

They say the waters play

And trifle in the hearts who love the fallen.

Oh lands of Nalzambor, take them home from whence they came.

Oh, Rivlenray of Escalay, lead the fallen down the path of the next rising sun, and beyond.

Samaz sang verse after verse, and several minutes later, it was over.

"Well done, Samaz." Rerry thumbed a tear from the corner of his eye. "Well done." He faced Scar. "I think it's high time you told us what's going on. You imprisoned us, and we hadn't even committed a crime. What's going on, Scar?"

"I don't answer to you," Scar replied. His shoulders drooped. He shifted his wounded arm in his sling and grimaced. "I answer to my superiors. I follow orders."

Standing taller than Scar, Rerry said, "Even when they have broken away from protocol? No justice. No representatives. Surely in your heart you had to question that."

"Don't pretend to bluff me, child."

"I'm no child. And what do you mean by bluff? What do I have to bluff about?"

Fingering the white scar on his chin, Scar replied, "You can't be that stupid."

Rerry looked at Samaz and found Samaz looking at him with an expression just as perplexed as he must have been making. He opened his hands up and said, "What in Nalzambor are you talking about?"

"Laedorn of the High Council is dead. Assassinated, months ago. Nath Dragon is the killer! All who have ever been connected with him are to be captured and detained."

"Are you mad?" Rerry said, rising up on his toes. His cheeks warmed.

Even Samaz's jaw dropped. "Nath Dragon didn't kill anybody! Least of all Laedorn. Only a madman would accuse him of something as ridiculous as that!"

"There were witnesses," Scar fired back, neck straining. "Dozens. He shot him with the bow the elves gave him, Akron. And that's not all. He's accused of killing Uurluuk Mountainstone of the Dwarves as well. Two entire races are hunting for him. You should consider yourselves lucky the elves found you before the dwarves did. They'd put you in the belly of a mountain so deep the world would forget about you."

Rerry shrank away. Scar seemed convinced whatever he was told truly had happened. Holding his head, he said, "What is going on? This truly is madness. Samaz?"

Expressionless, his brother shrugged.

"We have not seen Nath Dragon since the end of the war, Scar." Rerry poked the soldier in the chest. "You need to leave us be."

"Then what are you running from?" Scar said.

"Running? We're not running from anything. We seek a cure for our mother, Sasha. She has fallen under the power of the wizard's dementia. It's our quest to find a cure."

Scar's taciturn face softened. "I've heard that's a terrible thing. The elven council will have her brought in too. The same goes for your father. Any allies of Nath Dragon are considered with suspicion."

"Nath has hundreds of allies, if not thousands," Rerry argued. "Are they going to bring them all in?"

"Just those closest to him. You'd be wise to surrender and wait until this all clears up, or…"

"Or what?"

"Or until Nath Dragon is dead."

CHAPTER 10

"THAT WAS SOME FIGHT," BEN said, hours later. The storm had passed and the entire party had moved on from the Temple of Spires. They were all back on the woodland path that had brought them there to begin with. Boots covered in mud, they trudged on.

Chin up, Nath said, "It was, wasn't it?"

Brenwar glanced at his hand and said, "Costly. Mmmm, I've never seen a man fight like that. Not on his own merit. Rybek cheated." He scratched his beard with his skeleton hand. "Evil's never truthful. I think he would have lied to you anyway if you beat him."

"I did beat him," Nath said to Brenwar. "You don't think I won?"

"He was more intact than you when I last saw him," the dwarf said.

"Don't listen to him, Nath," Ben said. The older warrior hobbled along, using a stick for a cane. "You had him. I saw it with my own eyes. I've never seen a sword move so fast. I just wish when you flicked his helmet off, his head was with it."

"Well, he's gone now." Nath shook his head. "And the whereabouts of my father with him."

"I'm sure we'll be able to find your father, Nath," Sasha said to him. Her pretty, bright eyes had a sparkle in them.

Bayzog walked with the aid of his staff in one hand and the fingers of the other locked with hers. With most of his black hair now gray from the battle with the phantom, he looked as old as her. "There's always more than one way to accomplish anything. You'll find him."

"With friends like you, no doubt I will," he said. Sasha's face became sympathetic and distant. "What?"

In a raspy voice, Bayzog said, "Our sons, Nath. They search for a cure for Sasha. We need to find them. Given the nature of what I've seen and heard, these times are perilous. We must go to them."

"Aye," Brenwar agreed. "You aren't getting any younger. The dirt you tread on has more youth to it than you do."

Violet eyes still filled with endless strength, Bayzog replied, "Well, at least it's not smarter."

"What? Why you rigid little elven trickster. I'm as smart as any elf, particularly in all things dwarven."

"That hardly matters in the grand scheme of things," Bayzog replied.

As everyone bickered back and forth, Nath's thoughts went elsewhere. To his father's whereabouts, and to Selene. It seemed like forever since he'd seen her, and he had no idea about her condition. She'd fallen into a slumber, and there was no telling when she might awaken. And if could happen to her, then it could happen to him. Again.

Nath thumbed the stump of his missing hand.

I want my hand back, but I can't let it happen at such a critical time. I have to find . . . I have to help Father.

He turned his attention back to his friends. "I don't think the two of you are equipped to go it alone. With all the wurmers and giants scouring the countryside, it's too big a risk. We should stay together."

Sasha walked over to him, rested her forearms on his shoulders, looked deep into his eyes, and said, "When you have children one day, you'll understand. My sons lost me once, but now they need to know I'm back again." She kissed his cheek. "I have faith in you, Nath. I always have. And I'm oh so grateful to your father for lifting the curse from me. I think I'm doing right by him in going after my sons. Family. It's the most important thing of all."

"I know." He clasped her hands and watched her and Bayzog go. All the wizard did was wave.

"Dragon." Ben the durable warrior stood beside him now. "I'll go with them."

"Ben, you can hardly walk."

Ben opened up his hands, revealing several clear but colorful potion vials. With a devilish grin, he said, "I'll make it." He squeezed Nath's shoulder. "Margo, Tristin, and Justine will kill me if I don't."

Brenwar pushed the chest over to Ben with his boot. "Take this."

"No, I couldn't."

"You'll need it," Brenwar argued.

"Perhaps, perhaps not." Ben's eyes were wide on the chest full of magic. "I'm certain you'll need it as much as we will."

"Nath?" Brenwar said with a perched brow. "Help him make a decision."

Rubbing his chin, Nath gave it more thought. His father had given the chest to Brenwar to help them. But it was to give aid to anyone, not just them. He opened it up and removed several items. He gathered them up into a small sack hidden within his clothes. "There, we have something, that's better than nothing." He closed the lid and handed the chest to Ben. "You and those sorcerers need to make the most of it. And take the horses too."

Ben smiled, then burped a puff of smoke. "Sultans of Sulfur! Did you see that?"

"Yeah, I did. Don't overdo it on the fire-breath potions," Nath said. "They stick with you."

"Will do, Dragon," Ben moved on, horses in tow, after Bayzog and Sasha, who had veered down a steep split in the path. It left Nath, Brenwar, and Laylana with only one another's company.

The dark-haired, green-eyed elven woman dressed in the leather garb of an elven warrior said to him, "If you like, I'll go with them, too."

"You would?"

"Yes. As much as I've enjoyed your company, I find my questions have been answered. You're a good man—dragon—Nath. It's been nothing short of an honor to fight by your side." She gave him a warm embrace and a kiss on the cheek. "I know you were a true friend of my grandfather Laedorn, and that like your eyes, you have a heart of gold. But now my instincts beckon me to return home. And it wouldn't surprise me in the slightest if the elves were still in pursuit of you, Nath. They won't rest until Laedorn's slayer is found. It's best I get some sense of what's going on. There must be clues to who did this. You don't need any other distractions while you look for your father. The world's dangerous enough as it is."

Nath wrapped her up in his arms and lifted her off her feet. He liked Laylana very much and found it difficult to let go. "I'll miss you. Be well." He let her slip out of his arms.

Arms still draped around his neck, her eyes held his with a deeper passion. Slowly, she looked away. "Farewell, Nath." She waved. "Farewell, Brenwar."

With a grunt, Brenwar said, "Uh, goodbye, elf lady."

Moving with the grace of a swan and the strength of a lion in her strides, Laylana vanished down the path the others had taken.

"I guess it's just the two of us versus the world again," Brenwar said.

Nath looked at his missing hand. "What's left of us, anyway."

"Har!" Brenwar showed a fierce smile. "By the time it's over, nothing will be left of us but my beard and those flaming locks of yours."

Nath lowered his satchel over his shoulder. "True, but you know what?"

"What?"

"We're still going to win."

"Now you're talking like a dwarf."

CHAPTER 11

ATH AND BRENWAR MOVED NORTH at a brisk pace.

"I don't think your father should be hard to find."

"Why do you say that?"

"He's too big to hide. Someone or something will have seen him." Brenwar grumbled, "Besides, Balzurth would never get himself into a situation he couldn't handle."

"No, but he's not himself. Not since he cured Sasha. I saw darkness in his eyes when it happened."

"Your father will be fine." Brenwar stroked his beard. "I'm certain of it."

"Of course you are," Nath replied.

There wasn't much else for him to say. Part of him didn't want to help—not because he didn't love his father. He did. But in the back of his mind, Nath kept thinking maybe he should be working on something else. For one thing, he needed to find out who Laedorn and Uurluuk's assassin was. Every elf and dwarf, aside from his friends, thought it was him. There were the titans to worry about, too. He needed to stop them. They and the giants had taken over every town they had passed. The world was a disaster. Evil had it by the throat again.

"Brenwar, what do you think I should do? I'm not even sure I should be looking for him at the moment. You said it yourself: he knows what he's doing. But … I don't fully believe that in this case."

"We'll find him. Besides, wherever he is, we'll find the heart of the trouble. You're kind of like him in that manner." A pair of deer bounded through the woods right in front of them and vanished into the brush. "See, a good sign."

"Deer crossing one's path is not a good sign. It's just deer crossing a path." Nath took his scabbard filled with Fang from his back and lay it on the ground. He sat down.

Brenwar came to a stop and looked down at him. The dwarf had plenty of recent scuffs and scars to show for himself. A gash in his leg. New dents peppering his breastplate. A wurmer's claw marks in the leather of his tunic arms. "What are you doing on your backside? We need to go."

"Go where?"

Shaking his war hammer, the dwarf said, "To the heart of the fight!"

Nath huffed. "That's a fine idea, except we don't know where the heart of the fight is." He grabbed a pine cone and slung it hard into the woods. "It's hard to fight an enemy we can't find."

"What are you talking about? They're giants. Huge! They aren't hiding. They're out in the wide open. We're the best trackers in the world. How can we not find them?"

"I'm not as much of a tracker as I used to be. Guzan!" Nath held up his missing hand." What am I supposed to do with half of my hand missing? The enemy gets stronger. I get whittled away a hunk at a time."

"You'll get used to it." Brenwar scratched his nose with his skeleton fingers. "Besides, you should be tired of looking like you've never been in a fight before. Heavy scars put the fear in people."

"I know." With a stick, Nath stirred patterns in the ground. His thoughts were heavy. Something inside of him just didn't feel right. "Brenwar, do you ever feel like sometimes I go about things the wrong way?"

"Like how?"

"Well, like fighting. I feel like maybe I'm always doing it the hard way."

"Fighting's not supposed to be easy." Brenwar huffed. "If it was easy, it wouldn't be any fun."

"I just feel like I'm working harder and not smarter. I mean, is the fate of the world only up to a few of us? Shouldn't we have more help? We can't count on the elves and dwarves, because they're hunting us. Leaves us with the humans and halflings. Maybe some gnomes."

"Har!"

"Why just us? There has to be a smarter way to go about things. I like to fight. I love to fight. Not only do I want to fight harder than ever before, but I feel like I need to fight smarter as well. What am I doing wrong?"

Eyeing Mortuun, Brenwar spun the great hammer in his hands. "I've been fighting and feuding in one way or another for hundreds of years, Nath. I've never fought with anybody like you. You have instincts only a few who ever lived had. Trust your instincts. What do they tell you?"

Nath brushed his hair from his eyes. "They tell me I need more help than you and me." He looked at what was left of his missing hand. "Clearly."

"If you need help, then ask for it."

"I can't drag Bayzog and Ben back into this. Did you see them? They looked like a bull dragon chewed them up and spat them out. No, I've asked plenty from them. I've asked plenty from you. I'm tired of seeing my friends hurt."

"You can't protect them always, Nath. They're in this fight too. But they aren't the only friends you have. And you have family, too." Brenwar took a quick look up into the sky. "Lots of family."

Nath lifted his chin. Puffy white clouds with gray at the bottom drifted through the rich blue sky. Flocks of birds crossed his line of sight and disappeared into the great beyond.

I sure miss flying.

"Are you saying I should call for the dragons?"

"No, I was thinking you should call out for the dwarves." Brenwar puffed his moustache out. "Of course I mean the dragons!"

Nath eyed him.

The dwarf's chin dipped. "Sorry, Your Highness."

"It's fine. Any other suggestions?"

"Maybe Fang has some answers. He's a friend as well, is he not?"

Nath ran his fingers over the finely crafted scabbard. The leather over the wood was weathered and soft. He partially drew the weapon. The dragon-headed crossguards were exquisite. Each of the dragon's eyes had perfect little gemstones in them, ruby and emerald. There was a living sparkle on both of them. Only recently had Nath been able to figure out how to call upon the sword's abilities. He'd summoned vibrations, fire, ice, and even teleported Nath forward in time. Sometimes Fang even did as Nath asked, but most of the time he still didn't.

Sword crossed over his lap, Nath held the handle firmly. "What other mysterious powers do you think Fang has?"

Combing his skeleton fingers through his beard, Brenwar suggested, "Why don't you ask him?"

If any friend of Nath's had been neglected, it was Fang. His sword had bailed him out as much as anybody. He slid the magnificent blade all the way from its sheath. The brilliant steel showed like silver. He could see the sky above in the metal. Nath felt a little guilty. Perhaps he should have taken more time getting to know Fang. Training, talking, or something. He said to the blade, "Fang, I'm sorry for any neglect, and I hope you'll forgive me, friend." He gave Brenwar a quick glance and continued. "Fang, will you help me find Father?"

CHAPTER 12

SELENE'S EYES CRACKED OPEN. SHE was in a glorious domed room with wondrous murals of dragons and the lands of Nalzambor filling the walls. Every scene looked real, as if she were standing right there. Stiff limbed, she rolled off the bed of satin pillows in which she lay. She swung her feet onto the floor. The bed was so soft and deep she could barely get out of it.

Where am I?

It was a question she asked herself, but she was certain she knew the answer. She was in Dragon Home—or, to its enemies, the Mountain of Doom. The dizzying display of surrounding artistry left her head a little woozy.

How did I get here?

The last thing she remembered was fighting alongside Nath. For some reason, it felt like a dream or something that had happened ages ago. She pushed herself up to her feet and traversed the mosaic floor. Each tiny tile was painted a different color, but overall it looked like a meadow filled with splendorous wildflowers in a multitude of colors. A breeze came from somewhere, and a gentle melody of music hummed in her ears. The environment was comfortable and soothing. It was clear she had been well cared for. But what had happened? She rubbed her head.

Perhaps something smote me from behind. I must have been blindsided, but I feel fine.

She moved about the room, violet eyes straining to see where the exit might be. It only made sense that whoever had brought her to the chamber would not know of her awakening. Certainly someone would check on her at some point, but she didn't want to wait. She moved toward the nearest painting on heavy feet. Her limbs seemed more cumbersome than normal. She stretched her back and rolled her shoulders.

I feel like I gained two hundred pounds.

She stood in front of one of the murals with her arms outstretched but not touching the wall. It was a painted green forest, with tall trees and a path splitting the middle, leading to a mountain range she recognized from the northeastern part of Nalzambor. She couldn't see one single flaw in the painting. It appeared as real as if it were a window.

Whatever creature painted this is a marvel.

A little uncertain if the mural was real or not, she leaned forward to touch the wall with her fingertip.

It can't be real. Selene, something's missing.

Her breath quickened.

She touched the surface and let out a sigh. She felt the stone under the paint. "Ah, that's better. For a moment I thought I was going to have to pinch myself." Marveling at the extraordinary painting, she continued to run her hands over the surface of painted trees, leaves, and even the dirt path. But something in the scene wasn't right or was missing.

Her gut twisted.

What is out of place here?

She ran her black-scaled fingers over the smooth stone once more. The golden claw of her index finger pecked on the face of a brown squirrel nestled in the branches of one of the trees. It winked at her. Her brow furrowed.

"What in Nalzambor is going..." Her voice trailed out.

Her eyes became big as saucers, fixed on her scaly fingers.

She rotated her palm back and forth.

Her jaw hung.

She lifted her arms and gazed.

Coal-black scales covered her from her fingertips to her elbows and beyond. "Great Guzan!"

She'd transformed, like Nath had. Her arms were sleek and marvelous. There was power in them too. She brought her tail around and draped it over her shoulder. She stroked it with a caressing hand and smiled. "I'm glad you remain. I wonder what else has changed." Her fingers found her face, touching around the eyes, cheeks, and chin. The soft flesh of a human was underneath, but she still wasn't sure. She lifted up her lavender-and-white lace gown, revealing her legs. They had scales on them. Even her abdomen did. Not all over, but mostly. She jumped up. Her feet propelled her so high her head almost hit the sky-painted ceiling.

"Oh, Nalzambor, is this right? Have I become a dragon again?" She tossed her head from side to side. Her jet-black hair was still there. "I need a mirror." She searched the room, but there were only the bed and the murals. On the floor she noted a pond of clear water. It looked so real she swore she would be able to see her reflection in it, but that was impossible. It was just a mosaic. On a hunch, she took a knee and gazed. Her reflection appeared on the surface of the water. She gasped, "Huh!"

Her face was what it had always been as a human. Her high cheeks and pale skin contrasted well with her maroon lips. She was filled with relief—and disappointment. This was nothing quite like having the full power of a dragon, but at least she had more scales—and they were exquisite.

She caught another image appearing behind her in the reflection. She twisted around and gasped. It was Grahleyna, Nath's mother. She was beautiful on beautiful, and in the form of a woman. But scales, gold and white with hints of red, adorned her limbs where they weren't covered in silky robes, like jewelry.

"How do you feel, Selene?"

"Grahleyna," she answered, taking a bow. "I-I don't know exactly. Why am I here?"

Brushing the honey locks of wavy hair aside from her shoulder, Nath's mother replied, "You fell into a dragon's slumber quite some time ago. Do you feel rested?"

"Dragon slumber?" Selene took a seat on the bed and put her face in her hands. "How long have I been asleep? Please don't tell me the world has turned upside down again." She recalled moving forward in time on account of Fang's transportation, and she was aware of the many long slumbers Nath had fallen into in his lifetime. Looking up at the dragon queen, she said, "Please don't say a century, please."

Grahleyna let out a delightful laugh and sat down beside Selene. "No, nothing like that. Weeks, I believe. Months, perhaps. Barely a nap."

Selene let out a sigh. "So, what happened? Why am I here?"

"Nath had Sansla Libor bring you here for your protection. He went through an awful lot to have you rescued."

"Rescued?"

"From the nuurg, a strange sort of giant breed which now plagues the lands." Grahleyna studied her gold fingernails, which Selene now saw were peppered with flecks as white as snow. Nothing was out of place with the dragon queen. She was perfect. "They've run amok, the giants have. How do you like your new scales?"

"So I was kidnapped? Where?"

"Oh, you'll have to have Sansla explain to you. I've been rather busy in the absence of Balzurth. The males of our kind," Grahleyna nudged Selene's shoulder with her shoulder. "They're drawn to danger, and nothing makes them more happy—or miserable—than carrying the world on their shoulders."

"So where is Nath?" Selene asked with a frown. She was concerned about the answer.

"I can't say, Selene. He, like his father, could be anywhere. No doubt they are trying to take down Eckubahn before Eckubahn takes down them." Grahleyna took Selene by the hand and squeezed it. "I'm worried about both of them. Right now, it's taking everything I have to stay here and keep Dragon Home safe. Our kind are restless without Balzurth in his home. And as much as I hate to admit it, they don't mind me the same as they mind him." Her beautiful face, which had a dragon-like quality about it, frowned. "And I feel there is something very, very wrong."

Selene patted Grahleyna's hand. "I can help, can't I?"

With a nod, the dragon queen said, "You couldn't have woken up at a better time. Come." Grahleyna led her to a mural shaped like a stone tunnel going into a mountain. They passed right through the opening and walked up a spiraling walkway illuminated by the torches painted on the cavern walls. They walked for miles, maybe leagues, until they arrived at the top of Dragon Home. A stiff wind tore through both women's long locks as they stood just beneath the clouds.

"It's quite a view, isn't it?"

The top of Dragon Home was the highest point in all of Nalzambor. The view was crystal clear, and whether it was from her own power or something radiating from the rock on which she stood, Selene could see for miles, leagues even. Her eyes were more open then they'd ever been before.

Grahleyna pointed north. "What do you see?"

Over a league away were giants by the hundreds. With huge axes, they chopped down trees. There was fire. Great fires in the middle of a camp made up of the giants. Huge rocks made for the bellowing of forges and furnaces. There, they made tremendous weapons of iron and steel. And there were men, like toddlers among them, following their every command. Giants by the hundreds, orcs and men by the thousands. In the distant hilltops she could see more were coming. An army building like Selene had never seen.

"What are they doing?" she asked.

"They are preparing for an invasion," Grahleyna replied.

"Where?"

"Here."

Chapter 13

Brenwar's head cocked from side to side like an old hawk's. "Well, is Fang coming to our aid or not?"

Nath shrugged. He'd run through an entire list of commands with Fang. He'd barked out orders, and then he'd asked politely.

"Fang, take me to Balzurth."

"Fang, please take me to Balzurth."

Nath tried many other phrases.

"Fang, bring fire. Summon rain. Lightning. Ice!"

Holding the sword over his head, he said, "By the power of Balzurth!"

The blade did not charge up in his hand. Its metal and pommel remained lukewarm to his commands and promptings.

Leaning on his hammer, Brenwar said, "You know, when I command the thunder of Mortuun, I never have any trouble." He patted the war hammer's fat head. "He does exactly as I say."

Nath held his great blade in his arms and flipped it around. "Well, I guess those powers only unleash when they are needed. Truly needed. In the meantime, Fang is still the finest sword ever made." He flashed a smile. "And you know what, he's always been there for me whenever I've really needed him. Maybe he doesn't turn it loose until the danger is truly imminent. Perhaps he's wiser than I and preserves his power."

"Perhaps." Brenwar hefted Mortuun over both of his shoulders and rested his hands on the ends. "Can we start walking now? All of this standing around feels a little silly. We need to move, whether it's an inch or a mile. That's progress."

"I suppose so." Nath took the lead. "North it is, then. We'll just have to do what we normally do and find more clues along the way."

"Aye. That's the way I like it."

They walked for the better part of the day. Storm clouds rumbled overhead. Light drops of rain splatted off Nath's scales. He carried Fang in his arms like a small child, talking to the blade from time to time, trying to connect. Fang was like a brother in some ways. Not a servant but family. His father had often said, "Take care of the little things, and then you can be trusted with true riches." Perhaps Nath hadn't cared for the blade as he should.

"We are nearing some towns. We might need to get some supplies and horses," Brenwar said. "What do you say?"

"One horse should do. I don't mind running." He took out a cloth he had and started rubbing it over the blade. "I don't know if this feels good or not, Fang, but I hope you like it. I never saw the need to clean a blade which always shines and never nicks, but that's no reason not to give you the care any other fine sword would get."

Brenwar held Mortuun out before himself and said to it, "You like the dirt, don't you. Heh-heh." He head butted the flat of his hammer. "I like the dirt, and busted-up orcs and giants, too."

A couple of miles later, they crested a hill and surveyed the town resting on a flat plain between the steep hillsides. Night was falling on the small wood-framed homes and stone buildings. Men and women were finishing up their day and gathering the children inside. Firelight could be seen through the windows.

On one knee, Brenwar said, "I can't help but be suspicious." He took a deep draw through his nose. "Should I go, or should you go?"

Nath gave a little shrug. He never would have had the slightest trepidation going into any town of any kind before. That had changed. Now, he couldn't go anywhere without some sort of suspicion. He had enemies of all sorts, and no one could be trusted. It was a sad time. A dark time. "Probably not the best time to go in there. Not in the dark of night. We could wait it out until morning… or just keep moving."

"Eh, I'm fine walking. I wouldn't mind a bite to eat though. Can't remember the last time I ate as a matter of fact." Brenwar pounded his armor over his stomach. "It's hard to admit that."

"You must be hungry then. I've never heard you mention it before."

"All the fighting works up the ol' dwarven appetite. I miss the feasts that used to come at the end of the battle." Brenwar peeled a piece of bark from a tree and chewed on the end. "Not bad. Could use some salt and pepper."

Nath couldn't help but chuckle. "You'd eat dirt if it would fill you."

"I'll have plenty of dirt to eat in the grave."

"Brenwar, I'm pretty sure I can rustle up some game. We can cook it on an open fire. We're pretty far away, so I don't think anyone will take notice." He tipped his chin at the town down in the valley. "Or I can scurry down there and get some eggs from the chickens. Just like a weasel. It'd be stealing, but we are pretty hungry."

"Dwarves don't steal. Dragons shouldn't either."

"True, but I could leave some coin. More than enough."

Brenwar's dark eyes were fixed on the village. His lips twitched. With an eyebrow perched, he said, "Nath, I'm tired of hiding. Let's just go down there and ask. They can't all be bad." He sniffed. "Besides, something good is cooking."

Nath got up on his feet, patted his belly, and said with a smile, "Well, I have to admit, I like your direct approach. Let's follow your nose."

Brenwar led. He ambled down the hill right into the very heart of the small town. No more than a couple hundred people could have lived there. The barns were small and the livestock few. Smoke puffed out several of the small chimneys, and the smell of baked bread and hot stew lingered in the air.

Nath's mouth watered. He didn't admit it, but he was just as hungry as Brenwar. He wasn't going to mention it. He still couldn't believe Brenwar had.

He had better not be going soft on me.

Many of the small, gabled houses had empty porch fronts, aside from one, where three men were standing outside, talking and smoking their pipes. The talking came to a stop as soon as Nath and Brenwar crossed their line of sight. Nath's keen ears picked up one man's whisper to another, "Fetch the magistrate."

A lanky figure scurried across the street and vanished into the shadows. It left the remaining two men on the porch all alone to face Nath and Brenwar.

"Let me do the talking," Nath said softly to Brenwar.

"Aye."

CHAPTER 14

Rerry and Samaz were faced with a difficult decision. What to do with Scar and his men? The choice was simple: knock them out and leave them or bring them along. Bringing them along would only slow their pace. Letting them go would bring more elves in pursuit. It was a no-win situation, but in the end, Rerry and Samaz took the elves as their captives.

Once his hands and his soldiers' hands were secured behind their backs, Scar said, "You two don't know what you're doing, do you. Have you even taken anyone prisoner before? I venture to say no."

"Just because you haven't done something before doesn't mean you aren't any good at it." Rerry kept Scar's own sword lowered on the elf's back. "Just keep walking and stop talking."

"It might help if you mentioned where we were going," Scar fired back. "And remember, you're going to need to feed us."

"Feed you!" Rerry said. "You left us to starve to death in that dungeon back there."

"Orders are orders."

"I've got an order for you." Rerry sliced the rapier through a branch, cutting the limb clean. "Mind your tongue or lose it."

Scar started laughing. "You're a child. You wouldn't hurt anybody."

Rerry lifted his arm to strike the elf in the back of the head.

"Rerry!" Samaz said.

"What?"

"Are you planning on dragging him through the woods? Leave him be. He's just trying to be annoying." Samaz had the other two elven soldiers at sword point.

"He doesn't have to try," Rerry replied. "He just is."

Scar let out another chuckle. His voice wasn't as elegant as those of most elves. He was gruff. "Fine, boys. I'll cooperate. But it wouldn't hurt to mention where we're going." He eyed the sky. "South is good. South is Elome in the furthest, but I can't imagine why you'd be going there."

"It's not your concern where we're going." Rerry shoved the soldier forward.

Scar stumbled onto a knee. Slowly, he got back up again.

A pair of hummingbirds with bright green feathers zipped by Rerry's face and into the trees. "That was strange."

"That's a bad sign," Scar said.

"You're a bad sign." Rerry shoved the man in the back again. "And quit buying time by falling down. You're an elf. Elves don't trip, especially not in the woods. A deer would trip before we did."

"As you say." Scar moved on, head down, stepping up his pace.

Rerry didn't mind the faster pace. Behind him, Samaz and the other soldiers weren't having any trouble keeping up. They weaved their way through the forest, dodging the trees and ducking the branches. In all truth, Rerry wasn't entirely sure what he was doing. He wasn't equipped to handle this situation. It was encumbering. Beyond encumbering.

What have I gotten us into?

He got a closer look at Scar's backside. The man's hands were tied behind his back with elven twine. The soldier's palms were showing swordsman's callouses thicker than Rerry's. He felt his own. His callouses were small bumps by comparison. Scar's hands were rough as cowhide, his muscles thick in the arms and shoulders, a bit more so than a typical elf's. Scar moved with purpose and determination, but there was still the graceful ease of a fencer in his step. Rerry couldn't help but feel he wasn't in control. Scar still was, somehow.

I need to be careful. An enemy never shows his true intent until it's too late.

They made it a few more miles, but then as they crossed through a thicket-filled gulch, the briars jabbed into their knees.

Scar spoke up again. "You know, it would be best if you remembered the farther south we go, the more likely it is we'll run into elves. If they come upon us as your prisoners, it won't go well for you." Scar's neck craned. His eyes were fixed in the trees. "It'll be too late once you run into them. It's best you turn yourselves over. As a matter of fact, I'll even take you to Elome rather than back to the dungeon." He walked around a low-hanging branch and turned around so he was walking backward, facing them. "I'll be truthful. You'll get better treatment there in Elome than you did back in the hole where I had you."

"I'll be making the decisions, thank you."

Scar stopped, shaking his head slowly from side to side. "Boy, you don't know what you're doing."

"Keep moving." Rerry still had the rapier out, keeping Scar an arm and sword length away. Something crawled up his spine. He kept his eyes fixed on the elf. "I'm not playing games with you, Scar. Move."

"You aren't going to harm me. You aren't going to harm my soldiers, either. You're incapable." Scar pursed his lips and let out a sharp whistle.

The two elven soldiers exploded into motion. Hands still tied behind their backs, they hopped up, bringing their knees to their chests and slipping their hands under their feet so that they were in front of them. Heads low, they bolted into the woods.

"Samaz!" Rerry's head twisted back and forth between his brother and Scar. "Go after them!"

Samaz gave chase, but it was clear to Rerry his brother would never catch the leaner and quicker elves. Samaz wasn't slow for a man, but he was for an elf.

"Ha ha ha!" Scar belted out a wicked laugh. "You'll never catch them. At least not your brother. They're gone. Long gone. It's only a matter of time before they bring more after you, foolish boys."

"Well, we still have you." Rerry's confident voice was now shaken.

"You don't sound so sure of yourself, Rerry." Scar walked right up to him and stared him in the eye with the sword right on his chest. "Make me march somewhere now, child."

"Don't tempt me, Scar. I might not kill you, but I won't hesitate to maim you if you try to escape."

Brows high, Scar said, "Really? Like your brother did? Do it."

Rerry swallowed. Sweat rolled from his hairline into his eyes. The salty sweat stung. He blinked.

Scar struck. A leg sweep took Rerry from his feet and landed him flat on the ground. Before he could bounce back up, Scar's boot collided with his ribs—once, twice, three times.

He curled up and groaned.

That did not just happen!

Rerry sat up just in time to see Scar standing a bit away under a tree with his rapier back in his hand. How Scar had slipped his bonds Rerry would never know.

With a grunt, the rugged elven soldier banged his shoulder into the tree, making a nasty *pop*. Pain filled his eyes, but it was quickly replaced with victory. "My shoulder was out of joint, not broken. Your bindings were weak. Your mind is as slow as a human's." Scar walked up and lorded over Rerry with his rapier. "Tell me, Rerry, who's in command now?"

CHAPTER 15

A MAN STEPPED OFF THE PORCH with a curled wooden pipe in his hand. He was a rangy fellow, tall, with the broad shoulders of a farmer or a smith. He gave Nath a double take, looking up a little in his eyes and stepped back on the porch, meeting him at eye level again.

"Good evening, travelers." Broad faced and fish eyed, he broke out in a sweat. "Pardon my directness, but what do you seek?"

"I apologize for the late intrusion, but we only seek to purchase some food and maybe a horse, and we'll be on our way." Nath smiled. "It certainly wasn't our intention to cause a stir, and we hope we don't."

The rocking chair groaned as the other man on the porch shrank back in his seat. His fingers fidgeted with the chair's arms, and he kept looking up at his friend and Nath's sword.

The man with the pipe then said, "We don't have much means these days." He let out a stream of smoke and sucked on the end of his pipe. "It's hard enough to feed ourselves. The crops aren't what they used to be." Sweat dripped down the side of the man's cheek. "And truly, as much as we'd like to help out, we have a standard here where we take care of our own."

Brenwar shifted on his feet. His mouth opened and shut twice before he finally spoke. "You're telling me you can't use any coin? Coin can buy you more food. Our offer will be generous."

Looking down at Brenwar, the man said, "We can't spare it."

Brenwar stiffened. His fists balled up.

Nath wedged himself between the dwarf and the man with a polite nod. "We'll be moving on then."

With an air about him, the man said, "I think that's for the better. As you say, you don't want to create a stir. And folks are pretty jumpy around here." He let out another stream of smoke. "We bid you safe travels." He pointed at a pair of buildings, the rising moon visible between the two and added, "That avenue makes for the most discreet exit."

Nath nodded, and with Brenwar at his side, headed down the alley.

"People aren't very friendly these days," Brenwar said under his breath.

"Or honest either," Nath replied. "They do have food to spare, and I've never seen small places like this turn away anyone in need. Something's going on."

"We, I might be hungry enough to eat a four-tusked boar, but I'll live."

"Me too." Nath took a look over his shoulder. The men from the porch had gathered around another figure who was little different than the rest of them—aside from a broadsword hung from his hip. He assumed it was the magistrate they'd sent for. All of their eyes followed him and Brenwar as the men argued in hushed voices. "It seems we caused a stir after all, didn't we."

"Aye."

He and Brenwar passed between the buildings into where the open fields awaited. Nath pulled Brenwar aside, and the pair of them paused with their backs to one of the buildings. Under his breath, Nath said, "Let's give it a moment and see what happens."

Brenwar nodded.

Nath had a couple of concerns. As harmless as the simpler people of the country could often be, it didn't always take much for them to get riled up and do something stupid. Second, given the nature of Nath's enemies, there was no telling whether or not his enemies were among them. It wouldn't surprise him a bit of a giant, a nuurg, or a flock of wurmers exploded out of one of the storehouses at any moment. It wouldn't be the first time.

A drizzling rain began, dulling the sounds around them. Head tilted, Nath tried to make out what the men were saying. It wasn't easy, given the vast distance between them and their use of lowered voices, but he could tell they were still arguing. It must have gone on for at least ten minutes before it came to a stop. There were some murmurings and the scrape of boots on the wooden porch and the faint creaking sound of a door opening and closing.

Nath peeked around the corner. The men on the porch were gone.

"Seems they've had enough excitement for one night," Nath said under his breath. He eased away from the wall. "No eggs and biscuits tonight. I guess we're going to have to head back to the woods and rustle up some possum."

Shoulders slumped, Brenwar started his trek back into the woods. "Eating from a table is soft, anyway."

A scuffle of dirt caught Nath's ear. He grabbed Brenwar by the elbow and pulled him back into the shadows.

Someone on light feet was making his way down the alley. A man emerged from the alley and into the open plain. His eyes were forward, scanning the outline of the forest. He wore a cloak over his shoulders and held a broadsword at the ready. He moved well, with the technical craft of a seasoned soldier. He turned from side to side. Something dangled from his neck. It was metal, a whistle or something.

That must be the magistrate.

Staying low, ready to spring, the magistrate started toward the forest on soft feet.

Out of nowhere, Brenwar's stomach rumbled like rolling thunder.

The magistrate whipped around. His eyes locked on Nath and Brenwar. He grabbed the whistle and put it to his mouth.

CHAPTER 16

RERRY, GET UP!

But Scar said, "Stay put, fledgling."

Rerry rested back on his elbows. "I underestimated you."

"Oh, that's an understatement." Scar tossed the elven rope to Rerry. "Now we get to see how well you fare on an ever-so-long march back to Elome. No food. No water. Just one long stiff march with a needle at your back."

Rerry's chin fell to his chest. After all that hard work, he was right back where he'd started. A captive. A failure. He wanted to scream. He picked up the rope and said, "So what do you want me to do, bind myself?"

"No, save it for when your brother returns at the hands of my men. They'll have him wrapped up in no time, I'm certain." Scar admired his sword. "It really is a fine piece of weaponry, and yes, it is enchanted. All of the captains of the guard receive blessed weapons when they survive the test and make the rank. I even helped to forge it myself. Me, the smith, and a pair of lovely elven enchantresses." His fingers caressed the blade's edge. "I don't think I could live with myself if I ever lost it. And the thought of your kind even touching it makes me want to wash it." His face soured.

"What is your problem with me? I may not be a full-bred elf, but you act like I'm an orc!"

Without looking at Rerry, Scar cut the blade through the air a few times. "You might be."

Rerry's lips tightened. He glared at Scar. The elves were possibly the most sophisticated race in Nalzambor, but their snobbery was often overbearing. He and Samaz hadn't done anything wrong, and his parents hadn't either, aside from love each other. His eyes found the sword Samaz had been carrying. His brother had dropped it before he went to pursue the other elves.

Every little bit makes him faster, and he doesn't know how to use a sword anyway.

Scar caught him looking at the sword and said with a confident air, "Go ahead. You say you're a swordsman, pick it up."

"Why, so you can try to kill me?"

"Oh, there won't be any 'try' in it. If I want to kill you, I will. But that's not my plan. I was just planning to teach you a few lessons." Scar flexed the rapier behind his shoulders. The steel bent a little between his hands. "This blade won't break. It's like a living thing in my hands."

Rerry crawled over to the sword on the ground but didn't pick it up. He considered himself a fine swordsman, but the truth was he was self-instructed for the most part, though he had spent some time with the legionnaires. "You sound like someone who relies on his sword more than he does his own skill."

"Oh, it took ample skill and the sword to kill a giant with one blow. Just imagine what I could do to you."

Rerry picked the elven longsword up and stood.

Scar's green eye brightened. The patch over his left eye darkened. "You really do have the fire of a fool in you, don't you."

Eyeing the man's patch, Rerry said, "And you have a blind spot."

Scar lifted up his eye patch, revealing a solid milky white eye. "Do you know what blinded me, boy?"

"I couldn't care less." Rerry tested the heft of the longsword. The fine elven steel was well balanced, but it was still heavier than the rapier Scar carried. "So, are we going to spar or not?"

Scar flipped his eye patch away. It left his appearance unsettling. Menacing. "A blade caught me, in a sparring match such as this. They told me my career as a soldier was over. They washed me out of the ranks. But I practiced and practiced and practiced until I overcame my disadvantage. I climbed back up the ranks." He flicked the blade around in a twirl of blinking light. "I defeated my own master."

Rerry swallowed. There was truth in Scar's words. He didn't doubt a single syllable. Rerry was the bigger of the two, looking down at the smaller elven man whose presence yet seemed as big as his own. A sparring match seemed impractical, but his pride wanted to take a shot at the cocky elven captain.

Just one mark. I'll give him a scar he'll remember.

"I tell you what, Scar, let's fight for blood. If I nick you three times, you have to leave us be."

Scar huffed. "I can't do that. An elf releasing a prisoner? Shame myself? If I lose you, I have to suffer the fate they had in store for you, and I'd rather not know what it is."

"You sound like you fear you might lose."

"Hardly. I'm just giving you an education. I should have known it wouldn't have been a custom you were aware of, seeing how horrible a captor you are."

"Well, if I win, you can be my indentured servant. At least then you could be on the right side of things."

"I'm on the right side when I follow orders." Scar eyed his sword's keen edge. "And what are you offering me when you lose? Oh, that's right, you have nothing to offer. But maybe, just maybe, you could give me one of those eyes of yours."

"That's just sick."

"That's life with an edge. So, do you want to spar, surrender, or just fight? The truth is, Rerry, your only chance to escape and help your mother is to beat me. What are you willing to lose to save your mother?"

Rerry readied his sword. "Everything."

"It sounds like we have a fight then." Scar's feet twisted in the dirt. He lowered himself into a swordsman's stance and waved Rerry over. "Let the steel dance."

Rerry rushed in swinging. He delivered hard, fast blows.

Scar parried and shifted. Metal smacked on metal. Scar batted Rerry's sword from his hand and cut his forearm open.

Rerry jumped away, holding his bleeding arm.

"It was a fine attack. Fast. Powerful." Scar took out a cloth and wiped the blood from his sword. "But you lack refinement. Finesse." With the tip of his rapier, he flipped the fallen longsword up into Rerry's hands by its crossguard. "This time, don't try to kill me. Just use what you know and fight."

Grimacing and with a flutter in his ear, Rerry poised his sword. Staring Scar right in the elf's bad eye, he said, "So be it then."

CHAPTER 17

"THAT'S AN AWFUL LOT OF giants," Selene said to Grahleyna. "And the wurmers. Their numbers will only grow. You need to strike fast if you're going to strike at all. Scatter those forces before their numbers become even stronger."

"No army has ever penetrated Dragon Home. No army ever will."

"I don't mean any disrespect," Selene said. "But have the dragons ever had to fend off an army so big?"

"Selene, we'll stay on the defensive and seal all the entrances. But I'm not going to send the dragons out to attack. Not without Balzurth or Nath." Grahleyna stood out on the very edge of the mountain. The wind tore at her elegant robes. Hair streaming in the wind, she said, "I'm not willing to risk the dragons in a fight right now. Not if I don't have to. Balzurth is King. Nath is the prince. The battle is up to them.

But in their stead, I'll certainly do what must be done in defense. Between now and then, I need you to find them."

"I'd be glad to track them down, but the search would go quicker with wings beneath me."

"Getting out of here will be easier without them." Grahleyna's eyes scanned the horizon.

Wurmers flocked through the air like birds. Selene couldn't count them by the hundreds. The insect-like dragons made an evil humming sound, swarming like locusts. They weren't the biggest dragons—only the size of large dogs or small horses—but there were so many it didn't matter.

"Couldn't you send dragons out to search?"

"I could send a flight of dragons out and hope some of them squeezed through the ranks of those foul things, but I've made my decision. No dragons are going out. There are some in Dragon Home, Selene, but not many. I have to wait things out. It won't be easy."

Selene found it hard to breathe. A dreadful feeling overcame her. Her failures haunted her. She was part of the reason the wurmers thrived, and she hadn't yet figured out how to stop them. A strong part of her wanted to resume that quest. "If the dragons can't leave, how am I supposed to get out of here?"

"There are other methods." Grahleyna turned.

Something caught Selene's eye: a flock of small dragons whose wings beat with rapid fury. "Oh my!"

They were young crimson dynamos, cinnamon scaled and very deadly. The three of them formed a wedge. The one in the rear fought to keep up, with its damaged wing. The dragons must have slipped through the wurmer ranks undetected.

But the wurmers caught the burst of wings and scales beating through the sky. A sea of the evil creatures let out a shrill sound, splitting the air. They gave pursuit. And closed in fast.

Crimson dynamo dragons were not known for their speed. They were a breed strong in power. And this group was young.

"Come to me, brothers and sisters, come to me!" Grahleyna cried out. Her body shimmered. She was transforming into her dragon self.

Selene caught her by the arm. "No, you can't go out there. It's just what they want. We can't lose you, Grahleyna."

In a voice wroth with anger, Grahleyna yelled at Selene, "Unhand me!" With eyes like fire, she jerked her arm away. Wings sprouted from her back.

But Selene knew it was too late. Just as she lifted her gaze into the distance, the wurmers caught up with the young crimson dragons. Swarmed the three of them. Claws and teeth flashed. Fire exploded in the sky. Wurmers crackled and sizzled, but not enough of them. The fires of the young dynamos faded. The wurmers latched onto them and tore them to shreds.

Grahleyna screamed, "Nooooooooooooooooooo!"

Selene held her back by the waist. It was difficult.

Suddenly the sky darkened. Wurmers were everywhere, blanketing the sky like clouds.

"We must get back inside!" Selene felt Grahleyna sag in her arms.

The three young dynamos' broken bodies hung from the jaws of the wurmers, which flew away in triumph and dropped the dead dragons into the waiting arms of the giants.

Above, the wurmers circled in a taunting formation, hundreds of them all at once. The hum they made was deafening.

"We must go inside, Grahleyna, we must!" Selene urged. "Come. They need you inside."

Wurmers landed on the peaks of Dragon Home.

Selene's own blood stirred. An enemy dragon landing on the peaks of Dragon Home was like an orc planting an orcen flag in Morgdon. She was appalled. Finally leading the reluctant Grahleyna back inside, she said, "We're going to end them, my queen. We're going to end them!"

But how?

CHAPTER 18

ATH SMACKED THE WHISTLE AWAY from the man's lips before he had time to blow. The metal whistle spun around the man's neck and whacked him in the side of the head.

"Ow!" The man reached up to rub his temple.

Brenwar knocked the man down to his knees and put him in a chokehold.

"Urk!"

Nath peeled the man's sword from his fingers. Seeing the man's eyes bulge from their sockets, Nath said to Brenwar, "Ease off a bit. Let's at least question the assassin."

Brenwar let off just enough so the magistrate could manage to speak.

He sucked for air and said, "I'm not an assassin. I'm here to help."

Holding the man's own sword up, Nath flicked the metal with his claw.

Ting.

"With this?"

"I'm a legionnaire. What did you expect? I'm not going out into the dark unable to defend myself." The magistrate coughed. His sagging jaws shook from the effort. "Please, let me breathe some more. At my age, breathing's hard enough as it is."

Nath took a careful look at the man. His wavy hair was grey, his muscles were softer than a legionnaire's, and his wrinkly skin had age spots all over. He must have been sixty, maybe older. But Nath could tell he used to be iron strong. He gave Brenwar a nod.

The dwarf released the magistrate.

He fell onto his hands and knees, wheezing. "Sorry, I'm trying to keep it quiet. I guess I should have known better than to try and sneak up on the likes of you two." He looked up into Nath's face. "My, it really is you."

"Pardon me?"

The man's focus shifted between Nath and Brenwar. Hands up, he said, "Nath Dragon and Brenwar Bolderguild. In my town." His voice rose. He covered his mouth. "Sorry, I need to keep it down. Too many light sleepers around here." He extended his hand. "It's an honor."

Nath shook the man's hand.

Many of the man's fingers were missing, but he still had a strong grip and shook vigorously.

Nath asked, "You know us?"

"Well, we've never met before, but you'd be hard to miss given the description. The hair and eyes alone are a dead giveaway, even in the dimness. Both of you. The rest wouldn't know it so much, but I do. I've been around."

"You say you're a legionnaire?" Nath said.

"I am." He pointed at his sword.

Nath noted the eagle image crafted into the pommel. He handed it to the man. "A fine piece of steel."

"It served me well against the throngs of Barnabus, but my steel's not as quick as it used to be. And my joints burn like fire if I move too fast—and when it rains." He wiped the rain from his face. "I'm Timothy. Call me Tim." He shook hands with Brenwar. "Gah! What happened to your fingers?"

"I got hungry."

Tim looked at Nath with bewilderment.

Nath said, "It's a long story, Tim. Now, you say you came to warn us about something."

Tearing his glance from Brenwar's skeleton hand, Tim said, "That fellow you talked to on the porch, that's Malden. He's a rat. I tried to talk him out of doing what he's about to do, but it won't stick."

"What's he going to do?" Brenwar grumbled.

"The nuurg oversee this town and many like it. They have quarters a few miles away. It's a sad situation, but we survive by feeding them." Tim sheathed his sword with a click. "Well, a fair part of this town worships them. They turn my stomach. It's as if people's minds are turned inside out. Well, the nuurg demand that if any stranger passes through, we let them know about it. I tried to convince Malden to let you be. We have plenty of people pass who are hungry. He agreed, but he's a liar. He'll slip out of here at first light, if not tonight."

Tim peeked down the alley between the plank wood buildings. "He doesn't like me much. He was magistrate before I was, until the people spoke. You can bet your boots he'll have those giant fiends on their giant horses riding after you in no time." He rubbed his eyes. "And I thought I'd seen all there was to see in the war on Barnabus. Now we have giant orcs. Giant trolls. Giant ogres. Giant everything."

"Thanks, Tim," said Nath. It was good to know the good people could still conquer their fears and do the right thing. Tim, an old soldier, was bound by that. Whether he was still a soldier or not, he had a sense of duty, the duty to take care of his people. It was clear Tim was ever willing to risk his life to do that. "Tim, have you heard the saying 'Sometimes the greatest battles are won from the smallest victories'?"

"Wars are won one battle at a time." Tim's eyes gleamed. "What are you getting at?"

"I think it's time for the nuurg to have a little surprise."

"Really? There's an awful lot of them."

"How many?" Brenwar asked.

"Ten nearby. They scour the towns in pairs." Tim took a breath. "Boy, my blood's churning. I'm ready to stick it to them."

"I don't want your departure to rouse suspicion. Just tell us where they are." Nath patted Tim's shoulder. "We'll do the rest."

"But I can help."

"You could really help by grabbing us some food," Brenwar said. "I can't sneak through the woods with my belly growling."

"That wasn't a growl I heard, more like a roar." Tim shrugged. "I'll do it."

Somewhere in the town, a horse whinnied.

"Did you hear that?" said Nath.

"I did. Come on." Tim led them toward the eastern face of the town and huddled behind the split fence of a barn. The man, Malden, led a horse out of one of the stables and outside. Once he got out of earshot, he mounted the horse and trotted away. "Yep. Malden the overgrown rattle snake is going to report to the nuurg."

"How long will it take them to get here?"

"As fast as those big monsters move? They'll be here in an hour, and you'll hear them coming a mile away."

"Good," Brenwar said, "That gives us plenty of time to eat then." He patted his belly and said to Tim. "Now go fetch food."

CHAPTER 19

IT WAS A HEATED SPAR. Rerry attacked, blocked, shifted, and foot shuffled. Sweat dripped down his face and stung his eyes. He labored for breath.

"Chin up! Shoulders back! Eyes on me!" Scar the master swordsman picked his way through

Rerry's defense and tore the longsword from the part-elf's hands. He put his blade right at Rerry's throat. "I thought you said you were good."

With the blade nicking his skin, Rerry lifted his chin high. "I'm just getting warmed up."

"I can't help but say I'm shocked you made it this far in your journey." Scar backed away. "You aren't horrible. You have the same skill level as many of my students. Given a hundred years of practice, you might be half as good as me. Oh, but you won't live that long, will you. As a matter of fact, you might not even live through the day. You're bleeding everywhere."

Rerry touched his neck. Blood smeared his fingers, making things look worse than they were. But his forearm was pretty bad and needed treatment. Shoulders drooping, he bent over and picked up his sword.

Everyone has a weakness, Rerry. Find his.

"Oh, so you don't want to surrender. I almost admire that." Scar twisted his torso from side to side and made a couple of thigh lunges. "I think I'm now warmed up. Let's let the new lesson begin."

I'm not bad. I'm not bad.

Rerry had always been confident that he was a fine swordsman. He'd been practicing since he was old enough to hold a blade. But Scar was hundreds of years old. His sword arm was like a living piece of iron. Rerry had never encountered anyone so masterful.

But he had to beat the master or be imprisoned, and deep inside him there was fear. He might not see his mother again. He might not see anyone again. He pulled his shoulders back, set his stance, and caught his breath. "This time, you attack me."

Scar almost smiled. A deadly delight showed in his good eye. "So, you want to test your defense. So be it then." Scar shuffle stepped but then stopped.

Samaz appeared out of the woods. He had both of the elven guards who had escaped slung over his brawny shoulders. The elves were out cold.

"What is this?" Scar was gaping. He shifted his focus onto Samaz.

Rerry couldn't believe his eyes. Somehow, his weak brother had impossibly managed to roust out two formidable elves on his own. He made a silly smile. "By the trees, Samaz, how did you pull that off?"

Samaz set the unconscious elves down. "I have skills."

"Clearly you have more than your brother." Scar's eyes slid back and forth between the two. "Don't get any clever ideas. Both of you are still my prisoners. Alive, barely alive, or dead, I'll have you both." He gave Samaz a once over. "Back away, rotund one. Your brother and I have business."

Hands on his knees, Samaz asked, "What sort of business?"

"Assuming he doesn't bleed to death first, after I beat him into submission, he's going to surrender."

Samaz wrinkled his brow and looked to Rerry, "Is this true?"

With a little shrug, Rerry said, "I don't have much of a choice."

Watching the blood drip from Rerry's arm, Samaz said, "You can beat him." He sat down on the ground and crossed his legs. With a nod at Scar, he said, "Do it, Rerry."

"Your brother believes in you. Both of you are lacking in judgment. So, shall we resume the bout?"

With a nod, Rerry readied his stance again. "Come on, Scar. Attack me."

Scar didn't hesitate. He jabbed right at Rerry. The tip of his blade was on a course to impale Rerry's eyeball.

Rerry's instinct, more than skill, deflected the blow. For the next several seconds, he fought for his life.

Scar came at him, hard and fast.

If the elven guard was holding back, Rerry couldn't tell. Every blow he parried was a finger's breadth from cutting him open. He must have beaten ten solid whacks off with his own blade. His arm was like lead.

Though in actuality smaller, Scar's tireless arm was as strong as a warrior's twice his own size, and the elf's rapier struck quickly but heavily.

Rerry's lungs soon burned again.

"I admit, your defense is much better than your offense. Good for you." Scar broke off his attack and took a breath. "Whew. I'm actually enjoying this. It's been a while since I had a half-decent workout."

Rerry wanted to reply but didn't have the breath in him. He actually did feel a little good about himself. He was learning from Scar. He could now anticipate the elven guard's attacks. A dip in the shoulder. A shuffle to the side. A twist in the neck. All of them were signs of the next attack. The problem was, he didn't have any energy left to keep up. He looked at his forearm. His sleeve was blood soaked and still dripping. Nearby, his brother sat on the ground with his eyes closed, head lifted toward the sky. He looked so peaceful.

Samaz, you are so strange!

"So, are you going to surrender now, or do you want to see if you have a few decent strokes left in you?" Scar swished his rapier through the air. "I can do this until the rooster crows."

The wind picked up, rustling the leaves and cooling Rerry's body. It somehow rejuvenated him. He received a charge of power he didn't understand. His heavy breathing eased. Strength returned to his weary arms. His blood coursed through his body.

I feel wonderful!

Rerry's thoughts were clear. He focused on Scar, and with a wave of his fingers, he beckoned the soldier forward.

"It seems someone has gotten a second wind. Well, it won't last long." Scar attacked.

Steel collided with steel. The fine elven blades danced like metal snakes.

Scar attacked. Rerry parried. The exchanges went back and forth for a few more seconds.

And then without warning, Rerry counterattacked. He deflected Scar's attack and twisted his sword down and under Scar's defenses and cut through the chest of the soldier's black leather armor.

Scar gasped.

Rerry pressed the attack.

Now Scar was on the defensive. His face became a mask of concentration. Brows buckled, Scar said, "Impossible!"

Rerry used his heavier sword and bigger body to his advantage. He beat Scar's sword down.

Bang! Bang! Bang!

Scar counterattacked.

Rerry swatted it aside. He attacked.

Scar retreated.

Rerry wasn't sure what was going on. He could anticipate Scar's moves before they happened. And his strength and skill had increased. It was as if something else, something vaguely familiar, had become a part of him. A presence. He went with it. Seeing an opening, he cut Scar across the shoulder, drawing blood. "That's one!"

Scar let out a howl.

Rerry cut the elf's thigh. "That's two!"

Scar took his sword in two hands and said, "You are not going to beat me!" He attacked in an unorthodox style, chopping at Rerry like a woodsman cuts a tree—only with ferocity. "I'm going to kill you!"

Rerry saw blood in Scar's eye. The elven soldier meant it, but Rerry caught every stinging blow on his blade, shrugging aside the jarring impact.

Scar didn't let up.

Clang! Clang! Clang!

Anticipating the next move, Rerry jumped aside.

Scar's sword bit into the ground.

With Scar overextended, Rerry smacked him hard with the flat of his sword.

Sprawled out on the ground, Scar twisted around only to find Rerry's sword at his throat.

Rerry nicked the elf's neck. "That's three."

Chest heaving and with an eye of contempt, Scar said in a voice full of denial, "I don't know how you did what you did, but this is not over."

"You gave your word," Rerry said, poking Scar in the chest with his sword. "Are you taking it back?"

With a sneer, Scar said, "No."

"Good." Rerry's boundless strength fled his body. The world spun. He was falling without control, and the day turned into night.

CHAPTER 20

THEY CAME, STARK AGAINST THE night. The nuurg. The pair of monstrous humanoids rode on the backs of the colossal horses called wrath horns. Rain splashed off of them, splattering the muddy streets. Their spiked hooves made huge puddles. They trotted into town, stopping in the middle of the main road. Behind them was Malden. The man seemed insignificant among the towering ten-foot-tall monsters. Malden spoke, gestured, and pointed.

Nath could hear door bolts sliding shut. Shutters closing. The light of oil lamps dimmed, and many were extinguished. Fear was in the air, heavy as the rain. The mood of the tiny town was brooding.

The presence of evil had taken over.

The nuurg resumed their advance. They were covered from head to toe in heavy armor. One carried a spear longer than a man was tall. The other nuurg had a spiked flail far too big for an ordinary man to wield. Their faces were ugly, like those of orcs or ogres. One was a cyclops, and the other, with the flail, seemed more man than orc.

Malden led them down the street and pointed down the alley where he'd sent Nath and Brenwar earlier.

The nuurg paid him no mind. With awful nickers, the wrath horns, shaking the tusks on their faces, snorted and veered toward the alley.

Nath's blood stirred. He stepped from the shadows into the rain-soaked street and called out, "Pardon me! But I think I can save you some time. I'm the one you're looking for!"

Malden's jaw hit the saddle. Visibly gathering his thoughts, he pointed, saying, "That's him! That's him! That's the stranger I told you about!"

The nuurg pulled back on their reins and backed up. Facing Nath, they spread apart and continued their advance.

Out of the night from the backside of the nuurg, Brenwar bellowed out, "And don't forget me. I'm the one you're looking for as well!"

The nuurg with one eye, the cyclops, slowly turned his horse around to face Brenwar. He lowered his massive spear. The wrath horn snorted. Its front hoof clawed at the muddy ground.

"You know, you might not want to do that," Nath said in a loud voice. "Dwarves don't like to be poked or trampled."

From the far end of the street, Brenwar said, "I can speak for myself!" The dwarf didn't even have Mortuun in hand. He was nothing but soaking-wet beard and breastplate. "Come on, one eye, what are you waiting for?"

The wrath horn reared up and charged. Its great hooves thundered down the road on a path to overrun Brenwar.

All eyes were on the event.

What in Nalzambor is that crazy dwarf doing?

The naked end of the spear's metal tip was right on course to skewer Brenwar like meat on a stick when Brenwar slipped to the side. His powerful fingers grabbed hold of the spear and yanked the nuurg right out of the saddle. Strengthened by the bracers of power that he wore, Brenwar pummeled the giant of a man into the mud with his skeleton hand.

Wham! Wham! Wham!

Covered in grit, Brenwar stood up and waved. "He's finished."

The nuurg with two eyes turned his attention to Nath. He drew his flail. His head swiveled on his shoulders. His dark eyes pierced Nath.

"Looking for me?" Nath said from behind the nuurg, in its blind spot. And smacked the horse hard on its backside.

It reared up.

The nuurg rider, no longer having its hand on the reins, toppled. It hit hard with a splash and a thud. The big humanoid scrambled up to his feet and came out swinging. The flail ripped over Nath's ducking head.

Without hesitation, Nath ran the nuurg through with Fang.

The monster died in the rain.

Nath shook his head. Killing wasn't what he wanted to do.

Brenwar came along and said, "Don't doubt yourself. You can't keep evil in prison. It will get out. You did what had to be done. This is war."

"What have you done?" Malden yelled, clutching his head and hair as if the world was crumbling down. "You've doomed us all. The other nuurg, they'll kill us. They'll kill us all!"

Brenwar walloped the man in the gut with a quick punch.

Malden sank to his knees. He groaned.

"Listen to me, farmer! The only ones dying are them! But if you side with them, you'll die with them. Tonight we turn the tables."

Tim rushed over, feet splashing through the water. He carried Mortuun in his arms. He handed it over to Brenwar. Catching his breath, he said, "That thing's heavier than it looks."

"It's supposed to be," Brenwar replied.

"I-I couldn't believe my eyes. The two of you made such quick work of those giant beasts. You both truly are what the songs say you are." Tim shook his head. "I never would have believed it if I hadn't seen it for myself."

"That was nothing," Brenwar remarked.

Nath had one of the wrath horns by the reins and said to Tim, "Do you think you can handle one of these things?"

Staring up at the huge beast with wide eyes, Tim said, "Are you joking?"

"They aren't as mean as they are ugly. You just have to take command." Nath handed the man the reins. "Just imagine if the legionnaires had horses like these back when."

Tim petted the horse between the forehead and muzzle. It snorted. Stamped its hooves. With a nod, he said, "I think I can manage." He climbed into the saddle. Looking down at Nath, he said, "Whew, this is different. So where are we going?"

"You say you know where the other nuurg reside. Brenwar and I want to pay them a visit." Nath put his fingers to his lips and whistled. The other wrath horn walked over with its head down. Nath mounted the creature and held down his hand. Brenwar took it and climbed up behind him. "It's going to be our first and final visit."

Knees deep in the mud, Malden said, "You'll doom us. You'll doom us all. Tim, don't be a fool."

Tall in the saddle, Tim said, "If I weren't so darn set on being a good guy, I'd trample you into a mud hole."

Malden smirked.

Tim dug his heels into the wrath horn. It reared up.

Malden cringed.

The hooves crashed down right in front of the country man.

Up on his feet, Malden took off running.

With the look of a hardened soldier firing in his eyes, Tim said, "Let's go get them."

CHAPTER 21

RERRY AWOKE. HE WAS LEANED against a rock, head spinning. Something tugged at his arm. Eyelids flickering, he slowly made the image of Samaz form in his vision. His brother had him by the forearm. There were at least twenty stitches in the wound. Samaz was wrapping it up. "What happened?" Rerry asked.

"You passed out."

Rerry's heart fired. He lurched up. "Where's Scar?"

"He'll be back. He and the other two are out scouting for food. It's been a busy day. Everyone is hungry."

"What are you talking about, Samaz? Are we their prisoners again?"

"No, they're our prisoners." Samaz finished up the wrap. "Keep it clean." He tried to get up.

But Rerry held him down. "Samaz, I don't see any prisoners. You must mean they're our escaped prisoners."

"You beat him, Rerry. Scar is honoring his debt. He's in your service, and his men are in his." Samaz traced his finger along the cut in Rerry's neck. "That might scar. I'll see if I can find some of nature's loam for it."

Scratching his head, Rerry looked around and said in a whisper, "I did beat him, didn't I. For the life of me, I don't know how. Something just … overcame me. I felt like two men in one. It was strange, very strange."

Making sure no one else was around, Samaz said, "It was me."

"What do you mean, it was you?"

"We became one. I was merged with you. I can't explain it. It just sort of happened."

"You don't know anything about fighting with a sword." Rerry leaned back against the boulder and closed his eyes. "But something happened, for certain. What do you mean, you merged with me?"

"I've always felt something, a connection. I've talked to Mother about it before. She says that, being brothers born with magic in our veins, we might bear special powers. She says that if we do, one day these powers will reveal themselves." He sat down shoulder to shoulder with Rerry. "That revelation came today. I don't know what happened, but you were fighting, and I felt it. I tingled from head to toe right before I said you could beat him. Besides, I dreamed it."

"Dreamed it? When?"

Samaz caught a colorful butterfly on his finger. "At least ten years ago."

"I'd have trouble believing you if you weren't so strange." Rerry sighed. There wasn't any reason for his brother to lie, and he'd indeed felt something. There wasn't any better explanation. Scar should have cut him to ribbons, but he hadn't. He hated to say it, but he did. "Let's not let Scar know about this. He'll want a rematch."

"Don't worry, I won't."

"So, how did you catch those elves? Did you use some kind of spell on them?"

"I'm faster than you think."

They helped each other to their feet.

"Well, I'd hope so."

Scar and the soldiers returned. They had some dead rabbits and a sack of small green apples. The captain had a hard time looking at Rerry when he said, "We'll get the meat cooked. These apples are sour as an elven elder, but they'll fill your gut and quench your thirst."

"I'm famished," Rerry replied.

Scar tossed him a pair of apples.

He caught them both with one hand. "Thanks." His lips puckered as soon as he bit into one. He pitched it away. "No thanks. I'd rather eat a rock."

Scar took a big bite out of his own apple. "I'll gather you all the rocks you want to eat. Mmmm, that's good."

What's he up to?

Rerry was far from comfortable having Scar as his indentured servant. He wasn't even certain to what extent he could order the elf around.

Time to push.

"Let me see your sword, Scar."

Scar unbuckled his sword belt. "It's yours to have. All I have to offer is yours. Even my life. The same goes for my men. We'll keep our word." He handed Rerry the sword—belt, scabbard, and all.

Rerry examined it.

The working of the scabbard was of the finest craft. The leather of the belt was worn and soft but well maintained by the natural oils of the lands. Countless hours must have gone into crafting the sword. It had been forged by the finest blacksmiths.

"Put it back on. It's yours to keep for a lifetime. I have to be honest with you, Scar, I'm not comfortable having henchmen."

"Then you're releasing me from my word?"

"No, you are not released. As soon as I do that, you'll be right back after me again. Instead, you and your men shall accompany us on our quest. I didn't say I wouldn't get used to it." He gave a nod to Samaz. His brother was making a fire while the soldiers skinned the rabbits. "And it might just last forever."

Scar adjusted his eyepatch. "I couldn't have cared less before, but seeing how your quest involves me now, enlighten me some more."

Rerry filled him in on his mother's problem with the wizard's dementia and went even further back to the final battle of the Great Dragon War when the elves and dwarves teamed up and turned loose the Apparatus of Ruune on the Floating City.

Scar and his men hung on every word.

Without realizing it, Rerry captivated himself. He just kept going on and on until the sun dipped behind the trees and the darkness came. When he finished, the campfire crackled and all the rabbit meat was gone. He wiped his fingers on the grasses. "It was something."

"I must admit, I'm envious." Scar stirred a stick in the ground. "I wasn't doing anything when all that went on. As for your mother, I sympathize. But going into Elome to acquire the Ocular of Orray? Hah! You look more human than elf. You'll never acquire the gem. I don't think you can even find it. It offers no guarantees it can heal her anyway." He broke the stick in half and tossed it into the fire. "'There's more than one way to do anything,' they say. But some things can't be undone, Rerry. Listen to me. You too, Samaz. I don't think your mother would want you to die on her account. Go home. Abandon this quest."

Rerry stiffened. "That won't happen! You just want to be free."

"You aren't going to slip through the elves' and dwarves' clutches forever. You should turn yourselves in. See what happens. If Nath Dragon truly is who you say he is, his name will be cleared."

"Not if they kill him."

"That's easier said than done, based off what you've told me. For the love of Elome, he's a dragon. I've never heard of a dragon being put on trial before. But they'll make it happen."

"Nalzambor has enough evil in it. Nath Dragon is the least of their worries. He's the one fighting the danger lurking out there."

Scar rubbed his hands over the fire. "The greatest danger is what lurks within the hearts of all. We're all quick to judge one another, Rerry. We always want a scapegoat. I hate to admit it, but your friend's enemies will only pile up."

"Why do you say that? It doesn't make any sense."

"There's a flaw in all of us. If there weren't, we'd all get along." Scar lay down with his hands behind his head. "You're young. You've much to figure out yet. Now, get some sleep. Your human side needs it. I can see the blackness under your eyes where if you were an elf, they'd still be bright as day."

"I don't need any sleep. I need to help my mother."

"Things will be clearer once you get some shuteye. Be a soldier. Take a moment. You never know when you'll get another chance to rest." Scar closed his eye. He breathed easy and slept. The other elves did the same.

The glow of the dying fire showed on Samaz's face. He looked wide awake. He always looked wide awake. "I never sleep," he said. "Take some rest."

"What do you think we should do?" Rerry asked.

"I might abandon Elome, but I won't abandon Mother."

"I'm glad we agree." Rerry lay down, but he couldn't sleep.

There has to be another way to help her, but I don't know where to start.

CHAPTER 22

THE NUURG. THEY MADE NATH's skin crawl. He could see one of them standing outside a small fortress made from logs and rock. It had heavy orcen features and only one eye. It chewed meat from the bone of a stag near where a metal urn filled with burning firewood blazed. The animal's rack of antlers lay nearby. The nuurg stuck the meat in the fire, cooked it, then pulled it out of the flame and ate some more.

Concealed in a spot of higher ground fifty yards above Nath overlooking the distant open plain where the nuurg's fortress stood sentry, Tim fidgeted.

The rain had stopped, but the humidity was up. Everything outside was quiet.

In a low voice, Tim asked, "What are the nuurg? I understand giants, but these are bigger, are they not? These monsters are something else."

Nath couldn't really explain it himself. There were plenty of creatures in this world he hadn't seen before. He hadn't even seen most of the dragons. But one thing was certain: the nuurg were a twisted abomination brought about by the titans. He rubbed the neck of his wrath horn. "I believe they are a mix of orc and giant blood. Maybe there's dark magic behind it. We were in Urslay, the giant home in the mountains, not so long ago. There were faces from all of the races as big as them. Somehow, the titans are building an army of giant races."

"Are you telling me there's going to be a lot more of them?" Tim thumbed the sweat off his brow.

"They war with the dragons, not men."

"I say it's man's fight as much as any. We're slaves to those beasts." Tim's grip tightened on his reins, making a squeaking sound. "So what's the plan?"

"We ride in and take them out, but you don't need to come," Nath said. "You've done enough by leading us here. I thank you."

"I might not be as young as I used to be, but there's still plenty of fight left in me. I can't just stand here, watch, and do nothing." He pulled out his sword. "I want to fight."

Nath nodded. "I know you do. So, you said there were ten that patrolled the towns?"

"Yes. And you've killed two, so now there'll be eight. They stay in at night and make plenty of noise in the morning. But they aren't alone in there. They keep our people, who need to be freed."

"Oh." Nath noticed Brenwar's eyes on him. "That changes things."

"Aye," Brenwar said. His eyes were intent on the nuurg fortress. "We can't just storm in there and bust their bones up. We'll have to be more careful. I don't like being careful."

The nuurg sentry crunched through the bone, chewed it up, and swallowed it down.

"I suppose the nuurg expect company before long." Nath readied the satchel he'd put the contents from Brenwar's chest in. "We should just give them what they expect then." He took out a potion vial. A tangerine-colored fluid swirled within.

Tim's eyes enlarged. "Is that magic? What are you going to do with it?"

"I'm going to make Brenwar drink it."

"No you are not!" the dwarf objected.

"Well, I'm not drinking it, and I'm in charge, so there you go."

"What does it do?" Tim asked.

"It's a polymorph potion. It will turn you into whatever you want to be, for a short time." Nath held the vial up against the sky. Mystic fragments twinkled within. "The idea is Brenwar drinks it and turns himself into one of the nuurg. As a disguise. He waltzes me in there as his—"

"I'll drink it! Let me drink it!" Tim's fingers grasped at the air.

"Aye, let him drink it. He's volunteering for it. Let the soldier have at it." Brenwar pumped his skeleton fist. "It's a good idea."

"But they'll be expecting two nuurg, not one," Nath said.

"You didn't say that."

"We have to do it right if we want to pull this off."

"What do I do?" Tim asked.

"Think of the nuurg that come into your town. The one I slew. Can you picture it?"

Tim nodded.

Nath handed the legionnaire the vial. "Then drink half of this and concentrate on its image."

Without hesitation, Tim took the vial and slurped half of it down then handed the vial back to Nath. "I tingle."

"Oh, you'll tingle," Nath said. He gave the vial to Brenwar and sat behind him. "Your turn, faithful friend."

"Hah." Brenwar frowned, closed his eyes, and swallowed the remainder of the potion. "Happy?"

"Delighted." Nath dismounted.

"Oh my stars," Tim said. His hands were outstretched. He gaped at them. The man's body contorted and grew. His face became mean and ugly. His body filled the saddle. In mere moments he'd gone from man to man-monster. His one eye blinked. "Did it work?"

"Perfectly." Nath turned to Brenwar. The dwarf was now a nuurg like the one he'd slain, but something wasn't right. "We might have a problem."

"You can say that again. I look like an orc again. A giant one at that."

"That's not it. The problem is you still have more beard than face."

Chapter 23

Transformed into nuurg, Brenwar and Tim rode on the wrath horns. They took a road that led straight to the fortress with Nath in tow behind them, hands bound up by a rope.

Brenwar grumbled under his beard, "I even smell as bad as they do." He caught Tim smiling and glowered at the man-turned-giant. "The nuurg don't smile."

"I can't help it. I still tingle."

"Nath, what do I do if they say something about my beard? Can I bash them then?" asked Brenwar.

"I don't know. Let's hope it doesn't come up." It wasn't that the nuurg didn't have facial hair. Many of them had plenty, but not to the extent it looked like a black bush beneath their faces.

"I can do the talking," Tim suggested. "I've communicated with them plenty of times before. I have a feel for them."

Brenwar drifted back and said, "That's fine by me."

Closing in on the fortress, Nath caught a glimpse of the nuurg sentry. It tossed the stag's antlers aside and picked up its spear, barring the gate that led into the fortress with its body.

Tim and his wrath horn came to a stop several feet away from the sentry. He didn't say a word. The sentry didn't say a word either. Its single eye bore into Tim. Spear ready, it moved by Tim and gave Brenwar a longer look. Brenwar glared right back. With a grunt, the heavy-footed cyclops made it over to Nath. A bunch of men's skulls made up its belt.

Here we go.

The cyclops stood a full three feet of muscle taller than Nath. It leaned down, nostrils flaring, and sniffed him. With its finger, it poked Nath in the chest, knocking him down.

Nath got up but kept his eyes down and didn't say a word.

The nuurg poked him harder.

Nath shuffled back without falling.

Someone's going to lose a finger!

"Quit fooling around with the prisoner! Let us in. I hunger," Tim said.

The nuurg sentry touched Nath's cheek with its fingers and said, "He's pretty like a bauble. I want his head. Humph. That hair would look fine on my belt."

"We'll cast bones to see who gets what. Now open the door," Brenwar interjected.

The sentry waggled the spear in front of Nath's eyes. "I bet those eyes would make a fine seasoning for people stew." He breathed on Nath.

Nath coughed.

Sultans of Sulfur, that's awful.

The cyclops walked away. A pair of twelve-foot-high doors still barred the entrance to the fortress. The brute put its back into it and shoved both doors open wide. With a quick look back at Nath, Tim the nuurg led them inside.

The fortress wasn't very big. Square and straight on all sides, it would house about fifty men in close quarters—or ten nuurg. The middle was an open courtyard, and the rest of the establishment was nothing but barracks and stables.

The nuurg sentry made its way over to one of the barracks. It was taller than the doorframe. The nuurg pounded on it with its fist, saying, "Bruke! Bruke! Wake! A meal awaits!" The sentry stepped back.

A loud moan stirred within the confines of the wooden barracks. The door swung open, smacking against the frame of the building with a loud *whack*. A big body filled the doorway, ducked down, and squeezed beneath the frame. It was a nuurg, a huge one-eyed orc with small knuckle-like horns on its head. Bare chested, but furs and hides covered it below the waist. "Why did you disturb me? What is it?"

At least they speak Common.

"What do you mean?" the sentry said, irritated. It pointed with its spear. "See for yourself."

Bruke rubbed his eye and yawned. He peered beyond Tim and Brenwar. Spying Nath, he blinked. Warily, he leaned over and grabbed a halberd that was leaned against the barracks. "That one is too fast to be fooled." He gave Tim and Brenwar a look. "How did you catch that one?"

"Caught him hiding. Hemmed him in and overpowered him." Tim shifted in his saddle. "He's slippery. Not slippery enough. Heh heh."

In a fierce voice, Bruke said, "There was mention of a dwarf. Where's the dwarf?"

Brenwar the nuurg held up Mortuun the war hammer. "Dead by his own hammer."

Studying Brenwar and the weapon, Bruke said, "Something smells about your story."

More of the nuurg emerged from their barracks. Each carried a heavy weapon crafted from iron and steel. In a few long strides, they had encircled Nath and his companions.

Nath counted heads.

...Six, seven, eight. The full welcoming party has arrived. Unless Tim's count is wrong.

He noted the faces of people crowded back in the shadows of the barracks. He felt their hearts racing.

These people are terrified.

"I don't remember you having a beard," Bruke said to Brenwar the nuurg. "And where's your weapon?"

"It got lost in a mud hole, but this one is fine." He held the hammer in front of Bruke's face. "Just fine."

Bruke's nostrils widened. His shoulders tensed. "You don't talk like yourself. You don't smell like yourself. You smell...dwarven."

Nath caught a look from Brenwar. He gave a quick nod.

"Do you want to know why I smell like a dwarf?" Brenwar said.

The nuurg sentry said with confidence, "Because you killed one."

"No," Brenwar replied. "Because I am one!" Powered by his bracers of strength, the dwarf-turned-nuurg cranked Mortuun back and dotted Bruke smack dab in the middle of the forehead.

Crack-Boom!

The entire fortress shook.

Bruke dropped to his knees. Knuckles dragging on the ground, the nuurg collapsed backward, dead as a stone.

Timothy wheeled his wrath horn around and snapped the reins. The bestial mount charged over the nuurg nearest him, horns down with ram-like force.

The flat-footed nuurg recovered their senses. Two of them focused their efforts on Nath. They rushed him.

"Brenwar!" Nath yelled. "I need Fang!"

The dwarven warrior in nuurg form had another nuurg pinned down to the ground by the neck. He bellowed, "Get him yourself."

The nuurg collided right on top of Nath and drove him into the ground.

This is not part of the plan!

Chapter 24

While Tim was turning the wrath horn around for another charge, a huge body collided into him, knocking him from the saddle. He barrel rolled back up to his feet, sword poised to strike or defend against his attacker. His sword, a fine broad blade, didn't fit in his hand as it usually did. It was awkward but light as a stick. He slashed back and forth.

I can make this work.

He took in a deep breath. His body was alive, more so than it had been in decades. His muscles were strong and powerful.

"Oh, what a body!"

A nuurg fighter wheeled into his path. It held a flail with both its hands and swung it over its head. The steel-spiked ball whistled through the air in wide circles. The nuurg rushed in, bringing the flail head down with wroth force.

Tim caught the chain of the flail around the length of his sword.

The pair of giants stood chest to chest, shoving one another back, snarling and growling.

The nuurg enemy puffed and spun.

Struggling for balance, feet sliding through the dirt, Tim held on for dear life. The monster was strong. Fierce. Its force unrelenting. He'd never faced such power before.

Come on, soldier. You're as big as him. Act like it.

Hard knuckles punched Tim in the ribs.

He groaned. His body might have been as big or as strong, but he wasn't used to it. The size was awkward.

The nuurg bent him backward. Its shovel-sized hand fell to a knife inside its belt. It snaked it out and tried to stab Tim.

With combat experience coming back to him, Tim locked his fingers over the monster's wrist.

The blade edge nicked his flesh.

The old fires of battle within Tim ignited. He rammed his forehead into the nuurg's nose.

The cartilage gave way.

Crunch.

The nuurg bellowed. Its grip released its flail. It held its nose.

Big mistake.

Tim slung the flail from his sword and closed in, piercing the nuurg right through its heart.

It dropped dead.

He hoisted the sword high. "Victory!"

A nuurg with two eyes close set together rushed into his path with a machete matched to its size and body.

Flashing his sword, Tim said, "Have at me then! I've got a body as big as yours, and now I'm used to it!"

His stomach churned.

He belched.

His body collapsed to its normal size.

With two colossal bodies piled on top of him, no sword in hand, Nath fought back with the only available weapon he could think of. He bit the one-eyed nuurg in the leg.

With an angry howl, it punched him in the side of the head.

Stars burst forth.

Nath's teeth clattered.

The one-eyed nuurg grabbed a handful of Nath's long red hair and jerked Nath up off his feet—and practically out of his boots.

"Now you've done it!" Nath said, kicking and flailing. "Nobody touches my hair!" He dug his golden-yellow claws into the flesh of the giant's hand and raked them down.

One-eye moaned and released him, but Two-eye stabbed at him with a knife made from a solid piece of iron.

Nath sprang from the strike. He jumped at the giant orc and punched it hard in the throat.

Two-eye choked and gurgled, but One-eye charged from behind, swinging its anvil-like fist.

Nath ducked.

The fist collided with the choking nuurg, flopping it to the ground.

Nath unleashed a flurry of punches in One-eye's heavy gut, hard and fast. The nuurg might have been bigger and heavier than him, but they weren't any stronger. He was a dragon who just looked like a man. Well, and had to walk like a man rather than fly. He hit as fast as his heart beat.

One-eye crumbled under the assault.

Nath wrenched its arm behind its back and called out, "Brenwar, I need Fang!"

"Hold yer horses! I'm coming!" Brenwar had resumed his normal form.

"Don't you mean hold your wrath horns?"

Brenwar dashed his war hammer against the head of the nuurg.

Nath punched it in the throat.

Whop!

Brenwar marched over and said, "Hold him still, will you?"

"Are you serious?"

"No." The dwarf cocked back and smote the wriggling giant in the skull.

Neither giant moved again. The nuurg lay scattered in heaps all over the courtyard.

"Where's Tim?" Nath said. A scuffle caught his ear.

Tim was pushing himself out from under a nuurg's big body. With his legs still pinned beneath the giant, he held up his sword and said breathlessly, "Victory."

Regaining his feet, Nath rolled his sore jaw and combed his fingers through his hair.

Four, five, six, seven …

"We're missing a nuurg, the sentry with the skulls for a belt."

Outside the fortress, the shrill sound of a metal whistle ripped through the sky.

Nath rushed out the front gate.

The sentry stood there blowing an iron whistle the size of a curled ram's horn.

"I'll stop him!" Brenwar slung Mortuun head first into the nuurg's chest. Bone cracked. It hit the ground. He ran over and tore the whistle from the wheezing nuurg's hands. "What is this for?"

With a smile on its crooked lips, the nuurg said, "They come."

Against the deep blue sky with their black wings, the wurmers came like great bats of the night.

CHAPTER 25

"INCOMING, EH? WELL, I'M STILL itching to fight. Let them come. Let them all come." Brenwar moved away from Nath, twirling Mortuun around his body and yelling into the sky, "I'm right here, insects!"

Timothy lumbered over, shoulders sagging. He had his shoulder in one hand and Fang in the other. Blinking, he looked up in the sky. "It's like my old soldiering days. Never enough time to catch your breath between the battles." He took a deep breath. "I can still do this."

Nath took Fang. "Not with ordinary steel you won't. They have hides hard as iron, Tim. Get inside with the others and take cover."

Tim nodded. "If it weren't coming from you, Dragon Prince, my pride wouldn't let me retreat, but I'll follow your order." He took another look above. The wurmers dove like black lances in the night sky. "Yes sir, I'll follow your orders."

Fang warmed in the palm of Nath's hand. The blade hummed with angry life.

Me and you, Fang. Me and you.

The swarming wurmers closed in. There looked to be ten of them, a hundred yards away. Fifty yards.

Nath and Brenwar cocked back.

Something whistled overhead. With blinding speed, streaks of silver slammed into the oncoming wurmers. It was a collision of scales followed by roars of fury. Dragon fury.

Nath's heart wanted to burst from his chest.

Silver dragons. Man sized, quick, and powerful. Their claws shredded the wurmers. They clamped onto the insect-dragons. Tore off wings. Locked jaws on necks.

The stunned wurmers shrieked and spun out of control.

Several wurmers hit the ground.

Nath and Brenwar, quick to strike, pounded them with hammer and sword.

Above, the battle raged like fireworks in the sky. Light coursed through the bodies of the silver dragons, shocking the wurmers. The monsters fought back with their hot, glowing breath. Blasts of deep purple erupted from their mouths in balls of energy. The silver dragons slid by the attack, quicker than the wind.

One silver dragon, marvelous from the tip of his nose to the end of his tail, locked up in battle with the biggest wurmer. The dragon's tail coiled around the wurmer's neck, and its body charged like living light. Lightning fired from its mouth. The wurmer exploded. Smoldering scales showered the sky. A burnt, crispy smell lingered in the air.

Standing back to back with Brenwar, Nath said, "They're dead. All of the wurmers are dead." He blinked. "Those silvers really wiped them out." A couple more wurmers dropped dead from the sky. "Cloudy with a chance of wurmers."

The silver dragons circled like a spinning windmill.

Nath waved. "I guess this is the part where they save us and leave us. It would be great if once, just once, they'd stick around long enough for me to thank them."

"Aye." Brenwar gave a dwarven salute. He pumped his fist and thumped his chest. "Unlike you, they're not much for talking."

Nath eyed him.

Brenwar shrugged.

The circle of dragons broke. In a V formation, wings flapping in unison, they shot off toward the moon. All except for one. He landed, the biggest of the group. The leader. His lean, serpentine body clung low to the ground. His long neck undulated like a fish's body.

Nath spoke to the silver dragon leader in Dragonese—an ancient language, melodic, a combination of sounds and words. "Thank you, brother."

The dragon skulked forward. His eyes were bright blue. Penetrating. He had seemed bigger in the sky, but up close, the silver dragon was no bigger than Nath. Coming closer, he reared up onto his hind legs and stood like a man. He crossed his front paws over his armored chest. Holding his chin high, he stood a full head taller than Nath. Then he bowed and said, also in Dragonese, "I might be your brother, but you are my prince."

Nath's jaw dropped. He was speechless. He reached out and, with his hand under the dragon's chin, he lifted his eyes to meet his. "Slivver?"

"At your service," the dragon said in Common.

Nath hugged his brother.

Slivver hugged him back. It wasn't an awkward hug by any means, just two brothers embracing after a hard-fought battle. Slivver was all dragon but carried himself, at this moment, like a man.

Breaking the embrace, Nath exclaimed, "I've missed you!"

"Of course you have. Everybody has." Slivver's sleekness and charm matched the wondrous scales of his body. He held his elbow in one hand and gestured as he spoke with the other. "I have to admit, I've missed out on many exciting things." His ice-blue eyes drifted to Brenwar.

"Where have you been hiding, Slivver?" Brenwar said.

"Well, if it isn't my old, old friend Brenwar. Old, old, old friend." Slivver stretched out his arms. "Hugs?"

"Dwarves don't—"

"I know, I know, dwarves don't hug." Slivver laughed, shaking the bearded flap of skin under his chin. "Hugs, thugs. Watch out behind you."

Nath had completely forgotten about the nuurg sentry blowing the whistle and alerting the wurmers. It rushed the backside of Brenwar.

Without turning, Brenwar socked it in the gut with Mortuun.

"Oooof!" The monster sagged.

Brenwar cranked back for the finishing blow.

"No, wait!" Nath said. "Bind him up. Let's see what he knows."

"Still learning mercy, are you?" Slivver said.

"I've learned plenty since you've been gone."

"It's an abomination."

"I know, but I need information. I need to find Father. He's gone rogue."

"It wouldn't be the first time." Slivver's long tail swished behind him. "Tell me about it?"

Nath caught Slivver up with how their father Balzurth had healed Sasha of the wizard's dementia and then disappeared from the Temple of Spires.

Slivver shook his magnificent dragon head. "And ever since, you've been trekking the earth by foot and hoof? Why not call for the dragons?"

"I have called. They didn't answer."

"Just because they don't answer doesn't mean you stop calling." Slivver chuckled.

"Oh," Nath said.

Throwing his paw over Nath's shoulder, Slivver said, "I got here in the nick of time. Now let's go find Father."

CHAPTER 26

SELENE WAS BACK IN THE bedroom with all the murals. She wasn't alone. Grahleyna was with her, as was Sansla Libor. The winged white ape stood in front of one of the murals, staring at a distant view of Elome.

"Do you miss being among the roamer elves?" she said.

"I'm the Roamer King. It always hurts to not be among my people." His ape face was long. "It's not easy being an outcast, but I've learned to accept it."

"In time, your people will learn to accept you," Selene said.

"The elves aren't even accepting of one another at the moment. Their hearts have been twisted."

Grahleyna sat on the edge of the bed with her head down. She hadn't said a word in hours. "It's the titans' fault," she said under her breath. "Those evil spirits poison everything. I can only hope my overzealous husband puts an end to this. He went out there because he loves me, perhaps too much, if that's possible. But he hates Eckubahn even more. I can't blame him for what he did." She slapped her knees and stood. Pointing at all the murals, each as real as the next and divided by a network of honeycomb columns, she said, "You need to decide where you want to start."

"What do you mean?" Selene said.

"I mean, in what part of Nalzambor do you want to begin your search for Nath and Balzurth? It's not possible for us to fly you out of here, and it isn't safe to tunnel out." Grahleyna straightened and fluffed the pillows on the bed. She moved as if her mind was far away. "There is deep magic here. You feel it. With my aid, you can walk through to the place you see in an instant. You won't be coming back through once you cross, however. It'll be a one-way trip."

Selene gazed at all the different mural portals which filled the wondrous room. She could see the village at Dragon Pond. Tiny fisherman, like insects, fished from the piers. In a corner above her head, the orcen city of Thraag loomed. Part of its own mountain and carved from within, Morgdon of the dwarves waited with stark banners whipping stiffly in the wind mounted on enormous poles. Narnum, the Free City, was anything but. It stirred Selene within. She'd done horrible things there. Now it fared even worse than she'd left it. Giants of all the rogue races roamed the streets like men. Soaring wurmers crested the building tops.

"Where the trouble is, Nath will be." Selene stroked the tip of her tail, which rested over her shoulder. "That's the spot, but I don't want to be too close."

"That's not a problem. Just think of a spot you've been before and go."

Selene said to Sansla, "Are you coming with me?"

"I gave Nath my word I'd look out for you."

Selene hugged Grahleyna. "I'll stay if you wish."

"I'd like that, but under better circumstances. Now go."

Heart thumping hard in her chest, Selene grabbed Sansla and stepped into the mural.

CHAPTER 27

"TIMOTHY, YOU'VE BEEN BRAVE AND excellent. I thank you." Nath shook the veteran's hand. "Can you handle him?" He spoke of the last living nuurg. The nine-footer's arms and legs were shaking in heavy chains.

With a smile, Tim said, "I feel like I can handle anything. We'll put this monster to work back in the fortress if we have to. Probably let him bury his own dead. The people are happy. The fortress holds more supplies than I expected. It'll help us. Thanks, Dragon Prince. It's been an unbelievable honor fighting by your side. I might even have to come out of my retirement." He stepped forward, jabbing the air with his sword, but then he grimaced and held his shoulder. "Ohhhhh. I'll think about it."

Nath, Brenwar, and Slivver departed. Nath had allowed Brenwar to spend the better part of an hour interrogating the nuurg. That had been an ugly sight. Not so much the howls of pain, but seeing a cyclops cry was just uncomfortable.

Narnum.

Regarding the whereabouts of Eckubahn, all the slobbering crying nuurg could say was "Narnum." The very heart of Nalzambor.

It stirred a lot of bad memories for Nath. He'd seen the worst of the worst in Selene there. So much so, it made his heart ache. "I guess the titan den is pretty obvious," he said, rubbing the back of his head. "Evil seems to have an affection for the place. I wonder why."

"Location, location, location," Slivver said. He walked on all fours now.

"You always have a good answer for everything."

Brenwar huffed.

"No offense, Brenwar. You have good answers too. Sometimes."

Nath's thoughts drifted to the time he'd spent more than a century ago with Slivver. Unlike most of his brothers and sisters—who resented Nath for being named Dragon Prince when they were all older—Slivver was a friend and a mentor. The silver dragon had taught him much when he was younger about the different breeds of dragons and their ways. The two of them had even gone adventuring together, back when Nath was barely a century old, a youngster. Slivver shared Nath's fascination with the races. Like it was supposed to be for Nath, when Slivver didn't look like a dragon, he could easily pass for a man.

"So, Slivver, where have you been all this time?"

"Sleeping. You know how it goes." The silver dragon, now on all fours, moved more like a cat than a lizard. His lean body snaked through the bushes they passed. "When the dragon sleep comes, it comes."

"So you weren't part of the Great Dragon Wall?"

"I can say with glee my time on the wall has passed."

"Oh, I didn't realize. Of course, I never knew there was a wall to begin with. I can only imagine how many other secrets I don't know." He gave Slivver a look. "I don't suppose you're going to tell me."

"And let you miss out on the excitement of discovery?" Sliver flashed all of the fangs in his pearly-white teeth. "Fret not, Nath. For the most part I only know what I have seen. The rest of the dragons know even less than that. You know how they are."

"Yes, I know."

The odd group stayed on the country roads and wended their way through the rolling hills. It was still nighttime, and there wasn't a single passerby.

Nath had opted not to take the wrath horns along. The last thing he wanted to do was arouse suspicion. "Feel like picking up the pace?" he said to Brenwar.

"Aye."

"Surely you don't plan to continue walking to Narnum," Slivver said with his dragon face aghast. "That's preposterous."

"In case you hadn't noticed," Nath hitched his thumb over his back, "I don't have any wings."

"Then ride a dragon," Slivver suggested.

"No offense, but I don't think you're big enough. We tried before, remember? Ha ha."

"Oh, ho-ho," Slivver said. "My back still aches from it."

With moonlight shining on his face, Nath said, "Slivver, how did you come by me? By us, back there?

Was it by chance? Because to me, it seems unlikely you'd show up at the right place at the right time so conveniently."

"Like I said, I've been asleep for quite some time. I've not been awake very long, and when I did wake, I sought you out." Slivver rose up on his hind legs and walked upright beside Nath. "Dragons are nestled all around. Some of them helped me. Besides, you've always been my charge, by Father's request." He whispered in Nath's ear. "I have to tell you, I'm surprised the bearded stump is still around."

"I heard that," Brenwar said. "Giants' whispers are quieter than that."

"As I was saying," Slivver continued, "I was close when all this happened. I caught up with you and have been watching since before you made your way into the small town of Timothy."

Nath stopped. "Why did you wait so long to reveal yourself?"

Oddly, Slivver rolled his ice-blue eyes. "I was waiting for a dragon call. I'm not supposed to intervene without the call. But you don't call. You're the Dragon Prince. Use the call." He huffed on his claws. "But there's nothing holding me back from ripping those dreadful wurmers apart whenever given the chance. Never seen such disgusting things." He eyeballed Nath. "Well?"

"Well what?"

"Will you summon a dragon so we can expedite this quest? You don't imagine the titan horde taking a stroll through the green valleys, do you? No, it's devouring everything in its path as fast as it can."

Nath cupped his hands to his mouth and took a breath.

"I don't want to fly," Brenwar interrupted.

"Of course you don't. If dwarves were meant to fly, they'd have wings," Slivver replied.

"For a change, I agree with you."

Slivver got back down on all fours and faced Brenwar, "I'll believe when dwarves fly."

"Enough of the bickering, you two. Here goes." In a voice with the strength of a vast and flowing river, he made the call. It was like the roar of the tide, blended in with nature. One would not know they heard it if they didn't know what they were listening for. Still, Nath tried to focus. His summons needed to be sincere.

"RrrrroooOWwwwwwfffFFFttTHhhhhrrrrrruuuuUMmmmmmmmmmmmmmmm!"

After a minute, he stopped. The night skies remained clear. "Well, that's it. Should I try again?"

Slivver shook his head. "The call must travel. The dragon must travel back. It's not teleportation."

Moving on, Nath doubted anything would happen.

CHAPTER 28

BALZURTH WAS SUNK KNEE DEEP in mud thicker than ogre pudding. His hands were shackled above his head in dwarven irons. Scraped up and bruised, head pounding, he looked up at the light in the sky. Clouds drifted by the moon. Slow. Tedious. There was red—like blood—in them. He drew in the stuffy night air. The scent of evil was strong. The oil and sweat of giants. The presence of evil was even worse. Nearby somewhere, innocent blood had been spilled. Not of men and women but of dragons.

He snarled at the giants who filled the massive coliseum. It was the same group that had tried to drag the life out of him into the city of Narnum. Somehow, he had managed to make it back to his feet and walk into the town under his own power. The people's eyes were heavy on him, their stares familiar. He knew of the feats his son Nath Dragon had accomplished in the Contest of Champions. Now he was here. The people knew other things as well. How Nath, the form Balzurth had taken, had saved the world. He saw the hope fade from their eyes when they saw him shackled and broken.

Anger stirred within his breast. A deep hatred built. The titans were nothing but destroyers of everything good in the world. He had to put an end to them. It took everything he had to not burst free of his bonds, hunt down Eckubahn and Isobahn, and blast them into the netherworld once and for all.

I am close. So very, very close. Eckubahn, you will be mine. Vengeance for all the innocent is at hand.

CHAPTER 29

Selene rubbed her shoulders. They were ice cold from the teleportation from Dragon Home to where she'd just arrived. She'd known where she was the moment they arrived. After all, she'd targeted the destination. The towers of Narnum were a league away. Urns filled with fire burned on the rooftops. They hadn't been there before.

"The titans have a new home. Perhaps Urslay is abandoned." She laughed. "Maybe all the people should move there."

"What do you want to do?" Sansla shook the frost from his wings. The eight-foot ape stood with his knuckles on the ground. "I can't take to the air or waltz inside."

Selene's robes covered her wrists and ankles. "I can still pass for human. I should be able to go in. It's not as if the giants have any special defenses. There's nothing for them to defend against, aside from the dragons." She searched the skyline. Only wurmers passed overhead. "I'm only going in for a look. Maybe ask a few questions. Give me a day."

Sansla nodded. "There will be temptations."

"I know." Selene made her way out of the field and onto the road. Step by step, she headed back into the city she'd once conquered. A dangerous thought lingered in her mind.

Perhaps I can turn the titans on my own.

CHAPTER 30

Nath and company hadn't even made it half a league when a great shadow blotted out the moon. Every head turned up.

Above, a massive dragon circled with wings spread wide. Gliding through the wind, he slowly spiraled downward. His front and rear legs bore great talons. A pair of tremendous horns formed a U on his head. An orange glow in his eyes resonated with what must have been a great fire within. He was a bull dragon, mighty in size and frame. He landed with the softness of a dove, blocking the entire road and then some.

Slivver somehow formed a smile on his nonexistent lips. "I told you so."

The bull dragon, red scaled with a hint of green, let out a snort and lowered his head. His body was scales over huge muscles, his breastplate like steel. His huge claws could rip a giant in half.

Nath approached on soft feet and rubbed the bull dragon's neck. It was like petting a hot anvil.

The dragon's eye remained fixed on him. The burning orb was as big as his head.

"Thank you for coming."

The dragon snorted a blast of heat.

That was as good an answer as Nath was going to get. Bull dragons weren't talkers at all. They were beasts of action. It was a temperamental brood too. Private. Difficult. Of all the dragons who could have arrived in reply to Nath's summons, a bull dragon was at the top of the list of least expected.

Nath had been in a fierce fight with them before, years ago, just outside of the Floating City. He eyed the sharp talons on the tips of its wings.

I hope he's not here to eat me.

"I'm Nath, and you are?"

The bull dragon clacked his teeth really fast and shook his head, knocking Nath backward.

"I see." Nath glanced at Slivver. "Could you make that out?"

With a nod, Slivver said, "Yes. He says his name is Waark. Well, for short. If you don't want him clacking like a beaver all night long, I'd stay with that."

"I can go with that. Waark, shall we ride?"

The big dragon's belly flattened on the ground. He held his head low. Nath used the hard, scaly ridges to climb on his back. He wedged himself between the armor scales running down the dragon's spine. Getting a grip on a dragon of such massive girth wasn't easy. Riding would be even more difficult.

"Uh, Brenwar, do we have a rope or something?"

Arms folded over his chest, Brenwar said, "No. You need to be walking."

Waark spread his massive wings. They flapped, and then, bunching back onto his back legs, the dragon launched himself up into the air.

"Whoa!" Nath yelled. He dug his nails and heels into the dragon's armor.

Up, up, up they went. Wedged between the dragon's ridges, it wouldn't be too difficult to hold on, assuming the flight was level and Waark didn't go into any barrel rolls, which was unlikely. Bull dragons weren't the fleetest. As a matter of fact, they were some of the slowest, if not *the* slowest—aside from the dragons who didn't have any wings at all.

Below, Brenwar shook his fist and screamed, "Get down here, Nath. Get back down!"

Nath shrugged and called out, "I'm just going to scout ahead. You know me. Do you want to ride?"

"No!" Brenwar became a speck on the ground, and in a few moments, the dwarf was out of sight.

Nath eased back into the strange seat, and before long, wind tearing at his face, he smiled.

Ah, it feels good to be part of the wind again. How I've missed it!

Before long, they were soaring through the clouds of the night, and Nath said in Dragonese, "We're headed for Narnum, but avoid the wurmers."

The dragon's wings beat slow and steady. There was enough power in them to hold at least ten more of Nath, if not twenty. The strength of the bull dragon fed him. Its heart beat in unison with his. They connected. Scaled brothers.

Out of the deep blue sky, Slivver came. His wings beat with the ease of a feather falling. He landed right on the back of the bull dragon, in front of Nath. "Enjoying the ride?"

"Absolutely."

"I don't think the dwarf is very happy."

"He'll catch up. Eventually." Nath chuckled. "He always does."

The bull dragon soared higher than the distant snow-capped mountains that spiked the drifting clouds. The chill air normally would brittle a man's bones, but it didn't. The bull dragon huffed out a warm wind, like off a campfire, every time his wings made a downward stroke. The fire from his belly was warm and soothing.

Taking a look at the quiet lands below where only sparkles of fires burned like fireflies in the night, Nath said, "This is really something, isn't it?"

"Adventure always is." Slivver managed to somehow make himself look extremely comfortable on the bull dragon's back, yet he seemed more man than dragon. "Sometimes it's fun to just enjoy the ride, though it is a slow one. For a dragon, Waark moves at the pace of a dwarf."

Waark's body tremored, jostling the riders.

Nath and Slivver clung on.

"Take no offense, Waark!" Slivver winked at Nath. "It seems no one appreciates being likened to Brenwar's sort."

Like Nath, Slivver was one of a kind among the dragons. He was a silver dragon, but there were many types. There was the larger breed, some of which grew to a size rivaling the bull dragons, and then there were the smaller, more petite sort, quick and powerful with their magic. Not all dragons were old because they were bigger, and not all dragons were young because they were smaller. There were fire bites and pixie dragons who were more than a thousand years old. But even among the rarest of rare was Slivver.

Unlike the rest of their kin, Nath and Slivver were both fascinated with the races. Most dragons didn't care at all. Ever. But Slivver did. If his brother could change into an elf, Nath had no doubt he would. For a while at least.

"Slivver, it's good to have you back. It makes me think of the good old days. You know, back when I was little more than a century. Boy, I was so cocky back then. It's a wonder I made it this far." Nath brushed away a lock of red hair that had drifted over his eye. "I really missed you when you left."

"I missed you too. Even in my sleep, I dreamed of our quests. Now they begin anew."

Nath glanced back. The bull dragon's tail swished behind them. Even at this slower flying speed, it wouldn't take much longer to get to Narnum. A few hours at most. He felt a little guilty leaving Brenwar behind. "Perhaps we should turn around."

With a flip of his paw, Slivver said, "Do as you wish. I can do the scouting ahead if you want. Besides, if the wurmers catch wind of Waark, he won't be able to escape them, but they'll never catch me."

"Eh, he'll be fine."

CHAPTER 31

SELENE DONNED HER HOOD JUST before she entered the formerly Free City of Narnum. She'd almost forgotten the people would recognize her. Thinking back on all the atrocities she and the other Clerics of Barnabus had committed, she had no doubt the people would mob her if she showed her face.

She walked by a pair of giants, each of whom was covered in coarse hair and patches of armor. They were full bloods. Twenty feet high, their bodies filled half the stone-paved street. They poked at one another, jesting and laughing. Their bellies shook when they laughed. Women scurried back and forth, rushing in and out of a tavern. They held pitchers of ale in their arms and filled the huge tankards the giants set on the ground. Every time a giant spoke, the women shouted praise. Their painted eyes were wild with adoration in most cases, but not all.

Music, exotic and dark, blared from horns, voices, strings, and drums. It echoed throughout the city. Sounds from band after band collided with one another.

Selene weaved her way toward the sound of where the masses gathered, fighting the urge to cover her ears and moving with the flow of the raucous crowds filling the once-glorious streets, now rough and shambled. Above, nested in the spires and lying on rooftops, were the dark-scaled wurmers. Their eyes bright, bodies never resting, they were like lizards bathing in a moonlight sun. She could see dozens, but there must have been hundreds.

She pressed through the knots of people who waded among the giant men as casually as they did their own. Men and women who stood ten and more feet tall. Each had a flock of followers behind them, and for every ten small giants, there was one full blood. They lounged and frolicked with one another. The normal-sized people behaved with wild abandon.

This is insanity.

A woman caught Selene by the elbow with both hands. "Come, sister! Come with me!"

Selene pulled away.

The young woman's grip remained firm. "Why do you hide your face, sister? We are all beautiful here."

A second woman blindsided Selene and jerked the hood down. "You're so beautiful! A true maiden for Eckubahn. He must see you!"

Selene shoved the women aside. Heart racing, she covered her head and ran.

The women called out after her. "Eckubahn will have you! He'll take your heart."

Ducking into an alley, Selene cut from one street to another and waded into a different sea of people. They all moved in one direction. Hands and arms waving, they were chanting and praising Eckubahn. The giants. The titans. She followed the sea of people into the arena where the Contest of Champions had been held. It was bigger than it used to be. The giants had expanded it to have seats to hold their kind. Within the entrance tunnel, Selene couldn't see what it was inside the arena that had the crowd so excited. Everyone pushed and shoved.

These people are wild!

Finally, the throng of cajolers squeezed out of the tunnel and filed into the seats of the oval ring. On ground level inside the arena, Selene looked up and caught her first glimpse of the colossal giants. There were many. Bare chested. Armed in some cases. All of them were full blood.

Seated on a throne made from the bones of dragons sat the biggest one of all, Eckubahn. His head was aflame. Beside him stood another titan with a long ponytail and burning green eyes.

A sick feeling stirred inside the pit of Selene's stomach. She made her way up the steps of the coliseum. The seats were filling fast. She made it up high enough to see down into the arena.

Time to see what all of this ludicrous commotion is about.

She turned. Immediately her heart jumped. She gasped and clutched her chest.

In the center of the arena, Nath was chained up to a wall of iron, waist deep in sludge.

CHAPTER 32

ECKUBAHN. THE TITAN KING.

Staring at him, Balzurth knew he was every bit the menace Gorn Grattack was, but worse in other ways. Gorn was a dragon. Even a good dragon once. He didn't hate dragons. He just hated the good in them. That's where Eckubahn and Gorn differed. Eckubahn hated all things good. The giants hated all things dragon, good or not. Eckubahn was the worst of all atrocities: an evil spirit in an evil body commanding an ever-growing army of oversized fiends.

"MY PRIZE. MY PRIZE."

Eckubahn's cavernous voice hushed the crowd. He turned his flaming head to face his fellow spirit, Isobahn. Together, the pair of titans was more formidable than every person and giant in the arena put together. Brawny and mystical, the titans emanated uncanny, wicked power.

"My servant Rybek did well. Did you send for him?"

"I did," Isobahn replied. He stroked his ponytail. Isobahn was the leaner of the two titans. His face, shaven and scarred, might have even been handsome at one time, for a giant. He didn't seem worried about a thing. "I imagine he'll be here soon. I see no reason to wait for him. Let the games begin."

Eckubahn shifted his focus to Balzurth, who was still disguised as Nath. The dark, glowing pits of the titan's eyes bore into Balzurth, searching. The titan's fingers gripped the dragon skulls that made up the chair arms. His long fingernails pecked the dragon-skull foreheads.

Two wurmers as big as horses lay at his feet like dogs. Their hungry eyes were fixed on Balzurth. Claws scraped at the stones below the dragon seat.

"Nath Dragon. Today your heroics end."

Time to sell it, old man. Say something smart-alecky like your son would.

Balzurth stared right back at the titan and said, "Why thank you, Eckubahn. I can't tell you how much I appreciate the celebration. And to think you went to all this trouble to throw a retirement party for me. I'm elated." He looked from side to side. "And a bit baffled. I don't see any cake."

Isobahn sat up, eyes wide, brows lifted. A confused expression filled his face. He chuckled. Others in the seats chuckled as well.

Eckubahn's flaming head brightened. His fists went up and came down hard, shattering the dragon-bone chair arms.

"SILENCE!"

As Nath, Balzurth shrugged. The chains on his arms rattled.

That's it. Get in his head a little. Distract him.

Sweat trickled down his cheek. Balzurth, as mighty as he might have been, could still worry. At the moment, he was faced with the two most powerful titans, Eckubahn and Isobahn. The rest of the spirits were scattered all over Nalzambor. In addition to that, a host of giants surrounded him. He couldn't fight them all. Not at once. Not without help. But he didn't need to fight them all. He only needed to take the fight to one, Eckubahn. Balzurth's nostrils flared. He had his wish. He was close enough to kill the titan king.

"I know what you're doing, Eckubahn." Balzurth jerked his head and blew at the long, red Nath hair in his eyes. Not having any success, he said, "You want to draw my father out. But let me tell you, he's too wise for that."

"He'll come," Eckubahn said. "He'll hear your cries. Feel your pain. The only way to save yourself is to get him to exchange his life for yours. Let me assure you, Balzurth is mine."

Balzurth shook his head, this time managing to get the hair out of his eyes. "No, no. I don't think it will happen. I'm my own dragon now. He knows this. I got myself into this, and I can get myself out. Besides, my father never listens to me. He's stubborn like that."

Eckubahn leaned forward and said with authority, "Call for him."

"Eh, my father is all knowing. If he wanted to be here, he'd be here by now. Sorry, but we'll just have to have the cake without him." Balzurth tried to cross his arms over his chest, but his restraints wouldn't let him. "Imagine me folding my arms over my chest right now."

Eckubahn sat back on his throne and gave Isobahn a nod. "You are a fool, Nath Dragon. For I am all knowing. Perhaps your father is not here, but someone else who cares for you is."

Isobahn's head swiveled over his shoulder. He pointed toward the audience in the stands and said, "Seize her!"

A commotion erupted in the stands. Men and giants converged on a single figure in the crowd. Oversized limbs and hands the size of shovels locked on the legs and arms of a lone robed figure.

Who is he talking about?

The giant men roughly dragged a woman kicking and screaming over the benches, but her cries were from anger, not fear. They dragged her in front of the throne. The giant yanked down the woman's hood. A black-scaled tail lashed out, smiting the giant in the head.

Balzurth got a glimpse of her face.

Selene!

Without holding back, the giant force of men clubbed her to the ground and dragged her across the dirt floor of the arena in front of Balzurth.

She moaned.

A giant hit her again.

"Quit, you monster!"

The giant drew back its club.

"Stop," Eckubahn said. There were no visible lips to be seen behind his speech; just his eyes showed on his face. "Harness her to the stone."

Standing twenty feet high, a cyclops walked over with a block of stone the size of an ox cart. The chunk of granite must have weighed tons. Rectangular in shape, the slab was bloodstained, like a sacrificial altar. With muscles bulging in its arms, it set the block between Eckubahn and Selene. The smaller giants shackled Selene by the wrists with dwarven iron and secured her to the pillar of stone. She lay flat on her back.

"What are you doing, Eckubahn?" Balzurth yelled. "You have me. Let her go! I demand it!"

Eckubahn's flaming head brightened when he spoke. "No one makes demands of me. I make demands of you. Your woman, this Selene, I know of her and her darkness. It still flows through her blood. I can sense it. But the good in her is strong. So much I don't like it." The titan nodded.

An earth giant hairy as a caterpillar walked over. It held a tremendous axe in its hand. It was an executioner's axe with a single, one-sided blade. Covered in dried blood.

Balzurth could smell dragon blood on the metal of the axe and on the stone slab. His temper rose.

How many dragons have died by this monster's hands? No more!

The giant executioner stood over Selene and the slab. Lifting the axe over its shoulders, it turned its head to Eckubahn.

"I don't delay, Nath Dragon. Call for your father, or she shall surely die right before your golden eyes."

The deranged crowd chanted, "Kill her! Kill her! Kill her!"

Every syllable the crowd said felt like a dagger in Balzurth's chest. It hurt. It angered him. His chin trembled with fury. For centuries, he'd been fully composed. There'd been no circumstance he couldn't handle. But the gorge of madness now surrounding him infuriated him. The twisted, evil minds disgusted him.

His temper, long dormant, rose some more.

And this time, he didn't tamp it down with wisdom.

Sasha's darkness now dwelled within him, and it stoked his fires. Fanned the flames. Urged him to let the rage against evil come forth.

It's time!

He locked eyes with Selene. The weary dragon woman's eyes widened.

He spoke into her mind. *Get ready.*

With a snarl, he spoke to the titan, "Fine, Eckubahn! Fine! If you want me to call my father, I shall call him!"

"Make it quick. Hope he arrives soon. The axe will fall at any moment."

Balzurth's golden eyes burned brighter than the stars. He said, "You don't have to worry about that. He's already here." Balzurth called out in an all-powerful voice that could be heard by the dragons to the five great cities and beyond.

"BAAAAAAAAAHHHHHHHHROOOOOOOOOO!"

CHAPTER 33

INGERS CROSSED BEHIND HIS HEAD, Nath said to Slivver, "You know, I'd probably have this adventure completed by now if I could get Brenwar to ride on a dragon. That's probably why, when I call, they don't come. Maybe my heart's not in it because he doesn't like it."

"Perhaps," said Slivver. The beard of skin under his chin waved in the wind atop the bull dragon's back. "But you need to remember you're a dragon, Nath. You can't do as the other races of people do. You're different. Being among them too much holds back your dragon development. That's been your problem all along."

What? Really?

This was exciting news that gave him hope, but on the outside, Nath played it cool. "I know. It's hard, though. After all, I was born a man. I've walked, eaten, breathed, and drunk as a man all my life. It's so hard to be something else." He stretched out his arms, letting the high winds caress his clawed fingers. "Besides, they're so entertaining. I tell you, Brenwar makes me laugh, and he's never even trying to be funny."

"Well, you know how I am about it. I share your fascination with the world of men. Much of that comes from my relationship with you. To mentor you, I've needed to comprehend your dilemmas. But Nath, the dragons, your brethren, are far from bland. You would find as much joy among us as anyone else. Take me, for example. Think back. You had friends back when."

"I know, but I'm so attached to people. I love them."

"There's no wrong in that."

"I'd hope not."

A sound filled with vibration rushed through Nath's body. His scales stood on end.

Waark lurched beneath him.

It was a dragon call. One much like the one Nath had used to summon the bull dragon, but at least a hundred times more powerful.

Nath was on his feet.

Slivver's eyes were staring into his. The silver dragon's jaw hung.

Waark's wings beat faster.

"That was Father! It came from Narnum!" Nath about jumped out of his boots. He'd never heard anything like that before. Nothing in the entire world could have equaled it. The earth-rocking bellow echoed through all the lands and stirred the snow in the very mountaintops. It was a dragon call for not just one dragon but all. It was a call to war. He could hear the voice of the people cry out in alarm as if the world were about to end.

Spreading his wings, Slivver hopped into the air and glided alongside Nath. "I'm going ahead. See you there." And with that, Slivver took off like he'd been launched out of a sling.

"No, wait!" Nath said.

Slivver was gone. His host of other silver dragons joined him, streaking through the air like bolts of lightning in a stormy sky.

Nath crawled up to the top of Waark's neck and said, "Faster! Faster!"

Waark moaned. His wings beat with new fury, neck stretched ahead.

Nath guessed it would take an hour to get to Narnum at this rate.

Might as well be an eon.

His muscles tensed and flexed. His body was ready to burst from his skin. He needed to get there now. Something big was happening, and he knew what it was. Balzurth battled Eckubahn. His father was ready to break the evil titan once and for all.

He needs me! I can feel it! Something's wrong. I feel he can't do it alone!

With the wind tearing at his face, he urged Waark on. "Faster! Faster! Balzurth needs us! The entire world needs us!"

CHAPTER 34

Selene couldn't believe her eyes. It wasn't Nath chained to that slab of stone, it was Balzurth! His powerful roar strengthened her limbs and knocked the grogginess from her mind. She felt ready to fight every giant and wurmer in the land.

Axe in hand, the giant executioner quavered. The axe fell from its fingers.

Eckubahn shrank in his throne. The bones of its frame rattled.

Balzurth enlarged. The chains cuffed to his wrists popped and snapped. The body of Nath Dragon transformed.

The crowd screamed in terror.

The king of the dragons emerged. Forty feet of brick-red and bronze scales. His neck was a pillar of iron. His tail was a great cedar. A true natural-born behemoth of armor and brawn. The sun was a lantern behind his back. His shadow cast over both Selene and Eckubahn. Brilliant illumination came from his eyes, filled with anger and judgment. Balzurth shook his grand horns and said to Eckubahn:

"TODAY IS JUDGMENT DAY, TITAN! AND I AM THE JUDGE!"

The giant executioner's fingers stretched for its axe.

Balzurth's tail snapped like a clap of thunder, striking the giant dead.

Filled with a new strength she'd never imagined, Selene strained at the iron chains. The dwarven metal groaned. She didn't know if it was her newly scaled body or Balzurth's presence, but the strength in her limbs was that of a dragon. With a roar bursting from her lips, the chains snapped. She was free. Poised to strike from the slab, she surveyed her enemies. Giants and wurmers of all sizes converged from all directions in a maddened frenzy. It was her and Balzurth versus the world. She punched her fist into her hand. "To the end!"

The overwhelming sea of evil came by the hundreds.

And then it rained.

But it rained dragons.

In a wave of teeth and claws, dragons of all colors tore into the enemies with their tantalizing scales winking in the sun. Fire shot from their mouths, covering giants in flame. Blue razor dragons sent shards of lightning through the wurmers. Jaws locked on wurmers and tore them apart.

A sky raider dropped from the sky, crushing the giants in the stands. He stormed forward, horns down, stampeding a bewildered horde of smaller giants.

Indeed, it was judgment day on the back-biting citizens of Narnum.

Under a compulsion she could not explain, Selene grabbed the only weapon she could find: the giant executioner's axe. Somehow, she lifted the unwieldy thing and swung it into the back leg of an earth giant that was locked up with a bronze dragon. The giant toppled. The dragon blasted flames into its face. With a two-handed swing of the axe, she ripped into a flock of wurmers. Scales and claws were sliced and scattered.

All around, the ground shook and tremored. The battleground was hazy. Fire and smoke. Burning scales and sizzled flesh. Roars. Bellows. Screams. It was carnage.

Wave after wave of dragons dived down into the arena from the sky. They unleashed their breath weapons, pelting the giants with wroth heat and pain.

The enraged giants howled. They grabbed people and hunks of stone from the stands and hurled them at the dragons.

With ease, the dragons swerved in midair to avoid the huge flying hunks of stone, only to attack with more fire again and again.

So many dragons were there, and in such a multitude of colors, locked in a mortal battle. Blue razors, bulls, bronzes, green lilies, orange blazes, crimson dynamos, ivory sliders, yellow streaks, fire bites, grey scalers, and dozens of other colors attacked from all directions. It was an onslaught. They had the giants on the run.

An orange blaze was locked on a giant's head. The giant beat at it with fury. A second orange blaze unleashed a white foam from his mouth, coating the giant from neck to toe. The foam disintegrated the giant's skin to the bone.

A bronze dragon, grand in frame, swooped down from above. Its tail locked around a giant's neck like a whip. Wings pounding the air, the bronze dragon lifted the giant into the sky like a hawk snatching a rabbit from the prairie. Up, up, up the dragon went, a speck in the sky. The giant thrashed, arms flailing and legs kicking. The bronze dragon's neck bent, and it let out a gust of fire. The giant burned. The dragon uncurled his tail from the giant's neck. The burning giant fell like a falling star and crashed on two of its brethren.

Standing among the fray of chaos, Selene tossed the axe aside, pumped her arms high, and said, "Yes!"

The tide of battle was in the dragons' favor. Narnum was moments from being liberated.

And then a strange hum rose among the growls and the roar of fire. A storm cloud rolled in like a swarm of locusts. They came from the west. A deep purple glow was within the cloud.

A chill doused the fire in Selene's bones.

Evil's cavalry was coming. Wurmers. Not by the hundreds but by the thousands.

"Balzurth!" she yelled. "We need more dragons!"

Whether the Dragon King heard her she didn't know.

Balzurth, towering above all, battled Eckubahn. A crushed throne of dragon bones lay beneath them. Balzurth coiled his tail around the titan's neck. The titan king's fists hammered at Balzurth's body.

Boom! Boom! Boom!

Selene did a double take between the sky and the battle of kings. Balzurth needed to finish Eckubahn. He needed to finish Eckubahn now.

A second titan that Selene didn't recognize at first was on the move. Oh, it was Isobahn, the muscular, oily, tattooed brute with the long ponytail. The titan had slunk away from the fracas, only to reappear with a spear the likes of which she'd never seen before. At the huge spear's tip, six strips of twisted metal came to a razor-sharp point. The weapon was big enough to skewer three giants at once, more than capable of running Balzurth through, in one side and out the other. A dark aura flowed around the metal spearhead with a life of its own.

What is that?

But even though she had never seen the weapon before, in her heart she knew what it was. Before her time, her father, Gorn Grattack, had been the evil enemy in the first Dragon War. In the final battle, Gorn had been beaten and subdued by a man, a special man who wielded a weapon that could kill anything. A special man whose legendary name Gorn had twisted into a lie to turn the races against the dragons.

"Barnabus!" she cried out.

Selene knew she beheld that same weapon now. Isobahn had it poised at Balzurth's back. The titan had a gleam in his eye as if this moment had been planned all along.

Nalzambor, have mercy!

"Balzurth! Watch out behind you! He wields the Spear of Barnabus!"

CHAPTER 35

ATH HUGGED A LARGE FIN of armor jutting up from the bull dragon's back. His claws dug into the bull dragon's rocky hide. Jaws clenched, stomach in knots, he couldn't shake off the spiders crawling up his spine.

I need to be there! I need to be there now!

Still leagues away, he could make out Narnum from the sky. There was a deadly jubilation of fiery activity below. Dragons dive bombed from unseen heights. It sent a charge through his scales into his bones. He could sense the battle's full scale. The victorious shrieks of the dragons carried through the skies.

Nath couldn't imagine anything or anyone in the world surviving such an onslaught. What could possibly withstand a legion of dragons led by Balzurth?

The dark fear in his heart enlarged the moment he spotted a sea of wurmers moving in from the west like a rain-heavy storm. He clutched his head in his hands.

Oh no! Oh no!

The wurmers were on course to blindside the ranks of dragons. The foul insectoids not only had strength, they had strength in numbers.

Nath let out another dragon call, screaming a warning.

"MaaaaaaAAARRRrrrrrrrrrOOOOoooooooooooooooooooooo!"

It carried. But would it carry far enough, fast enough, and into the ears of the battling mad dragon fray?

"Faster, Waark! Faster!"

Nath felt his heart sinking in his chest.

I can't be too late!

CHAPTER 36

ITH THE SPEAR OF BARNABUS in hand, Isobahn closed in.

Selene propelled herself into the towering titan's path, waving her hands above her head, shouting, "Take me, coward."

Eyes fixed on Balzurth's back, the titan's steps did not falter.

Out of the corner of her eye, she could see that Sansla Libor came, blasting through the chaos. Wings beating, arms outstretched, the great ape's fists collided with the titan's jaw with ram-like force. The blow staggered the titan. The spear tip dropped. The metal bit into the ground.

Selene coiled her body around the spear and held it with all her dragon strength.

Growling, Isobahn lifted her from the ground along with the spear. He tried to shake her off, arms flailing back and forth, side to side.

All the while, Sansla Libor stood on Isobahn's shoulder, punching the titan in the face with blows that would have dropped an ogre.

The bone necklace on the titan's neck rattled, but he didn't flinch. "I will not be stopped!" Isobahn's huge legs churned forward again.

Selene called out in Dragonese, "Help! Help! Your king needs your help!"

A small host of silver dragons zipped through the battle. Bolts of white-hot light shot from their mouths, striking the titan.

Isobahn convulsed. Bellowed. His furrowed brow darkened his once-omnipotent expression. "Fleas! I am a titan! You are fleas!"

The silver dragons latched onto the evil giant from head to toe. Claws and teeth sank into the mad titan's skin.

Any normal creature on Nalzambor would have fallen. But this was no ordinary giant. He was a titan, fueled by more than just flesh and bones; he had an ancient dark and evil magic as old as the world itself.

Surging ahead like a juggernaut, the Selene-covered-spear-wielding titan said with sinister glee, "Ho-ho-ho, nothing can stop a titan like me." With a single hand, Isobahn wrapped his fingers around Selene's body and squeezed her like she was part of the spear itself. "Fledgling, prepare to witness front and center the death of the once mighty Balzurth!"

With her body being crushed like it was stuck in a blacksmith's vise, Selene let out one final cry:

"Balzurth, watch out!"

CHAPTER 37

THE TIME HAD COME. THE moment had arrived. Balzurth was locked up in combat with his mortal enemy Eckubahn. It had been more than a thousand years, and the hatred they harbored for one another had only grown.

It showed. The two thrashed through the arena like a pair of rabid savages. Balzurth's claws sank into the flesh of the earth giant's body that hosted the evil spirit of the ancient titan. Balzurth's tail coiled around the flaming neck of the fiend. The kings conversed silently, from mind to mind.

"It's over, Eckubahn! I showed mercy before, but I show mercy no more!" Balzurth drove the titan into the ground, smashing a wurmer and giant beneath him. "And all of your foul brood are going down with you!"

"Never!" Eckubahn's fist slugged Balzurth in the jaw with thunderous impact.

The Dragon King's talons held firm, sinking deeper into the titan's thick hide.

Eckubahn squirmed, twisted, and wrestled with all his might. He threw dirt in Balzurth's eyes. Spat fire in his face. He clawed at the ground, straining. The titan couldn't escape Balzurth's grasp.

The Dragon King locked on with fire in his eyes and a volcano ready to erupt from his chest.

Striking Balzurth with anything and everything he could get his hands on, Eckubahn unleashed another deadly defense. "You cannot win, Balzurth! You are already defeated! See my wurmers! See my giants! They are turning back your pathetic surprise attack!"

Balzurth sensed the presence of the swarm of wurmers. He'd even anticipated it. That was why he'd put his plan in motion long before he arrived. The dragons had gathered high above, far from sight and suspicion, the moment he'd arrived in Narnum. It was all on account of a very tiny dragon who had been with him all along, hiding behind his locks of hair. A lizard wisp. Small but faster than a hummingbird with wings that beat a hundred times faster than an eye could blink, the tiny creature had carried out Balzurth's orders. The dragons had come and waited for his call. Now he just had to do his duty. Finish off Eckubahn. If not, he'd be lost. All of the dragons who had come would be lost as well.

"Again I say it's over, Eckubahn! Stop squirming and accept what's coming!" Balzurth rolled on top of Eckubahn. He pinned the titan's shoulders down to the ground. "Look me in the eye and face your doom!"

Eyes squeezed shut, the titan pushed back, shoving Balzurth's face up with his palms. "You can't destroy me, Balzurth! You weaken! I strengthen! You couldn't destroy me before. You doubt you can destroy me now! I can feel it!"

"I DOUBT NOTHING!" Balzurth drew his horns back and head butted Eckubahn in his flaming face.

CRACK!

The titan's body shimmered. His mighty limbs loosened.

Balzurth freed his front talons from the titan's body. Faster than a wing, his talons seized Eckubahn by the throat and squeezed.

The titan's head turned from orange to red to purple flames. His hands chopped at Balzurth's powerful arms. "You will not win, Balzurth! You will not win! You have a blind spot!"

Balzurth dug his talons deeper into the mounds of neck muscle. He searched for the titan's evasive eyes.

The fiend wriggled and thrashed. His huge head rolled from side to side like a spoiled child trying to avoid healthy food.

"You will face the truth, titan! You will face it now!"

"Never!" Choking, the titan's eyes popped wide. Balzurth's eyes bore right into him. "No! No! Never!"

Balzurth, fully aware of the chaos that surrounded him, sent out a silent message to all of the dragons.

Go! Far and fast!

He sent another message to his son, Nath. Mind to mind, Balzurth's final thoughts mingled with his son's. "Nath, save Selene. Save yourself. Get out of here. That is my final wish. Live on, Son. I love you. Live on."

CHAPTER 38

"FATHER! FATHER!" NATH CRIED OUT. The message his father had sent confused him.

What's going on?

For a moment of the fleetest sort, he and his father had been connected, mind to mind. He had felt Balzurth's fury and rage building. Had sensed the deep love within his father too. There had been that final command from father to son, and then the connection had just gone.

Nath barked an order. "Dive, Waark! Dive!"

Narnum rested in their path, only seconds away now. He'd be in time to help his father win the battle. But Selene was in danger? Where was she?

The dragons scattered in the air in all directions.

The wurmers gave chase.

Nath's keen dragon eyes zeroed in on the battleground. The arena of the Contest of Champions. More than half of the arena's stonework stands were nothing but dust and rubble. Thousands of bodies of giants, dragons, and wurmers lay still, but many others still battled. In the middle of it all, his grand and glorious father Balzurth had the titan held fast to the ground.

Nath pumped his fist. "Yes, Father! Yes!" Balzurth had Eckubahn right where he wanted him: in an unbreakable death grip. His father's plan had worked.

I should have known!

"End it, Father! End it!"

Wurmers came at him like bats bursting from a cave.

Waark plowed through them.

The wurmers cracked against his mighty frame. They spiraled toward the ground with their wings busted.

"Go, Waark! Go!"

Scanning the ground with the winds ripping at his face, Nath caught a glimpse of another battle. Another titan stormed toward Balzurth with a monster-sized spear. A woman hung onto the shaft. The ugly ponytailed titan plucked the female from the shaft and slung her hard onto the ground.

"Selene!" Nath cried out.

The titan lifted the spear over its head.

"Waark!" Nath ordered. "Attack! Now!"

The bull dragon shifted direction the slightest bit, maneuvering away from Balzurth and toward his and Selene's attacker.

Now I know what Father meant. But I want to help him.

Nath caught a glimpse of his father's grand breastplate turning the color of flame. Time stopped around him. In his mind, he got it. He understood.

Waark plowed into the spear-wielding titan, knocking it flat on the ground.

Nath hopped off Waark's back, rushed over to Selene, and picked her up in his arms. "Selene, Selene!"

Blinking, she said, "Nath?" She wheezed, coughed, and shook her head.

Sansla Libor landed by his side.

A wurmer rushed in.

Sansla cracked its skull with his fist.

"We must go!" Nath said. He ran toward Waark carrying Selene, Sansla with him. "Father is going to turn this place into an inside-out volcano!"

"Understood." Sansla gave a nod and leapt into the air, flying away.

With Selene in his arms, Nath climbed back up onto the bull dragon's back. "Go, Waark! Go!" It ripped him up inside, not rushing to his father's aid. He wanted to help with the victory. But he understood what his father was doing. And he needed to obey.

Finish him, Father! Finish him so I can celebrate with you!

The bull dragon lifted them into the sky.

Selene came to her senses. "What are you doing? Let me go, Nath! Let me go!" She fought in his arms.

With great effort, he held her fast, saying, "My, you've gotten stronger. Now stop squirming, will you? My father's victory is at hand. Watch it unfold. But you might want to shield your eyes."

"No, Nath, no!" Her eyes were filled with terror. They got bigger the higher they went. "You don't understand. It's a trap! The titan has the spear!"

"No spear can pierce my father's hide."

"That's no ordinary spear. That's the Spear of Barnabus!"

Nath watched the titan pick up from the ground the huge spear that had fallen from its grip. The titan resumed its march on Balzurth's exposed back.

It all came together. The doubt that had been pushing at his mind blossomed. Eckubahn was ready. The vile monster was ready for anything.

Nath slapped Waark on the neck. "Down! Down!"

Fire erupted from Balzurth's mouth, filling the arena with blinding, white-hot flames.

CHAPTER 39

Balzurth loosed all of his power.

BOOOOOM!

His fury. His fire. Wave after wave of orange, yellow, blue, and green flames blasted from his mouth. The fires pounded into Eckubahn. A blast wave of his raw power tore through the arena, shattering the stonework and beyond. The closest surrounding buildings of Narnum collapsed. Everything the mighty dragon's breath touched caught fire. It spread. The wicked turned to ash.

Eckubahn screamed, writhed, and howled. The flames exposed everything he was and the harm he meant to bring on others like those who already suffered a thousandfold. The flesh of the giant body he inhabited flecked away like paper, burning in Balzurth's fire.

The titan's spirit fought against the flames consuming it. It clawed and squealed, trying to tear away from the inescapable fires.

"Mercy, Balzurth! Mercy!"

The flames kept coming.

"I will do anything! Anything!"

The endless stream of unbridled disintegrating heat did not slow. Balzurth would not let up. He had to destroy the evil spirit once and for all. "You still spin lies in your last moment of life. You lived a liar, you'll die a liar, forever."

Eckubahn swam in the flames. Separating from the body, the titan's spirit bucked and flailed. Its energy crested over the fire only to be pulled down again. Eckubahn shrank in his futile struggles.

Sensing the end, Balzurth huffed out the final gust where his flames were hottest.

In the very back of his mind, he heard someone yell, "Watch your back, Balzurth! Watch your baaaaaaaa….."

The Spear of Barnabus pierced Balzurth's scales and bore right through his heart.

His fire extinguished.

Only his last cry remained.

CHAPTER 40

THE BLINDING BRIGHTNESS CLEARED. NATH could see the battle of a lifetime unfold. His father's fire destroyed everything but the titans. Isobahn dropped to a knee on the shaking ground, but in a moment the titan was back on his feet, poised to strike.

Eckubahn fought against the dragon flame but could not overcome it. The titan was like a man drowning in a storming sea. Doomed.

With the artifact over his head, Isobahn drove the Spear of Barnabus right through Balzurth's heart.

Nath clutched his head again and screamed. "Nooooooooo!"

Balzurth's flames turned from fire to the fury of sound.

"MAAAAAAAAAROOOOOOOOOHHHHH!"

The Dragon King's voice sent shock waves through all of Narnum. Its tallest tower cracked in half. It toppled. Five hundred feet of stone crashed on top of the city.

"Get down there! Get down there!" Nath ordered Waark. He pumped his finger at the ground.

Face white as a sheet in his arms, Selene said, "He's gone, Nath. He's gone. We must go."

The wurmers thickened in the sky.

Nath could barely see the ground beneath them. The last thing he saw was his father's body. The Dragon King lay still, surrounded by smoke and flames for a grave.

Nath jumped off Waark.

"Nath!" Selene yelled.

He sailed toward the ground like a falling meteor, hair billowing over his shoulders like the meteor's tail.

The ground rushed up to meet him.

A wurmer glided into his path, jaws wide.

Fang out, he split the beast in half. Still falling, he saw more wurmers coming after him.

Sansla Libor swooped in. The roamer king caught him under his arms and bore him away. Slivver flew nearby. The silver dragon and his host battled away the wurmers.

"Let me go! Let me go!" Nath screamed and kicked. Tears streaked down his face. "Release me!"

"I am sorry for your father, Nath," Sansla said. "But you are the Dragon King now. Take it from one king to another. You must be protected. The world still has hope so long as it has you. We can't lose you too." Sansla dropped him back onto Waark's back and then joined a regiment of dragons to fight off the wurmers.

Waark flew on. The distance between them and the enemy lengthened.

Now Selene held Nath in her arms.

Head down, Nath sobbed and sobbed.

CHAPTER 41

Eckubahn breathed. The titan's spirit remained in the same body it had been hosted in. He stood, a mountain of a person, more skeleton than flesh. He peeled off the smoking skin from his forearm and flicked it aside. His eyes burned with deep orange flames. He faced Isobahn.

The brother titan glowered down at Balzurth's dragon body. All of the hair was burned from the titan's body. Boils covered his skin.

"That was close," Eckubahn said.

Isobahn nodded.

Eckubahn took a knee in front of Balzurth's face. By the horns, he turned the Dragon King's eyes toward him. "Finally, my greatest enemy has fallen. I told you that you had a blind spot. The sacrifice you made for a woman. Compassion. Mercy." He spat. "For weaklings." He eyed the spear. "Make sure he's dead."

Isobahn took the spear in hand, set his foot against Balzurth's body, and gave it a twist. The dragon body didn't move. The titan yanked out the spear. With a grin, he said, "We did it." Spear high, he shouted. "WE DID IT! WE KILLED BALZURTH!" He pounded his smoldering chest.

Only the wurmers were gathered. All that remained of the others were dead piles of ash and bone.

Still talking to Balzurth, Eckubahn said, "And you called me a liar. Well, I didn't lie about everything. I told you to watch your back, didn't I?" He stood, grabbed the Spear of Barnabus from Isobahn, and stabbed Balzurth himself. "Didn't I!"

EPILOGUE

Sharing a saddle behind Sasha, Bayzog the elven wizard swooned and fell from his mount.

Sasha jumped off the horse. "Bayzog!" She grabbed him up in her arms. His limbs trembled.

Birds scattered in the trees. Vermin darted back and forth. The horses whinnied and nickered.

"Bayzog, what is it?" Sasha said.

A dragon's roar, like a spirit, ruffled the leaves with a wind of its own.

Dismounting, Ben's nape hairs stood on end. Sadness filled him.

Bayzog's violet eyes moistened.

Sasha started crying. "Oh my, oh my," she said. Her chin quivered. "What happened? What happened? Is Nath all right?"

"I did not foresee this. Who could have?" Bayzog cradled the Elderwood Staff in his arms. He closed his eyes. A tear dripped down his chin and fell to the ground. Mystic words formed on his lips for several minutes. The clouds darkened, and Ben didn't feel it was because of Bayzog but something else. A buzzing *ree-rah, ree-rah* sound permeated his ears. It became louder. Covering his ears, he watched above.

A flock of wurmers soared overhead, heading south.

In a loud voice, Ben said, "That's not good! Not good at all!"

Sasha shook her head. Her hands were on Bayzog's. "I don't like this."

The wurmers passed.

Ben's hands fell from his ears.

Bayzog's murmurings stopped, and he spoke once more in Common. "He's gone. He's gone."

"Who's gone?" Ben demanded. His blood rushed through his ears. All he could think of was Dragon. "Is it Dragon? Tell me it's not Dragon!"

Bayzog's spacey violet stare cleared. "No, it's not Nath." The wizard's shoulders sagged as the truth became too much to bear. "It's Balzurth. The Dragon King has fallen to the titans."

Sasha gasped.

Ben fell back on his haunches. "Impossible," he whispered. "That's impossible, isn't it?"

"Death is the enemy of all who live, even Balzurth."

Sasha began crying uncontrollably. She babbled. "It's my fault. It's my fault. I know it. He lifted my curse and took it upon himself. It weakened him. It must have." She clutched clumps of grass and ripped them from the ground. "I did this. I did this."

Setting the staff aside, Bayzog hugged her from behind. Holding her fast, he said, "Balzurth was wise. He would not have done something without knowing the consequences. This is not your fault, Sasha. Do not think of it like that. What he gave you is a gift. Accept it. Enjoy it. Live right by it."

Shuddering, she said, "I didn't deserve it."

Ben took her hand in his. He rubbed her palm with his thumb and said, "Sasha, just like Nath, Balzurth would have done the same for any one of us. Now is the time to be strong."

"Why?" she said, half hysterical. "Why?"

"Nath is the Dragon King now. He's going to need us."

She wiped her nose and eyes. Sitting up straight, she said, "Forgive me. I know you're right. Nath will need us, but what about Rerry and Samaz?"

Bayzog kissed her on the cheek. "It's been revealed to me he'll need them too." He helped his wife to her feet. "Every one of us. You know how he is."

She giggled a tiny bit. "How can you make me laugh at a time as dark as this? You never make me laugh."

Bayzog cupped her face in his hands and thumbed the tears from her eyes. "There's hope. There's always hope. That's why we laugh at death."

Ben slapped Bayzog on the back. "I like it! I don't know where that came from, Bayzog, but I like it!" He pointed toward the sky with his sword. "It's time to avenge Balzurth! Come back, insects, come back." He winced. His hand went to his ribs. "Something still hurts. Something everywhere still hurts."

Bayzog patted Ben softly on the back. "That's a good thing. It wouldn't hurt at all if you were dead."

"I don't know if he's being cynical or funny," Ben said to Sasha.

"Me either, but it's refreshing." She climbed into the saddle. "Let's find our sons before the world ends."

TRIAL OF THE DRAGON

-Book 6-

Craig Halloran

CHAPTER 1

NATH SAT IN THE THRONE room of Dragon Home. He was alone, sitting on the very throne from which his father, Balzurth, had lectured him countless times. His body was ten times too small to fill the seat. That was how he felt, too small to fill his father's clawed footsteps. He was still a man, not a dragon. He scooted over and leaned on the golden arm of the grand chair.

Father, you can't be dead. Why did you die?

For weeks he had relived his father's death. Over and over, he'd seen the crafty titan Isobahn run Balzurth through with the Spear of Barnabus. It happened just when Balzurth was moments away from eliminating the head titan, Eckubahn. His father's powerful breath had been cleansing the world with fire at that moment, only to be cut off by the tip of a spear.

He can't even have a burial.

His claws dug into the soft metal of the throne arm.

I don't even have his body!

Nath hopped off the chair, landing hard on the array of coins that jingled on the ground. Scattering thousands with a sweep of his foot, he stormed through the grand treasure-filled chamber and snatched up the precious figure of a wild bear wrought with silver. The ornate figure was bigger than his head. He glared into the green emeralds that made up its eyes for a moment and then hurled it from one side of the chamber to the other. The figurine struck one of the huge support columns, skipped off the wall, and landed in the pile with a crash of glass.

Nath perked up.

What was that?

Wading through the piles of treasure and countless valuables, he stormed over to the source of the sound. Brows knitted together, he muttered to himself. He'd done much of that lately. "Why do you need all this treasure? All people do is fight over it. Why hoard it all, because it's pretty?" He scooped up a diamond bigger than his knuckle then flung it aside. "If all this treasure can't bring my father back, then what good is it?"

He stopped at the spot where he had heard the crash. The sound shouldn't have surprised him. After all, there were plenty of vases and statues in the great hall. Still, he couldn't fight the bad feeling that he'd broken something that wasn't his. It wouldn't have been the first time.

Aw, I'm the Dragon King now. I can break what I want. Who's going to punish me?

He caught a glimpse of himself in a broken piece of mirror. It had been part of an oval mirror that had sat half buried in the treasure ever since he could remember. It was bigger than he was.

"Huh?"

He pulled the mirror out and leaned it against the column, gazing at the shattered image of himself. Several pieces were missing. The longer he looked, the more his image contorted.

"Yes, I look just how I feel: broken, with many pieces missing. Sometimes it stinks to be me." A piece of mirror fell out of the frame. "Oh, and it keeps getting worse. I just can't stop falling apart."

Shoulders hanging, he sluffed through the coins, circling the throne room. He had spent so much time walking around in the chamber that he had made a track through the treasure. He came to a stop behind the throne and stood looking at the great mural filled with dragons. All of them were painted as real as life itself. In the bright sky the dragons flew, so real that he swore he could touch them. Yet something was missing.

Eyes watering, he said, "Father, you should be here. I should be dead."

Nath again recounted his mistakes, reliving his errors.

If I had been able to handle my responsibilities to begin with, Father would still be safe in the world beyond the mural. If I had just listened more, I wouldn't have made so many stupid mistakes. Now you're lost to me, Father, when I need you most.

He touched a fingernail to the mural in a spot where the sky was icy blue. It was warm on his scales beneath his index finger. The images shifted. The dragons painted on the sky faced him with angry eyes. He took his finger away and moved on, pacing in deep thought for hours. He couldn't recall the last time he'd talked to another person, but he knew the last words he'd had with his friends and family were ones of anger.

I'm still mad at them.

Nath wanted to go back to Narnum. He wanted to find his father's body and bring it back. He didn't care if he needed a thousand dragons to pull it off. It was the right thing to do. However, his friends had different ideas. They had overpowered him and taken him away. Despite all the great strength he had as a man, it was no match for Selene, Sansla Libor, and Slivver. They had held him fast until his temper cooled enough that he could be reasoned with. However, he still simmered. After the last bout with all of them—including his mother, Grahleyna—he'd holed up inside the throne room, giving them all a final order:

Do not disturb!

After all, he was the Dragon King.

It was a hard time. There were many things in the throne room that made him think of his father. Countless things. When he was a boy, the throne room had been his favorite place to play. Balzurth would sit on his chair, which was really more of a gigantic stool than a throne, and chuckle. His rumblings and hot breath gave the extravagant room special life. All the while, Nath would dress up in the variety of clothing and assortment of armor that were scattered about. There were weapons too—knives, swords, maces, and bows. He mastered them all, imagining himself conquering one monster after the other. One time he'd picked up a wizard's wand. Not understanding how to use it, he had shot his father in the rear end with it.

He laughed. He cried. He felt like he was dying inside. Finally, after he'd wallowed in self-pity up to his ears, he recollected something his father had said a thousand times and that he had never heard.

"It's your life. You have to live it, not me."

Nath pushed himself up off the coins that slid around his feet and headed for the towering doors. Taking a deep breath, he pushed them open.

CHAPTER 2

In southern Nalzambor between the Mountain of Doom and the dwarven home of Morgdon were the settlements, a rugged stretch of land filled with small towns put together by one race or another. Farmland was scarce, making it tough on the people, who thrived on their privacy but openly traded with everyone in the lands. The settlements were in the valleys and hills, made of wood and stone buildings that blended in with the rock and land. The resilient people were a quiet lot, hard at work, tilling what little fields they had and feeding the livestock. Most of them were human, but occasionally a halfling would pass by. Sometimes dwarves and elves passed through. They traded, refilled their supplies, and moved on.

Such wasn't the case at the moment. A group of dwarves—eight in all, covered from their necks to their toes in beards and armor—were sticking around. They asked questions. They were obviously searching for someone.

Rerry and Samaz sat inside a small farmhouse on a pair of stools, eating some eggs and grits. Rerry smiled at the dark-headed farm girl who served them. She tore her eyes away, giggled, and hurried off after he flashed his teeth.

"Stop drawing attention to us," Samaz said to him. Head over his plate with his shaggy black hair covering his eyes, he spooned in a mouthful of grits.

"Oh, don't be so jealous." Rerry lifted up out of his seat, peeking after the woman. "She's a fetching little thing. I might ask for her name."

"Fine, get her name. Maybe she will bring us a meal after the dwarves capture us and throw us in one of their league-deep dungeons."

"Try not to worry so much. They aren't looking for us specifically."

Rerry stood up and made his way over to where the barn's entrance stood open to a full view of the surroundings. The small barn sat on an overlook of the valleys below. From its unique vantage point, he could see the buildings that wound through the valley. About fifty yards away he saw Captain Scar and his men talking to the dwarves that had been hanging around longer than they—according to Scar—would normally stay.

He shooed a chicken away with his foot. "Go away, or I'll have my brother scarf down more of your children." The chicken clucked and moved off. With his eyes intent on Scar and the dwarves, he tried to imagine what they were saying.

Pretending to read Scar's lips, he said, "Hello, Mister Dwarf. My, that is a fine beard. Can I cut it off and make a blanket out of it?"

Imitating the dwarf, he said, "Touch my beard and I'll poke your other eye out."

"Then I wouldn't be able to see how short and ugly you are."

"Ugly? Say it again and I'll make a belt out of that scrawny body of yours!"

"No you won't!"

"Yes I will!"

Rerry stopped talking to himself at the sound of girls giggling. He peeked up, seeing some little kids in the hayloft. They covered their mouths, but the laughing still came out. "The show's not free, you know. At least give me some applause."

Someone clapped. It was the farm girl. On ginger feet, she walked up to him, a little shy, and said, "Mother says I need two silvers for the meal. I'd give it to you for free if I could."

He placed three coins in her warm hands. "There's no need for charity… Uh, I'm sorry, I don't know your name."

Her cheeks flushed. "Nell."

The children in the loft made kissing noises.

She yelled up at them, "Stop that, you little monsters."

Rerry couldn't help but laugh. Still holding her hand, he said, "I'm Rerry. You know, we shouldn't have waited so long to have a formal introduction."

"Why is that?"

He noticed Scar coming back. The hardened elven soldier wore a mask of concern. The dwarves eyed his back every step of the way. Scar moved into Rerry's line of sight, blocking his view. He was mouthing the words, "Get inside!"

"Nell, it's possible I might be moving on today, and it pains my heart to know we might be parting company so soon."

"Mine too." The comely young lady with locks of honey and brown dangling half over her eyes lifted up on her toes, kissed his lips, and hurried away.

Agape, he watched her vanish and said as he touched his lips, "What was that?"

Samaz turned on his stool, got up, and said, "I'd call it a kiss goodbye." He wiped his mouth with a handkerchief. "Or maybe it was just a polite thank-you for the extra coin you gave her. That's how these pretty girls make a living."

"Are you saying she wasn't sincere?"

"Yes."

"You're just jealous."

"Of what, having more coins left than you?" Samaz slapped Rerry on the back. "Don't be so defensive. I'm only teasing you."

Scar arrived and practically shoved them both inside, saying, "Why don't you just walk down there and kiss the dwarves! For all the trees in Elome, you can't keep your head tucked in, can you, Rerry."

"Those walking beards couldn't make me out from that far. I look like nothing but a commoner. From a distance, that is."

"Hah. Have you ever been interrogated by a dwarf?'" Scar said.

"No."

"And you don't want to be. He grilled me. Me! Who is he to grill me? A dwarf has no right. With that said, he let out plenty about the search for Nath Dragon." He poked Rerry in the chest. Eyeballing his surroundings and noting the children above, he switched his speech to Elven. "He mentioned Nath Dragon's allies: Brenwar. A man called Ben. Oh, and this name might sound familiar: Bayzog. Funny, they also mentioned his wife Sasha and his sons Rerry and Samaz. As a matter of fact, they even gave descriptions. Very accurate, I might add. To be clear, he didn't seem convinced that I hadn't seen you. With that said, it's time to go. Plenty of people have seen your faces, but at least they don't have your names."

Rerry blanched. His fingers fidgeted at his side.

"You didn't blurt out your name, did you?" Scar said.

"Well, she wouldn't say anything if I told her not to."

"Don't be a fool. She will if someone offers her so much as a piece of gold. These people can't afford to turn that down. Would you blame her?"

Rerry shook his head. He searched the barn with sad eyes, but he didn't see her. "Fine, then. Let's go."

CHAPTER 3

Across from one another, Bayzog and his wife sat in a grove of holly trees, holding each other's hands. They'd been doing so awhile now. Nothing stirred them—aside from the wind that rustled the leaves from time to time, whipping them into their faces. A pinkish amulet glowed on its chain around Sasha's neck. Bayzog's Elderwood Staff lay across his lap, also glowing with a life of its own at the top. Mystic energy from the objects swirled together, uniting them in an array of beautiful colors.

Standing guard among the trees, Ben was transfixed. The hypnotic energy filled his eyes and added new strength to his limbs. He squinted and finally turned away. Rubbing his temples, he blinked several times, clearing his head.

Well, I stood it longer this time than last time.

Bayzog had told him not to linger around and stare at what they did, but Ben couldn't fight his fascination with magic. It was especially tempting now that he was older, getting on in years. His joints ached to the point where it always hurt to bend over. His knees cracked when he squatted. A little magic here and there to hopefully save his behind in battle was something he thought about often. He'd asked

Bayzog and Sasha to teach him a few things, and Sasha had made a few attempts, but he didn't have it in him. He rolled his aching shoulders.

Maybe I should have stayed a farm boy. Nah, my back would still ache. And I wouldn't want to miss a day with Nath Dragon.

Nath was quite possibly the best thing that had ever happened to Ben in his life. The fascinating warrior had left him awestruck the first time they met. He had wanted to be like Nath, but even better, they had wound up becoming great friends. Now Nath needed all the help he could get, and Ben didn't want to let him down. Instinctively, he reached over his shoulder, grasping for the magic bow, Akron. He found empty air, but the bow always seemed to linger on his shoulders. He shook his head.

How did I lose it?

Nath had trusted him with the powerful weapon, and now it was gone, stolen by thieves—and even worse than that, it had been used, allegedly, to commit murder in Nath Dragon's name. Ben lost plenty of sleep over it, trying to recall every detail of his life from the time he had last seen the bow until he discovered it missing. There just wasn't any evidence—except one thing.

There had been a day when his wife, Margo, was acting strange. Even his daughters, Tristan and Justine, thought so. Margo didn't recall anything out of the ordinary at all, but Ben's gut told him she'd been in two places at once. That was the hard part to swallow, because it didn't make any sense.

If I hadn't lost the bow, neither of those leaders would have been killed. The elves and dwarves wouldn't be blaming Dragon. They wouldn't be hunting after him.

He cracked his neck from side to side. Shaking life into his stiff arms, he made his way over to Brenwar's chest, which sat on the ground against a pile of mossy stones. He peeked over at Bayzog. The part-elf wizard's face remained a mask of concentration. Ben enjoyed taking a look inside the chest from time to time. He undid the hasp and opened the lid.

Small wooden racks of colorful potion vials unfolded like they would in a fisherman's tackle box, filling his eyes. In the bottom of the box—which seemed deeper and wider than it looked—were several strange objects. A bag filled with carved marble pieces. A folded sheet of black cloth. The horn of a ram, curled up with a brass tip on the small end. He picked up a tiny lantern and set it in the palm of his hand. A yellow ember pulsated within. He fished through some other items. A wand of carved black wood, a thread and needle, a bejeweled dagger with a stubby blade.

I bet Brenwar would have a fit if he knew I was rummaging through this.

He fingered the potions one by one.

I love these things. I want to drink them all. I wonder what would happen if I used two at once.

They were marked with lettering he didn't understand, but he was pretty certain about the yellow ones. They healed. He shook one up, watching the little sparkles twinkle within.

I could use one of these about now. My back's aching. Just a sip.

He started to twist off the cork.

"Ahem!"

Ben jerked around. He found Bayzog's penetrating violet eyes boring a hole right through him. With a sigh, he put the vial back. "I wasn't going to drink it." He closed the lid. "Did you find anything?"

With a straight face, Bayzog said, "Maybe."

CHAPTER 4

LAD TO SEE YOU AMONG us, Dragon King." Brenwar took a knee and bowed as soon as Nath walked out the throne room door. He remained there, unmoving, and he wasn't the only one who bowed.

Slivver, Nath's brother the silver dragon, was on one knee and had his head down as well.

Noticing no one else was around, Nath said to them, "Friends, there is no need for such formalities unless we are in the presence of others or it's a formal occasion, from here on out." Nath pushed his hair back. "Please rise and just be my friend and brother, the same as you have always been. I mean it."

Brenwar rose first and looked around the cavernous hall. "Good. Do you have all of your pouting out of your system?"

"I was mourning, not pouting."

Dragon arms crossed, Slivver stood seven feet tall in his brilliant coat of silver scales with the look of grand nobility. With his long chin up, he said, "Any time that bottom lip is out, it's a pout. Yours still hangs a little."

"It does not." Nath tightened his lips. The last time he was among them, he'd been arguing with everyone. He wanted to go back and recover his father's body. They had all told him no, which had infuriated him, because he was the king and they had defied his orders. It wasn't so much that they stopped him from doing what he wanted but the fact that they convinced him not to do it. Grahleyna and Selene had been adamant. They had made a strong case, but he still stewed over it. Sansla Libor had sided with the women, and so had Slivver, though he hadn't been very vocal about it. The only one Nath hadn't argued with was Brenwar. "I still want to retrieve my father's body. He deserves a burial."

"Aye." Brenwar stated. "He deserves a grand funeral. One that lasts for weeks. I'm all for going back after him. I was to begin with. I'm ready."

"And what do you think, Slivver?" Nath said to his older brother.

Slivver's icy blue eyes stared into his. "He's my father too. And I agree about the burial. But I don't think Balzurth would make that a priority when there was only one king left. That one is you, Nath. But you've had plenty of time to think about it. I'll stand by your decision as your servant, your brother, and your friend."

Nath put his hand on Slivver's shoulder. "You'll never know how much that means to me. I'm elated to have you by my side." He dropped his hand. "Both of you—like old times, but with a thousand times more responsibility." He tossed his long red hair back and allowed himself a smile. "One way or the other, we will get Balzurth back, but after days of thought and careful consideration, I think I need to consider a different strategy. How do we stop the wurmers and titans once and for all? How can I do that and run a kingdom of dragons at the same time?"

"We take them down one at a time," Brenwar said. He punched his fist into his hand. "The same as we always do."

"Nath, I know you think the dragons won't rally around you, but they will. They are ready. I've spoken with many of them, and they see what's going on. They are more than ready to fight." Slivver smiled. "Besides, at this point, they really don't have a choice."

Nath started to walk with his friends in tow. The cavernous tunnels inside the Mountain of Doom wound, turned, dipped, and bent. They passed chamber after chamber as they walked. Most of the huge alcoves were open for all to view, but some had beautiful woven curtains hung on iron rods. He made his way to the outside top of the mountain, where the stiff winds greeted his cheeks like icy kisses. The clouds soared more than a thousand ells below his feet in some places. Beyond the greenery were the surrounding lands of Nalzambor. Nearby, scattered in the rocks, dragons of all sorts were perched. Their eyes were outward, wings closed behind their backs, as they studied the enemy that lurked in the distance.

"No wurmer attacks?" Nath asked.

"Every once in a while a few rogues will fly too close, but our brethren have been quick to take them down." Slivver's wings stretched out for a moment and folded behind his back again. "Things have been quiet the last couple of weeks."

"Too quiet." Brenwar clawed his skeleton fingers through his thick locks of beard. "Something's brewing. They are stacking up fortifications all around the mountain. Their armies are building. I've never before seen so many giants in one place. It should be a feast for Morgdon when the real battle comes."

"Assuming the dwarves show up," Slivver commented.

"What's that supposed to mean?"

"You know what I mean."

Nath stepped between them. "It sounds like you both know what you mean, but I'd like to be filled in." Brenwar and Slivver turned their backs on one another. "As your king, I command you both: out with it!"

CHAPTER 5

"YOU'RE THE ONE FLAPPING YOUR lizard lips, Slivver, so go on with it." Brenwar's brows furrowed as he crossed his meaty arms over his chest.

Slivver stretched his neck over Brenwar, glowered at him. "Call me a lizard again and I'll roast you like a chestnut."

"Go ahead and try it, fish bait."

Nath pushed them away from each other. "Just tell me: what's going on?"

Slivver the dragon put his fist to his mouth and cleared his throat. "It seems that the dwarves and elves are becoming more obsessed with your capture these days."

"What do you mean?" Nath suddenly recalled the other dilemma. "Oh, they're still looking for Laedorn and Uurluuk's murderer. Am I still the only one accused?"

"Both the dwarves and the elves have sent messages to Dragon Home, demanding your surrender," Slivver continued.

Exasperated, Nath said, "And how in Nalzambor did they get messages to us through all that?" He pointed out toward the distant and growing armies of the titans. "Do they not know that my father is dead? That I am the Dragon King?"

"The letter came from a mystic envoy, signed by both the elves and the dwarves."

"Did we send them a reply?" Nath asked, eyeing Brenwar.

"I sent them a reply, all right. Now I'm out of sorts with them and them with me." Brenwar made a long face. "It doesn't sit well with me, being at odds with my kin. You know how they are when it comes to justice. They won't stop until they find Uurluuk's assassin."

"Dwarves do have one-track minds," Slivver commented.

"Well, the elves and the dragons aren't any better!" Brenwar picked up a hunk of rock and punted it off the mountain ledge. He wagged his finger at Slivver. "Next time, it's going to be you going over the cliff like that."

"I can fly, you know."

"You're not going to fly!"

"Enough," Nath cut in. "We should all be happy about one thing." They looked at him with perched brows. "At least the elves and dwarves are working together for a change." His friends remained expressionless. "Fine, no more levity, even though I could use some. So, have we had any luck finding Bayzog and his family?"

"I'm afraid I don't have anything to report," Slivver said. "I've dispatched dragons by the dozens to find them, but it's been difficult communicating with our brethren. There's just so many wurmers dominating the skies. Any time a dragon is sighted, there's no hesitation. They attack. Bayzog and his family have enemies coming from all sides. Wurmers, giants, dwarves, and elves are all searching for them now. The elves and dwarves are determined to bring anyone close to you in for questioning at their high tribunal."

Brenwar started shaking his head.

That guilty feeling seeped into Nath's heart. His friends were in danger because of him. It ignited a fire inside him, because—this time—they were in danger for something he hadn't done. "We need to find them. We need to find the murderer. Someone somewhere knows something, and we must be overlooking it. Honestly, Gorlee is the only living person I can imagine imitating me and pulling it off."

"There are many ways to deceive the eyes," Slivver reminded him. "There are dark resources capable of such things. Magic disguises. Objects of transformation. Even a potion could do such a thing for a little while."

"And let's not forget that the witnesses could be lying," Brenwar added. "I hate to admit it, but even some of the dwarves can be bribed."

Nath nodded. "True, but they have Akron. Whoever stole it must have been close to us at one time or another. That's why I think of Gorlee. One of his kin could have fallen under the spell of the titans." Nath pushed the hair out of his eyes. Now was one of those times he wished he could turn back into a dragon. *If it's not one dilemma, it's another. How did Father deal with all this?* "We are at war, friends, and we are going to need the help of the dwarves and the elves to get through it. I don't think we can rely on any help from them until we get this resolved. Somebody needs to find this assassin." He sighed. "I'm not going to lie to you. I'm tempted to just turn myself over to them. After all, I am innocent. A trial will find that."

Slivver shook his head. "No, you can't do that, Nath. We don't know who is driving this. I agree with Brenwar: perhaps the leadership is jaded. Too many evil spirits abound that are corrupting the minds of the races."

"You are as wise as you are silver. Let's put all our heads together and try to figure out what we need to do to get a handle on this mess. It's sad to say, but I think we can use Father's death to our advantage. Perhaps we can regain our old allies while the titans revel in it." Nath started back inside Mountain Home. "Let's go advise Selene and my mother."

Brenwar and Slivver stopped in their tracks behind Nath.

Nath turned. "Don't tell me. She's gone again, isn't she."

CHAPTER 6

"WELL PLAYED, RERRY, WELL PLAYED," said Scar.

They'd spent two days breaking free of the settlements by moving a league west around the mountains, beyond the edges of the lava lakes. Heavy downpours came on and off, making for sloppy footing. The rain was pounding at the moment, splattering muddy drops up to the small band's knees.

Rerry and Samaz slogged through it, having a little trouble keeping up with Scar's brisk pace. They'd both become hardened in their early adventures, but they weren't soldiers accustomed to long marches without breaks. Rerry wiped the water from his face and said back to his brother, "All this because I gave a woman my name?"

Samaz nodded his rain-drenched mop of black hair. "Your lips are too loose with the ladies." He grinned. "You need to be more the strong and silent type, like me." He took a long look over his shoulder as they moved across the rain-slicked bank. "I'm still not sure where we're going. I thought we were going to take our chances in Elome."

"That's what I thought," Rerry said. His fingers grasped the branches as he hauled himself up the bank. At the top, he found himself face to face with the one-eyed Scar. "What?"

Scar grabbed his hands and opened them up. There were pieces of green leaves in them. Aggravated, Scar said, "What's that?"

"Leaves. Why?"

"No, it's a trail!" The elven warrior smacked the leaves out of his hands.

"What do you mean? They can't follow us in this rain."

"Of course they can. You're making it easy. If you were all elf, you'd know that."

"I knew it," Rerry fired back. He hadn't, but he certainly wasn't going to admit that to Scar, even though they were getting along much better. "Where are we going, anyway? Wouldn't it be easier to lose them in Elome? I still want to take a crack at the Ocular of Orray."

"We aren't going to pursue anything until we lose our pursuers. And that won't be easy. Those dwarves will march nonstop until their feet fall off. Even then, they'll probably keep going."

"We're much faster. I don't see how they can even stay close. Certainly by now we've put a great distance between us and them. We need to relax."

"I'll tell you this, you'll have plenty of time to relax after you're captured if you want to wait up for them." Scar started after his waiting men. "But if you don't want to experience life behind dwarven bars, you'd best follow me."

"Fine, but where are we going? Listen to me, Scar. I want to help my mother. There has to be a way."

Scar resumed his pace with the others. "I can't believe you two made it this far. What you're looking for is like looking for a needle in a haystack the size of a mountain. You can't just leave home thinking 'I'm going to find a cure' and have it happen."

"Why not?" Samaz said.

"You need a better... Actually, you need a plan."

"We had one," Rerry said.

"Yes, to steal the Ocular of Orray. But what was your back-up plan?" Scar stopped and poked both of them in the shoulders with his gauntleted hands. "And now you have me caught all up in it. Lucky for you, I do have a plan."

"I like it so far. Wandering aimlessly through the mud is so much better than what we were doing."

"You're funny, Rerry. And look how far it's gotten you. Believe it or not, once we shake these dwarves, I know a seer who can give us a better idea about your situation. She knows much about everything." Scar pulled his booted foot out of a section of mud that made a sucking *pop*. "Watch out for the darker patches of clay. Some of them are sinkholes."

"Who is this seer of whom you speak? I always heard that seers were misaligned people," Samaz stated.

Scar shrugged. "Maybe so, but even misdirected people can be beneficial. Besides, there's no guarantee she'll reveal herself. She's a real crone."

"How far away is she?" Rerry asked.

"She's on the other side of the Flooding River, west of Harm's Way."

"Harm's Way?" Rerry gave his brother a concerned glance. "Are we supposed to believe that's a real place?"

"I didn't name it. It just is."

They marched, trotted, and ran through the slop and the slick grass on and off for another day and night. Rerry's legs felt like lead. Samaz's chin sagged. Even the remaining elven guards were puffing. Finally, just after nightfall, the rain subsided. They stood on the soft bank of a rushing river. The strong current was half a mile wide.

"We can't swim that with our gear on," Rerry said. "Even without, it would be a challenge."

"There's a bridge, more than one." Scar gave his elven guards a whistle. They sprinted down the riverbank, vanishing among the reeds. He pointed upriver. "We'll check the next crossing north of here. Last time I came through, it was guarded."

"You're well-traveled for an elven guard," Rerry said. "I thought most of your stations were in Elome."

"I made plenty of rounds when I was younger. The elven merchant trains were a good way for a young soldier to cut his teeth." Scar smirked. "I was young and had some adventures of my own. You'd be surprised." He picked his way through the thickets that hugged a bend in the river. "That's how I learned about the seer. My leaders sought her wisdom once. It was a strange thing but beneficial."

The group ducked under the rain-soaked branches without disturbing a drop of water until they found themselves in a clearing that overlooked the river. Up the rushing stream, a long, dark bridge snaked over the watery expanse.

"Hah!" Rerry smiled. "It looks like we have an easy walk over the river." He started toward the bridge.

Scar stuffed his palm into Rerry's chest. "That's what scares me."

CHAPTER 7

An army of orcs marched down the muddied road heading south. They carried banners of black and red that waved in the brisk wind with the cut edges snapping. Among the hundreds of them were all the races, double in size. They stood out among the ranks like walking trees. Their weapons were made of steel and iron. Great chains hung from their necks.

They chanted in Orcen, "Death to the dragons! Death to men! Death to all who oppose the titans!"

The centipede of steel and death pushed up the hill and vanished on the other side. It took several long moments before their bellowing chants were no longer heard.

Alongside the road was a clump of rocks piled up with the bushes. The image shimmered. Three forms took shape, and they were Bayzog, Sasha, and Ben.

The rangy soldier Ben rose to full height and stretched his limbs. His eyes followed along the muddy wake in the road left by the terrifying army. "Great Guzan, I was certain we were going to be stepped on. That was close!" Ben pinched his nose and shook his head. "Oh my, I wonder how long this stench will linger. Have you ever smelled such a thing?"

Sasha and Bayzog were getting to their feet.

The pretty woman's face was drained. "How did I do, Bayzog?" She tingled from her fingertips to her elbows. It had been the first real spell she'd summoned without Bayzog's help in quite some time. She put her trembling hand to her head and started to get up.

"Sit a moment, Sasha." Bayzog brushed her wet hair from her eyes. "You did well. Exceptionally well considering the short time you had to prepare for it. I can't believe an army like that slipped in on us. I should have sensed it."

Ben stepped into a boot print three times the size of his. "I wouldn't feel bad, Bayzog. We live. If it's anyone's fault, it's probably mine. I think I'm going to need a bigger sword."

"Now is not the time for us to cast any kind of blame on one another." Sasha took Bayzog's arm and pulled herself up. Seeing the crease in his forehead, she said, "I'm feeling better."

"Are you sure?"

"Yes." She wiped her hands off on her robes as best she could, but it didn't make much of a difference. She couldn't remember ever being so dirty. Bayzog either. The part-elf wizard's usually spotless robes were sullied with mud and grass stains. Ben was the worst of the three. His beard was layered in dirt, with patches of grey where the rain had washed it. Still, she guessed he wore the grime the best of them all. "Shall we continue our journey then?"

"As long as it takes us away from that smell." Ben fanned his face. "If we wouldn't have been upwind from them, we couldn't have missed it. Listen, you two keep focusing on your sons. I can keep a better eye out. I swear it."

"We know, Ben." Bayzog shuffled over the rough road. "West. I still feel it."

"I do too," Sasha added.

Together, the pair of them cast a location spell to detect their sons, using some personal items they had brought from each of them. One item was Rerry's small whittling knife he had carried as a boy. The other item was a lock of Samaz's thick hair. These were things Sasha always kept close to her heart. However, all attempts to contact them had been unsuccessful. The guilt within her continued to rise, seeing how her sons had set off on a foolish errand to help her. But now there was some hope. A shadow of movement of both boys brought a smile to her face. They were alive.

"Let's keep moving then. It will be dark soon." Ben led the way in a steady stride, arms swinging loosely at his sides.

The veteran soldier and adventurer had become their devout protector. None of them were young anymore. From time to time, Ben had to help them over the difficult spots in the terrain. Sasha and Bayzog had slipped and skinned their knees more than once. Horseback would have been much easier, but it would have drawn more attention to them, too.

The armies of the titans snatched up every able horse they could find. They moved with great herds of stolen livestock. Nalzambor's surface was no longer a place of wonder and exploration but a place of danger.

The party cut through the high grasses and wildflowers of the prairie until the sun fell and the moon rose high in the air.

Stopping where the flats hit the forest, Ben said, "We should be safe within the edge. Let's get some rest and hope we don't get another downpour in the middle of the night. I'll fix something to eat if I can find it."

Sasha took a seat on the ground beside Bayzog and leaned into him with her shoulder. "You look as tired as I feel."

"I'm certain that I am." His violet eyes still burned with the life of cooling embers. He clasped her hands. "We're going to find them. We have to before the elves and dwarves do."

"And what happens after that?'

"We'll need to reunite with Nath. There are titans that need slaying and wurmers that need slaughtering."

"Mmm, I like it when you talk like that." She turned his face toward her and kissed his lips. "Now that we have a moment, maybe we should take advantage of it."

"Sasha," he stammered, but he didn't pull away.

"Oh, I just wanted to embrace the human in you, like you used to when we first met."

"I need to focus and control my passions."

"Sometimes you need to let them loose. The time will come when you can't afford to hold back." She kissed him again, and this time he embraced her soft lips with his own.

Ah, that's better.

"Gaaaaah!" From somewhere in the forest, Ben cried out in the night, "Ruuuuuuun!"

CHAPTER 8

E NEED TO FIND A better way to keep track of her," Nath said to Grahleyna. His beautiful mother was in full dragon form, elegant in her powder-white scales with touches of cinnamon. She was the most graceful dragon he ever saw. "Why did you let her go?"

Inside the grand chamber that was nothing more than a cavern inundated with precious metals and stones that glimmered against the carved rock, she said, "She feels guilty, Nath. The young woman is determined to find the source of the wurmers on her own. And I can't blame her. If anyone can discover the queen's location, it would be her. After all, she did give life to those foul breeding insects."

"Someone should have let me know before she left."

"You two are made for each other," Brenwar scoffed. "She's just like you. Now you know how it feels."

Nath shot Brenwar a look. "Yes, yes, I get the idea. Mother, tell me, did she go alone?"

"Sansla Libor aids her."

"And how did they manage to slip out of here?"

"The same as last time. They used the Chamber of Murals." Grahleyna made a clever smile. "It keeps us one step ahead of our enemies. You remember using it, don't you?"

"I do. Though it's been a while." He held his stomach. Passing through a mural always left him queasy.

"So, my king, what course of action are you going to take?"

"We need to get the murders of Laedorn and Uurluuk resolved. It's becoming a huge distraction, allowing Eckubahn to gain stronger footholds. If we don't sort it out soon, we'll have the entire world against us."

"I wish I could go with you, but I assume you'll need me here."

"I do, Mother, but I hate to make it a command. It seems strange for me to be ordering you around."

"Think nothing of it, but if it makes you feel any better, I volunteer." Three times bigger than Nath, she put her winged arm over his shoulder. "Son, you are a special man. If anyone can do this, you can. But try not to be gone long. The dragons will need their leader when the time comes. You're the Dragon King now. Remember that."

"I know."

"Slivver, I can't tell you how much it thrills me to see you united with your brother. He needs you."

Slivver bowed quickly. "I'll look after him with my life."

"Dragon speed then—and Brenwar?"

The old dwarf faced her with his head down. "Yes, Your Majesty."

"Keep them both out of trouble."

"You have my word to Morgdon on that."

Nath, Brenwar, and Slivver stood in the Chamber of Murals. Images from all over Nalzambor captivated them with a life of their own.

Brenwar gawped at an image of Morgdon, the city of great stone and iron, built into a mountainside. He licked his lips. "I swear I can smell dwarven ale."

"Brenwar, nothing is holding you back from returning home," Nath said. "Perhaps one more crack at your dwarven diplomacy."

"Nay, I've given your mother my word. I know the kind of trouble you two get into when you're together."

Nath and Slivver grinned at each other, but it was only a brief moment, because Nath returned his attention to the murals. His golden eyes were fixed on the City of Narnum. That was where his father had fallen. The view shifted from place to place depending on where he stared. His eyes searched the towers and the streets. Overall, the view was still distant, but his eyes found their way to the coliseum. It had been the battleground of his father's fall.

Slivver stepped in front of him. "I know where your mind is headed. I don't feel any different than you, but you can't afford to let your emotions get all stirred up. Eckubahn and Isobahn want that."

Nath's jaws clenched. He heard Slivver's words, but they didn't register. No, he had to see what had befallen his father's body. "Step aside."

Slivver obeyed.

Nath zoomed in on the mural until it was as if the three of them were on the street in Narnum. Their view followed the people, who made their way to the coliseum, where a crowd gathered. Dead center in the arena, Balzurth's great body had been propped up for all to see. A framework of iron held Balzurth upright. Tremendous chains suspended his outstretched arms. Chains with hooks like the ones used to catch a fish were sunk into Balzurth's wings. His mighty body filled the arena. His red scales still had their luster.

That should be me, not you, Father.

A collar of chains held Balzurth's head upright. A giant was sawing the last great horn from Balzurth's head.

Nath's fist clenched.

"That's abominable," Brenwar muttered. "Cutting off a dragon's horns is as bad as shearing a dwarf's beard off."

"I know."

To make matters worse, the Spear of Barnabus still stuck out of Balzurth's back. Nath couldn't fathom why the weapon hadn't been removed. Certainly Eckubahn would want it as part of his arsenal. Nath's blood boiled. People were throwing trash and other foul things at Balzurth. The expired Dragon King was speckled in filthy grime. Many of the giants guarding the body stood by laughing.

Nath stepped forward. "I've seen enough of this."

CHAPTER 9

T THE SAME TIME, SLIVVER and Brenwar shouldered their way in front of Nath. Slivver was the first to speak. "Once you go in, there won't be any retreat. I'll back you up, but do you have a plan?"

"Sure he does. Kill all those giants and the rest of their rotten ilk," Brenwar advised. "The sooner they're all dead, the better. But I do admit, it's a tad spontaneous even for me."

"Dwarves were never ones for surprises," Slivver commented.

"Sure we are, just slow-developing surprises. Eh, what's it going to be, Nath?"

It took every ounce of willpower he had not to jump into the mural and start ripping into the callous hordes of evil. Finally, Nath stepped back. The image of his father faded. "Now is not the time to be vengeful, but it's coming, and the mural of chambers gives me a plan." As horrifying as it was to gaze upon his father's abused corpse, it still gave him an idea that he tucked away for later.

"Let's get this chore done with first." Nath returned his focus to the other murals. "There has to be a better way to find one another. The murals make it easy to look where we've been before, but finding someone who wanders off in an unknown direction is impossible. It could take weeks, maybe months to find them, and that's assuming they're someplace where they can be seen."

"Aye, they might be captured underground." Brenwar's foot started tapping. "But we sure have a fine view of our enemy's forces that are gathering." He pointed his stubby finger at the ceiling. The painted portion was the land surrounding Dragon Home, where armies of titans gathered in the tens of thousands. That didn't include the wurmers that grayed out the blue sky like swarms of bats. "There are so many."

"It's no wonder Selene did what she did. The titans wouldn't be nearly so powerful with the wurmers gone. It's the only way to fight an army that keeps on growing. She's going after the source."

"You want to help her, but you're just going to have to have faith that she can handle it herself, Nath.

She's proven herself more than capable." Slivver slapped Nath's back with his tail. "Just focus on one thing at a time. We can't be everywhere at once."

"Well, it would be a lot of help if we could find Gorlee. He was supposed to be helping my father anyway. He's vanished."

"The spirits might have him, Nath," Brenwar said. "Remember what Selene did to him? It may be he's been taken over again."

"That's what I was thinking. Still, with all this power," he said, spreading his arms wide, "one would think we could find some answers to our plight. I wish Bayzog were here. I bet he could make the most of this."

"Yes, if only the murals could reveal what was hidden." Slivver stood beside Nath with this arms crossed over his chest just like Nath's. "Perhaps the mural teaches patience. I have a strong feeling that the more we watch, the more will be revealed."

"I used to watch the world for days on end from here, but I never before saw so much danger. Things were better then. It astounds me how quickly it ran afoul."

"The races can easily be deceived. That's why the dragons are here to protect them," Slivver stated. "One step at a time, Nath. What is your command?"

Nath studied the murals, trying to make his best guess as to where his friends might be. He had never learned enough about Gorlee to know where his home was. As he understood it, the shape changers were very secretive. Gorlee had once mentioned that sometimes they had trouble telling one from another.

He took his eyes away from the murals for a moment. His friends stood by his side, and they weren't alone. Slivver had brought in a dozen other silver dragons loyal to Nath. They were similar to Slivver but a bit bigger, and they didn't talk but behaved like dragons. They sat back, tails wrapped around their legs, heads high and proud. They all gave approving looks to Nath.

Each of these new silver dragons was slightly different from the others. Their horns varied. Most of the differences were minute but noticeable. He walked up to each one of them and touched their chests in a respectful manner. Each snorted in good grace. They'd all sworn to be Nath's personal guard.

"Oh, if I could only fly among you," Nath said. Seeing the murals, he was dying to take flight again. "I'm tempted to summon Waark, but I don't think that bull of a dragon will fit inside here." He snapped his fingers. "I know what we need. We need some seekers."

Slivver nodded. "There we go, a plan. Your patience is paying off. I'll send for some. I just hope we can find any." He gave a command to one of the silvers in Dragonese. It slunk out of the room.

All of them studied the murals for several more hours, but nothing caught their eyes. Hours later, the silver dragon returned with three small dragons on his back. The small dragons, no bigger than raccoons, all had wings that buzzed like a hummingbird's.

Nath reached out. The dragons, colored like honey bees with bright green eyes, landed on his arms. They sniffed and licked him with their long snouts and tongues. He made his way over to a black spot on one of the walls that had a tapestry of colors like a painter's swatch at the bottom. Using his finger, he drew and colored in an image of Bayzog, Sasha, Selene, Sansla, Rerry, and Samaz. He had them down to every last detail.

The seekers' eyes widened on the image. They absorbed every bit of it and spoke in a funny language back and forth. They floated up toward the murals and crossed over.

Nath strapped Fang over his shoulders and said, "Follow them."

CHAPTER 10

NATH AND COMPANY PASSED THROUGH the murals into a soft spot of Nalzambor where the enemy's activity was low. It pained his heart to leave his father's body where it lay in ridicule, but something within held him back. Now they were far west of Morgdon, on the other side of the Valley of Bones.

A drizzling rain came down, splattering his scales. The tiny drops had the chill of the changing seasons. Nath tied his hair into a ponytail, trying to blot out the image of his father, but it was eating at him.

"I see that look on your face," Brenwar said. The dwarven warrior adjusted the buckle on his magic belt. "We'll take care of your father's burial when the time comes. Now we must do what must be done."

Nath nodded. With a flick of his fingers, he waved the little dragons called seekers over to him. The small, bee-colored dragons were the only ones faster than the fabled blue razors. They darted like hummingbirds through the air. "You know who to look for. Be safe. Be careful. Stay low. There's too many wurmers out there."

The seekers zipped out of sight in a buzzing of wings, splitting off in three different directions.

"If anyone can find our friends quickly, it's them," Slivver said.

"Let's just hope it's quick enough. I've got a bad feeling in my scales. You'd think I'd be used to it by now, having the entire world chase me down."

"So why did you choose this to be our starting point? It's quite isolated," Slivver said.

"We have to start somewhere. Besides, I just had a feeling. The major cities are hives of activity. The titan armies attempt to invade Dragon Home." Nath kneeled down and tightened the laces on his boots. "I know Bayzog is wise enough to avoid all that. The others are too. And I wouldn't dare get close to the elves or dwarves."

Brenwar slung Mortuun over his back. "We'll find a trail. We always do."

"Nath," said Slivver, "there's no reason the silvers can't scout ahead. You know that would be faster."

"Let's just pound the ground for now. They can scout ahead, but stay out of the skies." Nath searched the darkening clouds. "It will be more difficult to see the wurmers prowling the air. No, we'll be patient. We can use our speed when the time comes."

Brenwar started marching forward. "Let's go then." He came to a stop. "Where are we going?"

"Let's try the smaller farmlands in the south. Perhaps they will have encountered something useful." Nath followed after Brenwar, with Slivver and the squad of silver dragons in tow. Despite the darkening weather, he had a spring in his step.

There was nothing quite like marching with his brethren dragons. They'd be more than a match for just about anybody. In the meantime, he put his faith in some of the other dragons, the seekers. They wouldn't have any trouble finding Nath and company on their return. They were a hundred bloodhounds in one, and they could have made his life a lot easier if they would have worked with him before. Now they were, and having command over them was exhilarating. In the coming days, he knew he'd need all the help he could get.

It was late in the day when they came across the first village. He and Brenwar made the approach. Nath donned the hood of his cloak and tucked his hands into his shirtsleeves.

Brenwar did the talking, but the villagers didn't have anything to say.

Nath and company passed through three other farm towns before nightfall, but no one knew anything. The people were quiet. Fear lurked behind their eyes.

The party made camp in the woods but didn't start a fire.

"The people are about as talkative as a sleepy dwarf," Nath commented as he stirred a stick in the mud. "At least they haven't been overrun by enemies."

"Not yet," Brenwar said. "But those villages used to have more livestock. A flourish of wheat and greens. The titan army is sucking the marrow from their bones. They won't last long."

Nath shook his head. The long faces of the people stuck in his mind. Hungry children holding their bellies had tugged on Nath's cloak, asking for food and coin. Not being able to help them was heartbreaking.

I can't let this happen to Nalzambor again.

Sitting on the fallen brothers of the dripping leaves above their heads, Slivver said, "Aside from the dwarf, there really isn't much need for us to rest if you wish to press on."

"Dwarves don't need rest," Brenwar said, "other than a rest from those flapping jaws of yours."

Nath grabbed Fang and stood up. "Huh, I see your point. I guess I've been with men so long, I tend to mimic their habits. Let's get on with it."

They walked through the night, cutting through the brush until they hit a path in the woods. The passageway led them out of the forest about two miles from a small town. The buildings were small, no higher than two stories tall. Only the barns and storage silos stood higher. Nath picked up the sound of a large stream that turned the wheel of a gristmill.

"It's a little too early to go knocking on doors. The people should be up with the sun in an hour or so." He took a knee. "Let's just wait."

A breeze started up in the valley, pushing down the grasses coming south from the direction of the village.

Brenwar rubbed his nose and sniffed. "I smell something rotten."

Nath's nostrils flared. The oily stench of an evil brood permeated the air.

Hanging over Nath's shoulder, Slivver said, "Something is amiss that is fouler than ever the weather was."

They waited.

A golden ray of sunlight burst out over the hilltops, giving off a dim illuminating effect. The village began to stir. So did one of the silos.

Brenwar lifted up to his feet. "That's no silo, that's a giant."

A rooster crowed. The crack of a whip sounded. People woke from their slumber on the muddy streets.

CHAPTER 11

THE BRIDGE THAT TRAVERSED THE flooding river creaked and groaned against the surging waters that rushed beneath it. Scar led the way, testing the planks. With the wind and rain in his face, he said to the others, "It's been a long time since any workmen saw this bridge. There's probably a better one." His foot pushed through the softened fibers of a wooden plank that cracked beneath his feet. "Avoid that one."

Rerry tiptoed from plank to plank. The bridge was wide enough for two wagons, but there were plenty of holes. "This bridge is more than serviceable if you go around the few bad spots. I don't see any reason to move so slowly. Let's just get across."

"Feel free to lead the way if you wish, but don't come hollering to me when you get swept downriver. If you don't drown, the current will take you a day away." Scar skittered over closer to one of the side rails. "And I'm not coming after you."

"You have to. You gave your word," Rerry laughed. "Come on, we can make it." He hopped from one plank to another. The wood gave way beneath him. *Snap!* "Gah!" He found himself up to his armpits in the hole he'd just made. His feet dangled over the water.

"What did I tell you?" Scar yelled. "Just stay still! If you wriggle, more wood will give way."

"I can pull myself up, thank you," Rerry replied.

"Just stay put," Samaz said. The bigger of the brothers inched toward Rerry. "I can feel this entire bridge shift under my feet."

"I can manage. It's only a hole. Lesson learned. Ha-ha. You were right, Scar." Rerry planted his hands on the planks and started pushing himself out of the hole. "I can see this happening to you, Samaz. You're beefy. But me?"

"It's the human in you part elves. It's dead weight." Scar had almost made it to Rerry. "Just be still until I get ahold of you."

"I'm fine." Rerry pushed up out of the hole. Suddenly, his eyes widened. "Eee-yah! Something's got me!" His body lurched. He clawed at the planks. Something powerful was sucking him downward. "Help!"

Scar dove with his hands outstretched and locked his hands on Rerry's wrist. He pulled, yet at Rerry's feet, something more powerful than both of the elves reeled them in. One by one, the elven guard locked their arms around their captain. Their efforts were futile.

"It's tearing me in half, Samaz!" Rerry screamed. "Help!"

Samaz had never seen Rerry with a panic-stricken face. It horrified him. At the same time, it spurred him into action. Without thinking, he scrambled over the rotting planks, leaned over the edge of the bridge, and took a peek below.

A bulging monster like a limbless toad waded in the deep. It was a husk of slimy flesh wedged between the river boulders. A mouth big enough to swallow cattle hung open, and out of it stretched a long tongue-like tentacle, which had coiled around Rerry's waist and legs.

"I see it! I see it!" Samaz yelled.

"Then kill it!" Rerry replied.

It was clear that the monster had the upper hand. It was nothing but a bulk of flesh and muscle. More tendrils began to snake out of the gaping jaws, reaching for Rerry's dangling toes through the busted-up planks.

Here we go!

Samaz summoned his energy and dropped into the water. The racing river carried him speeding into the monster. Arms wide, he slammed into its bulk. Lips sputtering in the foaming river, he unleashed a charge of energy.

The flabby flesh of the monster juddered. Its gawping mouth let out a screech. It let go of Rerry, and with its tentacles wriggling, it sank back into the river.

Samaz's fingers searched the slippery rock, fighting to find a grip. The rushing water beat against his body in an angry tide, determined to sweep him away.

"Hang on, Samaz!" Rerry yelled from above. The younger brother hung head first out of the hole that had almost swallowed him up earlier. "We're going to lower a rope." He turned back. "Where's that rope, Scar?"

Samaz's fingers slipped.

The river took him away and left Rerry screaming, "Samaz!"

CHAPTER 12

"RUN!"

Bayzog and Sasha sprang to their feet. Doing exactly the opposite of what Ben urged them to do, they rushed after his voice. Bayzog let the glow of the Elderwood Staff guide him to the scuffle that had erupted in the woods. With Sasha at his back, he muttered a protective spell. A glowing shield of soft white lingered in front of them. He called out in the growing silence that had fallen over the night. "Ben, Ben, where are you?"

"Ah, Ben. A fine name for a meal. Brothers, we eat Ben tonight." The voice was foreign, but it had a deep richness to it.

The shield and staff cast light on the voice's source. Ben lay on the ground. Something long and sharp had pierced his thigh. A ring of men with stag antlers on their heads surrounded him. They were over six feet tall, closer to seven feet with the horns, giving them a towering effect. Their muscular builds and hairy chests gave them a more than formidable appearance.

Sasha gasped, and her fingernails dug into Bayzog's elbow. "What are they?"

"A twisted side of nature," Bayzog said of the strange men. The stag men appeared all around them, clacking their antlers together. There were more heads than he could count in the dimness. "Stay close and be still. I'll do the talking."

"At least they speak Common," Sasha whispered.

Some of the stag men glowered at the shield with tilted antlers. They bucked their horns into the object, each taking turns, making a clatter.

The leader—who displayed the most points on his rack—stepped over to Bayzog with his brown, hairy chest stuck out. "You seek to attack us with this sorcerous thing? It shall be your death."

"I will be glad to extinguish it if it would make you feel safer."

"Safer? You dare insult the staagan!" The leader cocked back a wooden club that had a sharp knot on the end. "We are invincible! Soon we will take over this world." He came at Bayzog. The club smote Bayzog's shield. The force behind the swing cracked through.

Bayzog reeled. He felt the force of the blow inside his temple. He stepped back on Sasha's toe.

"Bayzog!" she said as she offered him support from behind.

"I'm quite well," he said. "Just surprised is all."

Sasha's face flushed. She stepped forward, and with fury she said to the leader, "What business do you have attacking us unprovoked?" With her hands balled up and shaking at her sides, she added, "Explain!"

The odd herd of staagan recoiled, shuffling back with weapons bared in front of them. "Don't accost the staagan!" The leader pointed at Ben. "This man's flesh will be roasted the same as those that hunt us. Yours as well."

"You're going to eat us?" Sasha said. "That's savage."

"No more savage than your hunters who enter our forest to trap and skin our kindred. Nay, it's time you were taken as well."

"I've never known you to eat meat," Bayzog said, carefully. The staagan were as dangerous as they appeared. Just as stubborn too. He needed to reason with them, and if that didn't work, he could try to outwit them. "Eh, mighty staagan, we're not hunters. We're just passing through in search of our children."

The leader approached, towering over Bayzog. "I don't care. You will be eaten. If we find your children, we will boil them in the pot as well."

"Great, I needed a bath anyway," Ben said. He was keeping pressure on his bleeding thigh with his hand. "Can I at least get a bandage on this? I'm getting blood all over your grass."

"Let him bleed."

"We are not hunters!" Sasha yelled. "And you aren't going to eat us! Now let us pass, in the name of Nath Dragon!"

The leader threw his head back and laughed. His men imitated him in a chorus of animal-like chuckles. After he stopped, the leader said, "You invoke an unknown name. The laughter you bring will only bring flavor to our soup." He reached over, grabbed Sasha by the shoulder, and shoved her forward. "We will cook you first."

"Bayzog," Ben growled, "I'm starting to think they're serious."

"Be silent!" The leader marched over to Ben and lifted him to his feet like a rag doll. "We shall roast you like the deer you slaughter."

"Well, which is it? Are you going to roast us or boil us?" Ben fired back.

The leader seemed confused. Bayzog got the feeling the staagan weren't certain what they were doing. If he had to guess, fear was driving their strange behavior. "Certainly there's something we can offer you in return for our freedom."

"I have some jerky," Ben said.

Sasha shot Ben a look. "Will you behave yourself?"

"Why should I? They stabbed me. I'd expect that from orcs, not men."

"Orcs!" The leader puffed out his chest. "You dare compare us to those upright pigs!"

"Did I say orcs? Let's not forget the ogres too!" Ben's words had some bite to them. "And the bugbears. I bet you play cards with the bugbears."

The staagan clacked their horns together and stomped the ground with the hooved shoes they wore. "You dare compare us to the likes of them!"

Bayzog let Ben do the talking. He seemed to have a feel for the staagan, a skill he didn't have.

Ben continued, "You mean to tell me you're not part of that army that just stormed by? I assumed if they were your enemy, you would have fought them all. I thought you were scouts for the titan's armies."

"Never! You are the ones who are with them."

"Us? No! We try our best to avoid them. They're the ones feeding the giants everything in their path, not to mention the wurmers."

Standing tall, the staagan leader remained silent, tilting his head from side to side and grumbling.

Bayzog felt a glimmer of hope stir inside him.

Finally, they listen to reason.

At long last, the staagan leader broke his silence. "Bind them up. It's time to march."

CHAPTER 13

"People are sleeping on the streets, in the dirt." Nath was up on his feet staring right beneath the rising sun. "I've never seen the likes of it!"

Brenwar grabbed him by the wrist and pulled him down. "No need to make yourself a target, King Nath. There are far worse things than a gritty slumber. It's never bothered me a wink."

The distant crack of a lash followed by a painful cry sent shivers up Nath's scales. Ogres worked with the giants, rounding up people like sheep. The ominous figures were truly giants among the haggard people who shuffled over the muddy ground. And there was no quarter. Men, women, and children alike splashed over the sloppy spots in the road.

Nath could see their long faces and scrawny limbs. All of them were covered in grime as they threw their tired backs into their work. "Look at that. The people wither away while the bellies of the ogres and giants bulge. I've had enough of this."

"Me too," Brenwar agreed.

"A little prudence should be exercised, brethren." Slivver put his arms around the shoulders of both of them. "The silvers and I can circle this town and get a feel for it. There's no telling what other dangers are nestled among the men."

"What are you suggesting? That wurmers sleep in the haystacks?" Brenwar said. "I volunteer you to check them."

"And what about the giant? Are you saving him for yourself?"

The leather that wrapped up the handle of Mortuun creaked in Brenwar's bony grip. "Exactly."

Nath made a quick head count.

There was one giant—a twenty footer with coarse hair that coated its body like armor. Tusk-like teeth jutted out from the bottom of its mouth. It wore a crude leather skull cap made from hide over its face and swung a section of fence railing from side to side. The railing slung mud all over the people.

The giant was accompanied by six ogres. Each of them was built like a barn, with long arms that swung like hammers at their sides. Standing just over eight feet tall, they were more than a match for the farmers.

It didn't take Nath too long to assess the situation. The town was being milked by the titan army. Once the supplies were used up, the town would dry up and its people with it. If they stayed put, the people would starve to death, so they'd be forced to move to the bigger cities and give up the peaceful life they had known here for centuries, only to fall prey to the titans.

Nath said to Brenwar, "One village at a time, right?"

"Aye!"

Slivver and the silver dragons broke away from Nath and Brenwar. The dragons moved like cats through the meadows, all but vanishing to the naked eye in the tall grasses. On one knee, Nath gave them several minutes as he watched the people being driven like cattle by their oppressors.

How can they do such things to others? Why does evil turn everything to chaos?

He saw a man who'd been shoved into a mud hole by an ogre push himself up and face his aggressor. The ogre slapped the man so hard the man spun around in a full circle. Nath felt the blow in his scales. He let out an angry sigh.

"Not yet," Brenwar whispered. "Just let that anger build. That's what I'm doing."

At least they're fighting.

Seeing the man stand up for himself gave Nath even more purpose. There were plenty of villages where the people fell on their faces in worship of the enemy. It had spread in the larger cities first, and only now were the smaller places succumbing. Now was the time to turn the tide on evil. If the people in this village could be saved, then so could their legacy.

But sometimes you need help.

Nath perked up. The soft call of dragon sound caught his ears. It was a murmuring that mixed with the wind and could travel for miles undetected. Not all dragons could do it as well as others, but it was one of the silver dragons' many gifts. Nath had that gift too, even when he was a boy, but up to now, few dragons had heeded his calls—or even thanked him when he rescued them. He flipped his hand against Brenwar's shoulder. "It's time."

"Good." Brenwar stood tall. "Let's run in there and make thunder happen."

"No, let's stroll and see what they have to say."

"Walk or run, it doesn't matter to me. I'm bringing the pain like rain."

Nath and Brenwar walked right toward the heart of the village. The hapless people didn't look up long enough to even notice. By the time they did, Nath and Brenwar stood among them like two bristling warriors born of a burning forge. The crowd slowed. Some of the people gaped.

The odd moment was enough to capture the ogre overlord's attention. The burly humanoid with powerful meaty arms blinked several times before his eyebrows knitted together.

The people's eyes slid back and forth between the ogre and the bold interlopers.

Breaking the silence, Nath cleared his throat. "Ogre, I'm going to give you and your unwashed kin one chance to abandon this place in one piece." He huffed on his fingernails and cleaned them off on his cloak. "I repeat. One chance."

The ogre let out a gusty laugh, catching the attention of his kindred, who turned. Their beady eyes grazed over Nath but locked on Brenwar. Some of them snarled; others pounded their chests.

Brenwar puffed through his lips, stirring his long moustache. He began winding Mortuun up in a slow windmill. He growled, "One is one more chance than I'd give."

The ogre nearest to them cracked his whip with a loud *snap*! "We will feed on your bones, Dwarf! You too, Red Hair!" He let out a call that caught the attention of the giant. The monster stood alongside the barn, overlooking the livestock. The giant was about to stuff a sheep in its mouth when it turned. The white of the giant's eyes enlarged behind the hide mask. The giant flung the sheep aside, and with long heavy steps that shook the ground, it came their way.

Nath gave a whistle. The six silver dragons flew into the village, wings beating and bellies dusting the ground. Letting out shrieks that could scare the hair off a bear, they encircled the giant like a flying buzz saw of silver fury.

The giant howled. It cocked back its arms with its fists balled up with might.

Bolts of flame and silver erupted from the silver dragons' mouths. The white-hot blasts ripped into the giant, who screamed so loud the ogre's back hairs stood on end.

The giant's painful bellows fell silent. What was left of its incinerated body became dust on the earth.

"Aw, I wanted to kill that one," said Brenwar.

The ogres' lips flapped and quivered. In a panic, they locked eyes on the bristling Brenwar and charged.

CHAPTER 14

"COME ON, OGRES! IT'S TIME to kiss my hammer!" Wearing his magic bracers, Brenwar slung Mortuun.

The hammer careened through the air, smiting the first ogre with a clap of thunder. The powerful force knocked the ogre backward into a second ogre. They landed in a heap of limbs. The first ogre was dead, the one beneath scrambling to its feet.

"For Morgdon!" Brenwar yelled. He charged the monsters, snatched his hammer up, and started swinging again.

With Fang in his hands, Nath sprang at the next two assailants.

The brutes' eyes widened when he crashed into the side of one of them.

The charge knocked the ogre off the path to Brenwar. It stumbled.

The whistle of a whip caught Nath's ear. Quicker than a cat, he spun just in time to catch the tail of the snapping whip.

"I guess you've never seen anyone so fast before, have you, Ugly!" Nath gave the whip a yank.

The swift move caught the ogre off balance. The ogre's arms flailed.

Nath smote the ogre in the chest with Fang. Two ogres were dead. "Four to go!"

Brenwar clobbered the next ogre in the head with Mortuun.

The beast of a man staggered, wobbled, stumbled, and finally dropped to both knees. Drooling, it swayed from side to side.

Brenwar strolled up to the drooling monster.

Even on its knees, the ogre was still almost twice as tall as the dwarf. Its eyes were wide. It scratched the dent Brenwar had put in its head.

With a shove of the head of his hammer, Brenwar pushed the ogre over.

It landed on its side, unmoving.

"Go ahead, breathe your last foul breath."

"Brenwar, look out!" Nath yelled. He'd just finished off his second ogre when he turned in time to see another one rushing toward Brenwar.

The ogre slammed into the dwarf at full speed, with its full weight behind it. Brenwar was plowed deep into the mud. The ogre pinned Brenwar's face in the wet dirt.

Nath rushed in.

The two remaining ogres stepped into Nath's path, one of the brutes loosing a windmill chop with its oversized hatchet.

Fang clashed into the metal head of the axe. *Clang!* The blow rocked Nath's arms down to the elbows. Ogres hit like a mule kicked.

Guzan! I felt every bit of that!

Behind his assailant, Nath could see Brenwar's arms and legs flapping under the other ogre's superior weight. He held Fang back in one hand, pointing at the ogre with the other. "You should have run when you had the chance."

The ogre let out a savage scream with jaws so wide that could swallow a watermelon whole. It took one step forward.

A bolt of lightning ripped through the ogre's chest. Tendrils of energy crackled all around the beast. Ears smoking, it fell face first to the ground, splashing mud all over Nath.

Slivver walked over to the scene and lorded over the charred remains of the ogre. "My, are they thick. I was hoping it would explode."

Nath wiped the mud from his eyes. "Thanks, Slivver. I had this under control. You should have helped Brenwar."

"Who?"

Nath pointed to the mud wrestling going on several feet away.

"Ah." Slivver chuckled. "I seem to recall Brenwar liking the mud."

"To sleep on, not to breathe in." Nath marched over to the ogre and tapped it hard on the shoulder.

It turned its giant ball of a head toward Nath and showed as inquisitive a look as an ogre could possibly make.

Nath punched it in the jaw with everything he had in him. *Whop!*

The ogre fell over sideways and lay still.

Brenwar popped up. He was more mud than dwarf, with brown sludge dripping from his beard. "I had him right where I wanted him." He shook his head, flinging mud everywhere. "Never doubt a dwarf!" He kicked the ogre in the ribs. "I win."

There weren't any more signs of enemies. The villagers' eyes were big as saucers. Many of them trembled. Others grumbled.

Nath put away his sword and raised his arms high. "People, you are free from these monsters. They will oppress you no more. Now enjoy your labors. Eat and be fulfilled."

It took some goading, but after Nath spoke with some of the leadership, he convinced them they were safe, for now. He even offered them protection the likes of which they never could have imagined. "It's time the people of Nalzambor learned to trust in the dragons again. Slivver, I want some of the silvers to stay and protect them until this war is at an end."

"As you wish, Dragon King."

By midday, smiles began to form on the faces of the people again. Along with full bellies, the warm sun lifted the people's spirits. Nath spoke with many of them. He received hugs and well wishes. Even Brenwar got some hugs from some of the town maidens. They ignored his "Never hug a dwarf" rumblings.

Nath sat down to a feast of meat and eggs fit for a king. He and the others ate with merriment. There was nothing quite like being among people who looked forward to the days ahead. They were more than ready to rebuild all they had lost. He watched a pair of mules drag all the dead ogres away.

Brenwar said to him, "Today was easy. It won't always be this easy. Remember that."

"I will."

A couple of hours later, Nath, Brenwar, and Slivver departed with four silver dragons. They had only traveled a league when one of the bee-like seeker dragons appeared.

CHAPTER 15

ONCE THEY MADE IT ACROSS the bridge, Rerry and Scar raced down the riverbank, searching for Samaz. Rerry's heart pounded in his temples as he called out in the night, "Samaz! Samaz!" Scar and the elven guard kept silent, but their eyes were searching. They'd spread out along the bank in a long line, searching the river brush in the hope that Samaz might be caught up in there.

In the dim light, it was difficult to see anything alive, even with his keen elven sight. Rerry, being only a quarter elf, could see some of the smaller living critters that burrowed and scurried on the ground, but his vision wasn't so good from far away. He had hoped to see a warm lump in the river by now.

"Come on, Samaz, where are you?"

About fifty yards upriver, one of the elven guard called out. The soldier was knee keep in the waters and waving his hand.

Rerry took off at a full sprint, traversing the difficult terrain like a jackrabbit. Finally, he came upon the scene. Samaz floated haphazardly in the river, hanging onto the branch of a tree that had fallen. Rerry waded into the water, and with the help of the elves, he pulled Samaz onto the slick bank. Lightly smacking his brother's face, he said, "Samaz, can you hear me?"

"Well enough that I couldn't catch any sleep from it." Samaz coughed and wheezed then looked up at his brother. "You know, it's really hard to swim with clothes on."

Rerry gave his brother the strongest hug he'd ever given him. The warmth of his brother's body ran through his arms to his head and toes. "Samaz, you did the bravest thing I ever saw when you jumped in the river to save me. And you attacked that monster! I know I've been difficult, but I've never felt more like your brother than I do now. Thank you."

"Well, I am the elder. I'm supposed to watch out for you." Samaz hugged his brother in return.

Rerry felt the iron strength in his brother's limbs as he patted his back. "I suppose it's time to get back on with it then. Scar, we aren't too far off course, are we?"

"Actually, we're closer. Follow me."

They made their way west until hundreds of feet of hillside appeared. Scar led them through the hills until they hit a clearing in the forest. He pointed at a small fort made of stone about halfway up the next hill. "That's it."

Rerry could see smoke billowing out of a chimney that made for an eerie lingering haze. The closer they marched toward the small fortress, the more his limbs itched. He whispered to Samaz, "Do you make anything of this?"

"It seems like an odd place for an elf to go."

"Agreed, but I was hoping for a little more insight than that from you. I figured that much out."

"Well, my eyes haven't rolled up into my head yet. That's a good sign."

Rerry rubbed the chill bumps creeping up his arms. A fog crept over his feet. The hoot owls stopped hooting. Only the sound of their footfalls remained, and those seemed unusually loud. Up the hill they went, barely able to see the person in front of them, with Scar somewhere ahead, leading the way.

"Whoa!" Rerry said in a very audible whisper.

They stood right in front of the gateway that led into the small fort. The stone archway entrance was a black mouth waiting to swallow them whole. Rerry couldn't see a thing on the other side. Scar stood half in and half out of the light. Rerry's hand fell to his sword.

This is unbearably strange. I've trusted Scar too much.

Adjusting his eye patch, Scar said, "If we're going to find any help at all, it will be in here." He leaned back into more light. "You look spooked. You don't want to turn back, do you?"

Samaz gave Rerry a nod. He moved forward. "No. We've come this far. Besides, I wouldn't mind seeing what's cooking within." He sniffed. "It smells like stew."

"Don't get your hopes up. If she eats, she doesn't eat much, unless it's people."

"What?"

"A jest. You just never expect one from the likes of me." Scar went in with his elves.

Rerry and Samaz followed. The fort was more of a small home built from stone in the form of a tower. They ventured into a chamber, where dark curtains hid the faint light behind them. He smelled oil, burning wood, and other things that weren't so bad and weren't so good.

From behind the curtains came a voice that sounded as ancient as the tallest tree in the forest. "I've been expecting you."

Rerry's heart skipped a beat. Something scurried over his toes, sending chills up his spine. "What was that?" he whispered to Samaz. His eyes darted all around. The floor was hidden by smoky yellow vapors. Webs with large spiders hung in every corner. He imagined an old crone with a nest of bugs in her hair.

Scar pulled the curtain back, making for a passageway, and stepped aside. "After you."

Rerry gave Samaz a little shove forward. "You go first. You're the oldest."

A woman sat with her back to all of them, facing the fireplace. She was slender and clothed in a set of robes older than she was. Her hair was long, gray, and braided, running the length of her back. Her leathery arms were stretched out to her sides.

The room itself was medium in size, with small cupboards and a table upon which sets of pottery were either neatly stacked or in orderly rows. Strange growth covered the walls, a mix of yellow and lavender moss. Little critters moved among it.

Her head moved a little. "You seek somebody. All who come here are seeking someone or something. But with you, it's someone. Eh, Captain Scar?"

"Yes."

"But you are not the seeker. Those with you are." She cackled. "I'm flattered that you thought of me, but there is much you are unaware of."

The flames in the fireplace grew brighter. Something swirled within, making a pulsating effect in the room. She turned to face them.

Rerry's fingernails dug into his palms. He stayed behind Samaz's shoulder. *I can't look, I can't look.* He tried to close his eyes, but they were frozen open. The rest of him seemed fastened to the floor. The first things he saw were her eyes. *Sultans of Sulfur!*

CHAPTER 16

BEN SAT ON THE GROUND, tied to a tree. Nearby and bound to other trees were Bayzog and Sasha. Brenwar's chest and the Elderwood Staff were nowhere to be seen. A half dozen staagan stood guard.

Ben's leg throbbed, and he was thirsty. "Say, can we get some water?"

The staagan didn't move. They didn't even blink.

"That's wonderful. We have mute—uh, what did you call them, Bayzog?"

"Staagan."

"Oh yes, staagan. They are some strange creatures. And they aren't very hospitable." He wriggled in his bonds. "Come on now, staagan. Bring us some water. We've been tied up for hours."

"Bayzog, we should have done something when we had the chance." Sasha's hair half covered her face. She kept trying to shake it from her eyes. "You should have just used the Elderwood Staff and blasted them."

"The staagan aren't aggressive creatures. We will talk them into letting us go." His violet eyes flicked up at Ben. "I thought you did quite well making our case, Ben. You certainly did much better than I have so far. They didn't buy the pitch is all."

"Well, I'm sorry. I should have seen them coming." Ben banged his head against the tree, shaking some of the raindrops off the leaves. One splashed into his eye. "I'm getting old, I guess."

"Stop blaming yourself," Sasha said. "The world is full of trouble. And quit whining. It just reminds me how old I am."

"You don't look half as old as me. That's for certain, and you still look younger than Bayzog."

Sasha made a weak smile. "That's because he's always looked old."

Ben laughed. The more he chuckled, the more the ropes tightened. The coarse material was rubbing his skin raw. His stomach growled. "Great, thirsty and hungry." He looked at the staagan and yelled, "Not to mention still BLEEDING!"

The longer he sat, the more sore he became. His joints ached. He felt his heartbeat in his temples. He closed his eyes and tried to forget about everything.

Just pretend you're out camping with friends.

Earlier, he had felt confident that things would go in their favor. The staagan didn't appear threatening, even though they were formidable. The problem was they weren't very smart. Stupidity mixed with fear was a deadly combination. If they felt threatened, then they would eliminate the threat. That was how most creatures survived.

The guards stirred.

The powerful staagan leader returned—with Bayzog's staff cradled in his arms. He said to his men, "Bring them."

The guards untied the three of them from the trees and brought them to their feet.

All of their hands were still bound behind their backs. The odd party began another long march, winding through the forest like a snake, mile after mile.

Ben's leg burned with each and every step. He tripped on a root and hit his knee hard on a rock. "Ow!"

Sasha and Bayzog stopped and turned. "Ben, how are you?"

A staagan picked him up by the armpits and lifted him to his feet with ease. The stag man shoved him forward.

"I'll make it. If not, I assume the horned brutes will carry me. Great dragons, I've never felt so worthless."

"You should know by now that you are priceless." Sasha gave him a wink.

Ben enhanced his stride and caught up with her. "Thanks. You always know the right thing to say."

"That's because I can read men's minds."

"Oh really, then what am I thinking now?"

"That you need a drink and that Bayzog should have blasted them with his staff."

"Wow, you truly are a marvel."

They forged ahead another mile, coming to a stop inside a grove of pine trees. In the middle was a large ring of stacked stones about ten feet wide. Ten of the staagan, with muscles bulging in their necks and arms, lifted a giant slab of stone that covered the well. They walked it aside and set it down with a chorus of grunts. One of the staagan rubbed his back.

That's when Ben noticed Brenwar's chest lying off to the side. The staagan leader pointed at the chest. One of the guards picked it up and walked it toward the well.

"No! What are you doing?"

The staagan guard dropped the chest in the well.

"Nooooo!" Ben cried out. "Are you out of your mind?"

"That strongbox is evil," the leader said. He walked over to the edge of the well. "So is this cursed thing." He tossed the Elderwood Staff in the well.

Bayzog dropped to his knees.

Ben's pounding head felt like it was about to explode. This was madness.

The leader waved his hand at all of them. "You are all evil. You are going in the deep well to feed the belly of the world." He pointed at Sasha. "Start with that one."

CHAPTER 17

The seer's eyes were pitch-black orbs that gave her a haunting appearance. At one time her appearance might have been lovely, but her once-lustrous skin was now weathered and gray. Her high cheekbones were pointed knots on her face. She smoothed her hair back behind one ear, revealing the smallest point on the top.

She's part elven.

In an elderly voice, she said, "You are very observant, Rerry."

"How… how do you know my name? And you read my thoughts!"

She waved in a relaxed motion with her hand. "I'm a seer. It's what I do. Be at ease, men. You've had a long journey. Now is the time to settle yourselves and listen."

Rerry and Samaz looked at each other.

Samaz shrugged and took a seat, crossed his legs, and gave the seer his undivided attention.

Before Rerry sat, he asked, "What—"

"—is my name?" she replied. "I'm so old it no longer matters. But they used to call me Saree. Saree the seer. Yes, that is what they would call me after I discovered my gift." A smoke-colored cat slipped onto her lap, and she petted it. "This is Cat. I've had too many pets to bother naming them anymore, and this is far from the first one I've called Cat." The fireplace continued to warble behind her with a strange life. "Please, men, take a seat. Then I'll be more comfortable answering your question."

Taking his place beside his brother, Rerry said, "We only get one question? It's one question each, I hope."

"You are a feisty one. Every bit the problem I foresaw." She placed her hands on her knees. "Well then, first things first. A warning. Nalzambor reels after the death of Balzurth."

In unison, Rerry and Samaz sat up and said, "The death of Balzurth!"

"Yes, the Dragon King is dead, at the hands of Eckubahn and his brother Isobahn. The Dragon King was killed by the very Spear of Barnabus that he forged himself." She hugged herself. "Oh, it broke my heart. I felt it the moment it happened. It was as if glass was shattering. Now the world quakes. Evil builds its forces and strikes from all directions. Honestly, I'm surprised you made it this far. All that matters is that you did. The west is the safest place to be right now. And no one comes to visit my creepy place." She leaned over and touched Scar on the knee. "But you remembered. Never will you forget that last adventure, will you, One Eye. Tee-hee!"

Rerry felt like he was floating at sea without a rudder. Hearing that Balzurth was dead had hit home. If the titans could kill the Dragon King, then they could kill anybody. His concern for his parents grew. He needed to get to them, and fast. "Can you help us find our parents?"

"That's why you were brought here, isn't it?"

Looking around the dreary room, he said, "I can't imagine any other reason why I would enter this place."

"That might change after you try my stew," she said.

Rerry gave a sniff and replied, "I doubt it. So, can you tell us where they are?"

"The answer will be revealed in the fires if they are willing." She lifted the cat off her lap and shooed it away. With a little shake, she loosened up her hands and arms then offered them to Samaz and Rerry. Beckoning for them, she said, "I need something that is close to them. There is nothing closer than you. Come, come and sit by my side."

With hesitation, they took spots on either side of her, facing the fire. It didn't crackle or pop, and it was more warm than hot.

Saree closed her eyes. "Just let your guard down and trust me. Think of your parents. Reflect on your strongest memories. That will strengthen the spell." She began to speak strange words in a rhythmic pace that would speed up and slow down.

Rerry felt strength flow into him from her warm, leathery hand, and he leaned forward. He found Samaz looking at him for a moment. Samaz gave his broad shoulders a shrug, closed his eyes, and leaned back. Rerry gave in and did the same. He thought about walking in the gardens of Quintuklen with his mother. They had a favorite spot on a granite bench surrounded by purple tiger lilies.

I miss those days. Wherever did they go?

Saree the sage's grip fastened like a vise on his hand. It was like a tree branch had grabbed ahold of him. Wincing, he lost his train of thought.

How'd she get so strong?

The seer wailed and moaned. The fire roared with new bright light that swirled in their midst. She started to speak out loud. "Oh, so strong! They are so strong! It is delightful! You've done well, Scar. Oh so well. I didn't think you would ever repay me."

Unable to pull free of her iron grip, Rerry turned toward Scar and said, "What have you done? You owe me a life debt, and now you betray me."

Without a shred of concern, Scar replied, "I owed her a life debt first." He saluted. "So long, Samaz and Rerry. I'll sleep well knowing I can't repay the dead." He and the others vanished.

Rerry screamed after him, "You'll never sleep at all!" He tugged with all of his might. Each passing second drained him from top to bottom. His eyes fell on his arms and hands. Saree's skin now had a youthful luster, and his own skin clung to his bones like a venerable old man's. On the other side, his formerly meaty brother's eyes and cheeks had sunken into his bones. He'd never seen Samaz so thin before, and his brother's coal-black hair had turned white. "Let us go," he managed to say.

Saree sat in full form. Her body and hair had been restored to their youthful appearance—that of a wild and comely woman. She showed a smile of pearly-white teeth. "I would, but you're both too delicious."

The last thing Rerry heard was his head bouncing off the stone hearth of the fireplace.

CHAPTER 18

"NO! NO! STOP!" BAYZOG SURGED in front of Sasha, blocking the staagans' path to the well. "Spare her and throw me in."

Ben tore out of the clutches of one of the monsters and bustled over. "And take me next, or first, it doesn't matter! What kind of horned savages are you, throwing the woman in? It's despicable."

"It makes no difference." The leader snorted and stamped his hoof. "You are all a meal, nothing more and nothing less."

"And you are nothing more than the orcs and ogres, I'll tell you that much!" Ben yelled.

The staagan seized his arms and picked him up by the legs. They took him to the edge of the well. Wriggling against his restraints, Ben took a glance in the well. It was pitch black. "I swear if I survive this, I'm going to start hunting again and mount your heads on my wall. We are innocent!"

As Ben fought with everything he had in him, Bayzog's fingers kept working at the cords that bound his hands. If he could only get them free, he could cause some sort of distraction to get them out of there. He felt terrible guilt about his gamble. He had bet on the more reasonable nature of the staagan, had thought they'd free them, but with all the world falling apart around them, the staagan had chosen to rid themselves of any potential enemies. *Sasha and Ben were right. I should have blasted them when I had the chance.* He found his wife's eyes. She blinked at him several times.

"Hold on a moment!" Ben yelled just as the enemy were about to throw him in the well. He glanced all over the forest. "Do you hear that? I can smell it! *Sniff! Sniff!* Orcs are coming!"

The staagan froze. With a wave of his hand, the leader sent several of his men. All but one let go of Ben and ran out of sight.

Ben was buying time. Bayzog acted. Seeing Sasha's signals, he understood her idea. He said to the leader, "Can I at least have one last moment with my wife?"

With a nod, the staagan said, "No."

"That looked like a yes to me!" Ben shouted.

Bayzog made his way to Sasha. The staagan cut him off. "Please," he begged.

The leader shook his head this time. "No. I smell trickery."

Bayzog's shoulders sagged. "As you wish."

The staagan search party returned from the woodland. They shook the racks on their heads.

"See, there are no orcs." The leader pointed at Ben. "You prove my point by trying to deceive."

Once all of their attention was focused on the leader, Bayzog took action. He squirted between two staagan on quick feet. He kept going until he ran into Sasha and her captor. In the tussle, the husband and wife found themselves back to back and locked fingers. Together they summoned energy they couldn't get on their own. Tingling raced up his arms. Energy filled his body. The cords that bound them started to release.

Almost free!

The sharp blow of a fist hit Bayzog in the side of the head. His fingers slipped from Sasha's. He dropped to the ground with bright spots in his eyes.

The leader stood over him, nostrils flaring and snorting. "Deceiver! Throw this one in now! Throw them all in now!" The staagan clacked his teeth. "I'm tired of this."

The staagan carried him to the edge of the well. Bayzog strained against them, but it was futile. The staagan were every bit as strong as they appeared. He found Sasha's eyes and said, "I'm sorry, dear."

"Don't blame yourself," she said. "We all failed."

"I can't believe I'm going to die for such a stupid reason!" Ben said, kicking at his captors. "We didn't even do anything!"

The staagan leader stood where they could all see him. With his fists on his hips, he said, "No one is innocent."

"If that's the case, then throw yourself in!" Ben said.

"That would be foolish."

The staagan raised Bayzog, Ben, and Sasha over their heads. Bayzog felt his stomach empty. With all of his study and intelligence, he couldn't overcome blind stupidity fueled by fear.

The leader raised his arms.

The wind tore through the trees. Except it wasn't the wind. It was dragons. Silver dragons with scales that shone like the stars in the sky. The five dragons surrounded the well with wings spread and a dangerous look in their eyes.

The staagan leader let out a bellow.

A powerful figure with flame-red hair lifted the leader overhead.

Ben let out a shout. "Dragon!"

CHAPTER 19

"JUST WHEN I THOUGHT I'D seen everything, I see this?" Nath said. Looking up at the staagan leader, he said, "If my friends go in this well, then you're going in too."

"You dare!" the staagan huffed.

Nath edged closer to the rim. "I dare!"

The staagan swallowed. He gave a nod to his guards. They backed away from the well and set Nath's friends free.

"I'm going to set you down," Nath said to the staagan, who was every bit as big as him. "But you had better not try anything else stupid, or I'll rip those antlers from your head. Agreed?"

The staagan eyed the silver dragons. His lips smacked together. "Agreed."

Nath set the staagan down.

For the first time, the staagan got a look at Nath dragon. His eyes blinked repeatedly. With a snort, he backed away, made a bellow, and said with his chin high, "This time, we go." Together, the staagan all vanished into the woodland.

Ben let out all of his glee. "You did it, Dragon! What a sight for my aging eyes. I thought we were finished!" He hopped around wincing, wriggling his bound hands. "Do you mind?'

Nath slit the cord with his fingernail. "You're wounded."

Ben gave him a strong embrace. "I'll live."

Brenwar teetered over to Ben and looked at the bloody gash in the old soldier's leg. "It's barely a scratch."

"You would know."

Nath made his rounds to Sasha and Bayzog. "It's so good to see you both."

Sasha gave Nath a hug. "Your timing couldn't have been more remarkable. I have to admit, my hope was fleeing." She looked up into his eyes. "Nath, I'm sorry about your father."

Nath's throat tightened. "Thank you."

Bayzog put a hand on Nath's arm. "Me too, Nath. We'll find a way to make this right. I swear it."

"I know we will. Words can't explain how thankful I am to be among such great friends. I had my doubts that I would fix my eyes on you again."

"How did you find us?"

Nath took a moment to explain the journey from Dragon Home through the Chamber of Murals. He called for the seeker who had aided them.

He landed on Nath's shoulder. Sitting like a bird, the black and yellow dragon cocked his head from side to side.

Nath stroked the beard of skin under the seeker's neck. "He found you, and others like him are searching for Rerry and Samaz. Oh, and there's someone I want you to meet."

"Really, who?" Sasha asked.

"My brother, Slivver."

"You have a brother?" she said.

"I have many, but Slivver is the one most like me, or I'm like him." He waved Slivver over. "Here he comes."

Unlike the other silvers, who stood on all fours, Sliver walked over with a wide, leggy gait, dragging his tail behind him. With an air of nobility, he nodded at Bayzog and Sasha. "It is grand to meet you." He took Sasha's hand and kissed it. "Your beauty is exceptional, and I've heard so much about the both of you."

Blushing, Sasha said, "Nath, you never told me you had a brother. And he's all dragon? And so exceptional?"

"Yes, my much older brother is quite exceptional for his age," Nath joked.

"Ha-ha," Slivver said.

"So I take it the search for Rerry and Samaz is not going well?" Nath said.

"We sense they are west of us." Bayzog frowned. "I don't have much more to go on than that."

"Keep your chin up. We found you, and we'll find them." Nath continued to pet the seeker. "It's a shame that it's taken so long for these little guys to warm up to me. They would have come in handy back in the day, but they are pretty elusive. We were fortunate that when he alerted us, we weren't that far away. Not even a league. Anyway—"

"What do you mean you lost my chest?" Brenwar blurted out.

Everyone turned. Ben and Brenwar were arguing.

"It's not your chest as I understand it, and it's not my fault. Those stag men did it!" Ben replied.

"What's going on?" Nath said.

"Ben lost my chest down into this hole!" Brenwar started fishing out some rope. "And I'm sending him down after it."

"I'm not climbing down there! I almost met my doom in that pit of blackness. It's your chest, you go."

"Oh, so now it's my chest." Brenwar rolled his eyes.

Slivver stepped forward. "I'll go get the chest. I can fly, after all."

But Nath stopped his brother with a hand on his arm. He stuck his other hand down inside the hole. The air was icy, and his fingertips disappeared. "This is not an ordinary hole. Certainly you can tell that much. There is magic here. Dark magic. Things are not as we perceive them. The chest is down there?"

"They tossed down the Elderwood Staff as well." Bayzog was unable to hide his long look.

Nath shook his head. "The staagan are so stupid. If they only had brains as big as their horns. So how deep is it? How long did it take before you heard the chest hit the bottom?"

Bayzog, Ben, and Sasha all looked at one another at the same time. Ben said, "I didn't hear anything hit."

"Me neither," Sasha added.

Bayzog sighed. "The staagan said we were to feed the belly of Nalzambor."

Brenwar picked up a rock and tossed it in the well. Cupping his ear, he leaned over the rim on his tiptoes. Seconds passed. Then a minute. He clawed at his beard. "That's deeper than a dwarven diamond shaft. I suppose we'll just have to do without." He started pulling the rope up, eyeing Bayzog. "It's just a stick. I'll whittle you up another one."

"And you're just going to leave your chest behind?" Ben said.

"Aw, it's like you said, it's not my chest anyway. I've got Mortuun. I'll be fine. The rest of you will have to adapt."

Nath slid Fang out of his sheath and stuck the sword blade first into the well. The blue light lit up the edges, but that was it. Nath felt a chill on his arm like a cold breeze. "This is odd. It's a hole, but it doesn't feel like a hole."

"I sense something odd too." Bayzog waved his hands over the rim and closed his eyes. One brow perched. He started to mumble something.

Sasha reached for Bayzog. "Don't you—"

Bayzog jumped into the hole.

"—dare!"

CHAPTER 20

SAREE THE SEER HOPPED AND skipped about her home, singing and laughing. Rerry and Samaz both lay in front of the fire where she had drained them. Rerry could barely manage to lift his arms. With effort, he held them up, looking at his bony hands.

Samaz rolled over on his side, facing Rerry. He started laughing in a raspy chuckle. "You look dreadful."

"No more dreadful than you." Rerry gave Samaz a feeble punch in the shoulder.

Saree hopped over between them. Her dark-green eyes were filled with restless energy. Excitement was in her voice. "I see my little old men are getting feisty. I can't have that now. You might hurt yourselves." Hands on her hips, she said, "I had better tie you up."

"Tie us up? We can barely move. I don't even want to move. Everything hurts. What did you do to us?"

"I took all of your youth and made it mine. I should last a couple hundred more years now." She rummaged through her cupboard until she produced a ball of twine. "Ah, this should do."

"Couldn't you have just drained an orc or something?" Rerry asked.

"Oh no, that wouldn't work. You see, my curse is more interesting." She combed her rich brown hair over her head. "You see, like you, I am part elf. Only a part elf will do. Part elves are hard to come by, and dear old Scar brought me two." She tied up Rerry's ankles. "What a feast. I haven't felt so well in decades."

Samaz rolled over on his back and asked with an upside-down look, "What is the long-term plan for us? Are we to be indentured servants?"

"No. It's more of a short-term plan. What's left of you will be dinner for the wolves."

"Wolves! You feed people to wolves?"

"Certainly. They are my pets."

"Shouldn't you have fed us to them before you sucked the marrow from our bones?" Rerry said.

"I see you still have spirit. I can't have that. It's dangerous." She bound up Samaz by the feet and tethered them to another section of rope she fetched, then patted down their clothes and looked inside their palms. "Just making sure you don't have any tricks up your sleeves."

"I think you're the one with all the tricks," Rerry said.

"Humph, I think you're right, but you have to give Scar some credit. He marched you right on inside a witch's haven, and you both followed him blithely." She hefted the bigger rope over her shoulder and began dragging them out of the room. "Scar. How could you trust an elf named Scar? So young and naïve. So delicious."

Rerry's feeble fingers clutched at a chair he passed. His grip only lasted a moment. Dread overcame him.

I'm so stupid! I can't believe I trusted Scar!

Saree dragged them outside and down the hill without an ounce of care as they jostled over the hard roots and rocks. They might as well have been dead already. Rerry grasped at everything they passed with no effect, but one time her efforts did come to a halt. Samaz had tangled his arm up in a thick patch of ivy. With a scowl, she stormed over and gave him a swift kick in the ribs.

Samaz groaned.

She took up the rope and resumed dragging them down the hill. They came to a level overlook with a backdrop of stone. Rainwater trickled over the layers of rock. Old bones lay on the ground, picked clean. Rusting chains were fastened to the rock. The depressing area was partially overgrown. The smell of death and decay seemed to keep nature at bay. Saree shackled them by the wrists.

A wolf howled.

Saree howled back. Her eyes slid over both of them. "I'm grateful. The wolves will be grateful too." She squatted in front of them. "Don't be so sad. This is just a part of life's cycle. Besides, you didn't think you'd live forever, did you?" She winked. "But you could if you were me. Bye bye, part elves."

Rerry didn't even try to stop her. He just tugged at the twine.

Samaz did the same, saying in his old-man voice, "We have a better chance of sprouting wings than of getting ourselves untied."

But Just as Saree was about to vanish around a bend down the path, she stopped and said, "What are you doing here?"

A sword cut through the air with a whistle. Saree's head left her shoulders and bounced down the hill. Her body fizzled, and ghostly tentacles emerged. The mystic fibers drifted over to Samaz and Rerry.

Rerry lurched in the mist. His essence filled him. Color and strength returned to his lips. It was beyond exhilarating. The next thing he saw was Scar untying the twine that bound his wrists and ankles. "You traitor!"

"And savior," Samaz said. He was free and up on his feet, rubbing his wrists.

Rerry jumped to his feet and hauled back to punch Scar.

Samaz stepped in the way.

Scar handed his sword to Rerry. "I couldn't do it. I just couldn't. You boys didn't deserve this, and I'm sorry. I hope you'll understand one day."

Rerry snatched away the sword. "I should chop you to bits!"

With a dead stare, Scar said, "It wouldn't make any difference. I'm dead anyway. That's the choice I made. I should have made it long ago, but I was a coward."

"What are you talking about?" Rerry asked.

The sky darkened.

"Just go! Go now!" The leaves in the forest started to tremble and shake. Wolves that sounded like a hundred howled. "Just get across the river. The wolves won't follow that far. None of her minions will." He shoved the both of them. "Don't waste my sacrifice. Go!"

With the forest agitated as in a thunderstorm, Rerry took off at a sprint down the hill with Samaz on his heels. Every branch they passed seemed to claw at them.

And then they heard Scar's scream over the racing wind, cut off with a loud *snap*.

Rerry started to look back, but Samaz pushed him forward, shouting, "Don't you dare! Onward!"

They cut through the trees until they hit the bottom of the hill. Running for the river, they could hear the wolves barking in the forest.

Rerry's eyes caught sight of the bridge. "It's there! It's there!"

With the wind whistling in his ears, his toes touched the first plank. Remembering to soften his footfalls, he skipped from plank to plank. They groaned but never gave. Samaz followed him step for step until they made it to the other side. Rerry turned to look at the pack of wolves gathered on the other side, howling in the wind. After a long moment, they vanished up the hillside.

Hands on his knees and sucking for breath, he patted Samaz on the back. "We made it."

Samaz didn't reply, just tapped Rerry's shoulder.

Rerry looked up and found himself facing a host of dwarves. Catching his breath, he said, "Perfect timing. This bridge is in desperate need of repair. I can assure you, my—"

A dwarf clubbed him in the back of the head. The world went dark.

CHAPTER 21

SASHA CLIMBED UP ONTO THE rim of the well. Nath took her by the waist and set her back on the ground. "No you don't, Sasha. If he wanted you to go, he would have taken you."

"Let me go, Nath!"

Peering over the rim, Brenwar said, "It's a black hole. Not even a dwarf would leap into the likes of that. That part elf has gone squirrely."

Nath was dismayed. He'd never seen Bayzog do anything so impulsive before.

"We have to do something, Nath!" Sasha said. "He'll certainly need our help if something evil is down there."

Slivver stepped up again. "I'll go in after him."

"I say we both go." Nath prepared to make the leap. "On three?"

Bayzog erupted from the hole. With the Elderwood Staff in one hand, the gem at the top burning like morning light, he slung Brenwar's chest to the ground with the other. His robes were in tatters. He was scraped up from head to toe and panting for breath.

"Bayzog!" Sasha rushed over and hauled the reeling man in. He collapsed in her arms, trembling. "He's ice cold," she said, brushing his face with her hands. She leaned over his shivering lips. "He's speaking, in Elvish."

Nath leaned over the both of them. Interpreting Bayzog's words, he said, "Put the lid on. Put the lid on!"

The ground shook. A howling moan erupted from the well.

Brenwar scrambled over to the giant slab of stone. "I could use a hand."

Nath, Slivver, and the rest of the silver dragons picked the stone up with ease. Together they lifted it high over the well's rim, walked it over the top of the hole, and set it down.

The quaking and moaning came to a stop.

"That was weird." Brenwar's bone fingers drummed on the slab. "Weird as a bugbear wizard." He made his way over to the strongbox and sat down on top of it, eyeballing Ben. "I'd better keep it."

"You look like you just laid a dwarven cackleberry." Ben turned his attention to the others.

Nath and Slivver had gathered around Bayzog. The part elf's rosy hue was returning. He stared up at Sasha. "I missed you."

She gasped. Her eyes became misty. "Missed me? But you were only gone a few moments, my dear."

"No, I was gone much longer than that. It seemed like years, but now I'm not so sure. "

"Look at your hair," Nath said in awe. "Gray has overtaken the black. Bayzog, what happened down there?"

"Everything." He reached up for Nath. "Please, help me up." Back on his feet, he gave his surroundings a once-over. "I fully didn't expect to see you when I made it back. Actually, I was surprised when you didn't leap in after me."

"We were about to, but then you came back."

The light of the staff extinguished. Bayzog said, "Trust me when I say those few precious moments lasted months in that dimension, maybe longer."

Sasha kissed her husband's hands. "Bayzog, what did you encounter down there? You looked like you were being spat out by a giant."

"Another time, my sweetest." He took a breath. "I'm just so relieved to know that no time has been lost here. Let's find our sons."

"You need to rest, Bayzog," Nath said. "The journey can wait. I'll send the silvers to scout things out."

"No, it can't wait," Bayzog replied with anger in his tone. "We need to save our sons. Especially after what I've seen. Every moment counts from here on out. I aim to make the most of each one."

Nath found Sasha's eyes searching his. She was as perplexed as he was.

Whatever happened down there has changed Bayzog. Maybe even scarred him.

Brenwar offered Bayzog a vial of golden liquid. "Drink this, part elf. We can't have you bleeding and leaving a trail behind."

Bayzog gave him a look.

"Well, do you want to find your sons or not? Drink up. I'm ready to march."

Taking the vial to his lips, Bayzog drank it down. And then he closed his eyes, pulled back his shoulders, and took a deep inward breath through his nostrils and released it through his mouth. "Thank you, Brenwar. I needed that." He slung his arm over Sasha's shoulders and gave her a squeeze. "Let's march."

Nath shrugged his eyebrows.

I'm not sure what to make of this, but I had better keep an eye on him.

Limping over to Brenwar with a hand on his pierced thigh, Ben held out his hand.

Scowling, Brenwar gave the aging soldier a yellow potion too.

Ben drained it and watched the hole in this thigh visibly close. He smacked his lips. "Ah!"

Nath threw his arms around both of his healed friends. "Onward, then."

CHAPTER 22

Selene trekked with Sansla Libor through the Valley of Bones. For weeks on end, she and the winged-ape Roamer King had scoured the skies with their eyes, following the flight patterns of the wurmers from the Chamber of Murals. The flocks of the dragon-like insects that hummed like locusts with a mind-jangling *ree-rah, ree-rah* sound had led them to where they now stood.

Squatting with the sun at her back, she picked at the scales and bones of a dead dragon. It was a gray scaler, little bigger than her. Its body had been torn apart, its flesh devoured and burned. It was one of many loners she'd come across in this search. "There was a time when this wouldn't have even made me sad."

"Are you sad now?"

"No, I'm angry."

She stood up. Selene no longer wore the robes that hid her tail. With the help of Nath's mother and Dragon Home's vast array of storage rooms, she had opted for a different look, embracing what she was: a dragon in the form of a woman. She wore a steel breastplate similar to Nath's that covered her torso. A skirt of iron links covered her legs to the lower thighs. Her arms and calves were bare of clothing but covered in black scales with sparkles of gray when the sunlight hit them right. Two daggers rested on her hips. A sword was strapped to her back. She wasn't just a princess now but a warrior princess.

Sansla's nostrils flared. "The surroundings of this valley decay. It didn't used to be this way." He touched a branch where portions of the green leaves had wilted. "Something sucks the life out of the lands beyond the valley."

The Valley of Bones wasn't a graveyard as the name suggested but rather a small stretch of land among the hills and valleys that had once all been a massive graveyard. Many races had buried their dead here long ago, but it hadn't been a place of mourning, rather celebration. The grounds had always remained green and fertile year round, the soil rich and hallowed. But now the greenery had become sparse, and the varmints that darted from tree to tree and chuck-hole to chuck-hole had vanished.

All over the hills, plains, and savannas, there were caves. Many were in the hills, but others were fresh holes in the ground, where the resting dead head been disrupted. These caves were marks of burrowing wurmers. The mindless things desecrated the dead.

Selene and Sansla had spent day after day searching the caves, trying to find the hive of the queen wurmer.

With the tall grasses licking against her knees, she bent her ear to the sky and stopped. The droning sound of the wurmers came from the northern hills. She and Sansla hunkered down. Wurmers by the hundreds flew overhead like a swarm of bees. The *ree-rah* sound was so deafening that she fought the urge to cover her ears. She remained still until the danger passed and the terrifying sound was gone.

"It seemed like they burst from the mountain," Sansla said. "A new flock, perhaps."

"They were smaller than some of the ones we've seen." Selene patted a leather satchel that was strapped over her shoulder. "Maybe we're getting close to the queen. I remember the last time I went to the sea, they combed the sky by the dozens nearby. Oh, Sansla, I never imagined what a terror I'd unleashed."

"The terror would have come one way or the other. It always has and it always will," he said, stretching his massive jaws in a yawn.

She gave the great white-winged ape a puzzled look. "You don't believe evil can be entirely defeated?"

"The roamers have a belief: Evil will fall when Nalzambor ends and a new world begins." He winked. "I try not to think about it too much. In the meantime, I do my best to do the right thing."

Resuming her trek, she said, "It makes me wonder if there's any purpose in what we do at all."

"People know what is right and wrong. Some accept it and others don't. You've seen what happens when people are consumed by their selfish will. They're left with nothing but destruction and misery."

"I know that now. I just can't believe I was so blind to it before."

"You were taught wrong. In that regard, you were like many in the world. But Nath Dragon's actions opened your heart, didn't they."

She nodded. Her heart fluttered. "I feel bad for leaving him behind, but I understand his mourning. I just can't believe Balzurth fell. I didn't think it possible."

With his long arms swinging through the grass, Sansla said, "The sting of death is unavoidable. But remember, there are yet many miracles in this world."

"What's that supposed to mean?"

He forged on without answering.

They spent the better part of the day searching their way up the mountain. The higher they went, the more trees had fallen in the forest. The greens turned to browns. Leaves crunched under their feet. Not even a bug crawled, but Selene's scales did. Near the peak, there was fog coming from her breath.

"Interesting," Sansla commented. Near the top of the mountain, a seam had ruptured between the rocks, big enough for a small army to march through. The wind moaned between the cracks. "Shall we take a look inside?"

Selene had gotten comfortable with Sansla. His savage beast appearance starkly contrasted with his mannerisms. He carried himself in long easy strides and talked with the highest character of a nobleman. There was nothing gentle about him, though. He remained stern but reserved. She enjoyed that quietness about him. Eyeing the seam, she gestured forward. "After you."

He stepped aside with a bow. "I insist."

Their trek led them deep down into the mountain several hundred feet until the light of the sky dimmed. Close to an hour later, the seam widened into a cavern more than a hundred feet deep and ten times as wide. Standing among the rocks and debris were two stone giants, tossing back and forth a rock as big as the two of them put together. Their clubs were propped up against the mouth of a side cave. A soft glow of fire pulsated from a source somewhere deep in there.

"That's it," she whispered.

"Now we just need to find a way around the giants," Sansla commented.

"Or kill them."

CHAPTER 23

MOVING AT A FAST PACE, Nath and his companions headed west on the advice of Bayzog and Sasha. A steady rain beat them like drums. The grasses were slick and the paths muddy. More than a day in, the journey had them climbing up the hillsides when the earth began to quake and he heard powerful roars through the rain.

"What in Morgdon is that?" Brenwar said.

"I don't know, but I'm going to be the first to find out." Nath took off at a sprint right in the direction of the danger. Reckless, he ran at full speed through the woods. Behind came Slivver and his guardians, hot on his tail. Nath couldn't help but enjoy the moment, yelling back at them, "You might beat me in the air, but you can't keep up with me on the land."

Slivver closed in.

In a surge of strength, Nath lengthened his long stride, speeding through the forest like the fleetest white deer. The branches smacked against his face, but he didn't care. He felt especially alive for some reason. And then new sounds of battle sent his blood racing. He burst onto the scene frozen in his tracks. His jaw dropped.

A two-headed ettin was engaged in mortal combat with a sky-raider dragon. Both of them were beasts of brawn and muscle. The towering thirty-footers were tangled up in swinging limbs. The ettin pounded fists the size of boulders into the sky raider's ribs. The dragon's tail coiled around one of the two ettin necks. The ettin clawed with a free hand at its constricted head. The other hand of the ettin pounded harder and harder. The dragon let out a painful roar that turned angry.

Nath drew his sword. Fang's blade glowed like blue flame. "I'm going to help."

But Slivver hooked his arm. "And insult our kin? I think not. It is our kin's fight, and his fight alone."

"What do you mean? That's ridiculous. He could die, and I'm not going to let another dragon die."

"Have you forgotten yourself? Sky raiders have too much pride to accept help. If you help him win, he will turn on you. He'll turn on all of us." Slivver shook his head. "It's one on one. Let them have at it and see what happens."

"I don't like it." Nath lowered his sword, watching them pound away on one another. The ettin wrestled with the ferocity of a wild ogre. The humongous man had moved. The ettin slipped out of the dragon's tail and put the dragon in a headlock. The dragon let out a roar that scattered the pouring rain. "I can't just watch this!"

"You must!" Slivver said.

The sky raider shook and shivered until, with the burst of a kicking mule, he shook the ettin clear off his neck. The ettin landed flat on its back. The dragon pounced on the ettin's chest, pinning it to the ground. The dragon's jaws opened. The armor-like scales on his chest glowed with lava. Fire spewed out of the dragon's mouth, coating the ettin and sizzling the rain. The ettin was flayed. Its fists hammered the ground. It let out a moan so horrifying Nath almost turned away. Finally, the ettin twitched and spasmed no more. Its body became a pyre of flame. Smoke billowed. The air stank. The dragon let out a roar of elation.

Nath caught his breath.

Oh, what I wouldn't give to be able to do that again.

"Next time we find a giant, I had better get to fight it!" Brenwar pounded Mortuun's handle on the ground. "I mean it."

"We heard you," Ben said as he hobbled up to see the battle site. "Great dragons, that thing is big. What kind of dragon is that?"

"A sky raider," Bayzog answered. "Otherwise known as a flying fortress."

"You can say that again," Ben said, watching the sky raider stamp out the burning pile of giant with his tail. "Why's he doing that?

"Part of the celebration," Slivver said.

"Great Guzan, we could all ride on him, couldn't we?" Ben asked. "Dragon, why don't you ask?"

"We'd better wait until his temper cools before we say anything. I might be the king, but I still respect my kindred's privacy. Let's give it a moment. And by a moment, I mean it's probably not going to happen and we need to get moving. He knows what he's doing."

The sky raider caught a glimpse of them. His bright-green eyes, like burning emeralds, locked onto Nath. He gave a nod, let out a roar, and took to the sky.

Watching the dragon go, Nath said, "At least he said hello. I wish he'd given me time to say well done."

"I think he understands," Slivver said. And then the expression on his face changed, and he pointed somewhere else in the air. "Look."

One of the seekers buzzed down, landing on Nath's shoulder. The raccoon-sized thing chattered in Nath's ear.

Nath's golden eyes turned to saucers. "He's found Rerry and Samaz!" His excited tone sank. "But the dwarves have captured them. They march for Morgdon."

Sasha came right up to Nath and said, "How far away are they?"

"Not far enough, if we make haste. Slivver, you know what to do. Just don't let the wurmers see you. Go!" Nath ordered.

Slivver saluted. "We're gone."

CHAPTER 24

SELENE AND SANSLA SLUNK INTO the cavern, keeping their bodies hidden in the grooves and fallen hunks of rock. The hairless, solemn-faced stone giants tossed the boulder back and forth. They goofed and rumbled in their strange language to one another. The giant with long steel hoops in his ears picked up a second hunk of stone while the other one wasn't looking. Hurling the object like it had been launched from a catapult, the one giant crashed the rock into the other giant's head with a notable *thud*.

The smitten giant rose up to his feet with a snarl on his face and grabbed a handful of rocks. He flung them with all of his might, pelting the one with rings in his ears. The friendly game of catch had turned ugly.

"Now's our chance," Selene said. Using the natural cover for as long as she could, she snuck toward the entrance to the side cave. The giants beat on each other like drums. Bellows echoing all around, they had turned their backs, which were each broad as a trout stream. She and Sansla dashed for the mouth of the cave, but her foot clipped a stone, rolling it into a crevice with a loud clatter.

The tussle of the giants ceased. Like the trained soldiers they doubtlessly were, they bounded over on loud footsteps to investigate.

Selene and Sansla slipped just inside the confines of the cave entrance, but the floor was irregular, so they had to slow down. Backs pressed to the wall, they hunkered in the shadows as they carefully made their way.

The giants snorted and sniffed, saying, "I smell something. Do you smell something?"

"Aye, something is amiss. I smell dragon. I smell," *sniff-sniff*, "elf?"

The giants moved toward the cave entrance. All Selene could make out were their pillar-like legs. She shoved Sansla deeper into the tunnel. They rounded the edge, and just as she looked back, she saw one giant lowering itself to peek in. Clear as a bell, she heard the giant say, "What goes in must come out. We'll wait!" *Sniff!* "We'll see."

"I don't think we fooled them," she said as she crept deeper into the catacombs.

"Giants aren't smart, but their instincts are rarely fooled." Sansla skulked after her. "At least we made it this far."

She silenced him with a hand signal. They hadn't made it very far inside the catacombs when she all but stumbled on a nest. The eggs of the wurmers covered the lair like the grass of the open steppes. They had an eerie glow. Small wurmers the size of cats crawled among the eggs on the floor. Many of them were hatching. Selene felt her heart pounding inside her ears. She'd found nests before but none as big as this one.

There must be a queen in here.

She crept deeper into this new cavern with Sansla right at her heels.

Slow and quiet, Selene. Slow and quiet.

She understood enough about the wurmers to know they weren't yet ready to attack when they were this young. That came later. Once they imprinted on the older wurmers, they would seek and kill what they were trained for. Staying as far away from the eggs and wurmers as she could along the outside edge of this second cavern, she made her way deeper and deeper. All she saw were eggs and baby wurmers, scraping over the rocky floor with their mouths opening and closing.

Right in front of her an egg split open. A wurmer squirted out covered in a sticky purple goo. Her lips puckered.

The long minutes had turned into an hour when she heard the sound of a large dragon slithering over the cave floor. A long, thick tail snaked by in front of her feet. It was every bit as big as Balzurth's. Just as the tail passed, she edged in closer. There, with its head on a long, scaly neck reaching the top of the cavern, stood a wurmer more than thirty feet tall.

How did that thing even get in here?

The wurmer queen was one of a kind among the rest of the insect-like dragons. Her scales were the color of black iron. Her wings were those of a hornet, and they buzzed from time to time. Clinging to her massive frame were dozens of tiny wurmers with their claws fastened between the scales. Underneath the monster, fresh eggs were being laid one at a time. Other tiny creatures picked them up and moved them out of the path.

Selene knew what the hairy little people were the moment she saw them: black gnomes. They moved with purpose, carrying the eggs in the crooks of their arms and moving them to safety.

"Creepy," she said.

"I didn't think any of them still lived," Sansla replied.

The black gnomes were hard workers but mute. They made the perfect slaves for a task such as this.

"I would have suspected goblins."

Somewhere beyond the wurmer queen, a gas-like steam released into the air. Selene covered her nose and fought back a cough. The pungent, tangy smell lingered. The coolness of the cave heated up. Whatever the gas was, it clung to her like a nasty fog that did not rise. She caught Sansla rubbing his watery eyes and gave him a nod.

The queen moved deeper into the cave and out of sight.

Selene led them deeper toward the steam. Cutting through the yellow fog, she came across a small crater that boiled with a colorful and angry light. Deep inside its translucent goo, a gemstone the size of her head beat with fiery life.

Selene swallowed. "This is what we came for. That gemstone, a life giver, is the source of their beginnings. It is the heart of the queen. No life stone, no wurmers. That's how the ancient wizards set it up. That's what we must destroy." She pulled her satchel around to the front of her waist and unbuckled the leather straps. She was reaching into it when a voice filled the cavern.

"Welcome, Selene and Sansla. I've been expecting you."

Before she could blink, the black gnomes had them surrounded.

The queen wurmer returned, and the voice spoke again. "Don't look so surprised. I know all."

Chapter 25

Nath left his friends behind. It wouldn't be possible for them to keep up with him by any stretch of the imagination. He did see to it that one of the seekers stayed with them to guide them. Running at full speed, his dragon heart didn't falter. His lungs were as strong as ever, and so was the rest of him. As best as he understood it, the dwarves that marched with Rerry and Samaz were only a few leagues away.

Barring any unforeseen encounters, I should be able to cut them off in time.

With his fleet feet traversing the steppes, he followed the first seeker dragon, who flew in front of him. The little black and gold dragon seemed annoyed, flying back and forth and making little roars at him.

"I'm going as fast as I can. It's not my fault I don't have wings, speedy one."

The dragon buzzed ahead, only to zoom back again. It made Nath feel like he hadn't moved at all.

I've got to become a dragon again! This is getting old.

Another mile into the run, he crossed into a thick patch of woodland filled with briar bushes and low-limbed trees.

"Great dragons! Why'd you take me this way?"

Nath forged on, hurdling or tearing through every obstacle in sight. He broke free of the woodland and found himself standing on an overlook. A few hundred feet below him, twelve dwarves were huddled up on the road between one patch of woodland and another.

Slivver and the other silver dragons had the dwarves surrounded.

The dwarves reminded him of Brenwar, but they had a slightly fiercer look. Wearing a black breastplate and carrying a long-handled mace with a studded ball of iron on the end, one dwarf yelled up, "You! Nath Dragon! You're coming with us!"

Nath had a clean look at Rerry and Samaz. They were on their feet, with their arms bound behind their backs. Other than being scraped up and smeared with dirt, they seemed fine. He yelled down to them, "Rerry? Samaz? Are you well?"

"Aside from being very hungry, we're fine. It's good to see you, Nath."

"Quiet, prisoner!" The dwarven leader pointed his mace at Nath. "You're coming with us. Now be wise and surrender."

Noting the other dragons with his eyes, Nath said, "I don't think you're in any position to make demands. I respect your skills, but you are no match for dragons."

"So you seek to rob us of our charges, eh?" The dwarf stroked his beard. "We'll die first. And that will prove you are the murderer of Uurluuk, as accused."

Nath wholeheartedly believed the dwarves would die before they released their prisoners. *I need to figure out a way to extract them without hurting the dwarves. Well, maybe I can hurt them a little.* He started down the hillside and came to a stop a few dozen yards from the road. He could see in the hard eyes of the dwarves that they were ready to fight to the bitter end. "Perhaps we can negotiate their release?"

"Dwarves don't negotiate."

"You most certainly do. Everyone does." Nath went into a historical tirade of all the negotiations that the dwarves had been involved in. More than an hour later, the dwarves hadn't given an inch.

The leader said, "You presume to give me a history lesson on my own people? Again, Dwarves don't negotiate. Now if you know what's good for you, you'll surrender."

"I can't do that."

The dwarf gave his troopers a command in Dwarven. Four of them fell from the ranks, brandishing battle axes. They marched up the hill, spreading out to flank Nath.

The leader came right at Nath.

Brenwar, Ben, Bayzog, and Sasha appeared behind him. Brenwar jogged down the hill, passing Nath and barring the path between Nath and the dwarf.

The dwarven leader's eyes widened at the sight of Brenwar, and he stopped. "Out of the way, Father. I have orders."

"Out of the way? Don't you dare speak to your father that way, Glenwar. You're on the wrong side of things!"

"Glenwar?" Nath exclaimed. "I thought there was a similarity, but he was so young last time I saw him."

"Oh great, there's two of them," Ben commented.

"No, Father, it is you who are on the wrong side of things. You stand by the side of a murderer." Glenwar took another step up the hill.

"Don't you dare, Son. Don't you dare."

Glenwar stopped. "What would you have me do, Father? I have my orders. I shall follow them through. Wouldn't you do the same?"

Brenwar paused. Pawing at his beard, he replied, "Glenwar, I was with Nath Dragon the entire time. It's not possible that he did what he is accused of. The dragons have been allies since before you or I ever existed. Certainly you can see that?"

"Nevertheless, he is accused. There have been witnesses. Piigliin was one of them." He pointed to a dwarf among the ranks with a soft yellow beard. The dwarf nodded, pointed at Nath, and said, "He's the one I saw. For certain. I'll never forget those scales and that flaming hair."

Glenwar eyeballed his father. "Have you ever known a dwarf to lie about such a thing?"

"Things are not always as they appear," Brenwar said. "Do you not know that the evil spirits have been released into the world? The titans have returned. War is waged in air, land, and sea. People are amiss. Even the blind squirrel can see it. You've been taught better than this."

"I've been taught to follow orders. As for those spirits, I've yet to see them. I believe what I see."

"You believe what you want to see. That's dangerous, Glenwar. I've always told you about that, but you never wanted to listen. There's a war going on." Brenwar's bony thumb went over his shoulder at Nath. "We need Nath Dragon. We can't afford to have him locked away in the dungeons, not for any amount of time. We all need to engage the same enemy."

Glenwar stood toe to toe with his father. "I have my orders. Step aside, Brenwar Bolderguild, or be dealt with."

Chapter 26

With the air rife with tension, Nath broke the silence. "Glenwar, don't cross your father. You'll regret it."

"I have to follow orders. Father should respect that and step aside."

"I'll step aside when you come to your senses, Son."

With intent in his dark eyes, Glenwar said, "It will be the hard way then."

A high-pitched whistle sounded from the woodland on the other side. Elven archers dressed in brown and ivy-colored leather woodsman's garb emerged. There must have been a hundred of them that Nath could see lined up in the trees. Many of them came forward, quiet as ghosts, fanning out until all the dwarves and dragons were surrounded.

Glenwar backed off. "Sound our horn, Piigliin!"

Piigliin put a brass horn to his lips and blasted out a call as loud as a dragon's roar. The sound blast must have carried for leagues.

Brenwar shook his head. "They'll hear that all the way to Morgdon. You've really done it now, Son."

"I've done my duty. You should expect that." Glenwar lowered his weapon. "It's only a matter of time now, Father. A host of dwarves is only a league away." He turned his back. "Let's see what these elves have to say."

The elven commander made his way front and center on the road, wearing the same garb as the rest of his elves. The only noticeable difference was a pair of golden bracers on his arms. He called up the hillside, "Glenwar Bolderguild, you have done well. The elven avengers of Laedorn are here to aid you in your endeavor." He gave a courteous bow.

"Well met, Axillis," Glenwar said. "Your aid with the fugitives is welcome."

"Taking aid from elves? Pah!" Brenwar said. "Can you not see what isn't right with this?"

"Nath Dragon is the enemy of both races. He—"

"He is the enemy of no one but the titans and all who oppose freedom in this world!" Brenwar pulled Mortuun around. "I will not fight my fellow dwarves, but I won't hold back against the elves. How do you know they aren't behind all this?'

"Why would they be?' Glenwar asked.

"Why would Nath Dragon be? Or any of us!"

This reminded Nath of an old proverb: *Duty is blind.* As Brenwar and Glenwar went back and forth, memories of his father swelled up inside his chest. Arguments with his father had been similar, but this smelled different to his dragon senses. Something about Glenwar's body language made Nath uncomfortable. The son of Brenwar didn't seem himself. Judging by his shifting feet, he wasn't one hundred percent behind what he was doing. But he was a dwarf. Stubborn. He would do it anyway, even if it killed him.

Bayzog and Sasha came up on either side of them. "I have to be with my sons," she said.

"I don't see any way out of here without someone getting hurt," Nath admitted. "I'm open for ideas."

"I was prepared to handle the dwarves," said the part-elf wizard, "but not all these elves. There are far too many."

From the middle of the road, Axillis said, "Nath Dragon, this is a surrender-or-die moment, meaning if you don't surrender, we will fight and many will die. Of course, being the murderer you are, I'm certain that won't bother you."

"It bothers me plenty." He started back down the hill. His hope had been that they could rescue Rerry and Samaz before the elves and dwarves found them. They were too late. The elves wouldn't let up any more than the dwarves. "I'm not guilty of the bloodshed I'm accused of, and I won't be held responsible for any more bloodshed." He unhooked Fang from his back. Elven bowstrings tightened. He handed Fang to Slivver, who took a spot by his side.

"Dragon King, you cannot do this," Slivver whispered.

"I wish I had a choice." Nath lifted his hands. "I'll come willingly on one condition."

"You are in no position."

Nath gave the elf a hard stare. "Let me be clear. We could wipe all of you out in seconds if we wanted to."

Axillis blanched.

Nath continued, "Someone has to fight the titans, so let the boys go, let my friends be free, and you can take me."

"And me," Brenwar growled. "If anyone is as not guilty as he is, it's me."

Glenwar and Axillis locked eyes. Glenwar gave a nod. Together the dwarf and elven leaders said, "Done."

As the elves bound Nath's feet to his neck with elven elotween, Rerry and Samaz hustled up to him.

"Thank you, Nath," Rerry said to him, "but it hardly seems fair, and I don't feel worth it."

Nath gave him a wink. "You're worth it. Now go up there and hug your mother."

Unable to hide the sad look on his face, Samaz gave him a quiet nod.

"Samaz, stay close to your parents. Your father has been through something horrendous, and I don't know what the consequences may be."

"I will."

CHAPTER 27

"WHO ARE YOU?" SELENE ASKED. She saw the queen wurmer and the gnomes, but the source of the voice in her mind was unseen. "Reveal yourself."

The female voice laughed. "I am one of the titan spirits, released from the Great Dragon Wall courtesy of your dearest Nath Dragon. For centuries I've seen many things from beyond. Your life has been quite interesting, Selene of Gorn Grattack. Ha, you think you can walk away from your evil deeds and replace them with good ones? It's entertaining."

Selene and Sansla stood back to back. She looked from side to side, saying to him, "Do you see anyone?"

"Can't say I do," he replied. "Of course, this gigantic wurmer blocks most of my view."

The newborn wurmers creeped in among the black gnomes. Their tiny claws scraped over the rocky floor. Selene shivered. There weren't many things that startled her, but the thought of being covered in wurmers sent chills up and down her scales. "You must have something to fear if you won't face us, eh? What's your name?"

A cold wind blew through the warm room. The unseen spirit whispered in Selene's ear, "I am Tylabahn, sister of Eckubahn and Isobahn."

Misty vapors coiled around Selene's neck like gentle hands. The air thinned. Her breathing became shallow. Chin up, Selene said, "If you seek to scare me, you will fail. I do not fear your monstrous ilk."

The ghostly vapors moved in between Sansla and Selene, caressing and probing them from head to toe. Tylabahn continued, "Your heart races, dear Selene, High Priestess of Barnabus. But of course you don't fear me. It takes a monster to know a monster." The spirit made a hair-raising chuckle. "I find it so amusing that you stand right in the heart of the monsters you awakened. You, the high priestess, awakened the wurmers for your own purposes. And now you seek to destroy them? Why, Selene? Why don't you use them to finish what you started and help us?"

Selene swallowed. Sweat beaded on her forehead. "I've seen the error of my ways. Soon you will as well."

Tylabahn's voice became angry. "Don't presume to judge me, Selene! You have as much blood on your hands as I do. Do you really think you can redeem yourself? The people of Nalzambor will never forgive you, nor forget you." The spirit embraced Selene like the hug of a loving mother. "Join me, Selene. Shed that make-believe nobility and embrace the warrior who resides within. You are meant to be more than a shadow, but instead a ruler of this world. You were so close, Selene. It was Gorn Grattack who failed, not you."

The burning desire to fight simmered and boiled within Selene. The power she'd lost had been awesome. She had controlled all who surrounded her. Ever since she gave that up, she had felt lost, trying to fit in and scrape by. She wasn't sure who she really was.

"You cannot undo what has been done, Selene. This world is already conquered. The dragons and the races don't know it yet, but they will come to that realization soon enough." Tylabahn's voice was a welcoming purr. "Join me. Join us. Be an everlasting goddess."

"Don't listen to her, Selene. The spirits are liars." Sansla clawed at the vapors. "They make promises they will not keep. Do what must be—*urk*!" Sansla clutched at his throat. His powerful arms flailed.

Swaying in a trance, Selene watched Sansla struggle against his unseen bonds.

"I am going to kill him, Selene. He has no power against me. I am ten of him. But you, Selene, you can end this. Show mercy. Take out your sword and kill him. A quick death is much better than watching him suffer. Besides, he'll make a great meal for the wurmers. They'll be thankful to have you as a second mother. They'll be loyal to the end."

Without even realizing it, she drew her sword.

Sansla's elven eyes enlarged. "No, Selene, don't let her seduce you." He tried to scramble away, but the vapors lifted him off the ground and spread his arms and legs wide. Wings beating, Sansla strained against his bonds.

She approached with her blade pointed at his chest. The anger that had once made her queen of the world bubbled over. She wanted that power back. She wanted it all.

But she wanted it on her terms. With the tip of her blade inches from Sansla's exposed chest, she said, "If I kill him, can you make me a whole dragon again?"

"You will become more powerful than you have ever been."

With the growing hunger within, she said, "I'd like that." She drew the sword back to strike.

With compassionate elven eyes, Sansla said, "I forgive you."

The words came to Selene like a cold slap in the face. The spirit of Tylabahn shuddered within her. Selene lowered the sword, shaking her head.

"Finish him!" Tylabahn commanded. "He might forgive you, but the rest of them won't!"

Selene shrugged off the unseen bonds and put away her sword. "Some of them will, and some of them won't. I can live with that." She reached into her satchel and withdrew an orb that filled her hand. It pulsated and throbbed.

"What is that?" Tylabahn hissed. Ghostly tendrils came at Selene.

"It's an Orb of Destruction!" She sprinted to the burbling pool of goo as a gem of life beat within.

Tylabahn's tendrils licked out, tripping her feet and dragging her away from the pool. "You fool, you would kill yourself!"

Selene clawed at the rock floor with her free hand. "Not to mention you, all the wurmers, and these useless little gnomes." She muttered an enchanted word. The orb in her hand pulsed faster. A tendril locked up her wrist, trying to wrench it free. The orb fell from Selene's grip.

"Hah! Now you'll only destroy yourself. The gem of life is protected."

Out of nowhere, a black gnome rushed over. He picked up the orb, slipped through Tylabahn's tendrils, and slammed the orb into the boiling crater.

The spirit of Tylabahn went wild. She released Selene and Sansla. The ghostly vapors of her body dug into the gooey pool, slinging slime everywhere.

The black gnome took Selene by the hand, saying, "Come, come. I know a way out."

"This mountain will collapse on us in seconds," Selene said, racing after the scurrying gnome.

He replied, "Then you had better make the most of them!"

CHAPTER 28

ATH STOOD STILL WHILE THE elves secured his feet to his neck. "I think you're being excessive, seeing as I've turned myself over to you."

"We're not going to have you running away," Glenwar said. "We know how fast you are."

"So my reputation precedes me."

"I don't think you should be making light of your situation, murderer."

"Alleged murderer. Aw, I can't believe I'm even saying that. I didn't kill Laedorn and Uurluuk!" He rattled his chains. "I can still run faster than you, even in these things."

"I'd like to see you try." Glenwar marched away, leaving a dozen dwarven spearmen standing guard.

Nath sighed. Nothing seemed right about the elves or the dwarves. He understood they had a duty to bring him in, but they didn't seem right. Not the way he was used to seeing them. The worst thing had been seeing Glenwar challenge Brenwar. That had been downright unnatural. Now the father and son couldn't even look at each other.

The dwarves and elves lined up in two separate columns and started to march. They headed east, just beyond the distant peaks of Morgdon. Brenwar and Ben stayed by Nath's side, talking to him from time to time, but they were without their weapons.

"I think you'd be better off fighting the real war that's going on," Nath said, holding his chain so it wouldn't choke him, "not fooling around with this farce."

"I'm not taking my eye off you. Not with them holding the other end of that chain. I don't like it." Brenwar's hot glare scanned the ranks of his kin. "It's weird."

"Dragon," Ben said, "If it gets too wooly, you have to get out of this."

"Don't even talk like that," Brenwar warned. "They'll shackle all of us."

"No, Ben. Don't be antsy. That's just what the enemy wants. They want to take us all off the game table. We can't let that happen."

"Who is they?" Ben asked.

"Good question. Let's just hope we know them when we see them."

"Well, if I were you, I'd summon the dragons to free me." Ben dusted off a bug that landed on his shoulder. "I wouldn't toy around with them. They should know better."

"I'll be curious to see who the other witnesses are." Brenwar did a half step, getting his feet in sync with the other dwarves. "So far, there's only Piigliin that I know of. He was always trouble. It's hard for me to speak against my kin, but we have our share of rotten eggs. They were always swiftly dealt with, but now it seems they are turned loose."

"There is bad in everybody."

The conversation fell silent. The steady rhythm of boots hitting the ground stayed with them all through the day until nightfall. Nath wasn't surprised when the torches were lit and they kept on going.

As Glenwar had mentioned, they joined ranks with even more dwarves. Another host of elves came as well. By morning, Nath was marching with a full army thousands strong.

All this over me?

The next day, the army came to a halt at a military outpost called the Corridor. The fortress had been crafted by dwarves and elves, and it was extremely well fortified. A twenty-foot-high wall stretched over one hundred yards, and it was half as deep. They entered through a steel portcullis on the side closer to Morgdon, guarded by dwarves. They heard that elves guarded the side facing toward Elome. The facility had been built when the dwarves and elves battled the orcen hordes together. In recent years, it was all but abandoned, so far as Nath knew, with only a skeleton crew to watch over it. Apparently, now it served another mutual purpose: his trial.

Thousands of soldiers lined the walls and the parapets, half facing outward and the other half inward. The banners of the dwarves and the elves snapped in the high winds. The four round corner towers rose forty feet in the air. At the very tops were elven archers and dwarves on ballistas.

In the center of the courtyard, a court hearing area had been built with slabs of cut stone and wood. Five throne-like chairs made from highly crafted steel sat upon a stage, empty. In front of the stage was a large cage made from steel bars.

Glenwar and Axillis hooked Nath by the arms and put him in the cage. "The trial comes when the trial comes," Glenwar said as he and Axillis departed, slamming the cage door shut behind them.

"I could use a meal," Nath said.

Axillis waved his hand at the army. "After we feed all of them, then we will feed you. Maybe."

"I'll find you something, Dragon," Ben offered.

"No, I'm not really that hungry. Just testing the waters. And they're foul." He pressed his face against the bars. "They couldn't possibly find me guilty, could they?"

"The dwarves better not, but I can't speak for the elves." Brenwar tugged the bars. "Dwarven. Well made. You'd have a hard time getting out of this."

"Thanks, Brenwar." He lifted his chain. "Care to comment on this?"

"The best."

CHAPTER 29

VER THE NEXT COUPLE OF days, the dwarves hauled in lumber and built bleachers that rose from the flagstone courtyard floor to the top of the parapet wall. With the assistance of the elves and Brenwar—who'd gotten bored standing around—they turned the fortress courtyard into an arena.

Nath waved at his old friend, who was pounding in nails with his skeleton fist. "Thanks, Brenwar. Make sure everyone is comfortable."

Ben returned with a platter of food and took a bite of apple pie, which oozed juicy glaze. "Do you feel like eating yet?" Also on the platter were sausage links, a small brick of cheese, and a tall tankard of ale.

Nath shook his head no. "What's going on out there? It smells like an elven festival."

Ben lifted his brows and nodded. "You'd be surprised. It's as if word has spread all over. The elves and the dwarves are pitting their arrays of food and ales against one another. Slabs of meat, tasty cakes, pies with raspberry jelly jam whip oozing out of the rim, and hors d'oeuvres." He licked his lips. "I can't remember the last time I ate so well."

"Ben! If they find me guilty they're going to kill me."

"I think that's part of the draw too," said the aging farm boy-turned-soldier, wiping the juice from his mouth. "Oh, sorry, Dragon. I guess I got caught up in the moment. You know they won't find you guilty. It's impossible."

Clasping the bars, Nath said, "Do you remember the floating city?"

"Of course I do."

"Did you always think such a thing was possible?"

Ben chomped down on the crust of the pie and said with a mouthful, "No, but that was magic."

"Yes, that was magic, and what do I always say about magic?"

Ben's eyes slid up. "Uh, you say 'with magic, anything is possible.'" He nodded.

"Yes, and that includes my conviction."

"Oh, I see."

"Ben! Quit eating that food. It's doing—Ben?"

The old warrior had set the tray down, picked up the tankard of ale, and walked off as if he hadn't even been part of the conversation. He disappeared into the crowd.

"What in the name of Guzan is going on?" Nath turned and slid down against the bars, holding his head. Everyone was acting strange. That hadn't initially included Ben and Brenwar, but now it did.

It has to be the titan spirits, but how? They couldn't possibly possess so many people. Or could they? And if the people are under a spell, won't the judges be, too?

He banged his head against the bars. "Great dragons."

"What did those bars ever do to you?" said a female voice.

Nath found himself gazing up at Laylana, the granddaughter of Laedorn. Remaining seated, he said, "Please tell me you still have your wits about you."

"Excuse me? That's an awfully strange way to address your defender." Her jet-black hair hung in a long braid over her shoulder. Her beautiful eyes were deep pools of green. "I assure you I have all my wits and more. You'll need them."

Getting up on his feet, he reached through the bars, pulled her body in, and kissed her forehead. "I can only hope so. Everyone here is going mad! They celebrate before my trial. Laylana, a curse has fallen over the people."

"Keep your voice down." She gave their surroundings a glance. "I got here as soon as I found out you were in custody. I was afraid this would happen."

"What do you mean?"

"Whatever has afflicted the minds of the elves, I can't explain. It started up weeks ago. They all started acting off, or silly. Some are affected and some are not." She held up her hand. She wore a silver band on her ring finger that was engraved with leaves. "This ring was worn by Laedorn. It protects me from many things. I hope this madness is one of them."

"It's affected my friends, Ben and Brenwar. Maybe something they ate or drank."

"I admit I'm not the most knowledgeable when it comes to magic. I'm a warrior, as you know, but I'll keep investigating."

"Bayzog could help if you could reach him."

"I'll see what I can do. Perhaps the warden will let me speak with him."

Taken aback, Nath said, "What do you mean, the warden?"

"Didn't you know? They're held captive in the Corridor's dungeons."

"They were supposed to be set free. I had Glenwar and Axillis's word on that!"

"I'm sorry, Nath, but it was discovered that they plotted your escape. They had to be brought in, but they surrendered willingly." She touched his hand. "Stay calm. I'll look into it. I thought you knew."

"I'll tell you what I know. This isn't a trial. It's a farce!"

CHAPTER 30

FOLLOWING BLIND INSTINCT, SELENE RAN after the black gnome.

Behind her, Sansla called out, "Are you sure this is best?"

"I'm sure we only have a few seconds left!"

The black gnome skipped and skittered through the cavern, making for a slit in the wall.

Behind them, young wurmers gave chase, nipping at their heels. They were outnumbered a hundred to one as they ran loose through the pits, stepping on wurmers and knocking over eggs. The ground trembled under her feet, tripping up her steps. She crushed one of the eggs with a splatter.

The wurmer queen became angry.

Sansla pushed Selene up to her feet. They made a full-speed dash, with baby wurmers latching on to scales and skin. Beckoning them with his hand, the black gnome jumped into the split in the rock and disappeared.

BOOOOOOOOOM!

The jarring explosion heaved the ground up beneath them. A wash of mystic energy bore down on them like a tidal wave. The energy wiped out every baby wurmer and egg in its path. The wurmer queen reeled against the force while at the same time making the most awful sound Selene had ever heard.

With the explosion sizzling their toes, Selene and Sansla dove for the gap together. She popped out of the portal and landed on Sansla. They were back in the two giants' huge cavern. The black gnome stood nearby, rubbing the back of his shaggy head. Across the cavern, the cave mouth that led into the wurmer nursery was burning with fire. The stone giants were staring at it.

Selene poked the black gnome in the back. "Who are you?"

He spun around and slapped her hand away. "There's no time for that now. Let's get out of here while those giants are distracted. They'll sniff us out, you know." The black gnome plucked a wurmer spawn off her leg, threw it down and stomped it, then took off.

Without objection, Selene followed the gnome back into the seam and up out into the hills. Her chest was tight and her knees were a little wobbly, but she felt safer in the dying forest than she had down in the chasm that haunted them from behind. "There had better not be too many queens. Fortune found favor with us today."

"Indeed," Sansla said. The winged ape had bite marks all over. Parts of his white fur had clotted red.

Selene said to him, "I almost killed you. I don't know what came over me, but I was going to do it. I felt that old hate rising in me."

His big paw engulfed her shoulder. "But you didn't. Now you've seen the power of forgiveness. Its cleansing can break curses."

Something about his words made her heart swell. She hugged him. Tears ran out the corners of her eyes. "I just thought of all of those horrible things I did. I felt like I couldn't escape my past."

"If others forgive you, then you can learn to forgive yourself. Tylabahn almost got you because your faith in yourself is weak. Be strong." He broke the hug. "You've grown. Shown you were willing to die to save others. I can see that. Look." He held up her hand. The black scales of her palms had turned white. "The same thing happened to Nath."

Selene studied her hands. She fingered the palms. It was different. Much of the guilt she carried was gone for some reason. "I-I didn't do that much."

"There aren't many people who would have dared to drop that Orb of Destruction into that well. You did it with no self-regard whatsoever."

She wiped her tears. "That sure took care of that, didn't it? Ha! I only wish I could have seen that titan's face when she realized it was over. Say, where did that gnome go?"

The black gnome was nowhere in sight. Aside from them, the forest was empty.

"How did he do that, Sansla?"

The winged white ape's nostrils flared. "His scent is gone."

Eyes narrowed, she headed in the direction where she last saw the little guy. She bent over and touched the small footprints in the ground. They went on for a few steps and vanished. "We didn't imagine him, did we?"

"Certainly not, though I am perplexed as to how we came across that portal. I'm grateful while at the same time dismayed."

"Woohoo!" said a voice far up in the trees.

Selene's head snapped up. A figure sat in the branches, slender and humanoid, hairless, with odd pinkish skin. Nothing like the black gnome she'd just seen. He waved at her with long, agile fingers. His face was expressionless.

Her eyes brightened. "Gorlee!"

"At your service."

CHAPTER 31

ANOTHER DAY PASSED WITH NATH sitting, standing, and pacing in his cage. The oddness of his surroundings had reached a point where he was too uncomfortable to eat. And anyway, he didn't trust the food. His stomach growled. His temper flared.

I should summon the dragons, but would they get to my dungeoned friends in time?

Aside from the soldiers who stood watch by the thousands and only moved to relieve one another, the people reveled. They were singing, drinking, and carrying on like the trial was a celebration. Elves and dwarves walked arm in arm, complimenting one another. They patted one another on the back and played music together.

Nath tried to flag Brenwar down.

The old warrior was at the top of the stands, putting the finishing touches on the railing. People had filled up half the seats. They ate and talked—males, females, and children—as if they were on a picnic. The children would stroll by and make faces at Nath.

Finally, he called out, "Brenwar! Brenwar! Get down here!"

Brenwar waved his bony hand. "In a moment. This railing isn't quite straight."

"Your head isn't quite straight!" Nath tossed his mane of red hair. He wanted to scream. He hadn't seen Ben or Laylana since yesterday. They'd vanished. He wondered if they'd been taken prisoner too.

I could have sworn turning myself in was the right thing. It spared lives and prevented injury. But the entire gesture has turned backward on me. I can't believe it!

Two of the biggest dwarves he ever saw carried a stone table between them. Their hair was so thick he could barely see their faces. Wearing only sleeveless leather armor, they were all muscles that bulged in their snakelike arms. The powerful duo set the table down between Nath's cage and the judge stand. Its heavy legs hit the flagstones with a *bang!* The two dwarves took a glance at Nath. One wiped his nose. The other spat. They moved on.

What is that table for?

From the tops of the corner towers, trumpets blared. The music stopped. The bustling crowds went still. Behind Nath was the entrance on the dwarven side. The soldiers parted ranks, making a path. In front of him behind the judge stand, the elves did the same thing. A team of black horses eight deep pulled an alabaster and ivy-colored carriage under the elven portcullis and down the runway of grass.

On the dwarven end of things, the dwarves themselves pulled a dwarven-crafted carriage. On its roof, smoke puffed out of a chimney stack, giving it the look of a tiny cottage on wheels.

The crowd murmured. The stands filled. Excited faces commented, "The judges are here."

To the right of Nath, the dwarven carriage came to a stop. On the left, across from the dwarves, the elven carriage did the same. A small set of wooden stairs was carried in front of each carriage door. The doors opened.

Standing with his nose between the bars, Nath watched the occupants of the carriages come out. Three dwarves with grey and white beards almost touching their toes marched out. They weren't dressed in armor but instead wore heavy leather gowns stitched together with intricate patterns of golden threads. Though simple, their chestnut-colored ensemble appeared fit for kings.

Across the way, the elven judges came, in soft blue robes sashed with kelly green and maroon. They were older, with crow's feet showing in the corners of their eyes. Their once-lustrous hair had become thin and faded after centuries of life. Together they walked front and center facing the dwarves, who did the same on the other side of the lengthwise table. They clasped hands.

"Nath. Nath." He turned. Laylana stood behind his cage, motioning for him to come over. "The trial is beginning."

"Thanks for the warning. I thought you were defending me. Where have you been?"

"There's no need to get snippy."

"Snippy? Me? My trial's about to start, and we haven't even discussed strategy! You vanished on me. I was worried."

"I was interviewing the witnesses."

"And?"

She shrugged. "Many of them claim to have seen you do what they say you did. It will be difficult to sway the judges unless I can discredit them all."

"Laylana, are you sure you're up to this?"

She touched his hands. "Nath, I've never been more ready."

"What about Bayzog? Did you talk to him? What did he say?"

"Uh, oh, yes. He'll be able to give a good account in your defense. He speaks very highly of you."

Nath slapped his face. *This is a disaster! She doesn't know what she's doing. None of them do!* "Have you been eating the food they're serving?"

"Only a little bit." Her brows knitted. "I was hungry. Why?"

"Never mind." He turned toward the judges. They were exercising a strange ritual with their hands. "What are they doing?"

"As you can see, there are six judges. But only five can hear your case, so that there can be a majority vote." She counted them with her fingers. "Yes, there are six."

"I can clearly see that."

"You really need to be nicer to me. I'm trying to free you from the bind you're in. Anyway, they are deciding if the majority will be elven or dwarven."

Rubbing his temples, Nath said, "Why don't you just bring in an orc to be the tie breaker?"

"How rude," she said, keeping her attention on the judges. The dwarven judges let out an angry grunt. One of them stormed back into the carriage. "Ah, the elves win. A good thing. I should have more sway with them." She winked at Nath. "See, have a little faith, Nath. Things are starting to go your way."

The judges took their seats on the stage, overlooking the table and Nath's cage. An elf judge sat in the center, with the dwarves on the right and the elves on the left. The center judge looked very much like Laedorn.

Nath kept his voice low. "What's his name?"

"That is Lindor. He was a dear friend of Laedorn's. I take it you've never met him?"

"No, I don't see a face I know aside from yours and those of my other fair-weather friends."

"Well, Lindor is firm but fair. Be glad of it."

With his slender elf hand, Lindor picked up a ball of obsidian marble that glinted in the sun and banged it on the judges' stone table like a gavel. The world fell silent just before he said in a slightly shaky voice, "Let the trial of Nath Dragon begin."

CHAPTER 32

To Nath's right, the bleachers were filled with dwarves. Brenwar sat in the front row with his hands on his knees. Ben was at his side. Both of them kept their eyes on Lindor. They looked like they'd woken from a dream. All the people did.

Nath tried to get his friends' attention with a gesture and a harsh whisper. "Brenwar. Ben. Get over here." Neither of them responded. Brenwar steadily combed at his beard with his skeleton fingers. Ben worked a toothpick between his teeth.

Lindor the elven judge banged the gavel again. "We have a unique situation. It has been centuries since the elves and dwarves held mutual counsel, so I'll take a moment to explain the proceedings." He cleared his throat. "There are five judges. If at least four judges find Nath Dragon guilty, then he will be hung by the neck."

Someone in the stands shouted in Elven, "Kill him!"

Holding up a finger, Lindor said, "Guards, control these outbursts. Remove the interrupter from the congregation. We are civilized people."

The elven guards removed the intolerable elf from the grandstands. He kicked and screamed like a wild man. "You're guilty, Nath Dragon! Guilty!"

Nath looked away.

At least Lindor seems reasonable. I just wish he'd remove the rest of these squirrely people.

"If three judges are in favor of a guilty verdict," Lindor continued, "then Nath Dragon will be imprisoned in the Dungeons of Morgdon for five hundred years or until he expires, whichever comes first."

There was some grumbling among the elves.

"In the event Nath Dragon lives beyond five hundred years, he will be taken to Elome and held prisoner there until the day he dies. His remains will then be returned to the Mountain of Doom for a proper funeral and burial among his kind."

Laylana leaned toward Nath and said, "That sounds reasonable."

Nath moved away from the elfess. Judging by her chronic lip picking and blinking eyes, she'd become just as uncharacteristic as the others.

She used to be as hard as iron. Now she's as looney as a crystal gnome. For the love of Balzurth, is there anybody here I can count on?

Nath's breathing became heavy.

Lindor moved on. "In the case of a majority three or better not-guilty verdict, Nath Dragon will be set free."

"Boooooo!" yelled the crowd on both sides of the stands.

Nath had never seen nor heard the elves and dwarves more unified.

Banging the round marble gavel on the table, Lindor calmly said, "Quiet, please, quiet. I will not hesitate to throw the lot of you out. This is court. A place of order. Settle yourselves."

The dwarven judges stood. The dwarves in the stands fell quiet. The elves followed suit. The judges returned to their seats.

Lindor caught Laylana with his eyes and waved her to the table. "Are you and your client clear on how the decision will be made?"

She nodded. "Certainly."

With a flip of his hand, Lindor motioned over another person whom Nath had not noticed, another female elf who had been sitting in the front row of the stands. She was lanky and well dressed in dark purple robes that matched her eyes. There was something sinister in the way she moved. With her chin up, she stepped to the table in a soft stride and bowed.

"Ah, prosecutor Anlee Couso." Lindor snickered and elbowed the dwarf beside him. "A student of mine. Possibly the best." He cleared his throat again and looked around. "Could I get some refreshment? The long ride left me parched."

An elven maiden with a tray of decanters slunk over to the judge stand. She set down five metal goblets and began to fill them. Nath studied her closely. Dressed in the pink-and-white garb of a server, the elven maiden had white hair that ran down the length of her back. She was on her tip toes.

But her toes weren't touching the ground. The top of the grass barely licked them.

Nath's neck hairs stood on end. *There's something familiar about that maiden.* "Laylana! Laylana! You need to object!"

Everyone looked at him.

Lindor banged the marble orb on the table. "Laylana, counsel your client."

Laylana stormed over. "Nath, what are you doing? Keep that up, and you won't be present for your own trial."

"You need to object."

"To what? The proceedings haven't started."

He pointed through the bars at the serving girl. "Don't let them drink that. It's enchanted, I tell you."

"Don't be silly. I've been drinking from those decanters since I've been here." She twirled her hair with her finger. "I'm not under any spell."

"You wouldn't know it if you were." Looking over Laylana's head, he watched the serving maiden depart. She walked the same as anyone else, but he swore her feet only grazed the ground. She looked at Nath and made a smile. Her eyes were lavender. She blinked them both. Her eyes were black as coal. Batting her eyelashes one more time, she made her eyes turn lavender again. With a victorious smile, she disappeared into the ranks of elven soldiers.

"Lotuus!" He hollered at Brenwar and Ben. "That was Lotuus! Can you hear me?"

Brenwar cupped his ear. "I can hear you just fine. Now behave yourself."

Laylana rushed out in front of him. "Nath, you have to stop this."

"No, you have to stop this trial. I'm telling you, a bewitching is going on here."

Lindor banged the gavel. "Nath Dragon! One more outburst and you won't see your own trial. I suggest you behave yourself as a testament to your character, which at the moment seems to be lacking."

He cocked his head and whispered to Laylana, "Can a judge say that?"

"He's the judge. He can say whatever he wants."

"Anlee Couso," Lindor said, "Do you have any questions about how the judgment will be made?"

Hands behind her back and with a prudent tone, she said, "I argue that any majority decision of a guilty nature should mean immediate hanging."

CHAPTER 33

LAYLANA OBJECTED. "YOU'VE EXPLAINED THE rules, Lindor, and they are more than reasonable. They cannot be changed now."

Lindor rubbed his chin. "You are right. The agreement we have in place will not be altered. Anlee, your proposal is dismissed."

"Judge Lindor, I believe you should take counsel with the other judges—"

With a whack of the marble gavel, he said, "That will not happen."

Nath breathed a sigh of relief. Things seemed to be going his way.

The elven judge with sideburns that were only seen on the older elves bent Lindor's ear.

Now what's going on?

Judge Lindor took a drink from his goblet. "I've reconsidered. All of the judges in favor of hanging with a majority decision, raise your left hand."

"What?" Nath exclaimed.

Every one of the judges raised their left hand. The crowd on both sides let out a hearty cheer.

"This is insanity!"

"Nath, be quiet. Your outbursts are not helping your case," Laylana said.

"Your lack of an outburst isn't doing anything for me either, Laylana. This is outrageous!"

Lindor pounded the marble ball like a hammer on the stone table. "Silence! Silence!"

The people cooled.

"Anlee, make your case."

"Thank you, Judge Lindor." Anlee motioned to an elven soldier wearing an almond-shaped helmet on his head. He marched forward with a bow in his hand. It wasn't any ordinary bow. It was an exceptional one. She took the bow and held it up for all to see. "This is the murder weapon, which is more fondly known to the accused as Akron."

"Ooh!" said everyone in the audience.

The soldier also handed her a quiver filled with arrows and two separate arrows that were not inside the quiver. Anlee set the bow on the stone table and the quiver beside it. She kept the two arrows in her hands. Raising them high, she said, "The arrows that pierced the hearts of Laedorn and Uurluuk!"

"Boo!" said the people. The outcries were angry.

Lindor banged the stone. "Silence! Silence!"

Anlee respectfully set one arrow down. She pointed the other one at Nath Dragon. "Witnesses—and there were many—saw a man fitting Nath Dragon's unique description firing these arrows, unprovoked, into the very hearts of our leaders." She reached over and caressed the finely carved elven ash wood of the bow. "And the most sickening thing is that this weapon—a gift from the elves to Nath Dragon—was used against them in a dark twist of fate."

"I did no such thing!" Nath said with his head stuffed between the bars. "Haven't you ever heard of an imposter?"

"Silence, Nath," Laylana said in a warning. "I can handle this."

"Can you?"

Laylana walked away and approached the table. "Judge Lindor, may I speak?"

"Anlee, is your opening statement concluded?"

With a quick look at Nath, she said, "That will do."

Nath fought the urge to pull his hair out. He'd witnessed court judgments before in Nalzambor among many of the races. But he'd never seen a court that was so informal.

This is a joke. I have a bad defender, addled judges, and even my friends' minds are elsewhere. They should be going after Lotuus. She's behind all this.

Laylana began her opening statement, circling the table. Her eyes slid back and forth between the judges and the weapons as she spoke. "Judges, we certainly have a tragedy in the loss of our invaluable leadership. But we have something else as well. Mystery! Nath Dragon has always been a friend of the elves and the dwarves. He has been admired by them. What we have before us is the instrument, the weapon Akron. What we don't have is motive." Her fingers dusted over the table. "Why would Nath Dragon do something so uncharacteristic? To what gain? But by the end of this trial, I assure all of you that in your heart you will know Nath Dragon is not guilty of this crime. Somebody else is."

The elven judges beside Lindor nodded. Nath found himself nodding as well. The tightness in his chest eased.

Maybe Laylana isn't so affected as I thought.

"Any other remarks from either one of you?" Lindor asked.

The elven women shook their heads.

"Ah, proceed then," the judge said with a yawn.

Laylana backed away and stood near Nath.

"You did well," he said under his breath.

"I can get you through this. Trust me." She gave him a nod.

Anlee approached the stone table. Using her hands and a mouthful of confidence, she made her case. With a finger up, she said, "Fact: Laedorn and Uurluuk are dead. Fact: Witnesses say a man fitting Nath Dragon's description slew Laedorn and Uurluuk. Fact: The weapon Akron was described at both scenes and retrieved by the dwarves when the assassin fled. Fact: There isn't a description of any other suspect." She turned her back on the judges and faced Nath. "There is an old saying that goes, 'If it looks like a unicorn, it's a unicorn.' Look at Nath Dragon, those scaly arms, that flame-red hair, and those golden eyes. There's no mistaking Nath Dragon for anyone else but Nath Dragon."

"Whoa," Laylana said back to Nath, "that was really good."

All of the judges behind the bench were nodding. With a dry throat, Nath replied, "Yes it was."

CHAPTER 34

THE FIRST WITNESS THAT ANLEE called forward was the dwarven soldier Piigliin. Still in armor, he stood a full head shorter than Anlee. Nath couldn't make out the dwarf's eyes from behind all the hair. The only skin he could see on the dwarf was his turned-up nose. He listened to the dwarf's convincing story after Anlee asked him what happened.

"I was part of Uurluuk's escort—not that there was need for such a thing in Morgdon, until now at least, but it has always been customary." Piigliin teetered back and forth on his feet. "So we marched as we always do to the square to have our fill at the Festival of Meads and Meats. We have those at the beginning of every changing season. We'd taken our places at the table when a wooly feeling went right up my beard." He crawled his stubby fingers up his beard like a spider. "I took a gander in the spires, and there he was."

"There who was? Can you show us?" Anlee asked.

Piigliin jabbed his finger at Nath. "I saw him, Nath Dragon. Plain as day because it was day. I was about to wave, thinking I'd offer a greeting. That's when I noticed the bow. We'd just heard about the falling of Laedorn, but it hadn't registered with me yet as to what was going on. By the time my wits caught on, it was too late. Nath Dragon pulled back the bowstring and fired. The arrow pierced the armor that covered Uurluuk's chest. I'll never forget that sound. Metal piercing metal. It was the sound of the world ending." He sniffed and wiped his eyes. "Uurluuk died instantly, but he didn't spill a drop of his mead. Like a statue, he held it right up to his lips. It was some fine mead."

Nath rubbed his neck. He'd been around the dwarves plenty enough to know they weren't liars. What Piigliin said he saw, Nath believed.

This isn't good. If I'm *convinced, how can the judges not be?*

"Thank you, Piigliin," Anlee said, patting his shoulder. "I don't have any other questions for this witness."

Lindor lifted his chin up from his chest, blinked his eyes, and said, "Yes, yes, any questions from the defender?"

"A few," Laylana said. "Piigliin, how far away from the assassin were you when you saw him, her, or it?"

"Objection! The defender is misleading in her statement. The assassin is clearly a man," Anlee said.

"And we know this how?" Laylana argued. "My own investigations have revealed that no one was closer to the assassin than a good fifty feet."

"Overruled," Lindor said. "Please continue."

"Piigliin, how far from the assassin were you when that infamous shot was made?"

With a shrug of his shoulders that rattled his chest armor, Piigliin replied, "I'm certain it was fifty-seven yards. I'm good with distances. Just ask Glenwar or any of my kin."

"I see. Fifty-seven yards is a fair distance." Laylana walked away and up into the stands. Nearing the top, she said at the top of her voice, "About this far?"

"Close," he yelled back.

"Interesting." Looking right at him, she said, "Can you tell me what color my eyes are?"

He leaned forward. So did the judges. Piigliin's features squirmed under his hair. Finally, he pushed his bangs up, revealing his brow and his own eyes, and said, "Blue."

Laylana marched back down the steps, stood in the center of the courtyard for all to see, and said, "Clearly they are green, yet you say you saw golden eyes. You couldn't have seen that."

"Those golden eyes are bright. No one can forget them."

"I believe you made an assumption. I argue that you didn't even see scales—black arms, yes, but no scales. The hair, well, I'll give you that, but anyone can wear a wig. After all, we know that assassins are masters of disguise, correct?"

With a grunt, Piigliin said, "I suppose. But I know it was him."

"Or you hope it was him."

Stamping his feet, Piigliin yelled, "There must be justice for Uurluuk!"

"Aye!" the dwarves yelled.

Lindor banged the round gavel on the stone table. "Order! Order! This festival-like behavior is for beyond the walls. There is no place for it within this courtyard!"

Nath stood back in the center of his cage, hanging on every word that was said.

Anlee brought forward witness after witness, dwarves and elves alike. Each of them recounted the same believable story, but when it came to the details, Laylana picked them apart. Witness by witness, she imparted doubt about what they had seen.

As it turned out, Laylana was right. Not one single witness had been closer to the assassin than a good fifty feet. The only caveat was that when the dwarves gave chase, the bow and quiver had been left behind.

When the last witness departed, Lindor stood up, pounded the stone on the table, and said, "Let's take a brief recess."

Laylana made her way over to Nath's cage. "How do you think I'm doing?"

"Truly great. I'm thankful."

"Well, we have a long way to go, but I might be able to turn the tide when I call your friends to testify."

"I just hope they've regained their wits by then," Nath said, referring to Ben and Brenwar. Both of them had departed. "Something has gotten into them, Laylana. I swear, you have to listen to me. Fairy Empress Lotuus is here."

"Nath, I have people looking into it."

"Who?"

"People. Now keep silent while I work. The quieter you are, the better I do."

The judges who had briefly departed returned to their chairs. They whispered to one another and made quick unsettling glances at Nath.

Feeling the tingling in his fingertips, he said, "I will."

CHAPTER 35

As THE PEOPLE REFILLED THE empty seats in the stands, Laylana got caught up in a conversation with the judges and Anlee. Nath overheard every word of it. Anlee made the case that Bayzog, Sasha, Rerry, and Samaz could not be called as witnesses since they were incarcerated for conspiring to free Nath. Laylana made the case that neither Nath nor his imprisoned friends had been found guilty of anything, hence they could witness.

Among themselves, led by Lindor, the judges deliberated on the argument. They returned to their seats, and Lindor quickly said, "No, the witnesses brought to our attention will not be allowed to testify."

With her brows knitted together and her cheeks turning red, Laylana stormed over to Nath and said, "I'm sorry, but I didn't see that coming. You're right, Nath. Something is amiss, but stand with me."

"I am. Do your best."

Lindor banged the marble gavel. "Defender, call your first witness."

Laylana motioned to the first row of the dwarven stands and said, "I call Morgdon's very own Brenwar Bolderguild."

Applause erupted among the dwarves when Brenwar stood up, waving his skeleton hand. His face almost made a smile.

That's unsettling.

"Brenwar," Laylana began, "you are on the record stating that during the time of the assassination, you were with the accused. Can you explain?"

"I'd be glad to." Casually, he clawed through his beard. "We were fighting our way out of Urslay, the giants' home, in the windy mountains with snows deeper than a bugbear's thighs. We'd been corralled by the titan leader himself, who was hosted in an earth giant's body. Death swarmed around us. Mortuun and I took down giant after giant, but there came that moment when the tides that fill the graves swept in. Somehow, on Nath's command, his sword Fang transported us to the Elven Field of Dreams. It was there that we encountered the wilder elf Slavan and the guardians. He informed us of the assassination." Brenwar shook his head. "The accusation is impossible. I can't explain how, but we found that we'd traveled forward in time, one year to the day."

"I see. I admit that is a unique story, but far from impossible." Laylana reached under the stone table and pulled out some wooden crates. She took out a pair of leather-bound tomes and held them up. "These are elven histories. Tales from our past. There are many examples of elven heroes and enemies moving through time that we are all well aware of. I'd like you to admit that these are evidence."

With a bored look, Lindor gave a wave of consent.

Continuing, Laylana said, "Brenwar, you've traveled with Nath Dragon for over a century. Can you share an example of him showing ill will toward the elves or the dwarves?"

"I cannot say that I ever have known him to, but he does have a hard time listening to one particular dwarf from time to time."

Oh please, Brenwar, are you lecturing me from the courtyard now? At least he seems to be himself.

"I see," Laylana agreed. "But there is no ill will that you know of between Nath Dragon and the dwarves or the elves?"

"No."

"Good. Now, Brenwar, can you tell me about a creature called Gorlee the chameleon?"

"Now that's an odd bird if there ever was one. He can put on the likeness of any person in this court. I've even seen him change—more than once—with my own eyes."

"So, what you are telling me is that this chameleon can even change into the likes of Nath Dragon."

"I've seen it with my own eyes."

Laylana gave a quick smile to the judges. "No further questions."

"Er, Anlee, do you care to cross-examine?"

Anlee pushed her sleeves up past her elbows, walked in front of Brenwar, and said, "I would, your honor. Brenwar Bolderguild, have you ever seen Nath Dragon kill anyone in anger?"

"Objection!" Laylana shouted out. "She's attempting to mislead the judges about the witness."

In a smooth reply, Anlee said, "I'm merely painting a picture of the true nature of the accused."

"I'll allow it," Lindor said.

Huffing, Laylana briskly walked up to Nath and said, "She's a snake."

"I'll ask the question again. Brenwar Bolderguild, have you ever seen Nath Dragon kill anyone in anger?"

Brenwar replied with uncharacteristic casualness. "Oh, lots of times. Back when he was younger, he had a really bad temper. A real hothead. That's a big part of the reason I got stuck with him. He needed that temper tempered."

"And this is the truth?"

Brenwar's chest puffed up when he said in a growl, "Dwarves don't lie."

"So, Nath Dragon is a killer?"

"Regarding the orcs and the rest of that foul brood, I'd certainly say yes. But we dwarves don't really count the orcs as people. Killing them is the equivalent of cutting down briars."

"Nonetheless, he's good at killing things?"

"He's Nath Dragon, the most renowned warrior in the land. It goes without saying that he is."

Nath felt a slight out-of-body experience. Part of him took what Brenwar said as a compliment. The other part began to sink back into the quagmire of his troublesome past. What got him was that he *had* killed in anger. It left a bitter taste in his mouth.

No matter how fast you run, you can never outrun yourself.

Anlee hammered at Brenwar with more about Nath's personal history. By the time she finished, Nath felt like he'd been drummed on by a pair of ogres, the things she asked were so deep and personal.

How does she know all this?

He noticed some elven maidens offering drinks in the stands. One of them, clad in clothing that was unusually revealing, refilled the judges' cups. It wasn't Lotuus, but this one's toes didn't touch the ground either.

I smell the stink of Lotuus's treachery.

CHAPTER 36

NEXT, BEN WAS CALLED IN front of the judges by Laylana. He walked over with a bit of a limp.

"Ben, can you tell us how you came to be in possession of the bow Akron?" she asked.

"Certainly. Ever since I met Dragon, er, Nath Dragon, I've been fascinated with the bow. I was just a farm boy when we met all those years ago. Well, as time passed, and with a lot of pleading on my part, Nath let me shoot Akron. I guess you could say I earned his trust." He tugged at his shirt collar with his finger. "So, over time, I used Akron many times during our adventures. As a matter of fact, he let me have the fine weapon when I returned to Quintuklen after the last Dragon War."

Pacing with her hands behind her back, Laylana said, "I see. So, it's been a very long time since Nath Dragon has been in possession of Akron."

"A very long time. I'm not going to lie, I took a great deal of pride in keeping the weapon with me. It was an honor."

"Did Nath give it to you?"

Ben shook his head. "That was never the understanding. I think Nath allowed me to use it to help protect others in my home city, Quintuklen. My family too." He gave Nath a little wave. "I'm grateful."

"So, tell us what happened to Akron. When and how did it end up missing?"

With a long expression, Ben said, "I can't say when or how exactly, and that's hard for me to admit. But over a year ago, we battled the wurmers just outside of Quintuklen. That was the last time I used it. Nath departed after that, and I held onto Akron. I secured the bow in my home, in a locking chest. I'd check it every month or so."

"And when did you notice it missing?"

"Several months ago."

"Did you tell anyone?"

"No, I was embarrassed. It wasn't until I met with Bayzog that I mentioned it again. That's when I found out about the assassinations." With a guilty look at Nath, Ben added, "If anyone should be accused, it should be me. I didn't do it, of course, but I know Nath didn't either."

"Ben, do you have any idea who might have stolen the bow?"

"I really don't. No one in my household remarked about anything strange."

"Thank you, Ben."

Lindor asked Anlee if she wanted to question this witness.

"Certainly, Judge." She marched right up in front of Ben and asked, "Did the box you secured the bow in have a lock?"

"Yes, a good one."

"How many keys are there to the lock?"

"Just one."

"Do you keep the key with you at all times?"

"No."

Anlee gave Ben a quick smile. "Ben, do you think it's possible for the key to be stolen or the lock to the strongbox to be picked?"

"I suppose."

"You know Nath Dragon well, right?"

"Yes."

"Do you think that if he wanted to, he'd be clever enough to retrieve the bow from your strongbox?"

"I suppose. If anyone could do it, Nath could."

"Objection!" Nath shouted out.

"Shush, Nath," Laylana said.

"Why didn't you object to that absurdity?" Nath glared at Laylana. "She's putting words in Ben's mouth."

"Order! Order!" Lindor said. "Laylana, control your client's outbursts."

"Apologies, your honor." Laylana bowed. "To all of the panel. It won't happen again." She eased over to Nath and talked under her breath. "You're making this worse. I'll handle this. You might not see it, but this is going much better than expected."

"Even a mole could see that you are losing."

Aghast, she said, "You aren't making it easy. I'm the only hope you have left, you know."

"Laylana, is there a problem?" Lindor asked.

"No, your honor. There is no problem at all." She moved away from Nath. "Please, continue."

With a smug look on her face, Anlee said, "No further questions, your honor."

"Does the defense have any other witnesses?" the judge said.

With a disappointed look at Nath, Laylana said to the judge, 'No.'"

"I see. Then we will allow for the closing arguments after a short recess." Lindor banged the table. "Adjourned."

Nath tried to get Laylana's attention, but she moved on. Brenwar and Ben disappeared among the soldiers and the citizens. Standing in the cage surrounded by thousands of people, he had never felt so alone. He could see now that his outburst against Laylana hadn't helped him any. Guilt dug between his ribs. Everything around him was so surreal. It didn't seem like anyone was on his side at all. He rested his head against the bars.

Some of his father's words came to him. "Often, there's a veil over the eyes of the races that clouds their judgment. They can't always see the truth like a dragon can. They are flawed and prone to error. Their hearts can be easily manipulated."

Nath watched the judges begin to reconvene. They were so casual. They drank and jested with one another as they sat down.

They are flawed, and my fate rests with them.

CHAPTER 37

The sun was setting, casting gray shadows over the courtyard. The dwarves lit the oil lanterns and hung them on tall posts. Wavering yellow light cast shadows on the people's faces, giving them a disturbing look. Many of them jested and frolicked.

Elven and dwarven cajolers unified together. Madness!

Nath rubbed the chill crawling up his scales. He'd always felt like he had all the time in the world. Today was different. Time was running out. His fate now rested in the hands of people whose reasoning had been diluted. He scanned the faces in the crowd and those of the soldiers who manned the walls. There wasn't a friendly face among them. The only person on his side was himself.

Every seat in the stands was filled. Laylana and Anlee stood before the judges with their chins down. Laylana hadn't so much as acknowledged Nath.

Lindor clonked the stone table again. "We have heard all the evidence, and now we will hear your closing arguments. Anlee, you may begin."

Laylana stepped aside.

Anlee stood tall. She brushed her robes behind her back and spoke with conviction. "Judges, the defender is making the case that Nath Dragon is not the murderer by using nothing short of deceit and misdirection. I've called a dozen witnesses, all credible elves and dwarves who are pillars in their communities. Every last one of them described the murderer of Laedorn and Uurluuk as a man fitting Nath Dragon's description. Look at the man, the assassin himself. There can't be any mistaking his identity. His flaming mane of hair. Those insidious black scales."

Anlee pointed right at Nath. "As the old saying goes, if he looks like an assassin, he's an assassin. But that's putting it nicely. Don't be fooled. He's nothing but a cold-hearted murderer. A villain who took the lives of our heroes."

She held her stomach. Her dark eyes watered up. "It makes me sick. It makes me sorry. And now, the granddaughter of the slain Laedorn steps forward to defend his murderer. It's unthinkable. But who am I to judge what kind of relationship she developed with Nath Dragon in their foreign travels together? Perhaps she is more than just counsel. Perhaps she has been dazzled by his golden eyes—which she spoke so fondly about."

Nath noticed Laylana's fists ball for a moment before loosening again. She still didn't look at Nath.

Anlee went on. "Laylana has cleverly concocted a defense that would even stretch the imagination of a ten-year-old halfling." She began to prowl around the table. "She claims that a person with chameleon-like powers, called a changeling, shifted into the image of Nath Dragon, stole his precious bow Akron from a secret location, and, without any motive whatsoever, invaded Elome and Morgdon and killed our leaders. She claims this assassin is still out there, on the prowl. Hah, perhaps this shape shifter is among us, but the funny thing is that no one else has been assassinated. Once word got out about Nath Dragon, the killing stopped."

Putting her hands together as if in prayer, Anlee continued, "And finally, to take the theory into another realm of wonder, she brings forth two of Nath Dragon's dearest friends. One of the friends, Brenwar Bolderguild—who's probably taken more hits in the head than a one-armed orcen brawler—claims that they time traveled. What a convenient alibi. Now, don't suppose that I don't believe in magic. I'm an elf, so of course I do. But traveling in time at the whim of a magic sword which," she spun around arms wide, "is unaccounted for? Maybe if we had it, we could travel back in time and prevent the assassinations. Perhaps Nath Dragon should have thought of that. Oh wait, why would he want to bring the dead back to life? If he's the hero he says he is, wouldn't he have done that?"

Nath rubbed his chin.

Is that possible?

"So, in closing, judges," Anlee said, "all you have before you is the most convicting testimony of all. Eye witness testimony. As sure as that man stands before us all, the witnesses testified that he indeed is the heartless, cold-blooded murderer they saw." She moved toward the elven side of the stands and stood quietly.

Lindor gave Anlee such an approving look that Nath thought the judge was going to stand up and applaud. Finally, the elven judge gathered himself. "Laylana, we are ready for your closing arguments, if you please."

Laylana smoothed some wrinkles out of her skirt. "With intent and purpose, the opposing counsel has created the biggest illusion of all. Like a house of cards, she has stacked one paper-thin witness testimony upon another and another, hoping to build a wall of conviction. The problem is that none of the witnesses, after careful dissection of their testimony, could discern whether or not the assassin was indeed Nath Dragon or just someone who looked like Nath Dragon."

She took a breath and calmly let it out. "In addition to that, we have the murder weapon, the bow Akron, which was conveniently left behind in Morgdon. The dwarves testify that the bow was found in plain sight, long after they'd lost track of the assailant. This is a remarkable coincidence. If Akron is so precious to Nath Dragon, why would he leave it behind? No, honored judges, this was done with intent. It is a set-up against Nath Dragon, the greatest enemy of the wicked."

She paced back and forth in front of the stone table. "Again, I can't emphasize enough that Nath Dragon does not have any motive to harm the elves or the dwarves. Personally, I will admit that when I myself sought vengeance against the accused for the murder of my dear grandfather Laedorn, I had nothing but blood in my eyes. I confronted Nath Dragon, and he confronted me with something I didn't expect: action. I personally witnessed his own sacrifices for his friends, for myself, and, on a broader scale, for all of Nalzambor."

She faced the judges. "We cannot rule out the involvement of magic or the powers of our unseen enemies when so much is on the line. The titans, the spirits, the hordes of evil want Nath Dragon gone. They will stop at nothing to end him. While we stand here and argue an absurd case against one of the greatest champions of good and freedom, the real murderer runs free. That isn't justice. That is injustice. No one has even given a shred of thought to the fact that it could have been someone or something else. How can we ignore that?"

She turned and paced again. "Finally, I say this. Nath Dragon, a friend to all that pursue right over wrong, has a target on him because he's the easiest to blame. It's all so convenient to blame him rather than ourselves now that we have realized the true assassin has slipped through our fingers. Nath Dragon is our friend, and he is not guilty."

Lindor nodded. "We will deliberate." He banged the gavel. "Adjourned."

Nath caught Laylana's attention.

Grudgingly, she came over. Without looking at him, she said, "Yes?"

"Laylana, you did well." He reached through the bars, lifted her chin, caught her eyes, and said, "I'm sorry."

Her eyes flicked from green to solid black to green again. "You're going to be sorry soon enough." She licked her teeth and floated backward on her tiptoes. "And I can't wait."

CHAPTER 38

"PLEASE EXPLAIN WHAT IN NALZAMBOR you are doing here," Selene demanded. She had her sword drawn. For some reason, the appearance of Gorlee was unsettling.

The changeling was a fragile creature in his normal appearance, little more than pinkish skin and bones, giving him a translucent look. His head was bald and a little bit veiny. "A thank-you would be appreciated," he said.

"Thank you." She poked the sword at his throat. "Now tell me what you're doing here. And change form. You look like an aging newborn."

Gorlee sprouted brown hair on his head, his color tanned, and common clothing formed over his body. He appeared to be a middle-aged man, somewhat like Ben. "Is this better?"

"It's better than a dark gnome. Now out with it."

"I suppose I could ask the same question of you, but I'll go first," Gorlee said with a confidence that belied his appearance. "I know Balzurth is dead, but I was his servant. I've been keeping an eye on things, particularly the wurmers." He turned into the form of a green lily dragon. "Believe me when I say that I have been coming and going from Dragon Home for quite some time. Like you, I presume, I used the Chamber of Murals to map the locations of these nests. I've found many and made note of them. My mission wasn't to seek and destroy but rather to find their weakness and see how they operate."

Selene put her sword away. "I'm not sold. Why not destroy them?"

"I posed the same question to Balzurth myself. He believed that once one wurmer nest was destroyed, the others would be alerted. They'd move. Once they moved, there was no telling how long it would take to find their new locations." He transformed back into a man. "Ideally, we wanted to find all the nests and take them all down at the same time. Much the same way as you did, using Orbs of Destruction against their life stones."

She caught Sansla nodding and said to him, "Thoughts?"

"I'd be curious to know if Gorlee learned anything else that is helpful."

"On a good note, you managed to destroy one of the life stones. That's quite a blow to their ranks. But it will only trigger more devastation and make it even harder for us to find the others."

As they walked through the Valley of Bones, Gorlee tore off a small dying branch. His arm turned into the size and texture of the branch. He tossed it aside, and his arm went back to normal. "The wurmer queen was paired up with a titan spirit, as you encountered. I remained undetected, because I'm getting really good at being me. I imagine the queen is dead, but the titan spirit probably survived. We survived because of the dimension portal I set up. It came from a scroll from Balzurth's treasure room. I set it up in case I found myself in a pinch. Then the two of you came along."

"So we can only assume the spirit Tylabahn will warn Eckubahn," Selene said.

"Exactly. But in order to do so, she'll need a host body. I learned that much about the titans. They lose strength if they aren't close to a body. It's as if another force reels them in. They have power, but they need flesh to thrive."

"Perhaps we need to capture one," Sansla suggested.

The distant branches quaked. Pushing through the trees and coming down the hill, the stone giants from the crater came. One of them had eyes red as fire.

Gorlee stepped between Selene and Sansla. "Speaking of capture, did anyone bring a really big net?"

"Maybe you should turn into one," Selene said.

"If I could—eh, I probably wouldn't."

Standing as tall as some of the leafless trees, the giants were still far away. "What do you think, Sansla?" Selene asked.

"If they have our scent, I imagine they'll be coming right for us. Or as Gorlee says, they might be moving on to warn the others."

The giants shoved through the trees, splintering branches of deadwood with their brawny shoulders. In longer, heavy steps, they made it to the base of the Valley of Bones in seconds. There they stood, surveying the land and sky with long looks. The giant with the burning eyes looked right in Selene's direction.

She leaned back behind a tree trunk.

Tylabahn. She's in that thing.

She peeked back. The giants were on the move, away from them, north. Her breathing eased. "Gorlee, what's to stop her from taking the body of a bird and flying away from here?"

"Unlike the minor spirits, she's a titan. Her body has to be strong enough to hold the spirit."

"I see."

"What do you want to do, Selene?" Sansla said.

"I want to stop that titan."

Chapter 39

"Isn't this lovely? All the little heroes of Nalzambor wrapped up in steel like holiday gifts. I do agree that it's certainly high time for celebration." The Fairy Empress stood in the dungeons below the fortress where the trial was taking place. She had the appearance of an elf, but her hair was cotton white. The feathery gown she wore was a mix of black, white, and pink. Hovering around her were winged fairies no bigger than a man's hand. They moved through the air with little impish faces, decorated in many bright colors. "Of course, the celebration has been going on for quite some time, and it will go on forever when Nath Dragon is gone like his father, Balzurth."

Crammed inside a small dungeon cell, Bayzog stood with his family. All of their hands were bound up in leather so thick that he couldn't see his fingers. His mouth was covered too. So were the mouths of his family. Staring at Lotuus, he knocked on the bars with his fists. He blinked at her.

"Oh, Bayzog, you are such a flirt. And shamelessly in front of your wife. I'm flattered." Lotuus reached through the bars and pinched his cheek. "It's adorable."

Bayzog continued to blink.

Staring at his lips with hungry eyes, she said to him, "What a shame. I thought you were flirting, but you're talking." She squinted. "I see. You want to know what is to become of you and your family after Nath Dragon dies. No, wait. Oh, this is so dated. Ah, congratulations on fooling the elves." She shook her head. "I'm not saying what you want me to say?" She looked confused.

Bayzog gave up the attempt.

Lotuus threw her head back and laughed. "This was easy, Bayzog. A well-planned effort for me to redeem myself with Eckubahn. We managed to get the elves and dwarves in such a lather that all they wanted was the blood of Nath Dragon. Here they gather, only to be duped by the fairies. Everything they eat or drink is tainted. It's our specialty. We've had some help from the lesser spirits. They host the weaker dwarves and elves. It worked to perfection. The best revengeful planning always does. And once the trial is over and Nath Dragon is dead, so will fall all of those elves and dwarves up there. The wurmers are close. Nestled by the thousands, waiting nearby, hungry for the slaughter."

She backed up to where the Elderwood Staff leaned against the wall. She caressed the long staff with the back of her hand. "Another prize for Eckubahn. An artifact that he will enjoy, the same as the bow, Akron." She kicked Brenwar's treasure chest. "This hunk of magic will prove useful too. The only item left to round up is that troublesome sword, Fang. Care to tell me where it is?"

Bayzog shook his head.

"I didn't think so. But I'll find it. Just like I did Akron. I quickly learned that I was an amazon shot with that thing. Just ask Laedorn and Uurluuk. Oh, but you can't. They're dead." She picked up the staff and hung it over her shoulder. "I just wanted to mention that you have a lovely family. I'm sure the wurmers will find you more than satisfying. Now, if you'll excuse me, I have the final verdict to attend to. Goodbye." Lotuus departed, and as she left, one by one the fairies took the forms of elves and fell in step behind her, carrying Brenwar's chest.

Rerry jumped forward and beat on the steel bars. Samaz managed to pull his brother back. Bayzog looked into Sasha's eyes. He hadn't ever seen her so worried. Now though, he had answers. Lotuus had given him the information he needed when she revealed herself.

Evil never passes up the opportunity to gloat.

Clearly, the fairy empress carried much more power than he originally estimated. Enough power to change her form—and all the other faeries did, too. It was powerful magic indeed. Now they had poisoned the minds of thousands of elves and dwarves. The question was how long it would last. Judging by the sound of things above, it had lasted long enough.

We've got to save Nath. We have to warn them all. But will they listen?

He faced his family. His sons both stood taller than he did and had the weathered look of seasoned adventurers. There was great strength in their eyes, much like their mother's. He stuck his elbows out. Together they all locked arms, huddled together, and put their heads down. Bayzog searched for the magic he commanded with lips, thoughts, and fingers.

Let my mind be my fingers and my lips. In this desperate hour, come to me, magic, come.

CHAPTER 40

SWEAT BEADED NATH'S BROW. HE wiped it away with his finger and eyed the thick layer of moisture.

If scales could sweat, I'd be dripping from my elbows.

He found himself alone again as dusk settled over the hilltops and the day became early night. He'd lost sight of Laylana, but her black eyes were now etched in his mind. At first he had thought she was Lotuus, but he'd since come to the conclusion that Laylana was possessed by one of the spirits that had escaped from the Great Dragon Wall.

The presence of evil lingered in the air like smoke from burning incense. He wasn't sure why he hadn't noticed before, but Lotuus and her brood of faeries hid their evil well. They had duped thousands of elves and dwarves.

Now I'm going to pay for it. I'm going to pay for it with my life.

After hours of no contact with Brenwar and Ben, the pair of them finally approached.

"Well, look who's here. What's the matter, did they run out of food and mead?"

Ben patted his belly, which had popped out over his belt. "No, I just don't have any room for more." He sucked on a toothpick. "You should have tried some, Dragon. You certainly must be hungry after all this."

With plenty of bite in his tone, Nath replied, "Sure, Ben, why don't you go and fetch me my final meal? Make it dandy."

"Why the heat?" Ben said, backing away with his hands up.

"Because I'm about to be hung by the neck!"

"You aren't going to be found guilty, Nath," Brenwar said. "You're not guilty. Who's not going to believe my testimony? Things are as I say they are."

"No, Brenwar, that's the problem. Nothing is as you think it is. I told you Lotuus was here. Remember her? The fairy empress? The reason you lost all the skin from your hand?"

"Of course I do." His head swiveled back and forth. "I don't see her."

"That's because you've been drinking cursed ale all day. Great Guzan, Brenwar, I'm about to die. I'd thought you'd be up in arms about it!"

"The dwarves won't vote against me, Nath. You know that. No four votes. That will save your skin. Or scales, rather."

"Weren't you paying attention? They don't need four votes to hang me. They only need three."

Scratching his forehead, Brenwar said, "That seems unfair."

"Very unfair," Ben agreed. He tapped his chest with his fist and burped. "Excuse me."

Nath looked them both square in the eye. He saw a watery glaze there. It reminded him of the time he battled a former ally who had turned against him, long ago. "Do either of you think you can remember something long enough to take it to Dragon Home?"

"Certainly, Dragon, I'll tell them."

"If either of you live to see Selene or my mother Grahleyna again—which, once I'm gone, I kind of doubt—tell them I'm sorry for failing. That I'll miss them. Tell them I'm gone because my friends turned from stalwart to nitwit."

"Hold on, I think I might need to write this down if you keep going." Ben yawned. "Just say it one more time."

Nath smacked his chain against the bars. His dander had risen, and his nostrils flared. "Listen, the both of you! I'm the Dragon King, and I'm giving you one final command. Bayzog, Sasha, Samaz, and Rerry are in the dungeons somewhere. Brenwar, do something with those stubby little legs of yours and find them!"

"Don't take that tone with me," Brenwar said.

"Will you just move?"

"Nath, your nostrils are smoking," Ben commented with his eyes filled with marvel.

"Good!"

Whack! Whack! Whack!

Lindor pounded the sphere on the judges' table. The banging sound felt like a hammer striking Nath's head. He tasted burning sulfur in his mouth.

Oh, if I can let out some fire, let me let it out now.

He took a deep breath, filling his lungs, and exhaled a puff of smoke weaker than a small campfire being doused. Nobody even noticed.

Ben and Brenwar resumed their seats in the stands.

What are they doing? I told them to find Bayzog!

Lindor remained standing while the other four judges took seats. He beckoned Laylana and Anlee. With the kind eyes of a caring father, he said to both of them, "The two of you represented the greater good well. It made for a difficult decision. I thank you both for the preparation and effort. With that, the judges are prepared to render their decisions."

A stiff breeze blew in that rattled the lanterns hanging on the posts. Nath blew his hair from his eyes.

I can't believe it's come down to this. I thought when I went down, it would be in a fight, like Father. Instead, I fall into a web of lies and deceit.

He pecked on the bars with his index fingernail. The tiny divots he made seemed so significant for some reason. It was a detail he normally wouldn't have paid any attention to at all. It was as if something was missing.

This can't be real! Somebody pinch me! This must be an illusion!

Lindor resumed his seat. With his elbows resting on the table, nestled in the blossoming folds of his sleeves, he said, "In case of a tie, I will be the determining vote." He held up a finger. "Let me remind the audience once more. Remain quiet. Respectful. A vote of guilty by three or more judges is a hanging verdict. If the vote is not guilty by three or more judges, Nath Dragon will be given his freedom, and for this crime, he will never be tried again. If he is found guilty, he will be hung by the neck shortly thereafter. His remains will be returned to Dragon Home, otherwise known as the Mountain of Doom." His eyes slid over to Nath for a long moment, then he eased back into his chair. "We will start with the elven judges if there is no objection."

Nath's throat tightened. Sweat dripped into his eyes.

Great Guzan, this is really happening!

Lindor rolled the marble sphere down the judges' table to the elven judge at the other end. The judge with flowing white hair covering his shoulders and back slowly stood. He took the sphere in hand, lifted it chest high, and smote the bench. In a baritone voice, he said, "Guilty." He rolled the gavel to the next elven judge.

Taking the sphere in hand, the elven judge who appeared the youngest of them all, with half his short hair mostly brown mixed with white, dropped the sphere with a resounding clatter. In elegant speech, he said, "Guilty."

I'm doomed! I'm doomed!

The marble sphere rolled down to the dwarf furthest to the left.

Oh please, Brenwar! Please be right! Let the dwarves be on my side.

The white-bearded dwarf with a balding crown of hair scooped up the gavel as he stood, lifted it high over his head, glared at Nath, slammed it on the bench, and said in a voice that could startle a statue, "Guilty!"

Nath's heart sank into his toes when the rousing cheers from both sides of the aisle erupted.

Ben and Brenwar sat with perplexed looks on their faces, shaking their heads. Quickly, the excited crowd took up the chant that was suggested by the soft whispers of the elven serving maidens.

"Hang Nath Dragon! Hang Nath Dragon! Hang Nath Dragon!"

CHAPTER 41

BEFORE NATH COULD SAY THE first twenty-seven syllables of his actual name, the dwarves and elves began building the gallows. The structure was built over the stone table where Akron lay like a forgotten piece of history. Plank by plank, nail by nail, one mind-jarring crack at the head of a spike after the other, Nath watched the last minutes of his life go by.

He pointed at a spot in the scaffolding where a nail head wasn't flush. "Eh, bearded one, it looks like one of the elves isn't too proficient with a hammer. I don't want the platform coming down before the show gets started. Can you imagine the embarrassment if your craftsmanship fails?"

The dwarf stopped, backed up, and eyed the bent head of the nail that protruded. He clawed it out with the hammer, plucked a shiny new nail from his pouch, and hammered it home with one strike.

With his thumbs up, Nath said, "Well done! I feel much better now. The dwarven reputation for being the finest craftsmen in all Nalzambor is still intact."

With tiny chisels and knives, the elves made ornate carvings in the support posts and railings that followed the steps to the top. Within an hour, the entire contraption was complete.

"Well, it looks like you have everything you need but a rope," Nath commented. He was numb from head to toe. The only thing still running was his mouth. Some sort of bizarre denial of what was happening.

Brenwar appeared with a long stretch of dwarven rope and knotted up a noose.

"Brenwar!" Nath cried, "What in Balzurth's name are you doing?"

"If you're going to hang, you're going to hang right." Brenwar gave the rope a few tugs. With a nod, he handed it to his son Glenwar, who ran the rope to the top.

Nath startled when the lock to his cage turned with a grind of metal. His arms were locked behind his neck and the metal collar removed. He was flexing his muscles when a black-eyed elven soldier whispered in his ear, "Fight this, and your friends in the dungeon die before you do."

Shoulders sagging, he let the soldiers march him out of the cage.

I bet Bayzog isn't even captured. Everything else is a lie, so why wouldn't that be? Perhaps I should make a break for it. I'd get these chains off eventually.

Out of the corner of his eye, he caught a wink of light. He turned his head. Proud as a peacock, Lotuus stood in fully elven form, holding Bayzog's staff. She winked. She waved.

I hate her.

He began the long march up the steps. Not a single board creaked underfoot on his way to the top of the gallows. Twenty feet off the ground, he found himself looking down at all the judges and people. They slung the noose over his neck and pulled the rope tight. Below him were only the trap-door platform and twenty feet of air.

"Nath Dragon," Lindor said, "you have been judged guilty. Do you have any last words to say?"

He eyed the dwarven soldier who held the handle to the trap door. He made an uncomfortable swallow and said, "Yes I do."

Perhaps I'll take this moment to summon the dragons. I have to do something before it's too late—but what about my friends? I'll just say something really long. Delay until I think of something. For the love of Balzurth, somebody do something!

"You might hang me, but know this: you will have hung the wrong man. You'll regret it."

The now-black-eyed Lindor cut him off. "That will do."

The dwarven soldier yanked back the lever. The trap door dropped open.

Weightless for an instant, Nath fell through. The rope went taut with a snap. He bounced. His neck muscles bulged and flexed. His head and neck retained their iron composure.

The judges, particularly Lindor, couldn't have been more startled when Nath's neck didn't break. All of their eyes were as big and black as raccoons' as he hung swaying in the wind with the rope groaning above his head.

In raspy, strong-willed words, Nath said, "This is awkward."

JUDGEMENT OF THE DRAGON

-Book 7-

CRAIG HALLORAN

CHAPTER 1

SELENE THE FORMER HIGH PRIESTESS of Barnabus, Sansla Libor the cursed elven roamer king turned white winged ape, and Gorlee the changeling in the form of a middle-aged man slunk through the forest. Leaves gently fell from the trees they passed. A soft rain came from above, and an eerie evening fog began to rise from below. Selene couldn't see her feet. She slunk through the trees, eyes alert on the ground and branches. They'd been chasing after the titan Tylabahn. The evil spirit now possessed the body of a stone giant and moved toward Narnum to warn the lead titan, Eckubahn, that one of the nests of a wurmer queen had been destroyed. They'd been chasing after the giants for hours, but the trail had gone cold.

Where could that giant be?

Swishing her tail over the ground, she cleared the fog away. She could feel impressions in the ground with her tail the same way she might feel cuts in a table with the swipe of her finger. The black tendril eased over the landscape, side to side. Selene's eyes scanned the ground as well. She was hoping to see a footprint. Instead, there was only a rut where the trunk of a tree lay rotting. "Certainly the giant didn't sprout wings and take flight," she said.

Standing nearby, Sansla inspected the branches with his hands. Gorlee wasn't far from Sansla, following suit. Bright-green eyes looked up, piercing the high branches. He blinked several times.

"This is truly perplexing. I don't claim to be a tracker of any sort, but the thought of losing a giant, a man the size of ten, is…er…embarrassing?"

"That's an understatement." She scratched her temple with her index finger. "Especially considering there are two of them. Sansla? Anything?"

Sansla approached her. His hulking seven-foot-plus build dwarfed that of Selene and Gorlee. He extended his open palm, revealing a handful of small green leaves and red berries.

"You found something."

"I'm an elven roamer, one of the greatest trackers in the world. It's natural that I found something." He took a berry, stuck it in his mouth, and chewed. "Anglon berries. They are a great sustaining substance and very rare." He offered his hand. "Refresh yourself with some? The leaves make a great thirst quencher, too."

"This is all you have? I'm not hungry. I want to stop that monster."

"This substance will help clear your thoughts. It will gain you more focus."

"Am I to understand that you have lost the trail as well as I?" she said, watching him slowly chew.

Sansla swallowed. "As difficult as it is for me to admit, yes."

Clenching her fists, Selene said, "Ugh! This can't be happening." She certainly wasn't a tracker the likes of Nath Dragon, Sansla, or Brenwar, but she'd still grown better than most. "I can't believe this."

Gorlee stepped into the group. "May I try some of those, er, what do you call them?"

"Anglon berries," Sansla replied. "Please, help yourself."

As the changeling reached for the food in Sansla's paw of a hand, Selene slapped the berries and leaves up into the air. "Forget your precious substance! We need to find those giants!"

Shrugging, Sansla dusted his hairy hands off with the mannerisms of a noble. "Certainly, Selene. Perhaps it is time I took a bird's eye view of things."

She stroked her tail, which rested over her shoulder. The last thing she wanted was for them to be sighted by the wurmers that dominated the skies, searching for dragons. But with night coming, it might not be such a bad idea. "Let's keep moving while I think on it a bit."

"Certainly. I think we can all agree that the titan moves toward Narnum. That was the direction we went until the trail went cold. I've lost trails before, but persistence has always paid off." Sansla bent over and picked up some of the leaves and berries. He handed them over to Gorlee. "That's assuming the titan hasn't summoned some other trickery we're unaware of. The stone giants don't make a scent, and like so many giants, they have unique powers. We need to move quickly but be wary."

"Then start moving quickly." Selene gave Sansla a shove. "I don't care for all this talking."

Gorlee perked up. "Mmmm, these berries really are good. Sansla, what did you call them again?"

Selene slapped the berries out of his hand. "Keep the lips shut and the feet moving."

With a frown, Gorlee moved after Sansla, with Selene following in the rear. She didn't like how things were going. At the rate they moved, they should have caught up with Tylabahn an hour ago. Now, it felt like she'd only gotten farther away. *What if Tylabahn isn't going north? Perhaps she went another way.*

On soft feet, the small group weaved through the trees and brush. The night fog thickened and rose. Selene lost track of Sansla and Gorlee from time to time, only to catch them in her sight moments later. Sansla was so quiet she had to focus to even hear him breathe. Gorlee, on the other hand, was a little sloppy with his movements, but still quiet nonetheless. She wandered up to them. The ape and changeling studied a river of fog that barred their path. She wouldn't have known it was a river if not for the sound of water rushing under the fog. It was at least fifty feet from one side to the other.

"Have you ever crossed through here before?" she asked Sansla.

"I've traversed countless rivers in my travels. Some run very deep, but most of them don't." Sansla eased forward. "This one I'm not so sure about. I can fly you over."

"There's no need for chivalry, Sansla. I can handle getting a little wet." She surged in front of him. "Besides, my scales shed water."

"Ladies first then, but I will be close behind."

Selene waded ankle deep into the water. The icy stream filled the rim of her boots. She kept going until she was knee deep. Sansla was her shadow. Gorlee sloshed in behind both of them, saying with a shiver, "Now that's chilly!"

Selene shushed him. "What did I say about those lips of yours?"

"Sorry," Gorlee replied.

The farther she went, the higher the river surged around her waist. At what Selene felt was the halfway point, she slowed. The direction of the waters shifted. She glanced backward. Sansla's head was cocked to one side. Gorlee was nowhere to be found. "Where's Gorlee?"

Emerging through the fog, Gorlee said, "I'm here."

"Stay close and keep moving." Selene pushed through the water a few more feet and came to an abrupt stop. A pylon of some sort jutted out of the stream, blocking her path.

"What is it?" Gorlee said.

"I don't know. We'll go around."

The pylon moved.

She froze. A shiver went up her elbows.

The water erupted. Huge arms blasted out of the water and scooped up Gorlee in one swipe.

In a flash, Selene snaked out her sword. "It's the giants!"

CHAPTER 2

LOTUUS HAD LEFT.

Locked up arm in arm with his family, Bayzog reached deep into his mind, searching for a fragment of the magic that resided within him. His elbows were looped with Sasha on one side and Rerry on the other, with Samaz right across from him. He envisioned a spring of energy coursing from his stomach and feeding the rest of his body. His brow knitted. Sweat ran from his temple to his chest. The minutes passed without a spark. He opened his eyes and sighed through his nose.

Samaz was looking right at Bayzog. His son was a beefier version of him with the same violet eyes and far more meat on his bones. The young adult was mysterious, even to Bayzog. Both of them were quiet people, but Samaz operated on a deeper intuitive level. There was power behind his violet eyes, deep and unsearchable.

With a grunt, Sasha leaned into him. Her pretty eyes were saying it was fine, to have faith. He was looking up when a clamor arose above. Bits of debris drifted onto their heads and into their gazing eyes. It wasn't a good sound. There were cries and cheers that brought doom.

I have to do something!

He squeezed his eyes shut.

Reach deep, Bayzog! Reach deep!

With his hands tied and his lips gagged, and without some object to focus through such as the Elderwood Staff, it was unlikely he could summon his power. And even if he did, he wouldn't be able to control it. That would be dangerous.

Unbridled magic could destroy me or, even worse, my family.

Samaz grunted.

Bayzog remained in deep thought. He started to block out everything and imagined himself before a cauldron of fiery power.

This is my magic. I will take it.

Rerry gave him a hard tug. His eyes snapped open. Glaring at his son, his widened eyes asked, "What?"

His fair-headed son cast his gaze at Samaz.

He looked. Samaz's eyes had become violet infernos. The burning irises of energy sought Bayzog's own. He looked right into Samaz's eyes while at the same time clutching Sasha's hand. Her amulet lit up, and they all three connected. The magic inside Bayzog awakened. His own eyes flared up like the violet stars in the sky. Their energies merged. Samaz's power was a stampede of wild horses.

Samaz, can you hear me?

I can! I can't control it, Father!

Listen to me. Follow my voice.

A sharp crackle caught Bayzog's ear. His face started to heat up. Samaz had unlocked his magic, and it began to run wild in the dungeon cell. The rock walls trembled and split. With their eyes locked together, Bayzog added, *Feed your power to me. I will shape it. Give it purpose. Give it form.*

Samaz loosed more of what he had.

Bayzog's head kicked back. His knees wobbled. Samaz's seeping power started to pour into him. His body trembled. He raced through the spells he knew by heart, summoning the words in his mind, syllable for syllable. He became the hands and lips of his son's power. The mystic power groaned, trying to tear away at him, but Bayzog's sharp mind corralled it. The violet power swirled around the four of them, tearing at their clothing and bonds. Bayzog turned the unleashed energy into hands. Wildly, the mystic hands clawed at the air, threatening to tear them all apart.

I'm losing control, Father.

Bayzog ignored the words. Focusing on the hands he'd created, he grabbed the gag that filled his mouth and yanked it free. Taking a quick breath, he spoke a spell in Elven. His powerful enunciations brought Samaz's fires under control. The mystic hands Bayzog commanded ripped free the gags and ate away the leathers that secured their hands.

Bayzog jumped forward and wrapped Samaz in his arms in a strong embrace. "Close it off, Son! Close it off! You can do it!"

Bayzog had brought forth his powers, but Samaz's still spun around the dungeon, gathering speed and out of control. Face wroth with pain, the young man screamed.

"Aaaaaaaaaaaaaah!"

With the power tearing at his clothing like a mighty wind, Rerry cocked back his fist and smote his brother square in the jaw. The power faded. Samaz sagged in his father's and mother's arms.

Rerry rubbed his knuckles. "I always wanted to do that."

Bayzog smirked. "You did well. Just don't ever do that again." He slapped at Samaz's cheeks, but his older son didn't awaken. "He's out, but he should be fine. And you're going to have to carry him."

Rerry looked at the dungeon door that sealed them in. "Carry him where? We're still stuck inside."

Bayzog pointed his finger at the door and uttered a command in mystic Elven. The door burst off the hinges and into the adjacent wall with a clatter. "We were stuck, but now you're stuck carrying your brother."

The cries above them rose to an all new crescendo.

"Let's go!"

CHAPTER 3

Still hanging by the neck, struggling for words, Nath stared down Lindor and the other judges and said in a raspy voice, "If you try to hang me and I don't die, what happens then?" He wriggled. "Do I go free?"

The elves and dwarves in the stands gawked and gasped. The murmuring rose.

Lindor and the other judges huddled up. They spoke in low voices.

Nath could hear every word that sputtered from their fumbling lips. They were completely baffled about what to do.

"Hang him again," one of the dwarven judges suggested.

An elven judge offered to keep him in prison. Another suggested they just wait and see if Nath choked to death. They all turned and looked at him.

Nath's neck muscles continued to thicken and harden like roots from a tree. The stretch of rope groaned above him. He said to the judges, "Do you mind?" The roughness in his voice started to ease. "You could at least cut me down while you talk about it. This is a bit cruel, you know."

Lindor held up a long, shaky finger. "The prisoner will be silent." He next snapped his fingers.

An elf in rose-colored robes rushed up the steps with a leather tome almost as big as himself. The elf dropped it on the judges' stone table and hustled away.

Lindor began leafing through the pages. "This will take a while. Hmmm…let's see. What happens when you hang somebody and they don't die…?"

"Free him!" Brenwar marched toward the judges. "That's what happens!"

"Oh, so now you stand up for me," Nath said. "Thanks, Brenwar. Have you finally come to your senses?"

"I've always had my wits."

"No you haven't."

"Yes I have!" He scratched his head. "I think."

Laylana stormed toward the judges. "I call for a mistrial!"

"Yes! A mistrial!" Brenwar agreed.

The elven prosecutor, Anlee, came forward. "The penalty is death. It must be adhered to, whether it is by the rope, the guillotine, or a squadron of archers."

Chanting broke out among the dwarves. "Free Nath! Free Nath! Free Nath!"

Ben was pumping his fist in the air and leading the chorus.

On the other side of the fort in the stands, the elves chanted, "Death! Death! Death!"

Nath managed to turn his chin far enough to see an elven woman who resembled Lotuus in the stands, leading chants. Wearing silky layers of black, pink, and white, she carried the Elderwood Staff. "Brenwar! That's Lotuus. You need to end her!"

Brenwar was caught up in the cheering for Nath. His bony fist pumped in the air. "Free Nath! Free Nath! Free Nath!"

The elves and dwarves began to argue back and forth. They pushed and shoved one another, even dwarf against dwarf and elf against elf. The Corridor fort became a sea of confusion.

Nath watched Lindor and the other judges comb the pages of the tome, also arguing with one another. Stubby dwarven fingers poked at the pages. The elves shrugged the argument off with their noses stuck in the air. Between blinks, Nath caught the changes in their eyes from time to time, from black to their natural colors. He was pretty sure they were going to find a way to kill him, one way or another.

Finally, Lindor lifted the marble gavel. He slammed it hard several times on the table. *Whack! Whack! Whack!*

The sound shivered Nath's scales. The courtyard fell silent. The elves and dwarves returned to their seats and sat down, quiet. Even Brenwar and Ben sat still.

Straining to get a better look at his surroundings, Nath searched the faces in the crowd.

What's going on? What made them sit down like that?

He understood the spirits had taken over some of the people, and he knew the fairies had used food and wine to weaken the minds of many others, but something else was happening. There was another powerful force at work. He could sense it.

What is it?

In Lindor's hand, the gavel—an obsidian ball with flecks of stardust that faintly twinkled—caught his eye.

That's it! I'm not sure what it is, but it is controlling them!

Nath called out, "Laylana! Laylana?"

His elven defender was nowhere to be found.

Lindor closed the tome, and the judges took their seats. Lifting his arms high for all to see—aside from the view being blocked by the gallows—the high elven judge cleared his throat. "Ahem." He took a sip of wine and remarked, "That's better. Now, according to the annals of law, if the accused fails to die by the first method, then another method will be tried, and so on, until death is final. We will now deliberate as to what that method will be."

The dwarves and elves started shouting out suggestions.

"Stones!"

"Swords!"

"Bury him alive!"

"Guillotine!"

Over the rising chaos of suggestions, Nath said to the judges, "Can you at least cut me down while you decide?"

Lindor looked right at him with coal-black eyes and said, "No."

CHAPTER 4

ATH STRAINED AGAINST THE MOORITE shackles that held his arms fast behind his back. His temper rose.

I'm surrounded by a sea of idiots. I'm not going down like this.

He'd faced an unfair trial and an absurd hanging and still lived. Now, the possessed judges were trying to decide how to kill him again.

I've held back long enough.

There was sadness in his heart, mixing with anger. Lotuus had Bayzog's staff, and he figured that meant his half-elf wizard friend was dead. He had to move on if he could.

Bayzog would have understood. I'd want him to do the same.

He flexed his arms while twisting and turning his wrists. Moorite was the toughest steel in Nalzambor, but nothing was unbreakable.

There's a weak link in every chain. Find it, Dragon. Be bigger. Be stronger!

Lindor caught him fighting against his bonds. "Stop doing that. You've been sentenced to death. You must accept it!"

Still fighting against his shackles, Nath felt the infernos deep in his bowels begin to ignite. "I've been judged by dwarves and elves, but I am a dragon! I am the Dragon King!" His voice got louder as he spoke. "You have no right to judge me!"

Lindor pounded the gavel. "Stop! Stop what you're doing!"

Nath ceased to struggle. He wasn't able to break the chains. His body slackened. He could feel the power of the sphere in Lindor's hand trying to subdue him. However, it was too late. The inner inferno within started to leak out. Staring down Lindor, Nath let the smoke steam from his nostrils.

"Stop doing that!" Lindor ordered. His elven features became dark and angry.

"What's the matter? Do you have a problem with me smoking? I like smoking!"

"Cease your efforts!"

"You know what they say, Lindor. Where there's smoke, there will be fire!" Feeling the inferno within that he'd missed so much, Nath spat a stream of fire upward out of his mouth. The bright orange flames raced up the rope fibers of his noose and incinerated them. Nath's feet hit the gallows. As soon as they did, in a gust of breath, he set the gallows on fire. It didn't burn him. "Sultans of Sulfur! I have my breath back! It feels great!"

Many of the elves screamed. The dwarves barked orders, rushing from the stands and searching for pails.

With the flames of the wooden gallows roaring all around him, Nath hopped high in the air, knees high. In the same motion, he looped his cuffed hands from his backside under his feet to the front side. "That's better."

With the gavel in his hand raised high and an elven face contorted into an evil grimace, Lindor shouted, "Seize him, soldiers! Seize him!" The orb came down. It cracked on the stone like a clap of thunder.

Nath pounced onto the judges' table. Wrists still cuffed, he wrenched the gavel from Lindor and shoved the elven judge into the others.

Lindor shrieked.

"This trial's over," said Nath, "for good."

He could feel the power of the orb pulsating beneath his fingers. All the while, the soldiers crowded him. He hit the orb on the table and said, "Back off!"

The forces kept coming.

From out of the sky, Lotuus landed. She was in elven form, with fairy wings sprouting from her back. She let out a wicked chuckle. "You cannot control the Orb of Command. It doesn't know you, fool! Now what will you do, Nath Dragon? Fight all of these elves and dwarves to the death? Tsk, tsk, you wouldn't want that on your conscience."

A spear careened right at Nath. He slid his head out of the way, all the while staring at the black sphere.

An Orb of Command. Hmmm, I've heard about these things. Very powerful indeed.

He spewed out flames, making a circle that separated him and the judges from the soldiers. The wall of flame rose ten feet high.

"Fool! The dwarves and elves will rush right into your flames. They follow blindly!" Lotuus said.

Behind her, the elderly elven judge came back to his feet with the spryness of a young man. He cackled. "You'll have no victory here, Nath Dragon. Your efforts are temporary. The titans have already taken measures to thwart any extraordinary circumstances." Possessed by an evil spirit, Lindor's body jumped from the bench into the flames.

"No!" Nath cried out in horror as Lindor's body perished in his inferno.

"Oh, boohoo," Lotuus said with a smirk on her face. She still hovered over the ground. "Surrender, Nath Dragon. Accept your death, or even more of them will perish in your flames!"

"The only one going down in flames here is you!" Nath filled his lungs with air and let out a gust of wind. No flames came, only a stream of smoke.

Lotuus fanned the smoke from her face, coughing a little. "How pathetic. The little dragon is out of fire." She flew upward out of his reach. With a wave of her hand, she ripped the Orb of Command free of Nath's grip. It sailed right into her palm. Her other hand held Bayzog's staff. "After what's about to happen, Nath Dragon, you'll wish you had died. Maybe these weakling elves and dwarves can't kill you," she pointed the staff high into the air, "but I'm pretty sure they will."

High in the air, wings beat, circling like a storm. For the first time, the droning *ree-rah* sound of the wurmers caught his ears. They flew by the thousands.

He said to Lotuus, "Is that all? I can handle that batch all by myself."

"Maybe you can, Nath Dragon, but none of the rest can." She tossed her head back and laughed. "Not even you can save all those dwarves and elves."

"If you just wanted to kill me, why go to all this trouble? Why the charade?"

"I wanted your death to be amusing. Life, death—it's all entertainment to me."

"You're a monster, Lotuus."

"No," she held out the staff and orb, "I'm a winner. And you, dear golden-eyed Nath, are a loser."

Chapter 5

Selene jammed her sword under the stone giant's kneecap. The blade slid right into the stone-hard skin, drawing forth a pained howl.

Gorlee slipped out of the giant's grip and splashed into the water.

Selene unleashed her fury on the giant, chopping at the exposed leg like a lumberjack hewing down a tree.

The tremendous hand of the giant lashed out. Its log-sized fingers sent Selene sprawling into the water.

With her hand buried in the soft sand of the stream, she pushed up, twisted around, and emerged. Water cascading over her body, she stood in the fog with the water swirling around her. The giant was gone. The sound of the monster's angry voice and huge legs sloshing through the water was not. The giant was close but moving away.

"Selene!" Sansla called out from beyond the fog. "Help me!"

Sword bared, she walked through the stream, eyes searching through the cloudy bank of fog. Catching sight of Sansla, she froze where she stood. The pair of giants had Sansla's arms locked up between them. They tugged him like a rope. Agony filled the great ape's face. She rushed right for him.

The titan Tylabahn, whose spirit was hosted in the other stone giant's body, stopped Selene in her tracks. "You seem awfully eager to watch your dear friend's arms get pulled off. I'd be more than glad to do it. Just give me an excuse, Selene."

She eased back. "Just let him go and we'll leave you alone, Tylabahn."

The titan leered at Selene. "Oh, I doubt that. After all, you are trying to be a hero, aren't you, dark-hearted Selene. No, no, no, I'm not fool enough to take you at your word." She pulled hard on Sansla's arm. It popped from the socket. Sansla groaned. "I'm not fool enough to let this cursed roamer king cut off my mission, either. No, I'll be clear: I'm going to kill you all. But if you like, you can run, Selene—and you won't have to watch his blood run through the waters."

Selene tensed. Her stomach turned over. Tylabahn wasn't one to make veiled threats; she was a killer. The only life that meant anything to the titan was her own. "Would you be willing to exchange my life for his? I'd make a fine prize for Eckubahn."

"I don't see the point in it. You are worthless. As I said, I'm going to kill you both."

"Nath Dragon would come for me."

Tylabahn's eyes widened to the size of wagon wheels. She hissed through her teeth. "Tempting, but no. The more dead heroes, the better."

Selene held out her sword. Crafted of the finest steel and blessed by powerful magic, the fine blade was right out of Balzurth's throne room. The blade shimmered like living lightning. The gilded pommel pulsated in her hand. "This sword has a name: Stone Cutter, the slayer of giants. Forged by the hands of Balzurth himself to take down the giants. Look at your limping friend." She eyed the giant's dripping knee. "If you kill my friend, I promise you, I'll turn you both into lumber."

Eyeing the blade, the wounded giant took a half step back.

Tylabahn leered at him. "Don't be a coward. Live like a giant, die like a giant." She turned to Selene. "Besides, you cannot kill me. I'm a spirit."

"You're a spirit in need of a willing body, and if you don't have one that can hold you, Tylabahn, then what happens? You fade away, like sand washing away from the riverbank. Now, wouldn't that be a fitting end?"

"Neither fitting nor likely. I'll never go out—and even if I do, it will be in a blaze of glory." Her eyes flared up with an angry emerald green. "Say goodbye to the roamer king, Selene." She put her back into it.

Sansla wailed.

"No!" Selene cried out. She rushed through the water, watching agony take over Sansla's face.

Out of the water behind Tylabahn, a monstrous figure emerged. Rising twenty feet tall and covered in plate-like scales, spikes, and horns, the gigantic humanoid walloped Tylabahn in the jaw.

She lost her grip on Sansla.

Quick to react, Selene sliced into the wounded stone giant's wrist.

The giant jerked his hand away and dropped Sansla into the waters.

Selene pressed the attack. She raced up the giant's chest, wrapped her tail around his neck, and held tight.

The giant hammered at her with flailing fists, screaming, "NO! NO! NO!"

Selene struck the giant point first in the skull, right between the eyes. The stone giant's body seized up, making a loud splash. She pulled the sword free and raced toward Sansla. The lifting fog revealed him wading knee deep in the water. He held his damaged shoulder, eyeballing the battle that raged right before their eyes.

"What is that thing?" Selene said as she watched Tylabahn, in a stone giant body, exchanging thunderous blows with the other monster. A waterfall splashed them both.

Sansla replied, "I can only assume that's Gorlee, but he's taken an awfully large form, the likes of which my own eyes have never seen."

"That makes sense. Perhaps he can turn into whatever he wishes now." She moved straight toward the battle. "But he'll still need help."

Sansla caught her by the elbow with his good hand. "Selene, I could use your strength. Please take my bad arm and hold it fast. Quickly, now."

She hugged his arm like it was the trunk of a tree. She planted her feet firmly in the water the best she could by wedging her feet against the rocks. "Hurry up then. The battle rages!"

"I don't want to miss it either." Sansla jerked back. His shoulder popped into place. "Ah! That's better. Thank you, Selene. Now, let's finish this titan." He took to the air, wings beating, and flew right into Tylabahn's face, covering her eyes.

Gorlee's fists looked like spiked anvils in his colossal form. He pounded the stone giant's body with devastating bone-jarring blows.

Selene cut through the water. The smallest of the four of them, she hacked away at Tylabahn's legs, shins, and knees.

"Nooooooooo!" Tylabahn yelled. She swung wild haymakers.

Gorlee rocked her with a punch so hard that her entire body shook.

Tylabahn went down into the water in a shambling heap.

Sansla darted aside just as the changeling jumped right on top of the titan.

Gorlee held her head under the water by the neck.

Massive limbs kicked, clawed, and slapped at skin and water. A big shudder came, and then Tylabahn, in the stone giant's body, moved no more.

Chapter 6

The dragon flames that broiled inside Nath's body might have been extinguished, but his fiery will hadn't. Eyebrows knitted together, muscles knotting in strain, he made the moorite cuffs that bound his wrists groan. The metal links started to give. Flexing the muscles in his back and shoulders, Nath took a quick breath and let out his fury.

"Huuuuuuuuuurk!"

The chains gave way to his growing strength with the sound of snapping metal.

Chink!

Drifting in the sky above, Lotuus's eyes popped wide open.

Nath got his legs up underneath him. He sprang high in the air, with his clawed fingers reaching for her toes.

She lifted out of harm's way in the nick of time, laughing as Nath descended to the ground. "Hahaha, an impressive try, Nath Dragon," she gloated. "If only you could fly, then maybe you could catch me. If you did, I might even give you a kiss."

Chest heaving, he replied, "Why don't you just come down here and kiss me now? You know you want to."

"I think I'll watch you die first. If there's anything left of that handsome face of yours, I might just keep it. I'll definitely save your hair, and those golden eyes will make an excellent source of illumination for my lanterns."

With the fires roaring all around, Nath noticed the wurmers diving. The elves and dwarves were oblivious to the slaughtering horde descending on them.

I have to do something!

A shadow rose up behind Lotuus. She didn't even notice the form closing in on her. She caught the flicker in Nath's eyes and whirled around in midair. She found herself face to face with Bayzog. The part-elven mage locked his hands on the staff.

"Bayzog!" Nath yelled with delight.

If his friend heard him, he didn't acknowledge it. Instead, the Fairy Empress and Bayzog spun through the air in and angry knot of fury and faded beyond the flames and out of Nath's sight.

"Let her have it, Bayzog!" He stood flatfooted for a moment, gathering his thoughts.

The *ree-rah* sound of the wurmers increased. The entire brood circled down from the sky like a pinwheel of living death. As the circle of flames that surrounded him started to diminish, the elves and dwarves prepared themselves to strike at him.

"Wake up!" Nath yelled. "Wake up!"

Wurmers dove and plucked unsuspecting elves and dwarves from the ground.

"Sultans of Sulfur! I need help!" Nath filled his lungs with a gust of air and let out a mighty dragon call. His voice amplified a hundredfold. Ten giants couldn't have been louder.

A streak of silver slipped through the sky and landed right beside him. It was Slivver. He stood beside Nath and said, "I was beginning to think you would never call. You really are pushing it."

"So you've been keeping an eye on things?" Nath said.

"As you said, it's been very amusing. I really liked the part when they tried to hang you. Hang a dragon?" Slivver snorted. "Who does that? It gave me a chuckle."

"You could have stepped in a little sooner, you know."

"Again, it was your call. So, have you vetted the enemy?"

"Yes," Nath said, watching the circle of flame extinguish. "Slivver, these dwarves and elves need to snap out of this. How can I wake them from the delusion?"

"Use the same voice you used to call me. Deliver the truth to their ears, quickly!"

Facing his aggressors, Nath let out a roar that rattled the flag poles in the stands. The fires extinguished. The advancing elves and dwarves stopped in their tracks. A moment of silence fell. Blinking eyes were rubbed. Heads were shaking.

A bold voice cut through the silence. "What's all this yelling about, Nath?" It was Brenwar. He moved through the dying fires toward the judges' platform.

"You had better come to your senses, Brenwar. Look!" Nath pointed to the wurmer-filled sky.

"Morgdon's peaks! Where did they come from?"

"That hardly matters now. Rally the dwarves!"

"Glenwar! Glenwar! Fetch my Mortuun now!" Brenwar hustled into the quickly forming ranks of his dwarven kin.

"Speaking of weapons, where's Fang, Slivver?"

"Ask and you shall receive." Slivver barked a command in Dragonese. Silver dragons soared beneath the belly of the dropping wurmer. One of them dropped more than a full yard of gleaming steel.

Nath snatched Fang out of the air. "Ah, that's better. Thank you, Slivver."

"My pleasure."

Nath called out, "Laylana! Laylana!"

The elven woman appeared. She'd buckled on a suit of elven chain armor. An almond-shaped helmet like those of the other elven soldiers was tucked under her arm. A sword of fine elven steel filled her grip. "I'm here, Nath!"

"I hope you're in control of your wits now."

She nodded. "I am. So sorry, Nath, but things can be confusing."

"Can you lead the elves?"

"Better than anyone." She stuffed her helmet onto her head. Raising her sword high, she shouted, "For the honor of Elome!"

A wurmer dropped right onto the platform where Nath and Slivver stood. Its neck coiled back, ready to unleash its fiery breath.

Nath struck. Fang sliced clean through the monster. "Guzan, that felt good!"

"May every swing of yours be as deadly as the last." Slivver took to the air, joining the other silvers. Lightning bolts shot from their mouths and ripped into the enemy.

Wurmers dropped from the sky like rain. Some dead. Most alive. The entire fort had become a battlefield of swinging steel and lizard tails. Balls of energy blasted from the wurmers' mouths, downing dwarves and elves in heaps.

Nath battled wurmer after wurmer. Fang's edge dismembered heads, claws, and tails.

The acidic blood of the wurmers sizzled on the ground and burbled on Nath's own scales. The durable elves screamed and shouted. The dwarves hammered away with the fury of a storm. Nath could barely make out what was going on from the swarming activity. But he saw enough to see that some of the elves and dwarves were possessed by the spirits—and fighting alongside the enemy.

Sultans of Sulfur, there are too many enemies. This is a disaster!

CHAPTER 7

BAYZOG HELD ONTO THE ELDERWOOD Staff for dear life.

Lotuus screamed with fury as the pair of them spun through the air like a slow tornado. With eyes hot as fire, she shouted in his face, "Unhand me, you fool! Unhand me!"

The commanding words were a strike in the face filled with arcane power. He reeled. His fingers loosened on the staff.

No! Don't let go, Bayzog! You can't let go!

Lotuus, though fragile in appearance, was a powerful being and strong as a warrior. It took everything he had to hang onto the staff.

Using the Orb of Command, she walloped him in the temple. "Let go! Let go!"

The stunning blow drew spots in his eyes. One of his hands slipped. The other hand barely held on. Using his free forearm, he blocked her swings, all the while maintaining his concentration for his flying spell.

I'm not letting go of this staff. Not for anything!

With the orb still colliding with Bayzog's body, Lotuus said, "You are a fool, wizard. You are nothing but a mortal being, not an all-powerful creature of Nalzambor like me." Her iron grip remained fastened on the Elderwood Staff. "I will dine on the flowers that decorate your grave and use your staff as my lantern." She started into another swing at his ribs.

Bayzog lowered his arm to block her.

In a swift move, Lotuus countered. Pulling her swing from down to up, she clipped him hard in the chin. His fingers slipped, and he sagged toward the ground—half flying, half floating, and fighting to gather his wits.

From out of nowhere, Sasha sailed through the sky and collided into Lotuus's body.

The Orb of Command fell from the Fairy Empress's fingers. Shrieking with rage, she grabbed Sasha by the hair and slung her aside, then lowered the Elderwood Staff at Sasha and discharged a bolt of power.

The energy hit Sasha square in the chest. Her back arched. She gasped, "Gah!" Her body went limp as she tumbled from the sky and hit the ground with a smack.

Fingers outstretched toward his wife, Bayzog screamed, "Sasha!"

His wife lay on the ground. She wasn't moving.

Lotuus cackled. She stuck out her bottom lip and said, "What's the matter, Bayzog? Did your little wife fall and go boom? Too bad. I'll be sure and put your grave right next to hers."

Bayzog's brows buckled. His violet eyes turned into storms. He pushed up his sleeves and flew right at Lotuus. "You will pay!"

"I hardly think so." She turned loose a bolt of power from the head of the staff. It sailed right into his body and lit him up with webs of energy.

He bucked in the sky. His robes became smoking tatters. Suspended in the air, he hung like a dead thing, with his eyes half closed.

"Marvelous. He makes a fine ornament." She descended on him but kept her distance. "Certainly, it will take more energy than that to kill the likes of you." Her eyes narrowed. "You're playing possum, aren't you."

Bayzog opened his eyes. "No, I'm absorbing *my* staff's power and turning it against you! See?" He winked one eye and sent a blast of energy out of the other. The bolt hit Lotuus square in her face.

She tumbled head over heels through the air, screaming.

Bayzog chased after her. He locked his hands on the staff, planted his feet in her gut, and wrenched it free. He summoned the power in the staff. It coursed through his veins like a stream of lava.

Lotuus recoiled. Her wings came to life. She clawed at the air, flying for escape.

Mixing mystic words with the staff's power, he turned loose a bolt of lightning that turned the night to day. The beam hit Lotuus square in the back.

Her wings fluttered and crackled. Still flying, she soared higher in the air, crying out in a language Bayzog didn't know.

"You aren't going anywhere, evil one!" He blasted her again.

Sssrazz! Boom!

And again.

Sssrazz! Boom!

Lotuus's body shrank from the elven form to her smaller fairy form. She spun around to face him and said through her broken features, "A curse on you!"

Dozens of colorful fairies arrived in a mob of colors like candlelight. They surrounded Lotuus and swept her out of sight.

Bayzog dropped from the sky and landed by Sasha. He held her broken body in his arms. Tears dripped down his face onto hers. "Nooooooooo!"

CHAPTER 8

The wurmers came in a variety of sizes, from dogs all the way up to cattle. Brenwar and Glenwar chased after the bigger ones.

Brenwar unleashed a haymaker. The blow collided with a wurmer skull, shattering its bones and horns. "That's how you do it, Son!"

Glenwar, with the girth of a small grizzly bear, brought his battle axe down into the meaty flank of another wurmer. "Like this, Father?" he shouted. He hit the reeling wurmer again. "Dwarven steel likes the taste of this foul fiend's flesh!"

"Watch out for the splatter!" Brenwar warned.

"The what?" Glenwar replied just as he sank his axe into the beast again. The dark blood of the wurmer splashed out onto Glenwar's face and skin. "Morgdon! Its blood burns!"

"I told you to watch out! They have acid for blood. Very nasty stuff." Brenwar fought through a heap of smaller wurmers, bashing their skulls on his way to his son. "That's going to leave a mark."

Glenwar pounded his axe into another wurmer. "I hope it's a scar! A big ugly one!"

Brenwar beamed. Together they smote the same wurmer at the same time. *Krang! Bang!* He shouted, "That's my boy! Hit 'em where it hurts!"

"Where's that?"

"Everywhere!"

Father and son clashed with beast after beast. Bones were shattered. Horns were broken. Wurmers dropped dead on the ground.

The monsters fell fast, but for every one that fell, there came two live ones and sometimes three. Whipping tails struck at the dwarves. Claws ripped at them. Teeth bit into the dwarven metal that coated their bodies. Every able body—and some not so able—fought the wurmers with equally matched ferocity. It reached a point where the dwarves couldn't swing without hitting a wurmer.

Brenwar grabbed a wurmer that latched on to his leg by the neck. He ripped it free and slung it into the air.

Glenwar chopped it asunder, saying, "For Morgdon!"

One of the larger wurmers dropped from the sky and hovered over them. It spat a ball of energy that hit Glenwar square in the back. The dwarf's back caught fire. The smell of burning hair permeated the air. He kept fighting.

"Glenwar! You're on fire!" Brenwar said.

His son twisted his head over his shoulder. His brows buckled. "Nobody burns a dwarf!" Two handed, he slung his axe into the assaulting wurmer. The axe sailed hard and fast, spinning head over handle to bury itself in the wurmer's chest. The beast's wings beat the air for a few long-lasting moments.

Staring, Brenwar had his head cocked to one side when Glenwar said, "Wait for it."

Glenwar's axe blade started to glow red hot. The wurmer let out a bloodcurdling roar. Glenwar made a powerful clap.

The wurmer exploded.

Kah-Poompf!

As chunks of wurmer showered the sky, Brenwar patted out his son's flaming back. "I like it! What is the name of that axe?"

Glenwar opened up his fist. The battle axe flew back into his grip, and he said, "Guulton!"

"Ah, Dwarven for Angry Steel. I like it!" With wurmers and dwarves falling all around them, he said. "Well, stop admiring your weapon. We've got plenty of work to do." He lifted Mortuun high.

Glenwar joined him with Guulton. "For Morgdon!"

"Laylana, how are you holding up?" Nath fought the tide of raging wurmers, devastating them with one chop after another. Fang's razor-keen edge found its home in the hearts of the evil monsters.

Nearby, up to her waist in wurmers, Laylana skewered one monster as she replied, "I'll fight as long as my limbs allow me!"

Nath's arms were tireless. His attacks were quick and precise. He wasn't sure what had happened, but he'd strengthened when the noose tried to take him. His body had reacted, amplifying his power.

I might be stronger, but it's not doing anyone else much good. There are too many. We need more help.

The clash of battle rang out in all directions. Elves and dwarves fought with the wurmers and even with one another in one of the most bizarre battles Nath had ever witnessed. The spirits that possessed some of the people were creating chaos. He saw one elf stab another elf in the back, and elves considered it immoral to kill one another.

"Nath!" Laylana cried out.

A dog-sized wurmer was latched onto her arm. She poked at its scaly hide with a dagger, but the metal didn't bite.

"I'm coming!" He dragged the wurmers hanging on his legs through the wake of battle. At Laylana's side, he grabbed the alligator jaws of the wurmer on her arm, pulled them apart, and flung the monster aside. "You're bleeding bad!"

"Just fight with me to the end," she said while taking a hard swipe at the snapping jaws of another monster.

Nath redoubled his efforts. Nostrils flaring, he tore into every wriggling enemy that skulked within a few feet. The bodies piled up. Acid blood splattered. The wurmers kept on coming. "Great Dragons! If we ever needed help from my brethren, now is the time!"

Above, the silver dragons led by Slivver more than had their hands full. They were faster and stronger, more powerful in magic, but the sheer numbers were overwhelming. It wouldn't be long before the entire fort at the corridor was dead.

Ree-Rah! Ree-Rah! Ree-Rah! Ree-Rah!

The twirling sound of the wurmers became a deafening chant of victory. One right after the other they came.

Laylana moaned, "Ugh!" Her body collapsed under the strike of a wurmer's tail.

Nath hacked the thing in two. "No!"

The elves fought. The dwarves brawled.

It didn't matter. The wurmers wore down the soldiers one rank at a time.

Nath screamed, "GUZAN!"

CHAPTER 9

THE GROUND SHOOK. NATH'S FOOT slipped. A wurmer pounced at the perfect time and slammed right into Nath's chest. He stumbled backward, tripped over a corpse, and landed flat on his back. The wurmer, bigger than Nath, snapped its dripping teeth at his neck. The wurmer's head coiled back and struck, again and again. Its teeth clacked together like collapsing steel traps.

"Get off me!"

The wurmer's jaws clamped down on Nath's arm. The teeth chomped on his scales. Nath released his sword. The battling pair thrashed all over the courtyard. Using his free hand, Nath punched the monster in the head repeatedly.

Whap! Whap! Whap!

Nothing shook the monster. The more Nath hit it, the harder the monster's jaws clamped down. If not for Nath's steel-hardened scales, he would have lost his arm. Rolling over the short grasses of the yard, he wrestled his way toward Fang. The blade lay in the grass, all alone among the fighting masses.

If I can just get my hands on Dragon Claw, I can put an end to this foul beast.

His fingers stretched. They came just inches from the sword.

Almost there!

A wurmer dropped from the sky, landing right on top of Fang. Nath lost sight of his sword completely.

"Of all the lousy breaks!"

The ground trembled again.

"What in Nalzambor?"

The earth moved.

Wurmers screeched.

Suddenly, from the sky above, a hand big enough to engulf him and the wurmer reached down. "Oh no, not giants too!"

The gigantic hand scooped both him and the wurmer up off the ground. A second hand appeared. With a thumb and index finger, the hand pinched the back of the wurmer's neck. The jaws locked on Nath's arm opened. Nath freed his arm. The wurmer's neck snapped, and its body was casually flung aside.

Nath stood up in the giant's hand, turned to face the giant, and said, "Samaz!"

In a loud, slowly drawn-out voice, the eighty-foot-tall Samaz calmly said, "HELLO, NATH."

Nath's heart leaped. "I can't believe it! How did you—"

Samaz cut him off, quickly lowering Nath to the ground, saying, "NO TIME TO TALK. HAVE TO KEEP FIGHTING."

Nath hopped to the ground. He pushed away the wurmer that lay dead on his sword and snatched Fang up. All the while he watched the eighty-foot-tall Samaz go to work against the wurmers. "Go, Samaz! Kill them!"

The wurmers looked like little scaled black birds attacking a man. Samaz swatted them down. He plucked two from the air and smashed them together. They flew right at him like a swarm of stinging bees. He crushed them in his hands—one by one, two by two, and three by three.

Nath pumped his sword in the air. "Take it to them, Samaz!"

Rerry appeared beside him. The young part elf's body shimmered. His eyes were wild with excitement. He shouted alongside Nath, saying, "Yes, take it to them, brother!" He zipped away with blinding speed, goring wurmer after wurmer with his sword. Even Nath's dragon eyes had a hard time keeping up with him. Rerry's furious assault rallied the reeling elves. The hard-fighting soldiers came to life with swinging steel that mowed down their aggressors.

With Fang arcing high in the air, he brought the blade down on a slithering wurmer. "Rerry, I don't know what's gotten into you, but I like it!" He spun to attack a charging wurmer coming at his flank. Halfway into his swing, Rerry breezed in and slew the thing.

Talking really fast, Rerry said with a wide smile, "It's the potions! It's the potions!" He sprinted away again.

Nath almost felt that his swings were clumsy compared to Rerry's superfast strikes. The son of Bayzog was slaying wurmers two to his one.

I can't have this! I need to up my game!

He pulled Dragon Claw free of Fang's pommel. Two handed, he started dropping wurmers at double the pace. Just as he finished up killing four more wurmers, Rerry ran up to him and said, "Ah, two weapons at once. Great idea!"

Rerry filled his free hand with a second sword from a fallen elven soldier. Moving from wurmer to wurmer, he killed them while saving one life after another.

"Rerry," Nath called out, "Did you get those potions from Brenwar's chest?"

Sneaking up behind Nath while downing a wurmer, Rerry replied, "Yes."

"Where—"

In a blur, Rerry sped in front of him, dropped the chest at his feet, and sped away again, saying, "Whooopeeee!"

A wurmer dropped from the sky, landing on the chest. It spat a ball of energy at Nath.

He knocked it aside with the flat of his blade. With Dragon Claw, he killed the wurmer with a shot to the neck. That was when he noticed Laylana fighting off three wurmers at once. She was cut up and bleeding in several places. "Rerry! Help Lay—"

Rerry rushed in with dazzling speed. He cut down two. Laylana finished the third.

Nath popped the chest open. His fingers fumbled through the racks of potions. He grabbed one filled with a sparkling swirl of yellow fluid. "Rerry—"

"Got it!" Rerry said, snatching the vial from Nath's fingers. He took it to Laylana.

"That was for me," Nath said.

Rerry came back with his head tilted to one side. "Really?"

"No, I'm just teasing."

THOOOOOM!

Nath turned. Behind him, the gargantuan Samaz was stomping wurmers to death beneath his sandals. They made a crunchy squishing sound.

"They crunch like cockroaches!" Rerry shouted. He cupped his hands over his mouth. "Keep it up, brother!"

"How did he get so big?" Nath asked.

"I gave him two of them!" Rerry said. He was beaming. His head seemed to turn all directions at once. "Got to go!" He dashed away like he had been shot out of a crossbow.

Nath was smiling all the way up to the point where Rerry slowed down and stumbled. Above him, Samaz let out a loud *hiccup* and started to shrink.

Oh no, the potions are wearing off!

CHAPTER 10

SENSING THE COMING CHANGE OF the tide of battle, Nath met up with Laylana beside the strongbox. He rummaged through the vials. "Aw, I'm never sure which potion does what."

"Let me give it a look," a newcomer said. It was Ben. He was puffing for breath. His sword rested on his sagging shoulders. He had nasty wounds all over. "I could really use one of those yellow ones."

Nath flicked a vial over to Ben. "You really are a glutton for punishment, aren't you Ben?"

He drank down the vial and said, "What can I say? No one can take a better beating than me. Nath, what are we going to do? There are still too many."

"I have a feeling that even if we drank all of these potions, it still wouldn't be enough."

Stepping forward, Ben said, "I volunteer."

"Volunteer for what?"

"To drink all of the potions."

"Don't be silly. That would kill you."

"Look!" Laylana said. She pointed at the sky.

The wurmer forces that still dove and attacked broke off the aerial assault. Their long necks twisted toward the black clouds. Their loud, intimidating *ree-rah* sound fell silent when the clouds lit up with fire.

Nath lifted up on his toes. "Can it be?"

A dragon dropped out of the clouds. He glided with a host of other dragons behind him, but none were bigger than him. His scales were armor of many metallic colors, his wings were huge and black. He was larger than the flying fortress sky raiders but smaller than the tremendous landlocked Hull dragons.

"Guzan!" Nath Screamed. "Yes! It's Guzan!"

The wurmers, led by the biggest of their buzzing brood, spearheaded an attack on Guzan. Even the ones that battled on the ground broke free of the melee and launched themselves into the air with angry shrieks.

But Guzan wasn't alone. Behind him were dragons of all sorts: cinnamon-colored crimson dynamos, steel dragons with scales like plated mail armor, golden flames... There weren't just dozens of them like the last time Nath encountered Guzan. This time there were hundreds.

In a gust of fiery breath, Guzan set dozens of the much smaller wurmers on fire. They dropped from the sky like flaming raindrops.

The elves and dwarves let out a rousing cheer. The slaughter of the wurmers in the sky became jubilation.

"Oh, if I could only be up there!" Nath said. Rerry and Samaz had returned to normal and gathered by his side. Also with him were Ben and Laylana. "I want to fly! I need to be a dragon again!"

The golden flame dragons wove a path of destruction through the wurmers with the agility of cats. Their long golden claws fileted the evil spawn. Their breath weapon—a cone of radiant energy—knocked the scales from the wurmers' backs.

The steel dragons—every bit the size of bull dragons but a bit leaner—ripped up the wurmers with devastating effect.

The sky became fireworks of death and devastation. The colors were so bright and the sounds so thunderous and powerful that the people around Nath shielded their eyes and covered their ears. A burning wurmer crashed through the stands. Another one fell on top of it. It wasn't all wurmers, though. Many dragons met their doom. Dozens of them spiraled from the sky, covered in the vicious wurmers, driving them to the grave. When they hit, they hit hard. The elves and dwarves went to work, finishing off any wurmer that might have survived the fall.

Nath and his comrades did what they could.

When the frightening battle ended, all of the wurmers were dead, but hosts of the dragons still remained.

Guzan glided down from the sky. He made a soft landing in the middle of the fort. His body crushed all of the dead beneath him. Guzan's magnificent form was very much like Balzurth's.

"I can't thank you enough, Guzan. If you hadn't come to our aid, we would have been slaughtered."

Guzan shook his head up and down. With a quick flick, he slung a gored wurmer from his horns. With his thoughts, he spoke to Nath. *My name parts from your lips many times. I came by to tell you to curb your use of it.*

"Guzan, I apologize, I never meant any offense by it."

The grand dragon's throat rumbled with laughter. *I tease with you, young king. The honor is mine. Nath, I am sorry for the loss of your father. He was always a dear brother of mine. The truth is, I was more than eager to lock my horns in this battle. I was more than eager to come to your aid. I'm glad you called.* With his head, he gestured toward the other dragons. Some had landed. Others roamed the skies. *We all are. The death of Balzurth left a foul taste in all of our mouths.*

Nath took a moment to soak in the heat that radiated from Guzan's body. It was like bathing in the warmth of the sun. "So, I can count on you then, to help in the fight against the titans and to take back Dragon Home? I'll need your help convincing others to fight. Certainly there are more of us than them. We must rally."

Nath, I will do what I can, but know this. The dragons, possibly the better part of them, will struggle to follow a dragon who is still a man.

Nath frowned.

Guzan tilted Nath's chin up with his claw. *Keep your head up, Nath. Even your father had trouble corralling the dragons when he needed them, and he was all dragon.*

"If he couldn't do it, I can't imagine how I'm going to do it." He shrugged and looked over his arms and legs. "Not like this, for certain."

Nath, I've never seen Nalzambor in the midst of such peril. This outlandish horde threatens to destroy the entire world. Nothing will survive. Nath, whatever you have to do, you must do it. All of the good in Nalzambor depends on it. Guzan's wings spread out and beat against the wind. His clawed feet lifted from the ground. *Find a way, Nath Dragon. You must find a way!*

As all the dragons departed through the smoky vapors of battle in the sky, Bayzog approached. He had Sasha's limp body cradled in his arms.

Rerry and Samaz rushed over to their father. "What's wrong with Mother?"

CHAPTER 11

"She lives, children." Bayzog's smooth skin was crinkled behind the eyebrows. Sasha, on the other hand, looked like she'd been struck by a bolt of lightning. Her robes were seared. Her hair was frizzy. "She took a very deadly shot from Lotuus."

In a gentle grip, Nath took Sasha by the wrist. "Her heartbeat is very strong. No surprise, seeing how she is such a strong woman."

"Indeed," Bayzog replied. He lowered Sasha to the ground. Rerry and Samaz tended to her. The sons were on either side, patting her arms and holding her hands.

"Will she wake up, Father?" Rerry asked. "And where is Lotuus? Tell me you killed her."

Leaning on his staff, Bayzog shook his head. "I'm afraid she escaped." The wizard's robes were tattered and had several burn holes in them.

Nath gave Bayzog a little nudge in the shoulder. "Don't feel bad, Bayzog. We'll get her. The important thing is that your wife lives."

"I know, Nath, but I had her. So close." Bayzog made a fist and shook it. "It's too dangerous to leave one like that living."

Sasha coughed and sputtered. Her eyes opened. With a lazy look, she said, "I feel like all of my bones are separated from the joints. Tell me it isn't so, children."

With his hair hanging in his eyes, Samaz said, "You're fully intact, Mother."

"I don't feel like I am." She squeezed her eyes shut. "Oh, my head hurts. It hasn't felt this bad since the first and last time I drank dwarven ale."

Rerry chuckled. "*You* drank dwarven ale? *You?*"

Sasha shushed him with a feeble motion of her hand. "Please, don't speak so loud."

With his finger digging in his ear, Ben walked up and said, "I know what you mean, Sasha, my ears are ringing too. Boy, the things we go through for the ones we love. It's painful sometimes, isn't it?" He handed her a yellow potion.

She drank it down. "I couldn't have said it better myself, Ben. Love hurts, but it's worth it." Sasha took her sons by the hands. "Help me up now."

Gently, they brought her to her feet. "Thank you." She hugged them both. Bayzog joined them.

"Ah, isn't that touching," Brenwar stated. He and Glenwar marched right toward them. The father and son were splattered from head to toe in wurmer guts. Patches of beard and the coarse hair on their arms were missing. "The fight isn't over yet."

"What do you mean, Brenwar?" Nath asked.

With a thumb over the shoulder, Brenwar said, "Look yonder. Many of my kin and the elves are possessed. What's left of us are trying to corral them without killing them." He grumbled. "There aren't so many left of us, however."

Across the field of corpses—dragons, dwarves, elves and wurmers—a nasty scuffle broke out among the two races. Black-eyed elves and dwarves struck out against their brethren.

Nath's jaws clenched. "That's a problem, all right."

"I think I know what to do, Nath." Bayzog held out the Elderwood Staff and something else: the Orb of Command. "I believe I can dispel them."

"That's an awful lot of power in your little old hands, Bayzog." Nath studied the eerie swirl in the black sphere. "Ofttimes, things that powerful do more harm than good."

"I know, but what choice to we have? I…we have to try something."

With Fang still in hand, Nath said, "Do what you must, but I'm staying close. Glenwar, Laylana, have your forces corral the possessed. Quickly. I don't want any of them escaping."

It took less than an hour for the soldiers to corral their brethren who were possessed by the spirits. The soldiers had them encircled. Dwarves and elves hissed like snakes and hurled foul insults at their kindred. Facing the angry throng, Bayzog took to the stands and spread his arms wide. The Elderwood Staff was in one hand and the Orb of Command in the other. He began to speak in mystic Elven.

A chill wind picked up, standing up the hairs on Nath's neck. A tingling sensation ran up his arms. *I'm not sure I like this.*

An arc of energy leapt from the orb to the staff, connecting them. The fiery jewel mounted in the top of the Elderwood Staff burned like brilliant starlight. The courtyard was washed over in light as bright as day. Bayzog's eyes were fires of violet. In ancient Elven, he spoke with power. "Begone, evil spirits! Nalzambor take you! Begone!"

The possessed elves and dwarves howled, moaned, and screeched.

Laylana wrapped her arms around Nath. Eyes big as the moon, she trembled.

Apparitions floated out of the bedeviled bodies, swirling and twisting in the air. The shapeless ghosts howled in ear-piercing screams that could freeze the marrow in men's bones. Bayzog's light became stronger, the spirits' wailings weaker. One by one, the spirits turned into puffs of smoke.

Pffi! Pffi! Pffi!

Bayzog's words of power ended. The crystal in the Elderwood Staff faded. The glow of the Orb of Command went out. Bayzog's shoulders slumped. He wobbled and fell.

Samaz caught him just before his head hit the stands.

Brenwar grunted. "Humph, a little bump on the head might have done him some good."

CHAPTER 12

Selene, Sansla, and Gorlee sloshed their way to the other side of the stream. The fog had finally lifted. Gorlee had returned to human form. The changeling clutched at his side and rubbed his ribs.

Selene gave him a hand out of the water. "How are you, Gorlee?"

He didn't reply. Instead, he sat down on the bank a few yards away from the stream, gawping at the stone giants lying dead in the water that rushed over their protruding heads, elbows, and knees as if they were part of the rocks of the landscape.

"They're stone giants. Now that they're dead, they'll petrify and become one with the lands." Sansla flapped the water from his wings. "All of the fallen return to Nalzambor from where they came."

Selene scanned the sky. "Do you think Tylabahn is gone?"

"It's difficult to say, but if she survived, it wouldn't surprise me one bit if she revealed herself in some monstrous form. Perhaps she'll show up in a bear or something. Though I doubt such a creature could hold her for long." Sansla kneeled down beside Gorlee and laid a hand on the changeling's shoulder. "That was impressive, what you did."

Jerking away, Gorlee said, "Get off of me!"

Hands up, Sansla said, "Easy now." His eyes slid over to Selene's.

She saw his uneasy look. "Perhaps he needs a drink. I imagine the battle was very stressful."

"Sorry," Gorlee said, shaking his head. His body quavered. "Sansla, I apologize. I just have the jitters. My skin… Oh, how should I put it? …is sensitive. I'll be fine. Just give me a few moments."

"Certainly." Sansla backed away and shrugged his eyebrows at Selene.

She'd dealt with Gorlee before and had a good grasp of his powers. She'd even gone as far as taking control of him. Had used him to fool Nath Dragon by having Gorlee pretend to be Sasha. Before that, Gorlee had fallen into her hands when he posed as Nath Dragon. He hadn't fooled her then, and if something was wrong with Gorlee, he wouldn't fool her now. "Gorlee, when the titan fell, did you notice anything strange? Was there a shudder or a separation that you felt?"

"There was something." Gorlee combed his fingers through his hair. "It was like what you say. The entire body shook when I took it down. Something angry passed right through me, turning my stomach inside out. Then it was gone." He rubbed his mouth. "I don't remember a few of those seconds after the battle. I just remember wading in the water." He looked up at Selene. "I was following the two of you. I'll tell you this though, I'm bushed." He fell back in the reeds. "Just give me a few minutes to rest my eyes."

Before Selene could get another word out, Gorlee started softly snoring. "Well, that was easier than putting a baby down to sleep." The sky cleared in several places, and the distant stars twinkled from beyond. Scattered rainclouds moved quickly through the night, with a rumble of thunder here and there. "Any thoughts on the next step, Sansla?"

"Perhaps we should continue toward Narnum. If Tylabahn survived, she'll certainly head that way. There should be some signs of her if she makes it very far, which I imagine a spirit as powerful as her could. At least fortune is on our side, putting us in such a remote area."

"I agree. No doubt she'll try to take over any varmint she can, but I don't think they can control much of those mindless things. We just better hope that she doesn't find anything formidable from here to there. As a matter of fact, we must see to it." She cracked her neck from side to side. Looking at Gorlee, she said, "I hate to admit it, but I could use some rest myself. What about you?"

"I don't sleep," said Sansla. "Please, take your rest. I'll keep watch over the both of you."

"How is your shoulder?" Selene said, taking a seat in the tall grasses.

Rolling his shoulder, Sansla's lips curled a little. "It's been better. It should be healed by morning."

"Good. Sansla, I don't normally require rest myself."

"I thought all dragons were known for their long slumbers."

"Some, yes, like Nath, but not all. If I haven't awoken before dawn, don't hesitate to shake me. And if Gorlee wakes, wake me as well. I just need for my mind and eyes to relax a few moments. It shouldn't take too much time."

Sansla gave her a firm nod and politely said, "I understand, Selene."

She lay back with her sword resting over her chest, staring up at the sky. Sansla's hulking form moved away and vanished from the corner of her eye. She'd begun to trust Sansla. He was stalwart, honest, and brave. Despite the curse of his scary appearance, he still chose good over evil. It was clear that he could have gone another way. Certainly, he must have been tempted to.

His own kind rejected him, yet he still cares for them. I can't say I would do the same.

She curled up in the grass and used her tail for a pillow.

I want to trust people, I really do, but I must redeem myself before they trust me. Even then, there won't be any guarantees.

CHAPTER 13

THE WRECKAGE AT THE CORRIDOR was mortifying. Elves and dwarves by the thousands had died. Their broken bodies were carried away, with great care, into the surrounding plains. The dwarves were taken beyond the boundary of Morgdon. The elves hauled their dead off through the gates of Elome. The preparation had gone on for days.

Nath and Ben stood inside open graves, shoveling out the dirt.

"How are you feeling, Ben?" Nath asked as he scooped out a shovelful of dirt and flung it aside.

Wiping the sweat from his brow with his forearm, Ben stopped what he was doing. "I hate to complain, Nath, but my back feels like it's on fire. I'm tempted to stop digging, but the aching is another reminder that I'm alive." He looked around. "Heh, I didn't want Brenwar to hear me saying that. He might think I was taking a shine to him."

"Dwarves don't shine," Nath said, making a grim smile. "Don't worry, I don't think you'll see him on the side of the elven graves. He'll have his hands full on his side of the boundary." Nath noted the hollow look in Ben's eyes. The old soldier's gaze followed the endless rows of graves. "You've dug many graves, haven't you."

"Huh? Oh, yes, too many. When you were gone all those years, I did plenty of soldiering. I buried more dead than most could count. I can only name the ones I knew, but I never forget any of their faces. I had troubled sleep for years because of it. Nath, is it a good thing to harden your heart so that you are not disturbed by those things? So many are dead, but I haven't shed a tear. It doesn't seem right."

"It's not right or wrong, Ben. We all deal with grief differently so that we can cope with it." Nath felt a flutter in his heart. His throat tightened. "It hurts me knowing that so many died and I couldn't stop it. All I know is that the elves and dwarves had faith. They lived life based off what they believed, and they were ready to die for it. I find comfort knowing they're in a better place now." He looked up into the clouds. "I'm sure they're watching, so do them honor and make nice graves for their bodies."

"Honor the dead," Ben said. He dug his shovel into the soft dirt again. "And they will honor you."

They dug for another hour and made two more graves, talking on and off about many things. Life, death, love, and family.

"You know, Dragon, I'm going to assume I'll die before you, seeing how you're a dragon and live ten or twenty years to my one, but would you do me the honor of burying me when my time comes?"

"I'd rather not think about it, but it will be my honor."

"Will you see to it that my funeral is grander than Brenwar's funeral?"

Nath started laughing. "One thing's for sure, Ben. I'll miss your sense of humor."

Ben stopped digging. "I wasn't joking."

"Oh."

"No, of course I was." Ben resumed digging with a smile. "If Brenwar is there, make a spectacle of it, like some dragons and a parade. That ought to get him riled. Ha! I can see his cheeks puffing up now." He imitated Brenwar's voice. "What kind of man gets a dwarven funeral? He doesn't even have a beard, by Morgdon!"

Nath laughed so hard his belly hurt. Some of the other elven diggers cast him impolite glances. He took a long breath and let it out slowly. "Ben, I admire your candid attitude toward this. It's uncommon but refreshing."

"I know when my time comes I'll be in a better place. In the meantime, I'll fight the good fight, until that time comes."

"Hear! Hear!" Nath was just finishing up the grave when an approaching elf caught his eye. It was

Laylana. She looked as tired and marred as the rest of them, but her green eyes were still bright. "How are we doing, Laylana?"

"Nath, it isn't necessary that you complete this task. The elves will handle it, and more help has been sent for." She grabbed Ben's shovel and took it away from him. "You either, Ben. Please, rest a moment, the both of you. I bring good news."

Ben crawled up out of the grave with a groan. "Is it a cure for a backache?"

"We have maidens who can—"

"No more maidens. Those last ones took my mind away. I still can't remember the better part of yesterday. No, I'll just take the pain and keep my wits, thank you."

"What is it, Laylana?"

"I've spoken with the elven judges. They have spoken with the dwarven judges. They came to a majority decision that your name will be cleared, and it will be announced that you are not guilty of the murders of Laedorn and Uurluuk."

"Huh, I suppose that is wonderful news. Do you have it in writing?"

She handed him a scroll.

Ben limped over. "What does it say, Dragon?"

Nath unrolled the parchment. "I'll be, I am no longer accused—not that I should have been in the first place." He handed the scroll back to Laylana. "I just wish it had never come to this. Laedorn would be proud of you, Laylana."

"Thank you. He would be proud of you too." She flagged her elven escort down with a wave of her hand. He marched right over and presented her the bow Akron and a quiver full of arrows. She dismissed the soldier with a nod. "I think this belongs to you, Nath."

"It's been too long." Nath took the weapon and slung the quiver over his shoulder. The bow was compact in size. He expanded it to full length. *Snap. Clatch. Snap.* A bowstring unraveled from the grip and fed itself from the notch at the top to the notch at the bottom. Nath tested the string. "Akron feels good." He tried to hand it to Ben.

Ben shrank back. "No, Dragon. I lost it last time. I won't risk it again."

"Ben, everyone deserves a second chance, and in some cases a third or fourth, even. Besides, it's not like you misplaced Brenwar's anvil."

"No."

Nath let it go and said to Laylana, "So, now that we know Lotuus is the murderer behind it all, are the elves and dwarves going to pursue, or should we?"

Laylana showed a pretty smile. "I'm glad you asked."

CHAPTER 14

Night had fallen again. Just outside the fort at the Corridor, Nath stood by a bonfire on the dwarven side of the boundary. In the background, the dwarves pounded funeral kettle drums with a gentle, steady beat among the sound of the chirping crickets. Laylana, Bayzog, Sasha, Rerry, Samaz, and Ben were with him. The fire cast shadows on the edges of their faces, giving them all a hard and haggard look.

"I don't know, Laylana," said Nath. "Capturing Lotuus won't be easy. She's a fairy, and she's leagues from here by now. Besides, they fly. It's difficult to track a creature whose feet don't touch the ground."

"The elves and dwarves insist that she be brought to justice. They'll need your help, Nath. You're the best tracker in Nalzambor."

Bayzog stepped away from Sasha. "He's also the Dragon King, Laylana. His shoulders already bear the burden of countless responsibilities. Lotuus is neither the first nor the last of the murderers in this world to run free. There are more than we can count. The elves and the dwarves should focus on fighting this war against the giants, titans, and wurmers. You need to convince them of that. Lotuus is nothing but a distraction."

"How can you say that?" Laylana argued. "That evil fairy was more than a distraction. She took down our leaders. Without leadership, we are a ship without a rudder. What happens when she uses another clever disguise and strikes at us again?"

"I find that unlikely. This was a setup to frame Nath Dragon," Bayzog continued. "Besides, the elves and dwarves are now privy to her tricks. It's unlikely she'll attempt something like that again. It would be a perilous task, even for her."

The elven princess's emerald eyes narrowed on Bayzog. She started to say something then looked away.

"Laylana," Nath said. "I want justice for your grandfather as much as you do. Please believe me when I say we all do, but right now, we need to focus on the bigger picture. As much as I hate to say it, for now, let bygones be bygones. Once we win this war, we'll be able to bring all of our adversaries to justice. Especially Lotuus." He put his hands on her shoulders. "Laylana, if there is anyone for you to direct your anger toward, it's me. I'm the one who freed Lotuus."

Her eyes flashed. She pulled away. "What?"

Nath quickly recounted the story of how Lotuus had been freed when he and Brenwar began the search for his mother, Grahleyna. "I never imagined it would lead to all this," he finished.

Laylana stood silent with her jaw clenched. She was a strong-willed woman. A true warrior. It was clear that a battle raged inside her. With her hand gripping the pommel of her sword, she said, "I think it's best that we part company. Enjoy your endeavors, O Dragon King. Hopefully they won't unlock any more troubles."

"Laylana, please," Nath said, reaching for her.

She slipped his grasp and stormed away.

He stood shaking his head. That guilty feeling swelled inside him. No one was speaking, but everyone was looking at him.

Do they all blame me for this?

"She doesn't have any more right to blame you than I do," grumbled a voice on the other side of the blazing bonfire. It was Brenwar. He marched around with Glenwar by his side. "Those elves are a touchy bunch. They always think the fault is with someone besides themselves. As if they never made a mistake. No, the dwarves know what happened. They accept it. The elves should too. Instead, they point fingers."

"I appreciate the words, Brenwar, but she's hurt from her loss."

"She needs to get over it. If they want to chase Lotuus and her fairies, let them. The dwarves, we're in this one to the end. Right, Glenwar?"

"Right, Father!"

Even though Brenwar's words made Nath feel a little better, Laylana's angry departure still ate at him. They'd need the elves to win this battle. The last thing they needed was for the elves to be against him. He needed Laylana. "I'm going to go try to talk with her again."

"No, Nath," Sasha said, coming to her feet. She eased up to him. "Let her be angry. She'll be easier to talk to once her flames have cooled."

"Are you certain she doesn't want me to chase after her?"

"In most cases, you'd be right, but not this time. This time you might get a sword stuck in you. Leave her be. We have much to discuss." She pulled him away from the fire. "Please, sit."

"Yes, Dragon, sit," Ben said. "My legs get tired from watching you stand."

Nath sat down between Ben and Sasha. "Your legs get tired when you sleep, old man."

"I'm not that old, but now that you mention it, my legs do get a little restless in my slumber. Heh-heh."

"Dwarves' legs never tire," Glenwar said.

"Aye," Brenwar agreed.

"That's because they aren't legs, they're tree stumps," Rerry commented.

Glenwar bulled up. "Nobody calls a dwarf a stump."

"Apologies, I meant bearded stump," Rerry replied.

"Or bearded boulder," Samaz added.

Glenwar reached down and grabbed both sitting brothers by their collars. He picked them both up off the ground. Rerry and Samaz's eyes grew bigger. "What did you say about my beard?"

"It's a fine beard," Rerry said.

"Yes, very distinguished," Samaz said.

"That's what I thought you said." Glenwar set them both down.

Nath swore by the proud gleam in Brenwar's eyes that he was smiling inside.

Clawing at his beard, Brenwar said, "So, what's it going to be, Nath? Do we resume our quest to find Selene?"

"I'm leaning that way. But it will be weeks before the dwarven funerals end. I hate to depart on the next leg of the journey without you."

"You aren't going anywhere without me!" Brenwar bumped Glenwar's ribs with his elbow. "Glenwar will represent my family in my stead, won't you, Son."

"Aye."

"That's good to know," Nath said. Slivver came forward from out of the darkness. The silver shade dragon whispered in his ear. "Everyone, please, excuse me."

CHAPTER 15

ATH RESTED HIS HANDS ON a dead golden flame dragon. The beautiful creature was bigger than a horse and twice as long from horn to tail. "He's so magnificent. None of our brethren even look dead. Have you ever noticed that, Slivver?"

"I have. That's one of the differences between the dragons and the other mortals. Dragons don't decay as soon. Their scales keep them stitched together until the last of their magic fades."

"I know." Nath traced his fingers over the dragon's golden scales. There was still warmth within. "So, you believe the fetchers should have arrived by now?"

"The fetchers are never late. That's what worries me. They are as steady as the rising sun and falling moon. My concern is that something happened to them. It's not a good sign."

"No, no it isn't. Perhaps there is too much fear in the skies."

"It didn't stop Guzan."

Nath closed the eyes of the golden flame, saying to him, "I'll make sure you are given the proper burial that you deserve. All of you."

Burying dwarves and elves was one matter, but with dragons, it was entirely different. It wouldn't be possible for men to bury dragons, at least not the large ones. No, death with dragons was treated differently. Many dragons, when they lived to be venerable and had few days left to live, would pass through the murals of Dragon Home, never to be seen again. Other dragons, such as the ones fallen in battle, were taken to the Necropolis of Dragons. Nath knew of it, but he'd never been there.

The Necropolis caretakers were the dragons called fetchers. They were behemoths of the sky, quiet and somber, with scales that were a ruddy gray and brown. The last time Nath had seen them was after the last dragon war at the Floating City. Scores of them had floated down from the clouds and plucked up the dead. With powerful wings, they lifted off into the air and carried the dead away, never to be seen or heard from again. It was a somber and sobering event, just like being in the presence of his dead kin was now.

Nath wiped the tears that formed in the corners of his eyes. "We can't leave them like this."

"We won't, but if you must leave, I'll be honored to stay and guard them. We won't let any scavengers or poachers get to them."

"I know you won't. Perhaps I should call the fetchers."

"It is within your authority to do so, Nath. You are the Dragon King. Honestly, I would like to see you exercise your authority more often. Though I agree with what Guzan said, that many dragons will have trouble following you in man form, there are still plenty who will."

"The truth is, I'm still not used to commanding."

"You're a natural, Nath, just like Father."

"Let's hope." Nath rubbed his chin with his index finger. "Hmmm…you've actually given me an idea." He made a little whistle. Two seekers showed up in an instant and hovered right in front of his eyes.

"What do you have in mind, Nath?"

"I think it's high time I started taking more of your brotherly advice. I might not be able to be everywhere at once, but I can certainly make better use of my allies."

"You mean your subjects."

"Yes, my subjects." He petted one of the seekers that landed on his shoulder. "But I serve them the same way I expect them to serve me."

"So, what's your plan for them?"

"Eckubahn has done a much better job of using his resources than I have. It's given him a huge advantage. Lotuus has fed off that too. Perhaps it's time we started spying on them."

Arms crossed in front of him, Slivver said, "I like the way you think."

Nath spoke in Dragonese to the seekers. He gave them a description of Lotuus and the fairies. He told them about her black, pink, and white features, down to the very last detail.

The little bumble bee–colored dragons nodded. Their tongues flickered out of their mouths. Seconds later, they buzzed away on their hummingbird wings.

"Well done," Slivver said.

"That should satisfy me, and hopefully it will ease things with Laylana. Those seekers will be able to find the fairies faster than we ever could."

"Indeed. Now what?"

Nath looked over the field of his dead dragon kin. "I'm going to see to it that they are buried, and that my father gets a proper burial, too."

Chapter 16

Eckubahn sat on his throne made from dragon bones. His grand chamber—built in the center of Narnum—was silent. Many giant warriors stood guard in a protective circle around him. Their backs were facing Eckubahn. Huddled on the floor were people bowing in worship. They brought gifts. Baskets of food. Boxes of gold and jewels. They laid the objects at his feet while singing his praises—until he silenced them with a command that froze the marrow in their bones. No one dared to move. Except one.

A lone man wearing the black robes of one of his priests lifted his head toward the throne.

Eckubahn tilted his head in the man's direction, catching his eye. His flaming head flared. In his chamber-filling voice, he said, "You, stand."

The priest did. His fingers clutched the sides of his robes. He averted his stare and licked his sweating upper lip.

"You cast your gaze on me, priest," Eckubahn said. "Tell me, what gives you this right over all the others?"

"I only mean to appease you, great one." The priest tried to stop shaking, but he couldn't. "I'm sorry. Your countenance delights me."

"My countenance." Eckubahn's voice rose. "This horrifying wreck of a body that I possess? It's disgusting. My true appearance is ten times beyond magnificent. Why do you mock me, oh servant of mine? Why do you dare?"

"I-I-I meant—"

"Fool!" Eckubahn slammed his fist on the throne's newly reconstructed arm, chipping away some of the new stone. "I say what you can and cannot admire!" He leaned forward. "You are a weak little servant. You lack discipline. You did not look up at me out of respect but out of a lack thereof. You fear me, yes, but you tire of bowing. You weakling. Bowing before me was too much for your fragile body to bear. I need strong followers with strength in their backs. You are not one of them."

"I adore you, Eckubahn. I swear it on my family! Let me remain your servant."

"You want to be my servant?" Eckubahn scooped the cringing man up off the floor with one hand. Holding the man before his eyes, he said, "You may serve me by being an outlet to my anger." His eyes flashed. The hand that clutched the cleric caught on fire.

The cleric screamed. His robes turned to hot yellow flames. His skin turned from ash to dust, leaving only a body of steaming bones.

Eckubahn slung the skeleton across the chamber. It smashed into pieces when it hit the wall. "Does anyone else care to take a look at me? Or your fallen brother? I have plenty of anger that still needs a release."

Every human bowing on the floor balled up even tighter, aside from one. A single person stood up among the rest. She lowered her hood, revealing her tattooed face, and looked right at him. "O great Eckubahn, allow me to be the subject of your wrath."

"Come forward."

Long and slender, the bald woman glided over with the ease of a snake. She looked right at him, but not in the eyes—instead, the chest.

"What is your name?"

"I am your servant, Forever."

His brow arched, "Forever. I like that name."

"It is yours to command, Grand Titan."

He leaned close and sniffed her. "You reek of devilry. I like it. Your body is weak, but your spirit is strong. A rare thing among the mortals. Forever, you will command my fragile flock. Make them stronger than iron."

She took a knee and bowed. "It will be done."

"Hear this, servants. Forever is now your commander, imbued with power accordingly. To cross her is to cross me."

Isobahn, the brother titan, entered the chamber. His great body was a little bigger than those of the other giants in the room. Bones of men and dragons jeweled his neck and wrists. His features were cruel and terrifying. "Have you received word from the trial of Nath Dragon?" he asked

"I'm well aware of it, Isobahn. My flock shrinks—by my own hand as well as those of my enemies. But I've found promise in this little one." He patted Forever's head. "Isn't she a marvel?"

"No. If you want to marvel me, then we need to finish off Nath Dragon."

"Nath Dragon will be ours soon enough."

"I don't share your confidence, Eckubahn. Lotuus assured us that the trial would be the nails in his coffin. But he survived. Again."

"An enemy the likes of him should not be so easy to kill. I'm not happy, but I'm not surprised. Tell me, dear brother, how did you learn of his survival?"

"I could ask you the same." Isobahn walked right up to the throne. He leered down at Forever. "Move, puny creature."

She remained in place.

Isobahn lifted his foot above her head.

"Brother," Eckubahn said, "Please don't harm our most willing servant. Forever, you are dismissed. I'll summon you later. Now, take your tribe of weaklings and punish them, thoroughly."

"As you wish, Lord Eckubahn."

The priests departed the chamber, leaving only the giants. Isobahn scowled. "Your fascination with these mortals is wasteful." He kicked the treasures laid at Eckubahn's feet. "It makes you weak."

Striking like a snake, Eckubahn locked his fingers around Isobahn's throat. "Weak! You dare call me weak, brother! You would still be burning chattel behind the Great Dragon Wall if not for me!"

Isobahn managed to sputter out, "Bunk! If not for me, you would have died at the hands of Balzurth! You would be dead in body and spirit then. How quickly you forget."

Eckubahn squeezed harder. "I'm not going to kill you now, brother." He shoved his brother to the floor. "Consider the debt repaid."

Isobahn rubbed his throat. "You can't kill me anyway." He swatted away more treasure. "Your fascination with worldly things was always your weakness."

"We are conquering this world." Eckubahn sat back down. "I'll enjoy the spoils all I wish. I did not ask for these things."

Isobahn rose. "What is to be done with Nath Dragon?"

"Brother, now is your time to shine. If you want Nath Dragon so bad, then go and get him. But I want him alive."

"I can't promise that. A live enemy is a dangerous thing."

"Then stay here and I'll send some of my pets."

"No, I'll do as you wish. I'll gather some forces."

"No, Brother, I want you to do it, and I want you to do it alone."

"You jest?"

"Are you scared of the little dragon?"

"No, I'm only scared of bad decisions. That's what got us trapped behind the wall last time." He headed out of the great chamber. "Goodbye, Brother."

"I'm unclear. Are you going to fulfill my request, or not?"

Isobahn exited the chamber.

With his head aflame, Eckubahn brooded.

CHAPTER 17

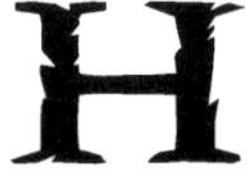

HARD RAIN CAME DOWN SO heavily that Selene couldn't see her hand in front of her face. Soaked from head to toe, she stood in the entryway of an abandoned outpost. With its glory days centuries behind it, the old stone building was just big enough to host a few dozen soldiers. The stony spires were thick in moss and ivy. Two sections of the walls had fallen inward, making a pile of rubble and overgrowth. There were several places, however, that provided shelter from the heavy rain.

Sansla eased in behind Selene. With a few quick flaps of his wings, he shook off the water from underneath the archway. The rain was so loud that she could barely hear his low voice when he said, "The rains have been more frequent and heavier this season. I don't recall one such as this in my lifetime."

"Me neither." She stood proudly in her glorious skirted armor, wringing water out of her hair and cloak. "It's nothing to be concerned about, is it?"

"The weather in Nalzambor has always been steady. Storms come and go, and there are even dry spells that occur in the seasons, but these storms disturb me. I've never noticed so many dark clouds in the sky before."

"I've heard that weather like this comes every thousand years or so."

"Perhaps. I've never paid much attention to it. But there is a saying among the elves that in Nalzambor's last days, the world will be in travail. There are even scrolls that speak to great wars and horrible famines becoming commonplace." His chin dipped. "We are in the midst of a second great war within only a few years of the last."

"What are you saying? Is the world going to end?"

"Nothing we know of lasts forever in this world. Everything, everyone passes and fades." He stuck his open palm out in the rain. It filled quickly. "I feel that if we don't triumph in this war, this time there won't be anything left worth fighting for." He brought his hand in and sipped the water from his palm. "Indeed, the world will end as we know it."

Selene rubbed her shoulders. She felt a little cold for some reason. Not so long ago, she had tried to take over Nalzambor. She had been determined to destroy everything good and replace it with something else. She had honestly thought Gorn Grattack's way would be better.

How could I have been so blind? How could I have been so wrong?

People had been miserable under her father's oppression. Starving and depressed. Fear had ruled their lives. In the end, all it had done was make the wicked more powerful—and the powerful were the most miserable. She had hated everything during those times, but most of all, she had despised herself.

A picture of Nath Dragon formed in her mind. He wasn't perfect, but he stood for good. He would do what was right, even if he had to die for it. She had tried to break him, but she had failed. His faith in the good of Nalzambor was too strong. She had tried to change him, but in the end, it had been he who changed her.

Nath, wherever you are, I miss you.

The pounding rain started to lighten. She tilted her head. She swore she heard the clink of metal coming from down the hill. She looked at Sansla. His widening eyes were on hers. "You hear it too then?"

He nodded.

She looked back into the fort, searching for Gorlee. The changeling had been unusually quiet during their journey. *I don't see him anywhere. I haven't seen him since we arrived.*

Another rattle of metal caught her ear, along with the sound of horseshoes scraping over stone. Coming up the hillside, the faint outlines of men appeared in the wind and rain.

"We have company," she said.

Squinting, Sansla said, "Very large company."

The closer the travelers came, the larger they appeared. The first person up the hill led a horse by the reins. He was much bigger than a man, but he was not a giant. A sword that would take two men to swing hung from his belt. Behind him were more men of the same size. The horses they led were tremendous.

Selene blinked, wondering if it was the rain and wind playing a trick on her eyes.

Under his breath, Sansla said to her, "It's the nuurg and their horse-spawned wrath horns."

"Why in Nalzambor are they coming up here? Do you think they found our trail?"

Sansla shrugged. "What do you want to do? If we move now, we can slip out of here undetected."

"We need to locate Gorlee first." She started backing out the entrance into the pouring rain. Before she turned to see where she was going, she bumped into somebody.

"I'm here, Selene," Gorlee said.

"Stay close. We have company."

"I know. I saw them and heard you and Sansla. I have very good eyes and ears, you know."

"If that's the case, then why didn't you tell us they were coming?"

"Oh, well, that's why I came down from the wall—to warn you. But I was glad to see you had already caught on to it." Gorlee shielded his head from the stinging rain. "So, should we stay, or should we go?"

Sansla rushed over from the archway. "I say we go. Their numbers are growing."

"This way." Selene led them toward an exit where the outer wall had fallen in. Just as she crossed the threshold, she saw and heard more of the nuurg soldiers coming right at them. She slipped behind the inner wall, dragging Gorlee with her. "What in the world are they doing here?" She could hear the heavy breathing of the nuurg and the snorting of more wrath horns.

There must be a dozen of them.

The rain eased up from heavy drops and turned to steady drizzle.

She frowned as she said under her breath, "Now it stops raining, just when we need it most."

The nuurg spread out and surrounded the fort. Their weapons slid out of their sheaths. They positioned themselves in front of all the exits.

Selene and company hunkered down behind the rubble. To Sansla, she said, "They move as if they know we're here. I know we didn't leave a trail so bad the rain wouldn't wash it away."

Gorlee leaned over her shoulder and whispered in her ear in a familiar voice that was not his own, "You didn't leave a trail, Selene, but I did."

CHAPTER 18

FINALLY, AFTER THE ELVES AND dwarves departed, the fetchers arrived. The special dragons—big as small buildings with ruddy scales—didn't have horns, but their wings and paws were oversized. They landed on the ground with a gentleness about them. Their faces were smooth and pleasant. With the ease of a mother cat taking away her kitten by the scruff of the neck, they scooped up the dead dragons and flew them away.

Everyone who remained, from Brenwar to Bayzog, watched the fetchers fly into the horizon with bated breath.

Sasha clung to Nath's arm and said with tears in her eyes, "They seem so sweet and gentle, and they're beautiful."

"They are." He let out a sigh. It was more a sigh of relief than of sadness. He was glad that the fallen would be well cared for now. It had been worrying him. "I guess they weren't so comfortable with so many others around."

"I'd say so," Slivver replied. "I learned something new about our kin today. They are so full of surprises."

"Are we going to stand here gawking at the sky, or are we going to retrieve Balzurth?" Brenwar said. "I think we've been standing around long enough since you made the announcement."

"I still don't agree that it's the best course of action," said Bayzog. He was standing just outside of the fort's edge with Rerry and Samaz by his side. Behind them, a portion of the fort's wall had been knocked clean through. A handful of dwarven masons had begun repairs with tools such as hammers and chisels. "And I don't believe Nath's made a final decision."

"It sounded final to me." Brenwar had been a little more irritable than normal since Glenwar had departed. "You and your little clan are more than welcome to do whatever elves do. Maybe you can plant some flowers or something while we do the fighting."

"We'd be happy to plant the flowers that will one day dress your grave," Bayzog said.

Rerry and Samaz gave their father a surprised look, and with a glance at each other, they chuckled.

"No one—not man, dragon, elf, nor dwarf—better put any flowers on my grave. Unless they're made of steel and iron." He rubbed his jaw. "Dwarven steel and iron, that is. I don't want that elven steel that rusts."

"Elven steel doesn't rust." Rerry pulled free the sword he'd been given by Scar and thumbed the blade. "It doesn't nick either."

"Is that so?" Brenwar held out his hand. "Here, let me try it."

Rerry put the sword back in his sheath. "I'll pass."

"Scared to put your metal where your mouth is, huh? No surprise there. Ho-Ho!" Brenwar spun on his heel and headed north. "I'm heading to Narnum."

"My mind's made up, Bayzog. I'm going after Father." Nath adjusted his sword belt, which crossed over his shoulders and back. With a somewhat grateful look at Ben, he snapped Akron into place in the special notches on the back of his armor. "You don't have to come along if you don't wish to. I'll understand."

Digging his staff into the ground, Bayzog headed north as well, saying, "If you think I'm going to stay behind and let Brenwar get all of the glory over us part elves, then you're mistaken."

Watching Bayzog go along with his sons and Ben, Nath said to Sasha, "What do you make of Bayzog's swagger?"

"So far, I like it."

"Have you noticed anything odd about him? There's been something amiss with him since he came out of that well."

"I know," she said, "But I trust that he'll tell me more about it when the time comes. I've probed a little, but he's not ready yet."

"I see." Nath found Slivver. "So are you walking or flying?"

"We silvers will take to the air and keep an eye out for the wurmers or any other adversaries. I'll meet you back on the ground soon enough. I'd just like to stretch my wings."

"I swear, one day, you and I are going to finally fly side by side, Brother."

"I look forward to it." Slivver took to the sky, with the other silvers flying right behind him. They quickly disappeared over the trees.

"I sure miss that."

"I know," Sasha said. "I feel for you, Nath. How horrible it must be to be a dragon and not fly."

"I keep reminding myself that not all dragons have wings, but once you've had them, it's never the same without them."

"Yes, I can remember losing my ability to use magic. That was so hard, and a very confusing time. I'm grateful for what your father did for me, Nath." Walking by his side, she gave him a serious look. "But do you really think this is the right time to do the right thing?"

"It's always the right time to do the right thing."

"Yes, but I feel like he's using your father as bait." She stopped and sucked air through her teeth, holding her side.

Nath steadied her in his hands. "Sasha, what's wrong?"

Grimacing, she said, "I'm fine. That jolt from Lotuus had some lingering effects, even with the healing potion. This isn't the first time that's happened." She let out a breath. "Let's keep walking. Hopefully, my old knees won't give out next."

"You aren't that old. You make it sound like you're ancient."

"Right now my muscles are so stiff, I feel like I am."

"You know, if you'd been born a dwarf, you wouldn't have all these problems."

"Haha, don't change the subject. Nath, are you certain this is what you want to do? The world can't risk losing you."

"Sasha, I don't plan on storming into Narnum like my head's on fire. I know it's hard to believe, but behind my handsome exterior, there's a brilliant mind to match."

Holding her gut, she laughed. "Oh, don't make me laugh, Nath. It awakens my aches and pains."

"You need another vial."

"No, I'll be fine. That chuckle you gave me has me feeling better already. Please, continue. I believe you were about to unveil your brilliant plan."

He gave her a suspicious look. "Depending on what we discover when we get there, it's possible I'll ask Eckubahn for a parlay."

"A parlay. You would negotiate with such evil? I don't like the sound of that, Nath."

"I don't either, but I'm willing to do what I have to do to get my father's body back."

Chapter 19

With forceful hands, Gorlee shoved Selene out into the open. She drew her sword. "You traitor!"

Gorlee's body took the form of a taller and thicker man, much like the nuurg but more human—and female. "Oh, no, I'm not a traitor. No, I am the captor of this exquisite body of your changeling friend, Gorlee."

"Tylabahn!"

The titan woman clapped. "Very good. Was it my voice or my pouty lips that gave it away?"

Selene watched the nuurg move in. The eight-foot-tall one-eyed orcs were more than a handful of ugly. One of them dangled a spiked mace with a ball and chain bigger than her head by his side. He sneered at her as he lowered his head and stepped through the hole in the wall.

Selene backed toward the center until she stood back to back with Sansla. "You should go while you can. Get help."

"Come now, Selene," Tylabahn said. "You must know that I'm too clever to let that happen." She pointed her finger upward. Wurmers streaked through the rain. "I'm afraid you don't have anywhere safe to go. You know, you should have just left me alone." Her hair grew longer. Fingernails stretched out of her fingertips like claws. Her jaws widened, and her skin became shaggy. "But now, part of me wants to thank you. This new body that I host has unlimited potential. I can be anything I want."

"Could you at least turn into something more pleasant to look at? You're making the nuurg look handsome."

"Jest all you like, Selene, but I am what I am, and I'm not ashamed to hide it—like you. Look at the both of you monsters. You're a murderer, Selene. Sansla, you are an abomination. Embrace your identity, like I do mine. Only then will you make peace with the killer that lies within."

"We don't walk down that dark path anymore, Tylabahn," Selene said.

"You will again, trust me."

As Tylabahn faced off with Selene, more of the nuurg lumbered inside the fort. They surrounded

Selene and Sansla in a wide circle. She counted nine of them in all, not including the wurmers that landed on the broken parapets of the abandoned outpost.

"We don't surrender."

"Never," Sansla agreed.

"Pity. We'll just have to tear you to pieces and feed you to the wurmers." Tylabahn's shaggy hands clutched in and out. "Of course, if you kill me, then you'll be set free. I see that dangerous twinkle in your eye, Selene. You want to run that sword right through me. The problem is, the only way to stop me is to kill your friend Gorlee." She threw her head back in evil laughter. "This body is worth all the gold in Narnum. I'm unstoppable."

Selene sheathed her sword.

Tylabahn's eyes brightened. "Oh, you've come to your senses and decided to surrender. A wise choice. Nuurg, bind them up."

"Did you not hear me when I said 'We don't surrender'?" Selene summoned her magic. "I thought I was perfectly clear."

Tylabahn gave Selene a funny look. "But you put your sword away."

"I did, because with it, I can only attack one foe at a time. With my magic, I can strike many." Her violet eyes flashed. Her fingertips glowed with mystic fire. "Let the battle begin!"

Tylabahn's jawed dropped.

Selene fired off a bolt of power that sent Tylabahn flying into the wall.

CHAPTER 20

MARCHING INTO THE STIFF WINDS of the changing season, Nath said to Ben, "How are you feeling?"

"I'm feeling good, but the last three decades of fighting, I have to admit, are catching up with me. These long marches don't come as easy as they used to." Ben drank from his canteen. "But don't worry. The older you get, the tougher you are."

"You aren't that old, Ben. How old were you when we met anyway, sixteen?"

"No, I was seventeen, thank you. I just looked young for my age back then. Now I look old for my age."

"You don't look old. If anything, you look as old as you really are, in your forties, I guess. And look, your hair is as rich and brown as ever."

"Have you not seen the gray hairs in my chin?" Ben scratched at his jaw. "I shouldn't make a fuss about it. Margo likes it. You know, my father's was mostly gray as long as I remember. It must run in the family. Dragon, why do you think men don't live as long as the other races? I just don't understand that. It doesn't seem fair."

The discrepancy in age expectancy of the various races was one of the topics Nath felt guilty about. Humans, pure humans, didn't live very long, and Ben was right. It didn't seem fair. Some elves lived a thousand years, dragons a few thousand, and even dwarves into their late hundreds, but most humans didn't live to be a hundred. "I don't know, Ben, but if I ever figure it out, you'll be the first to hear."

"I guess I shouldn't complain. At the rate I'm going, I probably won't make it much longer anyway." Ben stopped, took off his boot, and dumped the grit and pebbles out of it. He did the same with the other before stuffing it back on. "Ah, that's better. It shaves a year off at least. Do your feet ever ache?"

"No, I can't say they do, but sometimes my ears ache."

"Your ears?"

"Yes, whining does that to them."

Ben made a perplexed look. His eyes suddenly brightened. "Ah, I get it. I suppose I am being whiny. It's just that I like doing this, and you'll be doing it much longer than I will. I really want to be around to see all the marvels that happen."

"Our *marvels* have been filled with nothing but danger and treachery. You enjoy it?"

"Well, I can't say I enjoy it in the moment when I might perish, but at the same time, I never feel more alive than then. When the fighting stops, I miss it. It makes me restless. Don't get me wrong, I don't want to set out and hurt anyone, but at the same time, I can't stand the thought of sitting around and not fighting the good fight. The time will come when, if I survive, I won't be able to fight anymore. I'll just be sitting in a rocking chair growing old."

"You have it all wrong, Ben. You'll have something that young warriors never have: wisdom. There is no greater weapon than that."

Ben's brows lifted, and he nodded. "You know, Dragon, that actually does make me feel a little better. But if wisdom comes with age, can you explain to me what happened to Brenwar?"

They both laughed.

Out front, Brenwar—who still led the way—slowed and turned. "What are you two roosters clucking about? I'm certain I heard my name."

"We were just talking about all your years of wisdom," Nath said.

Ben covered his mouth while holding in a laugh.

"Years? You mean centuries," Brenwar corrected.

"Exactly," Ben said, laughing.

"I don't see what's so funny about it."

"No, nothing is funny at all, Brenwar, we were just admiring you, so to speak." Ben sealed his lips shut.

Brenwar's freshly scarred black brows lifted. "None are wiser than the dwarves. As a matter of fact, I know a song about that. Perhaps I should sing it to you."

"No!" Nath and Ben objected together.

"I see, but you'll hear it soon enough, the ballad of Onaar Cleeven." He cleared his throat and marched away, singing under his breath.

"Well, he still has his hearing. That's for certain." Ben said.

"Agreed."

"So Nath, I've been meaning to ask you something for quite some time."

"What is it, Ben?"

"Well, dragons live a very long time, and I imagine a relationship like the one we have might be difficult, because we humans pass away so young. I just wonder, have you lost many friends like me? I mean, I can only assume you've had many. I couldn't be the only one, aside from Sasha, that is."

"Boy, Ben, you're really on a morbid streak today, aren't you?"

Ben eyed the sky. "Maybe it's the weather."

Nath's thoughts drifted back to his past. He didn't reflect on it often, because he wasn't proud of it. For decades, he hadn't been even close to the person he'd become now. He had walked the world with good intentions but had been young and self-centered. He'd had many friends back then, but none as close as those he cherished now—aside from Brenwar and Slivver. He had been more of a loner in his younger days, full of bull with a chip on his shoulder. There had been good times but just as many bad.

"You know, Ben, I had friends, but most of them were just acquaintances. Some of them are still around, but most of them have long since passed away." He pictured many faces from his past in his head. "I don't think you would have cared for me so much then, Ben. I was cocky."

Ben grinned, "More so than you are now?"

"Oh, much worse. I was more man than dragon. I was obsessed with saving the dragons and myself, but looking back, it was more about myself. It took me a long time to learn my lesson—at least a century, I'd say—before I woke up and realized how selfish I was being." He lifted his arms. Even in the dim light of day, his black scales had an oily shine to them. "Actually, this happened right around the time I met you. That's when I realized I was on the wrong path. I like to think I'm on the high path now, but sometimes I'm not so certain."

"If you always thought you were on it, then I'd say you weren't. I bet that's how you felt in your younger days."

Nath gave Ben a friendly shove. "You couldn't be more right. You, Ben, are going to be a walking and talking fountain of wisdom. I can feel it in my scales. So—" He stopped in his tracks.

Slivver and the handful of silver dragons darted through the dark skies toward them. Slivver landed as the other dragons circled in the air. His ice-blue eyes were filled with warning. "We have trouble."

CHAPTER 21

ITH A PAIR OF NUURG closing in on him, Sansla Libor set his feet for the charge. The armor-laden monsters swung their steel right into his chest, but their blades skipped off of his coarse hair. Sansla gave them a smile. The nuurg fighters recoiled and gave one another blank stares.

"He doesn't bleed," one nuurg said to the other.

"Not from the likes of those old blades, but I'm certain that you do. Let's see." Sansla drew his legs up underneath himself and pounced. Both of his fists collided with nuurg jaws. Their thick legs became noodles. They fell down in two heaps. On instinct, Sansla ducked.

Whoosh!

A studded club just missed his head.

Sansla grappled with another nuurg with a ring of brass in his nose. Breast to breast and equal in size, they grappled back and forth with the club. With wide jaws slavering and murder in the nuurg's eyes, the monster matched Sansla's own savage power. They rolled over the muddy ground and smashed into the rubble.

The nuurg's head butted Sansla square in the nose.

With a snarl, Sansla head butted the nuurg in the bridge of his own nose.

Crack!

The nuurg let out a pained howl and lost his grip on the club.

Sansla wrenched it free and slung it away. He unloaded on the nuurg with punches so hard that the force broke ribs.

The nuurg's hard body sagged. His ugly face became a painful grimace.

Sansla hit the helpless nuurg again and again until it flopped to the sloppy ground and moved no more. Sansla's chest heaved. His temper flared. He snorted through his nostrils.

The elven roamer king within—cool and in control—began to fade away. The curse of the monster Sansla fought so hard to control came out. He made an animal-like growl. His fists pounded his chest.

A nuurg with a sword stepped into Sansla's path and attacked.

Quick as a snake and more powerful than a lion, Sansla charged into the sword-wielding nuurg.

The nuurg's sword came down hard on his shoulder.

Sansla didn't feel a thing except rage. He snatched the nuurg up off the ground and hoisted it over his head. With a savage howl, he hurled the nuurg into a stone wall with ram-like force and broke the small giant's neck.

As soon as Selene unloaded her bolt of power on Tylabahn, she drew her sword. Just as the steel snaked out of the scabbard, she parried a two-handed chop from the closest nuurg. The blow jarred her arms, sending sharp pain up into her shoulders.

"Pretty woman going to die," said a one-eyed nuurg with a long black beard and a bald head with a second eye tattooed over his real eye. He cocked back the sword over his shoulder.

Selene sliced deep into his leg.

Howling "Aaarrggh!" the nuurg chopped at her, as durable a fighter as any orc but bigger and quicker than it looked.

She sidestepped the sword tip that bit into the ground. Jabbed her steel deep into its knee.

The nuurg enemy towered over her.

Selene used her smaller size to outmaneuver the monster. She slipped in behind it and stabbed it in the back.

Its back arched. Its arms flailed behind it. "You will pay!" the nuurg screamed as it dropped onto both knees. Its head twisted back over its shoulder and found her preparing to strike. "No, wait," it pleaded.

Selene hesitated.

A nuurg soldier riding a wrath horn stormed into the fortress and trampled her.

Elbow deep in the mud, Selene pushed herself up out of the muck, spitting mud from her mouth, just as the nuurg prepared for another charge. With her bones aching beneath the scales that had saved her body from certain death, she faced her aggressor.

The wrath horn and rider charged.

She raced right at them with her sword high. At the last possible moment, she leapt high, clearing the wrath horn's head. She kicked the nuurg rider in the face with both feet, knocking it from the saddle.

The nuurg splashed onto the soft ground.

Selene landed beside it. Her tail slithered over the giant's shoulder and coiled around its neck.

"Urk!" the nuurg clawed at her tail until its screams were silenced.

Selene's eyes searched over the battlefield. There had been nine nuurg fighters to start. She'd fought two, and right before her eyes, Sansla was fighting all of the others. She'd never seen him like she saw him now. He fought like a caged animal. The blue in his eyes was molten lava. He killed without remorse. It sent a chill through her.

His curse has awakened.

She started forward to aid him but froze in her tracks when Tylabahn said, "You! You dare!"

Selene spun around.

Tylabahn stood with her back against the wall, rubbing the scorch marks on her chest. She'd grown from eight feet to every bit of twelve.

"I see you've given me a bigger target." Selene spun her sword around. "I thank you."

"You would kill the changeling just to kill me?" Tylabahn's lips curled back. "I don't believe you have it in you!"

"I know the changeling well enough to believe he would rather die than be a device of evil." She twirled her sword and started forward. "If I have to kill my friend, then so be it."

Tylabahn snatched up a hunk of stone and hurled it at Selene. "You fool, you cannot kill me!"

Selene dodged the boulder. "With this enchanted sword, Spirit Slicer, I can destroy anything in any form."

Eyes on the sword, the titan woman said, "You are lying. Your entire life is a lie. You are not good. You are bad. A killer."

"If you think I'm lying, then come closer, and we shall see."

"I know you're a liar. There is no sword known as Spirit Slicer. If there were, the titans would know of it." Tylabahn clacked her teeth. "I will have you, Selene. You are outnumbered. And I have no desire to part with this body. It can be used for so many terribly clever things. Who knows, maybe I'll take your form so I can entrap Nath Dragon."

Selene charged.

"Wurmers! To me!" Tylabahn ordered.

The wurmers dropped out of the sky like bats, covering Selene.

Fighting for her life as the monsters tore at her scales, she caught a peek at Sansla. Apparently, rage could only feed the elf king-turned-flying ape's awesome strength for so long. The nuurg hit him from all directions with clubs, swords, and chains. He sank to his knees. It was the last she saw of him. She ran her sword through a wurmer's ribs. With a chop, she took the head off another. Hungry jaws clamped down on her sword arm. One by one, they locked up her arms and legs in their jaws. Only her scales saved her. She wriggled and screamed. They stretched her out.

Looming over Selene, Tylabahn stood with her hands on her hips. "Tsk! Tsk! Tsk! You have plenty of fight in you, but not enough."

"Believe what you want."

Tylabahn made a crooked smile and leaned down. With her massive fist, she walloped Selene in the face.

The sky went black.

CHAPTER 22

Nath ran, leaving all the others behind except Rerry, who managed to keep pace with him for about two miles before he finally faded back. With the tall grasses and wildflowers licking his waist, Nath raced after Slivver, who led him from the sky. For a moment, he lost the silver dragon in the pouring rain, but he found him again once he entered the storm.

Slivver's news had been dire. He'd come across the seeker dragon who'd found Selene. As Slivver understood the information conveyed by the little dragon, Selene and Sansla had been in a great fight with the nuurg, a host of wurmers, and another strange creature. Not wanting to risk being caught by the wurmers, the seeker had sought out Nath and Slivver as the battle raged.

Hang in there, Selene! Hang in there!

The details were vague, but based on what Nath had heard, it sounded like Selene and Sansla were severely outnumbered. That was the bad news. The good news was that they were close, only a few leagues away.

Sultans of Sulfur! If I could only fly! I would rather have my wings than my fire!

He ran with all his heart. Slivver sent the silver dragons ahead to give aid. Nath hoped they would be enough to fend off the wicked forces. He knew how formidable Selene and Sansla could be.

It wouldn't surprise me one bit if those nuurg got more than they bargained for. I wouldn't want to tangle with either one of them, not again.

In lengthy strides, he rushed through the pouring rain, leaping small gulches and creeks. The running stint seemed to take forever. Finally, he followed Slivver up a steep hill that was slick with mud and pine needles. He lost his footing once, only to snag a branch and keep surging forward without slipping. The rain had died down to a drizzle, and a fog rolled in. Nath reached the top of the hill but had lost sight of Slivver. He stood in front of an abandoned outpost. He could smell fresh blood in the air. The stench of nuurg sweat too. On the ground were the massive hoof prints of wrath horns.

He placed his hand in a muddy print. *There are so many.*

Slivver called out for him. “In here, Nath.”

He made his way through the doorway. His jaw dropped. Nuurg soldiers lay dead on the ground. Their bodies were busted up and broken. A sword lay on the ground, bent. One nuurg had a chain wrapped around its neck. They weren’t alone. There was a handful of wurmers that had been sliced up with a sword. The only dead he saw were the enemy.

The four silver dragons were perched on the four parapets. Nath eyed Slivver, who milled about the dead like a man.

“The battle was long over when they arrived here, Nath. I’m sorry, but the enemy is gone.”

“The enemy is never gone.” Nath picked his way through the battle scene. His keen eyes absorbed all the details. He noted a spot on one of the walls that had a new crack in it. Something or someone as big as a nuurg must have hit it. There was a strange set of footprints too, different from the others. Plus, there were Selene’s, which he knew for certain by the size. He sniffed the air.

She was here. And fighting for her life.

Nath noticed another set of tracks moving away from the battle. A person or beast of some sort had crawled through the mud and grass and into one of the storehouses. Nath caught Slivver’s attention with a soft word in Dragonese. He pointed at the storehouse. Drawing Fang, he crept toward the facility. With Slivver following behind him, he stopped just outside the door frame. His nostrils flared. He didn’t catch the scent of anything. If it were a nuurg or something else, he would have known it. He put away his sword.

“What are you doing?” Slivver said.

“I don’t smell anything, but something living made this trail.” He pointed to the rut in the road.

“There are many monsters that don’t carry a scent.”

“And I have allies like that as well.” Nath stepped through the storehouse threshold and softly called out, “Sansla?” Inside, his eyes caught the backside of a hulking figure crouched in the corner. Wings were folded tight over the creature’s back, but one of them drooped. *That’s Sansla for certain.* He reached out and laid his hands on Sansla’s back.

Sansla lashed out with a mighty swing that took Nath from his feet and sent him sailing through the wall.

CHAPTER 23

ath! Are you all right?” Slivver rushed and helped Nath up off the ground.

“Ugh,” Nath moaned as he clutched his chest. “That certainly stung a little, I’ll say that much. Sansla sure packs a wallop.”

Sansla stormed out of the storehouse with his blue eyes filled with blazing fury. He looked at Nath and Slivver like a starving wolf smelling fresh meat.

Slivver stepped in front of Nath and said, “Stay back. I’ll handle this.”

“No, Slivver. We can’t hurt him. We have to find out what’s wrong. We need to subdue him.”

Sansla’s jaws opened wide and let out a frightening roar. “Raaawwwwrrrrrr!”

The white ape was splattered in mud and full of fury. Nath wondered what had happened to the level-headed elven roamer king who resided within. The calm blue eyes were now blazing storms. The wild beast had been unleashed. Sansla pounded his chest like a drum and roared again.

"I'm curious as to what you have in mind to subdue him," Slivver said, "because I don't think he wants subduing."

Nath calmly shuffled forward. "Just don't make any sudden moves." He eyed the silver dragons poised to strike from the walls. "Keep them at bay."

With his palms out, he made his way toward Sansla.

Sansla roared and snorted.

Speaking in Elven, Nath said, "Sansla! Sansla! I am your friend, Nath. You know me, and you know that I won't harm you in any way. Please, Sansla, show me that you hear me." He searched Sansla's eyes. Saliva dripped from the ape's huge jaws. *Guzan, if I didn't know any better, I'd say he would eat me.* But then he saw the storm in Sansla's eyes begin to calm, and he crept closer.

The winged ape shook himself, bared his teeth, and withdrew two steps.

"Good, good, Sansla. Listen to me. We are here to help. Just trust me." Nath stretched out his hand.

Sansla snarled. His eyebrows knitted.

Looking up into Sansla's face, Nath said, "Easy, friend. Easy. You don't want to do anything you'll regret. That's not like you. Let me help you."

The wrinkles between Sansla's eyes eased. He reached out while snorting the air and grabbed Nath's wrist.

"Good, Sansla, good. You see, I am your friend."

Sansla's grip tightened. The frown in his brows returned.

Worried, Nath said, "Sansla, what are you doing?"

Sansla jerked Nath up by the arm and slammed him down hard into the ground.

"Nath!" Slivver called out.

"No! Stay back," Nath said. "Oof!"

Sansla pounded Nath in the back with his fists. He picked him up again and slammed him into the ground. Then tossed him into the wall. He kicked and beat Nath all over the fort.

"Are you mad, Nath?" Slivver said.

Caught up in a bear hug, Nath managed to blurt out, "Stay your ground. I can take it."

Sansla body-slammed Nath. He kicked him up off the ground. He punched again and again.

Nath felt his face swell. His eyes bulged and his bones rattled, but he wouldn't fight back. He just continued to say in Elven, "I know you won't kill me, Sansla. We are friends. Always have been and always will be."

Sansla unleashed rage and frustration on Nath's body.

On pins and needles, Slivver shouted, "He's going to tear you apart, Nath!"

"No, he won't. *Urk*!"

Sansla lifted Nath's busted-up body from the ground by the neck. He started choking Nath.

Not this again.

Sansla stared right into Nath's eyes and let out a terrifying scream. "Eeeeeiiiiiieeeeeeeeee!"

Nath felt his consciousness fading. His eyes weakened but remained fixed on Sansla. If his eyes could speak, he was saying, "Come on, Sansla, you're better than this. Don't give in to the curse. You can't let it win!"

Chapter 24

Sansla shook Nath like a rag. His bulging arms trembled. Suddenly, his body sagged. His eyes softened. He released Nath.

Nath gulped in lungfuls of air. *Oh, thank goodness.* He rubbed his neck. *This choking thing is getting really old.* He found Sansla kneeling beside him. The winged ape's shoulders were slumped over as he stared at the ground drawing with his finger in the mud. He made an elven symbol for peace.

"Nath, are you well?" Slivver was staring right at Nath and Sansla, but he kept his distance.

Nath coughed a few times and said in a raspy voice, "I think we're out of danger." He waved Slivver over. "Help me up."

Keeping an eye on Sansla, Slivver did as Nath requested. "I have to admit, out of all of the stupid things I've ever seen you do, that might have topped them all. Did insanity compel you?"

"I just knew, deep down, that Sansla wouldn't kill me." He rubbed his ribs. "He was holding back, or at least he was holding part of the beast back."

"It certainly didn't look like it." Studying Nath, Sansla said, "I'm curious. A younger Nath would not have been able to control himself like that in the heat of battle. Did you feel the rage?"

"Huh, you bet I did. It took plenty of effort not to loose my fire, especially considering this wasn't the first time Sansla and I clashed. I just hope it's the last time."

"Honestly, I have to say I would pay to see that fight."

"Slivver!"

"Come now, you know I'm too civilized to indulge myself in such events."

"Yes, I know." Nath wrapped his arm around Slivver. "Thanks for looking out for me."

"It's always a pleasure."

"Nath." Sansla rose from his muddy seat. His eyes once again showed the calm of the elven roamer king within. "I am sorry."

"Though there isn't any need for apologies, I accept, old friend."

"I owe you a great debt of gratitude, Dragon King. More than you'll ever know. If you hadn't come along, the curse would have consumed me." Sansla's wings unfolded from behind his back. He grimaced and stretched them out wider until something popped. His drooping right wing straightened. "Ah. I could see myself fighting you as if I were a spectator watching a horrible battle. You're right, I did resist, perhaps more than I realized, but what sanity I had left was fading."

Scratching this scales on his neck, Nath said, "I did feel that squeeze strengthen toward the end. So what happened? How did I get to you? Was it the Elven speech?"

"It wasn't your words, Nath. It was your eyes. That golden luster was hypnotic, like the warmth of the rising sun, until I was able to hear your soothing words. Your friendship brought me peace. That peace quenched the fires of the beast. I've never seen or felt anything like it. It is another one of your many gifts."

"I noticed something too," Slivver said with approval. "There was a glow in your eyes that I had never seen before. To be truthful, whatever happened was beautiful."

"I don't know how I did it, but I hope I can remember how if I ever need it again." He rubbed his swollen jaw. "I just hope it doesn't have anything to do with you."

"I hope so too," Sansla replied.

"So, can you tell us what happened? Where's Selene?"

Sansla gave Nath a long look. "I failed to protect her, I'm afraid. When the nuurg attacked, I lost all control." He shook his head. "My memories are dim. Forgive me."

"Take your time, Sansla. Just start wherever you're comfortable."

Gathering his thoughts, Sansla told them about everything that had happened since he'd been with Selene. The wurmer den where they'd encountered the wurmer queen and the titan Tylabahn. The battle in the deep stream with the stone giants and how they had come across this fort, only to be tricked as Tylabahn took possession of Gorlee.

Soaking it in, Nath scratched his forehead. "That's bad. Really bad."

"What's so bad?" said a newcomer.

Nath turned. Brenwar and company were walking in through the fort's archway. "Everything."

"I'm not bad," Brenwar said. "What happened to your face? It's all swollen and puffy." His eyes popped wide when he saw the fallen nuurg. "You fought more giants without me! You didn't even save me a one?"

"Brenwar, you'll get your opportunity. Right now we need to find Selene. One of the titans has taken her hostage. At least, I hope that's the case." Nath turned to Sansla. "You don't suppose the titan killed her, do you?"

"No. I think she has an insidious purpose for Selene."

Nath's brow arched. "Such as?"

"I think Selene will be bait so they can control you," Sansla replied.

"That's horrible," Sasha said. She and Bayzog entered the outpost last. Rerry and Samaz were already within.

"Judging by all of these tracks, it shouldn't be difficult to find them." Brenwar's eyes followed the wrath horn tracks leading out of the fort. "And they don't have much of a head start. Let's go fetch them and put an end to them."

"Let's not be too hasty," Bayzog advised. With one hand, he kept the hem of his robes out of the mud. "We are getting close to Narnum. The enemy's forces will thicken in that area."

"That's why we need to get after them right now, before they get too far ahead," Brenwar said.

"The silvers and I will scout ahead," Slivver said. "We have a seeker on their trail too. It wouldn't surprise me if he reported back at any moment, seeing how they can't be far away."

One of the silver dragons barked out a warning. All four of them took to the sky. A lone wurmer flew high in the air. It held something in its mouth. Flying over the middle of the fort, it dropped the object.

Recognizing what it was, Nath raced beneath the object and caught it. It was the seeker dragon. His heart sank. His eyes became misty. Everyone gathered around just as he said, "They killed him."

CHAPTER 25

NATH LED THE SEARCH FOR Selene at a brisk pace while fighting the urge to run. Slivver had taken to the sky as a lookout. The silver dragons wouldn't be much help tracking Selene in the woodland from above, but hopefully they'd see any wurmers before the wurmers saw them. In the meantime, he couldn't get the image of the little seeker dragon out of his mind, such a small and innocent thing. Not to mention the fact that the wurmers and nuurgs had been able to catch it, which disturbed him.

They must have an awful lot of tricks I never suspected. No, it couldn't have been. It must have been that titan, Tylabahn.

That part made the death of the little seeker worse. The wrath horn–riding nuurgs couldn't have been any easier to track. They left a trail in the woodland that even a blind man could follow. There had been no reason for them to kill the seeker.

Either that act was pure evil—which I can't rule out—or the seeker saw something they didn't want it to see.

Nath pushed some pine branches aside, spooking a deer as he passed. The oversized riders had left broken branches all over. The trail was so obvious that it was insulting.

Rerry caught up to Nath. He didn't say anything for the first mile or so. Instead, he followed Nath and did everything he did.

Nath considered pointing out a few things about tracking to the youngster, but he didn't feel like talking.

If he wants to know something, he can ask Brenwar.

He kept moving on with a head of steam until Rerry finally broke his silence.

"Ahem, Nath, er, is tracking supposed to be this easy? If you don't mind me saying so, something seems amiss."

"Perhaps." He slowed to a stop and pointed at the ground. "If you'll notice, the stride of the wrath horns changes from time to time. There's more space between their tracks when they move quicker, suggesting a trot or a gallop. And," he kneeled down over one of the hoof prints, "you can see here where the hooves dig in deeper. See these pointing impressions, like needles?" Rerry nodded. "Well, those are the spikes that are shod around the wrath horns' ankles. The faster they move, the deeper they dig. They're in a hurry. Any questions?'

Rerry shook his head. "No."

"Good, because I don't feel like answering any." Nath forged ahead until the woodland ran out and became the open plains again.

Standing right behind his shoulder, Rerry said, "Narnum's the next stop, eh?"

"We've leagues to go, but yes, there isn't much cover between here and there." He searched the cloudy skies. A wink of silver. He pointed and said to Rerry, "Can you see that?"

Squinting and leaning forward, Rerry said, "The silvers are coming."

"You have good sight."

Ben caught up with them next. A little winded, he said, "What are you looking for?"

"Can't you see them?" Nath said.

"No, I don't see anything at all."

"You'll see them soon enough."

Ben drew his sword. "I'll be ready then."

"No, you can put that away, Ben. It's Slivver. He'll be here any moment." He nudged Rerry. "Do you see how the grasses have been plowed over?"

"Yes. The trail disappears over that knoll and just over the next, but I can't see beyond that."

"That's pretty good, Rerry. I wouldn't expect you to see through a hillside. Sorry for being short with you earlier."

"Let some of your burdens be mine as well, Nath. We'll get Selene back and avenge that little dragon."

By the time Slivver flew in, the rest of the party had caught up to him. "Well, what did you discover, Slivver?"

"We caught sight of them riding hard in the saddle, but we had to break off when we saw wurmers with them. The closer to Narnum you go, the thicker they become. But for certain, they head for Narnum at full speed."

"Did you see Selene?"

"Yes. She was draped over a saddle. I couldn't tell if she was alive or not, but I think it's safe to assume she was. Why else take her?"

"They'll do just as it's been said, to bait me. But I believe you're right, Slivver. She's alive. I can feel it in my heart of hearts. I would know if she died."

Brenwar set down his strongbox and sat on it, dashing the sweat from his brow. "So what are we going to do, Nath? This is an awfully small army to storm in there, though *I* am more than ready for it."

"No, we aren't going to be able to use force in this one. I'm still going to try and parlay, but now the stakes are even higher. I'll be negotiating for both Selene and my father. In the meantime, I'm open for suggestions on the best way to go about this."

He saw growing concern in everyone's faces.

Bayzog intervened. "I think it's high time we got a better look at what we're up against. Perhaps we can get a better look at our enemy if some of us can slip into the city."

"We'll stick out like glowing gnomes if we go in there," Brenwar said.

Unable to hide his excitement, Rerry said, "You might, but not all of us. I can certainly blend in."

"So can I," Samaz agreed.

"I like the idea, but let's not be too hasty. It's getting late. Let's sleep on it." Nath moved into the edge of the forest. "Please, make camp. Slivver, come with me."

CHAPTER 26

"WHAT'S ON YOUR MIND, NATH?"

The brother dragons had found a spot to talk between four large dogwood trees that stood out in the forest. Nath leaned back against one of them and plucked a green leaf. "You're a dragon. Tell me, am I thinking more like a man or more like a dragon?"

Scratching above his earhole, Slivver said, "I can't think of anything more dragon than rescuing dragons."

"I guess I just needed a little reassurance."

"Truth be told, Nath, I'd like to think my advice would be some of the best, but even I can lose my level head sometimes. I'm another dragon who likes to walk among the races."

"I don't think you'd like losing the power of being a dragon, Slivver. Trust me, it's ugly."

"But you seem to do well without it."

"Remember, I was born this way. You were born that way. We are what we are, but I'll tell you this, I can't wait to be a full dragon again one day. I think if I was a full dragon now, I could finish off Eckubahn that same way I took care of Gorn Grattack."

"Perhaps, but you can't count on that, Nath. This time, you just might have to do things the way you are." Slivver lashed his tail into a tree with a whack. "When the moment comes, you must be willing to strike."

Nath pushed off the tree and nodded. "Slivver, I have to ask, can you tell me why you want to be one of the races so much? It seems truly abnormal."

Slivver locked his hands behind his back and started to pace. "What I am about to say might banish me from your sight forever, O king. Over the decades I've been on a search to make myself mortal. It's one of the reasons you haven't seen me in so long, Nath. I know what I am about to say is impossible, but the truth is I've fallen in love with a mortal woman."

Nath's jaw dropped. The ring of truth in his brother's voice stirred him up. He seized his brother by the shoulders. "It's not a bad thing to love someone, even though it's forbidden, but who?"

"You know her."

At first Nath thought of Sasha, but he and Slivver went way back. Then it hit him. With a gasp he said, "Its Ericha, isn't it."

"She is the star and sun of my dreams. Nath, how did you know?"

"I remember how you looked at her in our travels. I never saw you so stricken before, and we'd been in the company of many gorgeous women. But Ericha was the only one you ever spoke to. Do you know where she is? Elome, I assume?"

"I've spied on her over the years. Yes, she is still there. I caught a glimpse of her not so long ago. I was so close I could smell the unforgettable scent of her honey-colored hair. And her eyes, as soft and beautiful as the petals of roses. She's the most wonderful thing in Nalzambor. I love her, Nath. I truly love her."

Smiling, Nath said, "I see what your problem is: you're a rebel and a romantic. I'll tell you this much: I know mortal women like that." His smile widened. "A lot. Have you told her how you feel?"

"I dare not." Slivver spread his wings. "Nath, I'm a dragon. She would laugh at me."

"Why, you loving her is no more absurd than her loving you."

"I never thought about it that way."

"That's because you're a male dragon. We don't think the same way women do. But I've learned a thing or two hundred over the centuries." He looked Slivver in the eye. "I'm glad you told me. Now, I'm not certain what the answer is, because it's weird, but we need to get through the war with the giants first. And assuming we survive, you have to promise me you'll tell her."

"I will, Brother."

"Good, now get your dreamy eyes out of the clouds and help me figure out how to deal with Eckubahn."

"I actually thought the wizard's idea was a good one. The only thing I didn't like about it was that I wouldn't be able to attend." Slivver sat down on the ground. With his dragon-claw fingers, he ripped out a patch of weeds, revealing a small patch of clover-like flowers. "Evil suffocates all that is good in this world. It quickly spreads. The last thing you want to do is become the yeast in the bread."

"Evil rises, huh. I know that. I think we are well beyond the spread. It's everywhere now. What I need is something to barter with. Aside from my head, what is there to barter with? I can't give them more power."

"Perhaps you should evacuate Dragon Home."

"That's madness. Would the dwarves and elves give up their homes?" His long fingers dug into his palms. "They'd die first. So would we. We'd be scattered. The whole point is to bring us together again."

"It was just a suggestion. No, Nath, this is a mystery. I could go into the city, feel it out and see what they want. At least figure out where Selene is."

"I'll consider it." Nath feigned a yawn. "And if you don't mind, Slivver, I'd like some time to myself."

"Certainly."

CHAPTER 27

THE FIGHT AT THE OLD fort on the hill took it out of Selene. She hung in there as long as she could, but the overwhelming forces of nuurg and wurmers proved to be too much. Her dragon-strong limbs gave way. The brutes subdued her.

"Welcome home, Selene!" Tylabahn said. The titan in Gorlee's body rode a wrath horn and led in the front. She wasn't as big as the last time Selene had seen her but still the size of a nuurg. The titan's shaggy hair covered her back like a muddy waterfall. She was ghastly, like a mystic field hag from the north. "I look forward to seeing how the citizens greet your return."

I don't.

Selene's hands were bound with the type of rope orcen poachers used to bind up trapped dragons. They called it iron cord, which was a dwarven version of the elven elotween rope. The fibers were hard to cut or break, rendering her sharp claws useless. A second rope was wrapped around her waist and linked to one of the wrath horn's saddles. She was by far the smallest among them all. She felt like it, too.

I hope Sansla survived.

Tylabahn led the group down one of the main roads that led into the once-Free City of Narnum. Every face they passed was long and tired, grubby and dirty. In the skies, wurmers circled in clusters. There were hundreds of them. Everywhere she looked, she saw dozens of them. Inside the city, the ugly insect-like wurmer dragons were perched on rooftops and ledges. The locust-like *ree-rah* sound was a constant annoyance.

Tylabahn gave an order to one of the nuurg soldiers.

The brute nodded. Digging his heels into the ribs of the wrath horn he rode, he galloped toward the city.

Tylabahn looked back at Selene. "I'm letting Eckubahn know that I'm bringing you. Just imagine how excited the people will be to see their former queen. As I understand it, you were awfully good to them."

Selene didn't show any expression. She toiled along, lifeless, determined not to give Tylabahn anything to feed on. The remarks, however, ate at her. Selene had been anything but kind to the citizens of Narnum. She'd been a dictator. Cruel and malicious. If anyone dared to speak against her, she hadn't hesitated to put them in prison or silence their treasonous tongues with death. Reigning by fear, not love, was all she had known back then.

About one hundred yards away from the main entrance of the trade city, Tylabahn came to a stop. The brisk winds dusted through her wavy ribbons of hair. She looked at Selene from the corner of her eye. There was an evil glimmer there.

What's she up to now?

Tylabahn's disturbing shambled appearance ate at Selene. She had figured Tylabahn would take on a more comely form—which evil often did. Instead, her appearance was repellent. The word "lummox" was an understatement when describing the brutish hag, but somehow fitting. Selene kept her eyes forward.

Giants marched out of the city, twelve feet tall and wearing heavy coats of chain-mail armor. One of them waved his hand.

Tylabahn jerked the reins. "Ah, Eckubahn awaits us. Let's not waste his precious time." The wrath horn she rode reared up and whinnied. She took off in a thunderous gallop.

The nuurg riders followed suit, including the one Selene was tethered to by the wrists. She was jerked off her feet. They dragged her face first down the muddy road into the city. She fought all the while to regain her footing, but it was impossible. She was at the mercy of the powerful wrath horns. For the first mile, it took all she had just to keep spitting the mud from her mouth. If the mud was bad, the next mile of cobblestone roads was worse. The hard surface jarred her limbs and clacked her teeth. Halfway into the city, they slowed to a trot.

There wasn't anything to be thankful for. She was still scraping over the road on her hands and knees. The wrath horns' long strides allowed them to move fast enough even at a walk so that she couldn't gain her feet.

She quickly realized she didn't want to. People lined up on both sides of the streets shouted insults at her. The anger spread as word came out that Selene had returned. Children hurled rotten fruit and vegetables. Rocks were flung that skipped off her head and back. It was nonstop misery all the way into the center of the city.

I deserve this. Every bit of it and worse.

She could feel the rage of the families she'd destroyed. She saw the people's faces. Anger. Hatred. Misery.

But that wasn't the worst of it. There were people in the crowd who weren't normal. Their faces were contorted into unnatural shapes, and unusual sounds came from their mouths. They danced and screamed like wild things.

"We hate you, Selene!"

"Kill her!"

"She's an abomination!"

"Cut that tail off of her!"

The harassment stopped when she was dragged into a great cathedral that had been built after she'd left. The people could still be heard on the outside, demanding that she be put to death.

I knew my time would come. It's only fitting that this be the place where it happens.

Coming to her feet, she studied the huge circular chamber. The grand cathedral ceiling was suspended more than fifty feet above her by stone columns. There were paintings on the ceiling, of giants slaying dragons in a massive war.

Tylabahn dismounted. She walked over to the wrath horn Selene's rope was linked to and unhooked it. She reeled the rope in until it was taut and gave it a jerk.

Selene shuffled after her, noting the surrounding guards. Between the ten columns that held the ceiling were twenty-foot-tall giant soldiers in full armor. Each was beastly, and the armor they wore was crude and not the best fit. It seemed to have more of a ceremonial purpose than a practical one, seeing how giant skin in many cases was too thick to cut.

Tylabahn approached the dais.

Eckubahn, bigger than all the rest with his head covered in fiery flames, sat on the throne of dragon bones. His dark eyes were fixed on Selene.

"Greetings, Brother," Tylabahn said with a slight bow. "I come bearing gifts and some bad news. The wurmer nest I occupied has been destroyed, by this one's hands. Our enemies grow wiser."

"Sister, it is disappointing, but we can deal with that. Wurmers multiply fast. We'll triple the protection of the nests. As for bringing me this one, well, nothing could please me more—aside from Nath Dragon. You have done well."

He leaned forward and said to Selene, "Your presence has upset my people. When my people are upset, then I am upset. I will give them satisfaction. Prepare, Selene, for judgment."

CHAPTER 28

"BAYZOG," SAID SASHA, "I NEED to go in with them. I can protect them."

"We can't risk them detecting your magic, dear. You're too strong with it. I fear they'll smell you out." Bayzog was leaning over Brenwar's chest. The lid was open. With a soft touch, he rummaged through the potions and items within. "They'll need magic, but something a bit more subtle."

"Nath has far more magic than I do, and he's going in," she said. "What's to stop the titans from sensing him?"

Nath shrugged.

Bayzog replied, "You raise a good point. I won't lie. I really don't want any of my family going in. Not without me, at least. That's the belly of the beast in there."

"But you would send your sons?" Sasha said.

"Mother, we'll be fine." Rerry kneeled down by his father. "It's just a scout mission. Perhaps if Samaz stays behind, you'll be more comfortable?"

Samaz scoffed. "No, I'm going. You'll need me in case you get into a jam."

"No, you stay with Mother and Father. You're too slow to go!" Rerry said.

"Enough!" Nath said. "I'll decide who comes with me. I'm more concerned about going in there without any weapons." He patted Fang's pommel. "I think I'll need my blade in case we get into a mess."

"If you get into a mess, just call out. The silvers and I will come," Slivver said.

"I don't know." Nath removed his sword belt and tossed it to the ground. "I'm certain that if we go in, we'll be searched. I'm just going to have to use my wits—to get in and out."

"I thought we were going to sneak in," said Ben.

"Ha!" Brenwar remarked. "Not with all of those wurmers. You could be the size of a field mouse and still not get inside."

Nath's eyes brightened. "Except they won't be looking for field mice, will they."

With a puzzled look, Brenwar said, "I don't suppose, unless their cats are hungry."

"That's not what I mean. Bayzog, can you shrink us?"

"Oh, I've always wanted to do that," Ben said. "Well, that and be a giant, and a dragon. I think I saw a potion for that."

Rerry plucked a vial out of the box. "I think this is it."

Bayzog snatched it away. "I know what's what!" He eyed the lavender fluid. "Yes, this is the one. I'm not sure how you knew."

"I can read the little labels," Rerry replied, touching one vial lid after the other. "Polymorph, winged feet, fire breath, iron skin, sea gills…"

"Why don't you turn into a bat again, Nath?" Brenwar said.

Nath smirked. He'd done that to escape Brenwar in Morgdon. It hadn't gone too well. The real bats had almost killed him. It was then that he had discovered his inner flame and scorched them. "I have a feeling the wurmers eat bats, so I'll pass. Besides, shrinking sounds like a good alternative."

"The vial only has two doses within, Nath," Bayzog said. "That's only enough for two people. It won't last that long, either, when you split it."

"I guess it's just you and me, Ben."

"Oh, cackleberries!" Rerry said. "I wanted to go!"

"Maybe next time, Rerry. Bayzog, will the potion shrink our gear?"

"It should."

Nath contemplated taking Fang, but he had a feeling that in the new Narnum, if you weren't a soldier or a giant, then you weren't carrying any weapons. Rubbing his chin, he said, "Ben, we're going in with only our wits for weapons. Are you comfortable with that?"

"Certainly." Ben took off his sword belt while he watched Nath unlatch Akron from his back and set the bow aside. "Of course, you can still breathe fire if you have to, can't you?"

"I suppose."

"Hopefully there won't be any need for that during this reconnaissance mission." Bayzog started filling Nath and Ben's pouches with mystic vials. He told them what each did by their colors. "Just get in and get out. But once you shrink, you'll be very small, and your journey from here will become miles long. How do you propose to get in before the magic dissipates?"

"I never thought about that. Hmmm… how much will we shrink?"

"I'd say you'll be at most a hundredth of your weight."

Nath searched the vast distance between them and the entrances to Narnum. The city had channels that tapped into the river that rushed nearby. "I have an idea."

Brenwar, Ben, Rerry, and Nath slunk over to the river bank. The water seemed harmless but moved fast.

Brenwar dug a piece of driftwood out of the sand. "Do you think you can hang onto this?"

"I suppose," Nath replied. He nodded to Rerry in thanks. Gathering Rerry's traveling cloak around him in order to blend in once the shrinking potion wore off, he held up the lavender vial and drank down half the contents, then handed it over to Ben.

"Bottoms up!" Ben said in Samaz's traveling cloak, nodding to Samaz and then gulping down the rest of the potion. "Mmm, it has a bit of a cherry flavor to it that tingles the tongue. How long until it takes?"

"I don't know. Brenwar?"

"Why would I have any idea?" All of a sudden, Brenwar's voice deepened. His words became loud and slow. In a long, drawn-out voice he said, "Nath?"

Right before Nath's eyes, Brenwar started to grow, slowly at first, then it sped up. Nath felt his stomach sink into his toes. Arms out, he steadied his footing. Brenwar looked to be over a hundred feet tall, perhaps two hundred. Rerry was even taller. "I must look like a chipmunk beside him." He swung around. Ben wobbled. Nath reached out and steadied him. "Just stand still until Nalzambor stops spinning."

"Good idea."

Nath saw Brenwar pointing at the hunk of driftwood. It now looked like a barge. "I guess we need to get on then. Are you ready, Ben?"

"I suppose, but I hope you don't regret taking me over Rerry. I may be getting too old for this."

Together they climbed onto the driftwood. Brenwar picked them up and waded into the river. The winds were much stronger and faster than Nath remembered them being before they shrank. The waters swiftly passed under them like wild rapids. Brenwar set them down in the river.

"Ready?"

They nodded, and the dwarf let them go. In a whoosh, the waters took them toward Narnum at a frightening speed. Ben was screaming.

CHAPTER 29

THE SWIFT RIVER TOSSED NATH and Ben back and forth, jostling them all over the driftwood barge they clung to. With water splashing his face, Ben called out to Nath, "I'm slipping!"

Digging into the soft bark with his claws, Nath inched his way toward Ben. He wrapped his arm around Ben's waist and said, "I've got you. We're almost there."

Spitting water out of his mouth, Ben tried to speak. Only splutter came out.

The river ran outside the city's boundary, but man-made channels fed the fresh water into the city. Nath kicked his legs against the current, guiding the strange watercraft toward the next split that led into the city. He turned the hunk of wood just enough by using his swimming legs like a rudder. They sailed into the foaming gap where the river and the channel met and made rapids.

"Hang on to me, Ben!"

They splashed into the surge. Fully submerged, he held onto Ben until they popped up again. The water here wasn't quite as swift but a steady flow heading into the city. Ben started coughing. Nath slapped his friend on the back. "That was fun, wasn't it?"

"I'd like to say so, but admittedly, I can't. Nath, I don't think I want to be small anymore."

"I have a feeling you soon won't be."

Narnum lay ahead. An aqueduct system covered in archways fed the city. The arches looked like gigantic bridges when they passed under them. Looking backward, Ben said with chattering teeth, "Where do we get off? This water is cold."

"I have to admit, Ben, I haven't thought it that far through."

"Good plan."

Back in the day, Narnum had been one of Nath's favorite playgrounds. He knew the city like a local. "Don't worry, I'll know where we are when we get there. I'm just not used to coming in on the river."

"That makes sense enough. Nath, look!"

Nath's head whipped around.

A muskrat bigger than two of Nath put together slipped off the bank and swam right for them. "Guz—er, Great Dragons! Looks like someone is hungry. I have to let go of you, Ben. You have to hang on!"

Ben nodded. "Go, go. I don't want to die by vermin."

The muskrat cut through the water with alarming speed. Nath climbed to the back of the piece of driftwood. He waved his hand. "Come and get me, little beast!"

The hungry-eyed little scavenger closed right in. As soon as the varmint came within arm's length, Nath punched it square in the nose. It let out a squeak, splashed, and spluttered. Then it swam back toward the bank.

"How's that, Ben?"

Ben shook his head. "Exhausting."

They floated a few moments longer before hopping off and swimming to the stone rim of the channel and climbing out. They were just inside the edge of the city, early in the day, shortly after the sun had risen. Like a pair of rats, they raced over the pavement and found shelter in the morning shadows.

Nath wrung the water out of his hair and combed his fingers through his locks.

Ben looked at him. "Really? Do you think we'll run into someone special down here?"

"You never know who you'll meet wherever you go."

"Like a muskrat?'

"Or a rat and a cat." Nath pointed down the backside of the alley, where a cat was chasing a rat into the street. "Heh, and we thought giants were problems."

"All we have are giant problems." Ben dumped the water out of his boots one by one. He shivered. "So now what, do we wait to be big again?"

"There's no telling when that may happen. I think we'd better move. It will help you shake the chills."

"So would the sun."

"It's early and it's fall. I know where we can find some coals nearby."

"Lead the way."

Everything inside Narnum was gargantuan. The cracks in the roads were trenches. The wagons and carts hauling trade were tremendous machines of destruction. And the people busy with the chores of the day made the giants Nath had fought look like children. Being so small was a different reality altogether. It made Nath's perspective change in regard to the smaller creatures of the world. But there was something peaceful about it too, even among all of the racket and clutter. Freedom.

Hah, it wouldn't be half bad to nestle out of sight for a while and avoid all this commotion. Besides, with my breath, I think I could fend off most of the predators small enough to notice me.

Ben grabbed Nath by the arm. "So, where did you say we were going?"

"I'll show you." Nath led the way, sticking close to the walls. People were busy in the streets: buying, selling, eating. A single misplaced footstep could crush him or Ben if they weren't careful. Nath stopped at the corner of one building and pointed across the street. "There!"

"The stables? It looks like it's at least a mile to get over there." A woman led a black horse out of the barn door. "And what happens if we spook one of those mighty beasts? Not to mention we're surrounded by giant people a thousand feet tall. Surely one of them will see us."

"I see your point." The intersection Nath wanted to cross was a hive of activity. Even as small as they were, chances were someone might see them. Maybe not. But it would be hard to avoid those big feet clomping by. "Just give it a moment. Something will reveal itself."

"Like a wild-eyed child?"

"A wild-eyed child? What are you talking about, Ben?" Turning, Nath saw exactly what Ben was talking about.

Leaning against a wagon, a wild-eyed boy stared right at them with a tilted head. His rumpled, long, dirty hair hung over to the side. He had a shovel in his hands. Without taking his eyes off Nath and Ben, he started across the street.

"He doesn't look like a friendly boy."

"No, he looks like the kind that sets a cat's tail on fire. What do we do, Nath?"

"Come on, we'll hide." He gave Ben a shove. Together they scurried away and slipped into a stack of wooden crates stuffed with small red potatoes. "Hungry?"

"I've never been this hungry. There he is."

Through the wooden slats in the crate, he could make out the rough-looking boy. *At least he's alone.* The gargantuan boy crouched down. His stubby hands pawed over Nath and Ben's path. Nath squeezed deeper into the potatoes.

The boy lifted up the crates one by one. Not seeing anything underneath, he looked inside the next crate, giving each a hard shake. He hoisted up the crate with Ben and Nath within.

"Oh my!" Ben said.

"Hang on."

"I'm not worried about hanging on, I'm worried about being turned into smashed potatoes."

The boy shook the crate. The jarring force was like being in the middle of an earthquake. Ben fell out, screaming, "Dragon!" He hit the deck hard.

The boy slung the crate aside with bone-jarring force, smashing Nath between the potatoes. He gathered his wits and squeezed out of the crate just as the giant boy's hand closed around Ben.

CHAPTER 30

A GROUP OF MEN WHEELED A unique contraption into Eckubahn's throne room. It was a heavy-duty cart on a wagon-wheel platform. Like a small stage, it was big enough to hold a handful of men. On top were two heavy beams crisscrossed in the shape of an X. Shackles dangled from chains embedded in the wood.

"I like the people's name for this," Eckubahn said. His voice was a low rumble. "The Podium of Judgment." He snickered. "As I understand, it's a creation of yours, isn't it, Selene?"

Selene didn't acknowledge the titan.

Tylabahn shoved her to her knees. "Answer him!" She kicked Selene in the ribs. The blow lifted Selene off her feet. She skidded across the floor.

Selene's tail licked out, snagging Tylabahn's ankle. She jerked the woman to the floor along with her, knocking Tylabahn's head into the hard floor with a loud *smack*.

Tylabahn jumped to her feet. She rushed Selene with murder in her eyes.

Eckubahn stretched out his tremendous hand between them. "Stop, Sister." His stomach muscles tightened from laughter. "Let Selene have her strength. She'll need it."

"Let me rip her eyes out first."

"No, I want to see her tears before you do. Bind her onto the podium and begone."

With downcast eyes, the burly soldiers hooked their arms under Selene's and dragged her onto the podium. She didn't fight them. They locked her feet at the base of the beams. Her arms were spread out over her head and hooked to the cuffs. They even managed to secure her tail.

Selene could feel the men's hearts pounding in their chests. Their perspiration was driven by fear. They dared not cast a glance at Eckubahn under penalty of death. Testing the bonds with hard tugs, they nodded at one another and, without a word, departed.

"Now what are we going to do to her, Eckubahn, tickle her for more of your amusement?"

"No, I'm going to do something else that I find amusing. I think you'll enjoy it as well." He grunted.

Giant sentries opened up another set of doors adjacent to the front of the throne. A slender woman in priestly robes entered. Her face was pretty, and her bald head was covered in colorful tattoos.

Selene's lips drew tight. The woman was a cleric of Barnabus. One of her very own. The clerics had been disbanded, but many of them had fallen into the service of the titans. To make matters worse, Selene recognized the woman. And she recognized the rectangular case made from polished amber wood that the woman carried. Her chest tightened as the woman took the small set of stairs onto the podium. "It's been a long time, Forever."

"Not that long," Forever coolly replied. She smiled at Selene. "It does my heart well to see you."

"They know each other? What good is this, Eckubahn?" Tylabahn pulled at her ragged locks of hair. "Did you arrange this reunion?"

"No, but it is a pleasant surprise." He tapped his fingers together in a contemplative fashion. "Forever has my eye. Today, she's going to prove her unfailing loyalty. Aren't you, dear?"

Forever bowed her head then looked right up at him. "With an unquenchable passion. Master, may I proceed?"

"The podium is yours."

Kneeling down, Forever set down the rectangular box and opened the lid. Resting inside on a pad of red velvet, slender metal instruments gleamed. She picked up a needle as long as her forearm. "Do you remember giving me this, Selene? What did you call me then, your precious acolyte? You remember that, don't you?"

"You know I do." Selene inhaled through her nose and breathed out slowly. She knew each of the objects intimately. The slender needles, tongs, and tiny saws brought back disturbing memories. "You don't have to do this, Forever."

"Do what? What you taught me to do, my former queen?" Forever poked a needle between the scales on Selene's arm. "Interesting. I've never operated on black scales. Anyway, I hope you don't hope to dissuade me from what you taught me. Especially since I was so, oh, how did you say it, *gifted* at it?"

"We all have gifts, good ones only, not bad. You need to believe me when I tell you that."

"Didn't you tell me once that the only good in the world was death?"

Eckubahn chuckled. "What a shame that you've changed your way of thinking on things, Selene. You would have been a fine asset. But every asset can be replaced. Continue, Forever."

Using a scalpel, Forever started to slice through the layer of Selene's scales. The sharp instrument slipped between the scales. "I've penetrated. You know what that means, don't you, Selene?"

"Of course I do. It means you're about to do something you'll regret."

"And do you regret torturing all the dragons you tormented and experimented on?"

"Absolutely!"

Forever looked Selene right in the eyes. "I don't believe you. I saw you delight in it. And I will delight in it the same way you did, Selene." Her expression darkened. "You abandoned me. You turned your back on all of us. Now you are going to pay for it."

"Everyone has a choice to make. You could have turned away as I did."

Nose to nose, Forever said, "You were my queen! You were my everything! Now I see that you are weak. Now I serve Eckubahn. And just so you know, I hate dragons as much as I ever did." She took a pair of tongs that had small, jagged teeth out of the case. "Especially you."

"Do what you want with me, but that won't change anything. You'll lose in the end."

"Says the one shackled to a tree. What did you think, Selene? That after all of the wrongs we committed, Nalzambor would forgive us? What about you?" She clacked the tongs in front of Selene's eyes. "What punishment did you reap? Nothing. While we died and bled from deeds ordered by you, you started another life for yourself in the dragon realms. How, I ask you, is that fair?"

The very thing that had been eating Selene up all along was now being spoken.

Forever is right. I have this coming.

"I don't hear you saying anything, Selene. I accept your silence as proof of guilt." Using the tongs, Forever clamped down on one of Selene's black scales and said, "This, as you know, is going to hurt." She yanked.

Selene screamed.

CHAPTER 31

NATH HUSTLED OUT OF THE broken crate just as the gargantuan boy snatched up Ben. The boy's eyes were filled with a wicked gleam.

Ben's arms were pinched to his sides in the boy's fist. With pain exploding in his face, he yelled, "Dragon, help me!"

At ground level, Nath stood helpless. *What am I going to do?*

The boy let out a cruel "Hee-hee-hee."

Seeing Ben's fear-stricken face, Nath's inner fires came to life. *Use your wits, Nath.* He let out a puff of smoke. *Use your fire.* He took in a deep breath and let out a whoosh of fire. The bright-orange stream of flame caught the boy's boot ablaze.

It took a few eternal seconds before the boy caught on as he started his trek back across the street. Nath gave chase. Finally, the boy stopped, looked down, hopped, and screamed. His fingers opened up. Ben slipped free.

Nath rushed forward and caught his friend.

The screaming wild-eyed boy patted at the flames. The commotion stirred the crowd.

"Perfect," Nath mumbled.

"What's perfect about being trampled?" Ben replied.

"The diversion, pure and simple. They won't even notice us, so stay close and don't get stepped on." Nath wove his way through the crowd, whose focus was on the hollering boy. As the people rushed to see what was going on and give aid, the road emptied.

Nath and Ben raced into the stable and out of sight.

Ben huffed for breath. "Thanks, Dragon. That was close. The boy was going to use me for a plaything, and he clearly wasn't the kind that would play nice. I'm glad you set his foot on fire. That was brilliant."

"Who knows, maybe he'll become a better man one day for it."

"I doubt it." Ben scanned the barn filled with stables. "So, what are we here for?"

Nath pointed toward the back. An older man in the rear of the stable was leaned back in a chair sleeping. "An old friend." He started walking, covering his nose and avoiding the piles of manure they walked by.

Ben pinched his nose too. "Guzan, that's ripe. It smells ten times worse when you're smaller." A fly as big as his head buzzed right by his face. It landed on the pile. Ben started running. "Gah!"

The old man in the chair wore a pair of bib overalls and no shirt. The hair on his corded limbs was white. Standing at the man's boot, Nath said, "Stay out of the way."

"But—"

Nath climbed up the man's pants leg and didn't stop until he made it to the top of the snoring man's shoulder. He pushed aside the man's graying locks of hair and spoke into an ear as big as he was. "Guthrie." He didn't get a response. He cupped his hands over his mouth and summoned his dragon voice. "GUTHRIE!"

The old man jumped up out of his chair.

Nath latched onto the man's hair.

Guthrie snatched a nearby pitchfork and wheeled around, looking in all directions. "Who's there? Who's there? Stay back! I warn you!"

Nath spoke into the man's ear again. "When's the last time you cleaned your ears, Guthrie? Yuck! They're filthy!"

"Who said that?" Guthrie demanded.

"It's me!"

"Me who?" Guthrie's eyes searched over the barn high and low. "Oh me, oh my, I'm getting possessed by one of those spirits. I knew this would happen."

"You aren't possessed, Guthrie. It's Nath. Nath Dragon!"

Guthrie went still. "You sound like Nath, but your voice is so tiny."

"That's because I am tiny. Listen to me, Guthrie, and don't get all jumpy. I shrank, and I'm on your shoulder."

Guthrie turned his head to the left. "I don't see anything."

"Your other shoulder." Nath stepped to the other side of Guthrie's overall strap and waved.

Guthrie turned his neck. His bushy brows lifted as his eyes fastened on Nath. "Oh my, it is you. Why are you so small? Never mind. I know the answer to that. There's nothing but trouble here, and here you come. I should have known you'd show up, but I was worried."

"You know me," Nath said, studying his old friend's face. Guthrie was a lantern-jawed blacksmith who slept a lot but always looked tired. "Say, you don't look half bad, Guthrie. I'd figured that with me out of your hair, you'd have caught up on your sleep by now. How long's it been, forty years?"

"Forty-two years and as many days." Guthrie yawned. His mouth was so big he could swallow Nath whole. "I didn't think I'd ever see you again, Nath. Especially with all the trouble in the world. It's no surprise you're right in the middle of it, though, aren't you."

"Of course." Guthrie, like Ben, had been a young man when they'd met and adventured together long ago. Guthrie hadn't changed that much aside from the grey hair and added wrinkles. The blacksmith still had plenty of iron in his limbs. "So, are you still putting plenty of sting in the metal, my friend?"

"No one in this city can smite the iron like me. I lie low about it these days, by slinging hay in the stables. I've no desire to aid the enemy." He set the pitchfork aside. "So Nath, how can I help you?"

"Us, actually. I've a friend along." He pointed down at the ground and called out. "Ben, it's safe now. Eh, watch your step, Guthrie. Ben is no bigger than I am."

"Certainly. Ah, I see the wee little fellow. Hello, Benjamin."

Ben waved and let Guthrie pick him up.

Guthrie shuffled away and closed the barn door, cutting off their view of the outside. He moved deeper into the barn, behind the stables and into the back, where a well-equipped forge was set up. The coals inside were banked, warm but not hot. He set Ben down on the warm opposite edge, where he turned around and around, warming and drying every bit of himself. Nath hopped down beside Ben. Guthrie dragged over a chair and sat down. "Tell me what's going on, and leave out the bit where the world is falling apart. I'm keen to that already."

Nath filled Guthrie in about the wurmers, giants, and titans. He explained why they had shrunk down—to slip into Narnum the way they had.

Guthrie nodded. "Oh, that was a clever idea. You were always full of those, Nath. So Brenwar's out there, is he? Any chance he'll swing by? Always good times with Brenwar in the smithy."

"Perhaps when all this is over," Nath said.

"Good. I'd really like to master that seventh layer of metal before I die. There's something I'm missing. It's been forty years, and I still haven't figured it out yet. You tell him I'm waiting."

"I will. So, Guthrie, while we're small—and mind you, it could wear off at any moment—we could use a guide around the city. We need to make haste and avoid treachery. I need to get my father. It's imperative that he be given a proper burial."

"Aye." Guthrie's durable expression softened. "So sorry about your father, Nath. I know how that goes, losing a parent to a monster. Pah!" Guthrie spat. "These giants and those nasty insects have so many minds fooled. The people are as addled as when that evil Selene ruled here. But she's going to finally get what's coming to her. I heard the good news buzzing in the streets this morning. She's on the block." He moved away toward the wall, where a huge, single-bladed battle axe hung. He removed it from the pegs and said, "And I'll have the gratifying pleasure of supplying the axe."

CHAPTER 32

Nath looked at Ben. "Don't say anything."

Guthrie took the axe over to a grinding stone and began sharpening it. The axe was a crude-looking device designed for only one purpose: the swift removal of heads from shoulders.

"Nath, what are you going to do?"

"He doesn't need to know. Let's just see how this plays out."

Guthrie ground the axe's edge against the turning stone. The blade turned red hot and sparked. "Yes, if there is any good in the evil that the giants do, it's putting an end to that nasty Selene. You know, Nath, I was there, at the Contest of Champions, when you won. That was some battle. I've always wanted to tell you how proud I was of you when you prevailed over Kryzak. I thought that would put an end to the streak of evil, but it's back. But some vengeance will be had. That Selene, she killed my mother and father. And they were elderly. Harmless, but they spoke against her. Killed for treason right before my eyes." He held up his axe. "Not with this thing. No, they were some of many who faced the crossbow squad."

"So Guthrie, when is this execution to take place?"

"Sometime between now and when it happens. The giants have an odd way of going about things, so one must remain alert." Guthrie thumbed the edge of the axe blade. "I imagine you won't mind seeing justice dispensed yourself."

Nath wanted to defend Selene. But that would take some explaining. And in the case of Guthrie, it would take a lot of explaining. Guthrie was the kind of man who made his mind up about something and didn't change it. Nath decided to wait for the right time. "Guthrie, can you take us to the arena now?"

Guthrie gave a lazy nod. He hung the axe on the wall. Eyeing his reflection in the blade, he brushed the scruff of his beard. "Sharp enough to shave with. Old Razor Beard can cut anything alive."

Guthrie didn't have any trouble concealing Nath and Ben on his trek through the streets. He loaded them into the pockets of his heavy belt pouch. The only scary thing about the trip was passing the giants in the city that were two to three times bigger than Guthrie—and he was a strapping man.

The crowds thickened the closer they got to the arena. Nath could hear voices shouting out and yelling from inside. Guthrie even fished out some coins and paid for entry. Once inside, he forced himself into one of the front seats that looked out over the arena grounds. Nath's heart broke when he gazed at his father. Ben gasped beside him.

Oh, no, no, no, this is even more horrible now that I'm here in the flesh!

Just as Nath had seen in the mural, Balzurth's great frame was stretched out over a metal rack. His brilliant scales were tarnished in grime and dirt. People down on the arena floor paid money to throw rocks at him. Paintings of the fallen dragon were being sold. Actors in costumes of dragons and giants staged a reenactment of the great battle. The people in the stands cheered and chanted with wicked glee.

Standing up inside the leather pouch with his arms over the rim, Ben said, "This is sickening, Nath. Your father doesn't deserve this. We'll do something, Nath. We must."

At least twenty giant soldiers stood watch around Balzurth. In addition to that were the wurmers that perched on the outer wall of the coliseum. There were hundreds. There would only be two ways to remove Balzurth from Narnum: by force—which Nath didn't have—or by negotiation. His eyes found the Spear of Barnabus, which still stuck through Balzurth's sagging body. A chill went through Nath.

I'll think of something, Father. I promise.

Dropping his chin, Guthrie said to Nath, "Have you seen enough?"

"The evil of this place has filled my eyes forever. Let's go, Guthrie."

"Where to?"

"Can you tell me where Selene is being held?"

"Why?"

"We need to talk, Guthrie."

CHAPTER 33

Using the tongs, Forever dropped one of Selene's scales into a small green crystal bowl. Forever set the tongs down and lifted the small bowl up before Selene's eyes. It was a quarter full. The scales rattled inside when she shook it. "We'll take a little break, Selene. But I do intend to fill it. Just imagine the street value of this. Black scales? Why, this little bowl will be worth a fortune. Isn't that how you taught me to finance our quests?"

Selene panted. Her arm burned like fire. The bridge between her eyes stung. Sweat drenched her hair and dripped down her face. She said nothing.

Using another bowl, Forever caught the sweat that dripped from Selene's chin. "I can sell dragon sweat. The alchemists will pay handsomely for its alluring qualities. Oh, Selene, you taught me so much that I feared I'd never have the pleasure of using again. It thrills me. It's even more exhilarating having you as my subject."

"Why the torture?" Selene managed to say. "You haven't even asked me a question."

"We don't have any questions." Forever gave Eckubahn an approving look. "We already know everything." She picked the tongs back up. "No, I'm just enacting vengeance and showing my loyalty one scale at a time... and it's personal."

"It's not too late to change your ways, Forever. What I taught you was wrong. You can still make things right."

Stepping away from Selene, Forever replied, "You're jesting. At a time like this. I think the strain has gotten to you, Selene." She clicked the tong teeth together, making a clacking sound. "Let's see. You changed your ways, and now you're being tormented. I have not changed my ways, and I still delight in it. I don't think it should be my wisdom in question but yours."

"Yet here I am, standing my ground. Torment me all you want. In the long run, all you will have is pain and regret."

"Eckubahn isn't looking back. He seems quite content."

"Look closer. Didn't you notice his head's on fire?" Eckubahn and Tylabahn were busy talking in words Selene didn't understand. "How much longer before it's the rest of him?"

"That won't happen."

"That's what Gorn Grattack thought."

"Humph. No more talking." Forever grabbed another one of Selene's scales with the tongs. "Only your screaming is allowed."

CHAPTER 34

Guthrie covered his ears while shaking his head, saying, "I don't want to hear any more, Nath. I can't believe what you're saying! You want to help that monster, Selene?"

Nath and Ben were both standing on the anvil inside Guthrie's smithy. The aging blacksmith uncovered his ears and began stoking the fire of the coals. The warmth quickly filled the room, and the glow darkened Guthrie's features.

Nath called to his friend, "Guthrie, you have to let me explain."

"No. No. No!" He stuck his fingers in his ears. "I don't want to hear it, Nath. Not one more word of it. That Selene—*gah*—I hate to even say the name! She's a killer. Forget about her, Nath. What she has coming to her, she deserves. My parents, Nath, you met them, remember? Old and Sweet you used to call them. They were turned into targets. You didn't see them die. You didn't see!"

Guthrie was a hard-headed, loyal hound. It was one of the qualities Nath liked about him. If you crossed Guthrie, you'd never get a second chance. He wouldn't have anything to do with you. And now, Nath was asking Guthrie to help him find someone who had crossed him.

Scratching at the back of his neck, Ben said, "Dragon, I can see the guilt building in your eyes. I understand what Guthrie's going through. I was bitter for a long year after I lost my first wife and children in the war against Barnabus. It took a long time before I came to grips with war and what it is. Selene was behind all of that too, just like she was behind what happened to Guthrie's parents. But Gorn Grattack drove it all, not her. She was a soldier following orders. Somehow, I was able to reconcile that and move on."

"Thanks, Ben. That makes me feel better, but if it took you a year to get over it, it will take Guthrie ten. He's got a lot of stubborn in him, and I can't expect him to help if he's not right with it." He eyed the ground. "We're going to have to do this without him, I suppose. I just wish this shrinking potion would wear off. It should have by now. Do you feel anything?"

"I'm hungry." Ben's face lit up. "Imagine what a plateful of buttery biscuits would look like right now. Imagine swimming in warm butter and dipping that soft, chewy bread. Maybe if we eat something, it will help."

Nath hopped off the anvil, landing on a nearby stool. "Come on. We'll fetch you something somewhere, I suppose. We'll just have to fend off the cats and the rats." He cupped his hands over his mouth and said, "Guthrie! We're leaving!"

Guthrie stopped stoking the coals. "What do you mean, leaving?"

Helping Ben down from the anvil, Nath replied, "I understand why you don't want to help, and I respect that. You've done plenty. We'll find Selene on our own."

Setting the fire poker aside, Guthrie began wringing his hands and coming closer. "Nath, do you remember what you once told me about the wickedness? You said the best way to deal with it was to extinguish it."

"Yes, I do. I was vastly more cavalier in my ways of thinking in my youth."

Guthrie pulled up a stool and sat down. He looked right at Nath and Ben. "It's been over forty years since you said that, and I'm fairly worn with age now. But I've lived by that. I've used it as a simple measuring stick. A standard. Are you telling me it's wrong now?"

"Even the worst of us deserve another chance."

Guthrie leaned closer. "Even orcs?"

"It's not likely that orcs would ever seek redemption, but I suppose it's possible."

Easing back on his stool, Guthrie folded his corded arms over his chest. "I can't believe my ears."

Nath watched Guthrie's eyes become glassy as he turned and fixed them on the glowing coals. Not only had Selene's past come back to haunt her, but Nath's foolish youth had followed him as well. He had followed his own code back then. It hadn't been the best one either. "Guthrie, we're leaving. I hope you understand."

Guthrie's slumped shoulders shook when he let out a weird chuckle.

"I have a feeling we *need* to go," Ben whispered to Nath.

"Yes, I'm getting the same feeling. Can you make the climb back down to the ground from here?"

Ben looked over the edge. "I can manage it."

"I'll go first, in case you slip. I can handle the jump."

Just as he started to hop down, Guthrie turned. "Here, let me help. It's the least I can do before you depart."

Not liking the tone in Guthrie's voice, Nath made the jump.

Guthrie scooped Nath out of the air with surprising agility before he hit the ground. His fingers closed around Nath like a vise. With his free hand, he picked up Ben.

Nath hollered at the gargantuan man. "Guthrie, what are you doing?"

"I'm not going to let you free her, Nath. I can't allow it. That would be wrong, and you know it."

"Listen to me, Guthrie, please!"

Guthrie carried them both tight in his hands. "Don't try anything, Nath. You might be able to escape, but you won't be able to free your friend. So behave. I'm taking you back out of the city."

"No, the wurmers will find us if we grow back, Guthrie. You can't do this! Guthrie, you have to trust me."

"I do trust you, Nath, but I don't trust the likes of Selene. You shouldn't either." He emptied nails out of two clear class jars and dropped a man in each jar. He put corks on the jars, eyeballed them both, and said, "Sorry."

CHAPTER 35

FROM ONE JAR TO ANOTHER, Nath stared helplessly at Ben. His friend pounded on the glass, yelling. Nath could barely hear through his own glass prison.

Glass is much thicker when you're smaller.

He scratched an X into the jar with his fingernail. He punched it, but the thick glass was harder than steel to a dragon his size.

I think I can make it out of here, but I don't know about Ben.

Waving his arms overhead, he tried to capture Guthrie's attention. His friend didn't even look down. Guthrie was headed out of the stable. Ben pounded on his jar with fists that doubled in size. His head grew bigger as well.

Nath punched his own glass. He was yelling at Guthrie, "Let Ben out! The potion has worn off! He'll be crushed to death!"

Guthrie paid him no mind and kept on walking.

"I don't have time for this!" Nath took a quick breath and exhaled a stream of flame. The fire melted a perfect hole in the side of the glass. Nath stuck his head out of it and said in his dragon voice, "Guthrie! Let Ben out now."

Guthrie stopped in his tracks. "What did I tell you about that, Nath?"

Ben's body filled the jar.

"Whoa?" Guthrie said, lifting Ben's jar before his eyes. "He's getting heavy."

"You have to let him out of there! He'll be crushed to death."

Guthrie popped off the lid, turned the jar over, and tried to shake Ben out. Ben's head was out of the jar, but everything else was squeezed inside. He was choking to death. Guthrie shook the jar harder. "I'm trying, Nath. I'm trying!"

Ben's face turned beet red.

"Smash the jar, Guthrie!"

Guthrie dropped the jar hard. It didn't break on the dirt floor. "It's dwarven tempered. Hard to break. I'll get a hammer." He ran back toward the smithy.

"Hang in there, Ben!" Nath wanted to use his breath, but he couldn't risk roasting Ben to death. "We'll figure it out."

Ben moaned.

Guthrie was nowhere in sight.

Nath didn't see anything that could help him at all. He ran over to the jar, balled up his fists, and prepared to hammer away. The glass shattered, showering him in tiny pieces. Ben kept growing. His body returned to normal size. He held his throat in a fit of coughing. The color in his flushed face had returned when Guthrie came back with a hammer.

"He's big again?" Guthrie dashed the sweat from his eyes. "I'm glad for it."

Nath stood on the ground looking at the humongous men. "If he's back, then I ought to be back at any moment! I hope!"

The door out into the street slid open. The wild-eyed boy who had chased them earlier stood at the threshold. A group of soldiers carrying spears and wearing breastplates accompanied the boy. The boy's quick eyes flickered to solid black and locked on Nath.

Spiders crawled up Nath's spine. *Sultans of Sulfur, he's a spirit!*

With a voice not of a child but more like a terror from the darkness, the boy pointed at Nath and told the soldiers, "Catch him! Kill them!"

The first guard advanced. He jammed his spear into Ben's ribs.

"Noooooo!" Nath screamed. A pair of soldiers jabbed at Nath in an attempt to roust him out into the open.

Guthrie rushed in with alarming speed. He clobbered both men upside their helmets with his hammer. Both men stumbled and fell. "That felt good!"

Ben snatched the spear from the soldier who had stabbed him. A blank look fell over the soldier's eyes. Ben butted him in the face with the spear. The soldier collapsed.

"Ben, you live!"

The old warrior searched the ground until he found Nath. "That iron skin potion sure came in handy. I feel great." He broke the spear in half and tossed it aside. "Strong, too!"

The wicked boy who had called them out was gone, but Nath could hear a stir outside. Heavy feet pounded the ground. People in the streets scattered. "Sounds like bigger and badder company is coming." Crawling up Ben's traveling cloak onto his shoulder, Nath shouted to the blacksmith, "Guthrie, is there another way out of here?"

"Follow me." Guthrie ran back into the smithy and opened a panel covered in tools. Ben slipped inside. Guthrie followed them into the secret passage. He shoved the door back. "This will get us into the alley. I'm not sure where you can run after that. Sheesh, that little fiend wants my head on a platter too." He punched Ben's shoulder that Nath stood on. "Ow!" You are harder than iron. Anyhow, I was going to say, just like yesteryear, eh, Nath?"

"Yes, aside from being a thousand times smaller. I have to say, I tire of everyone getting bigger but me. Let's go."

Guthrie led them down the passage and opened up another door that led into an empty alley. They hustled to the opposite end, away from all the noise. "Perhaps it would be best if we split up, Guthrie. You don't have any fight in this. I just want to find Selene."

"It seems I'm in the thick of it whether I like it or not. No, Nath, I'll stay with you."

"I'm going to see where Selene is."

"She's not hard to find at all. You would have already found her, if not for your size. She's been taken to the titan cathedral. The people wait outside to hear her sentencing."

Nath shook his head. A wurmer squawked above them. Everyone looked up and found many wurmers' eyes looking right back at them.

"Guzan!"

CHAPTER 36

"DON'T MAKE ANY SUDDEN MOVES," Nath said. "They're nesting up there. They aren't after us."

"I hate those things," Guthrie said.

The paired-up wurmers dropped their necks below the roof line. Their heads swayed from side to side.

"Ben, just ease into the streets. We might get lucky," Nath said.

"I'm going," Ben replied. He took two steps backward.

The hound-sized wurmers split up, slunk down the walls into the alley, and cut off the exits. Their eyes had a deep purple glow in the dimmer light. Each of the monsters opened its mouth and hissed. Head and long necks low, with tails swishing behind their backs, they advanced.

Holding the hammer in his hand, Guthrie said, "I always wanted a crack at one of these things." Back to back with Ben, he lifted his weapon high.

A wurmer came at him with the speed of a hungry alligator. Jaws snapped at Guthrie's legs.

He brought the hammer down hard on the top of the wurmer's skull.

Crack! The beast recoiled, with its tail flipping back and forth.

"It lives? After that lick? My, they have hard heads!"

The wurmer facing the weaponless Ben and Nath charged at Ben's legs.

Ben sidestepped the enemy's bite.

The wurmer's tail lashed out, swiping Ben from his feet.

He hit the ground hard on his backside.

The agile wurmer clamped its jaws on Ben's leg.

"Gah!" Nath hopped to the ground. He felt helpless with his small size. Everything he did seemed insignificant. "Ben, are you all right?"

With his arm locked around the wurmer's neck, Ben punched the monster in the face. "The iron skin potion is doing the trick. Its claws are tearing the lining out of my traveling cloak, though." He pounded the wurmer harder and harder, stinging its eyes and nose with his iron-hard fists.

The beast broke out of Ben's grip.

Guthrie was fighting hard with the other wurmer. The old blacksmith pounded the wurmer as if he was straightening a piece of steel.

Nath turned back toward Ben. He found himself facing the wide jaws of a wurmer. The monster scooped him up inside its mouth. Its jaw locked down. Nath's world went black. "Great Dragons!"

The wurmer's tongue tried to knock Nath down its throat. He jammed his hands into the roof of the creature's mouth and pushed upward. Its locked jaws didn't give. With saliva dripping down his arms, Nath summoned his fire. His golden eyes lit up. He could see down the black tunnel of the wurmer's throat. He let loose his breath. The golden flames ignited everything inside the wurmer's soft interior and spread. Its jaw widened. It writhed and sucked for air. Nath jumped out of the mouth and landed softly on his feet. Now standing, he watched the monster burn from within. Smoke and flames came out of its nostrils and eye sockets.

Standing high above, Ben said, "That's an eyeful. Well done, Dragon."

Guthrie stood over the other dead wurmer with his smith hammer in hand, laboring for breath. "That was the hardest egg I ever had to crack."

Ben reached down to pick Nath up. His hand started shrinking. His entire body did.

Elated, Nath realized he was growing again. He looked down at the wurmer he'd killed. It seemed small now. "Oh, thank goodness. Being small was really wearing me down." He put his hands on Guthrie's brawny shoulders. The strapping blacksmith was almost as big as him. "It's much better to see you from this point of view."

"I can say the same. Now what, Nath?"

Peeking into the streets and seeing that the commotion had cleared, Nath raised the hood of his cloak. "I still need to see what I can do for Selene."

"Yes, I know. I'm sorry, Nath. This is as far as I go. Thanks to all this stir you created, I'm going to have to see to the safety of my family." He shook Nath's hand. "I hope when we meet again it will be in more peaceful times."

Nath nodded. "Thanks, Guthrie." He watched his friend disappear into the crowded streets. "Come on, Ben."

Narnum wasn't anything like the smaller towns spread out all over Nalzambor. Those places were the backbone of the world, but Narnum was different. The once-Free City was filled with dozens of mighty towers that were hundreds of feet tall. People walked the streets during the day in tens of thousands. It was the biggest city in all Nalzambor, filled with countless people. Once you were in, blending in was easy in a cloak—so long as you didn't create a stir.

Nath and Ben navigated the streets with their heads low. Nath even slouched over a little, even though there were giants far bigger than him roaming the streets. At the moment, he was elated to be back to his normal size.

I don't think I'll ever complain about being small again.

Careful to avoid the prying eyes of the wurmers that scoured the rooftops, Nath and Ben slipped through the streets. After a long haul, they reached the cathedral that Guthrie had spoken about. Impossible to miss, it was a monolith made from huge blocks of cut stone encircled by tremendous archways. It rested beneath the grand tower that Selene and Nath had once called home. Thousands of people were gathered. Many held signs. Others chanted for the death of Selene.

Jaw set and stomach stirring, Nath pushed his way to the front. Giant metal doors stood within the main arches that surrounded the cathedral. A giant sentry stood on each side of the doors. Smaller giants, massive orcs, and ogres kept the angry throng at bay. They pushed people back and off the stone partitions that guarded the entryway. Nath and Ben watched the closed doors.

He said to Ben, "They'll have to open sometime."

"I hope you're right. I'm still hungry."

Nath gave Ben a look.

"What? Those elixirs take it out of you." Ben bit his finger. "But I think I'm still iron hard."

A small knot of soldiers surged through the crowd, led by the boy who had tried to kill Nath and Ben earlier. The giant sentries pulled the doors open enough to allow the boy and soldiers inside.

Craning his neck, Nath caught a glimpse of Selene stretched out on a rack. He gasped.

CHAPTER 37

Nath felt sick to his stomach. He'd never seen Selene in such bad shape before. She hung in the shackles with her head cast down. Sweat drenched her face and sagging neck. The luster in her vibrant body was gone. She seemed lifeless. The giants closed the door, sealing her inside like a tomb.

"You look like you swallowed a green toad, Nath. What did you see?"

"Selene," he muttered. "Come on."

He shoved his way through the people, jostling anyone who didn't move out of his way. He marched to a tavern he knew called the Wyvern's Spur. It was a low-key establishment he'd taken a shine to decades ago, located in one of the poorer areas of the city. The door was open. The boards creaked under his feet when he entered. About twenty men and women were spread out inside. Not a single one of them glanced his way.

Nath found a table in the rear but sat down with his back to the wall. Ben sat across from him with a full view of the bar. He flagged the waitress over. She was a heavyset woman who made the boards beneath her groan as much as Nath had.

"Two ales, darling. Big ones," said Ben.

"Right away, sweetie." She hustled off and quickly returned with two tankards of ale with a creamy froth running down the sides. "Enjoy."

Ben scooted one of the ales over to Nath, then hitched his arm over the back of his chair and took a long drink. "Tell me what's going on, Dragon."

Nath couldn't get the image of Selene's crumpled form out of his mind. The sympathy and anger building inside him wrestled each other. "I'm ready to kill something, but I feel powerless to do so." He took a long drink. The oatmeal stout brought back many memories from his past. "Narnum was always such a fascinating city. Now it's a den of evil."

"Almost everywhere is these days. I just do my best to find the good people." Ben wiped the froth from his mouth. "But sometimes I feel like we're the only good people left in this world. So many of our allies are confused."

"I'll drink to that." Nath finished half of the tankard and set it aside. "I'm not sure what to do, Ben. I need to get Selene out of there. Now."

"You need to stick to the plan, Dragon. You know that. We found her. That was the mission. We just need a way out of here so we can tell the others. I'm certain that when we all put our heads together, we'll come up with something. No doubt Bayzog will."

Nath closed his eyes and breathed in slowly and easily. Ben was right. He'd gotten what he wanted. He knew where Selene was and what was going on. The tough part would be getting her out. The only thought he had was to use Fang. The blade could teleport them through space if Nath could control it, but there was always a risk of losing time as well. It made for an altogether dangerous adventure.

Ben's right, I'll need more ideas on this one.

The city was huge, but it was well defended by the wurmers that covered the skies. In addition, there were all the giants. Getting back out to tell the others was one problem, and getting back in again undetected was another.

"Dragon, I hate to say it, but maybe you should consider only trying to rescue Selene. Balzurth's burial can wait. I'm sure he would understand. Wouldn't you?"

Nath nodded. "Ben, what kind of vials do you have left in your arsenal?"

Ben produced two vials, one yellow and the other a filmy green. "I have some healing, and I believe this one is polymorph. Say, that means I can turn into anything. What about you?"

Nath checked his pouches. There were two mixtures that swirled with mystic color. "Fire breathing and blazing speed. I'm not so certain I need this last one."

Ben snapped his fingers. "I know what we can do. I'll turn into a wurmer and fly out of here, and you can just run back at blazing speeds."

"That helps us get out, but it won't help us get back in. But I like the idea. Ben, you need to trust me."

"Uh oh, what are you getting at, Dragon? I'm not leaving you here alone. Brenwar would kill me."

"I have to stay close to Selene in case anything happens, Ben. You know I can't leave her in the hands of this mob. I have to save her."

"You're right. I say we work together and just snatch her now, Nath. This might be the best shot we get. Let's see. We have speed, polymorph, fire, and healing. Two doses in each. I drank all of the iron skin in a gulp because I was so frightened. Sorry about that."

"No, I would have done the same thing, I'm sure." Nath finished off his ale. "Ben, I like the way you think. It's a good plan. Let's see about our options. I bet we can put something together that the titans will never see coming."

Ben held up his tankard. "Free Narnum."

"Free Selene."

CHAPTER 38

Selene's arms showed small patches where scales were missing. The skin underneath was scabby and swollen. It was even worse in places where Forever stuck in hot, painful needles. The pain got worse and worse. There was no getting used to it.

Finally, the torment stopped when a boy with solid black eyes entered. He told Eckubahn he'd seen a tiny man matching Nath Dragon's description in the city. Eckubahn ordered the boy away and told him to resume his search for Nath Dragon. At the same time, he ordered the soldiers to shut down the entry points in and out of the city.

Putting away her tools, Forever said to Selene, "Don't get your hopes up. The titans know everything. Whatever Nath Dragon does, it won't come as a surprise. The surprise will be on him." She put the lid on the full jar of Selene's scales as quietly as a ghost and vanished behind the cathedral's parlor doors.

Sweat dripped from Selene's chin onto the rolling platform were she stood. She could barely hold her head up. She slung the hair out of her face over her neck. It gave her a clear view of Eckubahn. The broad-chested titan sat on his throne, eyeing the doors. His huge fingers were locked on the arms of his chair. His lips curled back from time to time.

He sits there like Nath is about to come through those doors any moment. How could he even know? He must have better resources than I ever did. It's so hard to tell whose side anyone is on anymore. She squeezed her eyes shut. *Nath, leave me be and save yourself. I deserve what I have coming. You don't.*

Tylabahn returned. The giant, haggard woman glowered at Selene, while at the same time she said to Eckubahn, "You summoned me? I hope it's so I can scale the rest of those black diamonds from that one over there. Why let that little woman have all the fun?"

"I have better plans for you," he said aloud, and then he whispered something in Tylabahn's ear.

Tylabahn's eyes lit up. "I like it. I like it a lot."

CHAPTER 39

NATH AND BEN DIDN'T COME up with any great ideas. The potions Bayzog had given them were just enough to help them get out of the city. Nath had a better idea: use the potions to get Selene and Ben out of the city.

"Listen, Ben. We go in. I'll attempt a parlay. You work your way toward Selene. I'll distract Eckubahn long enough for the two of you to use the polymorph, blend in with the residents, and escape the city."

"What about you? You won't be able to slip the giants."

"I will if I'm fast enough." He held up the speed potion. "I'm fast enough, but with this, I can vanish and they'll never find me."

"I think this is the worst plan I've ever heard. Eckubahn will just kill us. I'd kill us."

"You don't have to go if you don't want to, Ben. Just drink the potion and slip out. Tell the others what's going on."

"No, I'm too far across the border. I'm all in, as always." Ben rolled the vials in his hand then tucked them away. "Let's go."

Nath led the way out of the tavern. He didn't know if Eckubahn would be willing to parlay with him or not, but it was worth a try. Evil people were often overconfident. They tended to gloat about everything. Nath was counting on that to buy all the time he needed.

He sucked down the vial of fleet feet as he approached the crowded cathedral. Again, he pushed through the masses right up to the partition.

An ogre and an eight-foot orc stopped him from climbing over the stone barrier. Nath grabbed the ogre by the nose ring and said to the towering orcs, "Tell Eckubahn that Nath Dragon requests a parlay."

The great doors parted wide less than a minute later. Escorted by giant soldiers, Nath and Ben were led inside. Eckubahn sat tall in his throne, a colossal, muscular giant whose very presence overpowered them all.

Selene hung in her shackles. Her eyes were weak. She seemed disappointed that he'd come.

Eckubahn's jutting chin dropped when he said, "You request a parlay, Nath Dragon? I can only assume it's a trick. I see no reason to honor it." He stroked his chin. "But my curiosity is getting the better of me. What do you have to offer me?"

Nath counted ten giants in all. Each of them had their backs turned. The grand doors had closed. Beyond the columns were parlor doors to many other rooms inside the massive building. Aside from that, it just seemed to be the four of them: Eckubahn, Nath, Selene, and Ben. The chamber echoed when he cleared his throat.

"Ahem. I'll be happy to express my offer while my friend Ben tends to Selene."

"Your friend is not worthy of my presence. He has nothing but mortal blood in him. It's an insult to bring him."

"I know better than that, Eckubahn. These humans tend to many of your needs. They tend to mine as well."

"Beware, Nath Dragon. One false move will be your end, but I'll begin with me. My giants delight in the flavor of bones and flesh."

Nath gave wide-eyed Ben a nod. He climbed the steps up onto the wheeled podium and tended to Selene's wounds. Nath cleared his throat again. "Eckubahn, I'm here to give you an opportunity to surrender."

Eckubahn's head burned bright green. "Do not toy with me, Nath Dragon!"

Nath held his hand up. "Don't get red behind the ears. If you were in my throne room, you'd demand the same. Besides, it never hurts to ask." His laughter echoed and died. "I want Selene and Ben set free, and you can take me in their place."

"Such a childish offer. I have no need to make you a martyr when I already have all three of you."

"They don't wield any power, Eckubahn. I'm the Dragon King. Take me…over them."

"And have you slip free of my grasp the first chance you get? Do you take me for a fool?"

"Well, you are on the wrong side of things."

"Don't mock me, Nath Dragon, or you will wind up in far worse shape than your father."

"Speaking of my father, I want a proper burial for him. In the Dragon Graveyard. I want the fetchers to come in and pick him up and take him away."

"Do you think I would dare part with my most treasured prize? I came back here to kill him. Now I have him on display for all to see. His very appearance crushes the hopes and dreams of those who thought they had free will. No. No to all your requests." Eckubahn snapped his fingers. The giant soldiers did an about-face toward him. "Take them," he ordered.

"Whoa, Eckubahn, this is a parlay. You're supposed to let me return to where the parlay was requested. Certainly you want your people to see that you're honorable."

"I'll honor half the deal. Your useless assistant may depart, but I offer him no protection outside of this hallowed ground. You, Nath Dragon, are staying with me and will be my special guest at the judgment of Selene." Eckubahn pointed at the doors. Soldiers pulled them open.

Nath's eyes slid over to Ben. He gave his friend a wink. Facing Eckubahn, he said, "Fair enough. I wouldn't leave Selene anyway." He started to cough. With the potion of fleet feet surging through his veins, he couldn't hold it back any longer. He summoned his fire and let out a stream of smoke. The smoke covered him, Ben, and Selene in an instant.

Eckubahn roared. "Treachery! You'll regret this!"

Nath moved through the smoke as fast as he'd ever moved on two legs. He hopped up onto the platform and snapped Selene's chains. Ben drank half of his potion and fed the other half to Selene. "It's polymorph. Blend in and flee," Nath said.

"Close those doors!"

Nath bolted into the gap between the doors and wedged his body there before they could be closed. He strained against the giants that were trying to close them. "Hurk!"

Selene and Ben dashed through the crack. Nath's strength gave way to the giants. He got trapped between the doors with his head on the outside.

The crowd ignited when they cast their eyes on Selene. Nath let out another blast of smoke. In the confusion of smoke and mist, he noticed Selene and Ben changing into a pair of orcs. They wrestled with the crowd for a few moments and finally disappeared.

Trapped and wriggling between the doors, he said, "Well, two out of three's not bad."

CHAPTER 40

FANNING THE SMOKE FROM HIS face, Eckubahn said, "Clever, Nath Dragon. You almost managed to pull it off." The titan remained seated on his throne with little change in his expression.

Two giants held Nath up by the arms. His feet dangled high over the ground. The potion of fleet feet had worn off. The use of all his fire and smoke had left him drained. He still had enough energy to say, "I disagree. I did pull it off. My friends are free."

"They'll never make it beyond the wurmers and all of my spies."

"I made it in. It will be even easier for them to get out."

A rumbling sound came out of Eckubahn's throat. "You are overconfident, Nath Dragon. We titans know everything. When we were trapped behind the Great Dragon Wall, we still heard and saw everything that went on. We've seen every trick mankind has ever pulled. We are always ready for anything."

Nath didn't like the way the titan said it. Eckubahn was entirely too calm. "So what are you going to do to me?"

"That's a good question. Now that I have you, I'm not sure if I want to torment you. I missed that opportunity when I killed your father. I was looking forward to that. Or should I take your life and be done with you once and for all?"

"I can see your point about not wanting to let me hang around." Nath kicked his feet, which dangled in the air.

"Silence."

"Sure, I always do my best thinking when it's quiet." He started to whistle.

Eckubahn looked right at Nath and grinned.

It sent a chill right through him. Something was wrong. The only ones in the room were him and the giants. There wasn't anyone else left. *What is he hiding? What am I missing?* Nath told himself the only thing that mattered was that Selene and Ben were safe. He was confident that the two of them together would get out of Narnum. They had to. But something else was eating him up, raising his scales on end.

Draw him out, Nath. Use your wits. Think of something.

"Say, Eckubahn, it seems rather pathetic that you aren't willing to take me on in a straight-up battle. Would you prefer to settle the matter of conquest on the field? As a matter of fact, I challenge you to a contest in the open plains and skies."

Eckubahn's eyes flashed. His chin lifted. "The battle is already won. I've taken the general from the field."

"Face it, Eckubahn, the dragons will never surrender if I don't. The only way to take this world is through my submission. I'm offering you an opportunity to prove yourself. You should take it. Or are you scared of losing again, like you did against my father?"

Leaning forward with his hands crumbling the stone armrests of his throne, Eckubahn said, "Your father deceived me! That is why he won." His voice shook the room. "He took the coward's way out when I challenged him to a head-on battle."

"That's not how I understand it. Didn't he defeat you on your own terms in your hive? You and your spirits were in the belly of Nalzambor when you lost…"

"Silence!"

The flames covering Eckubahn's face fluctuated. His expression darkened. The fires brightened and dimmed.

Nath could feel the heat rise in the room.

I've gotten under his skin. I'd better not overdo it, lest these giants pull my arms off.

He could see that he'd hit a sore spot, however.

Grahleyna had revealed how Balzurth had defeated the titans. They'd lured Balzurth into a battlefield deep in the core of the earth, where their spirit-like forms had strength and a great advantage. The only way to finish them off completely was in their realm down there. Balzurth led the dragons to the threshold of the titan netherworld. Instead of taking the bait of Eckubahn's challenging calls, Balzurth—in his great wisdom—had sealed the titans inside the netherworld by forming the Great Dragon Wall.

Nath smiled. Not only had the Dragon Wall vanquished the spirits, it had saved countless dragons as well. The battle had been won without shedding a single drop of blood.

No wonder Eckubahn's furious at the mere mention of it.

Still dangling, he said to the silent Eckubahn, "Unlike my father, I will face you above the ground in an all-out battle. You have the giants and wurmers, and I have the dragons. Come now, Eckubahn. You're a warrior. You can't tell me that isn't exactly what you want. Let's finish the fight once and for all. Dragons against titans."

"You are all bluster, Nath Dragon. From my side of things, it is very amusing. You see, the spirits know everything, but you don't. But now a portion of that mystery is going to be revealed to you. You'll have plenty of time to contemplate it." He gave his giants a hand signal. "In the Deep."

Chapter 41

The Deep of Narnum was a well that waited below the city's tallest tower. It was more than a thousand feet down, so they said. Nath knew of it. Gorlee had talked about his experience of the deep, including his encounter with the triant Bletver and the Phantom—both of whom Nath knew were now dead.

Nath stood in the sublevel below the great tower facing the entrance to the deep. Giant soldiers surrounded him. One of the giants—bald and smelly with sagging skin—held the line of iron cord that was wrapped around Nath's neck. Nath's hands were bound behind his back. Another soldier kept a spear on his back. Every doorway he passed through was heavily guarded and sealed.

The giant holding the rope shoved him forward. "Go."

Nath shuffled ahead. Hanging over the twenty foot-wide-hole was a cage similar to the ones miners used to be lowered into the mines. A crank-and-pulley system was manned by an ogre. Nath stepped onto the big oversized platform, joining the one-eyed ogre that stood within. The ogre held a lantern with a flickering eye of flame inside.

Looking up at the ogre, Nath said, "Down, please."

The ogre's lips curled. He grunted words in Ogre to his kin at the crank, who pulled back a lever, unlocking the gears with a grinding of metal. Slowly the ogre began turning the handle with a note of strain in his face. The caged platform started down.

As they descended, more ogres poured barrels of black oil down the edges of the well. Nath could see the surface was as slick as black ice.

I should have negotiated for better quarters.

The cage descended at an agonizingly slow rate. The air became stale and chill. The heavy breathing of the ogre was accompanied by the steady *click click clack* from the crank above. Nath could see the oily stone walls. No one would be climbing out again like Gorlee had. Nath marveled that the changeling had managed that feat.

Almost an hour later, the cage neared the bottom. There was a faint illumination in the corridor below them, of an unknown source. The ogre let out a loud grunt. The cage stopped ten feet above the ground. The ogre took the noose from Nath's neck, grabbed him by his cloak, and slung him out of the cage.

Nath hit the ground with a *thud* then forced himself up to his knees. The cage began to rise. His hopes began to fade. Oil dripped in his face from the inner core of the well that hung thirty feet above his head. The ground was slick with black oil as well.

"Yeck!"

Up on his feet, Nath moved down the corridor. He knew the Deep harbored the worst of the worst of Narnum's criminals. He imagined someone ruled down here—like Bletver, but even worse.

This must be what Eckubahn had in mind. Imprison me like Father imprisoned him. Or have me devoured by some vicious monster down here.

The corridor was illuminated by a type of rock that glowed when crushed into gravel or powder. Called Alsium, it filled the cracks in the walls. It was more common in the world of dwarves and gnomes. The corridor sloped upward, then bent to the left up a crudely cut set of wide steps in the stone. He followed the path in eerie silence until a grand chamber opened up before him. It was a sunken cavern surrounded by several levels of small caves. It must have housed hundreds of people before. Now there wasn't a soul to be found. It looked abandoned.

Nath tried to smell for people, but he found it hard to breathe.

Don't tell me I'm here alone. I can't think of anything more miserable.

He hopped off the overlook unto the cavern floor. His eyes scoured the interior and froze on a figure lying with its back to him just inside the mouth of one of the small caves. The person shifted. Nath's instincts ignited as he crept forward.

Careful, Nath. It might be some sort of marrow-sucking monster in disguise.

A tail licked out and swept him off his feet. Something strong and powerful pounced on top of him and pinned him down.

Nath found himself face to face with the unexpected. "Selene?"

"Nath?" Her weary violet eyes couldn't hide their surprise. Then her expression changed. Her voice filled with concern. "Nath, you look like you've seen a ghost. I know I look bad, but it can't be that bad."

"No, Selene. That's not it." He had trouble finding his breath. He shook his head. "Oh no, oh no!"

"What is it, Nath? Tell me."

"If you're down here, then who did I rescue up there?"

Selene said the dooming word, "Tylabahn."

"Sultans of Sulfur! Ben's in trouble. They're all in trouble!"

EPILOGUE

POSING AS ORCEN SOLDIERS WITH an orcen search party, Tylabahn—still disguised as Selene using Gorlee's body, but temporarily transformed into an orc with a potion—and Ben managed to slip outside of Narnum. Letting the old human lead the way so he wouldn't ask the wrong questions, she told the rest of the search party in Orcen that the two of them would expand the search to the southern part of the city.

Taking them on a fork off the main southern road with Narnum a mile behind them, the bony old man sighed.

"That was close. If you didn't speak Orcen, I'm not so sure we would have made it out of there." He stared right into her face. "I know you're wounded. Do we need to stop and rest?"

"No, keep going, please. The sooner we get to the others, the sooner we can find a way to help Nath."

Shuffling along with his arms swinging, he said, "We almost made it. All of us. I hated to leave him. It will haunt me until we get him back."

"You did well, Ben. You followed his orders. I'm grateful for it. We'll get him back." She patted his back. "Trust me."

Ben nodded.

Inside, Tylabahn was laughing. *Fool. All of the races are full of them.* She kept up the conversation. "How long do you think this potion will last?"

"Hours, maybe. By the Sultans, I'm glad you said something. Let me know if you see me change. We can't just walk right up to the others like this. They might kill us." He rubbed his head. "I'm so weary I wasn't thinking."

"Who awaits us, Ben?"

"Brenwar, of course. Bayzog, Sasha, Rerry, and Samaz." He counted on his fingers. "Oh, and Sansla. He had quite a story to tell about your battle with the nuurg." He showed her a grin. "You made a lasting impression."

"I have a knack for that."

The old fool led them down the path to where the distant woodland started. Deep into the tree line, he stopped and checked his hands. "Huh, still an orc, I guess. I think it's best we wait."

"Wait for what, you stupid orc?" Brenwar stepped into full view. Mortuun was cocked behind him, ready to swing. "For me to put a crater in your head?"

Rerry and Samaz appeared with their weapons drawn. The three of them had Ben and Selene surrounded.

"No, wait, Brenwar, it's me, Ben, and this is Selene." He motioned over toward her with his hands. "We're polymorphed."

"You speak awfully funny for an orc, I'll grant you that, but you sure look like one." Brenwar looked Ben and Selene up and down. "Tell me something only Ben would know."

"Uh, well, Nath Dragon wields Fang and Akron. He stood trial at the Corridor, where we just left. Er…"

"That's good enough. Come on, the both of you. Just stay ahead of me where I can see you."

"Come on, Selene," Ben said.

Brenwar led them deeper into the woodland and inside the cover of a cave. Bayzog and Sasha were waiting inside. They stood up with wide eyes.

"Wizard, they say the potion did this to them." Brenwar shoved them both forward. "I'll let you vet them."

Bayzog's eyes locked on Ben's with an entrancing power. Ben blurted out the whole story of the ride down the river, a meeting with Guthrie the blacksmith, and finally escaping with Selene. During the duration of his speech, he felt himself change back from orc to Ben.

He also saw Selene change back while he talked. She held her shoulders and shivered.

Ben caught her out of the corner of is eye. "Selene, you're back." He checked his fingers. "I'm back as well!"

"You still smell like an orc if you ask me," Brenwar said.

"No I don't." Ben sniffed the air. His face soured. "Aw, maybe it's the orcen sword belts we wear. We stole them as part of the disguise."

Sasha got up and draped a blanket over Selene's shoulders. "You look like you've been through a lot. Let me help."

"Thank you," said Selene.

Bayzog stood in front of her now, staring at her with penetrating eyes.

Coughing, she averted her eyes. She coughed really hard.

Bayzog reached out to help her. "Please, sit down and refresh yourself. We'll discuss our plans when you're ready."

She eyed his exposed chest. "That won't be needed. My plans have been fulfilled. Good-bye, Bayzog." She plunged the dagger into his chest.

Everyone around her screamed, "Nooooooooooooo!"

Selene laughed.

Wrath of the Dragon

-Book 8-

Craig Halloran

CHAPTER 1

"Noooo!" Rerry screamed. His eyes were locked on the impaled form of his father with Selene's dagger poking out of his chest. Blood dripped down her hand.

Bayzog's violet eyes dimmed. His eyelids fluttered. Before his body sagged to the ground, Samaz caught him in his arms.

Sasha rushed over and helped Samaz lower Bayzog to the ground. His eyes were glassy. "Bayzog, my love, stay with me. Stay with us." Her hands caressed his peaked face. Her head turned over her shoulder. "Someone get a healing potion!"

Brenwar stormed at Selene with Mortuun gripped in his hands. "I knew you were a traitor! Hold her fast, Sansla! I'm going to end this one."

Sansla seized Selene in his powerful arms. The winged ape held her in a bear hug from behind. A grave expression ran through the wrinkles of his face. He said, "How could you? How dare you? Why?"

Ben's stomach churned. His knees weakened. He staggered back into the cave wall.

Selene dropped the blood-wet dagger on the ground. She laughed. "The wound is fatal!" Her face filled with triumph and glee. "It's delightful!"

Brenwar's fist smote her in the belly, knocking the wind from her lungs. "There'll be no laughing, witch!"

"Get a healing potion!" Sasha screamed.

Listless, Ben's fingers found the healing potion in his belt pouch. He walked it over to Rerry's awaiting hand.

Rerry put the potion to Bayzog's lips. "Drink this, Father." Tears streamed from the young part-elf's eyes. "Please."

Bayzog sputtered and spat. If he got any of the potion down, it was hard to tell.

"Just pour it on the wound," Sasha ordered.

Rerry complied.

Selene huffed in Sansla's vice-like grip. "It won't do any good. That strike was the strike of death. See the glaze over his eyes? He is taken. Ooomph!" She doubled over beneath the power of Brenwar's hard fist.

"You murderer!" Brenwar's eyes were ablaze. He puffed the whiskers of his long moustache. "Your end will be just as swift! You'd better pray that he lives!"

"Why would I do that? I want him dead. I want you all dead."

"No, Bayzog, no, no." Sasha cradled her husband in her arms. She was hysterical. "You can't die! You can't die like this!"

Looking into Sasha's eyes and taking his sons' and her hands in his, Bayzog's last words were, "Be strong. Be faithful. Where this life ends, another begins." Bayzog expired.

Rerry sat on his knees with his hands covering his face, crying.

Samaz remained by his brother's side, stark, sad, and silent.

Sasha's sobs echoed in the cave as she clutched Bayzog to her chest. "Why?" she whispered. "Why did you do this, Selene? He was your friend."

"None of you are my friends. All of you are fools. I delight in your misery. I always have." Selene tossed her head back. "Besides, Bayzog only bought you time. Without him, your doom is inevitable."

"Your doom is inevitable," Brenwar said, poised to strike her with Mortuun.

"I hardly think so. Look around you. Not here, per se, but outside. The wurmers will come. The titans and the giants will come. They know you're here. Nothing but death awaits all of you out there." Selene's sneer grew. "I'll enjoy seeing you all devoured."

"How could you do this?" Ben yelled in her face. "Dragon and I risked everything to save you, and this is how you repay us!" He was mortified. His skin was clammy and cold. He hadn't seen this coming. No one could have. The entire event was bizarre. "I thought you were one of us."

"I stand with the true victor. I always do, once I see the handwriting on the wall. You see, this is your problem, all of you so-called heroes. You think you can do anything, but at what price?" She stuck out her chin at Brenwar. "Death. Your pitiful little band has reached its limit in the department of good fortune. How long did you think you could slip bad fortune's grasp, forever? Hah! If anything, I did Bayzog a favor. I ended his prolonged misery of a life on Nalzambor."

Rerry jumped to his feet and pointed at Selene. "You won't fare any better! You're a murderer! What you'll face will be far worse than death!"

"I'll take my chances," she said.

The cave quieted. The dirt walls closed in. Ben struggled to breathe. He couldn't make heads or tails of what Selene had done. The titans had tortured her, and now she was siding with them. *This is madness!* With watery eyes, he walked up to her. "How could you do this to Nath after he gave up all of his powers for you? No one can be that sick!"

"You'd be surprised what one can do in the interest of self-preservation. None of you are any different." She glared at Sasha. "You'll wish that you shared a grave with him before it's all over. Of course, once you are truly pressed by the likes of Eckubahn and his forces, it wouldn't surprise me one bit if all of you switched sides. Narmum is full of people not so much different than all of you, who caved to Eckubahn quicker than they caved to me."

"Speak for yourself, not me!" Brenwar said. "Not any of us, you black-scaled fiend!"

"You're such a stupid dwarf." She looked away from Brenwar. "And your stupidity has worn off on the others."

Brenwar turned to his comrades. "Listen to me, all of you. We witnessed this black heart committing murder." He spun his war hammer in his hand, revealing the bladed side. "I'll deliver the execution myself. There is honor in it, both dwarven and elven. But we cannot let Selene live a moment longer. It's too dangerous."

Selene chuckled. "You won't kill me. You're too noble. And what would Nath say? Do you think he would approve of you killing me?"

Glaring at Selene with hot eyes, Sasha said, "I know he would. You have my support, Brenwar."

"Mine too," Rerry said.

Samaz nodded.

Ben stepped away from the wall. "None of us can speak for Dragon, but he's not here. So what he thinks doesn't matter. She's too dangerous to keep alive. Execute her."

Brenwar looked up at Sansla Libor.

The winged-ape said, "As the king of the roamers, I concur."

Selene's eyes popped wide open. "But…"

CHAPTER 2

"I don't expect anyone to watch," Brenwar said as he thumbed the edge of the war hammer's back blade with his skeleton thumb, "but what must be done, must be done. Sansla, hold her fast."

"You're really going to go through with this!" Selene gasped. "I almost admire you, dwarf. You aren't as feeble as I presumed you to be. I'm shocked you're willing to kill a woman."

"You aren't a woman. You're a monster."

Selene struggled inside the grip of Sansla's mighty arms. She kicked her heels back into his shins. "Let go of me!"

Sansla lifted her off the ground. He squeezed harder.

Selene's eyes bulged. "Gah!"

Brenwar brought the edge of Mortuun to her neck. "Any last words, Selene?"

Selene's violet eyes turned black. Her lips curled. "You are fools! Every last one of you! I cannot die! I never could!" The black scales on her neck pulsed and stretched. She flexed her arms.

"She's getting stronger, Brenwar," Sansla said. The powerful ape's joints cracked. "Make it quick!"

Selene's body lurched and convulsed. Grew. With her feet now touching the ground, her toes dug into the dirt like claws. Her shoulders widened until she reached Sansla's own great girth. She let out a shrill cackle as her black hair spread out over her shoulders in a rich shade of gray. Breaking free of Sansla's grasp, she hip-tossed the winged-ape over her shoulder.

Brenwar dove out of Sansla's path. Lifting his beard off the dirt, he yelled, "Stop that thing!"

Selene transformed into a towering hag. With a swipe of her long, powerful arm, she knocked Ben into the wall. "I'm not toying with you little wretches any longer!"

Coming to his feet, Brenwar growled, "Who in Nalzambor are you?"

"It's Tylabahn!" Sansla replied. "I knew something didn't smell right."

Rerry burst in front of Tylabahn and stabbed her in the chest with his sword. "Vengeance for my father!"

Tylabahn staggered back. Gripping the sword buried in her chest, she said with dramatic flair, "Oh, you got me!" With the back of her hand on her forehead, she swooned and dropped to a knee. "I'm dying, I'm dying! My strength flees me. The light grows dark within."

"Good," Rerry said as the room fell quiet.

"I confess, I'm, I'm so sorry for what I did. Eckubahn made me do it. I had no choice in the matter. I never wanted to be evil. Really." Tylabahn sagged a little farther. "This elven steel in my chest burns me. My heart fails." Slowly she pulled the sword from her chest. It was a small thing, more like a wand, in her hand. She tossed it at Rerry's feet. "Take it, brave young elf. You will need that special blade to vanquish Eckubahn. It's the only way."

Rerry's head tilted. "Huh?" He glanced back at the others.

Seeing a dangerous flicker in Tylabahn's eyes, Brenwar said, "Rerry, watch out!"

Striking fast, Tylabahn's clawed fingertips ripped through Rerry's back and spun him completely around. The part-elf hit the deck screaming, "It burns! It burns!"

Brenwar and Sansla sprang into action. The pair of men stormed Tylabahn with hammer and fist swinging. A strike from Mortuun sent Tylabahn sailing out of the mouth of the cave. Her body bounced over the ground and smacked into a tree.

She rose to her feet, clutching her side with one hand. "Is that the best that you can do?"

Sansla flew into her face fists first, rocking her jaw.

She let out a howl. Now out of the cave, her body expanded even farther. The trees became saplings beside her. Standing at twenty feet, the all-powerful titan hag scooped Brenwar up with one hand and smashed him into the ground.

"Brenwar!" Sansla called out. He pounced onto the titan's neck and put her in a choke hold.

She lurched back, gagging.

Brenwar pushed up and spat the grit from his mouth. "Dirt never tasted so good." Hammer in hand, he charged, unleashing a deadly strike to her knee.

Whack!

Tylabahn let out a furious howl. She grabbed ahold of Sansla. "Get off me, you furry tick!" She flung him into the treetops.

Brenwar hammered her in the belly. A second sharp blow from Mortuun cracked her in the face.

She stumbled backward. Eyeing Brenwar, she scowled. "I'll have you skinned alive, you little bearded pig."

"Nobody skins a dwarf!" He charged.

Tylabahn fled on foot, swift as a giant stag. Birds burst from the treetops at the sound of the shrieking wail she made as she disappeared out of sight.

Sansla hopped down out of the tree. "I can go after her."

"No." Brenwar eyed the sky. Through the tree limbs he spied large flying creatures high above. "Wurmers. She's alerted every last one of them. We need to get out of here."

Ben and Rerry were standing in the mouth of the cave, grimacing.

Eyes squinted, Ben said, "So you scared her off?"

"Only to scare up other things. We need to get out of this forest before it's too late."

Ben held Akron in hand. He nocked an arrow. "I'm more than prepared to make my final stand. In a way, I'm just relieved that wasn't Selene. Which means she and Nath are still inside that city somewhere. I failed. I was supposed to bring back at least one of them, and I lost both of them."

"If you want to sulk, go sulk somewhere else," Brenwar said.

"I wasn't sulking. I'm mad at myself. Can't I be mad at myself? Aren't you always mad at yourself?"

"No, I'm a cauldron of joy inside." Brenwar turned at the sound of huge bodies crashing through the branches.

Several wurmers landed. With fierce glowing eyes the wurmers scurried straight for them.

Brenwar squeezed Mortuun. "It's time to dance."

CHAPTER 3

URMER AFTER WURMER CRASHED THROUGH the branches like a plague of giant insects. Sansla snatched up a pair of wurmers by the necks. He crushed their heads together. Beside him, Brenwar was up to his beard in them.

Ben fired moorite arrows into them, one by one. The first shaft zinged through the hearts of two of them. "Top that, Brenwar!"

Grunting, Brenwar replied, "Nobody tops a dwarf!" With the flat of his hammer, he pulverized a wurmer's skull. With a backspin of Mortuun, he broke the back of another. The foul creatures writhed like worms. Brenwar stopped them. "I hate these things as much as the giants!"

Many wurmers spat glowing fireballs at them. The spitballs singed the fur on Sansla and burnt Brenwar's beard. At the mouth of the cave, the bold men and Rerry fought them off with deadly swings.

Rerry's elven blade that was once Scar's sheared through the hard scales of the wurmers like wheat. Gutted open, their acidy innards spilled and bubbled on the ground. The brave part-elf had smoking flecks all over him. "And I hate these creatures more than I hate orcs!" He hacked a small wurmer in two with a double-handed chop. "And titans!" He cut again. "And Tylabahn!" He swung away. "I will avenge my father!"

The wurmers continued to fill the forest like falling leaves.

Ree-rah! Ree-rah! Ree-rah!

The hollow, disorienting sound was deafening.

Sasha's voice cut through the horror. "There are too many, Brenwar! We must flee!"

"There's nowhere to go except fight!" Covered in burning wurmer grit and busted scales, Brenwar pounded away. "If we all go to the grave today, so be it. I'm certain that Bayzog misses my company!"

Sasha's amulet glowed with a radiant pink fire that shimmered like rose blossoms. It traveled down her arms and rose on both of her hands. Her eyes glowed white-hot. She marched into the throng where flesh met scales, metal, and meat.

"Get back in the cave, Sasha," Brenwar ordered. "Find a way out of here for us, if there is one to be had."

"NO!" Her voice was amplified. The amulet hanging around her neck became a beacon of angry starlight. "I am angry! They will feel it!" A blast of power burst from her hand. The burst tore a hole clear through the wurmer ranks. She then unleashed one ray of power after another. Wurmer wings were singed and blasted apart. Scales flaked from their bodies. Holes of light were punched clear through them.

"Yes, Mother! You're doing it! Have at them!"

Brenwar blinked for a moment, as a path cleared. The wurmers fell under Sasha's power in heaps. "You've got an awful lot of fight in you, lady."

"I've been saving up!" She hit the next landing wave of wurmers. Some of them burned. The trees caught fire. Smoke filled the air. Tears streamed down Sasha's angry face. "Burn, demons! Burn!" The rosy-pink flames firing from her fingertips ripped through the scaled masses. And then as suddenly as Sasha's fire had started, it went out. Her shoulders sagged. Her body swayed.

Ben scooped her up just before she fell. "Sasha! Sasha!" he said, tapping her face. "She's out, Brenwar!"

The wurmer ranks regenerated as fast as they'd taken them out. Now they were down another fighter. Still fighting with wurmers all around him, Brenwar roared, "Let them have it, Mortuun!" Wearing his special bracers, he raised the great war hammer high over his head and brought it down with wroth force. The ground shook.

KRANG!

A shockwave of energy knocked the wurmers backward. The branches in the trees cracked and snapped. The field of the enemy cleared, if but for a moment. Everyone backed toward the mouth of the cave as the wurmers began to drop from the sky once more.

Samaz had the Elderwood Staff in one hand and his father's dead body over his shoulder.

"What are you doing?" Rerry said to him.

"I don't know, but get Brenwar's chest, Rerry," replied the shaggy black-haired Samaz. "There has to be something inside it that we can use." Rerry ducked into the cave. "And grab Nath's sword too."

Rerry quickly reemerged. With his own sword sheathed, he had Fang in one hand and was dragging the strongbox with the other. Eyeing Fang's blade, he said, "I suppose I can fight with this. I always wanted to. It will be a fine way to go down before we join Father."

"That's not what I had in mind," Samaz said.

Turning his hot stare on Samaz, Brenwar said, "What did you have in mind, boy? Time is pressing."

"See if you can use it like Nath did, to teleport us," Samaz suggested.

Ree-rah! Ree-rah! Ree-rah!

Wurmers hit the ground and crawled through the smoke.

"They're coming!" Brenwar yelled.

"I can't do that!" Rerry responded.

"Try!"

Holding the sword out in front of him, Rerry closed his eyes. His brows knitted together as he said, "Fang, take us away! Fang, take us away!" He repeated it several more times. "It's not working!"

Samaz fished through Brenwar's chest. "Keep trying. It has to work!"

Brenwar and Sansla Libor were fighting off the horde of wurmers with everything they had. Brenwar called out, "You think of something! We fight! There has to be something in that chest!"

Ben set Sasha down beside the fallen Bayzog, reloaded Akron, and started firing. He yelled out a battle call that was not his own. "Dragon! Dragon!"

Rerry repeated it. Sword high, he charged into the frenzied fray, screaming at the top of his lungs, "Dragon! Dragon!"

It was music to Brenwar's ears. They fought on, taking down the wurmers one, two, or three at a time. But at long last, his powerful limbs met with exhaustion. His last drop of sweat hit the ground. He let out his final battle cry. "For Morgdon!"

CHAPTER 4

THE JAWS OF THE WURMERS clamped down on Brenwar's legs. He groaned. Mortuun's swings became sluggish. Knowledge of the iron dwarf's mortality sank in as his powerful endurance expired. Beside him, up to his neck in wurmers, Sansla Libor labored against the gnashing forces. The winged ape's body was full of gashes. Mats of his fur flew. "There will be no shame in you falling before I do," Brenwar said to Sansla.

"Ha! You're practically buried already, dwarf!" The ape grinned. "It's been a good fight, has it not?"

Still hitting anything scaled that moved, he replied, "One of the best. I just wish it was giants." A silver streak of light caught Brenwar's attention. Silver dragons landed in their midst. Slivver was among them.

"Did someone call for dragons?"

"Where've you been? Oh, I know. Where the fight is, you aren't," Brenwar said.

"I'm here now." Slivver barked a command in Dragonese. The silver shade dragons that accompanied him snaked through the frenzy. They picked up Bayzog, Sasha, Rerry, and Samaz and took flight. Others gathered the chest. Ben was plucked up next, leaving Brenwar, Sansla and Slivver. "It's time, dwarf."

"I'm not flying!"

Slivver's tail coiled around Brenwar's ankle. "I know. You're being flown." With a fierce beat of his wings, he took to the air.

Brenwar yelled, "Put me down!" He watched Sansla slug a few more wurmers.

The great ape's legs coiled. He jumped high, beat his bat-like wings, and flew right after them. The wurmers screeched and pursued with tenacious ferocity. Taking the wurmer clamped on his ankle by the wing, he slung it off. Then he said, "You'd better fly faster, Slivver! They're gaining!"

"It's difficult to reach top speed with all of this deadweight!"

"What kind of crack is that?"

"A true one."

With the high winds tearing at his beard the higher they soared, Brenwar watched the wurmers close in. They moved south of the hilltops beyond Narnum. The chase went on for miles. "Just drop me, Slivver. I'm too heavy. All I'm doing is slowing you down."

"Don't be foolish, you're slowing every one of us down. But if you insist." Slivver released Brenwar. "Goodbye."

"Aaaaahhhh!" In a total free fall, Brenwar watched Slivver wheel around in the sky to face the wurmers. Bright shards of lightning erupted from Slivver's mouth, tearing through the flock of evil. The energy spiked clean through the wurmers that dared to dive after Brenwar. Spinning in the air, he caught a glimpse of the hilltops rushing to greet him. With his beard flapping in the wind, he said, "This isn't fair. I'm supposed to die fighting, not failing at flying!"

Below him a black swirling portal caught his eye. Like the trees below him, it grew bigger and bigger. He swam in midair. The black hole swallowed him.

"Noooooooooooooo-*omph*!"

He landed hard on something but not too hard. Shaking his head, he blinked away his distorted vision. He was inside an exquisite cavern that he knew to be the Chamber of Murals. All of his comrades including the silver shade dragons were there as well. His eyes caught another friendly gaze. It was the beautiful countenance of Grahleyna in full dragon form. He took a knee and bowed his head. "Your Majesty."

CHAPTER 5

SELENE SAT WITH HER HEAD between her knees. Her long hair spread out over her back. There were patches on her arms where the scales had been plucked out.

Nath was on one knee, rubbing her arm. "I can't believe they did this to you. I'll make them pay for it."

"No, I deserved every bit of it. Even worse." She shuddered. "If you only knew more about what I did to so many people, innocent people, you'd understand."

"That's in the past."

"The past is never so far away as you'd like to think. It's always chasing me, Nath. Can't you see that?" She lifted her head. Her eyes scanned the dreary, tomb-like cave walls. A green slimy algae dripped down through the seams in the stone. "The only thing I'm doing is putting more lives in danger. You're trapped. Ben and the others, probably dead."

He poked her in the forehead with his finger.

"Ow, what did you do that for?"

"Despair?" he said almost sarcastically. "That's not like you, Selene. Quit your sulking. It's making this glorious room more, er, gloomy." His voice echoed a little when he spoke. "The Deep was chock-full of prisoners. Especially when you were in charge. Where are they?"

"I can only assume that Eckubahn freed all of the miscreants to do his bidding on the surface." Selene took a long breath and sighed. Rising from the floor, she wobbled a little.

Nath caught her by the elbow and helped her up. He put his arm around her waist. There was warmth in her body nuzzled into his. A natural vibrant power. He kissed her on the head just above the temple. "At least we're alone for a change."

Selene's eyes narrowed on his. "You find pleasure in such a bleak situation? Perhaps your mind is wounded."

"I guess I'm just happy to see you. I was worried, you know. Please forgive me for reveling in the moment."

"You are a peculiar person, Nath." Her features softened. She pressed closer to him. "But that was what drew me to you. That never-failing optimism you bring. You're a light that I'd never seen before." She kissed his cheek.

Nath moved his lips toward hers.

Selene slipped away. "Not now. After we're no longer doomed, maybe."

Holding her fast by the wrist, firm but gentle, he said, "You toy too often with me."

"We need to find an exit, Nath, even though I'm certain there isn't one. The only way out is up."

The cavernous chamber remained dimly lit by the alsium ground between the stone. Even without it, Nath's and Selene's dragon sight would have allowed them to see the outlines of the rock. Dragons roamed the nether regions below the ground as well as the skies above. There were plenty of wingless dragon types who burrowed in the ground. The red rocks, ivory sliders, and squawkers were a few that came to mind.

Staying close together, the pair moseyed through the different levels of caves and chambers. Nath brushed against Selene's vibrant figure from time to time.

"You don't need to stay so close," she said, hiding a smile in the corner of her mouth.

"But I must. You're wounded, and I plan to catch you when you fall."

"I'm regenerating quite well, thank you." She patted his back with her tail. "I appreciate the thought, but mind you, I'm a very independent dragon."

"Yes, I know. That's how you wound up here in the first place."

She turned to him. "You accuse me!"

Hands up and palms out, he said, "Easy, Selene. I've been there myself. I'm not the most innocent man in the world. I've run off plenty of times with that chip on my shoulder. But I have to admit, you're worse than me."

"I'm not worse than you at anything." Her fiery violet stare subsided. She punched his shoulder. "And you know it."

"If you say so."

They scoured the caves and tunnels. It seemed like every nook and cranny was lined with rotting filth and bones. Tiny little bugs crawled the floors. Cotton-white wool worms inched over the piles.

Nath kicked through a pile of bones. There was a shiny thing in the deteriorating clothes. The octangular badge was brass and had the arcane markings of an agent of Barnabus. He plucked it out and flicked it over to Selene. "Looks like one of your old acolytes fell out of your favor."

Studying the badge in the palm of her hand, she shook her head. "I'd rather you didn't remind me." She dropped the badge on the floor.

"Sorry. So, how did they survive down here? We haven't been given any food."

Selene gave him a look.

It sank in. "They ate one another?"

"Like dragons eat the herd."

"That's different."

"Is it?" She ducked into a tunnel with a low ceiling and vanished.

Nath hustled after her. "Of course it is. People shouldn't eat people. It's sick. The herd was made for dragons and the races."

"Everything is fair game to be devoured by evil. Do you think we can stop talking about this? Or will I have to remind you again before we reach the next cave?"

"Boy, your scales really are getting thin. But I'll do my best to mind my clever tongue."

"It's not that clever. Clumsy is more like it." She slipped into a cavern where some crude tables and chairs still stood. There was packaging of iron rations scattered on the floor. "There, you see. Not everyone ate everybody. Blatver had handled these items. The triant had made for a fine manager." She took a seat on a wooden chair. "Nath, you don't seem so eager to get out of here. Time is pressing, I imagine."

"I'm just trying not to panic." He pulled up a chair that was leaning against the wall and sat down across from her. "The truth is, I'm a bit surprised at myself. Normally, I'd be pulling my hair out by now. Not that I would ever actually do that."

"Of course not, but I might."

Nath laughed. The truth was, he was enjoying being in the company of Selene. Her beauty captured his heart, and something about all the scales on her sensuous figure drew him to her more. He wanted to be with her now, as much as ever.

With her arms folded over her chest, she said to him, "Will you stop looking at me like that?"

"Like what?"

"Your eyes are devouring me as if I'm some kind of meal. Perhaps we should separate."

CHAPTER 6

The chair groaned under Nath. "What do you mean, separate? Separate where? There isn't anywhere to go."

"I just think you're having a little trouble controlling yourself right now. Your passion is blinding your reason. It's common in men."

Leaning forward on the table, Nath poked at his chest. "I can handle my passions just fine, frost breath. It's not as if you're the first woman I've ever wanted."

"I know that," she replied flatly.

Nath got up. "And you won't be the last, either. I'm going to see to that."

Raising her voice, she said, "Good, that's exactly what I want you to do!"

"Good! That's what I'll do then." Nath stormed out of the room. He didn't understand what Selene's problem was. He just wanted to spend some time with her. Flushed, he admitted to himself maybe he wanted that a little too much. He headed back to the main chamber, up the steps and down the corridor where the shaft was where he'd been lowered down inside. Oil continued to drip down the sides of the tunnel that led to the world above. There was a wink of light, high at the top. He coiled his legs under him and leapt high. He swiped at the stone, missing by less than a foot, before landing softly on his feet. "Sultans of Sulfur," he muttered.

He jumped again, still coming up short. He flexed his fingers. Eyeing his golden-yellow claws, he came up with another idea. The corridor's wall was high, but the oil pipe jutted out a bit at the top, a black pipe to freedom. Nath took off his boots one at a time. *I've never tried this before, but there's a first time for everything.* He stuck his fingertips into the hard stone of the wall. The claws poked into the wall like a pick. So sensitive was Nath's touch that he could find the hair-sized imperfections in the seemingly smooth stone and use them for a better grip. Next, he sank his toes into the wall—and like a spider, he began to climb. *Not bad. I'm so amazing.*

With his flame-colored locks dangling toward the stone-tiled floor, he traversed from wall to ceiling. "Ha-ha! I knew I'd figure this out." Movement farther up the corridor caught his eye.

Selene came his way with a sliver of a smile on her face. She stood on the stone floor right under him, shaking her head.

"What?"

"You look silly and creepy. Congratulations."

"I'm going to get us out of here. I thought you'd be excited."

She caught the dripping oil with her eyes. "We'll see."

"You don't think I can do it?"

"As I said, we'll see."

"Well, thanks for the encouragement!" His fingers and toes dug in hard. Jaw set, he moved toward the oil-slick pipe. *I'll show her!* He made his way to the lip that led upward. Hanging by one hand with two feet firmly planted in the ceiling, he reached into the mouth of the pipe and jammed his fingers into the greasy wall. The thick oil ran down to his wrist. *I hope I don't get this in my hair. That would be awful to get out.*

"How are you doing?" Selene said from below. Her chin was up and tilted to one side. "That looks difficult."

"I'm doing just fine, thank you. As a matter of fact, I just about have it. Watch this." He freed his hand from the ceiling and waved at her. "See, I'm dug in like a—" His grip inside the pipe gave way. "Ahhhh!" He plummeted thirty feet and landed hard on his back. The wind was knocked out of him in a *whoosh*!

Selene leaned over him. "That was interesting, indeed. What were you saying about being dug in? Dug in like a what?"

"Oh, be quiet." He sat up. Oil dripped from his arms and elbows. "Great, just great. I don't suppose you installed a bathing facility down here?"

"You never know. The Deep precedes me. There's no telling what secrets it keeps."

"Well, one thing's for sure. The awful smells that lurk within aren't any secret."

Selene laughed. "You make me laugh, Nath." She helped him up.

"Thanks, glad you got a chuckle out of it." He ground his teeth. His brows buckled. "How in Nalzambor are we going to get out of here?"

She patted his cheek. "That's what we need from you. A little more fire."

"So now you're going to show some kindness to me. When I'm mad. Your timing couldn't be any worse."

"If we go too hungry down here, chances are we might end up hibernating. Who knows, we might wake up in a different age."

"I don't want to go through that again. Well, I sort of do. Perhaps if I did, who knows, maybe all of my dragon powers would be restored and I could fly right out of here."

"Maybe we both could. Not all wars are won in days, months, or years, Nath. Remember, you were asleep for twenty years before. Gorn thought he had that war won, but you came back." She brushed his hair aside. "I'm glad you did."

"Yes, I did come back, but there were so many lost in the meantime. I can't let that happen again. No, Selene, we absolutely have to get out of here. There must be a way."

"Let's just keep looking, then, huh? While we look, my powers will renew. I might be able to summon something." She started back down the corridor with her tail dragging behind her. "Coming?"

He looked back up in the hole above. "I guess. I thought Eckubahn would just kill us. Why didn't he?"

"We are prizes. Besides, I believe that he wants us to surrender. Perhaps he thinks that given enough time, maybe you will do it publicly. Who knows, he might call on us in a few years."

"Now you are starting to sound like you enjoy it down here." He followed after her.

"I suppose I should make the most of it."

I'll never understand her.

CHAPTER 7

Being underground posed interesting problems. Without seeing the sun setting in the sky, a sense of time was lost. What might have been minutes also might have been hours. Most dragons were used to this in the sense that it didn't bother them. Dragons lived so long that they didn't have much worry for how much time was spent.

Nath was sitting with his back against the wall inside a small cave. He'd managed to clear out the debris, making the nook somewhat cozy. For what he assumed to be days, he and Selene had scoured The Deep. It was troubling. Most places had a back door, a way of escape. But in the case of The Deep, there was only one way out, and that was up.

He scratched at the dirt floor. With his fingernail, he drew the face of Selene. The two of them had come to a point that required giving one another space. They'd settled in somehow, like an old married couple. Nath didn't go after her unless she needed him.

"How are things going, Nath?" Selene called up from the main chamber below. "Have you found a way out from that cave yet?"

He didn't even crawl out to look at her when he replied. "It's giving me plenty of inspiration. As a matter of fact, I think we could dig from the bottom to the top. It's all dirt. I don't see why not."

"That would take months, possibly years."

"It's not as if I have anything else going on. Perhaps I should give it a try. Say, why don't you fetch me a wheelbarrow?"

"A wheelbarrow?" Selene sounded astonished. "That's a silly idea."

"Well, I can't do it without a wheelbarrow."

Selene popped up in the air and landed in front of Nath's cave. She'd just leapt the equivalent of two stories. She eased inside, eyeing the ceiling. "I don't see any evidence of your tunnel."

Nath poked his nose into the ceiling. "But I can see it right here. It leads straight up through the earth until it touches the clouds in the sky."

"Ah, it sounds marvelous. I can't wait to see it when it's finished."

Nath shrugged. "It will be impossible without a wheelbarrow."

"What about a shovel, would that help?"

He flicked a pebble into the back of the cave. "No, that would only make things more complicated. I'm not very good with shovels."

She kicked him. "You're a silly man." His finger drawing on the ground caught her eye. "Is that me in the dirt?"

"That's you."

She crawled over and stared at it from an inverted angle. "It's lovely, even though it's dirt. I can't tell if I'm smiling or not."

"Yes, I have the same problem."

She gave him a playful little slap in the face with her tail. "And I can't tell if you're joking or not."

"Me, joke?" He wrapped his fingers up in the end of her tail. The snakelike appendage squeezed his hand like the strong grip of a blacksmith. "I wonder why I never grew a tail in my moments?"

"Perhaps you wouldn't have been smart enough to use it. It's like having another limb, you know."

"Yes, I know, I've been a dragon before: tail, wings, and all." He shook his head. "Not that I mind your little visit, but you seem to be brimming for a change. Did you find a way out?"

"No, but much of my strength has returned. Follow me, I have an idea."

Together, they walked back to the entrance to The Deep.

"This again?" Nath said. "What exactly do you have in mind?"

"I'm going to lift you up."

He looked at her and then up at the entrance to the well. "On your shoulders?"

"No, with my magic. Levitation."

"You can do that?"

"We'll see."

"I'll never understand why you got powers that I don't have. I'm the Dragon King. One would think that I'd be able to do just about anything."

"Remember, I was a priestess before. Harnessing the realm of magic came from my training. There are many things I can do. Besides, you're all brawny, a warrior, more used to using your body instead of your mind."

"With a body like this, who needs brains?"

"You're the only dragon I know who can flatter himself."

Nath tossed his hair. "I can, can't I?" He looked up into the portal. "Let's get on with it then. What do you need me to do?"

"Be silent and still." Selene closed her eyes and filled her chest with air. "And if you can do that, then anything is possible."

"Haha—*ack*!" An unseen force lifted Nath off the ground. Invisible cords and tendrils seemed to be pushing and pulling him at the same time. Up, up, up he went, high into the well, moving slowly at first before gaining speed until his hair rustled. "You're doing it, Selene! You're doing it!"

This is great! Finally we're going to get out of here. My, won't Eckubahn be surprised the next time he sees me!

He sailed up at least halfway before his ascension began to slow. His head glanced down. "Uh, Selene, why am I slowing?"

The mystic force that held him began to sink. His body bounced downward like a bad elevator in a rickety shaft. Sinking faster, he started swimming in midair. "Seleeeeeene!"

Nath plummeted downward. He stretched his arms out until he hit the greasy stone walls of the well. Somehow, he dug in enough to slow his fall. He slid down the pipe, digging in his claws with all his might. It wasn't enough. "Aaaaaaaaah!"

Covered in grease and oil, he hit the floor of The Deep so hard he lost his breath. He had painful stars swirling above his eyes when Selene leaned over him.

Eyes wide, she said, "I'm sorry, Nath. I didn't have enough strength in me. You're too heavy."

Wincing, he pushed up to his elbows. "So it's my fault?"

"No, certainly not. I'm…I must not be strong enough." Her face sagged. "I've failed."

Nath pounded the ground with his fists. "I really thought we had it. Blast my scales! We're never going to get out of here!" He let out a roar into the well that made the oil drip like rain. Even Selene recoiled. Chest heaving, he stood up, and with head down he walked away.

An all-powerful voice sounded in his head.

"Settle down, Nath."

Nath's head snapped up. "Father!"

CHAPTER 8

THE VOICE IN NATH'S HEAD dropped him to his knees. He stared down the corridor in a trancelike state. "Is that you?" he whispered.

"Nath, what is it? I don't see anyone," Selene said, following his line of vision.

He held up his hand. "Be silent."

The voice of Balzurth sounded off again as clear as a bell. *"Nath, you must free me."*

"Father, you're alive? I've seen your body." The scales on his arms tingled. "I tried to take you to the Dragon Graveyard, but I failed."

"No, Nath, listen to me, my body might have fallen, but my spirit is alive and well." Balzurth let out a pain-filled roar. *"Help me!"*

Perspiration coated Nath's face. A searing pain wedged itself in Nath's mind. He teetered in his stance, finding support in Selene's strong arms. "Where are you, Father? Tell me!"

"The Dark Plane. Find me, Son. Find me!" Balzurth let out a howling moan, and his voice faded away.

"Father, come back! How do I find you?" Nath jumped to his feet and wheeled around, searching in all directions. "Father!" Sweat dripped from his chin to the floor.

Selene caught his arms. "Tell me, Nath, what do you see? What did you hear?" She squeezed his arm. "Your scales are so hot."

"I know. I felt the heat. His pain. It was Balzurth. He was suffering. Running and hiding. A great wall of flame and black smoke swallowed him whole. Or his essence. I have to find him, Selene. He's alive!"

"Nath, are you certain? The spirits can play many tricks on the likes of us. You have to be sure."

"No, I know it was him. No one else has a voice like that. Trust me, I'd know." Every fiber of his being was ready to spring. He took the cool cave air into his lungs. "I've got to do better, Selene. I can't let the enemy get the best of me anymore. Father is counting on me. I just wish he would have told me more."

"What did he say?"

"He says he's in the Abyss. His spirit, that is." He looked into her eyes. "Do you know anything about the Dark Realm?"

"Very little. I don't know that it's a real place so much as the realm between life and death. Every race has a different name for it, I believe. Some call it the Abyss and others the World of Spirits." She clasped his hand in hers. "At least we know he's alive, so to speak."

"Yes. Between life and death. He said it was his spirit, perhaps something like Eckubahn. Father never destroyed them, he trapped them. They were harmless without their bodies, at least in this world."

Selene's face paled.

"What is it?"

"I'm sorry, Nath. Perhaps I know more than I care to admit. The spirit realm is where Gorn Grattack came from. He stayed there, manipulating the world until he drew enough power to return."

"You don't think he's still there now, do you?" Nath said. "I thought I killed him."

"I did too. Perhaps that's what your father is running from. There is much evil in the Dark Plane."

Pacing the corridor, Nath raked his claws through his hair. "Why would Father's spirit be there? If anything, he should be resting in the realm beyond the murals. The Dark Plane is for the wicked, isn't it?"

Selene shrugged. "I wish I knew more. Perhaps there is still life in your father's body. As long as he lives, his spirit can't pass elsewhere. Maybe, he didn't want to pass from Nalzambor and he ventured into another plane to buy time. Perhaps he's still fighting from within."

"I don't know very much about such things, Selene. All I know is what my gut is telling me. Father won't last much longer there if we don't help him. I've a very bad feeling that his spirit can perish there. I felt him…dying."

"We can't let that happen, Nath. There has to be a way out of here. Certainly there's something you have buried deep inside that handsome skull of yours." She drilled her finger into his temple. "You are the Dragon King. You have knowledge of this world others don't have. Find it. Harness it."

"But I've lost so much of my power. If I only had wings, we could fly right out of this hole!"

"No more doubts, Nath. You have what you have. Use it. How did Gorlee get out?"

"He turned himself into a triant and was big enough to crawl out, as I recall. The phantom was there too. The foul creature could float its prey up and down. I can't do any of that. I've tried to change into a dragon, like I used to. It's just not happening."

"I must admit that I can't either, and believe me, I've tried." Selene tied her hair back in a ponytail. "Perhaps we should try it together."

CHAPTER 9

Inside Dragon Home, also known as the Mountain of Doom, Brenwar finished chiseling away on the lid of the stone sarcophagus. Dragon Home was equipped with all the finest tools and had workshops that rivaled those of all the races. Every item was organized and like new. It was an odd thing from a time long lost, back when men and dragons often worked together. That time was long before Brenwar. Sweat dripped onto the stone image he carved.

"Are you crying?" Ben asked. The old warrior stood beside the stone sarcophagus, dabbing his forehead with a rag. The furnace behind him glowed red-hot. "I don't know why you insist on doing masonry in the smithy. Certainly it would be preferable to work somewhere cooler."

"Dwarves don't cry," Brenwar murmured. "And if you're here to be comfortable, then I suggest you leave."

"I'm not going anywhere. I just don't see the purpose in working in these insufferable conditions. It's been days. I can only stand so much."

Brenwar stopped hammering and eyeballed Ben. "If it makes you feel any better, I'm about finished. Hand me that whisk."

Ben reached on the worktable behind him and picked up a small broom. "This?"

"Yes, that."

"Catch." Ben tossed the whisk.

Brenwar snatched it out of the air. "You'd think you'd know your way around a forge better."

Arms tucked under his armpits, Ben mocked, "You'd think you'd know your way around a forge better." He sighed. "Sorry, I shouldn't do that. Whether or not you'll admit it, I'm sure this is a hard thing for you."

"No, it's not. Bayzog's dead. I just want to give him a proper burial."

"It's a sad thing, really, that we can't take him to Elome to be buried. I'm sure his family would have a wonderful glade where they could lay him to rest with all of the proper ceremonies."

"Maybe." Brenwar dusted the stone debris out of the cracks and lines he chiseled. "His family has strange ways with him being only part-elf and all." He scratched his head with his skeleton hand. "I don't think it would matter to him one way or the other where he was buried. But this chamber I'm making will hold him for now. Once this war is over, we'll see to it he gets a proper burial."

"You're a true friend, Brenwar. I'm sure he appreciates it."

Brenwar blew the dust out of the cracks. "Maybe."

Ben took a closer look at the image on the lid. Squinting, he said, "I'm sorry, but what exactly did you carve? The stone is dark and foreign to me. I can barely make anything out but elven or dwarven lines."

"You'll have to wait for it."

"Huh, how long?"

The door leading out of the forge swung inward and banged against the wall.

"Sorry." Rerry was accompanied by Sasha and Samaz. All of them were dressed in white robes, a type of elven ceremonial garb. Sasha carried the Elderwood Staff and led the way down the platform of steps into the forge. She walked right up to Ben, who was standing by the sarcophagus, and kissed him on the cheek.

"Oh, you shouldn't do that." Ben blushed. "I'm all sweaty."

Brenwar grunted. "It's not from working."

Sasha offered a warm smile. "It's fine, friends. It's certainly a sad time, but we are ready. I was, well, I just wanted to see the both of you. I'm very thankful for what you're doing." She stared into the sarcophagus. "I think he would like it."

"It's not complete." Brenwar wandered over to the furnace. He put on a set of heavy leather mittens and drew a stone pot out of the flames. Cradling the pot in his arms against his apron, he walked back over. "This is the final step. I hope you're pleased."

With the head of the lid propped up at a slight angle, Brenwar poured from the stone pot. Rerry and Samaz gathered around the coffin. Molten silver slid from the cauldron into the top seams of the lid, snaking through patterns as natural as nature itself. Every groove Brenwar had carved in the coffin lid came to life, swirling from top to bottom until every crevice filled.

Sasha gasped. Her sons' eyes misted up as they gazed at a perfect silver image of Bayzog. "He's absolutely beautiful," she said in awe.

Ben's tears ran freely now. There was not a better testament for Brenwar's adoration for his friend

Bayzog than this. The image in the coffin lid was so refined and realistic he blinked several times, wondering if it was real. *Brenwar did this? Unbelievable.*

Rerry and Samaz shouldered up to Brenwar. "'Tis truly magnificent. Thank you so much, Brenwar," Rerry said with his eyes aglow. "It makes me feel like he yet lives."

"He'll always live in our hearts." Samaz gave Brenwar a shoulder hug before easing away. "Mother, I don't mean to sound impudent, but do you intend to bury him with the Elderwood Staff? It seems fitting."

"No, don't be silly, Samaz. Mother can use it, certainly," Rerry replied. "Mother, you must use it. We'll need its power."

"The staff is elven craft and magic," she said, shaking her head. "No, I'm not capable of controlling its power." She walked over to Samaz and handed the staff to him. "This is your legacy, Samaz. You will need to learn how to master it. That's all I can say."

Samaz ran his hands up and down the smooth wood of the staff. The gem mounted inside the carved wood at the top twinkled. "I have so very little elf in me. I'm not so certain even I can harness the power within, yet I feel its warmth between my fingers."

"You'll do just fine, Samaz. Bayzog would be proud of both of you."

Scratching the back of his neck, Rerry said, "I wish I was a bigger part of his legacy. But I'm a swordsman. I always felt Father was a little disappointed in me and my craft."

Touching her son's cheek, she said, "Never, Rerry. You have your father's eyes and the feisty arrogance that dwelled deep within him. You are much more like your father than you think."

Brimming, Rerry said, "Yes, much more than Stone-face, for certain. I can live with that."

"Well, I suppose it's time to begin the ceremony, now that the coffin is ready." Sasha gave Brenwar a nod then shook her head. "Sorry, I don't mean to sound hasty. I love Bayzog and miss him dearly, but I want to get after the monsters that did this to him. I hope you understand."

"Completely," Brenwar said.

"Yes, I want vengeance too, for him and for Dragon. Those titans must pay," Ben said.

With Sansla's help, they'd been able to surmise that Tylabahn had taken over Gorlee.

That was another problem in addition to the loss of Nath and Selene. They'd tried to find a trace of them through the Chamber of Murals, but they hadn't had any fortune at all. Now, another search needed to begin. Chances were they'd have to go back to Narnum, and without a doubt, the titans would be ready.

Ben mopped the sweat from his face. "I'd better get changed into something more appropriate." He eyed Brenwar. "I suggest you do the same."

"I know how to dress for a funeral. Go on, then. I'll catch up with you."

CHAPTER 10

DOWN IN THE DEEP, NATH and Selene spent countless hours trying to combine their powers so that they could leave the buried prison. Selene's sorceress powers were strong, but it didn't come so easily to Nath. At the moment, they stood inside the main chamber.

Concentrating, he tried to lift her up from the ground the way she'd done to him. She made it several feet off the ground before he dropped her again. She landed softly on her feet.

"I just don't have the knack for it," he said. "Can't you just lift yourself out of the pit?"

"No, I've tried. I guess since dragons have wings, that wouldn't be a power I needed. Even lifting you was a different practice than what I'm used to. I'm more comfortable blasting things apart."

"Wings. Maybe in a few decades, at the rate we're going. If only I hadn't lost so much power."

"Having regrets, are you? I told you I wasn't worth it, but you didn't listen."

"No, now don't start that again. I don't have any regrets saving you at all." He put his hands on her waist and lifted her off her feet. "You've made it all worthwhile."

"Put me down, you oaf," she said, smiling. "Mind you, I'm every bit as strong as you are. How would you like to be plucked from the ground like a daisy?"

"I'd like to see you try it." He felt Selene's tail snake around his ankle. "Oh no, you don't." He let go of her, quickly took a knee, and started to peel her tail from his ankle.

Selene slipped behind him.

Before he knew what hit him, he was up off his feet with Selene grappling him from behind the waist.

"I told you I could do it."

"I let you do it. I like the feeling of being in your arms."

"Oh, please." She set him down. "You know what your problem is? You still use your body too much more than your brains."

"I suppose, but that's what I have you for. After all, you are much, much older. I lean on your wisdom."

Easing up to him, she put her hand over his heart. "I don't know everything about you that makes you tick, Nath. You're the Dragon King. You have powers and command that I'll never have. You need to dig deep and find them."

"It's not as if I'm not trying." He looked at the scales on his hands. "I'm trying to transform into something else."

"That's the problem. You're trying to change, but maybe that isn't the answer. Perhaps you need to try another angle." She bit her lip. "Tell me about the powers you commanded."

"Well, I've had smoke and fire come from my breath. I flew when I had wings. There's the Dragon Call—or Roar, rather. I can make a lot of noise with that."

Selene's eyes lit up. "Maybe that's it. Perhaps you should summon dragons?"

"From down here? I don't think so. Besides, the giants will hear the roar. Anything that comes, they'll kill. I can't have that. I don't want any more dying on my account. I won't summon them. It would be their deaths."

"I see your point." Selene started pacing the floor. The pair of them had worn a path in the grimy floor. The path circled the exterior of the huge audience chamber. "But you know, more will die so long as the titans have the upper hand. Many are probably dying now."

"Don't say that," he said so loud that his voice echoed. "You won't guilt me into it."

"They are your subjects. They are yours to command," she said with clear irritation in her voice. "Take command of them!"

Nath took a seat on the floor facing the opening that led toward the main entry corridor. He crossed his legs and closed his eyes. He started humming.

"What are you doing?"

"Sh, sh, sh," he said. "I'm doing as you suggested. I'm summoning dragons."

"By humming?"

"It's my gift, not yours. It's just been some time since I used it. When I was a boy, I used to sing with my brethren, didn't you?"

"Sing? Me? No, never," Selene said. A frown formed on her face. "Another thing I missed out on."

"Why don't you be quiet so you don't have to miss out on it again."

Selene fell silent as soon as Nath's lips started to move. There was something about the way he talked that had a hypnotizing effect on her. His voice was quiet like a morning wind that caresses the dew-speckled leaves of dawn. The words were Dragonese. His words penetrated her body, through the scales and into her pounding heart. She'd never seen Nath like this before. Peaceful, radiant, and handsome. It melted her from the outside in. She swooned.

Lathered up in his music, tears began to run down her face.

How can he make sounds that are so beautiful? How can they come from lips that are so difficult?

The dragon song went on for minutes that became an hour. The rich sound of his voice lifted the dreariness from the walls. The glowing alsium pulsated in rhythm with his words. It made for a fascinating spectacle that went on for another hour and ended. He opened his eyes to find hers. She wiped her face.

"You liked that, didn't you?"

"It was wonderful, Nath." Selene felt elated, like a new person inside and out. "I didn't realize you could do that. Do you think it will work?"

"I felt something when I sang. I know another heard my call, but I don't think it was a dragon."

Selene stood up. Her jaw dropped.

"What is it?" Nath turned his head.

Lying on the ground in a scabbard a few feet behind him was a magnificent sword with dragon heads on the cross guard. "Fang!"

CHAPTER 11

"I CAN'T BELIEVE IT!" NATH EXCLAIMED.

"Believe it!" Selene rushed by his side. Her eyes were as wide as moons. "The sword heard your call. How intriguing."

Nath reached out for the handle but stopped inches short of the grip. "You're certain that you see it too? Sometimes I get a little addled after singing."

"No, I see Fang."

Nath grabbed the sword by the fine leather wrapped around the grip and slid it from the sheath. The warm energy of Fang coursed through his body. Nath let out a delighted gasp and hugged the great blade. "Ah, my dearest friend, you came for me." He stepped away from Selene and began cutting the blade through the air in artistic stabs and blurring motions. "He's like a third arm. A sharp one. You know, Fang has many powers, some of which I feel haven't even been discovered yet."

Selene stood with her hands on her hips, watching Nath cut the weapon in the air. "I'm not certain I'm familiar with them all."

"There is the sonic ring that comes from a tap of his tip." He rested Fang on his shoulder with both hands on the grip. "He's turned giants to ice before. That and, ah!" His face brightened. "Teleportation. Perhaps that's our way out of here. He teleported here, right?"

"He has a mind of his own." Selene came closer with her eyes studying the blade. She traced her finger through the groove in the flat of the blade called the fuller. "I wonder how he got it."

"That's a question for Father, who forged Fang. I can't imagine the secret behind it, but one would think that I'd know something about it."

"You father is old, Nath. His knowledge was tempered over centuries. I'm sure what you need to know and learn lies within Dragon Home. Be patient."

"Haven't we been patient enough? It's time to get us out of here. I've got a strong feeling that Fang is here to do just that."

"Remember how that turned out the last time," she warned. "He took us forward in time and gave us a bellyful of trouble. Do you recall hanging by the neck?"

"You don't need to remind me about that trial. I'm just glad it's over. As for moving through time, that makes me wonder." He held Fang before him. "If he took us forward in time, perhaps he can take us backward in time as well."

Selene tensed. "I don't think that's a very good idea, Nath."

"No? But I could save Father. I'd be a step ahead of everything. I'd already know what the titans were doing and what to expect. I could end them once and for all."

Shaking her head, she said, "Don't focus on the past, Nath. Focus on what we can do today to be victorious for tomorrow. Besides, there's no guarantee that the outcome would be any different."

"I suppose. So, where should I ask him to take us outside of Narmum, Dragon Home? Perhaps he should land me right behind Eckubahn. I'll take his head from his shoulders with one long hard swipe."

"I like the way you think, but let's weigh all the options. We know there are more nests that we need to destroy to stop the wurmers. Your father is trapped in the Dark Realm. Tylabahn possesses Gorlee. Dragon Home is surrounded by the armies of the wicked, preparing for a mass invasion. My, my, my," she said. "There are many burdens for us and Fang to bear."

"True enough. Let's just hope I can control Fang."

"Don't you think it's high time you did? He's another one of your subjects, isn't he? He should do as you command."

Nath spun the sword through the air. "We haven't gotten to that point yet. Perhaps I haven't proven myself worthy of that command. When I'm ready, he'll probably be more willing."

"So now what?"

"Well, last time this happened, I wasn't asking for it. He decided where we went. He took us to the Elven Field of Dreams. It's quite possible we will wind up there again. I don't know." He reached for Selene. "Take my hand."

Selene complied.

Nath held the sword high and said, "Fang, without taking us forward in time, or backward, we need to get out of this well. If our friends are in danger, take us so that we can aid them. If not, then somewhere else we are needed." He brought the sword tip toward the ground. It hit the stone and made a ringing *ting*.

The walls swirled and spun. Nath's body raced through space and time. The fabric of his being stretched and screamed. He came to a stop with just his stomach spinning. He and Selene held one another upright.

On wobbling knees, she said, "Sultans of Sulfur, I hate that."

As the spinning in his mind came to a stop, he gazed at his new surroundings. They stood inside another cavern filled with stalagmites and stalactites. Shallow pools of water made echoing *plop plop* sounds around their feet as they were filled with drips from above. "It appears we are still subterranean. Thanks, Fang, I think."

Selene's nostrils flared. "Something seems familiar about this place."

It was dark, but Fang radiated a faint blue glow. A strange hum surrounded them as if the caves were filled with living and breathing things. On cat's feet they moved toward the sound, with water from above dripping down on them. They stopped at the edge of a large chamber filled with knee-high eggs planted in the ground. There were thousands of them.

"What are those?" Nath said.

Selene clamped her hand over his mouth. Her eyes flitted toward the ledges above.

Nath followed her intense stare. Wurmers, small ones, were nestled in the nooks and ledges, by the hundreds.

Way to go, Fang!

CHAPTER 12

ATH FELT INVISIBLE SPIDERS CRAWLING down his spine. He'd never seen so many tiny wurmers crawling around like a sea of giant ants before. It mortified him, thinking about the danger they posed if they became bigger. He looked at Fang.

Why in the world did you deliver us here of all places?

There was a rumble deep in the cavern. The wurmers' wings fluttered for a moment, but they quickly nestled back into their spots in the stone.

Taking Nath by the arm, Selene led him back toward the cave where they had arrived. With her voice low, she said, "This is a lair. I'm certain of it. It's much like the ones I've encountered before. I think Fang brought us here to destroy the life gem."

"Life gem?"

"Yes, that's what Sansla and I were doing. I brought orbs of destruction into chambers such as this, and once I found the life gem, we destroyed it. That's where we discovered Tylabahn. She was living inside a wurmer queen. Certainly another one lurks inside here." She smiled. "I think Fang bringing us here was a good thing."

"I'm not going to complain, but how are we going to get past those wurmers? There looks to be a thousand of them out there."

"They aren't trained to hunt the likes of us just yet. That doesn't happen until they get a taste of our hides. If we're careful, we can walk right through them."

"Certainly they'll alert the guardian."

"Maybe, maybe not. I'm not sure we have much of a choice at this point." She again started back toward the main cavern.

Nath caught her shoulder. "Hold on." He slid Dragon Claw out of Fang's pommel. "I'd feel better if you'd hang on to this. More than likely you're going to need it."

"Thanks, and keep your thoughts to yourself as best as you can. If a titan spirit resides in a wurmer, it's very possible it might hear us. Be mindful."

He shrugged. "Lead the way."

Selene crept back into the fullness of the cavern, minding every step she took. Eggs were scattered all over the cave floor by the hundreds. Here and there, baby wurmers were slowly clawing their way out of them, coated in a sticky goo. It turned Nath's stomach. The unnatural movement of the insect-like dragons put his senses on high alert. Seeing a wurmer pop out of one of the egg-like pods soured the taste in his mouth. *That's so alien.*

Following a narrow channel between the eggs, Selene climbed onto a ledge along the outer wall that made for a clearer path. Her eyes darted all around. Like bats in a cave, the wurmer spawn didn't pay any mind to their presence. She moved from one chamber to another, each not very different than the one before. Only Fang's and Dragon Claw's faint blue light gave them a glimpse of all that was around them.

Nath would rather not know. He fully expected the wurmers to drop on him at any moment, but they didn't. A wurmer did crawl over his toes. *I'll never get used to that. For some reason, they're a lot creepier when they're smaller.*

A new light source glowed ahead. Nath and Selene headed right for it. She came to a stop and pointed. There was a natural stone well that glowed with a mystic yellow-green light that throbbed and pulsated within. Fog and mist spilled from its mouth.

Whispering, Selene said, "That's where the life gem lies."

"How do we destroy it?"

"I don't know. Perhaps with a blade."

"Perhaps." Nath's golden eyes searched over the new surroundings. It was nothing but eggs and wurmers. A separate tunnel on the other side of the cavern appeared to slope up. "There's no sign of a guardian. It can't be that easy, can it?"

"Maybe Fang knows something we don't." She crept toward the throbbing light of the well.

"I'm certain of that, I just wish I knew more about what it was."

They made it to the rim of the well and peered within. A bright stone twice the size of Nath's fist pulsed with life within. Its power had a hypnotizing effect. The well was filled with a translucent goo that wobbled a bit on the surface. "So you blew up the last one?"

"I planted the orb with it. It takes a lot of power to wipe it out." She wielded Dragon Claw over the jellylike goo. "It's like a heart. Perhaps I can pierce it."

"Let me try with Fang. I have a bad feeling that you don't want to touch that goo. It just looks a little too sticky to me." He held Fang out over the rim. "Old friend, you brought us here, so I hope you're up to this." Tip first, he pressed the blade into the goo. The entire cavern rumbled and shook. Nath fought for balance. The wurmers came to life.

Ree-rah! Ree-rah! Ree-rah!

"Quick, Nath! Stab it quick!"

"I'm trying." Fang's blade was held fast in the goo. The life gem within sank deeper into the well. "That's a problem."

"It's only one of two." Looking behind him, she gasped. "Look!"

Still holding Fang, Nath turned his head.

The small wurmers were gathering together into one mass of bodies. As a single unit, they began to take form, growing into a towering figure whose head, arms, and legs began to take shape.

With its head high in the stalactites, the humanoid made from wurmers spoke in a loud and wicked voice. "Welcome, strange guests. Time to die."

CHAPTER 13

"JUST WHEN YOU THINK YOU'VE seen it all," Nath said, standing on the rim of the well, straining to yank Fang free. "I hope you can handle him."

With a body consisting of wurmers, the monster spoke again. "I am Many, the all-powerful guardian of the life gem. All intruders shall perish. All mortals shall die."

Selene spoke up. "We are here under the authority of Eckubahn and Tylabahn. We are testing you, Many. You let us in. You have failed."

"What?" His great slithering and grinding form of the dragon-insect bodies paused from advance. "I don't believe you."

"How do you think we got in here? We are not some wanderers of the enemy. No, we wield great power and easily slipped through your defenses. You are lazy, Many. You are a failure. I am to be your replacement."

"But you are not a spirit? You are flesh. You cannot control—"

"Silence, or I will sever your spirit with my dagger, Spirit Render!" She held Dragon Claw high. The blade shone with radiant purple.

Under his breath, Nath said, "Keep it up, but I'm not getting anywhere. This goo holds Fang fast. I didn't think that possible. Don't stop talking." Nath tugged harder. The jelly would not give.

Selene pressed her conversation. "Back off, Many. You are inches away from your own death. I will not hesitate to use my authority given by Eckubahn. Seek a host elsewhere. This cave is no longer under your care."

"There are none that can hold me. It takes many." He glided forward. "I don't believe you. Your scent is sweet like the saplings that gather by the rivers. No, you are not one of us. You are one of them." His glowing eyes narrowed. "That item winking in your hand cannot kill me. Nothing can." He extended his hand. The fingers were wurmers that gnashed and spat.

"I warned you," Selene said. She struck out with Dragon Claw. The blade hit home in the meat of a wurmer that made for a loud crackling sound. Ice spread out over the knot of bodies. The ice spread up the arms and over the chest, up to the neck and down the abdomen.

Many bellowed, "Nooooooo!"

Ice over took his mouth and face. He crystalized from top to bottom.

But at the same time, the wurmers that weren't part of his body attacked. More of them popped out of the eggs. The floors and walls were alive with the writhing creatures.

"Get that gem out, Nath!" she yelled.

The titan began to crack out of his ice-crystal trap.

She blasted away a small knot of wurmers with a flick of power from her fingertips. "Quickly!"

Nath tugged and tugged. The blade didn't budge. The life gem continued slowly sinking. While Selene fought off one wurmer after the other, he pleaded with Fang. "I'm going to need a little help here. What do you want me to do?" Nothing came to light. The blue glimmer in Fang's steel went cold as if the blade was suffocating. With muscles bulging underneath his scales and rippling all over, Nath gave another tug with all of his might, spitting and groaning.

Shards of ice cracked away from the guardian titan's mighty frame and crashed to the ground. "You have made me angry! You will suffer much for your insolence!" His entire head burst out of the ice.

Wurmers swarmed Selene.

Fighting for her life, she yelled out, "Nath!"

He gave another heave. A hot bit of dragon saliva shot from his mouth, hitting the gel. The material warbled as if in agony. "I'll be!" Nath said. He spat a small ball of fire into the well. The gel sizzled. In its own living way, it screamed. He unleashed a full stream of fire. Fang was freed. The gem sizzled, lurched, and bucked. The flames reached another level of intensity. The well went up in a *whoosh*!

Nath fell onto his back. Wurmers climbed all over him, biting and clawing at his body.

Covered in wurmers so thick she could barely be seen, Selene cried out, "Get the gem, Nath. Destroy it!"

With the horde latched onto just about every square inch of his body, he surged toward the mouth of the well. Fang in hand, he crawled inside, falling deep toward the bottom. There, twenty feet deep now, rested the life gem. It throbbed and beat like a hardened heart. Wurmers poured into the well, filling it like a busted dam.

"Noooooooooooo!" the voice of Many screamed. "Stop it!"

Straining against the wurmers that tore at his flesh, Nath lifted Fang high. He stabbed the blade down.

Chink! Booom!

An undertow of energy erupted all around and exploded out of the hole. Wurmers were incinerated. Others flopped and died.

Nath shook his head. His body was smoking, and his iron limbs trembled. "Selene?" he called up with his ears ringing. He wriggled his jaw. "Selene?"

"Yes?" she said, leaning over the upper lip of the well. Her frazzled hair hung in her eyes.

"You really need to do something about that hair. It looks horrible. What kind of a queen goes out of the castle looking like that?"

"As if your glorious mane looks any better?" She sighed. "They're all dead. Congratulations, but we'll still need to track that spirit. He'll be looking for another host. Let's hope he doesn't find one."

Nath sheathed Fang and climbed out. The cave walls, floors, stalactites, and stalagmites were splattered in the debris of the wurmers. "Yech." Nose crinkling, he added, "They smell as bad as they look, don't they?"

"You're one to talk."

"I don't smell. I never smell."

Selene rolled her eyes and headed toward the other tunnel. "I saw his essence go this way."

Nath shuffled after her. The blast had been ten times as concussive as it would have been outside of the well. It hurt to walk. He winced when he breathed. "Don't walk so fast. No need to be hasty."

The tunnel made a steep slope upward, where the enormous mouth of the cave waited. So did the cave's guardians. Huge white yeti growled and hopped in a lather.

CHAPTER 14

Selene looked back at Nath. "Looks like friends of yours."

Nath's shoulders slumped. "I don't remember loaning any yeti money. I don't suppose you'll be able to reason with them with that silky tongue of yours? You did such a great job with Many."

"We'll give it a try."

"No, I'm not going to toy with them. It's been a bad enough day." Brandishing Fang over his head, he took off at a full sprint, yelling, "Dragon! Dragon!"

The hungry-eyed yeti waited for him with clacking teeth and sharp claws. Each of the four bestial snow monsters stood at least fifteen feet tall, layered in white fur over packed muscle.

The first yeti pounced right into Nath's path with great arms stretching out.

Nath chopped clean through the beast's wrist. He dove underneath the yeti's leg and stabbed the exposed gut of another.

Savage as animals can be, the burly brutes howled. Each of them flailed at Nath.

With Fang's keen edge, he removed fingers and toes.

The monsters didn't flee. Instead, they went into a greater frenzy. Striking from all directions, the frenzied horde climbed over one another like a pack of wild dogs.

A fist smashed Nath in the back. The blow sent him sprawling on the hard, cold cave floor. Before he could turn, a yeti landed on top of him. It hammered his body with giant fists that sent shockwaves through his body. The yeti whose one hand he had turned into a stump got ahold of Nath's hair. The monster jerked him off the ground and smacked him into the wall.

"Guzan!" Nath yelled.

The yeti pummeled him with heavy blows. The one-handed yeti continued to yank Nath by the hair. The beating he took came with the power of angry mules kicking. They walloped him blow after blow. One of the yeti got in his face and tried to bite his nose.

Nath let out a stream of flame, turning the yeti's head to fire. It fled through the mouth of the cave only to collapse in a ball of flame. Nath loosed the rest of his fire on the others. Their thick fur ignited. They hopped and bellowed while desperately trying to pat the flames out. The almighty fires turned them into stinky bonfires of crispy flesh and bones. Nath stood up from the ground he'd be plowed into, saying, "Nobody touches my hair!"

Selene stood by with a satisfied look on her face. "Does that include me?"

"Yes!" He shook his head. "No! You know what I mean." He covered his nose. "Guzan, that smoke is awful. Have you been watching me fight them the entire time?"

"Of course. I enjoyed it."

"And you didn't help?"

"I didn't think you needed any. They're normal creatures. I don't think their claws could hurt you."

Holding his side, he said, "Yes, well, tell that to my ribs that are floating over my innards. They might not be able to cut me, but that doesn't mean their hits don't hurt."

"Oh, poor little dragon. Do you want me to kiss your wound?"

"Yes."

She slapped him in the chest with her tail. "You'll be fine. Come on."

Once outside of the cave, they were surrounded by gray skies, snow-capped mountains, and waist-deep snow. It wasn't nice, but it might as well have been.

With frosty breath, Nath said, "I'm not certain where we are, but it's above the ground not in. I like it. What do you think?"

Selene stood inside some tracks that looked to have been made by a yeti in the snow. "I think Many took up a new host. We need to catch up with him before he alerts the titans to our presence. We have a clear advantage being out here when they think we're still in The Deep. We must press the advantage."

Nath glanced back at the smoking cave mouth. "Too bad we won't be able to revel in our victory. This time. I'll lead, you follow."

"After you."

Nath took off at a sprint. The yeti's tracks were easy to follow, but there was a problem. It was snowing, and it came down heavily. If they didn't catch up soon, the tracks would be buried. *At least he doesn't have much of a start.* He plowed through the waist-deep tracks.

The titan's tracks led down the mountainside, beyond the icy hard rocks and into a rift in the snow that disappeared into darkness. Nath kept his eyes on the tracks, fighting through the slippery, troublesome footing, until they hit the next mountain's downward slope. Ahead through the downpour of snow, he caught a glimpse of a beast trudging through the snow. The lumbering brute's head swiveled back for a moment before continuing on. It disappeared into the folds between the mountain peaks.

"Selene! I see him. We're closing in! Can you keep up?"

"Of course I can," she said, slipping for a moment before regaining her balance. "Hurry!"

Nath moved as fast as possible, given the treachery of the terrain. He slipped and slid a little with every step. Before long he caught up to the spot where he'd seen the titan that called himself Many. The tracks followed a snow-covered ledge that plummeted into a steep hillside whose bottom was nowhere in sight. The natural road was plenty wide enough for the likes of Nath but would be troublesome for a yeti. He pressed on to a place where the tracks came to a stop then paused.

"What?" Selene said as she settled in behind him.

"His tracks are gone." He looked over the edge. "I've a feeling he might have leaped."

"Down there?"

"Well, the snow would make for a soft landing, especially for a yeti."

Clots of snow slipped down off the ledge above them.

Nath looked up. "Selene!"

Many the yeti stood on the icy ledge. His feet stomped the snow-cake. A huge bank of snow broke free from the rock. Inescapable, the avalanche hit the flat-footed Nath and Selene flush. The momentum carried them off the ledge. They plummeted into the icy abyss.

CHAPTER 15

There was a long free fall and then a few hard bounces followed by a feathery drowning under tons of snow. Nath was face-planted upside down in icy blackness. His limbs were pinned under the mass of the avalanche. Barely able to breathe, he wriggled. He managed to pack the snow around him, giving himself just enough space to begin moving his fingertips. He didn't fare well. Even worse, what about Selene? She'd be trapped underneath the snow as well.

I've got to get to her.

Nath had seen the effects of avalanches before. Entire parties of people had been buried in either snow or earth. It was a foul trick of the giants', and of the ogres in particular. They were notorious for using such traps. Cruel and crafty, they'd set up prey time and again, by luring them into this deadly demise.

Gaining some arm room, Nath punched his fist into the snow. The problem was, he didn't know how far down he was.

This might take forever. I need to try something else.

After a moment of thought, he decided to summon his flame. He drew in a difficult lungful of icy air and blew. Eye-watering steam came up, but no fire. His inferno had extinguished in the battle with the yeti.

Great. Looks like I might be here for a while, but I have to get to Selene.

Strong hands punched through the snow behind him. Strong arms yanked him out of the snow. He shook the snow out of his hair and gazed up at Selene.

"What were you doing, taking a nap?"

"Huh? I guess I was facing downward. And not so deep either. It's a good thing you came around. I might have dug myself back into The Deep."

Selene stood there shaking her head. "I worry about you."

"Well, it's not as if I was stuck in there for hours. I'd have figured it out."

"I don't know about that." She stood on a mountain of snow looking up at where they'd fallen from. There was nothing but black mountain above. "I don't think we're going to find that titan now. And I thought you had him. You should've seen that coming."

"Me?" Nath thought about it. "Yes, you're right. I should have. It happens, though. Let's just head for the bottom of the mountain. After all, he's a yeti. It's not as if he'll be able to hide from anyone."

"Catching up to him won't do a lick of good once he crosses with others. Once he communes with another spirit, word will travel back to Eckubahn faster than the wind."

Nath pulled his foot out of the snow. "There's no reason we can't still at least try to catch him. Will that make you feel better?"

She gave him a look.

Nath shrugged and started moving again. Based off where they had landed, he gave it his best guess as to where Many might be going.

If I were an evil, smelly, stupid yeti, where would I go?

His journey had angled him in the direction they'd been traveling before. The mountaintops were much like the area that surrounded the giants' home, Urslay. At first Nath thought that might be where they were, but he was relieved they weren't. The possessed yeti would have a direct path to that. He surged on, with Selene right behind him. The icy winds bit into his cheeks. Snow coated the small red beard he'd begun to grow in The Deep.

He caught an odd sound in the wind howling through the channels. He paused his trek.

"What is it?"

Nath held up a finger and cupped his ear. Somewhere on the mountainside, creatures growled and groaned.

Selene pushed his finger down. "I hear it too."

With knees high, they tromped through the deep snow and climbed the rocky ledges. Sure enough, the farther they went, the louder the sound became. They raced up a ridge until they found the source of the sound. The yeti-titan, Many, was locked up in a battle with a full-sized white dragon who blended in with the snow.

"She's a blizzard fury!" Nath said with a smile as wide as a barn. "I've never seen one so big before."

The dragon and yeti crashed over the ground, bouncing from berm to berm. One was just as fierce as the other. The yeti's hands choked the dragon. The dragon's claws scratched hunks of fur from the yeti's chest.

In normal circumstances, Nath knew the snow dragon would be more than a match for a single yeti, but this yeti was more powerful. It was enhanced by the titan's spirit, making it a far more dangerous foe. The battle was still far away. The snow-colored dragon appeared to be losing. Under the grip of the yeti, the dragon began to sink in the snow.

With the wind whistling past his ears, Nath sped on. He pulled Fang free, and once he hit the higher ground, he moved in leaps and bounds. As the blizzard fury fought for her last breath of life, Nath cocked back and hurled his sword.

Fang sailed through the air like a javelin. The wondrous weapon slipped right into the yeti's ribs.

The monster arched back, jaws wide and roaring in great pain.

The blizzard fury acted. She coiled back her magnificent horned head, opened up her great jaws, and blasted out a cone of ice. The frosty attack covered the lurching yeti instantly. Its entire body turned into a block of ice. For a moment, Nath saw the yeti, Many, frozen inside, with eyes filled with horror, but then the blizzard fury unleashed her tail, striking the block of ice with a resounding *crack*.

The yeti burst into hunks and pieces. A wavering spirit hovered above the broken body, like an angry mist in the sky. The dragon hissed at the spirit. Without a serviceable host, the spirit moved on.

Selene caught up to Nath. "That might just do it." She kissed his cheek. "You did well."

He eyed the beautiful dragon and nodded. "No, we did well."

CHAPTER 16

AT THE BOTTOM OF THE mountains, Nath sat before the campfire he'd started with some dry branches and a ball of his fiery spit.

"Are you really cold?" Selene said, standing back and away from the fire.

"I don't know that I'm cold, so much. Not with the furnace that churns within me, but there's something about a campfire. There's more to it than the warmth and the wavering flames. It's the memories that come to mind from all of the adventures I've had." He patted the frosty ground next to him. "Come sit. Let's make some memories of our own."

"I think we have plenty to recollect. Much of it not so pleasant. You have to admit, our time together has been nothing short of difficult." She crinkled her nose. "I can't imagine why you'd want to recall any of it."

"We live a life that most people can only dream about. I'm thankful for it. Certainly, being a hero isn't a bunch of fun and glory as the bards tend to say, but nothing worth doing was ever easy." He rubbed his hands together over the flames. "Ah, to jump in the fire only to hop out unscathed. It never happens that way, does it?"

"No, I suppose not. I guess I'm not very accustomed to the role of the hero." She sat down and leaned her head on his shoulder. "Nath, you're my hero."

His heart pounded in his chest. He hadn't thought he was cold, but the compliment warmed him from head to toe. That admission from Selene was astounding. He put his arm around her waist. "Thank you."

They kissed until the campfire dimmed.

"Whoa," Nath said, with a broad smile on his face. "And that's another reason why men want to be heroes."

Then with a playful look dancing in her eyes, she rose up. "Just imagine how much better it will be once Nalzambor is free."

"It can be better?"

"Maybe I was holding back."

"You could have fooled me." Nath kicked snow over the smoldering campfire. "I suppose we need to get moving and figure out what we're in for. I've got a better feel for the terrain now that the snow has broken. We're south at the peaks below the ruins of Barnabus. We'll head toward some of the townships and try to get a feel for things. I'd hate to find out Fang brought us too far into the future."

"I hope we're not in the future at all."

Walking in long strides, they came across a village just after dawn. Livestock roamed free. Most of the houses and barns were ramshackle. Overgrowth was everywhere. Nath and Selene hung back, observing the place for an hour. Men and women trudged along, heads down and in shabby clothing. Two women in sullied purple filled their buckets at the well. A durable young man pushed a plow in the fields. As best as Nath could tell, there were only thirty people in the village at best.

"It looks safe. I'll go speak with them."

"Don't be fooled, Nath. The spirits could possess any of them."

"I'll just make sure that I question one who is not a spirit. I think I have a pretty good feel for them." Evading the eyes of the discontented people, Nath angled between the barn and field where the young man pushed the plow. The barn shielded him from view of the others. He snuck up on the boy.

"Hello?"

The broad-shouldered young man kept plowing.

"Uh, hello, I said."

Still, the man kept at it.

Nath put his hand on the man's shoulder and stopped him. "Excuse me, I'm in need of assistance."

Slowly, the man turned to face Nath. His eyes were milky white. "I'm not much help to anybody, stranger. If you're wanting food, I suggest you go elsewhere. We all have a hard enough time feeding ourselves."

"I'm sorry, I didn't realize you were blind."

"Well, if you're sticking around, you best get used to it. We're all blind, and better off for it."

"All of you? Why? What happened?"

"Those titans." He spat on the ground. "They gave us a choice to serve or pay the price. What is left here, well, we refused. Some mystics came and took our sight with a stone brighter than the stars. We resisted, but the others, including my sisters and father, did not. They served the giants and left us to rot in the cold."

"Are there any giants or titans around?"

"I haven't seen any, heh-heh. That's a joke. No, we're left for dead. We live like this. Many of us starved to death." He took a handkerchief out and blew his nose. "Or got sick and died. The other towns won't help, not even for money. They worship those monsters. The truth is, I'm glad I can't see them, but I wish I could see my wife and child once more."

Nath wasn't sure he wanted to know the answer to his next question. "If you don't mind me asking, how long have you been blind?"

"You know, I don't really count, but nature tells me when it's time for night or day. Of course, there's a big difference between having the sun or moonlight on your face." He stuck his handkerchief away in his shirt. "Oh, and don't get spooked if you see our likes working in the middle of the night. We don't know any better." He scratched his head. "I suppose it's been a few years, though."

"A few years?" *Guzan! Not again!*

CHAPTER 17

NATH AND SELENE LAYERED UP in garb that the dead people of the village had left behind. Selene had paled when he shared the news that Fang might have taken them forward in time by a matter of years. To make matters worse, he worried about his friends. He wasn't there to protect them or give them warning. Worry ate him up inside.

The villagers were nice people. Even though they'd been stricken with blindness, they tried to be as helpful as they could. They had no idea who Selene or Nath were, which was helpful in case any of the titan overseers happened by. Nath thanked them and moved on, not making a promise to anyone.

From there, they headed from town to village, trying to get a better feel for things. The crops had died off in many places. Several of the small villages and provinces had merged together underneath the authority of the titans.

Heads covered in the midst of a steady snow, Nath and Selene ventured among the people. Many of them were dark-eyed, possessed, and as ornery as they were dirty. Depravity had set in. The people offered sacrifices of goats and cattle to the giants that oversaw the city.

It troubled Nath. Deeply. They moved on.

"I can't stand much more of this, Selene. Did you see those people? It's disgusting. All of them are blinded in worship to those, those shades!"

Selene led, picking her way through the forest, where even the varmints and birds had become scarce. "I never realized how evil corrupts people when I was so corrupt myself. I'm just glad my eyes are open now. It gives me strength on this journey, knowing we are fighting for a better world for all. Have you reconsidered summoning some dragons?"

"With all of those wurmers streaking through the skies? Not to mention the ones we encountered nestled in the woodland." He shook his mane. "No, not yet. I think it's best we stay on this path that no one will suspect."

"You think we can make it back inside Dragon Home?" She pushed a branch aside, allowing Nath to walk underneath. "You heard the people. They believe the titans have conquered it. Even though it seems incomprehensible, they act very certain of it."

"That's why I have to see it for myself." If Nath slept, he'd have lost sleep over it. Seeing Dragon Home conquered was unimaginable, but he'd also seen the armies that surrounded it before he last left. There had been wurmers by the thousands filling the skies like a sea of birds. Monstrous giants gathered by the hundreds. The armies of men, orcs, and the other willfully ignorant masses numbered in the tens of thousands. If taking Dragon Home was possible, that was the kind of force that could get it done. "Seeing is believing, you know."

"I agree."

Two days later they made it to a point high in the hills where Nath got his first glimpse of home. The tremendous mountain almost kissed the clouds in the sky. With his keen sight he could see the armies gathered all around the mountain. The enemy was small in comparison, though formidable. The wurmers were specks in the sky that swarmed in waves like angry bees.

"It doesn't look like the mountain is conquered to me."

"Me neither," Selene replied. "Let's get a closer look."

"Aye, but be wary for spies in the woodland."

"Let's just hope the woodland isn't a spy by itself."

Nath and Selene came within a mile of the mountain and hid among the hillside rocks. They nestled east, away from the surging army that seemed determined to bust inside the mountain by forming a wedge in the middle. Giants used huge mauls and picks where they dug into the base of the mountain. Rocks and boulders were tossed into the lava pools that had once formed a natural moat around the mountain's base. The giants had filled it with rock and made a huge bridge that led right to the mountain.

Farther back at a safer distance from the intense heat were the soldiers. All of them were armored from head to toe. The weapons they carried were sharp, heavy, and crude. The wurmers seemed to number like the snowflakes in the sky. Among the army was a giant bigger than them all. Dragon bones and skins covered his body. It wasn't Eckubahn, but another mammoth humanoid whose head was more monster than man. He stood watch over the bridge, barking commands at the soldiers and workers. He plucked a man that was teetering along in a casual manner up from the ground and stuffed him in his mouth then chewed the man up like a snack. The workers moved like they'd just felt the hot crack of the whip.

"That's disturbing. Perhaps we should take him down. I have Fang."

"It won't stop them."

"No, but it will slow them."

"I see that fire in your eyes, Nath. Now's not the time. We need to get inside. Do you know another way?"

"Oh yes, I know a way. There is always a way for me. The problem is, can we get to it?"

"Perhaps you should go it alone? I'd be safer here."

"No, we're both going. We'll just have to do our best to blend in."

CHAPTER 18

An orcen patrol of two chased after Selene about half a mile from the titan army's main camp. Nath waited behind the trunk of a white pinwood tree, staying concealed as she ran past. He stuck out his leg, tripping one who hit the ground hard in a metallic clatter. The other orc stopped in time to turn and catch Nath's fist smashing him square in the jaw. The orc dropped like a sack of oats with his eyes rolling up in his head.

The orc that Nath tripped brought a whistle to his lips. Selene's tail cracked him upside the head so hard it knocked the orc out cold.

"That was easy enough," Nath said. He started tugging the suit of mail armor from the orc he felled. "Well, what are you waiting for, Selene? Get dressed."

She kneeled down and began stripping off the armor with a sour face. "There needs to be a better way. They smell so rotten."

"Smelling bad is all part of the disguise. Not that I like it." He took off the orc's battle helmet that fully covered the pig-man face. It was a crude version of what the legionnaires wore, a metal face with many spikes. He covered his head. "How do I look?"

"Like an orc with red hair. I don't think you're going to fool anybody with that mane of yours."

"Oh, it will work. See?" It had been a while, but just like Nath was able to change the color of his scales, he could change the color of his hair. It turned from a rich red to ruddy brown. He held some of his long locks up to his eye. "Not very flashy, but we aren't going to a wedding celebration, are we?"

Selene struggled to pull one of the orcen boots over her scaly feet. "An orcen wedding, perhaps."

"Oh, that sounds disgusting. Do you know what they serve at those things?"

"Sadly, I do."

It took a few minutes for them to get into the orcen armor. They buckled one another's straps.

Nath wriggled around a little. "Constraining, but not a bad fit." Selene's armor looked a little big on her slender form. Nath tightened it up as best he could. "I'm impressed that you got your tail in there."

"My tail makes a nice filler around my belly." She patted her stomach. "See?"

"Well done."

"What are you going to do with Fang? You can't just waltz in there and not draw some attention. Will you leave the blade behind?"

Nath eyed his steel. "I don't know. Everything we do is a risk." He took his cloak he'd taken from the village of the blind and bound Fang up in it. "Let's just take it one step at a time."

Selene buckled on the orcen sword belt. "After you."

They made their way into the heart of the titan army's activity. Selene commandeered a pick and shovel. Nath managed to find a wheelbarrow. He put more digging gear in the wheelbarrow, burying Fang underneath.

Pushing it along behind her, he said, "See, I told you all we needed was a wheelbarrow."

"That's the easy part." She gazed up at the tremendous form of Isobahn, who overlooked the bridge of stone. "Don't be so certain he won't sniff us out."

"True, but hopefully the stink of the orcen gear will cover our scent." In most cases his scent was undetectable by even the keenest of noses, but titans and some of the giants were different. They could sniff dragons out more often than not. Nath realized that to cross the bridge, he'd have to be careful. With Selene hustling ahead, he said, "Wait, slow down."

She turned. "What? It's best to move right at him with our heads down."

"No, wait a moment. We need a distraction."

"We can't just stand here and do nothing. You've seen him. He's bound to notice that."

"Just give it a few moments."

Nath pretended to inspect the equipment in the wheelbarrow. In the meantime, he kept watch on Isobahn from the corner of his eye. The titan's heavy stare seemed to have an eye on everything in the camp at once. Nothing escaped his attention, coming in or going out. A train of laborers carrying gear similar to Selene's marched right by them, making headway for the bridge. Nath gave Selene a nod.

Both of them eased into the ranks. The foreman at the front of the ranks of workers led them right to where Isobahn stood. The orcen foreman said on a proud voice, "We are the next shift ready to work until we die for the glory of the titans!"

Head downcast, Nath could feel Isobahn's stare scouring over each and every one of them. Selene stiffened beside him.

He's going to see us. I know he's going to see us.

"Carry on until you die," the titan's cavernous voice said.

The work party of twenty durable bodies moved forward. The carts and wheelbarrows they pushed rattled over the massive bridge of stone and planks of chopped-down timber that dammed the moat of lava. The intense heat and steam had Nath sweating immediately. The strong smell of sulfur was an old friend to him. It was home. *Almost there. This couldn't be better.*

They were halfway over the bridge when Isobahn's voice called out in their direction. "Stop!"

The train of workers came to a complete stop.

Isobahn continued, "There are too many workers in your party. There should only be twenty. There are twenty-two. Explain that, foreman!"

The orcen foreman made a quick count with his finger. He stopped on Nath and Selene. Cocked his head to one side. "Those two I've never seen before."

Isobahn's angry voice shook the valley. "IMPOSTERS!"

CHAPTER 19

With intensity, Nath said, "Selene, run!" In a powerful surge, he put the wheelbarrow through the thick ranks of workers. He plowed them over, toppling them to the ground as they howled. While they were down, he slipped Fang out from the bottom of the wheelbarrow and sprinted side by side with Selene across the bridge.

"Stop them! Stop them!" Isobahn was crushing orcen workers with his feet in his rush to come grab them with his huge titan hands.

The workers at the base of the mountain came to a halt. Necks craned as they tried to see what was going on.

"Stay with me!" Nath said as they raced into the relative safety of a tunnel the laborers had made. At least Isobahn couldn't reach them in here.

Upon the hollering of Isobahn's voice, the laborers—orcs, ogres, and men—strained to see who they were supposed to be going after.

Once they were out the other side of the tunnel, Nath took full advantage of the moment of confusion, saying in his best orcen imitation, "They are on the bridge! On the bridge! I run to fetch the nets and weapons!"

Some of the workers turned away. Others did not. Covered in oily sweat and hairy brawn, ogres carrying mauls bigger than men cut off Nath's path.

I don't have time for this.

With a blast of his hot breath, Nath set the ogres on fire. Ignoring their screams, he raced right by them until he found the channel in the rocks he was looking for. The narrow pathway led right up to a majestic doorway that could only be seen by the eyes of a dragon.

"Hold them off," Nath to Selene. "This takes a little while." He could hear the pursuing forces scrambling and coming their way. He closed his eyes and placed his hands on the doorway that so elegantly blended in with the rock. In Dragonese he spoke words that came slowly at first before turning into song.

Keeping the forces at bay in the narrow channel with her powers, Selene yelled, "Hurry, Nath!"

Careful not to slip on a single syllable, he carried on, word after word, phrase after phrase until he was finished. The door in the rock didn't move. "Sultans of Sulfur, they've changed the passwords."

Using a shield of energy to hold back the forces as long as she could, she said, "You can't get in?"

Nath drew Fang. "I'm afraid not, we're doom—"

The door opened. Powerful hands grabbed Nath and pulled him inside. "Selene, come!"

"You don't have to tell me twice." She dashed after him with the spring of a gazelle and dove inside. The door sealed behind her, leaving only the appearance of rock and stone.

"Well," said a cheerful voice, "Look what the dwarf dragged in. Dragon!"

Nath erupted with elation. "Brenwar! Ben! You're alive!"

"No!" Ben said, hugging Nath with all of his strength. "You are alive! They thought we lost you, Dragon. But I knew better!"

"I never doubted it for a moment," Brenwar grumbled. "But how you got here is another question entirely! Not that I'm complaining, but how did you do it?" Suddenly, Brenwar's eyes filled with recognition. "Fang! We wondered what happened to him. He disappeared years ago."

"Years?" Nath said, noting the new gray hairs in Brenwar's beard. He gave Selene a look. Her brows crinkled. "How many years?"

"A little less than three," Brenwar said, squeezing Nath on the elbows with both of his hands. "It seemed much longer."

"Not for me." Slivver appeared in the corridor, as radiant as ever. "It might as well have been a thousand years. I began to worry whether you'd ever make it back. We tried to get to you, but The Deep made it improbable."

"You knew we were there?" Nath said.

"It took some doing," Slivver said. "After we lost you in Narnum, we managed to make our escape from Tylabahn's deception and make it back here. Using the Chamber of Murals, some of us went back to Narnum, where we learned you were in The Deep. Eckubahn guarded that hole like a prized possession. We couldn't get near it. So since you've been gone, we've kept spies in place, and kept an eye on it. It's hard to believe it's been so many years. The truth is, I'm having a hard time believing my eyes and ears."

"I can imagine so, seeing how for us, it's only been days, not years, since we parted." He waggled Fang in front of them. "I've a bad feeling that using Fang to move through time has a bit of a cursed effect. The more he's used, the further in time he takes us. It was a concern before I used him."

"Maybe you should have him take you back in time then?" Brenwar suggested.

"I thought about that. No, I can assume that would only make things worse. Believe me, I wanted to try. I thought maybe by going back, I could save Father." He grabbed his head. "Oh, Guzan. Father's been lingering in the Dark Realm all of this extra time."

"What do you mean, Nath?" Ben asked.

"In The Deep, Father called out to me. He told me to save him. He's alive. Or at least, his spirit is. He's in a place where he is hiding from his enemies." He shook his head. "It's going to take some time to get my head wrapped around this." He scanned the massive corridor that looked to have been hollowed out with fires that melted stone. The surfaces were smooth and shiny like glass. "Walk with me. I'd like to see Mother, and perhaps Bayzog can help with this. The Sultans know that if anyone can wrap their head about this, it would be him. Where is he, anyway? Please don't tell me Narmum. He's always so far away when I need him."

Walking alongside him, Brenwar, Ben, and Slivver came to a stop.

Nath's fingertips tingled as he faced them. "What?"

Brenwar cleared his throat. "Bayzog died."

CHAPTER 20

ITH MISTY EYES, NATH STOOD gazing at Bayzog's sarcophagus. His heart ached.

Selene stood with him, holding his hand. "Sorry, Nath. I know how dear he was to you."

"You don't know the half of it. Brenwar, what happened? It was Tylabahn, wasn't it."

Brenwar recounted the story of Ben and Selene returning to them as they waited outside of Narnum. Tylabahn had possessed Gorlee and used that power to her advantage, taking on the form of an orc and then Selene. The first chance she got to strike, she went after Bayzog. "None of us saw it coming, Nath. Once she sprang her trap, it was too late. The wound was mortal."

"We saw it coming, but I guess it was wishful thinking on my end. Selene and I figured that Tylabahn duped us." He looked at Ben. "I was mostly concerned you wouldn't make it."

"I wish it had been me. Bayzog was capable of much more than I am." Ben's eyes traced the silvery outline of Bayzog's figure. "I led that monster right to him. We all almost perished. I should have perished."

"At least we're all here now. Bayzog would understand. He would have given his life to save any one of ours. All of you know that, don't you?"

"Yes, but it still hurts," Ben replied.

"So where are Sasha, Samaz, and Rerry? I assume they're still here?"

"They are, and no doubt all of them will be glad to see you." Brenwar shoved the sarcophagus back into the tomb. "When we saw the disturbance outside, we didn't know it was you until I heard from your lips for myself. It's time we notified them."

"What about Sansla? Where is he?"

"He departed through the murals, looking for his rangers. That's been some time ago, and we haven't heard from him since." Brenwar marched back into the main corridor. Everyone followed.

The wide roadway spiraled upward into the great mountain. They passed dragon den after dragon den on their way up, along with a variety of dragons, who would stop and bow as Nath passed them.

He acknowledged them all. He was king. Being home again felt good.

Even with hallway tunnels big enough to march an army through, the journey to the top made for a lengthy trip. It gave Nath some time to think. He'd missed three years, and there wasn't any telling how many more had died during that span of time. All of the dragons and the races had to be reeling. He wondered how people had even survived. Now that he was here, he had to find a way to end it. He needed to find his father, locate Eckubahn, and kill the titan once and for all. He had hoped Bayzog could give some insight on that. Now that opportunity had passed.

Maybe Mother will have some advice on where to start.

They entered a dragon chamber that was as grand as any. Discs of wild energy were flying around the room. Rerry, with sword in hand, struck at the discs, which exploded in the air when he hit them. Samaz stood on the other side of the room from Rerry. He carried the Elderwood Staff in one hand with the gemstone glowing with warm light. Energy disks filled his hands one after the other, and he slung them at Rerry. The lightning-quick strikes of Rerry's sword chopped right through them.

Nath interrupted their training. "You swing steel like a striking snake. Well done, Rerry."

Soaked in sweat, Rerry turned. His eyes popped open wide. "Nath! Samaz, it's Nath! Nath's back!" He tossed the sword aside and rushed right over and hugged Nath. "I thought you were in The Deep! Haha! Welcome back!"

Samaz came over as fast as Nath had ever seen the older brother move. He poked Nath in the arm. "It really is you."

Rerry's and Samaz's faces were a little fuller than the last time he'd seen them. Rerry had packed on more muscle that showed well underneath his leather jerkin. Samaz had puffed a little more, but an even deeper intelligence glimmered in his dark eyes. "I'm sorry about your father."

"Thank you, Nath. But we will be avenging him in due time. We train every day for it." Rerry's gaze landed on Fang. "You found him!"

"More like he found me," Nath replied.

"I told you, Samaz. I told you Fang went to find him. I know how smart Fang is."

Samaz shrugged his eyebrows.

"It seems like there is a celebration and I wasn't invited. How rude."

Nath twisted around to face Sasha. She looked splendid in her lemon-colored and snow-flecked sorceress robes. His face lit up the moment he saw her warm smile. He clasped her hands in his. "I'm so sorry about Bayzog." He choked up. His body shook. He wrapped her up in his arms. "Forgive me."

"Sssh, sssh, sssh, Nath." Sasha hugged him back while stroking his hair. "We stopped mourning years ago. When we think of him, we celebrate the life that we lived with him. I'm not saying I don't cry from time to time, but my yearning for vengeance keeps my sheets warm at night." She pushed back. "I'm so glad you're back, Nath. Your presence alone fills all the empty rooms." She caught Selene looking at her. They hugged. "What happened? How did you escape?"

Nath filled her in.

"I suggest you make haste to see your mother, Nath," Sasha said, averting her eyes for a moment. "Uh, she'll be very excited to see you."

"Where is she?"

"She's been spending a lot of time in the throne room. I'm certain you'll find her there."

Nath gave everyone a quick goodbye before leaving the chamber.

Slivver caught up with him.

"Something bad is going on, isn't it."

"It's best that you hear it from Mother."

CHAPTER 21

ATH EMBRACED HIS MOTHER FOR the longest time. She was in full dragon form, but the same size as him, much like Slivver. Slivver hung back, waiting for him outside the throne room doors.

"I missed you so much, Son. I've been worried."

"I can hear it in your voice." He held her hands. Grahleyna was a most beautiful dragon, white scales accented with flecks of cinnamon. She walked, talked, and spoke like a true queen. "Everyone seems more troubled than they're letting on. Tell me what I need to know."

"I will." She led him through the glinting piles of coins that rustled beneath their feet to the base of the throne. "I sense you have something to share with me as well."

"It's Father. His spirit is alive. He reached out to me while I was in The Deep. He says I need to free him."

"Are you certain, Nath? It could have been the spirits playing tricks."

"No, it was him. I can tell the truth from a lie. Certainly in Father's case. But Fang took me forward three years. Father's been trapped in the Dark Realm that much longer." He scooped up some coins and gems and poured them back onto the floor. "It's tearing me up inside."

"Time in the Dark Realm is not as we know it here. It resides on another plane. I had a fleeting hope that your father's essence might have escaped to it."

"You knew Father might be alive?"

"No, I hoped." A warm smile crossed her face. "And hope prevailed."

"Mother, I don't know the first thing about traveling from one realm to the other. I hardly understand where the Dark Realm is. Speaking honestly, I've not heard any stories about it since I was a child. How can I be the Dragon King and still know less than anyone about all these things?"

"So long as your father remains, all the knowledge you need will not be fully yours. Consider that a good thing. You'll only have it all when your father passes into the next mural, or when you learn about it for yourself."

"Sometimes I feel like an infant. How can I fight things I don't know anything about?"

Grahleyna draped her wing over his shoulders. "Tell me, what do you know about the enemy now that you didn't know when you first crossed paths with them?"

"Hmmm…I suppose we know how to wipe out a spawn of wurmers with the life gems. Some of the titan spirits are too powerful to host a normal body. That's why they use the giants and wurmers. They need a host strong enough to hold them. If they can't find one, they perish, or perhaps they go back to the realm from where they came."

"You see, you've loaded some very deadly arrows into your quiver. Your experience has given you a powerful weapon: knowledge. With that, any enemy can be defeated."

"I just wish I had all my powers back. As a full dragon, I'd hunt down Eckubahn and tear him in half."

"Your size and powers are not what matters, Nath. That is all relative. It's your spirit, your heart that counts most."

Nath had heard a similar speech from his father at least a hundred times. Every time, it had pricked his scales, but it had never really sunk in. "I thought when I beat Gorn Grattack I'd mastered everything."

"You grew in mind, body, and spirit. That is all. You have to put it all together and use it to handle the next enemy that steps out of line." She sighed. "They will always come, Nath, always, until the end of times."

"Selene mentioned that Gorn Grattack might still be alive in the Dark Realm. Do you believe that's possible? He'd be trying to kill Father. Wouldn't he be more powerful in that realm than this one?"

"It's too hard to say, but we can search the libraries to see what we can find to help us out. In the meantime, as good as it is to see you, there is more troubling news to be shared."

"I guess I shouldn't expect any good news." He looked right at her. "Who else that I adore has died?"

"So many have passed. So many more will. We can't prevent the inevitable for much longer. The titan army is very close to penetrating Dragon Home."

Nath stood. "We can't let that happen! It's not possible. Certainly we can block every tunnel they build."

"You don't understand, Nath. They've been digging for three years. Once they penetrate the core, there won't be any stopping them. So many dragons have died plugging their holes and waging war in the skies. Our ranks are depleted. There are far more of them than of us."

Nath crouched low and clutched his head. "Ugh, this is my fault!" Quickly bounding back up on his feet, he paced through the mounds of treasure. "Look at this. All this wealth, and it won't do us a bit of good, will it? I don't suppose we could bribe them?"

"Nath, you know better than to barter with our enemies."

"Why do we store all of this up then?"

She swished her tail through the piles with a glint in her beautiful eyes. "You know it's because we like it. I remember times when your father and I would roll in it. There is just something about dragons and treasure. The colors are so radiant and so perfect. Besides, we are not invaders who stole it."

Nath never really thought of where the treasure came from before. It had always just been there. His head tilted when he said, "Where did all this treasure come from?"

"Didn't your father ever tell you?"

"No."

"Ah, I suppose that's why you lack so much knowledge that you should have had. Bear in mind, I was manning the Great Dragon Wall when your father was raising you. If I had been here, I wouldn't have let you venture into the world so early." She scooped up a small diamond chandelier with her tail. With a soft breath from her, its stones burned with mystic light. "I'd say you needed at least another fifty years of training."

"Tell me then, where did all this treasure come from?"

"The world is old, Nath, and every sparkle you see in this room was a gift."

"From who?"

"The races."

Chapter 22

Nath and Grahleyna spent hours talking about things. She explained how dragons and men had once been close allies. In some regards the gold and silver were gifts, and in others, they were tributes. Then too, dragons were notorious for creating their own gifts. They loved their kings that came over millennia and gave with cheerful hearts.

"There was a time when the throne room was filled with nothing but the murals and the thrones. But that time was long before me," Grahleyna said. "The dragons never asked for any of it. Eventually though, the dark times came. The races who came and saw the vast wealth became jealous. Word of the treasure spread throughout Nalzambor, and the men, dwarves, elves, and others stopped coming. To make matters worse, they turned against the dragons, thanks to the legions of evil. There came a point where we just decided to stay out of their way. In return, they decided to hunt us."

"So, there used to be peace in the land?"

"For the most part, yes. Men and dragons were united for the common good, but it only takes a grain of evil to tear the very foundations apart."

"That's sad, Mother."

"That's life. We live it by fighting to do what is right. I hate to admit this, but I was beginning to lose hope. I should never let that happen. But now, you are back, and the word from your father has lifted my spirits again." She let go of the chandelier. It floated toward the cathedral ceiling. "Nath, we are going to need to evacuate Dragon Home."

"What? We can't do that! The dragons would rather die first! I'd rather die first."

"Come now, Nath. You've hardly spent any time in this mountain. Would you miss it so much?"

"But this is a place of sanctuary for us. It's a testament to our power. As long as Dragon Home stands, the world has hope."

"Men call it the Mountain of Doom. They've done so for a very long time."

"No, Dragon Home needs to become a beacon of hope again. We need to change that. Mother, we have to hold off their forces. Just long enough to stop the wurmers and the giants. I just need more time. I can do this."

"We've waited long enough, Nath. We need to evacuate while we still can."

"But how? Wurmers fill the skies. We can't leave without some kind of battle."

"We can use the murals. As a matter of fact, I've already been dispatching many of the dragons through them."

"Where?"

"All over Nalzambor. They're hiding."

Nath couldn't believe his ears. "Mother, we need an army. There is strength in numbers! Now we have nothing, after summoning them back here to begin with."

"I'm sorry, Nath, I had to do what I thought was best—"

"No more dragons leave!"

"Almost all of them are already gone."

For the first time in his life, Nath almost pulled his hair out. An army numbering in the thousands was ready to invade, and they didn't have any forces to fight it. A skeleton crew wouldn't be nearly enough to stop the giants. Grahleyna might as well have given them the keys.

"Mother, they will have control over the murals. They'll be able to see everything. We can't give so much up."

"No, I'd never leave such a powerful tool under their control. We will destroy the murals, but someone must be left behind to do so. I volunteer for that."

The conversation was becoming maddening. Nath stormed out of the throne room, where he found Slivver waiting. "You knew all about this?"

"I'm ashamed to say that I did," Slivver said with his head cast down. "I tried to plead the same case that you probably did, but to no avail. The dragons were lost without a king. Mother did what she thought was best, and to be truthful, I'm not so certain she was wrong."

"But Dragon Home will be overrun with evil."

"It's a mountain, Nath. A pile of dirt that we call home. Perhaps we should let them have it?"

"I can't believe my ears! Let them have our home and all of that treasure! It is not theirs to take. They are invaders!"

"Our dwarven friend Brenwar had an idea."

"Good. I'm sure he wouldn't abandon Dragon Home any more than he'd abandon Morgdon."

"Yes, about Morgdon."

"Don't tell me it has fallen?"

"No, but the dwarves are fighting for their lives from within. They don't have any way of escape. Their ranks thin, and quite possibly they are starving. We bring them what we can through the murals, but that's about to end. They are so stubborn they refuse to let us fly them out. Nath, the titan army has grown every day since you've been gone. The people turn from their ways like a plague. If things were bad then, they are ten times worse now."

"I need to see this for myself." Nath didn't take his time. He ran up the corridor to the Chamber of Murals. There, he gazed at everything that was going on that he could see. Thousands of orcen soldiers boldly battled against the walls of Morgdon. The elven fields of Elome were in the midst of a similar invasion. The rich lands burned. Death and decay were rampant from one corner of Nalzambor to the other.

Nath's chest tightened. His fists clenched. He threw Fang away from him. "Why did you do this?"

CHAPTER 23

Sansla stood with his dark wings folded with the roamers gathered around. Hoven and Liam in particular had been scouring the land for the wurmer nests for years. Now, with frosty snow covering their backs, they spied what they thought was another nest. This nest was far north on miles of peninsula surrounded by the sea. With his breath misting in the cold air, he said, "It might be the last one, but we need to be sure."

A flock of wurmers streaked through the cloudy sky. They flew south, out of sight, but Sansla knew they were only circling the area. There was more than one group of them, also. It kept him grounded. Anything that flew too high in the air would be slaughtered.

With his hands clasped over his belly, Hoven said, "We'll carry on the same way we did with the rest of them. Liam and I will go. I need to move before my legs freeze over. It's cold up here."

"A ranger complaining?" Liam said with a shivering smile. "I never thought I'd live to see the day." His teeth chattered. "I think the weather is lovely."

"Exercise caution. If this is the last one, then the time to strike will come." Sansla gave them a nod of his chin. Hoven and Liam hustled over into the frozen woodland and vanished through the snow-covered branches. With the others around him in the dimming light of dusk, Sansla unrolled a sheepskin scroll in his hand. It was a map of Nalzambor, a bit crude for an elven hand. He fingered the top of the map where they stood. "I'm confident this is the last one. It has to be."

There were five spots marked on the map, and they weren't in any particular pattern. There were two nests close together near the Ruins of Barnabus: the one he and Selene had destroyed which ended up unleashing Tylabahn, and one they had discovered in the heavy snows behind the mountains of Morgdon. There was a nest near Thraag, the orcen city, and another west of that. This one they were at now, near the Dragon Pool, was the last. There weren't any south of Narnum. They'd looked, but the wurmers all came from the north, which was a good thing.

"Now that we've located them, we just have to destroy them."

"If you're confident that we've found them all," one of the roamers said, "do you want to try and destroy this last one since we're here?"

"We need to see what we're up against." Eyes on the distant peninsula with white foam waves crashing against the beach of stone, he said, "It seems very peculiar over there. I don't see any giants or wurmers. I'm certain the last nest would be even more heavily guarded than the others."

"The one in the icy peaks was only guarded by that treacherous terrain and a handful of yeti," the roamer said. "If we only had what we needed to destroy it then. I don't look forward to traversing those mountains once more."

The roamers meticulously rode through Nalzambor tracking down every sign of the wurmers they could find. Though many were becoming more and more distorted, people gave a good account of where the vicious flocks came from. The two hives near Thraag had been guarded by countless wurmers and a small army led by giants. Eckubahn wasn't taking any chances, not even now that Nath Dragon was gone.

"Let's see what they find out." Sansla produced an orb of destruction. "If we can destroy it, then we will destroy it."

Hoven and Liam snaked their way down the icy peninsula, using the frozen vegetation for cover. They headed toward the tall peaks of rock at the end. They moved with the gentleness of a deer on footfalls as soft as snow, barely disturbing anything they passed.

The end of the peninsula was a mountainous rocky cliff that took a beating from the salty wind and sea. There were trees, tall frosty pines that bent stubbornly in the breeze. They crept up to the top, eyes searching the grounds for the slightest unnatural disturbance. Crisscrossing the jetty of land, they tried to find any sign of a cave or entrance but found none. They made it to the edge of the cliff and looked down. It was a two-hundred-foot drop into the numbing waters.

"Perhaps Sansla was wrong," Liam suggested.

"He hasn't been wrong yet. You heard the sea folk. The fishermen report seeing them coming out of this area of seawalls like bats." Still looking down, he shielded his eyes from the wind. "There are seabirds nestled on the ledges."

Liam leaned over. "Yes, birds, but not wurmers. Of course, we can't get a clear picture from here, can we?" He lowered himself onto the lip of land. "Only one way to be sure."

"You're going to climb that wall of ice?"

"It's not so bad." Liam smiled. "Hoven, may I borrow your mittens?"

"At least let me tether you with a coil of rope," Hoven said, fishing a strand from his pack.

"I'll be fine."

Liam, son of Shum and Hoven's nephew, was the youngest roamer. Wanting to live up to his family reputation, he didn't hesitate to face the next challenge. With fingers frozen to the bone, he climbed down the rocks from one narrow ledge to the other. And found himself eye to eye with a seabird perched in a nest. It honked at Liam.

"Oh, mind your business. I'm hungry, mind you. I'd hate to take the egg you lie on during my trip back up, but I will."

The seabird honked again.

Liam moved on, foot after foot, hand over hand. He was halfway down the icy seawall when he caught a glimpse of a pitch-black hole swallowing up the wind. He waved up at Hoven, shimmied over, climbed farther down, and went inside. The hole was huge, a full thirty feet of doorway, and black as coal inside. The wind howled within the cave, making sharp whistles and shrieks. His elven vision adjusted. He could make the outline of the cave walls. Dozens of yards ahead, a seam of light caught his eye. He moved quickly, with the swirling sound of the wind covering his footfalls.

This has to be it. But I need proof. An egg, perhaps.

At the back end of the first part of the cave, Liam lowered himself down from ledge to ledge. The light grew stronger. The slopes and ledge angles steepened. Finally, he hit bottom, and with a strange mist hiding his feet, he headed for the light. A hundred feet later the sound of something cracking open caught his ear. He faced it.

A wurmer began to hatch. It squeezed out of the goo and shell like a winged worm. Liam slid out a dagger. His first instinct was to kill the little monster.

The fewer wurmers, the better.

He had only moved forward another foot when he felt the walls and floors coming alive with the mindless creatures. He saw more eggs: hundreds, perhaps thousands.

I think I have my proof.

He backpedaled, slowly at first, then picked up the pace. He put his dagger in his mouth and climbed back up toward the entrance. The wind started to moan louder. The hairs on his neck rose. It wasn't the wind. It was something else. Something huge inside. He took off toward the mouth of the cave. A huge body lurched up from the ground with glowing eyes.

CHAPTER 24

"I CAN'T BELIEVE YOU CAST YOUR sword aside," Selene said to Nath. They were in quarters designed more for men than dragons. Nath had stormed out of the Chamber of Murals, leaving Fang and Slivver behind. Selene had caught up with him. "That's no way to treat a friend."

Sitting on the edge of the bed, Nath said, "Friend? What kind of friend moves us forward in time so that we can witness the slaughter that we abandoned! He never does what I command him to do. Nor what I ask, for that matter. The Sultans know I've been more than polite about it. I can't help but think I would have been better off without him."

"Maybe Fang did what he did for reasons you don't understand? Did you ever think to consider that?" Selene straightened the pillows Nath had been punching earlier. "He took us to the wurmer nest and helped us destroy the life gem. There must have been a reason for that."

Nath stuffed his face in a pillow and screamed, "Yaaaargh!"

Patting him on the back, Selene said, "Feel better?"

"No. Selene, maybe you should go. I have to think."

"I think I'll stay."

There was a hard knocking at the door.

Nath rolled his eyes at Selene. "I'm not in the mood for any more company. Tell them to go away."

"Tell them yourself, mighty King."

The door swung inward. Brenwar stood small in the frame. "No disrespect, King, but I could hear your blubbering all the way down the hall. It's disappointing."

The words stung. Nath look a deep draw of air through his nose, closed his eyes, and gathered his thoughts. Selene and Brenwar were both right. This was no way for a king to act, nor even a prince. The worry on his friends' stern faces only made it worse. *Suck it up, Dragon. Your subjects are counting on you. Now's not the time to be part of the problem. You need to be part of the solution.*

He tossed the pillow aside and stood. "I apologize. I guess all the bad news was overwhelming. I suppose I should fetch Fang and make my apologies to him too. I can't believe I did that."

"Don't bother," Brenwar said. "He's gone."

"He's gone! What do you mean, he's gone!"

"I'm only teasing." Brenwar chuckled. "Just making sure you cared. There's no sense in slinging a fine piece of hardware around like that. Not now, not ever." He stepped back into the hall and came back with Fang. He held him out for Nath. "Moment of truth."

Eyes on the grand sword that had a shine in the steel that never dulled, Nath said, "I'm truly sorry, Fang. I hope you'll forgive me." He wrapped his fingers around the handle. The grip was cool. He lifted it from Brenwar. "I think he accepts." The grip turned white-hot. "Yeouch!"

Nath dropped the blade but caught him before he hit the ground again. With his forehead bursting out in beads of sweat, he hung on to the handle that burned his grip. "Yes, I deserve this. I'm not letting go. Not ever again." The scales in his palm smoked and smoldered. The pain raced up his arm and through his entire body. "Fang, you'll have to either forgive me or kill me!"

The blade hummed with anger, sending another shockwave of energy through Nath's body. His grip loosened, but using his other hand, he held on. The blade cooled. His hands steamed. "Ah, thank you, Fang." He blew smoke from one hand, switched hands on the grip, and fanned his other. "Guzan, that was hot."

"We noticed," Brenwar said. "But if you can handle that, you can help me scoop hot coals out of a furnace next time."

"Let's make sure there is a next time." Nath put Fang back in his sheath and slung him over his shoulder. "I think I need a good fight."

"It's coming. Follow me." Brenwar led them down below the mountain, humming a dwarven hymn. It took hours to get where they were going, wherever that was. "I've had plenty of time to explore the mountain since I've been stuck here and you've been gone. It's an interesting feat of natural engineering."

"Engineering? What do you mean?" Nath asked. In all of his life, Nath had never been in the subterranean levels below the mountain. He'd never given them any thought. The Mountain of Doom was vast, but he hadn't felt any need to explore it. At the base, it was over a league from one side to another.

"Give me a moment." Brenwar grabbed one of the torches along the corridor wall.

The road they were on came to a stop in front of a great black expanse. It was like looking into a void.

The grizzled dwarf stepped into the dark cavern, climbed up a set of rock steps, and lit another torch that hung on the wall. "Watch this." The yellow-orange flame from the torch danced with light. Then like it was some sort of fire sprite, it hopped away and lit another torch farther down.

"Flame fairies," Nath said with excitement. "I haven't seen the likes since I was a child." The flames jumped from torch to torch. As one lit, another jumped, then another. In moments, flame after flame came to life, giving shape to the vast room. There were gargantuan natural columns of stone lined up by the dozens. Each had torchlight all around it.

Nath and Selene ventured farther inside. He felt like an ant crawling within the walls of a castle. "Brenwar, why are there columns here? It looks like they support the entire mountain."

Smiling behind his beard, Brenwar said, "That's because they do."

Nath gaped up at the ceiling. It was over a hundred feet high. Centuries of stalactites lined the ceiling in icicles that hung like teeth. "Why are you showing me this? It's not that I don't have any appreciation for it, but I don't see how this aids us in our current dilemma." He ran his hands over one of the columns. There were words engraved in Dragonese. He traced the groove that made a number. "I don't understand. Was this once a ceremonial chamber?"

"No, even better. It's a trap. The greatest trap I've ever seen."

Nath read pillar after column. He began to put the order of the numbers together. It was something only a dragon could read. He studied two more columns and then exclaimed to Brenwar, "You can't be serious!"

CHAPTER 25

Hoven hunkered into a snow bank. Wurmers flew overhead, dipped in the air with their wings spread wide, and dipped out of sight along the sea cliff. His belly stirred. Liam had been inside the cave a little longer than he expected. The young roamer should have been out of there by now. To make matters worse, another group of wurmers had appeared on the northern horizon. He cupped his hands and placed them up to his mouth. Summoning his ranger sound—a mystic form of communication the roamers had—he let out a call. His howling mixed with the wind and other natural sounds only noticeable by the roamers' ears to carry a message back to Sansla Libor.

Satisfied the message had been sent, Hoven climbed down the sea bank and entered the frozen cave.

All of the roamers stirred around Sansla. The message from Hoven was clear. Liam was in danger. Sansla spread his wings out over his massive back. He'd seen the first patrol of wurmers disappear into the berm and not reappear. Now, another flock of the dragon insects was coming. "I'm taking to the air. We'll see how well I distract the wurmers. You go after Hoven and Liam."

"It will be so," the roamers said.

Sansla took to the air, remaining low at first, then picking up speed with wings beating fast and a few feet over the waters. He flew in a straight path that would lead him right underneath the wurmers. He'd stayed on the ground, avoided their probing eyes so far, but now it was his time for action. The distance between him and the wurmers closed to a few hundred yards. Flying them in a v-formation, the lead wurmer screeched. In a single unit, the wurmers descended.

Sansla aimed upward on a collision course for the purple-eyed fiends. In most cases, fully grown wurmers were as big as ponies, but there were plenty much bigger. This time, they were only pony-sized—not too powerful but plenty quick.

The lead wurmer spat a ball of energy at Sansla.

He swooped underneath the fiery orb, navigated back into the wurmer's direct path, and collided with the monster. Using his bare hands, he grabbed the wurmer, and with a twisting wrench, he snapped its neck. The wurmer fell out of his arms. After splashing into the waters, it sank like a stone.

The wurmers struck at Sansla from all angles. Claws ripped at his arms and chest. He shrugged them off and made speed through the biting wind, allowing them to give chase away from the sea bank. He'd caught a glimpse of the cave opening though. He needed to get back there. Assuming there was another titan guardian, the roamers would need his help.

He arced upward, firing toward the field of gray clouds, losing the wurmers momentarily in the mist. Upward he went, punching out of the cloud and into the setting sun. The bright light was blinding, just what he'd wanted. The wurmers, he'd learned, became disoriented in sunlight. He did a backward loop in the air and plunged back through the clouds toward the sea. Diving, his speed increased. So did the wurmers trailing behind him.

Fists first, he plunged into the seawater. The wurmers, hungry for Sansla's life and blinded by the brilliant sun, followed the new lead wurmer into the waters. They splashed one after the other into the sea, and wings flapping, they still sank like stones.

Submerged, Sansla watched them sink then swam to the surface. The rough water made it difficult to take to the air. He folded his wings over his back and swam for a boat filled with fishermen who were screaming and gaping. By the time they put their backs into the oars, it was too late.

Sansla climbed in. Towering over the frightened men, he shook the water from his wings. "I see you don't have much of a haul. Try casting your net on the other side." Knees bending, he sprang into the air and flew straight for the cave.

His eyes narrowed on the activity within. The roamers were engaged with a huge monster with many arms. *What is that thing?*

Wings pumping through the air, Sansla slammed into the monster's face. The monster's neck snapped forward. It let out a roar from a mouthful of fangs. The roamers' elven blades bit into the strange humanoid's flesh. Its eyes glowed in the dark.

A voice spoke inside Sansla's head. "You cannot kill me, Sansla Libor. I am invincible. I am the titan Carthage the Murderer!"

Sansla got his first close look at the spirit Carthage. His head almost hit the top of the cave. He had two faces, front and back, and was a giant covered in stone and flesh. He fought with eight arms and kicked out with four legs. He looked like four different kinds of giants that were once dead and brought back to life again, all sewn together.

"Carthage, let it be known your end is near!" Sansla drove his fist into one of the monster's jaws.

Carthage laughed. He scooped two roamers up in his hands and slung them into the cave wall. One of the roamers fell unconscious. Carthage stomped him dead. The other sprang away, chopping into the giant's wrist. The slice severed the hand at the wrist. "Argh!"

"You will die, Carthage, same as all the others." Sansla wailed into the giant's face with savage fury. He stung Carthage in the eyes while the roamers hacked into the unnatural mound of flesh. As a team, the roamers drove their elven steel into a weak point in the joints and sinew of the knees.

Carthage lost his footing. He tumbled with a crash. Unwilling to die, he rolled like a great worm, crushing bodies beneath him. Then the wurmers came, striking in the dark from all directions. Balls of fire hurled from their mouths. Roamers burned but fought on.

From the ground, the titan fought on too, laughing. "I cannot be killed. This body will die only to rise again. I can't say the same for yours. Let's find out." He scooped up another roamer and crushed the elf in four of his eight mighty hands. He dropped the corpse. "This is too easy."

CHAPTER 26

"THIS TRULY IS MADNESS, BRENWAR," Nath said, gaping at the columns. He continued to give them a closer look. There were dragons of all sorts carved in them. "Why would they go to all this trouble only to have it wiped out?"

"To sell it," Selene interjected. "It's quite brilliant actually. You know how meticulous dragons can be when it comes to doing things. It's not as if we don't have the time."

"Brenwar, you mean to tell me you like this idea?"

"We dwarves always say, 'There's nothing we've ever built that we can't build again—better.'" He patted one of the columns. "I like it!"

"You can't rebuild a mountain!"

Brenwar shrugged. "I don't see why not."

Nath marveled. Based off what he'd read, it was the stone columns that held up the mountain. *Unimaginable!* Dragons had hollowed out the core underneath making up the mountains. It must have happened eons ago. It made him feel small and young. Very, very young.

"But why would they do this? Who would even imagine it? If we knock out these columns, the entire mountain will collapse on us."

"On everyone inside," Brenwar added. "You could crush an entire army down here."

Nath puffed out a breath of air. "And the columns all fall like dominoes. The mountain drops and buries everything inside. And you both don't see the problem with this. It will destroy Dragon Home."

"It will destroy the titan army." Selene held his gaze. "That is what we want. My assumption is that long ago, the dragons foresaw this day coming. They knew it would be used at some point. Perhaps now is the time."

"There is no way we are going to lure that entire army down here. The giants aren't the most intelligent, but they are led by titans that are not fools."

"We don't have any other viable options. This one is good. We can sell it," Brenwar said.

"Selling it is an understatement. You're giving Dragon Home away. All of the treasure, magic, secrets will be buried. It's my kingdom, I cannot let it fall. Not like this!" His voice echoed and died away. Deep inside his chest, he realized how desperate they'd become. It angered him. At the same time, he didn't see another way out. The giants might take Dragon Home, but they'd pay a price for it. "It will be a river of blood down here."

"Bad blood. The more that soaks the rock, the better," Brenwar remarked.

"So we have to sell it." Nath moseyed deeper into the chamber. A plan started to form in his mind. "You're right, Brenwar. The titans will be suspicious if we just abandon it. No, we'll have to fight them with all we have and lead them down here. It won't be easy to get them all down at once. They'll straggle around in the halls."

"As I understand it, every tunnel in the mountain will collapse. We just need to keep them from the top level the best we can." Brenwar's eyes twinkled. "I have a plan."

"Brenwar, you can't read Dragonese, at least not that I've known. Were you really able to discern all of this by yourself?"

The dwarf's face shrank a little behind his beard. "Er, I might have had a sliver of help."

"No, you literally had a Slivver for help," said a newcomer. It was Slivver. "Sorry, but I've been eavesdropping. I couldn't let the dwarf take all the credit, even though it was his knowledge that led to this discovery, among other things."

Eyebrows up, Nath said, "What other things? Don't tell me it becomes still worse."

Brenwar waved his arm. "Let's keep walking. There are more than just columns down here."

"By all means. Lead the way."

They ventured two miles deeper into the strange cavern. In the center, glinting under the torches, were pieces of a broken statue. The metal segments were arms, legs, head, body, and wings of a dragon. It must have been a few dozen feet tall. Moorite horns adorned the solid gold head and neck. The chest was made of black iron. Silver arms, bronze legs, and a brass tail made up the rest of it. The claws and teeth were moorite, and bloodred gemstones made up the eyes. The wings consisted of steel covered with a dark fabric that Nath had never seen before. Scuffed up in many places, the body had dents, dings, and scratches all over. If it had fought one battle, it had fought a thousand.

Nath ran his fingers over the golden neck. "It's so wondrous. Why is it down here in the dust? It should be on display. Put together again." He hopped up on the stand with a smile on his face. "Slivver, do you know anything about this?"

"Only what we've learned over the past several months." Slivver's eyes had a curious sparkle in them. "It is more than what it appears to be, not just idle things of beauty."

"The detail is amazing." Nath ran his fingers over the bronze legs, feeling the detail in the scales. "So, it's not some broken-up statue that looks to have been discarded." He kneeled down. "Hmmm, this looks like a joint that hooks into the body. We can rebuild him."

"Aye," Brenwar said.

"I'm surprised you haven't done that yet, Brenwar. This is your kind of thing. Of course, it would take a lot of muscle to move it. Each section must weigh more than a tonne, especially the body. Slivver, you say it isn't just an idle thing of beauty. What do you mean?"

"It is called," he started in Dragonese but thought the better of it. "No, that will take too long. In short, this is Drolem the Guardian of the Mountain."

"It's a dreadnought. An automaton. A destroyer," Brenwar chimed in. "Metal brought to life to serve its master. The dwarves used to fashion such warriors in their own likeness, way back when. It's an old practice. A dangerous one."

"So we could turn the drolem loose if we only put him together and awaken him?"

"Perhaps, but the problem with destroyers like this is they are often hard to control," Slivver said. "The columns say, 'Beware of the metal that has no spirit.' Hence, our hesitation."

"Do you hear that?" he said to Selene.

She placed her hand on the drolem's chest. "I do. I feel a heartbeat."

Nath joined her. "So do I. He's alive. The drolem is alive." There was a flicker in the drolem's ruby-red eyes when Nath touched him. "I say we put him back together."

CHAPTER 27

THE ROAMERS TOOK A BEATING, as the titan Carthage showed no signs of slowing. The durable roamer elves were quick to strike, whittling off fingers and toes with their sharp elven blades. Carthage shrugged it off, perhaps with glee as he roared, "Nothing can stop me!"

The fight had begun with ten elves. They were down to six now, plus Sansla. He'd never seen so many of his roamers fall at once before. It was a rare thing when the roamers died. A defeating sight. They were being swarmed now by wurmers, full-sized and small. The hatchlings had now spilled out of the belly of the cave and started to attack. In seconds, the rangers would be covered in a sea of insects. The little monsters would devour them to the bone. "Hoven! Liam! Retreat!"

"No," Liam shouted back. He had wurmers crawling over his legs and shoulders. He stabbed Carthage's knees. "We will defeat him!"

Carthage would fall, only to rise again, laughing. "You fleas! You insects! It would be easier to stop the waves in the sea than me!" He brought a fist down, crushing a roamer's leg beneath it. The elf didn't scream, not even fallen and unable to move while the wurmers swarmed him. Their sharp teeth tore at his arm, rending sinew and snapping bone.

Sansla's voice rose, filling the entire cavern. "Retreat, brethren! Retreat now!" He took to the air and faced off Carthage. "Your end is near!"

"You are a fool, Sansla Libor! Your roamers fall like sheep. Your moments are numbered. The only escape for you is death. I'll find joy taking you there. All of you!"

Sansla hit the giant in the face with a series of punches. The thunderous blows cracked the giant's nose on each face. Carthage swatted at him with many arms. Sansla flew high and out of the way. The roamers scrambled out of the mouth of the cave with wurmers snapping at their heels. Sansla caught a glimpse of Hoven's gray eyes a moment before the elf pitched out toward the waters.

The wurmers spilled out of the cave mouth in pursuit by the hundreds.

"You bought your brethren time, but it will run out shortly." Carthage had been battling from one knee, but now he rose again. "Are you now going to flee as well, dear Sansla? What is your plan? To fight me one on one?"

With his eight arms stretched out like he was a giant spider, Carthage blocked the cave exit. There wouldn't be a way out for Sansla. He'd done just enough to allow the roamers to escape. "No, I'm more than comfortable being right here with you. I like to keep my enemies close."

"You will be close. You will be so close that you'll see the inside of my belly." Carthage stretched his jaws wide. They were a cave opening all of their own. He rambled forward. "Come, Sansla, feed me. I hunger for elven flesh."

Sansla darted at the monster, backtracked, and fled the other way through the air. He flew down where the ledges dipped into the lair of the wurmer eggs.

The thunderous footsteps of Carthage resounded through the walls of the cave. The stalactites shook. Many fell and crashed on some of the eggs.

Sansla landed. On his feet and hands, he searched the lair covered in small wurmers. The insect-like dragons covered him from his chin to his toes. Biting and snapping, they bored into his flesh. His hide protected him in part, but he still felt pain.

"Sansla! Where are you going? You cannot hide. There is no escape unless I give it to you!"

Plowing through the eggs and wurmers, he searched for the well that should have the life gem within. He went deeper into the cave. *Where is it?* He flung wurmers aside. Squirming necks were crushed in his hands and cast aside. Finally, with the loud footsteps of Carthage upon him, he spied a natural well, glowing from within, cradled in a corner of stalagmites. *That must be it!* He sprinted right for it.

The misty floor came to life. He lost footing. The fall took him into a nest of striking wurmers. Shrugging them off, he rose again. Rising in front of his eyes was a wurmer bigger than them all, the queen, over fifteen feet high. The queen wurmer hissed an angry rattle. Its neck coiled back to strike. Eyes glowing with raging purple fires, it opened its mouth gaping wide. An unavoidable spread of mystic fire came out, covering Sansla in flames.

His fur caught fire and burned. He screamed.

"Ah, that sound is so delightful," Carthage moaned. "How wonderful. I like my elves toasted."

With the strange fires searing his flesh, Sansla rolled on the ground. He wanted to take flight to the sea, but he was too close. The life gem was near. He fought the pain. Gripping the orb of destruction, burning from head to toe, he ran for the well.

A lash of the queen wurmer's tail took him from his feet. The tail came down again, harder and faster. The monster pounded his flaming body like it was trying to put him out.

Carthage's towering figure ducked into that segment of the cave. Both of the shrewd faces were smiling. "Perfect, scaly colleague. I shall devour him one appendage at a time. But beat him further. I like my meat tender."

The tail smacked on Sansla—*whap, whap, whap*—until the flames went out.

Sansla couldn't move.

Carthage picked him up in his arms. "I think I'll start with the head."

Chapter 28

Still in the Chamber of Columns, Nath and Brenwar had put the drolem together, with the help of several dragons who had remained. The dragon's metallic body groaned a little as it stretched its neck out, seeming to yawn.

"It's a beautiful creature," Grahleyna said. She was big for a dragon, but the drolem was still twice as big as her. "I can feel a heartbeat. I sense raw power. A dangerous power. Nath, you must be certain that you can control it."

"Him, Mother." Nath crawled onto the drolem's neck, where he found a spot behind the horns that made do for a saddle and sat down. "We need to treat him like family, the same as everyone else. Drolem, lie down."

The dragon hit the floor with metal scraping against stone.

"He's not going to sneak up on anyone, that much is certain," Brenwar said. "I could do better with pots and pans tied to my ankles and wrists." He looked around as if expecting to hear a comment from someone who wasn't there. Perhaps Bayzog. He grunted.

"Let's walk, Drolem," Nath ordered.

The huge metal beast made his way up and down the chamber with surprising grace. Nath felt the raw power under his seat. The drolem was more than a guardian. He was a juggernaut.

Everyone's eyes in the room were fixed on the metal dragon. Sasha, Rerry, Samaz, and Slivver were there, with a host of dragons numbering in the hundreds. Each dragon was grouped together with their own kind. Slivver stood with a score of silver shade dragons. Three dozen gray scalers hung around. Waark, Nath's personal dragon, made a baker's dozen of the bull dragons. All of the dragons varied from man size to bigger than horses, with some twice the size of elephants. Blue streaks, copper dragons, crimson dynamos, cinnamon spits, ivory sliders, green lilies, and bronzes were among the remnant army that should have numbered in the thousands. All of them were more than ready to fight through their last breath for Dragon Home, but that wasn't the plan. Not yet.

"Subjects, brethren, friends, the enemy is at the door. We will let them in, but it won't be easy." Using thought, Nath commanded the drolem to sit. He crawled up to a high spot between the horns. "The enemy does not know the size of the force that we have within, but we want them to believe it is formidable. I will lead the fight outside. When the time comes, we shall retreat within, battling them throughout the mountain. Luring them here, into this chamber, is a last resort." He brushed his hair back. "Though it seems inevitable, that doesn't mean we can't take as many of them down as possible while we fight. In the end, we'll have them all!"

A cheer went up among the men and women. The dragons let out encouraging roars. The cavern trembled.

Nath's heart thundered in his chest. The unity among the dragons overwhelmed him with joy. They accepted him as king. Nath raised Fang overhead, and the roars became even louder.

With his hands cupped to his mouth, Ben shouted out, "Dragon! Dragon!"

As much as he delighted in the glory, he knew that many would not survive the battle. It was a hard thing, making the decision to fight in a war such as this. The dragons mattered, all of them. So did his friends. Having found affection among his kin made it even more dreadful. Perhaps that was why Balzurth had always kept him at a distance. If the Dragon King became too attached, maybe he wouldn't be able to lead when the time came.

"Brethren, the time has come to avenge Balzurth. To vanquish our wicked enemies. Now, we will wipe the titans from one end of Nalzambor to the other! For Balzurth! For the mountains!"

Riding on the drolem with thunderous cheers at his back, Nath led them up to the top of the mountain. He got off the back of the drolem so he could slip inside the Chamber of Murals. Accompanied by his friends, he studied the titan and wurmer army that awaited them outside. Using his fingers, he zoomed in and out of the images. He focused on Isobahn, now standing on the other side of the stone bridge at the base of the mountain. The giant soldiers moved huge hunks of dirt and rock out of the way.

"I'm going right after him," Nath said, pointing at the burly titan. "The battle may slow them if anything. There are so many."

"I'm going out. Those giants are meant for me!" Brenwar adjusted the bracers of power on his wrists, spat in his hands, and picked up Mortuun, grumbling, "I'll even ride a dragon if I have to."

"Really?" Nath said, arching a brow.

"Extreme moments call for extreme decisions. Just find me one that won't throw me."

"We're going too," Rerry said, with Samaz stepping up by his side. Rerry was all lathered up with eyes filled with excitement.

"No, you'll remain as we discussed. But you won't be without some help." Nath made a little whistle. "The main objective is that everyone who needs to escape through the murals can do so. The two of you will help see to that when the battle within starts to rage."

White cat-sized wingless dragons with very long tails scurried along Nath's feet. They purred in their throats while their bodies pulsated. "These are ivory sliders. Very special. They'll enhance your skills and powers."

The ivory sliders crawled up the legs of Sasha, Rerry, Samaz, and Ben.

"That tickles," Rerry said with an impish smile. The dragon on his shoulder wrapped its long tail around the meat of his arm. "Whoa! What is it doing?"

"As I said, these little dragons pack a punch. You may need all the help you can get." Nath pointed to Brenwar's strongbox. "Don't forget about the vials. Everyone, it's critical, and if you want to take a mural out, then you can. There is no shame in it. Personally, I would prefer that you did, but I won't command it."

"It would be a waste of your breath anyway." Ben wore a suit of armor made from links and plates of moorite. He held a folded-up Akron in his hand, and the quiver on his back was full. "I'm finally healed up from the last battle, years ago. I'm ready to fight again. Besides"—he petted the dragon on his shoulder—"this little dragon has put a spring in my step I lost years ago. My knees aren't aching."

"Mine are over five hundred years old, and they never ache," Brenwar said.

"You wouldn't know it if they did."

"Dwarves don't ache."

"Of course not, Brenwar. Sheesh." Ben unfolded Akron. *Snap—clatch—snap.* The string twirled up the bow and strung itself in the notches. "Ready when you are."

Nath raced through his options. It was unlikely they would miraculously beat the horde back. There were too many. But that was only the first option. Perhaps they could fight them, use some surprise, and defeat them. The last option was to fall back into the mountain and fight the titan army within. To lead in as many as they could. Ideally, they'd retreat into the columns and spring the trap. The problem was whoever sprung the trap would be caved in as well. It was a sacrifice that had to be made—and most likely made by him.

"Mother, I want you to stay within the mountain. I hope you understand, but you will be more of a service within."

She spoke to him, mind to mind. "I can guide you from here, Nath. I will be your eyes. It's a shame the murals only take us far, far away. Otherwise, we could jump that titan from right here." Her eyes glared at the titan, Isobahn. "I certainly would like to rip him into pieces. But I understand. I must protect the secrets of the murals." She gave him a kiss on the cheek. "Fight with the fury of fire and the speed of the sultans."

Nath kissed Selene, hugged all of his friends, and departed the chamber. He climbed once more onto the back of the drolem. With help from Slivver, Brenwar scrambled onto the back of Nath's bull dragon, Waark. "Just drop me off at the nearest giant. I can take it from there."

The dragon army led by Nath marched to the top of the mountain, where a portal to the sky opened that was once concealed by magic. He crested the top of the mountain cap. There were dragons there by the dozens, guarding the spire from the wurmers that soared the skies at a distance. The dragons moved quickly behind him and onto the surface. The portal closed again. He said to the golden flares who guarded the spire entrance, "Wait for my signal."

The wurmers locked eyes with the dragons. Snarls and roars erupted from the dragon army.

The wurmers attacked.

Nath let out his battle cry, "Dragon! Dragon!"

CHAPTER 29

THE JAW OF CARTHAGE DROPPED open. Sansla strained against the viselike grip of the titan. Just as his entire body was about to be shoved into the gaping maw, the sharp swing of elven steel whistled through the air. Steel bit through the giant's flesh and bone at the wrists on both sides. The fingers fell open. Sansla fell.

Hoven and Liam had sprung into action. The leathers and skins they wore were in tatters. They fought on against the screaming giant whose hands were turned to stumps.

"What are you waiting for, Sansla?" Hoven cried out just as he skewered a pair of wurmers and slung them away. "It's time to kill these things! All of them!"

"I agree!" Liam said. It looked like part of his arm was torn off. "It was an awful fight getting back in here!" He batted one of the titan's lunging hands aside and sprang away like a deer. His blade stabbed one of the other hands a few quick times.

"FOOOLS! You cannot defeat me!" Carthage said. "You are the mouse. I am the great cat! I strike!"

Two hands came together so fast and big, Hoven didn't have time to jump aside. Hemmed in with nowhere to go when the hands smashed together, Hoven teetered on wobbling legs. The woozy elf's sword dragged through the mist. He hefted the blade up for one final swing. The clumsy swing cut the air. Wurmers raced up his body, attaching themselves in all places.

Sansla dove under the bite of the queen wurmer and dashed for Hoven, scooping the elf up in his arms just before he took flight and slipped through the titan's swings.

"Come back, little fly! I'll dine on you yet!" Carthage chased after Sansla.

The savage wurmer queen followed, leaving Liam behind to fight off the smaller creatures.

Wings flapping and head scraping the ceiling, Sansla beckoned them on. "Come, Carthage! Scaly queen! Try to stop the Roamer King!"

Carthage and the wurmer queen hemmed him in with his back to a dead end in the cave. "Where will you go now, boastful one?" The titan's ugly face showed a mouth of rotting teeth. "We have you now!"

"I'm right where I want to be, monster." Behind the giants, he saw the banged-up and bloody Liam crawling out of the well. The elven roamer held a glowing life gem that pulsated in his hand. Wurmers attacked from all over.

Liam shouted. "I have the life gem, Sansla! Hurry!"

"You're finished now, titan!" Sansla said. "The gem will be destroyed with the orb of destruction."

He slung the orb of destruction through Carthage's reaching arms. The titan missed it by a stump. The wurmer queen snapped at it. The orb sailed in a perfect arc into Liam's awaiting hands. "Ignite it, Liam! Ignite it now!"

"You'll slay us all!" Carthage shouted with his faces drawn up in worry. "Don't be a fool! We can bargain!"

"Death is the only guarantee for you!" Sansla said.

The wurmer queen and Carthage raced at Liam with the titan screaming, "Noooooooooooo!"

Sansla lost sight of his friend behind the broad body of the titan. He saw the eyes on the back face of the giant widen. He dropped to the ground with Hoven still in his arms and punched through the wurmers into a cleft in the rock.

KAAAAABOOOOOOOOM!

Sansla woke with a painful ringing in his ears. The world around him was black. He coughed dust from his mouth. A heavy weight was on his back, and something softer was underneath him. He knew it was Hoven. There was a heartbeat too.

On all fours, he pushed upward. The rock and stone gave. He burst out of the grave, chucking huge hunks of stone aside. There was light above him coming from a hole made in the cave ceiling. The stars were out. A few roamers stood high above, around the rim. One of them waved his hand and called down, "King Sansla, are you well?"

"I move. Always a good thing." He reached down and lifted Hoven from the rubble. Ragged breath came from the young roamer. The heartbeat was strong. He stirred in Sansla's arms. Stone dust caked the blood on his face and ravaged body. "Save your energy."

The remaining roamers climbed into what was now a sinkhole. Dead wurmers were strewn all over with their bodies blasted apart. The queen wurmer's head was nowhere to be found. The body had been ripped apart. Acid-like ooze dripped from the body all over. Carthage's body lay prone on the ground, charred hunks of flesh over a humongous skeleton.

The sea breeze whistled out of the massive sinkhole. Sansla snorted. It did little to carry the stench away. He meandered to the spot where he'd last seen Liam, hoping to get a glimpse of the brave roamer's remains. There was no sign of the roamer. Nothing. Sansla sighed.

Aside from Sansla and Hoven, only four roamers were left, and they made their way down. Using their swords, they made quick work of any surviving eggs. Some wurmer spawn struggled long enough to find the edge of a blade.

Determined to find some evidence of Liam, Sansla began moving the rocks. A burial was important to all of the rangers that had fallen. He would honor that. There was some sticky goo on some of the rocks, the ick that coated the life gem. He squatted down, got his hands under the rock, and with a tremendous heave, he shoved it aside.

"Finally. I was beginning to think I'd be living my last days in this dark and gooey place." Liam was neck deep in the goo of the well. "Sansla, if it's not too much trouble, I could use a hand. This goo is worse than quicksand. Not that I've ever been in quicksand. Well, there was one time, I was very young and tracking a bugbear."

"You live!" Sansla reached down and ripped Liam out of the pit. "How?"

Slinging the muck off him, Liam said, "I stuck the orb and gem together and tossed them into the queen wurmer. Its mouth was so wide I was certain it required a treat. I thought it was over, but in the last moment, I jumped into the well full of goo. It protected me from the blast, but my head hurts. Not that I'm complaining."

"Enough, enough, you've done well." Sansla hugged him. "Your father will be proud. Let's go find him."

CHAPTER 30

RIDING ON THE BACK OF the drolem, Nath flew down the face of the mountain. Brenwar, on the back of Waark, flanked him with his grizzled beard billowing in the wind. Behind them, the dragons came in a silent sheet of brilliant colors. The wurmers that caught sight of them gave chase, shrieking a warning through the skies.

At the base of the mountain the titan army came to life. Eyes widened like saucers, they scrambled from their work stations and picked up arms.

Across the moat of lava, huge siege machines and weapons of destruction groaned. Ballistae mounted on tall giant-made towers fired steel bolts thicker than ten spears. The massive needles of metal ripped through the air. Several hit the mark. Dragons skipped down the mountainside with metal protruding from their hearts.

Catapults launched nets into the sky. One whistled over Nath's head. "Brenwar, aim for the workers! Knock them away from the ballistae. I'm going right after Isobahn!"

Isobahn stood his ground, barking orders and commanding his troops. There wasn't an ounce of worry in his eyes. If anything, there was victory. The titan expected the last desperate stand of the dragons. The look in his eye told Nath Isobahn thought they were playing right into his hands.

Think what you want. I'll destroy you anyway!

Nath closed within one hundred yards. Fifty. Thirty.

Why is he smiling at me?

The titan vanished.

"Pull up, drolem!" Nath ordered. The metal dragon's belly scraped the ground. He plowed into a wall of giants. "Attack!"

The drolem's mouth opened, and white-hot flames came out. Two giants swinging wooden hammers caught fire and turned to ash. But where two of them fell, three more appeared. The drolem brought his spiked tail around. With a crash, the tail crushed the giant's chest. From all directions the giants and oversized men, ogres, and orcs came. The drolem went right at them. Huge and merciless, the metal beast crushed the smaller ones beneath his talons. Flames shot from his mouth, setting the side of the mountain on fire. From his throat came a roar so frightful, many ogres covered their ears and dropped to their knees. The drolem was a wild thing. A mindless, savage machine of destruction.

Nath gripped a horn with one hand and swung Fang with the other. Any enemy that got too close, he slew. There was no holding back. This was life or death. Survival. He could kill with a clear conscience. An orc scrambled up the raging drolem's back. Nath swung. The orc died in two pieces.

The drolem juggernaut ran roughshod through the work camp. For the most part, he did all the work. Nath took a moment, eyes searching for Isobahn. The titan was key to it all, but the titan had slipped away and vanished. *Where are you hiding, titan?*

There was no sign of Isobahn across the lava moat. He wasn't anywhere to be seen. It set off alarms in Nath's body. Using his thoughts, he called out to Grahleyna, "Mother, do you see Isobahn? I've lost him."

"Nowhere. Nath, there are too many. You've only hit a small pocket. Check the skies. It's day, but they blacken."

"I know, Mother. I know."

The dragons formed a wedge of destruction. Spitting flames, lightning, and strange fires, they flew in a single formation. They torched siege machines. Burned men. Scorched tents. A cry went up from the titan army as they scrambled to put one another out. The wedge took back to the sky, wings beating, and slammed into the flocks of wurmers. Balls of energy sizzled. Lightning streaked. Smoking bodies tumbled out of the sky. The dragons' impact was devastating. They dropped out of the sky and soared over the ground army again, setting flesh and earth on fire.

"Yes!" Nath called out. "Be victorious!"

But as charged with energy as he was, uncertainty lurked within. It was hard to stop an army without killing the leader. The scales on his arms tingled. Isobahn was out there, ready to strike, but where?

He fought on, strike after strike. The drolem wrought more devastation.

The giants rallied. Their huge weapons pounded into the great metal body in loud *bangs* and *clangs*.

The drolem reared up on his hind legs. He unleashed a bolt of lightning. It smote a giant full in the chest, passed through it into another, and kept going from giant, to ogre, to orc, to man. They all fell with their chests smoldering. Nath cheered the drolem on. "Let them have it! Let them feel chaos!"

Brenwar rode on the back of Waark, howling a dwarven battle cheer. The bull dragon plowed into two giants at the same time. Fire erupted from Waark's massive jaws, turning the giants into flames. The huge men fought on a few moments then crumpled like burning debris.

A giant swung a hammer into the side of Waark's head. The next giant up ran a massive sword through the dragon's wing. Taking no notice of Brenwar, the giants and dragon battled in a ferocious tussle of limbs and scales slamming together.

"Nobody ignores a dwarf!" Brenwar wound up Mortuun in a huge circle. "Nobody!" He flung the hammer at a giant that caught his eye, standing on the edge of the moat. The hammer sailed true and smote the chest of the giant with a clap of thunder.

BOOOOOM!

The giant pitched into the moat. The huge man screamed and splashed in the lava and finally sank into the steaming red murk.

Brenwar rushed to retrieve Mortuun.

An ogre carrying a spiked mace stepped into his path. "What's the hurry, bearded pig?" The ogre slammed the mace down.

Brenwar dove to the side, rolled back to his feet, and tackled the ogre in the legs, yanking it to the ground. Using his flesh fist and his skeleton fist—and strengthened by the mystic bracers of power—he pummeled the ogre to death. *Whap! Whap! Pow!* Strong as a giant, Brenwar picked up the five-hundred-pound ogre and hurled it into the moat then marched over and picked up his hammer.

Ogres and giants paused their advances for a moment. All of their eyes were wary.

With the charge of battle coursing through his veins, Brenwar said, "What are you waiting for? Who wants to fight next?"

A giant in full plate armor stepped forward. He carried a hammer in each hand. His eyes glowed behind a great iron helm. He banged the hammer heads together. "I'm next, little dwarf. I'll grind your bones into the dirt."

Brenwar charged. "For Morgdon!"

Chapter 31

The fierce battle raged on. Back and forth the dragons and giants went. Fire and steel clashed. The skies flared with magic and rained drops of blood. Nath rode the drolem over every foe, crushing men and orcs beneath its feet. The ball on the end of the tail smashed rib cages and legs with devastating effect. The enemy fell in heaps, but more continued to swarm and gather.

Ogres carrying ballistae fired bolt after bolt at Nath. Most of them skipped off the drolem's metal. He knocked one aside with Fang. Another he snatched out of the air and hurled into an ogre's chest. It died and fell on two orcs.

The drolem reared up again, took several shots in his silver chest from the giants, and brought down another wave of fire. The burning giants fought on for moments before succumbing to the flames. Using his great horns, the drolem swept them aside.

"That's it, drolem! You take the big ones, and I'll take the not-so-big ones!"

"Nath," Grahleyna said in his mind. "You need to return. There are too many. The dragons are depleting."

The ranks of the dragon wedge flying through the sky had thinned. The regiment of dragons was now half the size that it had been. He saw more bodies than he could count, lying on the ground. A golden flare fell from the sky with mindless wurmers all over it. With his blood up, the last thing he wanted to do was stop fighting.

"Yes, Mother. We shall return."

A monumental BOOM exploded from one of the mountain tunnels. Consecutive world-shaking booms followed. The titan army let out a cheer. Isobahn emerged from one of the tunnels and started waving the army inside. He yelled. "The mountain is breached! Fill its belly, brethren! Fill it with slaughter! Kill everything inside. The mountain is ours!"

"Mother, the army comes! Be ready!"

"Get inside, Nath! We need you here!"

"I'm coming!" He spied the army pouring over the stone bridge. *We need to slow them down.* Nath guided the drolem to the bridge. "Unleash the fire!"

The drolem let loose another geyser of flame. Some humanoids burned. Others were driven back. Nath searched for Brenwar. There was nothing but a knot of battle all around. He didn't see Brenwar, but he saw Waark goring a beastly earth giant. "Waark," Nath said in the bull dragon's mind, "get Brenwar and get out of here! Take him back inside."

Waark responded with a roar and a snap of his cedar-like tail that sent two ogres sailing off their feet and crashing hard into stone.

Between bursts of flame from the drolem's mouth, the army continued to advance. Three giants, shoulder to shoulder, marched forward with shields as big as a small barn roof. Flames from the drolem engulfed the hard steel shield. The giants marched on, carrying long spears. They jabbed at the drolem. Their spear tips skipped off the metal.

"Ha!" Nath said. "Nothing can stop the drolem, fools!" Nath earnestly thought if given the time, he and the drolem alone could defeat the entire army. Nothing in the enemy's arsenal slowed or hurt the drolem. The more the enemy attacked, the more dangerous the metal dragon became. "Show evil the same mercy it shows us, drolem. None!"

The drolem started into an attack with his tail and paused. His long golden neck turned toward Nath. His eyes bored into something beyond Nath.

"What is it?" Nath looked over his shoulder. Isobahn had locked up the drolem's tail in his muscular arms.

"This fight is over, Nath Dragon," Isobahn said. With powerful legs, he started pulling the drolem off of the bridge. "Surrender, and I might be merciful!"

"You're the one who should surrender. You're vastly outmatched by me and the drolem. Let go, and I'll be certain to show the same mercy that you've shown me."

"Fool." Isobahn took a quick look in the sky. "It is over for you."

More dragons spiraled from the sky. Wurmers filled it.

Nath faced Isobahn with Fang glowing in his hand. "If you want the mountain, you can have it, but you have to defeat me. I offered this challenge to Eckubahn, but he was a coward. Are you the same?"

"No." Isobahn grinned. "I'm smarter than that. Come on, little dragon." He beckoned with his hand. "Let's fight then. Me and you."

The armored giant hammered at Brenwar.

The burly dwarf skipped to the side and brought Mortuun down on the giant's metal toe. The bang of metal sent shockwaves that knocked the oncoming brood from their feet. Brenwar cocked back to strike again. A swipe from a giant hammer took him from his feet and sent him spinning through the air. He landed on the chest of an angry-faced ogre.

"What are you looking at, one-eye?" Brenwar socked the ogre in the face, sprang to his feet, and made headway back toward the giant.

The armored giant's hammers cut off his path with hard stone-chipping strikes in the ground.

Brenwar ran up the handle of one of the hammers and stuck the giant in the hand. Bone cracked, making the giant moan. Brenwar dropped to the ground and rolled away from the other hammer. The huge head of the metal hammer missed by an inch, twice. The third strike clipped Brenwar in the shoulder. Wincing at the grazing blow, he dropped to one knee, a little woozy. He shook his beard. The world spun. Spots were in his eyes, and his legs were numb.

Above him, the giant prepared another strike. The hammer went up over its head. It came down like a sledgehammer that was ready to drive a spike into the ground.

In a split second, Brenwar hoisted Mortuun up into the air to block the hammer. Metal collided with metal, jarring every bone in his body.

Krang!

Brenwar fell flat on his back. The hammer rose and fell again. He parried it once more.

Krang!

"Enough is enough!" Brenwar climbed back to his feet.

The giant, clad in twenty feet of steel, struck out once more at a dwarf not even five feet in height.

Brenwar knocked every jarring blow aside with Mortuun.

The perplexed giant backed away.

Brenwar, with the bracers' power surging though him, knocked the giant in the leg with Mortuun.

The giant fell as if hit by a man its own size.

Brenwar got after him. His war hammer hit the giant's armor in the joints, knocking it loose from the body.

The giant wriggled under the painful assault. His moaning kept the other fighters at bay.

A sharp blow to the exposed belly knocked the breath from the giant, and then Brenwar made a tremendous leap through the air, landing on the giant's face. "Say goodnight!" Bringing Mortuun down with savage power, he smote the giant between the eyes. *Crack!*

CHAPTER 32

ISOBAHN LET GO OF THE drolem's tail.

The metal dragon turned, looming, keeping his spiked tail swinging at the army that was trying to traverse the bridge.

Nath jumped off the drolem's back. He faced off with Isobahn. Fang became a blade of blue fire in his hand. "Today, you'll pay for what you did to my father."

The titan punched his fist in his hand. "You mean kill him? That was easy. The fool rushed into the jaws of death. I saw it coming leagues away. And just as he died, so will you." Isobahn stretched out his hand. One of the giants handed him a battle axe with twin blades on one side. The heads were black iron that glinted like busted coal on the edges. "A fine tool to wield. A real dragon slayer forged by the orcs just for me. I'll skin the scales from your flesh."

"Is that so? And here I thought you were just going to talk me to death. You're doing a fair job of it so far. I'd rather be dead than smell your malodorous breath."

Isobahn's brows knitted together. He struck out with the axe.

Nath ducked, sprinted forward, and swung for the titan's knee—summoning Fang's power as he did so. *Fang, help me make this quick.* The blade tore through the titan's knee.

Stumbling backward, Isobahn grinned. "It will take a thousand cuts to chop down this body."

"I've got time." Nath jumped at Isobahn. Fang struck with the speed of a snake, hacking and stabbing. In seconds, the titan's legs were covered in blood.

The titan didn't slow. He came at Nath with his full wrath. The double-bladed axe whistled through the air. Its blades bit into the bridge, missing Nath by a whisker.

He darted through the titan's legs and stabbed Fang into the bone.

With new fury, Isobahn whipped around and swept the blades in short strokes.

The attack kept Nath at bay. The sweeping strokes backed him toward the edge of the bridge.

"The wounds you make are far from fatal, little dragon. But one hit from me and you'll be finished."

Springing from side to side, Nath said, "You haven't come close yet."

"Perhaps." Isobahn made a loud grunt. Ballistae rocketed bolts through the air.

Besieged by a dozen missiles whistling right at him, Nath flattened on the ground.

Before he could get up, Isobahn stomped on him.

"Whooof!"

"I have you now, little dragon!" With Nath pinned under his foot, Isobahn put more weight on Nath. "Perfect. I can chop your head clean off."

Muscles popping out in his arms and neck, Nath pushed against the great weight.

The titan's foot lifted for a moment, only to shove him back down.

He squirmed from his back to his chest, took hold of the titan's foot, and pushed again.

"Ha! Ha! Your efforts are useless!"

With tons of weight pressing down on him, Nath huffed out a blast of fire. The blaze shot up the titan's leg.

"This is not my flesh you burn!" Isobahn put more weight on Nath. "I'll outlast you, oh Dragon Prince! Like your father's, your life is mine!"

"Never!" Nath screamed. With his dragon heart pumping a river of hot blood through his body, he pushed upward again. "Yeeeeargh!"

Dismayed, Isobahn cried out, "What?"

Nath squirted out from under the titan's foot, picked up Fang, and without stopping, he chopped into Isobahn's calf muscle. Ice exploded out of Fang's tip. It raced up Isobahn's legs, crystalizing him in crackles all the way up to his neck. Except for his face, his entire body had become a statue of ice.

Catching his breath, Nath said, "Thank you, Fang." He climbed up the titan's body, ready to deliver the lethal blow. The flames engulfing Isobahn's head had extinguished. Nath cocked Fang back for the final shattering blow, hoping the blade would destroy the titan's mind and spirit. "Any famous last words, Isobahn?"

With a dumb look in his eye and drool dripping from his lip, the giant murmured and said, "Huh?"

Nath's senses caught fire. *Something's wrong!*

Fang hummed a warning. The handle pulsated in Nath's grip.

Shaking his head, Nath said, "He's gone, Fang. Slipped away again."

"NO I HAVEN'T, FOOL!"

CHAPTER 33

NATH'S HEAD SWIVELED AROUND. HE was face to face with the drolem.

Only now, its golden dragon head was covered in the flames that had once adorned the head of Isobahn, and a new gleam of evil shone in the metal dragon's eyes.

"I can't believe you are so stupid, Nath Dragon. Now I possess the perfect body. The perfect weapon to destroy everything in my path." Isobahn, in full control of the drolem, let out an earth-shattering roar. "This fight isn't over yet. Let's finish it!"

"Fang, I hope you have something left. It's going to take more than my claws and clever wit to beat that thing." He dropped to the ground. "Fine, Isobahn. Let's go at it again. Apparently, you are too stupid to learn your lesson." He charged. "Dragon! Dragon!"

With a swipe of his metallic dragon tail, Isobahn knocked Nath from his feet.

He slammed headfirst into the statue of ice. Shaking his noggin, Nath picked himself up just in time to catch a blast of lightning bursting from the drolem's mouth into his chest. Sharp pain lit him up inside and out. Fang slipped from his grasp. Weak-kneed, he fell down, panting in aching lungfuls of air.

The drolem bounded forward. His golden head coiled back. The moorite horns were poised to gore him. "It's over for you!"

Nath held his chin up. "It's not over until the fat ogre sings." He cupped his ear. Ogres bellowed and jeered. "Uh, let me change that."

Isobahn struck.

Nath dived.

Out of nowhere, Waark plowed into the drolem's side at the last moment. The bull dragon and drolem locked horns and thrashed on the bridge. The drolem was much bigger than the bull dragon, but they were equally matched in ferocity. Flames erupted from their mouths. Angry snorts came with crashing horns.

Strong arms lifted Nath up to his feet.

"Taking a break, are ye?" Half of Brenwar's beard was ripped off. His armor smoldered. "What are you looking at? It'll grow back. Now let's kill this thing."

"No, Brenwar. We need to get out of here! We can't beat that thing. We have to go. Remember the plan."

"Retreat? Do you see any armor on my back? Dwarves don't retreat!"

"Come to your senses! Do as I say, that's an order."

Isobahn the drolem took control of the fight. He clamped down on Waark's bullish neck.

"We can't have that now, can we?" Two-handed, Brenwar hurled Mortuun. The war hammer smote the head of the drolem with the power of a giant. *Klang!* The metallic jaws loosened.

Waark burst free. The bull dragon put his head down and rammed the drolem toward the edge of the bridge.

"That's it, Brenwar!" Nath said, elated. "We need to knock him into the lava. That should stop him."

"I thought you said we needed to leave. Stop changing your mind."

Nath raced toward Isobahn and attacked. Waark pushed. Nath cut at the claws scraping for footing on the ledge of the bridge. The heavy, unbalanced metal beast was falling. Brenwar brought Mortuun to bear, hammering at the claws and toes.

"Keep hitting! Keep hitting!" Nath shouted.

"What are you doing? Stop this!" Isobahn cried out, clawing and scraping at the stone bridge. The rocky edge started to crumble. "Noooooo!"

All together, Nath hit, Brenwar struck, and Waark pushed. The drolem slipped off the edge and splashed into the moat of lava. His head vanished under the surface.

"Whoa, that was close," Nath said, with sweat dripping down his face. He noticed the army starting to crowd them again. He quickly searched the faces. *The drolem might be gone, which is a shame, but Isobahn could be anywhere.* "Brenwar, get on Waark. We have to go. Now!"

"I'm going, I'm going." Brenwar climbed up onto the bull dragon's back. Looking to the sky, he spun Mortuun by the handle. "By the looks of things, it's going to be a fight just to get back."

Nath cupped his hands together and let out a call of retreat. In his mind, he heard Grahleyna say, "Hurry, Nath, hurry!"

Waark spread his wings. He started to lift off, but Brenwar said, "Are you coming or not?"

Nath took another glimpse in the lava. Something burbled just below the surface. The drolem burst out, climbing up the rocky ridge. His body glowed red-hot. Almost at the top, he started to slide and melt. Nath turned away. Isobahn's tail snaked out over the rim, caught him by the ankle, and jerked Nath off his feet toward the lava.

"Noooooooo!" Brenwar screamed.

With a final command, Nath said, "Waark, get him out of here!" just before he splashed into the burning liquid rock, screaming, and sank like a stone.

CHAPTER 34

FLAT-FOOTED, SELENE STOOD BEFORE THE murals with her mouth agape. She wasn't alone. There were gasps and sobs coming from Rerry, Samaz, and most of all, Sasha. Ben dropped to his knees, holding his head. They all witnessed it, the grand battle of Nath Dragon fighting against the drolem. The moment was one to see: victory swallowed up in the jaws of death. Selene's heart throbbed with indescribable agony when Nath was pulled down into the lava.

"I cannot believe what I have seen." Grahleyna's long, beautiful neck sagged. "Not my son. I've lost both him and Balzurth now."

Selene was shaking, inside and out. She'd insisted on going out into battle with Nath, only to have him talk her out of it. *I could have saved him.* Someone squeezed her numb fingers. It was Sasha, with tears streaming down her face. They made Selene's heart ache more. All of the women in the room had now lost the men they loved. Sasha lost Bayzog. Grahleyna lost Balzurth, and now…see, all of them. Losing Nath made her want to quit. The guilt inside her that Nath had worked so hard to wash away began to rebuild.

"Selene, now is not the time to blame yourself. This is war." Sasha sobbed. "Death happens." She wiped her eyes. "Nath would trust you to lead us now. He would want that."

The great burden of responsibility shifted on to Selene. Her old life of not caring so much had been easy, but now she cared a great deal. All eyes were on her, even Grahleyna's. Taking a breath, she pulled her shoulders back, set her inner pain aside, and lifted her chin. "Nath Dragon did not die in vain. We will follow through with the plan. Death to the titans."

"Look," Grahleyna said as she gazed into the mural. "Brenwar comes."

Riding on the back of Waark, Brenwar led the surviving dragons back inside the portal at the top of the mountain.

"Ben, get up there and help Brenwar. Rerry and Samaz, the both of you go. Once the portal is sealed and secure, return."

The three men bumped forearms. "For Dragon!" They departed.

Together, the three women watched the titan army storm into the tunnel. The soldiers cheered wildly, pouring into Dragon Home at the base of the mountain.

"Look," Sasha said, pointing at the mural. The image of the giant's body that Isobahn had possessed had a head of flame again. The ice that encased him started to melt. With a shrug, the titan burst free of the ice. A broad smile crossed his face as he stepped over and peered into the moat of lava where Nath Dragon and the drolem had perished. With a single fist, Isobahn beat his chest. "The mountain is ours! Take it!"

"I thought Nath beat that titan." Selene's tail swished slowly and easily over the floor. "Now, we have no choice but to follow through with the collapse of Dragon Home." She eyed Grahleyna. "Are you certain of this?"

"You're right. We have no choice now. I'll see to it that all who can will make an escape. The murals, most of all, must also be destroyed. Too powerful a weapon in the hands of our enemies, they will be a great loss as well." Grahleyna laid her paw on Selene's shoulder. "I trust you to do what must be done. See it through. The world depends on it."

At the top of the mountain standing below the portal, Ben watched the surviving dragons soar in. For every dragon, he saw at least two wurmers tearing at the dragon's wings and neck. With Akron, he unleashed arrow after arrow, drilling the wurmers with deadly accuracy. "It's good! Very good!"

With the ivory slider attached to his back, Ben was filled with amazing power. He couldn't miss. He nocked an explosive arrow and unleashed the string. The arrow zoomed right by Brenwar and Waark and hit a wurmer in the face. The booming explosion knocked Brenwar off of Waark's back and sent the dwarf tumbling inside. He landed at Ben's feet.

"Which side are you fighting for?" Brenwar growled. He popped up to his feet. "Nath is gone!"

"I saw," Ben said. "No better time than now to avenge his death." He fired another volley of arrows. The dragons—only dozens left—were inside, and the portal door at the cap of the mountain was closing again. "You need to find Selene at the murals. It's time to take down the mountain. They'll need your help."

"Humph, I need to bust something up first!" Brenwar bashed in the skull of a wurmer. He started down the corridor. "Don't delay, Ben. We all need to stay together from now on. I'm not losing another. See to it that those two"—he pointed to Rerry and Samaz—"don't fall."

"I will."

Charged with the power of the ivory slider, Rerry moved on feet as light as feathers, hacking into the wurmers with deadly precision. Fighting with a sword in each hand, he lopped off two wurmer heads at the same time. He skipped aside from balls of energy that fired from one wurmer's mouth and poked holes through their ribs into the heart.

"Samaz!" he called out. "Do you see this? I'm amazing! Or whatever means better than amazing. Incredible, perhaps?"

Using the Elderwood Staff, Samaz sent wurmers crashing into the walls with telekinetic power.

A knot of the deadly insect-dragons came right at him.

Holding out his hand, he stopped them midmotion. Slowly, the three wurmers began writhing as Samaz closed his hand. The wurmer bunch balled up and hovered in the air.

A moment later, a crimson dynamo dragon set the crushed bodies of the wurmers on fire.

"Impressive!" Rerry shouted up to his bother.

Ben half emptied his quiver.

Thirty minutes of furious fighting later, the battle to secure the portal was over. Dead wurmers sizzled on the floor, but dragons of all sorts lay dead or wounded too.

Rerry wiped the stinging sweat from his eyes and said to Ben and Samaz, "Let's get back."

Down at the Chamber of Murals, Grahleyna waited. With a wave of her wing, she led many of the wounded dragons through the portal to distant sanctuaries. But some refused to leave. They were ready to fight. One of them was Slivver.

"We'll lead the chase in the corridors," Slivver said. "We need to find that titan. He's the key to it all. If we can lead them into the columns, we'll have them all."

"Slivver, you need to make sure all of you, as many as you can, come back. This entire mountain will come down. You'll all be trapped down there. The mountain will be your tomb."

CHAPTER 35

"MOTHER IS DOWN THERE. WE have to save her." Rerry started out of the chamber. The doors shut by an unseen power. Rerry spun around. "What's the meaning of this?"

"Your mother insisted that you stay," Grahleyna said, "both of you. I need you both here to help evacuate,"

"We've already lost one parent. We won't lose another. If we die, we die together. Besides, we all need one another." Rerry wedged his sword in the door. "I'm going."

Samaz hit the door with the Elderwood Staff. The doors parted. "We both are."

"We're a long way from the bottom," Slivver said. "It's going to take some time to get where we need to be. Everyone needs to ride a dragon."

"If you must go," Grahleyna said, "you must find them. They have another way to escape."

Rerry and Samaz climbed on the back of a crimson dynamo. Without a huff, Brenwar got on the back of Waark. Ben joined him.

"Lead the way through this giant catacomb," Brenwar said. "We don't have all day."

Much to Selene's surprise, the dragons were extremely helpful. Two winged red rock dragons the size of small horses scooped them up from behind and carried them swiftly toward the tunnels. They moved down where chambers and roads crisscrossed and spiraled. There were still dragons among them, clawing at the walls and forming barricades.

"What are they doing?" Sasha asked.

"It's part of the fortifications. The dragons' objective is to seal as many wurmers in the lower tunnels as they can. The barricades are designed so the titan army thinks we're seeking escape from below and not above."

"I don't suppose there will be a way out for us?"

"That's why Grahleyna gave me this." A rope chain of gold hung over her neck. A small gem twinkled in the center of the golden amulet. "It's supposed to take us back to the murals in case we get trapped in the columns."

A wicked cry of triumph howled in the tunnels. The *ree-rah* sounds of the wurmers became louder.

"I really hate that sound." Sasha ducked. A lone wurmer flew right over her head. A green lily dragon knocked it out of the air with its tail. A moment later, a weird dragon appeared. The feline fury was built like a lion with scales. Bigger than a horse, it tore the wurmer to pieces.

"Where'd he come from?" Sasha said with wide eyes.

"The fury is seen when he wants to be seen. A good ally to have."

They came to a barricade of heavy stones between a set of tunnels. Dragons gathered in small numbers. A surge of the titan army came at them, running along a sea of wurmers.

Sasha covered her ears. "There's so many of them!" she yelled.

The titan army came within a few dozen yards of the barricade. The dragons unleashed their fiery breath. The entire tunnel went up in a whoosh of flame. Men and orcs screamed. Giants battled through the wake of fire.

At the barricade, two fierce forces collided with one another. The dragons—quick, cunning and powerful—beat back the first wave of soldiers. Bodies piled up on the floor, making a second barricade of flesh and bones.

Beyond the mangled fracas, Selene spied the next wave. A huge giant with a flaming head was coming. His eyes caught hers. "Isobahn," she said.

"What?" Sasha said, trying to yell above the roars and the clash of battle.

Selene turned Sasha's chin with her fingers toward the titan.

"Oh. That's another level of ugly. For Nath, Selene. For Bayzog. We'll avenge them!"

"It's a good thing you weren't on my side, way back when. Gorn Grattack may have won. You're a warrior!"

As soon as Isobahn crashed into the sea of scales, fire, and armor with arms pumping like mighty hammers, the dragons shot out their flames.

Selene unleashed a blast of fire of her own. The bolt stuck Isobahn square in his face.

A dragon jumped into his chest and clamped its jaws onto his neck.

Isobahn grabbed it with two hands and broke the gray scaler's back. He slung it aside, pointed at Selene, and said, "Get them!"

"Retreat!" Selene said to the dragons, who followed her command. "Retreat to the column cavern! They'll never take that!"

On the backs of the red rock dragons, they burst out of the intersection so fast the wind whistled in her ears. They jumped another barricade of rocks that more dragons were building. It was all part of the design. The dragons built one barricade after the other, hoping the legions would follow them right into the trap.

Selene was worried, however. Isobahn was no fool. He might take the bait, or he might not. One thing was for certain. Either way, she would bring the mountain down.

For Nath!

Chapter 36

"Sultans of Sulfur!" Brenwar exclaimed. It was an odd thing for him to say. "Where do so many come from!"

They'd made it to the halfway point in the mountain when they encountered a flock of wurmers buzzing the tunnels. The dragons made quick work of the first batch, only to encounter hundreds more to follow.

"Quick, this way," Slivver said.

They darted into another corridor via a strange concealment in the wall. Even Waark managed to push through it. The magic veil covered them as the flocks of wurmers passed. Before long, the loud voice of the army sounded out in the caverns.

"They're going up," said Slivver.

"They should be going down," Brenwar said. "So many. We need to distract them. Take another turn."

"What about the murals?" Ben said. "It's the only way out of here for us or the dragons."

"We're at the point of no return now," Brenwar said. "Time to execute Nath's final wishes. It's the only way."

"I'm not going anywhere without Mother." Rerry stroked the tail of the ivory slider latched onto his back. "Can we get back down to the columns from here?"

"Yes," Slivver said. "There's more than one way to everywhere from here. Dragon Home is countless miles of tunnel. Follow me."

"Say, I'm not sneaking around when those vile things take over. We need to lead them down below," Brenwar said to Slivver. He started toward the tunnel they'd just departed where the titan army now roamed. "I don't plan on letting the dragons do all the fighting."

"We aren't going to do much fighting. We'll be doing more running." Slivver signaled to the silver shade in Dragonese.

The slick-backed dragon snaked up the tunnel they were in, sending word to the dragons who trailed them. The orders were simple. 'Slow the titan army's advance to the top. Force another chase down below.' For now, the golden flares would have to guard the Chamber of Murals before it was destroyed.

"Do as you must, Brenwar."

Brenwar tapped Waark on the horn. "Tell them hello."

Waark stretched his great neck out of the concealment and into the adjacent corridor. His great horned head startled the ogres marching up the walk with stone hammers. Waark's mouth dropped open. Flames spilled out, lighting the tunnel up like a chimney stack.

The wurmers screeched and sizzled. The ogres danced in the agonizing flames. Many died. Many more came.

"The chase is on," Brenwar said. "For Morgdon!"

Behind Brenwar, Ben fired arrows at their pursuers. Samaz shot balls of energy from his staff. Some of the dragons—particularly a pair of orange blazes—made a final stand. White-hot foam spewed from their mouths, coating the front ranks of the enemy. It slowed the army little, but it was enough for the company to stretch their lead.

Which didn't last. Slivver led them into another tunnel filled with the enemy.

Ree-rah! Ree-rah! Ree-rah!

Rerry cried out, "They're everywhere!"

Taking a split in the path, they ran down the winding tunnel, passing another opening where a distinct cry went up. All of them—dwarf, men, and dragons—skidded to a halt. A flare of magic and power lit up the middle of the monstrous hallway. Selene and Sasha were in the thick of it, fighting for their lives.

"Mother!" Rerry screamed. He led the crimson dynamo forward, plowing a path through the wurmers and army ranks. Samaz created a shield that pushed the enemy on the other side of the barricade back. Selene and Sasha, drenched in sweat, waved them away. "What?"

"Go, Sons! Go!" Sasha was screaming.

A spear passed right through Sasha's body. A giant wielding an iron mace smashed Samaz's shield. The horde piled on the women. Their bodies passed right through them.

"Guzan! An illusion!" Rerry said. "I don't think that was meant to fool us. We need to get out of here!"

The crimson dynamo let out a blast of cover fire, pushing the army back. Turning around with a lash of its tail, the dynamo busted up another wurmer. They joined up with the rest of the party with Rerry saying, "If that wasn't Mother, then where are they?"

Ben pointed. "There!"

Farther down the corridor, on the backs of dragons, Selene and Sasha waved them on. They followed in a rush of speeding dragon feet. Seconds later they caught up with the women.

With the fury of battle gleaming in her eyes, Sasha said, "Rerry! Samaz! What are you doing down here? I told you to stay back!"

"The family that stays together, dies together!" Rerry replied.

Still racing down the hall, Sasha said, "I want grandchildren, whether I'm dead or alive."

Selene led them into the subterranean levels of the mountain after minutes of riding through and over the enemy's wake. After being besieged from all directions, relief came once she hit the tunnel into the column cavern. The party poured inside—men, elves, dwarf, dragons, and all went into the expansive and wide-open chamber of the miles of underground arena.

With Slivver's help, the dragons stopped up the main pass leading into a corridor where a vicious battle raged. Dozens of other dragons formed a circle of protection around Selene and her friends.

"This is it," she said to all of them. Chests were heaving. Faces showed exhaustion. They'd all fought and scrapped to get down into the mountain tomb. With her hand on the amulet, she added, "Once they pour in, the only way out is with me. Everyone, stay close. Brenwar, how do we do this?"

"Believe it or not, it all starts with the center column." He marched up to the main support in the middle of the chamber. It was a little bigger than all the rest. He rubbed his palm on the arcane dragon symbols. "A solid strike right here should do it."

"Then what?" Selene asked.

"It's supposed to fall. They're all supposed to fall. Like dominoes. One at a time. I hate to miss it." Brenwar warmed up with Mortuun, making light swings from side to side. That was when Ben came forward with a frown on his face.

"There's a way out for us, but what about the dragons?" He patted Waark's tail.

Grim-faced, Slivver said, "They made this choice, Ben, to protect us and their brethren."

The titan army overcame the dragons and spilled inside, hundreds at first, then thousands. They filled the chamber in all directions, spreading out and encircling the party. Giants, men, orcs, and wurmers one and all made for a frightful sight. And then the most frightful of all came.

Isobahn entered with a smile broad as a river on his burning face. "That battle is over. Dragon Home is mine. In a great feast, I will suck your bones dry tonight."

"The only bones you'll be chewing on are your own!" Brenwar fired back. He uncorked a mighty swing into the heart of the main pillar with the sound of a thunderclap. Marble and stone chipped and flecked away.

Everyone looked at Brenwar.

He shrugged. Nothing happened. Studying the pillar, his eyes enlarged. "By Mortuun, I hit the wrong one!"

CHAPTER 37

"BRENWAR, WE MUST GO NOW!" Selene ordered. She held the amulet in her hand. "It's the only way out of here."

"I'm not leaving until all of those columns are down and the misbegotten enemy is dead." He climbed on the back of Waark. "Get me over there, dragon! We're taking down a pylon!"

Claws scraping over the stone, Waark lurched forward toward the pillar with his horns lowered and rammed it. The jarring blow shocked the room. Stalactites fell.

"No! No! Waark! You have to hit the sweet spot!" Brenwar jumped to the ground with Mortuun cocked behind him.

"Brenwar, look out!" Selene yelled.

A small boulder hurled by a giant collided with Brenwar. Mortuun fell from his grip. He wasn't moving.

With the titan army closing in, Selene tossed the amulet to Sasha. "Get out of here. Now!"

"No, wait," Sasha said, catching it in midair. But as soon as her fingertips touched the amulet, she vanished, along with Rerry, Samaz, Ben, Slivver, and a handful of other dragons.

Now Selene and Brenwar were trapped. She dashed over to Brenwar.

Groggy, he started to his feet.

Isobahn laughed. "You tried to trap us! You failed! The mountain is ours, Selene! You'll never spring the trap now. It might have slain us, but now it would kill you too!"

Around her, the remaining dragons fought back the horde with powerful fires and energy. Waark continued ramming the column.

Jaw set, Selene picked up Mortuun. She eyeballed Isobahn, cocked the war hammer back, and said, "Prepare to eat mountain, monster! I'm going, and you're going with me!" She swung Mortuun into the spot on the column.

Krang!

Powerful reverberations resonated all over the chamber. The titan army jumped backward as if hit by a forceful wind. Their eyes darted. They cringed and scrambled. The column Selene struck split in four great seams. The broken pylons fell in four perfect directions, striking the others adjacent to them. One pillar crashed into another, knocking all the columns over in a domino effect. The chamber collapsed fast.

BOOM! BOOM! BOOM! BOOM!

"Nooooo!" Isobahn bellowed with eyes stricken with fear. "Noooooooo!" His flaming head went out as a huge hunk of ceiling bounced off the top of his skull.

"Waaaaaahooooooooo!" Brenwar yelled. "Take them down, mountain! Take them all down!"

Waark huddled over Brenwar and Selene. Hunks of falling stone rained down on them. Brenwar stroked the dragon's neck. "It's been an honor, friend."

With the world shaking all around them, Selene handed Brenwar Mortuun. "It's been an honor for me as well."

Selene teared up when Brenwar said, "You gave all. You did well."

With the world crashing down around them, she hugged Brenwar tightly.

"Wait, wait, wait," he said. He revealed two potion vials in his hands. "Take this."

"What is it?"

Brenwar held his orange vial up. "A little something from the chest to ease the pain."

She clinked her vial with his. "To the end."

"For Morgdon."

CHAPTER 38

GRAHLEYNA USHERED ALL THE DRAGONS through the murals then closed the doors to the chamber. The magnificent and noble creatures had fought off the hordes of wurmers as long as they could. Now, she paced the floor, waiting.

Her heart ached. She'd lost Nath and now many others. Guilt settled in. Perhaps she hadn't made the best decision when she sent the dragons away. She wasn't certain. Matters of warfare had always been Balzurth's department, and now the decisions she made had lost her son as well.

What have I done?

A radiant wink of light flashed. One by one, Sasha, Samaz, Rerry, Ben, Slivver, and a half-score dragons appeared.

"Grahleyna, send us back. You must send us back!" Rerry demanded. "Selene, Brenwar, and many dragons are trapped down there!"

"I cannot. I will see to your safety."

"No!" Rerry screamed.

The ground shook. Everyone froze. The entire mountain trembled.

"It begins! There can be no hesitation. Slivver, aid me." Grahleyna's tail slid across the floor and snatched Rerry around the waist. "Forgive me, child, but you must go now." She slung him through a mural image of lightly covered snow fields. "He'll be safe there."

Samaz's body flared up with a glow of purple magic. He started to shimmer. "I'm going back."

Slivver locked his arms around the part-elf, walked him over to Rerry's mural, and hurled him through. "No, you're not."

"I implore you to go now," Grahleyna said to Sasha. "Watch over your children."

"What about you?" Sasha said.

"I'll manage." Grahleyna stepped aside. The floor cracked in a foot-wide seam. "You and Ben go now, please."

Ben took Sasha by the hand. Into the mural they went.

"Slivver, you and the dragons go. That's an order. Protect them."

With a nod, Slivver said, "As you wish, Mother." The metal doors began to grind and buckle. "Don't get trapped in here and die."

"I won't."

Slivver and all the other dragons departed, leaving Grahleyna alone in the chamber. With her tail, she smacked the stone frames around the murals. With spits of fire, she turned them to flame. All save one. The doors into the chamber collapsed. Wurmers spilled into the room. Grahleyna escaped through the last open mural a second before all the walls and floors fell through.

Using a battering ram, ogres bashed open the door to Balzurth's throne room. With eyes bigger than silver saucers, the dark forces rushed in and saw the treasure. They danced, they sang, they reveled in it. Their filthy bodies swam in the piles of coins. They hurled gems the size of stones at one another. They had taken Dragon Home. With victory came the spoils and control of the world. With piles of golden coins cascading between their fingers, they jumped up and down, laughing.

The chamber groaned. Their vile bodies froze. The floor dropped out from under them.

Tons of treasure crushed them.

CHAPTER 39

NATH HIT THE LAVA. EXCRUCIATING pain exploded over every single fiber of his being. From his toenails to the top of his hair, he burned. To make it worse, he lived. Suffering and suffocating, the only thing he could think to do as he sank into the molten rock was to hold his breath. His mind screamed, "Yeeeeeeooooouuuuuuch!"

With his body lost in another time and space that was incomprehensible thanks to the incessant fires that smothered him, he swam. His life flashed before his eyes. His childhood with his father. Time spent with his many friends. Selene, Brenwar, and Ben came to mind. Worse, the scowling, sneering, victorious faces of the titans. They would take over.

No! I can't lose! I won't lose! What kind of dragon dies like this?

Eyes shut, there was only a glowing orange darkness on his lids. He felt his toes hit rock bottom. The searing torment went on and on, seeming to last forever.

How do I live? Ah, the pain! No one should live like this!

Fighting the unearthly pain, he surged step by step at the bottom of the moat. He was trapped in a sea of inescapable agony. No torture ever could be so bad. He was on fire. He burned so hot he felt it inside and out. His blood boiled, but he did not die.

Impossible!

Somehow, he trudged through the burning liquid rock. With the scorching heat so bad that he could barely feel, he realized he still had Fang gripped in his hand.

Fang, if you can get me out of here, please, help me!

He moved on, fishing with the tip of Fang and trying to find a way out of the pool of hot wrath. Feeling his very own heart burn, his mind started to cave in to fear. That fear made the fires all the hotter. The intolerable heat triggered a moment of panic, followed by something else. Enlightenment.

If the red rock dragons can survive this, perhaps so can I?

When he was a boy, he had watched the red rock dragons that bathed in the lava pools. They rolled and basked in the hot murk like it was water on a warm summer day. They were dragons, special ones, and so was he. He was the Dragon King, after all.

He remembered sitting on a crag in the mountain one day, watching the red rocks play. Balzurth overshadowed him, a warm and protective fire. His father had said, "A day will come known as the immersion of flame. Don't give in to the flame. Own it…or perish."

Those words rang out in his head.

This is it. This is my immersion! I won't give in, Father! The Dragons need me! My friends need me. Nalzambor needs me! I'll do what I must, for them! In the heavy liquid rock, his chest started to heave. He opened his eyes into a burning sea of orange where there was no direction. Groaning, he forced himself forward with a new energy and bursting confidence.

Guzan! If I'm not dead yet, this molten lava must not be able to kill me.

He surged on until Fang hit rock. He dug the claws of his hands and feet in the moat wall. He climbed, slowly and agonizingly, hand and foot. His head emerged. The air felt like ice. He scrambled onto the bank, dripping in molten lava.

I'm out! Yes! I'm out!

The molten lava quickly cooled. It sealed him like a mummy in a crystal cocoon. The lava stiffened all around him, hardening into a shell.

Sultans of Sulfur!

Through a small opening at his mouth, Nath breathed. The cooling coat was refreshing compared to the blinding heat he had emerged from. He let the lava finish stiffening. Something told him to wait.

He recalled how the red rock dragons shook off the lava before they burrowed into the bank with the lava crust around them. With a shake, he broke free of his sulfurous shell. He dusted off the debris. He banged Fang on the rocks, freeing the blade of his ugly coating.

"Well done, Fang. Thanks. I know you played a part in saving me."

He started to climb up the bank, fully expecting to see the titan army attacking him from all directions. He was across the moat from the mountain, just outside the enemy's camp.

The place was abandoned. Wurmers no longer filled the skies. Only handfuls flew in flocks attacking the top of the mountain. There was quiet. He also noticed that Isobahn's giant body was gone. The ice had long melted away.

"Where did they all go?"

Scuffles of metal echoing out of the tunnels inside the mountain caught his ear. Squinting, he studied the giant holes.

They're inside! All of them! I need to help them!

He dashed across the bridge.

A stray bunch of wurmers came at him.

In three quick slices, he ended them.

He made it to the other side and came to a stop. The base of the mountain trembled. Rocks bounced down in an avalanche that started to grow. He stepped backward. Voices cried out in a loud panic. Members of the titan army stormed out of the tunnel. Huge hunks of falling rock crushed them.

With his golden eyes as big as the sun, Nath backed down the bridge.

TOOOOM!

The entire base of the mountain dropped over a hundred feet into the ground. A great cry came from within the mountain.

TOOOOM!

The level above the base collapsed. Another level crashed down, followed by another, all the way to the top.

TOOOOM! TOOOOM! TOOOOM! TOOOOM! TOOOOM!

Dragon Home looked like a pyramid collapsing into itself. Huge hunks of stone and boulder rumbled down to the ground. Trees were uprooted. Birds scattered. Varmints nestled within were crushed. The quaking went on for minutes. Nath couldn't believe his eyes. His thoughts went to his friends and fellow dragons. It wasn't possible that they all had made it out.

A storm of dust rolled down the great hill, coating him in smoky brown. He backed all the way to the other side of the bridge, watching the dust clear. Dragon Home still stood, but its peak was much lower. The very top had collapsed inside itself, appearing like the mouth of a volcano.

Nath blinked the grit out of his eyes.

I must get up there!

CHAPTER 40

ATH FELL TO HIS KNEES, holding his head. So many had died, good and bad. He felt the lives of many coursing through him in a fearful wave. It stood his hairs on end. It passed, leaving him in a cold sweat on his scales. His breath was frost.

Thousands of wurmers, orcs, ogres, bugbears, and giants had been crushed. It was a great victory that came at a great price. Hundreds of dragons must have died. Possibly, so had his friends. He had no idea. All he knew to do was climb. At the new base of the mountain, he started his journey toward the top.

Below him, at the mouth of one of the tunnels, the rubble started to shift. With hope in his heart, he eased down that way.

A giant pushed through the rocks and tossed them aside. The brute was covered in patches of hair. His shaggy head turned to green flame.

"Isobahn!" Nath said with fury.

The titan turned. Eye level with Nath, he said with surprise, "You live? Humph! Like me, you cannot die. Impressive, Nath Dragon. To my delight, I'm glad to inform you that your friends were not as fortunate as you. They all perished. Now, it's just me—including thousands upon thousands of our growing army—and you." He glimpsed at the mountain. "This setback won't stop us."

"Nonetheless, it is a victory. Our fight isn't finished yet."

"Pah!" Isobahn shooed him away. "If this mountain cannot take me, then you can't take me either. I jumped from body to body until I found this one. I made it. I'm invincible."

"True, but there aren't any bodies around for you to jump to now, are there."

Seeing no more giants in sight, Isobahn grunted. "No matter. You cannot defeat me. It's over." Isobahn's body shimmered. His spirit seeped out of his body. Wispy hands clawed at Nath. "I'll just take you over!"

Cat quick with a golden flash in his eyes, Nath jumped at Isobahn and buried Fang's hilt deep in the giant's heart.

The titan tumbled backward and fell. The flames on his ugly head went out. The spirit of Isobahn came out of the body with a howl. The spirit hovered and quavered for a long moment.

Nath made out Isobahn's eyes and heard the spirit speak.

"Beware, I will find another host."

On instinct, Nath stabbed the cloudy spirit.

It shrieked, writhed—and exploded into dust.

"Whoa." He looked at his weapon with new respect. "A sword that pierces the body and the spirit. That's more than impressive, Fang."

Nath resumed his long journey toward the top of the mountain, traversing the new landscape, hopping over new ridges and seams. He encountered two spirit-like visions before him. Brandishing Fang, he said, "Fair warning, go in peace or a thousand pieces."

The ethereal images solidified.

He gaped. "Brenwar! Selene!"

They were as wide-eyed as him. Woozy, Selene said, "Brenwar, what potion did you give us?"

"I don't know. I just plucked them from the chest. I just wanted to have something for a final salute. I didn't even think of them turning us into ghosts." He shook his beard. "Dwarves don't float."

"No, they're supposed to sink." Selene tousled his hair. "Either way, you saved us. I couldn't be gladder." She eyed Nath. "Nice scales."

"Huh?"

Nath took the first long look at himself. His legs and chest were scales. He touched his face and felt tiny scales on his chin. "Is my face covered?"

She nodded. "You look burnt, but still handsome. Too bad your hair is missing."

"What?" His fingers found his locks. "Aw, Selene."

She gave him a long embrace. "I don't know how you did it, but I'm thrilled you're back. You might want to cover up the rest of you, however. The wings are a nice change too."

"Wings? You're teasing again, aren't you?"

She stepped away.

Black wings stretched outward from his back. His heart leapt for joy. "I can fly again! I'll see you at the top of the mountain." He took off, flying with glee. He and Fang flew through the air, slaughtering every surviving wurmer in sight. He met up with Brenwar and Selene on the top of the mountain. "I don't suppose we know if the others came out of this alive."

"I think it's safe to believe they did. Grahleyna was well prepared," she said. "Your plan worked. The titan army lies dead."

"Yes," Nath replied, "this battle is won, but the war is far from over."

POWER OF THE DRAGON

-Book 9-

CRAIG HALLORAN

CHAPTER 1

STANDING AT THE BASE OF Dragon Home, Nath sang a long and sorrowful tune in Dragonese. Hundreds of dragons had died within the mountain grave. He hoped more had escaped through the murals, but he didn't know. Selene held his hand in hers. Her thumb rubbed the back of his palm. Brenwar stood on the other side, on one knee with his head down. Nath finished singing. Selene dried his eyes.

"That was a fine song, Nath." Brenwar rose to his feet. "Feel free to use it at my burial."

Selene kissed his cheek. "Mine too."

"Certainly, but let's not make any plans for the near future. I've lost enough friends today. We all have." There were still many dragons lying dead on the ground from the battle outside. It had been a day since the mountain fell, and now the fetcher dragons came. They dropped from the sky and landed softly by the fallen dragons. The tremendous, hornless beasts were smooth scaled, gray mixed with white, giving them soft feathers. They took the dragons in their claws, one by one, and flew them away.

"Won't the wurmers get them?" Brenwar remarked.

"They know a path in the skies only they dare follow. It's very high."

Selene gave Nath a puzzled look.

He shrugged. "What can I say? I'm enlightened." He started down into the moat's lava. Immersion in burning rock did more than change him physically. It gave him a greater awareness as well. He had gained knowledge of Nalzambor and the dragons that he hadn't had before. "We have to get back on track. I need to rescue Father. I'm not sure where to start."

"If you don't have any answers, perhaps we should head back to Morgdon," Brenwar said. "They could use our help, based on what I saw in those murals."

"We need to find the others too," Selene said. "Grahleyna and I spoke about a temporary sanctuary where we could rendezvous if we were ever separated. I'm certain they'll be there. Or close by. I can only assume they believe us dead. They may have moved on."

"No doubt they'll be looking for us, and we should be looking for them. We'll make haste." He faced the bridge that led across the moat. "I'd be interested to see the look on Eckubahn's face when he learns of all this." He swam across the moat in the molten lava, reflecting on the drolem Isobahn had possessed, almost killing him. It had been sad to see such a magnificent creation destroyed. He shook his head.

Together, they searched the camp for any supplies they might need. The titan army had been building for years. Even after the collapse of the now aptly named Mountain of Doom, the evidence of their labor at the base of the mountain was vast. Now abandoned, the dreadful encampment had become a ghost town. Along with a few varmints scuttling among scraps and skulking away, the tent flaps rustling was the only movement in sight. Any survivors had fled.

Nath ducked into the largest tent, centered in the camp—which was so large that this tent was a mile away from the base of the mountains. Scrolls and maps were piled at the side of the table. A layout of Dragon Home was spread out in intricate detail. The tunnels the titan army had dug were clearly marked. Nath could see several places where the enemy's efforts failed and they had to try again. "Huh, there's a lot of hard rock in that mountain. No wonder the siege took so long. They couldn't find a soft spot to dig."

"Dwarves would have done it in a tenth of the time."

"Then I suppose it's a good thing the dragons aren't warring with dwarves, then, isn't it?"

"I didn't mean any disrespect," Brenwar said. "Just making a point, sire."

Nath nodded. "Brenwar, so long as we aren't anywhere formal, let's keep it informal between us, shall we, dearest friend?"

"Certainly."

"Feel free to look around and see if there is anything useful." Nath rifled through some papers. "We might get a better idea of what their plans are elsewhere."

Brenwar grabbed a scroll taller than him, made from cloth, and rolled it out on the floor. "I don't see how they organized anything in this dung heap. They have plans scattered everywhere." He stood on the end of the carpet-sized scroll. "Look at this. A map of Thraag, home of the orcs. Look at how big they write. It's because they're stupid." He wiped his boots on the image of the city. "That's all this map is good for. It's too big to blow my nose on."

Selene picked through scroll after scroll, unrolling them and tossing them to the floor. "Supply lists. Inventory. This army wasn't bereft of organization. Hmm, now this is interesting."

Nath lifted his eyes toward hers. "What is it?"

"A list of cities and their leaders. The titan army's head count abroad. According to this, their forces number well over a hundred thousand men. Not including the force we defeated here. So many."

"Don't you mean orcs and the like?" Brenwar said.

"Men and the like. We aren't discounting the wurmers, either. According to this, aside from Morgdon and Elome, all of Nalzambor has been taken."

"We'd assumed as much," Nath said. "It would take all of the elves and dwarves to match a force like that."

"Well, they are spread out in a variety of forces," Selene added. She spread the scroll out on the table. "The largest portion was here at the mountain. I imagine once word gets out that the mountain collapsed and this force is no more, they'll change tactics. If I were them, I would unite my remaining forces and focus on either the dwarves or the elves. And their greatest force is already surrounding the elves."

Nath glanced at Brenwar.

"It's a likely idea for those pea brains," he said. "They won't be able to penetrate Morgdon as easily as Elome. The elves don't even have walls around their cities."

"No," Nath said, "but they're holding the enemy for now. We need to warn them, though. We need to be three places at once."

"Are you suggesting we split up?" Selene said.

"I'm not ruling out the possibility."

CHAPTER 2

BEN SAT UNDER A TREE with his head down between his legs. He and everyone else who had passed through the mural were fine, but all of their faces were long. Sasha sobbed with her sons. They'd lost great friends in Nath, Selene, and Brenwar, not to mention all the dragons, including Grahleyna. His chest rattled when he breathed. His breath was misty.

Snow came down, barely covering the green grass of the fields. Dragons of all sorts and colors lingered nearby. There had been more when they first arrived. Quietly and gradually, they were departing.

Ben noticed Slivver beneath another tree. The long-necked silver dragon stood on his hind legs, watching the other dragons depart. "Why are they leaving?"

Turning his neck a little, Slivver said, "They're going to hide, I suppose. That's what dragons do. They'll burrow into the rock and dirt. Carry on in their hidden ways."

"But there's still a battle yet to be fought, Slivver. We all need to stick together. Talk to them."

"I have been. They aren't listening. Dragons are stubborn. You should know that by now. It takes a strong leader to corral them, and even then, it's difficult." Slivver pointed at the other silver shades he led. "We'll stay with you, of course. Well, for a bit. I feel compelled to search Dragon Home for survivors."

Coming to his feet with a groan, Ben said, "I'd like to do that myself. The question is, how far are we from Dragon Home?" He slowly spun around. "I have no idea where we are."

"Can't you smell the salt in the air?" Slivver flicked his tongue out. "I can taste it."

"Please tell me we aren't near the northern seas."

"No, I jest. No seas are near. Judging by the greenery, I'm relatively certain we are far east of the Settlement, tucked between the mountains and rivers. We are south of Elome, and perhaps you could follow the river straight to it. That would be ideal."

Sasha and her sons sauntered over. She wiped the dry tears on her face and sniffled. "Sorry, I should be stronger than this by now. You'd think I'd be used to seeing the ones I love dying."

"Don't be silly," Ben said. "We've all lost, but we live for them."

"I know," she replied. "Slivver, you were saying we should make for the land of the elves. I watched the war going on there from the murals. I don't think they'll accept us, seeing how we aren't elves. I'm not, and my sons aren't full blooded."

"A dragon escort might have an impact on them," Slivver said, showing his teeth in a flashy smile. "I can be rather convincing."

"I'm sure you can." Ben adjusted his quiverful of arrows. "But I don't think we'll make it there without a fight. The titan army has formed its own border around Elome. We'll either have to punch our way through or fly, I guess."

"Or you could wait for me here," Slivver said.

"What do you mean?" Sasha said.

"I am truly compelled to check Dragon Home for survivors. I can make it from here to there in a day."

"Slivver, the past is in the past. We have to move on," Sasha objected. "We need to focus on fighting the titans—and"—she glanced at the sky—"the wurmers. We still need to take out those lairs. There's almost no point in fighting this war if we can't stop the wurmers. You saw how many of them there were. They fill the skies like rain. And truthfully, I don't like the idea of you leaving. What if they see you?"

"They might see me, but they won't catch me." Slivver spread his wings. "Trust me."

"I'm with Sasha, Slivver. I think we need to stay together. Let's head toward elven land. Perhaps they'll have some insight that we can use. Stay with us."

"What you want has no bearing on my decision. I'll do what I feel needs to be done. I'm a dragon, never inclined to take orders from humans. No offense, but I do what I do out of duty in honor of my mother and my brother. I suggest that you stay close to the river. Head north. I'll hurry back." Slivver leapt into the air. His shining wings beat. He flew out of sight in seconds.

Ben's eyes trailed after him. "I sure wish I could do that. Sasha, are you comfortable heading north?"

"I'll let you decide."

Rerry started to say something but closed his mouth. Samaz stood quiet as ever, carrying Brenwar's chest on his shoulder. The Elderwood Staff was in his other hand.

"North it is then." Ben led the way.

Sasha, Samaz, and Rerry fell in behind him. Faces to the northern wind, they marched alongside the river bank. Aside from being able to defend themselves, they had additional protection. Slivver's fellow dragons stayed close. There were other dragons in their midst, some bright and colorful, slinking through the waters and the tall grasses that kissed the bottom of the hills. The snowfall increased, coating the greenery in a soft, bright, white layer.

They had walked half a league when Rerry—who'd been oddly silent—spoke up. "I'm getting hungry."

Ben had been ignoring the nagging in his stomach. Grahleyna had sent them out of the mountain without any supplies. It was just them. He unhooked Akron from his back. *Snap. Clatch. Snap.* The perfectly crafted bow strung itself. Eyeing the hills, he said, "I imagine there must be some game. Rerry, are you in the mood to do a little hunting?"

Rerry patted his scabbard. "With a sword?"

"No, I'll let you take a shot or two with Akron, but no more. If you miss, then it's my turn."

The young elven warrior's eyes lit up. He took the bow in hand. "No, I'll do it in one shot, but I hope to do many."

"Sasha, we'll be back," Ben said. "Just keep heading north."

She showed him a smile. "Happy hunting."

CHAPTER 3

WITH HIS HEAD BURNING IN a bright-red angry flame, Eckubahn pounded on a giant sentry. His huge fists dented the metal armor the giant wore. Ribs cracked under his power. The giant gasped his last breath and died. The red flame surrounding Eckubahn's head cooled to a soft amber green. Sweat dripped from his mortal body. He returned to his throne. Five giants lay dead inside the throne room in Narnum, their huge bodies strewn over the floor—busted up, mangled, and broken.

He let out a loud sigh that echoed through the chamber. Some of the remaining giant sentries, backs to him, shuddered.

"Stand still!" Tylabahn said. The titan was still in the form of a giant hag of a woman. Her scraggly gray hair now hung past her waist. "What are you grinning at, Lotuus?"

The fairy empress was the bearer of bad news. She was the one who had delivered the message about the Mountain of Doom. The blow was devastating to Eckubahn. She delighted in it, but not because she wanted Eckubahn to lose. She just loved turmoil and chaos. "I can't help but find this entire scene entertaining. I bring news that a quarter of your army has been destroyed, and now you yourself destroy another portion of it. I thought you spirits were wiser than that."

Eckubahn took a swat at her.

Lotuus glided out of harm's away. "Please, don't kill the messenger. You've killed enough already." She hovered between Eckubahn, who sat, and Tylabahn, who stood. She was nothing more than a rodent between them. "It seems that Nath Dragon lives. Perhaps you should have killed him when you had him, like you did his father."

Eckubahn glared right at her. "It is impossible that he escaped. He should have been dead long ago."

"And yet, three years later, he reappears. Never underestimate the power of a dragon." Wings beating, she buzzed backward and out of reach. "There is a price for overconfidence, and now, not only is Nath Dragon back, but Isobahn is gone. Not to mention, you don't even have access to the Mountain of Doom. I have to admit, I never saw that coming. The dragons destroyed their own mountain. Brilliant!"

"Silence, Lotuus!"

She shrugged her little shoulders. "As you wish, my lord."

Lotuus had come back into the fold when she learned Nath Dragon had been captured and kept in the Deep. Since that time, she'd been serving as a go-between for Eckubahn and his forces. She had been about to deliver the good news that the mountain was about to be penetrated when Nath returned. From a distance, she had watched the entire battled unfold. The dragons fought the wurmers. Nath emerged from the mountain with a huge metal dragon that turned against him. She watched him fall to his death in the boiling lava. The Mountain of Doom collapsed. Nath Dragon emerged again and slew Isobahn with his sword.

And Nath Dragon had changed into something greater than he had been. She had considered approaching him for some reason but had thought better of it. She kept that to herself. After all, this was a war she had started. It wasn't likely he'd forgive her for it.

She'd fled back to Narnum and delivered the shattering news to Eckubahn. He'd been having a tantrum ever since.

"What do you want to do, Eckubahn?" Tylabahn ran a comb through her hair. Bugs fell on the ground with each stroke. "Shall we hunt after Nath again? He needs to be destroyed."

"I'm thinking."

"At least we can take comfort that many dragons are dead. The battle was not fought in vain. With the Mountain of Doom gone, well, the dragons don't have a base to rally from. They'll be scattered. We need to make sure Nath Dragon doesn't rally them. Keep him away from them, and the world will continue to be ours."

Tapping his fingers together, Eckubahn said, "Send word out. The titan army destroyed the Mountain of Doom. The dragons lost. I want it known from one corner of Nalzambor to the other. It will break the will of the people, especially those troublesome elves and dwarves. It's time to break them."

"The dwarves aren't going anywhere. The elves are the ones that need finishing. They are exposed." Tylabahn tucked her comb away. She moved closer to him, crunching the bugs beneath her bare toes. "Use the wurmers. I have an excellent idea…" Her expression faded into nothing.

Eckubahn leaned forward. "You were saying, sister?"

Lotuus watched Tylabahn's lids flutter. The ugly woman shook her head. *Something is very amiss there. The changeling fights within her.*

The glassy stare in Tylabahn's eyes cleared.

Eckubahn slapped his hand on the chair arm. "You had better have control of that thing you indwell, sister. I don't need any more failures!"

"I'm perfectly fine," she argued. "Can't a girl have a moment to gather her wits? As I was saying, I have an idea that will allow the wurmers to rain down devastation from above."

"I'd be interested to hear what you have in mind."

The giant sentries opened the throne room doors. The bald-headed priestess Forever entered, a former servant of Selene's. Robes dusting the floor as she crossed the expansive room, she came to a stop and bowed at Eckubahn's feet.

"What is it, child?" Eckubahn said.

"My lord, I am the bearer of horrendous news."

His head tilted. He cast a quick look at Lotuus. She faded back. "Out with it."

"I have confirmed that two more wurmer hives have been destroyed. That leaves only two. What would you have me do?"

Lotuus stopped breathing. Tylabahn stepped back.

"That's quite all right, child." Eckubahn extended his hands. He picked up Forever like a doll. "Quite fine." His green flames began to boil red.

Forever squirmed. "My lord! You're crushing me! Please," she begged. "Stop."

Bone and cartilage snapped.

Lotuus flinched. *Better her than me. I didn't care for her much anyway.*

Eckubahn chucked Forever's body over his shoulder. "We'll move on the elves. Now clean up this mess."

CHAPTER 4

"I WISH THERE WERE A WAY we could all keep tabs on one another," Nath said. He, Brenwar, and Selene began the journey east. He had decided it would be best to find the others and the surviving dragons. But there was still a gnawing in his stomach. Brenwar wanted to check in on his kindred, but it would be impossible for him to do so with the titan army swelling within their borders. "I'm tempted to fly back and see for myself, Brenwar."

The grizzled dwarf marched up the pathway, eyes fixed on the way ahead. "No, you made up your mind. I won't argue. Let's make Morgdon our next stop, though. The elves will surely need more help than we do."

"Well said." Nath lengthened his stride and broke into a trot for a long run. Finally, he said, "This is silly when I can fly." He looked back at his friends.

"We aren't stopping you." Selene glanced up. "Perhaps the wurmers are?"

"I can risk it. Besides, I haven't met a wurmer I couldn't handle. Just stay east until you cross the river. I don't want to lose you."

"Are you telling me you've forgotten how to track?" Brenwar said.

"No, of course not. I'm still the best tracker of them all. Just stay on course. I'll be back." Nath leapt into the air, wings beating, and started flying. Staying low, just above the treetops, he circled his friends once and waved goodbye. Then he shot over the treetops like a black bolt of lightning, cutting through the winds like a knife. A surge of exhilaration coursed through his body. *I haven't felt this good in, well, years! I love it! I love being a dragon!*

Scales covered every inch of his body except his head. He didn't have any horns. He was still part man and part dragon, but now dragon was the bigger part. While flying, he channeled more of his energy, trying to transform into a full dragon like before. The change didn't come. He shook it off. *I'm not complaining! I can fly again! And not only that, I have more scales!*

He started into a loud roar but cut it off. The wurmers still lurked in the open skies and were possibly dug into the forest below. It was the reason he hadn't called out to the dragons earlier. It was too risky. He stayed on course, drifting several hundred feet higher, where he was able to see farther ahead and more below.

Dusk was coming, but his vision was clear. It wouldn't be long before he made it to the river. He just hoped he'd find his friends alive and well. He was sick of all the needless death and endless suffering. It needed to come to an end. *With Fang, I bet I could kill Eckubahn.* He turned north for a moment and hovered in the air. *Fang slew the spirit of Isobahn, so why not him? One strike. Slice!* Fang burned hot in his grip. *You don't like that idea, do you?*

Nath resumed his journey east. Fang cooled. The essence of the sword seemed to guide him. There was more closeness between the two of them after his Immersion of Flame, yet something bothered him. Had Isobahn truly died, or had his spirit only been banished? The way Nath understood it, they didn't really die, not unless you killed them on their plane. Otherwise, they just lingered.

They need to be destroyed. All of them.

With the icy winds in his face, he flew on, hour after hour, into the night. With his toes almost grazing the treetops, he spied something ahead. A mile away, a flock of birds chased after a silver sparrow.

Birds don't fly at night.

He angled upward for them. The silver bird's wings beat with an unsteady rhythm. Nath got a closer look.

Those aren't birds, they're wurmers! That's Slivver!

Nath sped up. Streaking upward in the sky, he headed on an aerial collision course with the flock. Slivver labored through the sky with one wing half beating. He caught Nath's eyes.

"Nath, you live!"

"Yes, brother!" He soared right underneath Slivver. "And they die!" He chopped through the first wurmer in the V-formation. Striking mid-air, he detached two more heads from their bodies with the shimmering blade. Wurmer parts and bodies dropped toward the earth. Nath continued swinging.

The mindless creatures' pursuit of Slivver ended. The destruction of Nath Dragon had begun. In a frenzy, they swarmed him.

Spinning in a tight circle, Nath unleashed a torrent of fire from his breath. The burning fluid clung to the wurmers' bodies and spread. Their wings beat hard in the winds. His fires scorched their membranes. The wurmers spiraled downward, hitting the earth in small pyres.

Nath's head whipped around. All ten of the wurmers were gone from the sky. There was no sign of his brother. "Slivver?" On the ground, a small flash of lightning caught his eye. Slivver stood in the grasses, waving. Nath landed right beside him. "You're wounded."

"Only my body, but my heart is on fire knowing you still live!" Slivver gave Nath a great hug. "My brother of all brothers, I'm elated! Tell me everything!"

CHAPTER 5

THE SUN ROSE. BEN KICKED the coals of the campfire he'd made in the night. He and the others had camped just inside the tree line. Working through most of the night, roasting some meat on a spit and smoking the rest for later, they had cooked a small deer Rerry slew with Akron. It was enough to fill their bellies and keep them rationed for a few more days.

Sasha packed up some of the deer jerky in a bundle of deer skin. Her breath was frosting. "The sooner we move, the better. My toes are freezing. You did a good job with everything last night. I enjoyed watching you work with my sons. You're a good man, Ben."

"To be honest with you, last night was the closest to normal I've had in a long time. I enjoyed it." He stretched his arms wide and cracked his back. "It makes me think of my family. I know why I'm in this: to help end it so more fathers and sons and daughters can enjoy this world in safety."

"You make it sound like it's up to us to save the world," she said. "You're more ambitious than you let on."

"I'm just carrying the same torch that Dragon would. If we don't fight for the right things in the world, the wrong things will rule."

"That sounds familiar."

"It should. Bayzog told me that. He taught me a lot when I was confused. He was a great teacher."

Sasha teared up.

"Sorry, I didn't mean—"

"No, Ben. I'm fine. What you said, well, it does my heart well to remember him like that."

Rerry and Samaz returned from the river, where they'd filled skins with water. "Are we ready to go?" Rerry said, looking between Ben and Sasha.

"Of course." Ben grabbed what little gear he had and headed out of the grove. "The sooner we start, the sooner we get there." He made it to the river, turned north, and said, "Say, where are the dragons?"

"The only ones I've seen are the silvers." Rerry pointed ahead. "See? There are two of them just inside that line of trees. They're very quiet."

"I noticed a copper's head shimmering above the waters," Samaz stated.

"No you didn't," Rerry said. "I didn't see it."

"You weren't looking where I was."

"Either way, Ben, I'm certain they're around. They're here to look after us, aren't they?"

Ben shrugged. "That's what Slivver said. He should be back soon. I suggest we keep going."

The sun stayed out for the first hour before the clouds hid it. Snow started to fall once more. Ben marched on, heading toward the fascinating land of the elves. The last time he was there seemed like a lifetime ago. Now he had a chance to go back, if he could actually get there. He hated to imagine the titan army destroying another fantastic city.

The next thing he knew, the silver shades were back to escorting them. On each side of the small group, they walked in easy steps with their long tails dragging through the snow. Little bigger than Ben, the magnificent reptiles seemed at home in the frosty elements. He had to fight the urge to reach out and touch one. He didn't want his hand snapped off. As beautiful and graceful as they were, they were twice as deadly.

They'd marched into midday.

"We can stop if you like," Ben said to Sasha.

"No, it's too cold to stop," she replied.

"How about the two of you?"

"I'm part elf," said Rerry. "I can walk days and nights without sleep."

Samaz stared into the sky. A speck high in the air circled above. "What do you suppose that is, a wurmer?"

"Where there's one wurmer, there's at least a dozen," Ben replied. "Just keep an eye on it. Let's keep moving. If we have to take to the trees, we will." He thought he heard one of the silver shade dragons snicker, but he couldn't be sure.

The speck circled a few more times before vanishing into the clouds.

"It's gone now," Rerry said. "Probably one of our dragons."

"Yes, let's hope that's the case." Ben's heart pounded in his chest. They were a formidable group, but fighting a score of wurmers could be fatal. He didn't have the ability to control the dragons. There was no telling what they might do. He moved on, checking the sky from time to time. "Samaz, next time you see something, if you don't mind, please mention it."

Rerry punched his brother in the back. "Yes, big head little mouth. Say something."

The shaggy-haired Samaz walked on with his head down.

Ben let him and Rerry lead the way and drifted back to Sasha. "Samaz has been awfully silent. It troubles me."

"Yes, me too. I think most of it is just him mourning. He wanted to go back and fight for his friends." Sasha tucked her hands under her arms. "Grahleyna sending him to safety through the mural didn't sit well with him."

"I know how he feels. He carries that chest and staff like the world on his shoulders." Ben watched Rerry trying to take the chest from Samaz. The elder brother wouldn't give. "He needs to learn while he's young that you can't do it alone."

Sasha reached over and took his hand in hers. "Do you mind, dear friend?"

"Your warmth is more than welcome," Ben said, feeling half a foot taller. "I'd be honored."

"The honor is mine."

Just beyond a bend in the river, Rerry and Samaz came to a stop. Rerry's hand went to his sword. Samaz set the strongbox down. The silver dragons' heads lowered. Their tongues flickered from their mouths.

There was a dry stretch of river rock spreading out toward the bank. A black figure was balled up over the rocks, with wings folded over its back.

Ben readied Akron. *Snap. Clatch. Snap.* He notched a moorite arrow. "Stay here," he said to Sasha. Together with Rerry and Samaz, he crept forward.

CHAPTER 6

The creature on the dry river bed stood up. Wings facing Ben, the scaled man turned. Flame-red hair spilled out over the man's shoulders.

"Dragon?" Ben said. His fingers fumbled on the bow string. The arrow sailed.

Nath snatched the missile out of thin air with a broad smile on his face. "Nice shot, Ben, but save it for the enemy, not your friend."

Akron fell from Ben's fingers. Rerry and Samaz leapt forward. Rerry flailed his arms wildly and began yelling.

"Nath! You're alive! Alive!" He hugged Nath. So did Samaz.

Nath filled his long arms with the both of them. "I'm more alive than ever and glad to see you are also well." With nothing but black scales up to his chin, he waved Ben over. "Come on, get in here."

Ben joined in. So did Sasha. Tears streaked down all of their faces.

"How?" Sasha said with a trembling chin. "We saw you die."

"You saw me take a spill in the moat of lava, and the truth be told, it felt like I died a thousand deaths, but I survived." He gave them all a squeeze. "And there's even more good news. Look yonder."

Ben followed Nath's stare back toward the path behind them. Brenwar and Selene had arrived, along with Slivver. He pumped his fist. "Yes!" He ran over to Brenwar and picked him up, then he quickly set him down. He reached for his back. "Great Guzan, you weigh a ton!"

"And you leave a trail a blind orc could follow." Brenwar gave Ben a fierce slap on the back. "Don't make me look bad. I taught you better than that."

Selene gave Ben an unexpected embrace with arms as powerful as a grizzly's. His back popped several times.

"Uh," Ben said, holding his back and walking away, "good to see you too, Selene."

The group was back together. Everyone aside from Brenwar had smiles on their faces. In Nath's presence, even the chill air had warmed.

"I'm so glad you're alive. I didn't think I could save the world without you."

"Sure you could have, Ben. It just takes faith. With that said, I'm glad I'm back too."

They continued the journey, talking for hours about their plans. Everyone had a spring in their step. Better yet, more dragons appeared among them. Nath spoke with many of them along the journey. He now seemed as much one with them as he was with his friends.

By the end of the next day, they'd come to the edge of the elven lands. Spying from a hilltop, they saw that the splendid scenery of the elves had been invaded. The titan army had created massive camps that dotted the landscape. Huge pyres burned. Whole groves and even forests of trees had been chopped down. As far as the eye could see, the evil army was entrenched. And for every boot on the ground, it looked like there was a wurmer in the sky.

"There's even more here than there were at Dragon Home," Ben said to Nath.

"And more will be coming. The army has just been picking at the elves, but with a greater force, they'll advance. They'll squeeze the elves. Choke them." Nath put his hand on Ben's shoulder. "We can't let that happen."

"Even with you at my side, Dragon, I have to ask, how do we stop so many? We don't have a mountain to drop on them this time. Not that I would want to do that."

Selene eased into the conversation. "We won't win anything if we don't destroy those wurmer nests. They'll just keep hatching more, forever."

A lone, horse-sized wurmer flew over the elven plains. Carrying a net filled with rocks, it flew up over a remote elven settlement. The stones plummeted to the ground, crushing everything.

"That's diabolical," Ben said.

"That's just the beginning. It will get worse the longer we wait."

"Or the longer the elves wait," Selene said. "They should move out of harm's way."

"They'll never abandon their lands until the last one dies. And even if they did, the wurmers and titans would just follow. No, we need to get word to them and see what they have planned. Together, I'm certain we can help them."

"How are we supposed to get in there, Nath?" Ben asked. "Besides, I'm not sure I want to go in. I think it's safer out here."

"It's not safe anywhere. No, we need to offer whatever help we can, man and dragon. They'll need it. Where's that strongbox?"

Rubbing the back of his neck, Ben said, "You aren't going to shrink us again, are you?"

"We'll see."

Samaz set the strongbox at Nath's feet. Nath rummaged through with Rerry leaning over his shoulder. "Please, Dragon, let me sample that mystic fair. Ben got to last time—and remember, he shot you with your own bow."

"That was an accident."

Nath shook a vial in front of his eyes. "No fighting. Supplies are limited." He closed the chest. "There aren't enough items to get us all through the way I hoped."

Samaz bent down, reaching for the chest.

Brenwar stepped in the way. "I'll carry it. You just hang on to that staff of yours."

"Slivver," Nath said.

Slivver popped his head up from behind Selene.

"Here." He threw his brother a healing potion.

Slivver drank it down. "Somehow, I know you have something in mind," he said with a grin.

"I'd like to have you and the silver shades create a diversion."

"Let me guess, you want us to lead the wurmers on a chase? How riveting. I won't let them blindside me like they did that last time. When shall we get started?"

"Right away."

"And what are we going to do, Nath?" Ben asked.

"We're going to form a wedge and bust right into Elome."

"Suppose the elves don't want us?" Brenwar said with his foot on the chest.

"We'll learn the answer to that when we get there."

CHAPTER 7

Night arrived. Slivver led four more silvers into the sky, speaking to them in their minds, in their own dialect of Dragonese. "I want those wurmers divided. The whole flock won't follow us all. We need to split them up. We'll fan out: north, west, and south. Be careful, my brothers. Follow my lead."

Wurmers soared through the sky in the hundreds, but thousands more were on the ground. They crept over the plains and through the brush. Many nestled in the camps. More were perched on their hind quarters, eyes alert, watchdogs for the armies.

Giants of tremendous size milled about, barking orders. There were nuurg fighters, the one-eyes, riding on the backs of wrath horns. Ogres and orcs worked side by side with hosts of men. All of them worked hard, building and amassing armor and weapons. Wagon trains of equipment in the hundreds rode in. Great siege machines were built. Oversized orcs carried spears twice the length of normal men.

Slivver had never witnessed so many of the foul races working as a single unit before. His scales grew chill. There was more than enough of the enemy to wipe the elves from their thriving fields forever. He flew into the clouds. The ground disappeared beneath him. He had a sense of where his brethren were. They were all connected.

He tried to stay focused. In his flight back to Dragon Home, he'd been blindsided by a wurmer that came out of nowhere. For the most part, his mind was elsewhere, so the creature had caught him off guard. In an instant, a small host of wurmers had swarmed him. It would have been a nasty situation if Nath hadn't appeared when he did.

Now, it was time to summon powers of his own. He dipped out of the clouds. The other silvers followed suit. Spread out thousands of feet above the camp, they dove.

His descent increased with marvelous speed. He was knifing downward through the sky when an unsuspecting flock of wurmers blocked his path to land. His speed increased. The scales of his body transformed into a bolt of living lighting.

SCRAKOW!

He ripped three wurmers like they were piles of straw. The monsters exploded into ash. He eyed the ground below. Faces of the countless soldiers looked up. Their eyes widened at the sight of the silver meteor coming right for them. They went for their weapons. It was too late.

Slivver spread his wings, changing his direction a split second before he hit the ground. Wings wide and glinting with living lightning, he cut through the camp. His entire body was a weapon. His wings halved two nuurg riders. Heads of wurmers were clipped. He tore through over a dozen men and beasts on the ground before he took to the sky again.

"Upward, brothers! Upward! Fan out!"

He knifed through wurmers shrieking in the sky. Leaving a trail of carnage behind him, he flew west. His lightning power faded. His work was done. Below, he and his brethren had wrought shock and devastation. Scores were dead. Tents were burning. Smoke started to rise.

"If I could only do that a hundred times a day, this war would be over."

Wurmers of all sizes came by the hundreds in pursuit. The same amount went after the others. Slivver hissed at them. "Come and get me!"

"Uurluuk's Beard!" Brenwar exclaimed. "Will you look at that?"

Five trails of silver flashed in the sky like shooting stars. Each of the scintillating streams cut through the wurmers in a dazzling display of power. The lightning tore through the shocked ranks of the titan army, sending out howls of anger and fear. In a flash, the silver dragons shot back into the sky again. Wurmers gave pursuit from all directions.

"I don't think I've ever seen anything so amazing before." Ben's jaw hung open after he spoke.

Nath pushed Ben's chin up. "Slivver's a show-off. I expected nothing less, but I have to admit, that was more fantastic than I envisioned. Let's go."

Approaching Elome from the south, he decided to split between two camps that were entrenched about a hundred yards from one another. All eyes were on the sky. The distraction of the fires would give them a chance to slip through unnoticed. Poised in the mountains, he checked to see that everyone was secured on their dragons. Sasha rode with Ben on a steel dragon that was much bigger than a horse. Rerry and Samaz were gathered on a crimson dynamo. Selene rode a bull dragon. That left Brenwar. It was a fight to get him on top of a gray scaler that was every bit as stubborn as he.

"I don't like this one. I miss Waark," Brenwar said. The grey scaler hissed at him. "See, he's mean."

"I'd be mean too if you sat on me," Ben said. "You weigh a ton. Are you made of lead or something?"

"No, I'm made of dwarf."

"Enough chatter." Nath's wings unfolded. There were leagues of elven acreage ahead. He hoped to soar unnoticed over them. Initially, he had thought they'd have to fight their way into the elven lands, but Slivver's idea turned out perfectly. "We fly in low, while all their eyes are up. Follow me now. Quickly."

He jumped off the overhang. His chest dusted the treetops. At the bottom of the hill, he glided less than a handspan over the grasses. To his left and right were the enemy camps. Bonfires burned that would obscure their vision. Nath counted on that and how every head was tilted toward the sky.

Perfect!

His wings flapped, silently pushing him forward. He barely heard the whistle of the others behind him. In seconds, they cleared a few hundred yards from the camps. He kept going as far as he could. He took a glance over his shoulder. Everyone was together in a perfect formation.

Yes! We made it!

The tall oaks, elms, and pines in the distance thickened. Lights twinkled in the lush vegetation. His eyes narrowed. There weren't any signs of elven soldiers. Not even one heat signature.

That's odd.

Nath smashed face first into an invisible barrier. One by one, the others collided into it too, landing in a giant pile of scales, talons, jostled wings—and a grumbling dwarf.

"Dwarves don't crash!"

CHAPTER 8

NATH STOOD UP ON WOOZY legs. Everyone in the party was rubbing or craning their necks. He rushed over to help Sasha to her feet. "Are you injured?"

"Just rattled," she said. "What in Nalzambor did we hit?"

A wagon-sized copper dragon butted his horns against an unseen barrier. Next, he spat black acid on the invisible wall. The spit bounced and sizzled in the grasses.

Nath patted the copper dragon's neck. "Easy." He tapped the barrier with his knuckles. It was solid as glass, but it rippled, blurring the view on the other side when he hit it. "We might not be able to get through it, but I don't see why we can't fly over it. Only one way to find out, I suppose." He launched himself into the air, wings beating, tapping the wall all along the way. At thirty feet up he hit nothing. He dropped down on the other side.

"Now that's a wall," Rerry said. He stood across the barrier from Nath. "I didn't know elves were capable of this. It's amazing."

"It's magic. It won't last." Brenwar gave it a whack with Mortuun. The see-through barrier warbled. "The walls of earthen works are best."

"I don't know, Brenwar," said Nath, "this is pretty impressive. Perhaps the elves are in better shape than we thought." A few hundred yards away in the direction they had all come from, he noticed members of the titan army beginning to advance. "It looks like we're going to have company. Everyone, get over here. Make haste!"

They all mounted their dragons again. Wings spread, the scaled beasts took to the air. One by one, they landed on the other side.

"Let's move," Nath said, "Quickly." The moment he turned toward Elome, the ground came to life. Elven warriors popped up from the tall grasses. They wore almond-shaped helmets. Each carried a spear longer than themselves. The elven-steel tips gleamed. Great humanoids twelve feet tall made of bound-up grasses appeared from the trees in the forest. They marched forward.

"What are those?" Rerry whispered.

Nath could see the faces of elven soldiers peeking out of the chests of the shambling automaton bodies. The very elements of the earth had been turned into natural giant suits of armor. With bodies made up of bundles of long grass and hands and feet made from saplings, the shambling figures hemmed them in.

"That's the silliest armor I ever saw," Brenwar scoffed.

"I kinda like it," Rerry said, edging toward the soldiers. "It's the perfect camouflage—and huge."

Nath raised his hands. "I am Nath Dragon, friend of the elves. We are here to help. I request to see Laylana."

A soldier approached him. Sticking the spear in the ground, the soldier removed the helmet. Black hair spilled out over her shoulders. "And you have found her, Nath Dragon. Or rather, she has found you." She embraced him. "It's grand to see that you are well."

"My heart swells at the sight of you, Laylana." He pointed at the oncoming forces. "Are we going to fight?"

"No. Just be quiet. Watch."

An elf in a rich set of robes appeared among them and stood before the barrier with his arms spread wide. He began to chant in mind-bending syllables. The barrier shimmered. He stepped back, gave Laylana a nod, and said quietly, "It is done."

A small force of the titan army stopped several yards short of the barrier, looking from side to side, necks craning and eyes squinting. Nath's company and the elves were only a few dozen yards from them. The enemy soldier seemed to look right through them. Their leader, a one-eyed nuurg, snorted the air and spat on the ground. He turned and led his forces back where they had come from.

Once the enemy force was out of earshot, Nath said, "That was impressive. They couldn't see us. Were we invisible?"

"They only saw an image of nature's natural state, not us. It's something the elven mages like Inslay"— she put her hand on the shoulder of the elf beside her— "control."

"That's quite a spell, Inslay," Nath said to the droopy-eyed elf who appeared to be centuries old. "There's so much land to cover, though. Is all of Elome protected?"

"I wish I could say it was," Laylana continued, "but no. Doing what we do keeps us on our toes. The truth is, Nath, you couldn't have come at a better time. You bring me hope. I hate to admit it, but I was of the belief that you were dead. But you live, and, well, your new body is extraordinary."

Selene wedged herself into the conversation. "Are we here to discuss Nath's excellent figure or the fate of the world? Perhaps we can continue this conversation somewhere other than the wilderness. Some of these mortals are cold and hungry."

"I'm neither," Brenwar said. "And I'm in no mood for the elves' glorious assortment of fruits and vegetables. I could go for some black-horned stag, though."

"Please, come with me," Laylana said.

"All of us?" Nath said.

"Yes. Man, dwarf, dragon, I welcome all of you, but not all the others will. Come."

CHAPTER 9

NATH LEFT THE DRAGONS OUTSIDE the heart of the city. Elome was a vast network of small homes and shops built in the forest out of massive, carved-out trees. Suspension bridges crossed branch to branch in a network of walkways. The streets were wide and paved in natural stone. Every branch, road, hut, building, or storefront flowed together in a wondrous network that made up the divine city that seemed to go on forever.

Elven children hung on Nath's arms. They grabbed Selene by the wrist. Many of them made ugly faces at Brenwar. Nath tossed a boy high in the air and caught him upside down by the ankles.

"That's enough, children." Laylana shooed them away with her hands. "Sorry, but we don't get many strangers these days."

A group of elven citizens hustled by the group with wide eyes. Some of them sneered, but others showed delight. They moved into the market, where all sorts of buying and selling was going on.

"Uh, Laylana, your people don't seem too concerned about the enemy that lies at your doorstep," Nath said. "I'm curious as to why they're going on with business as usual."

"Because they're insane." Brenwar stomped his foot at some children. They sprinted away, squealing in delight. "They're born that way."

"Mind your manners, Brenwar," Nath said. "You wouldn't like it if the elves said the same of you in your land."

"I could not care less what elves think."

"It's fine, Nath. I'm plenty familiar with Brenwar's lack of courtesy. I think everyone is." Laylana wrapped her arm in his. Selene, standing on the other side of Nath, gave her a look. She held fast. "The elders don't want to panic the people. Don't get me wrong, they know what's going on. Most everyone has a relative fighting the enemy on one front or another. But the children, well, they go about life as they normally would, thriving in our sanctuaries. We will not cower or worry. That's weakness. That's what the enemy wants. We aren't weak—as the titan army has learned." She clenched her fist. "We are united and strong."

"I have to say, I've never seen a siege as pleasant as this—"

"There's nothing like this merrymaking in Morgdon right now, I'll grant you that, Nath." Brenwar stuffed his skeleton hand in the faces of a pack of children who had tried to sneak up on him. "Boo!" They scattered in more delightful squeals. "Stay away from me, you overly clean urchins!"

"As I was saying, it's bizarre." Nath arched a brow at her. "Are you certain that all of your minds are intact? After all, the spirits..."

"I know, Nath, and we've taken every precaution to weed out that invisible enemy. We seem free of it, but I can't be certain."

"I don't think anyone can be. So, where are you taking us?"

"To a place where you can rest and refresh yourselves while I notify the Elven Counsel of your coming."

"Wait!" Brenwar said. "This is the King of the Dragons. He waits for no one! I remember the last time we waited. It was months before we met."

"It wasn't as long as that," Nath said, referring to the time way back when they had sought the aid of the Ocular of Orray.

"It was to me. All that did was try to bloat me with sugary plants and vines. The wine was awful."

Laylana led them up inside a stone house much like the one they had visited decades ago. All the furnishings were chiseled from the very stone they stood on—tables, benches, beds, and chairs. All were padded in soft natural colors.

Elven maidens brought in trays of food and set them on the tables.

Ben nudged Rerry. "This is the best part of an adventure, the succulent rewards." He plucked a large, juicy, red grape from the vine and bit into it. Wiping the juice from his chin, he said, "Mmm… that's fantastic. I have to admit, suffering this long for another round back here was worth it."

Sasha, Rerry, and Samaz sat down together on one of the benches. Their eyes were at their feet.

"Make yourselves comfortable, everyone." With a wave, Laylana departed.

Nath made his way over to Sasha and her sons. "Er, Sasha, Rerry, Samaz, you should eat. Refresh yourselves. You never know when you'll have a chance to relish food like this again."

"Boys, you should eat," she said, slowly nodding yes.

"We won't if you won't, Mother." Rerry's eyes flitted up at Nath then down at his feet again.

"What's going on?" Nath asked.

"I'll tell you what's going on. It's this elven snobbery." Brenwar sniffed a clear bottle of wine. He frowned. "You didn't see the looks the elves gave them. You were too busy—"

Nath shot Brenwar a look.

"Apologies, sire." The dwarf took a seat on a bench with Selene. He propped his feet up on the chest.

"Is this true?" Nath said. "My apologies for not noticing. I'm certain you didn't do anything wrong."

"No, Nath, we're used to it. The high elves have always frowned on the likes of us," Sasha admitted. "Or at least Bayzog and my sons. It just isn't fair to them."

"If the elves are bothered by you, too bad. They'll just have to get used to you. There is nothing wrong with either of you. You should be proud of the blood that flows in your veins."

Inslay, the elder elven mage, crept into their sanctuary. He had the beginnings of crow's feet beside his bright green eyes. "Pardon me for eavesdropping, your majesty, but I couldn't help but overhear your conversation. I certainly hate to hear about this sadness, but the truth is, your perceptions are mistaken." His probing eyes landed on the Elderwood Staff that Samaz held upright at his side. "Bayzog is not disdained because of his split bloodline. It's because of what he did."

Rerry and Samaz bristled.

Sasha leaned forward and asked, "And what did he do?"

"Why, he did the impossible when he acquired the Elderwood Staff. Many elves have been in poor spirits about it ever since."

CHAPTER 10

SASHA GRACEFULLY CAME TO HER feet. "You wouldn't happen to be one of them, would you, Inslay?

"Heavens no, and it's Adept Master Inslay. I couldn't have been more proud of him. After all, I was his teacher."

Nath moved aside. Tears welled in Sasha's eyes. "Master Inslay, perhaps you don't know, but Bayzog was murdered by the titan Tylabahn."

The sharp features in Inslay's face softened. He scratched his cheek. "Are you certain?"

"I could only dream that I was wrong," she said.

"That's a shame. A shame indeed." Inslay took her hand. "You are very warm. It's no surprise why Bayzog was drawn to you. And both of his sons show his prominent features." He shook his head. "I just find it so hard to believe he's dead. He was special."

Rerry and Samaz crowded Inslay when he sat down. "Tell us about the staff. How did Father acquire it?" Rerry asked.

"Well, it was quite a feat." Inslay's eyes brightened. "You see, the Elderwood Staff is precisely what its name says: a staff made from Elderwood. You've heard of Elderwood, haven't you, Nath Dragon?"

Nath shook his head no. "I only know of the staff."

"My apologies, your majesty. Perhaps it was your father I was thinking of. You remind me so much of him."

"I know of the woodland of which you speak," Selene said. "As I understand it, the Elder Woods were destroyed in an age before the first dragon wars. Some of the wood was used for weapons, but almost all of it was burned. There are few remnants of the wood left. That staff is the only sample I've ever seen of it."

Inslay cleared his throat. "You are very correct, Selene. Yes, the Elderwood Trees thrived in a small grove far south of Dragon Home. The elves were some among many guardians of the unique timber. More often than not, they all fought over it. You see, Elderwood could store magic. It was priceless. But I myself never laid eyes on those trees. They've been gone since before I was young. But my mother said there was nothing like them, so tall and white, with leaves as beautiful as butterfly wings. The wood, well…" He stretched out his finger and touched the staff. "It's smooth and harder than steel, yet living. You, young Samaz, can you feel its power?"

Samaz frowned. "It feels like a fine stick to me." He leaned closer to Inslay. "Please, tell me how Father came by it."

"The staff is a remnant of another age. Like many such items in the elves' possession, it has been long preserved, protected, much like the Occular of Orray. However, in this particular case, the reason it was preserved was because no one could harness its power." Inslay chuckled. "You see, I'd even tried it myself. Much like with you, Samaz, it didn't work for me. But don't be discouraged."

"It makes perfect sense to me that elves made something that didn't work," Brenwar said. "The dwarves never have that problem."

"Of course not, Warlord Bolderguild. Dwarves are oblivious to anything they do wrong. For obvious reasons."

"You got that right," Brenwar said. "Er, hold on a moment. Say that again. It sounded like a jab."

Aside from Inslay and Brenwar, everyone fought back a smile.

Inslay held up his finger. "But you are mistaken, my dwarven ally, just as the elves were for centuries. You see, we always believed the staff was elven in origin. Do you see that spindle of woodwork webbing, which holds the stone within?" All eyes fell on the staff. "One would swear that was elven, but it's not. Nor could it be. We don't know who made it for certain, as the staff was discovered by accident. Elven pioneers found it in the Lost City of Borgash. It lay in an ancient hoard, guarded by a dragon known as Dark Wyrm the Hungry." Inslay gave Nath a glance. "Ever hear of him?"

Nath nodded. "Yes, he was one of the bad ones."

"That's an understatement. He ate elves like a halfling eating bits of candy. Dark Wyrm, every bit as grand as he was gory, sucked elven flesh right off the bones. He devastated Elome for centuries, snatching men, women, even the children. None could oppose him. He came without warning or cause, with years spanning between. Finally, a knot of willing elves—and one particularly brave dragon—tracked the flesh eater back to his burrowed lair deep in Borgash. The fight went on for days. The elves prevailed and found the staff among the treasure. Again, it was believed to be elven, but none could master it."

With his fingers clutching the staff, Samaz pleaded, "How did my father come by it, Adept Master Inslay? Please."

"Oh yes, well, every decade, elven masters of magic such as I and your father would have a tournament at the end of the sessions." Inslay fiddled with the buttons that dangled from his sleeves. "Every class had top students held in high regard. Your father, of course, was one of them. And make no mistake, despite the human portion of his heritage, he was treated quite well by the others. If anything, I believe many elves were jealous of his abilities. Bayzog, though silent, had great passion that burned down deep. He grasped that his days were limited and didn't take time for granted like the elves.

"So, the tournament came and all of the elven masters attended. It was ceremonial but still dangerous. The victor's spoils was the opportunity to grasp the Elderwood Staff, a chance at possessing its power. Up to then, not one elf had been able to draw a wink from it. As a matter of fact, a chance at the staff had become more of a ploy than anything else, to get adepts to work harder. The elder mages had pretty much given up on ever using the power.

"Finally, the tournament was on, and to no one's surprise, it came down to two young and very talented adepts: your father and Sindahl Suhn. Truthfully, Sindahl held the edge. His arcane bloodline ran back for centuries. It's older than mine. So, it came down to the two of them. The final contest was drawn from a chalice of marked stones." Inslay chuckled. "It was arm wrestling, the crudest test of them all. A test of will, stamina, and strength."

Rerry's chest puffed out.

"Don't be so confident yet, Bayzog's son. You see, at this point in the contest, both Bayzog and Sindahl were mentally and physically exhausted." Inslay touched Samaz's shoulder. "And it wasn't all about that brawny meat, either. There is a spell that allows you to enhance the physical limitations of your body. I cast it on both of them and let them go at it. No, in the end, it was a matter of who had enough left."

CHAPTER 11

"FATHER WON, DIDN'T HE?" RERRY said, wiping the sweat from his upper lip. "Didn't he?"

Inslay made a fist. "They locked hands. Elbows hit the table. Sindahl wasn't of slight build, either. No, he was taller than most. He matched up well with young Bayzog. I'd never seen Bayzog tired before. He'd barely made it to the final test, struggling in all of his matches. Sindahl, however, didn't have any trouble at all. His blue eyes were still full of energy. He was fresh. I was proud of Bayzog, but I didn't envision him going any farther. The Suhns had never lost."

Everyone present hung on every word the elder elf said, even Brenwar.

"They locked eyes. Clenched fists. I gave the signal. Their arms glowed with light of their own. Back and forth they went, but before long, Bayzog's arm was bent back toward the table. Sindahl's eyes lit up in victory. The next thing I knew—*wham*!" Inslay clapped his hands together. "Bayzog had pinned Sindahl down! It came out of nowhere. The shock, the dismay on Sindahl's—on everyone's face, even my own—must have been priceless. I'd never seen the Suhns so unsettled before. You see, your father, Bayzog, was bluffing. He played it close the entire way through, and when the moment came, he seized it."

"So he won the staff!" Rerry eased back with a smile on his face.

Samaz was breathing heavily.

"Well, not right away. Bayzog was accused of deception, or bluffing. Of course, there was no way to prove it. And why would anyone risk it against the likes of a Suhn? That would be foolish, but he did it. I know he did. Finally, after days of deliberation—"

"Days?" Samaz said.

"You know how elves are. We take our time about everything."

"Especially telling stories," Brenwar chimed in. He stretched his stumpy arms and yawned.

"The elven council ruled in Bayzog's favor, with some fierce deliberations on my behalf, mind you." Inslay's eyes rolled up in his head and back down. They flittered from side to side. "Sorry, I sense something, but that can wait. So, I had to convince them about the unlikelihood that Bayzog would be able to use the staff—or Sindahl, for that matter. They gave in. At the ceremony, Bayzog was brought forth to applause for his victory. The Elderwood Staff rested where it always did, lying on a slab of ivory. No one expected it to happen, but the moment his fingertip touched the staff, the jewel within lit up. No one alive at the time had ever seen this happen before.

"Well, as you can imagine, the air left the room. So did the Suhns. They were furious. All of them felt that it was Sindahl's power to possess, but I know better. It was destiny. You see, that staff takes great power to wield. But it takes something else as well—which I believe is a heart both human and elven. The Elderwood Staff was created by unbiased cooperation. It comes from a time when all the races—the good ones, that is—got along. It is a symbol of peace and power."

Samaz stiffened. His thick fingers stroked the smooth wood of the staff. "So only part elves can use it?"

"Or part men. Other magical creatures perhaps. However, hardly anyone believes it. As soon as Bayzog acquired the staff, the Suhns' campaign against him began. They were very powerful. They ran Bayzog off. They were just not able to come to terms with him having the staff and not their cherished son. But he wouldn't have been able to use the staff anyway. It's a shame."

"Poor Bayzog," Sasha said with her head sagging. "He never told me. He was so quiet about such things."

"No, he wouldn't complain. Instead, he chose to use the staff for the benefit of all. That, he did." Inslay patted Sasha's knee. "As you well know, he was special." He turned to Samaz. "I pray that staff will serve you as well, but one never knows. Such rare items tend to have minds of their own."

"You can say that again." Nath leaned Fang against the stone. "Be sure to honor them as much as any other friends."

Laylana returned. "I've met with the council."

"That was fast. What did they say?" Nath asked.

"They would like to deliberate with you, your majesty, and you alone."

"Lead the way," he said.

With his chin resting on his skeleton hand, Brenwar grumbled, "See you when the war's over, if even that soon. Hmph."

CHAPTER 12

The Land of Dim Light. That was what people called the portal between the real world of Nalzambor and the Dark Realm where Nath's father Balzurth was.

Other life forms thrived in the Land of Dim Light. Most of them weren't really people at all. People had bodies, touchable and tangible. Instead, vaporous beings moved through the grim and bitter landscape that seemed the opposite of Nalzambor. The trees bore no leaves. There was no sun, only a distant dreary citrine-sage light for illumination.

The ground was soft dirt and brown grass. There were few colors that blossomed in the thickets and vegetation. The tree bark was harsh and gray. No birds flew among the trees. Everything lived, yet it appeared to be dead as driftwood that had washed up from the river.

Day and night—though it wasn't possible to determine which was which—evil was calling. Wailing. Shrieking. Howling. The vaporous spirits glided through the miserable world, hungry and unhappy. They sought anything they could devour in the dark and depraved lonely place. Every so often, people of flesh made it into the world. Even if they survived the torment of the spirits, they thrived little, struggling for some semblance of peace that they yearned for on Nalzambor. Banished from the world above, the ones with flesh tried to cling together.

Rip Tippy was such a man. He'd burrowed inside the hollow core of a tree to shield himself from the chronic chill in his bones. He hid from the evil threats of the spirits that roamed between one world and another. He'd been in the Land of the Dim Light for a time that was impossible to remember.

The wailing in the winds came and went. The vaporous shades, searching for flesh and meat, moved on, rustling the dry branches they passed.

Rip Tippy stepped out of his hiding place. A constant mist swirled at his feet. His haggard face displayed a beard to his chest. The color of his eyes was hard to make out on account of the strange light. He wore the armor of a legionnaire. The leather on the breast plate straps was rotting. He had one set of thigh and shin guards left. His scabbard and belt looked like something a giant moth had eaten. The pommel of a sword, appearing black in color, was still stuffed in it.

There was a ceiling of clouds thicker than smoke that rolled high overhead.

Looking up, he spoke in a voice as polished as the finest metal. "Today is the day, perhaps."

Bayzog crawled out of the core of an oak that lay on the ground. He wiped the grit from his eyes and tousled his hair, which ran down to his waistline. "If we only knew whether it was a new day or not."

"Every time we avoid those shades, it's a new day by my account. What do you make of it, Bayzog? I don't see any holes in the mist this day."

Bayzog dusted himself off even further. His robes were in worse shape than Rip Tippy's armor. The hems were torn and loose. "No, but shades are still circling this area. They know better than we when a portal is opening. Trust me, I saw it."

"By my guess, I've been here a fair bit longer than you, but I never picked up on such things. I suppose I've been wandering around like a fool all this time." Rip scratched the corner of his mouth with a fingertip exposed through a chewed-up leather glove. "I admit though, I'm glad you showed up. So many of the others I came across have been nothing but fruitless. Do you really think we can make it out of this mind-numbing Abaddon?"

"I'd have my doubts if I hadn't seen it for myself." Eyes upward, Bayzog moved through the desolate woodland. "There's always a way out of anything."

"I don't know about that, but at least you've given me something to believe in. Glad you're here, Bayzog, even though it is to your detriment."

Bayzog had been trapped in the Land of the Dim Light ever since the staagan threw the Elderwood Staff into the Well from Nowhere. The moment he landed, he had searched for the Elderwood Staff. He had soon found a part elf like himself who had taken possession of the staff. Somehow, that part elf had absorbed Bayzog's identity. A fierce battle had ensued that drew the attention of the shades. Unfamiliar with the forces in the Land of Dim Light, Bayzog had retreated in hopes of fighting again. Before he got the chance, however, his doppelganger, aided by the staff, had found a portal back to Nalzambor and escaped before the flesh-hungry shades devoured him.

That was when Rip Tippy and Bayzog, along with a few others that walked with flesh and blood, had crossed paths. They'd stayed together for a time, fleeing and surviving, then been split up. Some of them hadn't made it.

The Land of Dim Light was unending. Being so vast, there was room to find refuge from the shades. Sometimes communities were born, but they never lasted long. Bayzog spent his time getting familiar with the world. He'd finally been able to harness its unusual powers. Now, he stored up everything he had for the moment when true light within the clouds came.

"I never thought seeking out the enemy would give us the doorway we needed," Rip said. "All this time, I've just been running. I should have known better. The only way I've ever known to victory was through fighting… one way or the other."

"If we didn't fight the good fight, there would be nothing left to fight for." The ground shook beneath their feet. Bayzog's hairs stood on end.

"What in the shades was that?" Rip slowly spun in his spot, drawing his sword. "The entire world just shook."

Bayzog took cover in a cleft. Rip did the same. A humongous vapor form that crackled with energy tore through the fabric of space and time, a horrendous beast with great horns, wavering in and out. Countless shades appeared out of nowhere. They flocked to the monstrous form. Its great head lingered.

Rip's eyes bulged.

Bayzog's heart trembled.

It can't be! He's alive! Gorn Grattack!

CHAPTER 13

IT HAD BEEN TWO DAYS, and Nath still hadn't returned from his meeting with the High Council. In the meantime, everyone seemed to be making the most of it. Rerry and Ben ate heartily. The both of them enjoyed the company of the refined elven women who refilled their plates. Sasha and Samaz spent the majority of their time in Inslay's company. The elder mage was a chatterbox when it came to talking about the craft with them.

Selene sat away from the conversation, but not too far away. What Inslay had to say piqued her interest as much as any. Nibbling on a morsel of cheese, she tuned in when Sasha asked, "Inslay, does that invisible barrier encompass the whole of Elome? It must be so vast."

"Dear Sasha, as much as my pride in the elven heritage would relish taking credit for it, I fear that is not the case." He looked around. There weren't any other elves within earshot. He eased a little. "I probably shouldn't share this, the council's noses would turn inside out, but I feel compelled to share. Those barriers are not permanent. They don't surround all of Elome by any stretch of the imagination. But that's all part of the deception. The enemy believes we're surrounded by that invisible wall.

"What we have managed to do is focus our energies wherever the titan army attacks. The soldiers in the field alert the likes of me, much like they warned us of your coming. I raise the spell." He gesticulated with his hands, like he was moving pieces on a game board. "The barrier moves from spot to spot, wherever it is needed, by my power and that of many others. For the lack of a better word, it's a bluff. So far, the titan army has been ignorant enough to fall for it. It's quite a delight seeing them be so ignorant, actually."

"That is fantastic." Sasha gave Inslay a slap on the knee. "I wish Bayzog would have shared more about his past with me. I so enjoy you, Inslay."

Inslay beamed. "I feel the same."

"It's a fine idea up until the titan army spreads so vast that they can't help but penetrate." Brenwar chewed on a piece of stag jerky that he'd pestered the elves for endlessly. "Then what, magic twister? What do your people do then? Will they continue to bounce balls off the walls and their heads?"

"When the time comes, we'll fight," Inslay said. "Or die. Either way, we won't abandon our home."

"You value your precious cottages in the trees too much, Inslay," Selene said. "That's always been the folly of all the races. You can't live without your precious achievements."

"Yes, what she said," Brenwar agreed.

"I could say the same in regards to the dwarves," said Selene. "You're as stubborn as the rocks you build in."

"I hardly think—"

"No, you don't. The dragons just abandoned their home and everything in it so that they could survive and fight again. Now the elves and dwarves stew in their homes, waiting for a better day. You hope and dream that this war will just end and you won't have to lose anything. If you want freedom, then you need to be willing to give up everything. Instead, you'd rather die defending your precious baubles in the trees or the hot iron in your forge. What legacy is that? It's a legacy of extermination and foolishness."

Brenwar's lips opened then closed shut. The sanctuary hadn't been so quiet since they'd been there.

Nodding, Inslay gave Selene an easy smile. "The High Council will make the decisions, and we will follow them. I'm not saying I disagree with you, but the elves are quite particular about the order of things. I know, I've often struggled with those inflexible complications, but as it seems, the older we become, the more proud we are. But I have faith, Selene, and you should as well. Elome has stood for millennia."

"So had Dragon Home."

Nath crept into the room. "Perhaps the High Council should have had you and not me speak to them, Selene. That speech of yours was very convincing." He walked up and put his arms around her. "Miss me?"

She gave him a gentle shove. "Like a hang nail."

From the same seat he hadn't moved from in two days, Brenwar said, "Well, what did they say?"

At that moment, Rerry wandered into the room. His eyes lit up. He choked on a piece of fruit before calling out, "Ben! Ben! Dragon is back!"

Ben sauntered in accompanied by Laylana. "I know. Great news. What did they say, Dragon?"

"I asked that already," Brenwar said.

"As you know, it was a long talk. I emphatically expressed Selene's same concerns. The High Council, however, didn't see it that way. They are of the impression that the titan army is under control. We went back and forth on those points for hours." Nath shook his head. "We had to move on. I shared everything I knew with them that they should absolutely know. For their own reasons, they seem to think this war is with the dragons, and they have a point—"

"That's ludicrous, Nath!" Ben said. His cheeks reddened. "How can they say it's against the dragons when giants are stomping on their doorstep?"

"Yes, I know, I wanted to pull out my locks too, Ben, but it's their choice. Regardless, we came to an agreement on one thing. The wurmers are the biggest threat. They want the nests destroyed."

The end of Selene's tail flapped impatiently on the floor. "We all want that. Anyone with sanity would want that."

"They are willing to equip us with whatever we need to finish off those hives. Any aid they can spare, they will. They are not so set in their ways as you would think."

"It certainly sounds like they are to me," Brenwar said. "Pah, once an elf, always an overbearing, high-minded, skinny-boned elf."

"You forgot to mention pot-bellied."

Every head turned.

Shum, Hoven, and Liam filled the doorway. Someone else filled the entirety of another.

Inslay gasped, "Sansla Libor!"

Chapter 14

"What in the dim light is that?" Rip said to Bayzog. His eyes were glued to the shimmering shadow image of Gorn Grattack.

Bayzog started to speak but caught himself. "I dare not speak its name."

Gorn Grattack let out an eerie combination of roar and moan. Without warning, he sucked many shades into his mouth and devoured them. His eyes became burning beams of light, searching the landscape.

Bayzog and Rip burrowed deeper into their hiding spot. The beast's shadow came over them and hung there for many long moments. Bayzog felt his heart in his throat. Beside him, Rip had his eyes squeezed shut. The light passed.

Another disturbing growl followed. It echoed far and away.

Together, Bayzog and Rip peeked over the top of the rocky threshold.

Gorn Grattack vanished through another rip in the fabric of time and space. The remaining shades scattered.

With his face painted in sweat, Rip said, "Whew. I really thought that was the end of us. Or me at least. I've never seen anything like that prowling around here before. What was it?"

"I'm certain I know, but I dare not say."

"And you are wise for not doing so, Bayzog."

Bayzog turned and faced a vapor-like figure that boasted a subtle wreath of golden light around his face. There was warmth in the shadowy figure's radiance. His voice was rich and gentle. "Balz—"

"Hush now. There is a reason why our old enemy appeared so abruptly. He's searching for me. He's quite angry that he hasn't caught up with me—or you. Of course, he's always angry."

Rip took a knee. He bowed his head. Bayzog followed suit.

Even in spirit form, Balzurth commanded a distinguished presence. He waved his ghostly hand. "Arise, my friends. In this world, we must be one to survive."

"You live. I'm so elated." Bayzog lifted his head to find the stare of Balzurth's eyes that were fathomless pools of wisdom. "How can I serve you?"

"By getting out of this cursed worm hole. I've been on the run, much like you, since I've been here. Much like our enemy that appeared, I too must return to the Dark Realm. But I was searching whilst I ran, looking for the thread of light. Thankfully, I caught wind of you, fair Bayzog, and a more-than-suitable ally in Rip. How have you been, old friend?"

Finally lifting his head, blinking, Rip said, "Barnabus?"

"Of course."

"But how did you… how can you?" Rip stammered.

"It's a long story, and there is no time for it now. Now, you must listen. Bayzog, bury this information in your mind. Keep it safe until the time comes."

Bayzog felt the all-powerful presence enter him. His body juddered all over. The moment passed, leaving him trembling in a cold sweat, gasping.

All of a sudden, Balzurth's talon-like fingers took form. He pointed upward.

A gap of daylight appeared in the sky. The howling began. The shades were coming.

"Go now, Bayzog. Use your power. Flee to the light while you still have a chance!" Balzurth's shadowy figure faded into a rift that sucked him in from behind.

Bayzog locked his grip on Rip's wrist. He drew forth all of his power, sprouted the wings of an eagle, and soared toward the skylight.

The moaning shades converged on him.

"Keep going, Bayzog! I can handle them!" Rip swung his long sword into the vapor-like spirits. The metal bit into them like flesh. At its touch, each howling shade burst into wisps of smoke.

Bayzog felt the icy touch of bony hands tearing at his clothing and digging into his ribs. He channeled everything he had left into his wings and rocketed toward the skylight.

Rip hacked and stabbed. A shade burst into smoke every time he hit.

Pffi! Pffi! Pffi! Pffi!

Claws tore at Bayzog's face and wrist.

"Don't you let go of me, Bayzog! Don't you let go!" Rip stabbed another shade. "Ever!"

Bayzog hit the light that shined in the bottom of a huge well. The shades screeched with fury and agony. They fell from his body, evaporating in the darkness below. With the wind in his ears, he emerged, flying out of the well into the rays of the bright orange sun and the gaping faces of the staagan. The brawny antler men bowed the moment Bayzog's feet touched the ground.

On his knees, Rip threw his arms up in triumph. Face to the sun, he screamed, "I'm out! I'm out! I can't believe it!"

Bayzog kissed the ground.

Rip jumped to his feet and brandished his sword at the staagan. "You foolish men with the brains of chipmunks! You threw me in there. I swore if I ever got out, I'd turn you into venison!"

The staagan reared up. With startling speed, each and every one vanished into the brightly colored folds of the forest. They left a bound-up man behind. The man wriggled in his bonds.

Sheathing his sword, Rip said, "What's this, another sacrifice?" Wary, he pushed the man over onto his back. "You're awfully odd looking for a man." He pulled the gag from the man's mouth.

The pie-faced man was older, with curly hair turning gray. He spat on the ground, "I'm not a man. I'm a halfling. My name's Pepper."

CHAPTER 15

"SANSLA, ALL OF YOU, IT'S great to see you!" Nath went to each and every one of them, shaking hands and patting backs. The roamers showed the rugged appearance of the durable outdoorsmen they were. Not a one of them was unscathed. "It appears Nalzambor's strikes have not been in vain."

"The peril is worth the price. We live." Sansla gave a quick bow. "It does my heart well to see you among us, your majesty. As I understand it, your valiant efforts were costly."

"That's an understatement. Please, roamers, sit and refresh yourselves. I must admit I am more than surprised to see you, here of all places."

"The Elven High Council and I have come to an agreement, given the circumstances. I'm a bit surprised myself, but here I am." Sansla didn't sit, but the others did. Liam started nibbling at the tray of food. "For the first time in decades, the roamers are welcome here."

"You seem confident of this. It does my heart well, Sansla. You were never deserving of the judgment you received," Nath said, referring to Sansla's past.

Sansla was the roamer king and one of the rightful heirs to the throne of Elome. A curse had fallen upon him, turning him from elf to winged ape. Innocent blood had been shed by what was believed to have been his hands. There was still a lack of clarity about the incident to this day.

"Since you and I parted ways, Nath, I've been on the same mission that Grahleyna sent me on. We've scoured the dying lands of Nalzambor searching out the wurmer nests. We've located them all. Two of them I've seen destroyed: one along with Selene and the other in the sea cliffs above the Dragon Pond. The other three—"

"Two," Selene corrected Sansla. "Nath and I were able to take down another when we escaped the Deep. It was in the mountains where the caps are covered in ice and snow to the west."

Sansla's blue eyes widened. "This is wonderful news. That leaves only two. One is north of Thraag. It appears the entire degenerate race guards it."

"You can say that again," Liam said, taking a bite of apple.

"Hear, hear," Brenwar agreed.

"The last one is tucked in near the Ruins of Barnabus."

"Are you certain? We destroyed one in that very area," Selene said.

"Yes, but this one is another dark gem guarded by giants the likes of which I've never seen before."

Sansla's wings expanded in and out a little. "The enemies in both locations are countless. The titan army continues to swell everywhere. Giant men now populate among the races. We need an army to greet them at every location. We don't have as many bodies as they."

Rubbing his forehead, Nath said, "We'll find a way. We don't have a choice."

"The roamers are here to serve, as always," Sansla said.

"Perhaps we should focus our efforts on one nest at a time. A large force to distract them, while a smaller group slips through their ranks," Nath said.

Brenwar picked up his war hammer. "It sounds like a fine idea to me. Lead the way, pot bellies."

Liam glared at Brenwar.

Clasped fingers resting on his stomach, Shum eyed his son. "Let it go. Brenwar is old and forgets himself. His insults, though at one time stinging, I now find refreshing."

"It builds thicker skin. Life's hard. You need it," Brenwar said to Liam.

"Nath, I'd be willing to lead a force to destroy one of the lairs while you lead another," Selene offered. "I feel that putting all of us in one place is a dangerous thing."

"The risk will be high no matter the path we take, but I concur, even though I hate to divide our forces." He searched the faces in the room. "And I don't believe all of us need to go. Some of us need to stay behind and assist the elves."

Rerry stood up. "I'm going. Don't you dare think you're leaving me behind. No offense, but this is not my home. My home is out there, among you."

Samaz stood up, staff in hand. "I agree."

Sasha joined them. "Where they go, I go."

"I take it everyone in the room, except our hosts, is determined to come? The problem is, with so many, it will be challenging to get us all out." Nath tapped his claws on the table. "I'll have to think on this. Laylana, Inslay, Selene, will you accompany me?"

They briefly looked at each other and followed him out of the room.

"What is it, your majesty?"

"I'd like a full view from the top of the grand trees. I need to see what you're seeing. I need perspective."

"Certainly." Laylana led the way through the streets, which had quieted now that dusk had come and gone. They made it to the bottom of a white oak tree with cherry leaves, wider than a dam. They moved inside, where soldiers waited by a round platform built like a giant bird cage. Long ropes higher than the eye could see were attached to a network of pulleys. They all stepped inside. In Elven, Laylana said, "Upward."

Elven laborers dressed in sky-blue and light-brown clothing each grabbed a rope. Hand over hand they pulled. Up the cage went, toward the top of the tree. At the top, hundreds of feet high, they came to a stop. Stepping out on the platform among the branches, they made their way to a balcony. It gave them a full view of the lands beyond.

Nath's keen eyes made out hundreds of the titan army's campfires. They had the entirety of Elome surrounded. "How did you see us when we came?"

"I'll show you." Inslay waved over one of the lookout sentries posted on the balcony. The lookout had a huge spyglass crossed over his chest. "I'll take that." Inslay offered the spyglass to Nath.

Nath put it to his eye. The magnification was unbelievable. Wherever he looked, the spyglass automatically focused. He could see the wart on a distant orc's nose as easily as the scales on Selene, who stood next to him. He searched beyond. He could see west for leagues. "This is fantastic. It's no wonder you saw us coming. It's quite an enchantment."

"Even better so for you, I imagine, as it amplifies the sight of its bearer. With your dragon vision, I imagine you can see three times farther than the elves can."

"It's probably ten times farther, but who's really paying attention?"

Selene gave him a slap. "Don't be a braggart."

"I can't help that I see well." Nath's smile faded. "Uh-oh."

"What?" Selene said

"Blast my great sight, but more titan army troops are coming this way. Whoa, that's a big force."

"How big?" Laylana asked. "May I see?"

Nath handed her the spyglass. While she looked, he rubbed his eyes. Squinting, he looked back the way he'd been watching before. He leaned outward on the rail. "I can't see them now."

"I can't see anyone at all either. Are you sure you saw them?"

"Plain as day—and it's night."

"I believe you, Nath Dragon," Inslay said with excitement. "It's possible you saw more than what can be seen."

"What do you mean?" Nath asked.

Selene borrowed the spyglass from Laylana. "I don't see anything either. If he can see it, I should be able to see it too. My vision is better than his."

"I doubt that," Nath said. "May I see the glass again?"

She handed it over.

Nath gave another look. "They're gone. I swear I saw them as plain as the nose on my face. This is troubling."

"My, the Eyes of Wolach have revealed their unique power," Inslay said with glee. "I believe you've seen the future."

Nath closed the spyglass. "If that's the case, I'll tell you this much, the future is starkly grim for the elves."

CHAPTER 16

In great detail, Nath described the oncoming army he'd seen to the Elven High Council. Shortly thereafter, he was dismissed and returned to his friends.

The core of Elome buzzed with newly purposed activity. Elven soldiers armed with everything from spears to swords and long bows took to the expansive fields. Within a few hours, they'd completely surrounded the heart of Elome by the thousands.

Nath waited in the fields where the dragons they had brought waited. He had Laylana and all of the others with him. Elven leather workers measured the dragons who were big enough to ride from head to tail with lengths of string.

Laylana stroked a copper dragon's neck. The copper dragon licked her face with her black tongue. "How many saddles should we make? One for each of them?" she said to Nath.

"That and more."

"More? Why?"

"Just make them adjustable," Nath said, speaking to one of the tanners. "You're going to need all the help you can get in case there's an evacuation."

"I thought we were going to be taking to the air and fighting against the wurmers."

"Have you ever flown on a dragon before?"

"No."

"Well, it's not any easier than riding a horse. And if you fall off, it's typically a long, long way down."

Laylana's eyes grew. "I just assumed, since the others made it, that we elves could manage."

"That was a short flight." He gave her a punch in the arm. "Don't worry, you and your people will figure it out when the time comes. After all, you don't have a choice."

Inside their sanctuary, Brenwar opened the war chest before all present. "Take what you need," he said to Ben and Rerry, both of whom were particularly wide-eyed. Ben's mouth watered. He stretched out his hand.

Brenwar slapped it away. "Don't get drool all over it. That's disgusting. It's not a pork chop."

Ben and Rerry rummaged through the chest. They grabbed vials and stuffed them into their pockets and sleeves. There was a ring and a small folded blanket. Ben took them both. Rerry grabbed a small dagger. "What's this?"

"A pointy blade," Brenwar said. "Are you finished?"

Rerry and Ben looked at one another. "I suppose," Ben said.

With a grunt, Brenwar closed the chest. He stuffed it into Samaz's arms. "Don't lose it, now. I have to go."

"Go? What do you mean?" Ben said. "You aren't sliding out with Dragon, are you?"

"I'm just going into the next room. I've got a letter to write."

Rerry and Ben laughed.

"Write? You? Are you certain you want to fool with a quill? You could put your eye out with it."

He stuck his skeleton finger in Ben's face. "Or I could just put your eye out. Now behave yourself."

Brenwar moved into a small alcove that served as a study. Rolls of parchment, a quill, and ink lay on the table. He sat down, picked up the quill, and dipped it into the small jar of ink. He started to write.

GLENWAR,

There comes a time in every dwarf's life when he knows the end is near…

CHAPTER 17

NATH MET WITH EVERYONE BACK inside the sanctuary. "Now that we are within, we just need to find a safe exit. Sansla, how did you circumvent the titan army—aside from the obvious fact you are roamers who typically slide by just about anything?"

"The dwarves aren't the only people with roads beneath the land. The subterranean levels of Elome are a well-kept secret."

"This I have to see," said Brenwar.

"I'll see you out." Laylana got up.

"We both will," added Inslay.

"I'm grateful, but I find it difficult to abandon you at the critical time, Laylana. I'd feel more comfortable if I were able to leave you with friends among you." He eyed several of his friends. Most of them were looking away. "I don't suppose there will be any volunteers, however, to keep an eye on things."

Not an eye was to be found gazing at him. Nath didn't like it. He didn't feel comfortable leaving the elves to themselves. He felt he needed someone there to keep an eye on things. The elves had been cooperative—maybe a little too much so. It gnawed at him.

"To be truthful, I'd feel better if some of you stayed within the safety of the elven realm. It would give me comfort to see you do so."

No one said a word.

"I could order you to do so."

"And we wouldn't listen," said Ben. "Sorry, but we're in this to the end—even though it pains me a little to leave this place. It's quite cozy here among the elves. Perhaps when it's over, I'll bring my family and settle down here, if they'll let me. I think Margo would like it."

"You can have it if there's anything left." Brenwar looked over at Laylana. "Lead the way. I'm curious about these gopher holes you dug. It won't surprise me one bit if it collapses on us."

The tunnel entrance was big and high enough to walk a herd of elephants through. Great beams of ash wood held up the tunnel walls and ceilings, much like the work one would see in mineral mines, but bigger. They all stood in a juncture where there were four tunnels in separate directions.

"This is impressive." Nath cast his glance from one mouth to the other. "I never suspected."

"The elves have made plenty of contingencies over the centuries. It's why the orcs never get an upper hand on us. We're always a league ahead of them," Inslay said.

Inside the junction, Sansla reunited with a larger group of roamers. There was also another group of elven soldiers about a hundred strong, all armed to the teeth in elven steel and wearing woodland battle garb.

"Who are they, Laylana?" Nath asked.

"Elven forces, at your service."

"To be frank, Laylana, the smaller our group, the better. I appreciate it, but you'll need them here."

"I'm sorry to say it, Nath, but they are sworn to accompany you at all costs." She clasped his hands. "Do me this honor and take them? They are some of Elome's finest."

"Thank you. Sansla, you take your group. I'll take mine."

They divvied up two satchels filled with orbs of destruction that the elves had crafted for them.

"We're splitting up then?" Selene said. "Are any of us accompanying Sansla?"

"There's no need," Sansla said, "though I appreciate the offer."

"Certainly you'll need spellcasting at your disposal?" Selene recommended.

Sansla had a second satchel strapped over his shoulder. He opened the flap and reached inside, removing a gemstone so brilliant it bathed the entire underground in light. Many shielded their eyes. "Behold, the Occular of Orray. It shall protect us." He put it back inside the satchel. His blue eyes slid over to the mouth of one of the tunnels. "We'll head north, to the hive near Thraag."

"Take fifty of Elome's finest with you, Sansla," Nath said. "And him." A tiny dragon with royal-blue scales that shimmered like metal crawled out from under Nath's hair and rested on his shoulder. "This seeker will be a go-between for us if needed. Take care of him, Sansla."

The seeker jumped onto Sansla's shoulder and nestled in his hair.

Sansla departed with his roamers and fifty more elves.

"We'll go west then, toward the ruins of Barnabus. How far do these tunnels go, Laylana?"

"More than half a league. Good speed, Nath Dragon."

"Once I get out, I'll send what aid I can. These tunnels can be a vehicle to victory or retreat. I hope you make use of them wisely."

"We will."

Nath motioned to the elven soldier in command of the small force. He was the only one in an almond-shaped helmet made from tanned leather. "Lead the way."

The elven commander gave a bow. "Yes, your majesty."

With a nod of his head, half of the remaining elven force marched quietly into the tunnel. Nath and his full company followed after them, with the second half of the elven force in the rear. It left him with a boxed-in feeling. Brenwar continued to look over his shoulder. He glanced up at Nath a couple of times.

Selene found his eyes more than once too. She whispered in his ear, "Do you have a strange feeling about this, or am I the only one?"

"I can't imagine we're about to be betrayed."

"Yes, but things are moving along a bit too perfectly."

"Agreed. Be ready."

CHAPTER 18

"PEPPER?" BAYZOG SAID. "I KNOW that name."

"Well you should," Pepper said. Rip cut his bonds away. Pepper dusted himself off and rubbed his wrists. "Now, what was I saying? Oh yes, you should know me. I'm Pepper, halfling extraordinaire."

"No, that's not why I know your name. Nath Dragon spoke of you."

"Who?"

"I'm fairly certain you'd remember Nath Dragon if you saw him."

Rip lay in the grass rolling back and forth, laughing in glee. "I can't believe I'm out! I can't believe it! After all these, well, I'm not sure how long it's been, but I'm free!" He sat up and pulled a daisy and blew out the seeds. "Oh, I can't wait to get back to Quintuklen. I'm going to feed on plates stacked up to my eyes. You're free, halfling. I suggest you let those little legs of yours take you as far as they can from here. You don't want to wind up in that pit."

Rubbing the thick patch of gray hair on his head, Pepper strolled over to the well. He pushed up on his tiptoes.

Bayzog grabbed him by the collar and hauled him back.

"Hey!" Pepper objected. "I'm my own halfling. There's no need to be tugging me by the shirt like I'm some child. I've lived eighty years, you know."

"That makes you a child in my eyes," Bayzog said. "I'm far past the century mark."

"Oh," Pepper said, noting Bayzog's eyes. "A part elf. How exciting. Well, see you around."

Bayzog held the small man fast. "What did the staagan want with you?"

"I don't know. I was just making my way through on the thunder beard when they came. The next thing I knew, I was bound up like a ham for feasting."

"I'll tell you why they snatched him. They're insane, that's why!" Rip came to his feet. He was an imposing man in his battered legionnaire armor and had a strong jawline. "We were having a polite conversation when they put the net on me. I was in the midst of a hunting celebration after the war. Never hunt alone. I won't do that again. At least not in these woods. My victorious celebration became a nightmare."

Still holding Pepper fast, Bayzog asked, "What war are you talking about?"

"What war? Why the war of all wars. The war against the black dragons." Rip patted his sword pommel. "I fought right alongside Barnabus himself, I did. Steel in hand. Hordes of evil over our heads." He paused. "How did Barnabus wind up down in that pit? It was him, yet it wasn't. He had claws. I don't remember him having claws."

"Who is this Nath Dragon fella you talk about?" Pepper asked. "I don't know any …oh, wait a moment. Is he that golden-eyed fellow with flame-red hair? He's a crafty one, that one is. He killed giants and made us move from one side of the world to another."

"You're talking about Barnabus," Rip argued.

"No, I speak of the man called Nath, I think. Can I go now? I have a family that needs feeding."

"And I'm heading back to Quintuklen. I'm most certain my family misses me." Rip rushed into the forest.

"Rip, I think we need to clear a few things up. The dragon war you speak about, well, that was over five hundred years ago."

Rip whirled around. He drew his sword. "You lie!"

"I wish that were the case. Which begs the question: if you've been gone for centuries, then how long have I been gone? Pepper, tell me, when was the last time you saw Nath Dragon?"

Pepper shrugged. "I don't know. Life is so hazy these days. A decade, I suppose. No, wait! No, I'm not sure."

Bayzog's spirits sank.

The color in Rip's cheeks vanished. He sheathed his sword. "If I've been gone so long, I need to see it for myself. I must. You coming?"

"I think at this juncture, it's best we stay together. Pepper, you're coming with us." Bayzog glanced back at the well. It was a gateway to other worlds that were dark and dangerous. It needed destroying. But for now, it was the only way to save Balzurth. The Dragon King had given him a mission to find Nath. He would do just that.

"I don't have my bearings, Rip. Are you still familiar with this land?"

"Like it was yesterday. Quintuklen, then?"

"Yes, but mind you, there are forces here now the likes of which you've never seen before. Giants roam the world like men."

"Giants, eh? I'd be more than happy to stick my steel in them. But I'd rather find something decent to eat first."

Following Rip's lead, they maneuvered through the woodland for miles before they slipped out of the woods and onto the steppes. The air was chilly. Snow dusted the grass field. A brown road wound north like a snake.

"The landscape has not changed," Rip said. "I find it comforting. That road is the same one I've known since I was a boy. Perhaps your summations are in error."

The road had deep ruts in it. Footprints in the grasses were huge. Rip was down on one knee. "No, you're right about the giants. There are many. Thousands have passed over this road recently. A full army. I thought the war of wars would have ended them all."

"War will never end so long as the hearts of the races are wicked," Bayzog said. "I'm not certain war will ever be eradicated. Not on Nalzambor, anyway."

"If we were all halflings, life would be better. We would desire quiet and peaceful lives."

A rumble caught Bayzog's ears.

Rip's eyes enlarged where he squatted.

A host of soldiers clad in armor and riding giant horses thundered down the road toward them.

"Not those things again," Pepper said.

Bayzog kneeled. "You don't think they've seen us, do you?"

Rip pulled his blade. "I fear they have."

Chapter 19

"We are almost at the end of the tunnel," the elven commander said to Nath. "I thought you should know that."

"I was starting to wonder. Thank you for your service, Eslin. I am honored."

"I'll make no bones about it, your majesty, it's an honor. I've looked forward to the day when I'd fight alongside the dragons once more." Eslin was a middle-aged elf with a seasoned look about him. He had the calloused hands of a weathered veteran.

"Am I to take it that you were in the last dragon war, or the one before that?"

"I was of early age in the Great Dragon War. Back then I could have sworn the world was about to fall around us. It was an ugly thing. But there stood Barnabus, taking the world on his shoulders, bold and fearless. You bear a remarkable resemblance to him, your unique armor aside."

"I've heard that."

The elves forged ahead at a quick pace until the tunnel narrowed into a smaller pipeline. Shoulder to shoulder, the small force pushed through. It opened up behind a waterfall.

Half a score of elves were already there and waiting.

"Guardians of the pipeline," Eslin said to Nath. "They protect our secret."

"Well done. I never would have guessed."

Nath followed Eslin and his men up a ridge of rocks that traversed by the river up into the woodland. They were well beyond the boundaries of elven land. Tall treetops stood between them and the distant Elome.

"We've got a long journey ahead of us toward the ruins of Barnabus. We should make haste, and I'd prefer to fly."

Selene took him by the arm. "Don't you dare fly off and leave us down here. You'll draw trouble to us. Be patient."

"The titan army's forces are growing, Selene. We need to know what we're dealing with. I need to keep the elves apprised."

"And how do you propose to do that? You can't be two places at once."

Another seeker crawled out of Nath's hair and onto his shoulder. The little dragon was bright green.

Selene's eyes lit up. She stroked the head of the little beast. "They are so rare. Where are they coming from?"

"Wherever I want. They've become very fond of me, and I of them. Aren't they adorable?"

"I've never seen one who wasn't."

Nath hung back with Selene while all the others headed into the wintery landscape.

"You have more up your scales, don't you, Nath."

"Let's just say I'm a lot more connected now than I once was. I can sense things in nature. I can hear the dragons hidden among the reeds. They respond to me now. Our forces are gathering, but I need to get word out to Grahleyna, wherever she may be. A seeker is after her now, and Slivver of course. I need to take to the air. I won't be long."

"I cannot deny you, but I can complain."

Nath noticed Brenwar hanging back from the others. He had a scroll in his skeleton fist. With his eyes closed, he spoke to the scroll in Dwarven. The scroll transformed into a large leaf. The wind picked up and took the leaf from Brenwar's open hands and carried it into the air—up, up, up, and out of sight.

Brenwar caught Nath and Selene staring at him. "My business. Let's go."

"I didn't realize you had a knack for spellcasting," Selene said.

"I don't. That's something from the chest. I sent word to Morgdon, if you must know." Brenwar stopped between them. He looked up at them both and moved on, saying, "Let him fly, Selene. That's what he has wings for."

Nath gave the emerald-green seeker a nudge. The little dragon darted into the air. Nath hung around a bit longer, walking with Selene. "I'll let the seeker check things out before I take to the sky. Will that make you more comfortable?"

"It's not you flying, it's me not flying." Selene ground her teeth. "I want to fly with you."

"It will come in time, Selene."

"Just go. I'll keep an eye on things down here."

Nath's wings began to spread. He stopped. "Selene, if anything happens to me, you need to see this through. Finish off the wurmer hole. If we defeat those demons, we can win this."

"Yes, well, they are only a fraction of the world that has turned its way from sanity on account of the spirits." She tilted her head. Nath gave her a soft kiss on the cheek. "Don't be gone long, Nath. A few hours at most."

"I'll return before night." He took to the air and saw Rerry and Ben waving from below. Wings beating, he circled a few times, then soared into the bottom of the clouds. He could see for miles now. The path to the west toward the Ruins of Barnabus seemed clear. They'd have to traverse the mountain range just north of Morgdon. It would make a long trip, even on swift feet.

Bright flecks twinkling in the sky caught his eye. The seeker was among those lights, flying in a zigzag pattern trying to lose the strange lights.

"That's not good. Anyone can see those lights, from the ground or the sky." Nath gave chase.

The swarm of radiant lights corralled the seeker toward the ground. All the lights vanished into snowy treetops.

Nath crashed through the branches, catching sight of the lights that surrounded the grounded seeker. The little dragon lay on the ground, squirming. His arms and feet were bound up with magical webbing.

The lights encircled the seeker. The colorful forms revealed their lithe little foot-long bodies.

"Fairies!"

"Not just any fairies, but my fairies," said a seductive voice.

Nath turned. "Lotuus!"

CHAPTER 20

"BY THE HILLS OF QUINTUKLEN, those are big horses," Rip said to Bayzog. There were five one-eyed orcs, huge in their saddles. They rode massive horse-like beasts. "What are those creatures riding them? Are those orcs? I never imagined they could be bigger and uglier."

"They are the nuurg," Bayzog replied, brushing his hair over his ears. "An abomination of giant and mankind. They are one of the many forms of corruption in this world." Bayzog held the gaze of the leading nuurg.

The nuurg leader lifted his hand. They came to a stop thirty yards away. The ram-horned horses called wrath horns snorted. They clawed their spiked hooves at the ground. Their harness jangled when they let out frightening whinnies.

"I don't suppose they're on our side," Rip said.

"No."

"I won't lie. I'm itching for a fight. It's been a long time since I sank my steel into an enemy of flesh and blood. I just figured I'd be able to warm up first. I hate fighting on an empty stomach." He patted his mail-covered tummy. "A hot meal first would have been nice. Bayzog, I hope you have some tricks up your sleeve. I'm going to need help with this."

"Lay down your arms," Bayzog suggested. "Let's see what they do."

"I'm a legionnaire. I don't surrender."

"I'm all for running," Pepper said. He was curled up in a bed of grass out of the nuurg's sight. "My legs may be short, but I can run fast. The willowwacks shall provide me with the cover I need. They won't find me there. You, maybe."

"Halfling, you won't make it to the woodland before they do. Just be still, I'll handle this. Perhaps we can parlay with them." Bayzog lifted his hands. At the same time, his fingers and lips moved the slightest bit.

The nuurg riders approached. The wrath horns moved in long strides. In seconds, they encircled the small group. Pepper shivered. Rip held his sword low. Bayzog remained exposed.

In front of Bayzog, the nuurg leader lowered his spear. His single eye narrowed beneath his thick eyebrow. He wore a full suit made up from plate mail and chain. Dragon scales strung like a necklace hung from his neck. Sweaty nostrils flaring, he spoke in Common. "You look lost, little people. Explain."

"No, just unfortunate. We travel to Narnum, to serve. We crossed some strange beasts in the willowwacks. We barely escaped with our lives."

The nuurg nodded. "I see. Describe these so-called beasts."

"They were tremendous brutes. Antlered men. Powerfully built. We managed to outwit them."

The nuurg laughed. His men joined in. "You speak in fables." He sniffed the air. "You have a strange scent about you." He stood in his stirrups. He spied Pepper. "Ah, a halfling. They make fine dinners. We are a day hungry."

Pepper clutched the grasses. He started to shake out of control.

"This one is old and sick, as you can see. He trembles from fever."

"He trembles from fear, liar." The nuurg stretched out his spear. With a nimble touch, he moved Bayzog's hair aside, revealing his ear. "You are a portion of elf, I see. Very tender meat." He withdrew the spear and stared down Rip. "That's a legionnaire insignia on your shoulder. I suppose you're traveling to serve the titans as well."

Rip gestured toward Bayzog. "I serve him. He saved me, now I owe a debt to him."

"Saved you? Interesting." The nuurg commander scratched the back of his head. "So, he saved you from those staagan, did he? We hunt those crafty people. They make a tasty meal. If this portion of an elf saved you from them, he must be quite formidable. Is that so?"

"I would say he's crafty," Rip said, looking at Bayzog with uncertainty. "A quick thinker."

"Thinking is dangerous. The titans don't care for it." The nuurg tugged the reins. The wrath horn turned. He spoke a command in Orcen. "*Gizzlit*!"

Bayzog knew Orcen as well as any tongue. "*Gizzlit*" was Orcen for "Kill them."

The nuurg riders dropped the tips of their spears. The one nearest Rip took a poke at him.

Rip cut the spear top off with his sword. "I knew talking wouldn't do us a lick of good! The only thing orcs respond to is death!" Moving with fluid skill, he rushed by the lowered head of a wrath horn. With a quick stab, he punctured it in the neck.

The beast reared up. Its rider tumbled to the ground.

Rip pounced on the humongous man. He ran his sword through the nuurg's heart.

A nuurg rider whipped his horned steed around. He charged Rip with the spear tip, ready to gore the man.

Rip jumped aside. The spear bit into the back of his thigh. "Gah!"

Bayzog flicked his fingers in the sky.

Two nuurg riders were ripped from their saddles and tossed high into the air.

The nuurg commander watched his men go up, higher and higher. With a twist of his great neck, he leered at Bayzog. "You!" Spear in hand, he cocked his arm back. "Die, deceiver!"

Bayzog stood on flat feet. His energy was spent. He swayed. All he could do was focus on the impending doom about to befall him. The nuurg's spear would go through three of him, if not more.

A startling sound sent shockwaves through the highlands.

"MAAAROOOOOOOOOOOG!"

The wrath horns reared up.

Bayzog fell.

The nuurg leader fought his reins and shouted commands in Orcen. He turned the beast toward Bayzog and snapped the reins, charging right at him.

Rip knocked Bayzog clear of the wrath horn's path. The veteran soldier jumped to his feet. He chased after the nuurg commander.

The nuurg turned his beast for a second charge.

Rip grabbed the harness and swung himself up into the saddle. He crushed the nuurg's nose with the pommel of his sword. Both of the fighters fell from the saddle. The nuurg landed on top of Rip.

Bayzog found himself with the last nuurg that had fallen from the saddle.

The nuurg charged with a spear.

Out of the sky, a nuurg fell on top of the one charging. Bone snapped.

The other nuurg hit the grass with a loud *wump*. None of the three moved.

Winded, Bayzog spied Rip.

The nuurg commander had the legionnaire pinned down with one hand. He punched Rip with the other. The heavy blows landed with jarring impact.

"MAAAAROOOOOOOOOG!"

The nuurg commander's back arched. He covered his ears.

Sword in hand, Rip sat up and stabbed the nuurg in the chest. He pushed the humanoid far bigger than he aside. His face was swollen and bloody. Using his sword for a cane, he stood. He limped over to Bayzog and helped him up.

"I'm the one who should be helping you, friend."

Rip laughed. "It's a grand day to be alive, isn't it?" He stuck his sword in the air and yelled at the top of his lungs, then fell down.

Pepper appeared on the back of a pony-sized bearded dragon. A big smile was on his face. He patted his wingless dragon's head. "Look, my thunder beard has returned. His timing is excellent, is it not?"

Sitting up on his elbows with a grimace, Rip said, "I could handle them. The bigger the orc, er, well, the more likely I'm going to kill them." His eyes rolled up into his head. He fell backward.

Bayzog leapt to his side. "Rip!"

Pepper rode over on the back of the thunder beard. "He looks bad. It's probably from the wounds that he suffered."

"That's a brilliant assessment."

"I know of something that can help. I saw it in the woodland. It's a root the halflings call moonsky. It will perk him up." With a nod, Pepper rode off into the woods. He didn't look back.

Bayzog had a feeling the halfling wouldn't be back. *Pepper is a strange person.*

"Guh, what happened?" Rip said out of his busted lips.

"You hit the nuurg's fists too many times with your face, I think. Can you walk?"

"A thousand leagues if I have to. Help me up."

Using both hands, Bayzog put his back into lifting the much bigger man.

"Where did that halfling go?" Rip asked.

"I think he travels far from danger."

"Well, I would too if I was trained to know better." Rip reached behind his leg that was gored. "Aw, will you look at that. My trousers are ruined. I can't walk around looking like this. Can we stop somewhere and get some new ones?'

"Certainly, let's find some shelter and stitch you up first." With a good deal of Rip's weight on him, they hobbled down the road the nuurg had come on.

CHAPTER 21

LOTUUS SAT ON A FALLEN dogwood tree, radiant as a rainbow. Her black eyes had a gleam to them. Her smile of bright-white teeth would freeze the marrow of a common man. Legs crossed and hands placed politely on her knees, she said, "Are you happy to see me?"

"The murderer of my friends Laedorn and Uurluuk? 'Happy' is the last word I'd use. 'Fortunate' might work, perhaps." He slid Fang out of the new sheath the elves had made for him. It fit perfectly between his wings. "Perhaps you came to give yourself up for execution. It's long overdue, Fairy Empress."

"Please, Nath, you wouldn't kill a woman as lovely as me. You like me. You know it. That's why you freed me."

"If I'd known you were in that tomb, you would still be there."

"Yet your father led you there, did he not?"

"What happened did happen for a good cause." He looked at the emerald seeker, who was still pinned to the ground. "Let him go."

"Why would I do that?"

"Because I demand it!"

Lotuus shrank back. She swallowed. With a quick motion, the fairies loosened the mystic webbing. Many of them kissed the little dragon a moment before he took off. "Are you appeased, young majesty?"

"Out with it, Lotuus. What do you want? You're far too arrogant to surrender, but that would be the advisable path if you want mercy."

"I stewed in that tomb for a thousand years, Nath Dragon. A thousand!" Her wings buzzed. She tossed her gossamer-like hair. "I simmered!" She took a deep breath. "But I've had time to mull things over since I've been back. In truth, I find myself viewing my actions from a new perspective."

"Are you telling me you have regrets?"

"A few. Nath, as delicious as making trouble is, I believe I've seen the error of my ways."

Nath stuck his sword in the ground. He held his hands over the dragonhead cross-guard. "Have you now? Do tell."

"Well, we are fairies, well known for our mischief. And we can't help but be drawn to power. I have to admit, I find Eckubahn entirely fascinating. The size, his brawn, and the cunning." She wagged her finger at Nath. "He is many steps ahead of you, Nath Dragon. The entire world is under his spell. He's magnetic."

"Yes, I've seen the oversized coward. The two of you make quite a pair. He wears his skin of evil on the outside, whereas yours is turned inward. So out with it, Lotuus. What do you want from me?"

"When it's over, I want freedom. I don't want to be stuck in that tomb again."

"You speak as if I've won this war. It's far from over."

She floated up into the air. Eye to eye, she said, "Your resiliency is astonishing. I've never seen the likes of it before. You took down Isobahn. You survived the molten flame. Your friends love you. I long for adoration like that, but I'll never have it. You are truly good. It changes people. I want you to win. I don't know why, but I do want that. But Nath, you cannot beat Eckubahn without my help."

"I suppose this is where I'm supposed to offer you a pass in exchange for your knowledge."

"Exactly."

Nath tilted his head. He needled his chin. "You're a murderer, Lotuus."

"My actions were by order. It was an act of war. Laedorn and Uurluuk were casualties."

"No, the way I see it, you killed them in cold blood. That's different. And I believe you acted not out of orders but rather out of malice. I can see right through you, Lotuus. Your heart is as black as your eyes."

She sneered. "Don't you dare talk to me like that, you pup! I am the Fairy Empress, and I—"

"And I am the Dragon King!"

Lotuus blanched.

"I tell you what, Lotuus. I'm going to show you grace today. I'm going to let you leave my presence alive rather than turn you into ash. When you go back to your master, you be sure and tell him I say his days are numbered. I'm coming for him."

Lotuus's jaw dropped. Her words became cross. "How dare you! You arrogant, bloated black lizard!"

Nath took to the sky, laughing when he heard what she said next.

"I gave you a chance, Nath Dragon! I gave you a chance! It's more than you deserve! I hate you, Nath Dragon! I hate you all!"

CHAPTER 22

NATH HUNG INSIDE THE FEATHERY folds of the snow clouds.

Hundreds of feet below him, a flock of wurmers sailed through the air. One as big as a bull dragon led the pack. The chronic *ree-rah* sound they made was disturbing and loud. It was the second time in the day that he'd seen the evil brood scouring the skies.

I should destroy them, take them out one at a time. No, they'll just keep breeding.

It was pretty clear that despite the victory at Dragon Home, the fight was far from over. The wurmers, even with three of the five nests destroyed, continued to multiply. The dragons were scattered and in hiding. Nath didn't know where his mother was. He needed more dragons but feared to call out for them.

That was where the seekers came in. He'd made a strong bond with the fantastic little creatures. They were out searching for more dragons. But there was a danger. Though super fast, the seekers were also fragile. If they were caught, they would die.

Nath continued west toward the ruins, farther than he had initially planned to go. He should have returned to Selene and the others by now.

She's going to be mad. Aw, I'd probably make her mad even if I was there. Hopefully, the little seeker I dispatched will win her over.

Nath picked up speed, shooting through the air like a black arrow with a flaming head. He didn't stop until dawn. He landed on a crag high in the hills, forgotten by most of the western lands. The temple ruin of Barnabus stood stark in the morning mist miles away. A tremendous ziggurat of rectangular stone built hundreds of feet high, it looked close to a mile long at the base. Smaller temples surrounded it. They all had multiple levels. On each level, wurmers were perched. In addition to them were men, orcs, ogres, nuurg, and giants, all guarding the walls.

Sansla wasn't exaggerating. If anything, they've doubled their forces since he came by. There's over a thousand of them. That nest wouldn't be more heavily fortified if it were in Morgdon!

Nath's chest tightened. His heart raced. It would take an army bigger than the one on the tremendous stone walls to take it down. The siege would last for months, possibly years. Eckubahn wasn't a fool. He'd planned well, had realized that so long as even one wurmer nest thrived, he'd be unstoppable.

A plume of infant wurmers burst out of an open mouth at the top of the structure, following a sizable one into the sky. There were at least a hundred of them in all. Their ugly wings beat against the stiff winds. They soared east, right over Nath, who stood hundreds of feet below them.

Nath remained in his position for hours, watching the army on the walls.

During that time, two more flocks of a hundred wurmers each departed from the nest.

There are so many.

He unsheathed Fang and took a knee. He closed his eyes and began to visualize himself penetrating the veil of evil that guarded the walls of the ziggurat. Should he fight his way through or just sneak inside was the question.

Fang, if you have any suggestions, I'll take them.

He was tempted to have Fang teleport him inside, but he couldn't lose any more time. The risk was too great. He'd need another way in.

Fang's grip pulsated in his hand.

Yes, perhaps there is another way in. Shall we look for it together?

Selene held the emerald seeker on her arm. Her brow furrowed.

"What is it?" Brenwar had just finished making a campfire. He blew on the kindling, bringing forth a stronger flame. "Let me guess: Nath isn't coming back."

"No, of course not. Not tonight at least. I should have known."

"What's the problem?" Sasha set some twigs down by Brenwar's fire.

"Nath is delayed. But he instructs us to keep marching." Selene gave the seeker a nod. The tiny dragon buzzed away and out of sight.

"Perhaps we should march through the night," Brenwar said. "I'm not one for stopping. Besides, nothing else moves on a cold night like this. That's why I think we should."

Sasha had dark rings around her eyes. She wasn't the only one, either. Ben, Rerry, and Samaz were all yawning and shivering as they spread their fingers over the fire. They hadn't stopped since they started.

Selene knew that unlike her and Brenwar, they needed rest. "Feel free to scout ahead with the elves if you like, Brenwar. I'm more than glad to keep company here."

Dusting his hands off, Brenwar said, "I don't know which would be worse, sitting still with part elves or roaming around with full elves." He grumbled. "I suppose I'll stay here. You probably need me to keep the fire going anyway."

Sansla Libor ducked into the woodland. He'd made headway north toward the orcen land of Thraag. The roamers, along with fifty of the elven finest, hid among the vegetation. Wurmers flew through the skies. The twirling *Ree-Rah* sound was a dead giveaway when the foul creatures passed.

The elves popped up from their spots.

Shum and Liam returned from scouting ahead. "The orcen lands are barren of soldiers," Shum said, untangling some briars that snagged his ankle. "People go about their business with toothy smiles on their faces. Their hogs are full of fat. They eat well."

Sansla gave Hoven a nod.

He sped off with two of the other roamers, taking lengthy strides until they vanished over the knolls. They'd traveled day and night without stopping. They opted not to use horses. With a group as skilled as this, it was easy to blend into the rolling fabric of the land.

"Let's keep moving then. Quickly. If the orcs get wind of us, they'll come by the thousands." He lifted his arm and motioned forward. "Onward."

CHAPTER 23

THE ELVEN SOLDIERS STOPPED THEIR advance at the base of the mountain range north of Morgdon. Brenwar and Ben caught up with Eslin. The elven commander was concealed in a grove with a few others. Their eyes were fixed on a break in the branches that gave a full few of the mountains.

Under his breath, Brenwar said, "Are there enemies afoot?"

"Perhaps. We caught sight of someone—or something—moving along the base. It was just a glimpse that one of my men reported." Eslin craned his neck. "There hasn't been any movement since we saw it."

"Maybe it was a mountain cat," Brenwar suggested. "The hills are thick with such creatures."

"Or it could have been a dragon," Ben suggested.

"No, my men would know. They've known many dragons and hunted more than their fair share of varmints. They have a sense of things. It moved as men move." Eslin drew an arrow from his quiver and held it in his teeth for a moment while he readied a bow made from short limbs with a gentle recurve at the top. "Whoever it is spotted us at the same time we spotted him. He's crafty. My men and I will handle him."

"Don't go hustling off anywhere just yet," Brenwar said. "I can track better than most."

"I'm no slouch either." Ben unhooked Akron. *Snap. Clatch. Snap.* He notched a moorite arrow.

Eslin's slender eyes widened. "That is a marvelous thing."

"Akron shoots better than he looks," Ben said with a wink.

"Apologies, I seem to have underestimated my present company." Eslin stepped aside. "Please, lead. I'll follow."

With his eyes ahead, Brenwar took off in the direction that Eslin pointed out.

There weren't any tracks in the snow leading up to the pine trees that made a skirt at the base of the mountains.

Pointing at a break in the trees where an avalanche of rock had come down decades ago, Brenwar gave Eslin a glance.

The elf nodded.

Staying low, Brenwar ambled forward, quiet as a cat.

Slipping into the trees, the three of them fanned out, putting ten feet between them. Making a search line, they headed forward.

Brenwar took a knee. He found a boot heel print that had dug a soft spot in a bed of pine needles. He brushed the needles aside with his fingers. The print was man-sized. Someone had come through this way. It was just a matter of flushing them out. With Mortuun on his shoulder, he got up and angled toward the mountain's snow-covered base.

Eslin and Ben moved toward the rock slide. There were portals between the stones all over, big enough for a bear to hibernate in. He watched for the longest time. They vanished into the rocks.

If there's a trap in there, they're going to spring it. I'll just wait for it.

Several minutes later, Ben and Eslin emerged from different holes. Ben waved at Brenwar and shrugged.

Whoever it was, they must have moved on.

Brenwar set Mortuun down on the hammer's head and leaned the handle against a tree. He took a knee again and started tightening the laces on his boot. Something wasn't right. He could feel eyes on his back. Weaponless, he moved back down the slope of trees. Neither Ben nor Eslin was looking at him, but he waved them over. When he turned around to retrieve Mortuun, he found a sword tip at his neck.

"Be careful. You might poke a dwarf's eye out with that," Brenwar said. The blackened steel in the armored man's fist was razor sharp. The warrior appeared more than capable of using it. "I'd hate to lose my eye. That would be fatal—for you, that is." Brenwar snatched the blade with his skeleton hand, locking his fingers tight as a vise.

The warrior tugged on his weapon's handle with two hands.

Brenwar wrenched the blade away as if the strong man had the strength of a toddler. "You have some explaining to do, vandal. He tossed the blade aside. "Out with it!"

Another voice came out of nowhere. "Perhaps he just doesn't like dwarves. Based off my experience, they are exceedingly difficult."

Brenwar's lips moved like a fish making bubbles as soon as Bayzog stepped into full view. "Uurluuk's beard! It can't be. You must be a shade!"

Eslin crept up behind Bayzog with an arrow pointed at his back. "Say the word, Brenwar, and I'll drop him."

Ben emerged with eyes filled with excitement. "No! No! Certainly not. It's Bayzog."

"Don't be a fool, Ben. You saw Bayzog die. You were there when we buried him." Brenwar's brow furrowed. "You play games that you shouldn't play, shade. I'll turn you inside out for it."

Hands up, Bayzog said, "I don't know what you think happened to me, but you of all dwarves should know you can't rid yourself of me so easily. I live. You'll just have to adjust to it."

Ben approached with a weird smile hanging on his face. "I know it's you even though it can't be you. How is this possible?"

"It's a long story, but I can explain."

Brenwar looked Rip up and down. "I suppose you're his alibi?"

"Yes, of course, son of Balor Bolderguild. I'm friends with your father."

"That's impossible."

"I can prove it. Do you see that sword? Check the mark on it."

Brenwar retrieved the blade made of blackened steel. He eyed a small dwarven smith stamp practically hidden in the pommel. "This is the sword of Rip Tippy! He died when I was a child."

"At your service—and I disappeared, actually."

Brenwar kept the sword. He turned toward Bayzog. The part elf's violet eyes said it all. The last Bayzog had been him, but off and somewhat strange. Brenwar had thought perhaps the spirits possessed him. "Well, there's only one way to know for sure. We'll take you to camp, cut you open, and see what's inside."

"I didn't miss your irrational way of thinking."

Brenwar led the way back to the others.

They were all huddled together less than a mile away near a small overgrown village. Selene, Sasha, and Rerry stood behind a shack out of the wind. The mother and her sons were bundled up in their robes. "I have a prisoner," Brenwar said, fighting back his own tears. "He says he knows you, but I'm not so sure."

Sasha gasped. Tears swelled in her eyes. On feet as fleet as a deer's, she tackled Bayzog, kissing him all over.

Rerry and Samaz piled on.

Brenwar wiped the corner of his eye. He caught Ben looking. "You didn't see that."

Chapter 24

Nath picked his way through the woodland with the quiet ease of a fawn. His senses were tuned to the creatures and varmints that thrived in thickets and red ferns—now burrowed in away from the cold and the invasion of evil. That made things a little more difficult for him. He hoped to exercise some of the powers he'd gained. He felt stronger in many ways. One of these was his connection with the natural world.

Soldiers approached. Their footfalls cracked fallen twigs.

Nath slid into the gap where an elm tree had split into a V-shape.

Three gnolls wearing furs and skins were patrolling the area. They carried hatchets fit for their hands. Their yellow eyes had a moody wink of evil to them. The leader, the biggest, carried a flail with a spiked ball and chain.

Gnolls, huh, I haven't seen their like in quite some time. One spitball would set the three of them on fire.

One of the gnolls started sniffing the air. His hard stare searched the trees. Like many of the fouler races, gnolls had a strong sense of smell. They were part bloodhound.

"What is it?" one of the gnolls said to the other with piqued curiosity.

"There's something odd in the air. It lingers." The gnoll's eyes bore right into the tree Nath was standing behind. "See? There, do you see it?"

Nath stiffened. It wasn't a matter of fear. He could cut the gnolls down in an instant, but he didn't want to draw attention to himself. That wasn't the only thing bothering him. The gnolls shouldn't be able to pick up his scent. It was one of his gifts. It took a nose far keener than a gnoll's to pick up a whiff of him.

The gnolls eased forward.

The leader said to the other two on either side of him in a low voice, "Do you not see it? There, among the branches."

The gnolls leaned forward with their eyes fastened on Nath's spot. All of a sudden, "Whack!" The leader smacked his two men on the backs of their heads. "Har, har, har!" the leader said, clutching his belly. "You hounds fall for that every time!"

The gnolls drew their hatchets back. "We should turn you into stew."

The leader was still laughing. "You're welcome to try, but you'll only embarrass yourselves."

The snarling gnolls jammed their hatchets into their belts. "It's time to end our patrol, is it not? Let's return. I'm looking forward to watching the giants sacrifice that dragon."

"Har, yes. Perhaps we'll get some more of those scales. Let's go then, stupids."

Nath's fingernails dug through the bark on the tree. His blood boiled.

They had better not be sacrificing a dragon.

He drew a deep breath.

Calm yourself, Dragon. Be wise, not hasty.

The gnolls moved on, disappearing among the trees but leaving footfalls a deaf orc could hear.

While he gathered his composure, something perplexed Nath. The gnolls had been looking right at him, and even he was surprised they hadn't seen him.

And then he noticed a change in his scales. They had changed colors to those of the bark, like he was some sort of chameleon. He pulled his hand away from the tree. The scales blackened. Nath smiled. He could change his colors again. Perhaps there were even more things he could do.

I should have spent more time with Father when I was young.

Nath shadowed the gnolls as far as he could. He took shelter in the forest and garnered a closer look at things.

The ziggurat was a tremendous block building. There were six levels. From top to bottom, wurmers and soldiers of the titan army crawled along the walls like ants. A huge staircase ran right up the middle. A sacrificial altar of stone was at the top. Earth giant sentries stood watch by it with their hairy arms hanging at their sides. Snow covered their shoulders.

The Ruins of Barnabus was one name for the fallen place. Long ago it had been a hive of evil, where men, beasts, and even dragons were sacrificed. As the legend went, it was Barnabus, Nath's father in human form, who took the temple of the wicked down. Now, it thrived with new life.

Regardless, Nath's heart swelled. It gave him comfort knowing that not so long ago, his father had called himself Barnabus and walked the world much like he did now.

We both trod the same ground.

Nath watched the gnolls take a path to the bottom of the ziggurat. They reported to a nuurg, who pointed them through an archway. They vanished inside. A few minutes later, another patrol party came out in full gear. It was three orcs and a pair of goblins. They marched right by Nath's position.

If I could get inside that ziggurat, I bet I could find the wurmer hive. A disguise, perhaps.

Sansla had never said with absolute certainty that the wurmer hive was within, but he'd reported what he saw. Baby wurmers by the hundreds pouring out. Nath had no doubt this was it. The ziggurat was the perfect stronghold for a hive.

A few minutes later, the ziggurat stirred with new activity. Wild cries and shouts went up. Soldiers pounded their weapons on their shields. On the northern end of the ziggurat, a bare-chested nuurg carried a bound copper dragon in his arms.

Great Guzan, no!

The nuurg had a headdress made from dragon bones, shiny scales, and talons that hung down over his shoulders. He was flanked by two ogres dressed much like him. Together, they began a long, slow march up the steps.

Nath drew Fang. His breath quickened. He squeezed the grip tight. He wasn't about to witness another dragon die. Not like this. The dragons had lost enough already. He wouldn't stand by and watch any casualties he could prevent.

Think, Nath. Not with your heart but with your mind.

The nuurg moved up the steps at a very slow, ceremonial pace. The *ree-rahs* of the wurmers started up in a steady rhythm. Somewhere on top of the ziggurat, kettledrums were beat.

On impulse, Nath hustled into the forest and came upon the orc and goblin patrol. He slipped in behind the goblins and banged their heads together.

The orcs turned. They launched into an attack.

Nath's fist smote their jaws like lightning. *Wap! Wap! Wap!*

All three of them hit the ground at the same time.

With his wings collapsed into leathery pods on his back, Nath donned the biggest orc's armor and furs. He removed Dragon Claw from Fang and stuck the magnificent sword inside a hollowed-out tree trunk. His scales changed from black to the green-hued orcen ruddy skin. His red hair turned brown. He tucked Dragon Claw under his skins, took the path out of the forest, and entered the excited crowd, pushing his way up the steps after the copper dragon.

CHAPTER 25

"SO IT'S AS YOU SAY." Rip combed his beard. "I'd hoped to go back to Quintuklen and see for myself. I wanted to… oh, surprise the legionnaires."

Bayzog had fully reunited with his family and friends. They'd all resumed the journey west up the mountains, ankle deep in snow.

Walking side by side with Rip, Ben said, "Wonders never cease in this world. I've seen the most amazing spectacles. Now, I witness a legionnaire brought back from a grave five hundred years old."

"I have a grave?" Rip said.

"More of a memorial, actually. There's even a statue of your likeness. That's why I was so shocked when I saw you. I knew your story well. I was a legionnaire myself, long ago."

"Once a legionnaire, ever the fair."

"I don't know, I was young and got caught up in some sordid business. Not my doing, but I lost my rank." Ben pushed a snowy pine branch aside and allowed Rip to step through.

"Sounds like politics, the soldier's worst enemy. I can tell you're good salt, Ben. No worries from me. I just wish to see Quintuklen standing tall again. I've missed that grand city." He tapped his heart with his fist. "I long for the faces of my family. They're long gone now, I suppose. I'm an old ghost, bereft of legacy."

"Look at you, five hundred years old and you appear to be a decade younger than me. You can start a new legacy. I did after I lost my family the first time around. I'm neck deep in this fight to see that it doesn't happen again."

Rip squeezed his shoulder. "Your words encourage me, Ben. Together, we'll send these devils to the pits. Tell me more."

Ben explained everything to Rip, from the arrival of the titans to the fall of Dragon Home. He saved the last part about Balzurth dying. Rip didn't seem to understand.

"You're telling me that Barnabus was actually Balzurth the Dragon King? I'm still having difficulty with that. Barnabus was such an amazing person, though, that perhaps I shouldn't be surprised. I was young when he and I met. He certainly managed feats that were extraordinary to me. This one time, we slipped into Thraag posing as a pair of orcen maidens." Rip guffawed. "I couldn't believe he talked me into it, but he did. Oh, it seems like yesterday, it really does. I'd love to see him in his full glory. You tell me his scales and bones rot in the arena at Narnum. That sickens me. I say we undo what has been done."

"We tried that," Brenwar interjected. The surly dwarf plowed through the snow and caught up with them. "And I'm all for going back, but now we're going after Nath. Apparently, our friend Bayzog has information that he doesn't care to share with us. Typical. Just keep marching and keep the yapping down. Those frozen overhangs can be sensitive."

"Apparently they aren't the only sensitive thing around here," Ben remarked.

Rip chuckled.

"Don't start with me, Ben." Brenwar surged ahead.

"He's a chip off the old anvil, that one is," Rip said. "Very much like his father, Balor." Ben and Rip guarded the rear with a handful of the elves.

The elven guard led them through a pass in the mountains. It wound a thousand feet up slippery trails before leveling off on a plateau that was miles of snow-covered fields. The elves fanned out, forming a wedge, with their faces down in the harsh winds that tore at their hair and clothing.

Bayzog walked with his hand clasped in Sasha's. She hadn't let him go since he'd returned. Rerry and Samaz were close by.

One of the elves lifted his fist. They all came to a stop. Another elf brought over a spear and started poking into the snow.

"I'd better go check it out," Brenwar said to Bayzog. "Looks like the snow has them spooked."

Ben and Rip eased up to the others.

"What do you suppose it is?" Ben said.

"Perhaps this lake of snow we stand on is not stable," Bayzog suggested. "I've heard many stories about expanses like this swallowing people into a frozen cavity below. Nature disguises many traps."

Brenwar twisted his head over his shoulder and said, "There's nothing but mountain beneath your toes. Trust me on that. I know. Apparently the elves don't." He turned back. A snowbank in front of him burst open. "Gah! Wurmers!"

A wurmer blasted Brenwar with a purple ball of fire.

Brenwar tackled it into the snow.

All around them, wurmer after wingless wurmer erupted out of the snow. One took an elf down with a quick bite to the neck. Two wurmers buried one elf in the snow. Blood was shed. Before anyone could blink, the party was fighting for their lives.

Ben fired a moorite arrow. It tore through an oncoming wurmer's chest.

With a single swing, Rip hacked the head off another.

Rerry struggled against a tail that coiled around his neck. His brother Samaz pounced on the wurmer's back. Tendrils of energy shot through his fingertips on a verbal command. The wurmer bucked. Its scales sizzled.

The Elderwood Staff gripped in Bayzog's hands ignited. An arc of energy cleared a clod of wurmers surging his way.

Steel bit into scales. Talons tore away flesh. The fight in the snow turned into a brawl of blood. The wurmers continued to appear. For every one cut down, two more came.

Brenwar pounded skulls like a hammer crushing nuts. "I'm sick and tired of these things!" *Whack! Whack! Whack!*

Finding mark after mark, Ben realized he'd be out of arrows soon if the wurmers kept coming. "There's too many!" he cried out. "We need cover!"

"There!" Rip pointed his dripping blade at a cave mouth uphill and west of their position. "We can defend better from there. Let's make a path!" His words spread quickly as fire.

Every able body fought its way up the path. Brenwar carried a gravely wounded elf on his shoulders. Bayzog sent waves of the fiends skipping over the snow. In ones, twos, and threes, they entered the expansive mouth of the icy cave.

From her fingertips, Selene loosed shards of energy that tore scales off the wurmers. "This opening is too big!" she declared. Wingless wurmers climbed up the walls and out of harm's way. "We've waltzed ourselves into our own trap."

"Fear not!" Bayzog lassoed the tip of the Elderwood Staff in the air, and a citrine yellow shield sealed off the cave entrance. Wurmers on the outside slammed into it. The ones inside, the elves and the party finished off one by one.

"A fine plan, but how long will it last?" Selene said to Bayzog while the wurmers piled up in a screeching and scratching wall of their own.

Bayzog shrugged. His face was a mask of concentration. "I don't know, but we'll see, won't we."

CHAPTER 26

THE TITAN ARMY BUSTLED ALL over the ziggurat with hungry activity. Their chants were as loud as they were foul. Every face was drawn up in an angry sneer. They wanted blood. They chanted death.

Nath's muscles were taut as bowstrings. He forced himself through the raucous crowd, fighting to keep his anger in check. Every fiber of his being wanted to lash out. Strike. Kill.

Settle down, Dragon. You still need to find a way to get her out of this.

"Her" being the female copper dragon tethered to the altar. The dragon's eyes were wide with fear. The long lashes over her beautiful eyes flickered. She was innocent, a sweet wondrous creature captured by the cruelest of beings. They had laid her on the slab of stone like a fattened calf.

Nath shouldered into the front row of the spectacle.

I can't let this happen.

Every eye was fixed on the copper dragon and the nuurg priest. This nuurg was a big one, standing a full ten feet in height. He unhitched a dagger sheathed in a gaudy ceremonial scabbard and raised it over his head. A thunderous roar of cheers seemed to shake the foundations of the ziggurat. The nuurg removed the blade from the sheath. The edge was razor sharp. It had a unique shine to the blade.

A dragon skinner! I should have known.

Now, it was up to him. At best, he could hop onto the slab and cut the copper dragon free. They'd be swarmed instantly. The copper looked weak. Nath wasn't sure she'd have the strength to fly to safety.

I won't stand here and watch her die, even if it kills me.

A gnoll shoved into his back. The dog-faced warrior was screaming, "Blood! Blood! Fill our cups with dragon blood!"

Nath shoved the gnoll backward into the crowd.

The gnoll tripped up and fell, then sprang back to his feet. "Why did you do that, orc?"

Speaking in Orcen, Nath said, "Because I don't like you yelling." He pushed the gnoll again. The surrounding crowd began pushing and shoving. The gnoll grabbed Nath's arm and tried to wrench it out of the socket. It would have been easy for the gnoll to twist a piece of iron.

The whites of the gnoll's eyes grew. "What kind of orc are you? I've never met an orc stronger than me."

Then, in a polite manner, Nath said, "Apologies, my friend. I didn't mean any harm. After all, today is a day of celebration. A time for peace. Harmony. Why don't you give me a hug?"

"What?"

Nath opened up his arms. He had the mob's attention. "You know, a hug, just me and you."

The gnoll's perplexed eyes slid over the other bewildered faces and tilted necks. "I'd never hug an orc. That's disgusting."

"Fair enough. How about a punch in the face then?"

The gnoll's chin shrank into his neck. "Huh?"

Nath popped him in the face really good. He merged with the throng, shoving and punching everyone. He was yelling absurdities. "The gnolls say they are better fighters than orcs! They get more grub."

Like wildfire, the chaos spread. In acts of lunacy, orcs, gnolls, goblins, and men broke out into fights.

The nuurg cracked whips, trying to separate the fighters in the frenzy.

In a voice that was unnaturally loud, Nath said in the guttural ogre tongue, "The nuurg say the ogres are worthless, that giant halflings would fight better."

An ogre with blood in his eye jumped down from one level of the ziggurat to the other. The ogre landed on a nuurg and crushed it to the ground.

Shoving his way through the crowd, Nath noticed he had the nuurg priest's attention. The priest belted out commands. The giants at the top turned their backs on the sacrificial slab.

Nath tore his way out of the crowd and snuck up to the slab. Cutting the bonds on the copper dragon with Dragon Claw, he said to her, "Do you have the strength to fly to safety?"

"More than enough, your majesty, but what about you? I won't leave your side. It wouldn't be fair. I'll fight to the end with you."

Nath cut the last of her bonds but held her fast. "No, you will go. That's an order." He spied the wurmers. They were everywhere. It would be impossible to avoid them. In his heart he knew the copper couldn't escape all of them. His distraction was good, but he needed an even bigger one. He noticed the flame and smoke coming out of the urns on the corners of the top level.

"That's it," he said to her. "Wait for my signal." Nath took in a lungful of air and let it out in a thick steady stream of smoke, spinning in a full circle as he did so.

Cries of shock and alarm went up. Many were screaming.

"Fire! Fire! Fire!"

The smoke spilled over the army and down the ziggurat in a thick, milky haze. Nath caught a glimpse of the giants turning back toward the slab. Their huge necks bent downward. They fanned the smoke, peering right at him. Nath kept blowing. The smoke thickened. He lost sight of everyone around him.

The nuurg priest swam through the smoke with the ceremonial dagger clutched in its hand. It caught sight of the copper dragon and lunged at her.

The copper loosed a stream of acid. The black liquid splashed into the nuurg's body.

Instantly, its armor and skin began to melt. Howling, it dropped the dagger and crumbled in a bubbling hiss.

"Go now," Nath said to the copper dragon. "Use the smoke for cover. Head for the woodland. There are too many wurmers in the sky."

"Thank you, your majesty. I can never repay you, but my service is yours, forever." The copper leapt from the slab with her wings spread out. She disappeared in the smoke.

Nath dusted off his hands. "Another thanks, from a dragon no less. I must be doing something right after all these years." He found himself reflecting on the time when he had lived to rescue dragons. They'd never thanked him back then.

Out of the smoke, a stone giant's fist came. The blow hit Nath flush in the chest. He bounced off the altar and hit the ground, sucking for wind. Bright spots floated in his eyes. The smoke thinned. Giant legs straddled the altar. Fingers as big as men clutched for him.

Nath jabbed Dragon Claw into one of them.

The hand turned to ice. The giant's limbs stiffened.

Holding his side, Nath forced his way through the blinding smoke and ran right into a nuurg.

"Get out of my way. Can't you see I'm going somewhere?" The nuurg took a swing.

Nath sidestepped and spat a flaming spitball on it. The flames spread quickly.

The nuurg fled into the crowd.

Using the smoke for cover, Nath spewed out a geyser of flame, torching everything in sight. Flaming bodies jumped from the upper levels to the lower ones. Panic spread. Still disguised, Nath converged with the stream of fleeing people trampling each other on their way down the great steps.

Nath didn't make any apologies for the ones he crushed beneath his toes, but he took a backward glance when he hit the bottom. The top of the ziggurat was a pyre of fire and plumes of yellow smoke. The giants and nuurg were tamping out the flames with anything they could find, including people. One stone giant was a block of ice. The other stone giant shoved it on top of the flames. The frozen giant shattered into huge chunks of ice that doused much of the fire.

"That's what I call teamwork." Turning his back to the chaos, Nath slunk back into the woods. He retrieved Fang with a broad smile on his face.

CHAPTER 27

Wurmer faces pressed against the shield Bayzog had created. Other wurmers bit and clawed at it. The translucent barrier warbled. His cheeks were flushed red.

Selene hung by Bayzog's side. "If you're going to give way, let us know before it happens. We don't need any more surprises."

"I will."

Sasha, Rerry, and Samaz huddled around Bayzog.

"Let us help, Bayzog," Sasha said.

Sweat dripped from his chin. He nodded. "Fasten yourselves to me then."

Rerry and Samaz locked arms around his legs. Sasha hugged him from behind.

"Now grab the staff."

All three of them clutched the staff at the same time. All four of them stiffened as if they were statues. A moon-white glow came from their eyes. None of them spoke. Their eyes were fixed on the barrier. They all became one.

"That's the strangest thing I've ever seen." Brenwar rested Mortuun on his shoulder. "I'll see if there's a tunnel out of here, but I doubt it. It's probably a tomb for the elves."

"Be quick," Selene said.

He waved her off.

The cave was wide. The giant icicles that hung over the mouth made it seem smaller than it was from the outside. Brenwar, Ben, and Rip wove through the fallen rock into the belly of the cavern. Rip's sword gave off a green hue. Aside from some small stalactites at the top, there wasn't anything. It went back about a hundred yards and ended.

Ben leaned against the back cave wall. "I guess this is a dead end. It seems we're going to have to make a final stand."

"Don't be sure." Brenwar ran his hands over the walls. "In my experience, none of these holes ever lead to nowhere. They always go somewhere."

"Maybe we can use a potion to get us out of this mess." Ben held a potion vial up to his eyes and shook it. Fiery orange and sparkling yellow swirled. "This one might do."

"You can't use that one in close quarters. You'll scorch us all."

"Oh."

Rip poked at the walls with his sword. "I beg your pardon, but this rock doesn't quite feel like rock. It's got some give to it."

Brenwar swung his shoulders around. "What are you talking about? I've never heard of soft rocks—aside from the ones in Ben's head."

"I didn't say soft, I said it's got give." Rip stuck his sword tip in the bumpy stone. Mushrooms were growing out of the rock. He sliced one off. "That's an odd thing."

"Let me see that." Brenwar snatched the sliver of mushroom from Rip and held it to the sword's dim light. "Ooh."

"Ooh, what?"

"I don't think this is a wall at all."

"If it's not a wall, then what is it?"

With Mortuun hanging in his grip, he backed away. "Ben, get away from that."

"Why?"

The entire wall lurched.

Ben jumped away and scurried over to Brenwar. Fumbling, he nocked another arrow. "Sultans of Sulfur, that wall is alive!"

An eye filled with a deep green glow opened up. It was bigger than Brenwar's head. A snort of hot air came out of nowhere in a hair-raising sigh.

All three warriors slowly backed away.

"I think we just woke something that's not ready to come out of its slumber," Brenwar said. "Well done, Rip. You poked a dragon. What kind of idgit pokes a dragon when it's sleeping?"

"I didn't know. You're the one who should have known."

The rocks cracked. Debris fell. The tremendous beast filled the entirety of the cave. The huge thing had crammed its entire body inside, and now it was coming out. It didn't seem happy. It snorted again. Its breath was bristling, hot steam.

Brenwar raced back toward the front. "Selene, we have company!"

Taking her eyes from the wurmer hole, she said, "What are you talking about?"

"I think my message is clear. You need to get in there and talk to that thing before we have another fight on our hands."

Ben and Rip were huffing for breath. The elves drew steel and nocked arrows. They braced themselves on both sides of the cave.

It sounded like the stone tunnel was bursting.

Something squeezed through. Its head appeared, almost filling the mouth of the tunnel. Its jaws were a cave all on their own. A powerful hulking beast of scales like rock, covered in another skin of natural vegetation, part of the mountain itself come to life.

"A stone dragon," Selene said. "I've never even seen one before. I never thought they grew so big."

The stone dragon's eyes flicked from person to person. He pushed through even closer.

Brenwar drew Mortuun back. "Is it on our side or not? Can you speak to it?"

"They don't talk." Selene crept forward with her hands out. "They're stupid."

"Maybe you should let Brenwar try talking to it then." Ben laughed. "Sorry, I get a little giddy when eminent death is upon me."

Selene called out in Dragonese.

The stone dragon's eyes fixed on her. Its thin lips drew back over its teeth. It snorted another blast of steam that bathed them all. Everyone was drenched in sweat. The tunnel became a sauna.

Brenwar eyed her. "What did you say to it, 'It's chilly, can you warm me up?' Need I remind you we've got another enemy still nipping at our backside?"

"You're the one who found this beast, not me. Dragon or not, he's not listening, and I'm thinking that after years of slumber, he's hungry."

"I've got some jerky," Ben suggested.

The dragon let out an angry growl. Its eyes narrowed.

"Take cover! Take cover!" Selene dove out of the way just as the dragon let out a cone of wet breath that coated the walls of the cave.

Brenwar's arms froze in mid-swing. His eyes were wide open. He couldn't blink. No one still moved but the dragon. They were paralyzed.

CHAPTER 28

AFTER A LONG RUN UNDER the cover of the trees, Nath took to the skies again. His smile hadn't left his face. It felt good, sticking it to the titans. He'd managed to free the copper dragon too, which made it even better. It was like old times. He wasn't so old, not for a dragon, but what had happened made him feel young again.

Those were the days. I'd forgotten how much fun rescuing dragons used to be.

Better yet, he had managed to beat the titan army's servants using his wits and not so much his powers. He was fairly certain that fight would have been a knock-down drag-out, but he'd come up with something and it had worked well. He was gleeful after seeing the army of the wicked scrambling all over the ziggurat in a full-blown panic.

I can't wait to share this adventure with Brenwar. He'll have a fit. The look on his face will be priceless.

He had made it another league when the green seeker appeared at his side.

Nath spoke to it. "Let me guess, Selene's mad. Well, feel free to tell her I'm on my way back, so there's no need to pitch a fit."

The seeker's wings made a warning buzz.

"What?" Nath said at the startling news. "Wurmers? They're trapped? Lead me to them."

The emerald seeker sped off.

Nath's wings took him as fast as they could. The first thing he saw when he got to the scene was the blood in the snow. Elves, many of them, lay dead. There were scores of holes that had popped up out of the snow bed like erupting volcanoes.

"No!"

Ree-rah! Ree-rah! Ree-rah!

The seeker hovered over the mouth of a cave that appeared to be filled with wurmers.

Nath flew right at them. He pulled up at the last moment, wings flapping, dropped open his mouth, and let out a torrent of flame. The fires slammed into the wurmers and spread. Snow melted all over the mountain, dripping over the cave mouth like a waterfall.

The wurmers twisted and burned. Their purple eyes found Nath. Many burned, many died, but the rest attacked like giant hounds.

Nath launched himself toward the burning fray with Fang pulsating in his grip. He removed Dragon Claw and dropped to the ground. He'd seen enough wurmers for a hundred lifetimes. He didn't want to see any more. He couldn't let any more hurt his friends. He plowed into them.

Slice! Slice! Slice!

Fang and Dragon Claw cut through the wingless monsters like hot knives through butter. He plunged Dragon Claw into their black hearts. The purple haze in their eyes went out. Their dark acid blood sizzled in the snow.

Fang split a wurmer from its skull to its tail.

Not fighting the angry dragon inside him, Nath hacked away with startling speed. His strikes were lightning, his fury a maelstrom. He launched into a spinning attack. The unorthodox move was like putting the wurmers in a meat grinder. They fell in heaps. They died in pieces. Nath was still swinging with the sting of acid in his eyes when he realized all of them, dozens, were now dead.

Stepping over the piles of bone and scales, he found himself face to face with a shimmering wall of citrine energy. Shoulders heaving up and down, he said, "I know this."

On the other side of the force field stood his friends and the host of elves. They were frozen. One of them in particular stood out. The Elderwood Staff burned white at the top. So did the eyes of a peculiar family. "Bayzog!" Nath screamed in elation. He pounded the mystic wall. "Let me in, you fool!"

The shield dissipated.

Before Nath crossed the threshold, the stone dragon moaned. Its great jaws snapped.

"How did I miss you, big fella?" Nath stuck Dragon Claw in Fang and Fang in the ground. With confidence, he strode right up on the leery dragon. Its long tongue had reeled Brenwar just inside its jaw. "No, no, no, no… you don't want to eat him. You'll get a bad tummy ache."

The stone dragon shook its thick head then paused, eyeing Nath with curiosity.

Nath knew stone dragons weren't much on reason. They had brains the size of walnuts. If you encountered one, you needed to treat him with great care. Like most dragons, all of them had something they liked.

Nath hummed more prettily than a songbird. The melody filled the chamber.

The stone dragon's slimy tongue uncoiled.

Nath stepped inside the monster's mouth and picked up Brenwar. Still humming, he moved away in slow, steady steps.

The stone dragon burrowed back into the cave.

Nath kept the humming up for several minutes. He set Brenwar on his feet and tousled his beard. "I know: Dwarves don't get eaten."

Nath helped Selene up to her feet. She was moving, but slowly. Her eyes said it all: she was fine, and glad to see him.

The Elderwood Light winked.

"Bayzog!" Nath leapt clear over to where the part-elf wizard was one with his family. Fists on his hips, Nath said, "Is it truly you?"

The Elderwood Staff's gem winked once.

"I can't be too sure. Not after what happened to you with who the others thought was Selene. You could be a spirit or a shifter. Is Brenwar your best friend ever?"

The light winked twice.

"No, that's too simple. Let's try another. Do I like orcs?"

Two blinks.

"Is my only vanity my multicolored scales?"

Two more blinks.

"Was I always in love with Selene?"

A pause, and then one blink.

Nath found himself relaxing more and more. This really did seem like Bayzog!

"Hm, some more hard questions. Did we always greet each other positively?"

Two blinks.

Wow, whoever this was knew of the game the two of them used to play.

"All right, one more, and let's make it count. Do you know your place in the scheme of things, that I am Dragon King and was Dragon Prince, above all?"

Two blinks.

"I'm convinced. With great joy in my heart, I'm convinced!"

CHAPTER 29

"I THINK I'VE BEEN HUGGED MORE in the last day than I've been hugged all my life," Bayzog said as he tried to squeeze out of Nath's bulging arms. "Granted, I find greater appreciation in it now."

Still inside the cave, Nath kept his arm draped over Bayzog's shoulder. It had taken over an hour, but everyone who had been paralyzed was now freely moving. "I never felt in my heart you were truly gone, my friend. You always lived in there. That other you was so much like you, but he was off a little. I thought that drop in the well had just changed you."

"Well, it was me, but it wasn't. It's difficult to explain how life works in the Dark Realm. Apparently I was down there three years, but it only felt like an endless day. There was a sun of sorts, which never rose nor fell. It was a wide stream of light that went all the way around."

"I don't care to see it. I'll take your word for it."

Rip sauntered over. He took a knee in front of Nath and bowed.

"Who is this?"

"Rip Tippy, legionnaire—a true knight of Barnabus, five hundred years ago. It's an honor to meet you." He held out his sword. "My service is yours."

"Please stand, Rip. The honor is mine. It's not very often I meet someone who fought alongside my father in the Great Dragon Wars. I'll be interested to hear what you have to say about him."

"You strongly favor Barnabus, sire. It does my eyes well to see the like of his stern visage again. We will free him. It must be done."

Nath gave the warrior a long, hard look.

Fully bearded, he appeared to be in his thirties, but he came across much older. The prominent jawline suggested his noble ancestry. He was a knight of knights.

"I'm curious to know what needs to be done. I'm eager to free my father from the darkness that binds him."

"Yes, we need to talk, you and I," Bayzog said to Nath. His violet eyes carried a burden within. "Sasha, Brenwar, Selene, can you give us some time? We'll catch up."

"Don't yap too long. We have a nest that needs destroying, and Nath still hasn't told us what he saw yet." Brenwar led everyone out of the cave, leaving Nath and Bayzog all to themselves.

"Tell me what you know."

"The well of the staagan was a portal to the Land of the Dim Light. It's a shadow of this world, and also a gateway to the Dark Realm. When I was there, your father reached out from the realm. He aided our escape."

Nath raised his brows. "So he's well then? My heart's been twisting in my chest. He reached out to me. He said I needed to save him."

"He survives, Nath. There are plenty of enemies in the Dark Realm. One such being Gorn Grattack."

"I didn't slay him?"

"He's banished, and he's weak, but still a match for Balzurth, who thrives little better himself."

"Is there nothing that destroys evil once and for all?"

"The spirits are only forever destroyed in their own plane. That's why they crop up again. Something or someone lets them out. The battle we fight stays in flux." Bayzog's gentle fingers, now showing signs of age, ran up and down the wood of his staff. "The only way to truly eradicate evil is to defeat it on its own plane. However, your father warned me—and you—that at all costs, we mustn't try this. The attempt will be in vain. Many have tried before but failed."

"But you made it."

"Yes, but look at the aid I received. There is no ally greater than Balzurth."

"How do we save him then? He called out to me, Bayzog. I must be able to do something."

"This is the perplexing part, Nath. I cannot reveal the answer to you. I won't. Balzurth was very clear. His priorities change. He sees the flux that Nalzambor is in. He'll hold out. But you must continue on your mission. You need to stop these wurmers."

Nath lifted Bayzog up to his toes by the neck of his robes. "You're not telling me?"

Calmly, Bayzog said, "Not under any circumstances. We must stop the wurmers first. Honor your father, Nath, and don't dishonor me."

He released Bayzog. "I'm sorry."

"Don't be. I understand how you feel, but for now, we need to focus on the wurmers. We have to stop them at all costs."

"I know, but you have to guarantee me one thing."

"What's that?"

"You can't die or disappear in the meantime, because I can't figure out how to free my father if you're dead."

Bayzog gave Nath a nudge with his staff toward the exit of the cave. "You make it sound like all I'm needed for is my precious information."

"That's pretty much the case. That and the fact that I might need you to help me wipe out a few thousand of the enemy."

"Well, it's a good thing I brought a mighty walking stick."

"Yes, you're going to need it."

CHAPTER 30

Ree-Rah! Ree-Rah! Ree-Rah!

A V-shaped flock of wurmers streaked beneath the clouds. There were hundreds of them. Sansla and Hoven watched them pass. They continued north. Sansla nodded.

Moving as one, the roamers and the elves strode through the orcen lands. Thraag wasn't so different than any other province. The orcs had their fair share of small towns and villages. It wasn't completely unheard of for them to do business with the other races from time to time. As long as there was money involved, they would deal with anyone, including dwarves and elves who walked on a shadier side of things.

Orcen farms were large stretches of land that grew root vegetables. Onions, turnips, and radishes were common in their diet.

The orcs, of which there were many, thrived in the company of gnolls and goblins. Even ogres could be seen pushing or pulling tremendous plows through the fields. For the most part, the orcs were not so different than any other race in their dealings. They were difficult, hard headed, set in their ways, and never thought anyone was more right than them. Their ruler was always the strongest, meanest, and cruelest. He tended to climb his way to the top through murder. Any other government would fall from this, but the orcen people admired strength above all.

Hoven's foot got stuck in a muddy onion patch they were passing through. He jerked it free with a sucking pop. "Even their fields remind me of them. Difficult and muddy. They even smell like orcs. How can that be? There are hardly any orcs around."

"It's the sacrifices they make that linger in the air," Sansla said. "They like the stench. It keeps their enemies away."

"They are so foul. How can an entire race of people thrive in slop?" Hoven pulled his leg out of another mud hole. "Even when they aren't around, they are treacherous."

Now they were east of Thraag. Much like the dwarven capital of Morgdon, Thraag rested in the mountains. A huge wall ran along the rugged terrain of the rocky mountain. The wall was made from huge cedars and tall columns of stone. Behind the gates and archways that led inside, stone-and-woodwork buildings could be seen. The dwarves hated Thraag. Orcen engineers had made it like Morgdon, but it was a mockery. The orcs didn't have the same skill for stonecraft. Their work was shoddy. Orcs constantly worked on repairing Thraag's great wall.

Red and black banners hoisted high on flagpoles waved in the wind. Chanting carried over the city's walls.

"They're in full celebration, it seems," Sansla said.

"Celebrating what? The war isn't over yet."

"No, but the orcs always have themselves convinced they won the battle before the first drop of blood is spilt." Sansla trudged out of the onion field onto harder land. "Have you ever known an orc that admitted to losing?"

"I don't think I've ever had a conversation with one." Hoven smiled. All the ones I know are dead."

Shum and Liam hustled back from the front of the scouting party. They both gave a quick bow. "The force that guards the entrance to the hive has been tripled since we found it, Sansla. Giants and nuurg guardians are fixtures in the rocks. The wurmers, however, are small in number."

"We're talking about a force of five hundred or so then," Sansla said. "It's manageable."

"That's about ten apiece." Liam was thumbing the edge of his elven dagger. "I can handle twenty."

"Let's move on." Sansla turned his shoulders westward. "I need to get a better look at this force myself."

The wurmer hive was straight north of Thraag. Two massive hills covered in rock and shale were shouldered together in the open plains. There were natural ridges lined along the rocks. The cave entrances were large enough for giants to walk through. The strange hillside and the openings that led to the hive gave it the look of an orcen face. There were three holes: two like eyes, a nose in the middle, and a ledge like a mouth, with jutting rocks for teeth. An eerie light illuminated the holes. The shadows of soldiers moved within.

"It's a fine hiding spot, right were anyone can see it," Liam said.

"It's orcen land. They wouldn't be expecting any visitors." Shum peered through a tiny spyglass. "They don't appear to be expecting anybody. I think they've gotten comfortable relying upon the wurmers that patrol the skies. That explains why we didn't encounter very many patrols."

"Our objective poses many challenges." Sansla cupped the satchel he wore slung over his shoulder. It carried the Ocular of Orray and many orbs of destruction. "The titan army can see their enemies coming from all directions. Once they spot someone, they'll launch missiles with those ballistas and shoot with those bows in heavy volleys. There aren't enough of us to withstand that assault. Additionally, once they are alerted, they'll send word to Thraag. Those forces will come quickly and, more than likely, in superior numbers." He shook his head. "This will be difficult, but it must be done."

"Sansla, you know we can make it inside that hive." Hoven brushed his braided hair over his shoulder. "We only need a distraction or three. We'll draw those soldiers out and slip into their blind side."

Hands over his belly, Shum agreed, "Yes, their force might be bigger, but the principle is still the same."

Eyeing the entrances to the hive, Sansla said, "We only know what we've seen so far. There's more to this picture. I can feel it. I need a moment to think on this."

Chapter 31

The wurmers Slivver had led away had long since returned. An aerial invasion of Elome had begun. Wurmers crisscrossed the skies in waves, dropping huge stones into the habitations of Elome. Rocks the size of people dashed wooden cottages to bits. Treehouses were rattled and busted. The elven children who had once laughed and sung were now crying and screaming.

Laylana and Inslay stood in the high tree where they'd taken Nath Dragon before. He'd warned them the titan army was coming. Now it had arrived. She stood helpless, watching the ugly lizards open oversized sacks full of rocks way up in the sky. They flew too high for archers or any sort of weaponry to hit.

"I believe we have reached the point where this is a crisis situation. Our city is being buried in stone." Inslay drew back his arm and opened up his fingers. His hand brightened. A missile of energy shot from his pinching fingers. The bolt of energy shot through the sky like a comet. A wurmer exploded. Its dark scales fell down like rain.

"You aren't supposed to be acting," Laylana warned him. "The High Council—"

"The high council can go kiss a toad for all I care. I can't watch this while our people are dying."

"And I thought you were firm in your belief that the elves must maintain order during the most chaotic times. We need to follow our leaders."

Inslay's wizened face crinkled. "I'm only acting on the decision they are inevitably going to come to."

"I like the way you think, Inslay." With her hand on the pommel of her sword, she marched to the shaft inside the core of the tree. "Are you coming?"

Inslay ambled onto the platform. It quickly descended. "I take it you have come to a rash decision."

Laylana's dark locks rustled in the breeze. She tied her hair back into a ponytail. "I wouldn't say that. I'd say it's logical."

"I'm curious to see what your version of logic is. I see that elven metal on your hip heating up. You're a fighter, much like Laedorn. He tended to be very direct about these matters."

"Yes, and I often catch myself thinking, 'If Laedorn were here, what would he do?' After all, he'd still be leading the council." The platform slowed to a stop. She and Inslay made their way into the streets. She turned her face toward the sky for a moment. "Come."

"It was a shame that you were not deemed a suitable replacement for Laedorn. But you are young. I suppose your time will come."

"Incoming!" yelled an elven soldier in a treetop. A tombstone-sized rock ripped through the branches, missing the scattering elves by inches.

Laylana broke into a trot.

Inslay had no trouble keeping up. He was older, not ancient, his legs still wiry and strong. They made it to the fields behind the grand barns that housed the livestock. The shepherds were moving herds of animals into the sanctuary in the carved-out stone. Many families that weren't part of the elven army made their way into the tunnels below ground. The fighting forces rushed from one spot to the other, aiding any in need. He lifted his eye skyward again on a gut feeling. "Laylana, move!"

A stone crashed right between the two of them and buried itself halfway in the ground.

Laylana lay sprawled out on the grass. She quickly popped back up and helped Inslay to his feet. Eyes on the stone, she said, "That would have hurt."

Shaken, he replied, "I'm pretty sure even a dwarf would have felt that."

They headed to the field where dragons were still being fitted with saddles and harnesses. Laylana's personal troops were doing the labor. All of her men were dressed for battle.

Commander Osslin, an elf with a taciturn expression, stood at attention and saluted. "Lady Laylana, please tell me you bring news that we aren't going to have to catch stone rain droplets anymore."

"Osslin, I don't have any news from the council, but I'm not going to wait another moment for them to arrive at the obvious decision. I'm going up."

Osslin's long jaw dropped open. "Without orders? It's abominable."

She studied his sour face. "You aren't under any orders. I'd go alone, but you're welcome to join."

"Lady Laylana, I must sternly advise against this. Please, Inslay, put that on my record."

"So you won't be joining me?" she said.

"On the contrary," Osslin's permanent frown turned into a disturbing smile, "I've been dying to get on one of these dragons."

Laylana stepped aside. Despite Osslin appearing to be the least accommodating of elves, she liked him very much. His frown fooled a lot of people. It also made him a formidable commander. The elven soldiers never wanted his cold stare landing on them. "Take your pick."

Osslin bowed. "Ladies first, I must insist."

The crimson dynamo was a magnificent creature. She rubbed his great neck with both of her hands. His warmth went right through her. She'd dreamed of riding a dragon before, but not in this dire situation. "You need to trust me." She stuck her foot in the stirrup and climbed into a saddle built for two. There was a quiver full of arrows and another with long spears.

Commander Osslin ordered the elves to take to the mounts. They all climbed into their saddles—two on the bigger dragons, others rode by themselves. There were only thirty riders in all.

"Inslay, aren't you coming?" she said, patting the seat behind her.

He shrugged. "Of course. I never figured I'd get this chance again."

"You've flown on a dragon before?"

"Yes." He climbed into the saddle. "The problem with riding on a dragon is, once you go up, you never want to come down."

"I'm eager to confirm that." She patted the dragon's neck.

The great beast lurched forward and took off running through the grasses. Its wings unfolded and flapped. Up and away they went.

Laylana's heart beat in her throat. "I love it!"

Inslay tapped her on the shoulder. He shouted in the wind. "There's nothing like it, but heed my warning." He pointed at the wurmers gathering in the sky. "They come!"

CHAPTER 32

"WHOOF," BEN STATED WITH HIS eyes set on the ziggurat. They were hiding on one of the distant bluffs. "There are so many."

"It wouldn't be bad if we had a few more dwarves among us. Instead, we have a bunch of lightfoots running around the woods with sharp needles. We need to do some damage. Real damage."

"I resent that," the elven commander Eslin said.

"I don't care. It's true, nonetheless."

"Fighting all of them at once is not what I had in mind," Nath said. "We just need to get inside. To be honest, I'm tempted to take this task on by myself. I fooled them once." Nath held out his arm. His scales turned to the splotchy skin of an orc. "I doubt they've put together what happened."

"You can camouflage?" Selene traced her fingers over his arm. "I admit, I'm very envious."

"You should be," he said. He clasped her hand. "I don't think I'd like seeing you in anything but your lovely black scales though."

"And I don't think you ever will. Not the way things are going with me."

"I suppose a grand distraction is warranted," said Bayzog. "Perhaps I can handle that, but I'd rather venture within. I have a feeling you'll need me."

"Where he goes, I go." Rerry shouldered alongside his father.

"We all go," Sasha said.

"That's too many," Brenwar argued. "I say Nath and I go in and that's it. We can handle whatever we need to handle in there."

"We didn't all come to be observers," Selene remarked. "We all came because we couldn't take any chances. What must be done must be done, whether we die or not." She hooked her arm through Nath's. "You aren't going anywhere without me."

"If it please you, your majesty," said Eslin, "my elves can turn the woodland into Bedlam. It would provide ample distraction, allowing you to slip in."

"How so?"

"A few fires will draw their eyes. We'll shoot them when they follow. The chase goes on."

"I'm all for a straight fight myself," Rip said. His long moustache was twitching. "This shrubbery is excellent for striking in the night. The dark will come. The deaths of our enemies will follow."

Nath contemplated the plan on the table. Less than two score men would only hold up so long against so many enemies. Eventually, the superior numbers would overcome them. It would be a wipeout.

"Your majesty, I see the concern in your eyes. Don't be alarmed. This is why we came. This is what we do." Eslin patted the elven High Guard insignia on his breast. "Have faith."

Nath nodded.

Akron in hand, Ben said, "I think I'll hang back too. Besides, if you're in there too long, someone is going to have to get you out."

"I know I can count on you, Ben. I'll hold you to it."

"Don't worry, I have plenty of potions. I'll be sure to keep it interesting."

"Fine. We'll go in, but we won't count on coming out again. The wurmers either," Nath said. "It will be us and them if it has to be."

Bayzog addressed his sons. "Listen to me. You need to stay out. Aid your friends out here and protect your mother."

"But Father—"

"No."

Bayzog took the hands of Rerry and Samaz and held them tight. He looked them both in the eye. "You must honor this request. My ears need to hear it from your lips."

Samaz, unblinking as always, said, "Yes, Father."

Rerry had a hard time looking Bayzog in the eye. "Yes, Father, I'll do it. But only for Mother."

"Promise me you'll come back," Sasha said, hugging Bayzog tight.

"I promise I'll do my best, my love."

The two companies headed down the slope. Nath spoke of their plans all the way down. The elven guard slipped out of sight first. The sun set like a burning eye behind the ziggurat.

Ben notched an arrow whose tip burned fire red.

Nath smiled at his friend. "I remember those days. It's been quite some time since I last fired one."

"Please, Dragon, take the shot," Ben said. "After all, it is your bow."

"No, the first shot is all yours, but dedicate it to me." He put his hand on Brenwar's shoulder, then pointed to the southern entrance at the bottom of the ziggurat. It was a knot of soldiers led by a squadron of nuurgs and a stone giant. "That is where we need to go in."

"I don't suppose you know the secret password?" Brenwar said.

"No, we'll try to fool them when the chaos starts."

"How do you propose to do that?" Brenwar asked.

"With one of these?" Nath held up a potion vial.

"You took that from me." Brenwar patted himself over and shook his beard. "No, no, no, I'm not turning my stomach into goo again. I'd rather stay out here and fight if that's the case."

Selene started laughing. "No surprise."

"I'll take it if she takes it," Brenwar said.

"Don't be absurd," she said.

"Oh no, Brenwar is correct. You need to take it too. All three of you do."

Ben started laughing. "This I have to see, but remember I'm a more than willing volunteer for it."

"Barreling in there without a show of force isn't something I'm accustomed to, Nath." Bayzog took the vial. "You've grown much since I've been gone. I like it." Eyeing the small glass decanter, he said, "Polymorph? A split between the three of us. We'll have to be quick about it." He drank his portion down and passed it to Selene.

"Only for you." She drank then dangled the vial before Brenwar's eyes. "Your turn."

Brenwar snatched it away. "Your turn yourself." He drank.

Within seconds, all three of them changed. Selene became an orcen woman, which wasn't anything uncommon in the enemy ranks. Bayzog appeared tall as a gnoll. Brenwar was as fat and squat a goblin as anyone ever saw—with a skeleton hand. It changed the appearance of their clothing to resemble armor and rugged clothing.

"That's interesting," Nath said of Brenwar's hand. "I think we can make use of it."

Ben said to Brenwar, "I've found a new appreciation for your old bearded face."

"Shaddup."

Nath changed the color of his scales and donned the same suit of armor he'd worn before.

It was an hour after dusk, and the first few fires had been set and were starting to blaze. The soldiers on the ziggurat came to life. Large search parties rushed into the woods.

The scales in Nath's hands felt a little clammy. He couldn't stand the thought of his friends covering for him. There was nothing he'd rather do than fight by their sides. "Follow my lead," he said to the others. "Ben, you'll know when to fire." He scooped up Brenwar underneath his arms. "You're a wounded goblin now. A heavy wounded Goblin. Selene, grab his legs."

"Put me down," Brenwar said, dragging his feet.

Selene scooped up his legs. Together, they carried Brenwar like a stretcher.

Bayzog led the way down to the base of the ziggurat by following one of the main roads. With the staff disguised as little more than a tall walking stick, he started waving his arms and speaking in orcen. "There are many! Many attackers come! The woods are filled with them. We have wounded."

Nuurg sentries cut them off. They carried battle axes in their hairy hands. "If there are enemies out there, then you should be out there fighting them!" The nuurg with tattoos all over his face shoved Bayzog down with a hard punch from his hand.

"No, you must see this wound," Nath pleaded. "I've never seen the likes of it before! Look, this goblin's flesh has been eaten. It rots away. We don't come to save this fowl giant's morsel. We come to warn you of the enemy in sight. Prepare yourself. What strikes cannot be seen!"

"You're very chatty for orc flesh." The nuurg bent over and sniffed Brenwar. "You look like a goblin, but you smell like something else. "Are dwarves out there?"

In a throaty voice, Selene replied, "I saw some husky two-legged rodents scurrying in the brush."

Chin jutted out, the nuurg said, "I see. But I smell better. You lie. We're privy to your tricks. Kill them!"

CHAPTER 33

GLENWAR STOOD ON THE PARAPETS of Morgdon overlooking the siege engines outside the great dwarven city's walls. Giants three times the size of normal men walked among the soldiers of the titan army. Six of them, earth giants, carried a great cedar with the iron face of a bugbear at the fore. They marched through the roaring soldiers, put their backs into the ram, and slammed into the great door.

The very walls of Morgdon shook. Notable tremors were underfoot. Glenwar, the younger likeness of Brenwar, shook his head. "They've been trying that for years. One would think they'd come up with something else by now."

Dwarven soldiers posted a hundred feet above Morgdon's entrance dumped vats of hot black pitch into channels that funneled outward. The hot pitch splattered all over the hairy, grizzled giants.

"Every day it's the same: they come, they try, they fail." Glenwar shook his battle axe in the air. He yelled down below. "You're stupid! We can hold out for decades in here, you ignorant giants!" He turned to the dwarf at his side, Pilpin.

Pilpin was the smallest full-grown elf Glenwar had ever known, but he was a dear friend of his father's. Pilpin looked more like a halfling than a dwarf. Indeed, if not for Pilpin's bushy beard, no one would know the difference.

"What's that?" Pilpin pointed with his short little fingers.

A big brown-green leaf floated down from the sky in a see-saw pattern. It landed at their feet and turned into a scroll.

Pilpin snatched it up before Glenwar could reach it. "Finders keepers, "the little dwarf said.

"It's enchanted. Open it up!"

Pilpin busted the wax seal. "That's an elven stamp. You can tell because the lettering is smooth and fanciful. I had penmanship like that before..." He held up his stump arm. "Well, you know."

Glenwar snatched the scroll away. He read, lips moving but silent.

"What? What? What? What does it say?"

"It's from my father."

"Did he ask about me?"

Glenwar turned his back. "Come, we're going to the council."

CHAPTER 34

THE SECOND NUURG BROADSIDED SELENE with the flat of its battle axe. The blow knocked her from her feet. The nuurg in charge took a jab at Nath.

Nath ripped the axe out of its hands.

"What?" the nuurg blurted out.

The quick movement caught the attention of the soldiers gathered at the entrance. Nath's plan started to crumble.

A streak of red light whistled through the air. It hit the corner wall of the ziggurat and exploded. Stone and bodies went flying through the air. Every neck twisted for a look except those belonging to Nath, Selene, Bayzog, and Brenwar.

As soon as the nuurgs flinched, the four of them struck. Brenwar tackled the nuurg leader in the back of the legs just as another exploding arrow rocked the ziggurat. Nath slugged the flat-backed nuurg hard in the jaw, making its eyes roll up into its head. He caught a glimpse of Selene with her arms locked around the last nuurg's neck. She choked it out.

The titan army forces were scrambling into action. They streamed into the forest in scores, howling for vengeance. Nath waved them on and pointed toward the forest. "That way! They struck from that way!"

"Now what?" Brenwar said.

The entrance was still guarded by a small force of men and a stone giant. Their eyes were on the carnage wrought in the stone temple. The giant moved. His massive legs blocked the entrance.

Nath slapped Brenwar on the back. "Come on. I'm sure you can convince him to let us in."

"I'll let Mortuun do the speaking for me!"

Selene cut Brenwar off. "We need to lure it away, not fight it."

An arrow whistled over their heads. The red bolt exploded in the giant's face. Its head smoked. The giant swayed. Like a great tree, it fell on top of six soldiers.

Nath sprang toward the entrance, shouting and yelling in Orcen. "We need reinforcements. We need reinforcements! They have an army of thousands in the forest!" His voice cleared out the area. He hopped over the giant's legs and shouted inside the ziggurat entrance using his dragon voice. "WE ARE UNDER SIEGE! WE NEED EVERY SOLDIER WE HAVE OUT THERE." His voice carried through the corridor.

In seconds, soldiers streamed out of the exit. Belts and scabbards rattled. Swords scraped out of sheaths. Nath and company stepped aside. The forest was burning in several places now, with black plumes of smoke drifting toward the grey clouds. The army poured into the forest by the hundreds.

Get out of there, Ben.

The last soldier sprinted out of the tunnel. Torches spaced several yards apart lit the tunnel up.

Nath led the way in. "I don't suppose anyone has a map leading to where the lair is?"

"I can find it." Brenwar ran his fingers over the stones. "There isn't anything so extraordinary about the design, just a maze of tunnels. Perhaps a secret passageway or two."

Selene sniffed. "I suggest we follow the stench of the soldiers. Clearly they were guarding something in here." She took the lead.

The corridor was as broad as it was high and plenty big enough for a wagon to roll through. The first room they came across was an abandoned barracks. Bed rolls were on the floor. Bunks were pushed against the walls. They found another like it on the other side of the corridor. There was room for hundreds to sleep.

"Let's move on, quickly." As far as Nath could tell, they were moving toward the center of the ziggurat. They passed by several more archways that led into alcoves. There were storage supplies and wooden barrels. There was a full armory and a smithy.

Brenwar took a sword from a rack. Eying it, he said, "Shoddy work."

"This isn't a weapons inspection," Bayzog said, "but feel free to tinker. In the meantime, I'll continue the search. There's miles of ground that needs to be covered in this labyrinth."

"True, and our allies outside these walls can't hold out forever." Following the dim wurmer scents that lingered in the air, Nath took off at a full trot.

The ziggurat was one continuous corridor that wound within the base. The turns in the corners were ninety degrees. They passed room after room, only taking a moment to peek in. Nath had seen the wurmers flying out of the top. It suggested the nest was in the center. It was possible that the only way to get to the nest would be by going to the top, level by level. The longer they ran, the more Nath regretted not taking a stab at finding the nest in the confusion the last time.

I should have trusted my gut!

Finally, there appeared an end to the long tunnel. He slowed. The corridor ended in an archway where the view opened up to an eerie light source. There was a faint hum too that vibrated the walls. Slowly leading the others, Nath walked forward.

"I don't like the sound of this." Selene placed her hand on the wall.

"There's no turning back now." Nath crept forward, stopping just short of the threshold.

The ziggurat was hollowed out. Stairways of stone led up to terraces on the upper levels. Terraces lined with wurmers. Soldiers were posted behind them.

Under his breath, Nath said, "Great Guzan, there are as many soldiers on the inside as out."

CHAPTER 35

NIGHT HAD FALLEN OVER THRAAG. The roamers and the elven guard spread out in the hills around the hive. In the cover of darkness, they low-crawled through the grasses.

Belly to the ground, Liam inched forward foot by foot. It was an agonizing pace. To the left and right of him were his father Shum and uncle Hoven. They were several yards apart, but all of them had the same purpose. In the cover of night, they would sneak into the cave.

Liam popped his head up. The fields weren't devoid of life. The titan army had patrols. Liam spied three guards wading through the ankle-high grasses. Metal rubbed on metal every time they moved. Each of them poked at the grasses with a spear. The soldiers murmured to one another. What they did was routine, mechanical. The spears dug into the dirt where the soldiers weren't looking.

Liam had been in the field for hours. He was more than halfway to the base hill. This wasn't the first patrol that had passed him, but the third. The others had walked right by him twice. He had his special roamer garb, a leather armor of blending, to thank for that, crafted by the roamers themselves. Its enchantments were special, making for perfect camouflage in the woodland.

The soldiers moved toward him, sticking the ground. Sticking, sticking, sticking. The spear heads enlarged right before his eyes.

Roamers, we have a problem.

One patrol had passed within a body length of him earlier, but this one was on track to walk right over the top of him. They wouldn't see him unless he moved—or they tripped over him. If they did, the roamer garb's blending effects would be spoiled.

Footsteps crunched over the cold and crispy grass.

Liam flattened out. Head down.

Go right! Go right! Go right!

A spear dug into his hand. Liam's jaw clenched.

Aaaaaargh! That hurts!

"Hold on a moment," a man said. "Something sticky here." The man's knees crackled when he lowered himself. "What's this? An odd lump of some sort. This grass is heaved up like a just filled grave."

"Look!" an orc soldier said.

A jackrabbit hopped out of its burrow. Liam could hear the rabbit's paws and the men's feet shift.

"That's a big one," the man said. "I haven't had good rabbit in ages. Do you suppose the three of us can catch it?"

"No, but I can. None of you can cast a spear like me." The orc's spear cut through the air.

"Ha! You missed."

The soldiers moved away from Liam. Their quick footsteps and voices faded.

Liam checked his hand. The spear had bit the meat between the bones. Blood oozed from the wound.

He tore a stretch of cloth from his shirt and wrapped it. *At least I still have my fingers.* He caught Shum's face and gave a quick nod. Shum eyed the sky, making Liam look up.

Something circled in the air. A twinkle like starlight went on and off in long and steady signals. Wurmers that had been perched on the ledges of the hillside took flight. The eyes of the soldiers guarding the hills were cast up and not on the field.

Shum took off at a dead sprint. Liam pursued. On feet graceful as a deer's and quiet as a rabbit's, all of the elves converged from their place of cover. Before the soldiers took another glimpse down, the elves had hidden themselves at the base of the hill.

Back pressed against the ledge, Liam listened to the soldiers. They mumbled and murmured over the strange light in the sky. Liam knew what it was: Sansla Libor with the bright stone of the Occular of Orray in his hands. He toyed with them from above.

Strong fingers squeezed Liam's shoulder. "It's time, son," Shum said softly. Liam swallowed. Roamers didn't get choked up, but he knew where his father was coming from, that Shum was proud of what he'd become. He rested his hand on his father's. "It's been a glorious life. I thank you for it."

Hoven slid in among them. "Don't be so sappy. We haven't even started, but there sure are many. I'm ready to get rid of them all." Hoven pressed into the ledge. It was a twenty-foot climb to the next level. "Let's go."

Shum climbed onto Hoven's shoulders. Liam climbed up the both of them. He spied the soldiers, looking up with their backs to him. He slid over the rim. Hand over hand, he help Shum and Hoven up. They stood in the midst of the enemy whose faces were turned toward the sky. In the same fashion, they traversed the next level, and one more. That was the plan for all of them.

When they were one level from the top, cries of alarm went up. Metal clashed. Somewhere on the hillside, the rest of the roamers and elves were now in the thick of it.

Scores of men posted on the jagged ledges pushed toward the sound of the battle. The problem was, there were soldiers moving away from Liam, Shum, and Hoven, but more soldiers came right at them from around the other side of the hill. Relying on their roamer garb, the three of them pressed into the hill.

The soldiers stormed by, but the last one, a burly nuurg with a huge eye in the center of its head, turned. His eye zeroed in on them. He cocked back his flail and opened his mouth to yell.

Striking like a cobra without the hiss, Shum thrust his elven blade into the nuurg's chest.

The huge, one-eyed orc went down easy, with Hoven and Liam catching his falling body.

But just then, more soldiers came around the side, led by another nuurg. Its eye popped out of its head at the sight of its fallen brother.

The nuurg yelled, "Slaughter those elves!"

CHAPTER 36

WITHIN MOMENTS OF TAKING FLIGHT, much like when a gallant horse thundered beneath her, Laylana became one with the crimson dynamo. But the exhilaration that raced through her veins was ten times stronger. Barely containing the shouts that built up in her chest, she guided the dragon through the air away from Elome—with a sea of wurmers nipping at their tail.

"You need to use some strategy, or else this is going to be a quick fight," Inslay yelled in her ear. "Use the trees. The mountain sides. Slow them in the crevices and ravines. At some point, we will have to fight with our back to the mountain. They'll eat us alive in the skies."

"I know. I just want to get them as far from Elome as possible. That doesn't mean we can't take out some of those wurmers in the meantime… Inslay." She leaned back and elbowed his ribs.

"Ooch, what was that for?"

"Are you just going to sit there, or are you going to do something? I didn't bring you along so you could enjoy the view."

"I might as well. After today, I'll never get the chance to appreciate it again." He leaned over the side. "Yes, the elven lands are truly a wonder in nature. I suppose once you've seen it, there is no need to see it again." His lips and fingers went to work.

Laylana turned in the saddle. Osslin flew behind her on a grand steel dragon with horns like halberds. A smile almost cracked his face. His eyes were filled with elation. In the saddle behind him was an elven archer who nocked arrow after arrow and fired with pinpoint accuracy. The missiles sailed true, dropping wurmers right and left. Other elven riders also shot from bows. The arrows plunged into necks, punctured hearts, and sheared through wings.

Wurmers died by the dozens, but the swarm's thick ranks didn't thin.

"I don't think we have enough arrows in our quivers to shoot them all. As a matter of fact, I'm certain of it," she said. "Inslay, you really need to come up with something."

Inslay opened his eyes. They glowed with a rosy hue. "I certainly hope you didn't expect that I alone could wipe out that frenzy."

"My expectations are nothing less."

"You flatter me. I'll do what I can." He flung his hands out wide. In Elven, he spoke words that were incomprehensible. His wrists rolled in tight rings. Rings of ambient light spun over his wrists and grew. He brought his hands together. A vortex twisted scintillating colors over his head. With a push from Inslay, the vortex held its position in the sky. Inslay kept his eyes fastened on it.

The dragons zipped right by the swirling powers of the vortex. The wurmers ran through it.

Inslay smacked his hands together and let out a powerful word of command.

Laylana shook in the saddle. Her ears rang. "What did you do?"

"Watch and see," he said with glee.

The vortex, small at first, began to grow. It sucked every wurmer into its angry winds. It became a maelstrom of wurmers. They shrieked. Their wings beat in a frenzy. Hundreds of them were mangled together. The wurmers that escaped the tornado of scales were shot down.

Led by Laylana, the dragon riders circled. "Will that kill them?" she asked.

"Probably just slow them down."

"Then what good is it?"

"It slowed them down, didn't it?"

Laylana patted her dragon's neck. "A little fire would be nice."

The crimson dynamo's body heated up under her saddle. It took the chill of the northern sky out of her limbs. And then the dragon spewed a gust of orange flame into the vortex. All of the dragons unleashed their breath weapons. Cones of fire, strings of lightning, and balls of energy turned the wurmers into a spinning inferno. Their roars were deafening. The vortex spun faster. The wurmers, several hundred of them, turned to ash.

"You did it, Inslay! I was only joking when I said it."

"I gave you all I had, but I fear it wasn't enough." He made a notable sigh. "Not nearly."

"Why would you say—oh..." Laylana's heart skipped a beat. The next wave of wurmers was coming. They were big ones, and they were saddled with nuurg riders too. "Oh, speckles."

The earth giants returned to the entrance of Morgdon. It was four of them this time, carrying the battering ram. The twenty-footers hit the iron doors with raw power that made the walls quake. The sound could be heard for leagues.

BOOM! BOOM! BOOM! BOOM!

The hinges groaned but held.

The earth giants labored. Shoulders heaved with bulging muscles and blue veins popping up like tree roots in their necks. Giants hated dwarves as much as dwarves hated giants. Anyone could see it their eyes a mile away. The dwarves fired crossbow bolts into their meaty bodies.

"Look at them! They look like oversized porcupines! Keep firing, bearded brethren! Let them feel our sting!" bellowed Anndee, a prominent dwarf known for his valor on the field. "Get off of our lawn, you stinking things!"

The giants walked the battering ram back, set their feet, sucked in wind, and surged forward for the hundredth time that day.

BOOM! BOOM! BOOM! BOOM!

The seam in the iron door popped open.

The giants paused, their heads tilted to the side.

The iron doors opened in silence.

"Say hello to our little friend," Glenwar shouted up at them. He was standing just inside the gate. Beside him was the Apparatus of Ruune. Two dwarves wearing dark goggles sat on the mystic cannon. The thunder stones lit up, charging the chamber of the apparatus's barrel. The brilliant gemstone light glared.

The earth giants charged forward.

Glenwar dropped his arm. "Fire!"

A bolt of energy shot from the canon's muzzle.

"TOOOM!"

The torpedo tore through all three giant bodies. It left gaping holes smoldering in all of them. They all looked at one another with disbelief. They started to fall.

"Timber!" Glenwar yelled.

The titan army stirred with rage. They beat their weapons on their shields. On order of the nuurg, they charged the main gate of Morgdon.

Ten thousand dwarves in full metal armor stormed out like a great metallic juggernaut rushing down the main gate's ramp. Like a hammer, they busted into the bewildered evil forces.

CHAPTER 37

"I'M ALL FOR FIGHTING," BRENWAR said to Nath. His brown eyes darted all over the massive numbers of the enemy glaring at them from the inner terraces of the ziggurat. "But this might be stretching it a bit."

"Are you suggesting we turn back?"

"It's not retreat if we haven't started fighting yet. However, I noticed something as we traveled down that corridor."

Trying not to look as out of place as he felt, Nath said, "And what was that?"

"There's an aberration in the stones of this corridor. I suspect it's a trap of some sort. But it hasn't been triggered yet."

"Trap?" Selene looked back. "I didn't see any trap."

"You're not a dwarf." Brenwar pointed back down the corridor. "Do you see that low spot in the ceiling?"

"You mean the one that is lowering?" she said.

A huge slab of stone began sinking in the corridor.

"Morgdon's walls! It traps us within!" Brenwar exclaimed. The corridor was sealed off by the huge slab of stone. Absentmindedly raking his bony fingers through his beard as if he were searching for something, Brenwar said, "I told you it was a trap."

"I get the feeling they knew we were coming." Nath eased out into the chamber. All of the faces were silent. The wurmers perched on the ledges no longer hummed. The purple in their eyes had a hot glow. Their hungry tongues flickered out. "Remember what we came for," Nath said quietly. "We need to find the life gem and end the nest."

The inner core of the ziggurat was a square fifty yards wide lit by a skylight hundreds of feet up. There was a rectangular wall that appeared to drop down into a pit in the center. Baby wurmers crawled out of the pit and scurried over the floor.

Still looking down into the pit, Nath said, "Remember, we have the appearance of them, so just act accordingly. It may buy us some time."

But Selene cleared her throat. "Ahem."

Nath turned around.

Selene, Brenwar, and Bayzog had all changed back to normal.

"Never mind. Just pretend you're my prisoners."

"You aren't going to be fooling anybody at this point, Nath Dragon." The throbbing voice that filled the cavernous chamber rankled Nath's scales. It felt like it was part of everything in the room. "Please, enter. Face your doom."

Nath shifted back into his normal form and led his friends inside. "If you don't mind, please reveal yourself, spirit."

"I am more than a spirit. I am I. I am you. I am all of you."

Apparitions rose up out of the dark pit, four in all. Floating forward, the ghostly forms stopped short of Nath and his friends. The smoke images took shape, forming mirror images of Nath, Selene, Brenwar, and Bayzog—clothing, armor, weapons, and all.

"I must say, I'd hate to fight an opponent with hair as gorgeous as mine." Nath flipped his locks over his shoulder. "Well, almost as gorgeous."

All four of the images spoke as one. "Nath Dragon, your end has come. There is no life stone here."

"My senses tell me there is. If you'd care to step aside, I'd like to take a look for it. You see, I have places to be. As a matter of fact, why don't you just lead me to it? You have to understand, I'm eventually going to find it either way."

Brows knitted on all four faces. "You jest too much."

"And you talk too much!" Brenwar swung at his twin.

The twin parried. Hammer hit hammer like a clap of thunder.

The dwarves went at it. Nath lost track of which was which. A problem of his own arose. With a sword the same as Fang in its hand, the mirror image of Nath attacked. He blocked the blow with Fang in a colliding sound of metal.

Great Guzan! This spirit is as strong as I am!

Selene socked her image in the face. Energy fired from her hand into its body. The image hit the ground then rose to its knees with a mocking smirk on its face. "You cannot hurt me, but I can hurt you." A blast fired from its fingertips, striking Selene in the belly. It doubled her over. A tail like Selene's coiled around her neck. It constricted. Selene's tail did the same. In a death roll on the floor, Selene and her mirror image choked one another. Selene's face purpled. Her twin's didn't.

Bayzog's twin jabbed its Elderwood staff at him.

Having the power of the Elderwood Staff already summoned to strike, Bayzog shadow-jumped away from the twin, then moved in behind his own image. He smote the flatfooted twin in the back with the butt of his staff. The striking power of the Elderwood Staff hit the mirror twin full force and slung the monster off its feet, sending it skidding over the floor.

It was up in an instant, saying, "I will kill you!" It shadow-jumped.

Bayzog, a split second ahead of it, shadow-jumped to the edge of the pit. He took a quick glance down. His fingertips tingled. The fine hair on his arms stood on end. There was a sea of eggs and wurmers resting in the basking glow and caressing mist of a life gem's powers. The glance cost him.

His twin locked him up, with its staff crushing his neck.

His eyes bulged. He couldn't see clearly.

Nath took a shot in the chin.

Brenwar's chest was busted with a hammer.

Selene was choking.

Surrounded by a horde of hate in the hundreds shouting wildly from the balconies, Bayzog realized something. They were losing.

CHAPTER 38

NATH LET OUT A STREAM of fire into his own visage. The flames washed over the image. Its handsome face was unscathed.

"You have no power over me," it said. "I am everlasting. I am invincible. Your mortal lives will end."

All four twins said the same thing at the same time. In a deadly fracas, they were beating the scales off Nath, the armor off Brenwar, and choking Bayzog and Selene to death.

But when he caught sight of Selene's eyes bulging from her sockets, Nath's energy surged. He let Fang go and hip tossed his twin. In a single leap, he made it to Selene's side. He punched her twin in the face with a flurry of punches.

Its face faded. The body shimmered.

Selene tore free of its tail that faded out for a moment. Coughing, she said, "Nath, that's it. We all need to attack as one."

The spirit resumed its solid form. "I will kill you."

Nath's twin tackled him. It shoulder drove him into the ground. Using its momentum, Nath rolled and flung his own twin into Brenwar.

The two twin spirits collided. They faded for a moment.

Brenwar slipped free, nose bloodied and eyes wild with anger. "I've had enough of this! For Morgdon!"

Attack as one! Nath thought.

As soon as Brenwar swung at his own twin, Nath loosed his flame on the same. Fire and metal clinched together in the breastplate of the dwarven twin. The spirit moaned. Its body faded to that of an apparition.

Before Nath's twin could react, a bolt of energy smote its face. Brenwar hit it with Mortuun. Nath hit it with a geyser of flame.

It let out an angry screech. "I cannot die. I will kill you!" it said, resuming the form of an apparition.

"Nath!" Selene yelled. She was limb locked with her twin. Their fingernails were digging into one another's throats.

"Brenwar, help Bayzog!" Nath scooped up Fang. He rushed over to Selene and did a double take. Selene and her twin had thrashed around so much, he couldn't tell which was which. "Uh, Selene." He caught the hot stare of one woman's violet eyes. With a quick swing, he chopped the head off the other. The blade cut through flesh that turned to smoke. Helping Selene up, he sighed.

"You know me well, Nath. Good thing."

Mortuun collided square in the back of Bayzog's twin.

The spirit hovered near them in ghostly forms that, for the moment, were harmless. Its words, however, were a different story altogether. The foursome rose up, facing the countless fiendish faces on the inner terraces and said, "Kill them all! Now!"

Men, orcs, ogres, and nuurg rushed down the steps. The wurmers dove right at them.

Rubbing his neck, Bayzog said, "The gem's inside the pit, Nath. I can feel it in my bones."

"I know. All of you, listen to me. Get out! I can take it from here."

"There is no out!" Brenwar said. He leaned over the pit. "It's the way it's always been. The only way is down." He jumped the wall into the pit, landing on a narrow set of stairs below. He crushed the smaller wurmers underfoot and crushed the bigger ones snapping at him with his hammer. "Are you coming?"

"Go, Nath. Selene!" Bayzog said. "I have an idea that should buy us time."

With a nod, Nath quickly led them in a jump down onto the steps into the pit. They hit the bottom dozens of feet below.

Wurmers flew right at them from above. Selene launched missiles into them. Nath sliced them into bits with his sword.

Bayzog shouted a word of command. The gem mounted in the Elderwood Staff turned a bright golden yellow. A force field of citrine energy sealed the pit over like a sheet of ice. Wurmers flew into it and bounced off. Within seconds, soldiers big and small were striking it with every heavy object they had.

With a deep crease between his eyes, Bayzog said, "What are you waiting for? That shield won't hold forever."

"Brenwar," Nath said. "Keep the wurmers off him."

With a skull-crushing swing, Brenwar replied, "Keep them off of him? Who's going to keep them off of me?"

The wurmers came at Nath and Selene in waves. It was just small ones the size of goats and sheep. Nath swung Fang in broad arcing sweeps. Blood and acid flew.

Energy exploded from Selene's hands. The radiant energy blasted away the scales and crackled the skin of the wurmers.

The insect dragons hummed an angry *Ree-Rah* chorus. It became louder and angrier the farther they ventured into the pit. The monsters clamped their jaws on ankles and wrists. If not for Nath and Selene's iron-like scales, they'd have been torn to bits and devoured in seconds.

Selene turned a dog-sized wurmer into a sizzling tower of goo. "Nath, it's good to see that you haven't forgotten how to show a dragon lady a grand time."

Nath ripped a wurmer from his arm and flung it away. "Yes, tell me about it." Together they slew wurmers by the dozens. There wasn't any sign of the life stone though. I'm starting to have my doubts, Selene. I can feel it, but I can't see it. Something's wrong. Maybe the stone isn't here after all."

"It has to be. Keep fighting."

CHAPTER 39

SANSLA FLEW IN THE NIGHT sky, dodging the wurmers that pursued him. He used the light of the Occular of Orray to draw their attention. It worked perfectly, but it also did something better yet. Its light kept them at bay. It allowed him to watch the scene below him unfold.

The roamers and elves advanced on the hive from all directions. Climbing up the levels, they engaged the enemy, except for three: Shum, Liam, and Hoven. Everything was a distraction so these three roamers could slip inside with the orbs of destruction they carried. Now, Sansla could see that the three roamers were boxed in by superior forces. They weren't going to make it.

It's time for me to engage.

Fist first, Sansla dropped downward in the sky. He plowed into three nuurgs, knocking them down another level. Now on his feet, fighting by his elves' side, he said, "Make haste! Take to the cave!" He led the way.

"Yes! Follow Sansla, our king!" Liam yelled.

Fighting as a single unit, they hacked their way to the highest level where the main cave mouth opened. The soldiers were no match for the blinding speed of elven steel. Swords and daggers in hand, Liam, Shum, and Hoven took the advancing enemy down in heaps.

Sansla picked up a nuurg and hurled it over his head. He beat his chest. "There!"

The mouth of the cave waited.

Sansla rushed toward the opening.

His roamers followed.

A giant that rivaled Eckubahn's great size appeared. It was long-armed, smooth, and black skinned, with teeth like a wolf. Its eyes were flames of amber.

"Watch out!"

The giant's hands were swift. It snatched Sansla off the ground, pinning his wings in its grip.

Sansla gasped.

"I am Sulker. Eater of all things!" Its burrow-sized nostrils flared. Saliva dripped from its jaws. "Ah, your flesh will be sweet. So divine!"

With his arms still free, Sansla waved at Shum. The roamer tossed up an apple-sized orb of destruction. Sansla scooped it up. "Dine on this!" He flung the orb down the back of Sulker's throat.

Sulker laughed. "You dare toy with me." He spat the orb out. It exploded on impact, shaking the very foundation of the cave.

The roamers momentarily lost their footing but popped back up quickly.

Sulker's brows knitted. "I'll squeeze you to death!"

Sansla's ribs cracked. "Argh!"

"Hurts very much," Sulker said, leering at him. "It won't hurt so much when you are dead."

With his arm hanging down at his side, Sansla flipped his fingers.

Hoven tossed him another orb. "We only have one left, oh king."

"I know," Sansla replied. When Sulker drew Sansla toward his wide-open mouth, Sansla jammed the orb deep into the giant's nasal cavity.

"What? What have you done?" Sulker dropped Sansla. With his long finger, he dug in his nose. "Get this thing out of me! I can't find it!"

"Give me the last orb, Liam," Sansla ordered.

Liam stuffed it into his hand.

"Now go. All of you flee. I must handle this." He shoved them all away. "I live to let live."

"We all do, oh king!" Shum said with a salute. He, Liam and Hoven jumped over the ledge.

Sansla spread his wings and flew deeper into the cave, right toward the snapping jaws of awaiting wurmers.

Sulker's last words echoed in the chamber, "No, no, no, don't leave me!"

BOOM!

The orb of destruction turned the giant into bits and pieces. The force flung Sansla forward. He collided with the wurmers. Using his powerful limbs, the wounded ape pushed his way into the heart of the hive. He stomped through the mist. Eggs were crushed under his feet. Gnashing teeth ripped at his fur and skin. He wouldn't be denied.

His ice-blue eyes locked on the throbbing heartbeat that illuminated the room. He stormed toward the glow. The life gem pulsed inside a murky cavity in the earth filled with red gel. With the last orb in his hand, he plunged it beside the gem and covered the cavity with his powerful body. The wurmers smothered him in a mass of inescapable bodies.

I live to let live.

The ground trembled. A thunderclap erupted out of the cave. With misty eyes, Shum, Hoven, and Liam watched the hillside cave in.

CHAPTER 40

NATH BIT INTO THE TAIL of a wurmer and slung it away with his teeth. "This is becoming ridiculous." The sublevel of the pit was a field of wurmer eggs as far as the naked eye could see. The nasty lizards burst from their eggs and crawled onto the misty floor.

Over the raucous battle, he caught Brenwar's voice. "You had better hurry up! This ceiling of evil is about to fall."

"Look!" Selene slung a wurmer right of his position. "That way!"

There were rows of stone sarcophaguses lined up on the floor. It all came together. The pit wasn't a pit at all but an ancient burial chamber.

Nath fought his way toward them. "There are so many. Do you think it's in one of these?"

"I don't know. Why don't you start looking?" Selene said, slinging wurmers off of her.

The first stone coffin was covered with a lid made from black stone. It must have weighed a ton. Nath shoved the lid aside. The bones of a large man lay inside. He shoved off one lid after the other. The results were the same. Old bones. No life gem.

"I'm growing tired, Nath," Selene said. The anguish was present on her face. The wurmers might not be able to kill her, but they could wear her down—which was more than Nath could say for Brenwar and Bayzog.

Nath spat out a stream of fire. It spread from one wurmer to another. They screeched and crackled. He took Selene by the hand. "Come on. Look for anything that might be helpful."

Every sarcophagus was identical, but he sensed the power of a life stone. It pulsated like a beating heart. He shoved a lid that cracked on a stone floor. Finally, filled with frustration and anger, he started flinging the lids at the wurmers. The onyx tablets crushed eggs and many of the little demons.

Selene shoved a lid off. A wurmer scuttled at her feet. She snatched it up by the neck, stuffed it in the coffin and pushed back the lid. "There's too many of these things!"

"Wurmers or coffins?"

"Both!"

Together, in the midst of fighting wurmers, they pushed aside more lids.

"Guzan! It has to be in one of these," Nath yelled. He batted three wurmers away with the lid and slung it aside.

Clonking wurmer heads left and right with Mortuun, Brenwar was yelling at the top of his lungs, "Find that thing, Nath! Find it!"

They'd cleared over a score of the lids and there were still dozens left. Every last one of them was marked the same. Stone coffins with black lids. One wasn't any more distinguished than the other. A pool of greater doubt formed in Nath's mind. If they didn't find the life gem soon, they wouldn't make it out of there.

"Selene, perhaps we should go! We're just wasting time."

She shoved off another lid. "We'll never get another chance. It has to be here. Keep looking!"

With wurmers nipping his knees, he kept pushing off lids at random. All of a sudden, the entire chamber was washed in pulsing illuminating light.

"I found it!" Selene shouted.

Nath bounded over to her in two great strides and looked into the great ruby's fiery light. "I'll finish it!" he said, raising Fang over his head.

Selene grabbed his arm. "No! You'll kill us all!"

"It must be done!"

"That's what I brought these for," Selene said, revealing the orbs of destruction from her satchel. She had two in hand. She dropped them inside the coffin.

"I'm not taking any chances." Nath shoved the lid over it. "How much time do we have?"

She shrugged. "Not long."

Nath grabbed Selene's hand. "I suppose we had better get out of here then. Brenwar! We're coming!" Stride for stride, Nath and Selene raced through the wurmers and flames.

Brenwar's battle-wearied face brightened. "It's about time! Now what?"

Nath noted the army of people pounding away at Bayzog's mystic shield. "Step aside and let it down."

"They'll land on top of us!" Brenwar said.

"Not if you get out of the way." Nath dragged them under the pit's overhang.

Eyebrows perched, Bayzog said to Nath, "Are you certain this is the proper course of action?"

"It's either this, or we'll all get a firsthand taste of the insides of an orb of destruction."

"Two orbs," Selene corrected.

"Good point." Bayzog's lips babbled rapid whispers.

Nath scooped Selene up in his arms.

She opened her mouth to object.

"Trust me," he said.

The citrine shield barrier gave. Hundreds of soldiers plummeted with frightened howls. They all hit hard in a loud clamorous thud.

"Grab my legs and hold on!" Nath ordered.

Brenwar and Bayzog latched on.

Nath's wings beat in a fierce fury. He lifted off the ground, higher and faster. He passed the opening in the pit.

Several soldiers launched themselves at him. Most fell short and tumbled into the pit. One, a long-armed gnoll, caught Brenwar's leg. The extra weight dragged Nath down a foot.

"Let go of my foot, you hound!" Brenwar cracked its skull with the butt end of Mortuun.

The gnoll fell.

Nath regained speed. He flew toward the skylight.

Wurmers darted right at them. They latched on with their claws.

Nath let out a booming roar. "NOOOOOOOOOOOOOOOO!" His dragon heart raced. A new surge fueled his veins. His wings beat quicker and without ceasing.

Two quick, muffled, yet all-powerful explosions came.

BOOM! BOOM!

After a gust of wind propelled him up and out of the skylight, Nath veered away from the gap, flying as far from the opening as he could get. He had made it twenty yards when a volcano-like explosion burst out of the skylight, flinging Nath and his friends farther away.

A huge geyser of life-rending lava gushed into the night in a steady stream. It spat up flesh and stone. Charred bodies fell from the sky. Burning bodies landed on the ziggurat and as far away as the forest.

The faces of the titan army were ashen. Their jaws hung to their knees. By the hundreds, they fled.

The geyser spewed for several long, scintillating seconds.

Nath had no doubt that everything inside the temple of stone had died a death worthy of the worst. He landed on top of the abandoned ziggurat. The stone was hot but bearable. "I can't say for sure, but I think that did the trick. Look!" Wurmers dropped out of the sky like dead flies. "It's raining."

Cradling Mortuun in his gashed-up arms, Brenwar said, "There's still plenty left to fight." The forest was burning. "And our friends are still out there." He headed down the steps. "What are you waiting for? The fireworks are over. Now it's time to clean up."

HOUR OF THE DRAGON

-Book 10-

CRAIG HALLORAN

CHAPTER 1

THE SKIES ABOVE THE ELVEN lands rained the blood of their people. The sea of pursuing wurmers washed over the elven dragon riders. *Ree-rah. Ree-rah. Ree-rah.* The wurmer riders were nuurg—one-eyed in most cases, each carrying a long lance.

Laylana, dark flowing locks flapping in the wind, watched in horror as a nuurg rider with a jutting lantern jaw impaled an elven soldier and his copper dragon mount. Elf and dragon plummeted toward the surface, both dead.

"We must stop this, Inslay!" Laylana yelled. Inslay sat on the back end of Laylana's dragon saddle. His droopy eyes hung on the battle scene. The crimson dynamo they rode swerved away from the tip of a nuurg's lance. "Inslay!"

The powerful mage was silent. He'd used a spell earlier, sucking the wurmers into a vortex while the dragons unleashed their fires. It had been a short-lived victory. This second wave of wurmers outnumbered them five to one.

Laylana withdrew another spear from the dragon's quiver. One with her, the beast tilted right. Just as a nuurg crossed into her line of sight, Laylana hurled the spear downward. The long projectile pierced the nuurg's wurmer mount in the neck. The monster bucked in the air, pitching the nuurg rider forward. The giant man and insect-like creature plunged headlong into the treetops hundreds of feet below.

Laylana drew another spear.

It was the fastest fight she'd ever been in. Unlike horses, dragons and wurmers were superior in agility. They looped and barrel-rolled all while unleashing breath weapons with uncanny ability. The majestic dragons fought with an intense passion against an enemy that was nothing short of an abomination to their kind.

The crimson dynamo dove down toward a wurmer and rider. The dynamo's great claws ripped the nuurg from the saddle. The dynamo's great tail slapped a second rider out of its seat. It all happened in seconds. It happened everywhere.

Laylana stayed focused on chucking spear after spear, some hitting and others missing. All the while, she couldn't help but notice the enemy's victories piling up.

Four wurmers latched themselves onto a single elven rider. The elf fought valiantly, but in the blink of an eye, the wurmers tore him up. The skies thickened with the falling dead. Arrows zinged through the air. The elven flyers, in tandem on their saddles, scored hit after hit. It wasn't enough. The wurmers outnumbered even the arrows.

A wurmer and nuurg rider came right at Laylana. A ball of fire erupted from the wurmer's mouth. The speeding globe of energy soared right over Laylana's head, searing her hair as the dynamo dipped. Dragon and wurmer skimmed right by one another with claws scraping at each other's bellies. They both turned for another joust.

For a short moment, both dragon riders hung in the air. The nuurg brute in the saddle lifted its lance and chin to the sky and bellowed a battle cry. Laylana withdrew another spear and rested its haft on her shoulder. The nuurg and wurmer were the largest pair she'd seen in the bunch. The wurmer was much bigger than the dynamo, a truly tremendous beast. Taking down their leader might slow the enemy and buy more time.

"This is it, Inslay," she said.

"It appears so." Inslay put his hand on her back. "I'll lend you all the strength I have left."

The nuurg lowered its lance. The wurmer rattled its neck. Wings beating, they charged through the air.

The powerful dragon came to life beneath Laylana. Wings beating, it bore down on the wurmer. A spring of energy coursed through Laylana's wiry body. With the spear cocked back over her shoulder, she waited until she saw the yellow in the nuurg's eyes. She'd have one shot. If she missed, the nuurg's lance would run both her and Inslay through.

Fifty yards. Forty yards. Thirty yards.

"Throw it! Quick!" Inslay blurted out.

Twenty yards.

Laylana let the spear fly. It sailed true. The missile hit the nuurg square in the chest. Arms flailing, the nuurg dropped the lance. The wurmer's entire body went limp. The crimson dynamo pulled up just as the wurmer started into a spiral descent.

The chronic, mind-jarring *ree-rah…ree-rah…ree-rah* fell silent.

"Watch out!" Inslay said.

The wurmers above them plummeted in lifeless corpses toward the earth. Laylana guided her mount out of the way. The nuurg riders were screaming. Many of them clawed at the air and awkwardly flapped like birds.

"They fall like rain." Inslay was looking at the mystic whips of energy on his fingers. He leaned over the side of the saddle, watching the enemy fall. "My, sometimes I can amaze even myself."

The surviving elves and dragons were the only creatures left riding high in the sky. The dragons formed a ring in the air and began flying a victory round, with the elves pumping their arms and weapons in the air and letting out unified cheers.

Laylana couldn't believe what happened. All she could say was, "They did it! They did it, Inslay! They destroyed the wurmer hives. That's the only possible explanation."

"I like my explanation better," Inslay remarked.

Osslin, Laylana's top commander, flew up alongside her. He was skinned up and bleeding, but the smile on his normally taciturn expression went from ear to ear. "I don't know what happened, but congratulations, Laylana. We have victory!"

Of all the elves and dragons who had rallied to the cause, it appeared little more than twenty of them survived. The losses were great. Many of Laylana's friends were gone. But Osslin was right, they had victory. They'd led the wurmers away from Elome. It had bought the elves time to make preparations against the titan army. Flying side by side with Osslin, she said, "We need to get back to Elome. Lead the way, Commander."

Jetting through the clouds in a unified string of victory, the elves were singing the entire way. It didn't take long before they were descending on Elome. They weren't the only ones closing in on the city, though. Even with the wurmers gone now, the titan army was advancing.

Laylana scanned her lands. She didn't see any elven troops on the ground. "What's going on, Inslay?"

The elven wizard pointed at white banners hanging from the high branches of the trees. "Sweet Elome! The High Council has surrendered!"

Laylana's heart jumped. "Madness!"

CHAPTER 2

Glenwar, son of Brenwar Bolderguild, sank the entire blade of his axe into an orc's face. The battle had been raging since he'd charged out of the gates of Morgdon hours ago. Every dwarf wore a full suit of plate armor, ten thousand in all. With long beards covering their chests like shields, they hammered into the titan army. Their piercing assault splintered the titan army's ranks. The dwarves became a machine of steel. Hammers, axes, and short broad-bladed swords whittled the enemy down…at first.

Sidestepping a savage swing from a gnoll twice his size, Glenwar hacked into its knee. A pair of goblins latched onto his arms before he could let loose with a finishing blow. "Get your dirty little hides off me." Glenwar head-butted first one, then the other. The goblins slipped from his arms, wailing. As they tried to crawl away, Glenwar hacked them down. "Goblins. I hate goblins. I hate orcs." He chopped. "I hate gnolls." He delivered a death blow with his war axe, Guulton.

The giants in the titan army posed the biggest problem. Their tremendous hands swept aside the dwarves like leaves. There were dozens of them. One in particular caught Glenwar's eye. Standing twenty feet tall, it was a husky earth giant covered in hair. The giant stuffed a dwarf inside its mouth. It laughed as it chewed, releasing tremendous guffaws.

"Dwarves! Cut that two-legged tree down!" Glenwar ordered.

A small force of gilded warriors shoved through the fray toward the giant. They bound a rope around one of the giant's legs. Hands locked on the rope, in a single heave, they yanked the giant's leg out from under it. The giant smashed face first into the ground, but the mighty-limbed man was far from dead. Covered in dwarves, it fought back with unbridled rage, scooping up dwarf after dwarf and flinging them aside like rocks.

"That's enough of that." Glenwar charged through the frenzy. He climbed up on the giant's face and split it right between the eyes with his axe. The giant's brows knitted together. Glenwar fought to wrench his axe free. "Uurluuk's beard!"

The giant clapped its hands around Glenwar.

The jostling blow crushed his armor into his body. He fell to the giant's chest, rolled, and hit the ground.

With the axe still stuck between its eyes, the giant stood. It lifted its foot over Glenwar.

With his bones tingling in pain, Glenwar crab-walked backward. He was too slow. The foot descended. "It's the warrior's boneyard for me!"

SHUUUUZZZBOOOOOM!

Ambient green energy torpedoed through the giant's chest, leaving a hole big enough for a dwarf to run through.

The earth giant looked down through the gap. Seeing the armies battling through his body-turned-portal, he lifted his arms to the sky and wailed. The giant's voice went silent. The light in its eyes went dim.

Regaining his strength, Glenwar popped back up to his feet and helped some other dwarves push the giant over. He went for his axe. With a few hard jerks and tugs, he wriggled the weapon free. "That's one thick skull."

SHUUUUZZZBOOOOOM!

SHUUUUZZZBOOOOOM!

The Apparatus of Ruune was making its second appearance. The dwarves let out a victorious cry. The weapon was rocking now. The mystical machine took long hours to recharge and three men to operate. The faces of the dwarves sitting in the weapon's chairs were lit up from the glow of the chambers that pulsated with energy from the thunderstones that powered the weapon. Now, the team gunned down the giants one by one.

SHUUUUZZZBOOOOOM!

SHUUUUZZZBOOOOOM!

One dwarf's iron-thewed arms pumped and cranked the handles and dials of the weapon. The barrel of the massive cannon swiveled left and right, up and down.

The giants caught a glimpse of the great weapon, which was newly mounted just inside Morgdon's gate. They converged. Five in all, they stormed the city.

Dwarves threw their bodies into the giants' path and were kicked, punched, stomped, and slung aside. The Apparatus of Ruune released its final charge.

SHUUUUZZZBOOOOOM!

The magic torpedo blasted the two front giants into bits, but the other giants kept coming. Seeing the opening in the gate, the titan army swelled into an angry tide.

Waving his arms over his head, Glenwar said, "Close the gates! Close the gates!"

Dwarven horns blared out the order. The Apparatus of Ruune was backed inside. The great doors into the dwarven city began to close, slowly.

"Don't let those giants inside, dwarves! Whatever you do, don't let them in!"

The dwarves climbed the giants like ants. Covering the huge men from head to toe, the burly fighting men stuck the giants with their weapons. They stung like a swarm of hornets.

The giants howled. Their momentous steps slowed.

"Keep fighting! Keep fighting!"

Glenwar cut into the soldiers attacking his men. He single-handedly made a channel between him and the giants. Arms over his head, he brought his axe down on a giant's foot. He cut its big toe off. The next chop bit into the giant's shin. The monster man tumbled backward. The doors to Morgdon closed. The battle raged.

Over the next several hours, every living thing that wasn't dwarven died or fled.

Without taking a single minute to revel in the victory, Glenwar gathered his troops. Thousands of dwarven soldiers, banged up from head to toe, had fought with everything in them. Fire burned in their eyes. Glenwar stood on a mound of the fallen giants. Piplin climbed up beside him with the grit of battle all over his face. Glenwar pulled out a parchment that was tucked underneath his armor. The parchment was stained with blood.

With his axe resting on his shoulder, Glenwar addressed the dwarven army in a strong voice much like his father's. "A note from my father, Brenwar Bolderguild."

The wind calmed. The soldiers fell silent.

"Glenwar, there comes a time in every dwarf's life when he knows the end is near. The elves believe the iron chalices of Morgdon have seen their final days. Elome believes no one can stop the titan army but them. That the dwarves are a lost cause. That only the elves can save Nalzambor. I say HAPOKKEE! It will be a cold day in a frost giant's bottom when the elves save the dwarves from anything. What are you waiting for? For Morgdon!"

Glenwar rolled up the parchment and stuck it back into his plate armor. "Dwarves, are the elves better fighters than we?"

Thousands of voices shouted out all at once, "Nay!"

"Then let's go show them who has the greatest army in the world! For Morgdon!"

All together, the dwarves jammed their weapons in the air, "Morgdon!"

CHAPTER 3

THE FOREST THAT SURROUNDED THE ziggurat was filled with giant campfires. Smoke drifted into the wurmerless sky and merged into the cloudscape. The titan army, once full and mighty, slunk off into the night.

Standing on one of the lower tiers with Mortuun gripped in his hands, Brenwar said to Nath, "We need to take the enemy down while they run."

"There're over a thousand, Brenwar, and only a few of us," Nath said.

"I can handle them."

"You couldn't catch up with them," said Bayzog. "Your legs are too short."

Brenwar eyed the part-elf.

Before he could speak, Bayzog cut him off. "Not that I could do much better. It's a simple truth that your legs are stubby."

"My legs won't tire. Theirs will," Brenwar argued.

"It's settled." Nath grabbed Brenwar by his plate armor before the determined dwarf could get away. "The only place you're going is to find our friends, Brenwar. Consider us lucky we aren't in the thick of another battle. We very well may have lost more of us."

"I'd rather be fighting than searching, but aye, as you wish." Brenwar marched down the steps with Bayzog right behind him, the pair of them bickering about something. A wurmer hatchling lay in their path. Brenwar kicked it down the steps, saying, "Looks like an elven wurmer if you ask me."

Selene's hand found Nath's. "You did well. I believe the tide has shifted in our favor."

"I can only hope so, but I'm not counting on it. The wurmers were only the means for Eckubahn's end game. They gave him the time he needed to taint Nalzambor from one corner to another. There might have been more wurmers than the eye could see, but at least with them, we could see the enemy. Now, with all the jaded minds the spirits possess, our enemies could be anyone."

"Will you please try to delight in your victory for a moment?"

"It's just that—*mrph*!"

Selene gave Nath a long, passionate kiss. When she finished, he was breathless. She said, "You're my hero, Nath. Thank you for cleaning up the mess I created."

"I—"

She put her finger to his lips. "Let's find our friends. All of them."

The falling night and the smoke made visibility poor inside the tree line. Brenwar and Bayzog scouted the hillside. There were tracks everywhere. Deep impressions were in the ground of the armor-laden soldiers who had trampled through the woodland.

Down on one knee, Brenwar said, "That army moves without discipline. Never seen the likes of it before."

"Perhaps they heard the mighty Brenwar was coming, and that was cause for alarm and panic," Bayzog said.

"I see your wit has improved. Too bad the rest of you didn't. Do you think you can do anything besides stand there and make snide comments?"

Bayzog whispered. The gem inside the Elderwood Staff came to life, leaving the immediate area clearly lit. "Does that help?"

"Perhaps. Follow me." Brenwar took the lead. There was smoke everywhere—like a fog, but heavier in some spots than others. He found a clearing where the rocks made for a steeper cliff. A stack of bodies lay on the ground, still burning. "There."

Shielding his nose with the hem of his sleeve, Bayzog eyed the pyre. The bones were small. It appeared to be three bodies. He choked.

Brenwar looked back between Bayzog and the fire. The elf was visibly shaken. At first glance, Brenwar thought nothing of the burning bodies. That was when something else caught his eye. A torn strip of cloth hung on a nearby sapling. Bayzog walked up to it. He plucked it from the tree.

It was Sasha's colors.

Brenwar's throat tightened. The bonfire of bodies could have been anyone, but his heart began to sink. They had been inside the ziggurat for a long time. More than enough time for the titan army to pin down Bayzog's family.

A small rock tumbled down from the stone bluff overlooking the flames. Brenwar glanced up. He found a pair of eyes looking right back at him.

"What are you looking at, Beard Face?"

"What am I looking at?" Brenwar replied. "What are you looking at? Get down here, Rerry."

"Oh, there's nothing I'd rather do, but I can't. My legs, well, my legs are broken."

"Son!" Bayzog rushed alongside Brenwar. "Your brother and mother, where are they?" Bayzog handed Brenwar the staff then climbed the rocks like a monkey.

Brenwar had never seen Bayzog climb anything. "Whoa, mage, don't fall. My hands are too full to catch you."

Bayzog vanished over the bluff. Rerry crawled out of sight. A moment later, Bayzog said, "Brenwar, get up here."

"Don't you order me around." He glanced at the staff and his war hammer. He couldn't carry them both and climb. "My hands are full."

Bayzog popped his head over the edge. "Oh, I see. Hang on to the staff." He waved his fingers. The staff carried Brenwar up to the top of the bluff.

"Why didn't you just do that to begin with?" Brenwar said as he waited for the staff to lower him to the ground.

"Even I can be impulsive when my passions get the best of me. I'm still part human, you know."

"Yes, well, I like the human side better." Brenwar took a knee beside Rerry. The young man's legs were smashed inside his trousers. "What in Flint's fire forge happened?"

"I think it's pretty obvious that a big rock hit me. I live. That's all that matters."

Holding Rerry's face, Bayzog said, "And your brother and mother?"

"They went for help the moment the enemy fled. To be honest, I thought we were dead, but when the wurmers crashed through the trees, hah, I just started laughing with joy. Hahahaha…ouch!"

"Stay with him, Brenwar. I'm going after them," Bayzog said.

"No need, Bayzog, your dearest love has returned."

Bayzog whipped around. "Sasha!"

CHAPTER 4

NATH HEARD THE DISTINCT SNAP of a bowstring. The whistle of an arrow followed. He snatched the missile out of the air inches from his face.

"Pretty quick." Selene darted toward the arrow's path. Nath was right on her heels. Another bowstring stretched then snapped. The arrow bounced right off of Selene's scales. They emerged in front of their aggressor. Selene ripped the bow out of an orcen archer's hand. She snapped it in half. "Look what we have here."

The orcen soldier stood with his back against a tree. The fish-eyed brute's glance slid between Selene and Nath. The orc's grubby hands fell to his sword.

Nath rested Fang on the orc's shoulders with the blade brushing against the orc's neck. "I wouldn't do that."

The orc sneered. His ugly face crinkled as he did so. With his coarse hair hanging in his eyes, the orc said, "Don't be a coward. End my life."

Nath looked at Selene. "They're always name-calling. Just for once I'd like to meet an orc with something nice to say."

"What would you like an orc to say?"

"I don't know, maybe something like, 'Your hair looks nice,' or 'I wish I was just a fraction as handsome as you.' That would just be so splendid."

"You're ugly." The orc spat on the ground. "You'll die ugly."

"See, there he goes again," Nath said.

"I see your point." Selene disarmed the orc. She tossed the sword aside, along with three daggers and a short knife. She snapped his bow in half. "Strange that this one didn't flee with the others. I wonder why that is?"

"Ah, a good question." Nath sheathed Fang behind his back. "Orc, why didn't you flee?"

"Orcs do not flee. The titan army rallies. We stay. We stand. We are the strings of death. Any enemies that cross our path, we kill them. We fight until they kill us."

"So there are more of you?"

"We are as many as the leaves in the trees." The orc glared at them both. "Our steel hungers for your deaths. You've fallen into a trap." He let out a throaty laugh. "You'll die like elves."

Nath pinned the orc to the tree with his forearm. "The strings of death, aye." He searched the trees. He had been fighting the orcs for decades. They were notorious for being fine hunters and even better ambushers. At the moment, Nath didn't hear, smell, or see any enemy aside from the one he had in hand.

"Nath," Selene quietly said.

Someone approached. Eslin, commander of the elven force, stepped out from behind the branches with a nasty cut on his scalp and dried blood on his face. "Your Majesty, it does my heart well to see you."

"You as well, Eslin. I see you live to fight another day."

More of the elven guard emerged from the brush. "Our numbers are still strong." He tipped his chin at the orc. "Many of them were found sulking in the willowwacks. Their foulness now fertilizes the soil. Shall we dispatch this one?"

"No, but of course I don't have any need for a prisoner. Perhaps you can deal with him elsewhere." Nath stepped away from the orc. "We've been away for a while. Have you come across Ben or Rip Tippy? Sasha or her sons?"

"Yes. The elves are with Bayzog and his family now. They huddle higher in the hills. Rerry requires a stretcher. His legs are broken."

"But they live?"

"Yes. But Ben and Rip Tippy, I've seen no signs of them."

The orc snickered. "They are dead. I saw them bleed myself."

"Is that so?" Nath said. "If that is the case, then what did they look like?"

"Dead men."

"Dead men, or dead elves?"

The orc's face clenched. "Elves?"

Nath shook his head. "Eslin, please scour the woodland. We need to find them, dead or alive." Nath's heart ached. He had a bad feeling.

Selene put her hand on his shoulder. "They're going to be fine."

The search went on for hours. Nath reunited with Brenwar, Bayzog, Sasha, Rerry, and Samaz. While Rerry's wounds were being tending to, Eslin returned with one of his elven soldiers. They carried Rip's sword, a quiver with a few arrows, and Akron. Akron was collapsed.

"Where did you find this?" Nath said.

Eslin replied, "There were signs of a skirmish where the rock mends with the woodland in the bluffs. These weapons were tucked inside a nook in the crags. I expected to find bodies, dead ones. Instead we found this." He opened his hand, revealing a severed ear and finger. "It appears they've been taken hostage."

CHAPTER 5

WURMERS LAY DEAD ALL OVER the streets of Narnum. The once-free city of Nalzambor had become the home of the titans. Eckubahn walked the streets, titanic in size, arms swinging. His knuckles brushed along the tall buildings, caving in the walls. His head was covered in bright-green flame.

Tylabahn walked one step behind him. She was a ghastly and oversized hag in tattered robes. Her crooked fingernails scraped along the walls. Some of the warts on her body were as big as people's heads.

Lotuus floated behind the both of them. She cast a glance at the wurmers scattered in the streets. People, men, and giants were dragging the corpses out into the fields. Their scaly bodies burned in heaps. Other than the foul tang in the air, Lotuus smelled something else brewing. Defeat. *I hate Nath Dragon.*

The last time she encountered Nath Dragon, he had treated her like a child. He'd laughed at her threats. Lotuus had never felt so slighted before, at least, not in over a thousand years. She'd taken his message to Eckubahn. Nath Dragon had said, "Tell Eckubahn I'm coming for him."

Lotuus normally would have laughed at such a statement, but at that moment she had realized she wasn't dealing with an overzealous hero. She was dealing with the Dragon King. Nath had made that clear. She hadn't believed it before, but now, after the wurmers fell from the skies numbering in the thousands, she was without any doubt. She landed on Eckubahn's shoulder.

"Mighty Eckubahn, I would give a golden dragon's wing for your thoughts," she said in his ear.

"Do not try to appease me," Eckubahn growled. "I can sense your doubt, Lotuus. I am disappointed. Do you now feel that Nath Dragon can make good on his threat?"

"Of course not, Mighty Master. You know I hate him every bit as much as you do. I desire only to see his death. Being one of your strongest allies, I would love to know what our next plan is."

"Plan?" Eckubahn turned in the streets. He made a straight line for the coliseum. "The plan has not changed. It still works to perfection. I own this world now. The enemy is defeated, whether they realize it or not."

"But without the wurmers, well, does that not pose a problem?"

"The wurmers were nothing more than a distraction. Has not Dragon Home been crushed? Aren't countless lives of our enemies now gone? The spirits now run every city in Nalzambor. All of them answer to me. With but a word, anyone that resists my will shall die." Eckubahn stepped through the gates that led to the coliseum where the Contest of Champions was held. His footsteps crushed dead wurmers. Scales and burning guts squished between his toes. "Ah, my greatest prize."

Balzurth's dragon body was still hanging from the rack. The bloodstained Spear of Barnabus protruded from the dead Dragon King's body. The dragon's skin still had the shine of new armor, but it continued to slip from the sagging flesh and bones. It made for a ghastly sight. Four stone giants stood guard. Many other giants and members of the oversized races remained. They all took a knee the moment Eckubahn and his host arrived.

Standing in front of Balzurth, he said, "It also delights me to come and see my old friend." He wiggled the sagging scales under Balzurth's chin. "He's never looked better. His inferior son will be just the same. I'll skewer that rodent like a hog. It's just a matter of time."

"Nath Dragon has been underestimated before. He still lives." Lotuus wished she had bitten her tongue, but the words had slipped.

Eckubahn's head slowly swiveled in her direction. He snatched her out of the air. She was no bigger than a doll inside his powerful grip.

"Please, Master, you are hurting me!" she cried.

"Yes, Lotuus, that is my intention."

She squirmed. The efforts were futile. "I am your ally, from the beginning. You need me!"

"Needed you. Past tense."

"I slew for you. I will slay again." Her temper turned hot. "I am the fairy empress! Loyal to the end! How dare you question me, Eckubahn? If I say Nath Dragon should not be underestimated, then you should heed my words. Did not his father imprison me a thousand years, and you even longer?"

The titan's grip tightened. The flames covering his head flared. He released Lotuus. She stood tall on his shoulder. "Your words are heeded, Lotuus, but be wise enough not to raise your voice to me again." He reached down and laid his hand on one of the kneeling giants' heads. Power surged through his arm. The giant's skin hardened and cracked. Its innards burst into flame. It crumbled into ash. "Ever again."

"Certainly not," Lotuus said. She had no doubt she would have died if she hadn't raised her voice. Eckubahn respected strength. "What are your wishes, mighty one?"

"See to it that all of our servants report anything suspicious. Nath Dragon will come. He slipped in and out of this city once, and I'm certain he'll try to slip in again. In the meantime, I will wait to hear word from Elome. With our spirits in their midst, it should fall any day now." He took one long look at Balzurth. "A shame you won't see your son fail, but soon enough, he shall join you, and all of the world will be mine."

"I shall summon my fairies. I didn't have any trouble finding Nath Dragon the last time. This time will be just as easy. Wherever he goes, we will know."

Eckubahn wiggled a tooth out of Balzurth's hanging jaw. "Keep me apprised, Lotuus. Tylabahn, come. We have business to discuss."

With a quick bow, Lotuus took to the air and flew out of the city. She watched Eckubahn and Tylabahn in the coliseum. *He's holding something back. I know he is.*

CHAPTER 6

Laylana stood inside the High Council's chambers. The grand room had cathedral ceilings and high archways. The marble pillars around the outer circumference of the room were ivory in color, matching the stony décor of the benches the elven council sat behind. She stood in the center, facing the half-moon ring of council members. There were twenty in all, each wearing a set of rich blue robes with white lace. All of them were elegant.

"We have defeated the wurmers, and now you fly a banner of surrender!" Laylana argued. Her fists were clenching at her sides. It took everything she had in her not to yell. Inslay was with her. He had his own fire simmering in his eyes. "The enemy is at our gate."

"It is a banner of peace, Laylana, not a banner of surrender. The titans come to talk, not fight," said one of the council members. His name was Andar. His silky black locks were combed over one eye. Gold rings set with onyx dressed his slender fingers. He had a ferret-like look about him. "There was a superior majority in the voting. The council has decided what is best for the elves. Peace and preservation."

"If they wanted peace, then why did they lay siege to our city? Why did the wurmers attack us in the skies? That's not peace. That is war!"

One of the elderly council members banged a round stone on the bench. "The council is no place for barbaric outbursts."

Inslay took Laylana by the elbow. Addressing the council, he said, "May I have a moment with Laedorn's feisty granddaughter, High Council?"

A female member spoke, saying, "Laedorn's legacy is the only reason we have honored this commoner's request."

"Commoner!" Laylana said.

"Shush," Inslay said. He pushed her toward an alcove designed for privacy inside the ornate chamber. He pulled the curtains. "It's more than clear their minds are addled. This is insanity. But they have the power over the people. It will be fatal to go against them. And that Andar, I've never seen the likes of him before. Haunting. The rest of the council are nothing but empty stares."

"I know those spacey looks," she said. "It's the spirits. The titan wickedness has permeated our very government. It was just like this at Nath Dragon's trial." She paced from one side of the alcove to the other. "It's almost impossible to break that spell."

"So it can be done? How?"

"Two things, well, maybe three. Nath Dragon's roar gathered the wits of some, but the other item was the Orb of Command. Your student Bayzog possesses one. That and the light of the Elderwood Staff. There is no other way that I can think of."

Inslay rubbed his chin. "Not even I have such an artifact. We need to get word to Nath Dragon, but it seems like an impossibility at the moment. We need to delay. Certainly we can talk some sense into these entities."

"I'm open for suggestions," she said, braiding a strand of her hair. "We wouldn't be in this dilemma if we were ruled by a true king and not the council. They've done nothing but frustrate the will of our people. We need a decisive leader."

"Yes, Laedorn was the pick, but his assassin threw our entire government askew. Now our enemies destroy us from within. Our once proud and determined people don't know what to do." Inslay sighed. "We need a king from the royal bloodline. There is power in the blood. The throne brings command."

"Aren't there other bloodlines that have the right to the throne?" she asked.

"Yes, your family's, a couple of others, and the age-old argument that's gone back and forth for centuries."

"You're talking about Sansla Libor, aren't you."

"Yes, the cursed elven king. But no one would ever accept a winged white ape to govern them. It sounds as mad as what we have now."

The curtain parted. Andar poked his head inside. "I believe you've had enough time to consult. The council becomes restless as we await the emissaries of the titan army. If you have anything else to say, then please, come forward and say it now."

Together, Laylana and Inslay stepped through the part in the curtain. They took their places in front of the long-faced council while Andar sat back down in his seat. Checking the faces of the other members of the council, he said, "Is there anything else you wish to add?"

Laylana didn't have a good idea how to delay the unfolding events. She said, "We would like to be present when these emissaries arrive."

"Is that all?" Andar said.

She looked at Inslay. He shrugged. She said, "Yes."

"Well, that won't be possible," the emissary said.

"But I'm the commander of the elven guard. I should be present for your protection, Andar. All of you. It's not safe out there."

"I assure you, we will be fine. Also, while you convened inside the alcove, we convened out here. With a superior majority, the council agreed on the best course of action regarding your command. You will relinquish your sword, Laylana."

"What! Why?"

"Because you and Inslay have been charged with treason."

The gavel struck the bench. The doors to the chamber parted. Elven soldiers carrying spears surrounded Laylana and Inslay.

Laylana whisked her blade out of her scabbard.

"Don't make this worse than it has already become, granddaughter of Laedorn," Andar said. He eyeballed her blade. "To fight would be senseless."

"I could cut you all down if I wanted to," she said to her men, "but I won't shed my brethren's blood." She tossed the sword down with a clank. "Ever."

Smirking, Andar said, "A wise decision."

She replied, "This isn't over."

CHAPTER 7

With all parties gathered, Nath said, "I'm going after Ben and Rip, alone."

Selene hooked his arm. "They have been taken by an entire army. This will take planning, Nath. You're going to need help. Don't risk it alone."

"I couldn't agree with Selene more, Nath." Brenwar set the strongbox down in front of him. "You'll need a bag of tricks, even though I don't tend to rely on this kind of means myself, it is best."

"No, the longer we wait, the greater chance I have of losing them. I can't let that happen," he said.

"They barely have a head start," Eslin injected. "My elves will catch up with them soon enough."

"No, they'll be looking for us. We are a small group. This is a plan to trap all of us. It's not as if the fight has fled them. They will regroup. Besides, I have a plan."

Selene locked up his arm in hers. "Nath, you are being hasty."

"They hurt my friends. They will pay. Remember, the skies are owned by the dragons once more. That's all the help I need." He gently fought his way out of Selene's grip. Bending at the knees, he spread his wings and launched himself into the sky. "I'll be right back."

Shaking his head, Brenwar said, "Some things never change."

"No, but he's brave. It's one of the many qualities I love about him," Selene replied. She noticed Sasha looking at her. The older sorceress was tending to her son Rerry. Bayzog and Samaz chatted quietly nearby. Selene approached. "How is our bold young Rerry doing?"

The young elf's face had broken out in a cold sweat. Sasha was wiping it away with a cloth. "He mends. I'm just thankful that I still have all of my family in one piece. Not to mention the rest of you. And how are you doing, Selene?"

"Unfortunately my relief of the wurmers was quickly dispelled. It's a hard road to victory yet." Selene yawned.

Sasha's skinned-up face made an awkward expression.

"What?" Selene asked.

"You yawned."

"Did I?"

Dragons didn't yawn unless they were about to go to sleep. The problem was, when they slept, it could be for a long period of time. Now would be the worst time for that to happen.

Selene said, "Don't fear, Sasha. Even I can get exhausted. I've been trying to end the wurmers for quite some time. It seems my efforts caught up with me."

"I should say, but I'll keep my eye on you anyway. Besides, we ladies need to stick together. It's up to us to keep these men straight." Sasha continued to pat down Rerry's face. The young warrior's eyes were closed. He breathed deeply. "The healing potion helps him rest. It will be difficult to keep him still wherever we go next. How long are we going to wait on Nath?"

Selene cast her eyes at Brenwar. His hard stare was hung up in the sky. "What say you?"

"We did what we came here to do. Now we need to head back toward Elome, I suppose."

"Agreed," she said, "but as for tonight, you should rest."

"And what are you going to do?"

From a squatting position, Selene stretched up to her full height. "I think I might do a little scouting around. Eslin, Brenwar, are you coming?"

Gliding on his wings a few hundred feet in the air, Nath enjoyed the freedom of the skies. There was nothing in the entire world like it. Despite his concern for Ben and Rip, Nath took a moment to stretch his wings. He barrel-rolled and dipped. He skimmed the treetops, letting the tops tickle his belly. It didn't take long before he came upon the fleeing titan army.

There they are.

Giants, nuurg, and the other foul races pushed their way through the dense brush and branches. They made no bones about their business. The giants at the forefront tore the forest, uprooting trees and knocking them over. It looked like a tornado had ripped a path through the brush. There was a lot of snapping, cracking, and grunting.

They certainly aren't being very subtle about what they're doing.

The army, well over a thousand strong, moved with purpose. The ranks in the back were made of soldiers that spread out among the trees, hoping that any pursuers would cross their path. Even giants and nuurg hid among them.

As I suspected. Ben and Rip are bait. Now all I have to do is find the hook.

The truth was, Nath was relieved to do this alone. It would allow him to exercise the full extent of his powers. At the same time, he didn't have to worry about others being at risk. Once he found Ben and Rip, it would be time to let loose.

Hanging in the sky, he made a few passes over the army. Relying on his keen dragon sight and hearing, he searched for signs of Ben and Rip. The soldiers were bunched together, making it difficult to discern one armed soldier from another. With armor creaking and weapons rattling, it was difficult to filter out anything discernible. After making several passes, Nath didn't detect his friends.

Not good.

Now he considered the possibility that the army was a distraction. He'd noted before that several other war bands had splintered away from the main pack.

Perhaps I should have taken Eslin up on his offer. I hate it when I'm wrong. But there is only one way to find out if I'm wrong or not.

Nath swooped down into the forest and landed a few hundred feet ahead of the army. It wasn't long before the giants shoved the trees between them and Nath to the ground with the loud snapping of popping wood. Two giants covered in hide and wearing necklaces of bones froze. Nath sat on the stump of an oak tree that had fallen years ago. One of the giants muttered to the other.

A nuurg marched right between them. The nuurg was a nine-footer of well-defined muscles. He carried a staff with a spiked steel ball on one end and a spear tip on the other. Without noticing Nath, he said, "Why did you stop?"

Both giants stretched out their long index fingers toward Nath.

The nuurg's neck snapped back. His single eyelid blinked rapidly.

"Don't try to gather your thoughts, one-eye. I just have a simple question. I'm looking for some comrades. One is missing an ear and the other a finger. Have you seen them?"

The nuurg's eye narrowed. His chest began to heave. The beast of a man started to slaver from his jaws and said, "Kill him!"

CHAPTER 8

LAYLANA AND INSLAY WERE MARCHED through the streets of Elome. There should have been a celebration after the wurmers had fallen. Instead, the elves cast long looks their way. Confusion had set in the elven people's eyes. There were tears too. The elves were scared. The distant drumbeats of the titan army were getting closer. No enemy had invaded their homeland so deeply in thousands of years.

"I don't suppose you have a way out of this?" Laylana said to Inslay. Their hands were bound in front of them with silky elotween cords. A score of soldiers accompanied them.

Inslay shook his head. "No. I was hoping you did."

"Silence," an elven soldier said. It was her top commander, Osslin. His almond helmet sat a little askew on his head. It had a dent in it.

"I am your commander," Laylana stopped and argued.

"Were," the sergeant said. He shoved her forward. "It hurts me to be in this position, but orders are orders, Laylana. We will obey them. You know that."

"Think for yourself for a change, Osslin!"

"Is that what you would have me do if I were under your command, Laylana?" His expression was as firm and impersonal as ever. "The world is chaos without order."

"Osslin, look around you. That army of butchers filled with orcs, gnolls, and savage giants waltzes right up to our doorstep. The elves will be slaughtered."

"There is no dishonor in dying for the sake of duty. We all have our reputations to think about." He gave her a firm push. "Keep moving. Don't make this any more difficult than it is. Go quietly."

Laylana's jaw hung. Inslay's did the same. Osslin was as fine an elven soldier as there ever was. He was a banner of elven high standards. For him to turn his back on the elven legacy when the elves liked him the most was appalling. At the same time, she fully understood where he was coming from. The elven standard was high. They lived by order. They resolved troubles by reason and only fought when they absolutely had to. But this was different. The elves faced elimination. The only sense that Laylana could make of it was that Osslin and countless others were now under the influence of the spirits. Osslin, however, had been fine just hours ago.

With one last look, she said to him, "I don't know you."

Osslin kept them moving at a brisk pace through the city. Seeing Laylana and Inslay bound was demoralizing. The council would want them out of sight and out of mind as soon as possible.

"The high order and its statutes are important, Osslin, but when the rules are perverted at the subjection of the people, good elves must rise," she said. "Right and wrong must be clearly defined in your heart. You must have discernment. Don't let this veil be pulled over your eyes. Our kingdom depends on it."

"Halt," Osslin ordered the company. He gave Laylana a stoic look.

Her heart lifted inside her chest.

And then it sank when he looked her dead in the eye and said, "Gag and blindfold the both of them."

CHAPTER 9

Compared to the races of men, time often stood still for the dragons. In the case of a powerful dragon, other people moved as if they were running in a swamp of molasses. The nuurg had called for Nath Dragon's death. Watching the bestial man unleash the order, Nath thought it seemed agonizingly slow. Nath would have yawned if his temper hadn't begun to spill over. The titan army had his friends. They'd killed or destroyed the lives of countless innocents. They were mindless murderers, one and all.

The nuurg was storming right at Nath.

He was left but one choice.

The only way to stop evil is to destroy it.

Nath popped up off the tree trunk he'd used as a chair. Fang gripped in one hand, he slid out Dragon Claw from the bottom of the grip. The gold in his eyes showed brightly in his enemy's eyes whose brows had knitted together.

The nuurg charged with a long shaft of wood. The unique weapon had a spear tip on one end and a spiked steel ball on the other. Its nasty design gave it an intimidating factor. "I will mount your head on my army's flagpole and march you straight into Narnum!" the nuurg said.

There was a time when Nath might have toyed with the towering soldier. Not today. He snaked away from the spear's point. His well-timed stroke with Fang cut the nuurg's leg off at the knee.

"Aaargh!" The nuurg's big body fell, and his blood spilled on the ground.

Nath didn't look back. Setting his teeth, he dashed toward the oncoming giants with his sword and dagger raised high. "Dragon! Dragon!"

Fingers clutching, the sneering giants lunged at Nath.

Nath came to a dead stop and spat balls of fire into their hands. The flames latched onto the giants' hands like dry kindling. The fire spread, burning the hair on the giants' arms and racing over their chests and toward their backs. Normal fire could not harm a giant, but dragon fire like Nath's could destroy almost anything.

The bestial men wailed. Their arms slung wildly in the air.

There was no time to watch the brutes perish.

Onward!

The vigor of battle got Nath's heart pumping. Unshackled from worry, he mowed down every evil creature that rushed into his path. No lone soldier nor any organized group was a match for the whirlwind of fury Nath turned loose on them. Fang and Dragon Claw struck out with dazzling speed. Not one living thing survived their lethal sting. The finest warriors the titan army had to offer were cut down. Belligerent bugbears were skewered and slain. Ogres swinging mauls that could crack a boulder missed the ribbons of Nath's flaming-red hair, time after time. The bite of Fang in their fat bellies left them dead.

The commanders scattered throughout the army sent in their fighters, wave after wave. They swung, stabbed, and dove at Nath. It was like trying to catch a wild jackrabbit. They'd close in only to see Nath skip away. Whatever direction Nath went, the enemy died.

"Kill that demon!" a gnoll commander shouted. Raising a hairy arm consisting of well-defined muscle, the dog-faced man open his mouth and roared, "He is one man! Pile up on him, you cowards!"

Nath ducked under the stabbing spear of an orc. The spear tip impaled another soldier. Nath killed the spear-wielding aggressor. It was instinct that caused him to move. He didn't need to dodge or dive. Their weapons weren't capable of piercing his hide. It took some getting used to. The battling horde parted. A row of soldiers with crossbows lined up in his path.

Nath spread his arms wide. "Bring it!"

"Fire!" the gnoll commander said.

The unified *clatch-zip* sound sent deadly missiles hurtling toward Nath's body. The bolts bounced off his chest and broke. He caught one well-aimed bolt between his teeth. Eying the soldiers, he took the bolt from his mouth and said, "You should be reloading, not gaping. Not that it will do you any good." He flung the bolt into the gnoll commander's chest. "I've heard enough out of you. All you are doing is getting your troops killed."

Nath's mind, once spinning with anger, began to calm. He cut his way through the ranks, saying, "It's never too late to surrender."

The titan army, despite their falling numbers, did not quit. They flung their bodies into Nath by the dozens. Nath stayed with the direct approach. Weapons skipped off his scales. Axe handles broke against his head. Nothing left a scratch. He didn't bleed. It was as if his baptism by flame had tempered his body. Made it tougher. Impenetrable. Even though he was in the form of a man, he felt like a fully formed dragon. He let out a triumphant, earth-shattering roar.

"RRRrrrrrraaaaaWWWWrrrrrrr!"

The sea of evil came to a stop. The soldiers' eyes were wide. They panted. Sweat dripped down their faces.

"Again," Nath said. "I'm giving you one last chance to surrender. All I want are your prisoners. Turn them over and live. Fight me and die."

A stone giant flung a boulder at him.

Nath hopped out of the missile's path. He gathered his arms around the rock. He hefted it over his head. "Last chance!"

A goblin slung a spear into his chest. It bounced away.

Nath tossed the rock onto the scrambling goblin. Its body crunched under the great stone. "Anyone else want to take a shot?"

All at once, the titan army let out a unified battle cry. As one, the blood-mad fighters threw everything they had at Nath. Bolts, arrows, rocks, axes, daggers, and spears ricocheted off Nath's dragon-man body.

He let out a gusty laugh. As the wind whistled through the tree limbs, his red hair flowed like a cape behind him. In a single bound, he spread his wings and took to the air just as the enemy surged beneath his feet. *There won't be any talking them out of it, I suppose.* Nath covered them all in a geyser of flame. The fire spread quickly.

Flying just out of reach, Nath flew from one end of the army to the other, calling out, "Ben! Rip!" His cries were met with howls coming from the army on the ground, calling for his death.

From behind the trees a giant jumped into Nath's path. Nath smacked into its chest. The earth giant caught Nath up in a bear hug. The giant threw its head back and roared. The monster's limbs began to constrict. Nath's eyes bulged. "Great Guzan!"

CHAPTER 10

BREATHING IN AND OUT OF her nose, Laylana fought to maintain her bearing. She might not be able to see or speak, but her acute hearing was as good as ever. The grip on the back of her elbows was firm as well. Her captors weren't taking any chances. Her heart sank some more. Her entire world had begun to crumble.

Keep the faith.

Four hundred years she had lived in Elome. Like most elves, she knew it like the back of her hand. If she had to, she could walk it blindfolded. She could even tell the type of tree she was near from the way the wind stirred the different leaves in the branches. At the moment, however, she was lost. The usual crowd of elves who bustled in the day was in hiding. The quiet march of soft leather boots on the cobblestone streets made an uncomfortable companion. The only familiar thing she heard was Inslay coughing from time to time.

Where are they taking us?

The elves weren't without their dungeons. As a matter of fact, many elves were incarcerated. They weren't without crime or problems, they just didn't experience it quite as much as other races. Crime in Elome was minimal and dealt with swiftly. The prison, however, wasn't in the heart of Elome. It was further out, north of the main city, set apart from the rest. It was a half-day's ride east to get there. Having walked for more than an hour, Laylana still hadn't heard the nicker of a horse. She had assumed Osslin would take her to a holding cell in one of the small garrisons posted throughout the expansive tree city. The problem was, she should have been inside one by now. That left an unsettled feeling in her belly.

Inslay let out a muffled cough in his gag.

A door creaked at the hinges.

Laylana was shoved forward. The daylight on her face turned to darkness. The warmth of a torch touched her cheek. The elven soldiers led her down a flight of steps that switched back and forth a few times. It was unfamiliar to her. Topside, Elome was easy to navigate, but inside the trees and stone walls were channels and burrows that could lead to anywhere.

There was a lot of scuffling at the bottom of the steps. All Laylana could make out was the smell of damp dirt walls. She wondered if it was a mass grave or a tomb no longer spoken of, from long ago.

With Inslay coughing more frequently, they walked underground for miles, changing direction several times before coming to a complete stop. All Laylana could hear was the soft breath of her captors. Her racing heart slowed in the silence.

But… Could it be?

The damp air had become familiar!

Strong fingers undid the elotween that bound her wrists. She removed her gag and blindfold. She stood in front of a large, gaping tunnel.

"I'm in the Corridors! I thought that was the case for a moment, but—" She searched out Osslin. The stark elven field commander had the slightest grin on his face. "You trickster!"

"I had to sell it, but it wasn't easy, Laylana. You're a difficult prisoner to manage." The elven soldiers were untying Inslay's bindings. "All I've done is buy you time. How much, I cannot say, but the Council is fooled for now. I distracted them. Well, committed treason, actually. Go now and find your friends. Get help."

"It will be slow going on foot to find them. Do you suppose you can get word to the dragons?"

"My first thought was to fly you out of here, but the High Council was already privy to that. The dragons we rode into battle scattered in the sky like spooked birds when the titan army's drums began to beat. They are wiser than we."

"Osslin, you should come, and all of our men."

"No, we will keep an eye on things. I await your return. Oh." He motioned to one of his men. The soldier brought forth her sword belt and filled scabbards. "You'll probably need these."

Laylana kissed Osslin full on the lips. "I thank you."

His brows peaked. He gave her a quick bow and said, "Be swift."

Together, Laylana and Inslay hustled into the tunnel.

CHAPTER 11

Ben and Rip marched among the titan army, dripping in sweat. Both men were bleeding from the wounds of battle. The army's stall up ahead couldn't have come at a better time. Ben's legs, stiffer than iron, throbbed and pulsated. The patch of blood where the enemy cut his ear off was hot and burning.

Rip wasn't much better off. He clutched at his hand that was bound up in a bloody cloth. The soldiers had been poking and prodding at them the entire way. Their chronic snickers were annoying. To make matters worse, they'd dressed Ben and Rip up in suits of armor that had been salvaged from their dead. It stank. It was, however, a good disguise on the titan army's part, keeping Ben and Rip hidden in plain sight among them.

Craning his neck, Ben rose up on the tips of his toes. Some unsettling activity was causing a commotion in the front of the ranks. He glanced over at Rip, who said to him, "What do you see?"

"Nothing."

An orc that stood well over seven feet tall swatted Ben on the back of his head. He dropped to his knees. It was like getting hit by a bag of sand. It left his head ringing. Rip helped him to his feet.

The soldiers shoved them back down and held their swords over them.

"Be still," one of them said. The soldiers cast wary eyes toward the front ranks.

Something burned. The stench was awful. On his hands and knees, eyes watering, Ben whispered to Rip, "Do you smell that?"

"Aye, how could I not?"

"What is it?"

A clamor broke out. The murmurings of the soldiers became louder. Feet shuffled in the dirt. Swords slid out of their sheaths.

"I don't know, but it's making our foul friends awfully skittish. Be ready," Rip said with a twinkle in his eye.

"I was born ready."

"Heh, we'll see."

A throaty roar louder than a thunderstorm carried through the ranks like a mighty gale. Every member of the titan army froze.

A new fountain of life sprang through Ben. Without any prompting, he and Rip busted out of the ranks and into the woodland. Ben was shouting out with excitement.

"That was Dragon! I know it was!"

"That was a dragon for certain! A big one!" Rip dashed through the branches that raked against his face. "Did you see the enemy's faces? Oh, what I wouldn't give to paint that!"

The victory was short lived. Their giant orc captors chased after them in heated pursuit. Each carried a hatchet the size of a battle axe in one hand.

"Let's keep running, Rip," Ben said. "We need to buy time."

"No, not running."

"We can't fight with our hands like this," Ben said. Both men were tied up at the wrists. "We need to at least get these bindings off."

Rip stepped into the clearing and waited for the orcs. The five-hundred-year-old legionnaire stood with a swagger about him, keeping his eyes fixed on the orcs. "The day I can't wipe a pair of orcs with my hands tied is the day I'm no longer a legionnaire."

Despite the extraordinary appearance of the half-giant orcs, Ben stood alongside Rip. "You're right. Let's tear them in half."

"That's more like it. Now, play along." As the orcs converged on them, Rip threw his hands up. "We surrender! We surrender! Can you blame us for fleeing that monstrous sound?"

Ben's jaw almost hit the ground. He hissed at Rip, "What are you doing? I thought we were fighting."

The nearest orc beckoned Rip over with the blade of his axe. "Get over here, human filth!"

"Immediately." As Rip hustled over, he tripped over a root and tumbled headlong at the orc's feet.

"Get up, fool!" the orc said.

"Yes. Immediately." Laboring, Rip fought his way back to his feet.

Ben couldn't believe his eyes. *What in Nalzambor is he doing?*

Rip stumbled backward and then, regaining his balance, he launched his boot into the orc's crotch. The orc doubled over. Rip wrestled the axe away from the orc and killed it in a single blow.

Jaw hanging, the last orc cast his eyes down at Ben.

Ben hauled back and kicked it right between the legs. Rip brained it as soon as its chin dipped. "Well played," Ben said. He held out his hands. Rip cut away his bonds. Ben did the same for him.

"So you think that was Nath Dragon's roar?"

Ben picked up the fallen orc's axe and smiled. "Only one way to find out."

Together, they raced toward the skirmish. Bursting out from underneath the low-hanging branches, Ben immediately spied Nath. A giant was crushing Nath in his arms. Together, Ben and Rip forced their way through the jostled ranks.

Ben called up to Nath, "Dragon!"

"Ben?" Nath's golden stare landed on Ben. "Ben! Take Fang and Dragon Claw! Get this monster off me!"

Fang and Dragon Claw slipped from Nath's hands, which hung uselessly at his sides because the giant was squeezing Nath so hard. Both stuck point first in the ground.

Nath's face turned purple. "Hurry, Ben! *Hurk*!"

Rip fought against the ranks swarming the giant's feet. "Yes, hurry!"

Ben grabbed Fang with two hands. Raising the magnificent blade high over his head, he stabbed it into the giant's foot, yelling, "Free Dragon!"

Poof!

The giant turned into a cloud of smoke.

Nath landed on his feet. He gulped in a lungful of air and took his weapons. "Thanks, Ben. Now, you and Rip get clear of here." Nath spat out a geyser of flame that scattered their enemies. "Now."

"What are you going to do?"

"They had their chance to surrender. They refused. A nasty storm's coming. Go!" Nath's jaws clenched. His golden eyes smoldered. Wings spread, he launched himself into the air.

Ben and Rip ran a good distance into the woods before they stopped and looked behind them. The howling masses were screaming at the sky. Dragon fire consumed them from one end to the other.

The wroth heat crinkled the leaves between them and the fight. Shielding his eyes, all Ben could say was, "Whoa."

CHAPTER 12

SHES DRIFTED IN THE AIR. The ground was covered in them in a long path that stretched out over a mile. The embers underneath held an orange glow. Steam rose up from them. Charred bodies were collapsed in heaps, but many stood upright, frozen skeletons on smoldering rickety limbs.

Brenwar looked up at a scorched skeleton that stood ten feet tall. Its mouth hung open toward the sky. It swayed in the gentle wind. He poked the bony knee and watched the once-great limbs collapse in the ash. Brenwar fanned the dust from his face. He clenched his jaws. "He should have waited for me. And this is cheating."

Selene chuckled.

Accompanied by Eslin, they stood at the back end of the wide runway of death, marveling. Nath had turned an entire army into dust.

Brenwar was a little beside himself. "Why are you laughing?"

"Our enemy has perished. You should be elated," she said. She was combing her long fingers through her hair with a playful smile on her face. "I'm envious. I didn't get to see this glorious work for myself."

"You're envious? He should have saved some for me!" Brenwar stomped through the ashes, knocking one toasted skeleton over the other. "I missed out."

With a perched brow, Eslin said to Selene, "You are certain Nath Dragon is responsible for this?"

"It could only be him. He breathes the fire that cleanses the world of evil."

"I never imagined any man could wield such power. He's created a graveyard. That army was well over a thousand strong."

"He's not a man. He's a dragon, and it seems he's coming into his own." Selene strolled after Brenwar, stirring up ashes. She rested her tail on her shoulder. "I'm curious to see him. Come on. He's bound to show up sometime."

They had walked a half mile when they saw three men strolling in their direction. One of them was waving. It was Ben. He walked on the right side of Nath. Rip was on the left. They were all smiling.

Stopping among the ashes, Ben circled in his spot. "Do you see this? Dragon wiped them all out. I never imagined the likes of it. Wings wide, he flew right over them and whoosh! He scorched them."

"Yes, yes, we understand what happened, Ben," Brenwar said. "We aren't blind." He inspected the side of Ben's head. There was caked blood on it. "Looks like you lost something. I don't suppose you're much good to us now."

"Aw, it's good to see you too, Brenwar. Even without my ear, I can still hear you clear as ever. And I must say, it's even more unpleasant than it used to be."

Brenwar fixed his gaze on Nath. His friend had the appearance of a knight in gleaming black armor. The radiance in Nath's golden eyes was unlike anything Brenwar had seen before in his friend. "Er, Your Highness, I suppose I should say well done, though I am a tad envious."

"There's plenty left to fight, Brenwar. The ones I didn't get scattered like varmints in the branches." Nath laid his hand on Brenwar's shoulders. "I really wish you could have seen it, though. It felt good destroying evil. Even better, we have our friends back. Most of them, that is."

Ben and Rip chuckled.

"It was worth it," Rip said. "It reminds me of those days in the Great Dragon War. The smell of the enemy's smoldered flesh. It gets my juices flowing. I feel like I'm twenty, not five hundred or so."

"Now what, Your Highness?" Selene said, cozying up to Nath. "Will you allow us to come along on your next triumphant journey, or will you get to take them all on your own?"

"As much as I wish this was a fight I could handle on my own, I know better. I've a feeling the elves still need us. But first, I need to talk to Bayzog."

The emerald-green seeker landed on Nath's shoulder. Nath patted its head. Softly, he said, "Find Grahleyna."

They'd begun their journey east toward Elome. Exhausted, they'd lumbered along with a smile in their voices among the low talking. Despite their wounds, they all lived to fight another day. All of their hearts were well.

Selene managed to stitch Ben's ear on with the help of a healing vial and a very thin thread that the elves carried. She offered to help Rip out with his missing index finger, but he would have none of it. His comment drew a respectful grunt from Brenwar.

As they walked, Nath took Bayzog aside. "The wurmers have fallen, old friend. Now will you fill me in on what my father said?"

"Certainly, Nath. And believe me when I tell you it was difficult to deny you this information the first time. But you needed to be focused. The goal is accomplished. Well done." Bayzog put some of his weight on his staff when he walked now. "I look forward to the day when we can revel in it."

"You, revel? Now that is something I'd like to see." Nath brushed his long red hair back over his shoulders. "Now tell me, how can I help Father? Can it be done?"

"Anything is possible given an adequate amount of time. If your father is able to see any of what happened, no doubt it will give him the strength he needs to survive." Bayzog stepped around a snow-covered tree stump. His robes got caught on new limbs sprouting out of the stump. He tugged them free. "Sometimes I wonder if there is any elf in me at all. I feel like a veritable fish in the woods."

"I couldn't have said it better myself," Nath said, his voice trailing off.

"Yes, well, continuing the discussion at hand. Your father's essence has been traveling between the Land of Dim Light and the Dark Realm. Chances are, by now, he's in the Dark Realm." Bayzog shifted the Elderwood Staff from one hand to the other. "His situation is not so much different than Eckubahn's or Gorn Grattack's. He needs a very strong host body in order to return. Given the all-powerful nature of your father, there is only one body powerful enough to suit him. His own."

"But his body, it's dead."

"Not according to him. You see, the Spear of Barnabus separated the body from the spirit, but it did not kill either one. This is where Eckubahn slipped. He keeps the body as a trophy. Perhaps he does not realize the possible danger he will face by not destroying the body. Or, it's all a clever trap to get you. Even so, in time, your father's body will deteriorate. It's not likely to hold up much longer."

"What am I to do?"

"You could try to destroy Eckubahn on your own. Send his spirit back to the Dark Realm. There would be no shame in that. Your father would be pleased."

"I want to save Father. I can't leave him there."

"Of course you do. So long as the Spear of Barnabus is in the body, for all intents, it is dead and cannot be rejuvenated. But if one were to remove it, that would create a tiny window. Your father would be able to pass through it. But the chances are very slim, and I can only assume the body is guarded. Most likely, Eckubahn anticipates this. After all, he's been right where your father is now."

"You know what I'm going to do."

"Of course. And I'm going with you."

CHAPTER 13

Laylana and Inslay traveled beyond the tunnel. Still on the far edge of the eastern elven lands, they moved at a brisk pace, glancing over their shoulders from time to time. Elome could no longer be seen. Its grand treetops were hidden by the dales that made the landscape go up and down like gentle waves. They waded through tall grasses and wildflowers that kissed their knees.

"You have to forgive me, Laylana. I'm no ranger, and the land is, well, quite expansive. How do you hope to track down Nath Dragon and his allies? Are we just going to march until we run into them?"

"Something like that." She brushed her hands over the petals of a bright-yellow wildflower. Blossoms in the early and late winter were something the elven lands were known for. The vibrant lands were practically in season year round. She pointed to a channel where the green stalks had bent. "See, there is the trail that I follow."

Inslay fluffed his robes and walked over, eyeing the spot Laylana pointed out. "You've been following a trail all this time? I thought this was a blind march filled with desperation. Hah, that gives me more confidence." Scratching the thinning hair on his head, he said, "Uh, how do you know you are on the right trail?"

"The greenery bounces back quickly after an interruption, but I can tell. Nath Dragon and his companions are the only fit. If it were the giants or their army, the impressions would be far deeper. Besides, Nath has not been so long gone."

"I suppose not. Again, I haven't been out and about in centuries, but long ago, I traveled with the best. Keen eyes and minds were among them." He nudged her with the back of his hand. "Laedorn being one of them. He'd be proud of you. Such a shame, the way he went. It made such a mess of things."

"The elves need a king. The High Council is a disaster. It's a wonder the orcs didn't take our lands using pitchforks the way things have been going," she complained. They came to a shallow stream. The waters rushed by and over stones standing below and above the waters. Standing on the bank, she said, "You should take my hand. It's nothing but bitter cold in that water."

"That sounds refreshing, considering my burning feet." He took her hand and gave it a firm squeeze. "But yes, I'll be careful." Inslay ambled over the rocks almost as easily as she did. He smiled at her after they crossed. "I couldn't have done it without you."

Together they climbed up the bank with Laylana leading the way. She dropped to her belly.

"What are you doing?" Inslay asked.

She jerked him down by his robes.

"*Bwwah*!"

Under her breath, she warned, "Sssssh. Soldiers."

Inslay gave her a thumbs-up. He closed his eyes and started speaking quick words and phrases.

Laylana crawled up the bank. Her heart was racing. She caught the eye of an orcen soldier that had more scars on his face than hair on his head. She couldn't count all the soldiers, but there were many, twelve or more if she had to guess. She parted the grass in front of her face.

Sons of Lindor!

Goblin soldiers skulked through the grasses. Their yellow eyes seemed to gleam in the dusk. Three in all came slowly, bearing down on her location. Behind them, the orc and a gnoll the size of two waited among their edgy brethren.

Laylana crawled back to Inslay. "Company's coming. Nowhere to run."

"How many?"

"It's a patrol. A dozen at least. One of them is big. A gnoll brute with muscles up to his earholes."

"Could be worse, I suppose. I'm ready. What do you want me to do?"

"Just stay behind me. They won't know what to expect from us. I'll handle it."

Side by side, the goblins appeared at the top of the bank. Then three wiry men carrying hatchets and small wooden shields. The one in the middle said, "Don't move, elves! Surrender!"

Laylana lifted her arms up over her head. Inslay did the same.

The goblin leading the small pack shouted back to the others in the scouting party, "Elves! Two fugitives from Elome, I'd say. A woman and a fragile male. Shall we slay them?"

"Nay!" Laylana heard the orcen leader say. His voice was distinct and gravelly. "Bring them forward. Different elves bring different bounties. At worst, we can have some fun with them before they die."

The goblins beckoned them up with their axes.

Laylana said, "Please, don't harm us." She pulled Inslay up the bank by the hand. He slipped and fell. She helped him back to his feet. He slipped again.

The goblins made wicked cajolings. The leader among them said, "The old one is not worth keeping, but the hair on the beauty shall fetch me a fair price. I cast claim on the raven's hair!"

"Shut your mouth and bring them to me," the biggest orc said.

Laylana reached the top of the bank with Inslay hanging onto her wrist. One of the goblins wrenched them apart. She got her first good look at the enemy patrol. There wasn't anything extraordinary about them, aside from the gnoll. His wolfish face and big body gave him more the look of a beast than a man. There was a collar on his neck fastened to chains gripped in the hands of two orcs.

Licking his lips, the orc leader said, "I can see she is fair, but she wears armor. Did you not strip her of her gear?"

The goblin's eyes fell on her sword. He shook his head.

The orc pulled his sword. "Fool! Take the woman's blades away!"

Laylana's sword and dagger whisked out of their scabbards. She stabbed two goblins in the belly simultaneously. The last goblin cocked back his axe. Inslay snagged his wrist. The goblin's skin lit up like a firefly with a crackling *bizzzap* sound.

The orc leader barked out an order. "Let loose the hound! Let loose the hound!"

The soldiers unlocked the chains from the gnoll's collar. They filled the slavering beast's hands with swords that looked like cleavers. The gnoll let out a howl as it advanced.

Inslay's fingers gently rested on Laylana's shoulders. "I'll let you handle this."

Chapter 14

"You know I'm going with you," Selene said to Nath.

"I'm counting on it," he said, "but I have a feeling it's going to be difficult to convince the others not to come. Especially you know who."

Her eyes glided over to Brenwar. He was marching along with the rest of the group, boots stomping the snow and Mortuun slung over his shoulder. She and Nath had hung back. Samaz and another one of the elven guard carried Rerry on a stretcher. Everyone else had their faces set against the chilling late-winter wind. "Are you certain you want to leave him out of it?"

"No, I don't want to leave him, but he's not very keen on flying. Besides, they'll need more protection for the march back to Elome. At least temporarily."

"What do you mean?"

"For the first time in a long while, we will have some help. Now that the skies are ours again, we'll have aid from the dragons." He scanned the firmament above. "We're just waiting now. They come. Soon."

"Your faith in our brethren has renewed. I can hear it in your voice. It twinkles in your eyes."

"I feel whole." Nath breathed in deeply through his nose. His lungs expanded. "I haven't felt this complete since I was a dragon. It's odd: I have the power, but not the form. But the flying"—he smiled from ear to ear—"and the sound of wood and metal snapping off my back, it's pure elation."

"And that small army you wiped out?" She caught his eye. "Did you have any reservations about that?"

"No. I actually pleaded for their surrender. I offered fair warning, but there wasn't any changing their minds. They made their decisions. What was done had to be done, lest more innocents die."

"I'm glad to hear that you feel that way." Selene held his hand. "Now is not the time to quaver."

"Quaver? Me? I am the Dragon King, more or less. I accept the burden heaped upon my shoulders."

"No, you relish it."

"Is that a bad thing?"

"No. Nalzambor needs you confident, not doubting yourself. You have quite a charge ahead of you if you want to finish off Eckubahn." Her grip tightened on his. "Nath, he's everything Gorn Grattack was and more. And I'll admit, I'm somewhat haunted that Gorn Grattack still exists, even if it is in another realm."

"Perhaps you shouldn't get in the thick of it then. It could be risky for you, Selene."

"No, it's not that. My loyalty is all yours. It disturbs me that he lives. I'd believed him gone forever, but deep down, I could feel his evil still. He'll always have a stronghold on weak people."

"Yes, the wicked thrive on that, don't they." He leaned his head into hers. "We've made it this far. We're going to get through the rest."

She nodded.

After a few minutes, Nath started to fidget.

"You're wanting to glide the firmament above, aren't you."

"Is it that obvious?"

"Of course. If I still had wings, I would want to do the same. Just try not to go too far."

"I won't. I'm just surprised I haven't seen any dragons as of yet. Certainly one or two would have crossed the horizon by now."

"Perhaps you should call them? There aren't any wurmers to fear now."

"I've considered it, but I'd rather not alert our enemies. They still abound, quite possibly in places where we cannot see them. I'll be back shortly." With a flap of his wings, he took to the air. Within seconds he vanished into the clouds.

Walking and watching, Selene almost bumped into Brenwar. He'd set his hard eyes on the clouds. "Where's he off to?"

"I believe our pace is too slow for him. He searches out a much quicker means of transportation."

"We're moving just fine. It's the part-elf that slows us down."

"I heard that!" Rerry shouted back from his stretcher.

"Well, it's true!"

"There's no need to give the young one such a hard time, dwarf—I mean, Brenwar. If you don't mind my saying so, you seem a little tense."

"Me, tense? Never." He clawed his beard. "I've got a feeling the two of you are making plans without me."

"Rerry and I?"

"No, you and Nath. I'm no fool. I felt your eyes on my back when you were talking. He's going after his father, isn't he." He blocked her path. "Isn't he."

"At the moment, no. He's looking for dragons so that we can be whisked back to Elome."

Brenwar set Mortuun's head on the ground. He rested his hands on the top of the handle. "I've been dealing with him a long time. He clams up when he's about to do something he doesn't want me to know about. What is it?"

"Brenwar, it's really a simple explanation. He figures you don't want to fly, is all. 'Dwarves don't fly.' I've heard that more than once from your lips. There are many things your kind finds objectionable."

"What! Is that his excuse for cutting me out of the battle?" His brows knitted together. "That's an excuse, and a poor one. There's a big difference between wanting to and having to. Do you think I bludgeon my enemies for pleasure?"

"Yes."

"Mmmm…perhaps that's a bad example. Uh, ah, I don't want to fight these wars. I'd rather be hammering away at my forge, building bridges, or walking the leagues with my family. I have to fight, because if I don't, the venomous races will only spread their poison. The point is, I do what I have to, not what I want to."

She crossed her arms and gave him the eye. "So you'll fly on the dragons and not complain?"

"Not complain? Of course I'll complain." He paced back and forth in a short path. "I'm a dwarf. I don't like things. I make my feelings clear. You can't expect me to hold them in. I'd crack like a cackleberry if I did. Besides, I've ridden on dragons. You've seen it." He rubbed his stomach. "It just makes me queasy. It's not normal."

Selene chuckled. "I'm convinced."

"That's grand! Now tell me what Nath's plan is."

CHAPTER 15

THE GNOLL FIGHTER RUSHED LAYLANA with startling speed. He swung his wide blade of steel with barbaric savagery. She backpedaled, slipped on the icy snow, and landed on a knee, then jumped aside just as the gnoll hacked into the ground with both blades. The metal bit deep into the snow-frosted ground.

The gnoll ripped his swords free, glowering at her. "Elven meat I eat." He gnashed his teeth.

Laylana planted her feet in the ground. Chin down, she eyed the gnoll. She'd trained for decades against Elome's finest elves. She'd battled her way through contest after contest. This game was different. Elves were light and quick. Their sword cuts came in flashes. They weren't anything like the raw savage in front of her. The gnoll was the size of three elves in one. His muscles were bunched up like knots in a tree. He was a beast.

"Come and get a taste, dog."

Swords wide, the gnoll rushed her.

Feet braced in the ground, she waited.

The dangerous swings of the beast's blade collapsed on her.

She struck and ducked. Her sword sank into flesh just as steel swished over her head.

The gnoll let out a pained grunt. He bowled her over.

Gnoll and elf were on the ground. His savage strength pinned her by the neck and wrist. Her sword arm was useless. Choking, she fought against his superior might. Saliva dripped from the gnoll's jaws onto her chest. With her free hand, she stabbed into the gnoll's side with her dagger. It bit deep. Howling, the gnoll rolled away.

Coughing, Laylana fought her way back to her feet. Spots danced in the air before her eyes. The gnoll's chest heaved. He bled. She wiped her busted lip. Her limbs were exhausted.

Panting, she said, "Round two."

Wary eyed, the gnoll lowered his shoulders and marched right at her. Using his advantageous reach, he attacked with hard and quick swings.

Laylana parried. *Clang!* Catching the savage blow—steel on steel—jarred her arm. Her grip loosened. Her arms lowered for a split second then sprang up again, catching another flurry of thunderous blows.

The gnoll hammered away. His powerful strikes knocked her sword and dagger aside time and again. "You will fall, weakling. You will die," he said with narrowed yellow eyes.

Laylana's blood boiled. She was a fighter, a skilled one, more than a match for the brute force of the gnoll. Yet he was beating her down. Exhausting her. Her skill was succumbing to brute force. *Don't go out like this, Laylana! He's an evil savage!*

"Prepare to fall, elf!" the gnoll snarled. He struck at her with hard hand-over-hand swings.

Summoning every ounce of strength she had left in her, she deflected one of the gnoll's swords, sprang backward into his body, and cracked him in the nose with the pommel of her dagger. With a quick slice, she cut the gnoll's wrist.

Dropping one of his blades, the gnoll shuffled backward.

She went in for the kill.

With his wounded arm dangling at his side, he swung hard with his sword.

Laylana knocked the lone blade aside. She coiled back, cocking both elbows for a lethal strike. Blades poised at the gnoll's exposed chest, she lunged forward.

The gnoll blindsided her with a haymaker. His fist collided with the side of her head.

She spun to the ground. Rolling to her back, she looked up just in time to see the gnoll lording over her with his sword high over his head. She was numb. Her body didn't respond to her commands. All she could do was watch the blade fall like a sliver in the sky.

"Nooooooo!" she screamed.

And then sitting up quicker than a wink, she sank both of her weapons into the gnoll's belly at the same time.

The sword slipped free of his fingers. It fell behind his back and stuck in the ground. The gnoll's jaws were frozen wide open. It died right where it stood.

Laylana removed her blades from the upright gnoll and staggered away. Huffing for breath, she searched for Inslay. She found him standing nearby.

Inslay's glowing hand was pointed at the burly gnoll's back. The mystic bands dancing off his fingers fizzled out. Sweating above the brow, he said, "That was close. I'm spent."

Laylana wiped her blades off in the snow and sheathed them. The orc commander and all of his men lay dead on the ground with smoking holes through them. "I should say. I'm spent myself."

"I won't lie, I thought I might have seen the last of you." He rubbed his fingers in his palm. "I can't make so much as a crackle. You're a true warrior, Laylana."

A shadow passed over them.

Laylana snaked her sword back out. But it was silver dragons that landed. Slivver was among them. Sheathing her blade, she let out a sigh of relief. She walked right up to Slivver and hugged him.

Hugging her back, he said, "This is a very welcome fanfare I wasn't expecting. Are you well?"

"Aside from my body feeling like it's filled with a bag of sand, I'm quite fine."

"Your body looks fine to me," Slivver said. "Aside from your face swelling. Were you stung?"

"Yes, by that." She pointed at the gnoll. He stood stiff as a statue. "He swatted me good." Holding a cloth packed with snow to her face, she explained to Slivver her problems with the elven High Council. "We have to find Bayzog and the Orb of Command."

"Perhaps," Slivver said.

"Perhaps? There's no other way that I can think of, Slivver. Unless you know something?"

"No, I don't." The handsome silver dragon turned his gaze north. "We have company."

Riders were coming. It was a small group that was too far away to make out from the distance.

"Who are they?" she asked. It seemed most likely to be another one of the titan army's patrols.

Slivver shrugged. "We'll find out soon enough when they get here."

CHAPTER 16

WITH THE ICY WINDS BENEATH his wings, Nath journeyed in a circular pattern that expanded outward. It wasn't long before the many heavy concerns that swam in his mind began to ease. The liberation of flight changed his perspective on everything. From high above, all the world's problems below seemed so small. It was hard to believe that the beautiful lands of Nalzambor were in such turmoil. From above, everything looked so majestic, from the mountaintops to the beautiful landscape of the forests.

I think I'd stay up here all the time if I could.

With icy bits of sleet kissing his face, he smiled and made a few barrel rolls and loops. It was just him and the skies and square leagues of freedom. It would be easy for one to lose himself. The skies were an entirely different world. Aside from the occasional harsh elements—which had little to no effect on him—it was bliss. However, after a few hours, flying became a little lonely.

I can't be the only dragon up here. I should have seen some by now. The skies belong to the dragons again.

It was odd. The skies were so vast that if you saw them from a distance, even the largest dragons appeared as specks. Nath, with his powerful vision, certainly should have seen something by now. The isolation began to gnaw at his stomach. Time began to tick faster. He needed to save his father.

A fleck of green caught his eye. The raccoon-sized emerald seeker came. It floated alongside Nath with its wings beating like a hummingbird's. Making dragonish chirping noises, it beckoned for Nath to follow.

"Lead the way, little one."

The seeker jetted off at a speed Nath struggled to keep up with. An hour later, the little bee-striped dragon dove toward leagues of high mountain ranges. The highest peak was covered in mist too thick to see through. Together they plunged through the vapors. Nath punched through the bottom and beheld a startling sight. It was a crater, miles wide from one end to the other and half as deep. He knew it instantly: the Dragon Graveyard.

The Dragon Graveyard was a forest, not thick in trees, but rich in soil and tall grass. Natural streams flowed from an unseen source. There were dragons too, not dead, but alive. Thousands of them lay on the grasses. Many of them were grazing. The most clearly seen were the fetchers. The huge gray behemoths' claws dug at the soft dirt and patted it down. There were countless fresh graves of all sizes.

Nath landed on a ledge of the crater's outer wall, marveling at the sea of colorful dragons. There were golden flames, green lilies, ivory sliders, steel bellies, red bulls, humongous sky raiders, red rocks, blue streaks, crimson dynamos, orange blazes, yellow streaks, thunder beards, lizard wisps, fire bites, silver shades… That was only a portion of the dragons, but it was the first time he'd seen so many in one spot.

Their ranks parted. One dragon, very large with golden scales streaked with white, came his way. It was Grahleyna.

"Mother!" He jumped from the rocks and clung to her great neck. "I was uncertain about you."

"I had my doubts too," she said. "But, we've managed."

"Why here, Mother? The wurmers are dead. All of them."

"We've been waiting on the king's word. Besides, there are too many spies. When we rally, we don't want them to see it coming." She nuzzled him with her cheek. "Trust me, I've been waiting eagerly for your return. Strategy in battle isn't my strong suit."

"I know you'd be great at it, Mother. There's not a smarter dragon than you."

"Thank you, Son, but this is your army to lead. What must be done?"

Nath slid off her back and stood before her. "It's Father. He lives. He can be saved. I'm going after him."

Her long lashes lifted. "You wouldn't toy about such a thing?"

"Never, Mother. There's a window of chance to save him, but it's closing. I need to get after him, and I need to do it now."

"Tell me more."

Nath explained to her everything that he knew about the Land of the Dim Light and the Dark Realm. A tear ran down her scaly cheek. Nath caught it. "Mother, we will save him."

"My heart aches when I think about him. He sacrificed so much for me."

"You're worth it." Nath grinned. "If you weren't, he wouldn't have done it. Together, Mother, we will put an end to this menace once and for all."

"You've grown so much, Nath. I believe in you and in your quest. Do you know how I know?"

"Because a mother always knows?"

She let out a charming laugh. "No. It's because you said *we* will save him and not *I*. You've learned that you can't do it all on your own. I'm proud of the dragon you've become, Son. There is much strength in numbers, Nath, and as you can see," she said, lifting her long neck and peering at the countless dragons, "our numbers are many. How will you use them?"

"Wisely." He moved toward a nearby sky raider. They were the biggest breed of them all. It sat with its head thirty feet high in the air. Nath started at the tail and walked up the spiny ridges on its back. He made it until he stood inside the crown of horns at the top of the flying fortress's head. Seeing all these dragons made his scales jostle. "Mother, the titan army has Elome. They attempt to drive the elves from their lands. I'll send part of our forces there."

She nodded.

"There is another task that needs to be taken care of. Urslay, the giant home, well, there is a stream there turning the races into giants. I think it's time the dragons paid them one last visit. Would you care to lead it?"

"I most certainly would. And what of you, Nath? Do you head for Elome?"

"No, I'll take a host of dragons to Narnum. No small force either. Eckubahn is there, waiting. I can feel it in my scales. I must face him again."

"Don't be anxious, Nath. Your father fell into that same trap. For centuries I nestled in the Great Dragon Wall and felt the spirits raging against it." She grimaced. "Their thoughts are dark and perverse. They seek to twist and deceive. They'll show no mercy. They thrive on cruelty. Be wary, Son."

Nath hopped down onto her back. He hugged her neck. "I will be."

CHAPTER 17

WITH HER EYES CAST IN the direction of the riders, Laylana started to pull her sword out of her sheath.

"There's no need for that. We can dispatch that little force in no time," Slivver said. He patted her on the back with his tail. "You should get your rest."

"I like the company of steel."

"Over the likes of me? I'm wounded." Slivver stretched his head up to his full height. "I can send my shades overhead for a closer look. Ah, never mind, it appears good company is coming."

"Who?"

"Roamers."

"Really?"

The riders vanished in the cover of the knolls. They reappeared a few minutes later, cresting the moderate slopes. They were large now, and she could make them out clearly. Six roamers in all rode high in the saddle. Their long hair was draped over their shoulders. Bows hung from their backs. They wore buckskin and animal furs. On their graceful stallions they moved like one with the land.

Tired as she was, Laylana couldn't contain her elation. She called out to them in recognition. "Shum! Hoven! Liam!" She waved. The riders broke into a trot. All three of them slid off of their horses and greeted her. "Your mission, it was a success, was it not?"

"Yes, in some ways," Shum said. "We made a wreck of things in the orcen lands but didn't stay around for a visit. The spirit we took down was a nasty thing, but the life gem was destroyed. When the wurmers tumbled from the sky, we knew we had victory, but that put the orcs in full alarm. We're blessed that most all of us made it out."

"And Sansla," she said, searching the skies. "Where is he?"

Shum's steady gaze held hers. "He paid a dear price, for all of us. It couldn't have been done without him."

Laylana teared up. She didn't know why; she never knew Sansla so well, but it hurt her heart. She peeked at the others on their horses. "His body? Did you bury it?"

"We tried, but could not find it. We lost the Ocular of Orray too. Perhaps both of them had served their final purpose."

"I, I'm sorry," she said. "For all of you. I know how close-knit the roamers are. I weep, even if you do not."

"Yes, thank you. If we had a body, perhaps he could be brought back as I was," Shum said. "But perhaps it wasn't meant to be."

Inslay angled in among the group. "Are you certain his body is lost?"

"As if it vanished altogether," Hoven replied. "There should have been signs of him, yet there was nothing. We have no answers. Regardless, we've moved on. Sansla would want that. How fare things in the land of the elves?"

"The elven High Council seeks peace with the titan army. They have waved the white banners. The spirits have deluded their minds. We are seeking out Nath Dragon, the Orb of Command, and Bayzog's staff of light. It's the only remedy I've seen. Nath Dragon's call seemed to shake them the most."

"The cleansing power of the truth is what the spirits need to see. It will vanquish them," Inslay added.

"It is the Council that needs their slates cleaned," she said with some bite in her voice. "If we can get them back to their senses, that will remedy much of the problem. I fear it might soon be too late."

"We've ridden hard to get here," Shum said. "We need to rest and seek refuge in a roamer haven not too far away. Our swords are yours, Laylana, but I'd like to take time to discuss things."

"I have to find Nath Dragon," she said.

"Laylana, we are more than capable of handling that," Slivver offered. "You should stay with your people. Strength and strategy. You'll need all you have for the battle at hand."

Taking Slivver's clawed hands in hers, she said, "I thank you, Slivver. Your presence gives me great comfort." She kissed his fingers. "Please, go quickly."

"Absolutely." One by one, he and the other silver dragons took off like shooting stars with wings.

Laylana and Inslay accompanied Shum and the others to their haven. The roamers had many sanctuaries scattered all over the lands. The casual eye would walk right past them and never know. This one was a burrow covered by prickly briars and vines. The foliage parted with a wave of Shum's hand. They filed inside, leaving the horses and a few roamers behind.

The soft white glow of moon worms, pretty caterpillar-like bugs that hung on the walls and ceiling, was the only source of light. The moon worms lit up the moment they entered. The haven had neatly fortified walls made from natural stone. Woven blankets with broad geometric designs and stitching covered the dirt floors. There were no tables or chairs, but shelving was built into the walls.

"It's not much but ample for our refuge and rest. Sometimes we go many weeks without sleep." Shum pulled back one of the blankets from the floor. There was a wooden trapdoor. Opening it, he removed some roots and bags filled with hard dried meat. "It's not much, but it will rejuvenate you. Skin those roots with your blades. It will taste better."

Taking the rations, Laylana said, "Thank you."

"I'll fetch some water. It's stored in the rear. I'll be right back," Shum said.

Laylana and Inslay sat down on the blankets. Hoven and Liam joined them. Liam snapped a root in half and began chewing it. He was smiling at Laylana as he ate.

"What are you smiling at?"

"We haven't had a female in the haven before. It's odd, is all." Liam picked a scrap out of his teeth. "No offense was meant. I find it refreshing."

"None taken. I feel welcome. This sanctuary is quite...cozy."

Suddenly, Hoven and Liam came to their feet. Shum was backing out of the tunnel he'd just entered. His sword was drawn. Laylana dropped her food and fumbled for her blade. Someone or something had invaded the haven. It came right at them.

CHAPTER 18

Nath caught up with Selene and Brenwar. He wasn't alone. An entire company of dragons was with him. The graceful scaled creatures cozied right up to the adventurers. The elven warriors petted the dragons' scales and horns. There were smiles all around. Rerry was jumping up and down. A pink blossom dragon had attached to his back and used her wondrous powers to mend his broken legs.

Rerry jumped up and clicked his heels together. He did a little jig where he flapped his elbows like wings. "I can dance again!"

"See if you can be quiet again," Brenwar said. The eyes underneath his knitted brows were on a bronze dragon. The beautiful beast had a head as big as him. "Am I supposed to ride this thing?"

"Be nice to him, Brenwar. I owe him a favor. Don't make it two." Nath patted the rustling scales on the dragon's neck. "Bronzie doesn't like being referred to as a thing. He's people, just like you and I."

Brenwar grumbled. "I don't think I'll be too comfortable riding on a sensitive dragon. I'm not suited for it as it is. Are you telling me this is a thin-scaled dragon?" He rapped his knuckles on the dragon's nose horn. "I want a tough one."

"Ask him yourself," Nath said.

Brenwar looked between Nath and the bronze dragon. He looked the dragon in the eye and said, "Well, are you tough or aren't you, Bronzie?"

Bronzie revealed long, sharp ivory teeth, then said in Dwarven, "I'd rather be called a thing than a dwarf. Now get on my back or stay here. I'm going where the fighting is, not the whining."

Brenwar leered at Nath. His huff stirred the long whiskers on his moustache. He said, "He'll do."

"Good."

Nath and Selene helped everyone out with their preparations. Not all the dragons had saddles and harnesses, but more than enough did in order to get Eslin's elves and the many others back to Elome.

Rerry mounted a steel dragon. Reins in hand, he yelled down to Nath, "We're off to Narnum, are we? Lead the way, Nath Dragon. I'm eager to follow."

"Uh, hold on a moment, Rerry." Nath sought Bayzog out. The wizard was helping Sasha climb onto her dragon. Samaz was with her. "Bayzog, have you explained to Rerry our situation?"

"No," Bayzog said matter-of-factly. He'd climbed halfway up to the dragon's saddle. Sasha and Samaz were sitting at the top. "I was getting to that."

"Getting to what?" Sasha asked.

"I'm going with Nath, to Narnum. It is there we can attempt to save Balzurth." Bayzog clutched Sasha's hand. "It is a critical time. I'd rather you stayed with our sons and the elves. Elome will need you."

"We shouldn't separate, Bayzog. It's too much. You've only been back with us a little time, and now you go again."

"Yes, Father," Samaz interjected. "We must stay together. We need one another."

Bayzog shook his head. "I realize how every moment of our lives is precious. I savor each one more now than ever. But I must do what is best, not just for us, but for all. I need you to understand that."

"Or course we do, Bayzog. We just don't like being away from you. We'll do as you ask. I won't even make you promise to return, because I know you will." Sasha kissed him.

Standing on top of his dragon a ways away, Rerry yelled, "Oh no! I've seen that kiss before. What's going on? Father, are you leaving us? I'm telling you now, I'm going wherever you're going. You and Dragon!"

"And leave your mother without your protection?" Bayzog admonished.

"She does just fine on her own," Rerry said.

"Rerry!" Sasha and Bayzog said at the same time.

"Well, she does," the young elven warrior replied.

Nath eased away, saying, "I'll let you get this sorted out." He didn't make it ten steps before he ran into Ben and Rip. "Oh, how goes it, warriors?"

Ben opened up his hands. "You tell us. We follow, you lead."

"Aw, Ben, you give my heart relief." Nath quickly recounted his plans. "What I need the both of you to do is search out the legionnaires. Any fighting force from Quintuklen. We're going to need them."

"With so many saturated minds, they won't be easily convinced," Ben said, shrugging his brows. "I'll give it a try. Rip might have better luck. Being five hundred years old should give him plenty of seniority."

Rip burst out laughing. Once he settled down, he said, "I like the way you think, Ben. Perhaps. Perhaps they'll think I'm a ghost, but they could just as easily think I'm an evil spirit. It will take some convincing."

"It's going to be a long journey on foot. I guess we had better get moving." Ben reached behind his back. "Uh, Nath, I suppose you will need Akron?"

"Not at this juncture. You keep Akron. As for the journey, you won't be going alone. You'll be flying on the backs of dragons." Two copper dragons with sleek black wings slunk over to the group. They were twice the size of horses. The hornless dragons lay on all fours. "They're ready."

Ben looked at Rip. "Take your pick, centurion."

"They're both real beauties." Rip shook Nath's hand. "I hope to see you on the battlefield."

"Agreed."

Ben gave Nath a brisk hug. "Get your father back."

Nath watched both men mount up and take to the sky. He sent another handful of dragons after them, mouthing the word, "Farewell."

Within the hour, Nath, Selene, Brenwar, and Bayzog had taken to the sky. Selene and Bayzog doubled up in the saddle of a steel dragon. Nath flew between them, and Brenwar rode the bronze. They headed in a straight line for Narnum. On the backs of dragons and accompanied by Eslin and the elves, Sasha and her sons flew for Elome.

Nath's mind ran through a hundred scenarios. He stayed focused on every possibility, but with only one theme.

Save Father.

CHAPTER 19

Blocking Laylana's view, Shum walked backward into the middle of the room. He took a knee. Hoven and Liam's partially drawn swords clicked back into their scabbards. They both kneeled by Shum.

Laylana leaned to the right. An elf stood in the entrance to the tunnel. He stepped out and rose to full height. His appearance was fully elven. He was an astounding specimen, taller than even Shum. His eyes were blue diamonds, his long hair coarse and black with streaks of white. Much like the roamers, he wore buckskin trousers, but he was shirtless. His muscles were thick and well-defined.

Beside her, Inslay's eyes were filled with wonder and recognition. She could see the elf was a roamer. Thick wristed and long haired, the stranger couldn't have been anything but one of the big-boned elves. But his familiarity had her at a loss. She choked for breath for a moment when the stranger's piercing blue eyes fell on her own.

"Don't be afraid," the stranger said. His voice was strong, rich, gentle, and commanding. "Only the good dwell within our havens."

At first, she thought she'd just encountered a roamer that she'd never encountered before. But the stranger's eyes told a different story. She'd seen them before, many times. With bated breath, she said, "Sansla?"

"Believe me when I say that I am as surprised as you are. I assure you, it is me. I'm just without the fur, fangs, and wings."

With a joyful cry, the roamers jumped up and threw their arms around Sansla. It was nothing but happy faces and tears. Laylana teared up herself.

"How, Sansla?" Hoven begged. "We searched for you. I swear it! You were gone!"

"Yes, I know," Sansla said as Liam placed a blanket over his shoulders. "The battle with Sulker was a detrimental one. We would have lost, I'm afraid. I did what had to be done." He opened up his large hand, revealing the starlight brightness of the Ocular of Orray. "I can't say for certain, but I believe my sacrifice lifted my curse. The Ocular of Orray transformed me back to myself. It transported me here as well. I've been waiting." He looked right at Laylana. "For you, I believe."

Her heart fluttered in her chest.

Sansla continued, "But that can wait. I am vague on things. My body's weak. It's been a bit of an adjustment. Until you came, I was lying on one of the bunks, asleep. The wurmers, have they been defeated?"

"They fell from the skies like lightning-struck flies. It was a glorious thing," Liam said. "Father, may I fetch a jug of honey wine? This calls for celebration."

"Certainly, Son," Shum said."

Liam scurried into the tunnel. He was back in seconds with two jugs of wine. The group sat on their knees in a circle on the floor. Liam passed the jugs, and all of them drank.

After Sansla drank, he said, "How are things faring in Elome?"

Inslay, now as bright-eyed as ever, injected himself into the conversation before Laylana could get her words out. "Since Laedorn died, the High Council has been in disarray. The titan spirits possess many. The Council is led by one called Andar. His words seize the dulled minds of our leaders." He gulped down a drink. "My, that's delicious. As I was saying, Elome is lost. It needs a king."

"Yes, and the royal bloodlines are maintained. But many believe one of them is tainted," Sansla said.

"Your curse is lifted, Sansla Libor. Not only are you the king of the roamers, but you are the rightful heir to the throne. The same as your father was meant to be, if not for all this nonsense."

Laylana's head turned toward Inslay. "If I may ask, who is Sansla's father?"

Leaning inward with excitement, Liam said, "Yes, who is it? I'd like to know."

Shum gently nudged his son.

"But—"

Shum gave Liam a look.

The young roamer fell silent.

Silence overcame the haven. Tension began to build. Eyes drifted between Sansla and Laylana. "Is there something I need to know? Who is your father, Sansla? Or is it some kind of secret?'

"It's been a secret from you for a very long time. I'm not surprised my brethren kept it so well." Sansla set the jug of honey wine down and looked right into her eyes. "Laedorn was my father."

"My grandfather? My grandfather was your father?"

Sansla nodded.

Laylana never knew her parents. She was raised by Laedorn. All she knew was that her father and mother had died tragic deaths at the hands of orcs. Shaking her head, she said, "Are you my uncle?"

"No, child. I'm your father."

CHAPTER 20

WITH THE WINDS LIFTING HIM at the wings, Nath hung in the air. It was night. The wind was chill and brisk. Below him was Narnum, previously the Free City. Iron lampposts with oil burning within lit the streets in a uniform grid. He reflected momentarily on the good times he'd had in Narnum, gallivanting among the people that came from all over the world. Now, it was home for despots. Straight ahead of him was the High Tower. The tallest building in all of Narnum was a monument of its success. It stood over a thousand feet tall. It was there Nath had lived with Selene for quite some time. Now, the sparkling spire was abandoned.

I shouldn't do this.

Nath had left Selene and the others a league away. He hadn't tried to convince them of his reason. He'd just told them he was going and that they just had to listen and understand. If he needed them, he'd call. With more than a thousand dragons in all shapes and sizes at his disposal, he was confident he could handle whatever trap Eckubahn might set.

He landed on Selene's old balcony of the High Tower that overlooked the entire city. The tiles on the patio had cracked. The flowers in the planters were long dead. Chairs and tables were busted. He had shared this balcony with Selene back in an evil time. But there had been order. Now, all he saw was in disarray. He could hear people of all the races cajoling wildly in the streets. The heartbeats of the good people raced. Their faces were long from lack of sleep.

With his hands on the iron railing, Nath looked downward. This was the very same spot Selene had hurled him from. He chuckled at the life-threatening moment.

Fly or Die.

Fortunately, things had worked out for him. In an odd way, he wondered why Selene had pushed him so hard. For the longest time, he was convinced that she wanted him to turn into a servant of Gorn Grattack as she was. But now, in this moment of reflection, he found a new perspective. Deep down, without even realizing it, Selene had coached Nath up. He was the key to defeating Gorn Grattack. He was the ticket to her freedom.

My girl is a clever girl. I wouldn't have her any other way.

Nath's nose crinkled. Huge bonfires burned on the outskirts of the city: north, south, east and west. Nath's keen dragon vision zoomed in on them. The bodies of wurmers crackled and popped over the flames. A filmy, eye-stinging smoke lingered in the air above as well as below. He spied a giant carrying a wurmer on each shoulder. The behemoth of a man marched the sizable wurmers outside the city, where the brute slung the wurmers like logs onto a fire. Bright orange sparks flurried up in the sky. Giants clapped and sang guttural songs in an odd celebration. There was frolicking and obscene confidence in the sprawling city.

A scuffle caught Nath's ear. A pair of racing hearts pounded nearby. He pressed back into a wall. A young girl, maybe eight years old, dressed in a night robe, stepped out on the balcony. Her hand was locked in the grip of a woman who trailed close behind. The woman carried a broken chair leg. They were an adoring pair that looked very much alike. Peering around, she lifted her crude cudgel and swallowed hard when she saw Nath.

The little girl hugged her mother's leg. She spoke up with a trembling lip. "Is he a demon sent to kill us?"

The fear-filled eyes of the pair said it all to Nath. They were survivors but terrified. He didn't sense the evil radiance of the foul spirits among them. He slowly shook his head and sank down into a squat.

The hard lines in the woman's face softened. She lowered the club. "You are—"

Nath held up a finger. "Don't say it. You are safe. Soon to be safer."

The little girl gave a curious look up at her mother. "He's a pretty demon."

"He's no demon," the mother said in a soft voice. "He's a friend."

"His eyes are like gold coins, and he has scales," the girl said. "Can I touch them?" Nath beckoned the little girl over. He cradled her in his arms and stood up. "He's warm like a quilt lying by the fire," she said.

"Yes," the mother said with a smile. "It is well known to many that he is."

Nath's head tilted. "And who have you been talking to?"

"Your reputation precedes you, Sire. I've heard many tall tales of your exploits passed down by my great-great-grandmother." She stretched her hand out toward his face. "May I?"

"You have me at a loss, but yes, you may."

She touched a lock of his hair and rubbed it between her fingers. "It's unlike anything I've ever felt before. It makes silk feel like sandpaper."

"I don't know about that, but I like how you say it." He gave her a quick wink. "Can you tell me anything about our common enemy?"

"The flaming one? Hah. He sulks inside his cathedral and dines on the people, so they say. I'm very careful how I travel." She let go of his hair, grazing her fingers over his chest as she did so. "I believe he's been pouting since his vile pets fell from the sky."

"Anything else?"

"The arena is filled with his finest soldiers. The nuurg stir at all times. I wish I knew more, but the more you know, the greater the danger it presents."

Nath whispered in the little girl's ear, "Yes, little one, obey your mother. Don't say a word of seeing me here." He placed the girl in her mother's arms. "Stay out of sight no matter the commotion. Seeing me has only put you in danger. Be still and stay silent as a frightened mouse."

"We will," the mother said. She kissed Nath's cheek. "You are warm as a biscuit. May good fortune follow this farewell." She took her daughter inside.

Nath took to the sky and soared over the arena. His father's body still hung on humiliating display. The arena was as the mother said: filled with dozens of stone-faced giants.

Eckubahn is no fool. He knows exactly what I'll do. I'm going to do it anyway.

Jetting through the skies, it wasn't long before Nath landed among the others and said, "I've seen all that needs to be seen and heard all that needs to be heard. It's time."

CHAPTER 21

LAYLANA WIPED HER MISTY EYES, looking at Sansla. "I-I believe you, but I don't understand how. This is not what I have been told." She looked at Inslay. "You knew."

Shamefaced, the elven wizard nodded. "As much as we pride ourselves on the truth, we pride ourselves on protecting innocent ones from harmful truths just the same. It's a flaw…for certain."

"A part of me is inclined to storm and brood," she said, wiping her eyes as she came back to her feet. She stood face to face with Sansla. "But I rejoice!"

Showing a broad grin, Sansla opened his arms. Laylana locked hers around his waist. Hugging him tight, she said, "Am I a roamer?"

"You take more from your mother's side, and her father, Laedorn, but yes, the roamer legacy is your legacy," Sansla said. "But many elves don't approve of it. It's always been a point of conflict going on for centuries. In our people's youth, the elves were a wild people, fond of the wilderness. Over time the elves became more civilized. As generation after generation passed, the elves leaned toward having a more permanent residence. They created Elome, the high elven city, every bit as splendid as the leaves on its branches. But our ancestors preferred to walk the world from one corner to the other, making their beds in the groves that would take them.

"As time went on, the other races grew in stature and power. The world was no longer free and wild. It became modern in buildings and facilities. There's no harm in that, but the naked world is not as it once was. The landscape changes. The roamers, however, make the most of it. We cherish and protect it as best as we can."

She broke off the embrace. "So what happened to my mother then?"

"The elves were divided. They feared that the roamer bloodline would ruin the civilization so many had worked so hard to create. We warred with the orcs endlessly. It took a thousand years to wrest ourselves free of their unyielding clutches. We held. Not so long ago I, a roamer, married your mother, Shaylan." Sansla's eyes became distant. His speech paused. "Many of the elves became nervous. We'd lost our king, Onlaay Rhyne, to the orcs. Laedorn led the Council of Advisors at the time, but his ties to his own royal blood—and now my tie to the ancient roamer kings of the elves—made too many of our brethren skittish. The roamers were called upon to complete a quest. It was my undoing. I became accursed. I lost my temperament."

"You killed my mother?"

"No, no, dear." He laid his palms on her shoulders. "But I was framed for it. Even Laedorn was fooled for the longest time. There was an accident, but I was given the blame for it. It haunts me to this day. It was a dark time. It fed my curse and boiling rage within. I didn't want to be king. I was young. I had no intention of turning all the elves back toward the lives of roamers, but someone feared I would."

"You are the rightful king," she said. "You can liberate the elves."

"Yes," Inslay said. "She is right. You must lead the elves."

"Perhaps the elves, or rather, the shades that work against us weren't counting on one thing." Sansla held up the Ocular of Orray and gazed into its bright star. "They made a mistake by giving me the Ocular. You see, the Ocular was used on me long ago for a cure. It didn't work. The spirits that inhibit the Council sent the Ocular with me on a fatal mission, assured that I would fail. They didn't count on two things. One, the roamers defeating the spirit Sulker, or two, the Ocular of Orray curing me. Now," he said with a twinkle in his eye, "it makes me curious."

In an excited voice, Inslay said, "The spirits fear the Ocular! It can dispel them, can't it!"

Sansla said, "There is only one way to find out. Elome, we're going home."

Outside the haven, Laylana found Slivver waiting. The dragon's silver scales gleamed in the moonlight. He was alone, so far as she could see. She hurried over to him. "Have you found Nath?"

"No, it seems my brother is off on another quest, but fear not. I found something just as good." Slivver took her by the hand. He glanced at Sansla and said, "I'm glad to see that you are back to yourself, old man. Sadly, now you're just a regular elf. A shame, that white pelt of yours was a glorious thing."

"It wouldn't have been so bad without the fleas," Sansla replied. He was in a full set of elven garb now. "I don't think I'll miss the scratching."

Slivver led Laylana up and over the knoll the hidden haven was tucked in. The sky full of clouds made the landscape dark. She made out numerous creatures scattered all over the fields. She gasped. They were dragons, hundreds of them. "What is this?"

"Why, Nath Dragon's army, of course," Slivver said. "Only the best. And not to mention many of his dearest friends."

Standing amidst dragons great and small, Sasha, Rerry, and Samaz waved at Laylana. She rushed over to greet them. "It's good to see you! All of you!" Captain Eslin of the elven guard was there. He saluted her. "Is this everyone? Where are the others?"

"They are with my husband," Sasha said.

Unable to hide her puzzlement, Laylana replied, "Bayzog?"

"Yes, he's quite the survivor."

Inslay shuffled in between the ladies. "You mean to tell me that Bayzog did not perish? It hurt my heart when I heard the news, but deep down, I didn't believe it. Tell me what happened."

Over a small campfire, Sasha made quick but thorough work of Bayzog's tale. In the meantime, Sansla and the roamers took to the sky on the dragons, along with Eslin's forces. They returned an hour later with concerned looks on their faces.

"What is it?" Laylana asked.

Grim faced, Sansla said, "We have our work cut out for us. The titan army's numbers are far greater than I imagined. They've encircled Elome in a tight wall. There are no skirmishes or fights, but the white flags still fly. It's painful for me to say, but if the elves haven't fully surrendered, then they are held hostage."

CHAPTER 22

BRENWAR MARCHED BACK AND FORTH, wringing his hands and muttering, "Trap, trap, trap, trap, trap…" He must have said it a hundred times since Nath returned from his trip to Narnum.

"Yes, Brenwar, the likelihood of it being a trap is high, but time is short." Nath polished Fang with a silk cloth Brenwar had given him from the chest. The chest was in the possession of Samaz now. Bayzog and Brenwar had taken what they thought was needed. "Perhaps were are giving Eckubahn too much credit."

"Better to overestimate your enemies than underestimate them," Brenwar said. "If we go in, we go in fast. Strike like a thunderbolt."

"Selene? Bayzog? Any thoughts?"

Selene's fingers toyed with a lock of her hair. "They know we are coming. They just don't know when. I say we strike when the sun rises. The giants hate the light. If we fly in from the east, they won't see us coming until it's too late."

Nath nodded. "Bayzog?"

"As soon as they get wind of you, that's where their focus will be." He stood leaning on his staff. "I believe we need to create as much confusion as possible. Just long enough to whisk your father's body away. It's a huge task. It won't be easy just to scoop him up and go. But I like the plan. I think we should try. Perhaps Eckubahn does not know your father can be revived."

Nath eyed Fang a long moment then slid him back into the sheath. It was hard to say what Eckubahn knew, but given the nature of the titan spirits, it was only safe to presume Eckubahn knew his every move. He hoped he could move his army of dragons discreetly, but the great numbers would be hard to miss. If one naked eye of the spirits saw them, then they all would. Nath's biggest advantage was the sky. It was the edge the dragons had always had over the giants.

The plan was simple. Retrieve Balzurth's body and extract the Spear of Barnabus. With the spear removed, it would be possible for Balzurth's spirit to return to his body. It was the only body strong enough to hold the all-powerful dragon. The difficulty would be fighting through the giants. Additionally, Balzurth's body was shackled on a heavy rack made of dwarven iron. It would be difficult to free him from those bonds. If Nath was successful, he and Balzurth would use the Spear of Barnabus and Fang to go after Eckubahn. Together, they should be able to finish him off once and for all. Nath had envisioned what needed to be done a hundred times.

"Any other thoughts?" Nath said, rising to his feet.

Brenwar, Bayzog, and Selene glanced about at one another.

Selene spoke up. "We follow your lead, Nath."

"Dawn it is, then."

Hidden nearby in the woodland, Lotuus heard everything Nath Dragon said. A part of her wanted to approach him. Strike a deal. She needed to do what was best for herself and her fairies even though she hated Nath and what he stood for with a passion.

It wouldn't be the first time I played both sides.

Sitting on a bed of daisies with her legs nestled beneath her, she watched and listened a little longer. A pair of fairy women, no higher than a foot in height, braided her hair. Nath was right. Eckubahn did know that he was coming, but not exactly when, not that it mattered. Eckubahn was ruthless in his preparation. Compassionless in combat. As formidable as Nath appeared, Lotuus didn't believe for a single moment that Nath could defeat the titan king. Even with so many dragons, all of Nalzambor was still jaded by countless spirit enemies. It would take more than a single battle to stop them all.

I suppose I should report Nath's whereabouts to Eckubahn. It is after all my duty. But why do I hesitate?

Long ago, she had crossed Balzurth. It had gotten her a thousand years in prison. It would have been longer if Nath Dragon hadn't come around. Possibly forever. In the first moments of freedom, she had vowed vengeance. Hatred still burned hot in her belly. But something gnawed at her. Why had Balzurth let her stay out? He could have told his son about the Great Dragon Wall to set his mother free. Instead, he had used Lotuus to tell him. It puzzled her. She heard soft laughing among the heroes. Her brows knitted together.

Enjoy the night. Tomorrow all of your laughter will be taken away forever.

"Let's go." In a single unit, they flew away to see Eckubahn.

Selene stood by Nath, following his stare. Her arm was hooked in his. "What do you see?" With her violet eyes narrowing, her head tilted. "Ah, I hear the wings of fairies. Lotuus?"

"I'm certain of it. I caught wind of her presence moments ago." His jaw muscles clenched.

"It's not too late to stop her. Send the blue razors to hunt her down."

"No, I've thought about that. We need to stay focused on what needs to be done. Lotuus is just a distraction. She always is. It's possible that she wanted to hear so she could divide our ranks. We'll do as agreed, but we're going to show up a tad early."

CHAPTER 23

Eckubahn sat on his throne inside his cathedral of worship. The green flames surrounding his head flickered cool. Lotuus hung in the air right in front of his face. She was no bigger than a bird compared to him. He leaned back in his chair with a lasting scowl on his face. He nodded his strong chin as she spoke. When she finished, he said, "You may go."

Lotuus blanched. "Go? I beg your pardon, Titan King, but go where? A battle is about to unfold. I am one of your highest officers, and now you dispatch me? I demand to know why."

One side of his mouth curled back, revealing his sharp teeth. He set his cold black stare on her. "There is no need for you to get your wings clipped, Lotuus. Do as you do and be my eyes. I require little else from you. There is little else you can do."

Her alabaster cheeks turned rosy. "You dare insult me! I am the fairy empress! My powers are as great as yours, despite my size! Don't you dare dismiss my power!"

Eckubahn backhanded her with a powerful swat. Lotuus bounced off the back of a stone giant and fell hard on the floor. She was up in an instant. Her body shook. "How dare you!"

With a powerful voice filling the chamber, he said to her, "Mind yourself, Lotuus! I am no fool. I sense the doubt in you. Do you think your weakness gives me comfort? Do you!" His fingers crackled as he closed his fists. "My plans for certain victory are not something you will be privy to. I know all about your little chat with Nath Dragon. I see all. I know all. My eyes are everywhere. If you know what is best for you, then you will stay out of my way. Once Nath Dragon is ended, you will have what you will. Vengeance. Power. Dragon skulls will be your footstool. What more do you want? Huh?"

She sank to her knees. Finding her voice, she managed to say, "What you have said is what I desire."

He leaned toward her. "Then earn it in these final hours."

Standing up, she regained her composure and floated up from the ground. "I just want to be a part of it."

"Everything is in place. Sit back and enjoy what the rising sun is about to bring: death to Nath Dragon."

"Yes." Eckubahn's voice filled her with elation. She believed what he said. "Death to Nath Dragon."

"Come." He waved her over. She sat on the arm of his chair. "Watch." His fingers clawed intricate patterns in the air. A globe of energy rose up out of the floor. The massive sphere was thirty feet around. It hovered several feet up. An image of Narnum's arena formed from it. Giants, nuurg, and soldiers armed to the teeth stood both inside and out of the walls. They even filled the stands.

"Magnificent view. It will be quite a fight."

"It will be quite the slaughter."

"Forgive me for not being so confident, but won't it be difficult for our forces to withstand the dragon flame? Nath Dragon laid waste to a thousand of your soldiers on his own. He turned them to ash."

"True, his flame, like his father's, is cleansing. But the giants can handle the flames of the other dragons. Their skin is thick enough. But as a precaution, they are fully equipped. Look closer."

Lotuus walked to the end of the arm of the chair. The giants and soldiers wore armor made from dragon hide and bones. Many of them carried crude weapons made from dragon horn. Small teeth and skulls rattled about their necks and wrists. A filmy mud with a grainy sparkle to it coated their faces and skin in a fashionable war paint. "What is that substance they wear?"

"The only weakness the giants have against the dragons is their breath weapon. Mud from the Dragon Pool mixed with the ashes from lakes of lava is enchanted by assorted necromancers. That, along with bones and scales, gives them all the protection they need. The battlefield will become a slaughterhouse soon after the fighting starts. I aim to enjoy it."

"It seems you've thought of everything."

"Perhaps. But strategy is one thing. Breaking the will of your enemy is another."

CHAPTER 24

Just before the dawn, Nath flew at the head of his dragon army. Narnum was in their path. Behind him, Selene, Bayzog, and Brenwar rode on the backs of their dragons. A full legion of scaled beasts flew behind them. There had been times when he thought the day would never come when he'd lead his kin into battle. Now, that day was about to dawn.

The lights in Narnum's spires twinkled in the distance. The wind howled in Nath's ears. Two thousand feet high in the bitter cold, he started his descent. He looked back to the others and said, "This is it! Be ready for anything!"

Everyone had their orders. Brenwar, Selene, and Bayzog would lead their own groups, distracting the giants and thinning their ranks. Of course, the dragons were more than clear on what needed to be done. But once the battle started, it would become unpredictable. The dragons and giants hated one another. It wouldn't take long for their passions to get the best of them. It would be a fight just to keep them all fighting together.

Nath drifted back between Brenwar and Selene. "It's time to see what Eckubahn has in store for us." With a wave of his hand, a score of bull dragons broke from the ranks. "Go!"

The huge brick-red scaled beasts power-dived toward the city below. Once they crossed the city's perimeter, a giant blew a great battle horn. The rooftops and balconies of the tall towers came to life.

Ballistas fired huge steel bolts that filled the skies like giant needles. One of the ballista bolts tore through a bull dragon's wings. The bolt's barbed end snagged the wings. A cord of metal rope was fastened to the bolt like fishing line on the hook. The bull dragon stretched the line taut. The dragon bucked in the air. Its wings were pinned together. It fell from the air and crashed into the streets. A wave of people rushed the dragon.

That was one battle out of many that were going on. The host of bull dragons barreled through straight for the arena. They were struck by mystic bolts, torpedoes, and the sting of the bolt-firing ballistas. The bull dragons knocked soldiers from the upper edges of the coliseum's ancient walls. Wherever soldiers fell, many more rose.

"There are many," Nath said.

The bull dragons circled the stone ring. Taking shots from all directions, they unleashed their dragon breath. The fires spread through the ranks. Soldiers screamed. A giant stormed up the arena steps and leapt onto the back of a dragon. The great weight of the huge man knocked the dragon from the sky. They hit the ground together, fighting with claws and fists.

The dragon fires made for an early dawn.

But the licking fires were extinguished.

"There is sorcery afoot!" Selene said. "Our brethren's fires are doused!"

"Yes!" Nath replied. "I've seen enough." He flew back to the dragons and spoke to them in Dragonese. "The titans have tipped their hand," he told them. "Your fire breath may not be effective, but we shall see. Let's go, brethren! Fight for freedom! Fight for Balzurth! Destroy the titans!"

All at once the dragon army dove. All of them roared at the same time. The glorious sound of a thousand dragons roaring together at once set Nath's blood on fire. The startled, horrified looks on the titan army's gaping faces made it all worthwhile. Nath crashed right into the nearest giant. He fed its belly with Fang's steel. He let out a roaring battle cry. "Dragon! Dragon!"

Bronzie dipped out of the sky, sank his claws into the meat of a small orc giant's shoulders, and took off like a hawk snagging a fish from a stream.

"What are you doing, dragon?" Brenwar yelled. "Get down there so I can hit something."

The dragon flung the giant head over heels through the air. The brute smashed into a host of soldiers storming down the streets.

With brows lifted, Brenwar said, "I like that. Looks like a good idea for a game. But get me down to the ground. In the middle of the action." He double-checked the cords that fastened the bracers to him. The leather bindings were looped in tight bows. The magic bracers fed him great strength. Now it was time to put the bracers and Mortuun to the test. Spiraling toward the ground, he watched the battle below unfold. Fire and lightning tore into men and giants. Some died, others shrugged the deadly breath weapons off. As dragon claws clutched for limbs, giants reached up and hauled them to the ground.

Bronzie rammed his horns into the backside of a two-headed giant. Brenwar jumped from the saddle and charged the first giant he saw. It was a hairy, potbellied brute who looked at Brenwar with disdain. The giant flung the gray scaler in his grip aside.

Brenwar ducked through the giant's fingers. He pounded Mortuun into the giant's shin. The weapon made the *krackow* sound of a thunderclap.

The giant dropped to its knees.

Brenwar spun on his heel and clocked the giant in the jaw full force.

The brute's head twisted hard, and its neck snapped. The giant died with its face thudding into the ground.

A surge of gnoll fighters bore down on Brenwar's position. Their faces were smeared in unusual war paint. Dragon scales and bones covered their bodies like armor. It was like that everywhere.

"Come! Come, dog faces! Mortuun has a kiss for you!" With a single swing, Brenwar sent three gnolls flying from their feet. Bones and armor were busted. He was hammering down on the rest of the pack when a shadow rose above him.

A giant foot from a beast of a man stomped him.

He dropped full to the ground, catching the foot in his chest. The foot entirely engulfed him.

"Nobody stomps a dwarf!" Brenwar shoved back against tons of weight. His muscles popped with strain.

The giant ground him under its foot.

Huffing and puffing, Brenwar pushed with all his might.

The foot started to give.

Brenwar gathered himself to his knees, gave a mighty shove, and squirted out.

The giant stumbled.

Bronzie's tail licked out of nowhere, smiting the giant in the chest. The blow knocked the huge man flat. Bronzie's jaws clamped down on the giant's neck.

Now, Brenwar stood in the midst of the fray, looking at his empty hands. His eyes searched the ground. Mortuun was gone. He spied a nuurg soldier dashing away with it. His eyes burned with rage.

"No one takes my hammer!"

CHAPTER 25

BAYZOG KEPT HIS FEET JAMMED in the stirrups of the dragon's saddle. The steel dragon he rode rocketed over the surging army's bellows, releasing cones of fire at spot after spot. The enemies scattered only to rebound. The flames that licked over their skin fizzled out.

Dragon fire nullified. Problem.

The dragon bent sideways in the air. Its sharp claws dusted soldiers off the bleachers. With a man snagged by its claws, the dragon took off higher in the air. It dropped the man in the streets.

The battle raged like this in all four corners of the arena. Dragons struck from above. Giants swung from below. Bayzog, Selene, and Brenwar's goal was to draw the giants away from the middle, where Balzurth's body stood shackled. The plan was effective. The titan army flung themselves at any enemy they could get ahold of.

But there were so many soldiers. For every one that died, five more streamed in from the city streets. They came like wild demons possessed.

A stone giant grappled a bull dragon in the stands. The giant had the beast in a headlock. It bent the dragon's horns, hoping to snap its neck.

Bayzog summoned a charge from the Elderwood Staff. An arc of energy tore right through the giant's back. The bull dragon clamped its mighty jaws on the giant's arms and dragged the giant over the wall of the arena.

Bayzog loosed a few more blasts from his aerial position. The bolts dropped the smaller giants dead on the spot. The bigger giants recovered. It was the same problem with the dragons. The breath weapons were muted by the war paint that sparkled on the enemy's flesh. It proved a formidable weapon. The titans were making absolutely sure that no one under any circumstances could whisk Balzurth away.

This battle is evenly matched without the power of dragon fire. I need to find a weakness.

A mystic bolt of energy rocketed from one of the nearby buildings. The steel dragon juddered. Bayzog's feet slipped from the stirrups. He locked his fingers on the reins. As he fought for his grip, the Elderwood Staff slipped from his fingers. "Nooo!" He let go of the saddle and fell after it.

Selene and her dragon skimmed over the battleground. Her dragon's claws raked at the flesh of the enemy. A pair of ettins pounced from below. Latching themselves to the dragon's paws, they hauled them down to the ground. The jarring crash left the dragon with a busted wing. Selene found herself flat on her back, shaking the stars from her eyes.

A smaller orc giant, ten feet tall, scooped her up by the waist. Its eyes were blacked with war paint that streaked down over its bulging nose. It laughed a heavy laugh. "Huh-huh-huh."

"Are you going to laugh or eat me!" she screamed in its face.

"No, I'm going to break your back and then eat you." It crushed her in a bear hug.

Selene covered its big ears with her hands and unleashed simultaneous charges of power.

The zap rolled the giant's eyes up inside its head. It fell away, head smoking through the eyes and ears.

By the time Selene fought her way out of the stiff arms locked around her body, she was surround by smaller soldiers who were quite big in size compared to her. She unsheathed her sword from her back and said, "Which one of you wants to die first?"

A nuurg charged with a long curved sword.

Selene shot it in the face with a bolt of power.

The soldiers crowded in, weapons swinging at different times.

Selene sidestepped the haymaker blows. Her sword punctured hearts through plate armor and chain mail. Every lunge and cut she made was precise. Their clumsy blows skipped off her hardened scales. Ten seconds into the battle, all of the small giants were dying at her feet. She finished the last one off with a head shot from the mystic power in her hands.

Without looking, she lashed out with her tail at a presence lurking behind her. A lean giant grabbed her by the tail. Twelve feet tall, the giant had a gaping hole in one eye. He glowered at her with the hunger of a jackal. Licking his lips, he jerked her from her feet and said, "Nice trick, snaky lady. But you'll have to be a lot quicker than that to beat me." With a twist of his hips and shoulders, he slung her into the sidewall of the coliseum then dragged her from the wall.

She spat out a mouthful of dirt and chopped at his fingers. The blade nicked his knuckles.

Letting go of her, he rubbed his bleeding flesh. "A nice clip, but it will take a thousand of those to defeat me." He drew a sword from a scabbard that hung from his leather belt. The blade had a hook on the end. The giant came at her with long, deadly strokes.

Selene sidestepped and parried. The blades clanged together with a jarring impact. Back and forth they danced, with sword tips kissing. With huge dragons and giants battling all around them, they fought between legs and snapping tails cracking overhead.

The giant smiled the entire time. "I'm the best sword master you've ever seen. Perhaps the best in all Nalzambor." He caught her blade on the tip of his. With a fierce twist, he wrenched Selene's sword from her hands. "Your sword skills are lacking. No surprise."

Selene fired at him with bolts of lightning from her hand.

A net of protective energy crackled on the war paint on the giant's face. He started laughing. "It will take more than cheap tricks to stop me." He lunged at Selene.

She grabbed his sword by the blade with her scaled hands and tore it from his hand. Right before his eyes, she bent the steel like lead.

His good eye grew. "You're tougher than a tick."

"And you're dead," she replied.

Just then a bull dragon snuck up behind the giant. In a quick strike, the dragon's massive jaws collapsed over the giant, swallowing him whole. With a nod to the dragon, Selene went after her sword.

As she bent over to get her blade, a huge earth giant came out of nowhere. He punted her head over heels and out of the stadium. Pumping his barrel-sized fists, he said, "It's good!"

CHAPTER 26

Nath led a herd of dragons right into the knot of giants surrounding his father. Fists met teeth. Claws ripped at giant flesh. Tails coiled around thick necks and squeezed until the eyes of the shaggy men bulged. Horns down, bull dragons, bronze dragons, and steel dragons slung the giants aside. The monstrous men pounced back time after time. They swung huge metal blades, hammers, and spiked maces. A steel dragon took a spiked flail to the jaw. It loosed its fire, covering a hairy earth giant in flame. The giant laughed. The flames extinguished into misty vapors. Not a single hair on his body was singed. The two ancient adversaries locked up. They thrashed over the grounds in a tangle of limbs. Battles raged like that everywhere.

Using Fang like a sickle, Nath cut down his enemies in large, arcing swings. He took it to the smaller giants, disassembling them from one appendage or another. Their weapons and armor shattered against Fang's powerful sting.

"Come, giant hounds of Urslay! Taste my wrath!" Nath yelled. The heat of battle raised Nath's inner temperature a hundredfold. The ancient hatred between the dragons and giants stirred. His blood churned like hot lava.

A nuurg crossed his path, swinging a battle axe made from bronze. The axe blade dented against the scales on Nath's chest.

He let out a wild laugh in the pie-eyed nuurg's face. A split second later he cut the soldier down like a tree. "More! Bring me more enemies!" He let out a booming roar. "DRAAAAAAAGON!"

Cutting loose never felt so good. He led the surge forward with golden eyes flaring and hair whipping in the churning wind. Every enemy he crossed made him madder. The dragon scales and bones they wore like foul decorations were abominations. He let into them like a tornado of fury. His lightning-quick strikes came in threes to their one. They were no match for Nath Dragon.

With a well-timed swing, a stone giant slipped in behind Nath. It swung a maul into his back. *Klang!* Nath splatted into the backside of an earth giant. His claws locked into a thick patch of back hair.

The giant was pounding a bull dragon's ribs with a bone-crushing stone hammer. Each blow came harder than the last.

Woozy, Nath labored off of the giant's back. Hanging by the coarse hairs on the giant's shoulder, Nath said, "Fang, do your worst." He slapped the giant in the side of the face with the flat of the blade.

The giant iced up all over.

The bull dragon's tail swatted the giant into a million pieces.

Nath landed on both feet. He spied the giant that had whacked him with the maul. In a rush, he hacked the giant down like a tree. All around him dragons and giants fought and died. Suddenly, Fang's pommel started smoking inside his palm. Nath dropped the blade. "Gah! Fang, what are you doing?"

The searing heat of pain brought Nath to his senses. In the heat of battle he'd lost focus on the mission: save his father. Rubbing his palm, he caught glimpses of his father's body hanging from the rack.

Nath let out a high-pitched dragon call. "Srrrreeeeeee!"

For all of the large dragons present, there were thrice as many smaller ones. They snaked over the grounds, attacking the enemy soldiers' blind spots.

Now, he'd summoned a small force of tiny dragons called iron eaters. The size of chipmunks, the iron-colored dragons gathered at Nath's feet. They smiled up at him with teeth that looked like polished metal.

"Follow me!"

Weaving through the fray, Nath charged headlong toward his father's chained body. The dragons were fully engaged with the last ranks that encircled Balzurth's body. Iron eaters in tow, Nath sprinted under the legs of a cyclops.

And ran smack dab into an invisible wall.

"Great Guzan!"

CHAPTER 27

Brenwar's eyes tracked his Mortuun. A nuurg wielded the great weapon with abominable action. It crushed the head of a copper dragon in a blindsiding blow. "You dare!" Brenwar yelled. He picked up a fallen orc. Hoisting it over his head, he hurled the orc through the air. The big body collided with the nuurg's legs. The crash took the nuurg to the ground.

Running as fast as his stocky legs could move, Brenwar lowered his shoulder and rammed his way through the ranks until he caught up with the nuurg, which had come back to its feet and was running. As soon as the nuurg lifted the war hammer, Brenwar locked his fingers around the handle. "Let go of my hammer."

"Take it if you can, bearded gopher," the nuurg said in a gloating sneer.

Brenwar tore Mortuun free of the nuurg's fierce grip as if it was a toddler. He wound the weapon up and clobbered the befuddled nuurg in the jaw. Without a moment of hesitation, Brenwar swung into every ten-, twenty-, and thirty-footer that moved. Every blow cracked bones from toes to shins. Giants toppled like trees. They slobbered angrily at the bearded demon that hit with strength and power as mighty as one of theirs.

"Kill that dwarf!" One giant pointed with a log-sized finger that trembled.

The giants hemmed Brenwar in only to see him squirt free time and again. The dragons fought alongside him with the same gutsy fervor. The giant ranks were rankled. Their teeth gnashed and lips were spitting.

Despite his enhanced strength, Brenwar's cast-iron body began to lather with sweat. He'd been knocked from his feet a dozen times only to spring back up again. He bled. He bruised. He spat dwarven curses. Putting everything he had into every blow, he focused on a single thought. *Just keep swinging. For Morgdon.*

Bayzog was in free fall with his eyes locked on the Elderwood Staff. Not losing concentration, he muttered a spell. His body turned feather light. Below him, an oversized ogre waited with open arms for the staff. Bayzog called the staff back to his hand. The staff slipped free of the ogre's clutches and returned to Bayzog's hands. The mage landed amidst many. They surrounded him with brooding faces.

"Elf! It's an elf," an earth giant growled. "His flesh is succulent when cooked, but he's hardly sufficient for one. I will have him still," he said, eyeballing the others.

"He's but a varmint," said an ogre. His eyes were sleepy but evil.

Encircling Bayzog were a massive earth giant, two ogres, and three nuurg. He was barely child-sized among them, but he was smiling when he said to them all, "I might not be much of a meal for you, but you'll be more than a meal for me. Or for the dragons."

The Elderwood Staff bathed their glowering faces in light as bright as the sun. The giants shielded their eyes with their meaty forearms. It had lasted but a moment when the nuurg said, "Hah, he thinks to scare us with that withered lantern. I say we skewer him on it."

With arms and weapons stretched out, the giants began to crowd him.

Bayzog shook his head and said, "Skewer this." He dashed his staff on the ground. A wave of radiant energy spread away from him. Touching the feet of the enemy, it raced up their limbs.

The giants shook. Their armor rattled. The skin on their bodies smoldered. A nuurg and an ogre fell flat faced on the ground. The earth giant drooled. He staggered away. Two bronze dragons dropped from the sky, hooked their talons into the giant's shoulders, and hauled him up and away.

It was a swift individual victory. Bayzog ran to his steel dragon, who had landed nearby. He hooked his hand in the harness, climbing into the saddle as the dragon took flight. It didn't take long for him to realize that the battle at large would be a long one. The giants were superior in number to the larger dragons. The streets were filled with giants. In fact, without the effectiveness of dragon breath's incinerating power, the dragons might not hold out much longer.

I have to do something.

Bayzog patted the dragon's neck. "Take me to the clouds."

Once Selene caught her breath, she screamed. Soldiers in the streets were all over her. Using the momentum of her tail, she spun in a quick circle, slapping her enemies away. It gave her enough space to leap from the street up onto the coliseum's back wall in a single bound. Through the portals, soldiers stabbed at her with spears. One by one, she grabbed the shaft of each spear and pulled each soldier through the portal. "Have a nice trip." They hit the ground, one after the other, with resounding thuds.

You'd think they'd be smart enough to let go of the spears once I grabbed them. She slid through the portal that led to the arena's bleachers.

The fighting was catastrophic. The skies above were filled with dragons, missiles, fiery breath, and explosions. The arena had become a battle royale. Of course, the fight was just a distraction, but Nath's army wasn't gaining any ground.

Selene searched for the banner of Nath's red hair. She found him among the masses, brawling around Balzurth's body. Her scales rankled. Something was wrong.

While she was lost in thought, a common orc soldier crept up on her. He hit her so hard in the back of the head with a hammer that the handle cracked.

Selene didn't budge. Irritated, she turned and punched his teeth out. "Orcs."

It became clear that something was wrong. Balzurth's great body, suspended on the rack, was shielded in a protective bubble. Now, the titan army focused its primary attacks on Nath Dragon. Selene bounded down the bleachers. In long, powerful leaps, she jumped from one giant to another, stabbing them critically as she did so. A few more lethal leaps and she made it to Nath.

While fighting his enemies, he chopped at an invisible shield with Fang. "A fine morning, isn't it, Selene?"

"What are you doing? You can't chop through that barrier like that."

Brows knitted, he hit even harder. "Do you have any other ideas?"

Selene kneeled down. She wedged an orb of destruction between the barrier and ground. "I need something to hold it fast."

Nath gutted a nuurg. He hooked his hand into the creature's belt and slung it toward Selene. "Try that."

Selene covered the orb with the nuurg's body braced against the shield. "That will have to do. Nath?"

"Yes?" he said as he slew an ogre.

"Run!"

CHAPTER 28

The concussive force of the orb of destruction's blast knocked every creature nearby from their feet. Giants, soldiers, and dragons were sprawled out on the ground. Nath and Selene had taken cover behind the body of the fallen stone giant. Before they could exclaim "Sultans of Sulfur," the war dragons and titans were knotted up, limb for limb, scale on bones, in fierce clusters.

Nath nudged Selene. "Let's go." Arms outstretched, he rushed forward. His hands smacked right into the invisible shield. "Noooo!"

Selene tapped on the invisible framework. "It holds. Perhaps it is a wall. Maybe we can enter from above?"

At a flick of his wrist, the iron eaters crawled up the mystic barrier. At the top, they rested on the curve that appeared to be a dome. "It's no use. We have to try something else."

From out of nowhere, a nuurg smacked headfirst into the barrier. Brenwar marched right at them. The hard lines of his jaws were set. The braids in his beard were tangled. Giant blood smeared the head of Mortuun. "What's the problem?"

"This magic barrier blocks our efforts to free Balzurth," Selene said. She blasted an ogre's face that lunged for her. They all fought as they talked.

"Let me give it a try. Make me some room." Brenwar ran his grimy fingers over the invisible surface. Setting his war hammer down, he spat into his hands and rubbed them together. He picked up the hammer and swung, saying, "By the power of Morgdon!"

Nath and Selene covered their ears.

KRANG!

The war hammer bounced off the shield. The reverberations sent Brenwar flying from his feet. He landed in the lap of a giant. Looking up at it, he said, "What are you looking at, ugly?" The giant growled. Brenwar crushed its nose with Mortuun. "That's what I thought."

Nath's scaled fingers fidgeted at his sides. A moment of desperation set in as he looked at his father's body hanging cold and lifeless from the rack. He closed his eyes and kneeled in front of the invisible dome. He put his hands on it. *There must be a way to take this down. What is it?*

"Nath, I don't know what you're doing, but we need to fight," Selene said.

"I need more time. I'll figure it out."

"You had better make it fast, or none of us will make it out of here." Selene was still fighting. "We might have to abandon this cause, Nath. I'm sorry. I don't have any answers."

Surrounded by the chronic pounding and thrashing of one beast striving against another, Nath rose. Hands still on the shield, he fought against saying the words, "Sorry, Father." He was so close, he couldn't give up. He called out at the top of his voice in Dragonese, "The moment is at hand! Help me, brethren!"

The clouds swirled and darkened above. Lightning flashed in the sky. A soft drizzling rain came down. Drifting through the skyline came a small flock of ghostly badger-sized dragons with lavender scales. With the nimbleness of hawks, they swooped through the barrage of missiles. They landed on the invisible dome shield. Spreading out their smooth and almost transparent wings, they latched on with their claws and mouths. Bat-like and eerie, they sucked on the energy of the shield. Their wings glowed with purple light.

Nath let out a shout. "Yeah! It's the lilac ravens! They came!"

There were so many types of dragons it was often difficult to account for them all. It had been such a long time since Nath last saw one, let alone a dozen.

The invisible dome warbled with angry colors that streaked through as it crackled, shifted, and sputtered. The lilac ravens grew in stature. The energy brightened their claws, tails, and wings like starlight. Within seconds they were as big as four tusked elephants. There was a loud *pop*.

Selene crossed over the singed ground where the barrier had been lodged. "It's gone, Nath!"

"Iron eaters! Get to work," he ordered.

The rust-colored dragons latched onto every chain and shackle they could find. Their sharp teeth nibbled at the massive locks and links. They devoured hunks at a time, but the going was slow. Nath hacked at the chains fastened to Balzurth's legs. Fang bit deep into the metal. He severed one link, but there were many.

"Nath, look out!"

Giants plowed through the ring of dragons that defended him. A smooth-skinned stone giant with spiked knuckles walloped a dragon so hard it cracked the dragon's horns. The dragons spat flame, foam, and coils of energy. The giants shrugged it off, surged forward, and plunged spears made from dragon horn into the dragons' bellies.

Nath screamed, "Nooo!" He leapt away from his father. He plunged Fang into the stone giant's chest.

The giant was laughing as it died. "You are losing," the giant said in a final gasping breath.

The giant was right. Time was closing in. Mighty as they were, the dragons were getting bludgeoned by a well-prepared force. With their breath weapons nullified, it was only a matter of time until their efforts collapsed.

"Fight, my brothers! Fight!" Nath yelled. He fought his way toward Balzurth.

Stone and earth giants, three in all, blocked his path. Dragon hide and bones covered their bodies like armor. The war paint on their faces and arms gleamed an evil gleam.

"Get out of my way or suffer the consequences! Aw, never mind. You're going to suffer them anyway." Nath loosed his fiery breath. Surely his own power would overcome the giants' foul magic. The flames washed over the towering brutes, consuming them from head to toe.

The flames extinguished moments later. With their skin and hair smoldering, the giants pulled their huge lips back over their rotten teeth. The tallest stone giant said, "Your father hangs from the rack. You'll be next."

CHAPTER 29

THE WIND PICKED UP. RAIN came down in heavy drops that turned into sheets. Nath's shoulders slumped underneath the heavy drops. As the giants came at him again, he caught a glimpse of his father. Water streamed down his horns and over the sagging scales on his face. It turned Nath's heart inside out. He sucked in deep draws through his nose and set his eyes on the giants. He slid Dragon Claw out of Fang. "Dragon! Dragon!"

Fang ripped out a pound of flesh from a stone giant's ankle. The giant let out an angry groan just before he brought his fist down. Nath jumped aside. A giant's fist blindsided him with a well-timed blow. On his hands and knees, he twisted around just in time to catch three giants diving on top of him. Their heavy bodies buried him in suffocating blackness. The wind was knocked out of him. They were giggling.

"The little dragon king is squished like a squash," one giant rumbled.

"I hate squash," said another. "I like meat with the crunch of bones in it."

Nath wrestled against the masses. He managed to twist onto his back, but it did him little good. His strength was great, but it was no match for the giants' superior size and girth. Struggling, he let go of Fang and Dragon Claw. The move didn't help. One giant grabbed his arms and another his legs.

The earth giants hoisted him up off the ground and stretched him like a blanket. "Look at this," the stone giant said. "We've got ourselves a catch. I wonder how this dragon tastes? Some taste like fish, at least most of the ones that I ate."

"You can't harm me!" Nath said.

"Oh, we'll see about that." The stone giant doing the talking picked up Fang with the tips of his fingers. His skin sizzled. "Grrrrr!" He dropped the blade. "You'll pay for that. Somebody find me a weapon with a keen edge." A nuurg trotted over. He held a huge knife with a razor-sharp edge out with his massive hand.

Nath could tell by the blade that it was a dragon scaler, made of the sharpened horns of a dragon. He swallowed hard. He wasn't sure if he could withstand its cut or not. Many of those blades were enchanted. He'd had the tip of one broken off inside his body before. It had almost killed him.

The stone giant, vastly bigger than the ten-foot tall nuurg, said to it, "You go ahead. Cut him open."

With the rain splattering in his eyes and no help in sight, Nath said in his dragon voice, "Come one step closer, nuurg, and I'll turn you into giant fodder."

The nuurg hesitated, but a glare from the stone giant sent it forward again. It thumbed the razor edge of the blade. "With delight." Coming forward, the nuurg cocked the dragon scaler back.

Looking the nuurg dead in the eyes, Nath said, "Last warning."

The nuurg stopped. A glare from the stone giant sent him forward again. Nath looked into the nuurg's eye. The mystic war paint had all but washed off of his face. Quickly, Nath scanned the faces of his enemies. The black war paint was mostly gone, washed by the downpour over their bodies into the sloppy puddles of mud.

Can it be?

Above, he spied Bayzog on the back of a dragon circling in the air. The mage was waving.

It can be!

The nuurg lifted the dragon scaler over Nath's chest. The stone giant said, "Any last words, Dragon Prince?"

"Yes. Burn, nuurgie, burn." Nath spat a small ball of fire into the nuurg's eyes. Instantly, the nuurg's head turned into flame. Dropping the dagger, it ran away screaming.

The startled giant's eyes grew to the size of wagon wheels. Nath covered the one holding his legs in flames. The fire shriveled every fiber of hair. The thick flesh dried and peeled away to the bone. A bull dragon's tail swiped right through the huge burning skeleton.

Nath put his eyes on the stone giant. With smoke rolling out of his mouth, he said, "You're next."

"Throw him!" the stone giant said to the earth giant still holding Nath by the arms. "Throw him away!"

An orange blaze dropped out of the sky. It spewed white foam all over the earth giant. The foam spread all over the giant's body, eating its flesh down to the bone.

Nath freed his arms and said to the stone giant, "No, you are."

The stone giant brought both of his fists down on Nath with wroth force.

Nath caught the blow on his hand and shoulders. He sank his claws into the giant's hands. Holding the monster man fast, Nath spewed out a geyser of orange flame. The dragon fire turned the giant into ash in seconds.

All around the arena, giants, nuurg, ogres, and titan-army soldiers burned. Lightning bolts streaked through their bodies. Black acid breath turned enemy skin to sizzling goo. The fighting continued, but the rout was on.

Nath turned his attention to his father on the rack. The iron eaters chomped through the chains. Links groaned and snapped. Balzurth's carcass hit the ground hard, landing on its shoulder. Nath rushed over to the body. The Spear of Barnabus was still firmly lodged inside.

Selene hustled over. Her worried eyes were fixed on Balzurth's body. With the battle still raging all around, she said, "Are you going to fly him out of here?"

"No," Nath replied. He grabbed the Spear of Barnabus at the neck just above the tip and set his foot against Balzurth's chest. "I'm taking it out now."

"Nath, you should wait."

"We've waited long enough. I can't pass up a chance like this. Watch my back." He set his shoulders and heaved. "*Urk*!"

CHAPTER 30

Accompanied by her father, Sansla, Laylana had moved south, where another tunnel entrance that led into Elome was hidden in the thickets and shrubs. Some of the dragons came with them, but the majority of the army, led by Slivver, took to the sky. It was a grim time in Elome. The very streets of the expansive forest city were overrun.

"Can you wield it?" Laylana said to Sasha.

Sasha held the Orb of Command that Bayzog had given her before he departed. It was a smooth sphere, granite in color, with arcane runes painted on it. Nodding, she said, "I've never used anything of this magnitude. It makes my hairs stand on end. But I will do what must be done."

Rerry put his hand on Sasha's shoulder. "You can do it, Mother. You are strong…like me."

Sasha let out a delighted chuckle. "Yes, I suppose that I'll be fine then. Sansla, Laylana, if you trust me, then I'm ready to go."

"Of course we do." Laylana squeezed Sasha's wrists. "The trust of the elves is with you, always."

"Thank you." Sasha found Inslay scratching his cheek and looking at her. "Having second thoughts?"

"No, the orb is your treasure to bear." He gave her a wink. "My hands are full enough already." Both of his hands were empty. "You're a sorceress. You know what I mean."

Laylana called Eslin over. "Are your men prepared?"

"Eager to serve," the elven commander remarked.

"Good. Father, shall we go then?" she said to Sansla.

Tucking the Ocular of Orray into his clothing, Sansla said, "At once." With a wave of his hands, the shrubbery that covered the tunnel parted. The elven guard bound up Laylana, Sasha, Rerry, Samaz and Inslay by the wrists. The cords were snug, but loose enough to squeeze out of. They did the same to the roamers: Sansla, Shum, Hoven, and Liam. Without dragons, they escorted them all into the tunnel.

Rerry said to his brother, "This is either going to be a bad idea or really brilliant."

The plan was for them to reenter Elome posing as prisoners. While the dragons scoured the skies above with mild attacks, the party, led by Sansla, would seek out the High Council. The challenge would be convincing the elven guard under the spell of the titans that they were indeed prisoners. Sasha would use the Orb of Command to convince the enemy they were. Once they were inside, they'd try to blend in and find the High Council.

At a brisk pace, they marched through the dark tunnel that bent left and right for miles. The party's footfalls were soft and silent. Near the end, Laylana spied elven guards fifty yards away. At thirty yards, the elven guards faced the tunnel's entrance with their spears lowered.

Eslin did all of the talking to the tunnel guard commander, who wore an insignia cloak over his shoulders. "We captured them on our way back from a scouting mission. They looked to use this tunnel for entry. Laylana and Inslay are fugitives. They should be taken immediately before the High Council."

The captain of the tunnel guardians sneered at Eslin. Laylana didn't know the elf. His close-knit eyes were shifty. The fine hairs on her neck stood on end. She knew it was the spirits.

"I don't know you, Commander Eslin," the elven tunnel guard said. He eyed all of the group and spoke with a bit of a hiss. "I find it very difficult to believe that your troupe managed the capture of four"—he craned his neck at the tall elves in the back—"roamers. And Lady Laylana, and I believe that is Inslay, is it not?"

With his brows knitted, Eslin said, "You underestimate the elves in my command."

"Are you overestimating your ability to lie? I know a liar when I see one." The elven guard licked his teeth and snickered.

Laylana eased forward. She got a better look at the guardian forces. Two dozen of them ready to die with a single command. The last thing she wanted was to see innocent blood spilled, even though she wanted to choke their commander. She nudged Sasha.

Sasha's hands were hidden inside the sleeves of her robes. She palmed the orb within. Her lips muttered.

Eslin spoke up. "The only ones armed are us. If you want the glory for yourself, have your way, Commander." He lifted his hands. "But if you challenge my authority that outranks yours, I'll cut you down."

"Clever. I suppose I would offer the same challenge, given the opposite circumstances." The tunnel commander blinked a few times. He pinched the bridge of his nose. "I don't know what it is, but something about you, all of you, gives me a headache. I won't be marching you to the High Council anytime soon, I assure you of that. I'll escort you to Elome's vaults. There, you can wait—forever, I hope."

"I wouldn't expect the protocol to be any different," Eslin replied.

The tunnel commander gave everyone a long, hard look. Shaking his head, he said to his men, "Take them away."

Laylana and company were marched up the tunnel steps and into the streets. She choked on a gasp. Elome's grand streets were filled with anyone but elves. Giants of all sizes strolled the cobblestones. Their hands were filled with food, and casks of wine were hooked under their arms. They passed haphazardly built gallows. The ropes groaned against the wind that stretched the necks of elves. One of the hanging elves was Osslin.

"No, no, no," Laylana mumbled.

Sansla leaned over. "Be strong, daughter. He did not shed blood in vain."

They were locked inside the stone vaults just outside of where Elome's stone road turned to turf. The cells were full of elves. All of them were long faced, beaten, scraped up, and bruised. As the tunnel commander escorted them into their cell, he said, "It will be the gallows for them too. That's the price for rebellion, the harsh kiss of a noose."

As the cell door slammed in Laylana's face, she said, "How can you stand by and let this happen? You are an elf. Elves don't kill elves."

The tunnel commander looked at Eslin and his men. Eslin's men were still crowded inside by the tunnel guards. "Well done, Commander Eslin. Please, stick around." He faced Laylana. "And in answer to your question, you are right, elves don't normally kill elves." He popped a dagger out of his scabbard. "Until now." He stabbed Eslin right in the gut. The tunnel guard slaughtered Eslin's men on the point of spears one by one.

CHAPTER 31

THE ANCIENT SPEAR OF BARNABUS snagged a few times inside Balzurth's wound. Hand over hand, Nath pulled the long spear out. On the head of the grand weapon were four barbs of metal, twisted at the ends to make tips fine as needles. That last foot of the ten-foot shaft came out with a sucking sound. Balzurth's body, a coat of scales clinging to a husk, sagged.

Nath set the spear down and laid hands on his father's neck. Balzurth's head was bigger than Nath's whole body. The king was the biggest dragon in the arena. Nath shot a look at Selene. "He breathes."

Balzurth's chest rose and fell gently. Cold breath whisked through his teeth. Nath shouted into Balzurth's ear. "Father! Father, wake up. It's your son, Nath!"

The Dragon King's eyelid popped open. Big as a plate and gold as the sunrise, the orb settled on Nath. The eye blinked a few times. In a raspy groan, Balzurth said, "Son, you saved me."

Nath snorted and blustered. He threw his arms around his father's great neck. Selene was sobbing. Brenwar stood nearby, wiping something out of his eye. Dragon skin and scales tightening and dragon fibers reattaching to muscle made a sickening sound. But Balzurth's body rejuvenated. Twitched. The great tail slowly fanned back and forth.

"Easy, Father. Don't rush yourself."

"I've never felt better, Son."

"Well, you've never looked worse, either. Pace yourself, Father."

Balzurth laid his heavy eyes on the battle. A snarl formed. His tremendous tail snapped like the crack of a whip. The blow sent an earth giant flying through the air.

Nath gave Selene a look. "I stand corrected."

"Agreed."

"Where's Eckubahn?" Balzurth demanded more than asked. "I want him." He rose to full height. "It's time to finish this once and for all."

"The cathedral!" From one knee, Brenwar yelled, "It's there or he runs somewhere. I would if I were him!"

Balzurth glanced at the rack that once held him. He shattered it with a swipe of his tail.

Nath picked up the Spear of Barnabus. "Father, will you need this?"

The great dragon's chin dipped. "No, but perhaps you will. Bring it along. The more weapons, the better." He plowed through the fiery fracas with the unified roars of the dragons. His gargantuan body created a corridor through the arena's wall. Down the streets he went.

Nath sheathed Fang. Carrying the spear, he took off after his father. Selene and Brenwar moved along by his side.

"Nath, are you sure this is wise?" Selene said. "He might not be ready for battle yet."

"There won't be any changing his mind. Be wary. We're going into this blind."

Balzurth charged down the street, crushing everything in his path underneath his feet and tail. With reckless abandon, he stormed the humongous cathedral in the heart of the city.

The great wide-open doors in the middle began to close. Picking up speed, Balzurth wedged his body between them. He shoved his way through. Nath, Brenwar, and Selene squeezed through just as the doors snapped shut.

Eckubahn sat on his throne, head burning with a quavering yellow-green fire. His elbows were on the arms of his chair. His fingers tapped together. Lotuus sat on the top of the throne's backrest. Her slender face showed no alarm. Giants sealed all of the doors that led into the cathedral with huge iron bars, including the ones they had entered through.

"I feel like the walls just closed in," Selene said

Nath's fingertips tingled. Balzurth's impulsiveness might have led them straight into a trap.

"Welcome back from the dead, Balzurth," Eckubahn said with an evil gleam in his eye. "Enjoy it. It won't last."

"I think you're mistaken, Eckubahn. My son has the Spear of Barnabus. It's only a matter of time before your undoing," Balzurth replied.

Eckubahn gave a quick nod. The giant soldiers guarding the doors came forward. There were ten in all. "You believe so much in your son, do you, Balzurth? He challenged me once before. Perhaps he wants to challenge me again. I've no fear of that spear of yours. What do you say, Nath Dragon? Do you want to see if you have what it takes?"

"This fight is between me and you, Eckubahn. Leave my son out of it." Balzurth stepped right out in front of the titan's throne.

"Balzurth, you are a fool. You're dead already." Eckubahn pounced from his throne. He socked Balzurth in the jaw. Balzurth reeled. Eckubahn got his arms around the Dragon King's neck. He locked the great dragon up in a headlock. Eckubahn leered right at Nath. "Your father is still weak. He's no match for me. I can't wait to see your eyes when I snap his neck."

"No!" Nath yelled. "I accept your challenge!"

In his gravelly voice, Eckubahn spoke into Balzurth's ear hole, "Do you honor this?"

"I do," Balzurth replied.

"Good, because once I finish your son, I'll permanently finish you."

CHAPTER 32

RINNING AND CLAPPING HER HANDS, Lotuus said, "This will be delightful! I can't wait to see you peel those scales from his perfect bones." Wings beating, she hovered in between the titan and Nath Dragon. "They are going to need to move."

Selene and Brenwar stood their ground beside Nath. "We aren't moving anywhere," Brenwar said.

Casually, Lotuus replied, "Oh, of course you aren't. But fair is fair, and we won't take any chances." She let out a soft whistle. Fairies with lithe little bodies appeared in an assortment of fantastic colors. Before Selene or Brenwar could move, the fairies blew sparkling fairy dust on them.

Brenwar's feet lifted up off the floor. "What is happening? Put me down, you evil pixies!"

Both Selene and Brenwar hung suspended in the air. The gleefully giggling fairies towed them away by their arms.

"Don't do any damage to them," Nath warned Lotuus.

"This is war, Nath Dragon. I'll damage them if I want. To the point of death even, but I want to see you die first." She winked at him. "Goodbye, Nath Dragon."

With his father looking on, Nath gave a nod. He readied his stance against Eckubahn. With more than enough room to brawl inside the dome of the cathedral, the two contestants circled one another. Eckubahn's fists swung at his sides. Nath kept the spear pointed at the titan's chest. Something rattled inside Nath's brain. An instinct. A deep warning.

Now is not the time to doubt yourself, Nath. It's time to finish this.

"What are you waiting for?" Eckubahn said. "Is it that you know you can't finish? Is it because deep down, you are a coward, a failure?" His dark eyes fastened on the spear. "Do you really think that little stick can stop me? You might have the Spear of Barnabus, but do you have the faith to wield it?"

Nath glanced at Balzurth. The grand dragon's body sagged on the floor. His eyes were on Eckubahn.

Lotuus let out a taunting cackle. "Look at his eyes, Lord Titan. He is lost. A leaf blowing in the wind. Oh, I suppose his father never took the time to tell him how the power of the Spear truly works."

"Don't listen to them, Nath!" Selene yelled. "She's a liar."

"Oh, be quiet, former black snake." Lotuus winked, and Selene's words went silent. Her lips were moving, but nothing came out. The same happened to Brenwar, who was red faced and yelling. "That's better."

Nath swallowed. "I know better than to believe anything you have said. You're both liars. Eckubahn, you want to fight, then let's fight." Nath charged. He heard his father whisper, "Aim for the heart."

Eckubahn sidestepped the charge. With alarming speed, he smashed his fist into the ground, missing Nath by a handsbreadth. He came at Nath, swatting the spear tip aside every time Nath jabbed. Against most of the giants, Nath could take advantage of their sluggish size, but not Eckubahn. The titan moved as fast as Nath did.

Nath jumped up and lunged at the heart.

Eckubahn backhanded him.

Nath hit the ground and rolled back to his feet. Shoulders low, he rushed again.

Eckubahn was laughing. "You're no match for me. You are but a child with a shiny toy."

"Am I now!" Nath snaked between the titan's swipes. Jumping into the air, he took flight. He'd been timing Eckubahn's patterns. Seeking a weakness. Toying with the titan's efforts. The titan lost sight of Nath.

The monstrous man spun around, saying, "Where are you, little flea?"

Nath hovered right in front of the titan, eyeing the titan's exposed chest. "I'm right here!" With all of his might, he stabbed the Spear of Barnabus into the titan's breastplate. He would never forget the shocking sound that came next. The spearhead bent. The shaft snapped. The spearhead bounced off the floor.

Eckubahn's thunderous laugh was deafening.

Nath hung in the air, gazing at the broken spear haft in his hand with dismay. "I don't understand!"

"Because you're a fool," Eckubahn said.

Balzurth rose up behind Nath. Nath's gaze hung on his father. There was a dark twinkle glimmering behind his eyes that he'd never seen before. "Father, explain."

"Certainly, Son," Balzurth said in a voice that started to change. "It's as Eckubahn said. You are a fool! A big one!"

Balzurth's eyes changed once and for all. His great body started to shift. Going for Fang that still hung from the scabbard on his back, Nath cried out in alarm, "Tylabahn!" His efforts came too late.

Eckubahn snagged his legs. He ripped the sword and scabbard from his back. The titan king used Nath like a hammer and beat him on the ground. Tylabahn and Lotuus taunted him while Eckubahn hammered him into submission. When the titan stopped, his chest was heaving. There was dragon blood on his fists.

Nath groaned. His body was in knots of pain. His face was swelling, and bones were cracked. His head lolled to one side. Tylabahn stood over him, a gangly twenty-foot-tall hag in ragged robes. He stretched out his fingers, saying in a wheeze, "Where's my father?"

Lotuus drifted down from her airy perch and landed on Nath's chest. With her legs crossed and a smile on her face, she said, "Yes, a good question. Don't feel bad, Nath. Even I was fooled at first by Eckubahn's brilliant deception." She looked to Eckubahn. "May I, or are you going to finish him right now?"

"Go on." Eckubahn took his seat on the throne. "I'll enjoy hearing it."

"Thank you, my lord. Now, Nath, you see—"

"I've figured it out. Get off me," said Nath. It was obvious now, what had happened. A forgery of the Spear of Barnabus had been made. Tylabahn, using the powers of Gorlee the Changeling, had taken the form of Balzurth on the rack. Eckubahn had sucked them in and fooled them all. "Where's my father's body?"

"Actually, I don't know. Eckubahn, where is the corpse of almighty Balzurth?"

"Right before your eyes, Nath Dragon." Eckubahn made a long arc with his hand toward the cathedral ceiling. The air shimmered. Balzurth's body took form. He hung suspended by bulky chains fastened to the arches in the vaulted ceiling. The true Spear of Barnabus was still lodged in his body. "I had my trophy moved. It served two purposes. I fooled you, and I get to see my trophy daily. I didn't realize until this very day that I'd enjoy it so much."

"I really like that, Eckubahn," Lotuus said. Moving away, with her fingers locked together, she said, "Please, please, please give me my own throne room with Nath Dragon hanging in such grand fashion as my treasure."

"I'll consider it."

Grimacing, Nath fought his way up to a sitting position. Brenwar and Selene were still suspended in silence. All of the great doors were sealed shut. The giant soldiers gave him cold, heavy stares. Eckubahn had beaten him to a pulp. Gazing up, he saw the spear jutting out of his father. There was stained blood on the tip. *I am a fool. How did I miss that? If I could only take the spear out.*

A hollow chuckle echoed in the chamber. Eckubahn stated, "I know what you're thinking, Nath Dragon. I've always known what you were thinking. For two centuries the titan spirits have watched your follies. You are predictable as an ogre. You need to be changing like the wind." He stood up on his tiptoes. His long arm stretched upward and grabbed the head of the Spear of Barnabus. In a fierce tug, he wrenched it free.

Swaying in the links, Balzurth's body hung as lifeless as ever.

"Your attempt was foolish. Your father has been trapped in the Dark Realm far too long. He's dead already, and now you'll be joining him." His jutting chin gave a nod. Two giant soldiers pinned Nath down to the ground by his arms and legs. With one hand Eckubahn held the spear over Nath's chest. "Today, Nalzambor becomes mine forever! Goodbye, Son of Balzurth!"

CHAPTER 33

ESLIN AND HIS MEN, EVERY last one, had been cut down. The blood drained from the faces of everyone in Laylana's cell. Her chest tightened. Her knees swayed. Never in all her life had she seen an elf take the life of another in cold blood. There had been trials, battles, and feuds, but never had she seen a bloody massacre like this.

The tunnel commander leered at her. "I don't know what you were up to, but soon, the High Council will find out. We are privy to your tricks." On his command, the tunnel guards dragged the dead bodies out of the vault. Many of the elven prisoners in the other cells sobbed and cried as the bodies of their brethren went by. With a foul salute, the tunnel commander departed.

"I'm so sorry, Laylana. So sorry," Sasha said in choking sobs. "It's my fault. I released my grip on them. I never imagined they were so vicious."

Hugging Sasha into her shoulder, she said, "None of us could have imagined it."

"Their sacrifice will not be in vain," Sansla said. "We'll see to it. We are just where we wanted to be. We are here, but the High Council doesn't know we are coming." He pulled Sasha to him. "Sasha, call for the jailer. Use the orb. Command him to hand over the keys."

With the orb clasped in her hands and her sons at her side, Sasha did as she was told. The elven jailer came forward with moony eyes and a ring of keys in hand. He slid the key into the keyhole and twisted. Sansla took the ring of keys. Sasha commanded the jailer to sit.

The elves in the other rooms let out sighs. "Free us, free us," they pleaded.

Using the Orb of Command, Sasha gathered up the other tunnel guards. Some of them were possessed, and others were confused. They hissed when they were hustled into the dungeon cell.

"Take their uniforms," Shum ordered Liam and Hoven. The roamers dressed in the emblematic cloth tunics, sword belts, and forest-green caps. Rerry and Samaz followed suit.

With Laylana beside him, Sansla addressed the elves.

"I am Sansla Libor, the no-longer-cursed elven king of the roamers. Our lands are invaded by a dark enemy from the netherworld. Our families perish to their madness right before our eyes. We've all witnessed it for ourselves.

"The High Council is under the spell of this wicked influence. We must stop this madness in its tracks. If I free you, you'll be captured again. I cannot risk your safety." He handed the keys to Hoven. "Protect them."

"No, Sansla," one of the elves shouted from inside the cage. "You must free us. If they come back, they'll surely slay us all."

"There is nowhere to run just now."

"Let's fight then," another prisoner said.

"When the time to fight comes," Sansla said to them all, "you will know. Until then, you must wait."

They departed the vault. While they huddled in the entryway, Laylana said to her father, "That must not have been easy."

"It was painful, but the last place they'll look for elves is in the prisons." Sansla poked his head outside. Titan army soldiers marched through the streets. From the trees, they launched missile weapons out of ballistas at the dragons in the sky. "We need to find the High Council, and quickly."

With chaos brewing all around, they marched into the streets in uniform fashion. Sansla, Laylana, Sasha, and Inslay kept their heads down, arms tied in front of them, as if they were prisoners. "We need to find someone in the know. They'll need convincing," Sansla said to Sasha.

A wary-eyed nuurg locked his eyes on them. "You! Where are you going?" he said to Shum.

Shum stopped the group. He saluted. "They are to be brought before the High Council and titan leaders. It's going to be a public execution."

The nuurg's numbers strengthened around them.

Sasha's knuckles turned white on the orb. Her face broke out in a cold sweat.

Laylana heard the woman softly saying over and over again, "Take us to the High Council."

Scratching his neck, the nuurg's single eye scoured over them all. He grabbed the sword hanging from his belt, drew it out, then slapped it back into the sheath with a hard *clack*. "Elves are such idiots. You're going the wrong way. Come, follow me!"

CHAPTER 34

JUST BEFORE THE SPEAR OF Barnabus plunged into Nath's exposed chest, Tylabahn said, "Eckubahn, my brother, let me have the pleasure."

Face contorting behind its flickering green flames, Eckubahn said, "Nay. The pleasure will be mine. Isobahn took out his father, but I will be the one to take out his son."

"It is not fair. I have earned the right as much as you have!"

"You are maddened. Back away while I do my work."

"Never!" Wild eyed, Tylabahn rushed Eckubahn. "Give me the spear!"

"Yes, give her the spear," Nath blurted out. "She's thrice the titan you are, Eckubahn!" The titans wrestled over the spear. Nath wasn't sure what was happening. He couldn't tell if Tylabahn had lost her mind or if Gorlee was regaining control. The glimmer of hope energized him. With giant hands still fastened to his arms and legs, he hollered at Lotuus. "You really know how to pick your allies, Fairy Empress. Won't you miss me when I'm gone?"

Lotuus landed beside him. Caressing his cheek with her tiny hand, she said, "Those soft lips, that silky hair and those handsome eyes." Her face turned demonic. "Never!"

"That's what I thought. I just wanted you to know that the feeling is mutual." He winked at her. "See you around."

"Have you gone mad?"

"No." His eyes flitted upward. "But you're sure going to be really soon."

"What?" She looked above. Bayzog hovered in the air with the Elderwood Staff pointed at her. Her lips curled back, baring razor-sharp fangs. "You! I hate you almost as much as the dragons!"

"I know," Bayzog replied coolly. "The feeling is mutual." A ray of light shot out of the staff. The bolt knocked Lotuus into the base of the throne.

Selene and Brenwar's bonds loosened. They hit the floor on their feet. The giant soldiers attacked the pair. Lotuus's fairies surrounded Bayzog. Tylabahn and Eckubahn wrestled on the floor over the spear.

Looking up at the giants that held him, Nath said to them, "You can either let go of me the easy way or the hard way."

Lotuus's wings came to life. She floated up off the floor. Yelling at the giants, she said, "Just pull him apart!"

The giants tugged at Nath like two dogs fighting over a piece of rope.

"Gah!" Glaring at them, he said, "It will be the hard way then." He spewed flames on the arms of the one that had his legs. Its fingers slipped free. The momentum of the giant tugging Nath's arms sent it sprawling backward. It crashed into a support column, shaking the roof. Still holding Nath fast, it lay momentarily still, backside to the floor.

Brenwar waltzed up to the giant with Mortuun in hand. "Hello, giant." He delivered a lethal skull-cracking blow. "Goodbye, giant!"

Free and on his feet, Nath held out his hand. "Fang, to me!"

The sword slipped free of the scabbard and flew right into his hands. The handle burned with a hungry fire that charged Nath's blood like lava. "Brenwar, Selene! Help Bayzog! I'll handle Eckubahn."

Tylabahn was sunk on her knees with Eckubahn lording over her. Her head was down with her blistered knuckles resting on the floor. She gave a sluggish glance back at Nath. Her eyes were Gorlee's.

Eckubahn stabbed Gorlee's transformed body straight through the heart. The changeling's head snapped back with his mouth hanging open.

"Noooooooo!" Nath shouted.

It was too late. The light in Gorlee's eyes went out. Tylabahn's spirit erupted out of the body with a shrieking howl. The ghostly essence jumped into a stone giant's body. The smooth stone body burst open with Tylabahn's shrieking spirit coming out. She jumped from giant to giant. Every titan soldier convulsed, spasmed, and died. No host could hold her powerful spirit. With a fierce wail, Tylabahn's spirit burst up through the cathedral ceiling and out of sight.

Nath turned his attention to Eckubahn. The titan removed the Spear of Barnabus from Gorlee's body. The changeling transformed into a hairless pink-skinned humanoid dressed in rags.

"How unfortunate, Nath Dragon," Eckubahn gloated. "Another one of your friends has died." He scanned his surroundings like a cornered rat. Eyes searching for escape, he spied Lotuus and her fairies battling for their lives against Nath's friends. "Perhaps we'll meet again."

"No, this fight between us is not over! I won't let you run now, coward!"

With a wave of Eckubahn's hand, the ceiling burst open. Hunks of stone fell, cracking the stone floor. Balzurth's body hit the floor with a deadening thud.

The titan started to leap. "Until we meet again!"

Nath flung Fang with all his might. The weapon shot out of his hand in a sliver of shimmering blue light faster than the naked eye could see. It pierced the heart inside Eckubahn's broad chest. The titan's jaw widened in a deafening howl. He landed feetfirst on the floor and collapsed. Groaning on the floor, he tried to pull the pulsating weapon free. His hands sizzled. His flesh smoked. "NOOOOOOOOOOOO!"

Eckubahn's spirit burst out of the juddering giant. In a hot flash of swirling mystic wind, the apparition hung before Nath's transfixed stare. Mind to mind for all to hear, the titan said, "You've slain the flesh, but the spirit lives forever!" In a whoosh, Eckubahn's spirit vanished.

Nath took a knee by Gorlee's body. He picked his dead friend up and cradled him in his arms.

Bayzog had captured Lotuus in a net of mystic fibers. She tossed her head back in laughter.

CHAPTER 35

SELENE POPPED LOTUUS IN THE side of the head with her fist. "Stop laughing."

Lotuus's eyes narrowed on Selene. "You dare!"

Drawing a dagger from her belt, Selene said, "I'll do more than dare."

"Your weapon can't hurt me."

"Want to find out?"

"No." Lotuus looked toward Nath. "So, mighty Dragon Prince—or King, should I say. What do you propose to do now? Are you going to revel in your hollow victory? Where's that dazzling smile lit up in celebration that should be expected in a precious moment like this? Oh, I suppose banishing Eckubahn to the Dark Realm isn't such a victory after all, seeing how your father, mighty Balzurth, is still dead." She almost started to laugh, but Selene's stare silenced the effort. "And your weird little friend is dead too. How sad…for you."

Nath barely heard Lotuus's words. He held Gorlee in his arms. The changeling seemed impossibly light even for a person of a medium frame. "I'm going to miss you, Gorlee." Brenwar found his way to Nath's side. Nath looked down at his battle-battered friend, placed Gorlee in his hulky arms, and said, "Let's put him to rest."

"Aye," Brenwar replied.

Balzurth's massive body lay in a heap on the floor. His scales still had a living glint to them. Dragon scales never lost their luster, even over the long ages. Nath laid his hand where the spear had pierced his father's heart. It was an ugly wound, bigger than his fist, where the spear had busted through. He swallowed the lump in his throat. Eckubahn was gone, banished to the Dark Realm, but Balzurth was there as well.

"Yes, he's quite dead, isn't he?" Lotuus said. "I told you that Eckubahn would win, Nath Dragon. The titan spirits now cover all of Nalzambor, and from the Dark Realm he still controls them."

"He and Tylabahn, you mean." Nath turned in Lotuus's direction. He wasn't certain Tylabahn was gone, remembering how she had spirit-hopped from giant to giant when the Spear of Barnabus had rousted her out of Gorlee's body.

"She made an effort to stay, but her spirit is wounded. Only time in the Dark Realm will heal it, but it's only a matter of time before they both return. In the meantime, you have quite a mess to clean up." She yawned. "The elven lands are in full collapse. Every city is run by evil. Even with your dragons, there is little you can do to loosen the titans' hold on the people. Besides, their minds are unwilling. They like embracing their dark side. The poison elates them."

"I'll find a way," Nath said.

"There is no way, Nath Dragon. The only way to loosen Eckubahn and Tylabahn's grip on Nalzambor would be to destroy them in the Dark Realm. A fool's errand. You'd have to die yourself to get there."

"That's what I thought. I just wanted to be sure," Nath said with a confident smirk.

Bayzog tightened the net around Lotuus. "Agreed, Nath. As for finding a way to the Dark Realm, you don't have to die, you just have to go through the Land of the Dim Light. I know because I've been there."

Lotuus scowled. "You only know what you think you know. You cannot survive down there."

"We'll see. Come, everyone," Nath said, picking up the Spear of Barnabus. He tossed it to Selene. "It's time to deliver Lotuus's sentence."

"What!" Lotuus cried out. She pressed her face into the webbing with her fingers clutching at the cords. "You cannot kill me, Nath Dragon. You are merciful."

"I am, but perhaps Selene is not, nor Brenwar. You killed Laedorn and Uurluuk in cold blood. The only justice for you is death."

"Give me the spear, Nath. I'd be honored to run this pixie through," Brenwar said.

"I am not a pixie! I am the Fairy Empress, a living part of this world. Nath, please, Eckubahn made me do it! He is the killer, not I! I was but a pawn. An unwilling one!"

"I know better." Nath led them to The Deep. Standing on the rim of the gaping black hole, he said, "This will be your home for a very long time. All eternity perhaps. But you won't be without company." Several gray scalers encircled the rim. Behind them were an odd breed of stone-skinned dragons with eyes that were citrine in color. He nodded at Bayzog.

"Goodbye, Lotuus." Net and all, Bayzog tossed her down into the well.

"Noooooo!" she screamed. Her loyal fairies dove after her.

The gray scalers slunk over the rim and scuttled down the wall after her. The stone dragons latched onto one another, creating a bridge over the portal. One by one they formed a tight lid over the well in a similar fashion to the great dragon wall.

"Do you think that will hold her?" Bayzog said to Nath.

"Long enough. There is only one way in and out of the well, unless you have Fang, of course." More dragons entered the chamber and stood watch.

"I would have killed her," Brenwar said, trying to peer through the lid made of dragons. There wasn't a crease for air between any of them. Subconsciously clawing at his beard, he said, "Pixies are nothing but good or paid."

"Brenwar, where is Gorlee's body?" Selene asked.

"I set him down over there. I wanted to see this." His eyes flitted over to Nath. "Sorry."

"It's fine." Craning his neck, Nath asked, "Where did you set him down?"

Brenwar turned on his heel and pointed. "Right there." Gorlee's body was gone. "Oh."

With a smile brimming on his face, Nath said, "We need to get moving."

"To Elome?" Selene asked.

"No, to the Land of the Dim Light. When I rested my hand on Father's chest, I felt a single heartbeat. Time is short to save Balzurth and put an end to the titans once and for all." He spread his wings. "Are you with me?"

Selene was the first to reply. "Until the end of time."

"For Morgdon!"

CHAPTER 36

Escorted by the nuurg and a squad of titan army soldiers, Laylana and company were marched to the top edge of a massive outdoor amphitheater. A swell of elves, orcs, gnolls, giants, and the like clustered on the green-topped terrace's seats that numbered in the thousands. Beautiful trees that had long sprouted from the grounds covered the amphitheater in a comfortable shade.

Laylana's stomach knotted up. Elves sat with orcs. Giants and ogres stood casually with their backs against the trees. They numbered in the thousands and talked among themselves. The elves had darkened expressions and a wicked glimmer in their eyes. They weren't elves as Laylana knew them. They were brethren possessed by spirits.

The crowd's attention hung on the High Council, who stood behind a table made from a granite slab of stone. They were having a conversation with an earth giant, a stone giant, and two nuurg commanders. Andar stood in the center of all of them. He wore the dark robes woven in the ancient symbols of the High Council. The rings on his slender fingers glinted. He held his arms up. The murmuring crowd slowly went silent.

"Now is not the time for war, but the time for peace," Andar said in a voice that carried over well. A rousing applause broke out. "The titan army has offered to let us live in peace among them in return for our surrender."

"This is madness!" Laylana hissed to Inslay. "We must do something, now! The High Council is giving our entire heritage away!"

Andar continued. "We cannot have any more resistance. As you can see by our once-fair brethren that sway on the gallows, that freedom they fought for was fatal. All elves, including myself, should surrender their weapons and strive for a peaceful transition. The titan king, his fine emissaries that he sent to help us"—he gestured to the giants and nuurg—"promise us no harm and a peaceful transition."

"Father, this has to end," Laylana said to Sansla.

The nuurg gave her a look and said, "Be silent, rebel."

Andar's fingers pointed at half a dozen elves who were bound up and sitting on the ground in front of the slab table with their heads down. "It is important that we have unity among the elves in order to preserve our heritage. As you can see, we have many of our kind that are creating trouble. These elves, sadly, are guilty of treason. Only their oath of loyalty to the High Council's decision can preserve them. And if there are any other traitors whose knees will not bend for the will of our kingdom, let them be ornaments for the gallows as well."

"This is appalling," Inslay said.

The nuurg escort called out, "Lords! Lords! I am Okar. I have brought more from the resistance. Their knees won't bend."

Every head turned in Laylana's direction.

"Bring them down." Andar combed his slender fingers through the silky hair that covered his eye. "We will give them a chance to publicly change their minds."

Disguised in the tunnel guards' tunics, Shum, Liam, Rerry, and Samaz escorted them down the steps between the terraces.

"Keep your heads down," Sansla said to Sasha, Inslay, and Laylana. "Be ready on my word."

Chin down and shoulders lowered, Laylana shuffled down the steps. Her heart was racing. Her entire world had been turned inside out. Too late, she realized that the spirits had been eating away at Elome's core for years. Now, the bridge of the entire community had collapsed. No one had been wise enough to see it coming. Not even her.

Andar stepped around the table and faced the new prisoners. "Let me see who we have here. Chins up, please." His eyes widened the moment he saw Laylana and Inslay. Many of the other council members gasped. Jabbing his finger at her, he said in a hiss that was anything but elven, "You! You! What are you doing here! You're supposed to be imprisoned!" He stared down their nuurg escort. "Are you responsible for this?"

Fumbling for speech, the nuurg said, "I was told to bring them here to you."

Laylana lifted up her bound hands. "We are still prisoners, Andar. Shouldn't you be happy?"

Andar's beady eyes darted over every single face in the group, including Laylana's friends dressed as tunnel guards. He shriveled back, bumping into the slab table. "You reek of deception. Foolish nuurg! These are not prisoners. They are interlopers! Kill them! Kill the interlopers!"

"Now!" Sansla ordered. He withdrew the Ocular of Orray and lifted it high over his head. The radiant gemstone became a living star in his hand.

At the same time, Sasha held the Orb of Command up in the air before the crowd. Tapping the boundless energy of the orb, she spoke out a single crystal-clear command, "Listen!" The amphitheater shook under the power of her voice. The captive audience froze: elves, orcs, nuurg, and giants. Even the faces of the High Council hung suspended.

"I am Sansla Libor: rightful King of Elome and the Elves, Ruler of the High Council, and wielder of the truth-bearing light of the Ocular of Orray." The light of a second sun washed over the crowd. "Cleanse my elves, one and all, of the abominable spirits that indwell their souls. Be gone, wretches of darkness. Away, curses that fear the light. Vanish, all enemies and defilers."

Possessed elves cringed in their seats. Angry, unnatural, haunting shrieks and wails exploded out of elven mouths everywhere. Shades and shadows rose up out of their bodies in the form of wispy gray shadowy mists. They howled and shrieked at the all-consuming light. Encircling the Ocular of Orray in a living web, spirits gathered from all around. They came from the seats of the amphitheater and beyond. They circled in a storm of energy and collapsed on the orb.

Sansla shook his fist with the orb in hand. "Let the pure power of the elves strike down our enemies that creep in the night!"

A ring of pure white light erupted from Sansla's hands. It sheared through the spirits like hot steel through wax. The spirits exploded in a series of smoking clusters that went *piff piff poof poof poof*. The winds carried the fragmented elements away.

The bright eye of the Ocular went out. Sansla and Sasha were shaking.

Andar regained his feet. His eyes were filled with the unsearchable depths of bitterness. He yelled up at the giants, "Kill them!"

CHAPTER 37

THE STREETS OF NARNUM WERE still in chaos when Nath took to the sky. Even with Eckubahn gone, the titan army and dragons were still going at it. The possessed townspeople were an even bigger part of the problem. He'd instructed the dragons to do their best not to harm them. The void in Eckubahn's departure made for disorder and chaos in the spirit ranks. They attacked with recklessness and wild abandon.

He circled the city a few times. Selene, Brenwar, and Bayzog were also in the sky, on the backs of dragons. Brenwar's voice cut through the wind. "It's a fine mess down there. You'd never see such clishmaclaver in Morgdon. I guarantee you that!"

"Look!" Selene pointed northwest. A long line of armored soldiers snaked over the dales, heading straight for Narnum. Their numbers were thousands strong. The bright banners waved in the wind at the fore and aft of each column. Lance tips pointed toward the sky. "Legionnaires!"

Nath spied Ben and Rip immediately. The two men rode side by side. Big grins broke out on their faces when they saw Nath gliding down toward them.

"Dragon! I don't know what you did, but you did something," Ben said. "The morning dew sings!"

"We've rousted Eckubahn. He's banished to the Dark Realm, but he's left behind a sea of madness. We need you to stifle this spirit of rebellion that's broken loose in Narnum, before they burn the entire city down."

"The legionnaires are more than equipped to handle damage control," Rip said. Stroking the long tails of his moustache, the hardened warrior said to Nath, "You're going into the portal, aren't you, Your Majesty."

"What portal?" Ben asked.

"The well that leads into the Land of Dim Light."

Ben looked perplexed.

"You know, that place where I came from," Rip said to Ben.

"Ah, well, I'm going too," Ben replied. "Right, dragon?"

"Ben, it's dangerous. We might go in and never come out."

"Or you might wind up trapped in there for five hundred years." Rip slapped Ben on the back. "But when you do make it out, your skin will look great. Look at mine. Hardly a wrinkle."

Ben put his fingers to his lips and whistled. The copper dragons that he and Rip rode swooped over the ranks from behind them. They landed softly. Before Nath could say Sultans of Sulfur, Rip and Benhad dropped off of their horses and saddled up on the dragons.

Rip shrugged at Nath. "No one knows the Land of Dim Light better than I. You're going to need a guide."

"Yes, Nath, and you know how much I love going to new places." Ben patted the quiver of arrows hanging from his side. "Besides, I have Akron."

Nath nodded.

Rip shouted out to the highest-ranking legionnaire, "Commander, I want that city in order by the time I return."

The commander, big and bulky in his plate mail, saluted Rip Tippy and said, "As instructed, High Centurion. It will be done!"

With the help of Brenwar, Nath removed the stone lid covering the Well from Nowhere. Gazing into the black abyss, he said, "This might be a one-way trip, everyone. Feel free to change your minds. Besides, I might need someone to haul me back out of there."

"Does he really think we would stay here?" Selene said to Brenwar. She stuck the point of the Spear of Barnabus into the black void. "I like spear fishing."

With Mortuun resting on his shoulder, Brenwar said, "You'd think he'd know he's not allowed to go anywhere exciting without us by now."

Bayzog climbed up on the well wall and dangled his legs over the rim. The Elderwood Staff was in his lap. "There's plenty of exploration yet to be done. I wasn't even a tenth into it when I came back."

Ben switched his quiver from his hip to over his shoulder. He opened up Akron. *Snap. Clatch. Snap.* He notched an arrow with a ruby tip. "The sooner we go in, the sooner I can be home for dinner."

Rip patted the pommel of his sword made from blackened steel. "I'm ready to kill something."

Nath had as much power and weaponry at his disposal as he'd ever want. But he had the feeling that even with all of their awesome unified power, it still might not be enough. He summoned an emerald seeker. It landed on his shoulder. He whispered to the little dragon. Its wings buzzed to life, and it took off like a shot.

"What did you say to it?" Brenwar said.

"I sent word to Grahleyna. In case we don't make it back, she'll need to know what's going on."

"Oh, I thought it might have been a eulogy. Mine's written, and I'd like to get word to Glenwar before I'm gone." He started pulling out sheets of parchment from inside the belly of his armor. The stack was over an inch thick.

Gaping, Ben said, "Great Guzan, that's your eulogy? It looks more like the deed to Morgdon."

Brenwar licked his skeleton thumb and leafed through the pages. "I've lived a full life. Maybe one day you'll get to read it." He set the clump of pages down and covered it with a large stone. With a grunt, he said, "Let's get at it, then."

With a perched eyebrow, Bayzog said, "The dwarf can write. Impressive."

"Watch it, elf."

"Watch it, dwarf," Bayzog shot back.

"Elf!"

"Dwarf."

"Elf! Bah, I'm ready to fight now." Brenwar climbed on the rim and jumped. "For Mooooooooorgdoooooon!"

Leaning over the rim, Selene said, "How long do you think we should wait before we join him?"

"As long as I'd like it to be, a minute might be forever down there," Bayzog said. "We had better go."

Nath drew Fang and waited a few seconds, then with a bob of his chin and a grin, he said, "Let's go."

CHAPTER 38

Something was wrong. The Ocular of Orray had dispelled the spirits, but Andar's evil intents were still alive and well. Laylana's mind raced to make sense of it all as chaos erupted all around her. The elves seated in the amphitheater rubbed their eyes. Slowly, they came back to reality only to have the soldiers of the titan army strike them down. The bleary-eyed elves were slaughtered on the grassy green tiers.

Shum and Liam burst into action. Swords out, they knifed down every enemy that crossed their paths. Sansla skipped through the hands of the earth giant's paws.

One of the nuurg leaders charged Laylana. It swung at her heart. She hopped backward. The hammer skimmed her chest. She hit the ground on her back, rolled, found the handle of a sword from a dead elven soldier's hand, and sprang back to her feet. The nuurg came at her. She stepped inside and gutted it.

Rerry's voice rang out from where he battled against a knot of orcen fighters. "Mother, watch out!"

Laylana lost sight of Andar. She found him. The elven High Council member launched himself into Sasha's blind side. They wrestled over the Orb of Command. "Sasha, I'm coming!"

The stone giant stepped in her path. Squatting down, it wagged its finger in her face. She stabbed it in the knee. "Get out of my way." A quick swipe of its hand sent her into the seats. She shook her head. All of the joints in her body cried out. On wobbly legs, she stood again.

Andar wrested the orb from Sasha's grip. He held it high in the air and shouted, "Elves, surrender!"

Laylana's strong will caved in. She lay down her sword and bent her knee. Andar's cackle pierced her soul. The elves—one and all including Sansla, Shum and Hoven—set down their weapons and took a knee. The brothers, Rerry and Samaz, swayed before Andar with spacey eyes. Sasha lay on the ground with her robes and hair in a tussle, knocked out cold.

Andar waltzed over the stage. He found a sword lying on the slab ceremonial table and picked it up. "Emissaries of Eckubahn, hold your vengeance. I'd like to deal with these instigators myself."

The soldiers of the titan army—orcs, giants, and nuurg poised to deliver fatal blows—stepped back with unhappy grunts.

Andar pointed his sword at Laylana first. "All of your little rebellion, front and center."

She led the roamers, Rerry, Samaz, and Inslay onto the stage.

"Take a knee and put your hands on your head," Andar said. "All of you!"

Grimacing, she did unwillingly as she was told. The orb's hold over her was unbreakable. She'd do anything Andar said.

With a devilish smile, the weasel-eyed elf said, "My, this is delightful. The power I have in my hand is pure elation. If I only had this before, I could have accomplished things much sooner. I could have done in a day what has taken a century."

Laylana wanted to ask him what he was talking about, but her tongue clove to the roof of her mouth. All she could do was obey.

Andar caught her eyes. "You are so young, Laylana. But your brethren know what I am. Inslay. Sansla.

They just didn't put it together until it was too late. Elves like me—and I am a pure elf, mind you—aren't spoken about in Elome's precious circles. We are ignored. I am a Caligin. An elf of the shadows." He tapped her cheek with his sword. "Our precious little sect has a different philosophy that runs contrary to elven tradition. We don't believe in one ruler, but the rules of many. Heh-heh-heh."

Struggling, Sansla managed to say, "Your ways are anarchy."

"Silence!" Andar said. Sansla clammed up. Andar plucked the Ocular of Orray from his hand. "Ah, more precious power to wield. It makes me invincible. Finally, the Caligin will rule forever."

Andar was right. Laylana knew nothing about the Caligin, but she knew of a handful of rebel sects among the elves that had to be dealt with from time to time. It sounded like the Caligin were the worst of them. It hurt knowing there was so much ill will among her people. The orcs weren't as dangerous as the enemy that lay within their own boundaries. She managed to clear her throat.

"You have something to say, Laylana? Please, go ahead. You may say it."

She looked him straight in the eye. "You're going to lose."

He got right in her face. "Even without the titans, I've already won. And now with you, Sansla, and Inslay in my grip, the Caligin will rule the elves forever." He stepped over to Sansla. "You think you're the king of the elves? So be it." He flagged down the elves who still lived among the audience. He motioned the members of the High Council over. "Elves, I command you, come down and listen. Stand, Sansla."

Sansla did as he was told.

Andar's amplified voice carried up and into the streets. "Elves of Elome, this is Sansla Libor, a member of the royal bloodline and a rightful heir to the throne. He and his colleagues have something to say. They want to pledge loyalty to the High Council. It will end the royal bloodline forever." He winked at Laylana, moved over to her, and said, "You'll make for an excellent mate, assuming you behave once this is over, or else, you'll be dead, like the others."

"You're going to kill them all?" she said of her friends. "Why?"

"It's the only way to wipe the traditional slate clean and bring forth a far better world for all. I will use the orb's power to bring my elven enemies to their knees." He massaged the stone with his fingers. "Yes, the orb's power will influence the actions of the elven bloodlines. With my focus, every elf will bend at the knee."

"You are mad."

"So sad you feel that way." Andar stood by Sansla. "Now, Sansla Libor, rightful successor to the throne, recite your oath of loyalty to the High Council. Elves, one and all, hear his words and heed my commands."

Trembling, Sansla opened up his mouth and started to recite the oath as more elven witnesses came down from the streets and into the amphitheater.

Chapter 39

"It's about time you got down here." Brenwar was sitting on a rotted tree stump with his fist under his chin. "I've been waiting for hours." He stood up as soon as everyone else's toes touched the ground.

"Sorry, Brenwar, but we just aren't used to you leading the way. You're usually last," Ben said. His eyes were wide. They searched the endless landscape that looked like Nalzambor turned inside out.

"Welcome to the Land of Dim Light," Bayzog said to Nath. He pulled the hem of his robe free from a crooked root that jutted up from the ground and snagged it. "Be careful where you step. The terrain is unforgiving."

"I can see that," Nath replied. The Land of the Dim Light chilled his scales. The air was stale, and there wasn't the slightest breeze. Vapors of mist covered his feet. The leafless trees and branches bent in different directions as if a gale passing through had frozen them. There was a dim horizon in all directions, like tainted setting sunlight under a dreary sky.

"This is one gloomy forest," Selene said. Her tail swished back and forth, stirring the fog. Little flecks of ash floated up. "The ground shifts."

"You won't get used to it," Rip said. "Keep your voice down and come on. I know where to go."

"Let's go quickly," Nath said.

The foul terrain proved to be watery, slippery, and rugged. Unseen creatures let out shrill cackles and cries that carried over their heads and died. Nath's scales rose from time to time. His belly quavered. The Land of the Dim Light was as far out of his element as he'd ever been. The Dark Realm would be much worse, he suspected.

Stay focused. Save Father.

Traveling to the Dark Realm was just as Lotuus had suggested. Only a fool would rush in. But that was exactly what Nath intended to do. Eckubahn wouldn't expect Nath to fight him on his own ground. The titan would be at his full power here. The only thing Nath had in his favor was the element of surprise. He didn't know if sneaking up on Eckubahn was possible, but he would try.

There was another issue too. Now that they had entered the Land of Dim Light, how much time would pass by up at home?

If we emerge, it might be a hundred years later. Longer. I can't think about that now. The only things that matter are that Father is saved and Eckubahn and his brood are defeated.

After walking for an impossibly long time, he noticed a gargantuan archway in the distance. It was made from huge blocks of stone with carved runes that glowed. Clouds hung over the archway, dripping down rain. Lightning flashed, and thunder rumbled overhead.

The group hung back behind rubble and stone from what might have been the remains of a city from a forgotten time. Their eyes were fixed on the arches.

Rip looked back at Nath. "I've done plenty of walking and hiding. I'm pretty sure that's the entrance to the Dark Realm. Fiends from these lands come and go." He hunkered down. Someone emerged from the archway. They were tiny underneath the arches that stood over a hundred feet tall. A skeleton in a hooded cloak pushed a wheelbarrow out. Five more filed in behind the first. The wheelbarrows were filled with bones and teeth. They moved away.

"Who were they?" Selene asked Bayzog.

"I couldn't begin to tell you. Judging by their hands, they might be relatives of Brenwar's."

"Har-har," Brenwar said.

Nath said to Selene, "Are you thinking what I'm thinking?"

"I'm certain you're thinking what I'm thinking."

"I see. I like what the both of you are thinking." Rip picked up a hunk of stone. "Be ready. Watch this." He clacked rock on rock.

The skeletons froze in their tracks. They let go of the wheelbarrows and dropped their hoods. Their heads twisted in the party's direction. Teeth clicking together, the shrouded skeletons ambled over at a brisk pace. Pupils burning inside their hollow eyes, they weaved their way into the ruins.

Brenwar stepped into their path, and clawing at his beard, he said, "Nice hands, but I don't care so much for the rest of you." He slung his hammer at them. Mortuun busted through the first skeleton and knocked the other five over.

Nath, Selene, Ben, and Rip bludgeoned the hideous skeleton spirits to pieces. Nath and Selene passed out the drab gray shrouds. "Put these on, everyone, and grab a wheelbarrow."

Everyone slipped on the shrouds. Brenwar's was a really bad fit, tight in the chest and draped over his feet. Heading for the wheelbarrows, he tripped every other step. "This isn't going to work." He turned the bones inside the wheelbarrow over and climbed in. He grabbed Ben. "Nobody pushes a dwarf, but since we are not in Nalzambor, this doesn't count. Now, grab those barrow arms and start pushing."

Ben looked at Rip. "I've got a bad feeling this might be a one-way trip."

Wheelbarrows in hand and Nath leading the way, they crossed under the archway and entered the Dark Realm.

CHAPTER 40

WHEN NATH GLANCED BACK, THE archway they had entered through wasn't there. Dead brown grass crunched underneath his feet. Flaming clouds lit the sky. The field they stood on went on for miles and miles. The forests were dead. No vermin crawled. A banshee-like howl carried in the winds that stirred the dust at his feet.

"Everyone stay close," Nath said, "and follow me."

"Are we upside down?" Rip said. The whiskers on his moustache hung in front of his eyes. He pushed them into his chin. "I feel odd."

Everyone's hair floated over their heads. Selene's ponytail hung up like the end of a mop. Bayzog's hair spread out of his head like a plume of peacock feathers. Brenwar clung to the wheelbarrow as if it was falling off the edge of a cliff. Nath reached up and felt his own locks. His stomach was pushing up in his throat. His queasiness compelled action. He shoved the wheelbarrow forward. The world underneath his feet flipped from top to bottom. His hair fell into his eyes. His limbs became normal and heavy.

"Start walking," Nath said.

One by one, everyone's hair fell over their faces. Brenwar clunked into the wheelbarrow. "Whatever just happened, it turned my stomach inside out."

Ben's face was green. "That was awful."

Nath continued his march, saying, "Hoods on."

The landscape of the Dark Realm wasn't so different than Nalzambor. There were trees and shrubs. Briar patches dotted the woodland. But here, it was all dead, devoid of life, and dark and unforgiving. They crossed over a dry riverbed. The rank air made Nath's eyes water. Time stopped on the journey. They walked the land, passing villages and towns. The people and livestock were skeletons. Their bones quivered with strange light. With picks, hoes, and shovels, they dug at fruitless land. They paid the trespassers no mind.

Nath fell back with Selene. "Any idea what we're dealing with?"

"They are a manifestation of what they were in Nalzambor. Spirits with new bodies created for them in the Dark Realm. They toil endlessly. Their work bears no fruit. They can only seek escape through the likes of Eckubahn."

"They must be working for something."

"I think they are digging for tributes for their masters." She pointed her scaly arm toward the next horizon. Underneath the flaming clouds was a city made from monoliths of black stone. A train of skeletons appeared to be filing into the expansive gates. The bright burning clouds clustered above the stark city.

"Looks like the perfect place for Eckubahn to spend his free time," Nath said. His nostrils flared. "As long as we're here, I suppose we should pay him a visit."

"Yes, there's nothing titans like more than a nice surprise," Ben said. Everyone gave him an odd look. He smirked. "Or so I hear."

"Just push," Brenwar said.

Ben hustled up beside Nath and Selene. "I can't tell if we've been down here for days, hours, or minutes, but I do find it odd that nothing is coming after us. Why is that, Nath? These disguises aren't that good."

"I can't say. Perhaps whatever is down here doesn't have anything to fear from us. They just exist. Either way, it's too late to turn back now. Are you having doubts?"

"I knew the journey would come to an end someday. I was just hoping there would be some pretty flowers at my funeral. I don't think they can grow flowers down here."

"So much for my parade, I suppose," Brenwar added. "I wish I'd brought some ale with me. But I'm not thirsty, nor hungry, and I can't feel anything. My extremities are stone cold."

They came to a stop at the end of the line leading into the stark castle. There were no windows, portals, nor parapets, just rugged walls of stone built from mortar and bones. The line of skeletal people crept forward at a slow and steady pace that kept their feet shuffling. Groups of other skeleton people dressed in the drab garb of commoners departed from another exit. They pushed wheelbarrows and carts filled with a hay-like mulch. The skeletons were all shapes and sizes, with the slender and thick builds of all the races. They stuffed handfuls of the mush in their bony mouths and moved on.

Up on his tiptoes and craning his neck toward the group exiting the castle, Ben said, "It looks like they're serving dinner. Strange that the spirit folk would eat."

Before long they crossed through a main gate that was big enough to swallow three sky raiders whole. There were no guards, just a massive courtyard on a bed of grass and stone with the constant fog swirling at their feet.

Selene reached out and squeezed Nath's hand. Figures thrice as big as the rest stood at the far end of the courtyard. Even with no flesh on their bones, their identities were easily defined. Eckubahn's head was flame. Gorn Grattack's tail lashed out at unsuspecting skeleton spirits. Tylabahn and Isobahn shoveled piles of mush into the carts and carriers. They hissed and spat and shoved the skeleton spirits away.

"It's him," Nath said under his breath.

Balzurth's skeleton frame was bound to a central dais by mystic chains. He hung suspended in the air, not bigger than Eckubahn nor Gorn. His body shook and convulsed every time the chains flared up with a searing new energy. Eckubahn laughed when Balzurth groaned.

One step at a time they moved closer. The skeleton-spirits kneeled as they dropped worthless offerings from countless hours of hard labor at the titans' feet. There were rusting weapons, corroded armor, marred coins, busted pottery, and worthless stones. In return, Tylabahn and Eckubahn loaded the skeletal people up with worm-ridden mush and sent them on their way.

"The more you suffer, the more you gloom," Tylabahn would say to them, with her ragged sleeves rolled up. "Enjoy your doom."

Isobahn was a brute of a skeleton. He punched several skeleton-spirits to the ground the moment they passed.

Nath took one last look back at his friends. He gave them a nod. They all nodded back. Fingers clinging tightly to their weapons, they moseyed up to the front.

CHAPTER 41

ATH AND COMPANY ROLLED THEIR wheelbarrows up in a row from left to right in front of Eckubahn and Gorn and set them down. Eckubahn's gaze fell on the empty wheelbarrows. Rubbing his bone chin, he said, "What's this?"

Gorn's head and shoulders swayed from side to side. His wings spread out like bony fingers behind his back. The purple glow in his eyes came to life. He hissed.

"Empty," Eckubahn said in his gravelly voice. "What sort of tribute is this?"

"We brought you a dwarf," Nath said. He motioned to Brenwar. The dwarf stood up inside the wheelbarrow. "A live one. See, he stands."

"All by himself," Ben added.

"I know that voice," Eckubahn said. He shifted his focus to Nath. "Can it be?"

Nath pulled down his hood. So did all of the others. "I felt bad seeing you go without giving you a hug. Did you miss me?" He revealed his sword. "And my little friend?"

Backing away, Gorn roared, Isobahn cursed, and Tylabahn shrieked. She said, "Eckubahn, they bring weapons into the Dark Realm. Magic ones!" Her bony fingers trembled as she pointed when she talked. "They can harm us! Get them out of here!"

"Huh-huh-huh," Eckubahn laughed. "I'm impressed, Nath Dragon. You are braver than I ever could have imagined. But twice as stupid, too." Fists on hips, he threw back his head and laughed a mocking laugh. "Yes, those weapons can hurt us. You are well prepared for that. The problem is, where are you going to go once the deed is done? You have entered the Dark Realm in your mortal body. There's no going back for you!"

Brandishing Fang's quavering blue blade before him, Nath said, "We didn't plan on going back. We just came to save my father. I'll give you one chance to let him go. Peacefully. Us for him. You don't want to fight me again. You know how that turned out the last time. One more battle with me will prove fatal."

"You've only doomed yourselves," Eckubahn said. "This is the Dark Realm. My powers are at their zenith here. There's no reason for me to give up anything when I have everything. Sorry, Nath Dragon, but you and your friends are going to be mine forever and ever."

Ben stretched back Akron's bowstring. Rip thumbed the edge of his sword. Brenwar hopped out of the wheelbarrow and wound his war hammer up. Selene aimed the Spear of Barnabus at Gorn. "I've been dreaming of this day a very long time."

"We aren't changing our minds, Eckubahn. We aren't here to save ourselves." Nath narrowed his eyes. "We're here to save my father."

Flapping her arms at her sides, Tylabahn said, "Do it, Eckubahn. I don't want to die! Make a deal!"

"Silence, you foolish witch! I don't make deals with my enemies, I slay them!" A dagger with flames snaking around the blade appeared in the titan's hand. He jab-stepped at Nath, turned his back, and dashed toward Balzurth's helpless form caught up in the magic net. "I've been holding off this moment, reveling in his suffering, but now, Balzurth dies forever!" He cranked his bony arm back and unleashed a lethal jab.

Everything moved in slow motion.

Nath was yelling, "Noooooo," while trying to fling Fang, same as the last time. He was cocking back to throw just as Eckubahn's fist was coming down. He wouldn't make it in time. All he could see was his father's ghostly heart beating inside the skeleton-shadow shell.

A bright-red missile streaked past Nath's eyes. The arrow rocketed into Eckubahn's chest. The titan's arms flailed backward. The dagger fell from his mighty grip. Nath's legs churned forward. Step by step he rushed straight for Eckubahn. Sitting on his haunches, the titan found Nath's eyes. He lifted his palm. A shield of energy popped up.

Gorn Grattack took in a lungful of air. His mouth glowed with a menacing lavender light. Selene jumped high. She rammed the Spear of Barnabus into the dragon spirit's chest. The spear lodged itself inside the rib cage. Gorn blasted out a final roar. The spasms shook his bones to dust, which lay smoldering on the floor.

Isobahn ran. Rip cut off his path to the exit. "I will wipe you out, little man!" the titan said. A flail of energy appeared in each hand. "Kiss your miserable life goodbye."

Rip flashed his sword back a couple of times. "Oh, I'm not here to fight you. I'm just a decoy."

"Ahem," Brenwar said.

The titan turned just in time to catch Mortuun in his face. His entire body turned to shards of bone and ash.

Sheathing his sword, Rip said, "I was hoping for a little more action than that."

"Maybe next time."

Tylabahn was cornered between two castle walls by the basking glow of the Elderwood Staff. Cringing, she pleaded with Bayzog, "Please, don't kill me. I wanted the deal. Not my foolish brother. I helped you. I told you that your magic weapons in this realm would be our death. You didn't know that."

"True, but that wouldn't have stopped me from destroying you anyway," Bayzog said. "I'm not a vengeful person, but you did murder me."

"No, that wasn't you, that was a doppelganger. You are not the same."

"True, but you thought it was me, so your murderous intent was still the same." Staff first, he closed in.

Waving her hands from side to side, she said, "You-you-you can't do this. You'll be trapped in the Dark Realm forever. I can help you escape. I know the way. The only way."

"I don't care." With a whack of Bayzog's staff, Tylabahn exploded.

The blast of energy erupting out of Eckubahn's hand splintered on the edge of Fang's burning blade. Nath let out his battle cry, "Dragon! Dragon!" He swung Fang in a wide, sweeping arc. Eckubahn shielded his face with his hands. Fang sliced the titan's hands and skull off. Eckubahn's head hit the ground and rolled. The flames went out. The skull crumbled to dust.

Wiping the dust from his eyes, Nath found himself, and all of his friends, inside the castle alone. All of the spirit-skeletons were gone.

"Nath, look," Selene said.

The mystic net that bound Balzurth extinguished. The Dragon King's spirit body was gone.

Nath said, "We did it, I suppose. Thank you, friends."

Ben put away Akron. *Clatch. Snap. Clatch.* Turning his head to survey the stark environment, he looked up at the fiery clouds. "This is weird."

CHAPTER 42

Andar's powerful words had created a fog over Rerry's eyes, but those words weren't binding. His mother's warm grip seemed to snap him out of his haze. His head sagged in her direction. Samaz's did the same. The gemstone in the amulet on Sasha's neck swirled with energy. With the bright light reflecting in his eyes, his thoughts became clear. His back straightened when he said under his breath, "Brother, we aren't elves. We are part elves. He focuses on the elves, not us."

From her back, Sasha nodded her head at him. Energy from the amulet ran through her body, down her arms and into her sons' ankles. Their eyes shone. Samaz linked up with Rerry, forming a bond that fed him new strength.

The light of their eyes shone on Andar's face. His head twisted at the brothers. Perplexed, he said, "What is this?"

Sansla's speech faltered.

Feeling strong as an ox, spry as a deer, and light as a feather, Rerry's body was propelled from his spot into Andar's face in a split second. "This is an end to your short reign of terror, Andar." He punched the elf in the face ten times a second with lightning-quick jabs.

Smiling gleefully, Rerry said, "That's face."

Andar threw his arms up as he collapsed. The orb and the ocular were flung high. Sansla snatched both objects out of the air. His fingers closed over both objects and he said, "Elves of Elome. Enemies dwell in our midst. Spread the word, there is once more a king of Elome, and it's time to fight!"

The dreary-eyed elves' softened expressions came to life. Their eyes lit up. Hands, mouths, and feet went into action. A rousing cheer shouting the name Sansla Libor spread with the speed of crashing waves. The elves turned whatever they could grab into a weapon then battled hard in the streets.

Together, Shum and Liam pierced the skull of a stone giant. Laylana hacked down a nuurg. Rerry pinned down Andar with his fingers locked around the Caligin's throat. The elf tossed his head from side to side, moaning, "No, no, no! So close. Noooooo!"

One by one, Inslay, Samaz, and Sasha coiled up all of the members of the High Council with magic nets and tendrils. A handful of them vanished in the chaos of the titan army and elves battling all around them. The three dragged them up by the mystic nets onto the stone table. Rerry hoisted Andar up and tossed him in with the evil brood. The magic net absorbed Andar into their ranks.

"Father," Laylana said to Sansla. She cut down a charging gnoll and stepped over it. "What would you have me do?"

"If you could do that a few thousand more times, that might do it." Looking to the sky, his shoulders heaved in a sigh. "I don't miss my curse, but I do miss my wings."

Like a silver dart, Slivver dropped from the sky as a great cry from the enemy went up. The titan army shrieked and wailed. Their soldiers went into a blood-mad frenzy.

"What has happened?" Sansla said to Slivver.

The ground shifted under Rerry's feet. It was an unnatural groan that came from the land. The screams became so loud he covered his ears. Sasha and Samaz stood with him, looking to Sansla and Slivver for answers.

"The titan army numbers in the thousands. Thousands more are pouring in," Slivver said. "They don't seek to fight so much as to destroy. It's as if the harness that held them back has been taken off. Nothing controls their madness."

"Father, use the Orb of Command on them," Laylana suggested.

Sansla shook his head. "There are too many, and unlike the elves, they are out of their minds. Draw your steel. It's time for the fight of a thousand fights."

The flaming clouds in the Dark Realm sky drifted quickly overhead. Nath strolled the barren courtyard with Fang clutched in both hands. He bounced the flat of the blade off his forehead. "Fang, take us home, please." He'd been pleading for hours that felt like an eternity. He'd made his case to the magnificent blade a hundred different times. "Gads! I really thought I had something up my scales, but I'm afraid I was wrong."

Ben and Rip sat near one of the mush piles with their heads in their hands. Brenwar talked to his hammer Mortuun in Dwarven. The light in the top of Bayzog's staff had waxed cold. The part-elf wizard said to Nath, "I'm certain there is another way out of here. We just need to look for it."

"Another journey. And I can only imagine we'll make it back home a thousand years later," Selene said. She dug at the ground with the Spear of Barnabus. "At least we aren't dead."

"No, I just feel dead. Look at this place. There's nothing. It's no wonder the spirits are so miserable."

Bayzog leaned on his staff. "This is a shadow of the world above, but without any love. I wonder how long it will be before our own endearing qualities fade. Just look what it did to Brenwar. Oh, never mind. Look at him, he couldn't be more at home."

Nath laughed, but it was hollow and void of joy. The depressing nature of the Dark Realm was slowly sucking the juicy marrow from his bones. How long would it be before he didn't care about anything? *This is miserable.* His eyes ran up and down Fang's blade. *Are your powers gone, my friend? Have I offended thee?* He shook his head. "We can't just stand here. We need to move."

"I don't feel like it, Dragon," Ben said as he rocked back and forth on his toes while holding his knees in his chest. "I'm tired but not sleepy. You go on, I'll catch up with you."

"Me too, eh," Rip Tippy said as he diddled a dagger in the misty dirt.

Nath's eyes flashed with golden fire. His voice boomed in the courtyard. "Get up!"

Ben and Rip popped up like they were shot out of a crossbow. They rushed over, hands fumbling for their weapons. "Sorry, Dragon," Ben said.

In a growl, Nath said, "Come on." He led the way out of the front archway. The black castle was surrounded by an endless sea of skeleton-spirits. If there were thousands, there were tens of thousands, spanning in all directions. Mighty monster spirits greater than Eckubahn and Gorn Grattack roamed among them. Their heavy steps shook the ground. They bellowed with gaping mouths that burned like infernos.

Nodding his chin, Brenwar said, "If I'm going to go out, then this is how I like it. It's been an honor, Nath. All of you."

"To the bitter end," Ben said while notching his first arrow.

With one long last look, Nath said to all of them one last time, "Thank you. Now, by the Sultans of Sulfur, let's have at these fiends." He lifted Fang to the sky and shouted out his battle cry. They all cried out together. "Dragon! Dragon!"

Fang's blade brightened. Nath's scales tingled. The Dark Realm army faded as Nath's stomach turned inside out with him yelling a long-drawn-out "Faaaaaaaaang!"

Nath found himself somersaulting in the summer sky. He unfolded his wings, catching air and swooping to a stop. Wings beating, he looked downward with a dizzy head. "Elome!" he gasped. A small flock of silver dragons zipped by him. They dove headlong into the titan army that was locked in battle against a small group of elves.

Dragon fire lit up the evil forces all over the land. The smoke of their oily flesh and hair left a notable reeking stench in the air. Nath circled in the air, eyes searching for his friends. Pounding the ground in full metal armor, hard-nosed dwarves ten thousand strong slammed into the back side of the titan army's forces. Brenwar had fallen in among the ranks. With his son Glenwar at his side, they sang dwarven fighting songs as they busted up the enemy.

"Nath! Nath!" Selene called out. She straddled the neck of a bronze dragon, hair flapping behind her, looking as glorious as ever. "I don't know what you did, but once this is over I'm going to thank you for it." She let out an exhilarating cheer. "Haha! I feel as alive as ever!"

The bronze dragon nose-dived. It unleashed its hot breath on a throng of orcs. The ravaging fire turned the orcs' metal armor molten.

Nath was about to dive right in when a storm of mighty roars erupted from down in the valley. "Mother!" Grahleyna led the thousands of dragons he'd dispatched to Urslay in a ground-level assault. He landed right on her back. "I take it things fared well in Urslay?"

A crack of her tail turned an earth giant upside down. Her breath turned the hulking, hairy brute to ash. She scooped the burning giant up with her horns and flung it aside. "Urslay collapsed with a shudder the moment we attacked. Their foothills heaved. The stream that turned the races into these oversized abominations vanished into crevices that cracked wide open. It was a glorious destruction. A shame you couldn't have been there, but I've a feeling you achieved something far more important." She winked at him. "I'm proud of you, Son."

From out of nowhere, a great shadow appeared that blotted out the sun. The roar of all roars came. The titan army's gazes froze on the scaled terror descending on them from the sky. Balzurth in his full glory—bigger than the biggest sky raider, with scales glimmering like the finest dwarven shields—turned the titan army by the hundreds into scorched chaff. The dragons, one and all, let out joyous roars of their own.

Pumping his fist in the air, Nath cheered, "Let them have it, Father!"

The titan army's forces scattered under the wrath of dragons, elves, and dwarves. The dark forces fell under dwarven axes, elven swords and bows, and endless waves of flames and spine-shattering tails. After long hours that went into the night, the elven lands were finally purged of the menace.

In the very heart of Elome, Nath waited for his father to land. The giant dragon's massive wingspan stretched from the end of one street to another. He folded his wings and made a windy rustle.

Nath was busy shaking hands, giving hugs and salutations. All of his dearest friends had gathered around. Sansla Libor and Laylana wrapped their arms around him at the same time. "We did it," Nath said. He let out a breath. "I kind of miss that fine coat of fur though, Sansla, but I understand you'll be wearing the crown instead."

Sansla threw his arm over his daughter. "For the time being, but I think we both know it's the roamer life for me."

"I look forward to it. Excuse me."

Balzurth and Grahleyna sat hip to hip with their tails twisted together. She nuzzled her lovely dragon face in Balzurth's chest. He smiled at Nath. "Come over here, my son, my liberator. With a joyful heart I tell you well done."

Nath took a knee and bowed his head. "Is it over, Father?"

"You can't destroy all of the weeds. They're always popping up as quickly as you stamp them out." Balzurth clacked horns with Grahleyna. "That won't stop until the end of time. Until then, all we can do is fight the good fight. You have excelled at that. All of your friends and brothers have."

"Dragon Home is in ruins. You don't have a home."

"The skies and fields are my home. They're all a dragon really needs. Besides, Dragon Home needed some renovating anyway. Isn't that right, Grahleyna?"

"I've been making that case for centuries, you ancient romantic. You still know how to thrill this dragon's heart." They nuzzled and kissed a little.

Nath cleared his throat. "Ahem." It caught their attention. "I still can't turn into a dragon."

Balzurth showed a handsome grin of fangs, patted Nath on the top of his head with his giant paw, and said, "You still have some growing to do. And I know just the thing to help you with that. Nalzambor's quite a mess. It will take centuries to clean it up."

"It sounds like quite a chore, Father," Nath replied, "but it will have to wait."

Balzurth huffed hot breath. "Oh really? And why is that?"

"We didn't celebrate our last victory, but this time we will, and I want it to be special." Nath sought out Selene, took her by the hands, dragged her in front of his parents, and took a knee. With all of his dearest friends gathered around, he looked into Selene's beautiful eyes and said, "Selene, will you be my bride?"

She teared up.

"Oh, great. Here come the waterworks," Brenwar huffed.

Selene sank down next to Nath, sniffled as she wiped the tears from her face, and said, "Yes, but only with your parents' blessing."

With approving looks, Balzurth and Grahleyna said together, "Certainly."

Brenwar clamped his hands together. "Dwarves! Roll out the barrels! Let the celebration begin!"

Ben and Rip lifted Nath onto their shoulders. Rerry and Samaz did the same with Selene. Slivver, Sasha, and Bayzog held hands and danced in the streets as one. All together, they sang praises in a wedding celebration that started in Elome, went to Morgdon, and finished up on the top of Dragon Home. It lasted for weeks.

By the time it was all over, Nath and Selene lay on the mountaintop alone, holding hands, flat on their backs, searching the stars.

"I love you, Nath."

"I love you too, Selene."

She rolled onto her side and started making circles on his chest with the light touch of her fingers. "Nath, now that we're married, I need to be really honest with you about something."

Nath turned his head and gave her a serious look. "Yes?"

"The past few weeks have been indescribably special. I loved it all, but…"

"But what?"

She bit into her lip and gave him the eye. "Since your father and mother have taken back their thrones, do you think we could…start pulling the weeds now?"

Nath sat up with a grin on his face. "Absolutely!"

Brenwar climbed up from the bottom of the mountain. "It's about time."

THE NEW NATH DRAGON/FROM THE AUTHOR

Yes! The very first story of Nath Dragon is here and this series takes place when he was only 100, just leaving Dragon Home. If you remember, Nath was 200 when he started way back in The Chronicles of Dragon, but I'm pressing on with bigger, longer, and even better adventures that I'm excited about and I hope you will be too!

His new book is on sale now!
Exiled: The Odyssey of Nath Dragon Book 1!

Regarding Tail of the Dragon, you just finished, boy, it was tough to wrap up and I hope you loved it. It was hard to do, but hey, I'm excited more adventures with the gang are coming.

Please leave a review. They are a huge help for me!
*I'd love it if you would subscribe to my mailing list www.craighalloran.com
*On Facebook you can find me at The Darkslayer Report or Craig Halloran.
*Twitter, twitter, twitter, I am there too. www.twitter.com
*And of course you can always, anytime, email me at craig@thedarkslayer.com

OTHER BOOKS AND AUTHOR INFO

Craig Halloran resides with his family outside his hometown of Charleston, West Virginia. When he isn't entertaining mankind, he is seeking adventure, working out, or watching sports. To learn more about him, go to: www.craighalloran.com.

Check out all of my great stories ...

CLASH OF HEROES: Nath Dragon meets The Darkslayer

The Chronicles of Dragon Series

The Hero, the Sword and the Dragons (Book 1) Free eBook
Dragon Bones and Tombstones (Book 2)
Terror at the Temple (Book 3)
Clutch of the Cleric (Book 4)
Hunt for the Hero (Book 5)
Siege at the Settlements (Book 6)
Strife in the Sky (Book 7)
Fight and the Fury (Book 8)
War in the Winds (Book 9)
Finale (Book 10)

The Chronicles of Dragon: Series 2, Tail of the Dragon

Tail of the Dragon
Claws of the Dragon
Eye of the Dragon
Battle of the Dragon
Scales of the Dragon
Trial of the Dragon
Teeth of the Dragon

The Darkslayer Series 1

Wrath of the Royals (Book 1) Free eBook
Blades in the Night (Book 2)
Underling Revenge (Book 3)
Danger and the Druid (Book 4)
Outrage in the Outlands (Book 5)
Chaos at the Castle (Book 6)

The Darkslayer: Bish and Bone, Series 2

Bish and Bone (Book 1) Free eBook
Black Blood (Book 2)
Red Death (Book 3)
Lethal Liaisons (Book 4)
Torment and Terror (Book 5)

The Supernatural Bounty Hunter Files

Smoke Rising (2015) Free ebook
I Smell Smoke (2015)
Where There's Smoke (2015)
Smoke on the Water (2015)
Smoke and Mirrors (2015)
Up in Smoke
Smoke 'Em
Holy Smoke
Smoke Out

Zombie Impact Series
Zombie Day Care: Book 1 Free eBook
Zombie Rehab: Book 2
Zombie Warfare: Book 3

You can learn more about the Darkslayer and my other books, deals, and specials at:
Facebook – The Darkslayer Report by Craig
Twitter – Craig Halloran
www.craighalloran.com

Made in the USA
Middletown, DE
08 March 2019